MARK OF THE HUNTER OMNIBUS

BOOKS 1-3

MORGAN GAUTHIER

Adalore

Taybourne Mountains
Northwind
Caelestis
Petram
Elisor
Black Forest
Oakenshire
Borg
Tree House Forest
Gomorrah
Bone Mountains
Sakura
Forbidden Forest
The Hollow
Fennor
Valley Pass
The Sisters
Hidden Tavern
Port Daelon
Trappers Bay
Dead Man's Lands
Enchanted Swamp
Jannat Sin
Caverns of the Undead
Isles of Myr
Numbio

Wolves of Adalore

Map by Gonzalo A. Mendiverry (IG: @gonzalom.art)

Cover and Character Artwork by Klára Dostrašilová (IG: @artzzofkae)

Edited by Ada Charlesworth

Interior formatting by Elle Beaumont (Book Savvy Services)

www.midnighttidepublishing.com

Library of Congress Control Number:

ISBN 978-1-7368282-0-5 (paperback)

ISBN 978-1-7368282-1-2 (ebook)

CHARACTER GLOSSARY

Northwind (North)

- Niabi, Queen, Mistress of Shadows
- Salome, Exiled Princess, The Hunter
- Crispin, Exiled Prince
- Gershom, Niabi's Second in Command
- Pash, Commander of Shadows, Gershom's son
- Ophir, Gershom's Brother, Pash's Uncle
- Rollo, Niabi's Son, Prince

Borg (West)

- Zophar, Crispin and Salome's Guardian
- Benaiah, King of Borg
- Ivar, Captain of the Drakaar
- Ragnar, Prince of Borg
- Lahki, Princess of Borg
- Korah, Village Boy
- Marta, Korah's Mother

Elisor (Andrago)

- Tala, Niabi's Most Trusted Advisor, Oldest Friend
- Leoti, Tala's Daughter, Niabi's Daughter-in-Law
- Dichali, Niabi's First Husband
- Chua, Dichali's friend

Gomorrah

- Matildys, Queen
- Cyler, King
- Thanos, Prince, Ranalda's Twin
- Ranalda, Princess, Thanos' Twin
- Thrak, Cannibal Soldiers

Sakurai (East)

- Jinn, Prince and Heir to the Jade Throne
- Kai, Ryoko Naga and Prince Jinn's Protection
- Kenji, King of Sakurai and Jinn's father

Caelestis (Immortals)

Ethereals:

- Harbona, Seer
- Lavena, High Counselor
- The Eldaar, King and Queen of the Immortals, Harbona's parents
- Keeva, Lavena's Daughter

Bellators:

- Kayven, Leader of Immortal Warriors
- Abba, Leader of Immortal Warriors

Numbio (South)

- Osiris, King
- Heru, Prince
- Rayma, Royal Healer
- Inaros, Rayma's brother
- Memucan, King's Advisor
- Amunet, High Priestess

Isles of Myr

- Nym, Queen, Grandmother of Niabi, Salome, and Crispin
- Zara, Princess and Heir to Bronze Throne
- Bilhah, Niabi, Crispin, and Salome's mother,
- Damaris, Princess and Oracle of Myr
- Mika, Princess and Red Maiden
- Marina, Princess
- Utara, Mika's Daughter
- Seraphina, Qata Vishna, Rosalina's Twin
- Rosalina, Qata Vishna, Seraphina's Twin

Pulau (Misfit Island)

- Uri, The Pirate King
- Nezreen, Shadow Wielder
- Palma, Diviner

The Sisters (Blind Order)

- Neempo, Sovereign
- Penn, Master of Keepers
- Balor, Master of Witnesses

Crew Members of the *Shadow of Death*

- Haldane, The Captain
- Rahab, The Stabby One

- Corwin, The Quiet One
- Phex, The Explosives One
- Ondrej, The Giant One
- Rafi, The Pint-Sized One
- Leeondris, The Missing One

Members of the Order (Rebel Force)

- Oden, Leader, formally known as Lord Maon
- Nubis, Stormcrag
- Ziggy, Call Girl from Borg
- Makeda, Manages *The Whispering Fox* Tavern

Stormcrags (Mountain Men Tribe)

- Cato, Scout
- Torrin, Leader
- Oifa, Torrin's Right Hand

Krazaks (Mountain Men Tribe)

- Gerd, King of the City of Bones
- Rune, Militia Leader
- Hanzo, Rune's Right Hand, Archer
- Orn, Giant Warrior

Other Characters

- Adonijah, "The Wanderer"
- Lykos, Prince of Northwind, Salome, Niabi, and Crispin's Brother
- Issachar, King of Northwind, Salome, Niabi, and Crispin's Father
- Odelia, Enchantress of the Swamp
- Vilora, The Old Witch of Endor
- Diron, Captain of *The Golden Rose*
- Anaktu, The Last Nephilim, Niabi's Iron Guard

WOLVES OF ADALORE

BOOK ONE

CHARACTER GLOSSARY

Northwind (North)

- Niabi, Queen, Mistress of Shadows
- Salome, Exiled Princess, The Hunter
- Crispin, Exiled Prince
- Gershom, Niabi's Second in Command
- Pash, Commander of Shadows, Gershom's son
- Ophir, Gershom's Brother, Pash's Uncle
- Rollo, Niabi's Son, Prince

Borg (West)

- Zophar, Crispin and Salome's Guardian
- Benaiah, King of Borg
- Ivar, Captain of the Drakaar
- Ragnar, Prince of Borg
- Lahki, Princess of Borg
- Korah, Village Boy
- Marta, Korah's Mother

Elisor (Andrago)

- Tala, Niabi's Most Trusted Advisor, Oldest Friend
- Leoti, Tala's Daughter, Niabi's Daughter-in-Law
- Dichali, Niabi's First Husband
- Chua, Dichali's friend

Gomorrah

- Matildys, Queen
- Cyler, King
- Thanos, Prince, Ranalda's Twin
- Ranalda, Princess, Thanos' Twin
- Thrak, Cannibal Soldiers

Sakurai (East)

- Jinn, Prince and Heir to the Jade Throne
- Kai, Ryoko Naga and Prince Jinn's Protection
- Kenji, King of Sakurai and Jinn's father

Caelestis (Immortals)

Ethereals:

- Harbona, Seer
- Lavena, High Counselor
- The Eldaar, King and Queen of the Immortals, Harbona's parents
- Keeva, Lavena's Daughter

Bellators:

- Kayven, Leader of Immortal Warriors
- Abba, Leader of Immortal Warriors

Numbio (South)

- Osiris, King
- Heru, Prince
- Rayma, Royal Healer
- Inaros, Rayma's brother
- Memucan, King's Advisor
- Amunet, High Priestess

Isles of Myr

- Nym, Queen, Grandmother of Niabi, Salome, and Crispin
- Zara, Princess and Heir to Bronze Throne
- Bilhah, Niabi, Crispin, and Salome's mother,
- Damaris, Princess and Oracle of Myr
- Mika, Princess and Red Maiden
- Marina, Princess
- Utara, Mika's Daughter
- Seraphina, Qata Vishna, Rosalina's Twin
- Rosalina, Qata Vishna, Seraphina's Twin

Pulau (Misfit Island)

- Uri, The Pirate King
- Nezreen, Shadow Wielder
- Palma, Diviner

The Sisters (Blind Order)

- Neempo, Sovereign
- Penn, Master of Keepers
- Balor, Master of Witnesses

Crew Members of the *Shadow of Death*

- Haldane, The Captain
- Rahab, The Stabby One

- Corwin, The Quiet One
- Phex, The Explosives One
- Ondrej, The Giant One
- Rafi, The Pint-Sized One
- Leeondris, The Missing One

Members of the Order (Rebel Force)

- Oden, Leader, formally known as Lord Maon
- Nubis, Stormcrag
- Ziggy, Call Girl from Borg
- Makeda, Manages *The Whispering Fox* Tavern

Stormcrags (Mountain Men Tribe)

- Cato, Scout
- Torrin, Leader
- Oifa, Torrin's Right Hand

Krazaks (Mountain Men Tribe)

- Gerd, King of the City of Bones
- Rune, Militia Leader
- Hanzo, Rune's Right Hand, Archer
- Orn, Giant Warrior

Other Characters

- Adonijah, "The Wanderer"
- Lykos, Prince of Northwind, Salome, Niabi, and Crispin's Brother
- Issachar, King of Northwind, Salome, Niabi, and Crispin's Father
- Odelia, Enchantress of the Swamp
- Vilora, The Old Witch of Endor
- Diron, Captain of *The Golden Rose*
- Anaktu, The Last Nephilim, Niabi's Iron Guard

To my fourteen-year-old self who had a dream to write stories. We did it!

PROLOGUE

NIABI

12 YEARS AGO

The Gate of Tayborne was underutilized and forgotten by most Northerners. She knew it would not be difficult to infiltrate, even on her own. Her green eyes glistened in the moonlight as she scaled the forty-foot-tall, white stone wall. As she neared the top, she hugged the wall to ensure the guards would not see her.

She expected a small company of guards to be on duty, but there were only six. Six was foolish. Six would require little effort to kill.

Slithering to the cobblestone street, the hooded intruder strutted up to the soldiers huddled by a flickering fire in the bailey.

"Halt," their captain stepped forward. "Who are you?" The soldiers drew their swords and encircled her when she did not answer. "I will ask you once more," he growled. "Who are you?"

Again, she did not speak, but she stretched her arms wide, level with her shoulders, fists closed and unarmed. Confused, the soldiers lowered their weapons. Then she struck.

With the flick of her wrists, she launched twin daggers in opposite directions, slicing the necks of two guards.

Two charged her. She whipped two lightweight blades from the holsters on her back, closed her eyes, and waited for them to reach her. The first soldier to get close enough swung his sword, but she dodged his blow, and as she rose stabbed him through his chest in one swift motion. She opened her eyes as the second soldier lunged toward her and blocked the incoming blow with her second blade. He thrust his weapon again but was unable to keep up with her speed. Losing control of his longsword, she sliced through his neck, nearly decapitating him.

Two remained. Both trembled at the sight of the assassin covered in blood.

"Who are you?" the soldier's voice cracked.

"One the North wished to forget." Her raspy voice caught them by surprise.

"A woman?"

"A demon," spat the taller soldier. "Come closer, so I might send you back to hell."

Even though she wore a black mask covering the bottom half of her face, the guards could see her smirk as she sprinted toward them. The tall soldier braced himself. She was quick. Their weapons clashed loudly as they dueled. The other soldier jumped in to take her down, but she ducked, dodged, and tumbled to elude them. They stood on opposite sides of her, one in front, the other behind. She remained very still as they circled her. With a nod signaling to attack, both Northmen charged. She waited until they were near and when they swung their swords, she dropped to the ground in a front split and watched as they struck one another down.

She retrieved her daggers and opened the gate where her elite squad of warriors, the Shadows, was waiting. Marching in four rows, their black robes concealed their leather armor and their black masks made them look more like executioners than a rival army.

"That didn't take you very long." Tala the Andrago kicked over one of the dead bodies.

"The Northmen have grown weak hiding behind their white walls." She sneered. She caught a glimpse of the ivory stone White Keep perched on a hill in the center of the city of Northwind.

For a moment, everything was quiet; everything was peaceful. She closed her eyes. She inhaled the crisp mountain air and listened as the waves of the Ignacia Sea crashed in the harbor. The white stone buildings and cobblestone streets glistened under the moon's glow. It was always a magical sight; it was just as she had remembered.

"Just six?" Tala rubbed his clean-shaven, bronze face. He never wore a mask. He wanted his enemies to know exactly who was about to kill them. "Why just six?"

"He always did underestimate me." She wiped her blades clean against her black leather pants. "Give the signal."

Tala reached for the war horn that hung from his hip. "You're sure about this?"

"I have come too far to turn back now." Her eyes narrowed as the horn sounded. "Now to kill the King."

CHAPTER I

GERSHOM

Gershom glared across the room at the chubby astrologer clothed head to toe in a flowing robe more expensive than he could afford. The astrologer stared into the heavens, mumbling to himself and jotting down notes forcing the Second in Command to wait in great angst to be clued into his findings.

Although most Northerners no longer believed in the prophecies of the Old World, Gershom had been a believer in the stars and their messages since his youth. The dark bags underneath his eyes were proof of the nightmares he had been plagued with for nearly two weeks and he wanted answers.

"What do you see?" Gershom growled as he scratched his scraggly beard.

"I see… I see…"

"I grow impatient," Gershom egged the old man to speak. "What is it that you see?"

Now frightened, the stargazer dropped his quill and spat, "My Lord, I see that the stars have moved."

"And?" He edged closer. "What does that mean? Speak," he shouted.

The white bearded man stuttered, trying to find the right words, but ended up saying what Gershom had feared most. "My Lord, I see the time of the prophecy has come."

"What?" Gershom leaned forward, wondering if the astrologer would dare utter that report again.

"The Year of the Hunter has come," the wrinkled servant shrunk back.

Gershom slammed his clenched fist on the arm rest of his high back chair. "Who is he?"

The astrologer trembled where he stood. "I do not know, my lord. His face is hidden from me."

"Where is he?" Gershom motioned to the grand solid oak table in front of him. A map of the Ten Kingdoms of Adalore had been carved into the top and the faces of bears were etched into the feet. Rumor was when Gershom was around fifteen, he crossed paths with a giant black grizzly and fought it off with his bare hands. For this reason, he was known as the Bear and he adopted the creature for his House sigil.

The astrologer unfastened his necklace and suspended the gold chain with a purple crystal tied to the end over the table. He muttered an incantation as he circled the table and stopped over the forests in the Western Lands, which was mostly inhabited by peasants protected by King Benaiah of Borg.

"He is in the Western Lands, my lord."

"Which forest?"

"I do not know for sure, sire."

"Then what do you know, old goat?" Gershom fumed. But the astrologer's sudden silence confirmed his suspicion. There was more he was not telling him. "Is that all?" His question was met with silence. "Is. That. All?"

"No, my lord," his voice cracked.

"What else do you see?" he squinted; voice low.

"I sense great danger for you." The elderly servant shook.

"What kind of danger?" Gershom approached him; he could almost smell the astrologer's fear with each step he took.

"He knows who you are and what you have done. He will kill you if he is given the chance." He stepped back.

"Is there anything else I need to know?" His voice softened; he rested his enormous hand on the astrologer's bony shoulder.

"No, my lord," he smiled slightly.

"Good." Gershom snatched him by the neck and lifted him off the floor. The old man's feet dangled as he struggled to free himself from Gershom's tightening grip. Crazed, he choked his servant until he stopped flailing. "Then I have no more use for your service." He threw the stargazer's body to the marble floor and stepped over him as he marched to the door.

The Bear whipped the door wide open and stared at the two soldiers guarding the entrance. "Bring me my son!"

Gershom grumbled as Pash, a tall, muscular man with dark chestnut hair and brown eyes, who was slow to respond to the summons, entered the room. The Commander of Shadows was always armed with a long blade and looked exactly as Gershom did when he was younger, with exception of their hair and complexion. Gershom had sported both sides of his head clean shaven with light chestnut locks, now streaked with white, slicked back into a bun atop his head since his youth. Pash, on the other hand, made sure his shoulder length hair was in a traditional Northern bun at the back of his head. Hairstyling was not the only thing they disagreed upon.

Pash stepped toward the dead body lying on the floor, not at all surprised by the sight.

"You sent for me?" Pash asked, formal in his tone.

Gershom was hunched over the oak table. "It seems that the Year of the Hunter has come."

"Is that what he told you?" Pash motioned to the dead astrologer.

"You always were cynical of the prophecies," he hissed.

"No one has seen a Hunter in over two hundred years. Frankly, I'm not sure they are anything more than stories told to frighten children," he shrugged off his father's superstitions.

"Then make sure the stories aren't true. Find him," Gershom ordered, pouring himself another glass of wine.

"I doubt the Queen will approve the dispatch of her Shadows for such a purpose," he reminded his father of who was truly in charge. "You have bannermen at your disposal. Send them."

"If I thought my men could handle this situation, do you think I would have involved you in this?" His nostrils flared, eyes wide.

He and his son had not seen or spoken to one another in almost two months, and he was beginning to remember why that was the case. Whenever they found themselves together, Pash was quick to smugly remind him, that he was *not* the King of Northwind, although he acted as if he was. In actuality, he also had a master to serve: The Queen.

"I cannot do what you ask without her -"

"I am her Second in Command," Gershom shrieked. "Everything she has I have helped her build."

"Even if this man did exist, why should you believe he would come for you?" Pash made himself comfortable in one of the chairs and kicked his feet up on the table.

"Believe it or do not," Gershom pushed his dirty boots off the table, "but mark my words: he will come for me."

He had never appeared so unsettled and by the look on Pash's face, Gershom knew it was obvious. He honestly believed his life was in danger.

"If I dispatched some of Her Majesty's Shadows to find your marked man, where would you suggest they start their hunt?"

"The western forests."

Pash's eyes widened, "The West is all forestlands."

"That is all I know," Gershom huffed, slumping into his seat.

"You want my men to search hundreds of square miles of peasant-infested forestland for one man you think might try to kill you?" The commander shook his head and chuckled. "Would they not better serve you here, where I am sure you have far more people wishing you dead?"

Normally Gershom would fire back with a snarky comment, but he said nothing, and that was far more concerning.

"You actually believe your life is in danger?" Pash rubbed the back of his neck.

"Yes."

Pash poured himself a glass of his father's finest wine. "Tell me what I need to know about the Hunters?"

"You never did pay enough attention to the tales of the old world." Gershom scoffed, taking the decanter, ensuring his son would not have a second serving.

"Forgive me, father. If I could go back to being a boy, I would have paid more attention to your stargazers' myths than to my sword masters."

The Bear eyed his skeptic of a son with great irritation as he pointed to one of the astrologer's drawings of the constellation of the Hunter. "The mark is in the shape of Orion the Hunter. Do not ask me where it should be on his person for each Hunter has been branded in a different spot since Malachi the First walked over a thousand years ago."

"Of course." Pash shook his head after downing his drink.

"It isn't water, Pash," Gershom crinkled his nose in disgust. "One should enjoy a glass of wine from the Isles of Myr."

He rolled his eyes. "Does it really matter?"

"You know it does," Gershom hissed through gritted teeth.

"Are you going to tell me what I need to know or not?" Pash motioned for him to get back to business, stifling a chuckle as soon as Gershom turned his focus back to the table.

"There have only been five documented Hunters and only one is marked at any given time," Gershom continued, although he wanted to chastise Pash further for his attitude. "Malachi the First was marked on the palm of his right hand; Tolemy the Red, the middle of his chest; Raego the Mighty, his left forearm; Lor the Meek was marked on his upper right thigh and Polantis the Peacemaker on the left side of his neck. Tale has it they were all marked for the same purpose: to avenge innocent blood."

"And you have spilled plenty of innocent blood, have you not?" Pash cocked his head to the side, knowing the answer to his question. "If there is a man who bears such a mark, he will be found." Swiftly saluting his father without allowing him to respond to his accusation, the commander left before he changed his mind.

With a new-found sense of relief, Gershom snapped his fingers alerting his guards to the body lying on the floor. "Do something with the astrologer."

CHAPTER 2

SALOME

Salome quietly drew an arrow from her quiver and took aim at the doe roughly twenty yards in front of her. She held her breath, and was about to release her arrow, when a tree branch behind her snapped, spooking the deer. She turned around, weapon drawn, ready to strike whoever had sneaked up behind her.

"It's me, Salome, it's me!" Jacobi yelled with his hands held above his head, eyes nearly squinted shut.

She lowered her bow. "Jacobi, I could have killed you. You know better than to sneak around in these woods."

"Did you kill anything?" The stocky, rosy-cheeked baker asked with a touch of excitement.

"It escaped."

She gathered her belongings to move to a different spot. For months, he had mentioned how he wished he knew how to hunt, hinting she could teach him, but she had no interest in teaching him. Honestly, she had no interest in spending time with him. Yet here he was.

"Don't worry, Salome." He patted her back gently. "Your skills will improve."

She rolled her eyes.

He followed her as she walked farther into the forest. She was not sure what irritated her more; the fact he made waste of the hours she spent stalking her prey or his failure to recognize he was the reason she missed her mark.

She whipped around, causing him to stagger backwards. "What is it you want?"

"Just ensuring my lady is safe in the woods," he flashed a boyish grin.

"I am not your lady." She shook her head and pressed onward. "How many times must we have the same conversation?"

"Once more," he replied sweetly.

"You say that every time. Do you not grow tired of rejection?" She ducked from hitting her head on a fallen tree.

"I am a patient man, Salome. I will wait every day until you agree to be my wife."

She stopped. *There it was,* she thought. He finally made his true intentions known.

"You are a good man, Jacobi," she faced him, "but I am not the woman for you."

He rubbed his hands together, eyes fixed on his feet. "I may not be who you imagined being with, but I can provide for you and I can… I can protect you," he plead his case.

"Does it look like I need protection?" she asked, covered head to toe in weaponry.

"Well, you can protect me then," he said with a chuckle. She was not looking at him anymore. "Please, just give me a chance to make you happy."

"You know what would make me happy?"

"Tell me." He stepped toward her, a glimmer of hope in his blue eyes.

"Being left alone."

"You don't mean that." Her words stung.

"Go home, Jacobi."

"How many times will you reject me?" he snarled.

"How many more times will you ask me to be your wife?"

"Ten thousand more times if that is what it will take for you to say yes."

"Then my answer shall be 'no' ten thousand and one more times," her nostrils flared. "Now leave me to my hunting."

"I may be the only hope you have of marrying. No man wants a sharp-tongued woman as the mother of his children. Remember every time you reject me, you grow older," his voice cracked.

She had wounded him, and she knew it. But she was not willing to spare him the truth to protect his feelings.

"I grow older, yes, but not desperate." As she walked away, she could feel his teary eyes glued to her. If she had not said something then, she would have said something eventually. She had reached her limit.

Finding a different spot to wait for her prey, she hid herself in a bush and calmed the blood that boiled within her. Jacobi had spent the last two years buzzing around her. At first, she was polite in declining his unwanted advances, but even someone as patient as she was had a breaking point. The baker tended to overshare with anyone who would listen, and she was sure when she returned to the village, she would be on the receiving end of a few dirty looks.

"You didn't need to be so harsh with him." Crispin bit into his apple with a smirk. "I think you hurt his feelings."

Her older brother was everything a brother should be: Protective. Dependable. Annoying. Very annoying. They were extremely close, being eleven months apart. When she thought about it, she realized he was the only real friend she had. And she was okay with that.

In no mood to ask him why he had perched himself in the tree above her like a gargoyle, she continued to focus her gaze straight ahead. "I don't need to waste his time with false hope, nor allow his unwanted feelings to plague me a moment longer."

"Just admit it. You have no intention of marrying any man." He allowed one leg to hang from the tree limb, clearly not as zealous about the hunt as she was.

"Did you come to hunt or to irritate me?" She glanced up toward her impetuous brother.

"Both," he smiled widely, smacking as he chewed. "Do you deny it then?"

"Deny what?"

"You have no intentions of marrying." He brushed loose curls from his face.

"I would rather die alone this very second than marry Jacobi." She shuddered at the very thought of being the baker's wife.

"That's harsh, sister. I think he loves you," he pressed with a twinkle in his eye.

"He loves the thought of me." She refused to take the bait, knowing he was just trying to get a reaction out of her. "It's no wonder you never kill anything when you hunt, smacking your lips as loud as you do."

"Fishing is more my speed." He leaned back against the tree and closed his eyes.

"And yet you are not good at fishing either."

"I live for the day you meet your equal." His mouth twisted into a half-smile.

"If there is such a man, I will marry him the moment he outwits me," she snorted, hoping it would silence him.

She was seventeen. Ripe for marrying. In truth, she was getting to the age where people started to ask questions of why she was not already married or at least betrothed. When she thought about her options in the village, it was not something to be excited about. Of the available single men in the Tree House Forest, she had exactly three options. There was obviously, Jacobi the baker. Followed by the Elder's son, Yosef, who was the village drunk, though his father did his best to keep that quiet. And rounding out her potential suitors was Old Man Canon, who was just as his name made him out to be: old. She shuddered again.

"The Almighty One bless the man who wins your heart." Crispin snorted, throwing his apple core on the ground. He jumped down and twisted left and then right to crack his back. "I think I'll head back."

"Empty handed again, I see," she muttered.

He rolled his eyes and huffed, "There are matters that require my attention."

"And what matters would that be?"

"If you must know-"

"How about whispering?" she cut him off with a hiss. "Some of us are actually trying to be successful today."

He whispered loudly, "I said, if you must know, Zophar asked me to fashion some arrow heads for our training session this afternoon."

"Even your whispers aren't quiet." Salome shook her head, hiding a smirk. He always made her laugh. Not on purpose. He was himself, and that was enough.

"Well, I will see you at home when you have either killed something or have grown weary in your failure," he bowed with a sarcastic grin.

"Be careful walking home," she teased, "wouldn't want to shoot you by mistake."

Once he was out of her sight, she trudged deeper into the forest. If there were any deer within a few hundred yards, they would have heard Crispin and hidden themselves.

She prided herself on not only being an excellent hunter, but a knowledgeable tracker. Stalking a deer was far more challenging than waiting for a deer to cross her path. And the reward was just as exciting. Other than the obvious reason for hunting, she was most relaxed when she was in the woods. Her mind quieted; she was focused; she was in control.

She tip-toed, following the tracks until she spotted a buck in the distance. A majestic beast: the largest one she had ever seen. With her back against a pine, she inhaled sharply and nocked her arrow. She slithered around the tree and aimed at the deer. Ready to release her arrow, a strong gust of wind rustled the leaves around her and she heard someone whisper her name.

"Salome."

She missed. She swore under her breath.

"Crispin," she growled, looking for her brother, confident he had been the one calling out to her. But as her eyes scanned the trees, she did not see anyone.

Maybe she *thought* she heard her name. She had not gotten any sleep the night before. She had been having nightmares for weeks and forced herself to stay up by cradling her knees to her chest and biting her lip.

She turned where the buck was standing and sure enough, he was gone. She swore once more, gathered her belongings, and pressed on.

After she and her brother narrowly escaped the Green-Eyed Raven's invasion of Northwind twelve years ago, she spent most of her childhood perfecting her skills. Hunting, fishing, surviving. All she had ever known was survival. She knew what it felt like to be prey and swore she would never taste it again. She learned to be the hunter. Patience was her strongest virtue and tenacity was in her blood.

She threw her disheveled brown curls up in a messy bun, revealing a small, red circular birthmark on her right temple. She tightened the holster around her left thigh and tapped on her most prized weapon, a dagger with an ivory handle carved in the likeness of her family sigil: The White Wolf. Before it was hers, it had belonged to her eldest brother, Lykos.

"Lykos," she whispered his name.

As she walked, she eyed the six black lines tattooed around her left forearm. Each ring represented a member of her family who had been murdered the night the city was attacked. Before refocusing on her hunt, she whispered each of their names and said a prayer for their souls.

"Salome."

She heard her name clearly that time and unsheathed her knife, now uneasy. She no longer cared for the hunt. It was the deer's lucky day.

"Crispin?" She did her best to sound brave, but her voice trembled.

Her name was whispered once again, except this time it was louder. "Salome."

Her grip tightened around the handle of her knife, "Who's there?"

"Salome."

The voice was familiar.

A strong gust of wind knocked her off her feet. She held her breath. She wanted to run, she wanted to scream, she wanted to hide. But she was frozen.

A bright white light appeared in the distance. It was coming toward her. She squinted as it drew closer. She thought she saw a silhouette of a man but did not really want to find out.

Scrambling to her feet, she sprinted home, hoping whatever was after her would not be able to catch her.

CHAPTER 3

CRISPIN

Crispin took maintaining his weaponry seriously. His knife, his sword, his bow and arrows; they were all an extension of him, a representation of what type of man he was. He was clean. He was orderly. He was strong. He was dependable. Lost in thought, sharpening his knife, he did not hear his guardian, Zophar, behind him.

"A rare sight indeed," Zophar leaned against the threshold of their tree house smoking his long stem pipe.

Crispin looked at his knife, his brow furrowed. "What do you mean?"

"Not that," he gestured toward the knife and exhaled a puff of smoke. "You hunting."

Crispin flashed a lop-sided grin, "And what is so remarkable about that?"

"You aren't what we call a morning person."

"Well, I happened to wake up early."

"You're not a very good liar."

Zophar had brought Crispin and Salome to the Tree House Forest as children. It was one of the most remote locations in the Western Lands that he could remember from his youth. Unless someone had prior knowledge of the lurking dangers of the dark forests, outsiders normally steered clear. The Westerner had aged well over the past twelve years. His blue eyes were still bright, and his red hair was wild as ever, but he was unable to elude the wrinkles that encircled his eyes.

Crispin clicked his tongue, "I'm a good liar, just not with you."

Zophar sat down next to him. "You had another nightmare."

Crispin was not surprised he knew. Whenever he had a nightmare, he would wake up screaming, dripping in sweat.

"Salome always goes hunting when she has a nightmare." Crispin tried to draw the attention away from himself.

"So, you thought you would do what she does?" he chuckled. "You know that hunting isn't your strength."

Crispin continued to sharpen his knife without looking up at Zophar.

"It's the same dream every time."

"What do you see?"

Crispin had not told Salome or Zophar what tormented him, but each time the nightmare visited him, the more real it became.

"I'm on some kind of battlefield and see a man staring at me from the other side." He stopped fiddling with his knife. "His hands are covered in blood. I try to draw my sword to fight him, but my sword will not budge. He charges; he swings his sword and..."

"And what?" Zophar gnawed on the tip of his pipe.

"Nothing." Crispin's voice cracked. "Nothing happens. I wake up."

A muscle in Zophar's neck twitched. "Hmm."

"What do you think it means?" Crispin glanced at him.

Zophar's eyes widened, and he sighed. "I am not an interpreter of dreams, Crispin."

"But you are the wisest man I know," he pressed, "surely, you have an opinion."

"Only a Seer can interpret dreams. Everyone in Adalore knows this." Zophar scratched his jawline. His bushy red beard could not fully hide the smile scars that extended from the corners of his mouth and nearly up to his ears. "All I know is that I am a soldier, nothing more, nothing less."

"You haven't been a soldier in twelve years." Crispin pointed at his belly. "Maybe there's a reason for that."

Zophar struck a match and relit his pipe. "Do I detect a hint of sarcasm?"

"Or truth?" he snickered, clasping one of his knees to his chest as he leaned back in his seat.

"Always the jokester." Zophar leaned back in his seat and rested his hands on his belly. "You know it's ok to miss them."

Crispin shifted his brown eyes to the ground. "What?"

"You don't speak of them -"

"Talking about them won't bring them back." Crispin had not talked about his family in years. He was six when they fled. Six when he lost everything. Six when he lost everyone, except Salome.

He ran his fingers through his short curly hair, beads of sweat dripped down his olive skin. "It's been twelve years..."

"Aye," Zophar sadly agreed, "twelve long years."

"Sometimes I wake up wondering where I am. I'm not supposed to be wasting away in this forgotten forest. I'm meant to be something more. Someone like my father was."

"Perhaps, if you got to know the villagers better -"

"This isn't my home, Zophar."

Crispin avoided getting close to most of the villagers as Salome and Zophar did. They had put down roots. He could not do that. If he befriended them, if he cared about them, if he, too, put down roots, he would then have to be content with staying. The Tree House Forest was as pleasant as the next village. It was quirky with its dozens of tree houses and wooden ramps and swinging bridges connecting each tree to the next. But it was not home. Northwind was home, even after all these years.

"What will it take to make you happy?" Zophar asked, with a heavy heart.

Crispin knew what Zophar was thinking. He had, after all, sacrificed everything to keep them safe and he had done everything in his power to make them happy. It was not his fault. In truth, Crispin would never be satisfied until he drove a knife through the hearts of those who had stolen from him.

"Seeing her dead body," Crispin growled. "That would make me happy."

"And what do you plan to do about it?" Zophar huffed, crossing his right leg over his left, a clear indicator he was uncomfortable. "Do you plan to march up to the gates of Northwind and demand your sister give up her crown? Do you intend to challenge Gershom to fight you for killing your mother and your brothers?"

"She is *not* my sister." Crispin's clean-shaven jaw tightened.

"Denying her does not change the fact she is your blood."

Crispin took a deep breath. There was a reason he never spoke of his family, his past. He had never met Niabi. She had been sent away from Northwind for an unspoken reason and by the time he was born, she was married to the King of Elisor. No one in Northwind spoke of her. It was as if she did not exist. That is, until she appeared twelve years ago and marched her army through the White City.

"Maybe I will challenge them," Crispin flashed a wry grin, shaking his thoughts free from his mind.

"They would strike you down before you had a chance to utter a word." Zophar exhaled a ring of smoke, noticeably impressed with its nearly perfect form.

Crispin just wanted the conversation to end. "I would welcome Death if it meant I tried to do something."

"Death would laugh at you," Zophar stifled a chuckle.

"I would welcome her like an old friend." Crispin stretched his arms wide, face turned up for the sun to shine upon him.

"May she be patient in her reaping." Zophar slid his index finger from the middle of his forehead down to the middle of his chest.

They sat in silence for a minute until Zophar said, "You don't plan on challenging them, do you?"

Crispin could tell by the tone in his gravelly voice there was more he wished to say. "If I did?"

"What good is it to your sister if you, too, are dead?" Zophar's eyes were fixated on him. His glare burned into his soul. "A lone wolf doesn't last long on its own."

Crispin mulled over his guardian's words, far too stubborn to admit he was probably right, so he changed the subject. "Are we still training today?"

"When your sister returns." He puffed another ring of smoke where he stood, pointing it out for Crispin to admire. "I'm getting better." He smiled proudly and walked across a swinging bridge to the main square.

Crispin shook his head, put his sharpened knife in its holster, and began crafting arrows. He enjoyed the work. He found he was quite good at carpentry, crafting, and whittling.

Toiling in silence, he was oddly caught off guard when a tiny hand tapped him on the shoulder. Only one person could ever sneak up behind him and that was a young, soft-footed nine-year-old village boy named Korah.

Korah always had a smile on his dirty face and had a knack for finding mischief.

His father had died before he was able to walk, so his mother worked at the one-room tavern in the main square to support them. During the day, the red-headed boy would spend his time watching Crispin train. Crispin knew by the look in his eyes that he imagined himself being a great fighter one day; Crispin had the same look when he was that age.

Crispin smiled at his blue-eyed friend, "Korah, what mischief are you up to now?"

"Will you teach me how to fight today?" Korah asked the same question every day.

"I thought we made a deal to wait until your tenth year." Crispin continued fashioning his arrows.

"I turn ten in a few days. You could teach me early," the boy begged as he sat down.

Crispin could not hide the smile that crept across his face. "I suppose we can begin with a simple lesson."

Korah was stunned. "Really?"

"Really."

"What will I learn first?" Korah jumped up in excitement. "How to shoot an arrow? How to cut off someone's head? How to -"

"Today you learn how to fasten these arrowheads to their shaft." He handed the young boy several wooden sticks he had fashioned.

"No fighting?" He crinkled his nose; the corners of his mouth fell downward.

"A soldier is only as good as his weapon. Now, string." Crispin patted him on the back with soft encouragement.

The boy stared at the arrowheads then looked back up at Crispin. With a smile once again on his face, he began to string the heads.

"Is Salome hunting?" Korah asked.

"Aye, she is," Crispin nodded, focused again on his whittling.

"Do you think she will teach me one day?"

"And why would I not teach you to hunt?" Crispin's left eyebrow rose.

"Because she is really good." Korah answered honestly.

"Am I not?" Crispin chuckled; hopeful his reputation had not already proceeded him.

Korah's eyes shifted. "String," he muttered. "String."

Salome stumbled up to the treehouse, short of breath.

"What? No kill? Did the deer elude you again?" Crispin teased. She appeared unhinged, as if she were being followed. "Salome, is everything alright?"

"I'm… I'm fine," she stuttered, wiping sweat from her forehead.

"Zophar is waiting for us." Crispin watched her intently, knowing something was wrong.

"I will be down. Just need... I... Give me a minute." She marched up the front steps to the tree house.

"What is wrong with her?" Korah demanded, without looking up from his work.

"I am not quite sure." Crispin watched her race up the steps two-by-two.

"Women," Korah sighed.

"And what do you know of women?" He looked down at the boy with a grin.

Korah stopped his work and eyed his teacher. "What would you like to know?"

"Never mind all that," Crispin clicked his tongue and shook his head.

"Can I at least watch you and Salome spar today? Please?"

Korah had a lisp he was teased over regularly, but Crispin never treated him differently. After a while, he did not even notice it anymore.

"Do you not already watch from the tree you perch yourself in?"

"Maybe." Korah blushed and stared at his feet. "I just thought I could get a better view this time?"

"Finish stringing and then you may come," Crispin granted his request.

"Really?"

"String."

"String." Korah returned his focus to the arrowheads with a wide grin.

CHAPTER 4
SALOME

As she grabbed the knob to the door, she was soothed with the feeling of safety. Slamming the door behind her, Salome heard a stack of books fall off a nearby shelf.

"Great," she mumbled.

Frustrated, she gathered them from around the room, hoping Zophar would not find her rustling in his private collection. She stood up to restack a handful when she caught a glimpse of her reflection in the mirror on the wooden plank wall by the crooked door. She grimaced at the sight of the dark circles under her bloodshot eyes.

Her eyes.

How she hated looking at them. From a distance, her eyes were brown. But upon closer inspection, her left eye had green speckles scattered around her pupil. She was teased growing up over the deformity; children and adults alike claimed she was cursed by the different gods of the Ten Kingdoms. And, for as long as she could remember, she thought their whispers might be true.

She felt hot.

She cupped water from a tin bowl and washed her face. Her olive skin glowed in the beam of sunlight that poured through the circular window. Her mother was from the southern Isles of Myr, so, she and her older brother had darker skin than most Northerners. Thankfully, the villagers could not place their origins based on their looks alone and did not care to ask where they had come from over a decade ago.

Putting the last of the books back on the shelf, she noticed a handwritten piece of loose parchment that did not belong with any of the texts.

"What is this?" Her curiosity got the better of her.

Zophar,

I hope you find your accommodations adequate in these troubling times. While not at all exciting or glamorous like the White Keep, the Tree House Forest is quiet, and the people are friendly.

I will find you again once the Year of the Hunter begins. Until that time comes, train them both well – their lives depend on it.

Keep them safe. Keep them hidden. Make sure they know the truth.

May the Almighty One be with you, my friend.

H

She had questions. Lots of questions.

"Who is H?" she whispered, turning the piece of paper to the back only to find it blank.

Zophar would not be pleased she had read the letter, but he would more than likely answer whatever questions she had about it. He had always been truthful as they rattled off a thousand questions a day when they were younger, especially about what happened the night they fled their home. They were well aware that the Green-Eyed Raven who had conquered their city was their sister, Niabi. They were also aware that Gershom, her Second in Command, had joined her to settle a personal vendetta against their father, King Issachar.

Was there another truth they did not know about?

Her thoughts were interrupted as she heard footsteps creaking up the front steps of their treehouse. She stuffed the note in one of the books, hoping Zophar would not notice they were not in their right order. He was extremely meticulous when it came to his collection. He had books varying in subject matter, so she would not even begin to know how to organize them.

"There you are, Salome." Zophar walked in the door, Crispin right on his heels, and greeted her cheerfully. Too cheerful if she was being honest. "You have returned early from your hunt. No deer?"

"I will try again tomorrow." Her stance was awkward, but she was unaware of how uncomfortable it made them.

"Zophar and I are going to the training grounds." Crispin broke the momentary silence. "If you aren't up for it today -"

"And miss another opportunity to beat you? Not a chance." She forced a smile, this time fully aware of how uncomfortable they were. "I will see you out there." She hastily brushed passed them before they could ask her anymore questions.

The moment the door closed, Crispin crinkled his nose. "I told you she was acting strange. Did you see how she was standing there?" He imitated her ungainly posture. "What was that about?"

"You said she came home looking troubled?" Zophar rubbed his chin.

"Aye," Crispin nodded his head. "As if she were running from something. She was spooked for sure."

Zophar scanned the room.

"What are you looking for?" Crispin turned around the small living space. "Is something missing?"

"Everything appears to be in order." Zophar lied; he had noticed the books as soon as he walked in. "We shouldn't keep her waiting. She might suspect something."

Crispin grabbed the training weapons by the door, "You ready?"

"I will meet you down there," he motioned for him to leave. Once the door closed behind him, Zophar quickly organized his books and papers in their proper order. "That would have bothered me all afternoon."

Zophar headed for their make-shift training grounds without noticing Salome backed against the side of their treehouse. Her head was by the window overlooking the living space. She heard everything they said.

Of course, Crispin noticed her odd behavior.

She could tell them what had happened in the woods. But what exactly would she tell them? *That a white light chased her?* She felt ridiculous even thinking it.

No. She would not tell them anything. She had to put the whole ordeal out of her mind. After all, she might have imagined the whole thing. She was exhausted. Lack of sleep can have a strange effect on one's mind.

That's it. She thought, rubbing her itchy eyes. *None of that actually happened. I just need sleep.*

CHAPTER 5
ZOPHAR

Living in one of the outskirt tree houses made it easy for the trio to set up a training area less than two hundred yards from their front door. Weather permitting, they would trek through the woods to their practice arena to sharpen their skills in the art of war.

Zophar took his time getting there, rushing was no longer befitting his lifestyle. Around one of the mighty pines was a large stump he used as a seat, but as he circled the tree, he noticed someone was already there. Young Korah had made himself comfortable on his stump and Zophar was having none of it.

"What do you think you are doing?"

Korah shrugged his shoulders. "Sitting."

Zophar's nostrils flared. "That is my seat," he snorted.

The two of them stared silently at one another until Zophar waved his enormous hand for the boy to move. Korah jumped off allowing his elder to sit.

"But where will I sit?" Korah crossed his arms over his chest.

"The grass appears most suitable for a boy your age." Zophar motioned broadly to the ground next to him.

Korah eyeballed the old soldier and muttered incoherent nothings as he slumped down next to him.

"And what is that you are mumbling?" Zophar scrunched up his face.

"Nothing, sir," Korah faked a smile, "just sitting."

Guardianship had been thrust upon Zophar in desperate times. His duty was to protect the crown. His orders were to lead two of the royal children to safety. He swore he would raise them, protect them, provide for them. He had kept his promise. Although, he was unsure of how successful he would be caring for royal children, for many reasons. The attitudes. The lack of survival skills. The constant state of needing something. But over the twelve years of rearing them, he found he had been wrong about them. He had grown quite fond of them. With all their challenges and ever evolving phases, there were more rewarding facets to them than he initially realized. Their unconditional love. Their quickness to forgive. Their eagerness to learn. In a way, they reminded him of his two sons…

He grunted and shooed the memory from his mind. "Take your stances."

Salome and Crispin stood ten feet apart in the cleared area, armed with blunt swords.

Zophar knew them well enough to know that Crispin's heart was beating fast. Whenever a duel was about to start, his breathing quickened. Salome however, never appeared nervous. She inhaled and exhaled rhythmically, keeping herself grounded.

They lifted their weapons to their faces and took their stances.

"Begin." Zophar set his wolves loose.

Crispin charged toward his sister the second Zophar spoke. She stood her ground, waiting patiently for him to reach her. Every clash of their dull swords kept Korah on the edge of his seat. They were quick and skilled in their movements. They were everything Zophar had taught them to be.

Crispin's attack was fast and aggressive. His sword was an extension of his arm. Bold, fearless. He was an unstoppable force.

Salome was defensive by nature. She read her opponent, learned his fighting style, and used his strengths against him. She was patient, she was cunning, she was a predator, which made her extremely dangerous for impulsive fighters like her brother.

Breaking free from his sister's counterattack, Crispin circled around her with his sword extended, keeping her at a safe distance. Flashing a twisted grin, he declared, "Impressive, Salome, you almost fight as well as a man."

"Funny, I was thinking the same of you," she fired back, smirking as Korah laughed. "I think the boy might agree with me."

"Whose side are you on?" Crispin gave him a once over. "Remember who is going to train you when you are old enough."

"And who will correct that training when he is through," she poked, causing Crispin to laugh.

"Enough talk," Zophar stifled a chuckle, demanding order. "Resume your starting positions."

The brother and sister waited for Zophar to release them again. The Westerner paused; he was unsure which one of his pupils would end up the victor that afternoon.

"Begin." He sounded, kicking one leg over the other.

This time, Crispin resisted the temptation to lunge toward his sister and waited for her to initiate.

Salome hurled her sword over Crispin's head. He carefully watched her weapon glide through the air and once it was close enough, he lifted his free hand and caught her sword.

He grinned. He was now armed with two blades, but when he looked for his sister, to his horror, she was nowhere to be seen.

"Salome?" He whipped around, but she was not there. "Where is she?" he asked Zophar and Korah.

"She is -"

Zophar covered the eager boy's mouth before he could reveal her position.

With Crispin distracted, Salome quietly jumped down from a nearby tree. She crept up behind him, just like prey in the forest and put her dagger against his throat.

"Yield," she hissed in his ear.

Crispin dropped his weapons. "Is this even allowed?"

Sharpened blades were banned from training sessions, but to Crispin's dismay, Zophar stated, "You took your eyes off her and it cost you this duel. Let that be a lesson to you, Crispin. Next time it could cost you your life."

Zophar beamed with pride. He had trained plenty of women in his homeland of Borg, because women, like men, were both expected to fight in the king's army. But he had never had a student like Salome. She did not have a soldier's mindset. She had a hunter's mindset. Instead of seeing an enemy, she saw prey, and he knew years ago she could be deadly, if she wanted to be.

"I have not had two better pupils." He patted Salome on the back. "And I love seeing you beat Crispin," he whispered in her ear and grinned.

"I can hear you, Zophar," Crispin chimed in.

Salome laughed and tossed him his sword. "Best two out of three?"

Crispin smiled and took his stance once more.

CHAPTER 6

NIABI

Niabi's green eyes scanned the city from Her Majesty's Tower as crowds of adoring citizens lined the cobblestone streets from the main gate to the White Keep steps.

Six months she had waited for his return. The White Keep seemed empty without him. In the blink of an eye, her small defenseless child had grown into a mighty warrior fit to rule the North. She had raised Rollo to fear nothing; to fear no one. He was her pride and joy, her saving grace.

Cheering from the crowd drew her attention to a nearby street where she spotted him. She ran to the mirror and brushed long strands of black hair from her face and tucked them into her intricately braided updo. Now presentable, the slender queen rushed hastily down the spiral staircase and through the castle to greet him at the front steps. Rollo was home; she could now stop worrying about him.

The White City was buzzing with excitement, not only for Prince Rollo's return from visiting the Andrago of Elisor, but for his Name Day Celebration. At his mother's request, Rollo spent six months learning the customs, history and traditions of his late father's people, the Andrago. Although Dichali had died a couple of years after he was born, Niabi wanted her son to know the former King of Elisor and to keep Dichali's memory alive in Rollo's heart.

The Andrago, also known as the Horse Lords, lived in the Valley of Elisor west of the Tayborne Mountains. They were the most respected tribal nation in the Ten Kingdoms and were famous for their incredible and elaborate braids, which showcased their bronze skin and high cheek bones; physical traits they all shared. Unlike other nations, they did not build stone walls around their city, but respected the land and lived off what they could hunt and gather.

The horn of Northwind echoed throughout the city as the royal caravan approached the White Keep.

Riding alongside the green-eyed prince was Tala, Queen Niabi's most trusted advisor and oldest companion. Tala had known Rollo's father from boyhood and the only signs of his age were the crow's feet creasing the corners of his dark brown eyes and streaks of white in his black hair. Sworn to protect Rollo from infancy, he rarely left the prince's side.

Rollo waved at the crowds who welcomed him home. "I had hoped for a quiet return before the festivities."

"You of all people should know your Name Day will be celebrated for at least a week, especially after your long absence." Tala the Andrago flashed a warm smile at the prince. "Your mother will be very excited to see you."

"Perhaps now that I have returned, she will tell me how my father died."

Tala sighed. Every day they were with the Andrago, he heard nothing but Rollo's plea to know more about his father's death. "Dichali's death was tragic for our people, but your mother, well… she never recovered."

"I don't understand the secrecy. I have a right to know," Rollo huffed. "I know it was you who instructed the Lords of Elisor not to tell me the truth."

"As your mother wished." Tala was unmoved. "After your eighteenth year has been celebrated, I am sure she will tell you what you wish to know. Until then, let it be."

"And if she doesn't tell me?"

"I have it under good authority that she will."

"But if she doesn't," he persisted, "swear, you will."

"My Prince -"

"He was my father, Tala. Please!" Rollo held his breath.

"If after all the festivities have ended, and she has not told you the truth, I swear I will." He held up his hand, putting an end to the matter.

The people cheered as Rollo turned into the royal courtyard. Once he dismounted his steed, his eyes travelled up the steps until he saw the familiar face he had been looking for: his mother.

"Mother!" The tall, lean prince bowed, bringing his right arm across to his left shoulder.

Niabi hugged her son, relieved he had returned to her safely. "Oh, how I have missed your face." She cupped his well-defined jaw in her thin fingers. "My heart and my soul, how you have grown."

She was stunned by how much his features had developed and how he had transformed from boy to man in just six months.

"And you have grown far more beautiful since I have been away." His kind eyes danced.

"Tala, how did he do?"

Tala's chest puffed up. "Dichali's blood runs through his veins."

Niabi smiled and squeezed Tala's hand. "Get some rest, dear friend, for tomorrow, we celebrate."

Tala bowed and left them to walk through the gardens.

The mother and son walked arm in arm as the attendants scurried around them to finish decorating.

"Are you excited for tomorrow night?" Niabi asked, with her eyes glued to him. Six months without him had been unbearable. She had not spent so much as one day apart from her son since he was little.

"Of course, I am," he flashed his boyish grin. "I know you have gone through a lot of trouble to ensure I enjoy my celebration."

"Soon it will be your responsibility to entertain the Lords and Ladies of the North." She was relieved at the thought.

He shook his head, "Not for many years."

She stopped and tugged at his arm. "That is what I wanted to speak to you about, Rollo."

Her tone was odd.

"Is something wrong, mother?" he grasped her hand tightly.

"All is well, my son." She patted his hand reassuringly. "Tomorrow night, I plan to announce your coronation."

By the look on his face, she could tell he was surprised.

"But that would mean..."

"I am abdicating the White Throne." She nodded her head, a smile on her face. "It is your time to lead our people."

"I... I don't believe I am quite ready."

She tenderly tucked loose strands of black hair behind his ear. "You will always have me here to support you."

"Mother, this is your kingdom."

"My time has come to an end." Niabi wrapped her arm around his and forced them to continue their stroll. "I have accomplished everything I set out to do. I made a promise years ago when you turned eighteen, I would let you rise and take your place at the table. It's time."

"I still have so much left to learn."

"Good kings are ready to rule, great kings are ready to learn." She kissed her son's cheek, sensing he was overwhelmed. "You will have to appoint your Second in Command tomorrow. Do you have someone in mind?"

"Yes," he said without a second thought, "Tala."

She beamed. "A wise choice."

Niabi noticed Leoti standing in the gardens and dipped her head toward her.

"I believe there is someone else who wants to welcome you home."

Tala's daughter stood with a shy smile. Her hip-length black hair, full lips, and round brown eyes were gifts from her late mother. Her honesty and calm demeanor were all Tala. Leoti was two when Rollo was born, and they had been promised to one another since that day. For them, it was not political. They were in love, and everyone could tell.

"Don't just stare at her," Niabi gently pushed him forward. "Go to her."

Rollo made his way down the garden path until he stood in front of her. She curtsied.

"Prince Rollo, it is good to see you." Her soft voice soothed anyone who heard her speak.

"My Lady," he kissed her tattooed hand. "Would you care to walk with me?"

She wrapped her arm around his. "I would be honored."

Niabi watched with fondness as they strolled through the gardens and remembered what it was like being with her late husband. Her heart always quickened when she looked at Dichali. He was everything she was not. He was calm, patient, forgiving. Not a day went by that she did not think of him.

"They make a handsome couple," Pash said.

She turned to face Pash who was standing next to her. "They do," she nodded. "I didn't see you in the courtyard when my son arrived."

"My apologies, my Queen. I had matters that required my attention."

"Is something wrong, Commander Pash?" She was good at reading people and noticed he seemed rattled.

"Nothing I need to bother you with," he forced a smile. "You must be relieved he is home."

His change of subject had not gone unnoticed.

"As his mother, I am relieved. As his Queen, I am proud. My son is now a man."

"The people worship him." He nodded, hands gripping the balcony railing. "He will make a fine king one day."

"Of that I have no doubt." She rested her hand on top of his. "Walk with me. There is an important matter I wish to discuss with you."

"Is something troubling you, my Queen?" he followed her.

"I have decided to announce my son's coronation, as I plan to step away from my duties as Queen."

His voice cracked, "You plan to abdicate?"

"I will recommend to my son he appoint you to be his Iron Guard." She watched him carefully to evaluate his reaction.

"Forgive me, my Queen, if I sound ungrateful, but I think my skills would be best used remaining with the Shadows." He motioned toward the silver masked Nephilim who lurked in the background. "Perhaps, your Iron Guard would be better suited to guard our future king."

Anaktu the Nephilim, the Queen's Iron Guard, was the last of his kind; born from the fallen Immortals, who had been banished from the City of Caelestis hundreds of years ago, along with the mortal men they had imprisoned. To most people, the Nephilim were mere fables, but all who knew of him knew the truth. He, too, was immortal but was cursed to a life of misery. Niabi saved him from his captors, and to repay her kindness, he swore an eternal oath to protect and serve her. A promise he had kept for two decades.

"Anaktu will stay in my services." She faced Pash, unwilling to accept anything less than his agreement. "There aren't many people I would trust with my son's life."

He hesitated. "If I accept, what will become of my position among the Shadows?"

"They rode before you and they will ride after you are gone. That is the way of the Shadows."

"But my men -"

"Are not yours to begin with." The fiery response startled him. "Or have you so quickly forgotten who their true master is?" Without giving him a chance to speak, she grabbed his arm. "Accept when Rollo appoints you." She released her tight grip and her gaze softened. "I will rest easier knowing he will have you by his side when he bares the crown."

His eyes narrowed. "Are you worried something will happen to him?"

"He is the only true Northern heir left. That alone places a target on his back."

His forehead creased.

"I have a certain reputation in the Ten Kingdoms that my son does not have. There may be some who wish to challenge him, oppose him." Her eyes bore into his soul. "So, when my son appoints you as Iron Guard?"

"I will accept." He had no choice but to agree.

CHAPTER 7

ROLLO

"Remember, don't take the blindfold off until I tell you to." Rollo held her long fingers tightly as he led her down the side of a rocky cliff.

"Where are we going?" Leoti asked.

The sounds and smells made it obvious they were not near the White Keep. The waves crashing indicated they were either near the docks or the white cliffs to the north of the harbor.

"How much farther, Rollo?" she giggled in anticipation.

"We're almost there. No peeking." He gently pulled her forward and positioned her in front of him. He untied the blindfold. "You can open your eyes."

Leoti opened her eyes and was shocked. They were not on the white cliffs nor by the docks. They were in a cavern with a circular hole at the top where the stars were twinkling brightly. She took her shoes off to feel the sand between her toes and allowed the water to envelop her feet. Turning toward him, she was surprised to see a basket of her favorite foods sitting atop a blanket. Torches surrounded the cavern interior just enough for them to see one another, but not inhibit the view of the stars above them.

"You did all of this for me?" She tucked her hair behind her ears with a smile.

"I hope you like it." He took her hand in his.

"I never knew this place even existed. How did you find it?"

"I used to come here a lot as a child," he admitted sheepishly, knowing as the sole heir he was not supposed to leave the White Keep unsupervised. "It's my favorite place in Northwind."

"It's beautiful."

"Sit with me." He guided her to the blanket where she sat between his outstretched legs. She could feel his heart beating against her back once he wrapped his arms around her.

"I missed you." She squeezed his arm.

"I missed you too, Leoti," he kissed the side of her head. "I have something else for you."

"What else could you possibly give me?"

He handed her a small book filled with dried flowers. "I know violets are your favorite and I knew they wouldn't make the long trip back from Elisor. But I wanted you to have a piece of your home."

She flipped through the pages. "You remembered?"

"I just wish you could have been there with me. They are far more beautiful in the valley than in this book."

She clutched it tightly against her chest. "I love it. Thank you."

He positioned himself to face her and took her hands in his. "You don't like it here, do you?"

"Why would you think that?" her eyes narrowed.

"Northwind and Elisor are different. I could only assume you prefer one over the other."

"It is different here, but I've lived here for ten years now." She shrugged. "I've grown fond of it in my own way."

"You're lying," he said softly.

"No, I'm not," she shook her head.

"Your nose twitches when you lie," he pointed out.

She touched her pointy nose and blushed. "I... I didn't know that."

"I think it's cute," he smiled warmly.

"I do miss Elisor." Her eyes met the ground, admitting what he suspected. "But I know where my duty lies."

"That's what I wanted to talk to you about." He pulled a simple turquoise beaded necklace from his pocket.

Her jaw dropped. "My mother's necklace. I haven't seen it since I was a little girl."

"I asked for your father's blessing."

"His blessing?" She stared at him wide-eyed. "For what?"

"I know our parents arranged our marriage when we were children. It has always been expected of us." He took a deep breath. "But I'm asking for myself now. Will you be my wife?"

"And if I say no, would I be free to return to Elisor?"

He was not expecting her to respond that way. "If that is what you want," he stammered. "Then yes. I only want you to be happy."

She smiled. "I am happiest when I'm with you."

His eyes lit up, he breathed deeply. "Are you saying yes?"

"Yes, Rollo," she caressed his cheek. "I love you."

He leaned in and kissed her forehead. "You nearly made my heart stop, woman."

She kissed his lips, "You're stuck with me."

He ran his fingers through her hair and whispered, "I'm ok with that."

CHAPTER 8

ADONIJAH

Travelling south toward the forests of the Western Lands at top speed, four Shadows on horseback left a cloud of dust behind them as they began their search for the Hunter. On one side of the dirt road were stretches of fields and on the other side of the road were unending acres of forestlands. Any villager who caught sight of the black riders immediately took refuge in their humble homes and prayed they were not the ones the mercenaries were sent to find.

Unlike the other frightened peasants, a hooded figure perched high in a pine tree waited for the four Shadows to pass his hiding spot. As soon as the last rider approached, the cloaked man jumped down, landed on the mercenary's horse, and stabbed him in the chest.

Ditching the body, the vigilante rode toward the other three mercenaries undetected. Approaching the next Shadow, he stood up on the horse and leapt onto the next one. The black rider did not have a chance to react before the vigilante snapped his neck and threw him from his mount.

He was noticed by the third Shadow who threw a knife at him. Being quite skilled with knife throwing, the cloaked attacker caught the incoming dagger and quickly returned it, stabbing the masked soldier in the neck.

One Shadow was left, and he was tackled to the ground.

The Shadow drew his sword while his mysterious enemy held two knives, one in each of his fingerless leather-gloved hands. Barreling toward the unknown figure, the last remaining Shadow swung his weapon with great force. Avoiding the incoming blow, the vigilante slid beneath the soldier and sliced the back of both his knees, rendering him incapable of escape.

The rogue fighter made his way to the survivor as he tried to crawl away. Stepping on his black cape made it easy to turn him on his back. He ripped off his black mask, but it was not him.

"I seek a Shadow who wears a mask to hide his disfigured face," the vigilante stated his purpose.

"We all wear masks," the Shadow hissed.

Dropping a knee on the wounded Shadow's chest, the hooded victor leaned in closer. "You see my dilemma then. More of you will die until I find the one I seek."

"I do not know who you seek."

Adonijah put a knife to the Shadow's throat. "Oh, but I believe you do know him. It is said, he is seven feet tall with burn scars all over his body and is missing an eye. We common folk know him as the 'Nameless Rider'."

"Who are you?" The Shadow squinted, trying to get a good look at the face hidden in the darkness.

"The last man you will ever see." Adonijah slit the Shadow's throat.

Rising slowly, his hooded face still a mystery, he retraced his path to unmask the three deceased Shadows. Coming up empty handed, he disappeared deep into the forest, leaving their bodies to rot on the main road.

CHAPTER 9
ROLLO

Rollo splashed water on his face then patted himself dry with a nearby towel. Hunched over the bowl he looked into the mirror that sat against the wall and stared silently at his reflection. He had not slept much. His mind had been flooded with a thousand thoughts. But there was one question that tormented him.

Was he ready to be King?

Consumed with his thoughts, he did not hear the knock at his chamber doors. It was only when Tala spoke, he returned to reality.

"It is time, Prince Rollo." Tala stood in the threshold with his hands clasped behind his back.

Rollo stared at the Andrago in the mirror. "I don't know if I can do this, Tala."

"Entertaining the Lords and Ladies of the court was never your mother's favorite obligation either."

"It's not that." Rollo rubbed his forehead.

Tala shut the door. "Then what troubles you?"

Rollo retreated to the bench at the foot of his bed and sat down. "I am not ready to be king."

The Andrago joined him. "Your father thought the same thing the night before he took the crown."

"I wish I had known him," he sighed. "Maybe I'd understand myself better."

"Dichali was the most patient and humble man among the Andrago," Tala smiled fondly. "And believe me, he had no reason to be. Even in our youth he was skilled with all kinds of weapons. We knew he was meant for greatness."

"But?"

"He didn't want to wage anymore wars." He leaned back and crossed one leg over the other. "He wanted a family and desired more than anything for the Andrago to live in peace. Marrying your mother was supposed to fulfill both dreams."

"Did it?" Rollo's eyes were fixed on him.

"For a time," he nodded. "During those few years, I had never seen him happier. He and your mother shared the same spirit. And he loved you more than anything. He would be proud of the man you have become."

The Prince rubbed his hands together and stared at the floor. "You think so?"

"I know it." Tala patted him on the back reassuringly. "He may be gone, but his spirit lives on in you. He will guide you during this next phase of your life."

"Will you be there too?"

He nodded. "Whenever you need me, I will be there."

"I told my mother I plan to appoint you as my Second." The prince squirmed, unsure of what he would say. "I'm hoping you will accept."

"It would be my greatest honor." He embraced the prince tightly, wiping a tear from his eye. "You will make a great king. It is in your blood."

"I still have so much to learn."

Tala pulled away from him and rested his hands on his shoulders. "A good king is ready to rule; a great king is ready to learn."

"My mother said the same thing to me yesterday." He was confused.

Tala's mouth twisted. "They are your father's words."

Rollo shifted his weight. "You still won't tell me how he died?"

"I still have a week of celebrations before I fulfill my promise," he smirked, smoothing his clothes as he stood. "I will give you a few minutes to finish up." He bowed and left the room.

Rollo breathed in deeply as he rose from his seat and opened one of the wooden drawers near his bed. Inside was a piece of paper, a sketch of his father.

He stared at the drawing then looked at his reflection in the mirror. Other than his green eyes, one would think it was a drawing of the same person. His mother drew it shortly before she gave birth to him. She kept it in her room until he was eight years old and only parted with it because Rollo begged her for it. He wanted his father to watch over him as he slept. He dragged the tips of his fingers across it.

"It's in my blood." He whispered Tala's words under his breath. "It's in my blood."

There was a soft knock on his door.

"Come in." He placed the sketch back inside the drawer and closed it.

He thought Tala had returned but was pleasantly surprised to see Leoti standing there instead. Her braided hair was adorned with pearls and her thin lips were painted a dark red. He had never seen her in a billowing gown before. She preferred simple dresses and even pants when she could get away with it. The off-shoulder white dress she wore left him speechless.

"You look incredible." He could not tear his eyes off her.

She ran her hands over her braid, "Your mother gave these pearls to me while you were away. She said they were from the Isles of Myr."

He took her hand and kissed it. "It's my Name Day, but I have a feeling all eyes are going to be on you."

"Stop it." She nudged him.

"It's true." He grinned, intertwining his fingers with hers. "The Almighty blessed me a thousand times over with you."

She kissed his cheek. "I need you to do something for me."

"Anything," he whispered.

"Would you help me with this?" In her hand was the turquoise necklace.

"Of course." He fastened it around her dainty neck and kissed her bare shoulder. "How would you feel about getting married next week?"

"Next week?" She turned around wide eyed. "So soon? Is that even possible?"

"Not soon enough if you ask me." He held her in his arms. "If I could marry you tonight, I would."

"You are too romantic for your own good, Rollo." She tapped the tip of his nose with her tattooed index finger.

"I'm serious." His eyes twinkled. "Being away from you for six months made me realize I want you by my side. I need you by my side."

"What would your mother say?" Her left eyebrow lifted. She was teasing him. She already knew the answer.

"You know my mother loves you as if you were her own flesh and blood. She's been praying for this moment since the day I took my first step." His giggle always put a smile on her face.

"And I love her like a mother." Her gaze fell to her feet.

"What is it?" He lifted her chin.

"I wish my mother could be here."

"I know you do." He embraced her again. "Our loved ones may be gone, but their spirits live on in us."

"And who told you that?" She wrapped her arms around his waist.

"This wise old man I know," he shrugged with a sheepish grin.

"Oh, is that so?" She rolled her eyes. "Which wise old man do you speak of?"

"Your father."

"Ah, I should have known," she chuckled with a sarcastic sigh. "He tells me that every night."

"Let's hope he's right."

Her gaze caused his heart to race.

"Why are you looking at me that way?" He brushed a loose strand of her hair from her round face.

She stood up on the tip of her toes and gently kissed his lips. "I love you," she whispered. "And I *would* marry you tonight if we could."

"Why don't we then?" Just by the tone of his voice she could tell he meant it.

"What about the party?"

"I suppose we will be a little late." His smile sent a warm sensation down her spine. "Should I send for the Elder?"

She nibbled on her bottom lip, failing to mask the smile that stretched across her face. "I think you should."

The Andrago Elder arrived shortly after being summoned and found the young lovers on the balcony. He bowed and touched the middle of his forehead with his index finger and floated it down to the center of his chest.

"Prince Rollo. My Lady. How may I be of service?" The wrinkles etched into his skin enfolded his narrow eyes, but his smile was as genuine as any.

"We wish to be married." Rollo patted Leoti's arm wrapped around his.

"My blessings, Prince Rollo," he nodded in approval. "When would you like the marriage ceremony to take place?"

"Now." He barely waited for the Elder to finish the question.

"Now?" He rubbed the back of his neck. "This is rather unorthodox. Royal weddings are planned well in advance."

"Please." Leoti's silky voice eased him.

The old man touched his chest with a tight-lipped smile. "Who am I to deny two souls becoming one?"

Standing on the balcony as the sun set, the Elder had them hold one another's hands as he wrapped them in red silk. Together, they recited the traditional vows of the Andrago.

You are my shelter,
You are my warmth.
You are my now,
You are my always.
You are my breath,
Until we breathe our last.
From this day forward,
You are mine and I am yours.
Forever my spirit,
Forever my soul.

"May the Almighty bless you." The Elder grasped their hands in his. "May the Almighty keep you."

CHAPTER 10

PASH

The Commander of Shadows made his way down the white stone hallway toward the queen's quarters. He was to escort her to the party, although he did not like public celebrations. He was a man of action and few words. Chatting with Lords and Ladies was never his strong suit but put a weapon in his hand and he would be noticed.

After a glass of wine and a good night's rest, Pash had come to terms with his promotion to Iron Guard. It was not a title he had desired, but he was a soldier, and obeying orders was what he did best.

"Pash." Gershom skulked around the corner and motioned for his son to approach him.

"Father," he greeted him with a sigh.

"What word from the West?" Gershom whispered.

"Nothing has been reported."

"They need to hurry their search," Gershom was visibly displeased, "my life is in danger."

"I will be ordering them to return immediately." Pash tried to walk by his father, but he grabbed his arm.

"What do you mean?" he hissed. "They haven't found the Hunter."

"And they won't," he jerked his arm back. "You will have to take your concerns up with the new Commander of Shadows. Perhaps, he will oblige."

"I grow tired of your games, Pash," the Bear growled. "I have told you how important this mission is. As Second in Command, I order you -"

"You don't know, do you?" Pash was giddy.

"Know what?" his eyes narrowed.

"The Queen plans to announce her abdication tonight. Prince Rollo will be crowned within the week."

Gershom shrunk back. He placed his hand on the wall for balance as his breathing quickened. "You're lying."

Pash shook his head; he was amused by his father's reaction. "She told me yesterday and informed me I will be the new king's Iron Guard."

"But..." Gershom rubbed his forehead. "I am her Second in Command."

"Not for much longer I'm afraid." He did not even try to hide the smirk that crept onto his face. "I have reason to believe that the prince intends to appoint Tala the Andrago as his Second."

The Bear furrowed his brow, his pale skin flushed.

Pash knew what he was thinking. His father had never liked Tala. It was bad enough to be stripped of his title, but for that title and all the power that came with it to be given to a foreigner was more than his father could swallow.

"Niabi can't do this to me." Gershom paced. "We made a deal."

Pash shrugged. "She is the Queen. She can do as she pleases." He brought his right arm across his chest with a slight bow. "I have matters that require my attention. Enjoy the party, Father."

"She won't get away with this," he muttered. "No one undermines the Bear."

CHAPTER II

SALOME

As night shrouded the Tree House Forest, Salome, Crispin, and Zophar were scattered around the living space completing their own tasks. Zophar puffed his favorite hand-crafted pipe, while Crispin carved a small block of wood into the likeness of a wolf by the fire.

Salome was obsessed with cleanliness in their tight living quarters and spent her evening organizing the small space as she saw fit. Maintaining the house was a peaceful task for her and kept her mind from wandering into troubled waters. But as routine as their evening seemed, there was an unexpected knock at their door.

"Were we expecting a visitor?" Crispin eyed the others.

"Not that I am aware of," Zophar shook his head and kept on smoking.

Salome walked to the door armed with a knife concealed behind her back, and slowly opened it. Before her stood a tall, clean shaven man with long platinum blonde hair under his hood and hypnotizing grey eyes.

"May I help you, sir?" she asked.

"The question is not what you can do for me, but what can I do for you?" The cloaked figure returned her question.

Confused, she tightened her grip on her knife. "I'm afraid I don't understand."

"You need not be afraid of me. The weapon you hold is not necessary, I mean you no harm." He spoke with such a gentleness that she believed he indeed was no threat.

"How did you know about the -"

"I am a Seer. I have come to speak with you and your brother," he interrupted. The old man's demeanor spurred Crispin to make his way toward the front door.

"I'm sorry, you must have the wrong house. We don't know a Seer." She attempted to close the door.

"Ah, but the Seer knows you, Salome," he smiled warmly, stopping Crispin dead in his tracks.

"How do you know my name?"

Zophar leapt to the door, battle axe in hand, "Who goes there?" He ripped the door wide open. "Harbona?" He took a step back. "Is it really you?"

"Zophar, my old friend," Harbona entered the house and embraced him.

The siblings stood in confused silence. For as long as Zophar had been their guardian, he had never entertained visitors.

"What is going on?" Crispin furrowed his brow.

"Crispin, Salome, this is Harbona the Seer," Zophar introduced the foreigner.

"How do you know each other?" Crispin's nostrils flared.

"I was one of your father's advisors many years ago." Harbona leaned his walking staff against the wall and made himself comfortable.

"You knew our father?" The prince shifted his weight.

"Oh, yes. I know all of you very well," Harbona smiled, knowing he was looking upon the heirs of Issachar. As he removed his hood, the banishment brand around his right eye made Salome realize she had seen him before.

"I know you," she took a step forward, visions of him walking around the Keep with her eldest brother flashed before her eyes. "You knew Lykos."

Yes" he nodded. The corners of his eyes crinkled. "Your brother was one of the finest men I have ever known."

"It has been far too long, my friend." Zophar patted the Seer on the back.

"I have kept my eye on you from afar to ensure your safety." Harbona's tone changed.

"You are here for a reason then." Zophar's breathing quickened as he glanced at his wards.

"I am afraid so," he confirmed.

"They know where we are?" The old warrior exhaled a puff of smoke, hoping to take the edge off.

"The time has come to reclaim Northwind." His eyes lit up. "The Year of the Hunter has begun."

"Year of the Hunter? What are you talking about?" Crispin scoffed. "There hasn't been a Hunter in over two hundred years. And even if that were true, what has that got to do with us?"

"*You* wrote the note," Salome figured out who 'H' was in Zophar's letter.

Harbona nodded. "What do you know of the Hunters?"

"Stories our mother told us – the first was Malachi over a thousand years ago. He was given the mark of the Hunter to avenge the deaths of the innocent." Salome recited all she could remember. "I'm afraid I don't remember much more than that."

"Have you ever wondered about the discoloration of your eye?" Harbona pointed a thin finger toward her.

"What about my eye?" Her shoulders tightened. *What a bold question,* she thought to herself.

"You believe you were cursed? That there is nothing more to the pattern the dots create?" He leaned forward, staring at her eye.

"If it's a curse handed down by some unknown god, then there's not much I can do about it." She shifted her weight, now defensive.

"What are you trying to say, Harbona?" Zophar set his pipe down on the small wooden table.

"You were not cursed, Salome." The Seer stared at her, even though he could sense it made her uncomfortable. "You were marked by the Almighty."

"Marked?" Crispin straightened from the wall he had been leaning against. "Are you saying -"

"She is the Hunter?" Harbona finished his sentence. "Yes."

"Me?" Her eyes darted around the room.

"You," the Seer repeated himself.

"Aren't Hunters male?" Crispin stepped toward the group. "There's never been a female Hunter."

"The Almighty does not choose his servants based on whether they are male or female. He chooses the heart," Harbona's eyes shifted back to a silent Salome, "and your heart has been chosen." He rested his back against the narrow wooden chair. "The Year of the Hunter has begun, and Gershom knows this. He fears this. He has dispatched a company of the Queen's Shadows to search these forests for the Hunter."

"So, he doesn't know who the Hunter is?" Zophar was only slightly relieved. "Does he know which village to find her in?"

"No to both," Harbona shook his head, "but we cannot stay here. It is no longer safe."

Crispin could not stop gawking at Salome's discolored eye. For years he teased her. He too believed she was cursed by one of the gods but now...

"Have you always known?" Crispin's tone was equally threatening as it was fearful.

"Of course not." She crossed her arms. "You don't actually believe any of this, do you?" Looking around the room she could sense she was the only one who had any doubt. "This is nonsense," she hissed like a cornered animal. "I am not a Hunter! I'm just... just me. I don't know what you want from me. I am not who you seek."

"Salome, listen to me." Crispin rested his hands on her shoulders. "We can avenge our family. Once I kill Niabi and Gershom, we can finally return home."

"As noble as that sounds," the Seer chimed in, "I am afraid that is not your destiny."

"You just said it was the Year of the Hunter; the time to take back our city. Are you now saying that is not the case?" Crispin's brow furrowed; he appeared as irritated as he was confused.

"Only the Hunter will avenge the blood of the innocent." Harbona sat stoically at the table with his thin fingers intertwined. "I believe you had a dream that needed interpreting?"

By the look on Crispin's face, he was clearly thrown by the sudden change in subject. How could he have possibly known about his dream?

"Tell me your dream and I will tell you what it means. Maybe then you will believe me." The Seer's piercing grey eyes did not shy away from him.

Crispin flipped a chair around and straddled it directly across the table from him. "I am fighting in a great battle in an open field outside of Northwind when I come face to face with a man."

"Gershom." Harbona identified and motioned for him to continue.

"He is mocking me, blood dripping from his hands. I reach for my sword to fight him, but it will not budge."

The Seer nodded his head as he stroked his chin, "You will indeed come face to face with Gershom during a great battle. In that moment, you will have a choice. Either you attempt to kill him and forfeit your life, or you leave him untouched and live to rule your people as King of the North. Taking Gershom's life is not your destiny. Your path is to forge the way for the Hunter."

Silence engulfed the room. Tension was thick and frustrations were at an all-time high until Salome spoke.

"Are you saying Crispin will die if he tries to do what is right?"

"Listen to him." Zophar's voice was raspy. "I've learned from years of experience to heed Harbona's words."

"You are afraid." Harbona saw right through her.

"Wouldn't you be afraid if you were me?" She was not normally one to pace around the room, but that evening was different. She could not sit still; her body would not allow it. "How can you be so sure about this?"

"Why do you think you happened to escape the night your sister attacked?" Harbona asked.

The question caught her off guard. *What did he mean by 'happened to escape'?*

"From the day you were born, any Immortal who looked upon your face knew of your destiny. Even your mortal brother knew. Your brother believed. Your brother understood his duty to ensure your survival no matter the cost."

"Lykos knew?" There was a lump in her throat. His face flashed before her eyes. She closed them, rubbing her hands against her forehead. She could hear the screams. She could smell the sulfur from her city burning. She could feel the fear as if she was reliving that night all over again.

"I know you are afraid, Salome." Harbona grasped her hand in his, snapping her out of her flashbacks. "Don't let your fear hinder you from fulfilling your destiny."

"I am just one person." Her palms began to sweat, and she struggled to breathe.

"But you are not alone."

She ripped her hand from his. "I cannot do what you ask of me." She darted up the creaky stairs.

SHE SAT with her knees to her chest on the roof of the tree house in complete silence, gazing at the stars in the night sky. They had always brought her comfort in the past but staring at them now only stressed her.

There he was: The Hunter.

Sparkling brightly, mocking her.

Why me? That was the only question she had and knew no one would be able to give her an answer that would satisfy her.

"I remember when we were younger all you ever dreamed about was being the North's first female warrior." Crispin interrupted her thoughts when he sat down next to her. "To have songs written and tapestries woven depicting your heroic conquests and countless victories against our enemies." He tried to hide it but could not help but stare at her discolored eye. "We all made fun of you and as it turns out, you're the only one of us meant for glory."

"Save your flatteries," her nostrils flared. "Say what you actually came here to say."

He took a deep breath. "We've spent years training, waiting for the day we could face those who stole everything from us." He leaned toward her; the tone of his voice more serious than sentimental. "Would you have us miss our opportunity due to your fear? Our family -"

"Is dead," she interrupted, the sharpness in her tone stung. "Nothing we do will ever change that. The North has forgotten us."

"If you really believe that then what was the purpose of Lykos sacrificing himself to save us?"

"For us to survive."

"For us to live." He rested his hands atop hers. "We owe it to him to do more than waste away in this forest."

"The North is not our home anymore," she whispered. "This is our home, and these are now our people. Why can you not see that?"

"Other than Zophar, you are the most tenacious person I know. You've never once backed down from a fight," he rubbed his temples, desperate to understand her hesitation. "What are you so afraid of?"

"I cannot lose you too." She touched his face, fighting back tears. "Have we not lost and suffered enough? How much more must we sacrifice?"

He moved away from her. "You don't believe we could defeat her."

"Why do you think we can? Because an old man with a staff told us we could? Because of this," she pointed to her marked eye, blood boiling.

"Because I believe in you."

"That is not enough."

"Why not?"

"Because," her voice cracked, "I do not believe in myself." She had never admitted that out loud before. She always carried herself in a confident manner, but she was rattled and could not hide anymore.

"Don't think for one moment you will be safe by doing nothing. Those who stand by and watch lose their lives the same as those who fight to keep theirs." He touched her hand. "I know you are afraid but know you will not fight alone."

She withdrew her hand. "Touching words from one who will not carry the burden that is being forced upon me."

"Salome, please -"

She scrambled to her feet, nostrils flared, "All you've talked about for years is killing our sister -"

"She is *not* my sister," he nearly shouted as he too jumped to his feet.

"Denying our blood does not make it less tainted." She stepped up to him. "Does it not anger you to know, you trained for years to challenge them, and you will never be able to touch them and live?"

"Does it not anger you to know, you are the only one who can do what is right and you would rather waste away in this forest?" He squared his shoulders up to her, staring down at her. "We all have paths we must follow."

"There lies our problem," she scoffed, not backing down. "You wish to fight them, but if you do you will die. I do not want a war, yet if I do not go, my life is forfeit. It seems the Almighty is playing a cruel game and we are nothing more than pawns."

"I would gladly be a used pawn in order to make a difference."

"I am no one's pawn!" Her eyes narrowed.

"Then take your place and fulfill your destiny!"

"I want no part in this." She retreated down the wooden steps and locked herself in her room, ensuring no one would bother her for the rest of the evening.

CHAPTER 12

NIABI

The Great Hall was filled with Lords and Ladies of the royal court who lined up to have but a moment with the young prince to wish him well on his Name Day. With Leoti by his side, Rollo stood taller and looked more confident. He looked ready to be king.

The royal trumpets blared bringing the room full of guests to a hush; their queen had arrived with Pash and her Nephilim Iron Guard following closely behind. She might have intimidated all who stood before her, but none could deny how radiant she looked that evening. In a form fitting dark green dress with a long train trailing behind her, her shimmering white crown was accentuated by the crystal embellished neck and waistline. Her raven black hair raised in an up-do exposed her bare back as she glided through the room of dignitaries.

Rollo met her in the middle of the Great Hall, kneeling before her with one arm crossed over his chest. As he rose, he extended his hand, inviting his mother to dance with him. The music began to play as mother and son shared the first dance of the evening.

"You look beautiful," Rollo whispered in her ear and smiled.

"A mother never did have a better son." She noticed the twinkle in his eyes. "Something is different about you tonight. What is it?"

"Why do you say that?" The slight tilt of his head confirmed her suspicions.

"I am your mother, Rollo. I have seen those dancing eyes before." She stroked his cheek. "You remind me so much of your father. He would be so proud of the man you are. Oh, how he loved you."

The shakiness in her voice made him hesitate before asking her what he really wanted to know. "Will you tell me how he died?"

Her smile faded, "Now is not the time for such melancholy stories."

"I want to know," he pleaded. "I need to know."

She was visibly unwilling to speak on the matter but humored him. "Your father was assassinated shortly after you turned two. The same blade was meant for you as well, but I made sure you did not suffer the same fate."

"Who killed him?" he urged her to give him details.

"All those responsible for Dichali's death have been dealt with." Her answer was sharp and by the tone in her voice, she was done answering his questions.

He furrowed his brow. "Why won't you tell me the truth?"

"Perhaps some truths should remain in the past." She maintained a smile and nodded her head toward the onlookers. As a royal, maintaining a certain appearance was vital.

"What are you afraid of me knowing?" He was not interested in what the Lords and Ladies thought of him and pressed further.

"There are things I have done that I am not proud of," her eyes narrowed, and her lips tightened. "If you knew the truth, you would see me as most Adalorians do: as a monster."

"You are my mother." He gripped her hand tightly. "Whatever you did, it wouldn't change how I see you."

"I wish I could believe that," she sighed. "I want you to know and remember me for who I am now. Not what I was."

Rollo was just as stubborn as she was. "If you don't tell me the truth before the week is through, I will deny my birthright, I will refuse the crown, and I will never sit on the White Throne."

Her mouth dropped. "Rollo, don't be -"

"How am I to be king if I do not know my own history," he interrupted. He softened his tone. "Nothing you have done would ever change my love for you. All I want is to know what happened to my father."

She could see learning from the Andrago had indeed impacted him; he was bolder. "Before your coronation, I will answer any question you ask of me. But not tonight. Tonight, we celebrate you." She caught Leoti's eye and noticed her blush. "Now what is it you have to tell me?"

The sudden change in subject threw him. "What do you mean?"

"Like I said before," she tilted her head toward the Andrago maiden. "I have seen those dancing eyes before."

"I can never hide anything from you," he smiled as his eyes met Leoti's. "I married Leoti tonight."

Her eyes widened; that was not what she was expecting to hear. "Married?"

"Married by an Andrago Elder at sunset."

The Andrago believed that by reciting marriage vows at sunset, it signified the death of two individuals and the birth of one spirit.

"I promise we will have a northern ceremony as is customary for northern kings but -" He realized her eyes were glossed over. "I hope you are not angry, Mother."

"Angry? How could I be angry?" She whispered with tears in her eyes and kissed his cheek. "My son, I couldn't be happier. You two now share the same spirit."

"You're really not upset?"

"All I ever wanted was for you to be happy with someone the way I was happy with Dichali."

"I am happy." The corners of his eyes crinkled as he smiled at his new wife. "She means everything to me."

"Then stop talking to me and dance with her." She nudged him in Leoti's direction.

Rollo kissed his mother's cheek and bowed. "My heart and my soul."

"My moon and my stars." She squeezed his hand and watched with a warm smile as the newlyweds danced. The way they looked deeply into one another's eyes reminded her of Dichali. It was as if no one else in the room existed.

Tala approached her, offering her a glass of wine. "It's almost time."

She guzzled half the glass. "Then maybe I will stop worrying about him."

"Are you sure you wish to abdicate so suddenly?"

"I swore an oath and I intend to keep it." She could not take her eyes off her son. "He looks so much like him, does he not?"

"Spitting image." Tala nodded his head, taking a sip of wine from his glass.

"My heart breaks that he is not here."

"We will see him again when Death comes for us." Tala touched his forehead and dragged his finger down to his chest.

"May she be patient in her reaping." She mimicked the same motion.

"They make a fine couple." Tala's chest puffed up.

"It seems," her velvety voice caught his attention, "that we are now family, my dear friend."

His sideways glance was filled with confusion. "What do you mean?"

"My son just told me he married your daughter before coming to the party," she grinned. "Married by the Andrago Elder at sunset."

His gaze settled on the couple. His mind was flooded with memories of Leoti as a child. She had grown up so quickly and now she was a married woman. Married to the future King of Northwind. "It seems like yesterday I was holding her for the first time."

"Our babies aren't babies anymore." She rubbed his back with a fond smile. "She will make a fine queen."

Her eyes caught sight of Gershom who had just slithered into the room. By the look on his face, she knew someone had alerted him to her plans. Once he spotted her, he weaved through the crowd toward her.

Tala's brow furrowed, "He looks like he has something to say." He had never cared for Gershom, and he had not bothered to hide his disdain for him.

"He knows." She finished her glass of wine and sighed.

"You didn't tell him?" His eyes bulged.

"Since when do I have to inform anyone of my intentions?" she snorted.

He placed his hand on top of the handle of his sword. "Let's hope he remembers he is in the White Keep and not in one of his favorite brothels."

Gershom reached them with fire in his eyes and throbbing temples.

"Lord Gershom," she greeted him with formality. "Have you wished my son a blessing on his Name Day?"

"Word has reached my ears that you intend to abdicate the throne," he growled.

Niabi noticed Tala's grip tighten around the handle of his blade and motioned for him to stand down. "You have heard correctly. I do plan to abdicate tonight and within the week have my son crowned King of the North."

"How can you give up the crown after everything we did to secure it?" He spat every word through clenched teeth.

"Surely you did not believe I would rule forever."

"What about my position?" He fidgeted. "We made a deal."

"You know the tradition of northern kings. My son will appoint his own Second." She lifted her chin. "Do not fret, Lord Gershom, you have more than enough money to live comfortably for the rest of your days."

"But our agreement -"

"Has been fulfilled!" She cut him off with a hiss. "You have prospered as my Second. When I step down, you shall too."

"Your son is not ready to be king."

She was silent. The look in her eyes was one Tala had not seen in years. She was no longer standing before them as Niabi, Queen of the North. The Green-Eyed Raven awakened within her. She flashed the tip of a hidden knife in the left sleeve of her gown.

"If you care even an inkling for your tongue, Lord Gershom, I suggest you remain silent and do as you are told." Her eyes narrowed and her speech slowed. "Remember it is *I* who rule the North, not you."

Knowing she never made idle threats, and aware Tala was more than eager to strike him down, he crinkled his nose and retreated to an unoccupied corner of the room.

Tala watched him intently. "He may end up being a problem."

"You know how we deal with problems, Tala." She refocused on her son who had once again started to greet people in the room. "Do not worry about Gershom. He has always been a man of many words with little action." She patted his arm. "Congratulate your daughter on her marriage. I am sure she wants you to know the good news."

Tala bowed and left the queen with her stoic Iron Guard, Anaktu.

A voice yelled from the crowd. "Speech, Prince Rollo, speech."

Applause echoed throughout the Great Hall as Rollo made his way to the small platform to appease his guests with a toast.

"I am honored to have you all here tonight to celebrate my name day. Over the past few months, I have come to appreciate you, my people, more than ever before. I spent the last half of this year with the Andrago, learning the ways of my father and all I could think about was when I would be able to return to my home. Now that I have returned, I am ready to be the leader I was born to be and lead us into the future." The guests applauded and hung on every word he spoke. "One day, I will bear the crown and responsibility my mother now carries, and I promise you, I will do all I can to ensure our people thrive, even though at times, I do not feel that I am ready to be king." The Lords and Ladies seemed uneasy with his confession. "Someone very wise told me that a good king is ready to rule while a great king is ready to learn. I am not perfect but this I can guarantee, I am ready to learn." The crowd once again erupted in applause. Rollo lifted his goblet. "And now, I would like to raise my glass to the people of the North and my mother, Queen Niabi for… for a…"

Something was wrong. Rollo started to sway from dizziness and his eyesight started to blur. His heart raced so fast, he thought it would burst from his chest. Dropping his goblet, the prince stumbled off the platform.

Niabi pushed through the crowd to get to her son as he clutched his chest. "Rollo!" She screamed, catching him as he collapsed to the floor. Tightly holding him in her arms she said, "Rollo, speak to me. Rollo." He continued to gasp for air. The queen looked around the room. "Someone bring the healers!"

"My heart," Rollo wheezed. "Mother, my heart…"

"Stay with me, Rollo, stay with me," she rocked her son in her arms.

Leoti dropped to her knees and grabbed his hand, tears streaming down her face. "Rollo."

He touched Leoti's face and forced a smile. "I love you."

"Don't!" she cried. "Don't leave me."

He weakly reached up and touched his mother's face, "My heart and my soul." His eyes closed.

"Rollo?" Niabi whispered in a panic. "Rollo?" He was gone.

Pash knelt beside her.

"Get them out of here," she demanded.

"Everyone out," Tala barked. "Everyone out." Noticing Gershom was the first to leave, Tala peered down at Pash, who tried comforting their queen.

Three healers arrived and scurried to the prince's limp body, but it was too late for them to save him. All they could do now was take his body to prepare him for a traditional Northern burial. One of the healers knelt and grabbed Rollo's arm which was met with Niabi's wrath.

She unsheathed the dagger hidden in the left sleeve of her dress and chopped off his hand. "The next one of you who attempts to touch my son will beg for Death before I have finished with them. Get out!"

Terrified, the healers scrambled from her sight, leaving only Pash, Leoti and Tala in the room while Anaktu guarded the entrance. Leoti rocked back and forth holding Rollo's hand in hers, sobbing uncontrollably.

"For eighteen years I did everything in my power to protect my son," Niabi choked. "As a parent, that was my first priority, and I failed." She brushed the hair from his face, tears streaming down her cheeks. "Tala, Pash. I need you both to make the necessary burial arrangements following the traditions of our ancestors."

"It will be done, my Queen." Tala wiped his face clean.

"She lied to me," Niabi muttered.

"My Queen?" Pash eyed her.

"Leave me."

Pash knelt in front of her with Rollo's body between them, "We must prepare him."

Her lip quivered when she realized she would have to release her son and accept that he was gone. "He never should have gone before me. A mother should never have to bury her child."

Pash gently rested his hand upon hers, but she withdrew.

"Forgive me, I meant no offense."

Her eyes were filled with a pain so palpable it caused him to tear up. Niabi gently kissed her son's forehead and released him from her tight embrace. She stood up and reached for Leoti's hand and squeezed it.

Tala wrapped his arms around his daughter and escorted her out of the room.

Niabi left the Great Hall, swearing she would never set foot in that room again.

~

NIABI ENTERED her chambers and headed to the stone hearth that sat in the middle of her room. She reached up to the right sconce and pulled it down. The stone hearth spun, revealing a dark room only she knew about. Since she had not used the room in years, dust had covered all the ancient texts and wooden furniture in the secret space. The grieving queen wiped clean the only book that sat out on the table and began flipping through the brittle pages. Once she found the incantation she was searching for, she pulled out her dagger and walked over to a pedestal filled with water. She ripped the left sleeve of her dress which revealed a black blotch that had the appearance of a spreading poison creeping up her arm. She took her dagger and sliced her left hand allowing the black blood to drip into the basin.

"Show me her face."

The blood swirled around the water until the image of an old woman was visible. Her wild white hair and weathered brown skin did not scream villainous, but Niabi knew her for who she truly was: The Old Witch of Endor. Niabi hunched over the bowl.

"Show me where she is hiding."

A beam of light rose from the bloody water and floated to the map of Adalore that hung on the wall. It illuminated a small area in the Black Forest. The Black Forest was now known to be inhabited by less than desirable folk that would not hesitate to skin you for your worldly possessions. Although these woodland dwellers were menacing, they would be no match for Niabi and her men.

"Anaktu," Niabi yelled for her nine-foot-tall bodyguard to enter the secret room.

She kept her eyes fixed on the reflection of her enemy. Her blood still dripped down the side of her hand, staining the floor.

Gritting her teeth, she gave the Nephilim his orders, "Bring her to me *alive*."

Anaktu, who never spoke, crossed his right arm across his enormous chest and left his master in the dimly lit room.

Enraged, she threw her dagger at the map of Adalore hanging on her dark stone wall, piercing the very spot the witch now inhabited. She screamed from the depths of her soul, releasing a sound she had never heard another human being utter before. She grabbed books, vases, trinkets, whatever was nearest, and smashed them against the walls and floor. She fell to the ground, exhausted; her heart was broken.

CHAPTER 13
CRISPIN

As the sun crept above the horizon, the usual routine the villagers carried out was interrupted by the sound of pounding hooves coming from the dirt path leading to the Tree House Forest. Every Adalorian's nightmare was now upon them. A troop of Shadows had trotted into their community and that only meant one thing: they were looking for someone, and they would not leave until they were completely satisfied with the results of their interrogation.

Kicking in door after door, the Shadows herded and dragged all the frightened villagers into the main square. Pushed into one group, Korah caught sight of Crispin and rushed over to him.

"What is happening?" The young boy grabbed Crispin's arm in great distress as the Shadows encircled the villagers.

"I don't know. Stay close to me. Everything will be alright." Crispin did his best to ease the young boy's nerves but knew if Shadows were in their village, it was more than likely going to end poorly.

He saw when Zophar and Harbona were ripped from their beds, but Salome was not with them. She was not in the house at all.

Once the last tree house was emptied of its occupants, the leader of the Shadows stepped forward to address the crowd.

Neth was a man of average height with broad shoulders and a sinister appearance. Although not as tall as the other Shadows, he was still an intimidating specimen and people feared the mere sight of him. His commanding presence brought the crowd to a hush before he had even uttered a single word. Once all eyes rested on him, he spoke.

"Lord Gershom, Second in Command of the Northern Lands, has issued a warrant for the arrest of one who bears the mark of the Hunter. Anyone who gives us any information toward the capture of this criminal will be handsomely rewarded." Neth waited for the quiet members of the village to speak up with the information he sought. "You have ten seconds, then my offer is void."

One brave villager finally spoke up. "Sir, we do not know anyone who bears such a mark."

Neth shot the most hateful expression in the villager's direction. "I know he is here in this forest. This is your last chance before I take my investigation further." An eerie silence fell upon the group. "Have it your way."

Neth snapped his fingers and ordered his men to sift through the terrified crowd and grab the first young boy they could find. They dragged the squirming child forward to the dismay of the crowd. Women screamed as Korah was thrust before Neth who now had his muscular hand on the young boy's shoulder. Crispin had tried to grab Korah before he made it to the front of the crowd, but one of the Shadows punched him and bloodied up the side of his mouth.

Neth unsheathed his dagger, alerting the villagers to impending doom. "The blood of this boy stains your hands." Without hesitation or remorse, he slit Korah's throat and dropped his body on the ground.

Blood curdling screams erupted from the crowd.

Crispin attacked the nearest Shadow, taking his weapon and running the soldier through with his own sword. Noticing the one villager fighting back, Neth ordered his men to bring Crispin before him, but before they could subdue him, Crispin managed to kill two more Shadows.

Zophar was restrained from helping his young ward by Harbona who was standing in the back of the crowd.

"Let me go, Harbona," Zophar cried, fearing Crispin would suffer the same fate as Korah.

"Trust me, my friend. Trust me." He refused to relinquish his hold.

Crispin was forced to his knees before Neth who leaned toward him, "You will pay for your rebellious act, peasant."

"You killed an innocent child," Crispin spat. He did not feel fear. He only felt anger, hatred, and a thirst for blood.

"And you killed three of my best men," Neth returned the sentiment.

"Best? If you say so," Crispin mocked. His eyes burned as he fought back tears.

"The penalty for attacking the Shadows of the North is death." Neth lifted the same blood-stained knife he killed Korah with and pointed it against Crispin's throat. "Any last words?"

"Go to hell."

Neth had every intention of slitting Crispin's throat but was shot down by an arrow from above. The two mercenaries that held Crispin on his knees were also swiftly struck down.

Crispin jumped up, grabbed a nearby sword and charged the two remaining Shadows. It felt like an out of body experience. Almost slow motion in his mind. All he could hear was the beating of his own heart, his rapid breathing. He sliced off the first Shadow's leg, then slit his throat as he fell to the ground. The last Shadow threw a knife at Crispin, but he dodged it, rolled toward him and stabbed him in the abdomen. Crispin did not stop pushing the sword until the tip pierced through his back.

Salome jumped down from the rooftop with bow in hand and ran toward Crispin who was kneeling next to Korah's lifeless body.

"Crispin?" She stopped when she saw the boy's neck had nearly been severed from his body. "They killed him? He was just a child."

"Gershom knows no limits. Kill or be killed." Crispin carried Korah's body to his mother, Marta, who had not stopped wailing since her son had been taken from her. The villagers mournfully took his body away to prepare for burial.

Crispin wiped tears from his eyes as he watched his young friend being carried away. "Today, he turned ten." He walked back to the tree house and wiped his bloody hands against his pants.

Salome tried to follow him, but Zophar grabbed her arm. "Let him go."

CHAPTER 14

SALOME

The villagers gathered again that evening to mourn the death of the young boy who had brought them so much joy during his few short years. Korah's body was carried out on a white sheet held by four elders. They escorted his pale and cold body down a path that led to a wooden platform. Laying him down carefully, the elders wrapped his body in the linen sheet, as was their burial custom. Korah's mother, Marta, was given a lit torch and she walked slowly toward her son's plat. As she faced her dearly departed, tears streamed down her cheeks. She laid the torch underneath his wooden pallet, allowing his spirit to be released to join their ancestors.

After the villagers watched the wooden pallet burn to ashes, they returned to their homes silently. Crispin, was the quietest of them all and retreated to his rooftop hiding spot, hoping to be alone for the rest of the evening.

Salome followed him up the creaky stairs and stood behind him in the doorway. "I know how much you cared for him."

Her comment was met with silence, which she expected. With an inkling of hope, she waited to see if he would respond, but he remained quiet. She turned to leave, knowing it was probably best to leave him to his own thoughts until morning, when he finally spoke.

"They were looking for someone with a mark." His words were filled with resentment.

She was surprised. "A mark?"

"No one knew anything except the people in this house and we said nothing." Crispin wiped the guilty tears from his face. "Korah's death was punishment for our silence." Salome touched his shoulder, but he wiggled away from her grasp. "Where were you? You saved me but not that innocent child."

"I know you're angry and you're hurting, but you cannot blame me for Korah's death. I would have done anything to save him. You know that, Crispin."

"All I know is he died today and nothing I do will bring him back. That is now my burden to carry."

"Crispin -"

"Leave me." His voice was icy.

She could not bear to see him this way. He was the strong one. He was the one who wiped tears from her face. She could not even remember the last time she saw him cry. "Listen to me."

"There is nothing you can say that will bring me peace." He refused to look at her.

"I am not suggesting peace," her tone changed.

"Then what are you suggesting?"

"That we kill them."

"Kill who?" He finally looked up at her.

"Niabi and Gershom stole our homeland. They sit at our father's table. They have taken everyone we love from us." Her eyes were filled with fury. She was ready. "No one else dies."

"You changed your mind?" Shivers ran up his spine at the thought of finally having her on board.

"Too much innocent blood has been spilled. Knowing what I know now, seeing what I saw today, I cannot turn a blind eye to this evil any longer. If a fight is what our sister seeks, then a fight is what she will get."

Their attention was suddenly drawn to a large mob of angry villagers stomping toward their front door. Armed with pitch forks and torches, they murmured amongst themselves. It appeared they had found someone to blame for the Shadows' unwelcome visit.

Zophar opened the front door to address the crazed mob of tree dwellers with Harbona by his side. "Friends, what is the meaning of this?"

Tiron, one of the elders of the village, spoke on their behalf. "Those Shadows came here only after that man came to our village." The elder pointed an accusatory finger at Harbona. Salome and Crispin worked their way to the front door just in time to hear Tiron say, "He is responsible for Korah's death."

The angry mob echoed their support for Tiron's words until Zophar was able to calm them down long enough to hear what he had to say. "I assure you, Tiron, this man is a man of peace."

"The death of a child is your definition of peace, Zophar?" Tiron continued to fuel the fire.

"We have lived here for twelve years without a problem -"

Tiron interrupted Zophar. "Until now. You must leave this village immediately. You are not welcome here any longer." The crowd cheered in agreement with his decree of banishment.

"Now, wait a minute -" Zophar's pleas fell on deaf ears.

"Look what you have done to our village," Tiron riled the community further.

Crispin stepped forward. "We saved this village. Those Shadows would not have stopped with Korah."

"Leave now before you bring death to us all." The villagers masked their fear with angry shouting.

"Do you really believe they would have let us live in peace had we not interfered?" Crispin shouted.

Zophar rested his hand on Crispin's shoulder, "Let it be. They are not going to listen."

"Leave! Leave us! Go now!" the mob shouted at them.

Salome turned to Harbona. "What will happen to them if we leave?"

Harbona was hesitant, "More Shadows will come."

"They will kill more of them?" She had a lump in her throat thinking of their future.

"Yes," he pressed his lips together, "more of them will die."

"We must warn them," she insisted, panic in her voice. "They must leave the forest."

"They will not listen," Harbona warned.

"You have seen this?"

"If I say yes, would you believe me?"

Salome asked, "Is there any hope one will listen?"

"There is always hope," the Seer nodded his head with a sad smile.

She pushed her way to stand before the men and women she had come to love and earnestly pleaded. "My people of the Tree House Forest, we received but a glimpse of the North's growing evil. The Shadows will return and once they see their men are dead, they will kill more of us. We must all leave this place and find homes elsewhere. It is the only way to survive future attacks. Please, think of your families. Save yourselves."

Though the mob had fallen to a hush, Tiron stepped forward once again and growled. "We are *not* your people. You and those men never belonged here in the first place."

"Please, you must listen -"

"It is because of you, my son is dead."

Salome was interrupted by the voice of a grief-stricken woman in the back of the crowd. Marta, Korah's mother, made her way forward.

Crispin stepped in front of his sister. "Marta, what happened to Korah was not her fault."

"She saved you," Marta scolded with a tear-stained face. "Why did you not save my son? Or do you only aid those who matter to you?"

"Marta, please -"

Marta refused to allow Crispin to speak. "She is just as guilty as the man who killed my son. She is a murderer with blood-stained hands."

"Leave this forest and do not return. You have brought nothing but pain and suffering to us all." Tiron capitalized on furthering his plan to banish them.

Salome was wounded. *Murderer? Blood-stained hands? Was that really what they thought of her now?*

Zophar wrapped his arms around her and escorted her inside. "Come, Salome."

Crispin followed them inside while Harbona addressed the angry mob one last time. "The Shadows will return, and they will not be diplomatic when they arrive."

"And why should we believe you, old man?" Tiron spat at Harbona, inciting the villagers to cheer.

"Heed these warnings or do not. The choice is yours." Harbona reentered the treehouse, leaving the crowd to disperse.

Salome sat by the fire, shocked by how quickly their community turned on them. She never expected the sweet men and women she had grown up with to reject them so viciously. Crispin cloaked his arm around her hoping to raise her spirits, but she shrugged him away.

"Salome -"

"Why will they not listen? They will die," she interrupted her brother.

"You have done all you can do; now you must let them go." Zophar drank his hot tea, his eyes fixed on the fireplace in front of them. "You cannot save those who do not want your help. We must prepare to leave before more Shadows arrive or our angry neighbors return for another round."

Salome focused her gaze upon the Seer. "Did you see their reaction?"

Harbona's eyes were filled with a warm kindness. "Yes, but I also saw if you did not warn them, you would have regretted it. Your hands and conscience are clean."

"Then why is my heart so heavy?"

Zophar lit his pipe and began to fill the small gathering room with smoke. "Where are we to go now?"

"We will make way to my house in The Hollow. From there we will plan our next course of action," the Seer assumed control of their future endeavors. "Take only what is important. Leave everything else."

"When do we leave?" Zophar asked.

"Tonight," Harbona answered to Salome's surprise.

"You would have us flee as cowards in the night?" she scoffed, unwilling to follow his orders.

"If you do not leave tonight, you will die here. Pack your things quickly. There is not much time." Harbona spoke with such conviction that no one dared to ask him anymore questions.

As quietly as they could, the fugitives packed their important possessions with great haste, saddled their horses and stood outside their humble tree house for presumably the very last time.

Zophar had tears in his eyes, which was a rare sight for a man born in the city of Borg. He stroked his red beard with a heavy sigh and mounted his chestnut steed.

The four travelers somberly rode out of the Tree House Forest. Zophar followed closely behind Crispin and Harbona, who took the lead positions in their caravan, but noticed Salome was no longer riding beside him. He turned and saw she had stopped right outside the village, taking in one last look of the place she had accepted as her home. He rode up next to her and looked with fondness at the village they had both found comfort in.

"I will miss it as well," he broke the silence.

"You trust Harbona?" she whispered.

"With my life." He did not hesitate.

"I hope he is right," she wiped a tear from her cheek. "This will be harder than I thought it would be."

"You feel like you are leaving your home behind?" He glanced over at her, barely making out her features in the darkness.

"I feel as if I am leaving myself behind and being forced to become someone else entirely." She admitted with a quiver in her voice.

"Trust in the Almighty One's plan, Salome." He patted her arm, hoping to comfort her.

"What if he is wrong? What if I am not who you think I am?"

"From the first day I met you, I knew you were more than just a princess. I noticed how strong and brave you were as a child and the warrior in me, saw the warrior in you. I think it's time you remembered who you are."

Salome continued to wipe the tears that streamed down her face as she stared at her home. She turned toward Zophar, knowing what she needed to do.

"What is your decision?" he asked her.

"We ride."

CHAPTER 15

NIABI

Every Northerner lined the main cobblestone street in Northwind to honor their departed prince as he was carried to his final resting place. Since the founding of the White City over a thousand years ago, every member of the royal bloodline had been buried in the mountain crypt just outside the kingdom gates. The carved tombs had only one way in and out and the one gate was heavily guarded day and night. Even Niabi's family members were given honorable burials according to the traditions of her people, all except her father, whose remains were burned.

The one royal she had not planned to bury was her own son. Rollo was her world, her light, and now she had to escort his lifeless body through their city to the Mountain of Kings. Her black gown boasted an eight-foot train and in keeping with northern tradition, she wore a sheer black veil to cover her face. The veil gave the queen a sense of privacy as she grieved the loss of her son as well as maintain a powerful image with her people. Her white crown sat upon her head as she marched down the street next to her son.

Rollo rested on top of a white golden plat, dressed in his favorite royal robes and furs; his crown was perfectly placed upon his well-groomed hair. The sword she had given him when he turned twelve rested on his chest. Even on his plat, he looked like a king.

Following closely behind the queen, Leoti, Tala, Pash and Gershom kept a steady pace. As the funeral procession progressed through the grieving city, citizens threw flowers on the path, paying their last respects.

A young little girl with loose brown curls dashed out of the crowd with a flower of her own, wishing to place it atop the prince's body. Her mother screamed and cried for her daughter to return before it was too late, but the young child did not listen. Instead, she pressed on and unexpectedly bumped into the queen. Niabi stopped, halting her entire entourage. A hush fell upon the citizens, knowing it was forbidden to touch a royal.

Niabi bent down and lifted her veil, revealing her tear-stained face. "Is that for Prince Rollo?" She pointed to the flower in the young girl's hand.

"Yes, my Queen." The brown-eyed girl's knees buckled as she stood before her.

Niabi extended her hand and led her to the plat that was being pulled on wheels by four armored horses and allowed her to honor the prince. Wide-eyed, the six-year-old respectfully placed her offering upon Rollo's chest and bowed before her queen.

Her face still unveiled, she once again took the girl's hand and escorted her back to her panic-stricken parents. With the girl now embracing her loving mother and father, Niabi whispered, "Your daughter is very kind."

Niabi locked eyes with the girl's mother. Pity. That is what she saw in the peasant woman's eyes. It hurt. She never wanted to be pitied. When someone wronged her, stole from her, harmed her, she would enact her revenge. She would protect and defend herself. But for the first time in quite a long time, she felt powerless. Vulnerable. Small.

Now mindful of all the eyes glued to her, she covered her face and continued her journey to the mountain.

Once the entourage arrived at the mountain crypt, six soldiers, including Pash and Tala, carried the plat down the dark hall to Rollo's burial plot. His body was placed in a white stone casket and would be covered with a statue of the prince once Niabi left the tomb. The soldiers disappeared so she could say her final goodbye.

"Tala, wait." She leaned over Rollo's body and cut several strands of his black hair, grabbed the sword on his chest and handed them to her friend. "See to it my son receives an Andrago burial, so he may ride with his father, until I meet them again."

"It will be done." Tala clenched the items tightly. "I will return as soon as I can."

Alone, Niabi placed her dainty hand upon the casket and cried. Feeling weak, she dropped to her knees and kissed the side of the coffin.

"I never should have had to bury you, Rollo," her voice cracked. "I never should have had to bury my son."

She wiped the tears from her eyes, a fire raged inside of her. She rose to her feet, grabbed his cold hand, and kissed it.

"I swear on the blood of our ancestors that I will avenge you, my son. Those responsible for your death will curse their mothers for bearing them. They will beg Death to take them, but she will wait, for I bend my knee to no one, not even her. The Ten Kingdoms will remember why they fear the Green-Eyed Raven."

Eerily silent, Niabi reclined in the White Throne as she drank her wine. She had not moved from her seat since her son's funeral and refused to see any member of her small council. Matters of importance would have to wait until she dealt with the old witch, she had sent her Nephilim to capture. Hatred boiled in her heart and the only memory she mulled over was the day she met the hag.

It had been nearly twenty years since Niabi wandered farther than she should have from her camp. Nagrom, the black stallion gifted to her by Dichali on their wedding day, became anxious as he trotted through the dark and mysterious forest, compelling her to stroke his neck, attempting to ease his nerves. They continued to trek through the spooky woods until they happened upon an old cabin with smoke rising from the chimney. With rain fast approaching, and no idea how to find her way back to camp, she reluctantly rode up to the house, fearful of what lurked behind the door.

Her horse was uneasy, and his body language hinted they should not stop.

"We are lost, Nagrom. Maybe they can help," she insisted with a false sense of bravery.

She dismounted her horse and cautiously walked to the cabin door. The stallion neighed and stomped his feet to prevent his mistress from continuing, but she kept moving forward despite his warning. Once she stood at the wooden entrance, she knocked, and the door opened. She did not see anyone, so she pushed the creaking door wide open to reveal a large room with furniture scattered around.

"Hello? Is anyone here?"

She entered the small cabin with trepidation. There was a stone hearth built from the floor all the way to the ceiling. A crackling fire roared while a large boiling cauldron hung above the flames and the aroma of myrrh filled the one room cabin. Two windows flanked the stone fireplace which allowed dim lighting to spotlight the long pine table in the center of the space. A rug was placed underneath the table which was surrounded by four high back pointed chairs. A large double door cabinet stood to the left wall and a small cot sat against the opposite corner. Quilts rested upon the single bed making the cabin very cozy.

Even though her eyes saw the innocence of the home, her heart was racing with the unshakable feeling of evil. She was soaking in her surroundings when the door suddenly slammed shut. Niabi could hear Nagrom whining outside urging her to return to him. She felt she was being watched, but no one was inside. She spun in a complete circle and still saw no one. Nagrom's wails did not cease. He stomped his hooves onto the ground demanding her immediate attention. Fear washed over her as she decided to heed her horse's warnings, but as she tried to open the door, she realized it would not budge. Terror set in as she pulled as hard as she could, but still failed to escape.

"What is your hurry, child?" A raspy voice behind her asked.

She whipped around and saw a petite white-haired woman standing near the fireplace. She had a ladle in her hand and began to stir the liquid in the cauldron.

"I did not mean to intrude. I was lost and needed direction," Niabi's voice trembled as she tried to explain her presence.

"Are you afraid of a little old woman, girl?"

"I am not afraid," she lied.

"Everyone fears something, Niabi. Why not be what they fear?"

Niabi suddenly realized her horse was not making noise. She looked out the front window and saw he was standing quietly.

"Your horse is fine, dear."

"How do you know my name? Who are you? What do you want?"

The old woman faced her. "My name is Vilora, but most Adalorians call me -"

"The Old Witch of Endor," she finished her sentence fully aware of the danger she found herself in.

"I see you have heard of me," the wild haired hag smirked.

Niabi's fear paralyzed her. All she could do was watch the witch. Everyone grew up being told stories about the Old Witch of Endor. How she was cursed from birth, scorned by her family, and rejected by her people. She had been sent to the smallest of the five islands that comprised the Isles of Myr. Consumed with anger, she used her darkness to sink Endor, killing every inhabitant. Niabi did not know exactly how Vilora escaped the Isles of Myr unscathed, or how she came to be hiding in a one room cabin in the foothills of Elisor, but what Niabi did know, was that the witch was not friendly to unexpected guests.

"Tell me, girl, what stories did they frighten you with?" She poured two bowls of what she had brewed in her cauldron and made her way to the table.

"That... That you were cursed from birth…" Niabi stopped. The witch's eyes were not filled with the evil she expected. They told a painful story, and in that moment, she pitied her.

"Go on, girl. What else have you heard?" Niabi remained silent. "Sit down," the witch instructed her timid guest. "I said sit down. Are you hard of hearing?" Vilora scolded.

Niabi obeyed and sat directly across the table from Vilora. She passed the young woman a steaming bowl filled with an unidentifiable stew. She looked at it and slowly stirred the mush attempting to recognize what she was offered to eat.

"What is the matter, girl? Have you forgotten your manners when offered food?" Vilora stared at her with icy blue eyes.

"Forgive me, I did not mean to offend you," Niabi said softly.

"If I wished you dead, I would not use poison. That is a coward's weapon."

Niabi realized she no longer feared for her safety. The witch was right. If killing her was her mission, she would have already taken her life. Niabi took a spoonful of the mush and swallowed it quickly. It was actually good.

"What is this?" Niabi asked, extremely curious about the odd colored stew.

"Human liver," Vilora burped.

Niabi choked as she did her best to spit out the mouthful she just consumed. The witch laughed which angered her. "What is the meaning of this?"

"Hush, girl. I spoke in jest. It is rabbit stew," Vilora continued to cackle as Niabi calmed down.

"It's not...?"

"Human? No, foolish girl," she chastised. "I may be many things, but a cannibal I am not. I leave that atrocity to the Thrak."

Niabi exhaled a huge sigh of relief as she took another bite. "It is good."

Vilora gazed at her visitor until she noticed.

"Is something wrong?" Niabi asked, taking another mouthful of food.

"What is it that you seek?" The witch's eyes twitched.

"What do you mean?"

"No one finds me unless they are meant to. So, tell me, what do you seek?" The elderly woman finally showed a hint of uneasiness.

"I... I found you by chance. I was… I was lost," Niabi stammered.

"Lost or not our paths have crossed for a reason."

"You do not truly believe that, do you?" Niabi did not believe in superstitions.

"Do you mean to tell me that there is nothing you desire?" Vilora squinted as she slurped from her spoon.

Niabi hesitated as she thought once more about the question posed to her. Slowly, she looked up at the nervous witch. "There is something I used to desire."

"Tell me, child." She leaned forward, sauce dripping down her chin.

"I wanted my father's throne. I wanted his kingdom, his crown. I wanted the North." Her response was chilling.

"To have your father's crown means he and all who would oppose your reign must die," the old witch explained rather callously.

"I know." Niabi had clearly thought about this before.

"You know all this, yet you do not seem bothered. Why is that?" Vilora realized she was not dealing with an ordinary woman.

"If you had the opportunity to exact revenge on those who shunned and banished you, would you take it?" Niabi turned the tables on her hostess, appealing to her emotions.

Vilora smiled. "I did take it. And I paid the price for it. Are you willing to do the same?"

Niabi was silent. She had not thought about her father in a long time; her desires had changed.

"No child of your womb will sit on the White Throne of Northwind until all other usurpers have been vanquished. But I warn you, you will pay a heavy price for victory and an even heavier price for failure," Vilora prophesied.

"I do not have a child."

"You carry him with you as we speak."

The young royal was surprised. "You mean to say that I am with child?"

"A son."

She rubbed her abdomen, "I am going to be a mother?"

"Born of both wolf and hawk blood." Vilora nodded her head. "He could sit on the White Throne if you choose."

Niabi mulled over her words. Northwind was envied by most Adalorians. Some would say it was the most powerful of all the Ten Kingdoms. To have her son sit on the White Throne...

"But you said it yourself," Vilora continued, "your desires have changed."

Niabi nodded, her eyes were glued to her bowl as she stirred the liquid aimlessly.

"Unless that was a lie," the witch watched her carefully.

"I am a different person now." Niabi snapped from her daze. "I love my husband, his people, and now I am to bear him a son." She once again rubbed her stomach. "Our son will bear his father's crown when the time comes."

Vilora shrugged, "And if that is not your son's destiny?

"What do you mean by that?" Niabi frowned, "What do you know?"

"Just a question, dear, just a question."

Niabi found herself deep in thought again. She was the first born of the Northern King. Northwind was her birthright, her son's birthright.

She shook her head. "I am a different person now," she mumbled.

Vilora slurped stew loudly, bringing Niabi back to the one room cabin. Niabi pushed the bowl away from her.

"If I claimed my birthright," Niabi enunciated each word, "what must I do to ensure my son's reign?"

Vilora's smile was unsettling. "Once more you will lose, then no one will forget your name."

Niabi looked confused, "What does that mean?" Vilora cackled which angered the green-eyed beauty. "Answer me, witch. Do not speak to me in riddles," she snapped.

"When the time has come, you will meet the one known as The Bear. But I warn you, do not underestimate him."

"Who is he?"

"That is all I can tell you."

Frustrated by the witch's lack of explanation, she asked, "Will you tell me how to get back to my camp?"

Vilora pointed outside. "Follow the path you were on, and you will find your camp."

"I was already on that path, and it did not lead me home," Niabi reminded her.

"No, but it led you to me. Now do not argue with me, girl. Just follow the path."

Niabi stood up quickly, slicing her left hand on the wooden table where she was sitting; some of her blood spilled onto the floor of the cabin. She opened her mouth to argue with Vilora when suddenly she was standing alone on the path with no evidence of the witch or her cabin.

"That is not possible!" She turned in a full circle looking for the hag, but she was gone. Her eyes rested on Nagrom, who stood quietly waiting for his mistress to return.

That was the first and last time the Green-Eyed Raven saw the Old Witch of Endor.

The queen was jolted from her trance when the throne room doors opened and Anaktu entered. She stood up, her black robes flowing behind her as she marched toward him. Her glistening crown sat gracefully upon her raven black hair that was pulled back in a loose braid. Deprived of sleep for days, she finally had a spark of hope.

"You found her?" Anaktu nodded without uttering a single word. "Take me to her."

She followed the Nephilim down the dark and ominous hallway that led to the damp and cold dungeons. Throughout the corridor echoed the screams of the tortured prisoners that had been held captive for various crimes against the crown. Niabi was unmoved by their pleas for mercy and continued onward to her most coveted prize. As she turned the corner, they came to a door at the end of the hall.

She peered around the small, windowless cell until her eyes fell upon the old, shriveled up witch who was chained to the wall.

Crumbled on the cold damp ground, Vilora opened her eyes and saw the young girl she had met years ago. She was now the most powerful Queen Adalore had ever known.

"I heard stories of the last Nephilim," Vilora sparked the conversation. "I never expected to see one with my own eyes."

"Leave us."

The giant obediently closed the door behind him. Two torches lit the dark, foul smelling, prison cell as the two powerful women stared at one another.

"How did you find me?" the witch asked.

Niabi lifted her left arm and pulled her sleeve back, "We have more in common than you know."

"My magic!" Vilora was surprised to see the discoloration of her arm.

"You know why you are here," Niabi stated matter of fact.

"I am your prisoner," Vilora lifted her shackled arms. "Perhaps, you should enlighten me of my crime."

Niabi squinted and hissed, "You dare test me, Vilora?"

"I assure you I do not know -"

Niabi lunged toward her, inches from the witch's face. "I did everything you told me to do, and you still took my son from me."

"You did not eliminate all usurpers that would oppose your reign. That was the price, and you did not pay it," Vilora remained calm.

"None of my siblings survived."

"I told you not to underestimate him," Vilora shook her head.

"Who?"

The witch smirked, "Two children slipped through the Bear's fingers that night."

With one swift move, Niabi unsheathed her dagger and put it against the Old Witch of Endor's throat. "Lie to me again, and I will cut out your deceitful tongue."

"The Witch of Endor does not lie." Her raspy voice irritated Niabi.

"They are all dead." She enunciated each word through gritted teeth.

"Did you see their bodies?" Vilora asked, knowing the answer.

Niabi thought back on the day she conquered her father's city and realized she had not seen her siblings' bodies. Nor her mother's. Per their agreement, Gershom would handle her five brothers, sister, and mother, while she took on her father. Gershom had the bodies cleared out before she even had a chance to see them. In truth, she did not want to see them. Her quarrel had never been with them; just her father. But for her to be queen, they had to go. He assured her they were dead. He swore to her.

Surely Gershom had held up his end of their deal. But if he had, Rollo would not have died.

"Crispin and Salome live. And because they live, Rollo no longer could." Vilora knew exactly what she was thinking.

Niabi lowered her weapon. Her eyes burned. *He had betrayed her.* She had given him power, wealth, a home, and he repaid her with lies.

Vilora kept her eyes glued on Niabi. "Am I free to go?"

The Green-Eyed Raven composed herself and stared so deeply into Vilora's eyes that it made the witch uncomfortable. Instead of releasing the old woman, the queen walked to the prison cell door and rapped on it three times.

"You cannot keep me here forever, Niabi," the witch hissed.

"Do not fret, Vilora," she smirked. "Soon I will have no more use for you, and you will meet the executioner's blade. Consider yourself fortunate to still be breathing until that day comes."

Niabi slipped out of the cell and had Anaktu lock the door behind her. "Bring Gershom to me."

NIABI STRUMMED her fingers on the armrests of her throne, waiting for Gershom to arrive. She eyed the door, rarely blinking, focused on the man who had betrayed her. Two soldiers stood guard on either side of the wide doors as their queen waited for her unsuspecting prey. The throne room doors opened, and Gershom entered escorted by the Nephilim.

The Second in Command confidently strutted toward Niabi, unaware of the lion's den he had just stepped into. "My Queen." He knelt before her.

"Save your pleasantries for someone who cares for them."

Gershom rose. "Is something wrong, my Queen?"

"You tell me." Her bloodshot eyes narrowed.

It was evident he was confused. He noticed Anaktu was standing in front of the door with two soldiers by his side. Panic began to stir inside him when he realized he was most likely in danger. "What is the meaning of this?"

"For twelve years, you have lied to me," she seethed. "I gave you power, wealth, and a kingdom to call home and you repay me with betrayal."

"Niabi, I have never lied to you."

"You will address me properly or your head will be brought to me on a platter." She slammed her fist down on her armrest, launching a thunderous echo throughout the vast room.

"Apologies, Highness," Gershom tripped over his words, unsure of what to do to appease her.

"Give me one reason I should not gut you like a pig," She slowly rose from her throne, fire raging in her eyes.

"My Queen, it has been a stressful week. Prince Rollo's death was an unexpected tragedy and you have been searching for the reason it happened. But I assure you, I have always been your faithful friend and ally."

"You speak as if we are equals and we are not." She stepped toward him. "We had a deal. I fulfilled my promise and you failed to hold up your end of the agreement."

"I have done everything you have commanded of me." He held his ground.

"You let two of my siblings escape the night we took the city."

His eyes shifted, "I swear I killed them all."

"Do you truly stand before me and deny it?"

"My Queen -"

"Stop lying!" Niabi's menacing glare struck fear into him.

Gershom knew his best chance of survival at this point would be to beg for forgiveness. "By the time we realized they had escaped, it was too late."

Furious with his confession, Niabi backhanded him, drawing blood. "Your betrayal has cost my son his life and you will pay dearly for it. Anaktu!"

The silent giant stepped forward, ready to obey any order she gave him.

Gershom's eyes darted back and forth between the monstrous Nephilim and the dangerous woman he called Queen. Falling to his knees he pleaded for mercy. "I swear I will find them."

"Finding them will not bring my son back," she shouted.

"Let me right my wrong, my Queen."

"Begging does not become you," she snarled at the pitiful soldier she once thought mighty. "I see now that you are weak, and I have no more use for you."

He stood in reckless boldness. "I am not weak!" He pounded on his broad chest. "The blood of the bear runs through my veins. Where are your wolves? Homeless, nameless, forgotten. The Bear has already conquered the Wolf."

Niabi raised her hand, halting Anaktu from coming any closer. She took another step toward her prey, thirsty for blood.

"You may think the bear is mightier than the wolf," she hissed, "but how many wolves have you seen dancing for peasants at their master's command?" Her words seeped from her mouth like a smooth poison. "The wolf is slave to no man; he lives and dies by his own choosing. It is time you knew your place."

Gershom stood in frightened silence.

She lifted her right hand exposing the long scar on her palm. "You know as well as I that I cannot kill you. Bring Crispin and Salome to me alive. If you fail me again, I promise you will beg for Death to take you before I am through with you."

"I will not fail you. I will send every man in my charge to each corner of Adalore if that is what it takes." He crossed his arm over his chest and rose to leave but Anaktu blocked his path.

She tilted her head, the corners of her mouth turned up. "Surely you did not believe you would leave this room unscathed."

Terror overtook his face.

Niabi nodded her head cuing Anaktu to force Gershom to his knees. She glided toward him; her freshly sharpened dagger clutched in her left hand.

"We swore a blood oath -"

"I never swore I wouldn't harm you." She knelt before him and touched his cheek with the tip of her blade. "Everything comes at a price."

She sliced his left ear off. Her hands were covered in blood as she held his severed ear. Anaktu released Gershom, who was screaming, from his clutches.

"Perhaps now you will learn to listen and obey. Get out of my sight, before I take your other ear."

He clawed his way out of the throne room holding the hole where his ear used to be, tears streaming down his scarred face.

Niabi handed Anaktu the ear, "Take care of this."

CHAPTER 16

NUBIS

When his watch ended, one of the guards from Niabi's throne room ditched his armor in the barracks and made his way to the docks. The dark alleys were packed with seedy characters and promiscuous women looking to earn their keep. Soldiers were known to frequent the area during their free nights to drink themselves into a stupor and hopefully, wake up next to a wench they never intended to see again.

However, Nubis was not like the other footmen in the queen's service. Originally born in Fennor, known to most Adalorians as the City of Bones, the Stormcrag tribesman had journeyed to the White City of Northwind several years earlier to serve the man who had saved him from a rival Mountain Men tribe, called the Krazaks.

The Krazaks were a brutal and bloodthirsty tribe who smeared ashen clay on their bodies and adorned themselves with the bones of their fallen enemies. Black and red war paint was always splattered on their skin; and they were ready for battle at a moment's notice. Both men and women wore their hair in braids; the longer the braid, the more battles they had won. Now in control of the Throne of Skulls, their sole purpose was to annihilate any member of the Stormcrags and fashion their skulls into prized helmets.

Being a Stormcrag was Nubis' greatest honor and safely kept secret. His kin were fur wearing, tattooed survivalists who spent their time killing Krazaks and Gomorrian Thraks, while guarding the sacred temple known as "The Tears of the Gods". Although his people all dyed their hair and painted their bodies in shades of blue, purple, and white, he had no choice but to maintain his shaggy black hair in a traditional northern bun and hide his blue ink tattoos. In contrast to the Krazak's long braids, Stormcrag men had two distinct beard braids to boast of their many victories, though he no longer participated in this tradition.

Boasting an impressive six-foot six-inch frame, Nubis never had any trouble with his soldier brethren. Though he had sworn an oath to protect the queen and fight her enemies, he had not come to serve her, but rather to spy on her and report his findings to his underground commander. With Niabi's feeble support of the Krazaks stopped, his people could once again assume control of the City of Bones. If that meant he would spend the rest of his natural born days in a foreign land fighting in an underground northern rebellion, then he was inclined to do just that.

As he turned the corner, he saw his destination: The Whispering Fox. Known around the Kingdoms of Adalore to be one of the most dangerous taverns, Nubis never feared for his safety because he was amongst his fellow rebels. Slipping in the bar unnoticed by the celebratory ruffians, the well-groomed, dark bearded insurgent carefully made his way down a steep, creaky staircase into the candlelit basement where he found him.

"You have news?" the voice in the darkness sounded out.

"Aye," Nubis stepped forward. "Prince Crispin and Princess Salome live. Gershom is searching for them now."

"Two of the royal children escaped?"

"Yes, my lord."

The underground warlord, who was masquerading as a tavern owner in the unsavory brothel district, stepped into the light. Oden, who was previously known as Lord Maon, now donned a thick long braid down the center of his back and rings on nearly every one of his fingers. For years, he had remained secluded in order to protect himself from the vicious, tyrannical queen who killed his king. Before the invasion, he had been King Issachar's Second in Command. Now, Oden was responsible for orchestrating The Order, a guerrilla brotherhood. No one truly knew if the rebellion existed or if they were just a hopeful legend, but the handful of members that were bonded in blood knew one day their band of assassins would overthrow the queen and all who followed her.

"Are you positive of their names?" Oden had to be sure.

Nubis nodded his head. "The Queen named them herself right before she sliced off one of Gershom's ears."

"She sliced off his ear?"

"Aye, said it was punishment for his betrayal. Said if it weren't for him, her son would still be alive."

"Rollo would be alive?" Oden said each word slowly, eyes closed.

"That's what she claimed. I don't know what she meant by it," Nubis shrugged. "And by the looks of it, neither did Gershom."

"She blames him for Rollo's death and let him live?" He scratched the stubble on his chin.

"She said he knew as well as she did, she couldn't kill him."

"See what you can find out." Oden paced. "Clearly, we are missing key information about her and Gershom's history."

"From what I know, the Nephilim was away from the city for a week on the Queen's bidding. Once he returned, she went to the dungeons and then summoned Gershom to the throne room."

Oden's eyes twinkled. "Who did she see?"

"No one knows." Nubis leaned against the wall, arms crossed over his broad chest. "According to the records, there is no one in that cell. Whoever it is, is meant to remain a ghost."

"We need to find out who she saw down there." Oden rubbed his hands together.

Nubis had seen that look before. He knew Oden's mind was racing trying to piece the puzzle together.

"In the meantime," Oden scattered pieces of paper on his desk and reached for his quill, "we must send word to the others. We need to find King Issachar's children before Niabi or Gershom do."

"They could be anywhere," Nubis reminded him with a scoff. "How do you expect to find two people who have gone twelve years undetected?"

"I still have many knowledgeable friends in Adalore who owe me a few favors," he smiled. "Seems it is time I pay them a visit."

"Are you sure it is safe for you to leave the city? Someone could recognize you."

"And how would that make me look to our brethren?" Oden shook his head. "Not burdened in issuing orders but too frightened to do my part in our fight. I would rather slit my own throat, than have The Order believe me to be a coward."

"At least have someone accompany you." Nubis knew Oden had not left the city in nearly six years and Adalore was a much more dangerous place than before.

"Where I am going, I must go alone." The commander shuffled around the room looking for his satchel. "If I do not return, you know what you must do."

"Aye."

"Good. Now go. There is much to be done."

CHAPTER 17

SALOME

"How much farther, Harbona?" Crispin huffed childishly, thoroughly exhausted from their journey.

"Not much farther." Harbona kept his eyes on the path.

"What is this place called?" Salome was in awe of the mystical forest they had entered.

"This is the Hollow." Harbona also admired the woodland he called home.

Wisteria trees in full bloom lined the dirt path and swayed in the light breeze. It almost seemed as if they were whispering as they rode by. Hypnotized by their airy song, she stopped to listen, convinced she could hear them calling her name.

"Do they speak?" She stopped the Seer dead in his tracks.

"You can hear them?" he asked.

When she saw their expressions, she realized they did not hear what she heard. "You don't hear them?"

"No, child." Zophar was wide-eyed.

"Not many can," Harbona chimed in.

"What does that mean? Not many can?" Crispin stared at his sister as if she had a contagious disease.

"It means they have something to say, and she should listen." The Seer stated. "What are they saying?"

"Just my name," she confessed sheepishly.

"Has this happened to you before?" Harbona pressed.

"Once."

"When?"

"Before you came to our village," she confessed. "I was hunting, and I heard my name. At first, I thought it might have been Crispin, but I was alone."

"Is that all that happened?"

The way Harbona looked at her, she felt like he already knew the answer. She could lie, but if the Seer did know, there would be no point.

"A bright light started to approach me," she felt silly admitting it, "but I ran before it could get to me."

"Sounds like dark magic to me," Zophar puffed.

"What would the trees want with me?" Salome pondered aloud.

"The trees are a mysterious bunch, but you needn't fear them." Harbona tried to ease her nerves.

"Needn't fear talking trees?" Crispin balked. "Am I the only sane one here? Trees are trees, nothing more."

"Trees are living beings," the Immortal countered. "Perhaps they speak to those who will listen."

"Maybe I just need some rest," Salome diffused the situation as best she could. "Do we have much farther to go?"

"We are here." Harbona pointed toward a wooded bend. The weary travelers saw a house carved in the hollow of a large Angel Oak tree.

The siblings had never seen anything quite like it. There was a yellow door and windows of different shapes and sizes scattered around the trunk and branches. Once they dismounted their horses, they walked into the warm and inviting house. Countless books and parchments were strewn throughout the main room. A narrow staircase, carved in the tree, spiraled to the second and third levels of the home. Harbona ignited the fireplace logs and set a cauldron above the flames to make supper.

"Please, make yourselves comfortable," their generous host smiled. He had not had visitors in years, so this was a pleasant day for him.

Salome and Zophar perused through all the Seer's books, while Crispin gazed at the weapons mounted around the small hovel.

"Why so many weapons?" Crispin questioned, genuinely intrigued. "What is it you fear?"

"Nothing at all, young Prince," he grinned.

Zophar's eyes fell upon a large book whose cover was made of solid gold. "Do my eyes deceive me? Is this the Book of Malachi? It is said this book was given to him by the Almighty One himself."

"Who exactly was this Malachi?" Salome walked toward her mentor, fascinated by the rare find.

"Over a thousand years ago," Zophar recounted, "a king rose to power and united all the citizens of Adalore. King Greygor was loved by the people and ruled them for ten years before his own brother, Phlias, consumed with jealousy and believing he was the mightier of the two, gathered his band of ruffians and attacked his brother's castle, Oakenshire. After overthrowing King Greygor and seizing control of his kingdom, with malice and pure hatred in his heart, Phlias murdered his younger brother and slaughtered all who opposed his illegitimate reign. Seven years passed and after numerous failed assassination attempts on Phlias' life, the Adalorian people accepted no one would be able to defeat the tyrant king.

In their darkest hour, The Almighty One heard their cries and sent a Seer to a poor farmer named Malachi, the youngest of seven brothers. Anointed to be his chosen warrior, he was marked with the symbol of the Hunter and was bestowed a golden sword forged by the Almighty himself. Having great favor, Malachi quickly gathered an army of peasants and noblemen alike to dethrone Phlias. Nearly two years after his encounter with the Almighty One, he came face to face with the vile self-proclaimed King of Adalore.

A duel ensued, both men were bloodied and bruised, but Malachi was the one who drove his golden sword through Phlias' chest, finally ending the evil reign his people had endured. The people demanded Malachi be their new king. But he knew one man should not have that much power and instead, spent the remainder of his life helping to establish the Ten Kingdoms of Adalore.

It took nearly fifty years for all Ten Kingdoms to be established, but once his task had been completed, the Almighty One called him home. Leaving his golden sword, this book, and a letter, he ascended into the heavens on a chariot of fire."

"How did you come to possess such a book?" Crispin asked suspiciously.

"Malachi entrusted me to protect it." Harbona poured himself a cup of tea.

"Wait, you are saying you were there?" He nearly choked on the question.

"Oh yes," Harbona's eyes twinkled, "I was there."

Crispin rubbed his temples. "But... But that would mean you were alive... over one thousand years ago."

"Yes," he nodded.

"You were the Seer who found Malachi," Salome chimed in once she put the pieces together.

"Yes, I was." Harbona smiled fondly remembering the victories he and Malachi achieved together.

"That is not possible." Crispin refused to believe the man who stood before him was over a thousand years old.

"Anything is possible, Crispin, if you only have faith." The Seer poured another hot cup of tea and offered it to the confused prince.

Crispin declined the beverage. "How old are you?"

"You would not believe me even if I told you."

"Are you immune to death?" Crispin asked, sounding like a little boy with a hundred questions.

"It is simply not my time yet; my work is not finished," the old man graciously answered as he sat in his favorite leather chair.

"And what of the sword?" the prince pressed. "Do you have that as well?"

He shook his head, sipping his tea. "Malachi entrusted another with its protection."

"Who -"

"Enough questions for now." Harbona offered him the tea again. "Eat. Rest. This is just the beginning of a long road ahead."

CHAPTER 18

LEOTI

Nestled between the winding Ameyalli River and the evergreen lined farmlands, the Kingdom of Elisor was comprised of thousands of lodgings made of wood, animal skins, and colorful woven tapestries. The city was unique because it was the only Adalorian capitol that was not enclosed by stone walls.

Tala, followed closely by his entourage, approached his homeland with a heavy heart. The citizens of the city stood outside their homes with streaks of black paint below their eyes down to their chins; a traditional gesture to pay their last respects to the prince they had only recently come to know and admire.

Although Rollo had spent most of his life in Northwind, as soon as the Andrago met him six months earlier, they knew his spirit was kindred to their own. As a descendant of both the Wolf of Northwind and the Hawk of Elisor, Rollo would receive a traditional farewell before his prized possessions were laid to rest next to his father's grave. The Andrago believed the father and son who had not gotten to know one another in life now had the opportunity to know one another in death.

Feeling their eyes fixated on her during the entire ceremony, Leoti maintained a fair distance from the women in the community. The last thing she wanted was to be pitied. Death had come for her mother and now her husband. The female elders would assume she was cursed – and maybe she was. She could only imagine what they were thinking or saying about her in the privacy of their homes.

Her eye caught sight of a familiar face. The color had faded from her eyes, but they were still warm and kind. She struggled to her feet, grabbed her walking stick, and hobbled her way to Leoti with a sense of urgency. Leoti stopped and waited for her.

"It has been a long time, sweet girl," Nokoma's smile caused her eyes to shrink into wrinkles. "I have prayed for years I would one day see you again. I just wish it hadn't been under these circumstances."

Leoti stared at the ground, smudging the black paint under her eyes while attempting to hide her tears. "I have thought about you often."

Nokoma lifted Leoti's chin. "May the Almighty be the wind that lifts you up. May the Almighty be your comfort during this heartache. May the Almighty be your light in this darkness."

She grabbed the old woman's hand in hers. "I believe the Almighty has forgotten me."

"He loves all of his children, Leoti, especially during their times of trouble."

Leoti's eyes burned as she fought back tears. "Why did this happen?" her voice cracked.

"When my sweet Tallulah passed into the next world, I asked Him the same question," she sighed, forcing a smile.

"And what did He tell you?"

Nokoma wiped a tear from Leoti's cheek. "She had served her purpose. It was time for her to rest."

Leoti whispered, "I don't really remember her."

Nokoma cupped her chin in her wrinkled hand. "Granddaughter, you may not remember her, but she lives on in you. And if she were here today, she would wrap her arms around you and remind you how loved you are."

Her eyes shifted to those hovering around them. "They think I'm cursed, don't they?"

"Why should you care what they think?" Nokoma snorted. "Only the weak lose sleep over the opinions of others."

"Perhaps I am not as strong as I once thought I was."

"Shedding tears does not make you weak, Leoti. Showing emotion does not make you weak. Taking time to be alone to heal does not make you weak." She grabbed her granddaughter's hand tightly. "What makes you weak is letting the whispers of lessers cause you to forget who you are."

Leoti lifted her head and met her grandmother's gaze.

"To the lessers you say, 'I am Leoti, daughter of Tala and Tallulah. The blood of the Andrago flows through my veins. The spirit of the doe guides my path. The Almighty breathes life into my soul. And when Death comes for me, I will greet her as an old friend, ready to start the next adventure.'"

Leoti straightened, confidence rushed through her. "May the fire that burns within you, fill me." She rested her forehead against her grandmother's.

"Who are you?" Nokoma whispered, eyes closed.

"I am Leoti," she whispered back.

CHAPTER 19
TALA

Nearly a week had passed since arriving in Elisor, and Tala had spent most of his time sitting on the banks of the river. He had not been persuaded to eat or sleep since he arrived. All he desired was to be left alone to grieve in his own way.

As she did every afternoon, Leoti brought him lunch, hoping he would finally break his silence.

"I brought you something to eat."

His eyes did not waver from the water rushing downstream. Instead of returning to her grandmother's, she sat down next to him. She closed her eyes and inhaled deeply. Together they sat in silence for close to thirty minutes before Leoti spoke.

"Rollo gave this to me the night he returned." She stoked the small book of pressed flowers. "Does the pain ever go away?"

"No," he sighed. "You just learn how to live without them."

"I never thought I would lose my best friend." She flipped through the pages with care and admired each flower pressed in its pages. "I will never understand why he was taken from me."

Tala's weight shifted and he cleared his throat. "Before Rollo was born, Niabi happened upon a witch who told her if she claimed her father's throne, she would have to ensure none of her siblings would survive to challenge her reign. If they lived, her son would never sit on the White Throne."

She was taken aback. "I... I thought she was happy with the Andrago," she stammered.

"She was," he affirmed. "She abandoned her birthright and the hatred she had for her father was forgotten once she realized how deep her love for Dichali was. With Rollo growing inside her, she was reborn. But once she lost Dichali..."

"So, when Dichali died, she decided to go back north?" Her furrowed brow caught his attention.

"There is much you do not know of that night, Leoti."

"Then what happened that night?"

"Rollo always asked me to tell him about how his father died." He stared at the ground. "He never did learn the truth."

"Why all the secrecy?"

"That is how Niabi wanted it." He rubbed his hands together and leaned forward. "She didn't want Rollo to know her as the Green-Eyed Raven."

"Then tell me," she pressed.

He hesitated. He had kept that night a secret for years. The Andrago did not like discussing how someone died; they only shared memories of how they lived. But he needed to tell someone; he needed to tell her like he should have told Rollo.

"When Niabi's father, King Issachar, heard she had given birth to Dichali's son, he was terrified the child would attempt to claim the White Throne when he came of age. Issachar would have rather died than have any child of Niabi's claim the North, so when Rollo turned two, he ordered all three of them to be killed."

"Her own father?"

"The night they were ambushed in their tent, Niabi had to make a choice to save either Dichali or their son."

Her swallow was audible. "What happened to those assassins?"

"Niabi tortured them." Tala's eyes were glassy, as if he were watching it happen all over again. "They lasted longer than I thought they would, but they finally told her who had sent them. Her hatred for her father pulsed through her veins once again and she swore that very night, covered in Dichali's blood, that she would avenge him."

"I still don't understand what that has to do with Rollo's death," she rubbed her forehead. "Niabi conquered the North. Her siblings are all dead. No one should oppose her reign."

Tala pulled a letter from his breast pocket. "I received this message this morning." He handed it to her to read aloud.

She ran her fingers over the broken seal of the Green-Eyed Raven. "Why would she not use the Northern crest?"

His eyes shifted and his fingers twitched. "This sigil strikes fear into the hearts of Adalorian men that the Northern crest does not."

She opened the parchment and read the message aloud:

"'My friend, truths have been uncovered since you left the city. Gershom, whom I once trusted, has betrayed me. He did not fulfill his oath the night we took the North and two of my siblings escaped. My Shadows are hunting them, and Gershom has suffered for his misdeeds. I need you to return as soon as you receive this. The Green-Eyed Raven.'"

Leoti gave the letter back to her father. "What oath is she talking about?"

Tala folded the paper and put it in his pocket. "Niabi and Gershom made a pact before attacking the city. Gershom was to kill all her siblings and in return he would be her Second in Command. He let two escape him, which means he signed Rollo's death warrant."

Leoti's nostrils flared. "He should be executed."

Tala bobbed his head. "I agree."

"She said he has suffered for his misdeeds." Leoti mulled over the words of Niabi's letter. "Why would she let him live?"

"Niabi and Gershom swore a blood oath that neither would die by the other's hand."

"You mean she *can't* kill him?" She was so enraged she nearly screamed.

"She forfeits her own life if she breaks a blood oath."

"Dark magic." She spat on the ground.

Tala patted her hand in an effort to calm her down. "Anger and blind desperation often lead us to make foolish and rash decisions."

"Do you think Gershom planned this so he could take the crown for himself?" She could tell by her father's silence that he was deep in thought. "If he let them go willingly, then he plotted his usurpation from the beginning. If they escaped as he claims, then he had twelve years to right his wrong, but he did not. Either way, Niabi has no heir. Gershom could take the throne as her Second, in the event of her death."

Tala's eyes widened. "And upon his death, his son Pash, would be the rightful heir."

"Treason," she hissed.

"It seems they are both far more clever than I gave them credit," he snarled.

"When you return to Northwind, I am going with you."

His eyes softened. "I thought you wanted to stay in Elisor to mourn?"

"I will mourn Rollo the rest of my days." She clutched the book to her chest. "I will heal once Gershom and Pash's heads sit on spikes at the main gate of Northwind."

Tala heard something in the tone of her voice that sent a shiver up his spine. "What are you suggesting?"

"There are many ways to kill a man, father." The fire in her eyes scared him. "Most look like accidents."

"Leoti, he is still Second in Command. His death would demand an investigation." He shook his head. "It is too risky. What if you are caught?"

"Then I will see my love sooner than planned."

Tala watched the river flowing and grasped his daughter's hand. "It seems like a lifetime ago that I married your mother at this very spot."

"What does that have to do with any of this?" She was caught off guard.

"Whenever I am angry, confused, lonely or in need of guidance, I always come to this spot. I may not be able to touch her, but I can feel her here with me. We buried Rollo's body, but his spirit is still with you."

"You always say that," she brushed him off.

"You are just like you mother." He looked at the necklace that hung from her neck. "She was much like this river. Calm, steady, and at times, wild and dangerous. What she would have given to be here with you now."

"I don't remember much about her," she admitted, fingering the necklace.

"You were four when she passed on." He wiped his eyes and whispered, "I should have been here."

"You were at war."

"Had I known what I know now..."

"What would you have done differently?" She rubbed his shoulder. "You did what needed to be done. You avenged Dichali."

"Yes, I avenged Dichali," he nodded. "What would Rollo say if he knew of the plotting in your heart?" His words were gentle and kind and humbled her. "What would your husband say?"

Her eyes stung as she fought the lump in her throat. "It's not fair."

"It isn't," he wiped her cheek.

"Did you ask Niabi the same thing when Dichali died?"

"If I had, Rollo would still be alive." He stared at his feet. "Do you plan on assassinating them?"

She turned toward him, and they locked eyes. "I cannot promise I won't have a hand in their deaths."

He knew he could not stop her. And a part of him did not want to. "Be mindful of your steps. They are predators, always anticipating an attack."

"Every predator has a weakness."

By the ferocity in her voice, he knew her mind was made up. "We ride at dawn."

CHAPTER 20
VILORA

The Old Witch of Endor's long white hair wafted as she was ushered through the back hallways of the White Keep. Not knowing whether she was safe, or her time had finally expired, Vilora held her head high, unwilling to abandon her pride.

"Where are you taking me?" she asked the Nephilim.

Anaktu stomped down the corridor without acknowledging his prisoner. He had his orders and interacting with her was not on the agenda.

"Are you silent because you choose to be or because someone cut that demon tongue from your mouth?" He was unmoved by her words, which was the expected reaction. "How long do you think she will be able to keep you alive?" She kept a watchful eye on the Nephilim. "She saved you once, yes, but what happens if she no longer lives?"

The giant swung around to face the witch who had spoken against his savior. Without any visible fear, Vilora stared deep into the black eyes of the monster, unmoved by his threatening stance.

"How unusual," one of her eyebrows lifted, "the monster has feelings."

As swiftly as he had turned toward her, he rotated once more to continue forward. Vilora had a way of finding one's weakness and using it to her advantage. Her purpose with the Nephilim was still a mystery to her, but she knew now how to control him.

Interrupting her plotting, the giant stopped in front of Niabi's royal chambers. Still in shackles, the witch slowly glided into the lavish quarters alone, amazed at the grandeur the girl she had met in the woods almost two decades ago now enjoyed.

"You were right," Niabi's voice echoed throughout the luxurious suite.

"About what?" Vilora peered around the room looking for the queen.

"He did lie to me." The Green-Eyed Raven stepped inside from her balcony with a small box in her hand. "Now he will know his place." She revealed

Gershom's severed ear as a trophy.

"Why am I here?" Vilora was not impressed.

Floating across the room, Niabi proudly placed the prized box on a nearby shelf surrounded by other similar containers.

"You have been honest with me, and for that, I believe you are owed a debt of gratitude. What is your price?"

"What I desire, you cannot give to me," the witch shrugged off the rare and generous offer.

"Try me."

The sorceress invited herself to sit in the nearest chair. "Remind me again of the story you were told of the Old Witch of Endor."

Niabi smirked as she poured herself a glass of red wine. "Are you so old you have forgotten your own history, Vilora?"

"Indulge me, my Queen."

Now seated comfortably in her high back chair, Niabi's eyes danced with delight at the thought of playing the witch's game.

The Old Witch of Endor,
How frightening is she.
The Old Witch of Endor,
How did they not see?

Her heart black as night,
Her eyes cold as ice.
With hatred so fiery,
That even her family,
Knew not the devil's wife in disguise.

Banished in fear,
All who were near,
Paid the deadliest price of them all.

The Isle of Endor,
Sunk deep in the sea,
Forevermore cursed for the dead.

The Old Witch of Endor,
Feared and hated by all men.

The Old Witch of Endor,
Worshipped and loved by all hell.
The Almighty grant you mercy,
If ever you see,
The Old Witch of Endor indeed.

"Does that sound about right?" Niabi sipped on her wine with girlish delight.

Vilora nodded her head, "You asked what my price for honesty was?"

"Tell me, what does the Old Witch of Endor desire?"

"I desire my sister's heart."

Niabi was stunned by the request; she never considered Vilora even had a family of her own. "Why do you need me to help you with that? You are the Witch of Endor, get it yourself."

"When I was a young child, my parents noticed a dark gift in me. They desperately tried to heal me, but you cannot fix what is not broken," Vilora recalled the beginning of her tale. "After my parents died, my sister became queen and fearing me to be a threat to our people, banished me to the Isle of Endor. Needless to repeat, you know what I did in retaliation for my sister's betrayal."

Niabi sighed. "I grow weary of your ramblings."

"My sister bore three daughters and each of them had a unique position. The eldest, Zara, is the heir to the throne and commander of the royal fleet. Damaris, the youngest, was christened as the virgin high priestess and she cast a spell, preventing me from ever returning home. Her middle daughter was the most beautiful one of them all," the old woman continued, not deterred by Niabi eyeing her. "My sister married her off to ensure a strong alliance with the mainland remained intact. Her name was Bilhah."

Niabi stared at the witch in complete disbelief, "You mean to tell me, your sister is Queen Nym of the Isles of Myr?"

"Your grandmother's heart is my price; nothing more, nothing less."

Vilora gave Niabi a moment to sift through all the information she revealed to her. The Old Witch of Endor was more than just a song parents would frighten their children with; she was her great aunt, her own flesh and blood.

"If I do this," Niabi leaned back in her seat, one leg crossed over the other, "you must also help me."

Vilora scoffed. "I thought this was your generous offer for my honesty."

"If your price for honesty is for me to have my own grandmother's heart ripped from her chest and given to you on a silver platter, then I will require more from you." The queen was prepared to make another deal.

"What is it you want?" She was intrigued.

Niabi spoke in a low voice. "You know how to raise someone from the dead, do you not?"

Vilora's eyes widened. "No one resurrects the departed. Kill or be killed, but do not bring back those who walk beyond the grave."

Niabi rose from her seat, grabbed a large leather-bound book from her shelf, opened it, and placed it on the table in front of Vilora.

"This is the Resurrection Spell," the queen continued, ignoring Vilora's reservations. "I know you have enough magic to complete the ritual. What I do not have is the Heart of the Righteous."

"You are mad to think you can save your son," she shook her head. She could not recall if anyone had ever successfully performed the Resurrection Spell.

"We can help one another," Niabi's eyes softened. "After all, we share the same blood."

"You said it yourself," Vilora smirked as she leaned back in her seat, "you do not have the Heart of the Righteous."

"No," she admitted with a grin. "But I know where I can find one." The queen bent down before the old woman and freed her from her heavy iron shackles. "I will give you your sister's heart if you give my son back to me. Do we have a deal?"

Vilora gazed into Niabi's eyes, sensing the danger they held. She knew there was a chance she would not be able to complete the Resurrection Spell and would face the queen's wrath, but her own deep-rooted desire for her sister's heart far outweighed her fear of Niabi. She nodded. "We have a deal."

CHAPTER 21

THE NAMELESS RIDER

The leader of the newly arrived group of Shadows ordered the dwellers of the Tree House Forest to be gathered for questioning. He was a burly man with a prominent jaw. The left side of his face had a deep scar that ran from his eye to his chin. Burn marks covered most of his body, but nothing was more chilling about him than his one, icy blue eye that was visible through his black mask. He never allowed anyone to know anything about him, not even his birth name, Pert. To keep his identity a mystery, he preferred being known as the Nameless Rider. He was a heartless man who slaughtered men, women and children. And anyone seeking revenge was added to his long list of victims.

One by one, villagers were brought before him to be questioned about what happened to his slain Shadows. He sat quietly peeling an apple with one of his many knives as the next peasant was thrown at his feet.

Jacobi was terrified of the disfigured warrior sitting in front of him, yet all he could do was hope he would not be the next villager to be added to the pile of dead bodies the Shadows had accumulated that morning.

"Name?" the Nameless Rider asked in a deep and raspy voice.

"Jacobi, sir," the baker whispered as loudly as he dared.

"Jacobi," the Shadow repeated, which sent chills down the young villager's spine.

"Yes, sir." Sweat dripped down his forehead.

"What is it that you do here in this hellhole?"

"I am a baker, sir."

"A baker."

"Yes, sir."

"You seem to be an honest peasant. Is that a fair statement?" the Shadow swallowed an apple slice whole.

"I try to tell the truth."

"I am seeking the truth about what happened here. Would you care to tell me what happened?"

Jacobi lifted his eyes from the Shadow's feet to the tip of his mask. "They were killed, sir."

He chomped down on another slice, "That part is clear, Jacobi. What I do not understand is how seven of my brothers were slaughtered in this... village."

"The one in charge murdered a child, so Crispin killed some of your men until they subdued him," the whimpering villager spoke quickly, hoping to appease the assassin.

"If they subdued him, then what happened to the other men?"

"His sister, Salome, killed them. She is an excellent marksman," he continued answering any question posed to him.

"You mean to tell me that two peasants killed my men? One being a woman?" The broad-shouldered man leaned forward, smacking another slice of his juicy apple.

"Yes, sir."

"Is that the truth, Jacobi?"

"Yes, sir, the truth. That is all I know," the trembling villager wiped sweat from his brow.

"I will determine if that is all you know."

"Of course, sir."

"Which tree house is theirs?" The masked leader stood up; his seven-foot-tall frame towered over everyone in the entire village.

Jacobi pointed to the tree house the Northerners had occupied. "That one there, sir."

The Nameless Rider peered down at the compliant peasant. "You have been most helpful." He turned to one of the Shadows standing nearby and pointed at the tree house, "Bring the villagers who live there to me, *alive*."

"They are not there," Jacobi chimed in. "They left."

"They *what*?" he growled.

"We did not want them here any longer because of their crimes against the North and we told them to leave."

The Shadow grabbed Jacobi by his throat and lifted him off the muddy ground. "This is why people like you are not worthy of touching the ground we walk on. Fools! Where did they go?"

Jacobi gasped for air. "I do not know."

"Where are they?" He tightened his grip around the villager's throat.

Tears streamed down Jacobi's face. "I tell you the truth, sir, I do not know where they have gone. I swear on my very life."

In a rare moment of what appeared to be mercy, the blue-eyed soldier released Jacobi from his death grip allowing him to fall back to the ground. He knelt in front of the baker, looking directly into his fearful eyes, "Would you be able to describe them in great detail?"

"Yes, sir," Jacobi rubbed his neck, knowing he barely escaped death.

"Good. You may be of some use to me after all, Jacobi."

"I will do whatever you say," the baker bowed.

"Tell me one more thing, Jacobi the Baker." He dropped his apple core at his feet. "Who was it who told these criminals to leave?"

In anguish knowing he was about to betray his neighbor, the baker lifted his face and stared at Tiron. The elder was waiting to be questioned; blood trickled down his head from the blow he had suffered that morning. "That man there."

Not bothering to look in the elder's direction, the commanding Shadow hissed, "Bring him to me."

"What do you intend to do with him?" Jacobi questioned without thinking.

"What will happen to you, if you disappoint me."

Frightened, Tiron was dragged up to the platform and thrown before the Shadow. "Please, my lord," the bald man pleaded. "I will tell you all I know, please do not harm me."

"Name."

"Tiron."

"Tiron." He repeated. "What is it you do here in this hellhole?" He rattled off the same questions.

"I am a farmer by trade, but I am also the elder of this community." Tiron attempted to look brave as he answered the seemingly harmless questions.

"A farmer by trade but also the elder of this community." He echoed in almost a whisper.

"Yes, sir."

"It has come to my attention, Tiron the Farmer, that you ordered a family who lived in *that* tree house," he pointed at Crispin and Salome's home, "to leave the village immediately following their attack on my men. Is this true?"

Tiron peered at Jacobi hoping to get a read of the situation, but the baker kept his eyes glued to the ground. "I did."

"You ordered them to leave?"

"Yes, my lord. We can't have murderers in our village."

"And where did they go?"

"I do not know." Tiron dripped sweat.

"You do not know?"

"No, sir."

"Thank you for your honesty, Tiron the Farmer."

"You will let me go?" The elder was elated.

"I will tell you what I am going to do," the Nameless Rider smirked. "You take this sword," he pointed at his own weapon, "and if you can beat one of my men in combat, you will be free to go."

Trembling head to toe, Tiron begged the Shadow, "Please, sir, I do not know anything about weapons."

"Are you refusing my generous offer?"

"No, my -"

"Then pick up this sword and fight."

Tiron glanced at his neighbor with tears in his eyes. "Jacobi?"

"What is Jacobi the Baker supposed to do for you? Fight in your stead?" The Shadow turned his focus to the shriveled Jacobi. "Is that what you want to do, Jacobi the Baker? Do you want to offer yourself in his place?"

Jacobi shook his head. "No, sir."

"I suspected as much." He shook his head. "You cannot ask a coward to fight for another coward."

"Please -"

"Tiron the Farmer, what do you intend to do?" the Shadow interrupted his pleas. "Will you fight for your life and die like a man? Or will you lay down and die like a gutless pig?"

With every villager watching, Tiron slowly reached for the Shadow's sword.

"Go on," the Nameless Rider motioned him off the platform. "Down there where we can all watch."

The elder shook as he walked to the open square where he was met by one of the Nameless Rider's men with two curved blades in his hands. Knowing this was going to be his end, he lifted the blade and swung with all his might toward the soldier. With a sidestep, the Shadow evaded his weak attack and in one motion, sliced the elder's head from his body.

The Shadow Commander snickered as Tiron's head bounced on the ground. "This hasn't been a total waste of a day after all." Turning his gaze once more toward Jacobi, he asked, "Does anyone else have any information that might prove valuable to us?"

Hoping to spare what remained of his village, the baker quickly said, "No, they do not know anything more than what I have told you."

"Good. I have grown quite tired of this village." The Nameless Rider stood up and stretched. "We ride out. You are coming with us, Jacobi the Baker."

Relieved he did not have to stay to face the judgment of his fellow villagers, Jacobi welcomed his prisoner status.

"Kill the others, burn what's left of the village," he ordered four of his men to finish the job. "The rest of us ride out."

"Wait!" Jacobi was horrified. "I told you they didn't know anything else. Why kill them?"

The Nameless Rider cracked his neck, "Why not?"

"Please, sir, please -"

"You can stay and die with them if it pleases you or you can ride with us to find these murderers." He mounted his horse as the villagers began to scream in terror. "I need an answer, Jacobi the Baker. What is it going to be?"

Unwilling to die with the rest of them, Jacobi hopped on the horse offered to him and left the village he had always known as home.

"You get used to it."

"To what?" Jacobi asked.

"The screams of those about to die. Most nights I won't even attempt to sleep until I have heard it." He smiled.

CHAPTER 22

NIABI

Smoth and calculated, every movement of her lean body was precise. Armed only with her two silver daggers, Niabi floated across the floor, a vision of fire, effortlessly sparring with three of her fiercest Shadows. Donning her black leather ensemble which afforded her the opportunity to wear pants, greatly increased her range of motion. Flexibility was her greatest strength. Roundhouse kicks, splits, and a wide array of flips were reasons why she was so deadly in combat. She had been trained by the Andrago and Myridians and her skills were no match for the structured battle techniques of other warriors in Adalore.

Her knives glistened in the beams of sunlight that poured into the courtyard as she swung her weapon at her approaching attacker. With a swift punch to his gut and cut across his face, the assailant stepped aside and allowed his two partners to advance. Both Shadows charged their queen, weapons drawn, instructed to strike if given the opportunity. As they drew near, Niabi sprinted toward them and slid in a front split between them, slicing the back of their nearest knees as she passed them. With two of them incapacitated, she turned her focus back on the Shadow with a cut across the left side of his chiseled jaw. He clutched his long blade and gritted his teeth, knowing he would suffer a similar fate, if he took his eyes off her for one second.

Circling one another, the last two standing warriors stared deep into one another's eyes. Once she spotted a hint of fear in his gaze, she pounced, flipping her daggers around her fingers. Blocking blow after blow, he continued to step backwards until his back hit a large column. Now knowing he had no choice but to charge her, he pushed off the wall and sprinted toward her. Niabi turned and ran across the courtyard until she reached a different column, ran up the side and backflipped over the Shadow chasing her. Landing on her feet, she pinned her opponent to the column with one of her daggers pressed against his neck and the other poking his left ribcage. He dropped his weapon, yielding the duel. She released him from her grasp.

Pash had slipped in undetected and watched as his queen sparred with the three Shadows for her daily training. Her knives were extensions of her two hands making her certifiably the most treacherous Shadow of them all.

It was in fact, Niabi, who originally banded the brotherhood together. Every member tattooed the symbol of the raven on top of their left hands to honor their master.

Having ravaged the three mercenaries, Niabi stood tall among the men scattered in the courtyard.

"You let my father live," Pash alerted Niabi of his presence. "Why?"

Her fierce green eyes peered up and down the commander's muscular body as she waved the other men out of her sight. "Does that surprise you?"

"Forgive me, my Queen, but you are not known to be merciful," he spoke boldly, standing between two large columns.

She smirked as she sheathed her two daggers and picked up a sword. "Spar with me. I could use the practice."

He walked down the steps into the sparring grounds and drew his sword. Both warriors took their stances as Niabi rubbed her weapon up and down the commander's outstretched sword. Circling one another, they began their duel.

"I let him live because he still serves a purpose," she exhaled, whilst landing powerful blows.

"And once he is no longer of use to you?"

"You know exactly what will happen."

"What will happen once you have tired of me?"

She dropped to the ground and knocked him off his feet with a low sweep kick. As he fell to the ground, she pressed her knee into his chest with her sword pinned against his neck. "Do you think I will grow tired of you?"

"You tell me, my Queen."

"I am cold," she softly breathed, "but I am not unfeeling."

"You took his ear," he pointed out.

"He is fortunate that was all I took," she spat.

His voice softened, "What do you intend to take from me?"

She gazed deep into his kind and gentle brown eyes as she kept him solidly pinned against the white stone floor. Leaning in, she kissed him, making her intentions known. Pash pushed the blade from his throat, spun her around and pressed her against the stone floor, furthering their passionate kiss.

"I thought you no longer cared for me," he whispered in her ear.

She ran her slender fingers through his long chestnut hair and admitted, "I do care for you, Pash."

"Then why have we not shared a bed in weeks?"

She pushed Pash off her and stood up, "You know why."

His eyes followed her as she retreated. "I loved him too, Niabi."

She kicked her sword up in the air and grabbed it. "Again."

Pash jumped to his feet, "Why do you push me away when you need me the most?"

"I do not *need* anyone," her eyes burned, nostrils flared.

He was unmoved by her menacing glare, "You are the strongest woman I have ever known but being strong does not mean going through life alone."

She threw his sword for him to catch, "Spar or leave."

"Niabi -"

"Is it not enough that I have told you I care for you?" she croaked, throwing her hands in the air. "Why do you push me?"

Pointing out the windows that surrounded the courtyard, he took a step toward her, "They may be afraid of you, but I know who you truly are, and I cannot abandon you to your own undoing."

"I entered this world alone and I will leave it alone, nothing you do or say will prevent that," she placed her sword on the rack. "You would do well to remember that I am still your queen, Commander, and I will be the one to determine my fate."

CHAPTER 23
MARTA

Shrouded in a long black cloak, Marta weaved in the dark and foggy forest hoping to find the Hidden Tavern on the river. With rain eminent, she knew if she did not find the dock master within the next few minutes, she would be lost in the swamp until morning if she managed to live through the elements. Her heartbeat hastened as she continued to fumble her way down the path, lit only by a small lantern.

"Halt! Who goes there?" A gruff voice echoed in the fog.

"I seek the dock master, sir. I fear I am lost," her voice trembled in angst, hoping she had not stumbled upon a troubled fellow.

As the fog cleared, a weathered man with long stringy hair stepped toward her with a lantern held above his head. With a tired sigh, he motioned her to step forward. "Fear not, woman. You have found the dock master."

She squinted her eyes and saw the boat that would take her to the Hidden Tavern bobbing alongside the creaky dock. The bar was secretly located in the middle of the swamp and the only way to get there was to ride in the dock master's boat. Relief overtook the wary woman when she stepped into the small vessel and silently rode down the river.

After nearly ten minutes, he pointed in front of him. "There she is."

The large wooden structure built on sturdy poles stationed in the middle of the lake was exactly as everyone had described it. Excitement swept over her as they docked. She would soon see the man she had travelled for days to meet. As quickly as she dared, she climbed the flimsy ladder to the wooden platform and made her way to the front door.

Once she heard all the rough and raspy male voices behind the door, she hesitated, but took a deep breath and walked inside. Deep in their beer drinking raucous, none of them noticed the newcomer, or the fact that she was a woman.

The bar keep was passing by with four large pints of ale when she stopped him. "Excuse me, sir, I am looking for someone."

"What's his name, ma'am?" he asked in great irritation.

"I am not sure," she answered sheepishly.

"You came all this way to meet someone you don't have a name for?" he chuckled, now amused.

"What I meant to say is I do not know his birth name."

"What name do you have, and I will tell you if he exists." His arms were beginning to shake holding the overflowing pints.

She leaned in and whispered a name she did not wish anyone else to hear.

The dirty bar keep's eyes immediately widened, and he looked toward the back, dark corner of the tavern. "That is the man you seek, but I warn you, he is not known to be an agreeable man."

Before she could ask him any other questions, he hobbled away from her, as if he did not want to be associated with her. She marched to the corner table where the dark hooded figure was seated. She could not see his face, but noticed he was smoking a small pipe and had fingerless leather gloves on both of his dirty hands.

"Sir, I am in need of your skill set," she blurted before she had a chance to change her mind.

"That depends on who is asking," a gravelly voice responded from beneath the hood.

Korah's mother uncovered her head. "I am a mother who was robbed of her son. I seek revenge."

"I assume since you know of my services, you know required fees," he ignored her passion and remained focused on business.

"I do not have much, but what I do have I will give you." She took a small coin purse from under her black cloak and placed it on the table.

The hooded figure did not even examine the purse. "That is not nearly enough to tempt me, woman."

"It is all I have. Please, sir, I beg of you to have mercy on a mother who has lost every person she has ever loved," she choked back tears.

"And why should I pity you above the rest?" He was eager to hear her answer but was surprised to see her rise and grab two wanted posters from the wall next to them.

"Where did these come from?" She inspected the wanted posters the Shadows had been posting throughout Adalore over the last day.

"Everyone knows the work of the Shadows, woman."

She handed him the wanted posters with Salome and Crispin's renderings printed with a reward. "The two responsible for my son's death slaughtered seven Shadows a few days ago in my village and there is a hefty reward for their heads."

He was now intrigued and leaned forward, still not allowing his face to be revealed in the light. "What are you suggesting?"

"If you kill them, you can keep the reward money. I will be satisfied knowing my Korah was avenged, and you will have your payment and then some. What say you? Do we have a deal?"

He exhaled a puff of smoke and pushed the coin purse toward her as he stood up. Disappointment set in. She believed he had turned her down but was shocked to see him fold the posters and put them in his cloak pocket. "I will take care of them for you."

"Oh, thank you, sir!" Marta grabbed the mercenary's hand and kissed it only to have him yank his hand away from her.

"We are finished here."

Marta smiled coldly as she watched her savior leave.

CHAPTER 24
GERSHOM

Just as the sun rose above the horizon, Gershom, and a handful of his most trusted personal guards, disembarked their small vessel and walked to the center of the uninhabited island of Petram. The tiny island was one large slab of rock off the eastern coast of Northwind. Thousands of years ago, Petram was used as a sacred place for ceremonial sacrifices. Gershom held this secret place in high esteem, believing in the ancient rituals of the Adalorians of old. Knowing the island now frightened people away, he used it to conduct private meetings which ensured his secrets would remain exactly that: secrets.

As he reached the middle of the rock island, Gershom spotted a short, elderly man with wrinkles that stretched across his dark skin sitting on a stone slab once used for sacrifices. The bald old man with a slight hunch in his back, stroked his well-manicured white beard, waiting for Gershom to sit down next to him.

His bony fingers reached across his chest and touched his left shoulder. "My Lord," his wheezy voice hissed from his dry lips.

"Memucan." Gershom returned the magician's greeting, observing the armored crew the old man had brought with him. "Why so many guards?"

"One can never be too careful, my lord." Memucan rubbed his weathered eyes, which had faded to a light blue color due to slight blindness, in angst. "Why have you summoned me?"

The Second in Command made sure no one would be able to hear their conversation. Being satisfied their guards were at a decent distance, Gershom turned his focus back to his companion. "What do you know of the old tales and prophecies?"

"Which tales and prophecies are you referring to?"

"Tell me what you know of the Hunters." Since Gershom now only had one ear, he had to situate himself properly, so he could hear what Memucan had to say.

"What we all know. There is only one marked as the Hunter and he is charged with avenging the blood of the innocent. Of course, there has not been one for over two hundred years." The magician stared at the earless warrior. "Most Adalorians no longer believe in such tales. Why do you?"

"He is coming for me." Gershom had never been surer of anything in his entire life. "The stars have spoken, and his time has come."

"Even if that were true, why would such a warrior come for you?" The sorcerer, who was rarely interested in anyone's tale, was now intrigued.

"When I was a child, I wandered away from my house and found myself lost in the woods of the Black Forest. I crossed paths with a fortune teller, and she told me of my fate."

"And what did she tell you?"

His chestnut brown eyes were filled with fear, "She told me that if I allowed myself to be seduced by the Mistress of the Night, I would betray my closest friend and the penalty for my sins would be the Hunter's blade buried deep in my heart." He rubbed his calloused hands together, staring toward the sun rising above the horizon. "According to the stars, he has come of age, and unless I find him first, my life is forfeit."

Memucan rubbed his chin, "Was that all she told you?"

"That was all she said, then she sent me on my way."

After a moment of silence, the wrinkled old man squinted his fading eyes. "What would you have me do?"

"I need to find him," Gershom hesitated, unsure how the next portion of his request would go over with Memucan. "And I need to find two of Issachar's children."

"You mean to tell me you let two of his heirs escape you?" he wheezed. "They could be anywhere in Adalore! They will not be easy to find."

"I recall helping you track down the elusive thief that stole your illegal book of dark magic." Gershom had no problem in reminding him of the favor he owed him. "I am now asking you to help me find those who threaten me."

Memucan realized the position he was now in and had no other choice but to agree to Gershom's terms. "I will see what I can do." He rose from his seated position and used his short wooden cane to help him limp back to his side of the island to board his awaiting ship. "Whatever happened to the thief?"

"He still rots in my dungeons." The fur wearing warrior stood up and flashed a sinister grin. "You know, I had nearly forgotten he even existed."

Memucan smirked, crossed his feeble arm across his sagging chest and hobbled away. Gershom knew he could count on the old man and although he had many enemies, foreign and domestic, he was determined to prove the fortune teller a liar.

CHAPTER 25
NEEMPO

On an island in Narrow Bay, between the Southern and Western Lands, stood two tall towers connected by an enclosed two-story bridge near the top of the dark stoned structures. Simply known as 'The Sisters', the self-sufficient fortress was home to citizens from every corner of Adalore, making it the only city to welcome diversity. However, there was a reason for the mixing of the races; every single inhabitant was born blind and sent in their infancy to live out their days amongst their own kind.

Adalorians born without sight had one of two gifts and were separated according to their gift and sent to their respective towers upon arrival. Witnesses were responsible for recording events, prophecies, and visions. Their recordings were stored in the largest library of the known world. Keepers were warriors who, although blind, used their heightened senses to fight those who would attempt to steal documents or treasures from the Blind Order. As a people, they avoided picking sides in the wars of Adalorian kings and remained neutral in order to keep accurate accounts of history. Both sects were faithful to their studies and disciplined in their everyday lives, so when it came to their city's defenses, they were superior to all who opposed them.

Oden, formally known as Lord Maon, had just arrived at the remote monastery, and was escorted through the gothic hallways by four Keepers to meet with the Sovereign in his study. In order to be the Sovereign of The Sisters, one had to be equally gifted as a Witness and a Keeper, which was rare. In fact, it was only when one Sovereign died that the next would be revealed.

The present leader of the Blind Order was fifteen when he was appointed the youngest Sovereign in the order's history, and he had now been in power for twenty-five years. Neempo was tall and slender with straight black hair and his alabaster skin was spotted with freckles across the bridge of his thin nose. Like most of the citizens of The Sisters, his narrow almond eyes were glossed over, but he tied a red cloth around his eyes to set him apart as the leader of the blind.

Oden cheerfully greeted his old friend, who he had not seen in nearly a decade. "Time has been good to you, my friend, you don't look like you've aged a day."

"And you carry heavier burdens than you did before." Neempo's swift and graceful movements through the circular room located in the middle of the two-story bridge showed his lack of eyesight did not hinder him in any way. "What do I owe the pleasure of your visit?"

The Sovereign sat in a low back wooden chair and Oden sat in an identical chair across from him.

"Whispers from my little birds have led me to believe there is a storm coming for the North."

Neempo smiled, "You speak of Issachar's children."

"So, it *is* true. They did escape." The reports Oden had received were now confirmed.

"Prince Lykos's last selfless act was to see his siblings survive." Neempo weaved his fingers together as his smooth voice shared what information he knew. "But that is not why you have come to see me."

Oden never could disguise his true motives for journeying to The Sisters. "Rumor has it that the Year of the Hunter has begun. It seems Gershom is afraid of this news and has dispatched some of the Queen's Shadows to find the Hunter before he can pose him any threat."

"And afraid he should be."

Oden's eyes danced with delight, "Where can I find him?"

The Sovereign shook his head, "I am sorry, but I cannot answer that."

"Neempo, please! I must find him before Gershom does," Oden pleaded. "I need your help."

Neempo poured two cups of tea. "The Sisters does not concern itself with the trivial pursuit of Adalorian crowns. We solely exist to keep honest records and maintain order in our own city. You know this."

"Would you sit idly by once again to the suffering of the innocent?"

Although insulted, Neempo did not allow his voice to show any resentment. "What happened in the North twelve years ago was not due to our neutrality. Issachar was given report by his Seer, and he chose not to heed this warning, ultimately paying a heavy price."

Oden accepted the cup Neempo extended to him. "You do not understand -"

"I know how much you loved Bilhah, and I realize this is more personal for you than for most, but my people will not involve themselves with this matter." He could sense Oden's heavy heart just by listening to him breathe. "Issachar's children are the key. Find them and they will lead you to the Hunter."

"I don't know where to even begin to look for them." Oden rubbed his bloodshot eyes. "No one does."

"Perhaps looking *for* them would not be wise. But thinking of where they might be headed..." Neempo smiled, knowing that clue would be enough for his companion to figure out.

Oden rose with a newfound determination. "Thank you, Neempo."

"Go," Neempo embraced Oden as he bid him farewell. "They will need your help sooner than you realize."

"I will find them." Oden patted him on the back.

"And perhaps," Neempo chuckled, "don't wait another ten years before visiting with me again."

"Take care, my friend."

Once the door closed, Penn and Balor, masters of the two sects of The Sisters, entered from the adjoining room, having heard the entire conversation.

"You trust him?" Originally from the Andrago, Penn was the first female Master of Keepers and in keeping with the ancient custom, wore a black wrap around her eyes as their counselor. Her snub nose and full lips were prominent when the wrap was tied around her bronze face. Although, she had not spent much time in Elisor, she maintained tradition by intricately braiding her long, silky black hair.

"He has a good heart." The Sovereign sat back down in his chair to finish his tea.

"You did not answer the question," Penn pressed, sitting down.

"And he does not need to. He is the Sovereign." Balor's black skin was an instant indicator he was from the southern city of Numbio. Well into his sixties, his short white hair and manicured beard matched the white eye wrap he wore as Master of Witnesses. Sporting a wooden cane due to an injured hip, he limped toward the younger leaders.

"I beg forgiveness," Penn recanted. "I meant no offense."

"There is nothing to forgive, Master Penn," Neempo spoke softly as the masters sat with him.

"Will he find Issachar's children?" she persisted.

"When he is meant to." The Sovereign poured tea for them. "Why not speak on what troubles you?"

"War is inevitable," Penn spoke freely. "We will be forced to choose a side."

"We have never involved our people in Adalorian wars," Balor protested, stirring honey in his cup. "If they are bent on destroying one another, we should not take part."

"I have endured many sleepless nights as of late, Master Balor, due to disturbing visions," Penn was unmoved and did not accept tea. "Sovereign, we *will* be forced into this war." She felt his breathing pattern slow. "You have already foreseen this?"

"I have." Neempo admitted.

"So, war is coming for us." She leaned forward.

"We are a peaceful kingdom, neutral on these matters," Balor once again voiced his disapproval. "How else would the records of the Ten Kingdoms be accurate and impartial?"

"What good are your records if our halls are desecrated?" she argued.

Balor scoffed, "Our people are not trained for battle."

"Your Witnesses may not be," her nostrils flared, "but my Keepers certainly are."

"A haughty assumption from a soldier who has never engaged in true battle," Balor scratched his upturned eyebrows. "The blind fighting those with sight is ridiculous."

"Sight can be deceiving, Master Balor," she shot.

"Say we do send the Keepers to war," Balor sipped his tea, "what happens if you should fail?"

"We won't," Penn furrowed her brow.

"But if you do," he pressed.

"Failure is not a word I even comprehend," she pounded on her chest twice. "We were bred for this."

"Forgive me," Balor shook his head, "but I remain unconvinced."

"Do I question your Witnesses on the accuracy of their accounts? No. That is their purpose, their gift." Penn rested her hand on Balor's. "When war knocks on our door, for Death will come, we shall be ready to face her, sword in hand."

"Master Penn, Master Balor," Neempo set his teacup down on the end table. "Our neutrality has kept our people safe for hundreds of years, but I am afraid that is no longer an option." He sighed heavily, knowing their way of life was about to change. "Though the Shadow of Death comes, we will find our strength. Let it be so."

Both masters echoed, "Let it be so."

CHAPTER 26
SALOME

Salome spent most of the night staring up at the wooden ceiling, waiting for the sun to rise, so she could explore the Hollow. She quietly rolled out of her bed, grabbed her hunting knife, bow and arrows and slipped out of the cozy hovel before anyone noticed she was gone.

The Hollow had an ancient feel to it, as if the trees themselves whispered tales of the past. Mesmerized by the beauty around her, she abandoned the idea of hunting and decided to enjoy a lonely morning walk to clear her head. She inhaled the sweet air that whipped around her and pulled her long wavy curls back into a messy ponytail. This place was intoxicating, unlike any place she had ever been before. She closed her eyes and listened to all the sounds of the forest. Birds chirping, squirrels rustling around, the sound of a twig snapping.

Her eyes opened as she realized she was not alone. She turned to face him. The hooded man was armed with a long sword and walked toward her, noticing she was not armed with a blade.

"Who are you?" Salome stood her ground.

Adonijah held his sword up. "I thought it would take days to find you, but it seems fortune is on my side."

"Find me?" She was confused. "Why would you be looking for me? You must have me mistaken for someone else."

"If you come quietly, I will not harm you."

"It would be best for you to be on your way, stranger," she insisted. Although she had not unsheathed her knife and her bow was strapped to her back, it appeared to him that she had no means to protect herself, so he took a step forward. "Take one more step and I will slit your throat," she drew her knife from the holster attached to her upper thigh, forcing him to stop his advancement.

"Only if you are able to beat me."

"Take another step and find out."

"You are feistier than I expected," he smirked.

"Who are you?" She pointed her dagger in his direction. "What do you want with me?"

He sighed. "As much as I would like to explain everything in detail, love, I am on a deadline."

She started to circle, mimicking his movements. "Do you not understand how to answer questions?"

"I grow impatient, girl."

"As do I," she growled back. "Walk away and I will forget this ever happened."

"I am afraid I cannot do that." He pointed his sword toward her. "Hand over your weapon."

"The only way you will get my weapon is by prying it from my dead fingers," she spat at the ground by his feet.

He shrugged. "Have it your way."

He lunged toward her, but she deflected his attack with her knife. Swiftness was her greatest strength, having practiced with her much larger brother for years. Salome continued to spar with him, ducking and dodging his heavy blows. He left himself open to attack when he lunged too far, and she took advantage. She punched him in the face, hoping to knock him off balance. Enraged by her quickness, he swung his weapon toward her face and while she was distracted, he unsheathed his dagger and swiped at her torso. Retracting his dagger, he landed a powerful blow to her face, forcing her to the ground.

He stood over her as she wiped the blood around her mouth. "Are we finished?"

"Is that the best you can do?" Her dismissive tone signaled round two.

She rolled away from him and jumped to her feet. They sparred once again, evenly matched. Being blessed with the swift ability to read her opponent's pattern, she waited for the precise moment he would lunge forward to slash his chest. As predicted, he launched himself toward her. She cut him across his broad chest and kicked him off his feet. As he fell, Adonijah dropped his sword. She picked it up and knelt on his torso.

With a dagger against his neck she hissed, "Do you yield? Or shall I kick your ass again?"

Adonijah's hood now revealed the bottom half of his face so she could see his mischievous smile. "Not bad... for a woman."

"Stand up," she ordered, careful to keep a weapon pointed at him.

He stood as he was instructed, keeping his hands where she could see them. "Is this when you kick my ass again?"

Salome threw his sword back and he caught it with great confusion. "I never kill unarmed men."

This time he was unwilling to leave their duel up to chance. As they danced around one another, he kicked out his leg and tripped her. The fall surprised her, and she dropped her dagger out of her immediate reach. Adonijah bent down to grab her, but she scooped up a rock and smacked him against the side of his face, knocking him unconscious.

She took a moment to catch her breath. She looked at her attacker and saw his hood had fallen over his head. Adonijah had dark brown hair that fell just above his shoulders. His close-trimmed beard brought attention to his square jawline. She noticed with his eyes closed, he looked almost kind, but she knew better after sparring with him. The hooded man was a skilled aggressor, but she still had no idea why he assaulted her.

Looking through his pockets, she came across two pieces of paper and upon further inspection saw they were wanted posters with her and Crispin's faces sketched for all to see. Without delay, she picked up her weapons and raced back to Harbona's house to warn the others of the Shadows' warrant.

IT HAD BEEN an uneventful morning in Harbona's hovel as the three men lounged in the main room having just finished their breakfast. Crispin was obsessive about his weapons and as was his routine, he began to clean every item he possessed. He knew a soldier was only as good as the weapons he wielded, and he was determined to be at his best at a moment's notice.

Zophar and Harbona sat at the small table smoking their long pipes quietly. The older men were not known to be conversationalists but chose their words cautiously and wisely picked which battles they would fight.

Knowing Salome's routine, Zophar was not at all surprised by her absence when they woke up that morning. She desired time alone most mornings and he knew she would be able to defend herself, if needed.

Salome burst through the wooden door and slammed it behind her holding her bleeding torso. Crispin looked up at his sweaty sister and saw blood trickling down her mouth and jumped up to tend to her wounds.

"What the hell happened to you?" Crispin helped her to a chair.

She threw the wanted posters on the table in front of them. "This. This is what happened to me."

Zophar picked up the papers and saw Crispin and Salome's faces. "Where did you get this?"

"Off the bounty hunter who tried to kill me." She coughed up more blood as Crispin cleaned her stomach wound.

"He did this to you?" Crispin was enraged.

"I am fine."

"Where is he?"

"I handled it."

"You killed him?" Zophar asked after handing her a cup of water.

"No," she shook her head. "He was unconscious; I couldn't kill him in cold blood."

Crispin was furious she had not killed the bounty hunter. "Then what did you do with him? Could he have followed you back here?"

"By the time he wakes up, we will be long gone from here." She defended her decision.

"We had better leave." Zophar looked panicked that a mercenary was able to find them so easily.

"We cannot go together, Zophar." Salome grabbed his arm before he could leave the table. "Everyone is looking for us. Shadows, bounty hunters, greedy peasants; it is too risky."

"You are not suggesting we split up?" Crispin was dumbfounded at the very thought of them not being together.

"I do not see what other choice we have."

"We have never been apart." He refused to listen. "We have always been safer together, Salome."

"Not anymore. They know what we look like," she lifted the wanted posters. "If we stay together, it will be easier for them to find us. We are no longer safe together. At least, not right now."

Harbona, who had remained silent the entire time finally spoke. "She is right, Crispin. Your paths are going in two different directions."

Crispin's chest puffed out. "Where would I go?"

"You and Zophar shall travel south to Numbio to meet with King Osiris. He and your father were good friends," Harbona instructed the young prince.

"And what of me?" Salome asked.

"You and I will find the one they call the Wanderer. He will be an incredible asset to our cause. But we must do this quickly, for if one mercenary found you, then surely more will follow."

Zophar stood up from the table. "I will ready the horses."

"Wait, are we parting ways now?" Crispin was extremely uncomfortable with how quickly decisions were being made for him and his sister.

Harbona rested his hand on his shoulder. "It is time to fulfill your destiny, Crispin. You must walk without Salome for now. Gather your belongings, you have a long journey ahead of you."

When the horses were ready for the four travelers to part ways, Harbona sealed his tree house door and mounted his grey steed. "We must be on our way, Salome."

She turned toward her brother with tears in her eyes. "Please don't do anything stupid, Crispin."

"I make no promises." He smiled to keep from crying. "Take care of yourself." He kissed her cheek.

"We will see one another again," she promised him, knowing he was thinking the same thing she was.

He pulled his slender sister toward him in one last embrace. Fighting back tears he whispered, "I don't blame you for Korah's death. I was silent because in order to save him, I would have had to condemn you. I will never let anything happen to you, Salome. Even if I forfeit my own life in the process. I love you."

She tightened her grip around his waist. "I love you too." Before she had a chance to break down, she kissed his cheek and mounted her horse.

Crispin stared at Harbona. "Watch over her."

"I promise she will be safe in my charge," the Seer assured his prince.

The burly, red bearded man walked over to his young ward, grabbed her hand, and kissed it. "Remember everything you have been taught."

Salome leaned over and kissed Zophar's cheek. "I will."

A sad smile stretched across his pale face as tears filled his blue eyes. "Now, off with you."

As they rode in separate directions, not knowing when they would see one another again, they held on to the hope that their paths would cross again.

CHAPTER 27

NIABI

With her Nephilim by her side, Niabi gazed intently at the skittish scribe that knelt before her throne. The long train of her gown rested gently upon the white stone steps that led to her high-back chair. "Did you get all of that?"

The scribe skimmed through the message he had just recorded and nodded, semi-confidently. "Yes, my Queen."

"Good." She waved for him to leave her presence. "Now, see to it that message is sent to my servant in Myr."

He jumped to his feet and scurried from the throne room. Once he had vanished around the corner, Niabi rose from her throne and motioned for Anak-tu to step forward.

"See to it I am not disturbed."

Knowing her orders would be obeyed, Niabi left her Nephilim to do her bidding and made her way back to her private quarters to rest. As always, anyone who was in the hall as she passed by, would bow or curtsy and return to their tasks. The queen did not acknowledge a soul as she glided through the castle, desiring a moment to herself.

Once she reached her door, she suspected someone was waiting for her. Discreetly sliding her daggers from the long sleeves of her dress, she quietly slipped into her chambers. Eyeing every corner of her room, she finally noticed a man standing on her balcony.

"Enjoying the view, Pash?" She hid her knives.

"It is a beautiful view." He stared intently at the mountainous terrain that bordered the Ignacia Sea. "Of course, every window in the White Keep boasts a magnificent sight."

He seemed uncomfortable, as if he were waiting for the right moment to speak his mind.

"Why are you really here, Pash?" She poured herself a glass of wine. "Surely it is not to speak to me about the mountains."

"I know you did not summon me, but I needed to speak with you." He shifted his weight.

"Pash, please -"

"I ask my Queen for permission to speak," he bravely interrupted.

Reluctantly, since she knew what he was going to say, she permitted him an audience. "You may speak."

"I know your story and I have seen your heart broken more than once. I have cared for you most of my life and I will continue to serve you as you see fit," he hesitated, "but you must know, surely you must know, how much I love you."

She took another sip of her drink and nodded her head as she unclipped her black hair. "You know my past, and you have seen my brokenness, so you must know why I push you away. Why I will always push you away." She felt a heavy burden upon her shoulders as she exhaled. "I do care for you, Pash, but we could never be together the way you want us to be."

He was silent for a moment. "Did I do something to upset you?"

She set her glass down and started to brush her long hair, a nightly ritual. "Everyone I love has been taken from me and I do not wish that to be your fate."

She was genuine when she told him she cared for him. She had not felt this way since Dichali. But he did not need to know that. He could not know it.

Pash came up behind her and wrapped his arms around her waist. "You need not fear for me, Niabi."

She closed her eyes, rubbing his arm tied around her. "Why must you make this difficult for me? It may seem I am being cold, but I am doing what is best for you."

She broke away from him and stripped the armor from her left arm, revealing the blackness. He was one of the only people in the entire city who had seen what she hid beneath her custom-made armor and every time he saw it, he realized the decay, the poison, was spreading.

"It is still spreading." He gently grasped her arm to examine it.

"It will continue to do so until it reaches my heart," she spat flippantly as she set her arm band down in its case.

"You could die."

"Does not everyone?"

"A Healer might know how to stop this."

She flashed a serious glare in his direction knowing what he was about to do. "You will do no such thing, Commander. If I am to leave this earth it will be on my terms. I will not be dependent on any healer."

"So," his eyes met hers, "we are back to commander?"

She cupped her hands around his chiseled jaw and looked deep into his eyes. "Find a good woman and marry her before you have grown too old to enjoy her."

"Do you really believe I would listen to that command?" he squinted.

"It is not a command. It is my gift to you." She stepped away from his embrace. "Live your life before it is too late."

He caught her arm and pulled her back. "If I must live this one life, I choose to live it with you. And if you refuse me, then I will live my one life serving you until you change your mind."

"I told you the ones I care for are taken from me -"

"I do not fear Death," he interrupted her. "I fear living my life without you." He tilted her chin up and stared down into her eyes. "You love me too. I see it when you look at me. You may be my Queen, but you are also my lover -"

"Pash."

"Look me in the eye and tell me you do not love me, and I will never mention it again."

Silence overtook the lovers as they stared deeply in one another's eyes. Niabi breathed in the man she had grown to care deeply for and opened her lips to give him her answer.

"I…I…" Her eyes shifted away from him.

"You cannot say it." He leaned closer to her upturned face with the kindest eyes she had ever beheld.

"No," she whispered softly, "because it is not true."

Pash kissed her and this time she did not push him away.

CHAPTER 28

PASH

After several hours alone with her, Pash returned to his quarters with Niabi still on his mind. How he had fallen for the dangerous queen; how he wished their love did not have to remain a secret. It was in these private moments that he genuinely believed they had a fighting chance of having a lasting relationship. Of course, he knew how dark her heart could be, he was no fool, but he also saw the goodness that everyone overlooked.

The commander glanced around his dimly lit chambers to ensure his safety was intact. Every single time he examined the room he was alone, but this time he could feel someone's presence. He unsheathed his sword.

"You love her, but does she love you the same, I wonder?" The raspy female voice echoed through the dark space.

Weapon in hand, Pash turned in the voice's direction. "Who are you?"

With a flick of her tiny wrist, the Old Witch of Endor lit the space with an orb of fire she conjured, revealing herself. "Neither your friend nor your enemy."

"You speak in riddles of which I have no time for." He was leery of the woman who played with fire.

"Tell me, Commander Pash, how did you manage to find yourself in the Queen's bed?"

"You try my patience."

"Does she not scare you as she scares all those around her?" Vilora circled him.

Angrily stepping up to her, Pash spat, "I will cut out your tongue -"

A smirk spread across her weathered face as she waved her hand, forcing him to stop his advance. "Surely you would not harm an unarmed old woman, Pash."

Unable to move, he was frightened. "Who are you?"

"Very soon, you will be faced with a difficult choice to save the one you love most. Will it be her? Or will it be him?"

"Why do you say such horrible things?"

Vilora stepped forward. "I see you are a good man and I wanted to warn you of what lies ahead."

He tilted his head, still struggling to free himself. "You're wrong."

"The Old Witch of Endor only tells the truth."

Once he realized who she was, he was overcome with fear. He had heard tales of her since he was a young boy and knew he would be fortunate to make it out of their encounter unscathed.

"You need not be afraid of me," she assured him. "Your story does not end here."

"Get out," he gritted his teeth.

"Certainly, Commander," she smiled, "but first I have a question."

"Ask your question, witch."

"Are you prepared to die?"

Before he could answer, she waved her hand once more and disappeared, releasing him from his frozen position.

A knock on his door startled him; a guard entered his quarters. "Commander Pash, your presence is required in Her Majesty's throne room."

"I will be there in a moment."

The guard left. Pash looked around his room once more, realizing this time he was alone.

THE THRONE ROOM was dark except for bundles of candles scattered throughout the vast and impressive space. A light breeze blew through Niabi's cascading long black hair. It was extremely late, and every occupant of the castle was fast asleep.

When Pash entered, he noticed the grand wooden doors were not being patrolled by her guards and he became concerned: what was this emergency small council meeting about? Pash also realized his father was nowhere to be found. Apart from Niabi, Tala, and the Nephilim guarding the queen, there was one new face in the room he had seen just moments before.

Her white hair glistened in the candlelight, but that was the only softness the Old Witch of Endor possessed. She could not help but smile at the last arriving member. Pash clearly did not trust Vilora and was very confused as to why she was in attendance and his father was not. He marched up to Niabi and respectfully bowed, bringing his arm across his chest.

"You summoned me, my Queen." He sat in his designated seat.

Niabi gripped the armrests of her white throne, clearly something heavy weighed on her mind. "Now that we are all here, there is a matter of great importance we must discuss."

Pash was now certain Gershom was not informed of the meeting. "Forgive me, my Queen, but why is the witch here and your Second absent?"

Niabi glared at Vilora. "I see you the two of you have met."

"Briefly, my Queen." Vilora could sense her irritation.

"What of Lord Gershom?" Pash pressed the issue. "Is he to be absent while she attends?"

"*She* can be trusted," Niabi snarled. "He cannot."

Her words stung.

"But the witch -"

"Has been more honest with me than my own right hand." The irate queen rose from her throne, silencing him. "If you have a problem with my judgment, Commander Pash, then I will deal with you accordingly."

"I beg your forgiveness," Pash diffused the situation. "My intent was not to offend you, my Queen."

"He is right in not trusting me." Vilora's smooth voice calmed Niabi. "Commander Pash does not yet know me, nor does he understand our history. His entire existence is to protect you."

Niabi's eyes softened.

"He is behaving exactly as he should, my Queen." The witch looked at the soldier who seemed surprised by her defense of him.

"*This* is now my small council." The Green-Eyed Raven moved on to matters she wished to discuss. "Gershom has betrayed my trust and now word has reached my ears that he has been secretly corresponding with Southern Lords. His eyes are on my crown and that will be his undoing."

"Let me confront him about these accusations." Pash knew his father was indeed capable of such treachery, but hoped the whispers were untrue.

"Or warn him of our report," Tala spat, arms folded over his chest.

"What is that supposed to mean?" Pash's eyes narrowed.

"You are his son, his heir. How do we know you will not warn him? How do we even know you aren't conspiring with him?" Tala's long black hair blew loosely in the breeze.

Pash leaned forward, elbow on his knee. "Are you accusing me of treason, Lord Tala?"

"Stop it, both of you," Niabi's hiss silenced them. "I want eyes on him at all times. Every move he makes, I want to know about it. Every conversation he has, I want to know about it. Every time he eats, sleeps or shits, I want to know about it!" She slammed her fist on her armrest. "He will not be the only one to rot in my dungeons, but all who aided and entertained him as well."

Pash saw something in her he had not seen since she conquered the North. The vicious and strategic young Niabi had awakened after years of dormancy. Most would say motherhood had changed her for the better, but with her light snuffed out, her darkness once again thrived.

"Gershom is no fool." Pash rubbed his temples. "He will notice a tail."

"He will not be followed by a stranger, Pash." Her tone sent shivers down his spine. "You will be spending far more time with your father."

"Me?" He was shocked by her plan. "You want *me* to spy on my own father?"

"Will that be a problem for you, Commander?" Tala had not taken his eyes off him the entire meeting. "Our Queen has ordered you to report on a Lord accused of treason. If you disagree, say so now."

He had never been put in a position like this before. Gazing up at his queen, he saw by the expression on her face that she agreed with Tala on the issue. Pash was a soldier who had sworn an oath not only to protect the crown, but to do his queen's bidding. His entire life he always followed orders, but now being the queen's lover and being the son and heir to her now suspected rival, he found himself torn. Thinking, but for a moment on how he would respond, he made his decision.

"I swore an oath to protect the crown and that is exactly what I will do."

"We will see," Tala hissed under his breath. "We will see."

CHAPTER 29

SALOME

"How's my best girl?"

"Lykos!" A five-year-old Salome rushed to him with a smile.

Tightening his grasp around her, he planted a kiss on her cheek. "What are you doing out here?"

"Thinking."

"Thinking about what?" They sat together on a bench in the royal gardens.

"Things."

He had the warmest smile, the kindest brown eyes. "Must be important things."

Her smile faded. "Mother said you're going away."

"I will be back before you know it." He nudged her with his elbow.

"You promise?"

"I promise." He pulled his dark hair back in a traditional Northern bun and took off his pinky ring. "Here."

"But that's yours." She shook her head, refusing to accept it.

"While I am gone, you will need to keep it safe for me." He curled her small fist around the ring. "Can you do that for me?"

She stared down at the silver ring he had entrusted to her care and memorized every detail she could about the intricate piece. That particular ring had been given to Lykos by their mother after his first hunt. Etched on the inside of the band was the Myridian sigil of an octopus with the words, 'As Deep as the Sea'.

After a moment to think on his request, she smiled. "I will keep it safe."

"Remember," he lifted her to sit on his lap. "As long as you have this ring, I will always come back to you."

Salome's vision vanished and she was left staring at the dirt path she rode down. She glanced at the ring on her index finger. *Am I going mad?*

"Do you think of Lykos often?" Harbona asked, bringing her back to reality.

"How… How did you know I was…? I was thinking about him?" she stammered.

"I was there the day your mother gave him that ring." He smiled at the ring fondly.

She was silent. "Did you know him well?"

He nodded; eyes now fixed on the road. "He was one of my closest friends."

"I wish I had had more time with him."

"He loved you, Salome." His words bore right through her soul. "I hope you know that."

They were silent for a few minutes before Salome asked, in a hushed tone:

"You said he knew about me?

"Yes." He nodded.

She hesitated, taking a deep breath. "Did he know about my sister?"

"He knew about her, too," he cleared his throat. "But what you actually want to know is: did he know he would die the night he saved you?"

Her weight shifted while riding her horse. "Did… did he know?"

"He knew a few weeks before your sister invaded that Death would come for him."

"Why did he not leave with us?" her voice cracked. "He had a chance to live, why didn't he take it?"

"Had he tried to escape with you and your brother that night, it would not have made a difference. Death had called him; nothing could change that."

"Did..." she took another breath to suppress the tears. "Did he suffer... in the end?"

"He went quickly." He returned his gaze to the path ahead but stopped as they came to the bridge that connected The Hollow and the Swamp Lands.

"Is everything alright?" She noticed his hesitation.

"We are not alone," he whispered.

Three men came out of the woods, blocking the path.

"Who are they?"

"Greedy peasants looking for you and your brother," he huffed, trotting toward them. "Let me do the talking, Salome. Perhaps they will not be trouble."

The bounty hunters waited for the riders to get close enough to them before ordering them to halt.

Rozdale, the leader of the group, stepped forward. Shorter than his two companions, the squinty eyed mercenary wiped his dirty mouth, revealing his right hand was missing two fingers. The foul-smelling peasant licked his dry lips. "What was your business in The Hollow?"

"Just passing through," Harbona answered calmly.

"Where are you headed?" Rozdale pestered.

"To my brother's house," the Seer lied.

The dirty gang leader turned his focus on the hooded woman who had remained silent. "And who are you?"

"She is my niece -"

"I asked her, old man," Rozdale cut Harbona off, spitting on the ground. "Now," he drew closer to Salome, "Who are you?"

"I am his niece." She followed Harbona's dishonest lead.

Rozdale squinted his already tiny eyes, not believing a word he heard, but was deciding if he would let them pass. His two associates: Jethro, a tall, gangly man with a fresh black eye, and Morta, a stocky man with a round face who rarely spoke, started to encircle the two riders.

Jethro stood next to Salome and boldly caressed her leg. "I bet you could keep us company." The simple looking man flashed a lustful smile at the first woman he had seen in weeks.

"Do not touch me," she hissed.

Since he was missing a few teeth, Jethro's chuckle was more like a whistle. "Feisty one she is."

"Jethro," Rozdale rebuked. Looking back at Harbona, he stepped out of his way. "You can go."

Salome breathed a sigh of relief as Harbona nodded his head in gratitude. "Thank you." Their horses had barely moved forward, when the three men blocked the path again.

"I said, *you* can go," Rozdale smirked. "She stays with us."

"I am afraid that is not going to happen." Harbona was unmoved by the weapons they now wielded.

Rozdale pointed his sword at him. "I said move along, old man. She belongs to us now."

"Move or be moved," Harbona snarled.

Flashing his decaying smile, Rozdale held up the wanted poster with Salome's picture. "Not without our prize."

Morta and Jethro tried to yank her from her horse, but she expected an attack. She punched Jethro and kicked Morta out of her way. She and Harbona took off over the bridge. The three mercenaries were not about to let their biggest payday get away. They mounted their horses and pursued them. Morta snatched his bow off his back and launched three arrows at the riders.

Salome, who was better with a bow than a sword, shot arrows back at them. Twisting her torso backwards, she released an arrow, piercing Morta in his left arm, just missing his heart. He fell from his horse, but that did not deter the other two bounty hunters from their wild pursuit.

"Harbona, we have to fight them. We will not be able to outrun them much longer."

In agreement, they turned their horses around and charged at them.

The scrappy princess stood on top of her steed, balancing as he stomped along the uneven path. As soon as she was close enough, she jumped from her horse and tackled Rozdale off of his. They both scrambled to their feet; he drew his sword; she unsheathed her dagger. With a loud screech, the leader of the gang rushed toward her, but before he could reach her, she threw her knife, piercing his left thigh. He fell to the ground, squirming in pain. Cautiously, Salome approached her assailant, turned him on his back and retrieved her dagger.

Rozdale eyed his sword which was just out of his reach.

"I wouldn't, if I were you," she warned.

Not one to heed the warnings of a woman, he desperately lunged for his sword, but was stopped short by her knife, which penetrated his already deformed right hand. He screamed as she dug her knee into his spine.

"I warned you." She smashed the blunt end of his sword on the back of his head, knocking him unconscious.

The only one who was left unscathed was Jethro, which Harbona easily handled. Using his staff as a jousting spear, he unseated his enemy from his horse. Terrified, the scrawny man scurried away as fast as he could, hoping they would leave him untouched.

"We must hurry," Harbona insisted. "We do not have far to go."

~

SALOME COULD BARELY STOMACH the smell of the swamp as they dismounted their horses.

"You didn't tell me we needed to take a boat." She stood on the rickety dock, disgusted by the murky water.

"This is no ordinary tavern." Harbona sat in the small rowboat with the weathered and smelly dock master. "Hurry up, we do not have all day."

"What do you mean a tavern?" Her eyes widened. "Are we going to a bar?"

"Bar, tavern, all the same." The Seer shrugged off her concern. "It is there we will find the Wanderer. Now please, get in."

Although Salome knew how to swim, she was leery about the muddy waters, unsure of what may be hiding beneath the stagnant stream. "Perhaps, I should stay here."

"Trust me." He extended his hand.

Reluctantly, she grabbed his arm and sat inside the boat.

The normally quiet dock master began paddling through the swamp. "You said you were looking for the Wanderer?"

Salome glanced up. "You know him?"

"Aye, I know of him." He kept his pace steady. "Dangerous feller, that Wanderer. No one has ever seen his face. It's as if he does not really exist. Like he's a ghost among men."

She scrunched her nose, glanced at Harbona, and whispered, "A ghost among men?"

"You need not be afraid of him." He patted her hand.

"How far is the tavern?" she asked, ready to disembark that small rowboat.

"It's right in front of you." The dockmaster's gruff voice sent shivers up her spine.

"Wait for us." Harbona handed the withering old man a shiny coin. "We will not be long."

The Hidden Tavern was exactly that, hidden. Defying all odds of being considered a solid structure, the bar built on stilts was a popular destination for mercenaries, criminals, and all other undesirables. Walking up the rotting staircase, Salome soaked in her surroundings. She had never heard of this place and was now wondering how Harbona knew about it. As they neared the wooden door, he turned to his young companion and blocked the entrance.

"Make sure to keep your hood on. There are less than honorable men in this tavern who are looking for you and I want to ensure you are safe."

Salome pulled her hood down further, making sure only the bottom half of her face would be visible to suspicious eyes. Once they entered the dark tavern, she glanced around the large room and saw nothing but dirty scoundrels drinking, gambling, and smoking.

"Are you sure about this?" she whispered.

"Why do you doubt me?"

"I do not doubt you. I doubt the Wanderer." She looked around the room. "Is he even here?"

"He is here." He stared at a dimly lit corner. "Do not mention your name; the North has spies everywhere."

She glanced in the direction he was looking and saw a hooded man sitting by himself. Smoke rose from under his cloak from the long pipe he clutched in his fingerless leather riding gloves.

"Would you grab us three drinks?" Before she could object, Harbona started to walk toward the ruffian.

Nearby eyes shifted to catch a look at the old man who dared to approach the deadliest man in the room. The Wanderer sat stoically as he took a sip from his large pint of ale.

"Can I help you?" he asked, unmoved by the unexpected visitor.

"Yes," Harbona lowered his voice, "you can fight for us."

The hooded mercenary set his drink down and smirked. "I guess I can't help you then."

"May I join you?"

"I sit alone, old man."

Harbona sat down anyway.

"You test my patience," he snorted. "Leave me."

"I seek the Wanderer."

"And you have found him, but it doesn't help you."

"Let me introduce myself. I am Harbona -"

"That means nothing to me," the dark figure interrupted the introduction. "You are now wasting my time."

"I do not believe I am wasting your time, Adonijah." He leaned back in his seat with a huff. "And I certainly would not dare waste my time."

The Wanderer was silent. "What did you call me?"

Harbona moved closer to his reluctant host and whispered, "I know who you are, Adonijah, and you were never meant to be a wanderer."

The clearly rattled mercenary pushed into the little bit of light the candle on his table projected, exposing the bottom half of his face. "I chose my path."

"Maybe so," the Seer stared into his shadowed eyes, "but you can redeem yourself by helping us; helping her."

Adonijah looked over at the bar where a hooded woman stood. "And why would I want to help someone I have never met and fight a battle I have no business fighting?"

"On the contrary, you do know her."

Confused, Adonijah once again examined the woman. "I do not know her." He was cautiously confident.

"She is the daughter of Issachar, King of the Northern Lands."

"That is not possible," the young warrior whispered. "The royal family was murdered years ago."

"All but two," Harbona spoke softly. "She and her brother escaped."

"Issachar's *son* still lives?"

"Yes, but I cannot say anymore. It is not safe." The Seer squinted, "It is time for justice; I know that is what you desire most."

"I do not desire justice." Adonijah gulped down his ale. "I desire revenge."

"We need your help, Adonijah."

"I have nothing I can give you."

"It is your destiny."

"You don't need me, old man," the young man scoffed. "I know the old prophecies and I don't bear any mark that would give you victory against the North."

"You are right. You do not bear the sacred mark," Harbona agreed. "But we have the one who does."

Intrigued, Adonijah leaned forward once more. "You have the Hunter?"

"The time has come for the prophecy to be fulfilled and you have a part to play in this war."

"Who is he?"

"Patience, patience, my friend. Revealing their identity would be foolish, especially since the man to your left has been trying to listen to our conversation for some time now." Adonijah turned to look at the eavesdropper, but Harbona grabbed his arm. "We will leave now, and you will get a good look at him. Remember his face because you will see him again."

Adonijah nodded and rose from his seat, casually turning to see the spy as they walked toward Salome. She had just received the drinks she had been instructed to order when he grabbed her arm and escorted her to the exit.

"Time to leave," Adonijah pulled her.

"What is going on?" She stared at Harbona. "I thought you wanted drinks?"

Adonijah set the drinks down on a nearby table where two drunks started drinking them. "No time for questions, we have to leave now."

"Halt!" The spy stood up from his table and walked toward the three fleeing companions.

"Is something wrong?" Harbona turned to face the armed bald man.

"I am placing you under arrest for conspiring against the northern crown by order of Lord Gershom," Ophir declared, eyeing his prize with great delight.

Enraged, Salome pushed past Adonijah and stepped up to Ophir. "May he beg for Death before she takes him," she spat on the ground.

Unsheathing his sword, Ophir gritted his teeth. "Bite your tongue, foolish girl, before I take it from you."

Adonijah stepped forward, shielding Salome. "If you want her, you will have to go through me first."

"With pleasure." Ophir swung his blade at the hooded mercenary with great force. After ducking, Adonijah tackled him to the ground and repeatedly punched him.

Unaware of who started the fight, the drunks in the tavern began fighting one another, tearing the small bar apart. The added raucous caused Adonijah to lose sight of Ophir leaving him vulnerable to attack. Out of nowhere, the older soldier leapt over an overturned table and struck Adonijah across his jaw, sending him flying across the room. Ophir grabbed his sword and stomped toward his younger opponent, determined to slice his throat open. Before he was able to reach him, Salome smashed a wooden stool over his shiny bald head, knocking him unconscious.

The newly banded trio escaped the brawl, jumped into the awaiting boat, and headed back to shore.

As soon as they reached land, the three wanted fugitives paid the dock master and made their way to their horses. The sun was setting; Harbona knew they had to find somewhere to camp for the night, but Shadows and mercenaries were looking everywhere for them, and he had to be sure it was safe to continue traveling.

"Wait here," Harbona instructed. "I will see if anyone is lurking along the roads."

Once Harbona disappeared, Salome looked at her new traveling companion. Adonijah wiped his brow, revealing his face. Her wide-eyed expression caught his attention and they realized they *had* met before.

Simultaneously they cried, "You!"

"You tried to kill me," she snorted, furious at the very sight of him.

"*You* are Issachar's daughter?" His jaw dropped.

"This must be a mistake." She took a step toward him, fingers tickling the handle of her dagger just in case she needed it. "We were looking for the Wanderer."

He took a step forward. "And you found him."

"*You* are the Wanderer?" she rested her hands on her hips, eyebrow raised.

"I am." He seemed amused by her.

She scoffed. "There has clearly been some kind of mistake."

"No mistake." Adonijah leaned up against a tree with a smirk. "You sought me out and found me."

"Why would I agree to travel with you after you tried to kill me?"

"I wasn't going to kill you, love." He rubbed his chin. "I needed you alive to collect the reward money."

She furrowed her brow. "My name is Salome."

"I know what your name is," he hissed.

"Then use it," she fired back.

"Whatever you wish." He shrugged, unbothered.

"And keep your distance, unless you are up for round two." Her blood boiled at the thought of them traveling together.

"Woah, woah. I am on your side now." He raised his hands to the level of his eyes. "I'm not going to turn you in, nor will I harm you."

"I would kill you before you had the chance."

"If you were going to kill me, you would have done it when we first met." Adonijah's crooked smile normally enamored any lady that crossed his path, but she was not falling for his charm.

"I took pity on you," she sneered, stroking her horse's head. "I won't make the same mistake twice."

"Took pity on me?" He snorted. "You cheated me."

"Cheated?" she whipped around with a shriek.

"You hit me with a rock," he reminded her.

"Any skilled fighter knows to use their environment to their advantage. Or did they not teach you that in the Swamp Lands?"

He waved his fingers in the air. "Like a bar stool in a tavern brawl, for instance?"

"You're a quick study, you are," she hissed. "Perhaps you're not as dumb as you appear, Wanderer."

Adonijah extended his hand. "My name is Adonijah."

Salome stared blankly at his hand. "What are you doing?"

"I thought," he stammered, not expecting that reaction. "I thought we could start over since we may have started off poorly."

"May have?" she choked.

"Look," he sighed, "I didn't know who you were when I found you the other day. If I had -"

"You would have done the exact same thing," she interrupted.

"I am trying to make this right."

"You're doing great."

He lit his pipe. "Has anyone ever told you that you are incredibly stubborn?"

"Me? Stubborn?" She placed a hand on her chest, pursing her lips.

"Aye, stubborn," he spat back, mimicking her tone. "Or are you unfamiliar with the word?"

"You think you are far more clever than you actually are."

"All I want is for us to get along." He exhaled in her direction. "Do you think we can do that?"

She swatted the smoke away from her face. "No."

"You can call me Adonijah."

She stared at him until it was awkward.

"Or not," he squinted.

She continued to watch him in silence.

"Hello?" He snapped his fingers in her direction. "Have you finally run out of words to say?"

"I'm thinking." Her eyes narrowed, still staring at him.

"Dare I ask what thoughts are running around that head of yours?"

"I think I should have killed you when I had the chance."

He was unfazed. "If you had, you would've missed out on all the fun."

"I'm still waiting for this to be fun." She crossed her arms over her chest.

"Well, that's a shame." He exhaled another puff of smoke. "I've been enjoying myself."

She scoffed and refocused on her white mare.

"What's her name?" He pointed, sliding down the tree to sit on the ground.

She did not look at him. "Snow."

"Snow?" he muttered disapprovingly. "Why would you name a horse Snow?"

"I haven't seen snow since I left Northwind. I have fond memories of..." Salome furrowed her brow. "Don't."

"Don't what?" Adonijah threw his hands up in the air. "Don't be polite?"

"Don't try to get to know me," she hissed. "Harbona might trust you, but I don't."

"Why didn't you?" He changed the subject abruptly.

"Why didn't I what?" She turned to face him.

"Why didn't you kill me when you had the chance in The Hollow?" his voice softened. "You see, I've mulled over that question since our run in and never thought I'd see you again to get an answer."

"Like I told you before," she eyed him carefully, "I never kill unarmed men."

He wagged his finger with a crooked grin. "I think you're upset because you finally met your equal in both wit and skill."

"You are hardly my equal," she rolled her eyes. "Was one ass beating not enough for you?"

"I already told you." He hopped up and stood in front of her, looking down into her eyes. "You cheated me," he whispered.

Salome was tall, but he still towered over her. She pushed up on her toes and snarled, "I would gladly beat you again."

"Tell me when and where, love."

"My name is -"

"Salome. I know," he remarked flippantly. "How could I forget?"

Their faces inches apart, they soaked one another in. For years she had dealt with the unwanted affection and attention of Jacobi, and he was far less irritating than Adonijah.

Why did he bother her so much?

Why was she suddenly uncomfortable being this close to him?

Harbona reappeared. "The path is clear for us to -" His eyes shifted between the two of them. "Is everything alright?"

"Perfect." She broke her gaze to mount her horse.

Shaking his head and muttering under his breath, "Women," he mounted his brown stallion and chased after his new companions.

CHAPTER 30

NIABI

The Green-Eyed Raven stomped through the hallways of the White Keep, focused on one person in particular. With Anaktu closely in tow, Niabi burst through the door that led to Gershom's private quarters. Her unexpected visit stunned the Second in Command, as he was presently entertaining a female companion in his bed.

"My… my Queen?" he stammered, covering himself with sheets.

The young woman, a highly paid prostitute by the look of her expensive clothes, was terrified to see the queen staring at them. "Your Majesty." Her lips quivered as the words left her pouty mouth.

Gershom tried to shove her out of the bed. "Get out."

Niabi lifted her hand in protest. "Stay exactly where you are; my intrusion will be but a moment."

Furthering his discomfort, she sat at the foot of his bed and stared at him intently before she addressed the issue she had come to discuss.

"It has come to my attention that eleven of my Shadows are dead." Every word she spoke was venomous. "Do you have any idea why *my* men were killed in the forests of the Western Lands?"

His gulp was audible. "My Queen, I can explain -"

"Please do," she interrupted with a snarl. "Because the way it appears to me is you abused your power and dispatched my Shadows without my permission. Surely, that is not the case."

Stammering once again, the scruffy soldier pulled himself together. "I assure you, Majesty, I can explain."

"I am listening." She crossed one leg over the other.

"The Shadows I dispatched were searching for your missing siblings and were attacked by rogue fighters," he told a half truth.

"Lies." Her eyes narrowed.

"I swear to you -"

"You dare look me in the eye and continue to lie to me?" she hissed. "You dispatched them before I even knew of their survival, something you were not in the least bit concerned about until I brought it to your attention. I shall give you one last chance to tell me the truth." She unsheathed one of her daggers and laid it on her lap.

Fear blanketed his face, his fingers brushing where his ear used to be. "My astrologer informed me the Year of the Hunter has come and he will come for me, so I sent the Shadows to find him before he could reach the city."

"You are far too superstitious for your own good, Gershom." She shook her head. "No one believes in the Hunters anymore."

"But the astrologer -"

"Believes in what the stars tell him," she laughed. "Only a fool believes in the stars."

"And if the stars are right and he does come?"

"Then let him come," she growled, leaning forward. "I believe in what is in front of me and right now, all that sits before me is a rat."

"My Queen, please -"

"Silence," she whispered through gritted teeth. "If you continue to think yourself mightier than you are, it will cost you your life."

Gershom leaned forward resting his hand over his heart. "I have only faithfully served you -"

"You have served yourself and have become careless in hiding your agenda to usurp me."

"You are mistaken."

Her eyes were cold and vicious. "I would have forgiven your foolish lapses in judgement had your mistakes not cost my son his life."

"Rollo's death was not my fault!" He protested.

"You have gone from friend to foe and as the Almighty is my witness, I shall destroy you with every piece of my broken heart."

She rose from the edge of his bed and glided out of his room.

Gershom was equally afraid and angry by the unexpected visit. He no longer had the appetite for his female companion, and he shooed the hired girl from his sight. All that concerned him now was his own survival.

CHAPTER 31
ZIGGY

Scurrying out of his quarters, the freckle-faced redhead made her way through the dimly lit underground corridors that led down to the city streets. For the last eight months, Gershom had her sneak in the White Keep so their relationship would remain secret but with the queen now aware of their rendezvous, it was sure to become a problem for both of them.

The second her feet hit the white cobblestone street, she exhaled a huge sigh of relief. Pulling her curls into a messy bun, the petite, fair-skinned escort ensured she was not being followed as she weaved down the alley.

"You're early tonight," a deep voice whispered from a dark corner behind her. "Is something wrong?"

Her blue eyes shifted. "The Queen surprised us."

"Were you hurt?" Nubis stepped into the moonlight revealing his towering muscular frame.

"I'm fine." Ziggy patted his hand reassuringly, exposing the hooked shape scar on top of her left hand. "I need to see him."

The duo slithered through the alleys of Northwind, avoiding all patrols on their way to The Whispering Fox. Once they stood outside the front door, Nubis knocked four times rhythmically. A small rectangular pocket of the wooden door slid open, and a pair of hypnotizing grey eyes stared back at them.

"Nubis?"

"Makada, we must speak to him," he whispered as he looked up and down the abandoned street. The door unlocked and creaked open to allow them entry into the tavern.

"Follow me."

Ziggy and Nubis followed her through the empty bar. Makada had hip long black braids, a curvaceous figure and three hooped nose piercings in her right nostril. Shorter than both of them, the dark-skinned maiden led them down the stairs to Oden's quarters.

"Sit. Wait here," she instructed as she quietly slipped into the adjoining room. A few moments later, the bangle adorned Makada reemerged with Oden following closely behind her.

He sat across from Ziggy and Nubis in his high back chair and asked his spies, "What news do my sparrows bring?"

Ziggy crossed one leg over the other and leaned forward. "The Queen barged into Gershom's chambers unannounced and found us together."

"Were you made?"

"No."

"Good." Oden nodded. "Did they speak of anything of importance?"

"Eleven of Niabi's Shadows were found dead in the Western Lands," Ziggy reported. "At first Gershom claimed he had sent them to find her missing siblings, but then admitted he sent them to find one he called, the Hunter. He did this without her knowledge or permission."

"Did they find him?"

"No, my lord, but the Queen threatened him. She said he was responsible for Prince Rollo's death."

"They are unraveling." Oden looked up and smiled at Makada who stood by his side. "Ziggy, continue to make yourself available to Gershom. Perhaps you will learn more."

"Are you sure that is wise now that the Queen has seen her face?" Nubis protested. "If she is set on destroying Gershom, Ziggy could get hurt."

"A risk we all agreed upon when we joined the Order," Oden brushed him off. "You know your assignments. Nothing changes. Is that understood?"

"Understood." Ziggy and Nubis both nodded their heads.

"Now keep your ears to the ground on the whereabouts of Issachar's children. We need them to lead us to the Hunter before the Shadows find him." Oden rose from his seat. "Be watchful, for the night is long and a storm is coming."

Just like that, their meeting had ended. Ziggy and Nubis saw themselves to the door and stood outside the tavern in silence. The broad-chested Mountain Man stood more than a foot taller than the redhead, making them an odd-looking couple. Normally one could not tell what Nubis was thinking, but when he looked at her, she could see the angst in his face.

"You should not see him again," he broke the long silence.

"Oden is right," she stared into the distance, eyes glossed over. "I knew what I was getting myself into."

"The Queen has seen your face; returning is too risky."

"It has always been a risk being so close to Gershom, but how else would we know what the inner circle is doing?"

"Ziggy, it has gone from being risky to being life threatening. You will be harmed if you do not tread carefully."

She glanced up at him and smiled. "Is that concern I hear?"

"Don't tease me."

"I'm sorry, Nubis." She grabbed his hand and rested her head against his muscular arm. "I promise I will be careful."

"Please don't return to him," he pleaded. "We have already lost so many."

"And if I too am lost, remember me as I am in this moment. To lose my life fighting for the freedom of our own would be an honorable departure." She cupped his face in her petite hands. "If one day you wake up and I am no longer here, know that I lived bravely and died with purpose."

"Ziggy -"

She gently pressed her fingers against his lips and kissed his cheek. "Until we meet again." Before he could protest, she vanished into the darkness of Northwind.

CHAPTER 32
ZOPHAR

The tiny village of Jannat Sin was a welcome sight. Dozens of tents pitched in the middle of towering sand dunes surrounded the only oasis in Dead Man's Land. Lush palm trees were the only source for shade from the scorching sun.

Crispin and Zophar had traveled through the Sand Lands for days and were in need of rest and supplies. Crispin had done nothing but express his liking for the dry air, endless sand dunes and the sense of adventure, much to Zophar's dismay. Zophar was a man of forests and lakes. The desert did not suit him, and his sunburned skin was proof.

Before parting ways, Harbona told them the people of Jannat Sin were some of the most hospitable in all of Adalore and they would welcome them for three days without asking any questions.

Sheikh Ibrahim was exactly as Harbona had described him. He was a tall man with dark eyes and dark facial hair. His brown skin seemed even darker against his white flowing robes and matching keffiyeh. His smile was warm and his embrace firm, as he ushered the weary duo into his tent where a spread of food awaited them.

"Please, sit," he motioned to the multi-colored cushions scattered on the ground. "Eat, make yourselves comfortable. You must be tired from your journey."

They sat cross-legged on the cushions and ate as the women continued to bring in new dishes for them to try. Lamb, goat, wild berries, bread, dates, and milk. Zophar had not seen this much food displayed at once since he lived in Northwind and although he and Crispin had not eaten food prepared in this manner, they were starving and were excited to put anything in their growling stomachs.

"Thank you for your hospitality." Crispin was so hungry, he swallowed some of his food whole. "I have never seen anything like your village. It's beautiful."

Ibrahim nodded with a smile, "It is paradise."

Zophar cleared his throat, "A friend of ours told us you would allow us to stay the night on our journey to Numbio, if we asked."

"Well, your friend is correct." Ibrahim nabbed a handful of dates and ate them one at a time. "You are welcome to stay as long as you like."

"Thank you," Zophar said, gulping down a mouth full of mutton.

"Is there anything else you will require for your stay?" their host asked, clapping his hands.

"A place to sleep and food to eat is more than generous -"

Crispin's voice trailed off when a woman adorned with bangles on her arms and ankles slowly entered. She wore a sheer black veil to cover the bottom half of her face and a beaded headdress sat upon her long dark hair. Black liner accentuated her dark and exotic eyes. Her robes floated around her as the music began.

Ibrahim grinned, "Entertainment."

The way she danced was hypnotizing. So fluid, so enticing. Even through the veil, they could see the outline of a smile. She locked eyes with Crispin who had not stopped staring at her since she had entered. Zophar nudged him and clicked his tongue.

"Where will we be spending the night?" Zophar asked, doing his best not to ogle like his young companion.

"You wish to retire now?" Ibrahim asked.

"We should get some rest if we are to make it to Numbio by tomorrow," Zophar nodded as he stood and cracked his back. "If that is alright with you, of course."

Ibrahim clapped his hands and the dancer bowed and left. "But of course." He smiled warmly. "Follow me."

As he left the tent, Zophar grabbed Crispin by his sleeve and whispered, "Must you stare like you've never seen a woman before?"

"I've never seen a woman like *her* before," Crispin chuckled, gently elbowing Zophar in the gut. "I love the Sand Lands."

Ibrahim led them to an empty tent, like his, near the water. He pulled back the curtain and motioned them inside.

"There is water inside for you to bathe. Should you need anything else, please, let me know." Ibrahim bowed, "Rest well, my friends."

Zophar and Crispin both bowed, and their generous host released the curtain, enclosing them inside the cozy tent. Crispin was grinning ear to ear. Zophar knew exactly what he was thinking about.

"It would do you well to just forget about her." He shook his head. "Women are not on the agenda."

Crispin sunk into one of the beds and cradled his head in the palms of his hands. "Oh Zophar, how long has it been since you entertained a lady companion?"

Zophar snorted, furrowing his brow. "That is none of your business."

"That long, huh?" Crispin snickered.

It was true. It had been a long time since Zophar had been in the company of a lady. When he was young and still living in the City of Borg, Zophar had a beautiful wife named, Siv. How he loved her. Her red hair, her blue eyes, her freckles, her smile, her warrior spirit, and the two sons she gave him, Bjorn and Ivar. No one, not even Crispin or Salome knew anything of his life before Northwind, and that is the way he wanted it.

Women in Borg were highly skilled warriors, equal to men in every capacity. Siv died in battle when pirates from Pulau invaded their villages. He gave her a warrior's burial: a fire lit boat sent out to sea. And his sons...

He did not want to think about his family anymore. It was still too painful. But he never took another wife; he never engaged with another woman after Siv's death. She was his best friend and he lost himself when he lost her.

"Zophar?" Crispin brought him back to reality. "Are you alright?"

He forced a smile, wiping the back of his neck with a wet towel. "Just tired is all."

Crispin sat up. "Can I ask you a question?"

Zophar was willing to answer any question Crispin and Salome asked. In fact, he made it a policy once he became their guardian. The only topic that was off limits was his family. He held his breath, hoping that was not what Crispin wanted to know.

"What is your question?" He eyed him in the mirror on the small table in front of him.

"Why was he banished?" Crispin sipped from one of the sheepskins left for them.

Zophar faced him, "Who?"

"I may not know much about the Immortals," Crispin wiped his mouth, "but I know enough to recognize their banishment mark."

Zophar washed his face. "I thought you better than to judge someone before knowing their story."

"So, I should blindly trust him because you do?" Crispin took his sandy shirt off. "He doesn't even have the Immortal glow."

"When he was banished, he lost his aura," he explained.

"What is he then?" Crispin scoffed. "Is he still an Immortal?"

Zophar finished bathing, undeterred by his line of questioning. "Banishment has not stripped him of his identity. Are you any less a northern prince for not living in your ancestral home?"

"One is not banished lightly," the prince fired back. "Why won't you tell me what he did?"

To Crispin's irritation, Zophar dodged answering the question. "It is not my story to tell."

"That is your response?"

"Understand this," Zophar sat down on the pillow-adorned bed, "I would entrust my own life in Harbona's hands. Had I one suspicious thought Salome was in any danger, I never would have parted ways with her."

After a moment of thoughtful silence, Crispin asked, "He said, he knew my father?"

"Aye," he nodded. "He and I served on your father's small council, along with your brother, Lykos, and Lord Maon, his Second in Command."

"Yet none of you knew of Niabi's plan to attack the city," Crispin's words oozed with judgement. "What kind of Seer cannot see a black storm?"

Realizing his tone had turned, Zophar tried to redirect the conversation. "You are clearly under a lot of stress, my young Prince, perhaps sleep -"

"I will have answers *now*," Crispin snorted. "How did a Seer on my father's small council not forewarn of her impending attack?"

"I think you should rest -"

"Tell me what I want to know," he snapped. "Tell me the truth," Crispin stood over Zophar. "Why did he not warn my father?"

"He warned your father," Zophar jumped up from his seated position, "but your father did not listen!" His deep voice frightened Crispin.

Crispin shook his head, bottom lip trembling. "My father would have heeded the warning. He never would have jeopardized my family or our people."

Zophar softened his approach, seeing the confusion in Crispin's eyes. "I begged your father to listen, we all did, but he refused. You were six years old, there is no way you would have understood any of this."

"If what you say is true," he crossed his arms over his chest, "why did my father not listen to Harbona's warnings?"

"Simply put," Zophar rubbed his forehead, "your father underestimated your sister."

"She is *not* my sister," Crispin growled, retreating to his side of the tent.

"Deny her if you like," Zophar shrugged and lit his pipe. "That does not change what is true."

"Then what of Gershom? Surely, he would have known about him."

Zophar exhaled, silent for a moment, reflecting on memories he wished he could forget. But it was time Crispin knew the truth. All of it.

"As I have told you before, Gershom was once the commander of your father's army. He refused to obey one of your father's orders, so your father sentenced him to be executed. There were many soldiers loyal to Gershom, so the night before he was supposed to die, his men freed him from your father's dungeons, and they escaped to the Black Forest."

"So, he waited until he had enough men to attack my father." He paced back and forth, chewing on a date.

"Truth be told," Zophar kicked his feet up on the bed and exhaled a puff of smoke, "Niabi is your father's first born and according to the laws of your ancestors, rightful heir to the White Throne. She has the true claim in Northwind."

"But Gershom -"

"Was a soldier fighting in *her* war."

Crispin was quiet. He closed his eyes deep in thought. "Why didn't he just listen?"

Zophar squirmed, unsure of what to say to ease Crispin. "Your father did not believe she was capable of an attack of that magnitude. Northwind's walls had never been breached. He did what he thought was best."

Crispin started to gather his belongings. "We should press forward."

Zophar clicked his tongue. "I know you want to see King Osiris, but we need to rest. We must regain our strength, or we will never make it."

"We have important matters to tend to." Crispin's stubbornness was in full swing.

Zophar grabbed Crispin's forearm as he passed by, "Important matters that have waited twelve years, one more day will not hurt. Besides, we would not want to insult our host by leaving in the dead of night. We will leave in the morning."

The royal was reluctant to listen, but knew the Westerner was right. "Fine," he snorted, "we will wait until morning."

"Perhaps you should think about that dancer." Zophar exhaled.

"Oh?" Crispin laid on his bed and stared at the ceiling of the tent. "And why's that?"

"Far better dreams with her on your mind."

Crispin half-smiled. "Maybe so."

CHAPTER 33

SALOME

With his back against a tree, Harbona pressed his lips to his favorite wooden pipe. He inhaled deeply and exhaled a generous puff of smoke toward the small fire Adonijah had started in the middle of their camp.

"Well, that was quite an exit yesterday," the Seer grinned.

Perched in a tree, Salome looked down at Adonijah who sat stoking the flames of their fire. "You're welcome, by the way."

His identity no longer a mystery, Adonijah looked up at the icy princess. "Are you talking to me?"

"A simple thank you will suffice."

"Thank you?" he chuckled. "Thank you for what?"

"What do you find so amusing?" She jumped down from her lounged position and stood over the crouching mercenary.

"You." He did not flinch when her feet hit the ground next to him. "If you are referring to the fight at the tavern, I was fine on my own."

His attitude made her blood boil. "Not from where I was standing."

Adonijah stood up slowly, maintaining eye contact with her. "You expect me to thank you for grabbing a chair?"

Not to be outdone by his sharp tongue, Salome stepped toward the tall, muscular swordsman. "That chair not only gave us time to escape, but also spared your pretty face from being disfigured by your superior opponent."

He clicked his tongue. "I am more than just a pretty face, love," he smirked at his own cheekiness.

"Let me know what that is when you figure it out," she tilted her head, squinting her eyes.

"You have a sharp tongue; I will grant you that." Adonijah lit his pipe and exhaled. "I would have been fine in the tavern without you. I always am."

"Forgive me," she half-heartedly curtsied, "next time, I will just watch you get your ass kicked."

"Please do," he shot back, "you might learn something." Adonijah laughed with each step he took toward her. "I don't even know why you, a woman, would be here in the first place. You're a liability."

"I have more of a right to be here than you do." Enraged, she squared her shoulders to his. "It was my family who was murdered, not yours."

"I may end up losing my life to save you," he leaned over her, "I need to know you are capable of handling yourself. Perhaps you do not know, but there are no chairs for you to use on the battlefield."

Circling around him, she studied him as if he were prey, ready to strike. "Don't flatter yourself, Adonijah. It is you who should be worried about the battlefield. After all, I not only saved you in the tavern, but I bested you in The Hollow as well when you came to collect my bounty. You tell me who is the better swordsman."

"If you are so sure of yourself then what do you need me for?" He stood as still as a statue while she circled him.

"All I need is for you to do what Harbona has recruited you to do and stay out of my way." Salome grabbed his shirt and leaned into his face. "You are a means to an end, nothing more." She released him and pushed past him, stomping into the Swamp Lands to calm down.

He watched as she walked away and once she was out of his sight, he glanced over at the quiet Seer. "Is she always this stubborn?"

Harbona, who had not been deterred from smoking during their heated encounter, finally looked up and said, "Oh, yes."

"Great," he shook his head, "women."

Furious, Salome marched through the Swamp Lands, hoping the walk would calm her nerves. "Who does he think he is?" she mumbled to herself. "He probably won't make it to any battlefield, I might kill him."

The sudden sound of a twig snapping caused her to whip around to see who was following her, but no one was there. This was the type of game Crispin would play when she walked in the woods of the Tree House Forest, but she knew it could not possibly be him. With an eerie feeling she was not alone sending chills up her spine, she reached for the dagger she kept sheathed to her thigh but realized she had left it at their campsite. She knelt to retrieve a small knife she hid in her right boot, when she was struck from behind and knocked unconscious.

After some time, Salome started to regain consciousness and realized she was tied to a large tree. Her three captors were the same men she and Harbona had scuffled with. They were huddled around a slowly dying campfire and appeared to be tending to their wounds from their first encounter. Morta turned to check on their prisoner, prompting Salome to close her eyes, pretending to still be unconscious.

"When is she going to wake up?" Morta grew impatient.

"Well, if you hadn't knocked her out, we wouldn't have this problem," Jethro chimed in, spitting on the ground.

"Oh, so now this is my fault?"

"All I'm saying, Morta, is there was no need to hit her that hard."

"Now let me tell you something, Jethro -"

"Jethro, Morta, would you two shut up!" Rozdale huffed. "She'll be awake soon enough and then we'll hand her over to Ophir."

Morta clenched his teeth, "And that's another thing. Why is Ophir not working with us? He should do his own dirty work."

"Watch your tongue," Rozdale hissed, hands over the fire. "Ophir is our master, and we shall do his bidding."

"What if she wakes up before he arrives?" Jethro picked at his few remaining teeth with his knife.

"Then we question her about the whereabouts of her companions," Rozdale spat on the ground.

"And if she doesn't answer our questions?" Morta furrowed his brow.

Rozdale unsheathed his dagger with a smirk. "She'll answer one way or another."

Jethro's stomach began to growl loud enough for his companions to hear. "I'm hungry. When are we going to eat? We haven't eaten all day."

Grabbing his axe, Rozdale rose to his feet. "Fire is about to go out. I'll chop some more wood."

As he left, Morta reached for his bow and arrows. "I'll get you something to eat; anything to stop your whining."

"What should I do?" Jethro never liked being left alone.

"Watch the girl." He disappeared.

Salome slowly opened her eyes to assess the situation and saw only Jethro remained, and he foolishly had his back to her. Keeping a watchful eye on the sulking bounty hunter, she sliced through her binds with the small knife she wiggled out of her boot. Conflicted as to whether to kill her captor or just sneak away, she carelessly stepped on a twig alerting Jethro of her impending escape.

"Oi!" he shouted as she sprinted. "Rozdale, Morta! She's getting away!"

Light on her feet, she easily kept a safe distance between them as she weaved in and out of the trees. As she ran downhill, she avoided the bogs and ducked behind a bald cypress. She looked around and saw a fallen tree limb and bent down to grab it. Once he ran up to her hiding place, she swung the branch with all her might, knocking him backwards.

Jethro scurried to his feet with his sword drawn, only to see Salome running toward him with a knife. He swung his weapon, but he was not fast enough. She easily dodged the incoming blow and swept him off his feet with a low kick. Jethro backhanded her to buy himself some time. She lunged for her dagger, which flew out of her hand when he slapped her, but he tackled her to the ground before she could reach it. Sitting on top of her with his sword to her throat, he believed he had neutralized her.

"You have caused me more trouble than you're worth," Jethro gnashed his teeth as blood oozed down the side of his dirty mouth. "You'll regret trying to escape once Rozdale gets ahold of you."

She managed to stretch for her dagger without him noticing and with a swift motion, plunged her knife into his neck, killing him.

Knowing it was only a matter of time before the other two goons found her, she pushed Jethro off her, grabbed his sword and placed her dagger back in her right boot.

"There she is!" Morta caught sight of her.

"Get her." Rozdale charged toward her, weapon drawn.

Frustrated she had been found so quickly, she started running through the wooded swamplands hoping to escape them once and for all.

Morta launched arrow after arrow at her and she managed to dodge several of them, but one of his arrows landed near her foot and tripped her. Closing in on her, she flipped to her back and began to crawl away from them. The sword she had swiped from Jethro was now beyond her reach, and her two captors had caught up with her. She glanced at the sword and hoped she might be able to snatch it in time.

"Ah, ah, ah," Rozdale clicked his tongue with a triumphant grin. "I wouldn't try that if I were you."

"She killed Jethro," Morta growled.

"And she will pay dearly for it. You should not have tried to escape. Especially after we took such good care of you."

"Took care of me?" she hissed, unafraid of the blade she now faced. "A horse could have taken better care of me than you three idiots."

"Get up," Morta ordered.

"No."

"I said, get up!" Morta viciously pulled her to her feet, shoved her toward Rozdale, and they led her back to their camp.

Knowing she still had her knife hidden in her boot, her mind raced to formulate a plan to escape when Adonijah stepped out in front of them with his sword drawn.

"Who goes there?" Rozdale addressed the man who blocked their path.

"Release her and I will not harm you." Hooded, Adonijah's tone was chilling.

Rozdale laughed the deepest laugh a man could laugh and directed Morta to, "Kill him."

"With pleasure."

Morta stepped up to the mercenary and the two swordsmen began to duel. Rozdale firmly restrained Salome and held a knife to her throat, just in case, anything happened to his last remaining companion. The two men sparred quickly and ferociously, both knowing the one to fall had much to lose. In the end, Morta was no match for Adonijah, who was far superior with a blade, and was stabbed through the chest.

Turning his focus to the lone bounty hunter, Adonijah issued one last warning. "Release her and I will let you live."

Rozdale swiftly sliced Salome's upper right arm, hoping to show his enemy how serious he was. "Drop your sword or I'll kill her." His voice trembled even though he clearly had the upper hand.

"Don't listen to him!" Salome ordered as blood trickled down her arm.

"Don't test me." Rozdale shoved the knife deeper against her neck, drawing blood. "Drop your sword or I'll kill her."

"Don't do it!" Her eyes were filled with a rage that surprised Adonijah.

Unwilling to risk her life further, he dropped his sword. "I've done as you asked. Now let her go."

Rozdale cackled, "Did you really think I would let her go?"

Never without a knife clipped to the back of his pants, Adonijah slowly moved into a position to throw it. "I thought you would be a man of your word."

"I am collecting the bounty on her head and if you try to stop me, I'll run you through."

"Suit yourself."

Adonijah launched his knife at the unsuspecting goon, and it sliced into Rozdale's forehead. Rozdale fell to the ground dragging Salome down with him.

Adonijah rushed over and knelt next to her, wiping the blood from her cheeks. "Are you alright?"

"I'm fine," she breathed heavily.

Focused on the deep cut across her right arm, he began to examine the damage. "It could be worse."

Not liking the attention, she shrugged off his concern. "It's just a scratch."

He applied pressure to her arm.

"Ah!" She winced and pushed him away. "Why would you grab my arm?"

"Only a scratch?" He tried to wipe the dirt and blood from her face, but she slapped his hand away. Once again, he turned his attention to her arm. "Let me take a look at that cut."

"I said, I am fine," she insisted, twisting her shoulder away from him.

He squinted his eyes at her. "That is a deep gash and if it's not cleaned, it could get infected."

"I can take care of it," she once again refused his help.

"Salome" he said softly, "let me help you."

"I said not to worry about it."

"I think you might be the most stubborn woman I have ever met," he rubbed the back of his neck. "Just let me help you."

"No."

"I promise I will be careful."

They stared at one another silently, for the first time truly taking one another in. His dark eyes, which she once found menacing, were actually quite warm and kind. He too, found himself in a daze, soaking her in until he noticed she released her arm and allowed him to clean her wounds.

"Who were they?" he asked, eyes focused on her arm.

"Bounty hunters Harbona and I had a run in with earlier." She grimaced as he fiddled with her wound. "They were waiting for a man named Ophir."

"Ophir?" Adonijah stopped what he was doing and stared at her.

"Do you know him?"

"I have heard the name before, but I haven't met him," Adonijah refocused on her arm. "From my understanding, he is one of the founding Shadows."

"That is who they were going to hand me over to; they called him their master."

"We should be heading back to camp before he arrives and finds you here." He wrapped her arm with a piece of fabric he had torn from the edge of his cape.

"Thank you."

He was surprised by her gratitude. "You're welcome."

They walked back to their camp site, exhausted and hungry.

After a moment of silence, he looked down at her and smiled, "I won't hold rescuing you over your head." He tried to lighten the mood with his version of a joke, which surprisingly, rendered a smile from his stubborn companion.

"I am sure you won't."

The weary duo finally laid their eyes on Harbona's friendly face. The Seer leapt to his feet and welcomed them back to camp. "Are you hurt?" His eyes examined her blood-stained clothes.

"Just some cuts and bruises." She smiled at him as he exhaled a sigh of relief.

"Thank the Almighty One you are safe."

Salome turned to the hooded figure that followed her. "I am glad you found me in time."

He was waiting for her to finish with a snarky comment or break out into laughter, but she didn't.

"You're welcome," he fumbled over his words. "I should have thanked you earlier for what you did for me in the tavern."

"Don't mention it." Perhaps, she could trust him after all.

CHAPTER 34
OPHIR

As the sun set, Ophir rode up to where his minions had set up camp, but upon inspection, realized it had been abandoned. Dismounting his horse, the Shadow looked for any clue that would lead him to the three bounty hunters who had disappeared. Finally finding fresh footprints, he followed where they led; his horse closely behind him. Not far from the campsite, he found Jethro's dead body. Now suspicious, he unsheathed his sword, in case he encountered any mischief.

Continuing forward, he found Morta and Rozdale lying on the ground in pools of blood; the sight frustrated him.

How could this have happened? He had given them the simple task of capturing a woman, but even they turned that into a life and death ordeal.

About to mount his horse once again to leave, he heard a faint cough escape Morta's beaten body.

He coughed up blood. "Master."

Ophir knelt next to him, keeping a watchful eye on his surroundings, "What happened?"

"We failed you."

"Tell me who did this." The bald Shadow was enraged.

"We captured the woman just like you asked, but she got away."

"*She* did this to you?"

"She killed Jethro." His pale face, stained with blood, now had tears streaming down his cheeks. His friends were dead and now it was only a matter of time before he too slipped into the afterlife.

Ophir grimaced at Rozdale's disfigured face. "Who killed Rozdale?"

"There was a man that came for her," he gasped for air.

"Did you find out what their names are? Where they were headed?" Ophir milked him for any information he could get, knowing there was nothing he could do to save him. Not that he would have bothered in the first place.

Having great difficulty breathing, he managed to whisper, "Salome."

The name sent a shiver up his spine, knowing exactly who she was and how dangerous the situation had become. "And the man? What was the man's name?"

"Forgive me, Master," the dirty bounty hunter cried. And with one last breath, the last member of the trio died.

Ophir released his limp arm, brushed himself off, and mounted his horse. A proper burial would not be necessary in the swamp. There were far more creatures living in the wetlands than even he knew about. Their bodies would be gone within three days, leaving no memory of their existence.

CHAPTER 35

PASH

Pash marched to Niabi's chambers unsure of why she had summoned him. Oddly, four soldiers were standing guard outside her door.

"Is our Queen alright?" he asked.

"She has been expecting you, Commander Pash." One of the guards stepped in front of him. "Follow us."

He was escorted inside, which had him on high alert. She was standing in the threshold of her balcony staring at the city below, sipping a glass of wine. She did not bother to turn when he entered.

"You sent for me?" he bowed.

At the snap of her fingers, her guards encircled him with pointed spears.

He raised his arms showing he was unarmed. "What is the meaning of this?"

"Seize him." They obeyed her orders. "Wait! I have changed my mind. Release him." They let him go. "Leave us."

"Niabi -"

"Did you notice how they obeyed my orders? Listened to my voice?" She whipped around, glaring at him indignantly as they walked out of her chambers.

Pash was confused. He brushed himself off, his fingertips grazing the handle of his sword. "What is going on?"

"If you ever consider obeying your father's voice again, remember mine. I am your Queen. I have the power to give life or take it," she growled. "My Shadows are never to do Gershom's bidding again or I promise it will cost you your head."

"Niabi -"

Eleven raven sigil pins hit the floor at his feet. "They are only of use to me alive."

He exhaled deeply. Losing men was never acceptable. "I never thought they would be in any danger."

"You are their commander, but *I* am their master," she grated her teeth behind tightly sealed lips. "It would do you well to remember your place. From this day forward, I expect to know every time my birds set flight."

"Do you not trust me after all my years of loyal service?" He boldly stepped forward.

"A man cannot serve two masters, Pash. To truly serve me, you cannot do your father's bidding."

"As I said before, I did not believe they would be in any danger."

"Slaughtered!" She shouted, shattering her glass against the wall behind him. "They were slaughtered by peasants!"

His voice cracked, "He is my blood."

"Blood means nothing. They are often the very ones to betray you." She walked over to him and cupped his face in her hands. "You are a fool to think he wouldn't do the same to you, given the opportunity."

"You speak of him as if he were some sort of monster," he whispered, eyes locked on her.

Her fingers slid from his face to the decanter of wine on the table behind him. She poured herself a fresh glass.

"Monsters are not figments of our wild imaginations. No, no. You see, the truth about monsters is they are real. They are those we once loved, once trusted, and maybe still even care about. They will stop at nothing to steal our happiness. They play on our fears, exploit our weaknesses, and plot our ultimate destruction. Monsters are not just creatures in fairytales told to frighten children at night. They are people. And if not careful, we could become the very creature we fight." Her glassy eyes homed in on him. "If your father should require your services again..."

"You are my Queen. In life or death, I serve you and you alone." He knelt before her with his arm crossed over his chest.

"Mind your steps." Her eyes narrowed, running her fingers through his hair. "I will not show mercy again."

"Niabi -"

"That will be all, Commander."

Dismissed, Pash bowed and left, unwilling to risk angering her any further. After her door closed behind him, he saw Tala round the corner with a smug look on his face.

CHAPTER 36
TALA

"It would appear you have once again failed our Queen," Tala cooed. "I would tread lightly, if I were you."

"Is that advice or a threat, Lord Tala?"

"What good are threats from me, when you are your own worst enemy?" The Andrago smirked. He no longer hid his animosity for him.

"You have always envied me."

"You confuse distrust with jealousy, Commander."

"What is your issue with me?" Pash spat.

"I will not stand by and watch you betray her as so many others have."

"She is just as much my Queen as she is yours. We are on the same side."

"You are more like him than you even realize." Tala circled around him; arms secured behind his back. "You think she does not see it? You believe she can truly trust you, while you defend him?"

"Spying on my father and executing him are vastly different." Pash stood very still as the Andrago circled him.

"Both of which you object to, or am I mistaken about that as well?" He stopped and faced him.

"I will do as my Queen commands."

"And when she demands his head?" Tala asked the question he truly wanted answered.

"What is it you would like me to say?" Pash shot him a vicious look. "That I would execute my father for her if she asked? She is my Queen. I swore an oath to serve and protect her. I know my duty."

"Did you not also swear an oath to serve your father's house? To wear his sigil?" Tala pressed, knowing he was getting under Pash's skin. "Yet I see no symbol of the bear on your arm. It would seem you are good at swearing oaths of loyalty, but following through, that remains to be seen."

Pash's eyes narrowed. "You sit on her small council and hold a high position among the Andrago, do I question your loyalty?"

"The difference between us is the Andrago have not failed nor betrayed her." Tala stepped up to him and hissed, "If your father should ever think of attempting to usurp her authority, I wonder where your allegiance would fall. One day soon, you will have no choice, but to truly pick a side. Will it be her or him?"

"What did you just say?" Pash had heard those words before.

"You look pale, Commander. Perhaps, you should consult a Healer." Leaving Pash in the hallway, he entered the queen's chambers for a private audience of his own.

She sat in her chair, sipping from the glass of wine in her hand.

"I heard about your Shadows." He closed the doors behind him.

She looked at the eleven raven pins scattered on the floor. "Gershom is a fool."

"Yet you let him live." He crossed his arms over his chest.

"You know that my hands are tied," she growled, staring at the silver scar running across her right palm.

"He cannot be trusted and therefore -"

"He must die," she interrupted. "I know the Andrago way."

"He still lurks in your halls," he looked at the shelves filled with boxes, "more of a threat now than before."

"You heard about his ear, I gather." She smiled and looked up at the box containing his ear that she proudly displayed on her shelf.

He sat across from her. "Is it wise to poke a sleeping bear?"

"If only to watch him dance." Her tone of voice could not disguise her delight.

"He is dangerous." Tala cautioned, preferring Gershom dead than agitated. "He should be dealt with."

"When his time has come, he will suffer greatly before Death takes him. But until then," she leaned back in her seat and stared out the window, "he is not to be touched."

Tala cleared his throat and whispered, "Would you have already executed him if you and the Commander were not involved?"

"You know about us then." She set her goblet down. "You think me to be weak?"

"I believe your mind is clouded." By the wrinkles in his forehead, she could tell he was worried about her.

"You took no issue when I murdered my own father on account of Dichali."

"Your father had to pay for his crimes," Tala poured himself a glass of wine, "as does Gershom."

"You are my most trusted friend and advisor. Your opinion bears much weight, but I ask you to trust me now, as you trusted me all those years ago." She reached for his arm, looking deep into his sunken brown eyes. "It takes great strength to allow your enemy to live, knowing he still serves a purpose."

After a slight hesitation, he nodded his head in agreement. "Tell me what to do and it will be done."

She leaned back in her chair and smiled. "Gershom has been sneaking a red headed prostitute into the castle. Find her and bring her to me unspoiled. She and I have much to discuss."

CHAPTER 37
SALOME

"Why are you crying, Salome?" Lykos asked. "Were Elias and Mosgalath picking on you again?" She nodded her head, affirming his suspicions. He picked her up, sat her on his lap and kissed her forehead. "You should not be sitting here crying."

"I shouldn't?" Her chest rose and fell with rapid breaths.

"No," he wiped a tear from her cheek. "You should defend yourself."

"How?" She fidgeted with her ringlets.

"I will show you." He flashed the training sword he had been practicing with. "I will teach you everything you will need to know."

Wide-eyed Salome shook her head, refusing to take the weapon. "Girls are not allowed to fight."

"Women of the North should know the way of the sword."

"But father -"

"You learn how to fight," he interrupted; the sternness in his voice surprised her. "A woman can fall to a sword just the same as a man."

She hesitated. "Am I a woman?"

"Of course, you are," Lykos smiled. "Just a short woman." He extended the sword to her, and she accepted it. "Lesson one: never underestimate your opponent."

He noticed her admiring his dagger with the handle carved in the shape of a wolf, so he unsheathed it from his hip and handed it to her.

"Take it."

"But father gave it to you," she protested.

"It is mine to give to whom I please and I could think of no one worthier than the North's first female warrior."

The vision faded away and Salome was left holding the unique gift in her right hand. She had spent years training herself not to dwell on the memories of those she had lost, but for some inexplicable reason, she found herself unable to stop the visions. They felt so real. As if she had stepped back in time to relive that moment. *But why? Why was it happening?* She did not understand, but perhaps it was best that way.

Jarred from her quiet moment by the sound of approaching footsteps, she threw the knife. The dagger struck a tree, barely missing Adonijah, who had come to check on her.

"That was close." His eyes darted toward her.

"What are you talking about?" She rolled her eyes and grunted, "I missed."

He pulled the knife from the tree. "I have never seen a blade like this."

"It belonged to my brother." She took the knife from him and sheathed it in its holster on her thigh.

By the tone of her voice, he could tell she did not want to speak of him any further and decided to let it go.

"Harbona sent me to find you. We must cross the Enchanted Swamp before dark if we are to reach Port Daelon in two days."

THE THREE COMPANIONS travelled as quickly as they could through the wetlands. Usually, travelers avoided the Enchanted Swamp due to the countless people who went missing. Harbona knew the risks of the misty lands, but knowing they were being hunted by the Shadows, decided to take his chances.

Although dark in the swamp, Harbona had a small orb that he kept in his breast pocket. Whenever he needed a light to guide him, he would breathe on the orb and it would float in front of him, glowing so the path would be easy to follow.

Salome never imagined anything so remarkable possible. She was tempted to ask him a bunch of questions about the orb but seeing how focused he was on getting them through the swamp unscathed, she held her tongue.

"Tell me again why we are going deeper into the swamp." Adonijah kept a steady eye as he walked beside his skittish horse.

"It is the quickest way to Port Daelon, and Shadows avoid the swamp, fearful of what might be lurking," Harbona answered with a shortness.

"That I understand." Adonijah's eyes dropped to the murky water.

Harbona whipped around and hissed, "Do not look at the water. Focus on the lit path and we shall make it through."

Craving to know why they should avoid looking at the water, Salome once again wrestled with whether she should ask about it or just obey and press forward. She decided on the latter but felt she would burst if anything else spiked her curiosity.

Even with the orb leading them, the further they walked, the darker the Enchanted Swamp became, making it difficult to see what was before them. That is when Salome's foot caught the top of a thick root protruding from the ground, causing her to fall. Adonijah knelt to help her up when they both noticed their odd, warped reflections in the cloudy water and instantly disappeared.

"No!" Harbona's risky trek through the Enchanted Swamp backfired; he knew if he wanted to see them again, he would have to find *her*.

Adonijah and Salome were swept into another dimension of the Enchanted Swamp and although they had both peered into the mysterious waters, they were not sent to the same place.

Salome found herself in a meadow filled with tall grass that swayed in the light breeze. The wildflowers that adorned the field were familiar to her; they were lavenders, her mother's favorite flower. Suddenly, as if thinking of her mother made her appear, she saw her standing across the field. Dressed in a billowing white gown and a crown made entirely of lavender flowers, she extended her hand to her daughter. Without any hesitation, she sprinted toward Bilhah, but as she approached the former queen, she stopped a few feet short, not knowing if she was real or not. Her mother handed her a flower and upon taking it, sniffed it. As soon as a familiar comfort set in, a dark storm tore through the peaceful meadow, leaving an evil aura all around her.

Salome blinked and saw she was now atop a high mountain, encircled by her deceased family members. "Mother? Father?" Tears welled in her eyes at the sight of her loved ones.

"Avenge us," Issachar instructed his daughter.

"Avenge us," Bilhah echoed.

"Avenge us. Avenge us." Her four brothers joined her parents' chant.

It was then that a masked warrior dressed in black from head to toe, walked toward her carrying a bloody sword with blood-stained hands. Frightened, she backed away, unsure of what she was supposed to do.

ADONIJAH WAS WALKING through the wheat fields of the Farmlands, north of Gomorrah, when he saw a small, wooden farmhouse in the distance. He recognized his childhood home and entered the front door expecting to find his mother inside, but no one was there. Walking around the humble abode, he caught sight of his old toys, his mother's favorite quilt and a battered vase of fresh flowers sitting on the wooden table in the center of the common room. He closed his eyes and heard his mother's breathy voice singing a lullaby she used to sing to him every night. He opened his eyes when he heard footsteps behind him, and he drew his sword. He turned around and found himself face to face with a Shadow.

HARBONA HAD NEVER MOVED SO QUICKLY before, but he knew he had a limited amount of time to save his companions from a brutal and excruciating fate. Nestled in the misty clearing was an old wooden and metal bungalow with a rickety front porch. On the eastern side of the small house was a body of murky water and a raft anchored to the dock. The Seer finally saw the woman some believed to be a myth. What was unanimous amongst all Adalorians was whether she existed or not, she was to be feared.

The Enchantress of the Swamp sat on her front porch with her large, black boxer resting loyally at her feet. Upon seeing the visitor, Reaper alerted her of his arrival with a deep howl. Her beautifully hydrated brown skin showed no sign of her age, but her white, hip-length long braids revealed she had walked Adalore for many years. Her petite, curvaceous figure was adorned with gold jewelry and her round nose boasted an ornate septum ring.

She stood with a smirk plastered across her square-shaped face as soon as she saw him. "I have been expecting you, Harbona."

"Where are they, Odelia?" Having known her for quite some time, he was not in the mood for her games.

"No proper greeting?" She shook her head. "Is that any way to greet your hostess?"

"I will not ask you again. Where are they?"

"Somewhere in the swamp." Her voice was smooth as honey and could hypnotize just about anyone who would listen. "But you already knew that."

"Release them."

"You are in no position to demand anything of me, Harbona. The last time I saw you, my hair had not yet turned white."

"Is that what this is about?" he roared. "Because I left?"

"Do not flatter yourself," she brushed him off with a chuckle. "This is the Enchanted Swamp. You know what happens when you look into the murky waters."

Feeling completely helpless, he appealed to her good nature. "Surely there is something you can do to save them."

"Rules are rules," she shook her head and stroked Reaper's muscular chest. "The only way you will see your companions again is if they defeat what they fear most." Odelia walked inside her dark house and waved her hand over a black metal cauldron. "Come, see for yourself."

Harbona realized all he could do at that point was watch.

SALOME'S FAMILY did not stop chanting for her to avenge their wrongful deaths, all the while the assassin circled her. She drew her sword, trying her best to look confident. The fighter initiated their duel and Salome realized she was no match for her skill level. Salome caught a glimpse of the mercenary's green eyes through her mask. Distracted, she left herself open to attack and her left thigh was sliced. Salome crumbled to the ground, writhing in pain. The warrior raised her sword, dripping in Salome's blood, and was about to strike her down when Lykos broke from his chant.

"Salome," his voice was warm, just like she had remembered it, "you are greater than your fear."

"I am greater than my fear," she whispered his words under her breath. "I am greater than my fear."

With the little bit of strength, she still possessed, she rolled away from the impending strike and swung her sword with all her might, cutting her enemy's head off. Her mark began to sizzle, burning her eye. She had never felt pain so excruciating in her entire life. She covered her left eye and watched her family members, one by one, fade from existence.

"No," she whimpered, reaching out to them, "do not leave me again."

Lykos knelt in front of her and smiled. "We never left." And he faded away.

ANGER SWEPT over Adonijah at the very sight of the Shadow standing in his mother's house. He began to fight the intruder with a ferocity he had never exercised in battle before. Landing blow after blow on the Shadow's shield, Adonijah hardly noticed the Shadow was not putting up much of a fight. Swiftly knocking the warrior clad in black to the ground, holding his sword against his throat, Adonijah ripped the mask from the soldier's face to reveal his identity. The face staring back at him was his own. Terrified, he stabbed him in the chest and screamed in pain as if he felt the brunt of the blow.

~

FOLLOWING THEIR ENCOUNTERS, Adonijah and Salome both reappeared in the Enchanted Swamp where they had last seen Harbona. They were both trying to catch their breath, just a few feet away from one another.

He crawled to her. "Are you alright?" He wiped sweat from his forehead.

"I will be," she leaned against a tree. "What happened?"

He hesitated, kneeling in front of her. "I came face to face with what I fear most."

"I did, too." She was somewhat relieved to know they had experienced the same thing.

He leaned against the same tree, sitting next to her. They sat in exhausted silence for what seemed like an eternity but was only about a minute.

"What did you see?" She pulled the loose strands of her curly hair back into a ponytail.

He shook his head, "I can't say."

"Can't or won't?"

"Both," he spat. "What I fear is between me and the swamp."

"Feared," she corrected. "What you feared. You must have conquered it. How else would you have made it back?"

"Then why am I more afraid now, than I was before? What was the point of this?"

"That is your answer." Odelia walked up to them with Reaper by her side and Harbona following closely behind. "The girl is wise beyond her years. Everyone fears something or someone, but only a few face them."

"Who are you?" Salome was not in the mood for any more surprise encounters.

"I am Odelia," she smiled, "Enchantress of the Swamp."

"So, it is *you* we have to thank for this?" Adonijah hissed.

Odelia bent in front of him with a tight-lipped grin. "It is not *I* who peered into the murky waters, Adonijah, the Wanderer. But it is *I* you have to thank for your enlightenment. Now come, you both must be hungry, and we need to take care of your wounds."

Both of them stared at her, still unsure if she could be trusted.

"You need not fear me." Odelia motioned them to follow her. "You are now my guests and will be treated as such. Now come."

CHAPTER 38

CRISPIN

Crispin stood in awe of the limestone walls that soared thirty feet into the sky. Two giant, black alabaster statues guarded either side of the main gate of Numbio. One of the protectors was fashioned in the likeness of the late Queen Zulu and the other was carved in the image of King Osiris.

The city appeared to be one large marketplace, filled with a constant flow of people buying and selling goods. The Southern people were not afraid to dress in attire that showed skin. Crispin had never seen such beautiful and vibrant colored fabrics before. He and Zophar were definitely noticeable standing in the sea of brown smiling faces with their dull, worn-out clothes and Zophar's fiery red hair.

It did not take the weary travelers long to notice the majestic palace in the distance. Weaving through the markets, they passed the crystal clear Umpoco River where fishermen brought their hauls back to the docks. They finally found themselves at the bottom of what had to be a hundred stone steps up to the front doors of the palace of Osiris.

"I am too old for all these stairs," Zophar huffed as they neared the top.

"I never thought I would hear you admit to being old." Crispin flashed a smile at him.

"I am not too old for battle," he fussed, "but I am too old for climbing these steps."

Crispin could not help but chuckle. Once they reached the top, they were met by four guards and one elderly attendant of the royal court.

"Who comes before the throne of His Majesty King Osiris?" the feeble man asked in a gravelly voice.

"I am Crispin, son of Issachar, and this is Zophar, son of Nen. We were sent by Harbona the Seer to have an audience with King Osiris."

The attendant stared at the two dirty men and with a slight nod of his head, he entered through the two large doors, leaving them with the fearsome guards.

"Wow!" Crispin turned to admire the view of the bustling kingdom. "I've never seen a city like this. It's beautiful."

Zophar was eyeing the steps they had just climbed and shook his head. "So many steps. Why? Why so many steps?"

Crispin patted him on the back reassuringly, "You made it though, old man."

"Barely, my boy." He leaned as far back as he could and cracked his lower back. "Barely."

His focus returned to the palace. "I hope this works," Crispin whispered.

"It will." Zophar nodded. "Trust Harbona."

"But -"

"It has to work," Zophar interrupted and pointed downwards. "I don't intend to touch those steps again, until absolutely necessary."

The attendant reappeared and motioned them to follow him inside. "His Majesty will see you."

Crispin and Zophar followed the old man as he led them into the royal throne room. They were in an open courtyard with no roof, surrounded by ten colorful columns documenting the history of their ancestors.

At the end of the long courtyard, King Osiris sat stoically on his golden throne with a black onyx and ivory scepter in his right hand. Even in a seated position, Crispin could tell he was tall with wide shoulders and powerful arms. His elaborate gold crown sat upon his dark bald head and his white goatee highlighted his strong chiseled jaw. Osiris' wide nose sat evenly between his dark brown eyes that bore neither kindness nor fear. He had been King since he was nine years old; nothing and no one intimidated him.

To his right stood an equally impressive royal, his son and heir, Heru. In his physical prime, the tall, broad chested prince wore colorful robes that draped over his left shoulder, exposing his toned brown abdomen. His black beard was perfectly manicured to compliment his dark hair. Although the prince facially appeared to be the exact image of his father, his kind hazel eyes were given to him by his late mother.

Queen Zulu had married Osiris when they were teenagers and bore him two sons. Their youngest son, Duale, died two years ago in a chariot racing accident during Numbio's Festival of the Fallen, an annual celebration honoring their ancestors. Having lost her son was more than she could bear, and her mourning manifested into a disease their healers could not cure. Heru was by her side until the very end and he now wore her favorite jade necklace in her honor. Everywhere you looked in Numbio, you could see statues, paintings, and other pieces of art erected so the people would always remember the beautiful and compassionate queen who spent her whole life serving her people.

"Your Majesty," Crispin bowed.

"Rise." Osiris' deep voice boomed as he rose from his golden seat and descended the steps. "So, you are the son of Issachar; you have his eyes. Your father was my friend, his death was difficult to bear. Harbona told me to expect you." He extended his arm, "Welcome to Numbio."

"Thank you," Crispin grasped his arm.

"I feared his children dead. Though, I had heard rumors that one of his sons had escape." Osiris could not hide his curiosity.

"My sister and I escaped with Zophar by means of an old tunnel."

"Three very brave and blessed people. The Almighty One has surely smiled upon you." He motioned for his son to step forward. "This is my son, heir, and commander of my army, Heru. The old man lurking in the shadows is my advisor, Memucan."

Crispin turned toward the feeble old man who stepped out from behind one of the colorful columns and hobbled his way to his King's side. With a slight nod, he showed the visiting men respect.

"It is an honor to meet you, Prince Crispin." Heru extended his arm for Crispin to grasp.

Crispin had not been referred to as a prince in a long time and it felt weird to hear the title before his name. He grabbed Heru's arm. "The honor belongs to me, Prince Heru."

"Why have you come to Numbio?" Osiris asked, taking a cup of wine from his cupbearer.

Crispin took a deep breath. Confident. He had to be confident. "I intend to challenge Niabi for my father's crown."

"War with the North?" Heru's eyes darted back and forth between Crispin and his father.

"I have come to ask for your aid." Crispin locked eyes with the king.

"You are indeed your father's son." Osiris gripped the arms of his throne as he sat back down. "I understand your desire to avenge your family and take back your home, but to battle the North, to battle the Green-Eyed Raven, is suicide." He lowered his head. "Many have tried, and all have failed to assassinate her and that rat of a Second, Gershom. Those taken alive by the Northerners paid the price for their rebellion." Osiris sighed. "Your father was one of my dearest friends, but I cannot risk anymore of my people's lives for this crime."

"What if there *is* a way to defeat them?" Crispin was not deterred by the ruler's first response. Harbona had instructed him not to take 'no' for an answer.

"A sure way to defeat a monster is wishful thinking." Osiris sipped his wine.

"What do you know of the Hunters?" Crispin asked.

"The Hunters are a myth at best," Memucan chimed in with a snarl. "Besides, no one has even seen one of these so-called Hunters in over two hundred years."

"That is true, no one has seen one for quite some time," Crispin pressed on, determined to win Osiris over. "But if I told you I have seen the Hunter of our age; would you join my cause?"

Heru and Osiris glanced at each other, unsure of how to respond.

"I cannot guarantee men will not fall," Crispin furthered his plea, "but I swear to you on the blood of my ancestors, I *will* take back my father's throne."

Silence. Five men said nothing for what seemed to be a lifetime.

Heru stepped forward, arm pressed across his chest. "I will join you, even if our army does not."

Osiris cleared his throat, furrowing his brow at his son. "You have seen the Hunter's mark?" His attention fell back on Crispin.

He nodded. "I have seen it."

King Osiris's stare was so intense, Crispin almost felt like he could read his mind. *Does he think I am lying?* Crispin did not blink. He held his breath, maintaining eye contact with Osiris. *How can I get him to believe me? What else do I need to say to convince him?*

"Harbona came to me many years ago and spoke with me about this day," Osiris broke his silence. "Years before you were born, your father saved my life, and I was never able to repay him. Even though he is gone, perhaps now, I can repay my life debt." The king crossed his scepter over his chest. "The Numbio will join you."

Lord Memucan did not even attempt to disguise his contempt for Crispin. Before the prince was able to express his gratitude, the hunchback advisor shook his bald head. "Your Highness, we have no quarrel with the North. Why stir up conflict when it is not in our best interest?"

"We have no quarrel with the North. But we have no allegiance to the North either." He focused once more on Crispin. "With him as King, we can rekindle the alliance. I have no daughter of which to bond our peoples in marriage, but we can be bonded in blood, like your father and I were many years ago." Osiris lifted his right palm where a scar sat.

Crispin extended his right hand. "Then let us be bonded."

Osiris smiled. "So much like your father."

"Majesty," Memucan stepped forward, "with all due respect, can you honestly believe what this Northerner says, to be true? Should we not see this Hunter with our own eyes?"

"Bite your tongue, Memucan," Osiris barked. "I am the rising and setting sun. What I say is final and I have spoken." His furrowed brow softened as he looked at Crispin. He lowered his head an inch to show respect once he rose from his throne. "I shall retire for now. Heru will make sure you are taken care of."

Crispin bowed, "Thank you, Highness."

"I, too, shall take my leave as I have matters that require my attention." The shriveling old man eyed Issachar's son as he left the room.

"I would be delighted to show you around, but I know you both need to rest after your long journey across the desert." Heru suggested with a smile.

"You will hear no arguments from us." Crispin noticed a woman standing in the shadows of the throne room but was unable to make out her face before she disappeared.

Heru waved his hand and one of his attendants stepped forward. "See to it our guests are given the finest rooms and have new robes sent to them." The servant bowed, obedient to do his master's bidding. "I shall see you both tonight."

CHAPTER 39

HERU

The wide palace hallways were decorated with beautifully painted images of Numbio royalty and the history of their ancient people. Columns of alabaster supported open archways looking onto the Umpoco River, the Golden Temple, and the hustle and bustle of the city below. Light linen curtains swayed in the dry breeze as Heru weaved his way through the endless hallways. He passed a courtyard with a pool surrounded by lush palm trees on his way to the last door on the right. Not bothering to knock, he made sure no one was nearby to see him enter the Apothecary.

Once inside, his eyes rested upon a curvaceous, dark skinned woman mixing potions on an enormous wooden table in the middle of the airy and bright space. Half of her ceiling was open to the light blue sky which allowed sunlight to beam down on her, highlighting the gold and turquoise beads she had clipped in her midback length braids. Her white robes billowed as he approached her. She did not bother to look up; she knew who had entered.

"I thought that was you in the throne room." Heru stood across the table from her and noticed her unwillingness to look up from her work. "You heard?"

She nodded her head. "Will you go with him?"

"It is my duty."

"You are the heir to your father's throne," she glanced up at him. "What happens if you do not return? What of your people? What of your father?"

"Is that concern for your future king I hear?" he teased.

"You know my concern for you runs deeper than that."

Heru rounded the table and wrapped his arms around her from behind. "I will return to you," he whispered.

"You should not promise such things," she fought back tears.

He gently kissed the back of her head. "Why not?"

"War claims many lives. It does not discriminate between soldiers and their generals."

Heru turned her around to face him and held her chin in his hand. "Rayma, do you trust me?"

"You know I do."

"Then know, I will return to you." He kissed her lips. "I'm sorry I can't stay longer but I must make arrangements for our Northern guests. I will see you tonight."

"I am going with you," she blurted.

He stopped in front of the door and turned, hand still on the knob. "What?"

"When you leave Numbio, I will be with you."

"The battlefield is no place for a woman, Rayma," he frowned. "It is far too dangerous."

"I do not go to the battlefield as a woman. I go to the battlefield as the best healer in the Southern Lands." She stepped up to him. "You cannot deny my skills."

She made a valid point. She was the best healer in Numbio. He had told her so on many occasions. She had been an apprentice for years under the former Royal Healer before his untimely passing and took his place. A year ago, Heru had fallen from his chariot and broke several ribs along with his arm. She eased his pain and helped him heal faster. During their short visits, he fell in love with her: her beauty, her intelligence, her fiery personality. She did not fear him, and she did not treat him differently because he was royalty. She kept him in line; she helped him grow up.

But to let her go into battle… He shook his head. "I cannot allow you to come."

"Give me one valid reason." She popped her hip to the side and crossed her arms over her chest.

"I don't want anything to happen to you." He clenched his jaw. "What if I am not there to protect you?"

"What if I am not there to protect you?" She cupped his face in her hands. "I would rather die by your side, than live in the shadow of your memory."

He knew she was not going to relent. "Before I say yes to you," he rested his hands over hers, "I must ask you something."

She narrowed her eyes. "What is your question?"

"When this war is over and we return," he took a deep breath, "will you marry me?"

"Ma… marry you?" she stammered, taking a step back. "You will be King one day and I am not of royal blood -"

"Our people need a queen again, and I can't think of anyone more suitable than the woman I love." He ran his fingers along her jawline. "So, when we return will you be my wife?"

"I will," her voice cracked.

Grinning from ear to ear, he kissed her. "I must go." He pecked her forehead. "I will see you tonight, my love."

Rayma busied herself mixing potions. Her blissful moment would not last long, A feeling she was being watched forced her to look up toward her door. Hunched over just inside her space was Lord Memucan, and she was not at all pleased to see him.

"That was quite the performance, Rayma," he cooed. "I almost believed you love him."

"What do you want?" she growled.

"I have not come to discuss what I want, but what we have agreed upon." The shriveled old man hobbled up to her table. "You know what must be done. The Northerners will not deter our plan."

"Do you not trust me to accomplish my end of the bargain?" She snarled, uncomfortable with him standing so close to her.

Memucan had a certain odor. At first, she thought it was because he was old, but that was not it. For years she could not place the smell, but as he stood there it finally hit her. Cheese. He smelled like cheese. When she thought about it, she realized he always had a board with cheese on display in his chambers. Her nose crinkled.

Memucan ignored the face she made. "I am afraid you have actually grown fond of our young Prince and that might cloud your..."

"Judgment," she finished his thought.

"Loyalty," he corrected with a hiss.

"You ask me to play the part, now you are worried I am too convincing," she scoffed, stopping her work. "Make up your mind. I grow tired of your games."

"You are in no position to speak to me in that manner," he snapped at the healer. "*You* are the one who has everything to lose, not I."

"Heru has agreed to let me accompany him when they leave Numbio, and I will report to you what I learn."

He glared at her. "Bantu will be going as well."

"You are sending your spy to watch me!?" Her eyes narrowed and her nostrils flared. She hated Memucan. But she hated Bantu even more. Sniveling little rat.

"It is for your own good, Rayma. Just in case you believe you can outwit me." He shuffled back to the door and halted for one last word. "Remember, I own you."

"How can I forget when you remind me daily."

Memucan smirked as he left. She grabbed the nearest glass vile and threw it across the room, shattering it against a column.

CHAPTER 40

NIABI

Niabi made her way down to the damp dungeons where Tala and Anaktu were waiting for her outside a cell door. Leading her into the small space lit by several torches, she sat down at the table in the middle of the room. Tala removed the sack that covered Ziggy's terrified face.

"Leave us," Niabi ordered. Her haunting gaze fell upon the red head. "What is your name?"

Her throat was so dry, she could only answer once she had gulped her own saliva. "Ziggy, Majesty."

"You are from Borg." A safe assumption from her features.

"Yes."

"How did you come to live in Northwind?"

"My parents were killed when pirates from Pulau invaded our village. They took us girls and sold us to the highest bidder. My master lived here in Northwind." Ziggy explained, breathing heavily.

"Slavery is illegal in the North."

"Illegal," Ziggy nodded, "but exists."

"And who is your master?" Her eyes narrowed, wanting a name.

"He was a ship builder named Bronn." Ziggy told the queen a truth most of her companions did not even know.

"Did he hurt you?" Niabi's voice cracked, she could not hide the compassion in her question.

Ziggy shifted in her seat. "I have lost count of all the scars on my body."

Niabi pointed, "Is that how you got that scar on your hand?"

She rubbed her hand, pulling it back from the table. "I tried to run away the night he bought me, but he found me easily. To remind me not to try to escape again, he sliced my hand open."

"How old were you?"

"I was twelve." Ziggy's eyes met the floor.

Niabi placed her elbows on the table and clasped her hands together. "Are you still his slave?"

Ziggy shook her head. "He went to a tavern one night a few years ago and after losing all his money playing cards, offered me up as payment. The man who won me gave me my freedom."

"And what of your former master?" Niabi pressed. "What happened to him?"

Ziggy hesitated. "He had an accident."

The queen leaned in closer, intrigued. "You mean to say you killed him?"

"He drank himself into a stupor and took a tumble off the dock." Ziggy's eyes showed no emotion.

"You didn't answer my question." The queen twisted a ring on her index figure absentmindedly. "Did you kill him?"

"My only regret is that I didn't do it sooner." She spat indignantly. She noticed a smile spread across Niabi's face. "Might I speak freely, my Queen?"

"Please do."

"Why am I here? Surely it is not to learn of my childhood."

Niabi leaned back in her seat. Ziggy was clever. She liked that. "I have suspected for quite some time now, that Gershom might try to usurp me." She paused. "You are his only female companion, so clearly he trusts you."

"What are you asking?" Ziggy mirrored the queen and sat back in her seat.

"Continue to see him and report to me what he confides in you."

The tone of the queen's voice frightened her. "You want me to spy on him?"

"Yes," Niabi confirmed.

"What if he finds out?" the red head's voice quivered.

"Anaktu and Tala have been instructed to keep a watchful eye on you." Her fingers tapped rhythmically on the table.

"Will Gershom not find their hovering odd?"

"So many questions," the queen growled.

"Forgive me, my Queen," Ziggy shrank in her seat. "I am nervous. I have never done anything like this before." She lied.

"Tell me everything he says and does." She rubbed her hands together, her eyes flashed. "Nothing is insignificant. Trust that Anaktu and Tala will protect you."

"Yes, my Queen." She agreed.

"Good. Now be off before someone notices your absence." As Ziggy stood to leave, Niabi grabbed her arm. "And if you betray me, Ziggy of Borg, I will give you to my Shadows until there is nothing left of you to be had. Do I make myself clear?"

"Yes, my Queen."

Niabi released her from her tight grasp, and she bowed once more before scurrying out of the queen's presence.

"You think this will work?" Vilora slithered around the corner. "What if she has feelings for him?"

Niabi's mouth curled into a smile. "She fears me more than she cares for him."

Vilora twisted a lock of her straw like hair, sitting in the seat Ziggy had occupied. "And your promise to protect her?"

"To ensure her loyalty." She stood up and looked down at the witch. "Her life means nothing to me. We are all pawns in someone else's game; I choose to be the one controlling the pieces."

CHAPTER 41
ODELIA

The trio sat at the large wooden table in Odelia's bungalow after eating one of the best stews they had ever had. Reaper stretched out underneath the Enchantress' chair, keeping a watchful eye on the front door. Harbona and Adonijah both lit their pipes and silently puffed, filling the small space with a hazy smoke.

"You look just like your mother." Odelia broke the silence as she stared across the table at Salome.

"Did you know her?" Salome's eyes softened as she set her cup down.

"Not personally," the Enchantress sipped some of her hot tea. "I knew her Aunt Vilora." Harbona glared at her. She knew by the look on his face that she should not say anything more about the witch.

"I'm afraid I don't know much about my mother's family or their history." Salome wiped some of the dirt from her face with the wet towel Odelia provided.

"You will learn about all of that very soon," Odelia smiled. "Is that not right, Harbona?"

Salome's eyes darted to the Seer who continued to smoke his pipe. "I thought we were going to Port Daelon. Are we going to the Isles of Myr?"

"I have arranged for us to have safe and secret passage from Port Daelon to Myr," Harbona confessed. "Your grandmother, Queen Nym, will be eager to finally meet you."

"Why did you not tell me before?" her voice cracked.

"I did not know how you would feel about going to your mother's homeland and it is vital we speak with your grandmother. Trust me." He exhaled a puff of smoke.

"How can you tell me to trust you, if you aren't honest with me?" She pushed back from the table. "I am used to being the hunter and now, I am the hunted. If we are going to be successful, or even make it through the night, we need to be honest with one another."

"You are right." He set his pipe down. "I should have spoken with you about my plans and from this point on, I will. For now, I ask you to accept my counsel and know that I will not lead you astray."

"You need not be afraid, Harbona," Odelia chimed in, knowing what was truly bothering him. "She is Issachar's daughter, not Issachar himself."

"What does that mean?" Salome glared at Odelia.

"Do not be offended, child." Her smooth voice brought a sense of ease with every word she spoke. "Your father did not listen to Harbona's warning and it cost him his life. He may not show it, but he is afraid of failing you."

"Harbona, what is she talking about?" Her shoulders tensed.

Odelia noticed how uncomfortable Harbona was, clearly unwilling to discuss what she had purposely brought up. Adonijah noticed Harbona's demeanor and leaned forward, now interested in knowing what he was hiding.

"Harbona?" Salome set her spoon down. "What are you not telling me?"

"Harbona was a member of your father's small counsel and before your sister attacked the city, he warned your father of her plans." Odelia spoke on the silent Seer's behalf. "He did not heed Harbona's warnings nor listen to the pleas of his small counsel to take necessary measures to protect not only the city, but to protect the royal family from certain death."

"That's not true," she stood up, shaking her head.

"He thought your sister to be weak," the Enchantress persisted. "He denied her. He underestimated her. Because of his stubbornness, he failed to act on the visions, and it cost your family their lives."

"Stop speaking lies!" The princess slammed her fist on the table. "It's not true." Her voice ebbed into a raspy whisper; repressing the tears that burned her eyes. She turned her gaze toward the quiet Immortal. "Tell me it's not true."

"I only hope you can trust me as your father could not. His death was not easy to bear." His eyes were filled with grief.

Silence enveloped the small bungalow.

Adonijah set his pipe down and eyed Salome. "I could use some fresh air and think it best not to walk the swamp alone. Walk with me?"

She nodded and left with him.

"How long have they known one another?" Odelia watched them descend the creaky porch steps.

"Not long at all," he answered, wearily. "A couple of days."

"Not long at all and yet he cares very deeply for her." She had a soft spot for potential romance.

He closed his eyes and rubbed his forehead. "I know he does."

"Curious, is it not, how two people can go from strangers to so much more in such a short time." The Enchantress sipped her tea with a coy smile.

"Everyone was once a stranger to another." Harbona shooed her romantic notions. "Such is life, Odelia."

"You know something." Her brown eyes danced with curious delight.

"I know a lot of things." He wiggled his back against his chair to satisfy an itch. "You will have to be more specific on what I supposedly know."

Her eyes rolled. He had not changed. "You know something about their future."

"I see many futures, you know that. It is my blessing and my curse." He exhaled a large cloud of smoke.

"You are not going to tell me, are you?" She leaned back in her chair, already knowing the answer to her question.

"There are many possibilities," he looked up at her, "their futures are not yet set."

"Yet you brought them together?" She tilted her head with a grin.

He narrowed his eyes with a sigh, "He was always destined to protect her."

"And what is *her* destiny?" she pried.

"To be his light in a dark place."

CHAPTER 42

ADONIJAH

Outside, a short distance from Odelia's bungalow, Adonijah and Salome sauntered aimlessly around the swamp. Reaper had followed them out and settled down on the creaky front porch where he kept watch. They welcomed his presence because it gave them a sense of safety in the strange terrain.

"Thank you," she said, now composed.

"For what?" He looked over at her, curious.

"It is not easy to speak of my parents. I didn't know them as others did." She rubbed her hands against her thighs. "I just have so many unanswered questions."

"Perhaps, travelling to the Isles of Myr will give you some answers." He comforted her as best he could, but his face flushed, and he immediately regretted his effort.

"Have you found the answers to your questions?"

"What do you mean?" He cocked his head, looking her up and down.

"I have lost many loved ones, Adonijah. I can see you too have suffered a similar loss." He stared at the ground. "You don't need to tell me what happened but know that you are not alone. I understand your pain." She reached for his hand and squeezed it, then headed toward the old wooden house.

"I found the answers I sought." His whisper stopped her where she stood.

"And?"

"The answers are just another form of pain." He glanced up at her, pulling leaves from a twig he picked up. "It did not bring those I loved back. It did not ease the ache in my heart. It did not bring me peace." He dropped the stick and sighed heavily. "I was reminded of how powerless I was to save them. It showed me how much hatred still fills my heart."

"I don't believe I could feel any more powerless than I am already. That I could hate my enemies more than I already do."

"You would be surprised at the depth one can hate another. You will see," he leaned against a tree and crossed his arms over his chest. "Myr will give you the answers you seek and break your heart all over again."

CHAPTER 43
SALOME

Early the next morning, Salome sat on the front porch and listened to all the unfamiliar sounds of the misty swamp. The day before, she found the wetlands abhorrent, but staying with Odelia and getting to know her better, made the spooky swamp seem quite nice. The land was truly alive with its own personality. The air was so thick, you felt you had walked into a wet cloud. She could see why Odelia loved it. It was quiet, peaceful, and private; every quality she held dear.

"I thought I was the only one who rose this early in the morning." Odelia's sudden presence surprised her. "Sorry, child, I didn't mean to startle you."

"It's alright." She smiled, noticing Reaper sat down next to the Enchantress' rocking chair, as if he were on duty. "I always wake up early to have time alone to think."

"And what were you up so early thinking about?" She plopped into her chair and rocked softly.

Salome shrugged her shoulders and changed the subject. "Why did you name him Reaper?"

"Because he is the Reaper of Lost Souls, of course," she smiled widely. "When the Swamp claims a soul, Reaper collects them. How else could he live to be forty-three?"

"Reaper is forty-three?" She did not know if she believed her tale.

"Aye, child, forty-three." Odelia nodded her head as she patted him on the head. "And as long as people continue to lurk into the Enchanted Swamp and look into the murky waters, he will keep on living."

He did not look menacing, but Salome looked at the enormous black dog with a newfound fear.

"Does he frighten you?" Odelia wiped the bubbling beads of sweat from her hairline.

She half-shrugged, "Normally, a dog wouldn't scare me but -"

"Not Reaper," Odelia interrupted. "Your male companion."

"Adonijah?"

"Aye, girl." She chuckled. "Does he frighten you?"

She shook her head. "No."

"Your eyes tell a different truth." Odelia's eyes danced.

"And what of your eyes, Odelia?" Salome sassed, bringing her legs up to her chest. "I see how you look at Harbona. Who is he to you?"

The Enchantress grinned fondly as she played with one of her dreads. "A memory."

"Now, it is *your* eyes that tell a different truth," Salome teased, finishing her tea.

"It is a pity you must leave so soon," Odelia cooed. "Me thinks we would have gotten along quite nicely."

Adonijah shuffled outside with his pipe pursed between his lips. "Ladies," he greeted once he noticed them and sauntered toward the horses to ready them for their journey.

Salome could not help but giggle. "He definitely doesn't frighten me."

"He *should* frighten you." Odelia's tone sent chills up her spine.

"Why?" Her eyes narrowed as she planted her feet on the ground.

"If I had a man that handsome look at me, the way he looks at you, I would find myself in a heap of trouble." Her eyes softened as Harbona stepped outside.

Salome stood and excused herself, knowing Odelia would want to say goodbye privately. "I will try to keep myself out of trouble."

"Or not." Odelia winked.

Odelia smiled as Reaper followed Salome down the steps. "She's a spitfire. Reminds me of myself when I was her age."

"You were far sassier." Harbona's eyes squinted as he flashed a warm smile her way. "You have not changed a bit."

She eyed the banished Seer, her tone serious. "I looked into her future, and it is not what I expected."

His gaze fell to his feet. "Odelia, you shouldn't have -"

"Harbona, if she should fail -"

"I know what would happen," he interrupted, rubbing the nave of his neck.

"Death will come for her," her voice cracked.

"I know," he whispered, eyes meeting hers. "Death comes for us all. But if she focuses on her own mortality, she will not live to see her victory."

The Enchantress could tell how much the mortals meant to him. He had advised many of them throughout his thousands of years walking Adalore and buried even more of them. But this mortal seemed to mean more to him than all those before her.

"It was good to see you, Harbona, after all these years." Odelia cleared her throat. "Perhaps, do not wait so long to visit me again."

He looked at her with deep regret. "I never should have left the way I did. You didn't deserve that."

"Ah!" she waved her hand in the air. "That was a lifetime ago."

"I *am* sorry, Odelia." He grabbed her tattooed hand in his. "When this is over -."

She gently caressed his cheek and examined his face. She did not know him before his branding, but the banishment mark did not cause her to treat him any differently. Although, it had been nearly three decades since she last saw him, his grey eyes were the same, except for the crow's feet around his eyes. His long platinum blonde hair pulled back revealed he had lost the glow of the Immortals. Emotions she had not felt in years flooded her heart as she stared at the man who held a special place in her heart.

"I will see you when I see you," she kissed his cheek. "May the Almighty One protect you."

She waved as they rode away and patted Reaper who had rejoined her on the porch.

"That man will be the death of me," she sighed.

THE TRIO ROAD through the rest of the swamp silently, simply because they had nothing to say. After hours of trotting through the misty wetlands, they finally arrived at the mouth of the Valley Pass, a narrow road nestled between two opposing mountain ranges. It was the only way to reach Port Daelon, which was at the very end of the pass. Any traveler who wished to survive the dangerous road, remained vigilant and made sure he made it to the city before nightfall or strange creatures, it was said, would attack.

"What is that?" Salome halted her horse to listen to a distant noise that sounded like the beating of a drum.

After listening to the echoing sound, Adonijah recognized the rhythmic beat and jumped off his horse. "We need to get out of sight. Now!"

Salome and Harbona both dismounted their steeds and pulled them behind a large cluster of boulders. Once they were securely hidden, she peered around the rocks to catch a glimpse of the incoming travelers.

Two men on horseback turned the corner and right behind them was a group of nearly two dozen chained men and women marching in single file, prodded by five slavers armed with whips, maces, and knives. All seven men were tall and broad-chested with unnaturally, bulging muscles and deeply scarred, bald heads. Their bodies were covered in white ash with black paint around their soulless eyes.

Salome could not take her eyes off their pointy ears and equally sharpened teeth, both filed in those distinct shapes by their masters. They only wore black, high-waistbands and loin cloths. The only armor they sported were spiked chest and shoulder pieces.

"The Thrak," Adonijah identified in a hushed voice. "Slaves to the rulers of Gomorrah, with one purpose: to hunt and enslave the Stormcrags."

"The Thrak of Gomorrah?" she whispered; eyes still glued on the villainous creatures.

"The very thought of that unholy city is more than I care to think about," Harbona spat on the ground.

"And the prisoners?" Her gaze switched to the men and women that marched through the Valley Pass in chains. They were of mixed racial backgrounds; clay and shades of blue and purple paint were splattered across their faces, arms, legs and chests to show which warrior clan they belonged to. Piercings adorned their faces, and their hair was left wild and untamed.

"Stormcrags. They are one of two rival tribes of Mountain Men, dwellers of Fennor of the Bone Mountains," Harbona explained.

"Sons and daughters of criminals," Adonijah said with contempt.

"They are known for their brutal attacks on caravans that travel around the mountains," Harbona continued. "To capture a Stormcrag is a difficult task, but there is a large price on their heads if brought back to Gomorrah alive. For hundreds of years, their peoples have battled, every attack becoming more sadistic than the last."

"What will happen to them in Gomorrah?" She spotted a small child among the prisoners, and it tugged at her heart.

"They will be questioned on the location of Bone City and their temple, Tears of the Gods, and when they refuse to answer, they will be tortured to death in the town square for all Gomorrians to witness."

Every word Harbona spoke weighed heavily on her. "We must help them," she declared, without a second thought.

"That is too risky," Adonijah protested, "Have you ever seen the Thrak in action? Because I have and -"

"You would rather have them tortured to death?" she cut him off with a snarl.

"They are none of our concern. If we are overrun and you are captured by either side, you will be lucky to have a quick death." Adonijah stood his ground.

"It is a risk I am willing to take," she fired back in a raspy whisper. "No one should be enslaved and brutalized for the pleasure of another."

Harbona finally added his input, "If we succeed in freeing the Stormcrags, they will owe us a life debt, something they take very seriously."

"But the Stormcrags are a vicious people." Adonijah continued to protest. "Who knows if we could truly trust them not to slit our throats in the middle of the night."

"The Stormcrags honor their word, unlike the Krazaks, who offer anyone up to the Thrak for sport." Harbona eyed Salome. "The Krazaks would slash our throats, no doubt."

"We have to help them," Salome insisted.

Adonijah was reluctant but knew he had been outvoted. "If we are going to do this, we must act quickly." He and Harbona unsheathed their swords and Salome nocked her arrow, ready for a swift strike. "On my mark, we will attack." Once Adonijah saw the Thrak had completely passed their hiding spot, he nodded his head. "Now!"

Salome jumped up and launched her first arrow toward the nearest Thrak, striking him between his shoulder blades. She ran to the fallen slaver and stood over him as he tried to crawl away. Clutching a mace in his right hand, he turned to strike her, but was met with a second arrow that pierced his thick neck, killing him instantly.

Adonijah found himself fighting the largest Thrak of the lot whose weapon of choice was a double-sided mace with spikes as long as knives. He had seen his fair share of fights but had never seen a weapon like that. At first, his main focus was defending himself as the Thrak swung the mace around in sporadic movements; ducking and dodging until he finally noticed a pattern and became the aggressor.

With swift and determined thrusts of his sword, Adonijah finally bested his ashen opponent, cutting his leg out from under him and stabbing him in the stomach.

Salome noticed a Thrak charging Adonijah from behind and shot him down. He turned and saw the dead Gomorrian face down in the dirt and nodded his head to show her his appreciation for her having his back. She caught sight of a ring of keys attached to the waistband of the slaver she had just killed and realized one of those keys had to unlock the prisoners' chains. She swiped the keys and started to free the Mountain Men.

"Go!" she shouted once their chains had been unshackled. "Run, you're free!"

Harbona had not been in true hand to hand combat longer than he cared to admit, but thankfully, he was not having difficulty in defending himself. Immortals were known for their agility and grace on the battlefield and although he had been banished, he still moved like an angelic being. The enormous Thrak grew tired as he swung his wooden spiked club toward the Seer and once he slowed, Harbona took the opportunity to strike. He slammed his staff on the ground causing the slaver to fly back and land on his back. Now disarmed, Harbona ended him quickly by slashing his throat.

As soon as Salome had finished freeing the last prisoner, she turned in time to see one of the horseback riding Thrak stampeding toward her and she dove out of his path. Instead of turning around to finish her off, he rode away to escape the Valley Pass. Harbona hopped on his horse and chased after the Gomorrian. If he were not caught, their whereabouts would be reported.

"You've cost me dearly, woman," the second Thrak on horseback hissed as he dismounted his steed.

She tried to hurry to her feet, but unable to scramble away, he kicked her ribs as hard as he could. Writhing in pain, she once again attempted to stand up, but he unsheathed his knife and slashed her face.

Adonijah was dueling the last Thrak and saw Salome was in trouble. He fought the ashen warrior as quickly as he could swing his sword, but this Thrak was armed with two swords and moved swiftly despite his large size.

Adrenaline kicked in and Salome grabbed her wolf blade from the holster on her thigh and blocked his incoming blow. She knew she was no match for him size-wise, but she knew she could beat him on speed. She swung her leg around, knocking him off his feet. Still in excruciating pain, she slowly stood to her feet watching to see what he would do next. To her surprise, he flipped up, drew his whip from his hip, and cracked it against her leg. He flung the whip back with every intent to strike her again, but Salome threw her hand in the air in a desperate attempt to halt the impending lash and grabbed hold of the end of the leather whip. The tip wrapped around her hand, stinging her, ensuring he could not rip it out of her possession. The Thrak cackled as he forcefully pulled her toward him, dragging her the entire way.

Adonijah whacked one of the swords from the Thrak's hand and took the opportunity to launch an aggressive assault. He whipped his sword around, knocked his enemy's second blade out of his grasp which exposed his stomach for Adonijah's kick. As he fell backwards, Adonijah took his knife from the holster on his back and threw it, slicing into his neck. He quickly retrieved his dagger and sprinted toward Salome who was a good distance away.

Struggling and failing to get to her feet, the Thrak pulled her closer to him. His eyes were crazed, almost possessed; she had never seen such blackened eyes. While being dragged on her belly, she tried to release her hand from the whip she was entangled in, but by the time she freed her bleeding hand, the Thrak had wrapped his calloused fingers around her neck.

"Now you die." The Thrak raised her off the ground.

Her feet dangled as she tried to pry his hand from her neck; now losing consciousness. Just before she blacked out, she dropped to the ground. When she opened her eyes, she saw the tip of a sword protruding from the Thrak's chest. The Thrak fell; he was dead. Standing before her, she saw her savior. It was one of the Stormcrags she had freed.

"Who are you?" She felt the loss of blood taking its toll on her. Instead of answering her question, he sprinted away.

"Salome!" Adonijah swept her in his arms and was instantly drenched in her blood. "Stay with me."

SALOME'S EYES fluttered as she woke, and a rush of pain flooded her body. When she was able to focus, she noticed all the bandages wrapped around her hand and leg.

"You're awake," Adonijah breathed a sigh of relief.

"How long was I out?" She eyed the makeshift camp as she rubbed the back of her head.

"A couple of hours."

Sure she had been drooling, she wiped the sides of her mouth when he turned to stoke the fire. "Where's Harbona?"

He rotated the rabbit he had caught over the flames, "One of the Thrak escaped. He chased after him."

She attempted to sit up, but the pain shot through her body. She grabbed her torso, wincing from an aching ribcage. Adonijah knelt in front of her and touched her non-injured hand.

"I feel like my ribs are broken," she scrunched her face.

"Not broken. But you took a beating." She eyed him before lifting her shirt to see bandages wrapped around her torso. "I had to bind your wounds. I'm sorry if that makes you uncomfortable," he explained.

She stroked her face and felt a nasty cut.

"Aye," he nodded with a grimace, "he got your face as well."

"I'm sure that will scar nicely," she mumbled. "Is it bad?"

"Since I tended to your wounds quickly, it should not be as noticeable. And even if it is, it will suit you fine." He hesitated before he said, "You have many scars."

She became uneasy. "No more than others."

"Where did you get this one?" He pointed at a small scar on her left forearm near her six lined tattoo.

"I was thirteen," she tugged at her earlobe, "I fell from a tree."

"And this one?" He motioned toward her collarbone.

"Crispin bested me during training a few years back. I think he did it on purpose after we got into an argument."

"And the one across your stomach?"

"I have you to thank for that one." She remembered that one distinctly from their first encounter in The Hollow.

"I'm sorry about that." He broke eye contact with her.

"It's alright." She pointed at a fresh scar on his chest. "I returned the favor."

"I suppose I deserved that." He smirked and cocked his head. "How many scars do you have?"

"Too many." She stood up with great difficulty.

"Where are you going?" He remained in his crouched position.

"I need to walk around," she breathed heavily. The pain was worse standing up than sitting down. "I need to clear my head." She leaned against one of the boulders their camp was hidden behind.

"You need to rest, Salome."

The way he said her name sent a tingling sensation through her body. It was just her name. She had heard it countless times over seventeen years, but it sounded different coming from his lips.

"I will be fine." She limped away from him keeping her hand against the rocks for support.

"Has your eye been like that since birth?" He scratched his beard, rising from his crouched position.

Her breath quickened. "Why do you ask?" The question fumbled out of her mouth.

The way he looked at her made her heart skip.

"Why are you looking at me like that?" She pressed her fingers to her lips, uncomfortable with his question.

"I know who you are." The words oozed from his lips.

She tried to hide the panic in her voice. "I am Issachar's daughter -"

"You are the Hunter, aren't you?" Their eyes met.

She lunged for her sword and pointed it at him. "Don't come any closer."

"What are you doing?" he flinched.

"I said, don't come any closer." She tightened her grip on her weapon.

He lifted his hands to where she could see them. "I swore an oath to protect you."

"A promise you made before you knew the truth." She felt trapped, cornered like a wild animal trying to escape its cage.

"I mean you no harm," his voice was silky, warm. "Please, lower your sword."

"I can't."

"Do you trust me?"

"I want to." She was sweating, unsure of what to do.

"Then trust me."

"This could be a trick."

"If I were going to kill you, would I have gone through the trouble of binding your wounds? Surely that counts for something." She still clutched her weapon. "I am the same Adonijah who swore to protect you."

"I am not the same Salome you swore to protect." Tears filled her eyes, her bottom lip quivered.

"To me, you are the same." He knelt before her and gazed into her shifting eyes. "You need not fear me, but if you do not trust me, take your sword and end me now. I will not live one more day with you fearing me to be your enemy."

She stared deeply into his caring brown eyes and lowered her sword with tears streaming down her cheeks. "I didn't want this."

"Are you afraid?"

Her nostrils flared, she whispered, "I am."

"I am too."

They stared at each other silently.

She sat on the ground across from him. "What do you fear?"

"Myself," he finally admitted out loud.

"Why?" She watched him intently.

"I fear I will become like my father. His blood runs through my veins, his weaknesses, his failures. I am afraid that if I let myself, I will live as he did, and I would rather be dead than be what I hate."

She rested her sword in her lap. "What did he do that frightens you?"

"He has brought more pain and sorrow than I dare talk about." Adonijah tore his eyes from her and stared at the ground.

"Who is he?" she asked, but as she expected, he remained silent. "Is that what you saw in the swamp?"

"Know your secret is safe with me." He rose from his seated position. "Nothing changes between us."

"Adonijah -"

"Stay down," he silenced her and ducked. Hearing horse hooves fast approaching, he readied himself for a possible altercation, but saw the rider was Harbona.

"Did you catch him?" Adonijah threw him a sheepskin filled with water.

"I tried my best – nearly followed him into Gomorrah itself – but it was as if he had wings." Harbona jumped from his exhausted horse and drank the refreshing water.

"It will not be long before the Gomorrian Lords set a bounty on our heads." Adonijah knew exactly what would be headed their way if they did not make it to their ship quickly. "The Thrak will not rest until they find us. We must reach Port Daelon by nightfall, or we may never make it to the Isles of Myr."

CHAPTER 44

MATILDYS

Racing through the dirty streets of Gomorrah, the Thrak that escaped Harbona swiftly made his way through the overpopulated kingdom that smelled of soot and manure, toward the menacing Black Tower that stood in the center of the circular city.

Gomorrah was completely enclosed by a black stone wall. Originally, the wall was a light color, but with the blacksmiths working on the outskirts of the city, it turned the structure black with dirt. Throughout the city hung the mangled bodies of tortured Stormcrags for all Gomorrians to mock as they passed by. An unhygienic people by nature, they were perfectly satisfied living in filth, if it meant they did not have to abide by any laws. All that was required of Gomorrians was that they honor and protect the crown.

Although the cannibalistic Thrak were considered barbaric to the rest of Adalorian cities, Gomorrians worshipped them and gladly committed their firstborn sons to the enslaved order. Thrak were not given names but were known only by the numbers that were branded into the back of their necks as children. Completely lacking in empathy, they were the perfect soldiers for King Cyler's army.

King Cyler was of the purest blood. Following the Gomorrian custom, a ruler could only reproduce with family. His blonde hair and blue eyes were his only redeeming features. He suffered from a plethora of diseases and the bulging hump on his back further weakened his feeble frame, forcing him to rely heavily on his wife and sister, Maltidys, to take care of daily affairs.

Maltidys was oddly beautiful and healthy for being a product of incest. Her wavy blonde hair cascaded to the middle of her back and her sunken, icy blue eyes were haunting. The queen's high cheekbones, narrow nose, and thin lips were the envy of all Gomorrian women. Because she never left her tower, her skin was extremely pale, and she appeared almost corpse like. Black and gold were the only colors she would wear, and she always fashioned her hair in the traditional Gomorrian way: half of her hair was twisted in two side buns, accentuating the squareness of her face, and the rest of her hair would lay flat across her back.

Most people in the Ten Kingdoms feared their kings, but in Gomorrah, everyone knew King Cyler was no true threat. Maltidys, on the other hand, was not only feared, but adored for her ruthless demeanor. She was their true leader and was grooming her fifteen-year-old twins, Thanos and Ranalda, to be just as merciless.

From their infancy, her son and daughter would watch as the captured Stormcrag men, women, and children, would be tortured for hours until there was nothing left of them to mutilate. After years of watching merciless torture, they had become just as cruel as their mother. Both Thanos and Renalda were in the dark throne room with their parents when the Thrak numbered 62198 appeared on bended knee before them.

"62198, your task was to find and capture Stormcrags for questioning, but it appears you have returned empty handed." The queen's chilling voice echoed through the circular stark room. "Why is that?"

The Thrak's black eyes darted around the room, not sure where to focus. "My Queen," his deep voice gurgled, "we captured many Mountain Men -"

"Then, where are they?" Maltidys interrupted with a shriek.

"We... we were attacked," he stammered. "I am the only Thrak to survive."

"Who would dare kill the Thrak of Gomorrah?" she wheezed in disbelief.

"There was a woman, highly skilled with a bow -"

"A *woman* did this to you?" Prince Thanos scoffed in disbelief.

"Hush, Thanos." The queen's eyes darted toward him, infuriated by his outburst. "A woman withstood the pain to birth you and if underestimated, a woman can easily take your life." She refocused on the Thrak. "Finish your tale of this skilled woman."

"She was not alone, my Queen. She had two men with her. One bore the banishment mark of the Immortals. They killed the Thrak and freed the prisoners."

Maltidys stroked her husband's bony hand in her own. "What do you think of 62198's report, my love? Should we believe him?"

The sickly king's hollowed eyes slowly lifted to stare at the Thrak who had returned empty handed. His hoarse voice whispered, "He knows the penalty for failure."

"Exactly what I was thinking." She eyed the quivering slave and flashed a sinister grin. "Take him to the Square."

Two Thrak grabbed their comrade and dragged him from the throne room down to the Square at the entrance of the Black Tower. A deep resonating horn sounded throughout the entire city alerting the people that fresh meat had arrived. Excitement pulsed through every citizen who rushed toward the infamous Square. The royal family made their way to a covered balcony two stories above the wooden platform which was quickly surrounded by eager civilians. Thrak 62198 was forced to his knees in front of an executioner's block while Maltidys stood to address the blood thirsty Gomorrians.

"Gomorrians," her shrill voice echoed. "Thrak 62198 returned to our great city having failed in his mission to capture our enemies." Her eyes fell on the condemned Thrak. "Gomorrians, what is the penalty for failure?"

"Death! Death! Death!" The crowd erupted in a thunderous roar as they pumped their fists in the air and stomped their feet.

"And Death he shall receive," she smiled.

With the slight nod of her head, the executioner swung his gigantic sword, claiming the disgraced Thrak's head to the delight of the dusty people.

Seeing her husband was exhausted from the day, Matildys motioned for her son to stand up. "Thanos, take your father inside. He needs to rest."

Obedient to his mother's commands, he helped his ailing father inside, leaving his sister and mother alone to watch the elated crowd.

"Ranalda, what is our creed?" Maltidys asked the elder twin.

"Kill, steal, destroy, but keep the blood pure," she beamed with pride. Ranalda had her mother's beauty, but she was not nearly as intimidating. Her rosy cheeks and boyish figure left her lacking the confidence her mother had.

"Very good." Her mother patted her thin fingers. "One day you will rule all Gomorrians -"

"But, mother, Thanos will be King, not I."

Maltidys smacked her daughter across the face. "Do not interrupt me again."

"I am sorry, mother." She rubbed her cheek, trying to hide the tears that welled in her eyes.

"Listen to me, Ranalda," the queen quickly moved on, "Thanos is weak and as long as I have anything to say about it, he will never rule our people."

"But our law states only a male can be -"

"You think your *father* rules the Gomorrians?" she hissed. "Do not be so naïve. He may bear the crown, but it is my voice the people obey. When I am gone, you shall take my place."

Ranalda was confused. "What of Thanos?"

"You want to be queen, do you not?"

"Of course, Mother."

"And queen you shall be. Thanos will pose no threat to your reign."

Before Ranalda could ask another question, Thrak 47134 bowed before them with a rolled-up parchment. Matildys snatched it and shooed him away as she read the papers.

"What is it, Mother?"

"The North is offering a hefty bounty if these two criminals are found and delivered to them alive."

Ranalda inspected the posters of Crispin and Salome. "They killed Queen Niabi's Shadows? How could peasants massacre such deadly mercenaries?"

Maltidys tapped her lips, deep in thought. "There must be more to this than meets the eye. No one would offer such a sum for peasants and insist they be captured alive." She examined Salome's poster once more and remembered what Thrak 62198 claimed. "A skilled woman…" A smile stretched across her pale face. "*She* killed the Thrak and released my prisoners. Ranalda, order Thrak 47314 to take a band of twenty to Port Daelon to find her."

"She may not be there."

"Tell him whoever brings her to me alive and unspoiled will be given their freedom." Maltidys could not tear her eyes from the poster. "She stole from me, and she will pay the price."

"But if you kill her, we will not receive her bounty," Ranalda pointed out.

"Revenge before riches," the queen glared at her daughter. "Revenge before riches."

CHAPTER 45

PASH

Gershom wiped the beads of sweat that dripped down his forehead. Breathing heavily, he was clearly exhausted, but refused to take a break from practicing with his sword. Any who watched could not deny he was highly skilled and even in his late years of life, he was still deadly. The Bear sparred with his personal guards daily for a minimum of two hours. Most thought he was trying to prevent old age from setting in, but Pash knew the real reason he kept himself trained was because he was always concerned someone he had wronged would one day come for him.

Pash had entered the room virtually unnoticed and watched as his father sparred. As fearsome a warrior as he was, he knew the true lethal threat was Niabi. After watching silently for several minutes, Gershom finally noticed his son lurking in the shadows of his private training room.

"What do you want?" Gershom hissed as he dismissed his guards.

Pash stepped forward. "I came to talk to you about the Queen's Shadows."

"Oh, she sent you, did she?"

"She does not know I am here," he lied. "Tell me how to help you."

"Why should I believe you wish to help me when everyone knows where your loyalties lie?" he scoffed. He sheathed his weapon in its holster and set it on the table.

"She never should have harmed you." He stared at the hole where his father's ear used to be. "Had I known what she had planned, I would have stopped it."

"It is the last thing she will ever take from me," Gershom growled.

"Tell me how I can help you and I will do it."

He stared at his son suspiciously. "I wish I could believe you, Pash."

"I know I have not lived up to your expectations, but you are my father, and blood is everything. You have been careless in your dealings with the Shadows, but with me behind you, commanding them, she will never know of my betrayal."

Before Gershom could answer, the Nameless Rider entered the private grounds. Crossing his right arm to his left shoulder, the Shadow began to report his findings. "My Lord Gershom, Commander Pash, I have returned from the village where our men were slaughtered."

"What has been done to those bold and reckless villagers?" Gershom fumed.

He grinned. "Most of them are dead, my lord."

His words struck Pash like a dagger. To think of the innocent being murdered did not sit well with him.

"Most?" The Second in Command eyed the Shadow in frustrated confusion.

"We spared one villager, Jacobi the Baker, who has given us detailed information about the two villagers responsible for the Shadows' deaths. He has proven himself useful. For now."

"Do you mean to tell me the two villagers responsible escaped you?" If Gershom still had his sword, he would have struck the Shadow down.

"They fled the night before we arrived."

"You have come all this way to tell me of your failure?" Gershom hissed.

"No, my lord." The Nameless Rider handed him the two wanted posters of Crispin and Salome that were circulating around Adalore. "To show you these."

"What do I care of their faces?" Gershom threw the two pictures on the ground without looking at them. "Find them!"

"We will find them, my lord," the Nameless Rider assured him.

Pash picked up the posters and examined them further. "Their names are Crispin and Salome."

"And what do I care what their names are?"

Pash glanced at him. "Those are the same names of the two children who escaped you twelve years ago."

Gershom snatched the pictures and immediately saw their resemblance to Issachar. "It cannot be," he muttered. "It cannot be." The longer he stared at them, the paler he became. "The villagers who killed the Shadows are Issachar's children?"

"We have posted these throughout the Ten Kingdoms. It is only a matter of time before we capture them," the one-eyed Shadow stated confidently.

"You will not find them in the Western Forests or the Swamp Lands." Ophir's voice echoed as he entered, still dirty from his long journey.

"What are you talking about?" Gershom whipped around to see his younger brother approaching.

"I don't know the boy's whereabouts, but the girl was headed toward the Enchanted Swamp." Ophir set his belongings on the table and poured himself a glass of wine.

"And how would you know that?" Gershom grimaced as he watched Ophir wrap his dirty fingers around the crystal decanter.

Ophir grabbed Salome's poster. "I saw her with my own eyes. And upon hearing her companions' plans to gather an army, I ordered my men to capture her."

Gershom's eyes brightened; he clapped his hands together. "Finally, some good news. Bring her to me."

Ophir cleared his throat, "She escaped."

"She what?" A vein in Gershom's neck protruded.

"By the time I made it to their camp to retrieve her, all of my men had been killed." Ophir tried to hide the worry on his face. Gershom was known for having a short temper and was always eager to strike down anyone who failed him.

"Am I only to receive reports of failure?" Gershom shook his head as he stroked the shaved sides of his head.

"There is one more thing they spoke of that you need to know," Ophir hesitated, fiddling with the now empty wine glass.

"Well," Gershom growled. "What is it?"

"The men she was with claimed to have the Hunter."

The Bear turned ashen white and stumbled to lean against the wall. "Are you quite certain?"

Ophir nodded. "On my life, I speak the truth."

As Gershom's eyes darted around the room, eyeing the three men that stood before him, a servant cautiously entered carrying a message sent by courier pigeon from Lord Memucan.

Pash took the piece of paper and handed it to his father. "A message from Numbio."

After reading the note, Gershom crumpled the parchment and threw it on the ground. His eyes raged. His breathing slowed. His teeth gnashed together.

"What news from the South?" Pash asked, offering him a glass of much needed wine. He tried to mask his disappointment that the rumors about his father corresponding secretly with foreign Lords was true.

He snatched the glass and drank every drop. Wiping his mouth, he said, "Crispin, son of Issachar, has arrived in Numbio seeking aid from Osiris." Gershom closed his eyes as he dropped into a chair, pale and feeling ill.

"Surely, they would not be so foolish as to join him." Pash's eyes darted between his father and his uncle.

Gershom rubbed his temples in a circular motion. "Osiris has pledged allegiance to him."

"Where did you say the girl was headed?" Pash turned his attention to Ophir.

"Into the Enchanted Swamp." Ophir sat in a chair opposite his brother. "If they find a way through, they could reach Port Daelon much faster than using the main roads."

"Why Port Daelon?" Pash joined them in a seat of his own and crossed one leg over the other. "That's Trader's Bay. Only merchants and seafarers travel there."

"Because -"

"They will seek aid from her grandmother, Queen Nym in Myr," Gershom interrupted Ophir with an exhausted sigh. "They must be stopped. Crushed before they can muster anymore hope." He leaned forward, elbows on his knees, "Find them."

"It will be done." The Nameless Rider crossed his arm over his chest and took his leave.

"I will send word to our assassin in Myr and have them handle our problem." Ophir was confident this would work.

Pash was taken aback. His father had an assassin living in the Isles of Myr? Was it possible his power stretched that far? This only confirmed Niabi was right to be suspicious of him. While collecting his thoughts, he sensed someone was watching him. Glancing up, he saw his father staring at him intensely.

"What would you have me do to help you?" If his father could read his thoughts, he would have struck him down where he stood.

Gershom shifted in his seat. He appeared reluctant to accept Pash's help. "These are trying times we now find ourselves in and I have run out of options, Pash." He sighed, "I believe there is something you can do for me."

CHAPTER 46

HERU

"We are to meet my sister at the abandoned fortress, Oakenshire, in the Black Forest to regroup." Crispin pointed at a large map of Adalore spread across an enormous table in the heavily stocked armory.

"It will be difficult to march our soldiers that distance without detection." Heru stared at the map and crossed his arms over his chest.

"What do you suggest?" Crispin glanced his way.

Heru inhaled, deep in thought. "I suggest we send a fleet by sea to the outer banks of Oakenshire off the coast of the Ignacia Sea."

"When could they be ready to leave?"

"It will take a couple of months before the ships could leave our port."

"We cannot wait that long to start our journey," Crispin shook his head. "My sister will be expecting us sooner than that."

"What if we take a small company of your fiercest warriors by foot and send the rest by sea?" Zophar proposed as he smoked his favorite pipe.

"When would we be ready to travel?" Crispin looked back at Heru.

"Give me a week and we will be ready to march." Heru nodded his head, flashing a proud smile.

"Then it is settled." Zophar scratched his red beard as he sat at the exceptionally wide table. "Do you suppose we could eat now?"

"I have never seen a man eat as much as you do and not get fat," Crispin laughed, stretching his back.

"We Westerners are fine specimens, indeed!" Zophar winked and patted his belly.

Heru discovered early on that Zophar was proud of his burly chest and hairy exterior, as was every Westerner. They ate plenty, loved often, and fought until Death took them; they were truly a people to be both feared and admired. And Heru was excited to have finally met one of them.

As the three men kicked up their feet to eat, a young servant hid in the shadows behind a large column with his bow drawn. He squinted one eye to aim at his target in the distance. Breathing slowly and methodically, he pulled his arrow back against the side of his cheek and exhaled as he released the arrow. The assassin watched as the arrow sliced through the room and pierced the prince.

The prince grabbed his chest as he fell to the ground; the arrow had pierced him directly above his heart. "Zophar…" he whispered, as blood oozed out of his chest.

"Guards! Guards!" Heru yelled as his soldiers rushed to search the palace. He caught one of them by the arm. "Bring Rayma."

Zophar covered in Crispin's blood, continued applying pressure to the wound. "Hold on, Crispin."

His eyes fluttered as the loss of blood began to take its toll on him. "Don't let me die," he whispered in Zophar's ear.

"Hush, my boy." Zophar gently patted Crispin's head. His eyes burned fighting the tears that slowly streamed down his cheeks. "You'll be alright."

"Please," a tear escaped Crispin's eye, "don't let me die, Zophar."

Rayma sprinted into the room with a bag full of potions and bandages. "What happened?" she asked as she tended to Crispin's wound.

"There is an assassin in the palace." Heru was enraged and on high alert. "Will he be alright?"

"He has lost a lot of blood," she examined him, "but I believe the arrow missed his heart."

"So, he will live?" Zophar wiped his face and held the prince tightly in his arms.

"Yes," she nodded her head. "I can heal him."

"See to it Prince Crispin is taken care of," Heru ordered as he stomped away.

"Where are you going?" she asked before he disappeared.

"I must speak with my father." His nostrils flared as he growled every word. "There is a traitor among us."

Heru found his father in his private chambers, heavily guarded due to the assassin running loose in the palace. The prince rushed toward Osiris and bowed before him.

"Father."

"My son," Osiris stood up as he entered. "Is he dead?"

"No."

Osiris exhaled, relieved, "Thank the Almighty One he still lives."

"I think it best we speak in private." Heru's eyes shifted to the guards.

The king waved them all out of his chambers.

"What is it, Heru?"

"Someone in the palace tried to assassinate Crispin."

"Surely it was not one of our servants." Osiris shook his head in disbelief. "They are all loyal to the crown."

"Which crown?" Heru spat harshly. "Someone has either been bought by the North or serves them willingly and we must find out who. What if there are more like him?"

"Our guards will find the perpetrator." Osiris patted his son's shoulder. "I will have Memucan investigate this matter. If there are more like this traitor, he will find them."

"Can Memucan even be trusted?" Heru hardly found the old advisor of upstanding character. "He was adamantly against us aiding Crispin."

"His duty as my advisor is to ensure the safety of our people, even if that means disagreeing with me."

"What if *he* is with the North?" Heru snorted.

His distrust of Memucan stemmed from his mother's dealings with him. Queen Zulu never liked him, and it was a fact she did not mask. She would always tell him, *'He's a serpent, my son. He is crafty and charming. But his words are coated with poison. Best to cut off a snake's head before it strikes.'*

"He has been a loyal friend and servant for many years, Heru." Osiris returned to his seat. "He would never betray the Numbio."

One of the Captains of the Royal Guard marched in and bowed. "Majesties, we found the assassin."

"Bring him forth!" Heru whipped around with a growl, fingers tapping the handle of his sword.

"He is dead, my Prince."

"Dead?" Osiris' voice boomed. "How?"

"We cornered him as he attempted to escape through a window, but instead of surrendering, the coward jumped to his death." The soldier shook his head, "There is not much left of him."

Osiris waved him off and turned once again to his son. "Whoever he was loyal to will remain a secret for now. This is one of many attacks that may cross Prince Crispin's path. Be vigilant, my son, for those who stand for their beliefs will surely be challenged to defend them."

CHAPTER 47
ADONIJAH

The beaten and weary trio arrived in Port Daelon just as the sun set. Under Harbona's advisement, Salome covered the bottom half of her face, just in case, her wanted poster had circulated through the enormous port. Ships from almost every kingdom in Adalore found their way to Port Daelon, for if there was trading to be done, it was done in Trader's Bay. Nestled in the mountains were a few local inns, taverns, and brothels at the disposal of sailors and merchants to help them relax and do business in the seaside village.

Salome and Adonijah followed their Immortal guide as he weaved around the dark and nameless floating dock streets with their horses in tow. Adonijah kept a watchful eye to ensure they were not being followed or recognized by bounty hunters. To his relief, the sea farers were too consumed with their liquor and female companions to even notice them passing by.

"We're here," Harbona announced as they stood before a large wooden vessel designed to transport spices.

"The Golden Rose." Salome read the ship's name aloud.

"Who goes there?"

Harbona looked up at the man who had called out to them. "Has it been so long that you do not recognize me, old friend?"

"Harbona?" The captain squinted his almond eyes, surprised to see him.

"Hello, Diron."

Diron waved them to come aboard his vessel. "I see you have not come alone this time." The middle-aged sea farer brushed his stringy dark hair out of his sun kissed face.

"These are my traveling companions." He embraced the captain and whispered, "We need passage to the Isles of Myr."

The narrow-eyed captain stared at a partially masked Salome with great curiosity but knew better than to ask about Harbona's affairs. "Then you are in luck. We are sailing for Myr at first light." He once again focused on the Seer. "Any chance someone might come looking for you?"

"Discretion would be appreciated."

"Follow me." Diron led them below deck, but instead of showing them to a room, he walked to the end of the hall and gently pressed the top corner of the wall and it opened. Inside was a cozy room equipped with two small cots and several shelves. "I hope this will be adequate for your journey."

"Thank you." Harbona extended a bag filled with gold coins, but Diron declined the payment.

"Consider us now even." He turned to leave. "I will see to it your horses find their way below deck. Rest, my friends."

As soon as the door closed, Adonijah eyed the Seer as he sat on one of the cots. "How did you come to be owed a favor from a smuggler?"

"He's a smuggler?" Salome uncovered her face.

Harbona nodded his head. "Diron was much younger when our paths first crossed. He had escaped from his cruel master in the Eastern Lands and asked to be hidden from his soldiers. I kept him safe for several weeks until he decided to sail with a crew based here in Port Daelon. Most know him as a spice merchant, but his true mission is to smuggle those who wish to be free from their oppressors to safety."

Salome sat on the opposite cot and rubbed her knees. "And his crew?"

"All slaves he helped free," he smiled. "He is a good man and will make sure we arrive to Myr safely. You both should rest. I want to smoke up on deck."

Once Harbona had left the small room, Adonijah laid down and stared at the planked ceiling. Noticing Salome was still sitting upright, with her eyes glued to the floor, he said, "You should get some rest."

"How can someone believe they have a right to enslave another?" she whispered. "That their life is somehow more valuable than another's?"

"You mean to tell me your father did not have slaves?" he yawned, rubbing his tired eyes.

"There are no slaves in the North." Salome lifted her eyes. "We are all free."

He was surprised by that. "But those who work in the castle -"

"Are free men and women who are paid for their work. In Northwind, it is not only an honor to serve one's king, but it is a paid profession."

He turned on his side and propped himself up on his elbow. "You realize that is not the same in most kingdoms."

"Were you born free, Adonijah?"

"Aye," he nodded, "I was born free, but too poor to matter."

Salome propped herself up on one of her elbows, mirroring his position, to face him. "Where are you from?"

"The Farmlands north of Gomorrah." No one had asked him that in a long time.

"Why did you leave?"

The way she looked at him; it felt like she could read his thoughts, see right through him. Her eyes. Those beautiful eyes that stared at him were filled with compassion. He was used to hiding under a hood, not letting anyone make eye contact with him, fearing what they would be able to see. She was not intimidated by him and that is what made him uncomfortable.

"It's complicated." He laid back down. "You should get some sleep."

She laid down and within a few minutes she had fallen asleep.

HER EYES FLUTTERED as the rocking of the boat stirred her from her slumber. As she rubbed her eyes, she heard an odd noise. She turned and saw Adonijah was gone and Harbona had taken his place. Careful not to wake him, she grabbed her knife and sheathed it against her thigh and went to investigate the sounds she had heard.

She found a staircase that led to the lowest level of The Golden Rose and upon her descent, she realized it was completely dark. She lit a lantern hanging by the entrance, being careful not to set the boat ablaze. The noise had stopped, but she continued forward. She came upon their horses.

She pressed her face to Snow's nose. Maybe it was just the horses she had heard. But then, she sensed someone was watching her. She was not afraid; she was confident she knew who was standing behind her.

"I never had the opportunity to thank you for coming back to help me." She slowly turned to face the shadowed Stormcrag who had saved her from the Thrak.

He stepped into the light; his tan skin was smeared in clay and blue war paint. His appearance would normally frighten anyone who laid eyes on him, but his soft brown eyes were kind and Salome was not like most Adalorians. Salome stood at five feet, eight inches, and he was not much taller.

"You have been following us." She stepped toward him, but he lurched back, unsure of her advances. "Don't be afraid."

"I am not afraid," he said.

She tilted her head. "What is your name?"

"My name is of no importance."

"Your name is the one thing no one can ever take away from you." She stroked Snow's face. "Are you hungry?"

He did not respond, but by the look in his eyes, he was starving.

She motioned for him to follow her. "Come with me."

As she passed him, he said, "My name is Cato."

"Cato," she repeated with a smile. "I am Salome."

ADONIJAH STOOD ABOVE DECK, he had never sailed the seas before and found himself to be quite seasick. Doing his best not to vomit, he clutched the railings as if his very life depended on it. He had not slept at all and his weary eyes were all anyone who looked at him noticed.

Diron patted him on the back, startling him. "A bit jumpy, aren't you?" The belly toting sea dog laughed the deepest chuckle Adonijah had ever heard. "First time out at sea?"

He nodded his head, "Aye."

"Take deep breaths and keep your eyes on the horizon," he pointed.

Adonijah burped. "Does that really work?"

"A lot better than staring down at the rippling waters." He chuckled once more and leaned against the railing. "Is she your wife? The woman you are traveling with."

"No." Adonijah did not like Diron asking questions about her.

"I meant no harm," the captain sensed he overstepped. "I noticed how protective you are of her and assumed she was your woman."

Adonijah was far too ill to try to intimidate Diron. He cleared his throat, eyes fixated on the horizon hoping it would help. "We had a run in with some less than desirable folk."

Diron nodded, "Understood."

Salome ascending the steps caught the captain's eye. Her presence was met with a friendly smile until he saw an unregistered passenger following her.

"Who is that?" Adonijah saw him, too.

"I do not know." Diron furrowed his brow as he approached them. "Who are you?"

"This is Cato." Salome stood between them. "He is one of the prisoners we freed from the Thrak on our way to Port Daelon."

Diron's mouth dropped in disbelief. "You *stole* from the Thrak?"

"If by steal you mean freed a person who was enslaved by his oppressors, then yes." Salome's eyes darted toward the captain. "We stole from the Thrak."

Diron scratched the stubble along his jawline. "To steal from the Thrak is unwise. They will surely be hunting you."

"You of all people should understand why we did, what we did." Salome held her ground.

Diron's expression softened as Harbona came into sight. "So, he told you."

Salome nodded, compassion in her eyes.

He whispered, "Aye, I do understand but -"

"But what?" she interrupted.

"The Mountain Men are the sons and daughters of exiled criminals," Adonijah said what Diron was thinking. "Their ancestors, Stormcrags and Krazaks alike, established a city built on the bones of both their enemies and the innocent."

"Should he be judged for the sins of his ancestors?" she quipped. "When I was in need of help from a Thrak that had bested me, this man saved my life. Surely that counts for something."

"He is right about us," Cato found the courage to speak. "The Mountain Men are a harsh people, but if we are not vicious, then all who wish to kill us would succeed. We are not hunted by only Thrak, but by the Krazaks, as well. It has been this way for as long as I can remember." His voice softened, "I lost both of my parents to the Gomorrians and my sister to our rival tribe. Without you," he turned to Salome, "my life would have been forfeited, and in order to truly repay you for your deed, I wish to join you on whatever quest you find yourself on."

"Join us?" Adonijah's words dripped with disapproval as he clutched the railing.

"When you return to the mainland, the Thrak will be searching for you," Cato warned. "I know their routes, patterns, and way of thinking. I also know my way around the Bone Mountains and can lead you where you need to go undetected. The Stormcrag owe you a life debt."

"If you know the Thrak so well, how did you come to be their prisoner?" Adonijah attempted to stand straight despite the queasiness in his stomach.

"I underestimated the Thrak." Cato's eyes shifted to his feet. "A mistake I do not intend to repeat."

"I believe he would be a great asset." Harbona stepped forward, resting his hand on Cato's shoulder.

Adonijah and Diron glanced at each other. Adonijah knew they would be fighting a losing battle, so he nodded reluctantly.

"Captain," Harbona lit his pipe with a satisfied grin, "perhaps, we could find some clean clothes for our new friend below deck?"

Diron nodded his head and muttered, "Aye," then followed Harbona and Cato down the creaky wooden steps.

Once they left, Adonijah leaned over the railing and stared at the horizon, breathing deeply. He closed his eyes and inhaled the fresh sea air. Suddenly feeling a presence, he opened one eye and noticed Salome standing next to him, eyeing him unapologetically.

"What did I do now?" his mouth twisted. From the look on her face, he already knew what she was going to say.

"Is Cato joining us going to be a problem?" Her tone was icy.

He rolled his eyes, gripping the railing tightly. "You and Harbona are the only Adalorians I know who seem to have a soft spot for the Mountain Men, and I cannot understand why."

"An entire people cannot all be bad -"

"For all you have suffered, Salome, you are far too trusting of men." He let go of the railing to light his pipe.

"And you aren't nearly trusting enough," she fired back. "There is more good in the world than you know." She rested her hand on his and whispered, "You told me you don't want to become like your father -"

"That is different." He ripped his hand away from hers, irritated she would bring that up.

"Is it different, Adonijah?" she asked softly. "You do not wish to be judged for your father's sins, so why do you judge Cato for the sins of his ancestors?"

He pondered her question. He had an inexplicable desire to argue with her, to fight her tooth and nail the remainder of their journey if he had to. But he knew she had trumped him by using his own past, his own fears, against him. There was nothing he could do or say to change her mind. She had won this round.

"Give him a chance." She leaned against the railing next to him, their arms touching. "He may surprise us."

"That is what I am afraid of," he whispered, exhaling a puff of smoke.

CHAPTER 48
CRISPIN

Crispin opened his eyes and felt the pain from his wound surge through his body. His shoulder and chest had been carefully cleaned and wrapped by Rayma while he had been unconscious. The weary prince turned his head to the right and saw Zophar sitting in the corner of his room, smoking his pipe. The dark bags underneath his eyes indicated he had not gotten much sleep, choosing instead to keep watch over his injured ward.

"You look terrible," Crispin winced as he sat up in his bed.

Zophar forced a smile, "Not as terrible as you." He placed the sword he had on his lap to the side of his chair and stretched as he walked over to the prince's bed. "How are you feeling?"

"Like I've been gutted." Crispin cleared his throat, "How long have I been out?"

"Three days."

"Three days?" Crispin grunted as he put his feet on the floor.

"You are not safe here," Zophar whispered.

"It would seem I am not safe anywhere anymore." He was now fully aware of the danger he was truly in but forced a smile to ease Zophar's frayed nerves.

"We must not stay here any longer." Zophar rubbed his bloodshot eyes. "Whoever sent that assassin will not hesitate to send another to finish the job."

"Good thing I have you to protect me." He winked, but Zophar did not laugh. He did not even crack a smile.

"I was not able to protect you from the arrow that narrowly missed your heart." His voice cracked so he cleared his throat. "We are not among friends."

"You worry too much. That's why you're starting to get those white hairs."

"Aye, and you do not worry enough," Zophar clicked his tongue, looking at his reflection in the mirror. "If I do have white hair, it's because of you."

"Me? And not Salome?"

Zophar pointed to the wrinkles around the corners of his eyes. "These are from Salome."

Crispin laughed, slowly standing to his feet, clutching his chest. "Glad to see we both gave you something permanent."

"Where do you think you are going?" Zophar huffed.

"I need some fresh air," Crispin muttered.

"Then I am going with you."

Crispin patted the burly man's shoulder. "I will be alright, I promise."

"Have you not heard a word I said?"

"Every word," he sauntered to the door. "Go to sleep. I will be back before you wake."

"Cheeky boy. Has a head as thick as they come," Zophar muttered under his breath, fighting the long overdue sleep that slowly overtook him.

Crispin shuffled through the hallways of the palace and gained strength the longer he walked around. He stopped at an enormous room filled with thousands of scrolls shelved from the ceiling to the floor. As impressive as the library was, the view from the three floor-to-ceiling windows nearly took his breath away. He never dreamt he would ever be standing in the great palace of Numbio, yet there he was. He could see the port on the Umpoco River and watched for several minutes as the seamen and tradesmen conducted business. When he was a young boy, he did not value the majestic view Northwind boasted, but being in Numbio, and after living most of his life in the Tree House Forest, he finally attained an admiration and appreciation for large cities.

Out of the corner of his eye he saw a figure pass behind him, sending him into high alert. "Who's there?"

"Walking the palace alone so soon, Prince Crispin? Are you not concerned for your wellbeing?" The mysterious voice spoke with a smoothness that made him feel at ease, even though he did not know who was speaking.

"Should I be?" His eyes darted around the library, hoping to catch a glimpse of the person the voice belonged to. "Who are you?"

"Why do you wish to know?"

"You know who I am, I think it only fair to know who you are."

"My Lord, life is not fair."

"Why not at least tell me your name?" He finally caught sight of a shadowed figure in a dark corner of the room.

"I am Amunet."

Still unable to make out her face, he said, "Step into the light."

After a moment's pause, Amunet stepped from the shadows into the bright light that poured through the windows. Crispin was in complete awe. She was beautiful and tall with wild tight curls. Attention was drawn to her hazel eyes by golden paint streaked around her eyes and cheekbones.

"Is this better?"

Crispin was rendered speechless but caught himself staring and pried his eyes from the dark-skinned beauty. "Who are you?"

"Follow me and all of your questions shall be answered."

Crispin hesitated only a second before he followed her down the hallway. Her long arms were adorned with gold jewelry that would be the envy of any royal in Adalore.

After several minutes of walking in silence, Crispin's curiosity got the better of him. "Where are you taking me?"

Amunet did not respond, but his question was answered as soon as they turned the corner. The Golden Temple was nestled between the palace and the Umpoco River and was easily the most stunning structure in the city, since it was constructed purely of gold, onyx, and ivory.

"You are a priestess?" he guessed once they entered the holy place.

"I am Amunet, the High Priestess of the Golden Temple."

Crispin was confused. "Why did you bring me here?"

"For this." She glided to an oversized golden mirror and ripped off the white linen sheet that covered it. Careful not to step in front of it, she waved Crispin forward. "What do you see?"

He stood before the mirror and silently stared at his own reflection. He shrugged, "I see my reflection. Is this a trick?"

"Look closely." Her serious tone amused him, and he once again stared into the mirror. "Tell me what you see."

This time, the mirror began to swirl until he was looking at a sinister version of himself. He watched as his heart slowly turned black, and in a panic, stared at his reflection's eyes and saw his brown eyes fade into total darkness. Every second that passed, his reflection grew more evil which terrified him. He tried to pry his eyes away from the horrific image, but found he was completely powerless.

"Make it stop!" Crispin yelled.

"Tell me what you see," the high priestess demanded, unmoved by his cries.

"I do not wish to see anymore."

"Now is the time your questions receive answers. There is more you must see before the mirror will release you." The mirror showed Crispin his homeland of Northwind and the White Throne he had coveted since his youth. "From the ashes, one will rise; to the ashes, one will fall."

Crispin found himself face to face with Gershom in the middle of a crowded and bloody battlefield. He remembered Harbona's warning but did not heed his instruction. The prince sprinted toward his enemy and with great force, swung his sword, initiating their duel. After a hard-fought battle, Gershom disarmed him and stabbed him through the heart. He could hear his sister's screams as his eyes faded to black.

Finally, the mirror released him, and he fell to the ground, clutching his heart. "What dark magic is this?"

"You have seen your future, my lord." She stood stoically as she looked down at him.

"That is not my future." His breathing was heavy. "The mirror lies."

"The mirror never lies. People lie." Amunet draped the linen over the mirror once again and turned her attention to the sweating prince. "If you do not accept it is not your destiny to battle Gershom, your life will be forfeit." Crispin sat on the ground, overwhelmed with the vision. "I see I am not the first one to warn you of this." She knelt in front of him and lifted his face toward her. "Your heart is fading, Crispin of Northwind. Do not let the evil that has consumed your enemies, fill your heart. Let your hatred go."

"My hatred is all I have." Tears filled his tormented eyes.

"If you lose yourself, then you have already been defeated."

Crispin shot up, "No! Stop saying such things."

She stood before him and gently rested her slender fingers on his chest. "You will be the leader of thousands. They will follow you into battle, but if you do not rid your heart of the poison that consumes it, you will not live to rule them."

He felt a deep and immediate connection to the priestess when she touched his chest and rested his hand on top of hers. "Come with me."

She shook her head. "I am needed here."

"I need your guidance."

The priestess unhooked her long pendant necklace and placed it around his neck. "As long as you wear this, I will be with you. May this be an everlasting reminder to follow your path and not wish for another's."

"I feel like I know you." He stared deeply into her warm hazel eyes. "As if I have seen you before."

"Perhaps, you have."

"Will I see you again?"

"When the time is right our paths will cross again." Her words brought him much needed comfort. "Now you must return to the palace before you are missed.

CHAPTER 49

PASH

On the same day for the last ten years, Pash drank himself into a stupor just to numb the pain of his mother's death. Shortly after Northwind had been conquered, his mother, Oona, was found dead in her chambers. There was no physical evidence of how she was killed. A full investigation was launched into her murder, but no one was found responsible and inevitably she was forgotten by nearly everyone in the city, except for him. Not a day went by he did not think of her, and wished she were still walking the halls of the castle, bringing joy to everyone she crossed paths with.

As he poured himself another glass of wine, he stared with teary eyes at a portrait he had painted of her. Oona had large round brown eyes, luxurious black hair that cascaded down to her hips and dark brown eyebrows. Her pointy nose and tawny skin tone had been passed down to him as were her long limbs. A smile was always on her freckled face and he could vividly remember she had the voice of a celestial being. As a child, he would only agree to go to sleep once she had sung him a song of her Southern ancestors, although now he could no longer recall any of the lyrics.

Oona had been sent on behalf of the Numbio to serve as their Ambassador to Northwind during King Issachar's reign. Due to Issachar's insistence of Gershom finding a suitable wife, the marriage between Gershom and Oona was arranged and blessed by both kingdoms. Pash would not describe their marriage as a happy one. His father had a wandering eye and dubbed monogamy a hindrance. But Oona had Pash, and that was enough.

"I miss you," his voice cracked as he glanced over her portrait with sad admiration.

"Has it been another year already?" Ophir startled his nephew. "Your mother was a wonderful woman, rest her everlasting soul."

"What do you need, Uncle?" Pash did not look up.

"I knocked; you did not answer. I wanted to make sure you were alright."

"Much troubles me, Uncle, but they are my burdens to bear. You need not worry about me. I will be fine by morning."

Ophir watched him guzzle the last bit of his drink and drop his goblet on the floor. "How much have you had to drink, Pash?"

"Why does it matter?" His eyes were glassy, his speech slurred.

"You are the Commander of Her Majesty's Shadows and the Second in Command's heir," Ophir reminded him. "You have a duty to conduct yourself in a manner befitting your titles or you will lose more than just your rank."

"Neither the Queen nor my father care if I live or die," Pash spat. "I am just a pawn they use at their convenience."

"Be quiet before someone hears you," Ophir whispered. "I know better than most, that something spoken in secret can cost you what you value most."

"Let them hear me!" he whipped around and shouted from his balcony. "Let all of Northwind hear my words!"

Ophir hushed him, trying to pull him back inside. "Think of your life, boy."

"I don't care for my life anymore." Pash ripped his arm from his uncle's grasp. "It has never been mine to begin with." The spitefulness in his voice did not go unnoticed.

"If you are not careful, your father will surely make you suffer."

Pash tapped both of Ophir's ears. "Are you not listening, Ophir? I no longer care. Let him take my life," he snarled as he leaned over his balcony. "It would be the first act of kindness I ever received from him."

"Pash -"

"I will never be good enough in his eyes." Pash's voice softened, tears in his eyes. "You of all people should understand."

"I do understand." Ophir poured himself a glass of wine from the decanter. He sat in a lounge chair and sipped his drink. "I helped my brother rise to his position of power and I will die to keep him there. It is our duty."

Pash turned around, fury in his bloodshot eyes. "You would let your own brother mistreat you and remain silent? After everything you have done for him. After years of loyal service. After everything you've lost?"

"He is my lord first and foremost, my brother second. You are his soldier first and son second. Learn this Nephew, it will do you well."

Pash stood only a few inches taller than his uncle but made a point to step in front of him to intimidate him. "What have you gained by selling your soul to the devil?"

"A home, wealth, power." Ophir was not fazed by the question.

"Do you sleep at night?" Pash's voice cracked. "Because I don't. I cannot sleep anymore."

"If you cannot sleep, then perhaps, you should consult a healer."

"What have we gained serving him?" Pash was on a warpath. "What has my father ever given us other than contempt and blatant disrespect? He has taken everything from us! Everyone we have ever loved."

"Pash, be silent," he hissed. "You need to collect yourself. You are coming unhinged."

"And what of Satara?" Pash knew by the mere mention of her name, he would get an honest reaction from Ophir. "Do you mean to tell me she meant so little to you that you would continue to serve him?"

Ophir's bald head turned a shade of red Pash had not seen before. Defensive and now enraged, he barked, "Never mention her name again!"

"You loved her, and my dear father took her for himself."

"Stop it, Pash."

"And when he had tired of her, had her killed." Pash would not relent. "And you did nothing to stop him."

"Pash, you are drunk -"

"I know my father had something to do with my mother's death." Pash paced the room, like a caged animal waiting to be set loose. "One day, I will learn the truth, and I swear before all the gods in the Ten Kingdoms of Adalore, that I will have his head for it."

"Enough, Pash," Ophir nearly shouted. "You speak of high treason."

"Why do you fear him?" Pash furrowed his brow as he faced him. "*He* is the one who should be afraid."

"Watch your tongue."

Pash scoffed. "Look at you, Ophir. You are just a shadow of a man I once respected. It is no wonder he took Satara from you. You're weak."

Ophir punched Pash, knocking him to the floor. "One day, Pash, you will push me too far."

Ophir retreated from the room, leaving Pash to sleep off his drunkenness alone on the cold floor.

CHAPTER 50
CRISPIN

Once night had fallen upon the vibrant city of Numbio, all the citizens donned their finest clothes and began to celebrate in the city streets, at the same time, King Osiris' banquet was underway in the palace. Having had limited time to organize the festival for his warriors, Osiris was pleased with the splendor of the great hall. The Southern Kingdom was known for their elaborate celebrations and Crispin was excited the tales were true.

"It is most unusual for pale ones to be included in our festivities," Memucan interrupted Crispin's moment of admiration. "I remember when your kind were forbidden from our halls."

"Your city is one I greatly admire, Lord Memucan, and your people are some of the finest in Adalore." The old man was visibly impatient with him. "Out of all the men and women I have had the honor of meeting, you have been the only one to show contempt for my presence. Why is that?"

Memucan showed no sign of embarrassment by the foreign prince drawing attention to his behavior.

"Prince Crispin, if I should even call you by that title," he sneered. "You have come to my city asking for the Numbio to fund your war against a queen who has done us no harm. The blood of *my* people will be sacrificed for a tragedy that most have nearly forgotten." The shriveled advisor hobbled closer to Crispin so only he could hear his whispers. "Let it be known that Memucan, son of Wentu, spoke against this alliance and opposed this war. The Numbio's blood will be on your hands. The wails of their widows and tears of their children will be on your head. Remember them as you command their husbands, brothers, fathers, and sons to fight your enemies. Remember them, for they will surely remember you."

Crispin did not know what to say. He watched silently as the advisor disappeared into the jubilant sea of smiling faces.

"There you are!" Zophar patted Crispin on the back as he ate some type of meat off the bone. "Why do you look so glum? This is a celebration, not a funeral."

Crispin mustered up a smile to please his friend, but deep down all he could think about was for some of these joyous warriors, it was their funeral.

Osiris stood from his throne silencing the music and the people in the room. After a deep inhale, the king's booming voice echoed through the vast space.

"Many years ago, I lost one of my friends. To know his life had been taken; that his murderers had claimed his throne and tainted the halls of his home was difficult to bear." With his gaze now fixated on Crispin, he continued. "Today, we have hope that a terrible wrong will now receive justice. By the grace of the Almighty One, Prince Crispin escaped the hands of his enemies and now seeks to sit on his father's throne. We remember the dead, and celebrate the living, who are willing to do what is right." Osiris lifted his golden cup in Crispin's direction; every guest followed suit. "Whether in life or death, we are with you, my brother."

Crispin drank with them, but he felt as if his eyes had been opened. All he had considered was himself, his family, his dead. In truth, he had not thought about anyone else. He had not weighed the gravity of the role he was assuming: Leader. The responsibility of that word gripped his heart. For years, this is what he wanted. Now that he was in the midst of it, he was unsure how heavy a price he would pay for victory.

After the king's speech, the jubilee resumed, and Rayma slithered through the crowded hall searching for one face in particular. Unable to find him inside, she knew exactly where Heru would be hiding. Out on a secluded balcony that overlooked the city, she spied him quietly observing his people dancing in the desert streets.

"Surely you must know I am not the only one looking for you." He turned his head toward her, smiled and extended his hand. She grabbed it and he pulled her close to him. The sound of his heart soothed her to the point she found herself closing her eyes to fully enjoy the rhythmic beat. "Why are you out here alone, Heru?"

"I have never left Numbio before and I am afraid that I may forget the sight of her."

"What you see is merely buildings constructed by men. That is not Numbio." She glanced up at him and placed her hand on his bare chest. "Numbio is here and that is something you will never forget."

The prince gently kissed her forehead and held her tightly. "If something should happen to me -"

"Do not speak of such things," she interrupted.

"Rayma," his strained whisper hushed her. "I need you to do something for me, if I should fall."

"Do not ask me to do what I cannot bear to think about."

"Please, just listen." He sweetly lifted her chin so he could see her face. "If I should fall, bring my body back home to my father so I may be buried with my ancestors."

Tears streamed down her cheeks upon hearing his request, but she mustered the strength to nod. "If you should fall, I will do as you ask."

THE FOLLOWING DAY, just before the sun began to set, the band of elite warriors made their final preparations before setting out on their long journey across the desert. Heru stood at the top of the palace steps that overlooked the caravan. He had been standing there for nearly an hour, mentally preparing to leave his homeland for the first, and possibly last time. Osiris joined him and watched Crispin ready his horse for the long trip.

"He looks just like his father," the king broke the silence. "Let us hope he is wiser."

Heru exhaled, "I will protect him."

"I do not worry for him, my son." Osiris embraced him. "Fight hard, Heru, and may the Almighty One bless and protect you."

"I will return," he saluted his father. "You have my word."

The war horn of Numbio sounded throughout the entire city, alerting all who heard that their warriors were about to depart. Every man, woman, and child lined the streets from the palace to the main gate to pay their respects. As the caravan made their way through the city, Crispin noticed all the people were dressed in red and held their left fists in the air with their right hands resting on their hearts.

"Why do they stand that way?" Crispin asked Heru who rode beside him.

"When we send our warriors from our homeland, we pay respect by lifting one hand to our Creator to ask for his protection and the other hand on our hearts to ask for his blessing. We wear red to signify that whether in life or death, we the Numbio, will forever be warriors."

Crispin was once again humbled by Heru's mighty people and realized how great a sacrifice they were making for him to reclaim his father's throne, to take back his home.

"To glory, my brother." Heru crossed his hand over his heart.

"To glory," Crispin touched his heart.

AFTER TRAVELLING THROUGH THE NIGHT, the sun peaked above the horizon signaling the caravan of an imminent stop. Ready to rest, the soldiers welcomed the dawn. Heru raised his hand and the Numbio stopped in unison.

"We shall camp here until nightfall," Heru announced.

Every member of the caravan knew their responsibility and began setting up their camp without further instruction.

Rayma pulled an apple from her bag and fed her exhausted horse, while the soldiers set up the campsite.

"You always spoil that horse." Bantu slithered up next to her, startling her.

"You know we are not supposed to be seen together, Bantu," she chastised Memucan's servant. "What do you want?"

"The master wanted me to give you this." The sunken eyed servant discreetly handed her a glass vile.

"Does he truly not trust me to -"

"No, he does not trust you," Bantu interrupted her. "Pour this in his drink at the right moment and the master will do as he has promised."

"And how do I know I can trust him?" She lifted an eyebrow. "Or you?"

"You don't." He smirked. "That is part of the fun."

"Get away from me before someone notices you," she spat.

"Remember," he taunted, "he is always watching you." Amused, he walked away with a grin spread across his dark face.

On the other side of the campsite, Crispin observed the endless miles of sand that laid before them.

"What do you see?" Zophar squinted in the direction Crispin was staring.

"Nothing," he replied, eyes still glued to the horizon. "Nothing at all."

"You make it sound as if that is a bad thing," Heru chimed in. Crispin's silence confirmed his suspicions. "What troubles you?"

"Something is coming. I can feel it."

"You have not slept well in days," Zophar drank water from his sheepskin. "You should rest while you can. I will take first watch."

At that moment, the entire caravan heard a thunderous rumble south of them. Staring toward the scorching desert, Crispin spied a billowing sandstorm headed directly for them at a frightening pace.

"Sandstorm!" Heru shouted.

Scrambling to their horses and camels, the group of travelers sprinted away from the determined storm. The winds whipped ferociously as they tried to escape. As the raging wall of sand neared them, Crispin could have sworn he heard a man's voice chanting in the distance.

His feeble arms stretched wide, Memucan's eyes were tightly shut as he chanted his incantation. On the table behind him sat a large black book filled with dark magic spells. Determined to destroy both Issachar's heir and Heru, he continued to recite the incantation passionately, knowing the more focused he was, the larger the storm would become. Despite his incessant shouting, he oddly started to feel weaker the longer he spoke. It seemed as if an opposing force was combating him, and he had no idea who it could be.

Feeling Crispin was in danger, Amunet stood in the Golden Temple and began praying for the warriors. She had never felt such evil before and feared her light magic would not be strong enough to defeat the unknown sorcerer. With her arms stretched wide, she closed her eyes and continued to fight for the Numbio's survival.

They swiftly galloped away, hoping they could outrun the storm, but they came to realize it had grown larger and was picking up speed. Crispin fought to keep his eyes open as sand swirled around them. He mumbled a quick prayer under his breath, hoping for some kind of miracle.

"We can't outrun the storm!" Heru yelled.

Crispin looked forward and caught sight of the mouth of a cavern. "Get to the caverns!"

The southern warriors rode toward their refuge. Sand continued to swarm them as they urged their horses onward. The storm claimed three warriors' lives, but the rest of the caravan made it safely into the cave.

MEMUCAN RAGED when he saw the vision of them escaping and screamed, which sent a bolt of lightning down to strike the rocks above the cave's entrance. Cascading boulders fell and completely covered the opening, trapping the remaining Numbio inside.

CHAPTER 51

RAYMA

"Where are we?" Zophar lit a torch and looked around the vast cavern.

"Some sort of cave." Crispin ran his hands on the rocky walls.

"This is no ordinary cave." Rayma joined the leaders. "This is the Cavern of the Undead."

"Cavern of the Undead?" Crispin repeated slowly.

She could tell by the way he looked at her, he had no idea what she was talking about.

"Out of the countless men who have dared to enter this place, only one lived to tell of its mysteries and he died from his madness," Rayma's words induced dread. "We must leave this place before it is too late."

"The way is blocked," Zophar reminded her.

"We must unblock the entrance," she insisted.

"That could take us far too long, Rayma." Heru rested his hand on her shoulder.

She gasped, "You cannot possibly be suggesting we go deeper into the cave." Her eyes darted from Heru to Zophar to Crispin. *They do not understand. If they did, they would be tearing those rocks apart.*

"That is our best option." Heru turned to Crispin who had been examining the blocked entrance. "What say you, Crispin?"

After a minute of weighing their options, Crispin agreed with Heru. "We must travel through the caverns."

"Forgive me, my lord," Rayma insisted her voice be heard once more, even though she knew her tone was dancing on the line of sounding disrespectful. "You don't know what creatures lurk in the darkness."

"I know that path is uncertain," Crispin acknowledged, "but that is our best chance for getting out of here alive. We do not have the tools necessary to remove these boulders and we need to conserve our strength for what lies ahead."

"Prince Crispin has spoken." Heru eyed Rayma in such a way that she knew fighting would be futile, so she reluctantly agreed. "We march forward," he announced to the warriors. "Stay alert."

~

THE CITY of Numbio had suffered some damage from the storm that had originated from their borders. King Osiris dispatched his soldiers to ensure the citizens were taken care of and their kingdom walls were secure. While they followed his instruction, the king rushed to the Golden Temple and upon arrival, he saw Amunet lying on the ground in exhaustion. He knelt next to her and helped her sit up.

"What happened to you, Holy One?"

"Someone has the Book of Noot," she gasped for air. "I have never felt such powerful dark magic."

"The Book of Noot?" Osiris exclaimed. "That cannot be. The book was destroyed."

"The book survived," she whispered, "and its servant is here in Numbio."

"Why would he conjure a sandstorm?" As soon as the question escaped his lips his eyes widened. "My son? Is my son alright?"

She nodded as Osiris rested her against the wall. "He is alive."

"Bless the Almighty One."

"My King," Amunet's weakened voice halted his celebration.

"What is it, Holy One?"

"They took shelter in the Cavern of the Undead."

"But that means…"

She mournfully grimaced, "They are beyond my sight. I can no longer help them."

"Rest easy, High Priestess." Osiris stood and looked out over Numbio. "We shall find the traitor who used dark magic in our city."

~

CAUTIOUSLY, the caravan pushed forward through the caverns for hours. Exhausted, they desperately searched for a safe place to set up camp, but the narrow winding pathways made that impossible. If they had not been concerned with remaining vigilant to a possible ambush, they would have been completely amazed by the wonderous beauty that surrounded them.

Rayma was still opposed to Crispin's decision and had kept to herself the entire time they journeyed through the unknown territory. Heru rode up next to her when he saw the path had widened.

"He did what he thinks is best," he whispered.

"Best for who?" Her tone was dripping with venom. "Why is he the only one making decisions for the Numbio? That is *your* responsibility."

"I pledged to fight with him," Heru looked at her, still speaking in a hushed tone. "I am not weak because I choose to follow. I am strong because I understand my place in this journey."

"He will lead us to our downfall," Rayma angrily disagreed.

"A leader is only as strong as his weakest soldier. He will not always make the right decisions, but he will never be victorious, if he must always battle his own."

"So, you wish him not to be questioned or his choices challenged?"

"Speak when you must, Rayma, but never undermine." Heru touched her hand as discreetly as possible and smiled. "You will make a great queen."

Before she could respond, a warrior cried out, "Water!" A short distance before them was a winding river.

"The River of Lost Souls," Rayma muttered under her breath.

Bast, the only man to have escaped these caverns, told tales of the creatures that lived in the darkness. The river that flowed through lured mortal men in, but it ultimately led to their doom. He told anyone who would listen, what he had seen; what he had endured. But the Numbio laughed at him. Called him mad. She was just a little girl when she saw him running through the streets in tattered clothes, a ghost of who he once was. Everyone mocked him, but she always believed. He died a broken and lonely man. All she could think about when she was growing up, was if she would suffer the same fate.

"We will set up camp here, until we have rested enough to continue," Crispin declared to the delight of the weary travelers.

Not having all of their resources because the sandstorm claimed their last campsite, the Numbio shared what they had and took shifts watching for the creatures that supposedly inhabited the caverns.

CHAPTER 52
CRISPIN

For the first time since Crispin left the Tree House Forest, he felt at ease. Even though, the unknown of the caverns frightened everyone else, he did not mind it. He was used to the "on edge" feeling. Never knowing if the villagers would learn who he really was or if Niabi and Gershom would finally discover they had escaped. But most importantly, he knew if he showed any sign of fear, those who followed him would feel hopeless.

Most of the camp fell asleep quickly after their long day. There were a few warriors guarding their slumbering companions, although, they did not expect an attack.

Zophar passed out the moment his bushy red beard hit the cot. His snoring could keep anyone up but having spent most of his life under the same small roof with the Westerner, Crispin was immune. Unfortunately, the young prince laid in the tent, wide awake; his mind was consumed with far too many thoughts to allow him to rest. He decided since sleep eluded him, he would relieve one of the night-guards. At least one of them would enjoy a restful night's sleep.

As he looked around the cold and damp caverns, he realized if there were any creatures out there, he would have no way of knowing they were there. The only light came from the campfire in the center of their encampment and that is where he spotted Rayma going through her apothecary bag.

"Can I safely assume you could not sleep either?" He broke her concentration as he approached.

Although she did not look pleased to see him, she politely responded, "I never sleep much, not even in Numbio."

"I have nightmares most nights," he sat down to warm his hands. "I have learned not to rely heavily on sleep."

She nodded her head and returned her focus to her bag.

"I have heard you are one of the best healers in all of Adalore. I am truly honored you are with us -"

"You may save your flattery, Prince Crispin," she interrupted. "I am not here for you, but for my people, who will more than likely need my services."

He smiled warmly. "You are not too fond of me, I gather."

Rayma softened her tone but remained bold. "I am sure you are a good man. There is no denying you have suffered greatly, but the North has no quarrel with us. I do not want Numbio blood spilled over a war we do not belong in."

Crispin nodded his head, having heard those words before from Memucan. "I agree with you."

"You agree with me?" Rayma was stunned.

"A few weeks ago, I was living in a humble tree house with no real hope of reclaiming my homeland. Then in a matter of minutes, my entire life was once again, turned upside down." Their eyes met. "I never wanted anyone to risk their lives for me. I just wanted someone to believe this wrong should be righted. That my family had not been forgotten by their friends. I am not a perfect leader, Rayma." He cleared his throat, "Is it alright if I call you Rayma?"

She nodded approvingly.

"Rayma, I will make many mistakes. But I will never ask any of you to do something I am not willing to do first." He hesitated before he continued. "I also know you are opinionated, and I value honesty. Crave it. My desire is that every member of our troop will one day soon, return home. I know you will help me make that happen."

"I am afraid I misjudged you." She reached out to him. "Although, I am against our involvement, the Numbio will always aid our friends in need. Just know if I need to speak up, I will."

He smiled. "I wouldn't want it any other way."

The horn of Numbio suddenly echoed through the caverns. Crispin and Rayma ran in the direction of the sound and saw a tall, pale, bone thin creature attacking the lone look-out. The hunchback assailant swung his sword, made from bones, with swift fury. His arms were as long as his legs and made running on all four possible. The soldier fought the pointy eared goblin as he continued yelling for back up. Crispin quickly joined the soldier and helped subdue the long, curved-nose devil. As they tied their prisoner, he growled, showing rows of jagged teeth.

"They are more frightening than I could have ever imagined." Rayma could not tear her eyes away from the beast who looked as if he used to be human.

Zophar and Heru rushed over to help and were shocked by the unsightly cavern creature.

"Hell!" Zophar could not believe his eyes. "What is this foul beast?"

"They are the Wagura," Rayma answered in a raspy whisper. "And I can guarantee you if it found us, its horde will not be far behind."

"It's a scout?" Heru asked.

Crispin knelt before the bound Wagura and stared into its yellow eyes. "Where is your horde?"

The creature cackled, "You stand no chance against the Wagura." His demonic voice was chilling.

"You underestimate us." Crispin showed no sign of fear, although, he was terrified of the nightmarish sight. "This is the last time I will ask. Where is your horde?"

"They are already here." It let out an unearthly howl signaling the awaiting horde to attack.

"To arms! To arms!" Heru shouted as a thundering swarm of Wagura charged at them from the darkness.

The captured cavern dweller howled once more, this time even louder. Fearing he would alert more creatures than they could handle, Crispin slit his throat and was surprised to see a green liquid ooze out of him instead of red blood.

Unlike the scout, the warrior Waguras towered over the tallest Numbio by nearly a foot. Even though they were bone thin, they were incredibly agile and strong. The Numbio fought with swiftness and great skill but there were so many creatures, they were concerned with being overrun.

Zophar sliced a creature across its chest and was splashed with green goo. Noticing Heru battling three Wagura, he let out a war cry and jumped to the prince's aid. The eight-foot-tall enemy squared up to the Westerner, who stood between him and his original prey. Enjoying every second of his first battle in over a decade, Zophar gritted his teeth and then cried, "Come closer, so I might send you back to hell!

Once Zophar evened the odds, Heru began striking down Waguras. Adrenaline pulsed through his veins. Unlike Zophar, a veteran, Heru had never faced an enemy in battle and was in survival mode. From the corner of his eye, he saw Rayma tending to the fallen Numbio, unaware of a Wagura rushing at her from behind.

"Rayma!"

He slashed his last victim and sprinted to save her. Making it in time to shield her, he took the blow. His arm was sliced, and blood gushed.

"Heru!" Rayma cried in horror as he yelled in pain.

Unable to shy away from his present clash, Heru switched his sword from his dominate, but injured arm, to his weak hand. Determined to protect Rayma, he battled through excruciating pain. The prince swung his sword and sliced off one of the creature's pointy ears, but it showed no sign of anguish, despite the flow of green goo pouring down the side of its weathered face. Heru dodged an incoming blow and quickly rolled behind the Wagura and stabbed it in the back.

Rayma was clearly shaken by the duel and threw her arms around Heru's neck, tears streaming down her face. "I thought I had lost you."

"I did too."

Near the River of Lost Souls, Crispin found himself covered in green 'blood', but unscathed. His eyes fell on the largest member of the horde stomping toward him wielding a five-foot-long bone sword. Its body was scarred from head to toe and it was the only creature who had black paint markings on its arms and chest. Crispin assumed the creature covered in human blood was the commander of the horde and prepared himself for the duel of his life. He was no longer practicing with Salome in the forest. This battle had consequences should he fail to defeat his foe.

The Wagura commander circled the young prince with a soulless glare. Crispin was trying to remember all the lessons Zophar had taught him as he stared at the demonic creature. Without warning, the Wagura swung his impressive weapon down on Crispin who sidestepped the blow. The ground shook where the large sword landed. Using his speed to his advantage, Crispin danced and skirted around the much stronger combatant.

Crispin grimaced when the creature's blade finally caught him, slicing his right thigh. He no longer had a choice, he had to become the aggressor, or this would be the end of him. Stumbling to his feet, he swung his sword and sliced off one of the Wagura's arms. He capitalized when he saw an opening and plunged his sword deep into the creature's chest.

Growling, the demon pulled Crispin toward him, and in a desperate attempt to kill the human, plunged them both into the rushing River of Lost Souls. The prince unsheathed his knife as he fought to keep his head above the icy water, and once the Wagura was close enough, he slashed its throat, nearly severing its head.

Zophar saw when Crispin was dragged into the river and ran as fast as he could down-stream to catch him before he disappeared into the dark cavern. Crispin was able to grab ahold of a large rock that protruded out of the water. Zophar extended his hand to him.

"Take my hand." They stretched for one another, but he was just out of Zophar's reach. "Reach, Crispin!"

"I cannot reach you," Crispin's tone was solemn.

"Don't you do it." The red bearded warrior saw exhaustion in Crispin's eyes. "Don't you dare let go!"

"Tell Salome, I'm sorry." His fingers slipped and the river claimed him.

"No!" Zophar watched as he disappeared into the darkness.

Heru approached him with his arm in a sling. The horde was defeated, and Rayma was tending to the injured Numbio. "Where is Crispin?"

Eyes glossed over as he watched the waters rush downstream, Zophar whispered, "He's gone."

CHAPTER 53

NIABI

Two torches lit the dark crypt. Niabi sat on the white stone bench in front of her son's final resting place. For hours she stared at his statue in silence, remembering him as a young boy. They had many wonderful adventures together – memories she was terrified she would one day forget. He had been her light when darkness consumed her, and with him gone, her past self, resurfaced. The queen faithfully visited her son, twice a week, but she found herself speaking to him less and less.

If Rollo could see what she had allowed herself to once again become... she cared not to finish that thought. He knew her as the best version of herself and that was all that truly mattered. She heard someone turn the corner.

"Your Majesty," Leoti stopped. "I'm sorry. I didn't realize you were going to be here."

Niabi patted the empty space next to her. "There's room for one more."

Leoti accepted the queen's invitation and sat down. She mumbled a short prayer under her breath.

"You still mourn him?" Niabi eyed her black ensemble.

"I will always mourn him. He was my best friend."

The queen looked at her son's statue again. Her smile was filled with sadness. "He was the sweetest child. My reason to continue living after Dichali..."

Leoti hesitated. "My father speaks of them almost daily. He misses them too."

Niabi grabbed Leoti's hand without looking in her direction. "Thank you."

"For what, my Queen?"

"For loving my son." She held back tears, gulping loudly, a knot in her throat. "I could always tell when he had been with you. You brought him so much joy." She turned toward Leoti who wiped tears from her cheeks. "My son may be gone, but you will always be my daughter."

Leoti's lip trembled, "I miss him so much."

"I know." Niabi nodded, fighting back tears as she held Leoti in her arms. "I know." She stroked Leoti's hair, fire raging within her, thinking about why her son had been taken from them. "Those responsible for Rollo's death will be dealt with."

The queen's gravelly whisper fueled Leoti. She leaned back and locked eyes with Niabi. "Yes," her tone deepened, "yes, they will."

Niabi was taken aback by Leoti's response. *What did she mean by that? What exactly did she know? What was she not saying?* Niabi noticed Pash standing at the end of the hallway and pushed the questions to the back of her mind. Maybe it was better if she did not know what Leoti was plotting.

She kissed Leoti's forehead and whispered, "If there is ever anything you need, you come to me."

She saluted her son's crypt and met Pash outside the entrance of the tomb.

"My apologies for interrupting -"

"Did he believe you?" she cut him off.

He nodded. "Yes."

"Good." She wrapped her black shawl around her shoulders. "What have you found out?"

He retrieved two folded up pieces of paper and handed them to her. As she examined the wanted posters, she intuitively knew who they were.

"He has Issachar's eyes." She flipped back to Salome's picture. "They are wanted by the Shadows?"

"It seems your brother and sister are the peasants who killed your Shadows in the Western forest."

Her hair was down without ornamentation for the first time in years. No crown, no jewels, just her natural self. The way he soaked her in did not go unnoticed by her. She felt him touch the tips of her raven black locks as they flowed lightly in the cool breeze. No one saw her in her natural appearance, except him. But that was only when they were alone. His eyes were filled with a longing that was undeniable. *He misses me*, she thought.

"What do we know?" She handed the pictures back to him, emotions now secondary to business.

"Your sister was spotted near the Enchanted Swamp," he cleared his throat, eyes shifting away from her. "Ophir returned with his findings when I was with my father."

"He found Salome?" Niabi's eyes beamed. "Is she here?"

"No, she escaped Ophir's men before he was able to retrieve her." The news irritated her, but he continued. "She was travelling with two men, neither fit Crispin's description. One appeared to be a mercenary for hire, while the second bore the banishment mark of the Immortals."

"Harbona," she whispered and tapped her lips. "So, the Seer is helping her. Where are they now?"

"Ophir believes they were going to Port Daelon."

"She is going to see Nym. Clever girl," the queen smirked. "Salome is not the only one with allies in Myr," she rubbed her hands together. "My sister is not my main concern. Find Crispin and she will come to us." She stepped toward the lookout point and together they gazed upon the White City.

"Crispin was last seen in Numbio with one companion."

"And how do we know of his whereabouts?" her eyes narrowed. "*I* have no servants in the Sand Lands."

He tilted his head. "It appears my father has allies in the South."

She straightened; a smirk crept across her face.

"You look... pleased?" He shifted his weight.

"Oh, I am." Her look pierced his soul. "You see, my suspicions of his misdeeds are now confirmed. Not only will he reap the benefit of these misguided alliances, but I too, will know everything he does. After all, knowledge is power."

"There have been no other sightings of Crispin." He rested his hand near hers on the white stone wall. "Without a lead, it may be difficult to find him."

"Do I look worried?"

After a moment of silence, he asked, "Do you trust the witch?"

"For now." She did not hesitate.

"For now?" he repeated. "How can you trust someone for a moment?"

"There was once a time I trusted your father." Her response was cold, but she had no problem speaking the truth.

Pash turned his gaze to the kingdom. The sun had just begun to set behind the Mountain of Kings and the White City was ablaze with the sun's orange glow. "What if they do come for the throne?"

"I sold my soul to take Northwind, and if necessary, I will fight until my very last breath to keep it. Let them come," she hissed, "I am ready."

THE RED MAIDEN

BOOK TWO

PROLOGUE

NIABI

14 YEARS AGO

Niabi trudged through the snow; every breath she exhaled was icy and stung the back of her throat. Winter was upon them. She never liked the winter months. Her father used to blame her dislike for the cold on the Myridian blood in her. But that was not the only reason she despised it.

Antilles. Dichali.

Niabi tightly pulled her enormous black fur coat across her chest to shield her from the brisk and brutal winds that whipped through the Black Forest. There would be time to truly mourn her dead, but first, she had to amass her army.

Deep in the woods was a well-hidden encampment of exiled Northern soldiers loyal to Gershom, the disgraced former friend and commander of Issachar's army. Stripped of his distinguished titles and life of grandeur, Gershom embodied his House Sigil and was now only known as The Bear. She was going to meet with him whether he liked it or not.

Dressed head to toe in a black robe and fur coat, Niabi strutted through the camp and entered Gershom's tent with an air of confidence that did not go unnoticed by the men scattered around bonfires trying to keep warm. With Tala the Andrago and her Nephilim bodyguard following a step behind, she stood before the brute she had spent a year tracking down. Her eyes scanned the back of the tent and stopped when she saw Gershom sitting on a humble, some would even deem pathetic, wooden throne.

Ophir, Gershom's younger brother, stepped toward her with his hand extended to halt her approach. "Bow before His Lordship."

Anyone who came to visit The Bear would kneel before him, intimidated by the mere sight of him. But Niabi knew her place as Queen of the Andrago, born of both Northern and Myridian royal blood, and with a vicious glance in Ophir's direction, she refused to bend the knee.

Gershom's eyebrows raised and he leaned forward. "You do not kneel." It was not a question.

"I bow to no man." Niabi stood her ground, maintaining eye contact with him.

"You will bend the knee one way or another," Ophir snorted as he reached for his sword.

Before Tala could unsheathe his sword, Niabi had already exposed her twin daggers hidden up her sleeves and held one against Ophir's neck.

"I said," Niabi hissed, "I bend the knee to no man."

Gershom waved them to stand down. "Forgive my brother. He is as zealous as he is loyal."

Niabi's narrowed eyes darted from Ophir to Gershom. She retracted her knives and lifted her head up higher. She was not one to be threatened or challenged. That was now clear to everyone in the tent.

With Ophir safely by his side, Gershom sipped his wine and oscillated his gaze amongst the three newcomers with disgust. "You march into my camp with a Horse Lord, and this damned monstrosity," he pointed at Anaktu the Nephilim with his goblet, "and upon first meeting me, threaten my brother, and insult me."

"Surely, a man with your reputation is not so easily offended," she sneered. "If so, the Green-Eyed Raven has been told falsely about your abilities."

Gershom licked his dry lips and smirked. "I have heard about you. You're prettier than I imagined."

"Should I take that as a compliment?"

"Take it as you wish." He placed his empty cup down on the armrest of his chair and leaned back. Pressing his palms together, he raised his hands to touch his chin. "Tell me, Niabi, daughter of Issachar -"

"Niabi, Queen of the Andrago," she corrected.

"You deny your Northern birthright?"

"I deny the man who denied me."

Gershom motioned for Ophir to bring a chair for Niabi. She watched Ophir as he carefully placed the chair in front of her, but she did not sit.

"What do you want?" Gershom asked.

"I have come for your allegiance." Her eyes returned to The Bear.

"Allegiance for what?"

"To kill the King of the North, of course."

Gershom and Ophir exchanged a bewildered look.

"Word has reached me of your husband's untimely death -"

"You mean his assassination," she interrupted.

Gershom cleared his throat as Ophir refilled his cup. "I know more than most your hatred for Issachar…"

"But?"

"But to plot his murder, is suicide. It cannot be done. Not that it should not. It cannot."

Niabi flipped the bottom of her fur coat behind her and sat down in the chair Ophir had offered her moments before. She stared deeply into Gershom's eyes until he blinked. She pointed at the three scars on the side of his face.

"Those scars, ordered by him, were they not?"

Gershom rolled his shoulders back and tilted his neck to the side until it cracked loudly. "Yes."

"Your ancestors' land, your title, your wealth – stripped. Your family forced into exile, ordered by him?"

His eyes narrowed as he leaned toward her, hands resting firmly on his knees. "I am sure you will make your point quickly."

Niabi crossed one leg over the other, revealing her leather pants. "Does revenge not interest you?"

"I have my methods of repaying him."

She scoffed. "You burn his crops and pillage his outlying villages and for what? He does not lose sleep over such nuisances." She slowly leaned forward and whispered, "You are nothing more than an irritating fly and eventually, he will crush you as such. We both know this." She watched him squirm in his seat. "Everyone fears something. Let's be what they fear."

Gershom laughed and straightened up in his seat. "Issachar does not fear me, nor your Andrago." He once again flashed a disgusted glance Tala's way.

"Maybe not," she shrugged. "But he does fear me - the daughter and rightful heir he tried to silence."

Gershom's face brightened at the realization of what she really wanted. "You don't just mean to kill him. You want the White Throne."

"And I will have it. Even if I have to burn his entire kingdom to the ground to get it."

"You would have us battle the North?" Gershom offered her a drink.

"Men go to battle." She refused the drink. "Women wage war."

Gershom sipped his wine in silence. "If I should join you – what is in it for me?"

"Pledge your allegiance to me and I will give you what Issachar wouldn't."

"Which is?"

"Second of Northwind." She knew by the look on his face she had won him over. "More wealth, power, and splendor than you can imagine."

Gershom's lips curled. "How do I know I can trust you?"

Niabi stood, grabbed the cup he had offered her before, and downed the wine. "I do not trust you. But the enemy of my enemy is worthy of my friendship."

"All this because he denied you?"

"My reasons are my own." She set the goblet down. "Are you with me or not?"

Gershom stood and stared down at her with a twisted grin. "Ironic, is it not, how you look so much like your mother, yet your father's words flow from your lips."

Niabi's eyes narrowed, and her nostrils flared. Her fingertips flirted with the blades hidden up her sleeves. She glared at him. "Careful. Unlike my father, I am not afraid to wear your blood like war paint."

He smiled. "And that is why you may very well survive." He lifted his cup. "To the Queen of the North."

CHAPTER 1
CRISPIN

Crispin opened his eyes and looked around the dark hovel. The last thing he could remember was being rushed down the River of Lost Souls. From that moment on, his memory was foggy.

He touched the loose long-sleeved white shirt that rested on his chest and realized he was not wearing his own clothes. He ripped the blanket off and sure enough, an oversized pair of brown pants had replaced his.

A fire was crackling near the bed he rose from. The entire house was one small room. There were no windows and only one wooden door to allow entrance and departure. As he paced around the foreign space trying to find a clue as to whose house he was in, he noticed freshly lit incense burning on a tiny wooden table in the center of the room. He spotted his clothes on a chair in the corner and eagerly put them back on, deciding it would probably be best for him to sneak out of the hovel before the owner returned. As he reached for the latch, a woman abruptly entered carrying a basket filled with freshly baked bread, fruit, and cheese.

Crispin had never seen anyone quite like her before and could not help but stare. Her brown complexion was flawless. Long, plum hair draped the right side of her body, while the left side of her head was clean-shaven, showcasing nearly a dozen ear piercings. Shorter than him by a foot, the petite fortune teller with haunting dark eyes and exposed midriff wore a stunning teal-blue robe adorned embellished with gold jewels. Her bare and dainty feet were adorned with toe rings and anklets.

The prince was clearly taken aback by her foreign beauty, but she did not seem to mind, as if she knew his thoughts were innocent.

"I see you have recovered." Even her accent was unlike any he had heard before. "You must be hungry. Come, sit, eat." She placed the basket of goods on a large, patterned rug surrounded by plush and colorful pillows as she sat cross legged in front of him. "Come."

Crispin did as he was told, confident that if he were in danger, she would not have taken the time to nurse him back to health. She extended a piece of bread to him, which he gratefully accepted.

"Who are you?" he asked.

"You are more concerned with who I am, rather than where you are? Interesting." Her eyes, outlined in smudged black kohl, danced as she continued eating the grapes that overflowed from her basket.

"Of course, I want to know where I am," he retorted, mouth full of food. "I suppose I was more curious as to why you helped me."

She glanced up at him. "You were in need of help, so I helped."

Such a simple answer. "What is your name?"

"Why do you wish to know?" She fiddled with her nose ring.

"So, I know who I am thanking."

"Why must you know me to thank me?"

Her questions frustrated him. "Listen, I am just looking for some answers. The last thing I remember, I was in the River of… I was in a river -"

"The River of Lost Souls." She knew more than Crispin gave her credit.

"Is that where you found me?"

"You found me."

"What?" Crispin raked fingers down the side of his face, more confused than ever.

"Your body floated to our shores, so I brought you inside before the others could find you."

"The others?"

She lowered her voice to a barely audible level. "You are in Pulau."

If he was not concerned before, he was now. Pulau was a cluster of small islands inhabited by bloodthirsty pirates, greedy gypsies, fortune tellers and halflings. Known as 'Misfit Island' to most Adalorians, Mainlanders stayed far from the wild, over-crowded kingdom

"Who are you?" Crispin asked again cautiously, wishing he had looked for his weapons sooner.

She pointed to the fireplace mantle where he caught sight of the handle of his sword resting inside a blanket. "My name is Palma," she revealed, sensing his anxiety. "I had a vision you would be coming. That is why I found you before the patrol did."

Crispin leaned back and arched one of his eyebrows. "You aren't going to turn me in?"

"If that were my intent," she nibbled on a slice of cheese, "I would have done so."

Her answer was acceptable. "How do I get off this island? I need to get back to my company."

"There is but one way, Crispin, son of Issachar, and that is by finding the Shadow of Death."

His breathing quickened. "How do you know my name?"

Palma smiled and brought out a folded up wanted poster from underneath one of her pillows. "I am not the only one who knows your name."

"Tell me what I need to do."

"I will take you to *The Dancing Lady* by the western docks. There you will find your way to the captain of the fastest ship in Adalore. He will help you escape Pulau if you agree to his terms."

"How will I get there unnoticed?" He scratched the fresh stubble along his jawline. "You said it yourself, there are other people looking for me."

"Put this on." Palma tossed a dark, hooded cloak to him. "If you keep your head down, no one will pay you any mind."

Crispin held the cloak but hesitated before putting it on. "What do you get for helping me escape?"

"I have already told you," she smiled, "you were in need of help, so I helped."

"The money on my head has no appeal to you?" He folded his arms over his chest, skepticism in his eyes. "I highly doubt you would risk your life sheltering me just for the satisfaction of helping someone in need."

Palma's eyes shifted toward the floor. "You are right, Prince Crispin, there is something I desire."

"What is your price?"

"There are whispers that you wish to take back your father's throne." Her toes tapped the floor. "If that is so, when you become King of the North, I ask that you allow me and my parents to live in the White City."

His eyes widened. That was not what he expected her to ask for. "You wish to live in Northwind?"

"My parents are growing old and are quite ill." She grabbed his hand. "I ask for a new life for us; a safe place where I can care for my family without fear."

Crispin's gaze softened and he gently squeezed her hand. "I wish I could give you more than just my word but -"

"You word is all I need." She patted his hand with a new-found hope. "Put the cloak on and we will be on our way."

As soon as Crispin's face was hidden, the duo made their way through the narrow, winding wooden streets. Pulau was composed of several small islands that had numerous canals running through the kingdom. The city looked as if the cliff-like terrain had fused with old wooden ships. The old-world structures were connected by ladders, suspended bridges, and ramps. Had Palma not been guiding him, he never would have found *The Dancing Lady*.

"Keep your head down," she whispered as four patrolmen turned the corner.

They were not at all what he expected. Not one of them resembled a soldier. One was skinny to a frightening degree with a hook nose while the other three sported tremendous beer bellies. Crispin could have sworn one of them was cross-eyed and wondered how he was able to even walk straight.

"*Those* are patrolmen?" he scoffed, clearly unimpressed.

"They might not look like much, but even rats bite." She motioned for him to keep quiet.

They passed the squad without prompting a second glance as they made their way through the humid city. *The Dancing Lady* was heard before it was seen. Dozens of tipsy sailors with semi-attractive, disheveled women hanging on their arms, were carrying on outside the tavern's signature red door. Loud piano music played daily, spurring the bar wenches to dance on the tables, making it popular amongst pirates.

Palma stopped abruptly. "This is where I leave you."

"Leave me?" Crispin whipped around; eyes wide. "What do you mean? You aren't coming inside with me?"

"I will no longer be of use to you, my lord." She leaned in as if to kiss his cheek and whispered, "Keep to yourself and find the Shadow of Death."

He wrapped his arm around her. "I swear your kindness will never be forgotten."

With a nod and one last smile, Palma disappeared into the bustling street, leaving him to continue his journey solo.

Crispin pushed his way into the crowded bar and sat on a stool at an abandoned table. While ensuring his hood was low enough over his face, he observed the pirates rustling about. Sitting quietly, he went unnoticed until the plump tavern owner came over to him.

"Kin I get ye anythin', sailor?" His chubby cheeks were flushed, and beads of sweat dripped down the back of his hairy neck.

Feeling compelled to blend in with the locals, he nodded, and in a muffled voice said, "Aye, a pint of ale."

"Comin' right up." The balding barkeep waddled away with a tray full of empty cups.

Crispin exhaled a sigh of relief but was still unsure of how he would find what or who the Shadow of Death was.

Suddenly, the pirates crowding the door parted, allowing three newcomers to enter without having to push their way in. The two men were accompanied by a woman wearing pinstripe trousers. As they walked up to the bar, three drunks gave up their stools.

The pirate on the woman's left was of average height with eyes as blue as the sea. The sides of his head were shaved. A strip of auburn, shoulder-length hair ran down the center of his head. Two thick strands of hair rested on either side of his black eyebrows and his chiseled face was framed with very little facial hair. Two silver cuff earrings graced his right ear and a hollow, circular pendant rested upon his hairless chest. Although he was consumed in a cloud of smoke from his reefer, Crispin could tell that under his navy, knee-length coat, he was heavily armed.

The pirate on the right had broad shoulders, wavy, black, chin=length hair which was mostly covered by a beige and red bandana. His cheeks, collarbone, and both arms were tattooed in the ancient runes of Pulau. The beastly seafarer was muscular from head to toe and carried at least six different types of knives in his leather belt.

The woman's brown complexion was as beautiful as Palma's. Her short, slick-back hair was icy blue, but her eyebrows were black. Her athletic arms were adorned with several gold pieces her crew most likely plundered. Unlike her heavily armed companions, she only carried a gold and ruby encrusted dagger which was tucked in her belt. By the way she carried herself, Crispin could tell she was more dangerous than her male counterparts.

Crispin watched the trio as an intoxicated sailor boldly, or stupidly depending on how one looked at it, marched up to the three newcomers. Puffing out his unimpressive chest, the drunk pirate leaned in and smiled at the female mariner.

"Lemme buy ye a drink," he burped.

The woman did not bother to look in his direction. "I have a drink."

"C'mon," he persisted. "Lemme treat ye."

She sipped her ale. "Get away from me."

"No need to be 'ostile," he turned toward his three mates and chuckled. "It's just one drink, milady." He bowed in exaggerated fashion.

She set her tin mug down. "I'll give you to the count of three to leave."

"And if I'm still 'ere at three?" He clicked his tongue at her with a wink.

"Stick around to find out."

The drunk laughed. "Ye got spunk, lass. I like that in me women."

"She told you to leave her alone," the blue-eyed pirate barked, a glint of violent mischief in his eyes. "Or do you not understand basic tongue?"

"Phex," the bandana wearing pirate said in a warning tone.

"Corwin," Phex hissed in response, eyes narrowed.

"A pretty lass like 'er wouldn't 'urt a nice fella like me." The drunk ignored the hot-headed pirate and placed his hand on the female's lower back.

"One."

"Uh oh! She's countin'," he smirked at his giggling buddies.

"Rahab." Corwin shook his head.

"Two."

"I suggest you leave," Phex warned him one last time.

"I ain't goin' nowhere."

"Three." In one swift motion, Rahab turned, pushed the drunk sailor away from her, unsheathed her dagger and stabbed him in the upper thigh.

"Ah!" he screamed. "Ye stabbed me!"

Rahab ripped her knife from his leg and wiped the blood on his pants. "You're lucky I didn't take your hand for putting your greasy fingers on me." She eyed his friends. "Get him out of my sight before I lose my temper."

As if nothing had happened, the trio turned their focus back to their drinks as the injured sailor was dragged out of the tavern leaving a trail of blood behind him. The music resumed and the rosy cheeked bartender hustled back to Crispin with a sticky goblet of ale.

"Who are they?" Crispin tilted his head toward the three buccaneers.

The bartender knew who Crispin was referring to and reluctantly whispered, "Corwin is the big one, and from what I hear, owns over a hundred knives from all over Adalore. Phex, is the one smoking; some say he has a crazed mind, inventing all sorts of unholy things. And the woman is Rahab. That's a black-hearted pirate if I ever saw one."

"It seems like everyone in here is afraid of them," Crispin said, still watching the three pirates from afar.

"Ye must not be from 'round here," the barkeep sighed, his arms beginning to shake from the weight of his tray. "They're crew members of the *Shadow of Death*. Not to be messed with, they are. Dangerous bunch."

"Did you say the Shadow of Death?" Crispin hid his excitement and kept his voice low.

"Aye, fastest ship in Pulau. Stay as far from them as ye can. No telling what they might do to ye for sport." Afraid they might catch him gossiping, he rushed back to his bar to tend to his other patrons.

Crispin took a sip of the warm ale and nearly spit it out. Pushing it away, he knew he wouldn't be finishing it.

He found where he needed to go, but was it really the only way to get out of

Pulau? While mulling over his options, the trio stood up and left the tavern. He had to make a decision: either follow them like Palma had instructed or find his own way off the island. He rolled his eyes and sighed. He was going to trust Palma. Hopefully, he did not find himself on the other side of the female pirate's blade.

Crispin slapped a coin on the table and tailed them from a safe distance as they walked down the ramps to the main harbor where their ship was docked.

From the exterior, the *Shadow of Death* was everything the name led you to believe. It was a black wooden ship with gold trim and skeletons mounted on the bowsprit. The black sails sported their emblem of a murderous mermaid etched in gold, ensuring once you saw them coming, you would know exactly who was chasing you.

He watched Phex, Corwin, and Rahab board the sleek ship and with a deep breath, he walked up the ramp. When he stepped foot on the main deck, the pirates he had followed were nowhere to be seen.

"What is your business here, stranger?" A voice boomed; catching him off guard. "Or have you lost your way?"

Crispin turned toward the odd voice and saw a halfling standing there. His straw-like, snow white hair was pulled back into a stubby ponytail. His moustache and beard ended in perfect triangular points which accentuated his round, sun-burned nose.

"I asked you a question," the pirate growled.

"I came to request an audience with your captain." Crispin's shoulders tight-ened. He lowered his head to make sure his face was shadowed in the safety of his hood.

"That can be arranged." The short pirate smirked as he motioned another crew member forward. "Ondrej, watch him. He wants to see the captain."

Ondrej was at least six-foot-eight, dark skinned, and had exceptionally long dreads all pulled into a bun atop his head. His bulky biceps were bigger than Crispin's thigh. The mere sight of him struck fear into the hearts of most men.

Crispin wondered if he made a mistake by boarding the *Shadow of Death.*

A few agonizing minutes later, the captain, followed by the halfling and the trio from the tavern, marched down the steps from the officers' quarters.

"Rafi tells me you're looking for the captain."

"Is that you?" Crispin asked, trying to keep all the pirates' names straight.

"I'm Captain Haldane," he nodded. "But by the looks of you," the captain sneered, "you're on the wrong ship."

"Is this the *Shadow of Death*?" Crispin asked, hood still covering most of his face.

"Aye," Haldane nodded, "that it is."

"Then I am on the right ship."

Haldane's raspy laugh echoed across the deck. "Do you know who we are, boy?"

"Pirates?" Crispin was confused by the question.

The captain roared in delight at his ignorance. "Pirates? We're not just pirates, lad! We're the Masters of the Seas; feared by Mainlanders and seafarers alike." He looked Crispin up and down. "If a job is what you seek, we don't need ye. If you wish anything more of us, look elsewhere."

"But -"

Haldane's narrow eyes flashed. "You're lucky, boy, that I'm letting you walk off my ship intact. Now get off before I throw you off." His shaggy blonde hair blew in the wind as he turned to head back to his quarters.

"I need your help," Crispin shouted.

"Did you not hear what I said, lad? Pirates aren't in the business of helping."

"I was told that you would help me if I agreed to your terms." Crispin took a step forward and stammered, "Perhaps… perhaps there is something you need that I can help you with?"

Haldane grinned, exposing three gold teeth. "I like you."

"So, you will help me off the island?"

"No." Haldane motioned Rahab forward. "Show the boy off my ship."

"Gladly." Her smooth-as-honey voice hypnotized Crispin for a moment as she glided toward him with every intention of throwing him overboard.

In a last-ditch effort to get Haldane's attention, Crispin grabbed Rahab, unsheathed the ruby encrusted knife from her hip, and held it against her throat.

"Don't move or I'll kill her!" Crispin stared intently at the green-eyed pirate. Testing his bluff, Haldane stepped forward only to stop as soon as Crispin pressed the knife into Rahab's neck, drawing blood. "I said, don't move."

"You've made a grave mistake, stranger." Haldane growled as he held his hand out to stop any other crew member from advancing.

"I need to get off this island," Crispin demanded through gritted teeth, "and you are going to take me where I need to go."

Haldane placed his hands on his hips. "And tell me why I would take orders from a faceless man on my own ship?"

Crispin yanked the hood off. "I am Crispin of Northwind; if you help me, I will see to it you are handsomely rewarded."

Haldane recognized the rogue prince the North was hunting. "You have my attention."

"You're hurting me," Rahab mumbled.

"Quiet, Rahab!" Haldane spat. "What is it that you want from me, Crispin of Northwind?"

"I was separated from my company and must rejoin them."

"Say I do what you ask." The captain stroked his scraggly beard with a smirk. "What's in it for me?"

"Enough gold for you to retire," Crispin promised.

"How do I know you're good for it?" Haldane tilted his head. "There is a hefty price on your head. Why not just take Queen Niabi's gold?"

"Do you actually believe she would pay such a sum? What would prevent her from executing you on the spot?" Crispin raised a good point. "I am good for the money; you will just have to trust me."

"Trust you?" Haldane cackled. "We trust no one, that is why we survive."

"Yet you will put your faith blindly in a black hearted queen?"

"Better a rich queen than an exiled prince."

"Palma was a fool for sending me here," Crispin muttered under his breath in frustration.

"Did you say Palma?" Rahab seemed surprised, rattled even, hearing Palma's name.

"Palma sent you here?" The captain's voice softened and if Crispin read his face correctly, he would have sworn Haldane's eyes were filled with longing.

"She told me you would help me, if I agreed to your terms." Crispin was cautious. He did not want to endanger Palma's life unwittingly.

"Well," Haldane hesitated, "that changes everything."

"How do you know her?" Crispin's eyes narrowed.

"Let Rahab go, and I'll answer your questions."

"No," he twisted Rahab's arm, "tell me how you know her."

"Twist my arm again and I'll rip your balls off," Rahab hissed in his ear.

"I'll tell you what you want to know," Haldane raised his hands and motioned for him to lower the weapon. "Just don't hurt her."

Crispin was taken aback by the captain's plea for Rahab's safety, so he loosened his grip. "How do you know Palma?"

The pirate took a deep breath. "She is my wife."

"Your wife?" The prince nearly choked.

Rahab seized her opportunity to escape his loosened grasp. She swept Crispin's legs out from under him and pinned him to the ground, her knee digging into his chest.

"Stop!" Haldane shouted. "None of you will lay another finger on him." The seafarer waved for Rahab to get off him, then helped Crispin to his feet. "Come. We have much to talk about."

Crispin extended Rahab's dagger to her as she stood up. "I believe this is yours."

She snatched it from him with a snarl. "Touch me again and I'll slit your throat."

Haldane led Crispin to a set of stairs. They could go up or they could go down. Instead of going up in the direction the group had descended when coming to meet the prince, they went down. They walked through a wood paneled hallway past the crew's bunks and the infirmary until they reached an arched opening where Haldane motioned for Crispin to follow him inside.

"Take a seat," Haldane tossed his hat on a long mahogany table. The sunlight streaming through the portholes lit the dining room. The scullery was just across the hall and Crispin could smell salted meat and a stew brewing.

Crispin obediently sat in a small chair opposite the middle-aged captain. After pouring himself a drink from the wooden wet bar, the pirate eyed the prince with great sadness.

"How is she?" he whispered.

"To be honest, Captain, I only recently met your wife and spent very little time with -"

"Did she look well?" Haldane pressed.

Crispin nodded. "She appeared well to me."

"Palma and I have been separated for several years now. She didn't approve of my choices..." The captain stared at his glass and tilted it back and forth to watch the liquid inside dance. "I'm not the man she deserves. Most days, I regret choosing the sea over her. Today, is one of those days."

"Perhaps you should tell her that," Crispin suggested.

"Aye, perhaps." Haldane snapped out of his depression, running his ringed fingers through his scraggly blonde beard. "But first, I will do as she promised I would. I owe her that."

"So, you will help me?"

The pirate downed the rum and poured himself another. He offered a second filled glass to Crispin. "Under one condition."

"What is your price?" Crispin accepted the glass.

"She is a clever diviner; she knew we needed to meet." Haldane shot the second serving and set the glass upside down on the wooden table. "My price is one rescued life for another."

"I'm afraid I don't understand."

"The *Shadow of Death* has never been boarded by an enemy, except for one time many years ago. I was a new captain, foolish and brash, and because of me stubbornness, we were overrun by the finest vessel from Borg. The commander of that ship was a young, fresh-faced boy who was under strict instructions to capture our ship and bring me to his king to be tried for me crimes against the West. To me surprise, he didn't arrest me – he befriended me and decided to let us go." Haldane leaned back in his chair. "He claimed his king had wronged his family and he had no intention of obeying any more of his commands. We abandoned his crew in rowboats, sunk his ship, and he joined us. After a few years learning our ways, he became more than just another pirate, he became family."

"What happened to him?" Crispin shot his drink and coughed; the rum burned his throat.

"He left. Unfinished business. Now word has reached my ears that he has been imprisoned, but by whom I am not entirely sure. Some say the Westerners finally caught up to him, others claim Gershom of Northwind had him imprisoned for attempting to assassinate him. No one knows for sure. That is where you come in, my new friend." Haldane's smile made Crispin uneasy. "I will get you out of Pulau, but before I return you to your companions, I need you to help us find Leeondris. I owe him."

"A pirate with a heart," Crispin chuckled, more nervous than anything. "Not at all what I expected."

"Even pirates live by a code, Prince." Haldane extended his ring filled hand to him. "Now, do we have a deal?"

Crispin realized he did not have much of a choice if he wished to make it off 'Misfit Island' in one piece, so he shook the pirate's hand. "We have a deal."

CHAPTER 2
SALOME

To the Sea, to the Sea,
The Sea is calling me.
Her mighty waves, her shapeshift ways,
The Sea is calling me.
All hail our Queen, she set us free,
Yet the Sea still calls for me.
When I breathe my last, send me to Death,
The Sea has called for me.

Salome did not have many memories of her mother, Bilhah, but the one memory she remembered vividly was on the nights she could not sleep; her mother would climb into her bed, caress her head, and sing her Myridian lullabies. As they sailed to the Isles of Myr, Salome found herself becoming more anxious. The only way to calm her ever-racing mind was to sing to herself, like she did growing up in the Tree House Forest. During her brief moments of peace, she felt as if her mother was still with her.

Every story Bilhah told her children about her homeland awakened a desire in Salome to one day visit the Isles of Myr. Maybe she could even learn to fight like the Qata Vishna. In Northwind, women were not permitted to learn about weaponry or politics, nor were they allowed to join the king's army. But the Isles of Myr was different.

It was known to the Mainlanders as 'The Woman's Kingdom'. Myridians were ruled by women. Their borders were protected by female warriors. Women owned and operated all businesses and if there was trading to be done, it was to be done with a woman. Property was deeded to females only and passed down to the first-born female heir.

What of the men? was always the question kings of other Adalorian kingdoms would demand to know.

And according to the Myridians, the answer was simple: Men were good for breeding and not much else.

After Malachi the First established the Kingdom of Myr, he appointed a king who stripped women of every basic dignity a human could have. They were treated as property – bought, sold, and traded. Being forced into servitude, raped, or beaten to within an inch of their last breath was common.

But one woman, named Arsinoe, stood up to the first and last King of the Isles of Myr.

Women outnumbered men three to one and in an act of defiance, they joined Arsinoe and waged war against the self-proclaimed stronger sex. For seven days and seven nights, the newly banded female warriors burned the tyrannical king's castle to the ground, sparing the king himself for their queen's blade. Queen Arsinoe beheaded the oppressor who persecuted them and established a new reign. A better reign.

After the war, men were free to choose to bend the knee to the queen or face the executioner's blade where Death could gladly have them.

For nearly a thousand years, women had ruled the Isles of Myr and the Adalorian rulers respected and feared angering the Qata Vishna.

Originally, five islands comprised the Isles of Myr, but Vilora sunk Endor, so only four remained. Single Myridian men were kept on Bullmar, while married couples raised their children on Antrope. The third isle, Delta , was used explicitly for training unmarried women for the Qata Vishna. And of course, the fourth and main island was Capitol, where all business and governing matters were conducted.

That was all Salome could recall her mother telling her. The small room on *The Golden Rose* started to feel cramped. She inhaled deeply and exhaled rhythmically. She was used to being around men. Now she felt as if she was being sent into the lion's den and she wasn't sure if she was going to walk out unscathed.

She twisted her brother, Lykos's, Myridian ring around her right index finger and closed her eyes.

"To the Sea, to the Sea, the Sea is calling me..."

The quick rap on the door startled her.

She cleared her throat. "Come in."

Adonijah entered, eyes heavy. He had not slept much due to seasickness. He and water were clearly not compatible.

"Still not feeling well?" She could not help but feel sorry for him.

He shook his head and slowly laid on the second cot, placing a damp cloth over his eyes. "I am already dreading the journey back to the Mainland. If I were not committed to you, I would consider staying."

Committed to you. The phrase gave her goosebumps. Salome knelt at his bedside with a feline grin. "I don't think you'd like to stay in the Isles of Myr forever."

"Oh," he mumbled. "Why is that?"

"Because." Salome plopped an elbow on the bed and rested her chin in her hand. "The Isles of Myr doesn't look favorably on *your* kind."

Adonijah lifted the towel exposing one eye. "And by my kind, you mean... handsome?"

She rolled her eyes. "Male."

"Ah, yes." His eyes twinkled of mischief. "I've heard all of that before."

"But?"

With great effort, Adonijah turned to his side and supported himself on his elbow. "I'm sure I can change their minds."

Salome laughed softly. "Is that so?"

"What?" He flashed a wry smile. "You don't think my charm will win them over?"

"And what charm would that be?"

"The same charm that won you over."

Adonijah's smile had not worked on her before, but this time it sent a sudden sensation of warmth through her body. Her lips parted as if she had a witty rebuttal, but nothing came out.

His eyes softened as he rested his hand on top of hers. "I'll take your silence as a good thing."

"Adonijah, I -"

Harbona burst through the door with excitement smeared across his face. "We are approaching the Isles of Myr -" He stopped when he saw how close they were. "Am I interrupting something?"

Adonijah cleared his throat and rubbed the nape of his neck.

"No, Harbona." Salome stood and wiped her hands down her pants. "We were just talking."

Harbona's eyes shifted back and forth between them. If he had something to say, he kept it to himself. He motioned for them to follow him. "You should come upstairs, approaching the Isles of Myr is not a sight to miss." He turned to head back to the upper deck.

"Maybe I should stay here," Adonijah said softly, his eyes meeting hers. "I'll see it when I see it."

"Are you sure? We can help you." She motioned for him to get up.

"He's gone." He nodded his head toward the door.

Salome whipped around and sure enough, Harbona was gone. "Then I can help you."

"If it's all the same to you, Princess," he rested his back against the wall, "I'd prefer to be down here."

"Please."

He was taken aback. "Please?"

She closed her eyes and pinched the bridge of her nose. "I could use some company."

"Harbona is -"

She cut him off. "Please."

That was not a word she used too often, and she had used it twice in the span of seconds. Her hesitation of using the word was not because she lacked manners, but because she was used to doing things for herself, by herself. She found herself in a world she was uncomfortable in. A world that had seemingly forgotten all about her. And now, she knew she needed support. Needed help. Needed a friend. Maybe even something more.

She blinked rapidly, realizing she had been staring at him. Longing for him. But then she noticed he was looking at her differently too. His eyes. So mysterious and yet so telling at the same time. His lips, his arms. Her eyes scanned down to his slightly opened shirt. His chest, his …

"So, what do you say?" she asked, shaking those thoughts free from her mind.

Adonijah inhaled; his tight lips curved into a smile. "You think I'm handsome?"

Salome's eyes widened and her heart raced. "What?"

"Earlier, when you said 'Myr doesn't look favorably on my kind' and I said, 'by my kind you mean handsome?'" He cocked his head to the side. "You didn't deny it."

Salome had never been in this position before. She was rarely lost for words. She stammered, hoping she could string together even the feeblest of sentences. But all she managed to say was, "Maybe I didn't want to hurt your feelings."

The sides of his eyes crinkled when he smiled. "Thank you for sparing my feelings."

"You're welcome." She crossed her arms across her chest, shifting her weight. She cleared her throat, "So, will you...?"

"Go with you?" Adonijah planted his feet on the ground and stood up. "How could I not?"

THE WARM SOUTHERN sea air enveloped her as she made her way to the upper deck. Crystal clear blue water crashed against the side of the ship, rocking it gently. Salome turned back to look at Adonijah, expecting him to be leaning over the railing ready to barf, but he stood tall with his mouth agape. Her eyes glanced in the direction he was looking and landed on the bustling capitol city of Myr.

Salome's eyes scanned from the white sandy beaches of the shoreline up the coastal cliffs where the ancient city was built. Cypress trees lined the stone streets that spidered through the kingdom. Tales of her mother's homeland painted Myr to be beautiful, but that was severely understated. There was truly no architectural rival in all Ten Kingdoms of Adalore.

Wine, spices, and bronze were in high demand from the Myridians. One of the few memories she had of her father was his thorough enjoyment of Myridian wine. She was allowed a sip as a child and had held on to the bold taste hoping one day, she would have a glass to herself.

The castle was built at the top of the cliff overlooking the sea and other small islands belonging to the queen. The rest of the city was built into the side of the same cliff. With the sun beginning to set, the Alhambra stone glowed red, and Salome finally understood why the castle was called the Scarlet Citadel.

"Are you alright?" Adonijah asked.

Salome inhaled deeply, stifling a cry. "My mother used to describe her homeland to us, and I always wanted to visit when I was old enough. I just wish she were here with me."

Adonijah rested his hand on top of hers after she gripped the railing. He did not need to say anything – she could feel his compassion the moment his hand touched hers and she breathed easier.

As the ship neared the harbor, she saw a royal committee waiting on horseback for their arrival.

Salome glanced at Harbona who joined them. "A royal convoy?"

Harbona smiled. "They knew to be expecting us."

"Who are they?" Salome's gaze returned to the bronze armored soldiers with Myridian blue and green banners wafting in the sea breeze; the Myridian sigil of the octopus etched into each with gold thread.

Harbona motioned to the woman positioned at the front of the pack. "That is your cousin, Princess Mika."

"Her armor is different than the others."

Salome was right. In fact, Mika was the only warrior in Myr who did not don bronze armor. Hers was red.

"They call her the Red Maiden."

"Why?"

"Since the reign of Arsinoe the First," Harbona explained as he lit his pipe, "there has always been a Red Maiden. She is the fiercest of the Qata Vishna – unbeaten in combat."

"Is she the Red Maiden until she dies?" Cato joined them. Now clean of the clay and blue paint that was caked on his body, and now dressed in traditional Mainlander clothes, he looked like an entirely different person.

"Traditionally." Harbona nodded at him and exhaled a puff of smoke.

Adonijah's interest was piqued. "What does that mean?"

"There is a Red Maiden that still lives but does not don the red armor." Harbona shifted his weight, as if he didn't want to say more.

"Who?" Salome asked.

Trumpets blasted as the ship docked.

"A story for another time." Harbona extinguished his pipe.

Harbona trotted down the ramp with Cato beside him, the Stormcrag's short, cropped, white hair gleaming in the sunlight. It appeared the Seer had taken quite a liking to Cato and spent most of the voyage catching up on the feud between the two Mountain Men clans. Salome, too, found Cato's people extremely interesting, and also terrifying. Hopefully, they wouldn't be running into the Mountain Men anytime soon.

"Salome?" Adonijah stood behind her, waiting for her to follow Harbona, but she was frozen in place.

"What if she doesn't like me?" Salome whispered.

"Who?"

"The queen."

"Why would she not like you?" Adonijah circled in front of her and lowered his head to meet her eyes. "You're her kin."

"Blood is fickle that way."

Adonijah reached out and squeezed her hand gently. "She will like you."

"You really think so?" Salome steadied her rapid breathing, maintaining eye contact with him.

He nodded. "Once she accepts you for the stubborn pain in the ass you are, she will love you."

She swatted at his arm and laughed. "You're horrible."

"Someone has to keep you humble," he shrugged with a grin.

"And you're an expert on being humble?" She rolled her eyes and planted her feet on the ramp to join Harbona and Cato at the bottom.

Adonijah followed closely behind her and whispered so only she could hear, "I am not just an expert on being humble."

"And what else are you supposed to be good at?" she teased.

"Apart from being an excellent swordsman?"

"Sure," she agreed sarcastically, "apart from that."

"I suppose if I'm as humble as I say I am, I'll have to let you tell me."

"I hope you also excel in patience," she snorted, "because that doesn't seem very likely."

"We will see." Adonijah flashed his mischievous smile. "We will see."

The four Mainlanders found themselves standing before a host of seven warriors on horseback. Up close, they were much taller than they had looked from the safety and distance of the ship. The craftmanship, detail, and feminine fit of their bronze armor was both impressive and enviable. Their helmets framed their olive and brown faces, and it was then Salome realized each of their head gear had different designs etched into it: flowers, sea creatures, landscapes, prayers, and tales of Myridian history.

The Red Maiden slid down the side of her armored white horse and greeted Harbona with a warm smile. "It's been a long time since you've visited our shores, Seer. It is good to see you."

"We thank you for your hospitality, Your Highness." Harbona bowed, then extended his arm to his companions. "This is Cato, Adonijah, and Salome of Northwind."

The Red Maiden's eyes rested on Salome. Green eyes. Myridian royalty were known for their green eyes and Salome had always wanted them. She suddenly became extremely aware of her two different color eyes and diverted her gaze from Mika's.

Mika tilted her head, "Welcome home, Cousin."

Home.

Such a simple word, but the concept seemed foreign to her. She had been forced to escape Northwind when she was five years old. She had been forced to escape the Tree House Forest just a couple of weeks ago. Was she going to be forced to flee from this new home too?

Harbona cleared his throat when Salome did not respond.

"Oh uh," Salome bowed her head. "It is good to be… home."

"Come." Mika remounted her steed. "You are expected at the Scarlet Citadel."

As soon as their horses had disembarked *The Golden Rose*, and they bid Diron and his crew goodbye for the time being, they joined the royal convoy weaving through the city streets. The path to the palace at the top of the seaside cliff zig zagged uphill from one side of the village back to the other side until it reached the peak. The breeze was much cooler up top, and the view was more spectacular than Salome could have imagined.

The Mainlanders were escorted inside the Scarlet Citadel. Salome thought the façade of the castle was breathtaking, but once inside, she was rendered speechless by the architecture. She stopped and turned in a full circle to admire the intricate lace-like carvings in the walls, archways, and columns made of stucco. The floors were a mixture of smooth stone and colorful mosaic tiles. The indoor-outdoor living aspect was what stuck out to her the most. She had never seen anything like it. In Northwind, the White Keep was a solid fortress with designated entrances and exits, even those leading to the impressive gardens. But here, she could not tell which rooms were considered indoor versus outdoor. The ceilings were either open to see the clear blue sky or were covered with mahogany wood with notches etched into it so light still streaked through to the floor.

How did mother give all this up for Northwind?

It was a haven. Every window boasted a dreamy view of the sea or of the Paraiso Gardens: a wonder of the known world. What she would give to wake up to a view like this every morning. Maybe she could. She shook her head, rattling that thought free. She was there for a reason and then she would leave for the next phase of the journey. She closed her eyes and listened to the waves crashing along the shoreline, the trickling of the countless fountains in and outside of the palace, the laughter of Myridian children running through the city streets... peace. It was the peace she craved. The type of life she longed for. The life she would most likely be denied.

As they continued to make their way through the palace, she noticed a small group of foreign dignitaries, consisting of mostly men, that looked like they were from the Eastern Lands. Their fine silk robes, their black hair, and their alabaster skin spared from the sun's scorn. She had never seen citizens of Sakurai before and found them to be not only a fascinating people, but beautiful as well. In fact, the man leading the entourage was dangerously attractive.

As if her thoughts had pierced through his head, he turned to meet her gaze, and flashed a handsome smile her direction. Her eyes darted to the floor, and she tried to regain her composure.

"Is everything alright?" Adonijah whispered after hearing her gasp.

She blushed, "Everything is fine."

He shot a glance down the hall and chuckled, "Have you not seen Easterners before?"

She shook her head, internally muttering every curse word she knew because Adonijah had caught her staring. "No. What do you suppose they're doing here?"

Adonijah shrugged. "Trade, diplomatic mission, marriage proposal... Who really knows with them?"

"Curious."

"What is?"

"They're mostly men. I only saw one woman with them."

"They aren't like Myridians, Princess. Women don't run things in Sakurai."

"We're here." Mika interrupted their conversation.

They had reached double bronze doors at the end of the hall. Mika took her helmet off once they reached the doors and saluted the guards who stood watch.

Mika extended her hand which halted the men from advancing. "Men are not allowed in the Inner Depths."

Salome looked at Harbona, slightly panicked. Harbona nodded his head reassuringly; his kind eyes motioned her to follow Mika.

"Wait here." Mika instructed the three men and escorted Salome inside.

Salome silently followed Mika through the bronze doors, and she found herself walking down a long colonnade hallway. Neither side of the passageway had walls. It was open to the queen's private gardens filled with red carnations, pomegranate flowers, bluebells, and gazanias lining the graveled pathway. Cypress and olive trees shaded the stone patios and ornate bronze statues and billowing fountains.

The breezeway was about a hundred feet in length, with red roses creeping up the colonnades, and led to a second pair of female warriors guarding another set of double bronze doors. These doors were different than all the other doors in the palace. Carved into them was the Myridian Sigil of a giant octopus with its tentacles crushing a ship.

The doors opened without Mika breaking stride. In the center of the Inner Depths was a rectangular pool of clear, still water with water lilies floating on top. In the reflection, Salome could see a woman seated on a throne which was set on a dais a few feet off the ground. Salome's, eyes rose from the water to the royal, but realized the woman before her couldn't be her grandmother. Although older, she was not old enough to be the queen.

"So," Zara's voice echoed, "you are the daughter of Issachar of Northwind." Although her foreign accent sounded melodic, her expression was chilly.

"And the daughter of Bilhah, daughter of Nym, Queen of the Isles of Myr." Salome responded, meeting Zara's menacing glare.

The room was quiet. Zara stared at the Mainlander, who looked very much like a Myridian, deep in thought before an odd smile stretched across her face. "You favor her."

"Thank you." Salome knew she was referring to her mother. She bowed slightly, not familiar with the traditional customs she was supposed to adhere to. "Forgive me, but I was under the impression I was going to see my grandmother."

Zara stood and descended the steps to get a closer look at Salome. "The Queen is indisposed. I am Princess Zara. Your mother was my younger sister."

Salome had noticed the similarities between Zara and her mother as soon as she entered the room. Long, dark hair, olive skin, green eyes, and their thick Myridian accents. The only difference was her mother's face was soft, kind, and gentle; Zara's face was hard, defined, and burdened.

"Tell me," Zara stood a foot in front of her. "Where have you been all these years?"

"My brother, Crispin, and I have been living in the Tree House Forest in the Western Lands."

"Instead of coming here?" Zara frowned. "Why?"

"It's where Zophar took us."

"And Zophar is...?"

"Our guardian."

Zara shook her head and looked her niece up and down. "He took you to live amongst boorish peasants instead of your own kin."

Salome could feel Zara's judgment oozing with each word she spoke. "How else would we have been safe?"

"The Myridians would have protected you. You bleed our blood." Zara's nose tipped upwards.

"And if my sister would have discovered you were harboring us and demanded you give us up, what would you have done?" Salome snorted indignantly. "I may have been a child when we escaped Northwind, but I am no fool. Northwind's fleet could overrun Myr without a problem."

"To attack the Isles of Myr would be foolish." Zara's eyes narrowed, her voice a bit higher in tone than it had been before. "Niabi would not dare bring war to our shores."

"Perhaps, you underestimate her."

"And perhaps," Zara clasped her arms behind her back, "like your mother, your tongue will land you in trouble."

Salome shrugged. "I'm used to trouble."

Zara smiled, which took Salome by surprise. "You were born in Northwind, but you are Myridian through and through." She motioned Mika to step forward. "Mika will see to it you have the finest rooms and robes while you stay with us."

"What of my companions?"

"You speak of the *men*?" Zara crinkled her nose.

"Yes."

Zara turned and made her way back toward the throne. "Naturally, they will stay in Bullmar, the male side of Myr.

"I would request they stay with me."

"Request denied." Zara's head nearly whipped off her neck when she turned to look at Salome. "Men are not allowed in our halls."

Salome stepped forward. "Unless they are foreign aides or dignitaries which permits them to stay in the Hall of Ambassadors."

Zara was clearly caught off guard by her niece's knowledge. "How do you know of the Hall of Ambassadors?" She shot her daughter, Mika, a cold look but was met with a shake of her head, denying any part in Salome's request.

"So," Salome chimed in, "they can stay in the Hall of Ambassadors?"

Zara growled, eyes still on Mika, "See to it her companions are accommodated." Her eyes floated down to Salome. "Rest, Niece. We will meet again soon."

Their first meeting was over. Mika led Salome back through the bronze doors they had entered. Once the doors were closed behind them, Mika finally spoke.

"How did you know of the Hall of Ambassadors?" she whispered.

"I saw men from the Eastern Lands head to a separate hall of the palace. By the look of their robes, I assumed they were ambassadors and were an exception to the rules. In Northwind, we had a Hall of Ambassadors, so I took a gamble you had one too."

Mika chuckled. "Very clever. My mother will be irritated the rest of the day that you outwitted her."

Salome blushed, "Your mother?"

Mika nodded, "Princess Zara is my mother."

"I hope I haven't offended you -"

"Sometimes she needs to be reminded she is not the smartest woman in the room." Marina interjected.

Marina was Mika's younger sister and was on her way into the throne room when she met them in the breezeway.

Mika side eyed her sister. "Salome, this is my sister, Marina."

"It is nice to meet you, Cousin." Salome bowed her head to pay respect.

"Tell me," Marina ignored her pleasantries. "The man in your company -"

"You will have to be more specific, Marina," Mika interrupted her with a snort. "There are many men in Salome's company."

Marina brushed off her sister's comment. "The handsome one with a pipe and leather gloves. What's his story?"

Salome's blood boiled and her cheeks instantly flushed. Upon first meeting

Marina, Salome could tell she didn't like her a bit, and it wasn't just because of Marina's interest in Adonijah. The way her cousin carried herself, the smugness of her head tilt, the mischief in her eyes – a girl trapped in a grown woman's body. She desperately wanted to tell Marina to stay away from him, but Mika kindly beat her to it.

"He's young even for you, Marina."

Marina huffed and crinkled her nose. "I'll have you know, if I wanted him, I'd have him."

"Perhaps, you overestimate yourself, Cousin," Salome steadied her voice. "Unlike Myridian men, Mainlanders are aware of their options."

Mika stifled a laugh. Marina's eyes narrowed. If she had a weapon in her hands, she might have challenged Salome, but Marina was not the warring type.

Marina composed herself and flashed a disingenuous smile. "Enjoy your stay in Myr. With any luck, our paths won't need to cross again." Marina stormed past them; her hands balled into fists.

Salome's gaze went from Marina's back to Mika's awaiting eyes.

"It seems I've been here a few hours and already I've offended both your mother and your sister."

"If you are about to issue an apology, don't." Mika clicked her tongue. "Marina deserved every word. And believe me, it's good for her." They pressed onward back to where her companions were waiting for her. "Now, out of curiosity, what is the mercenary to you?"

Salome was caught off guard by Mika's question and her knowledge of Adonijah's profession.

"Don't look so surprised." Mika smiled, "I've been to the Mainland before and have seen my fair share of sell-swords. So, what is he to you?"

Salome's cheeks flushed. "A hired sword." Even she did not believe the words that just spewed out of her mouth.

"Surely he is more than that." Mika kept her gaze fixed on the bronze doors ahead of them, nodding to the guards on this side of the breezeway to open them. "I saw the way you looked at him when you arrived to our shores."

Salome's breathing quickened and the tiny hairs on her arms rose. *What was Adonijah to her?* He might have started off as a sell-sword in the tavern but now he seemed to be more. He had to be more. The way she felt around him, the way he looked at her. But that didn't matter. She couldn't be distracted by him. She had a job to do and even he couldn't come before that.

The doors opened at the end of the hall and her eyes immediately met Adonijah's as he leaned against the wall smoking his pipe.

She felt a tingle surge through her body and for that moment, she wished she could read his thoughts. Mika was right. They had a connection. There was no use in denying it. But she was unsure if he felt the same way.

Mika cleared her throat, snapping Salome from her racing thoughts. "I see." Mika turned her focus to her young cousin.

"See what?" Salome refused to look Mika in the eye, afraid she would see right through her.

"Do you know if he feels the same for you?"

Salome shook her head. "Maybe it's better that way."

Once they reached the others, Mika motioned her arm down the hall to their left. "I have been instructed by Her Highness Princess Zara to show you to your rooms in the Hall of Ambassadors." Mika stated matter of fact. "Follow me."

Harbona's eyes darted to Salome, and he smiled. "Now, how did you manage that?" he whispered as they trailed behind the others.

"It's a gamble Crispin would have taken." She smiled.

Harbona nodded with a grin. "Good girl."

Salome hadn't thought about Crispin in a few days. She tried not to. But remembering his risky antics tugged at the corners of her mouth. She muttered a prayer for him under her breath and put him out of her mind. If she kept thinking of him, she would certainly break down in tears.

Mika swept her arms toward two doors on either side of the hall from each other and announced, "These will be your rooms for as long as you stay with us. You three," she spoke to the men, "will share these quarters." She pointed to the room on her left. "And this room," she looked to her right, "will be for you, Cousin. If you should need anything, do not hesitate to ask. Your ladies in waiting will make sure you have everything you need while here in Myr."

Harbona stepped forward and bowed, crossing his right arm across his chest. "You have been most generous. We thank you."

Mika nodded, "Get some rest." She walked back down the hall and once she turned the corner, Salome opened the door to her room.

Her mouth dropped once she saw her private balcony's view of the water. Clear sky, blue seas, and nothing but the horizon in the far distance. She teared up; it was the view she had dreamt of for years. And the room itself was massive.

This is bigger than our entire treehouse, she thought to herself.

White linen draperies, thick rugs, pillows of all shapes and sizes scattered around the room. It screamed luxury. Luxury was something she was not accustomed to anymore. She walked into the adjoining room and sank in the enormous bed, big enough for four people to sleep in comfortably, and exhaled a sigh of relief. She would definitely get a good night's sleep tonight.

There was a knock on her bedroom door.

"Come in." She pushed herself up from the bed to see who entered.

"I see you haven't wasted any time getting comfortable." Adonijah opened the door and peaked inside.

"Is this not the most beautiful sight you've ever laid eyes on?" She squealed in girlish delight and jumped up from the massive bed.

"One of them." He smiled and followed her as she ran past him to the balcony attached to her living and dining area.

"You have to see this view."

Adonijah joined her, but instead of admiring the view, his eyes were glued to her. "It's beautiful."

Salome closed her eyes and soaked in the sun beaming down on them, the sea breeze gently whipping the loose strands of hair around her face, the scent of salt and native flowers enveloping her. She was home. *Home.* She prayed she was home.

"Did you tell them?" Adonijah's voice snapped her back to reality.

"Tell them what?" she asked, looking over at him.

Adonijah rested his arms on the railing next to her. "About your eye."

Salome shook her head and frowned. "It didn't come up."

"Are you afraid of telling them?"

"No." She hesitated. "Maybe."

"Do you think they'll support -"

"You're asking a lot of questions," she interrupted him. Just when she finally had a moment of peace, she was dragged back to reality, back to the issue of who she was: the Hunter.

Adonijah straightened up from the railing. "Apologies, Princess. I'll be across the hall if you need anything."

He stepped inside, but she grabbed his arm. "I'm sorry," she said, "I know you mean no harm."

"You're right," he said softly. "I was asking a lot of questions; you have enough on your mind."

"I promise, you aren't what is upsetting me." Her eyes met his and she could see nothing but kindness in the brown eyes that looked back at her.

"I know." Adonijah scratched his jawline and shifted his weight. "As long as you are alright."

"I will be."

They stared at each other in silence until Adonijah said, "I should let you rest. It's been a long day." He turned to leave.

"Adonijah."

He spun around to face her. "What?" he whispered, standing close to her.

"Why did you come with us?"

"What do you mean?"

"I've been trying to figure it out since we met you at the tavern." Salome rubbed her hands together, squaring her shoulders to his. "Harbona didn't offer you any money, but you came with us anyway. Why?"

"You really want to know?" Adonijah's eyes floated from her mismatched eyes to her lips.

"Yes," she breathed softly.

Adonijah's hand glided up to her face and he gently tucked loose strands of hair behind her ear. "Outside the tavern, when I realized you were the girl who bested me in The Hollow, I couldn't come up with one good reason not to follow you wherever you went."

"Why?" she whispered, her eyes shifting toward his lips, inching closer to him.

"Because, I -"

A knock on the door halted their advance. Neither of them moved. Their faces were inches from one another. Salome's heart fluttered, she wanted him to kiss her. How she wished whoever was on the other side of the door would go away. But she would not have such luck. A second round of knocking was more deliberate.

"It might be important." Adonijah had not taken his eyes off her, though she had turned toward the door.

"It might be," she grumbled. She was resisting every urge to grab his face and slam her lips against his.

"Salome?"

"Yes?"

Adonijah started to lean closer to kiss her but stopped when a third round of knocking, followed by a gruff female voice on the other side, echoed through her chamber.

"Your Majesty, Her Royal Highness, Princess Zara, requests an audience with you. I have come to escort you."

Adonijah glanced from the door back to Salome. His hand slid from her cheek down her arm and grazed her fingertips. "You should go."

By the tone in his voice, Salome could sense his longing, and his disappointment. She nodded in agreement, although she was inwardly cursing her Aunt Zara. She reluctantly walked to her chamber doors and opened them to find two Myridian guards waiting for her.

"Your Highness." They saluted and started marching down the hall.

Salome could feel his eyes on her. She looked back at him before disappearing around the corner and saw desire in his eyes.

This had better be important, she grumbled to herself.

Odelia was right. The way Adonijah looked at her could get her into trouble.

CHAPTER 3

VILORA

Released from her shackles and given a spacious room in the White Keep with a view of the Tayborne Mountains, Vilora once again felt like royalty. For decades, she had scrimped, scrounged, and survived with only one motivation: revenge. She had been denied the life of luxury and power she was born to have by those closest to her and she swore the night she destroyed Endor, she would make them all pay.

Now a member of the queen's small council, she was able to move about the White Keep grounds as she pleased. Every morning, she would walk the royal gardens, inhaling the sweet floral and cold sea air. Vilora knew she had not earned Niabi's complete trust, but being in the queen's good graces was enough, for now.

Soon her sister's heart would be hers. A crooked smile spread across her weathered face. With Nym dead, there would only be two people left on her list.

"Any word from Myr?" Vilora poked her head in the queen's office.

Niabi did not look up from her daily correspondence. "Nothing yet."

"Do you think -"

"My orders will be obeyed?" Niabi's eyes shot up viciously. "Without question."

Vilora gave an exaggerated bow. "Forgive me, my Queen. Of course, your orders will be obeyed."

Niabi did not respond but continued to scribble with her quill. Vilora quietly walked around the room, even stopping to enjoy the queen's balcony view. Half of the view was the sea, and the other half was the Tayborne mountains. Equal parts Northern and Myridian. One land, one sea. It made sense to Vilora. Perhaps that's exactly the reason Niabi used these chambers. They weren't the chambers her father had used when he was king. Those had been sealed off and deemed off limits to everyone, including Niabi. It was as if Issachar's ghost would pop up one day to claim what was once his bedroom.

"Is there anything else?" Niabi growled impatiently.

Vilora turned to face her, arms secured behind her back. "What news of your siblings?"

Niabi took her signet ring off and stamped it into hot red wax to seal the envelopes. "My brother was last seen in Numbio, and my sister was headed to the Enchanted Swamp. We believe she was on her way to Port Daelon."

"They've split up?"

"It would appear so." Niabi reclined in her chair and crossed one leg over the other. "Clever really."

Vilora rubbed her chin, deep in thought.

"What thoughts are racing through that dusty mind of yours, Vilora?" Niabi sipped her goblet of wine with a smirk.

"Dusty mind?" Vilora snorted, furrowing her brow.

"The way you scrunch your face when you are lost in your thoughts makes it appear as if you're in pain." Niabi threw her head back and laughed. "So, what is it that plagues you, Auntie?"

Vilora did not care for the sarcastic way she said "Auntie", but knew better than to argue with the one woman who could track her down wherever she tried to hide and imprison her until she whittled down to nothing but bone and ash.

"You said your sister was seen going to the Enchanted Swamp?"

"Most Adalorians are quite superstitious." Niabi shrugged nonchalantly. "They would not have to worry about being followed on their way to Port Daelon."

"They?"

Niabi stared at the bottom of her empty glass. "She is in the company of a sell-sword and an Immortal Seer."

Vilora's eyes widened. "Harbona is with her?"

Niabi glanced up at her, her curiosity piqued. "You know Harbona?"

"It was a lifetime ago." Vilora tried to brush past her relationship with the Immortal but by the menacing glare plastered on Niabi's face, she knew she would not be so lucky. "I knew Odelia as well."

"Who is Odelia?" Niabi's left eyebrow arched.

"The Enchantress of the Swamp, of course."

Niabi leaned forward, surprise etched across her face. "She's real?"

"Very much so, my Queen." Vilora flashed a bitter smile. "And very powerful last I knew."

"You think Harbona took Salome to see her?" Now it was Niabi who sported an ugly thinking face.

"I would be shocked if he didn't." Vilora made herself comfortable on the velvet lounge in the center of the room, stretching her short legs as far as they could go and wiggling her toes in her sandals. "Harbona and Odelia are… close."

Niabi grimaced at Vilora's exposed toes on her furniture. "How close?"

"They are very much *committed* to one another."

"You sound bitter, Vilora." Niabi diverted her eyes from the old woman's feet to the peaceful view from her balcony. "I think there's more you aren't saying."

Vilora reached over to the end table and snatched a few grapes, popping them in her mouth one at a time. "I was fifteen when my mother, upon consulting with my father," she said "father" with great distaste, "summoned Harbona to seek his counsel on what could be done for me." She frowned, smacking the small fruit loudly. "My mother was weak. She *actually* loved my father; sought out his advice, she even wanted to spend time with him. It's no wonder she died well before her hair turned white. An embarrassment," she growled.

Niabi cleared her throat, demanding Vilora's attention. "If I cared to know about your mother, I would have asked."

"Apologies, my Queen." Vilora bowed again in an exaggerated fashion. "You wanted to know more about Harbona and Odelia. Well, Harbona did come to the Isles of Myr to meet with my parents. And upon meeting me, he suggested I journey with him to the Enchanted Swamp to consult Odelia. He convinced my parents that if I really wanted to change, Odelia's magic could draw my power like a poison."

"I am assuming it did not work."

Vilora shrugged and wiped the juice from her hands on her skirt, catching Niabi's disapproving eye. "I did not think anything was wrong with me. But I do remember travelling with Harbona. He was the first person who did not fear me, didn't avoid me."

Niabi stopped pouring herself another glass of Myridian wine and lightly chuckled. "You fell in love with him."

"I should have known better." Vilora leapt from her seat and paced the room, braiding her wild white hair. "Men are a weakness."

"And Odelia? Does she share your sentiments?"

Vilora flashed a hateful glare at the mention of her name. "She did her best to help me."

"Yet you hate her."

"Is it that obvious?" The witch caught herself and turned her frown into a sinister grin. "I caught them kissing – the way he looked at her – he never looked at me that way."

Vilora did not appreciate the look in Niabi's eyes. *Pity*. She despised being pitied.

"Is that when you returned home?"

Vilora nodded. "As soon as I returned, I was sent to Endor. Locked in the Tower of the Goddesses for two years. I was alone. Forgotten by everyone – abandoned by my own kin." She tossed her braid toward her back. "I swore one day, I would make them all pay. When my power was strong enough, I destroyed that pitiful island, sank it with everyone in it." Vilora poured herself a glass of wine and dropped in the seat across from Niabi. "Not a day goes by that I regret my actions. If I could do it again," her eyes raged, "I would not hesitate."

They sipped their wine in silence for a few minutes before Niabi asked, "What of this Enchantress? What magic does she possess that would aide my sister?"

"Nothing." Vilora downed what remained in her cup and set it down. "Unless used in battle."

Niabi leaned forward. "She is a weapon?"

Vilora tore a chunk of bread from the freshly baked loaf sitting with the afternoon spread and bit into it. "Rumor has it, she can control earthly elements."

Niabi pushed a cloth napkin across the table toward the witch. "Meaning…?"

"She can draw from the energy of the earth. She can summon earthquakes. Open the ground and swallow men, if not whole cities, if she feels so inclined."

Niabi tsked and waved her hand in the air. "Nonsense."

"How else could I have sunk Endor?"

The question clearly confused Niabi.

"During one of our cleansing sessions, I felt Odelia's power surge through me. I attempted to harness it, to keep some for myself."

"And it worked?" Niabi nearly screamed in shock.

"How did you know where to send your Nephilim to find me?"

Niabi raised her left dress sleeve, revealing her darkened arm. "My blood."

"Transferred power." Vilora corrected.

"Do you mean I could…?"

"Summon fire like I do?" Vilora nodded, using her sleeve to clean the crumbs from her mouth. "Yes. Have you never tried?"

Niabi stared at her arm as if she'd never seen one before. "No."

Vilora extended her hand toward the queen. "May I?"

Niabi allowed her to touch her arm and examine it.

Vilora hummed as she caressed the darkness that had spread up toward Niabi's bicep. "Unused power will consume you."

"If I use my power, my arm will heal?"

"No, my Queen. But the darkness will spread no further."

"Do you still possess Odelia's magic?"

The witch shook her head. "Sadly, I do not. The little bit of her magic that I managed to harvest, I used to destroy Endor. My magic transferred to you through blood. It is now part of you, whether you like it or not."

Niabi had that ugly thinking face again and Vilora guessed correctly what her next question would be.

"Could you drain Odelia of all her power?"

"Transference is possible if she were physically before me. But why -"

"Teach me to use my power." Niabi shoved her arm into her aunt's hands.

"That is the beauty, my Queen. All you need to do is envision how you want to use fire, and it will happen."

"Could it really be that simple?" Niabi mumbled to herself. She closed her eyes, pondered, and extended her left hand.

"Visualize it," Vilora whispered.

Niabi's eyes shot open, and a small flame appeared hovering over her hand. A smile stretched across her pleasantly surprised face. She wiggled her fingers, playing with the fire. "It doesn't feel hot."

"Flame cannot burn flame." Vilora was very pleased Niabi had so quickly embraced her power. "You are now fire."

Niabi looked at the logs in her fireplace, flicked the flame in her hand toward the hearth, and the wood ignited. She laughed in wicked delight.

Vilora smiled. "You learn quickly."

Niabi's joy vanished, and a serious expression overtook her. "Keep this between us." She marched to her desk, scribbled on a piece of paper, and sealed it with her sigil.

"As you wish, my Queen."

"Guard!" Nubis entered the queen's chamber and accepted the envelope she extended. "Take this to the Pit of Shadows and have my men set out immediately."

He bowed and left.

"You mean to have your Shadows capture the Enchantress?"

"Yes. We need her on our side."

"And if she won't cooperate?"

Niabi's eyes narrowed. "Then we will kill her after she has been drained of every drop of magic."

Vilora grinned. *Another name she could cross off her list.*

CHAPTER 4
ZOPHAR

It took four days to sift through the dark cavern to find their fallen brothers and burn their bodies. All but one: Crispin. Zophar had not eaten and had barely slept since Crispin slipped beyond his reach, claimed by the River of Lost Souls. He could still see the fear in Crispin's eyes as he let go of the rock he desperately clung to before being washed away.

Rayma told Zophar Crispin's death wasn't his fault and Heru did his best to stay positive and reminded Zophar that Crispin could have survived. But all Zophar could think about was how he was going to break the news to Salome. He had failed. Her brother was... gone.

He dragged the match he had been gnawing on across his chest and lit his long stem pipe. The first time Crispin saw him light a match that way, his jaw dropped. He thought Zophar was magical. He was six at the time, so Zophar cheerfully played along.

"I can teach you, if you like," Zophar smiled at the wide-eyed prince.

"Really?" Crispin nearly jumped out of his seat.

"Aye." Zophar nodded.

Crispin hesitated, a frown replaced the smile on his face. "Can you teach me how to kill?"

Zophar bit down on his pipe. "Why do you want me to teach you to kill?"

Zophar already knew the answer. They had only been in the Tree House Forest for a month after escaping the Green-Eyed Raven's invasion of Northwind. The battle was fresh and the wounds they bore would take a long time to heal; if they ever did.

"So, I can go back home." Crispin's teary eyes met Zophar's.

Those words haunted him.

The next day, he put weapons in the hands of two children, who without training, would more than likely die by the sword, or worse, if they were ever found by their enemies. He trained them. At first, the idea was for them to be able to defend themselves, if needed, but after several years, it turned into molding them into proper soldiers. And he knew one day, his soldiers would become generals. Northwind would be theirs' for the taking.

The rushing waters of the River of Lost Souls brought him back. Back to this lonely nightmare. The boy who could have been king, could have made it home, was gone. And Zophar never told him how much he loved him. Not just as his prince – not just as his pupil – but as a son.

Zophar had lost both of his sons, years before he met Crispin, and felt he had been given another chance to be there in a fatherly way. But he failed. Again.

The worst part of losing Crispin the way he did was he would never be able to say goodbye. He would not be sending him to the Almighty with a proper burial. The Caverns of the Undead seemed a little bit brighter with Crispin leading them. Now, it was exactly as it appeared: cold, dark, and lonely.

Zophar glanced over to the center of their encampment and spotted Heru and Rayma in what appeared to be a heated discussion. Of course, every conversation with Rayma seemed to end up that way. If by the grace of the Almighty they made it out of the caverns alive and reunited with Salome, he had a feeling the two, strongly opinionated women wouldn't get along.

The Westerner pulled himself up from the gravelly embankment and hobbled toward Heru and Rayma. Getting older brought about its benefits and challenges. In growing older, he gained wisdom and experience. But growing older also gifted him with crow's feet and bad knees. It was his right knee that seemed to flare up every so often and would cause him to limp around like a cripple. After seeing battle for the first time in over a decade, his knees were screaming.

Crispin was always the first to make a snarky remark about him shuffling around their tree house and Zophar would click his teeth in response.

"Another day older," Crispin would laugh.

"Another day wiser," Zophar would counter.

Zophar joined Heru and Rayma, muttering Western curses at his uncooperative knees. "What seems to be the trouble, Prince Heru?"

Heru broke his intense glare at Rayma and softened his brow. "Trouble, Zophar?"

"By your expression," Zophar frowned, "you seemed upset."

Heru's eyes shifted to Rayma and back to the burly Westerner. "Rayma and I were discussing what our next course of action will be."

"And what *is* our next move?"

Before Rayma could answer Zophar's question, Heru said, "We are going to honor our allegiance. We will make our way through the caverns and continue to Oakenshire to meet up with Princess Salome."

Rayma frowned; arms folded across her chest. "We should return to Numbio. We do not know what else lingers in the darkness. What if we are captured? What if we wander into their hive? What if we never make it out at all?"

"As I have already said," Heru's voice was steady, but his irritation was not hidden. "Your concerns are valid, but my decision is final."

"With all due respect, my Prince," Rayma popped her hip and spoke through gritted teeth. "Prince Crispin is…gone." She avoided looking at Zophar. "Your duty is to protect the Numbio -"

"I know my duty, Rayma," Heru barked. "My word does not become void because Crispin is gone. As long as Salome lives, so does our allegiance. Crispin -"

"Is dead!" Her voiced echoed through the cavern, drawing the attention of the Numbio warriors around camp. "Why do we continue to fight a dead man's war?"

The finality of her words pierced Zophar's heart. For as strong as he was, he found it hard to hide the tears that welled in his graying blue eyes.

Heru was fuming but took a moment before speaking, knowing his soldiers' eyes and ears were now fixed on him. "Forgive Rayma's wicked tongue and lack of honor, Zophar." He glared at her while he addressed Zophar. "She does not speak for the Numbio."

Rayma opened her mouth to spit her rebuttal, but instead, pursed her lips, bowed, and walked away.

"Forgive me, Prince Heru," Zophar whispered, "but she has a valid point."

Heru focused on Zophar once he ensured his men were no longer watching or listening to their conversation. "Thank you for your honesty, but the Numbio made a promise – a commitment to our Northern brethren – and we intend to honor that allegiance."

"But Crispin is…" Zophar did not have the strength or courage to finish that statement.

Heru rested his hand on Zophar's broad shoulder. "Northern law states a female heir can rule the North, yes?"

"Aye."

"Then Salome will sit on the White Throne. I will make sure of it." He patted Zophar's back and motioned to the tents being torn down. "I have already given the order to pack up and to move onward. I suggest you ready yourself, Captain." Heru sighed and rubbed the back of his neck. "I will depend on you to help me lead my warriors out of this darkness."

Zophar crossed his arm across his chest. "I will serve as needed."

After the caravan had packed their belongings onto the only cart that hadn't been destroyed by the sandstorm and run in with the Wagura, they moved as quietly as they could through the snaking cavern tunnels. They were not eager nor prepared to face another swarm of Wagura. But the further they travelled, the darker it seemed to become. The Numbio were not accustomed to darkness. Living in the Sand Lands, they were used to sunny days, warm weather, and cloudless skies. Down in these caverns, it was not only pitch-black darkness, but also damp and cold. The faster they found a way out and back to the surface, the better.

Zophar walked silently by Midnight, his black stallion, and strummed his nose to ease both of their nerves. Crispin's chestnut horse, Freya, trotted alongside them. *She knows,* Zophar thought, noticing the mare's downcast head and slow gait. He was cautious to reach his hand out to pet her. She was known to be a biter, except with Crispin.

When the time had come for Crispin and Salome to have horses of their own, Zophar took them to a farm north of Gomorrah where they picked their mounts. Salome was immediately drawn to her white mare, Snow, and from that moment on, they were inseparable. But Crispin's eye caught sight of Freya.

"She's not worth the trouble." The farmer snorted and spat on the ground. He pulled the

waistband of his trousers away from his belly to give himself a little breathing room. "That one is stubborn as hell."

Crispin smiled. "I want her."

The farmer furrowed his brow and shook his head. "I'm telling you, son, she is the worst horse you could pick. She bites anyone who approaches her. Watch." He walked toward the mare with wildness in her skittish brown eyes, stretched his hand toward her and was instantly met with the click of her teeth. "Told you." The farmer shrugged. "She's not worth it. Best to forget about her."

Crispin gently stepped up to the horse, maintaining eye contact with her, and holding his hands up by his eyes to show he meant her no harm. She stomped a hoof as a warning, but Crispin steadily pressed onward. He smiled. "You are beautiful."

"The horse doesn't understand these things." The farmer's hands flailed around with each word he spoke. He turned to Zophar and Salome who were behind him. "Is the boy crazy? The Almighty gave him ears, yet he does not listen."

Salome stifled a chuckle. Zophar kept his gaze fixed on Crispin.

"My name is Crispin," he slowly lowered his hand in front of her nose. "If it's alright with you, I'd like to take you home with me."

Her eyes shifted but she did not attempt to bite.

"I promise to take care of you. To treat you with respect. To protect you." Crispin gambled with his fingers and rested them on top of the white snip of her snout. "I know what it feels like to be forgotten."

"She does not bite him?" The farmer scratched his protruding belly, clearly taken aback by the horse's unexpected demeanor.

Crispin placed his forehead against hers and stroked her neck. "Let's go home, Freya."

"The boy," the farmer clapped his hands together with a wide set grin, "he is magic."

Zophar knew Freya needed comfort. Mustering every bit of courage left in his weary body, he exhaled, squeezed his eyes shut, then plunged his hand toward Freya's neck and stroked her mane. His eyes popped open when he realized all five of his fingers were still intact and that Freya had accepted his small offering of kindness.

"I miss him too," Zophar whispered in her ear.

"You are good with animals." Rayma startled him with a low whisper.

"Not normally."

"She misses her master."

"Aye," he nodded and patted Freya again. "She does."

Rayma was quiet for a moment then said, "Forgive me, Zophar. My outburst before… I was… I just want my people…"

"There is no need to apologize," he saved her from stumbling over her words. "I, too, was once in a position to advise my king." Her eyes met the ground. "You and Prince Heru are close, I gather?"

"I serve the Royal Family," she huffed, rattled by the insinuation.

"Of course," Zophar cleared his throat. "I meant no offense."

They walked their horses in silence until Rayma couldn't help but ask, "Did he say anything about me?"

"No," Zophar shook his head and brushed his bushy red beard with his sausage thick fingers. "But I am not blind, milady. I see how you two interact with each other." His smile quickly faded. "You two remind me of another couple I once knew."

"May I ask who?"

"My best friend, Lykos…"

"That name sounds familiar," she picked up when he trailed off.

"He was Crispin's oldest brother. When he met Lavena, everything changed."

"What do you mean, everything changed?" Her eyes widened. "Changed in a good way or … changed in a bad way?"

Zophar smiled fondly thinking of his friends. It seemed like a lifetime ago when he wandered the halls of the White Keep with Lykos and Lavena.

"King Issachar instructed Lykos to meet the new ambassador from Caelestis at the Harbor and escort them to the White Keep -"

"Caelestis?" Rayma interrupted him with a childlike grin. "The Immortals?"

Zophar nodded, "Aye."

"You've seen them? Up close? Do they really glow?" She rattled off her questions without taking a breath.

Zophar remembered when he first saw an Immortal. It was Harbona. But he didn't have the Immortal glow. He lost his aura when he was banished from his homeland.

"The Immortals have an aura," Zophar recounted how Harbona explained it years ago. "It is a glow of sorts. But they don't light up a dark room by any means."

"Was she on the ship?" she asked, more interested in the romance than the aura. Zophar realized then, beyond the tough exterior and serious expression that was always plastered on her face, she was a romantic at heart.

Zophar smiled. "Aye, she was. Lykos' heart was not interested in the political games the royals and their ambassadors played to his father's dismay. But King Issachar insisted if he was going to be king after him, he would have to learn to play the game of politics. Lykos dragged me with him anytime his father sent him on a mission, especially when it was a boring assignment. Meeting the new ambassador was one of those boring assignments, but we waited as the Immortals white ship docked. We fully expected to see another male elder disembark, but we were both shocked when Lavena led her entourage down the ramp."

"She must have been beautiful."

"Lykos was speechless, which was a feat in itself," Zophar chuckled. "Lavena seemed to float toward us. I still remember she was wearing a white robe and hood, her long platinum blonde hair cascading in front of her, and her gray eyes fixated on Lykos. They saw one another and just knew they had found the one they had spent a lifetime searching for." Zophar cleared his throat and sipped from his water canteen.

"What happened after that?" Rayma pushed him to finish the story.

"After meeting on the docks, they spent every minute they could secretly steal with one another."

"Secretly?" Rayma furrowed her brow. "Why secretly?"

"King Issachar was determined to marry Lykos to a woman of his choosing, to further the strength and power of Northwind. If I remember correctly, Lykos was supposed to marry Princess Anka of Sakurai."

"And Lavena?" Rayma looked at the ground.

"When Issachar discovered their love for one another, he ordered Lavena to return to Caelestis. He would never allow her to be the next Queen of Northwind."

"Well," she tried to wait for him to finish, but he was taking too long. "What happened to them?"

Zophar's voice cracked, "Uh, they..."

"Oh."

"Niabi invaded Northwind the night Lavena's ship set sail. Lykos made sure she was on the boat before the city was overrun. Before he ... died."

"What happened to Lavena?"

"I haven't seen her since."

Zophar didn't realize when he first started telling her about Lykos and Lavena, that it would be so traumatic for him. He felt like he was reliving every moment. He saw their smiling faces. He saw their love grow in secret, with him being their only help and confidant. He saw them on the dock the first day they met, and he saw them on the dock the night they parted.

"The point of the story is," Zophar forced himself to continue, "when Lavena and Lykos met, everything changed for the better."

Rayma bit her lip and looked ahead of them at Heru. "Better."

Zophar noticed who she was staring at nodded his head. "I pray your story does not end the way theirs did."

"Me too." She glanced back at Zophar. "Thank you."

"For what?"

"Sharing their story with me," she smiled. It was an odd sight for Zophar to see her smile. It wasn't something she did often. At least, around him. "Do you think you'll ever see Lavena again?"

"The Almighty willing, I might."

An eerie and unfamiliar sound echoed through the cavern and sent shivers up Zophar's spine.

"What was that?" Zophar stopped, his eyes scanning the darkness.

The group halted when Heru lifted his hand in the air. They stood in silence and listened.

Was that...breathing? A raspy, heavy growl?

Heru motioned one of the Numbio armed with a firelit torch in one hand and a sword in the other, to step toward the noise in the darkness. The soldier obediently did so with trepidation. Everyone held their breath, hoping it would turn out to be nothing but their wild and weary imagination. As the warrior made his way up the rocky incline, he stretched his torch forward and was met by the growling, jagged rows of blood-stained teeth of a Wagura. The beast howled a deep, guttural sound.

Fear struck Zophar like a knife to the heart when he heard more Wagura echo the battle cry. They had walked into a trap. They were surrounded.

"To arms! To arms!" Heru commanded, unsheathing his own sword.

Swords clashed as the Numbio and Wagura once again faced off. Before the Wagura launched their assault near Zophar's location, he grabbed Rayma's hand and pushed her under their only cart.

"You must stay hidden."

Rayma started to protest, "But -"

"Rayma," he interrupted forcefully. "No matter what happens to us, do not come out until this is over. You must get out of these caverns."

"Zophar -"

Long, bony fingers came into view, grabbed Zophar's shoulder, and dragged him deep into the darkness.

CHAPTER 5
NUBIS

Nubis sat in the circular office beneath *The Whispering Fox* waiting for the other members to arrive for their meeting. Ziggy normally beat all of them to these sit downs, but she was still missing. His heart ached at the thought of her being caught and tortured for being a spy. Gershom was known for his cruelty – Ziggy was not the first working girl to be in his bed and not seen again. Whenever Ziggy was with The Bear, Nubis didn't sleep.

When he first arrived to serve Oden, she was the first person to welcome him. She showed him around the city when she wasn't working, and they became fast friends. He was often homesick for the Stormcrag way of life but being in Ziggy's company was calming.

He knew from the beginning Ziggy was working her way to being Gershom's call girl, but he didn't realize how much it would sting when Oden helped secure her place in his bed. Not only was it dangerous, but she was with a man other than him.

Of course, he and Ziggy weren't romantically involved, but to him, there was no one that could compare to her. She was feisty, fearless, and her smile warmed the very depths of his soul.

His eyes kept glimpsing the entrance, hoping to see her fiery red curls bounce as she pranced in and sank into her favorite red velvet, high back chair.

Nubis heard footsteps coming down the stairs from the tavern and he stood, expecting to see her, but it was just Makeda. His smile faded and he sank into his seat, a simple wooden chair that no one else wanted.

"Don't look too pleased to see me," Makeda teased and dropped into a plush leather chair large enough for two people to share. She sat cross-legged and pulled her hip long braids to one side of her body.

"I'm sorry," Nubis cleared his throat, "I was just expecting…"

"A bubbly red head?" She flashed a pearly white grin.

He smiled, crinkling the corners of his hazel eyes. "Is it that obvious?"

"Absolutely," she nodded. "But as far as I know, she doesn't know how you feel."

"And Oden?"

"Oden knows everything, Nubis." She arched her eyebrows.

Makeda was right about Oden. He did seem to have the answers to every question. And if he didn't, he would find out. Knowledge was power. At least, that's what Oden always rambled on about as he formulated plans and planted the members of the Order in positions to learn what he needed to know to further the rebellion.

As if summoned by the mere mention of his name, Oden marched into the room with Ziggy following closely behind. Nubis exhaled a sigh of relief and allowed himself to relax in his seat.

Oden pulled his leather chair from behind his desk and sat down. Papers, maps, and empty glasses were strewn across the table. As organized as Oden's mind was, his workspace was the exact opposite. Without Makeda running the tavern upstairs, Oden's cover would have been blown years ago.

Although only four of them sat in the room for the meeting, there were a couple other members in the Order, but Makeda, Ziggy, and Nubis weren't privy to knowing who they were. All Oden would tell them was that they were in positions of power, and they would reveal themselves when the time was right.

"Brothers," Oden called the meeting to order. "I have just returned from consulting with the Sovereign of The Sisters, and I now know what we must do to further our agenda. To find the Hunter, we must find Issachar's children."

"And how do we do that?" Nubis crossed his muscular arms across his enormous chest.

"By going where they would go." Oden laid a map of Adalore in front of them. "If I were them. I would go where I knew I had kin."

Ziggy leaned forward and pointed, "The Isles of Myr."

"Precisely." Oden flashed an impish grin. "I have already sent word to our brothers to be on the lookout for Crispin or Salome."

"Are these the phantom brothers who are in positions of power?" Nubis ran fingers across his dark beard.

"They may not be here in person," Oden shot him a glance, "but they are doing their part in our fight."

"Forgive me, Oden," Ziggy cut through the tension with her sweet voice, "but do we have brothers in Myr?"

"We have brothers scattered all across Adalore." Oden didn't answer the question. "We also have brothers who will have a good chance of finding one, if not both of Issachar's children. We are a step closer to the Hunter. A step closer to ending this stain in our history." Oden placed his elbows on the tabletop and splayed his fingers together in front of his face. "Now, what news, brothers?"

Ziggy started. "The queen had me brought to her in the dungeons."

Nubis' heart nearly climbed out of his throat. "What?"

"What business?" Oden remained focused.

"She wants me to relay information to her about Gershom since I have access to him."

"She wants you to spy on him?" Nubis rubbed the back of his head, trying to hide his anxiety.

"What a blessed day!" Oden clapped his hands together and leaned back in his seat with a smile. "Good work, Ziggy."

"You don't think this is too risky?" Nubis cut in. "She is already jeopardizing her life by spying on Gershom for us. Now she is supposed to spy on Niabi and for her?"

"No risk, no victory," Oden said.

"That is your response?" Nubis scooted to the edge of his seat, his hands firmly placed on his knees. "At any moment, one of us could be found out and be executed or worse, tortured to death, and you don't seem to care."

"Everyone in this room knew the risks of joining the Order." Oden's tone remained calm, though his eyes burned with fury.

"We all owed you a life debt and came to serve you -"

"Do you not believe in our cause, Nubis?" Oden shot.

"Of course, I do," Nubis huffed. "But I don't see the point in us risking our lives more than we ought."

"Perhaps you care too much for Ziggy and it clouds your mind, Nubis." Oden glanced at the blushing red head.

"Better to care too much than not at all," Nubis countered.

Oden slammed his hands on the desk and jumped to his feet. "Is that a challenge to my leadership?"

Ziggy reached over and rested her scarred hand on Nubis' arm. "No, Oden, it's not."

"Good." Oden growled, still eyeing Nubis. "What other business?" He slowly sat back down.

Ziggy squeezed Nubis' arm reminding him he was the next to give report. "The queen has made some sort of deal with the Old Witch of Endor and has dispatched her Shadows to track down some enchantress."

Makeda perked up at the mention of an enchantress. "Which enchantress?"

Nubis shrugged. "The swamps, I think."

"Why?" she pressed.

"For her magic."

Oden narrowed his eyes at his assistant. "Is this of personal interest to you, Makeda?"

She shrank back in her seat which struck Nubis as odd. Makeda was not one to shy away from expressing her opinion.

"I was just curious about what the queen would need her for," Makeda answered.

"The Old Witch of Endor isn't real, is she?" Ziggy asked with an audible gulp. "I thought she was just a character in sad ballads."

Nubis shook his head. "She is the one the queen met in the dungeons – the one she sent her Nephilim to find. She now sits on the queen's small council."

"Which begs the question, why?" Oden rubbed his chin.

"I heard the queen refer to the witch as Vilora, her aunt."

"Her aunt?" Ziggy spat, shooting him a sideways glance.

Nubis shifted in his seat. "And that's not all, I'm afraid."

"How much worse can it get?" Ziggy rubbed her forehead so hard Nubis thought she would scrape her freckles clean off her face.

Nubis cleared his throat and resisted the urge to reach for Ziggy's hand to comfort her. "It seems the queen somehow… has powers."

Oden leaned over his desk. "Powers? What do you mean powers?"

"Fire."

"What?" Oden's eyes widened.

"She can conjure fire," Nubis explained.

"How is that possible?" Ziggy interjected.

"Somehow the witch's power is in the queen's blood. She didn't know she even possessed it, until today."

"Did you see her use fire?" Oden walked around his desk and sat on the edge closest to Nubis.

"No, but I could hear them discussing it on the other side of her door."

"That's why the witch wants the Enchantress of the Swamp," Makeda finally spoke again, twirling one of her braids nervously in her fingers.

Oden's attention was now fully directed toward her. "Share."

"They intend to drain the enchantress of her power and harvest it for themselves," Makeda explained.

"Harvesting powers?" Ziggy brought her legs to her chest. "How is that even possible?"

"Powers can be transferred to another through blood. A small dose of transference means you have a little bit of their power. Drain all their blood…"

"You harvest all of their power," Oden finished Makeda's sentence.

"But Niabi didn't take the witch's blood. Did she?" Ziggy posed the question to Nubis, who knew about as much as they did.

"I am not sure," he tapped his feet on the floor. "But if I heard them correctly, the queen's left arm is where she possesses power. They have a history. Maybe the witch gave her some power years ago."

"We must keep our eyes and ears open." Oden paced in front of his desk as the others watched him carefully. "If Niabi gains powerful magic…"

"We might need a different strategy to defeat her." Ziggy rolled her shoulders back and sighed.

"We will deal with that in due time," Oden said.

"We should send a word of warning to the Enchantress of the Swamp that a company of Shadows is headed her way," Makeda placed her feet on the floor and rested her elbows on her knees.

"And why would we do that?" Oden stood in front of her, arms clasped behind his back.

"Like I said," Makeda glanced up at him, "to warn her."

"No one knows where to find her. No one knows if she's actually real," Oden countered.

"The witch seems confident she's real." Makeda gritted her teeth.

Nubis stared at her. She was acting very odd tonight. What could be setting her off?

"Then let them chase fairy stories. We keep our focus on the queen and her witch." Oden had made his decision and started walking toward his private quarters.

Makeda jumped up, "Oden -"

"That is my decision." Oden snapped back. "Be watchful for the night is long and a storm is coming." He disappeared into his room, ending their meeting.

Nubis and Ziggy stood at the same time, and he looked down at her. He saw panic in her eyes, but she averted her gaze.

"Are you alright?" Nubis rubbed her petite shoulder with his massive hand.

The anxiety that riddled her face a moment ago was gone. She was very good at hiding her fears and emotions. She would have to be, in order to be the great spy that she was.

"Oh, Nubis, I'll be alright. I always am." She smiled up at him and gently patted his hand.

"You know how I feel about you being with him."

"I know," she stroked his cheek. "But he means nothing to me. He's just the assignment."

"If you weren't involved with him, would you …"

What was he doing? He thought to himself. He couldn't ask a working girl if she would give up her livelihood to live a nomadic life with him. She was a city girl, used to the finer things in life. Those luxuries she enjoyed were paid for by her clients. He had nothing to offer her. He was a Stormcrag. And once the rebellion was successful in dethroning Niabi and Gershom from the kingdom, he was confident he would return to his people in the Bone Mountains.

But what if he asked her to join him? Would she say yes?

"Would I what?" Ziggy's melodic voice cut through his thoughts.

"What?"

"You said, if I weren't involved with him, would I, and then you stopped. What were you going to say?"

Those blue eyes of hers. So alive. If she would but utter the word, he would give up everything he ever wanted just to make her happy. Just to have *her*.

"If you weren't involved with him, would you…" he took a deep breath, "would you leave the profession?"

That wasn't what he wanted to ask her. He wanted to ask if she would be with him instead, but of course, he couldn't brave the question. Couldn't brave the rejection.

She smiled warmly at him, as if she knew that wasn't what he intended to ask her, but sweetly answered, "No. I'm marked and once a girl has been marked, there's no respectable man who would want her to be the mother of his children."

The mark she was referring to was the tiny black rose tattooed above her heart. It forever branded working girls and she was right, respectable men wouldn't marry a woman like her, but they didn't have a problem sleeping with them in secret.

"A respectable man wouldn't let something as simple as a mark keep him from treating you right."

Ziggy wrapped her arms around Nubis' waist and rested the side of her face against his chest. "Oh, Nubis, you are one of the good ones."

He squeezed her as tightly as he dared, "Ziggy, I …"

"Yes, Nubis?"

"I…" He looked up and scanned the room. Makeda had vanished. Where had she gone? She was acting so strangely. He hoped she was alright, but he knew not to ask Makeda questions. She would say the same thing to everyone who tried to get to know her. *What's my business is my business.*

"Nubis?"

Nubis glanced down at the beautiful, freckled face that stared back up at him. "Promise me you will be careful when you're around Gershom."

She patted his chest. "Don't worry about me, handsome. I've got my back."

Although her words sounded confident, her eyes told him an entirely different story. She released him from their embrace.

"I should get going." She scrunched her curls in her dainty fingers.

"Let me guess," Nubis pressed his hands into his pockets, "you don't need me to walk with you."

"Goodnight, Nubis," she stood on her tip toes and pecked him quickly on the cheek. She wrapped her silky, green shawl over her shoulders, an expensive gift from one of her clients no doubt and slipped out the door. She was so light on her feet; he didn't even hear her walk up the stairs.

He touched the spot where she had kissed him. He would continue to do everything in his power to protect her and in due time, he would save her from this city filled with cruel men.

CHAPTER 6

SALOME

Salome's mind was racing as she followed the two guards down the corridors that led back to the Inner Depths where she first met her Aunt Zara. She didn't expect to see her aunt again so soon and couldn't help but wonder why she had been summoned.

I bet its Marina's fault, she thought to herself; her cousin's smug face flashed before her eyes.

The expression of utter disgust was evident on her face, and it did not go unnoticed by the soldiers posted outside the bronze doors that opened to the Inner Depths. There was no need to walk over the threshold with a sour look, so she relaxed her grimace.

Her aunt sat on the throne and was gripping the armrests tightly. Zara's eyes were as equally calm as they were wild. By her side, still dressed in red armor, was her daughter, Mika, who whispered something in her mother's ear.

Flat disks suspended around the intimate room hosted flames that lit the space. The first time Salome had been inside the windowless throne room, she failed to notice the five statues intricately carved into the walls. Her eyes bounced from one statue to the next, taking in their beauty. Each was carved in the likeness of the same woman, the only feature distinguishing one from the other was the type of bird perched on her shoulders.

She was amazed she knew who they were. Being in Myr somehow helped jog her memory of everything her mother had taught her about her homeland. These women were the Five Virtues. Wisdom was the first statue to her left, an owl on her right shoulder. Next came Strength with her eagle. Dead center was Love with her dove. Swinging around the right side of the circular room was Honor and her crane. Last, directly to Salome's right, was Rebirth with her dark eyed raven.

"Salome."

It sounded like the statues whispered her name. But that was impossible. She squinted her eyes, watching them closely.

"We've been waiting for you."

Their mouths did not move but she knew they were talking to her. How was that possible?

We've been waiting for you. What did that even mean?

Zara cleared the back of her throat, returning Salome to the present situation at hand. She tore her eyes from the Virtues and bowed before her aunt.

"I hope you find your accommodations satisfying, Niece."

"Most generous," Salome nodded, "but I assume that's not the reason you called me here tonight."

"How very intuitive of you." Zara extended her hand to her daughter, Mika, and grabbed two papers from her. "Actually," Zara held the wanted posters of Salome and Crispin up for her to see, "I summoned you here to see if you could explain this."

Salome froze. Tight-lipped, she exhaled slowly. There was no telling how much Zara knew about the posters, about the trouble she had escaped in the Mainland, but there was no reason to hide it. The Myrdians were a well-informed people. It would only be a matter of time before her truths would be public knowledge.

Salome shrugged, trying her best to appear nonchalant. "At least it's a flattering rendering."

"You don't deny this is you?" Zara's eyebrow arched.

"That would be a waste of my time and yours. Clearly, that is me." Salome admitted, relaxing her shoulders. It felt good telling the truth. Now to see what the truth would cost her.

"You are wanted for murdering Shadows of Nor -"

"Shadows who tore through our community and slit a ten-year-old boy's throat," Salome interrupted with a snarl.

"And why would the Shadows terrorize your peasant community?"

"They were looking for m... for someone."

"Who were they looking for?" Zara leaned forward; her attention piqued.

Salome took a deep breath. Harbona didn't instruct her not to tell her aunt who she really was, but it was still a title she didn't quite believe. When Adonijah figured it out, she felt cornered, trapped, vulnerable. Now she had a choice. She could tell Zara about her mark and the real reason the Shadows were in her village, or she could lie. But if Zara were anything like her mother, Bilhah, she would not fall for the deceit.

"Who were they looking for?" Zara repeated herself.

Moment of truth. "They were looking for... me."

"And your brother."

"Not Crispin." Salome raised her head high, her fingers intertwined in front of her. "Just me."

"I don't understand." Zara handed the wanted posters back to Mika. "Why just you? Crispin is Issachar's last living son."

"They weren't looking for Issachar's children. They were looking for..." Panic began to set in. She felt her heart beating faster and her breath quickening. She remembered being a child running around the Royal Gardens with her brothers, Mosgalath, Elias, and Crispin. She remembered them making fun of her eye. They thought something was wrong with her; that she might be cursed.

As if she was sent to save Salome from drowning in her own anxiety, Damaris stepped forward from the shadows. "Tell them, Salome."

Salome spun her head toward Damaris. "Who are you?"

"I am Damaris, the Oracle of Myr." She bowed her head.

"You're my mother's youngest sister." Salome put the pieces together.

Damaris smiled and the corners of her green eyes crinkled. "You are safe here, Salome, tell them who you are."

Salome couldn't stop staring at her Aunt Damaris. Her mind was running wild. She felt like prey and wished Damaris could hear her thoughts. *"I don't think I can."*

Damaris tilted her head and responded to Salome's thoughts with her own. *"It is time you are honest about who you are."*

"Wait!" Salome's eyes widened. *"You know what I'm thinking?"*

Damaris stared at her intently. *"Yes."*

"How?"

Zara cleared her throat startling Salome. Her Aunt Zara's nostrils flared, clearly irritated by the wait.

"It's alright, Salome." Damaris' thoughts sliced through her own. *"Tell them who you are."*

"What if they don't believe me?"

"It is not them you need to be honest with. It is yourself." Damaris reached for Salome's fingers and gently squeezed them. Her green eyes were kind, like Bilhah's.

Zara impatiently tapped her long fingers on the cypress armrests of the throne. "Well?" She finally had Salome's attention. "Why were the Shadows only looking for you?"

Salome turned to Damaris who nodded reassuringly. She took a deep breath and admitted, "They were looking for the Hunter."

"The Hunter?" Zara spat, her brows knitted together.

"Yes."

Zara's eyes narrowed, "Are you saying that you are the Hunter?"

Now was her moment to be honest with herself. To admit what she still didn't quite believe. "I am the Hunter."

"There has never been a female Hunter." Zara crossed one leg over the other and lifted her chin.

"Until now," Salome squared her shoulders to Zara's throne.

"Adalore has not seen a Hunter in over two hundred years." Zara waved her hand dismissively.

"I suppose it was time for one." Damaris clasped her hands behind her back, drawing her older sister's wrathful eye.

"And how do we know she is who she says she is?" Zara asked what most sane people would. Salome knew her question was valid and yet, she felt the sting of her unbelief.

"I knew as soon as she entered the room, she was the Hunter, Zara." Damaris' voice was gentle and seemed to soothe her sister.

"It is well known every Hunter bears the sacred mark... do you?" Zara motioned for Salome to prove herself.

Salome indignantly pointed to her left eye. The one thing she spent years hiding was now what she had to showcase, if she wanted anyone to believe she was the Hunter. "See for yourself."

Zara motioned with her head for Damaris to confirm. Damaris placed her hands on Salome's cheeks and stared into her eyes. It was certainly uncomfortable, but seeing the warm smile stretch across Damaris' face once she saw the mark, was worth it.

"We've been waiting for you," Damaris said, the golden, tentacle crown weaved through her black hair sparkled under the flame disks suspended in the room.

Salome's eyes widened. That was what the Virtues had said when she first entered the room. Damaris winked and tilted her head back toward Zara who had stood from her seated position, grabbed her spear, and marched down the steps to be at eye level with them.

"With this new information, your bounty should be higher."

Salome left most of her weapons in her quarters, but she still had a knife strapped to her thigh and a small dagger hidden in her boot. With her fingers twitching in anticipation of an attack, she was prepared to defend herself.

Zara stopped a foot shy of Salome, handed her spear to Mika, and smirked as she ripped the wanted posters in half. "It is a shame no one will be collecting it. You will need protection."

Salome breathed a sigh of relief, the tension leaving her battle-ready shoulders. "I have protection."

Zara shook her head, displeased. "Do not rely on men, Salome. Rely on yourself. You must learn to be the greatest weapon and your strongest protector. Your training begins tomorrow."

"Training?" Salome snorted, hands on her hips. "Training for what?"

"To become a Qata Vishna," Zara stated, matter of fact. "What other training could there be?" She retrieved her spear from Mika and tapped the tiled floor, the echo silenced everyone. "Mika will meet you at the docks at sun-up. It is time to embrace your destiny."

CHAPTER 7
RAYMA

Rayma hid underneath the cart like Zophar instructed. Terrified, and in total darkness, she lost all track of time. She commanded her body to crawl to search for a torch, but her body disobeyed. It felt like she was paralyzed; her limbs were numb from the cold, damp cavern ground and the darkness was so thick, she felt she could taste it.

As frozen and lifeless as her body was, her mind had been racing since their company was attacked by the Wagura.

I warned them.

I warned them.

They refused to listen.

I warned them.

Why did they not listen?

I warned them.

This isn't my fault.

I warned them.

The first time she had heard about the Caverns of the Undead and its horrifying inhabitants, she was no more than seven years old.

Bast was the only man to escape the Wagura. When he tried to warn the Numbio of the horrors of the caverns, everyone made fun of him, called him names, and refused to pay him any mind. Her people dubbed him "The Madman". But to her, he was just *Papa*.

When he returned from the caverns, she did not recognize him. He had been gone for almost a year; she and her family believed he had died with his troop who disappeared in the desert. She was ashamed to admit she was frightened of him. His unkempt hair, his matted beard, his shifting eyes, the scars along his arms and legs. But nothing scared her more than the night terrors. He would scream, convulse, sweat, and fight anyone that attempted to touch him.

She and her brother, Inaros, avoided him. Their mother did her best to bring him back to the living. She fought to heal his mind and to mend his body, but it was a hopeless endeavor. Bast was gone. To save her children from being branded untouchable and unwedable, she divorced Bast and put him out of the house they had built together.

How could Rayma ever become the best healer in Numbio with a madman for a father?

How could Inaros find a suitable wife from a good family if he came from an unworthy one?

Rayma was ten when her papa's body was found in a deserted alley – his neck broken. Suicide? Murder? A mercy killing? She would never know – she never wanted to know.

A month after Rayma celebrated her eleventh name day, her mother died.

"Broken heart," the Healer had said.

Broken for a long time in Rayma's estimation. Her mother crumbled the day they thought Bast had died in the desert. But putting Bast out of their lives to save their children's reputation – she never recovered. Rayma was convinced her mother's grief for losing her husband in more ways than one, was what took her in the end.

Had their parents not left them a small inheritance, Rayma and Inaros would have been out on the street, begging for a meal and place to sleep. But as luck would have it, or misfortune depending on who you asked, Rayma and her older brother Inaros were taken in by a man of means when their funds ran out. He sent Rayma to the best apothecary school when she was twelve and had Inaros learn politics, diplomacy, and business with him.

For the first couple of years, everything was great. They were well-fed, housed, clothed in the finest linens, and were receiving the finest educations money could buy. But once they were comfortable, things changed. In the beginning, they were told to refer to the man who saved them as Uncle, but that turned into Master overnight.

The Master never beat them. But the kindness he had shown them had run dry, and they were now expected to do his bidding, to pay off their debt to him.

But late one night, Inaros shook her awake and said they had to leave. He had stolen something from their Master. He said the Master was evil. That he had to be stopped before it was too late.

But Rayma was too afraid to move – too afraid to speak. Inaros looked crazed, just like their father. Inaros tried clawing her out of bed, but she dug her fingers into the sheets and refused to believe they were in any danger.

"Please, Rayma, please."

Those were the last words she heard him say before he leapt from her window and made a run for it – a small black book tucked under his arm.

Even after her brother had been gone for several minutes, she still clung to her sheets in a stunned stupor. That was how Lord Memucan found her when his guards kicked in her bedroom door.

"Where is he, girl?" Memucan smacked her across the face, drawing blood.

"I…I…"

"I…I…" he mimicked, furiously shaking her by her shoulders. "Where is your brother? He stole from me, and he will be punished."

"Please don't punish him, Master!" she wailed, clutching his robes.

He patted her head gently, the first kind physical gesture he had shown her in quite some time. "Tell me, child, where is he?"

"You must promise me that you won't harm him." She wiped the blood that trickled from her mouth.

"I swear I will not inflict harm to the boy."

She pointed a shaky finger at the window, "He jumped."

"I want him alive." Memucan instructed the guards. "You have done well, Rayma. As long as you obey my commands, your brother will be returned to you when the time is right."

She had obeyed Memucan's commands for four years. Now eighteen, she was the youngest Royal Healer in Numbio's history. That was partially in thanks to Memucan, and partially to her own skills and training.

When Memucan noticed Heru had taken an interest in her, his new command was for her to get close to him. Very close.

"If I do this, will you finally return Inaros to me?"

"Of course, child, of course." Memucan nodded, hobbling around her apothecary room in the palace. "And in a show of good faith, here is a letter from him." He placed the tattered, rolled up paper on the wooden table.

She lunged for it and soaked in every word. "Rayma, we will see each other again soon. Inaros."

"It's short today," she frowned, flipping the paper to see the backside.

"Is that ungratefulness I detect in your voice?"

"No, Master -"

"I would hate for Inaros' letters to stop finding their way to you." He planted his cane in front of him, balancing himself. "Get close to our prince."

"Then?"

"Then," he hissed, "I will inform you of your next task."

She and Heru had secretly been seeing each other for eight months. She had obeyed – she just didn't expect to fall in love with Heru. His compassion, his patience, his bravery – the way he held her…

A howl echoed in the caverns throttling her back to her reality. Her nightmare. She had allowed herself, allowed her fear, to paralyze her. If she didn't get out from underneath the cart – Heru, Zophar, the Numbio – they would all die. She was their only hope of survival whether she wanted to believe it or not.

Take the first step. Just take one.

She forced herself to crawl forward, dragging her belly across the ground, tapping her fingers in front of her to guide her in the darkness.

One step. Just one step.

She was out from under the cart and felt around for the wooden torches in a box inside the cart. The box was empty, except for one.

One more step, Rayma.

Rayma tip-toed around the wooden cart, fighting the thought that a Wagura could strike at any moment. Her breathing quickened as their terrifying images flashed before her. Her heart raced; her feet stopped. She clutched her chest; she was frozen again.

Heru needs me.

The Numbio need me.

Almighty, give me strength.

Just one more step.

She inhaled and exhaled rhythmically.

One more step. Just one more step.

She fumbled through a cloth bag filled with flints and used it to light her torch. It worked. She wiped sweat from her forehead with her sleeve and looked around at what remained of the battlefield.

She gasped and lunged back seeing several dead faces, Numbio and Wagura, staring back at her. She picked up a knife from a fallen Numbio warrior and tied it to her robes. As she danced around the bodies, she caught a glint of a blade and recognized Heru's sword. Green blood stained it. She picked it up and kept a tight grip around the hilt.

Rayma listened for any sound to indicate which way she should go to find her company. She strained to hear anything and caught the faintest sound of… drums?

She marched cautiously to the mouth of a tunnel and followed it. Patting the bag filled with her healing supplies strapped across her chest, she followed the narrow passageway. The noise grew louder with every step she took. After ten minutes of steady walking, she saw an opening at the end of a tunnel and shadows along the cavern wall. Flames from a bonfire projected the shadows making them look much larger than they actually were. She crouched and crawled to the opening.

Rayma's jaw dropped when she saw hundreds of Wagura dancing, beating drums, feasting, and fighting around a large bonfire. She scanned what appeared to be their city and looked for any signs of her company. She spied hovels made of mud and human remains, then she spotted the cages formed with the bones of fallen warriors enclosing the Numbio. Their horses were housed behind a bone fence. But she didn't see Heru or Zophar.

Panicked, she kept searching the encampment from her hiding spot above them, when her eyes finally rested upon Heru and Zophar. Keeping the commanders in a separate cage from their troops, she had to admit, was a smart move.

In front of the bonfire sat the largest hovel with a platform jutting out from it. She saw a throne made of some sort of material. She squinted her eyes and realized it had been formed with human flesh. Rayma shuddered at the thought of how cruel their leader must be, to use the torn skin of human victims to upholster a throne.

As if on cue, the Queen of the Wagura floated out of her hovel. She looked nothing like her hordes of demonic soldiers. She glowed – a bright, almost hypnotizing white.

The queen wore a long, black robe that made her look as if she were seven feet tall. The darkness of the robe clashed with the brightness of her illuminated pale skin. When standing, her six-inch-long fingers fell just past her knees. She was bone thin with a sunken face that Rayma was frightened to look at. Her eyes were solid white, as was her waist long hair. Her tresses floated around her. The crown on her head was forged of crystal, just like the dagger that dangled from her hip.

"My pets," Pyke's high-pitched voice sounded as if two women were speaking in unison. "After the sacrifice, we will feast on their flesh, build with their bones, and quench our thirst with their blood!"

The Wagura howled as one, which sent shivers up Rayma's spine. But as monstrous as the creatures were, their queen was oddly beautiful.

Pyke. That's what her father had called her. Pyke, the Demon Queen. She looked like a levitating spirit, but she was a physical being – meaning, she too bled. Her father had seen it – had seen her bleed – so, if she could bleed, she could be killed.

"Defeat the queen. Defeat Pyke. She can be killed. Defeat the Demon Queen." Her father would chant those words daily.

Once when Rayma had garnered enough courage, she asked how the queen could be killed.

"The dagger. Her dagger. It forged her," Bast said, *"and it can kill her."*

"How do you know this?" She asked, but he didn't answer her question. He started screaming, convulsing on the floor, and her mother pushed her out of the room before she could see anything else.

Rayma took a deep breath before she slithered down from her hiding spot and slowly sneaked through the camp, careful to avoid any Wagura not dancing by the fire.

Pyke disappeared into her hovel. Rayma didn't know how much time she had before the sacrifice, so she had to be quick. She scurried toward the cage where Heru and Zophar sat with their heads down.

"Psst," she whispered as loud as she dared, but they couldn't hear her over the drums.

She picked up a little rock and then thought better than to throw it. She had never been an accurate shot. Rayma dropped the stone and poked her head around the hovel she was crouched behind and when she saw the coast was clear, she sprinted to the cage and ducked behind the bars before a Wagura noticed her.

"Psst." This time, Heru and Zophar looked up.

"Rayma?" Heru jumped to his feet, but Rayma held a hand up to stop him.

"Don't draw attention to us," she warned, her eyes darting around.

"What are you doing?" Heru asked, slowly sitting back down.

"I told you to escape." Zophar fussed, arms crossed over his chest, eyeing her like a disappointed father.

"I couldn't leave you behind." Rayma meant the collective you, but her gaze was fixed on Heru. "I know what I need to do. You just need to be ready should I fail. Here." She pushed Heru's sword in between the bones used as bars. "If you should need it."

"What are you talking about?" Heru furrowed his brow.

"I need to kill the queen."

"You what?" Zophar puffed.

"Kill the queen? You have never wielded a weapon in your life!" Heru was clearly not a fan of her plan.

"Would you prefer to die an excruciating death instead, Your Majesty?" She knew by addressing him formally it would sting and by the flash of surprise on his face, she was right. "If I kill the queen, the hive will not have a life source – their existence is tied to her survival."

"How do you know this?" Zophar looked just as confused as Heru.

"Trust me," was all she managed to blurt out, hiding her shaky hands before they noticed.

Heru and Zophar turned to one another, then Heru nodded.

"Rayma," he pleaded, "be careful."

She couldn't afford to stare into his hazel eyes a second longer or she would lose the little bit of reckless boldness she had mustered. Rayma once again made sure there weren't any Wagura nearby and bolted hovel to hovel, working her way to Pyke.

Rayma was grateful the celebration of capturing the Numbio made the Wagura lax in their patrolling duties. Pyke's hovel wasn't guarded, so she slipped inside the curtains draped in front of the opening, undetected.

Now that she was inside, she began to question how she was supposed to lift the crystal dagger from Pyke herself and use it to kill her. But she didn't have to worry long – the queen was sitting on a throne, twin to the one on the platform, weeping.

"Are you here to kill me?" Pyke's gaze was on the crystal dagger on her lap.

Rayma stepped forward. "And if I am?"

Pyke's solid white eyes shot up. "You will need this." She offered the crystal dagger with both hands to the healer. "Take it. Please."

Rayma was stunned and was unsure if she should reach for it. "You want me to kill you?"

"Please, free me from this misery." Tears flowed from Pyke's eyes but seeped back into her skin, leaving no trace of emotion.

"Free you?" Rayma still hadn't taken the blade, fearing it to be a trap. "You are the queen -"

"I made a deal with the Grim – and this was the price I had to pay." She patted herself. "To become this… monstrosity."

"What did you ask the Grim for?"

"To be with the man I loved. He was dying but I begged the Grim not to deliver him to Death, to spare us. I asked him for time." Pyke's voices echoed through the hovel. "The Grim said he would let us live together peacefully for ten years, but when he returned, he would take us both."

"What happened?"

"The Grim kept his word. Ten beautiful years later, he returned to claim both of our souls. Though he delivered my love to Death, he kept me for a darker purpose – to replace the last Queen of the Wagura who had paid her debt."

Rayma took a minute to let the queen's story set in. "If I kill you…?"

"Then I can be reunited with my love in Death's arms."

"Why hasn't anyone else agreed to this?" Rayma was skeptical. "You have slaughtered hundreds, if not thousands, of men over your years as the queen."

"Because only a mortal woman can kill me." She exhaled deeply. "This is the Grim's cruel game, knowing women do not venture through the Caverns of the Undead. But you can set me free."

"What happens to me if I kill you?"

"Have you ever made a deal with the Grim?" Pyke stood and was much taller than Rayma originally assumed.

"No," Rayma stepped back instinctually.

"Then you can finally put an end to the Wagura – you can set our indebted souls free." She extended the knife. "Take it. Free us. Free me."

Rayma eyed the crystal dagger – she knew what she needed to do, but wasn't sure she could bring herself to do the deed. She swore an oath to heal, to protect, to save – not kill.

"I…" Rayma's bottom lip quivered, "I can't do it."

"Oh please, you must." Pyke floated toward her and pushed the dagger into her hands. "If you don't, I will have no choice but to kill all of your companions. To kill you. Please, don't let me do it."

"You don't have to -"

"I do not have a choice." Pyke whimpered and just for a brief moment, Rayma saw the human trapped inside the creature.

Rayma accepted the knife with trembling hands. "Where do I… put it?"

Pyke tapped her chest. "Run it straight through what is left of my heart."

Rayma pressed the tip of the blade to Pyke's chest. She had come to kill the Demon Queen but now that she stood face to face with the monster, she couldn't help but pity and even understand her. Rayma had spent the years repaying a debt to Memucan, yearning for her own freedom. There were days she even wished for Death to come for her; for someone to end her misery.

But she had also sworn an oath to heal and not harm. Could she really live with herself if she killed Pyke? Could she live with herself if she didn't and watched Heru and the Numbio die?

She had come to kill the Demon Queen.

She was going to set the Demon Queen free.

Tears slipped down Rayma's cheeks. "I'm sorry." She plunged the knife deep into Pyke's breast.

Pyke gurgled and her light began to fade. Rayma held her as she died, her own heart breaking as she kept repeating, "I'm sorry," to the queen.

Pyke grabbed Rayma's hand tightly and managed to say, "Thank you," before she turned into dust, leaving behind the crystal dagger and a key that had been tied around her neck.

Rayma stared at what remained of the queen – she had never taken a life before and the guilt that burdened her was almost unbearable. But she knew the Numbio needed her. Heru needed her. As she rose, she snatched the key – perhaps it opened the cage doors – and after wiping the dagger clean with her robe, she holstered it, claiming it as hers.

She inched toward the opening of the hovel, expecting to see the Wagura still celebrating, but instead, with their queen – their life source – gone, their strength began to fade. There was no more dancing. No more drums beating. But there was the sight of Wagura soldiers clawing for their weapons, grasping their chests in agonizing pain.

Rayma ran to the cages and used the key to free her companions.

"Rayma!" Heru scooped her up in her arms and she inhaled deeply, stifling the tears she desperately wanted to shed, now that she was safe in his arms.

Safe? Not quite.

Rayma reluctantly pulled away from him. "I killed their queen. They will be at their weakest."

Heru was surprised but nodded and ordered the men to kill the Wagura. To leave none of them alive. The Numbio armed themselves with whatever weapons they could get their hands on and battled the Wagura.

Heru ushered Rayma away from the fighting. He caressed her face and kissed her forehead gently. "I don't want to leave you…"

"Go," she pressed her hand against his chest, feeling his heart racing.

Heru clutched his sword tightly and reluctantly turned toward the raging battle. "Rayma." She met his gaze, her exhaustion kicking in. "I owe you my life." He slipped beyond her sight.

Rayma could hear the clashing of swords and the wails of Wagura dying as she leaned her head back against the hovel Heru had hidden her behind. She could smell the Wagura's bitter green blood. Her heart was pounding in her chest – her head spinning. She kept seeing the image of Pyke's dagger in her chest, how she turned to dust in her grasp.

But it wasn't Pyke's eyes giving her an icky feeling.

Rayma's eyes shot open, and her head turned to the side. There, gawking at her, was Bantu, hiding from participating in the fight. He wasn't frightened. He stared at her with a blackmailing smirk.

Kill the prince. That was Memucan's last command – the final task that would free her brother.

Bantu looked in both directions before scrambling over to her, kneeling inches in front of her. "You don't look well, Rayma." His slippery voice enveloped her like a malevolent embrace.

"Get away from me."

"I'm sure you're especially glad to see I survived this whole ordeal." His hands trailed up her arm to her neck.

"Don't touch me." She pushed him away and he smacked her across her face with his enormous hand.

"Who do you think you are to give me orders?" Bantu hissed in her ear; his fingers tightening around her throat. "Who are you going to tell? The prince? The Westerner?" He hummed. "I'll do whatever I want to do to you," his free hand slipped underneath her skirt, "and you won't say a thing about it."

His lustful smirk disappeared as a grunt escaped his parched lips. Bantu's eyes darted from Rayma to his stomach.

"May Death deny you rest," she hissed and ripped the crystal dagger out of his body, pushing him away from her. She watched as he thrashed in a pool of his own blood and felt no urge to heal him.

Rayma had killed twice in a span of minutes and was frightened that killing Bantu didn't draw guilt or remorse from her. She enjoyed that kill. And honestly, if given the chance, she would not hesitate to do it again.

Heavy footsteps approached. Her eyes sliced through the air and rested on Zophar. Truly grateful to see the burly Westerner rather than a grotesque Wagura, she exhaled a sigh of relief. A tear slipped down her cheek as she leaned her head against the wall. Zophar tapped his foot against Bantu's lifeless body.

"He…I…" she stuttered, unsure of how to explain what she had done.

Zophar crouched in front of her and whispered, "Are you alright?"

Her bloodshot eyes scanned his face, and she realized his question was genuine. She nodded.

Spying the blood on the crystal dagger, Zophar took the weapon from her hands and wiped it clean against his pant leg. "No one needs to know what happened here."

It was a statement.

Rayma couldn't resist throwing her arms around his neck and the tears she had fought before now flowed. She wept as he returned the embrace and only let her go when she was ready.

Zophar extended the crystal dagger back to her. "Yours, I believe."

Rayma shook her head. "I can't take it."

"You are its rightful owner now." Zophar insisted. "And if needed, now I know you can defend yourself."

"I'm a healer. I shouldn't -"

"Kill?" he interrupted. "I taught Salome to value life. And that included her own." He placed the knife in her palm. "Value your life as you save everyone else's, Healer."

She wrapped her fingers around the hilt. *Value your life.* She met his gaze. She was prepared to do just that.

CHAPTER 8

MATILDYS

Matildys glided across the black marble floors of the Black Tower with a sinister smile that could stop a heart from beating. Unlike her husband, her mind was filled with plans, with strategies, all with one goal – one purpose – to be sole ruler of Gomorrah.

She had been poisoning Cyler's food for nearly a year and took her already sickly husband and turned him into a useless invalid. Matildys had considered slitting his pale throat while he slept, but that would draw too much attention to who murdered the king. No, slow but steady, even if the brute was taking too long to die. No one would even suspect the dutiful wife, the loyal sister – she would be free of him, but not fit enough to rule the Gomorrians. Not with her son, Thanos, alive and well.

She didn't hate Thanos by any means, but she had no love for him either. Like King Cyler, Thanos was second born but because they were born male, they were named heir to the throne. Matildys was robbed of her crown – she would not allow the same fate for her daughter, Ranalda. In truth, Ranalda was mentally weak and Thanos was wicked but stupid, a true Gomorrian. But cruelty could be taught. Ranalda still had a chance to be a strong ruler, a mighty Gomorrian.

But there was still Thanos to contend with.

Matildys' eyebrows arched – a wicked glint in her icy blue eyes.

She could get rid of both Cyler and Thanos with one swipe of her blade. She would slit Cyler's throat, as she had wished to do for years, and use one of Thanos' daggers to do the deed. Thanos would be found guilty of assassinating the king and would be executed. It was perfect. The queen closed her eyes and exhaled a satisfied breath. Gomorrah would finally be hers.

"Mother?"

Matildys opened her eyes and turned to see her daughter standing in the hall.

"Stand up straight, Ranalda," Matildys clucked her tongue and swatted her bony fingers in the air. "You don't want an unsightly hump like your father."

Ranalda pulled her shoulders back, tipping her head upward. "Yes, Mother."

The queen tapped Ranalda's square jawline with the tips of her fingers. "That's better. What do you need?"

Ranalda's gaze faltered, not daring to look her mother in the eye. "The Thrak have returned from their hunt -"

"Tell me you look forlorn because they brought that bitch back to our mighty city dead and not alive as I instructed."

"Uh…" Ranalda cleared her throat, "not exactly."

"Ranalda, dear," Matildys cooed, "you look positively ill. What is it?"

"The Thrak didn't reach Port Daelon in time. The woman – Salome – was already on board a ship."

"Where are these Thrak now?"

"In the throne room awaiting your orders."

Matildys wrapped her arm around her daughter's shoulders and led her back down the corridor to the throne room. "My dear, it is time you handed down your first judgment."

Ranalda shook her head, "Shouldn't Thanos -"

Matildys dug her fingernails into Ranalda's upper arm causing her to wince. "If you want to rule Gomorrah," she hissed in her daughter's ear, "forget about Thanos."

"Yes, Mother," she cleared her throat as Matildys eased her grip.

"Soon, we will be free of our oppressors." Matildys spoke without looking at anyone in particular, her gaze fixed on the black wooden doors of the throne room. "Now is the time to take your place at the table."

The guards opened the double doors and the women walked through the awaiting Thrak to their thrones. Once they were seated, Matildys turned to Ranalda and tilted her head, indicating it was time to speak.

Ranalda gulped audibly but managed to say, "Thrak 47314, you and your company were charged with finding the peasant known as Salome, who is guilty of crimes against the crown. You have returned empty-handed. Why?"

The Thrak's soulless black eyes fluttered around the room. "The criminal had boarded a boat set for the Isles of Myr before we could apprehend her."

"So," Ranalda sat up straighter, mirroring her mother's posture, "you have failed your mission."

Thrak 47314 swayed side to side and sucked in a frightened breath. "We can still capture her, Princess. We know where she was headed."

"You propose to travel to the Isles of Myr?" Ranalda couldn't hide her surprise. She side-eyed her mother, searching for guidance but didn't receive any. She turned back to the Thrak commander, tilted her nose up, and lowered her voice. "Thrak 47314, you failed your mission, and you know the penalty for -"

"Go to Port Daelon and commandeer a vessel," Matildys interrupted, an idea sparked in her mind. "Sail to the Isles of Myr and bring me that girl, *alive*."

Thrak 47314 and Ranalda both breathed a sigh of relief. He bowed low spurring his band of thirteen men to do the same.

"But," Matildys continued, eyes narrowed, voice cold, "if you should fail the crown again, you know what the penalty will be."

The Thrak nodded with a grunt and snapped his finger in the air, summoning the pardoned company to follow him. They left before the queen had a chance to change her vicious mind.

"You…you let them live?" Ranalda croaked as soon as the doors closed behind them. "That is not the Gommorian way."

Matildys slithered from her throne, "No," she wiped strands of loose hair from Ranalda's face and tucked them behind her ears. "It is not the Gomorrian way, but do you remember what I told you when I first dispatched the Thrak to find this woman?"

Ranalda nodded, "Revenge before riches."

"Very good." Matildys flicked her index finger, beckoning Ranalda to follow her to the balcony behind the four thrones that overlooked the courtyard. "The same principle applies. They failed, yes, but how much harder will they push to complete this mission given this rare second chance?"

"You think their fear will motivate them?"

"The Thrak always fear – success or not." Matildys watched as the company of Thrak she'd shown mercy to saddle their horses and galloped out of the courtyard. "It is their hope of survival."

Ranalda shuddered at Matildys' tone. "You mean to execute them even if they bring that woman back, don't you?"

Matildys flashed a cruel grin. "How perceptive of you, Ranalda."

"But you said -"

"I never promised they would *not* die. They failed. What is the penalty for failure?"

"Death."

"And Death they shall receive." Matildys snaked her arm around her daughter's. "Now, off with you. There are some matters I need to tend to."

"I could help you -"

Matildys tapped Ranalda's arm and pecked her forehead with a rare kiss. "These are things I must do alone."

Ranalda's cheeks flushed. "Of course, Mother." She broke free from her mother's grasp and bowed.

Matildys watched her daughter disappear down the hallway. The sun was setting so she had to act quickly if she as to be successful in setting her plan into motion.

She turned on her heel and glided toward Thanos' quarters. Her son was especially careless when it came to his weaponry, leaving knives, maces, and ceremonial swords scattered around his chambers instead of locking them away in the armory or fastened on his person.

As she rounded the curved hall in the circular tower, she hastened her gait, and slipped into Thanos' unguarded room.

"Fool of a son," she murmured.

Thanos claimed he had no privacy when the Thrak were stationed outside his chambers at night, so he banned them.

His own undoing, she thought.

Matildys scanned her son's messy quarters and rolled her eyes in irritation. At least he wouldn't notice one of his knives missing. Until it was far too late.

She swiped the knife with a bone infused handle. "How poetic," she smiled. It was a well-known fact this dagger belonged to Thanos. It was given to him by his father for his Name Day the previous year. Forged with the ground bones of traitorous Mountain Men.

"For the future King of Gomorrah," Cyler had chimed, his chest puffed out like a peacock.

The next day, Matildys began to kill her husband. Slowly.

Hearing footsteps outside the door, she backed against the wall nearest the entrance, clutching the blade to her breast. She held her breath as the footsteps rounded past the room and continued down the hall. She exhaled.

Pity, she thought to herself. *I would have loved to have gotten in one for practice.*

Her gaze settled on the dagger in her hand. Matildys reached for the handle and pried the door open, slipping out unnoticed.

One step closer.

With the dagger securely hidden inside her billowing sleeves, she scurried to the chamber she shared with her husband. She waved her free hand sideways signaling to the two Thrak guards to open the doors.

Night was Maltidys' favorite time. She especially liked when the light of the full moon streamed through the windows, lighting up the black marble floors in the bedroom. She entered and heard Cyler, groaning like a wounded animal in bed.

"Matildys?" he wheezed, his weary eyes finding her in the dimly lit room.

"Yes, my love," she stepped forward, a wicked sweetness in her voice.

"You are early."

He wasn't wrong. Matildys couldn't stand the thought of being alone with Cyler for a minute longer than necessary, so she would occupy her time until he'd passed out.

"It's been a busy day," she sat at her vanity, carefully sliding the knife into a drawer, and began brushing her long blonde tresses. "Not to worry, my love, you just close your eyes and rest. Do not let my presence disturb you."

The king pushed himself up to a seated position with great difficulty and leaned his hunched back against the headboard. "It's been a long time since we've had some alone time, my sweet." He licked his dry lips, drawing a reproachful glare from Matildys.

Attempting to hide her disgust with the innuendo of having undesired incestuous relations, she let out a flirtatious chuckle and said, "You seem to have more vigor than I do these days, my love."

"Come, sit with me." Cyler patted her side of the bed with a lustful smirk.

"Perhaps another -""Now!" He might have been sickly and growing frailer by the day, but his tone was nothing short of menacing.

"Of course," she set the hairbrush down in the drawer and eyed the dagger. She had not intended to kill him that evening – but the thought of him touching her again made her retch. She snatched the knife, once again hiding it in her wide sleeve, and headed to his side of the bed.

"What are you doing?" He watched her approach with both excitement and suspicion. She roughly grabbed his hair and forced his head up to look at her. "Feeling feisty tonight, I see," he grinned. His appetite for her was obvious by his skinny chest rising and falling rapidly. "Do what you want to me."

"I intend to," she whispered coldly.

"Matildys?" A spark of realization ignited too late.

"I am no longer your slave."

"Matil -"

She sliced the blade across his warm, pale throat. It was bloody, but it was over quickly. She watched as the life drained from his eyes; she had killed many times before, but this was personal, intimate – and it was the most satisfying.

Releasing her grasp of his head, she let him fall back on the bed and went to work setting the scene. First, she dropped the knife where she stood. She changed into her nightgown, threw her bloodied gown into the roaring fireplace, and ensured the balcony door was wide open before climbing into bed next to her dead husband – her younger brother. She splashed some of Cyler's blood on her hands and nightgown. She held his limp hand in hers and took a deep breath.

It was time to finish this.

Matildys released a blood curdling scream so high pitched it could have been heard throughout the entire city. The two Thrak stationed outside her room rushed inside, spears ready to strike. Tears streamed down her cheeks as she held Cyler and wailed, "Our king has been murdered!" She pointed to the balcony. "He escaped."

One of the Thrak beelined to the balcony while the second knelt by Cyler's bedside and picked up the knife with fresh blood dripping from the tip.

"Do you recognize this, my Queen?" He held it up for her to see.

She gasped and slapped her fingers over her mouth, smearing blood across her face. "It cannot be!"

"My Queen?" Thrak 82419 stood up.

"That dagger belongs to my son, Thanos." She sucked in a breath, "He murdered his own father."

Thrak 26317 stepped inside from the balcony. "He got away, but we'll find him."

"We'll send the collectors to fetch his body, my Queen," Thrak 82419 began to follow his companion to the door. "Should we send for a healer?"

"I am not injured," she waved them off, tears pouring down her cheeks. "Find him," she rasped. "Find my son before he escapes."

They bowed and scurried out to the arriving Thrak, instructing them to close the gates and find the prince. As soon as the doors slammed shut, she stood up and walked back to her vanity, picked up her brush, and finished combing her hair. The deed was done. She smiled at the sight of her husband's dead body in the reflection of the mirror and at the sight of his blood smeared across her face. She was finally free.

CHAPTER 9
CRISPIN

Crispin had been on a ship once before when he was younger. He and his older brothers, Lykos, Mosgalath, and Elias, joined their father to examine Northwind's armada. It was purely ceremonial. They never left the harbor, but Crispin wished they had.

He was Issachar and Bilhah's fifth child – nowhere near threatened to be named heir to the throne – so he was determined to spend his days sailing the seas as an admiral in Northwind's navy.

He breathed in the salty sea air, his hair wafting in the breeze. A smile spread across his face, not caring a lick that the blazing sun was beating down on the deck mercilessly. For the first time in years, he felt at home, which was odd considering he didn't know the first thing about sailing.

Crispin scanned the ship's deck, taking in the motley crew of the *Shadow of Death*. Thieves, swindlers, drunks, gamblers, and murderers. Not his first choice of company, but at least they were on the same side. For now.

Captain Haldane was the sensible one.

Rahab was the stabby one.

Phex was the explosives one.

Corwin was the quiet one.

Ondrej was the giant one.

Rafi was the pint-size one.

Leeondris was the missing one.

Crispin shook his head. *A motley crew indeed*, he thought to himself. Salome would be fascinated by them. He wished she were there. He felt so alone. In truth, he had never been on his own before. What a strange, empowering, yet vulnerable feeling.

"Mainlander!"

Crispin glanced over his shoulder and saw Rafi waving him forward. He approached quickly since the halfling seemed to be in a hurry.

"The captain wants to see you in his quarters."

Crispin waited for Rafi to show him the way to the captain's quarters, but the pirate clearly had no intention of helping.

"Uh," Crispin cleared his throat and pointed up the steps, "I'm assuming it's that way."

"Maybe," Rafi stroked his pointy white beard with a mischievous grin, "maybe not."

"I'll show you the way to the captain's quarters," Ondrej's deep voice boomed behind him causing him to jump.

Crispin swung around, his face at direct level with the giant's bare chest. He never heard Ondrej come up behind him. He wasn't sure if he was more impressed someone, other than Korah – may his soul rest in peace – had managed to sneak up on him, or terrified that he had been caught unaware, like prey.

Crispin followed the enormous pirate up the creaky steps. Ondrej took three steps at a time while Crispin had to sprint just to keep up pace.

"You'll have to forgive Rafi." Ondrej ducked as he entered the hall leading to the back of the ship. "He doesn't take kindly to Mainlanders."

"And you?"

Ondrej shrugged. "I distrust everyone equally."

"Even your crew?"

Ondrej suddenly stopped and Crispin ran into him. "Especially the crew." He pointed at the wooden door at the end of the hall. "Go ahead, Mainlander. Keep your wits about you if you care to survive." He flashed a toothy smile and retreated the way they had come.

What an odd fellow. Crispin rubbed his temples. He faced the door and raised his fist to knock, but stopped, because he heard an angry voice on the other side. Knowing he shouldn't eavesdrop didn't deter him from placing his ear against the door.

"This is madness, Captain," Rahab spat. "We should turn him in, collect the bounty, and be done with it."

"Now, now, Rahab," Haldane's smooth as honey voice sounded, unbothered by her ranting. "You want us to get Leeondris back, don't you?"

"You know I do, but -"

"Then this is the only way," he interrupted. "You think those blind bastards at The Sisters will help pirates? No," Haldane set his glass down on his desk with a *clank.* "But they'll at least give the Prince of Northwind a chance to explain himself without turning him away at the gates."

"And once we find Leeondris, we turn the Mainlander over to the Shadows."

"I gave the boy my word. He helps us find our companion; I'll return him to his." Haldane's voice softened, "I owe Palma."

Rahab growled, "Fine. For Palma. But let it be on record that Rahab Montu was against helping this Mainlander."

"It is so noted." Haldane chuckled.

"What's so funny?" Rahab huffed as she leaned against Haldane's desk.

"You can come in now, Your Highness."

Crispin moved away from the door, unsure if he should really enter or not. Clearly Haldane already knew he had been eavesdropping. Crispin felt like he was about to be scolded by a parent for misbehaving. He drew his shoulders back, straightening up as tall as his six-foot frame could go, and pushed the door wide open.

"Would you care for some rum?" Haldane shoved the bottle across the table toward him. "It's a good year," he winked.

"No, thanks." Crispin sat down at the table, sliding the bottle back.

"You were eavesdropping?" Rahab hovered over him; arms crossed over her chest.

"I didn't want to interrupt," Crispin shrugged and flashed a smile up at her.

She lunged toward him, stabbing her ruby encrusted dagger between his fingers resting on the tabletop. He didn't flinch, although he was screaming on the inside.

"Very scary," Crispin purred.

"Enough," Haldane raised a hand in the air. "Sit down, Rahab."

"But -"

Haldane kicked a chair out. "I said, have a seat."

Reluctantly, with her eyes still pinned on Crispin, she uprooted her knife from the table and sank into the wooden chair, kicking her feet up on the desk.

"Now that we're all getting along," Haldane side-eyed Rahab until she planted her feet back on the floor, "we can get down to business." He cleared his throat and threw back a shot of rum. "We've set a course for The Sisters, where we'll have you," he set his gaze on Crispin, "arrange an audience with the Sovereign Neempo."

Crispin leaned forward, wiggling all his fingers before placing his hands to his chin. "And why would the Sovereign agree to meet with me?"

"You're the Prince of Northwind, are you not?" Rahab picked at her fingernails with her knife.

"I am," he ignored her flicking the dirt from under her nails in his direction. "But again, why go to The Sisters at all? Is that where your friend is?"

"We need access to their Hall of Records," Haldane said.

"You want to see if they have your friend's location on file." Crispin finally understood. "Ok," he nodded, scratching his sprouting facial hair. "I meet with him, find out where your friend is being held, we rescue him, then you take me wherever I need you to take me." His eyes rested on Rahab as he finished that last part.

"First of all," Rahab squared her shoulders to Crispin's, "you won't be meeting with the Sovereign alone. I'll be going with you."

"Rahab—"

"Someone should keep an eye on him, Captain," Rahab interrupted Haldane's protest.

"What's the second thing?" Crispin asked.

"What?" Rahab cocked her head to the side, confused.

"You said, 'first of all', like there was more to follow." Crispin stretched out his legs and reclined in his seat. "Was there something else you needed to say?"

Rahab looked gob smacked. Then angry.

"I'll go out on a limb here and say, no," Crispin's mouth curved, "there was nothing more you were going to say."

Haldane tried to mask his laugh as a cough. Rahab glared at the captain then at the Mainlander, fire in her eyes.

"Are we done here?" She stood up, holstering her weapon.

Haldane cleared his throat, "Aye, we're done."

"Good." She swiped her leather tricorne from the coat rack and plopped it on her head as she stomped to the door.

"Going so soon?" Crispin said sarcastically as he flashed an exaggerated sad face.

"If I don't, I'll gut you like a fish."

"You could try."

"Tread lightly, Mainlander," she hissed, her hands clasped both his armrests as she leaned closer to his face. "There is quite a bit of sea before we get to The Sisters. I would hate for you to fall overboard."

Crispin smiled, "You would miss me."

"I'd recover." Rahab straightened and walked to the door, slamming it behind her.

Crispin's gaze was fixed on the door until Haldane cleared his throat. "She won't really, you know," Crispin made a slit-my-throat motion.

"There's a good chance she might," Haldane nodded. "But there's an equal chance of her warming up to you."

Crispin flashed a boyish grin, "I'll grow on her."

"Let us hope so, my new friend." Haldane took one more shot, this time wincing with the burn down his esophagus. "I would hate to lose out on so much money on account of your untimely death."

"Me too."

Haldane waved him out. "Off you go, lad. Have my First Mate give you a rundown of the rigging."

Crispin stood from his seat. "Who would that be? Corwin?"

"No." The captain flashed a childish smile exposing his three gold teeth.

"Let me guess." Crispin looked Heavenward with a sigh.

"You'd be right." Haldane slapped his knee with a chuckle. "And a good First Mate she is."

Crispin made his way to the door, not looking forward to dealing with that woman again, but ready to make the most of it, seeing as he was stuck on a ship in the middle of the Obsidian Sea. He closed the captain's door and turned to walk down the hall to the deck when Rahab stepped into view, blocking his path.

"Miss me already?" Crispin strutted closer with a grin.

"Hardly." Rahab's arms were crossed over her chest. "I wanted to talk to you privately."

"How exciting." Crispin wiggled his eyebrows. "It just so happens the captain wanted me to talk to you, too."

Rahab moved forward meeting him in the middle of the corridor. In a flash she aimed her knee toward his crotch, but he anticipated the childish move and grabbed her knee, shaking his head with a tsk.

"Not nice."

"Wasn't supposed to be," she balanced on one leg while he held her right knee firmly.

"And not fair either," he released her and watched her stumble back a step.

"What can I say," she shrugged. "I'm a pirate. How did you know I'd try that?"

"I have a sister and have been on the receiving end of that move plenty of times."

Rahab smiled, "I see." She slithered up to the side of his face, grazing his ear with her lips, and whispered, "Did she ever use this move on you?" She swiftly swept his leg out from under him. Slamming him to the floor, she mounted him, and pressed a knife to his throat.

"Oddly enough," Crispin grunted from the fall. "Yes." He smirked. "But I don't seem to mind it when you do it."

"Don't do that," she crinkled her nose.

"Do what?"

"Enjoy yourself."

"If you're not enjoying yourself, you're living wrong." Crispin placed his hands on the side of her hips. "You seem to be comfortable since you're still sitting on me."

Rahab slapped his hands off her hips. "Let's get one thing straight, Mainlander," she growled, nostrils flared. "If you get cocky enough to try to lay a finger on me again, I will slit your throat."

"Before you even realize it," he propped himself up on his elbows once she stood, "you'll find yourself wanting me to touch you again."

"I doubt th -"

Rahab was abruptly slammed against the wall. Something had struck the side of the black ship. Rahab tumbled and landed on top of Crispin. Nose to nose, they could feel each other breathing.

"See," Crispin smirked. "I'm growing on you already."

"Shut up." She pressed on his chest to push herself to her feet and stumbled toward the main deck where the crew was yelling out attack orders.

Haldane's door flew open with a bang. He placed his hands on either side of the hallway, steadying himself as he stomped through the narrow corridor. He grabbed Crispin by the arm and hoisted him to his feet. "You alright, lad?"

Crispin nodded. "What was that?" He followed the captain onto the deck. As soon as Crispin emerged from the hallway his question was answered.

An unearthly high-pitched screech rendered him nearly incapable of hearing. He slapped his hands over his ears and squinted through the ice-cold water stabbing his face, finding the crew fighting off enormous tentacles wrapping around the hull of the ship.

"What the hell is that?" Crispin yelled to Haldane, who was drenched from head to toe already.

Haldane whipped around, his eyes sparkling with reckless abandon. "That there is Kubantu."

Kubantu. Crispin had heard tales of the sea monster but chalked it up to sailors' drunken exaggerations. But now, in the middle of the Obsidian Sea, the fabled creature was trying to tear the ship apart and drag them to their watery graves.

Crispin counted seven – no, eight – tentacles. When Kubantu rose out of the sea, Crispin saw its dark scaly torso. The human-like creature opened its mouth revealing long, razor-sharp teeth and a split tongue. His snaky eyes searched for prey, hissing loudly when he spotted them scrambling on deck. He lifted his scaly arms and fiercely dug its black fingernails into the ship.

Crispin tore his eyes from the monstrous creature and slid down the polished, wooden railing, and landed on the deck with a loud thud. He unsheathed his sword, and hacked into one of Kubantu's tentacles, extracting a ghastly howl from the beast as it released its hold on the ship.

Its eyes found Crispin.

Damn.

Crispin tumbled forward, avoiding an incoming blow from another tentacle. He heard the wood of the hull starting to split. If they didn't kill this thing quickly, no one would survive. The prince took cover behind the tallest mast where Phex was fiddling with a weird metal sphere.

"What's that?" Crispin pointed at the ball covered with spikes.

Phex's grin was truly menacing and sent chills down Crispin's spine. "A gift for the hungry beast." He twisted the halves together and the spiky ball began to tick. "Heads up!" Phex shouted before tossing the sphere over his head and toward the monster.

The blast rattled the ship. Kubantu squealed. Haldane cursed as he fought at the helm to keep the ship as steady as he could.

Crispin poked his head around the mast and saw a couple of Kubantu's tentacles hemorrhaging from the explosion. Crispin turned to Phex, but the pirate was gone.

Crispin watched as Haldane continued to hold them steady and was amazed at how Corwin used every knife on his person to stab close-by tentacles. Rafi and Ondrej quickly repaired and plugged any holes in the ship to ensure the beast's assault didn't sink them. Phex sprinted across the deck and lobbed more spheres at the sea monster, cackling with each throw and glorious explosion.

"*You'll* sink us before *it* does, you bloody fool!" Rafi spared a moment to fuss at Phex as he slammed his hammer down on the piece of wood he nailed to the deck.

"Better to go out with a bang, then be taken by force." Phex danced around the halfling with a grin so wide, Crispin thought for sure his face would split.

"Off with you, crazy bastard!" Rafi shook his hammer at Phex and went back to his repairs.

Everyone was accounted for except Rahab. Crispin looked all over the deck and didn't see her. He stood up and circled the mast slowly, not wanting to attract Kubantu's serpentine eyes. But as he looked up at the monster, he realized its soulless eyes were already preoccupied.

Rahab launched a harpoon toward the creature, but he caught it and let out a thunderous laugh. She took a step back when he hissed, thrusting his reptilian tongue at her; as if to say, she was its next victim. She ran toward the mast Crispin was hiding behind, unaware of the tentacle swinging to snatch her.

She's not going to make it!

Before he even realized what he was doing, Crispin ran to meet Rahab. He shoved her out of the tentacle's path, but in doing so, was swept overboard and into the raging sea.

Kubantu's tentacle had a tight grip around Crispin's legs, so he withdrew to the depths of the Obsidian Sea, wounded, but not empty-handed. Crispin felt himself sinking deeper into the dark waters. He opened his eyes and reached for his sword. With all his might, he sliced through the monster's tentacle. Blood encircled him, but Kubantu either tired of the hunt, or in severe pain, didn't go after him.

The prince spun around trying to figure out which direction was up. He was running out of breath. His lungs tightened. He felt himself slowly losing consciousness – the water was claiming him. His eyes closed and his mouth opened releasing a stream of bubbles. Crispin felt ice cold water fill his lungs as he sank deeper into the sea.

A hand suddenly grabbed his and dragged him back to the surface. Hoisted aboard the *Shadow of Death*, his body slammed onto the deck. He heard voices, but it sounded like they were miles away. Lips pressed against his and air filled his lungs. His eyes shot open, and he turned violently to his side to cough up water.

Once he finally caught his breath and wiped the film from his eyes, he saw Rahab lying next to him, her head tilted toward him. Her chest rising and falling quickly. She wiped the strands of wet hair that stuck to the side of her face behind her.

"You?" Crispin gasped when he realized she was the one who had saved him. "Why?"

"How else are we going to get paid if you're dead?" She stood up to hobble to her quarters.

"The *real* reason," he turned onto his elbow.

Rahab didn't bother to turn around. "A life for a life. We're even." She squished her way to her quarters, leaving Crispin with the rest of the tired and wounded crew.

Haldane patted his face dry with a rag as he squatted in front of the prince.

"She saved me." Crispin watched her disappear up the stairs.

"Aye," Haldane nodded, offering his hand to help Crispin stand. "I suppose that means she likes you."

"Or my bounty," Crispin pointed out.

"I don't care how much someone loves money; they would never jump in after a sea monster, no matter how grand the pay day."

Crispin slipped his shirt off and wrung it out. That blackhearted woman had saved him. He never expected a pirate to rescue him once he'd gone overboard, but to have Rahab save him was humbling.

"Should I go thank her?"

"Manners are wasted on pirates, lad." Haldane patted him on the back. "But if it'll make you feel like you did your mother proud by being respectable, then go ahead."

Crispin put his shirt back on and headed up the stairs to Rahab's room. As soon as he rapped on her door, he regretted it, and turned to retreat when the door opened.

"What do you want, Mainlander?" Rahab stood behind the half open door.

"I…I wanted to uh, thank you, for…" Crispin shoved his hands into his pockets, "for saving my life."

"Wow."

"What?"

"Did that feel as painful as it looked?" Rahab cocked her head to the side. Droplets of water splattered on the wooden floor from her wet hair.

"Can you just say, 'you're welcome', so we can move on?" Crispin rolled his eyes.

Rahab leaned lazily against the doorframe wearing just a bralette and pants, scrunching her hair dry with a towel. "I think it's more fun watching you squirm."

"Look," he tilted his head back in exasperation, "it's been a long day. I said what I came to say, now I'm going to lay down."

"You're welcome, Mainlander."

"You know I have a name."

"Your point being?"

Crispin shook his head and shrugged. "No point. Sleep well, Rahab." He could feel her watching him as he walked a few doors down the hall to the quarters Haldane had assigned to him in Pulau.

"That's Leeondris' room." Her voice was soft in tone but bitter in delivery.

Crispin glanced over his shoulder at her, "What is he to you?"

She frowned, "None of your business."

He nodded and lifted his arms in surrender. "Is there another room you'd rather me stay in during my time here?"

She straightened up and shook her head with a scowl. "No."

Crispin turned the knob and entered before she could say anything else, entirely too tired to play her games. She exhausted him more than fighting off that sea monster. He closed the door, leaning his back against it, and exhaled a long, weary breath. He spied the sparsely furnished quarters with gratitude. A bed and wash basin – it was all he needed. He peeled his shoes and wet shirt off before he heard a soft knock.

Crispin debated whether he should open the door or not, but he trudged over and cracked it open. *Of course.* Rahab was standing there looking like she had something else to say.

"What is it now?" He propped open the door and stood in the narrow threshold.

Rahab's brows arched and her eyes narrowed, "What?"

"Did you think of something else you wanted to say that couldn't wait until morning? How much you hate Mainlanders? How you desperately oppose me being here? How you should turn me in to the Shadows and collect my bounty? How -"

"Thank you," she interrupted him. "I came to thank you… for what you did out there."

"Like you said before," his gaze fell to the floor, "we're even."

She slammed her hand against the door keeping him from closing it. "I distrust Mainlanders because they banded together and shipped those they deemed *misfits* and *undesirables* to Pulau to die. But our people did what the Mainlanders did not expect – we not only survived banishment to islands made of solid rock with no greenery or chance to cultivate vegetation, but we thrived. We were given a death sentence years ago, but now, Mainlanders fear seeing our sails approach their shores."

"I'm sorry that was the origin of your people," Crispin's eyes rose to meet hers. "And I'm sorry for calling Pulau, *Misfit Island,* but you have to believe me when I say, I'm not like those who came before me. What they did was wrong. I hope I can help you see I truly don't wish to be your enemy."

"You saved my life, the one thing I never expected from a Mainlander," she said in hushed tones and tugged at her earlobe. "Leeondris is like a brother to me. The only Mainlander to earn our trust."

His heart raced at her revelation, but his face remained stoic. "Why are you telling me this?"

"Because I know you want to know if you're rescuing my lover. You're not."

"I don't care."

"You tilt your head slightly to the left every time you're uncomfortable," she pointed out.

Crispin straightened his head. "And you tug your ear the moment *you're* uncomfortable." He rubbed his eyes and sighed. "Whatever this Leeondris is to you doesn't matter. Once I help you and your crew track him down, I'm gone."

Rahab's lips tightened; her smile faded. "Right. Enjoy resting while you can. We should arrive to The Sisters tomorrow." She marched off; her fists closed tightly.

"Rahab," he called after her.

She whipped around, "What is it, Crispin?"

He was taken aback. "You called me Crispin."

She placed her hands on her hips and crinkled her nose. "Aye. What of it?"

A smile snaked across his face. "I told you I'd grow on you."

Rahab rolled her hazel eyes and headed back to her room, "Good night, Your Highness."

"That's worse than Mainlander."

Rahab turned around and bowed, sweeping her hand from her side down to the floor, her head nearly touching the wooden planks. "Apologies, Your Mightiness."

He muttered and rubbed his temples, "And now the bowing. Please stop."

She popped up and curtsied, "Whatever will please His Lordship."

Crispin pursed his lips and ran his fingers through his wet hair, "So is this what we're doing now?"

"Whatever do you mean, Majesty?" Rahab spread her fingers and fanned her face like one of the ladies of court.

"Look at me," Crispin closed one eye, gritted his teeth, and thrusted an imaginary sword around the narrow hallway. "I'm a scary pirate here to plunder your fields, drink your ale, and bed ugly women just because I can."

Rahab stared at him. He couldn't get a read on her. Was she amused? Offended? Angry? He holstered the invisible weapon and tilted his head slightly to the left.

"Too far?" he asked.

Rahab snickered. "Who were you impersonating? I'd like to meet that pirate."

"It's how we as children imagined," he cleared his throat, "how we imagined pirates talked," his voice trailed off.

Rahab laughed. It was a glorious laugh that made his heart soar. "You want to see our impersonation of you Mainlanders?"

"Absolutely."

She threw her hands in the air, shuddered in fear, and wailed in a high-pitched voice, "Oh no! What are we to do? The fearsome pirates of Pulau are here. We should just roll over like dogs. Maybe, if we're good, they won't spank us."

"Spank us?" Crispin roared; his deep laugh echoed through the passageway. "That's ridiculous."

"What?" she shrugged. "You've never been spanked by a pirate?"

He furrowed his brow, "You spank people you rob?"

"Nooooo," she slowly shook her head. "We would never."

After an intense stare off, they both broke out into laughter.

"You're funny," she said.

"You've got a great laugh," Crispin said without thinking. He rubbed the nape of his neck. *Was she blushing?*

Rahab sobered up at the compliment, her fingers scratching her earlobe. "Well, I suppose we should get some rest. Big day tomorrow."

"Right." Crispin nodded, realizing he'd been standing in the hall shirtless and barefoot. "Sleep well." He retreated into his room and sat on the cot. A smile inched across his face. He couldn't wait to tell Salome he battled a sea monster. She'd be so jealous.

CHAPTER 10
RANALDA

Thanos had been arrested and taken to the dungeon located underneath the Black Tower. Ranalda had never been this far underground before and had no intention of returning. Her hood draped over her blonde hair. Her black cloak dragged behind her, collecting bits of dirt, water, and sewage. Ranalda's pale hand shot up to cover her nose – the stench was unbearable. Blood, bile, waste, and rat droppings permeated the torch lit hallways. She passed cell after cell until she reached the end of the corridor. Two Thrak sat on either side of the iron door.

When they saw her approaching, one growled, "Who goes there?"

Ranalda quickened her pace without identifying herself.

The guards grabbed their weapons; one had a longsword, the other a mace.

"This hall is off limits!" The second Thrak screeched.

Within a few feet of them, she withdrew her hand from her cloak pocket and blew a white powder in their faces. In seconds, they both slumped to the ground, asleep. She scooped the key hanging from Thrak 87624's neck and unlocked the door to Thanos' cell.

The prince sat on the slab of rock meant to be a bed with his head buried in his hands. When he looked up, his blond tresses that had fallen forward swung back to cover the shaven parts of his head.

By the look in his weary eyes, Ranalda knew he didn't expect to see her.

"Ranalda?" He straightened up and fingered his hair back, though without the proper products, it wouldn't hold the structure he was so fond of. "What are you doing here?"

"Mother plans to have you executed in the morning for murdering Father." She leaned against the doorframe, flipping the key around in her fingers.

"I didn't kill the old man."

"I know."

"You…you believe me?" He sounded relieved.

"Isn't it obvious? Mother killed father and will not allow you to stand trial for

Gomorrians to find you guilty or not. She is preparing the gallows for you as we speak."

Thanos stood up and started pacing the tiny cell. If he wanted to, he could stand in the middle of the room, stretch his arms and his fingertips would touch either side of the walls. "I don't want to die, Ranalda." He stepped toward her, taking her hands in his and lifted them to his lips. "You have to help me."

"I intend to, Thanos." She gently retrieved her hands and motioned him to follow her.

As he stepped out, he noticed the guards hunched over. "Did you…?"

"Kill them?" She shook her head. "No. That's when people start asking questions." She patted her cloak, "Sleeping powder. It will look like you escaped while they slept."

His expression hardened. "Where did you get the sleeping powder?"

"Don't ask questions." Ranalda frowned. "Follow me."

The twins scurried through the prison halls, avoiding the patrolling Thrak because they were both unarmed.

"We should have taken the Thrak's weapons," Thanos whispered angrily.

"It has to look like they fell asleep while guarding you. If we took their weapons, it would look suspicious. Now hush."

They climbed up the black stone steps that led them to the street level. Slipping past more Thrak, they slithered through the sleeping city to the northern gates where a saddled horse was waiting for him.

"This is where I leave you." She untied the horse from its tether and handed her brother the reigns. "Get as far away from here as you can. Go where mother cannot find you."

"No guards?" Thanos glanced over at the oddly unguarded gate.

"I have taken care of them. But they will not abandon their posts for long. You must hurry."

Thanos embraced his sister and kissed her forehead. "I owe you my life, Ranalda." He mounted the horse. "I will return when I know I can defeat her. We will be together again. I promise."

"Then I will await your return." She wrapped her arms around herself and watched as he swiftly rode into the night.

Maltidys stepped out of the darkness and approached her daughter from behind. "You did well, Ranalda." Maltidys stood next to her and watched as her son disappeared.

"Thank you, Mother." Ranalda bowed her head. "What happens now?"

"When the Gomorrians learn the accused prince killed the two Thrak guarding his cell and that he escaped the city in the dead of night, they will know without a doubt, that he is guilty." She smirked, "No trial necessary."

"We are free," Ranalda whispered, a tear running down the side of her cheek.

Maltidys rested a hand on her daughter's shoulder. "Yes, Ranalda, we are free."

CHAPTER 11
ADONIJAH

Adonijah was fond of women and women were fond of him. It was a blessing, or curse, depending on how he felt that day. Visiting islands inhabited by mostly women, was nothing short of a dream come true – so, why could he only think about *her*? Salome consumed his thoughts; something he was unaccustomed to, but not upset by. She was different from other women he had met before. And his feelings for her were different.

Since leaving the Mainland, they seemed to have developed a… spark? Was that even the right word to describe what was happening between them? Was there *anything* happening between them? He wasn't sure, but the one thing he *was* certain of was his attraction to her was reciprocated. As much of a hard time as she gave him, as much as her tongue lashed out at him, her eyes betrayed her every time.

Her eyes.

Her eye.

Her marked eye.

The first day they squared off in The Hollow, he noticed something unusual about her eyes. They were different colors. It was strange, haunting even. From that moment on, he hadn't been able to stop picturing her eyes every time he closed his. He saw the crinkles along the sides of Salome's eyes when she smiled and how she scrunched her nose when she was deep in thought.

Her scars.

She had so many scars.

Even he had left his mark on her in The Hollow – and she had left her mark on him, in more ways than one.

If she only knew the power she had over him.

Adonijah shook his head as the bell tolled on Antrope, fondly known as Arena Island, and dragged him back to reality. Men weren't allowed on the training grounds, but because Salome pulled some strings with the Myridians, he and Cato were permitted to escort Salome as her protection detail.

Adonijah's gaze drifted to where Salome sat on the ground tying the leather sandals she had been given to train in. Her long, tan legs glistened as the sun kissed them. His eyes slowly travelled up her legs, up her body, to her face, to her lips… His chest burned when he realized she was watching him too.

There was that warm smile he had grown so fond of.

"How long have you known her?" Cato's voice interrupted his thoughts.

It was no secret Adonijah didn't like Cato, but Harbona insisted they spend more time together so they could get to know one another. He knew what Harbona was doing. Harbona wanted him to change his mind, to change his opinion about Cato and the Mountain Men. But that wasn't going to happen.

Adonijah knew Cato was a Stormcrag, therefore he couldn't be trusted.

What else did he need to know?

Adonijah realized he had been silently staring at the Stormcrag after he asked his question. Adonijah softened his brow.

"What was your question?"

"I asked how long have you two known each other?" Cato repeated his seemingly innocent question.

"Long enough," Adonijah snarled.

"Are you two…?" Cato motioned with his hands, touching both his index fingers together.

"Why do you want to know?" Adonijah's shoulders tensed.

"I'm not the only one who is curious."

"Well, it is no one's business." Adonijah tilted his neck to the side and cracked it. He knew it was probably Diron, Captain of *The Golden Rose,* who was the other interested party in the status of his and Salome's relationship. Another man he wasn't sure he trusted, even if Harbona did.

"So, that's a no." Cato stretched his arms above his head with a yawn. "Why do they have to train this early?"

"Hold on," Adonijah squared his chest to Cato. "What do you mean, 'that's a no'?"

"Simple really." Cato absent mindedly cracked his knuckles. "If you two were a couple, you would have just said so. Instead, you huffed your way through the question. I might not come from one of the more sophisticated kingdoms, but I'm far from stupid."

Adonijah knew arguing would be pointless. He hadn't known Salome long, but it seemed like they were meant to find one another. Or had known one another in another life? Cato didn't need to know all of that. He didn't deserve to know all of that.

Adonijah tried to push their first night in Myr to the back of his mind, but their "almost kiss" kept finding a way back into his thoughts – his desires. Maybe they could be more than what they were which was… friends? *Were they friends?* Or were they simply fellow soldiers? No. He swatted that idea down immediately. He wouldn't have this unquestionable yearning to kiss his fellow soldier. Unless that soldier was Salome.

What was she doing to him? Even his thoughts were nonsense. All he knew was he wanted to protect her.

Adonijah became very aware Cato was still watching him and he cleared his throat. "Why did you come with us?"

Cato reclined against the grassy hillside, resting his arms over his eyes to block the rising sun's rays. "I already told you. I owed Salome a life debt."

Adonijah lit his pipe and exhaled with a disgruntled huff, "As far as I'm concerned, you two are even."

Cato peeked one brown eye through his arms. "How do you figure?"

"She saved you from being held captive by the Thrak. You saved her from dying by the Thrak's blade." Adonijah shot Cato a vicious yet satisfied glance. "Even." Cato chuckled which irritated Adonijah. "What's so funny, Stormcrag?"

"Harbona told me I should ask you to train me how to fight. That you would be a good teacher. But now, I can see how ridiculous that was."

Adonijah held the tip of his pipe between his teeth. "I would make an excellent teacher if -"

"Then you *will* train me?" Cato interrupted, sitting up straight.

"If," Adonijah continued, side eyeing him, "I cared enough to teach you."

Cato released a defeated sigh. "How long are we going to be sitting out here?"

"Until she's finished."

They sat silence. Adonijah glanced at Cato, who seemed deep in thought, and remembered Salome's words. *"Should he be judged for the sins of his ancestors?"*

"Why do you want to learn how to fight?" Adonijah broke the stillness between them and immediately regretted reaching out.

Cato didn't look up from his twiddling fingers. "Had I known how to fight, the Thrak wouldn't have taken me prisoner."

"Did your Stormcrags not teach you anything?" Adonijah stretched his legs out and exhaled another puff of smoke, watching it float away. "I thought your people knew how to handle weapons."

"I'm too scrawny to be considered a worthy warrior."

Adonijah hated he detected genuine sadness in Cato's voice. It was true Cato was extremely thin; his ribs were nearly visible through his clothes. He was also clean-shaven when the Stormcrags proudly grew their beards in two sectioned pieces boasting of their victories in battle.

"My parents were taken by the Gomorrians when I was young," Cato said, "and my sister was captured by the Krazaks shortly afterwards." He hesitated. He seemed to be struggling with the memories deep within the abyss of his haunted mind. "If I had known how to wield a sword…"

"You blame yourself?" Adonijah rested his elbows on his knees. Cato remained quiet. "I lost my mother," Adonijah offered. "I was young and thought if I knew how to fight, I could have saved her."

"But?"

"But I did know how to fight, and she still died." Adonijah's misty eyes met Cato's. "You can spend the rest of your life blaming yourself, or you can get even."

"Have you gotten even?"

"Soon."

The Stormcrag nodded, shoulders hunched, defeat in his eyes.

Adonijah grumbled to himself, unsure if he was more irritated that they had more in common than he would have liked to admit, or that Harbona probably already knew that.

"Stand up."

Cato's light brown eyes flashed. "Are you going to fight me or train me?"

"Don't make me regret this," Adonijah rolled his head in a circular motion. Extending a hand to help Cato up, the Stormcrag took it and smiled as he jumped to his feet. "This doesn't mean I like you." Adonijah maintained eye contact as he stashed his pipe in his pocket.

"Of course not," Cato replied, rubbing his hands together in anticipation.

"And before I show you anything -"

"If I even think about betraying you or Salome, you'll kill me," Cato interjected and rolled his eyes.

Adonijah frowned and folded his arms across his chest. "Why would you assume that's what I was going to say?"

Cato took a step back. "Is that not what you were about to say?"

"No."

"Oh." Cato gritted his teeth. "What were you going to say?"

"I want you to answer my question from before." Adonijah stared down his nose at him. "Why did you come with us?" Before Cato could utter a word, Adonijah lifted his hand and said, "And I want the truth."

Cato stroked a hand over his short-cropped white hair, a scar zig-zagged along the side of his head. "The truth is," he clicked his teeth, "there are two reasons I joined your company."

"The first being?" Adonijah prodded.

"I have spent my entire life in the Bone Mountains fearing other Mainlanders. But then you rescued us from the Thrak, from certain death, and I had to know why."

"Salome saved you." Adonijah corrected. "I didn't want to." Cato swayed side-to-side, an immediate tell in Adonijah's mind of his nerves and discomfort. "And the second reason?"

"I noticed Salome's eyes."

Adonijah suppressed the panic rising within his chest; his fingers brushing the handle of his blade. He swore an oath to protect her. An oath he was intent on keeping. "What about her eyes?"

"Stormcrags believe in a prophecy that a woman with two colored eyes would one day bring peace to the Bone Mountains. She would be the only one to finally reunite the Stormcrags and the Krazaks," Cato explained. "So, when I saw her eyes, I knew she was the one. I had to follow her. Serve her in her quest and maybe when the time was right..." His gaze dropped to his feet.

"...she would save your people." Adonijah finished Cato's thought.

"I know you don't believe me -"

"I believe you."

"You do?" Cato whispered sheepishly.

"Aye." Adonijah nodded, unsheathing his long sword. Cato instinctively took a step back. "Here." Adonijah turned the blade so Cato could grab the handle. "Show me what you know, and I will teach you what you don't."

Cato stretched out his hand to take the weapon. His long, bony fingers wrapped around the hilt, and he raised it in front of him. He spied his reflection in the clean blade and saw a soldier. Sort of. Not really. But with Adonijah's help, he could be.

Cato smiled, "Does this mean we're friends now?"

"Don't press your luck, Stormcrag."

"What should I call you?"

"Adonijah."

"Well, that seems boring considering the fun nickname you've given me." Cato scratched his jawline. "Maybe, Northwind-er?"

"That's terrible," Adonijah deadpanned.

"Northerner?"

"Why are you doing this? Call me Adonijah."

"Will you call me Cato?"

"I prefer Stormcrag." Adonijah wasn't about to use his name. He didn't want them to be that friendly.

"Then I will call you.... Swamps." Cato flashed a gap tooth smile.

"Swamps?"

"Salome told me that's where you used to live."

Adonijah rubbed his temples, squinting his eyes. "Just... show me your fighting stance."

"As you wish, Swamps." Cato saluted before noticing Adonijah's serious expression. "Sir Swamps?"

"Your fighting stance."

Cato planted his feet wider than his shoulders and held the sword with both hands perpendicular to his thin frame.

Adonijah blinked. "What the hell is that?" He motioned his hand toward Cato's awkward posture.

"My fighting stance."

Adonijah groaned, "Almighty, what have I gotten myself into?"

"Well, that's encouraging," Cato rolled his eyes with a disgruntled huff.

Adonijah's fascination, or obsession, with weaponry began at a young age. He was from the farmlands north of Gomorrah, raised by a single mother. He hardly ever saw his father, but on the unfortunate occasion he did show up, Adonijah's mother would have him run into the fields to stay out of his father's reach.

During one of his father's unexpected visits, nine-year-old Adonijah snuck back to their two-room farmhouse, and saw his father strike his mother. The sight enraged him, and he vowed to kill his father the next time he came around.

He knew from his grandfather's drunken ramblings that his mother had been raped and he was the bastard that was the constant reminder of the attack. His mother had been seventeen when...

He didn't want to think about the cruelty his mother endured. Although his grandfather hated him, his mother loved him.

"You are my blessing," she would say as she combed her fingers through his hair while he fell asleep in their shared bed.

The next year when his father's entourage returned, his father was noticeably absent. Adonijah's mother sensed something was wrong and forced him to hide under the floorboards since he would be spotted retreating to the fields. He could still remember her golden hair in a single braid, smelling like wildflowers. Her warm brown eyes that emanated joy, and the freckles across the bridge of her nose he always wished he had.

But those memories were tainted when the disfigured Shadow – the Nameless Rider – kicked in their door and grabbed his mother by her throat, pushing his inebriated grandfather to the floor with his free hand.

"Where's the boy?" the Shadow growled.

"He's gone." His mother gasped, clawing at the soldier's tightening grip.

"Last chance, Satara. Where is he?"

"Tell him, he will never have my son."

"Have it your way." The Nameless Rider snapped her neck and dropped her lifeless body to the floor, shaking the floorboard dust and clouding his hiding spot.

His grandfather lugged himself up and threw a knife from the kitchen table at the Shadow. He caught the blade with little effort and launched it back at the old man, lodging it into his chest.

"Search the area for the boy." The Nameless Rider instructed the other two soldiers in his company. "I'll burn the house."

As flames engulfed the small farmhouse, Adonijah crawled on his belly to the edge of the house and kicked down the loose boards from under their shack and escaped.

Adonijah hid in the fields until the soldiers disappeared. With just a knife at his disposal, he wandered Adalore, doing odd jobs for a hot meal or place to rest, learning fighting techniques from strangers as he travelled. That's how he became known as the Wanderer. Now, nineteen, he had enough grief and experience to exact his final revenge. He would kill the Nameless Rider. He would kill his father. And then his mother could finally rest.

But first – he had to teach Cato.

Adonijah shook his head, rattling the sad memories from of his mind, and cleared his throat.

"Put one foot forward and one foot back. You will have better balance and a better chance to lunge at your attacker." Adonijah grabbed Cato by the shoulders and pointed to where his feet should be. The Stormcrag quietly obeyed. "Now, you look like a soldier." Adonijah nodded in approval.

"I feel… stupid."

Adonijah chuckled.

"So, you *do* know how to laugh," Cato snorted. "I was beginning to wonder."

Adonijah sighed and waved his hand forward. "Lunge."

Cato extended his front leg straight ahead and stabbed into the air with his sword. "Lesson one, complete."

"Is this a joke to you?" Adonijah crossed his arms over his chest and frowned. "Tell me now before I waste my time."

Cato sucked in a breath, "Sorry." He scratched the side of his head. "I'm nervous."

That wasn't what Adonijah had expected to hear. Mountain Men were ferocious in nature – some would say unfeeling. Cato wasn't like his kind in stature or attitude. It was almost difficult to dislike Cato. *Almost.* Adonijah had been deceived and hurt before. He wouldn't let that happen again – especially with Salome in the picture.

Adonijah wiped the nape of his neck. "Lunge." Cato once again obeyed his instructions. Adonijah nodded and clasped his arms behind his back. "Again."

He would make a soldier of him yet. And possibly a friend? Probably not.

CHAPTER 12
SALOME

Salome was glad Adonijah and Cato were only forty feet away. She was nervous – but not exactly sure why. It wasn't like she really needed any training. For over a decade that was all she and her brother did. Zophar taught them all about swords, knives, archery, hand to hand combat, and even setting traps to ambush their enemies. She had put in the training, and she had the scars to prove it.

As she strapped on the leather sandals Mika had tossed her, instructing she was to wear them per Qata Vishna tradition, Adonijah's gaze had not gone unnoticed. She saw desire in his eyes, the same desire from the other night when they almost…

She cursed under her breath, inhaling a deep breath of salty sea air wafting over the cliff where the training arena had been built.

Why did she care?

Why did she want to kiss him?

She had never concerned herself with the ways of men before but now – he was taking up too much time in her thoughts. Time and thoughts she really couldn't – shouldn't – waste on him.

Her task was simple. Defeat her sister and avenge innocent blood – her family's blood. She looked at her tattoo and their faces flashed in her mind. She lost four brothers: Lykos, Mosgalath, Elias, and Jepthudar. Lykos was the responsible one. Mosgalath was the smartest. Elias was the prankster. Jepthudar was the sweet one. Although, most of her brothers teased her about her eyes, Crispin included, she missed them terribly.

She missed Crispin. She *really* missed him.

Salome fought hard not to think of him or what dangers he might be facing. But every night before she drifted off to sleep, she would recite the same prayers she had spoken for the last twelve years. She would whisper the names of her fallen family members – blessing them in the afterlife and keeping their memory alive in the present – but after they parted ways in The Hollow, she added Crispin and

Zophar to her list; asking the Almighty to protect and watch over them because she no longer could. Praying she would see what remained of her family again.

Family.

Family meant everything.

Yet, family was what ripped hers apart.

Niabi had been married off to the King of Elisor, the Leader of the Andrago, before Salome had been born. The sisters had never met. At least, not formally. Salome saw her once, and it was the night Niabi attacked Northwind.

Salome remembered weaving through the chaotic city streets, sneaking past hordes of enemy soldiers undetected. Ducking into a dark alley, Zophar pushed Crispin and Salome against a white stone house and motioned for them to keep quiet.

"Wait for me here." Without another word, Zophar scurried off into the darkness.

Salome was too afraid to even breath. Neither she nor her brother knew their way around their city. In fact, they had only left the castle grounds a handful of times and hadn't bothered to observe their surroundings.

Heavy footsteps stomped on the main street. She sucked in a breath as the footsteps drew closer, hoping they wouldn't be discovered. The company of Shadows marched up the cobblestone path with the Green-Eyed-Raven leading them toward the White Keep. As they came within view, a soldier from Gershom's troop stepped forward.

"Lord Gershom has taken control of the White Keep," he reported flatly. "The city is yours."

"Not yet it isn't," the Mistress of Shadows hissed.

"The North belongs to you." The soldier narrowed his eyes and grunted, "Celebrate your victory."

Tala pointed his blood-stained sword toward the soldier, his tone too bold for his liking. "Shall I kill him, my Queen?"

"No." Niabi circled the soldier like prey. "The North still has a living king – one I must now deal with."

"He is in the throne room." The soldier's voice quivered and his breathing slowed. "They are waiting for you."

"How fitting he would be in his beloved throne room the night he dies." Even with ash and soot thick in the air and portions of the city burning, Niabi's focus on the White Keep did not waver.

"Should I show you the way?" The soldier asked, hoping to fall into her good graces for his disrespect.

"That won't be necessary." Facing him with a twinkle in her eye, Niabi stabbed him in the abdomen with one of her daggers and watched as he dropped to the ground. "I know the way." Looking over her shoulder at her Shadows, she said, "Move out."

As soon as the company was out of sight, the children sprinted down the street unsure of where they were headed. They rounded the corner and bumped into a soldier. Before they were able to scream, Zophar covered their mouths and whispered, "It's me."

"We saw her!" Crispin blurted.

"Saw who?"

Salome grabbed his hand, tears in her eyes, "She is going to kill father."

"We must get out of the city before she realizes you escaped." Zophar marched onward, dragging them forward.

"Why is she doing this?" Salome refused to take another step and ripped her hand from Zophar's grasp. "Who is she?"

"One day when we are far away from here, I will answer any question you ask of me, Princess, but today is not that day."

"But -"

"I need you to trust me." Zophar knelt before her. "If you don't, there won't be anything I can do to protect you."

Salome and Crispin followed him into a small house near the southwest side of the wall that encircled the city. Zophar closed the creaky door behind them and pushed the furniture to the sides of the room. Kicking a dusty rug up, they saw a door in the floorboards. He lifted the heavy latch and revealed a tunnel.

"Where does that go?" Crispin asked.

"Under the wall. It is the only way we can get out now."

Not needing any further explanation, Crispin descended the ladder into the tunnel. Zophar motioned for Salome to follow her brother.

"Lykos promised he would see us again." She took a step back from the hole.

"The Almighty willing, you might." Zophar once again motioned for her to follow the path.

Instead, she opened the door of the house and stared up at the White Keep in the center of the city with clenched fists. Ash rained down like snow and she no longer felt fear.

"One day when you least expect it," she hissed, "I will come for you, and I will kill you."

She was five. And she meant what she had said. One day she would kill her sister. It seemed it was now destiny for the sisters to face off. But Niabi had taken the impenetrable White City in a night. How could Salome compete with power like that?

"Salome!" Mika's voice ripped her from her thoughts. "Are you alright?"

Salome nodded, blushing, "I'm fine."

"I called out to you several times." Mika arched her brow.

Salome scratched the nape of her neck. "I guess I didn't hear you."

By the grace of the Almighty, Mika let the matter drop. "Are you ready?"

"I'm ready."

Mika led Salome to the center of the arena. The training grounds, located on Antrope, the smallest island of the Isles of Myr, was built atop of the cliff's plateau which overlooked the blue seas and the palace on the main island. Once again, Salome found herself catching her breath at the magnificent view and could feel the warm sea breeze wrap around her like a familiar and much needed hug.

Mika tossed Salome a sword with a bronze hilt. "You have skill with a blade?"

"I've been trained." Salome circled the handle around her hand.

"Trained by the Qata Vishna?"

"No, by -"

"Then you have not been trained," Mika clicked her tongue.

Salome's nostrils flared, "I was trained by Zophar of Borg, my father's Master of War."

"He might have taught you to fight," Mika conceded, "but the Qata Vishna will teach you to war." She cocked her head and flashed a confident smile.

"And there's a difference?" Salome's hand went to her hip.

"When you fight, you battle your equal. When you war, you defeat your lessers." Mika nodded her head to the weapon Salome held. "Show me what the Westerner taught you."

Salome took her stance and Mika shook her head in disapproval. "What?" Salome huffed.

"Your posture is that of a man."

Salome glanced at her footing, "It's a rooted position -"

Mika clicked her tongue again and shook her head, "You have been around men far too long, Cousin. Give me the greatest male warrior in Adalore and the least of the Qata Vishna will defeat him."

Salome straightened, "Bold talk for a people who have not seen battle in decades. "

"And why do you think that is?" Mika circled her cousin, arms securely fastened behind her back. "The Mainlanders do not pick fights with us because we are unbeaten. To war with us is a fool's endeavor."

"Unbeaten?"

"The Qata Vishna are at a level no man can touch." She stopped and stood face to face with Salome. "If you learn our ways, you will not be defeated."

"Is that how my sister defeated my father?" Salome's eyes narrowed; the words left a bitter taste in her mouth. "Her Qata Vishna training?"

Mika's expression changed, as if she was deep in thought. "Half-blood, yet she was the fiercest among us."

Salome crossed her arms over her chest, "You sound jealous."

Mika shook her head. "I would have followed her into the awaiting arms of Death…"

"But?"

"The world of men would not allow her to rise and take her rightful place at the High Table. Imagine what she could have been, had she stayed with us."

"She's a queen now -"

"Enough of your sister." Mika cut her off with what looked like sadness in her eyes. "It is not my story to share. I am here to train you. So," she pointed at the sword, "show me what you know."

Salome had so many questions she wanted Mika to answer, but the Myridian would duel her whether she was ready or not. She took her stance and Mika shook her head in dismay again. Salome grasped her sword with both hands, eyes fixed on Mika. The Red Maiden unsheathed her curved sword.

Mika reached her hand forward, fingers motioning for Salome to attack. "Begin."

Salome was used to defensive fighting, not being the aggressor. But with Mika's beckoning, she leapt forward, her sword swinging toward Mika with speed and fury.

Mika stood still and only lifted her sword to block the attack at the last possible moment. She didn't even look like she was trying.

They exchanged clashes of swords, side stepping one another. The difference between them wasn't the moves so much as the style. Salome was nowhere near as quick, seamless, and fluid as Mika was. Mika didn't appear to even be fighting – more like dancing. Her spins, twists, splits, and back bends astounded Salome. The most acrobatic move Salome had under her belt was a leg sweep and that wasn't perfect nor graceful.

Salome finally caught Mika's blade and flicked it from her hands, disarming her. Salome smirked, "It would seem Zophar taught me well."

"He taught you well." Mika leapt in the air, spun around, and kicked Salome's sword out of her hand and upon landing had unsheathed a pair of daggers that were strapped behind her back. "But he did not teach you everything."

Salome realized too late that her mouth was wide open and quickly closed it before Mika could comment. She snatched one knife strapped to the back of her pants and the wolf dagger from her thigh, flipping them around her hands.

"I'm better with my knives," Salome planted her feet and tilted her head.

"Let us hope so," Mika snorted.

Salome could feel Adonijah and Cato's eyes on her, but she refused to look their way. She didn't need to be distracted. She didn't need to lock eyes with *him.*

"You think he's impressed?" Mika asked, as if she could read her mind.

Salome attempted to keep a straight face, but the slight twitch of an eyebrow betrayed her.

Mika flashed a mischievous smile. "Let's give him something to think about later, shall we?" Mika lunged at her, blades whipping in separate directions to throw Salome off balance. Salome blocked both incoming daggers and kicked Mika away from her.

"Good," Mika cooed. "Knives are in your blood. The weapon of choice for the Qata Vishna."

Mika dodged Salome's blows, twisting side to side, flashing her back as she spun in a complete circle. Their knives sliced through the air so quickly, it didn't look like they were armed with weapons at all. Mika knocked one of Salome's knives from her hand, leaving just her wolf dagger.

Salome held the dagger tightly, the blade faced toward the ground. She hunched her body slightly, closing her chest off from attack, making herself a smaller target.

Mika flipped, kicked, swiped, and lunged to disarm Salome but she blocked the blows and held fast to her weapon.

Salome studied Mika's movements, and though they seemed chaotic and unstructured, there was a pattern. Mika lunged one of her arms forward, Salome locked her arm around Mika's, popped her elbow forcing her to drop her knife.

"Good," Mika nodded approvingly, back-to-back with Salome, arms still locked. "But I am afraid, you've lost sight of your footing."

"What?" Salome glanced down to see Mika's foot swipe Salome's leg, knocking her to the ground. Salome's dagger fell and as she reached for it, Mika's remaining knife sliced between Salome's outstretched fingers, lodging itself into the arena's grass.

Salome's eyes shot up. Mika's dagger was less than an inch from having stabbed her hand. "Did you miss?"

"Miss?" Mika planted her hands on her hips and frowned. "A Qata Vishna does not miss."

Still on her belly, Salome spat, "You could have stabbed me."

"If I meant to stab you," Mika crouched in front of her and withdrew her knife from the ground, "I would have stabbed you." She offered Salome her hand and helped her up. "Not bad for a Mainlander trained by a man from the West."

Salome retrieved her knives and holstered them. "Was my mother a Qata Vishna?"

Mika shook her head. "No. The eldest daughter is destined for the Qata Vishna. The second daughter for diplomacy. The third for the oracle."

"So, you being the oldest of your mother's daughters -"

"Qata Vishna." Mika holstered her weapons. "My sister, Marina, was meant for diplomacy. But you have seen how she treats those from the Mainland."

"I'm assuming she's not a great diplomat."

Mika laughed. "Not at all."

"Mother!" A young girl sprinted across the arena and jumped into Mika's outstretched arms.

"My little warrior! I see you outsmarted your guard detail again." Mika kissed her ten-year-old daughter on the cheek.

"It's not hard to get away from them."

"Well, I suppose that confirms what I already know."

"What's that?" Utara snickered.

Mika cupped Utara's face in her hands, "You are most definitely my daughter."

Salome was taken aback. She didn't know Mika had a daughter and she was dressed like a miniature Qata Vishna. Utara was the spitting image of her mother: long black hair, green eyes, olive skin, and a mischievous grin.

Mika stood behind her daughter, her hands resting on her shoulders and said, "Salome, this is my daughter, Utara. She has just made her tenth year and is now able to begin her training to become a Qata Vishna."

Just made her tenth year. Korah died when he turned ten. Salome had refused to think about the young boy from the Tree House Forest but seeing Utara so full of life reminded her of what sparked their journey. Korah.

"It's good to meet you, Utara." Salome managed to say with a sad smile.

"One day, when I'm older," Utara rattled off the words as fast as she could, brushing one of her feet against the back of the opposite leg, "I'm going to be the Red Maiden, just like my mother."

Mika beamed, clearly proud of the little version of herself. Salome didn't have much time with her own mother and seeing them together brewed fond memories, sad memories, too. She would give anything to have her mother back. To know if she was proud of the woman she had become.

When Salome was little, she would constantly find herself on the receiving end of a stern look and reprimand from her mother because she had been crawling through the bushes to scare the gardeners, or challenging her brothers to fight, or for ripping and setting fire to all her dresses in order to wear pants. After Bilhah fussed at her, she would flash a bright smile Salome's way letting her know how much she still loved her, though she was one of the reasons Bilhah's hair had begun turning white.

"Aren't you too old to be training to be a Qata Vishna?" Utara's question was met with an immediate frown from Mika.

"Our cousin is just the right age to become one of us, Utara."

"Sorry, Mother." Utara glanced up at her mother who was still holding her shoulders.

"We should head back to the palace." Mika wiped dirt off her daughter's face. "There is a lot to do before the festival begins tonight."

"Festival?" Salome's eyes widened. "What festival?"

"The Festival of Forbidden Fruit. Once a year, the men and women of Myr are gathered together to find a suitable mate," Mika explained as they walked toward Adonijah and Cato. "As royalty, your presence will be required, of course."

"I'm not sure I'll be any good in a festival setting," she protested.

"Don't worry," Mika tapped Salome's arm and winked. "You're not expected to find a mate tonight, unless you want to."

Salome's cheeks flushed, her eyes fluttering up to Adonijah's awaiting ones.

"We can go?" Cato stretched his arms high above his head.

"Yes," Mika affirmed. "Race you to the ship," she bumped Utara with her hip and together they took off down the hill. Cato followed them closely leaving Adonijah and Salome to make their way down to the awaiting ship.

"You held your own out there," Adonijah sparked the conversation once he knew the others wouldn't overhear them.

"I lost." Salome brushed dust from her clothes.

"Everyone loses at some point," he shrugged.

"Apparently not Qata Vishna." She didn't want to talk about the Qata Vishna anymore, so she changed the subject. "Are you going to the festival tonight?"

"Wherever you go, I go."

"It seems I have to go," she grumbled. "I'm afraid this might be the first of many royal engagements I will have to attend, if my Aunt Zara has her way."

"Ah," Adonijah clicked his tongue, "it can't be that bad."

"As long as they don't force me to wear a dress, I'll be alright."

Adonijah laughed the deepest, warmest laugh she had ever heard.

"What's so funny?" Her eyes narrowed.

"Picturing you in a dress."

She crinkled her nose, waving a hand in the air. "It isn't that funny, Adonijah."

"Someone as stab happy as you in a dress?" His eyes danced in delight. "I would break out of the deepest, darkest dungeon if it meant seeing *you* in a dress." Adonijah roared again.

"I hate you." She marched ahead of him; nose pointed upward.

"If only that were true." Adonijah took longer strides and easily caught up to her again.

"If my Aunt Zara has me parading like a peacock at this festival," she snorted, "I'll dive into the sea and pray the Almighty takes me."

Adonijah caught her arm and turned her toward him. His free hand gently stroked her jawline. "It doesn't matter what she has you wear; you will still be the most beautiful woman in the room."

Salome reached up and touched his hand, guiding it away from her face. "People might see you."

"Aye, they might."

"They might think we are…" she tilted her head side to side.

"I don't care what they think." Adonijah squeezed her hands. "I only care what you think."

Salome soaked in every bit of passion in his eyes and felt the strongest urge to kiss him. They had almost kissed the night before and she dreamt about how it would feel to have his lips pressed against hers. But before she could say anything, Cato yelled at them.

"Hurry up! We're ready to cast off."

Adonijah smiled down at her, "Come on, Princess. You have a festival to get ready for."

CHAPTER 13

NIABI

Niabi sat at her desk in her high back chair and sliced her daily correspondence open. The light breeze blowing through her office was evidence the season was changing from summer to autumn. She preferred the warm weather over the harsh winters of the north, but Rollo loved the cold, and this was going to be the first winter without him. She reluctantly pushed him to the back of her mind. If she allowed herself to dwell on him, she would never respond to any of the letters sitting on her desk.

She skimmed through the first six letters and they were of no importance. Invitations by lords and ladies of Northwind to join them for their parties, weddings, and funerals; all of which she would decline as she always did. She had never been one for attending social events and after Rollo died, she was even more determined to be a recluse. They would not get the satisfaction of hosting their queen when she was still in such a vulnerable state.

Niabi tossed the invitations back on the black wooden desk and reached for the last folded parchment. It bore no seal and was addressed to *The Queen of Northwind.* No formality like the others. She unfolded the letter and scanned the scratchy penmanship with curious eyes.

To the Queen of Northwind.

I offer you a trade. Your sister for my kingdom.

I am staying at the White Wolf Inn.

I request an audience with you as soon as possible.

Signed,

Prince Thanos of Gomorrah, Rightful and Soon to be King.

A twisted smile tugged at her lips.

How peculiar, she thought to herself.

Word had reached the White Keep that King Cyler was dead; murdered by his own son. The son that had escaped the impenetrable Gomorrian dungeons before he could be tried and executed. The same son who now requested to speak with her, to make a trade.

Your sister for my kingdom.

Niabi had never met the prince before, but she knew he couldn't be guilty of murder. She had the displeasure of meeting Matildys years ago and had no interest of socializing with the shrew again. Niabi couldn't prove it, but she was certain the murder was Matildys' handiwork.

But did she hate Matildys enough to help her son usurp the throne? Absolutely.

Niabi quickly jotted down her response:

Prince Thanos,

I will grant you an audience.

Signed,

Queen Niabi of Northwind

Niabi folded the letter, poured a glob of hot, black wax on the seam, and sealed it with her signet ring. After passing the message to the courier outside her door, she plopped into her chair with a well-earned glass of Myridian wine. She brought the sweet-smelling liquid to her lips and enjoyed the tingle in her mouth.

A knock on her door interrupted the first bit of relaxation she had had in weeks.

"Enter." She sighed and set her glass down.

Pash opened the door and bowed, his arm crossing over his chest and touching his left shoulder. "My Queen."

She waved him inside without turning to look at him. "What news do you bring me?"

Pash shut the door and slowly walked up to her desk; his arms firmly clasped behind his back. "We might have a problem."

Niabi leaned back in her seat and motioned for him to sit. "And what problem would that be, Pash?"

He sat down on the other side of her desk, legs shoulder-width apart, bouncing his leg rhythmically. "As you suggested, I offered my services to my father."

"And?" She pressed when he paused.

"He has asked for me to silence Lord Memucan of Numbio."

"Silence as in kill him." She took another sip of wine, not surprised by Gershom's request.

"Yes."

Niabi flicked her gaze up from her glass to Pash. "Do you intend to kill him?"

"That is what my father has asked me to do."

"That is not what I asked." Niabi poured a second glass of wine and slid it toward him.

Pash gratefully grabbed the cup and swallowed nearly half its contents in one gulp. "Do you want me to kill him?"

"I want any servant of your father's dead."

"So, that's a yes?" Pash's question seemed labored. As if it hurt him to say.

"Why does he want Memucan dead?" Niabi swirled the wine in her goblet. "He's old as dirt. Death can't possibly be far from claiming the codger."

Pash ran his fingers through his hair and scratched the back of his neck. "My father didn't give a reason."

Niabi strummed her fingers on her desk, deep in thought. She played through different scenarios as to why Gershom would want Memucan dead. *What was Gershom's game?* "What exactly did Gershom order you to do?"

"He told me to bring him Memucan's head."

"Wasn't Memucan the one who informed Gershom that my brother was in Numbio?"

"Yes," Pash nodded.

Niabi kicked her legs up on her desk exposing the black leather pants that were hidden under the billowing folds of her extravagant outfit. "Perhaps Memucan knows something Gershom does not want anyone else to find out. But why silence him now?"

"He has served his purpose?" Pash shrugged and finished his glass of wine. Niabi pointed toward the decanter for him to refill it.

"Or maybe," Niabi whispered, biting her bottom lip, "he does not want Memucan dead at all."

"What?" Pash asked, cocking his head to the side.

"It's clever really." Niabi tapped her nearly empty glass against her temple, trying to make sense of the chaotic thoughts running wild in her mind. "Gershom has a strong ally in Memucan. Even I don't have servants in Numbio." She straightened up and locked eyes with Pash. "If you go down there to kill the old man, one of two things will happen. Either Memucan will be waiting for you and will have you killed on the spot," she tapped one finger and then a second one on her desk, "or you will be brought before King Osiris for attempting to assassinate his advisor. Memucan tells him that I am the one who sent you, which would be seen as a declaration of war. With the Numbio supporting Gershom's plan to usurp my throne, he could attempt to take Northwind for himself. You would be executed, and I would be left fighting two wars. One with my siblings, and one with your father."

Pash was silent for a minute, digesting everything she said, before he responded. "I suppose it's safe to assume my father doesn't trust me."

Niabi crinkled her nose, lifting her glass to her lips. "He just wants to hurt me."

Pash leaned his head back against his chair, sighing as he stared at the ceiling. "I'm afraid I'm not as useful a spy as you thought I would be."

Niabi placed her empty glass down, stood up, and glided toward him. "You have found out enough."

"You don't seem upset." Pash's brows furrowed.

Niabi sat in his lap and walked two of her fingers up his arm. "You were only meant to be the decoy. My real eyes and ears already have Gershom's trust. No need to fret, Pash. We will know more soon enough."

Pash's hand rubbed up and down her thigh. It was apparent he was trying to process the new information, but she wasn't going to volunteer more on the matter.

"I received an interesting letter today." She changed the subject when his touch became too distracting.

"From?"

"The Prince of Gomorrah," she was delighted when his eyes widened.

"What does he want?" He crinkled his nose. Pash had never liked the Gomorrians and Niabi couldn't blame him. The Gomorrians were a cruel and vile people. Even she didn't want her mind to dwell too long on the abomination of the Thrak. She shuddered.

"Thanos has requested a meeting with me." Niabi pressed on. "And I want you to be there."

His hands tightened around her hips. "What could he possibly want with you? Surely he wouldn't be stupid enough to attempt to kill you like he killed his own father."

"Hardly," she scoffed. "He wants to make a trade. My sister for his kingdom."

"You would support a murderer?"

Niabi narrowed her eyes and pushed herself off him. "I murdered for the crown. Sometimes one must bloody their hands to get what they want."

Pash sat quietly as she walked to the other side of the room. He rose to his feet and saluted. "Forgive me, my Queen. I meant no offense. I will support whatever decision you make."

Niabi whipped around when his hand reached for the door. "Pash, don't go."

"Is there something else, my Queen?"

She stepped up to him, cupping his face in her hands. "Stay with me. I don't want to be alone tonight."

"Is that a command from my queen?" he asked, resting his fingertips on her waist.

"It is a request from the woman who loves you."

Pash tilted his head to the side, eyes soft, "You have never said that to me before."

Niabi kissed his lips, "Stay."

Pash kissed her and swept her up in his arms, her legs wrapping around his waist, and carried her to her bedroom in the adjoining room.

~

THE NEXT MORNING, Niabi rolled over on her side and opened her eyes. Pash was still lying in her bed. He looked peaceful. He looked happy. She cuddled up against him, resting her hand on his bare chest. He smiled as soon as he felt her touch.

"Good morning," he kissed her forehead, wrapping his arms around her.

"You fell asleep here."

Pash was never supposed to stay the entire night. She had made that clear from the beginning of their relationship. No one was to know about them, not because she wasn't happy being with him, but because he could be seen as a weakness in her. And if there was anything she worked hard at, it was to make sure her enemies did not see a weakness they could exploit.

Pash pulled away from her and looked into her awaiting eyes. "I can go. It's still early. No one of importance should be awake to notice me."

Niabi knew she should tell him to leave. But she hadn't woken up with someone by her side in years and she didn't realize how much she missed it until this very moment. Niabi kissed his cheek. "Stay."

His eyebrows shot up. "You want me to stay?"

"Don't make me change my mind, Pash." Niabi tucked her head so he couldn't see her smile. "I wish we could stay like this all day."

"We can." Pash chuckled. "You are the queen, you know."

"Being the queen doesn't mean I'm free."

The commander caressed her arm. "Would you leave the city and never look back, if you had the chance?"

"What?" She propped herself up on her left elbow to get a better look at him.

"We could go wherever you want." Pash twirled a strand of her black hair between his fingers. "We could disappear. Change our names. Start over."

"You make it sound so easy," she whispered.

"But?"

Niabi stroked his cheek. "I can change my name, leave this world behind me, but I will always be the Green-Eyed Raven. My sins will one day find me."

Pash sat up, covers dropping to his waist. "Niabi, we could do this. We could start over and have a life together. You said it yourself. Being the queen doesn't mean you're free."

"It's a dream, Pash. A sweet, wonderful dream that I was not meant to have." She slipped out of bed and tied a silk robe around herself. She walked over to her balcony and breathed in the sunrise.

Pash cleared his throat, still sitting in her bed. "Do you still think about him?"

Niabi glanced over her shoulder to look at him. "Who?"

"Dichali."

Pash saying her dead husband's name made her feel nauseous for some reason. Though Dichali had been gone for years, she still felt she had to be a dutiful and faithful wife. That was the main reason she never allowed her relationship with Pash to be more than what it was.

"If you are asking if I still love Dichali, yes." She nodded and returned her gaze to the sun rising over the Ignacia Sea. "I will always love him."

Pash fastened his pants and took a step toward her. "Could you ever love me as much as you loved him?"

Niabi slowly turned and rested both of her hands on his bare chest. "Pash -"

He placed his hands over hers and leaned in closer. "I love you, Niabi, but it is impossible to live in his shadow."

"I never asked you to be Dichali."

"No," he shook his head. "But when you think about the man you love, he will always be your first thought."

Niabi's throat stung, her eyes burned. "I cannot forget him."

"I am not asking you to forget him. I am asking you to make room for me." Pash took a breath. "Dichali is gone, Niabi. I am here with you now. All I want is for you to be honest with me. Will I ever be enough?"

Niabi yanked her hands from his and brushed past him, beelining for the wine decanter. "You are intimidated by a dead man." The words pierced her heart.

"I am intimidated by a dead man who is very much alive in your heart." Pash leaned against the balcony doorway. "I could never replace Dichali, but am I not also worthy of your love?"

Niabi stopped pouring her drink and swung around, locking eyes with him. "I do love you, Pash."

"But not the same."

"What would you want me to do or say to make you see that I love you?" Niabi rushed toward him, her robe wafting behind her, exposing her lean legs.

"Marry me."

She stopped. "What did you just say?" she whispered; not sure she had heard him correctly.

"I said, marry me, Niabi." Pash closed the gap between them and cupped her cheeks, "Marry me."

"I told you before, I'll never get married again."

"Then come away with me." He thumbed her jawline. "Leave all this behind."

Niabi so desperately wanted to say *yes*. But she couldn't. "I can't." Her eyes watered a second before fire took its place. "Not yet."

Pash's arms fell to his sides, and he took a step back. "Why not?"

"I have unfinished business."

"You mean to say, you have unsettled revenge."

"If that is how you would like to phrase it." She crossed her arms over her chest. "Yes, I have unsettled revenge."

"When will it be enough?" Pash rubbed the back of his neck and groaned in frustration. "When your siblings are dead? Or when my father is dead? Or how about when I'm dead?"

"Pash -"

"Revenge can consume you until your dying breath and for what?" he interrupted, a ferocity in his voice she hadn't heard before. "For your dead to be avenged? What about those who are alive who love you? Why do the dead seem to always outweigh the living?"

Niabi took a deep breath, unwilling to let one tear slip down her face. "The dead cannot fight for themselves."

"Would they even want you to fight for them?"

She circled away from him, angrily braiding her hair to keep her from snapping at him. "If Issachar had just left me alone…" she mumbled.

"You would still be married to Dichali with Rollo by your side." Even without looking at him, she knew he was wounded. She could hear it in his voice.

"Yes," she nodded.

Pash sucked in a breath. "Leaving me, where?"

Niabi finished her braid. She wasn't sure how to respond. She wanted to scream how much he meant to her. How it wasn't her fault she had all these conflicting feelings. But instead, she said nothing. And that was worse.

"Niabi," he walked up behind her and reached for her hand. "I fell in love with you the moment you walked into my father's camp in the Black Forest. And I will love you until the day I draw my last breath. I just hope you don't realize too late how much you sacrificed to still be unhappy." Pash squeezed her hand and slipped on his shirt and boots to leave.

Niabi caught his arm as he past her. "Don't go."

"It's probably best if I do." He didn't look at her.

"Pash…"

Pash grabbed the back of her head and pressed his lips to her forehead. She felt the tears coming. "These moments I have alone with you are honest reminders of the ghost you aren't ready to say goodbye to." He released her and walked out the door.

A single tear escaped her eye and then there was no stopping them.

CHAPTER 14
SALOME

Just as Salome suspected, Zara had a traditional Myridian gown delivered to her room minutes after she returned from training with Mika. Her two ladies in waiting burst through the door, dress in tow, to prepare her for the Festival of the Forbidden Fruit.

Seraphina and Rosalina, identical twins not much older than Salome, began listing everything they were sent to help her with right after introductions.

"We're here to do your hair."

"Make up."

"Lotions."

"Perfumes."

"Dressing."

"But first…"

"Your bath," they said in unison.

Salome put her foot down, both literally and figuratively, when they said they were there to bathe her. "I can bathe myself."

The sisters exchanged a sharp, disapproving glance at one another.

"I'll let you do everything you were sent here to do, without a fight," Salome bargained, "as long as you let me bathe myself. Let me have a shred of privacy."

"Fine," Rosalina was the first to agree, scratching the mole by her left eye. It was the only mark that differentiated the twin sisters.

"Alright." Seraphina raised an eyebrow, her hazel eyes bouncing from Salome's face to her dirty hands. She was clearly the harder twin to please. "But if you have one speck of dirt left on you, I will personally bathe you myself. You won't have us looking incompetent to Princess Zara."

"Deal." Salome stuck out her hand for a shake, but they groaned. "What?"

"Such a Mainlander." Seraphina crossed her arms over her chest.

"More like a man, if you ask me," Rosalina whispered to Seraphina loud enough for Salome to hear.

Salome retracted her hand, rolled her eyes, and marched into the bathing room where a large bronze inground tub awaited her with warm water. Adonijah thought *she* was stubborn. She almost couldn't wait for him to meet the twins. In fact, she relished the thought of them cornering him to spray perfume on him. She laughed.

"It doesn't sound like bathing."

Salome knew by the judgmental tone it was Seraphina. "I'm working on it."

She stripped quickly, throwing her clothes in a pile, and sank into the muscle relaxing water. She closed her eyes and leaned her head back. She had not been submerged in a tub since her days in Northwind. If she wanted to bathe in the Tree House Forest, she would use the wash basin in her room and a towel. Some days, she would get up early and bathe in the lake near their treehouse, but she stopped doing that when she noticed Jacobi would creep in the trees for a peek. The thought sent shivers up her spine, and she frowned.

Salome hadn't thought of Jacobi since she left. She wondered if the Shadows had returned. And if they had, if any of the villagers had survived. If Jacobi survived. Her nostrils flared at the thought. She didn't want to think of them anymore – think of Jacobi anymore – it was ruining her relaxing bath.

A sharp knock on the door made her jump. "Do you need help?"

Rosalina by the caring tone. Salome counted, *three, two, one*, and pointed toward the door.

"If you aren't out here in five minutes, I'm coming in."

Right on cue, Seraphina. Salome shook her head and quickly washed up, knowing Seraphina was counting down the seconds until she could break down the door separating them.

Salome wrapped the silk robe that was hanging from a hook on the wall around herself and tied it tightly at the waist. She flung open the door to the awaiting twins. Rosalina greeted her with a smile while Seraphina's eyes burned a hole into her soul.

"What next?" Salome motioned to Seraphina to take control.

Rosalina and Seraphina brushed and fashioned her wild curls with pearls to look more like Myridian royalty than a 'stab happy Mainlander'. They rubbed lotions and perfumes on her neck, arms, legs, and feet, which she had to admit felt amazing. The twins either didn't notice her scars or they didn't care because there was no mention of her body riddled with them. She was grateful they kept their mouths and opinions to themselves on that matter. Although, they were extremely talkative on all other subjects.

After Rosalina darkened her eyes with kohl and reddened her lips, Seraphina helped her slip into a flowy silk gown. It hugged her curves in all the right places and when she looked at herself in the full-length mirror propped against the wall, she froze, eyes wide.

"She's taken by her own beauty," Rosalina beamed, proud of their creation.

"She does seem speechless." Seraphina, too, appeared to soften with pride.

"I look…" Salome turned; her eyes popped when she saw her exposed back.

"Beautiful?" Rosalina filled in.

"Clean?" Seraphina shrugged her shoulders.

"Tempting?" Rosalina tried once more.

"Ridiculous." Salome finished with a snort. "I mean, look at me. I don't look like myself."

The Myridians folded their arms over their chests at the same time. Clearly, she had offended them.

"Perhaps, it is good you don't look like yourself." Seraphina's eyes narrowed. "Now you can see your potential, if you tried."

"No one is going to recognize me." Salome felt her appearance was the only thing she had any true control over, and that had been stripped from her too.

"That is the point of the Festival of Forbidden Fruit." Rosalina softened when she saw the sadness in Salome's eyes. "No one is what they seem." She walked over to Salome and grabbed her gently by her shoulders and turned her back to the mirror. "Everyone will be looking and feeling their best tonight. How else would we find suitable mates?"

Salome crinkled her nose. "I'm not looking for a mate."

"Well, not with that attitude," Seraphina snorted.

A knock echoed through the room and Rosalina scurried to answer it. Salome caught Cato's reflection in the mirror. His eyes shot to her and was taken aback at the sight of a dolled-up Salome.

"What business, Mainlander?" Seraphina snapped when he stared at Salome a bit too long for her liking.

"Harbona sent me to tell Salome it was time to go to the Grand Hall for the festival." Cato fought a smirk as he tugged at his festive robes, "Have you seen her?"

Salome rolled her eyes as Cato snickered.

"Her Royal Highness, Princess Salome of Northwind," Seraphina corrected him immediately, her nostrils flared in righteous indignation. "I suggest you address her properly or not at all."

Salome attempted to protest but Seraphina marched to the door and said, "We will bring Her Highness when she is ready, not a moment sooner." She slammed the door in Cato's face, ignoring his protests.

"Men." Rosalina huffed, shaking her head. "How do you even stand being around them?"

Salome was lost in thought and didn't hear her question. *Why didn't Harbona send Adonijah to check on her?* Maybe it was better he didn't see her in this ridiculous gown. He would probably laugh at her and hold it over her for the rest of their lives.

The rest of their lives? Where did that thought come from? Would he even stay with her after everything was said and done? Would they even be alive after facing her sister for the White Throne? She shook her head, bringing her back to Rosalina and Seraphina's awaiting faces.

"What?" Salome asked, sure she must have missed them saying something.

"Are you ready, Princess?" Rosalina smiled.

Salome swallowed and took a deep breath. "I'm ready." But she wasn't ready. She didn't know what she was walking into and for the first time in a long time, she truly felt alone.

~

THE FESTIVAL of Forbidden Fruit was more opulent than any event Salome had ever attended. The Grand Hall was exactly as it sounded. The room was three stories high with balconies overlooking the dance floor as well as the gardens. Candles filled the room and appeared like they were floating throughout the three levels where guests, men and women alike, were mingling, dancing, flirting, and coupling off, escaping to the empty rooms and romantic gardens.

Salome climbed up the stairs, more focused on not tripping over her long, silk dress than observing the male guests staring at her as if she were the prized cow at the fair. Once she reached the top level, she soaked in the entire room and gasped. The ceiling was elaborately carved into an arch with a perfect circle opening at the top to let the moonlight pour in.

As music played, she leaned over the thick stone railing and gawked as thousands of Myridians filled the floor. The light warm breeze wafted through the space and Salome was amazed it didn't blow out the floating candles.

She scanned the faces, searching for Harbona, Adonijah, or Cato. Rosalina and Seraphina had escorted her to the main doors of the Grand Hall and then disappeared, probably to ready themselves to enjoy the festivities. She found it difficult to picture Seraphina finding any male suitable enough for her liking.

"You look Myridian, but you're not from here."

Salome turned to her left as a strange man dressed in black leaned against the railing, two drinks in his hands. She could tell he was from the Eastern Lands. By the looks of his expensive clothes, he was either royalty or an ambassador. Once she accepted the drink he offered her, he raked his fingers through his short, satiny, jet-black hair. His well-groomed appearance, his almond eyes, and his alabaster skin were captivating, and she hated to admit she found him unquestionably attractive.

"You're not from here either…?

He tilted his head forward to show respect. "I am Jinn. Prince of Sakurai."

Salome reciprocated his bow, "It is an honor to meet you, Your Majesty -"

"There is no need for formality," Jinn interrupted. "Please, call me Jinn."

His smile nearly melted her. It was perfect. He looked absolutely… perfect. She couldn't even think of a different word to describe him.

"You must know who I am then," she caught herself staring and forced herself to take a sip of the fruity drink he had brought her, "if lack of formality suits you."

Jinn smiled again, "I admit, I was extremely curious to meet the surviving Princess of Northwind. But I was expecting to see someone more…"

"Regal looking?" She glanced at him.

"Pale," he chuckled. "But it seems you favor your southern kin."

Salome shifted her weight. His undivided attention made her uncomfortable. He wasn't doing anything wrong. He was just such an attractive man she found it difficult to maintain eye contact.

Pull yourself together! she internally screamed at herself before she managed to ask, "Are you here for the Festival of Forbidden Fruit?"

"I have been here for a few days on official business but didn't want to return home without attending this festival. It only happens once a year and normally Mainlanders are not allowed to participate. We Easterners call it 'The Great Fornication'."

Salome set her drink down on the railing. "I imagine in your city you don't host such festivals."

"Hardly." Jinn laughed, sipping his drink, a sparkle in his golden-brown eyes. "We are far more traditional. One's parents arrange a suitable match and that is the end of it."

"And you? Are you spoken for?" Salome spat out the question before she had a chance to think it through and immediately turned red. Had the twins not made up her face, he would have noticed her embarrassment.

"Not yet," he seemed amused by the question. "I suppose my father has not found a suitable wife of noble birth."

A woman several inches shorter than Salome with Jinn's same features emerged from the sea of faces. Her walk was slow yet purposeful and she headed straight for them.

"Princess Salome, this is Kai, my protection." Jinn motioned his hand to the petite warrior with black liner highlighting the shape of her almond eyes.

"Princess." Kai bowed, but her serious expression didn't waver. "My Prince." She bowed again, directly toward him.

"What is it, Kai?" He relaxed his back against the railing, downing the last bit of his drink.

"Your audience with Queen Nym is set for tomorrow."

Salome's eyes shifted from Kai to the prince. *How did he manage to get an audience with her grandmother, but she hadn't?*

"Anything else?"

Kai shook her head and he waved her off. Salome's eyes were glued to Kai's back when she turned to walk away. Her open back gown showcased her enormous dragon tattoo. It made Salome extremely conscious that her back was also exposed but knew it wouldn't garner the same attention. Feeling she was being watched, she turned her gaze back to the prince and found him smiling.

"Kai is known as Ryoko Naga to my people. She was one of the orphans that won the Dragon Tournament."

"Dragon Tournament?"

"Every royal is assigned an assassin to protect them. So, when a guardian is needed, we have orphans trained as assassins to compete in a tournament. Whoever is left standing at the end, is assigned to the royal. Kai is mine."

Salome crinkled her nose. "Forgive me, but that sounds rather cruel."

"What else are we supposed to do with the orphans?"

Somehow, he didn't seem as attractive to her anymore. Had they been in the forests, she would have punched him.

"Why the tattoo?" she asked politely, not wanting to cause a scene and risk Zara's wrath.

"Every winner of the Dragon Tournament has one."

"And her name, Ryoko Naga, what does it mean?"

"It means Dragon Queen." Jinn cleared his throat and stepped closer to Salome, their bodies now touching. "She is the only female ever recorded to win the tournament."

Salome caught sight of the girl as she slithered through the horde of guests. Although she felt compassion for Kai, she knew she had to be leery of her as well.

"And your tattoo?" Jinn lifted her arm, cradling her left hand in his.

"One line for each member of my family that… died."

"A tragedy." They looked at one another and Jinn stared at her left eye. "Might I be bold and ask about your eye?" He still held her hand in his.

Salome became indignant but couldn't hide the flush to her cheeks. "It's a birthmark.

"A curious birthmark." He kept his eyes locked on hers. "You are lucky Myridians are not superstitious like the Mountain Men or even the elderly in my city. They would think you were a witch."

The way he kept staring made her uncomfortable. Her shoulders tensed. Even though Rosalina and Seraphina insisted she not carry any weapons on her, she secretly strapped her wolf dagger to her upper thigh when they weren't watching her. If she needed to defend herself, she would be able to.

"Then perhaps, I will refrain from visiting either kingdom." Salome retrieved her hand from his grasp.

"You mustn't let a few batty old people keep you from visiting my homeland." Jinn rested his hand on her lower back and whispered in her ear, "I would be honored if you would accompany me to Sakurai as my guest."

"You flatter me, Prince Jinn." She stepped to the side, hoping he would withdraw his hand from her person, but he stepped with her, his face still unnecessarily close to hers.

"Dance with me," he glided his hand from her lower back and took her hand.

"Excuse me, Princess." Salome whipped around, her heart skipping a beat when she recognized Adonijah's voice. "Harbona sent me to escort you to meet with him on an urgent matter."

Salome pulled away from Jinn's grip. "You will have to excuse me, Prince Jinn."

"Of course," Prince Jinn smiled and brushed a loose strand of her hair behind her ear. "Another time."

Salome noticed Adonijah and Jinn exchange a look before Adonijah escorted her down two flights of stairs and through one of the side doors into the gardens. She looked around the garden lit by lanterns but didn't see Harbona anywhere. She turned around and saw Adonijah leaning against the doorway, arms folded over his chest. "Where's Harbona?"

CHAPTER 15
ADONIJAH

"Harbona didn't ask to see me, did he?" Realization sparked in Salome's eyes.

"No," Adonijah flashed a mischievous smile. "I saw how you were acting with the Easterner and thought you needed an excuse to escape him."

"How was I acting?" She squared her body to his, arms folded over her chest.

"I've not known you long, but I've known you long enough to recognize the look in your eyes when you're looking for a reason not to stab a man."

Salome paused before responding, a coy smile spreading across her face. "If you wanted to be alone with me, that's all you needed to say." She laughed.

Oh, how he adored her warm, silky laugh.

Adonijah curled up from the archway and stood in front of her. His eyes rested on hers – she looked different. When he spotted her in the Grand Hall, he couldn't believe his eyes. She was a vision, but he could sense how uncomfortable she was. If only she saw herself through his eyes. If she knew he was at her mercy. She looked like a true royal and it reminded him of the vast differences between them.

Salome's eyebrow arched playfully. "Don't tell me you were jealous."

"Of *him*?" Adonijah snorted. "Don't be ridiculous."

"Then why tell me Harbona wanted to see me when he clearly didn't summon me?" She popped a hip. Her white dress wafted in the light breeze exposing the slit up her leg to her thigh. He could have sworn he saw the tip of one of her daggers but dismissed it.

"Adonijah?"

He'd been staring. He blinked, returning to himself. "Like I said, you looked like you needed a break from him."

Adonijah knew Salome was perfectly capable of protecting herself, but he still felt responsible for her. And maybe, if he were honest with himself, he was a little jealous. Which was unfamiliar territory. Adonijah was not the jealous type – or at least, he wasn't before. It irritated him to have those feelings. But he saw how Jinn looked at her, how he touched her. Saw how all the men in the room watched her the moment she walked in.

"Admit it." Salome sliced through his thoughts.

"Admit what?"

"Either you wanted to be alone with me or you were jealous." Her smile was gone, the intensity of her eyes drew him in.

"Both," he whispered.

"What?" She seemed surprised by his admission. He was too.

Adonijah stepped to her, placing one hand on her hip and the other against her face, gently running his thumb across the curvature of her jawline.

"I know you didn't want to wear that dress -"

Salome's eyes dropped to the pavers, "You think I look better this way."

Adonijah lifted her chin, their lips so close they could feel the tension, the electricity, between them. "I know you didn't want to wear that dress because you were afraid no one would be able to see you anymore. But *I* see you. And even though you are a pain in my ass, I can't help wanting to be alone with you. Wanting to hold you. Wanting to kiss you. But seeing you with him… I'm not a jealous man, Salome…"

She rested her hands on his chest when he trailed off, staring up into his eyes, her sight drifted down to his lips.

Adonijah wanted to kiss her – to feel her lips on his, to run his fingers through her hair. And by the lack of space between them, he knew she wanted him, too. He moved his face to hers, his heart racing.

"Adonijah," she whispered.

He opened his eyes and felt her gently push him back. "What's wrong?" he asked, caressing her cheek.

Salome placed her hand on top of his. "I can't…"

Adonijah's arms fell to his sides, and he took a step back from her. "It's alright."

"It's not you," she reached for him but stopped short.

"You don't have to explain anything to me," he cleared his throat. He wasn't sure what happened, but he wasn't going to pressure her for answers.

They silently stared at one another; tears welled in her eyes – but why?

"Are you alright?" Adonijah asked.

Salome let out a half laugh, half groan. "I push you away and you're more interested to see if I'm alright?"

"Of course, Princess -"

"Don't call me that," she snapped.

"Alright." He rubbed the back of his neck. He'd called her that before, but it never drew that vicious of a response. "You realize that's your title."

"I am Salome. Just Salome." Her nostrils flared; she wiped her eyes. "Overnight, I became princess – her majesty – Hunter – chosen one. It's all too much." She turned her back to him and wrapped her arms around herself. "And now this," she flicked her dress and spied her reflection in the still waters of the pool in the garden. "I don't even look like myself anymore."

Adonijah braved being on the receiving end of another tongue lashing or worse, a physical altercation, to come up behind her and wrap his arms around her. Holding her, his face next to hers, he felt her exhale a deep breath and heard a muffled sob.

"Do you remember what I said to you in Valley Pass?" Adonijah asked in a raspy whisper.

"I have a lot of scars."

"Aye," he nodded, "but I also said that to me you were the same Salome. It doesn't matter if you wear dresses and crowns or if you run wild hunting in pants armed to your teeth in weapons." He kissed her temple, "You are always you." Salome released the tension in her body and relaxed into his embrace.

Holding her told him everything he needed to know. She was willing to let him comfort her, and she trusted him. It felt good to hold her, to feel her body wrapped in his. He could spend all night embracing her, but he released her instead.

Salome faced him, and grabbed his hand4. Adonijah wiped a stray tear that slipped down her cheek.

"I should go," he said.

Her eyes. Filled with such sadness.

She nodded and he walked back inside, letting her have time to herself, knowing it was important to her. But he didn't dare leave her unprotected. He sat on a bench on the opposite side of the wall and leaned his head back, gearing up for a long night.

CHAPTER 16
ZOPHAR

Three days.

It took the beaten down and weary warriors three days to find another way out of the Cavern of the Undead. With their resources depleted, half of their horses dead, and exhaustion setting in, the Numbio crawled into the moonlit sands of Dead Man's Lands with subdued happiness.

Relief washed over Zophar as he inhaled the deepest breath of fresh air his lungs could hold. He had never been so happy to see the Sand Lands in his entire life and that not only his horse, Midnight, had survived the Caverns of the Undead, but Crispin's horse, Freya, also made it out alive. Collapsing to the ground, he didn't care that sand seeped into every orifice of his body. He was just elated it wasn't the musty, damp rock of the caverns touching his skin.

Not knowing where exactly they were, Zophar could only hope and pray a rare passing caravan would catch sight of them and help them. If they were within walking distance of Jannat Sin, Ibrahim and his people would gladly welcome them to rest and regain their strength.

Zophar spied Heru sprawled in the sand and if he didn't know any better, he would have sworn the prince was kissing the sand.

"If we can make it to Jannat Sin," Zophar forced himself to stumble toward Heru, "we will receive aid. I know Sheik Ibrahim. He's a good man."

Heru's tired eyes found their way to meet Zophar's equally exhausted gaze. He nodded, his lips were so chapped Zophar could see dried blood around his mouth. "Then let's hope we can make it there tonight. I fear we won't last a day in the unforgiving desert sun without food, water, or shelter."

Agreed, they mobilized the Numbio to their aching feet and encouraged them onward. Zophar whispered prayers to the Almighty, asking for a miracle. It was all they could hope for at this point.

Walking slowly but steadily, the company trudged their way through the moonlit desert for hours until the dawn threatened to end their quest for the oasis village. One by one, Numbio began to fall to their knees until Zophar, too, couldn't take one more step. With the scorching sun rising, Zophar laid on his back, accepting that Death would be coming for them all before noon.

Extremely dehydrated, he closed his eyes, accepting the sun's burn upon his pale skin. He was wishing for a drop of water to quench his thirst when a splash hit his face. He squinted and saw a camel hovering over him.

A camel?

Zophar groaned as he propped himself up on his elbows, gazing up at the rider wrapped in black robes. "Please," Zophar's voice came out raspy and strained, "help us."

~

SOUNDS OF LAUGHTER, running water, and the smell of freshly roasted lamb filled Zophar's ears and nose. As his eyes fluttered open, he saw a familiar sight. It was the luxurious tent he and Crispin had shared in Jannat Sin.

They had made it. But how?

Zophar's mind flashed back to the camel that had slopped a watery kiss on his nose and its rider who had looked down at him with pity. Reluctantly pushing himself up from the soft and warm bed, Zophar rinsed his hands and face in the water basin and cherished the cool liquid sloshing through his hands.

Dressed in the clean clothes that had been left on a chair in the corner of his tent, Zophar ducked out of his quarters and made his way toward Ibrahim's dwelling in the middle of the village. As he passed other tents, he saw the Numbio eating their fill, drinking as much water as they could, and laughing. They were smiling for the first time in weeks.

Zophar caught sight of Midnight and Freya with the other horses in the fenced stables being tended to, looking healthy and strong. He whispered a prayer as he glided past, thanking the Almighty that both horses survived. Thankful that his last piece of Crispin was still living and keeping his memory alive.

"My friend!" Ibrahim's voice sang out to him as he approached the largest tent. His arms were stretched wide, and a friendly smile spread across his brown face. "It is good to see you."

Zophar embraced the Sheik and flashed a smile of his own in return. "I don't know how we got here but thank you."

"Some of my riders were on their way back from Numbio, having done some trading in the city, and happened upon you and your friends." Ibrahim ushered Zophar into the tent where a gluttonous feast was already out on display. Heru and Rayma were inside looking refreshed from a good night's sleep. "We are just glad we found you in time."

"How can we ever repay you for your generosity?" Zophar plopped down on the pillow Ibrahim motioned him toward.

"How could we let the desert claim you when we have the resources and good will to help?" Ibrahim shook his head and served himself a plate. "As long as my people can offer aid to those who are in need, we will continue to prosper. The Almighty blesses those who give."

"Thank you, Sheik Ibrahim," Heru chimed in, a hand over his heart. "The Numbio owe you a debt."

Ibrahim mirrored the prince's hand to heart motion but again declined payment or offer of any kind. "I just thank the Almighty you are alright." He dared a glance at Rayma. "Our healer said he wasn't needed. Despite the dire state we found you in, your men's injuries have been cared for."

Rayma nodded her head in gratitude for the compliment but something about her seemed haunted. Zophar had noticed Bantu creep toward her to assault her. He wanted to rip the man limb from limb but by the time he reached her, she had stabbed and killed Bantu. They hadn't spoken about it since. They hadn't spoken at all since the incident.

"Where is Prince Crispin?" Ibrahim asked between bites of mutton. "I am eager to see him again." His eyebrows bounced, "And I am positive he will enjoy tonight's entertainment."

The room fell silent, and Zophar met the Sheik's gaze. Tears pricked at the Westerner's blue eyes. That was all it took to convey the message.

"I am sorry," Ibrahim was somber as he trailed a finger from the top of his head down to his heart. "How did it happen?"

"He..." Crispin being swept down the River of Lost Souls flashed in Zophar's mind, and he couldn't utter another word.

"The River of Lost Souls claimed him," Heru said with great difficulty. "We don't know if he made it out alive or not."

"You were in the Caverns of the Undead?" Ibrahim's mannerisms were calm and graceful, but his eyes were filled with terror.

"When your people found us in the desert, we had just escaped." Zophar explained, his appetite now gone.

Ibrahim set his plate down, as if he also was no longer in the mood for food. "We shall keep our eyes open just in case the prince reappears. But as always, you are welcome here amongst our people. Rest, restock for your journey. I have a feeling you are not returning to Numbio yet."

Zophar and Heru exchanged a quick glance before the prince said, "We are headed north to Oakenshire. We are to meet Crispin's sister there."

Ibrahim nodded. "If I could offer you a word of caution..."

"Of course," Zophar motioned for the Sheik to continue.

"My scouts have reported quite a bit of movement from the Thrak of Gomorrah." Ibrahim's nose crinkled in disgust when speaking of the cannibalistic warriors. "They are looking for someone. From what we have gathered, they are searching for a woman."

"Their search stretches this far south?" Heru was dumbfounded.

"Where the Sand Lands and The Hollow meet and as far west as Port Daelon." Ibrahim crisscrossed his legs. "If you intend to continue your journey north, I would avoid the main roads and travel through the Bone Mountains."

"But aren't the Mountain Men just as cruel?" Rayma spoke for the first time in days.

"The Krazaks are," Ibrahim bobbed his head, "but the Stormcrags would help you if you asked. Their quarrel is only with the Krazaks and the Thrak."

"Thank you," Zophar put a hand to his chest, showing his respect and gratitude. "We appreciate the warning."

Ibrahim smiled at Zophar before turning his gaze to the prince. "Whatever you need, let me know and we will provide. I have a feeling the journey ahead will be a difficult one."

CHAPTER 17
ODELIA

Odelia's eyes shot open when she heard what sounded like footsteps outside her bungalow. It was dark, the middle of the night. She sat up from her bed and softly planted her feet on the creaky wooden floors. Having lived in that house for decades, she knew where she could step and not make a sound. As quickly as she dared, she hopped spot to spot until she reached her modest kitchen and grabbed the biggest knife she owned.

Reaper's growl rumbled low, but Odelia held her index finger to her lips to silence him. He stood alert; his nose pointed toward the front door.

Odelia's back was pressed tight against the wall with the door next to her. She inhaled and exhaled rhythmically to keep herself calm. If someone had come to kill the Enchantress, they would not leave the swamp alive. It was not the first assassination attempt, and it would not be the last. At least Reaper could claim another soul or two, adding to his own lifespan.

The intruder's feet stepped onto the front porch. Odelia clutched the hilt of the knife tighter and watched as the handle of the door turned. Going on the offensive, she sliced her weapon down to stab whoever was on the other side of the door: a Shadow, one of those grotesque Thrak, a mercenary for hire. But she stopped short of piercing *her*.

"Makeda?" Odelia stepped back, her mouth agape.

"Mother!" Makeda wrapped her arms around Odelia's neck. "Thank the Almighty I got here in time."

The Enchantress dropped the knife on the kitchen table directly behind her and returned her daughter's embrace. She pulled away to close the door and lit lanterns to get a better look at Makeda.

Odelia hadn't seen her in years, since she left the swamp for a life in Northwind. Makeda had wanted to join the rebellion in Northwind, to make a difference in the lives of the oppressed. A decision that left a sour taste in Odelia's mouth. The Northerners were not their people, therefore, they were not their problem, yet,

Makeda abandoned the swamp, abandoned her mother, abandoned her future, to pursue a life underground.

"What are you doing here, child?"

"Niabi dispatched Shadows to find you," Makeda accepted the seat Odelia motioned her to take. "She has instructed them to bring you to Northwind."

Odelia put a kettle of water to boil. "And why should she want me?"

"We think she wants to harvest your magic." Odelia furrowed her brow when Makeda said, "*we*". "There is no time for tea, Mother. I need to get you out of here before they find you."

"*If* they find me." Odelia smirked.

"They will find you."

"How can you be so sure?"

"It wasn't Niabi's idea to send them. She didn't know you existed until that witch told her."

Odelia's eyes widened, although she kept her back to her daughter as she fiddled with the tea bags. "What witch?" she asked calmly.

"The Old Witch of Endor. Apparently, she is Niabi's -"

"Aunt." Odelia finished the statement.

"You know of her?"

"I met Vilora a very long time ago." Odelia could see a young version of the witch flash in her mind. "It would seem she has never forgotten me."

Makeda slammed her palms on the table. "We need to go. Now."

"And where would we go? To your *friends* in Northwind where they can keep me underground? No, no. I am the Enchantress of the Swamp. No one invades my home and lives to tell the tale."

"Mother, please don't be stubborn." Makeda pleaded. "I am here to rescue you."

Odelia chuckled, patting Reaper on his square head. "It is not I who is in need of rescuing."

"Is this about me not staying?" Makeda hunched over Odelia. "Because I didn't want this," she motioned around the room.

Odelia knew she didn't mean the bungalow, but the swamp itself. "I should have known the swamp would never truly have your heart. After all, you are not fully mine."

"You still won't tell me where to find my father?"

"As I have told you before, Makeda, your path and his are destined to cross." The kettle sang, releasing its steam. Odelia snatched it from the heat and placed it on the counter. "Why spend time aimlessly searching when you were fated to meet?"

"Riddles. So many riddles." Makeda paced the small house, rubbing her forehead.

"I appreciate you warning me of the Shadows, dear." Odelia poured the boiling water in a cup but paused over the second mug. "Tea?"

"No!" Makeda lurched forward, pointing at the door. "Those Shadows can't possibly be far. They had a head start on me. Fortunately, I know my way around the swamp. Let me help you."

"I don't need your help, Makeda. You might have rejected the swamp, but I did not. The swamp fuels me, sustains me. I am strongest here. I am safest here."

"Have you used your magic recently?" Makeda popped her hip to the side, narrowing her eyes.

"Watch your tone, Makeda." Odelia blew the steam from her tea. "I am still your mother and won't hesitate to put you in your place."

"Is your boat still in working condition?" Makeda peeked through the drawn curtains toward the dock. "I released my horse before I arrived in the swamp so no one could follow my tracks."

"If you need it, take it."

Makeda squinted.

"What is it?" Odelia asked as soon as she noticed her daughter's sudden shift.

"I thought I saw something." She gasped and slid to the floor. "They're here."

"You saw them?" Odelia didn't bother to get down on the floor, instead remaining in her seat to enjoy her cup of tea. "How many are there?"

"Get down here!" Makeda whispered as she crawled over to the lanterns, blowing them out one by one.

Odelia sipped her drink. "I asked, how many are there?"

"I don't know," Makeda spat. "Could be one, could be a hundred. What difference does it make?"

"No difference."

"Then why ask?" Makeda rolled her eyes. "We can still get out of here." She felt around the wooden floorboards until she found the brass handle to a secret exit. "Come on."

"Go ahead, dear. I'll make sure they don't see you."

"Mother, please!"

Odelia was caught off guard by Makeda's unusual tone. She softened her gaze. "Take Reaper to the boat. I'll be right behind you.""Mother -"

"Trust me."

Makeda reluctantly nodded and patted her thigh for Reaper to follow. Reaper sat loyally by Odelia's side until she shifted her eyes ordering him to go with Makeda. Once the hatch closed, Odelia set her cup down. She cracked her knuckles then her neck.

"Let's have a little fun."

Odelia opened the front door and stepped out onto the porch. The moon lit the swamp enough for her to see the dark figures approaching. There were at least twenty of them.

"Consider this your only warning to leave my swamp." Odelia trotted down the steps and stood on the wet ground barefoot.

"We don't take orders from you," a voice hissed in the darkness.

"Then," she shrugged with a grin, "you will all die."

Odelia slammed her palms to the earth and a low rumble followed. She willed the ground to shake and heard the Shadows shouting orders at one another. She couldn't make out their words but knew she wouldn't have much time before the assassins reached her.

She dug her fingernails into the soft ground and yanked dirt up. Holes large enough to swallow some of the Shadows opened and claimed the soldiers. She slowly stood, lifting her arms with great resistance. As her arms rose, so did the roots she was controlling. They grew around the Shadows that remained. Odelia started closing her arms and the roots closed in on the men and entrapped them.

Odelia suddenly felt a piece of metal slice into her left shoulder and it relaxed her arms slightly. One of the Shadows had launched an arrow at her before the roots swallowed him. She heard Makeda shout from a distance. Pain or not, she had to finish this.

The Enchantress let out an unearthly scream and forced her arms to close, her palms meeting in front of her. The Shadows screeched in pain as the roots squeezed the life out of them. Odelia slammed her fists down to the ground and the roots pulled the Shadows into the earth.

Although it appeared she had killed all the intruders, she sensed one had survived. Her vision was blurry. The pain in her arm was slowly taking over all her other senses. In the moonlight, she caught the glint of the Shadow's sword as he slid down from his hiding spot in one of the trees. Blood oozed down her arm, and she was unable to stand up.

The Shadow in the distance lit his torch and dropped it on the ground, disappearing into the darkness, no doubt to inform his queen of what happened. The Swamp was thrown into chaos as the fire spread.

Her swamp. Her home. It was all burning around her and there was nothing she could do to save it. She didn't possess the power of water – just earth.

Odelia's eyes blurred to the point she couldn't see anymore, so she closed them. She felt the heat and smelled the trees burning. But she swore she heard the sound of rushing water spraying across the earth. She felt its coolness on her skin. She forced her eyes to open and used every bit of strength she had left to focus on what she could see. The fire had been extinguished. Billows of smoke stretched to the heavens, but there were no flames.

How was that possible?

"Mother," Makeda knelt in front of her and focused her attention on the arrow sticking out of her shoulder.

"Makeda." Odelia embraced her dripping wet daughter. "The swamp, it was on fire. What happened?"

"I put it out." Makeda wrapped her fingers around the arrow. "This is going to hurt."

"What?" Odelia screeched in pain as Makeda snapped the arrow shaft in half.

"We need to get you to a healer."

"Makeda, do you have magic?" Odelia grabbed her daughter's shoulders.

"Water." Makeda admitted.

"Why didn't you tell me?" Odelia felt herself fading. She grabbed Makeda's hand for balance.

"I've got you." Makeda's voice sounded as Odelia's consciousness faded to black. "I've got you, Mother."

CHAPTER 18

SALOME

If Salome hadn't attended the Festival of Forbidden Fruit, she wouldn't have believed it even happened. As she strolled through the Scarlet Citadel, after another grueling morning training session with Mika, there wasn't a trace of a party. It was still mid-morning when she returned from Antrope, and she managed to sneak out of her chambers before the twins arrived to dictate her schedule or Almighty forbid, try to make her up again.

Since arriving in Myr, she hadn't had the opportunity to go for her morning walks and was fully aware of how important they were to her. How necessary they were. Stretching her arms around her torso, she inhaled the sea breeze as the sun's rays lit up the castle. She wished for a split second that she could stay in Myr, but that wasn't her path.

"It's a beautiful view."

Salome jerked back from the banister overlooking one of the gardens. She never heard Jinn approach her and that was unsettling. What if he had meant to harm her?

"I apologize for startling you." Jinn said warmly. "I thought I was the only one walking in the gardens."

"It would appear we agree on something, Prince Jinn." She steadied herself, unsure of his intentions as he approached her.

Jinn gave her a look over and flashed a perfect smile. "So, this is what you really look like."

She glanced down at her loose-fitting green shirt, dark pants, and boots. Her hair was down and curly and whatever make up she had on her face was whatever she didn't wash off before tumbling into bed the night before.

"Surprised?" she asked, one eyebrow arched.

"Intrigued." Jinn leaned his elbows against the railing next to her. His fingers intertwined, the sun hitting him just right to make him look undeniably enticing.

Salome hated that she was attracted to him, especially since she found his personality grating. She found him arrogant, unfeeling, and invasive.

"You don't like me, do you?" Jinn asked, eyes fixed on the sea.

Was he a mind reader? How did he know what she was thinking?

"I didn't say that."

"But your eyes did." Jinn met her gaze. "It's alright. You're not the first woman to look at me that way. Despite my best efforts, I'm afraid I'm not good at first impressions." He shrugged. "Kai tells me I try too hard."

Salome flushed, heat rising through her body. She broke eye contact with him. "Prince Jinn -"

"Jinn," he softly interrupted. "Please, call me Jinn."

"Jinn," she complied. "Perhaps, I've rushed to judge you."

"It's because of Kai, isn't it?"

"What do you mean?"

"How Kai came to be in my service," he explained. "How my people treat our orphans."

Salome tried to hide her disgust thinking about children being trained to kill but it was impossible. He nodded, as if to say he understood her reaction.

"I don't like it either." Jinn rubbed his thigh. An obvious nervous twitch. "But it's tradition."

"Some traditions should be changed."

"Maybe," he nodded, gracious in his responses, just like a nobleman. "Might I ask you a question?"

Salome shifted her weight, leaning against the railing next to him, their elbows inches apart. "Sure."

"How old are Northern boys when they begin their military training?"

Salome felt her throat dry as soon as he asked his question. "All firstborn males begin training at ten."

"And how old were you when you started?"

"Girls aren't allowed -"

"Please, Salome," he shook his head with a chuckle. "I might not look like much of a soldier, but I can certainly identify one. And you carry yourself like a soldier." His eyes scanned her up and down. "You have at least four knives on you as we speak."

"Three actually," she admitted. The wolf dagger against her thigh, one sheathed to her lower back, and a small one in her right boot.

"So, when did you start your training?" Jinn asked again.

"I was five."

"And Myridians. How old are they when they begin training as a Qata Vishna?"

"Ten."

Jinn ran his fingers through his hair, slicking it back from his face. Such a beautiful, symmetrical face. "In Gomorrah, the firstborn son is dedicated at birth to become a Thrak. The Andrago teach their sons the way of the sword as soon as they take their first step. And I'm pretty sure the boys and girls of Borg are birthed clutching a weapon."

Salome smirked at the last one, thinking of Zophar as a baby armed with his battle axe.

"Families willingly offer their sons and daughters to honor their kingdoms and it is applauded. But children without a family: no one to feed them, shelter them, clothe them, protect them – it is wrong to have them trained in sword play? Housed in youngling barracks and given a purpose? What is so different about our peoples' traditions? You draw the line of training children to kill if they have parents?"

Salome dropped her eyes to her twiddling fingers. She didn't know what to say. He was right. What she scoffed at last night, she and her people were guilty of too.

Jinn placed his hand gently on top of hers. Their eyes met. His golden eyes were so warm, so inviting. It was as if she was melting into him, being drawn in by his spell.

"In Sakurai, to be a Ryoko Naga is the highest honor. To serve our kingdom, honor our people, and uphold our traditions. Without our ways, we would be lost. If you ever graced my kingdom with a visit, I would show you. You might actually like it there."

Jinn swept her hand into his. His fingers were calloused, a sign he might know how to wield a weapon. Based on appearance alone, she wouldn't have pegged him for a warrior. A politician, yes. A soldier, no.

Adonijah, although caring, had hands that matched his rugged appearance. When Adonijah touched her, she felt something surge through her entire body. A feeling that paled in comparison to how it felt when Jinn held her hand.

Why was she even comparing them?

Salome shook her head, retracting her hand. "I have to thank you, Jinn. You've opened my eyes to my own shortcomings and hypocrisy. I judged you and I judged your people when my people are not much different. Please accept my apology."

"There is nothing to forgive." He touched his fingertips to his chest, bowing his head. "Until our paths cross again."

"Are you leaving the Isles of Myr?" She hated that she cared.

"We sail to Sakurai tomorrow." His eyes were filled with expectation. "You are always welcome to join me."

Salome hesitated. An opportunity to see the first kingdom Malachi the First helped establish. A kingdom that still celebrated and upheld the traditions they were founded on a thousand years ago, whether she agreed with them or not. What a tremendous honor. What an incredible opportunity. A dream of seeing Adalore within her reach.

"Thank you," she whispered, "but I can't."

Jinn smiled. "It's because of your bodyguard, isn't it?"

"There are many reasons why I can't go with you." Salome kept a straight face, even though her mind was screaming at how it felt like he could see right through her.

"Him being one of them?"

"Have a safe journey home, Jinn." She wasn't sure what was going on between her and Adonijah, but it was not a topic she was willing to speak openly about, especially with Jinn.

Jinn nodded, folding his arms behind his back, and left.

"It would not be the worst match." Harbona walked up the garden steps to her right.

"How long have you been there?" Salome pushed away from the railing and squared her shoulders to his.

"Long enough to gather he is quite taken with you." Harbona's smile was meant to reassure her, but it made her feel guilty because Adonijah popped into her mind. "Come with me."

As he passed her, she asked. "Where?"

He flashed a toothy grin. "She is waiting for us."

"Who?"

But Harbona didn't answer. He pressed onward, weaving through the castle halls. Salome's curiosity got the better of her and she quietly followed him until they reached an enormous set of arched doors.

"We are here." Harbona reached for the handle.

"Wait." Salome touched his hand and was suddenly flooded with visions of what seemed like a hundred lifetimes. Faces, battles, places, all images she had never seen before. It happened so fast, within a split second, but she couldn't release her hold on him. She snapped out of her visions once they released her. She fell to the floor. Beads of sweat bubbled across her forehead.

How was that even possible?

Harbona stared at her wide-eyed, half curious, half pleased.

"What just happened?" Salome huffed, breathing rapidly.

"Remarkable." Harbona whispered, more to himself than her.

"What's going on?" She tried to stand up, but her legs wobbled as if she'd run ten miles. "What is happening to me, Harbona?"

"That has only happened to one other person who has touched me."

"Harbona!" Salome's fear consumed her. "What's going on?"

"What did you see?" Harbona reached to grab her hand, but she pulled away, keeping a few feet between them.

"Don't touch me," she hissed.

"What did you see?" he pressed, ignoring the panic in her eyes.

"Nothing," she whispered. "Everything. So many faces I've never seen before." She rubbed her eyes as if scrubbing them hard enough would erase what she saw. "Please, tell me what's happening."

"You saw the past," he said, simplicity in his tone. Like she should have known that. "You saw *my* past."

"How is that possible? I didn't see you in any of the flashes."

"Why would you?" Harbona smiled and took a step toward her. "You saw it through my eyes."

"Am I… am I going crazy?" she whispered after looking up and down the hall.

Harbona leaned forward and said, "Not yet, Princess." He turned on his heel and returned to the doors. "Come. She can tell us what we need to know."

Salome followed Harbona inside and saw an enormous circular table in the middle of a ceiling free room. Already seated were Adonijah, Cato, and Damaris.

"What is this?" Salome asked, still glancing around the atrium.

"Come, sit, Cousin," Damaris instructed and motioned to the seat beside her.

Salome was reluctant but was too exhausted to argue. She plopped down in the chair to Damaris's right and Harbona sat on Damaris's left. Salome could feel Adonijah's gaze on her from across the table and Cato's bouncing knee to her right frayed her nerves. She wanted to grab his thigh and force him to stop but she kept her hands to herself.

"Harbona asked me to meet with you," Damaris began.

Salome's eyes flashed in her direction. "About what?"

"What do you know of the Hunters?"

"Harbona already explained to me about Malachi the First." Salome shot her question down.

Damaris leaned closer to her, "Salome, what is a Hunter?"

Salome rubbed her eyes and groaned, "A Hunter is chosen by the Almighty, marked, and tasked to avenge the blood of the innocent." Damaris did not seem impressed. "What?" Salome shrugged, eyeing Harbona.

"Hunters are so much more than just one charged to avenge innocent blood." Damaris kept a fixed gaze on Salome, but her question was directed to Harbona. "You haven't told her everything, have you?"

Harbona shifted in his seat, "It is beyond my expertise, beyond my understanding."

Salome's nostrils flared, "More secrets, Harbona?"

"It is wise not to speak on matters one knows nothing about," Damaris came to Harbona's defense. "It is my destiny and my duty to help you understand your magic."

Adonijah and Cato's mouths dropped simultaneously when the word magic was casually thrown into the conversation.

"Magic?" Salome crinkled her nose. "I don't have magic."

Harbona cleared his throat, grabbing her attention. He nodded his head toward Damaris, as if suggesting she tell the oracle what happened just before this gathering.

"I *don't* have magic," Salome insisted, crossing her arms over her chest. "If I did, don't you think I'd know about it?"

"None of the Hunters knew they had magical abilities until they were called into the Almighty's service, Salome," Damaris said.

"You're telling me every Hunter before me had some kind of powers?" Salome was skeptical.

"Malachi the First was a creature summoner. Tolemy the Red could breathe underwater." Damaris seemed impassioned by remembering the old world and their Hunters. "Raego the Mighty could manipulate metal. Lor the Meek could read human aura, see people's emotions as colors around their bodies. And Polantis the Peacemaker controlled the weather." Damaris focused on Salome. "So, tell me, Cousin, what is your power?"

Harbona cleared his throat, louder this time, drawing everyone's attention. Salome's nostrils flared, irritated at the eyes that now drifted back her way. An explanation. That is what their faces demanded.

Salome grunted, "Sometimes, I hear..." she turned her head to the side and grimaced, "trees."

"You hear trees?" Cato tried to steady his voice, but Salome picked up traces of panicked laughter. "You can hear trees talking to you?"

"I... uh... Yes. No." She scraped her fingers down her face. "I don't know. But what I do know is it's not magic."

"A rare gift, indeed," Damaris mumbled, running her thumb across her fingertips.

"What do they say?" Cato leaned forward, resting his elbows on the table, cupping his jaw in his hands.

"My name."

"Your name?" Cato asked, disappointed. "That's it?"

"That's it."

Damaris turned her face toward her and smiled. "Salome, the trees themselves are not speaking to you, they are merely the vessel our departed use to communicate."

"The departed?" Salome blinked. "You're saying dead people are trying to talk to me?"

"The spirits of our ancestors, of our loved ones," Damaris watched Salome closely. "They are reaching out. But that is not all you have experienced lately."

Salome squirmed in her seat, feeling sweat dripping down the middle of her back. "I see things."

"What things?" Cato's eyes widened.

"You mean visions." Damaris clarified.

"Of the past." Salome nodded.

"How long has this been happening to you?" Damaris asked.

"A few months. At first it was just when I was asleep, but now," Salome leaned back in her seat, and puffed, "I see them even when I'm awake. When I travel, when I eat, when I hunt." Her voice trailed off, "They look so real."

Damaris reached her hand forward and gently rested her fingers on the six lines tattooed on Salome's arm. "Someone is trying to reach you. Have you asked what they want?"

"No," Salome furrowed her brows. "Why would I ask the trees or spirits or the dead what they want?"

"Next time you hear them call you, answer." She patted her arm and retracted her reach. "There is something they need to say."

Salome nodded, unsure if she really believed it was a departed spirit sparking a conversation, but she was willing to at least take Damaris's advice. What was the harm in responding to trees that whispered her name? *What an insane question to ask herself*, she shook her head. She remembered how Crispin looked at her when she told him the trees in The Hollow were speaking to her. As if she was diseased or had descended into insanity. She refused to meet Adonijah's gaze, she didn't want to know what he was thinking of her now.

"That's not magic," Salome said, bringing every eye in the room back to her.

"What do you mean?" Harbona spoke for the first time in several minutes.

Salome looked at him. "She said that Hunters have magic. Talking to trees or spirits can't possibly be all I can do." She bounced her gaze back to Damaris. "Can it?"

"Do you have other abilities you care to mention?" Damaris asked.

Salome wanted to ask Damaris about how they had spoken to one another with just their thoughts but clammed up at the thought of what the others would think. She shook her head. "No. But shouldn't I be able to, I don't know, be able to breathe underwater like Tolemy the Red or manipulate metal like Raego the Mighty? Something more powerful?"

"The Almighty gives the Hunters the abilities they will need to succeed. Perhaps, your strength will come from those who have already crossed into the afterlife." Damaris rose from her seat, signifying the end of their meeting. "Do not compare yourself to others. Peace and strength do not dwell there."

CHAPTER 19
CRISPIN

After fighting alongside the pirates and saving Rahab from being swept into the Obsidian Sea by Kubantu's tentacles, Crispin had earned some favor and respect from the crew of the *Shadow of Death*.

Rafi no longer shot Crispin dirty looks whenever he walked around a corner.

Ondrej was more than willing to show him every nook and cranny of the vessel with pride since he had reconstructed most of it over the years.

Phex eagerly showed him the secret, but terrifying, projects he was working on. At some point, all of them would go, "Boom!" the madman explained.

Corwin gave him one of his prized knives. Apparently having just a longsword wasn't good enough to be a member of the crew. The dagger looked like it was of Borgian design; a weapon Zophar would be jealous of.

Haldane was eager to share stories of their exploits and adventures. And Crispin wished for a fleeting moment to be able to have a life on the seas and enjoy the freedom and excitement that came with it. The captain even allowed him to take the helm for a couple of hours, igniting a passion in him for the sea.

But since their run-in with Kubantu, Rahab kept her distance from Crispin, and it had not gone unnoticed. He knew she was watching him. He could sense her eyes on him as he learned the rigging system from Rafi and Ondrej, even though he was supposed to be learning that from her, the First Mate.

Rahab stood on the quarterdeck next to Corwin as he steered them toward the cove where The Sisters was. Her hazel eyes homed in on him and he didn't back down from their stare off.

"She's pretty," Ondrej cut through Crispin's thoughts, causing him to lose the unspoken competition between him and Rahab, "dangerous. She's pretty dangerous."

"I've heard." Crispin sat against the mast and chewed a hunk of bread he'd snatched from the galley. "What is she to Leeondris?"

Rafi plopped down next to Crispin, resting his elbows on his knees. "You want to know if they are lovers?"

Crispin tried to hide his embarrassment by sinking his teeth into another piece of bread. "Are they lovers?"

Rafi furrowed his brow into a furry, white unibrow. "No."

Crispin nodded and accepted the one-word answer. He wasn't much closer to learning the extent of Rahab and Leeondris' relationship, though he wished he didn't care. At least someone other than Rahab confirmed they were not romantically involved.

Boots thudded toward the trio. Crispin looked up, holding a hand above his eyes to block out the sunlight beaming down on him. A dark silhouette stood in front of him.

"Captain wants to see you in his cabin, Mainlander." Rahab turned on her heel, expecting him to follow her without explanation.

Crispin hopped up and jogged to catch up with her. "You've been avoiding me."

"Hardly."

"Which begs the question," he ignored her feeble attempts at denial, "*why* have you been avoiding me?"

"I am the First Mate of the *Shadow of Death*. The fastest and most dangerous ship in the Obsidian Sea. I have more important matters to tend to than to worry about your whereabouts." Rahab didn't break stride as she hissed each word, refusing to look in his direction.

"Yet I've caught you staring at me several times."

Rahab didn't take the bait as she bounded up the steps that led to the hallway that housed their sleeping quarters. "Keeping a watchful eye on you is far from staring."

Once inside the narrow hall, Crispin slammed his hand against the paneled wall, not allowing her to pass. "So, you admit you can't keep your eyes off me."

"Move," she demanded hoarsely.

"Make me."

Rahab moved so quickly he had no idea what happened until it was too late. She grabbed his arm, whipped him around, and slammed his back against the wall.

"Are you always this stubborn?" Rahab hissed, holding her ruby hilted dagger against his throat.

"Are you always this aggressive?" Crispin fired back.

"I would have died a long time ago if I wasn't."

Crispin suspected she could feel his heart beating rapidly against the forearm she pressed to his chest. She had him pinned and therefore, had the upper hand.

"We don't have to be enemies." He rested his head against the wall, eyes still glued to hers.

"Who said we were enemies?"

"Don't tell me this is how you treat your friends," his eyes widened. "Your contempt for me couldn't be more obvious."

"What tipped you off?" Rahab relaxed her arm and tilted her head to the side. "When I told you, I'd slit your throat if you touched me again or that we should have turned you over to the Shadows the moment we had the chance?"

He smirked, mischief in his eyes, "The slitting my throat bit. So, either do it, or let me go."

Rahab's body tensed. Her lips curled, her eyes wild and vicious. What he would give to know what she was thinking that very second. Her gaze softened and she lowered her knife slowly.

"Letting me go," he was both relieved and surprised.

"With you dead," she holstered her weapon, "we don't get paid. And if there's one thing I value more than human life, it's money."

Crispin brushed the imaginary dust from his shirt with a smile creeping across his face. "See, I'm growing on you. I told you I would."

"What's to say, I don't kill you once you pay us? Or hand you over to the Shadows and collect on your bounty?" Rahab flashed a mischievous smile of her own – yet hers looked more menacing than playful.

"By the time money exchanges hands, you'll be in love with me." Crispin followed her as she turned on her heel to walk down the hall.

"Oh really?" she snorted. "Very cocky of you, Your Majesty."

"No," he shook his head, "just confident."

"Next thing you'll tell me is you've never met a woman who hasn't fallen for your charm."

"You think I'm charming?" He stepped in front of her, stopping her dead in her tracks.

"No, I find you annoying."

"If I'm being honest, I don't have very much experience with women. At least, not pretty women my own age. More like the wrinkled, old ladies who need help with odd jobs and ogle my body." Crispin rubbed his hands up and down his chest with a wink.

Rahab popped her round hip to the side, crossing her arms over her chest, and chuckled. "Funny."

Crispin ticked his fingers, "So, you think I'm charming -"

"Annoying."

"And funny."

"When I look at you, all I think is how -"

"Impossibly handsome I am?" He flipped hair from his eyes.

"How out of your element you are," she corrected.

"So," he lowered a finger, leaving two up, "not impossibly handsome?"

"You aren't..." she cocked her head to the side, examining his face, "...ugly."

Crispin slapped a hand to his knee and pointed his finger in her direction. "I'll take it. One step closer to you falling madly in love with me."

"For all your cockiness -"

"Confidence," he interrupted.

"Cockiness," Rahab held steady, her brow arched. "There is one thing you haven't taken into consideration about this whole 'me falling in love with you' ploy."

"Which is?" Crispin leaned his shoulder against the wall.

"You aren't my type."

"You mean, because I'm a Mainlander."

Rahab's eyes narrowed, "Unlike *your* people," she rested her hands on her hips, "skin color has nothing to do with who I love."

"My mother was from the Isles of Myr and married my father who was the King of Northwind. Skin color has nothing to do with -"

"You're a prince," she blurted. "And I'm a pirate. Our kind don't settle down to raise a family together."

"You think I'd be shallow enough…"

"Not to commit to someone like me?" she motioned up and down her body. "Absolutely. What do I offer? Nothing a princess or lady or ambassador with royal blood could."

"Rahab -"

She shot a hand up to silence him. "It's alright, Mainlander. I'm not offended, just realistic." She stepped up to him and whispered, "So, before you go through the effort of winning my affection, ask yourself if this is really what you want or if it's just a game."

Crispin grasped her hand as she tried to pass him and pulled her back to face him. "It is my choice who I love – and if that is you, then nothing and no one can change my mind."

Rahab's gaze bounced back and forth from his lips to his eyes.

"Tell me I really don't stand a chance of you loving me and I won't mention it again." Crispin dragged his thumb along her jawline, brushing over her mouth.

Rahab leaned in and closed her eyes. He lowered his head, ready to feel the touch of her soft lips against his, when he heard her laugh.

"What?" he whispered.

Rahab patted his cheek, "You really are good. You almost had me."

"What are you talking about?"

She smiled, inches from his face, "A lesser woman would already be in your bed. Thank the stars I am not a Mainlander wench."

This time, he didn't attempt to stop her from leaving. He smirked and ran fingers through his wavy hair as her hips swayed side to side. He didn't know why it mattered to him, but he was determined to change her opinion of him.

As Rahab lifted her fist to knock on Haldane's door, it swung open, and the captain filled the threshold. He smooshed his hat atop his head and Rahab stepped back, allowing him access into the hallway.

"What took you two so long?" Haldane's eyes bounced from Rahab to Crispin.

"I'm a slow walker." Crispin shrugged his shoulders. Rahab seemed to stifle a giggle. Maybe she did have a sense of humor after all.

"Well, no time for chit chat." Haldane marched to the end of the hall with the two of them fast on his heels. "We're here." He climbed the steps to the quarterdeck and motioned toward The Sisters.

Crispin turned toward the bow of the boat and sucked in a quick breath. The Sisters was breathtaking. He had never seen towers built so high before, and there were two of them inhabiting a small island with the pine trees of the Western Lands directly behind them on the Mainland.

Rahab pointed, "The left tower belongs to the Witnesses. The right tower belongs to the Keepers."

"And the bridge connecting them?" Crispin asked, pointing at the two-story connection at the top of the towers.

"That is where the Sovereign stays." Rahab inched closer. "He connects both sects, ruling them in harmony, keeping them balanced."

"He can tell us where to find your friend?" Crispin's eyes trailed down to hers.

"Aye." She met his gaze. "If he is feeling generous."

"And if he isn't feeling generous?"

"Let's hope that's not the case." Rahab stepped up to take her place on Haldane's right as they approached the harbor.

Once they docked, two Keepers approached their ship, spears pounding against the stone pavers with each step they took.

"State your business," one of the Keepers barked.

"We're here to meet with his Holiness, the Sovereign," Haldane's boots thudded down the wooden ramp toward the warriors.

The shorter Keeper crinkled his nose, "Pirates."

"You are ordered to leave our city immediately," the Keeper closest to the ramp commanded.

"You don't understand," Haldane protested, "we mean you no harm, oh mighty blind ones. Prince Crispin of Northwind is with us. See!" Haldane motioned with an exaggerated swipe behind him to Crispin but then smacked his palm against forehead. "I don't mean see as in actually... I mean see as in – uh." He exhaled in defeat, so Crispin jumped in..

"I am Crispin, son of Issachar of Northwind. I humbly request an audience with the Sovereign."

"And why would a *prince* keep the company of Pulauan pirates?" The Keeper folded his arms across his broad chest, his spear hugged against his body.

Haldane stuttered, clearly insulted, "L-L-Look here, we are -"

Crispin gripped Haldane's forearm. "These pirates rescued me when I was separated from my company. Please, allow me five minutes with the Sovereign and I swear we will be on our way."

The dark skinned Keeper sniffed the air loudly. "Smells like filthy pirate tricks to me."

"Be on your way!" The first Keeper demanded. "Or we will sink your ship and throw you in the dungeons."

Haldane growled, "Do you know who we are?"

"Does it matter?" The second Keeper scoffed.

"Now, listen here -"

"We're leaving." Crispin interrupted Haldane, silencing the captain.

Haldane's nostrils flared, ready for a good, old-fashioned fist fight, but he turned and marched back up the ramp. "Looks like we be leaving, lads!"

Rahab also fought spouting off and followed Haldane and Crispin up the steps to the quarterdeck. She took ahold of the helm, guiding their ship from the docks.

Haldane whipped around and pointed a finger in Crispin's chest. "You better have a damn good reason for overstepping your command and having us run like whipped dogs with our tails between our legs."

Crispin rubbed his chin, eyes still fixed on the towers as they sailed out of the cove and around the cliffs that bordered the Western Lands. "How hard would it be to break into The Sisters?"

Haldane's eyes nearly popped out of his head. "How hard? How har-" He slapped his tricorn hat against his leg. "I'd say it's impossible. Has the heat finally warped that brain of yours, lad?"

"Can you scale a wall?" Rahab asked.

"I don't know about walls," Crispin scratched the stubble along his jawline, "but I can climb trees faster than a monkey."

"You can't be serious," Haldane quipped.

"I'll race a monkey right now -"

"No, you twit!" Haldane waved his arms in the air. "No one cares about you racing monkeys. Are you two seriously considering breaking into one of the most secure cities in Adalore?"

"I made a deal to help you find your friend," Crispin leaned against the railing. "I will do what needs to be done to get back to my companions."

"Then I'm going with you," Rahab stepped forward, volunteering for the stealth mission.

Haldane took over steering when Rahab released the helm. "I don't like this. We're pirates, not thieves."

Crispin turned around to look at Haldane, "Do you even hear yourself? What exactly do you think a pirate is?"

"You know what I mean," Haldane snorted. "We belong on the seas, not breaking into fortified cities."

"How else do you expect us to get the information we need to find Leeondris?" Rahab asked. She grabbed Haldane's arm, drawing his gaze. "We can do this."

Haldane chewed on the inside of his lip. "Take Phex with you, just in case."

"Hell, Captain, we might as well just bang on the front door." Rahab shook her head.

Phex ascended the steps with a menacing smile that made Crispin shudder. He reminded Crispin of a sleepy fox, but a dangerous one that liked to blow things up. "I'll take that as a compliment."

"Take it however it suits you, Phex." Rahab watched as Corwin, Rafi, and Ondrej followed Phex up the steps to join them. "This is a stealth mission. Give me Corwin."

Haldane looked over at the crew and reluctantly nodded. "Fine. But any sign of trouble breaking in, you bail. Understood?"

"Aye, Captain." Rahab nodded in agreement.

Corwin flipped his knives around his hands. "Let's go rob the blind."

CHAPTER 20

ZIGGY

Ziggy laid in Gershom's bed, hating herself more than the last time they were together. Each time they rendezvoused, she felt cheap, dirty, and used. But no one else in the Order had gotten this close to Gershom or Niabi. They kept a close-knit circle and outsiders were rarely welcomed into the fold. Neither the queen nor her second in command trusted easily, so the fact she had been chosen, hand-selected by Gershom himself to be his female companion, was a reason to rejoice.

Oden had grinned ear to ear when she told him and the Order of her first encounter with the Bear. She had hoped Oden would tell her it was too risky being that close and in that vulnerable of a position, but he didn't. He just clapped his hands together, whispered a breath of thanks to no one in particular, and instructed her to see Gershom in whatever fashion he deemed worthy. Ziggy was to get close to Gershom, to learn everything she could, and report her findings.

"It is your duty," Oden had said, hands gripping her shoulders. *"You must do everything you can to please him so we might know his weaknesses."*

That had been nine months ago to the day, and she hadn't gotten much useful information. Instead, it had put her in the queen's sights and now service. Not only was Oden pressuring her to bring him intelligence worth his time, but the queen was too. And one would think Niabi would be far more frightening, but it was Oden's face that stopped her heart.

Gershom sat up in his enormous bed covered in furs, interrupting her thoughts. He planted his feet on the ground and turned his back to her. If she was determined and quick enough, she could snatch one of the swords he kept mounted above his headboard and strike him down. She could escape his calloused fingers roaming across her smooth, pale skin. She could tell Oden she eliminated one of their enemies and be reassigned to something less humiliating.

But as she tore her eyes from the three swords above her, her gaze rested on Gershom's battered back. For the first few months, he refused to let her stay the night, and warned her never to ask him personal questions. She learned to avert her eyes most of the time they were together. But tonight, she let her focus remain on his scarred body. Whip lashes by the look of them. There were so many. They were deep, too. She almost felt sympathy for him.

"Does my appearance frighten you?" Gershom's voice caused her to avert her gaze. He must have sensed her staring.

"No, my lord," she managed to spit out.

"You do not need to fear me," he twisted his torso so he could look at her. She sat up and leaned against the wooden headboard, pulling the furs up to cover her body. "I know of my scars."

"All great warriors have scars."

"Yes," Gershom nodded, "but most of my markings did not come from battle."

Ziggy opened her mouth but hesitated and snapped her lips shut. She knew she needed to ask him deeper, more intimate questions, if she was going to learn anything she could deliver to the Order, but she wasn't sure if Gershom would answer or smack her like past clients had.

"Go ahead." Gershom walked to a small table against the wall and poured two glasses of wine.

"My lord?"

"I can see it written all over your pretty face." He climbed back into bed, handing her one of the glasses. "You have questions. Go ahead and ask."

Ziggy couldn't mask her surprise. She had earned his trust. The poor fool. "If I may be so bold, my lord, where did you get those scars?"

Gershom gulped half of his wine down in one sip and cleared his throat. "Before serving the queen, I served her father. I was his commander, his friend. But something changed him."

"What changed him?" She sipped her drink, leaving a red lipstick stain on the rim of her glass.

"Her." Gershom polished off what remained in his glass and set it down. "Issachar did everything in his power to rid himself of a firstborn daughter. With plans to marry her off to the heir of Borg, he hoped he would never have to deal with or see her again. But King Benaiah wasn't interested in peace as much as he was in power. Knowing Northern laws, he understood Niabi's rightful claim to the White Throne and insisted his second born son, Antilles, marry her instead. Issachar was enraged by this proposal. When he learned Niabi and Antilles had grown quite fond of one another during one of the Westerners' visits, he ordered me to kill the young prince and make it look as if the Andrago had ambushed them during one of their northern hunting excursions. When I refused, Issachar had me arrested for treason and thrown into the dungeons." He cleared his throat and pressed on, as if he needed to tell someone or he would burst. "I was tortured for weeks until my brother, Ophir, rescued me."

Ziggy couldn't hide the horror in her eyes. Gershom had been mutilated for doing what she thought the Bear incapable of doing: the honorable thing; the right thing.

"But…" she scooted closer to him. "But you were his friend. How could he do that to you?"

Gershom rested his hand on her thigh and sighed. "Kings tend to forget their friends when it suits their agenda. Issachar was not interested in truth or honor – only power and blind obedience."

"Is she like him?"

Gershom's eyes shot up to meet hers. "The queen? She is far worse."

Ziggy shuddered, "She frightens me." A truth she would willingly admit to anyone.

"You would be a fool not to fear her." He mumbled to himself, "She will be my undoing when the endless night comes for me."

Without thinking Ziggy grasped his hand in hers and said, "I'm sorry that happened to you. I think you would make a great king."

Gershom glanced down at their hands clasped together and she instantly paled. She stammered an apology as she snatched her hand back.

"A man should never drink around a beautiful woman." He smiled. "He says more than he ought."

"My lord," her lips quivered. "Forgive me."

Gershom kissed her forehead, "You would make a lovely queen, Ziggy."

Her heart skipped a beat. "Such kind words -"

"Not just words," he grasped her petite hand. "If I bore the crown and sat on the White Throne, would you want to be my queen? To bear me sons? To be by my side?"

Ziggy's mouth opened but she didn't know what to say. She had to tread carefully because she was now wading in treasonous waters.

"I see you are speechless," he grinned.

"Of course, I am, my lord." Ziggy brushed rebellious red curls out of her face. "It is an honor to be by your side in any capacity."

"So, you would be my queen?" Gershom's eyes were filled with expectation, hope, if she dared to read into the emotion he had written across his scarred face.

She had a role to play. The Ziggy who Gershom knew wouldn't hesitate to accept this treacherous proposal. Ziggy mustered a bright smile and nodded her head.

"My lord," she whispered, "I would be your queen and I would bear you as many sons as I could give if you were King of Northwind."

Gershom squeezed her hand. "Soon, my dear, you will be dripping in gold and jewels." He brought her hand up to his lips where he planted a kiss. "When the time comes for me to bear the crown, I will send my men to ensure your safety."

"What of the queen?"

Gershom frowned at the mention of Niabi, "She will be forgotten. I just need more time."

Ziggy lifted a hand to his chin and gently forced him to look at her. "I will be here for you in whatever way you need me to be."

Gershom smiled and kissed her forehead, lingering a bit longer than normal. "That will be all tonight, Ziggy." He draped a fur over his shoulders, and left the room, allowing her to finish dressing in private.

For the first time in nine months, she finally learned of a potential plot to usurp the queen. She should have been excited to give Oden something to chew on, but she felt something for Gershom she never thought possible. She felt sorry for him. For a split second, she believed in his cause and pictured herself as his queen. Dressed in the finest clothes money could buy and dripping in beautiful gems.

Her thoughts were ripped from her mind when she heard Gershom and another man in the adjoining room in a heated discussion. She threw on her dress and as quietly as possible, tip-toed to the door, and dropped to her knees to listen through the keyhole.

Gershom sounded angry and was caught off guard by the unexpected visitor. She strained to hear what they were saying, so, Ziggy peeked through the keyhole to see if she could get a good look at whoever Gershom was talking to and was surprised to see a man from Numbio. Ziggy watched as Gershom pinched the bridge of his nose and snarled at his company. He pointed a massive finger at the bald, old man.

"You are a fool for coming here, Memucan," Gershom hissed.

"And what did you expect me to do?" Memucan asked angrily. "Stay in Numbio and have the king execute me for treason? Have him discover our plot to usurp him and Niabi?"

"Hush!" Gershom growled. "The walls have ears. Why do you think we have never met here before?"

"My life was in danger. The king and his priestess were putting the pieces together faster than I anticipated. I had no choice."

"And what do you think I will be able to do for you here?" Gershom shrugged his fur from his shoulders and made his way to the decanter of Myridian wine he loved so much. He shakily poured himself a glass but didn't offer one to Memucan. "If the queen doesn't already know of your arrival, she will soon enough. I cannot risk her wrath again. Not when we are getting closer to achieving our goal."

"I didn't sail here on a Numbio ship." Memucan sank into one of Gershom's leather chairs. "I came by way of Port Daelon. There is no way your queen would know of my presence. If anyone asks," the old man twisted his fingers to crack them one by one, "I am one of your servants."

"No." Gershom shook his head. "We need to find somewhere for you to hide. Maybe at one of the inns by the harbor."

"You want me to hide in this filthy city?" Memucan scrunched his nose in disgust.

Gershom squared his shoulders to face the door Ziggy was spying from. He tilted his head to the side and marched for her hiding spot. She scurried to the bed and started throwing more of her clothes on. When he burst through the doors, she was sitting on the bed tying her boots.

"My lord?" Ziggy feigned confusion. "Is everything alright?" Gershom stared so deeply into her eyes it made her skin crawl. "My lord?" she asked again, sure she had been made.

"Can I trust you, Ziggy?" he asked the question as if she were one of his soldiers.

Ziggy bobbed her head and flashed a nervous smile, "Of course."

Her answer seemed to satisfy him. "Do you know of an inn near the harbor that Her Majesty's soldiers don't patrol?"

She knew of several but the one she would recommend was a block away from *The Whispering Fox*. Whoever this Memucan was, the Order would want to keep an eye on him, and the proximity would make that easier.

"I could make arrangements at *The Black Lotus* if that pleases you." She finished tying her laces and stood up, his eyes roaming freely over her clothed body.

Gershom nodded. "See to it then. Send word when you have acquired a room."

With a quick bow, Ziggy slipped out of Gershom's chambers and made her way down the secret corridors to return to her small apartment in Northwind. She didn't know when Gershom would stage his coup, or who exactly Memucan was, but what she did know was she was now in dangerous territory. Up until this point, it was all hypothetical. Now, the game had truly begun, and she would have to be careful to remain on the victor's side, lest she die a victim's death.

CHAPTER 21
CRISPIN

Well after darkness had shrouded the cove, Crispin, Rahab, and Corwin disembarked the *Shadow of Death* anchored beyond the cliffs and swam back to The Sisters. They crouched behind a cluster of boulders near the harbor shores and scoped out the movement of the Keepers patrolling the perimeter of the Witness Tower. Being blind didn't hinder them. If anything, Crispin knew their hearing would be heightened. And if Corwin got too close, they'd be able to smell the mix of musk and tobacco easily.

"They have eight patrols, two Keepers in each." Rahab whispered near Crispin's ear, wringing her shirt. "There are seconds in between their paths crossing as they circle the Witness Tower."

"So, that's our way in." Crispin rubbed at the stubble growing on his face. He had made a point to keep his face clean shaven like Northern royalty, but he was liking the facial hair. Zophar would be pleased he looked more rugged.

Corwin scraped dirt from underneath his fingernails with one of his knives, his back rested against the boulders facing away from the Keepers. "I didn't spy any doors other than the main ones. How do you suggest we get in if we sneak by the patrols?"

Rahab turned from Corwin on her right to Crispin on her left. "Remember when I asked how good you were at scaling walls?" She smirked and nodded her head up the side of the tower.

Crispin's eyes followed hers and rested on the first of seven wraparound balconies. The lowest balcony was a good distance above the ground.

"How high do you suspect that landing is?" Crispin asked.

Rahab pursed her lips and scratched the side of her head. "If I was the guessing sort, I'd say fifty feet at least."

Crispin nodded, "I would have said the same."

"Well, good luck with that." Corwin huffed, folding his enormous, tattooed arms over his chest. "I'll let the captain know when you die."

"That's the spirit." Crispin forced a smile.

Rahab smacked the back of her hand against Corwin's bicep, clicking her tongue. "We all go."

"Oh, hell no!" Corwin shook his head.

"Corwin!"

"You said we were going to break in. No one said anything about scaling up the tower in the dark," Corwin snorted.

"Don't tell me you're afraid of heights." Rahab rolled her eyes.

"Not afraid." Corwin cracked his neck. "Just prefer to keep my boots on the deck of a ship."

"Look at it this way," Crispin offered, leaning closer to the pirates. "You won't be nearly as high scaling to that landing as you are on the deck of the *Shadow of Death*."

Corwin's brows formed a unibrow as he frowned at Crispin. "How do you figure?"

"Do you know how deep the Obsidian Sea is? More than fifty feet, that's for sure." Crispin squatted next to Corwin. "What happens if you fall into the sea? You sink and it's a long way down."

Corwin grimaced and Rahab rubbed her eyes with a sigh.

"I..." Corwin wheezed, wiping his sweaty hands down his pants. "I never thought about it that way. More than fifty feet, huh?"

"Great. Now you've done it." Rahab fussed at Crispin. "He won't be able to scale that wall or sail the Obsidian Sea now."

Crispin patted her hand which she ripped away. "Give him a minute. He might surprise you." He pointed with his mouth back to the pensive pirate.

"I," Corwin relaxed his face. "I suppose it isn't much different, distance wise.

Crispin nodded his approval. "See?" he whispered to Rahab with a smug smile tugging at his lips. "Just needed to give him a minute to put it together."

"You got lucky."

"Was it luck or was it my charm?"

Rahab thrust the rope they had brought with them into his chest. "Luck."

Crispin heaved the rope over his shoulder and followed Rahab toward the tower. Two patrols were crossing paths; his short window was about to open.

"Don't fall," Rahab side-eyed him.

"And hope *you* catch me?" Crispin chuckled. "I'm not that lucky."

She rolled her eyes and tugged at her left ear. "I'll be right behind you as soon as you lower the rope.

"Can't get enough of me." He noticed her nervous tell and tried to lighten the mood.

"You can't help yourself, can you?" she laughed softly.

"Where's the fun in that?"

"It's now or never," Corwin interrupted.

Crispin nodded and locked eyes with Rahab once more. Her lips parted as if she wanted to say something, but he took off before she had the chance. He hoisted himself up onto the stone landing and slipped behind the four Keepers walking in opposite patrol directions. He made it to the tower and exhaled a low breath, having held it since he left his companions. Crispin double checked to ensure the rope was still secure over his shoulder and across his chest before finding grooves to put his fingers to climb up the side to the balcony above.

Crispin kept a steady pace as he climbed up the side of the Witness Tower. He was about half-way when his fingers slipped, and he clung to the stones with his right hand. Fragments of stones fell and bounced off the pavers below. What would have gone unnoticed to Crispin's ears was magnified to the four passing Keepers who halted their patrol and turned around to investigate.

Grasping the building, Crispin picked up the pace. The last thing he needed was to draw their attention, hindering Rahab and Corwin from following him. He risked a glance downward just in time to see the Keepers resume their rounds. He exhaled a huge sigh of relief and focused on finishing the last ten feet to the landing.

The last few feet nearly took his breath away. That was the hardest and highest climb of Crispin's entire life. His forearms, biceps, and shoulders were on fire. His arms began to shake as he suspended himself just below the balcony to check for Keepers. Seeing it was clear, he hopped over the railing and ripped the rope from his chest, tying it around one of the columns that stood on the side of the open doorway into the tower.

Quickly and quietly, he lowered the rope for Rahab and Corwin to climb. Once Rahab sneaked past the Keepers and started her ascent, Crispin poked his head around the entryway and was relieved and surprised no Keepers were patrolling. He stared up to the top of the tower and was awed by the stained-glass ceiling that whisked moonlight inside.

His concentration shot back to Rahab as he heard her grunting near the top of the railing. She had scaled the wall faster than he thought she could and was impressed. He extended his hand to help her over, but she slapped his hand away and whipped her legs over onto the balcony.

"What?" Rahab huffed when she noticed Crispin's odd grin. "What is that smirk for?"

"You are an impressive climber."

"When you spend most of your time on a ship, you get really good at climbing up ropes." She turned her attention to the ground where Corwin had yet to appear. "Blast!" she whispered, a tinge of anger in her tone.

Crispin leaned closer to her, their arms touching. "What is it? Did the Keepers - ?"

"No," she shook her head. "If that brute of a sailor chickens out..."

"You'll make him walk the plank?" Crispin flashed a smile, elbowing her arm.

She flitted her eyes at him. "Is that what you Mainlanders think we do to cowards?"

"Ye-es."

Rahab rolled her eyes.

"So, that's *not* what you do?"

"No, we give them a big hug and hand them a pint." Before he could say anything, she smacked his arm and clicked her tongue. "Of course, they walk the plank! We haven't the time or space for cowards."

"Wait. But you just said -"

"I asked if that's what you Mainlanders believed. I never said you were wrong."

Crispin rubbed his eyes with a groan. "You are honestly the most frustrating woman I have ever met. Truly. You should be proud of your accomplishment."

Rahab saluted him. "An honor I shall cherish always, Your Mightiness."

"Again, with the titles." He squinted his eyes to see if he could spot Corwin. "How long should we wait -"

"Would one of you two jabbering fools help me up before I fall?" Corwin startled them as he heaved his arms over the railing. Their attention had been on each other, so they hadn't noticed Corwin scrambling up the rope with great difficulty.

Crispin grabbed ahold of Corwin's arms and dragged his heavy body onto the balcony, both falling to the tiled floor.

"Seven hells, Corwin!" Rahab wheezed as loud as she dared, a hand pressed against her heart. "You nearly caught a fist to your face."

"Thank the Seas, for once you kept those fists of yours to yourself." Corwin huffed, slowly standing to his feet. "Tell me we have another way out of here."

"Or what?" Rahab popped her hip and cocked her head to the side. "You going to stay here with the blind?"

Corwin turned to Crispin, a glimmer of hope and pleading in his brown eyes. "Tell me you have another way out of here."

"We have another way out." Crispin patted Corwin on the back. He could feel the trembling in Corwin's body. Heights was not Corwin's friend. Corwin inched his way toward the entryway, not daring a glance down to the pavers below.

"You lied." Rahab grasped Crispin's arm before he could follow Corwin inside. "We don't have another way out."

"I think you should say that a little bit louder, Rahab. I don't think the second tower heard you."

"What do you intend to do if Corwin refuses to repel from the tower?" She blocked his pathway, ignoring his snarky remark.

"We need him focused on our mission. There is no need for him to worry the entire time we're here. We need Corwin at his best and most focused." Crispin nodded back to the rope still tied for their return. "We will cross that bridge when we get to it."

The three intruders walked around the circular hall, open to the center of the tower, until they reached a set of spiral stairs. The staircase led them into the most impressive library Crispin had ever laid eyes on. Shelves that extended up the walls all the way to the ceiling at least a hundred feet above them. Crispin was taken aback at the grand space; it was hard to believe it even existed inside the tower. No matter which direction he turned, the rows of books, scrolls, and loose parchments seemed endless.

In Northwind, Crispin's mother had taken a special interest in the library. He spent many punishments helping her sort and restore book after book. What Bilhah never knew, or at least he assumed she never knew, was how he would purposely get into trouble so he could spend time with her. Books were their special thing. It's how he learned about the different Kingdoms of Adalore: their customs, their traditions, their laws. He never expected that knowledge to come in handy, but now standing in the middle of the Witness Tower, the ultimate library that housed the Hall of Records, he was awed by how much he still had to learn.

Rahab whistled a low drawn-out sound, pulling him from the memories of his mother. "This is going to be harder than I thought."

She was right. They had broken into the tower to find where Leeondris' was being held captive. Without a general idea of where they should look, there would be no way they'd find what they were looking for.

"Well, I guess we start here and work our way around?" Corwin scratched the tattoos on his cheeks so hard, Crispin was positive they'd peel right off.

"This is impossible." Rahab clasped her hands behind her neck, exhaling a sigh. "Maybe we should snatch a couple of the Witnesses from their beds and force them to find it for us."

"So now we're kidnapping people?" Crispin tsked. "Let's not disturb the hornet's nest, shall we?"

"Fine. No kidnapping." Rahab dragged her fingernails down her face. "But without some idea on how to look up information, we could be down here for years, and we obviously don't have that kind of time."

"It's your call," Crispin turned to her. "We either try to find what we came here for, or we leave and try to find him some other way."

"You'd do that?" She was surprised.

"My word is my word." Crispin nodded. "So, what's it going to be?"

Rahab didn't hesitate. "We find what we came here for."

"And what is that exactly?"

The trio hadn't heard the Keepers surround them in the library. The soldiers were hidden in so many places and because Crispin was distracted, he didn't check the room for Keepers.

"And what is that exactly?" The Keeper who appeared to be in charge stepped forward, asking the same question again. "You didn't think you would actually rob us, did you?"

Crispin stepped between her and his companions. "We were looking for information, Master…?"

She smiled, stretching the black wrap around her eyes. "Master Penn."

"From your wrap, you must be in charge of these Keepers."

"You are a well-informed thief." Penn nodded. "But that won't help you here. Without the help of a Witness, you would spend a hundred years in here and never find what you are looking for."

"Perhaps, you'd be willing to fetch one of them for us?" Crispin's snarky remarks didn't work on Penn.

"We are going to take a little walk." She snapped her fingers and twelve spears pointed toward them. "You are charged with trespassing and attempted robbery. The Sovereign will determine your fate."

An old man hobbled toward them; his cane echoed with each step he took. "It seems you have apprehended the intruders with little trouble, Master Penn."

"As I have told you before, Master Balor," Penn said, "we Keepers were bred for this."

"You are taking them to the Sovereign?"

"I am."

"I shall accompany you."

"If you like." Penn snapped her fingers again and six Keepers grabbed either arm of the three intruders. "But do try to keep up."

CHAPTER 22
ADONIJAH

Adonijah hungrily forked at the pork on his plate, shoveling bite after glorious bite into his mouth, as if he hadn't eaten in days. He had never eaten better than during his time in the Isles of Myr. He was going to miss the endless options paraded into his suite every day, but he was ready to return to the Mainland. He was growing tired of all the judgmental stares he received from the Myridian women, especially Seraphina, the mean twin. Although it was clear she despised every man that crossed her path, she seemed to have it out for him in particular.

He leaned back in his chair once his plate was cleared and lit his pipe. With a leg resting on his lap, he exhaled a puff of smoke across the table where Cato was scarfing down his second helping of roasted potatoes. Salome was pushing her fish aimlessly around her full plate, not having eaten one single bite since they sat down.

She hadn't said much since Damaris and Harbona told her about her magical abilities – or lack thereof. And for her not to devour her food like she normally did, signaled she was deep in thought, stewing in disappointment. Or anger. He wasn't quite sure.

Cato finished his dinner with a gratifying burp and sighed as he patted the small belly protruding from his skinny frame.

As much as Adonijah hated to admit it, and would never tell Cato because he didn't want him to get a big head, he had come to like the Stormcrag. Cato was entertaining and, on an island filled with man-hating-women, having him for a companion was oddly comforting.

Cato picked at his teeth with his golden fork. "What do you think your Hunter name will be?"

Salome only realized Cato was talking to her once Adonijah cleared his throat. "What?"

"Your Hunter name," Cato smiled with excitement. "Like Malachi the First or Raego the Mighty. What do you think yours will be?"

Salome tossed her utensil on her plate and shrugged. "I don't know, Cato."

Cato hummed. "Hmmm… Salome the…"

"Stubborn," Adonijah filled in the blank.

"Stubborn! Stubborn?" Cato gulped audibly, he glanced at Salome seated next to him. "Has a nice ring to it?"

Salome snapped out of her silence and glared at Adonijah across the table. "And you would be Adonijah the Ass," she snorted.

"Also has a nice ring to it," Cato chuckled, patting his mouth clean with his linen napkin.

"Aye." Adonijah kicked his boots up on the table and exhaled another ring of smoke above his head. "Salome the Stubborn it is. I'll spread the word."

She folded her arms over her chest, "You'll pay for that later."

"Oh, I'm counting on it, Princess." He flashed a mischievous smile, tucking a hand behind his head.

Cato's eyes bounced back and forth between Salome and Adonijah. "Should I give you two some privacy?"

Simultaneously, they said:

"No."

"Aye."

Cato leaned in closer to the table until his chest touched the edge. "What should I do in this situation?" he whispered. He turned to Salome, "Do what you say?" He turned to Adonijah, "Or do what you say?"

Adonijah's eyes were locked on Salome. "Always do what *she* says."

"So, I should stay." Cato reached for the bowl of green olives in the center of the table and popped one in his mouth.

Salome kept her gaze on Adonijah, as if she would lose some contest if she broke eye contact first. "Give us a minute alone, Cato."

"Right." Cato huffed and grabbed the entire bowl of olives. "Don't kill each other."

Once Cato disappeared around the corner of the suite's dining room, Salome stood up and slapped his boots off the table.

"Stubborn? Really?"

"Am I wrong?" Adonijah planted his feet on the tiled floor, his legs the same distance apart as his shoulders.

Salome slithered around the circular, wooden table and stood in front of him. Her thighs pressed up against his knees. "That's the best attribute that comes to mind when you think of me?" Her hip popped to one side and she rested her hand on it.

His sight floated from her hips up to her narrowed eyes. "Not the best," he rose from his seat and looked down at her, "just the first."

"So," she smiled, "you admit you think about me." She chuckled at her own cheekiness, and it warmed his face.

"Aye." Adonijah stroked her chin with his thumb. "I think about you."

Her voice softened, as if under his spell. "Do you think about our first night in Myr? When we almost…?"

"Kissed," he whispered and nodded. "Aye."

Salome slowly wrapped her arms around his neck. He rested his hands on her hips and leaned in to kiss her, but just before their lips touched, someone by the doorway cleared their throat announcing their presence.

Salome and Adonijah's heads whipped toward the arched threshold and spotted the twins, Rosalina and Seraphina, standing shoulder to shoulder. Rosalina blushed, looking uncomfortable with seeing them locked in such an intimate embrace. Seraphina, on the other hand, had her arms crossed over her chest and shook her head in palpable disgust.

How he had grown to loathe those meddlesome twins. Always appearing at the most inconvenient moments.

"Your Highness," Rosalina curtsied.

"Your Highness," Seraphina followed suit.

Salome released Adonijah and faced her ladies in waiting. "What is it?"

"Your grandmother, the queen," Rosalina started.

"Has requested you join her for an audience," Seraphina finished.

"When?" Salome tried to mask her irritation, but Adonijah knew her better than the twins, and by the tone in her voice, she was seething.

Please say tomorrow, Adonijah wished.

"Now," Seraphina flashed a satisfied grin.

"Now?" Salome scratched the side of her face, her eyes met Adonijah's.

"Yes, Your Highness." Rosalina nodded. "We are here to escort you."

"I'm sorry," Salome whispered up to Adonijah.

Not as sorry as he was. He kissed her forehead, drawing a grunt from Seraphina. Without looking at her, he knew the twin's eyes were rolling back in her head. "Go," he said softly.

All Adonijah could do was watch as Salome disappeared with the twins. He rubbed the nape of his neck with a heavy sigh. It seemed like the Isles of Myr didn't want to see them together. All the more reason to return to the Mainland. He would miss the food. He would miss the sea views. But he would *never* miss those damn twins.

CHAPTER 23
CRISPIN

Master Penn and her Keepers escorted Crispin, Rahab, and Corwin up what seemed like a never-ending staircase to the two-story bridge where Neempo, the Sovereign, dwelled. Once they reached the top of the enclosed bridge, they were able to see the Obsidian Sea on their right and to their left was the Mainland. The *Shadow of Death* wasn't docked in the cove, so it was safe to assume the Keepers hadn't tracked them down and brought them in for punishment.

The windows of the hallway ended on the right, and they marched another twenty feet before they were pushed up to a set of arched double doors. Two Keepers guarding the entrance slammed the butt end of their spears onto the wooden floors and the Keepers escorting the intruders echoed the movement. The doors swung open. Penn entered and Crispin, Rahab, and Corwin were shoved inside after her.

Neempo, dressed in his sleeping robes, sat stoically in his office, sipping a cup of late-night tea. It appeared he rolled out of bed for the sole purpose to sentence them, so the Keepers could execute judgment.

"The intruders, Sovereign." Master Penn announced, her hand resting on the sword that hung by her hip.

"Very efficient of you, Master Penn." Neempo blew the rising steam from his mug. "Master Balor, good of you to join us this very late evening. Or should I say, very early morning?"

Master Balor hobbled up and set his cane in front of him, setting both his hands on top to keep him steady. "Sovereign."

Neempo motioned toward the bonds around the prisoners' wrists. "Those bonds won't be necessary."

Penn tilted her head. "Sovereign, they could be dangerous."

"Cut their bonds." Neempo instructed. "Bonds are not necessary. None of them are foolish enough to attempt an assassination with both my Master of

Keepers and Master of Witnesses with me. No. We are simply going to have a nice chat."

Penn obeyed and cut their bonds. Rahab rubbed her wrists, her nostrils flaring.

"Please," Neempo motioned for them to take seats around the study. "Have a seat. There is much we need to discuss."

Penn and Balor sat on either side of Neempo, ensuring an attack would not be so easily accomplished. The Keepers backed away to the doorway.

"This will be a private conversation. Your services are not needed." Neempo dismissed the Keepers. Once the doors closed, Neempo flashed a friendly grin in the pirates' direction. "So, you were found trespassing in the Hall of Records. How very naughty of you."

"We beg pardon, Sovereign," Crispin leaned forward. "We are not here to harm you or your people. And we were not here to rob you."

"Then tell me, why would you risk scaling the Tower of Witnesses if not to harm or rob us?" Neempo didn't seem angry; he was amused more than anything.

"We were looking for a missing companion of ours. We figured…"

"You thought our Hall of Records could enlighten you." Neempo smiled, filling in the rest of what Crispin was trying to say.

"Yes."

"Surely you must know the penalty for trespassing."

Crispin shrugged. "Death, I'm assuming."

Neempo slapped a hand against his thigh and chuckled. "You speak without a trace of fear. And you don't sound like a pirate. Who are you?"

"I'm just a man looking for my companions." Not a lie, but definitely not the whole truth.

Neempo set his teacup and saucer down on the small table in front of him. "You are far too humble, Crispin, son of Issachar. Secrets do not exist here."

Rahab shot Crispin a look of panic. Crispin, too, was taken aback by how the Sovereign knew who he was.

"Do not look so surprised, Your Highness." Neempo continued, as if he could read his thoughts. "Perhaps, I can be of service."

"You…" Crispin scratched the back of his neck. "You want to help me?"

"Your visit has been foreseen. I have taken the liberty of having the information you need pulled from our Hall of Records. Master Balor."

Balor pulled a scrolled-up parchment from underneath one of his long sleeves and placed it on the table.

Crispin and Rahab eyed one another suspiciously. It couldn't possibly be that easy.

"What is it that you want in return?" Crispin asked, one eyebrow arched.

"I ask that you save my life."

Crispin saw both Penn and Balor tense up after Neempo's request. It seemed like they didn't expect that response either. "What do you mean save your life? What can I do for you that your own cannot?"

"They are coming for me." Neempo was calm. He kicked one leg up and crossed it over the other. "She has sent them, but she cannot succeed. I need to know that if protecting me fails, and if rescuing me fails, that you will be strong enough to do what needs to be done."

"Who is coming for you?" Crispin asked. "Who is *she*?"

"I think you know exactly who *she* is," Neempo said. "Do I have your word?"

Crispin risked a glance at Rahab. Her eyes were glued to the scroll sitting unopened before them. She made her decision. Anything for that information.

"Alright." Crispin nodded. "It's a deal."

"Good," Neempo stood with his back to the windows that faced the harbor and the Obsidian Sea. "Keep that scroll close. You haven't time to read it now."

"What do you mean?" Rahab spoke for the first time, growling each word.

"You have more important things to do."

"Like what?" She shot back.

"Fulfilling your promise to me." Neempo moved his head to face Crispin. "They're here."

The night sky erupted in explosions and the alarm bells rang. Crispin looked past Neempo and saw the harbor, which had been empty minutes ago, was now filled with pirate ships.

The Sisters was under attack.

Crispin walked up to the window and placed a hand against the cool glass. It rattled underneath his fingers as another explosion sounded. He felt Rahab join him.

"Did you know?" Crispin asked her, brows furrowed.

Rahab didn't look at him. Her eyes were wide, glued to the largest ship in the harbor. Crispin realized she was not only surprised by the attack, but she was afraid.

"Whose ship is that?" Crispin stared at the enormous pirate ship where the explosions originated from.

"That is *The Leviathan*." Rahab's fear-stricken eyes met his. "That is the Pirate King Uri's ship."

The Leviathan was three times bigger than the Shadow of Death and would easily require three to four hundred crew members. And if that wasn't enough muscle, the Pirate King brought seven more ships with anywhere between fifty to one hundred sailors aboard each vessel.

Crispin turned around. Master Penn was instructing some Keepers to guard this level from intruders. The remaining Keepers were sent to the other two towers to deliver her orders until she could join them.

"Is there a way to get you out of here unseen?" Crispin asked the Sovereign.

"There will be no need for sneaking." Master Penn shook her head and rejoined their group. "Our towers have never been breached. And they would be fools to attack us on level ground."

"And if they scale the walls like we did?" Corwin spoke for the first time in almost an hour.

"We allowed you to get inside our walls." Penn snipped, a snarl flashing from underneath her black wrap. "You really think you can outwit the blind?"

Corwin pointed a large, shaky finger toward the pirate ships in the harbor. "They won't stop at scaling walls. They will destroy these towers, stone by stone, until there is nothing left. Those are men you should be afraid of."

"I'll leave the cowering to you," Penn rolled her shoulders back and held her head high. She gripped the handle of her sword tighter and brought the blade up to tap her forehead. "Sovereign."

Neempo bowed his head, a silent thank you and good fortune. "Master Penn."

Penn stomped toward the doors to leave when an explosion shattered the wooden entrance and sent her flying.

Crispin had instinctually wrapped his arms around Rahab, shielding her from the shards of glass and wood that flew through the room. He looked around the Sovereign's chambers and saw everyone lying on the floor. The lights had been snuffed out, but Crispin was able to make out two dead Keepers sprawled over the threshold, blood pooled around their lifeless bodies.

Penn reached for her side. A piece of wood had sailed through the air and stabbed her. She grimaced but grabbed ahold of the spike and pulled it out with nothing more than a small groan.

Crispin ripped a piece of the curtain hanging behind him and slid over to her. "Let me wrap your waist to stop the bleeding."

Penn nodded, allowing him to help her. As he did, she whispered, "There is no way to slip past my Keepers. We have ancient magic shielding the Sovereign's chambers from invaders."

Crispin finished bandaging her wound and peered around the room. Master Balor was struggling to his feet. Neempo had found his seat and plopped down, blood trickling down his forehead from the impact. Rahab and Corwin had drawn their weapons, and had their eyes fastened to the smoke billowing in from the hall. Someone was coming. The pirates knew it. And they were afraid of who was coming. His eyes darted to the entrance as he heard boots stomping inside.

"Well, well, well," a deep, booming voice echoed through the decimated chamber. "It seems we have traitors in our midst."

Crispin saw the giant of a man staring directly behind him at Rahab and Corwin. Whatever fear had been in their eyes before was gone, replaced with anger and hatred. They had the appearance of cornered animals and were ready to launch an assault, if necessary.

Rahab's shoulders were rounded, her hand tightened around her dagger. She spat at the man, now surrounded by ten other pirates filing inside the room. "May your name be forgotten when your bones turn to dust."

The man stepped forward, a cruel smile stretching across his face. Now out from the haze, Crispin could see him fully. His dark skin was peppered with identical notched markings all over his body. He was bald except for three braids that reached down to his mid-back. By his commanding presence, and the terror on his companions' faces when they saw *The Leviathan* in the harbor, Crispin assumed he was the Pirate King.

Crispin stood up, helping Penn to her feet. "You must be Uri."

The Pirate King's blazing glare shot to him. He gave him a quick once over and if he recognized him from the wanted posters, he did not indicate it. "You seem to have the honor of knowing who I am. But who the hell are you?"

Penn reached for Crispin's forearm and squeezed it, warning him to keep his identity a secret. For once, Crispin heeded the warning.

"Take your thugs and get out," Crispin growled. "The Sisters is neutral territory."

"Not anymore." Uri rumbled a wicked laugh. "Don't worry, Masters." He mocked a bow. "We will leave your pathetic city intact. We only came for him." He pointed at the Sovereign, calmly sitting in his armchair.

Penn lifted her sword. "You will not touch him."

Uri sniffed the air and grinned. "Ahh, a challenge. I was hoping to bloody my swords tonight." He pulled two identical blades from their sheathes on his hips.

Penn dug her heels into the floor, ready to fight to her death, if need be, to protect her Sovereign.

"How did you get past our wards?" Neempo asked, no trace of fear or animosity in his voice.

"Hello, Neempo." A silvery voice sliced through the room. The woman dressed in a black, skin-tight robe floated to Uri's side. She had a thick strip of black paint across her eyes and gold liquid streaks from her forehead to her chin. "Miss me?"

"Nezreen." Neempo nodded. "I heard you died."

"A vicious rumor."

Crispin saw her eyes had a milky white film. She was blind.

"When you banished me," Nezreen wrapped her hand around Uri's outstretched arm. "My king found me and gave me shelter. Where you saw weakness in my gifts, he saw strength."

"All of this," Balor motioned around the destruction, "because you were not chosen to be Sovereign?" He rested a hand against his heart. "Nezreen, child -"

"I am no longer one of your Witnesses, Balor," she spat like a venomous serpent. "You are no longer my master."

King Uri smirked. His enormous, scarred hand stroked her petite, pale one. "Come with us, Neempo, and we will spare the rest of your order. Resist, and I will take delight in slaughtering all of your citizens one by one."

Neempo stood up slowly. "I will go with you."

Master Penn moved to protest but stopped. Her Sovereign had spoken.

As Neempo neared Crispin, he whispered, "You know where they will take me. If a rescue fails, you must do what needs to be done."

Crispin didn't dare a glance at Neempo. He didn't want Uri or that witch of his to ask what the Sovereign had said. Although, it was still as much a riddle to him as it would be to them.

Neempo stood in front of Nezreen and that's when Crispin's breath hitched. Something about them standing together sent an unwelcome shiver up his spine. Crispin felt eyes on him. The Pirate King was watching him closely. Realization hit Uri and a malicious chuckle erupted from him.

"Now I know who you are," Uri cooed, "Crispin, son of Issachar. Your sister might even reward me with a night in her bed for delivering you to her."

Crispin unsheathed his sword, taking a fighter's stance. "You'll have to fight me first."

Uri roared in wicked delight. He licked his chapped lips and took a monstrous step toward the prince. But he was stopped by Nezreen's voice.

"This is not your fight, my King." Nezreen's solid white eyes met Crispin's. "Not yet," she smiled.

Uri sheathed his swords without batting an eye. "Until we meet again, Prince." He cocked his head to the side. "I will take great delight in killing you when the time is right."

Crispin pointed the tip of his blade at the pirate. "I'll make sure to mount your head from the tallest tower in Northwind."

Neempo was shackled and dragged from the room. Nezreen followed the soldiers out but paused, waiting for Uri to fall in line.

Uri smirked at Rahab and sniffed the air. "Tell Haldane, Palma lasted longer than I expected her to." Rahab flinched; tears welled in her eyes. "Do you want to know what her last words were?"

Crispin stepped in between Uri and Rahab, halting his approach. His stomach was churning, picturing the kind woman who had saved him being tortured at the hands of this monster.

Uri snickered, "Her last word was *Haldane.* She repeated it over and over again, hoping he would save her from me."

"I'll kill you," Rahab rasped through tears. Corwin grabbed her arm, keeping her from attacking the Pirate King.

"Get in line." Uri pointed at Crispin. "I'll be seeing you again." He turned on his heel, joined Nezreen, and they vanished over the other side of the bridge.

CHAPTER 24
NIABI

The Royal Healer was instructed to tell the members of Niabi's small council that she was fighting off a cold and was instructed to rest, but that wasn't the truth. The truth was she was pregnant and only she and the healer knew. And that was exactly how Niabi wanted it. The Royal Healer obliged, being more afraid of suffering the queen's wrath than spilling the juicy gossip to her companions. She did as she was told and left the queen to rest, to process her thoughts.

That was three days ago and Niabi had refused visitations from everyone, including Pash.

How could this have happened?

What would she tell Pash?

Should she tell Pash?

She was still mourning Rollo – was it appropriate to be happy to welcome a new life?

Rollo would have been the first person she would have told. And he would have been overjoyed to finally become a big brother. He had begged her, year after year, to give him a brother or sister, but Niabi would kiss his face and tell him, *"Why should I have another child when the Almighty already gave me a perfect one?"*

She smiled fondly at the memory before softly sobbing and rubbing her swollen belly.

"Ivaylo if it's a boy and Suni if it's a girl," Rollo would say.

Niabi's pregnancy with Rollo was euphoric. She radiated joy and her vindictive and vengeful nature seemed to dissipate with every passing month. She never even suffered morning sickness; no pain plagued her. It was the perfect pregnancy with the perfect child. This second pregnancy, although still within the early stages, already had her suffering with nausea and lack of appetite.

But Rollo would be so happy.

Pash would be over the moon. All he wanted was for them to be together – to have a life away from all of this.

But who was she without her kingdom, her crown, her throne? It had been a long time since she was no one of importance.

Where would they be able to go and live in peace, unafraid of their enemies finding them?

If she asked Tala to take her to Elisor, he would. If she asked Tala to accept Pash into the fold, he would not.

But above all else, Niabi could never leave Rollo. She could never abandon her son, even in death.

After all, it was her fault Rollo was dead. She lowered her guard and gave her father an opportunity – a moment of weakness to destroy her; to take the man she loved. She believed in Vilora's prophecy. She trusted in Gershom. All of them were mistakes. Had she been vigilant when Dichali was alive, Issachar's assassins would never have gotten past her to kill him. Had she not listened to the witch, she never would have aligned herself with Gershom. Had she not sought out the Bear to help her get revenge, he would not have failed to execute Crispin and Salome, and Rollo would still be alive.

She jumped up from her chair overlooking her kingdom and snatched every glass cup and shattered them against the floor and the walls, one by one. She screamed. She wept. She allowed herself to wallow in misery, even though she hated herself for it.

Sinking to the white marble floor, in the midst of thousands of pieces of glass, Niabi swore no harm would come to her second born.

She would trust no one.

She would make deals with no one.

She would listen to no one.

Niabi would not make the same mistakes. She would not risk this child like she unknowingly did Rollo. She would not lose another baby. She would not fail again as a mother.

A knock echoed through her chambers. The sun had set and without any lights lit, the room was pitch black. She opened her left palm and let a flame flicker until she sent the fireball toward the fireplace, lighting it.

"Go away," she hissed feebly.

But the door opened anyway.

Niabi didn't have the strength nor desire to bark out more commands. She didn't bother to look over at the visitor who quietly shut the door and glided toward her. As always, she was armed with daggers underneath her sleeves; fearing assassins wasn't something she wasted her energy on. But she already knew who was approaching just by his footsteps.

Tala used his foot to push pieces of glass away from her and sat down beside her. He stretched his long legs in front of him and said nothing. Tala was a good friend, knowing when to speak and when to just be present. She placed her open hand down in between them and he grasped it. Neither of them spoke. His warm hand tightened around hers and she felt at ease.

Niabi lowered her head and rested on his shoulder, allowing tears to run down her cheeks. "I miss him," she whispered.

Tala kissed the top of her head and squeezed her cold right hand. "We will see them again."

Niabi knew when he referred to *them,* he wasn't just thinking of Rollo, but of

Dichali and Tallulah, as well. Riding their horses through the endless fields and valleys of the Great Beyond.

"There is something I have to tell you." Niabi wiped the snot from her nose with her sleeve.

Tala reached into his breast pocket, pulled out a handkerchief and handed it to her. "Rollo would have been the first to congratulate you, so allow me to be the second."

Niabi's eyes flicked up at him. Of course, Tala already knew she was pregnant. He wouldn't risk her wrath without reason.

"I will have that loose-lipped healer flogged."

Tala chuckled and patted her arm. "Spare your punishments, woman. I know you well enough to know you wouldn't allow something as simple as a cold prevent you from stomping through these halls."

"Then how did you know?"

"I could tell as soon as I opened the door and saw you."

She shot him a look; her lips pursed. "Are you insinuating your queen already looks to be with child?"

"You had the same fearful look on your face when you found out you were expecting Rollo."

Niabi inhaled a deep breath, commanding the tears welling in her eyes to stay put. "How can I be happy?"

"Because Rollo would be happy." Tala leaned his head back against the wall. "A new life is a blessing, Niabi. Consider this child Rollo's gift to help you heal." He squeezed her hand. "He is watching over you. So don't wither away in this room. Be the queen he always knew you to be. Make him proud and thank him for his gift."

"I won't make the same mistakes." Niabi vowed.

"If I might be bold enough to risk your wrath," Tala's eyes met hers. "Does the commander know, yet?"

Niabi shook her head. "And I'm not sure if I should tell him."

"Are you involved with someone other than the commander?" Tala asked, though he already knew the answer.

"You mean to say, whether I tell him or not, he will find out I carry his child." Niabi narrowed her eyes, drawing a chuckle from Tala.

"Of all the men in Adalore…"

Niabi laughed. "I chose your favorite."

Tala crinkled his nose in disgust. "What a disappointing statement. So, you'll tell him?"

"I'll tell him when the time is right." Niabi promised, although she wasn't sure when that would be. "Will you take me to see him?"

Tala escorted Niabi to Rollo's crypt but stayed outside so she could have a moment with her son. She slowly closed in on the white stone statue of her son guarding his final resting place. She ran her fingers over its face – such an incredibly accurate likeness.

"You always did look out for me, even before you could walk." Niabi's lip quivered. She cleared her throat. "No one could ever replace you, Rollo, my love. My sweet boy. But I thank you for your gift. I thank you for your continued love from the Great Beyond. I will make sure this little one knows all about you and never forgets you." She rested her forehead against the statue's and closed her eyes. "Tell your father, I miss him. And we will all be together again soon."

Niabi rested her hand on her belly and inhaled deeply. "Ivaylo if it's a boy and Suni if it's a girl."

CHAPTER 25

CRISPIN

As the sun rose, the harbor was once again empty and calm. If Crispin hadn't seen the forces of the Pirate King with his own eyes, he never would have believed The Sisters had been attacked.

Crispin nursed a cup of tea as he stared out the blasted windows at the docked *Shadow of Death*. "Who is she?" Crispin asked. "The witch?"

"Nezreen is Neempo's twin," Balor grasped his cane tightly. "They were brought to The Sisters as infants.""Both of them were born blind?" Crispin picked up an overturned chair and plopped down across from Master Balor and Master Penn.

Balor nodded his head. "I could sense great power in them the moment they arrived. When our last Sovereign died, his spirit had to choose who would replace him. Nezreen and Neempo were two of five potential candidates for Sovereign. I thought Nezreen would be chosen. She was more powerful than Neempo. But he was selected because of his kind heart. Nezreen was angry and for years she refused to speak with her brother. She poured all her time and energy into her duties as a Witness. But instead of accepting the visions as they were given, she tried to look into the future and that's when darkness grew in her."

"She tried to kill Neempo." Penn cut in. She reclined in her seat, massaging the freshly stitched wound on her side. "She tried to become Sovereign by force, believing her destiny had been stolen."

"Did you always hate her?" Crispin cocked his head to the side and flinched when Penn flashed him a menacing look.

"Hate is not a strong enough word to express how I feel about the witch." Penn cracked her knuckles before continuing, "Weeks before her attack, Neempo had been blessed with a vision into the future by the Almighty. A warning of her betrayal."

"Neempo did not wish to see his twin sister executed." Balor set his teacup down on the splintered table and brushed his fingers against his brow. "So, he banished her instead."

Crispin rested his elbows on his knees and leaned forward. "The Sovereign said he heard Nezreen had died. Couldn't he have checked by using his sight?""Witnesses are not Seers." Balor shook his head. "We see what we are meant to see for record keeping purposes. Seers can look into many possible futures, but even with their sight, nothing is certain."

"So, is Nezreen a Seer?" Crispin asked.

"She has limited sight as a Witness," Balor explained, "but whatever she does not see, her shadows whisper to her, warning and advising her along the way."

"Her shadows?" Crispin rubbed his hands over his face. Exhaustion was starting to take ahold him. "I thought that was smoke from the explosion."

Penn shook her head, "From what we know, the shadows are her closest companions. Wherever she goes, they go."

"It's rumored," Rahab marched into the room, drawing Crispin's undivided attention, "while wandering the shores of the Mainland, Nezreen made a deal with the Grim." Rahab sat in the chair next to Crispin when he kicked up to a standing position. "She sold her soul to him. She swore she would serve him for eternity in exchange for power to destroy her enemies."

Crispin strummed his fingers against the armrests of his wooden chair, deep in thought. "So…" he cleared his throat, "these shadows are the source of her power. How do we get rid of them?"

"One would assume by killing the vessel, the shadows would disintegrate." Balor scratched his beard. "But there is nothing to suggest that it would work."

"But in order to kill her," Crispin slid lower into his seat, tapping his foot against the dusty floor, "we would have to hide our plan of attack from her shadows. And from what you're saying, it's damn near impossible."

"Perhaps, if we found someone with cloaking magic, we could have the element of surprise." Rahab suggested, crossing one leg over the other.

Crispin looked at her. "Do you know someone with this ability?"

"The cloaker I knew is dead." She twiddled her fingers, eyes glued to the floor. Before Crispin could ask about the cloaker, she changed the subject. "The Pirate King said he had a dream of a powerful witch who would help him establish his kingdom. When Nezreen arrived on our shores, he welcomed her with open arms and a lustful smile. That was almost nine years ago."

"Are they a couple?" Crispin turned to her, kicking a lazy leg over the armrest of his chair.

Rahab grimaced and wiped her dirt-stained face. "Uri will never take a wife. His bed is open to anyone, willing or unwilling."

There was something about the way she said, "unwilling" that sent an unwelcome shiver down Crispin's spine. Had she been one of the unwilling ones in Uri's bed?

"Rahab?" Crispin whispered, but she waved her hand in the air, brushing him off.

"Do you have a plan?" she asked, not daring to meet his gaze.

"Not exactly," Crispin's gulp was audible to everyone in the room.

"The Sovereign said you would know where they are taking him." Rahab tilted her head, clearly looking for answers.

Crispin bobbed his head, meeting her calculating gaze. "Northwind."

"Why?" Rahab rubbed the back of her neck, looking defeated. She knew as well as Crispin did, that once Neempo was in Northwind, it would be a monumental task to rescue him.

"We have received report of a witch joining your sister's small council," Penn stated.

Instinctively, Crispin wanted to bark out that Niabi wasn't his sister, but he swallowed the argument. "Why bring Neempo to Northwind? Does he possess powers that Niabi would want to exploit?"

Master Penn and Master Balor tensed up at the same time. They knew something and seemed unwilling to speak on it.

"What is it?" Crispin pressed. "If I am expected to break him out of the White Keep's dungeons, I deserve to know everything."

"One of the reasons a Sovereign is chosen is because of their heart," Balor answered Crispin's question. "We call it the Heart of the Righteous."

"From what we understand," Penn added reluctantly, "your sister intends to use our Sovereign's heart to raise her son from the dead."

Crispin's eyes widened. He never thought resurrecting someone was even possible. "Sh- she can do that?"

"It's a difficult spell to perform." Penn stood and paced around the room with arms clasped behind her back. "But it worked once, a long time ago. With enough magic and the Sovereign's heart, it is possible."

Rahab exhaled as Balor continued. "For the resurrection spell to work, the heart must still be beating."

"You mean," Rahab brought a hand to her breast, "they are going to carve his heart out of his chest while he is still alive?"

Balor nodded in confirmation. "It is the only way."

An eerie silence engulfed the room. No one moved, no one uttered a sound. Crispin glanced at Rahab who went from looking ill to indignant. She angrily stood up, her chair falling behind her.

"Then we rescue the Sovereign," she said, "and kill Uri while we're at it."

"We'll need a ship," Crispin looked out the shattered window at the harbor.

"Then it's a good thing we have the fastest ship in Adalore." Rahab nodded with a cocky smile.

Penn planted her feet shoulder-width apart as she stood, and said, "I will bring twelve of our fiercest Keepers to rescue our Sovereign. We leave the Pirate King and his demon to you."

"Twelve Keepers?" Crispin was shocked at how few soldiers Master Penn was planning to bring to Northwind.

Penn tapped her fingers to her chin before bobbing her head slightly. "You may be right." Crispin breathed a short-lived sigh of relief. "Twelve Keepers seems excessive. I will bring our best six."

Crispin nearly choked, "What? No, I meant, shouldn't you bring as many Keepers as you can?"

Penn threw her head back and laughed heartily. "I haven't laughed so hard in ages." She collected herself before saying, "Six will be more than adequate, Prince Crispin. I will ready my Keepers and meet you aboard your ship." Penn squared her shoulders to Master Balor who slowly rose to his shaky feet. "Master Balor."

"Master Penn."

The Masters walked to the opening where a door once stood and went their separate ways to their respective towers.

Crispin walked up behind Rahab who stood by the windows overlooking the *Shadow of Death* docked in the harbor. "How is he?"

Rahab knew he was asking about Haldane. Her gaze didn't waver from the black ship whose deck was being scrubbed by the youngest crew members. "Shattered." Her lip quivered and she cleared her throat. "As shattered as a human can possibly be."

"I'm sorry about Palma." Just speaking her name made his heart ache.

Rahab turned around to face him, but he refused to meet her gaze. "Her death wasn't your fault." Her voice was soft and compassionate, but it did nothing to ease Crispin's guilt. Rahab's fingers grazed his and he finally looked at her. "Whether you had crossed paths with Palma or not, Death had called for her."

"She took me in, healed me, aided me," Crispin shook his head and withdrew his hand from her warm touch. "How am I not to blame for her death?"

"Uri and that witch weren't here for you," Rahab pointed out with a frown. She grabbed his chin, pulling his face toward hers. "Palma kept her knowledge of you hidden from Nezreen's sight. They were here for the Sovereign. This is not your fault."

"Then why go after her in the first place?" Crispin's nostrils flared. "Why kill her?"

Rahab tentatively stroked her thumb up and down Crispin's stubbled jawline. "When Nezreen came to Pulau, she convinced Uri that all diviners, fortune tellers, cloakers, and oracles on the islands were a threat to his power and should be eliminated. Hundreds of men, women, and even some younglings were slaughtered over the years. There were some of them, cloakers mostly, who hid, but eventually her shadows found them."

"Your friend?"

"His name was Desi." She rested her hand on Crispin's chest. His heart thundered underneath her palm. "He was fifteen."

"I'm sorry."

"Haldane blames himself for him and Palma separating. But the truth is, Palma distanced herself from all of us." Rahab's eyes were glossy as she remembered her friend. "She tried to shield us from any danger because of her gifts. Last I heard, she stopped using her power so her magic wouldn't leave a trail for Nezreen's shadows to pick up."

"She gave all of you up…"

"To save us." Rahab bobbed her head, a tear slipping down her cheek, which she quickly flicked away.

"But," Crispin cleared his throat, "Palma told me she saw me in a vision."

Rahab knew where he was going. "A vision she could have ignored but didn't. She believed in saving you more than she feared Nezreen."

Crispin thought back on his short time with Palma. It now made sense why her hovel didn't have any windows, why she didn't go into *The Dancing Lady*, why she refused to set foot on the *Shadow of Death*. And then realization sliced through him like a hot blade cutting through butter. Palma asked for her and her parents to be allowed to live in Northwind once he became king. But she knew

Nezreen's shadows would more than likely track her down before he even left Pulau.

Crispin's heart raced. He thought he was going to throw up.

"Your word is all I need." Palma's sounded in his head.

"Are her parents still alive?" Crispin opened his eyes and scanned Rahab's face. But he knew the answer before she spoke.

"She was the last of her name."

Crispin couldn't stop the tears from streaming down his face. Rahab gently wiped them away.

"I asked what her price was for helping me off of Pulau." Crispin rasped. "All she wanted was to live in Northwind with her sick parents, so they could live peacefully."

"Would you have followed her to *The Dancing Lady* had she not struck a deal with ye?"

Crispin hesitated. "I suppose I wouldn't have."

"Palma would have known that." Rahab interlaced her fingers with Crispin's, which caused his heart to skip a beat. "She knew her fate when she saved you. Don't let her death be a waste."

Crispin's eyes dropped to their hands clasped together. "What did the scroll say?"

Rahab's eyes widened at the sudden change in subject. Her free hand dipped into her coat pocket and retrieved the unopened scroll Neempo had given her. "I forgot I had this."

Crispin looked at her in anticipation, but she didn't unravel it.

"Whenever a girl in Pulau celebrates her sixteenth Name Day, the Pirate King has her snatched from her bed in the middle of the night and brought to his fortress. He is known to be cruel in his chambers but if you don't fight back, it won't be as painful."

Crispin tilted his head, horrified by her story and where it was headed. Rahab's eyes were glued to his chest where her hand still rested, fingertips caressing his skin.

"I was taken from my home four years ago. I didn't want his calloused hands roaming my body, so I fought back." She paused, inhaling a deep breath, "And he…" Rahab lowered the waistband of her pants an inch. There was a jagged scar across her lower abdomen.

Crispin reached to touch her but stopped. She grabbed his wrist and pressed his hand against the dark scar.

"The healers say I will never be able to have a child." Rahab's voice cracked. She tapped the side of her neck. "But I left a mark on him as well."

Crispin flashed back to Uri standing before them with a malicious grin and remembered seeing a long scar from the bottom of his earlobe to the center of his thick neck.

"And the notches all over his body?"

Rahab whispered, "One notch for every woman he has bed."

Uri must have had thousands of notches on him. Crispin shook his head trying to rattle the image of the Pirate King raping all those terrified women. He glanced down at Rahab, his hand still resting on her lower belly.

"He didn't rape me," Rahab shook her head, reading the question in Crispin's eyes, "but he had me thrown into his dungeons to bleed to death after I cut him." She lifted the scroll. "You want to know who Leeondris is to me?"

"He rescued you." Crispin pieced that part of the story together.

Rahab nodded. "He had broken into Uri's prison to free Phex. Phex had been captured and tortured for refusing to construct explosives for the Pirate King. After breaking Phex out, Leeondris passed by my cell and saw what Uri had done to me. He refused to leave me there to die, so he carried me to the *Shadow of Death* and sat by my bedside every night until I was able to walk again." Her eyes glistened with tears, but she held them back. "If he hadn't saved me that night, I would have died on that cold, damp dungeon floor."

Crispin fingered through her icy blue locks, moving hair out of her face and tucking it behind her ear. "I can't believe you suffered through all of that."

"I guess I'm a lot harder to kill than most people think," she flashed a smirk his way.

"I guess so," he said softly, removing his hand from her abdomen to cup her face, "I'm glad you survived, Rahab."

Her gaze lingered on his lips. "I am, too."

"If the Pirate King knows about you and Phex, then why hasn't he tracked you down?" His hands trailed down her arms.

Rahab motioned with her hand from her head down to her feet. "You dye your hair blue, change your name, and hide in plain sight, counting down the days until you can seek revenge." She cocked her head to the side with a wicked grin, "You really think Uri loses sleep thinking about people like me? People like Phex?" She shook her head. "The Pirate King looked me in the eye and there was no recognition, no realization, that I'm the one who gave him the scar he stares at in the mirror every day."

Crispin traced a circular motion in her palm, "He'll remember you the next time we cross his path."

"We will rescue the Sovereign. We will kill the Pirate King and gut the demon witch." Rahab's eyes were filled with a fire that made his stomach do somersaults.

"And Leeondris?" Crispin tipped his head toward the scroll she gripped tightly in her left hand.

Rahab thrust the parchment back into her pocket. "What if…" She inhaled and exhaled deeply. "What if he is not in need of rescuing?"

"You don't think he abandoned the crew -"

Rahab shook her head ferociously. "Leeondris would never abandon the crew." She tilted her head upwards, keeping whatever rebellious tears that stung her eyes at bay. "What if he is dead? I'm not sure I'm ready to find out what is in this scroll."

Crispin took both of her hands in his and clutched them against his chest. "We rescue the Sovereign. We kill the Pirate King and gut the demon witch. Then we open this," he eyed her pocket where the scroll was tucked.

Rahab shook her head. "What about your men?"

"I swore an oath to help you find Leeondris," he whispered, leaning closer to her, his fingers stroking from her temple to her chin. "I swore an oath to rescue the Sovereign. If I don't honor my word as an exiled prince, no one will trust me when I am…" He trailed off, for some reason he was unable to finish with…

"King." Rahab finished it for him. "When you're king."

Crispin nodded; eyes glued to hers.

"Does that frighten you?" she asked, leaning into his touch.

"Being king?" Crispin shrugged. His grip tightened around her hand. She was so close to him; she could probably feel his heart pounding in his chest. "I suppose I never looked at it as me being king so much as me killing my sister." He had never acknowledged Niabi as his blood before and the word *sister* felt bitter on his tongue when associated with her.

"But if you defeat her, you would be crowned king?"

Crispin arched an eyebrow. "Why the sudden interest? Are you inquiring into the position of queen?" He flashed a coy smile and she reciprocated with a grin of her own.

"If I ever need a pardon in Northwind, I know who I need to speak to." She retrieved her hand from his and lowered her eyes. "Besides, a queen would need to give you heirs."

Give him heirs. That phrase struck him like a knife to the chest. All the years he spent training and brooding in the Tree House Forest, not once did he think about being a father. His thoughts were solely focused on exacting his revenge, not being king. Crispin was his father's fifth son. He was never meant to sit on the White Throne. But now…

"I should check on the captain before everyone boards." Rahab's voice sliced through his thoughts.

"Right," Crispin bobbed his head, tucking his hands in his pockets.

"I'll see you down there." Rahab walked out before he could say anything else.

Crispin stood in silence, looking around the Sovereign's office that had been blown to bits. It was a wonder more of them weren't injured or killed in the blast.

Though he tried to push her to the back of his mind, he could still feel Rahab's warm touch on his skin. His eyes skimmed to the *Shadow of Death* and the longing for adventure on the high seas rippled through him. Being aboard the ship, finally living out his childhood dream, lit a fire in his heart that had been extinguished years ago. He never expected to be king. But that was now his future.

Why did Rahab make him question everything he thought he wanted?

"She's right."

Crispin whipped around and found Master Balor standing in the threshold, propped on his cane.

"What?" Crispin asked.

"A king will need heirs."

"Forgive my bluntness, Master Balor," Crispin hissed, "but you speak too boldly on a matter that doesn't concern you."

"Perhaps," Balor hobbled closer until he was standing a few feet in front of the hot-headed prince. "But I have lived for seventy-four years and have seen far too many lineages of good princes and great kings end with wicked men and women taking their place. Though battle is important for you to reclaim your father's throne, it is not the only priority."

Balor sank into the chair he had occupied earlier and set his cane to the side. He stretched his legs out and rubbed his wrinkled hands up and down his knees. "What a tragedy it would be for you to win your crown with ash and blood, only to lose it by loving a barren woman."

"I will do as I please," Crispin spat, shoulders tense like a predator about to launch an assault on its prey. "I will love who I please. I will rule how I please and I will die how I please. You, nor anyone else, will persuade me differently."

Balor shook his head in disappointment, "You really are no different than her."

Crispin knew Balor was referring to Niabi and his nostrils flared at the disrespect, the insinuation that he and his sister had anything, other than blood, in common. "For someone with age, you lack wisdom."

Master Balor smirked, crinkling the lines of the white wrap over his eyes. "And for someone with sight, you lack vision." He snagged his cane and struggled to his feet, shakily making his way back toward the chaotic hallway. "Marry the pirate and your line will end. Put your people before your own desires, and your sons and daughters will rule for an age." Balor squared his shoulders to Crispin who hadn't moved an inch and bowed his head. "Favor and fortune on your journey, Prince Crispin." He turned the corner and disappeared.

CRISPIN WATCHED as The Sisters faded from view and the open waters drew him in. In a few days, he would be home. Home for the first time in twelve years.

This was risky. Going not only into the heart of Northwind, but venturing into the belly of the beast, to rescue Neempo from Niabi's dungeons.

What if he saw her? Or came face to face with her?

He could possibly end a war before one was officially declared. He could avenge his dead and claim the crown and throne. He could finally return home for good. Crispin swore to himself right then and there, if he had the chance to kill Niabi, he would do it. He wouldn't hesitate. He would show her no mercy. He would do what needed to be done.

Crispin was going home. But a warm welcome didn't await him; vipers did.

CHAPTER 26
RAYMA

Dark shadows danced around Rayma, coaxing her to follow. She pushed herself up from the wet grass and found herself surrounded by lifeless trees that stretched upward farther than she could see. Grey skies and an eerie cold wind enveloped her as she let the shadows lead her through a graveyard filled with broken and crumbling headstones. She saw a crow perched on a tombstone covered in moss before a chilly voice beckoned her forward.

"So," the Grim sat on a floating throne comprised of shadows. "You're the one who stole from me."

Rayma tried but failed to tear her eyes from his skeleton face. His ruby red eyes flickered like flames and bits of flesh hung from his ivory bones.

"I…" she gulped to coat her dry throat. "I didn't steal from you."

"You killed Pyke," the Grim hissed through his lip-less mouth. "With her dead, you eliminated my Wagura. All those souls had years of servitude left to pay their debts to me."

"I had to free my friends," Rayma rasped, gripping her clothes tighter.

"Who is going to pay me now?" The Grim's bone fingers stroked the hilt of his scythe.

Rayma stifled a whimper. "Pyke said I could free her – free my friends."

"And you did." His red eyes flared beneath his black hood. "But now you must pay the price for their freedom."

Rayma clawed at Pyke's crystal dagger hanging at her hip and extended it to him. "Take it, it's yours."

The Grim lazily twirled his hand in a circle and another crystal dagger appeared. "You think that dagger is special? That it would be enough to tempt me?" He laughed, and the rattly sound sent a chill up Rayma's spine. "I care not for trinkets, jewels, or weapons. If I did, then many rich and royal humans would have escaped making deals with me." The Grim rose from his shadow throne and crunched the grass underneath with his skeletal feet as he approached her. "I deal in souls, Rayma. What is yours worth, I wonder?"

Rayma stood still when he circled her and his decaying fingers tugged her braids. "What do you want?"

"I'll make you a deal, Healer," the Grim stopped in front of her, whether he smiled she couldn't tell, but by his tone, she detected a wicked playfulness. "When Death calls for you, you can be the new Queen of the Wagura for a hundred years, a bargain considering all the years of servitude you stole from me."

Tears stung her eyes as she whispered, "Please -"

"Or," he continued, unmoved by her pleas for mercy, "you can offer Prince Heru's soul in your place for twenty years as a Wagura. After all, it was your love for him that got you into this mess in the first place."

"Don't touch him!" Rayma hissed.

The Grim stretched his cold, boney finger and touched Rayma's cheek; the contact made her skin crawl. "I will let you have some time to think it over before you decide. I look forward to doing business with you."

"No!" Rayma reached for the Grim, but he vanished, and she felt herself falling into a pitch-black abyss. "No! No!"

Rayma swung her arms to fight off whatever creature had grabbed ahold of her but realized it was Heru. His strong arms wrapped around her, pulling her against his warm, bare chest.

"You're safe, Rayma," Heru whispered in her ear. "I'm here."

"The Grim," Rayma squirmed out of his embrace, jumped up from her bed, and distanced herself from the prince. "It's the Grim. He's ... I... I stole from him. I stole all those souls from him."

Heru stood up and crossed the tent to her, but she threw her arm out to stop him from getting too close. "Please, don't get any closer. Don't you understand what I'm saying? I'm marked."

"Rayma, what are you talking about?" His eyes were wide, and she could tell he was afraid of her.

"I stole from the Grim," she hugged herself, eyes watering, "and he wants me to pay him back."

"It was just a bad dream," he said calmly, but she knew he didn't believe that. No one had dreams of the Grim unless he wanted something. Or someone.

"A hundred years." Rayma straightened, the gravity of the Grim's words hitting her all over again. "When Death comes for me, he wants one hundred years of servitude before I can pass to the Second Death."

Heru shook his head. "We'll find a way to get you out of this. I won't let that happen to you."

"I deserve it." Rayma sank to the carpeted floor and rubbed her face. "I deserve worse than one hundred years in debt to the Grim."

The prince knelt before her, clasped her hands in his, and forced her to meet his gaze. "No one deserves such a fate. You are a good woman with an even bigger heart -"

"Stop," she begged.

"I love you, Rayma," he kissed her hands. "I won't let you suffer this fate. We will consult every wise man, seer, oracle, and record keeper, if that is what it takes to find a way to defeat the Grim."

"I'm not who you think I am."

Heru sucked in a breath as if she had struck him across the face. "What do you mean?"

"I'm not who you think I am," she repeated. "I'm not the woman you love."

Heru dropped her hands. "What are you talking about?"

Rayma wiped tears from her cheeks and pulled her legs into her chest. "I was ordered by Lord Memucan to get close to you. When it was evident you had feelings for me, Memucan ordered me to return those affections, to earn your trust."

"No, that can't be true," Heru distanced himself and stared at her.

"Along the way I did fall in love with you, Heru. I do love you. I swear it. But…"

"But what?" Heru's voice carried a lethal tone. "What did Memucan want you to do once you earned my trust?"

Rayma didn't want to see his face when she revealed the entire truth, but she maintained their eye contact. "He wanted me to kill you. Slip something in your drink."

"You were going to kill me?" Heru rasped, but she didn't know if it was out of anger or pain.

She lowered her head, a lump rising in her throat, "If I killed you, he promised to return my brother to me. He's had him in prison for years. I didn't want my brother to suffer anymore. He's the only family I have left."

Heru paced like a caged animal, running a hand over his head, brow furrowed.

"Please say something," Rayma whispered.

"What do you want me to say?" Heru shot her a vicious look. "That it's alright you deceived me into thinking you loved me? That I forgive you for plotting my assassination? That I'm not angry you betrayed your crown prince and future king?" He sank onto her bed with his elbows resting on his knees. "What is it you want to hear, Rayma?"

Rayma's bottom lip quivered, and her voice cracked. "It might have started as a lie, but I do love you, Heru. I never intended to go through with it."

"I suppose you think that brings me some comfort?" Heru refused to look at her. After a moment of silence, the prince stood and said, "You are the only healer the Numbio has on this journey, so I won't order you to leave our company. But once this war is over, you will find a new home to return to."

"Heru -"

"It's Prince Heru." He interrupted, a brokenness in his tone. "Had you come to me with the truth about Memucan from the beginning, I would have done everything in my power to get your brother back to you." Without waiting for her to respond, he slipped out of her tent.

CHAPTER 27
SALOME

Rosalina and Seraphina walked Salome down the hall that led to the throne room but instead of stopping at the double doors to enter the Inner Depths, they walked past them. Salome was going to protest but was too irritated with them interrupting her time with Adonijah, so she followed them quietly. After a few more twists and turns down the mosaic tile hallways, they arrived at an archway that emptied into a garden Salome hadn't seen before.

It was much smaller than all the other gardens and by the stone wall and sizable hedges enclosing it, it was safe to assume it was the most private as well. Salome caught whiffs of roses, poppies, and pomegranate flowers. It was floral overload and yet, not revolting. Her nose welcomed the sweet smells, reminding her of what her mother used to smell like. She closed her eyes and allowed the moonlight to envelope her, not even noticing when the twins left.

"Salome," a soft voice called out.

"Yes?" Her eyes flashed open, but when she looked around the garden, she was alone. "Is someone there?"

"Salome." The voice grew louder. "Salome."

"I know your voice," Salome followed the voice.

"Salome," the sweet, breathy voice echoed.

She drew nearer, "Who are you?"

"Salome!" The voice wrapped around her in a familiar embrace.

"Mother?"

Salome found herself standing in front of a bronze statue of Bilhah. Maybe she was losing her mind. Maybe she was desperate enough to hope Damaris and Harbona were right about her ability to commune with the departed. Tentatively, Salome reached out and touched the statue's hand.

Salome blinked and was no longer in the Myridian garden, but in the White Keep. She was in her mother's chambers. A fire was roaring in the hearth, snow cascading like droplets of rain outside the window. Furs and bear skin rugs were strewn throughout the room. And then she saw her.

"Mother?" Salome exhaled, eyeing the dark-haired woman sitting on a tufted bench near the fire doing needle point. Bilhah turned to her with a warm and welcoming smile. Salome instantly felt the comfort of home envelop her.

"Hello, Sweetness." It was the nickname Bilhah had given her the moment she was born. "I've missed you."

Bilhah stood with her arms outstretched. Tears flowed from Salome as she ran to her, hoping unlike the Enchanted Swamp, she would be able to feel her mother's embrace.

Bilhah wrapped her arms around her daughter and whispered in her ear, "What took you so long?"

"What do you mean?"

"We've been calling you." Bilhah pulled away from Salome, tracing a finger down her daughter's cheek. "Why have you not answered us?"

"I didn't know it was you."

Bilhah flashed a sad smile. "You've forgotten our voices."

"No!" Salome denied it, even though she knew it was true.

"It's alright." Bilhah squeezed Salome's hand reassuringly. She spied the six lines tattooed around Salome's left arm. "You might have forgotten our voices. One day you might forget what we look like, but never forget how much we love you."

Trying to hold back the tears, Salome ended up making an unflattering grimace. "I miss sitting here with you."

Bilhah tapped her finger playfully on Salome's nose. "You hated needle point."

"I did," she nodded, "but I loved you. I loved our bench and the stories you told me. I loved how excited we would get during the first snowfall of the year. I loved how when I was scared, you would sing me Myridian lullabies and let me cuddle with you in bed. I wish that life wasn't over."

"I miss all of those memories too, Sweetness." She led Salome to their bench. Bilhah strummed her fingers through Salome's curls. "Northern curls."

"I always wanted your straight hair."

"Curls suit you. They're wild and rebellious, just like you." Bilhah cleared her throat. "Do you know why I called you?"

"You want me to avenge your death." Salome said confidently.

Bilhah shook her head. "To warn you."

"To warn me?" Salome tilted her head, confusion running rampant in her mind. "Warn me about what?"

"Soon, you will find yourself very much alone -"

"I'm not alone, Mother -"

"Listen," Bilhah interrupted her with the softest voice. "When the time comes and you find yourself standing on your own, you will have a choice to make. Rise from the ashes or crumble into dust."

Salome's mind was flooded with images of Crispin, Zophar, Adonijah, Harbona, Cato, and even Mika.

Would they abandon her?

Would they die?

Why, when surrounded by so many, would she have to walk alone?

"Will I be alone for the rest of my life?" Salome dreaded asking the question but dreaded the answer even more.

Bilhah smiled, cupping her face, "No, Sweetness, you will not spend the rest of your days alone. But the choices you make during your loneliest moments will determine who you will find on the other side."

"I don't understand." Salome looked into her mother's green eyes expecting her to explain but she didn't.

"Our time together is coming to an end. It's time for you to return."

"Please don't make me leave you."

"We will be together again, Sweetness. But when you hear us call you, don't be afraid to answer." Bilhah kissed her daughter's forehead.

Instantly, Salome felt a surge shoot through her body and upon opening her tear-filled eyes, saw her mother's statue crying.

"How can that be?" Salome whispered.

"Zara told me you favored your mother."

Salome whipped around to see an old woman standing stoically behind her with a bouquet of flowers.

"I am glad to see that is true."

"Are you…?"

"I am Nym." She flashed a half-smile, accentuating the wrinkles around her fading green eyes. The top layer of her long hair was white as snow, while the bottom layer was still raven black from that of her youth. Around her aging neck was a necklace of green aventurine fashioned in the shape of octopus tentacles. Nym's eyes were like Bilhah's and oddly enough, brought Salome comfort. "Our dead never truly leave us," the olive-skinned queen pointed at the statue's tears, not at all surprised by the sight.

"You are Queen Nym?"

"And your grandmother." She gently set the floral offering before her daughter's memorial. "I should have known Bilhah would eventually bring us together. All these years, I thought all her children had been killed. But when word reached my ears that you may have survived, I was both overjoyed and saddened that I had not been able to give you a proper home."

"My mother told us stories of the Isles of Myr." Salome faced her grandmother, who was just about her height. "Being here, makes me feel close to her again."

"Of course, you can feel her," Nym glanced at the statue. "She never left."

Salome looked at her mother's bronze likeness. "I would love to erect a memorial for her in Northwind."

"Northwind?" Nym shot a disappointed glance at her granddaughter. "Do you mean to tell me you actually plan to challenge Niabi?"

Salome was confused. "Yes."

"If you are to risk your life for a throne that is not rightfully yours, should you not know the truth?"

"What truth?" Salome scrunched her nose, taking a giant step back from Nym.

"Come with me. There is something you need to see."

Nym turned on her heel and glided down a set of steps Salome hadn't noticed were there. As they weaved through the labyrinth of hedges on the lower tier of the garden, they rounded a corner, and found a rectangular, inground pool.

"What is that?" Salome stared at the glowing waters.

"The Pool of Enlightenment." Nym ushered her toward the mystic pool. "If you wish to know the truth of what happened all those years ago, submerge yourself."

"I know the truth. I was there that night."

"You know what you witnessed but you know nothing of the truth."

Salome's eyes darted around the pool, looking for signs of a trap. She patted the dagger attached to her thigh, glad it was there. She would be lying if she said she wasn't curious about this so-called Pool of Enlightenment, but she was wary of the woman she just met.

"Well?" Nym ripped her from her thoughts, hand still motioning her toward the pool.

Salome slowly stepped forward and sat on the edge of the mosaic tiles that bordered the basin. Her grandmother hadn't moved, her eyes fixed on Salome. She slid her legs into the warm water and peered back at Nym. With a final nod from the old queen, Salome inhaled deeply and submerged into the water.

When she opened her eyes, she saw she was no longer in the Myridian pool, but in the White Keep years before her own birth. She sucked in a breath; she knew these halls. She reached out and ran the tips of her fingers over the white walls; a tear ran down her cheek when she felt the coolness against her skin.

The halls were bustling as the workers were talking about the birth of a royal baby. She followed one of her old nursemaids, Bertie, who looked so much younger than she remembered. She was carrying armfuls of blankets down the hall. Salome stopped dead in her tracks when she happened upon another familiar face. A decades younger Issachar paced outside her mother's quarters. Anxiety smeared across his unblemished face; the dark-haired king appeared frightened; a look she had never seen from him before.

"Father?" she called out, her voice cracking.

"He cannot hear you, Cousin."

Salome looked to her left and saw Damaris in white linen standing next to her. "What are you doing here?"

"You submerged yourself in the Pool of Enlightenment. There are truths I must show you."

Salome's gaze focused once more upon Issachar. "He looks frightened."

"He is," Damaris said. "That is what a man looks like when he is about to become a father for the first time."

"You mean…"

"Watch," she hushed her.

"Your Majesty," an elderly midwife bowed before the king. "The queen is ready to see you now."

Issachar barreled past her into the room and as he rounded the corner he stopped as he saw Bilhah holding the smallest baby he had ever laid eyes on.

"She looks so happy." Salome couldn't peel her eyes off her mother's joyful face.

"Bilhah always wanted to be a mother." Damaris' eyes were fastened on Salome. "It was her dream."

"Come closer, my love," Bilhah extended her hand to Issachar. He slowly approached his newly born heir with a proud smile. "The Almighty One has blessed us with a daughter."

"A daughter?" Issachar frowned.

"Is it not wonderful?" Bilhah was so happy she nearly sang. "The heir to the White Throne – the first Queen of the North."

"Queen?" He fumed. "Queen of the North? She will be no such thing!"

"What do you mean?"

"If you believe that girl will one day, be the ruler of Northwind then you are gravely mistaken."

"But Northern law states that any firstborn child can be heir to the throne," she protested.

"You were to bear me sons and you give me," he motioned with a snort toward Niabi, "this!"

"Issachar, please, just hold her -"

"I will do no such thing," he growled. "Until you bear me a son, you will no longer be in my good graces." Tears streamed down Bilhah's cheeks as she watched her husband disappear from her quarters, slamming the door behind him.

"He..." Salome was left speechless by what she saw. "He just..."

"He wronged Niabi from the beginning." Damaris stood beside her, knowing there was far more for her to see.

"All because she was a girl?"

"Never before had a daughter been born first in the North. Issachar had made a hefty wager with the King of Borg, that he too, would continue the tradition and have a son. He lost."

"Must I continue to watch my mother cry, Damaris?"

"Listen."

"Forgive your father," Bilhah whispered to her newborn. "He does not understand the power a woman possesses."

The bubbly midwife returned with fresh linens. "Have you thought of a name, my Queen?"

After a slight pause, Bilhah smiled. "Niabi. Her name is Niabi."

"A lovely name for a princess."

"Yes," Bilhah caressed her small, sleepy face, "and one day she will be queen."

In the blink of an eye, a year passed, and Salome found herself watching her father cuddling a newborn as he walked to the royal balcony that overlooked the White City. Two guards opened the double doors and Issachar proudly announced the birth of his son and heir, Prince Lykos, to the cheering citizens of Northwind.

"Your mother gave him his son," Damaris broke the silence.

"What of my sister?"

"See for yourself." The Oracle had her turn around to see her mother holding a one-year-old Niabi. "He never once held her."

"Even after Lykos was born?"

Six-year-old Niabi ran past them with a five-year-old Lykos nipping at her heels. Laughter filled the hall as they played together until their father turned the corner.

"Father, play with us!" Niabi attempted to hug him only to be pushed away.

"Go to your mother!" he barked.

"But father -"

"I said go!" Downtrodden, the children turned to leave. "Not you, my son. Come with me. I have much to teach you." Taking the young boy by the hand, he ushered him away with a smile.

Salome wasn't sure if she was more angry or heartbroken, but she wished she could wipe her sister's tears from her face. "Father never treated me like that."

"You were not his firstborn." Damaris grabbed Salome's hand and led her down a different corridor and as they turned the corner, she found herself walking the training grounds in Myr. "When your sister made ten, your mother sent her to Myr to be trained in our ways. She was a quick study and within a few years, earned the title of Red Maiden."

Salome suddenly remembered what Harbona told her when they first arrived in the Isles of Myr, that there was a living Red Maiden that did not don the red armor. Now, she knew it was Niabi.

A proud Nym stood off to the side as she silently watched her granddaughter spar with Zara and beat her in a duel. The Myridian female warriors cheered as the student had defeated her mentor; a rare feat to bear witness to in such a short amount of time.

"She had more Myridian blood flowing through her veins than Northern blood."

"Why didn't she stay with you?" Salome watched her grandmother bow her head to Niabi, showing her the utmost respect.

"Our queen appealed to your father, requesting he allow her to remain with the Myridians, but he refused. Issachar might not have loved Niabi, but he was not against using her." Damaris waved her hand in front of them, and they stood at the Myridian docks watching a teenage Niabi board a ship set to sail her to Northwind.

"Please," Niabi grabbed Nym's hand, "do not force me to return to Northwind. Please! He hates me. You know he does!"

Nym gently brushed her granddaughter's raven black hair behind her ear. "Never forget who you are, Niabi. You are the Red Maiden, Princess of the Isles of Myr and of the Northern Lands, heir to the White Throne of Northwind and one day, you shall be queen. Let him have this victory for it shall be short-lived." Showing an extraordinarily rare display of emotion, Nym embraced the teenager tightly. "Know that wherever you go, you are loved here in Myr."

Salome closed her eyes and the image of her sister faded. She emerged from the pool, coughing up water. Once she climbed out of the pool, she caught her grandmother's gaze and asked, "Why show me this?"

Nym knelt with a blanket and wrapped it around Salome's shoulders. "Your sister is not the villain in this story, child."

"You hated him, didn't you? My father?"

"Men of power are not to be trusted. He was one of those men."

"That is not true." Salome jumped up, hands tightening around the edges of the blanket hanging from her shoulders. "My brother is not -"

"What do you expect will happen, if by some miracle, you should defeat your sister for the White Throne?" Nym interrupted her, rising gracefully from her crouched position. "Your brother will be crowned King of the North. Do you think he will treat you as his equal? Do you think he won't turn out to be just like your father and use you as a pawn in his game? Do you think he would not marry you off to a foreign dignitary the first opportunity he sees to expand the reach of his power? Foolish, girl! You see Northwind as your home, but until now, the North has only been run by men. Do not do as my Bilhah did. You have Myridian blood coursing through your veins. Know who you are, Salome. You are meant for a far greater purpose than being in a man's shadow."

"How can you expect me not to challenge her?" Salome spat, the wetness of her hair and clothes dripping onto the stone pavers. "How can I allow her to live in spite of what she has done?"

"You believe she should die?" Nym arched her brow.

"For what she has done, she deserves to die."

"Your sister did what a true warrior would do. She rose from the flames meant to consume her and faced her enemy as a queen. For everything your father stole from her, she made him watch as she took it back." Nym straightened, her nose pointed slightly upward.

"She killed my family. She murdered your daughter! Surely you must see what she truly is!"

"I will never forgive her for what she did," Nym said sternly.

"But?"

"If you were Niabi, what would you have done?"

"I *am* Niabi." Salome fought back tears as she spoke. "What our father did to her, she has done to me. The pain, the suffering, the loss; we share the same story."

"Then do not follow in her footsteps." The queen took Salome's hands in her own. "There is an alternative to war. Stay here in Myr. Learn our ways. Take your mother's place in our high council. You belong here."

"You want me to forget about her?" Her was nothing more than a raspy whisper. "Forget about Gershom? Let them win?"

"Think, Salome, think!" Nym cupped her granddaughter's tear-stained face in her withering hands. "If you are anything like your mother, you would not want this war. So many people will die and for what? What is done is done, nothing will bring back your dead. Did you learn nothing from Niabi's past?" Nym sighed, "You can have a real life here; do not throw it away for your brother to reap the glory."

"But Niabi -"

"You speak of her as if she was some type of monster."

"Monsters come in many forms." Salome felt a lump of emotion bobbing in her throat. "Most of the time, they look like people."

Nym inhaled deeply before she spoke, her hands falling to her sides. "Consider what I have told you, and what you have seen, before making your decision."

As her grandmother began to walk away, Salome quickly extended her hand to stop her. "You are afraid."

Nym's brow furrowed, "Afraid of what?"

"When you look at me you don't see my mother, like you claim. You see my sister and that frightens you." Salome took her silence as confirmation. "Tell me I'm wrong, Grandmother. Tell me I'm wrong."

Nym sighed heavily as she sat on a padded bench overlooking the sea. "Niabi was a bright student; clever, kind, disciplined, hardworking. She deserved better than your father." She smiled slightly, "While she was here, she earned the honor and title of Red Maiden.

Salome sat next to her. Even though there was a warm breeze, she clutched the blanket tightly, still feeling the effects of the Pool of Enlightenment.

"Your sister was the deadliest warrior to walk the Isles." Nym studied her granddaughter's face. "Niabi was loved, respected, and admired. She belonged here, with us. I never should have let your father take her."

"You still care for her."

Tears welled in the matriarch's green eyes, regret deep within her soul. "If war can be avoided, and lives spared, should you not at least consider it?" Before Salome could answer, Nym stood to make her way back inside the castle. "The Isles of Myr can be your home. Consider my offer, child. Please." The queen walked away, leaving Salome to her thoughts.

CHAPTER 28

NIABI

Prince Thanos strutted to the throne with an arrogance that could be felt the moment he walked into the room. With his chin tilted upwards and his malicious, beady eyes fixed on Niabi as she lounged in her throne, the Prince of Gomorrah approached without giving Tala standing on her right, Pash positioned on her left, or Anaktu stationed at the bottom of the dais, a second glance. Niabi was thoroughly protected should the young heir mean her harm, but if he attempted to assassinate her, she would slit his throat faster than they could.

Anaktu lifted an enormous hand to halt the prince before he could ascend the steps to the throne. Thanos stopped and bowed, but his shifty eyes bounced from Niabi to her Nephilim.

"You seem frightened, Prince Thanos." Niabi purred from her white throne, a wicked grin stretching across her face. "You can't possibly be alarmed by one Nephilim, after growing up with the Thrak."

Thanos attempted to hide a gulp but failed. He reluctantly withdrew his gaze from the giant to look up at the queen. "The Thrak are flesh and blood. But that thing is -"

"He." Niabi interrupted with a hiss.

Thanos crinkled his nose but amended, "*He* is more demon than man."

Niabi shrugged lazily, bored by him. "You're right to fear him, but to be a king, you must never show it."

Thanos stiffened. "Have you considered my proposal?"

Niabi smirked, her eyes scanning him from head to toe. "I have considered it. But seeing you now makes me wonder why I should waste my time and soldiers on *you*." She threw the last word out with disdain. She was not impressed by the scrawny, haughty boy that stood before her. "Tell me, Thanos, why shouldn't I just kill you now and spare myself this aggravation?"

Thanos narrowed his eyes, "I am the Prince of Gomorrah!"

"Hair has not yet grown on your face, and you dare raise your voice to me, boy!" Niabi gripped the armrests of her throne, her eyes blazing. She leaned forward and rasped, "I wouldn't lose one night of sleep if I slit your throat."

Without realizing it, Thanos took a step back, distancing himself from both the vicious queen and her Nephilim. Thanos' voice was shaky, but his head was still held high. "If you kill me, my mother will wage war against you."

"Or would she thank me for ridding her of the one problem that stands in her way of being sole-ruler?" Niabi cocked her head to the side, the movement predatorial. "Clearly you are not her choice to rule. Your death would be the best present she could ever receive."

"You believe Maltidys needs a lesser reason to come for your neck?" Thanos spat, his fingers twitching at his side. "That woman won't stop until you are dead."

At the word *dead*, Tala and Pash drew their swords. Niabi threw an open hand in the air, halting them from approaching the hotheaded royal. She stood slowly and glided down the steps, her black train cascading behind her, and circled him like prey.

Niabi stopped behind him and whispered in his ear, "I welcome the challenge."

Thanos shivered as her breath touched his neck. "But I said I could help you."

Niabi let out a menacing laugh as she rounded in front of him, standing beside Anaktu. "If you live to be king, you will learn not to trust so easily." She stared into Thanos' eyes and said, "One battalion. I will send one battalion to claim your throne."

Thanos grinned and Niabi saw the features he had inherited from his wicked mother. "I will lead them to victory -"

"Don't be ridiculous," Niabi snorted and waved a dismissive hand. "Commander Pash will lead them." Pash stepped forward; sword now sheathed.

Thanos was nearly rendered speechless at the insult. "I should be the one to lead them if I am to be king."

"Commander Pash will lead *my* soldiers, or you can go elsewhere for aid." Niabi motioned for Thanos to come closer. "But before my men march, you must swear fealty to me."

Thanos wrinkled his nose, eyes burning as they bounced from the commander back to the queen. "I am to be King of Gomorrah. I will not bend the knee to anyone."

Niabi nodded her head in understanding, though her smile didn't falter. "You have so much to learn in the world of rulers and makers. You need me. I do not need you."

"But your sister -"

"Will be found with or without your assistance." Niabi interrupted with an iciness that sent shivers up Thanos' spine. "What will it be, *Prince*?" the word shot from her tongue like a poisoned dart. "Bend the knee to the woman who holds your future in her hands or walk away with your pride and no army to fight your battles."

Thanos gritted his teeth. "Perhaps the King of Borg -"

The queen erupted in laughter. Thanos' cheeks flushed with embarrassment. "By all means, go to all the other kingdoms for aid. Perhaps it will be a humbling experience for you." She clasped her hands in front of her and took a step toward him. "You came to me because you know I am not only your best chance at the throne, but your only chance. The West won't let you step one sooty foot before them. The Andrago," she motioned a hand to Tala, "answer to me. And quite frankly, none of the other kingdoms will care of your claim. They would delight in seeing you and that shrew you call a mother dead."

Thanos flashed her a dirty look. She had rattled him, and she enjoyed seeing the desperation in his eyes.

"Whenever you are ready to kneel…" She pointed to the floor before her.

Thanos hesitated before he slowly knelt before her, lifting his eyes to meet her awaiting gaze. "I, Thanos, Prince of Gomorrah, swear in life or death, my house shall serve yours."

Niabi clapped her hands together and grinned. "Now, was that so difficult?" She winked and Thanos flinched, as if she had slapped him. "Commander Pash, ready the battalion."

Pash crossed an arm across his chest in salute. "It will be done."

"I request to go along." Leoti's voice echoed through the throne room as she marched down the carpeted aisle.

Tala and Pash exchanged a quick glance before Niabi waved her to come closer. She was the only one in the room who didn't seem surprised by Leoti's unannounced arrival.

"And why would you like to join them?" Niabi asked.

Leoti bowed to Niabi before saying, "I have a set of skills -"

"Leoti, no," Tala whispered, panic in his eyes.

"I have a set of skills," Leoti continued, disregarding her father's warning, "that I have not used in quite some time, but I know can be an asset in this war."

"What skills could you possibly possess to help me?" Thanos refused to even look at her when he asked the question.

Leoti extended her leather-wrapped arm, and a falcon flew in the window behind the throne, perching on her outstretched limb. "This is Tiki." She handed him a treat. "Tell me what you wish to know, my Queen, and we shall tell you."

Niabi tilted her head to look at Thanos and flashed a vicious smile. "How many guards does Prince Thanos have in the courtyard?"

Leoti moved her arm and Tiki shot back out the window.

"Prince Thanos," Niabi instructed, "whisper to Commander Pash how many soldiers you have in your company."

By the look on Thanos' pale face, Niabi knew he was reluctant to admit how few men he had managed to scrounge up on his journey north, but he did as she bade him.

Leoti blinked and her brown eyes were replaced with solid white. They watched in awe as she sat completely still. At the right moment, she rose from her cross-legged position in time for Tiki to perch upon her awaiting arm.

Leoti smiled, her eyes back to their natural color. "Eight soldiers, Your Majesty."

Niabi eyed Thanos and Pash.

"Eight," Pash confirmed as Thanos nodded.

Niabi glided to Leoti, amazement and wonder in her eyes. "You are a warg."

"I am," Leoti bowed her head.

Niabi whipped her head around to look at Tala who looked ill. "Leave us," the queen commanded.

Everyone except Tala emptied the throne room. Once the doors closed behind them, Niabi's face softened, and she grabbed Tala's hand. "I didn't know."

"If word had gotten out that she had these powers…" Tala ran fingers through his hair and sighed. "I don't know who might have tried to get their hands on her for her power."

"Are you…?" Niabi whispered.

Tala shook his head. "No. Neither was her mother. There hasn't been a warg amongst our people in generations. The last one…" He forced himself to speak. "The Gomorrians kidnapped her."

"Looking for the Tears of the Gods and the City of Bones, I would imagine." Niabi pieced that bloodthirsty lot's motive together easily.

"And when she couldn't find it, they sent her back to Elisor in pieces. They kept her eyes though; a mockery and an insult of her gift."

Niabi cupped Tala's chin. "I won't send Leoti, if you do not wish it."

Tala had tears in his eyes, and it pained her to see him like this. "Thanos knows about her power now. If she doesn't go, he might try to come back for her, if he's crowned king. Not many people have magic like her anymore."

"Tala," she said gently. "There's something I need to show you." Niabi lifted her left hand and conjured a small flame to dance in her palm. Tala scooted back, eyes wide. "Vilora's magic is in my blood." Niabi shrugged with a half-smile. "I never knew."

Tala glanced to her arm, "The blackness…?"

"I didn't use my power and it began to consume me."

"You think Leoti may suffer the same fate?"

"That I cannot say," Niabi shook her head and closed her palm, extinguishing the flame. "But if she doesn't use her power, it may very well turn on her."

"I worry about her leaving my sight with this power," Tala said.

"But?"

Tala looked gutted to admit the next part but did anyway. "I am terrified of what she might do, if she stays here."

"Meaning?"

"I think…" Tala breathed in deeply. "I think she might attempt to assassinate *him*."

"I see." Niabi understood he meant Gershom. "I will have Pash watch over her. No harm will come to her."

Tala squinted and she knew exactly what he was thinking.

"I know you and he aren't on good terms, and I respect that," Niabi patted his arm. "But trust me once more, my old friend. If I tell him to protect her, he will give his life for her, if it comes down to it."

"Do you trust him?" Tala asked.

"Of course, I do," she narrowed her eyes, confused by the question.

"Then he knows of your magic? Of the baby you now carry?"

Niabi lifted her chin. If anyone other than Tala had spoken to her with that tone, she wouldn't have hesitated in claiming their tongue. She rolled her shoulders back and cracked her neck.

"He knows what I want him to know."

"Whether I like him or not," Tala rubbed the nape of his neck, "he deserves to know about his child."

"And he will know when I am ready to tell him." This was where she drew a line in the sand. The mountain she was ready to die on. She would not be pushed or pressured. Niabi felt heat in her left arm as it trailed down to her fingertips. She glanced at her balled-up fist and saw a faint orange glow.

"It seems I have upset you," Tala noticed it, too.

Niabi shook her hand to rid herself of the fire itching to erupt. "I… it's never done this before." She met his gaze and the worry in his eyes matched what she was feeling in her thrashing heart.

"For years you have stifled it," Tala tentatively reached for her left hand, "but now that it has tasted freedom, it craves more. That's the danger of magic. Once it is released, it has no intention of being caged."

"I can control it." Niabi retracted her hand before he could touch her.

"You are afraid." Tala knew her well.

"My fear will not cripple me." Niabi ascended the steps to her throne, flexing her fingers, the glow now gone. She sat, her train pooled around her leather boots and the hem of her black pants. "And Leoti? What would you have us do?"

Tala grimaced. "She goes."

Niabi nodded in agreement before calling for Leoti and Pash to come back into the throne room.

"Leoti, you will go with them." Niabi met Pash's gaze. "Consider Pash your commander and protector."

"My Queen," Leoti bowed with satisfaction.

Pash crossed his arm over his chest and the softness of his eyes nearly shattered Niabi's heart. She had to make sure her hand wasn't resting on her belly where his baby was now growing. She knew he understood she was trusting him with her daughter-in-law's life, and he wouldn't fail either of them.

Niabi turned her focus back to Leoti. "Is it just the falcon's eyes you can see through?"

Leoti smirked and looked every bit the predator as Niabi. "Any beast is prey to me."

Niabi smiled. "Good."

CHAPTER 29
SALOME

Salome left a trail of water from the gardens to her chamber doors. Though she had wrung her hair and clothes by the Pool of Enlightenment, she was still wet and uncomfortable, looking more like an angry cat than Myridian royalty.

I never should have let him take her. Her grandmother's words hovered over her like a dark cloud.

She pushed the door open to find her sitting room dark, except for the moonlight that glistened off the sea and filled the space with a silver glow. The door latched and a hand from behind her clamped down over her mouth, an attempt to stifle her screams. Salome elbowed the attacker in the gut, grabbed their forearm, and flipped them onto the ground. She snatched the wolf dagger from its holster, dug a knee into the intruder's chest, and put the tip of her knife against their throat.

"Salome, it's me!" The deep male voice rang out. "It's Jinn."

Her eyes began to adjust to the darkness and she saw his Eastern features. "What are you doing here?" she growled.

"I came to warn you."

"Warn me? You attacked me!"

"I didn't attack you," he spewed. "I didn't want your scream alerting your watchdog across the hall."

Salome knew he was referring to Adonijah and fury shot through her body. She poked her knife a little closer into Jinn's neck. "He is *not* my watchdog."

"Your protector, your lover," he waved a dismissive hand in the air. "It doesn't matter to me one way or another. But you need to listen to me. We don't have much time."

"Time for what?"

"Whispers have reached my ears of an attempt on your life."

Salome narrowed her eyes and hissed, "The only intruder in my room has been you."

"I'm not here to harm you." Jinn rested the back of his head against the floor, exasperated. "Do you really think an assassin hasn't been sent for you?"

"Perhaps," she scanned the room. "Perhaps not."

"I lied to you before." His statement caught her attention. "I'm not here on business. I'm here for you."

"For me?"

"I've been sent by one of your father's allies to help you."

Salome shook her head slowly, shoving her knee deeper into his chest, feeling nothing but solid muscle and hating herself for picturing him shirtless. "I don't believe you," she spat.

"Salome, please," Jinn pleaded. "You have to believe me."

"No, I don't."

"Salome -"

Her eyes scanned the room again, sensing they weren't alone. "And *your* watchdog? Where is she?"

Kai stepped out of the shadows on the opposite side of the room, moonlight flashing across her belt filled with knives of varying sizes.

Salome smirked and tightened her grip around the hilt of her dagger. "I have a knife to your prince's throat. Do you not care, Ryoko Naga?"

"She has been ordered not to harm you." Jinn whispered, a gentle calm in his voice.

"A mistake on your part." She said to Jinn, eyes fastened on Kai.

Kai stepped forward, her expression remained neutral, but Jinn extended his hand to stop her.

"Your father's Second in Command, Lord Maon, survived the invasion. He's been hiding for years while leading an underground rebellion against your sister." Jinn explained, a bit of blood drawn from the tip of her blade dripped down his neck.

"Everyone died the night Niabi attacked," Salome huffed before standing to her feet, releasing her hold on him, but keeping her knife pointed at him. "I did too."

Jinn slowly rose from the floor and wiped the blood from his neck with his fingers. Somehow, even in the dark, he looked devastatingly handsome. Dressed in black fighting leathers, instead of royal robes, he looked dangerous, like an assassin.

"Now, he goes by Oden." Jinn hesitated before taking a step toward her and was met with a disapproving look. He retreated a few steps showing her his empty hands. "He sent me here to help you."

"And how did he know I would be here?"

"Oden thought there was a chance you might meet with your grandmother."

By the tone in his voice, she was inclined to believe him. "And what do you gain by helping this Oden? Helping me?"

"Our peoples were once strong allies. With Niabi on the throne, that allegiance has been shattered." Jinn's eyes darkened. "My sister, Anka, was betrothed to your eldest brother."

Salome rested a hand on her hip and tapped her foot. "My patience is running thin. What do you gain in helping me?"

"An alliance between our mighty houses. Peace between our people."

"Is your sister still in the market for a Northern prince?" Salome scoffed. "I don't think Crispin would be too keen on that idea."

"Anka died a few years ago," Jinn lowered his head and Salome regretted her spiteful words. "But there is another heir."

Salome saw the desire in his eyes, sending a shiver down her spine. "I am not interested," she furrowed her brows.

Jinn seemed surprised, as if rejection from a woman wasn't something that happened often, or ever. "You – You won't at least consider my proposal?"

"If that's a proposal, it's a piss poor one."

Kai took a heavy step forward, but Jinn waved her off, keeping her at bay. *An insult to her master*, Salome noted.

"Come to Sakurai with me," Jinn slid his hands in his pockets. "My people, we can protect you until the time comes to face your sister."

His voice was enticing, and it took Salome a second to catch her breath. "I am safe enough here."

"One man cannot protect you forever -"

"I didn't say anything about Adonijah protecting me," she cut him off. "I'm the one who had a knife to your throat. I'm the one who held your life in my hands."

"Then perhaps," he risked approaching her, his hands once again showing he held no weapons to harm her, "I can be the one standing by your side as you conquer our enemies." Jinn reached her and although her knife was still a threat to him, he cupped her chin and gently brushed his thumb along her jawline.

She hated to admit it, but her heart began to race just from his delicate touch. "You need to leave."

Jinn's eyes were filled with disappointment, but he withdrew his hand. His gaze drifted from her fiery eyes to her full lips. "Is that what you want?"

Salome pointed to the door with her dagger. "Get out."

Jinn bowed his head. "Consider my offer. The Eastern armies for your hand in marriage."

Salome sucked in a breath. Jinn was serious about their houses being joined. Political allies. Strong ones at that. And she needed his army if she was going to defeat her sister in battle. As far as she knew, she and her brother still hadn't secured one. Maybe his proposal was worth considering. But he didn't need to know that. She kept her face neutral as she once again pointed to the door.

"Out. And take your pet with you."

Kai stomped by them and opened the door for them to leave, but he stopped and brushed his fingers against Salome's left hand. "I have extended my stay for two more days. If you change your mind."

"Don't hold your breath." Salome snatched her hand back and he slipped out, shutting the door behind him.

She exhaled a sigh of relief, having run on pure adrenaline since the moment his hand clasped over her mouth. She believed for a moment that someone was there to kill her, and it rattled her that she was right there for the taking. If it had been his knife that reached her throat instead of his hand…

She didn't want to think about it anymore and rushed to light her lamps. The curtains on either side of her open balcony whooshed and she felt someone's presence. She whipped around, ready for those assassins Jinn had warned her about, but it was Adonijah who had entered, dressed in all black, as if he were the night.

"I thought they would never leave," Adonijah puffed his chest out to crack his back.

"One of these days," she sheathed her dagger, "you're going to catch a knife to the chest sneaking around the way you do."

"With your aim, I've got time." Adonijah flashed a wicked grin.

Salome folded her arms over her chest. "What were you doing out there?"

"You think those two got into your room unnoticed?" His eyebrows lifted, as if he was insulted. "I've not survived as long as I have without embracing the darkness."

"Is it safe to assume you heard…"

"His attempt at a proposal was…"

"Adonijah," she warned.

"Painful. Truly, painful."

"Am I detecting a hint of jealousy?" Salome snatched an apple from the bowl of fruit left on the dining table and took a bite.

"More like secondhand embarrassment," Adonijah leaned against the wall lazily, crossing one ankle over the other. "Knocked on his ass and his proposal rejected. Bad day to be a prince."

Salome perched herself on the edge of the table, swinging her legs freely. "I recall knocking you on your ass, the first time we met."

The Hollow. It seemed like such a long time ago they had fought as enemies.

Adonijah shrugged. "And it was still less humiliating than his encounter with you tonight."

Salome rolled her eyes and took another bite from her apple. Once she swallowed the piece, she stared at her feet. "He's not that bad."

"Oh?" Adonijah seemed amused. "Do tell, Princess."

Salome furrowed her brow and shot him a vicious look. "You're a brute, you know that?"

"Aye," he pushed up from the wall and approached her. "And you like that I'm a brute."

"Is that so?"

"Aye." Adonijah stood in front of her and leaned forward to rest his hands on the table. Her legs were on either side of him, straddling his hips.

They stared at one another. She could feel her heartbeat quicken and noticed his breathing was raspy.

"Will you consider it?" Adonijah whispered, his brown eyes fixed on hers.

"Consider what?"

"His offer."

Salome knew the moment her body tensed up he sensed what was going through her mind. "Maybe I should consider it."

"Is that what you want?" Jinn had asked her the same question moments ago when she told him to leave. But from Adonijah's lips, the question carried pain.

Salome shrugged. "We need his army."

"Is that what you want?" Adonijah asked again.

"I don't think it matters what I want anymore."

Adonijah's hand scooped her face, his fingers tickling the back of her neck. "It matters to me." His gaze dragged from her eyes down to her lips. "What do you want?"

"It's stupid," she whispered, his hands hot against her skin.

"Tell me."

"I want a home," she admitted softly. "To finally find a place where I belong. A place where I can finally be at peace." A tear slipped down her cheek, and he thumbed it away.

"That's not stupid." Adonijah slowly shook his head, his free hand resting on her waist. "I understand."

Salome breathed him in. His tobacco and earthy scent filled her nostrils, which swept her away to a cozy cabin in the middle of winter. A fire roaring, a tea kettle whistling, his arms wrapped around her tightly as the snowflakes cascaded slowly to the ground.

"I would be a fool if I told you what to do," Adonijah's voice sliced through her thoughts, "but please don't marry him."

Salome's heart leapt to her throat. "Why not?"

"You're wild and strong and opinionated. And that tongue of yours always gets you into trouble." He leaned closer, his lips within inches of hers. "He can't handle you."

"And you can?" She arched an eyebrow, her eyes bouncing to his lips.

"Aye."

"You seem awfully sure of yourself."

Adonijah tightened his grip around her waist, pulling her toward him. "Aye," he whispered against her ear, and it sent shivers down her spine. "I am."

She closed her eyes, waiting for his lips that dragged from her cheek toward her lips.

"What do you want?" Adonijah asked one more time.

Salome turned her head slightly to meet his awaiting lips. *Him*. She wanted him. Her hands reached up and clasped the back of his neck as they kissed, pulling him closer.

Adonijah's lips were soft, his kiss passionate. His rugged appearance didn't match his gentleness. She bit his lower lip and he responded by slipping his tongue into her mouth. He cupped her face with one calloused hand and splayed the fingers of his other hand through her hair. She could feel the muscles in his arms tense, as if he was using every bit of strength he possessed to hold himself back.

"Adonijah…" Salome whispered his name, and he planted an open mouth kiss to her neck. Goosebumps stretched over every inch of her body.

"I've wanted to kiss you since the moment I realized who you were outside the Hidden Tavern." Adonijah muttered against her warm skin. "I find myself thinking about you every minute of every day. If only you knew the power you hold over me."

"I thought I was a pain in your ass?" Salome smiled against his kisses.

"Aye," Adonijah lifted her up from the table and she wrapped her legs around his waist. "But you're *my* pain in the ass."

Salome planted another kiss on his lips, her heart soaring inside her chest. She thought she heard something whistle toward them. A soft thud sounded, and she was falling out of his grasp. She opened her eyes and saw Adonijah grimacing. He melted to the floor, and she fought to keep him on his feet. Her eyes darted to the back of his leg and saw a black arrow sticking out of his hamstring.

Salome looked at the balcony where six Thrak had climbed over the banister. Armed head to toe in weaponry, she knew they had come for her.

Adonijah ripped the arrow out of his leg with a groan and wrapped the bloody wound with linen off the dining table.

Salome rose from her crouched position, standing between a wounded Adonijah and the enemy. Her eyes trailed right to left, from one Thrak to the next. She had never faced these many opponents at once. If she lived, she would have to apologize to Jinn for dismissing his warning. She flipped her knives out from their holsters on her lower back and thigh and circled them around her hands.

Adonijah struggled to his feet but took his place next to Salome. He drew his sword, squaring his shoulders to the Thrak and shook his head with a tsk. "Does no one use the door anymore?"

"You're coming with us." One of the Thrak cocked his head to the side, eyes on Salome, ignoring Adonijah.

Salome spat at the Thrak's feet. "I've killed your kind before, and I'll gladly kill the lot of you."

The Thrak commander cackled, flashing a mouth filled with crooked yellow teeth. "As fun as it would be to see you try, our queen ordered for you to be brought back to Gomorrah unspoiled."

"The only thing your queen is going to be getting is your head in a bag." Salome took a deep breath. With her gaze still fixed on the Thrak leader, she mentally sent out a cry for help, hoping her magic worked both ways. *"If anyone is listening, I need help."*

The Thrak commander bobbed his head and the warrior nearest her lunged at her. She blocked the incoming blow of his mace with her knives and swept his leg out from under him in a fluid motion, like a dance. Like a Qata Vishna. And as he fell to the floor, she swung her knives in opposite directions. One sliced his neck open and the second slashed a deep gash across his unprotected abdomen. He fell to the floor with a loud thud. With his blood splattered all over her face and clothes, she beckoned another demon to come meet his fate.

"Kill the man." The Thrak leader sneered, done with her taunting, "Maim the bitch."

Two charged Adonijah and two leapt toward Salome, leaving the Thrak leader to watch with a sinister grin across his scarred face. Even with an injured leg, Adonijah didn't miss a beat in fighting them with his longsword. Salome grabbed a chair and tossed it at one of the Thrak rushing at her, tripping him long enough for her to focus on one assailant at a time.

Even though she had only trained as a Qata Vishna for a couple of mornings, she was picking up on their techniques quickly and now realized how effective their movement was in defeating their enemies.

Before coming to the Isles of Myr, she had seen her enemies as her equals, if not her oppressors. But by learning the way of her mother's people, she now understood what it meant to be a woman who waged war. A woman who looked at her enemies as lessers. A woman who was an extension of her weapon. A woman men should fear. She would haunt their nightmares. She would invade their minds. She would destroy them bit by bit. She would rise from her ashes and her name would be whispered from trembling lips. Her face would be what terrorized them when they closed their eyes at night.

She was Salome. She had Northern and Myridian blood coursing through her veins. And she would no longer fear her lessers. She would be who they feared.

With five Thrak dead, and blood pooling all over Salome's chamber floor, their leader was still unimpressed.

"Your turn?" Salome cocked her head to the side flashing a malicious grin.

The Thrak leader laughed before he whistled. Eight more Thrak scaled the walls and slithered over the balcony banister.

"You were saying?" The Thrak commander taunted.

Salome glanced over at Adonijah. Blood was dripping down his wounded leg and his left forearm had a slash that would need stitches, if they survived.

Adonijah met her gaze and winked. A silent comfort. He had sworn an oath to protect her, to fight by her side. He had kept his promise and was willing to die fulfilling those words.

Salome hadn't thought much about death. She was never afraid of it, knowing whether in battle or in old age, she would leave this world for another. But standing shoulder-to-shoulder with Adonijah, having felt his lips on hers, his hands caressing her skin, she knew she wasn't ready to die. She wasn't ready to leave him.

"No matter what happens," Salome whispered so only Adonijah could hear her, "I will fight, live, and die by your side."

Whatever thoughts were flooding Adonijah's head, she wouldn't have the luxury of finding out because the second wave of Thrak launched their assault.

They braced themselves for eight rushing them at once, but before the warriors could reach them, two assassins dressed in black fighting leathers swung in from above the balcony and landed behind the Thrak commander.

Kai was already armed with two blades in her hands, holding one in front of her chest and the other over her head.

The Thrak leader growled and whipped around, drawing his longsword, but before he could unsheathe it completely, Kai flicked her blades and each one splayed into a seven-blade fan. She swiped the fans in opposite directions, decapitating the Thrak commander. His head bounced on the floor and Salome could have sworn the remaining eight Thrak flinched in unison.

Salome's eyes moved from Kai to Jinn. The light breeze blew loose strands of his jet-black hair across his face and the glimpse of danger she had seen in him earlier, was now full-blown fury. His golden-brown eyes blazed and if she had stared for any longer, she would have backed away, intimidated by the sight of him.

Jinn retrieved two slightly curved, thin blades from his back and held them at his sides.

After a moment of silence, as if the Thrak were trying to process what was happening, Jinn and Kai jumped toward the group, and joined the fight from the opposite side.

It was still four against eight, but they were far more skilled than the Thrak and made quick work of them. It was more of a bloodbath than a battle.

Realizing there was only one Thrak left, Salome stopped Adonijah from slitting his throat. "Wait! We need him alive."

"Alive?" Adonijah's knife was still against the Thrak's bobbing neck. His black eyes darted back and forth between them.

"To interrogate him," Jinn answered, holstering his tachi blades against his back.

"We need to find out if there are more Thrak on the Isles. If they were here just for Salome or if there were others -"

"I got it," Adonijah cut him off and lowered his weapon.

Kai flicked her fans and they retracted into daggers. She fastened them into the belt and quickly bound and gagged the last Thrak.

Salome's gaze met Jinn's. The assassin was gone, and the prince stood before her. She was relieved, happy even, to see him, and by the look in his eyes, he knew it. "How did you know we were in trouble?"

Jinn ran fingers through his hair and shifted his feet. "I wish I could explain it to you without feeling like a fool," he took a deep breath, blushing in embarrassment. "I thought I heard you calling for help. I mean, I didn't hear you out loud, but in my head. Like you were in my thoughts."

Salome's eyes widened. It had worked. Her mental cry for help was answered by Jinn. He had heard her. But how was that possible? She thought she could only communicate with the dead. But she *had* spoken with someone mind-to-mind before. Damaris. As soon as she could, she would talk to her aunt. Maybe there was more to Salome's magic than she originally thought.

"I know it sounds completely insane." Jinn rubbed the nape of his neck when she didn't respond.

Salome reached out and rested her hand on his forearm, catching Adonijah's watchful eye. "Thank you."

"You're welcome." Jinn seemed taken aback by her gratitude. "You don't think I'm crazy?"

Adonijah grunted behind her, but she ignored it, keeping her gaze fixed on Jinn. "I don't think you're crazy. I should have heeded your warning."

"Where do we take this monstrosity?" Kai asked, kicking the Thrak as he sat on the floor. He hissed through his gag and Kai hissed back.

"We take him to the queen. She will want to know about Thrak running rampant on her lands." And maybe, Salome hoped, this would sway Nym into joining her cause, joining her war.

CHAPTER 30

PASH

Pash did as his queen had instructed and readied the troops and an elite group of Shadows to travel to Gomorrah. Leoti, Ophir, and the Nameless Rider would be accompanying him and Thanos to claim the prince's kingdom. Pash thought it was odd the Nameless Rider insisted on bringing the villager from the Tree House Forest, but he wasn't interested enough to question or deny the Shadow's request.

Before the group left Northwind, Pash made his way to see Niabi in her chambers per her request. But as he rounded the corner of the longest corridor leading to her room, Pash was met by his father and uncle. And by the desperate look in his father's eyes, the commander knew he wanted something.

"Father," Pash sighed. "Uncle."

Gershom squared his shoulders to his son's. "Pash, your uncle informed me he is travelling south with you."

"He is."

Gershom's brow furrowed. "I see."

"Is there a problem?" Pash asked, though he wasn't really interested in his father's opinion.

"I assumed since you are still Commander of the Shadows that Ophir would head the search for the Hunter while you were away." Gershom folded his arms across his broad chest.

Pash pinched the bridge of his nose. "Again, you have assumed incorrectly. Ophir is needed with me."

"But -"

"The search for this Hunter of yours has cost too many Shadow lives," Pash interrupted his father. "The queen won't allow the Shadows to leave the city without her approval."

Gershom gnashed his teeth and balled up his fists. "So, that's it?"

"For now." Pash nodded.

Gershom took a step forward. "You are a commander in title only. I should have known you wouldn't come through," he hissed.

Pash shrugged. "I haven't the time for these games, Father. We can discuss this when I return."

"*If* you return," Gershom grumbled as Pash tried to pass by.

"Glad you have such confidence in me," Pash flashed a contemptuous smile. "Now, I have a meeting with the queen before our departure. Is there anything else?"

Gershom reluctantly stepped to one side of the hall and let his son pass. "Oh, Pash."

Pash turned with an exasperated sigh. "Yes?"

"Give my well wishes to Her Highness on her news." Gershom grinned when Pash wrinkled his brow in confusion. "I know something about her you don't? How delicious. I figured it was yours, but perhaps, I was wrong."

"What are you talking about?" Pash asked as he approached, an eyebrow arched.

Gershom clasped his hands behind his back and rocked on his heels. "Perhaps she never intended to tell you. It suits her cruel nature."

Before Pash realized he had done it, he smashed his forearm into his father's chest and nailed him to the wall. "Speak about her like that again and I'll…"

"You'll what?" Gershom rolled his eyes. "We both know you won't harm me. Your mother passed her weakness to you."

Pash unsheathed a knife from his belt and pressed it against Gershom's neck. "Do not speak of my mother."

Ophir's hand gripped Pash's shoulder. "Pash, don't."

His nostrils flared as he reluctantly lowered the knife, releasing Gershom from his grasp. "What do you know?"

Gershom straightened his clothes and laughed. "Our queen is expecting." Pash stood in stunned silence which provoked another hearty laugh from his father. "Look at him, Ophir, he really didn't know!"

Pash took off down the hall, no longer caring what his father said or did. The soldiers stationed on either side of Niabi's double doors opened them, so he wouldn't have to break stride. His eyes scanned the room quickly and spotted Niabi reclined in a lounge reading a book. He realized he hadn't seen her drink a glass of wine in a while. In fact, there were no wine bottles on her wet bar.

Niabi glanced up from her book and smiled at him. She looked relaxed and stressed all at once. "I assume you are ready for your…" She planted her feet on the floor, closing her book, and setting it to the side. "Pash? Are you alright?"

Pash marched toward her and knelt before her, gently grabbing ahold of her waist. "I – You – Are you?"

Niabi cupped his face, a spark of realization hit her. "I was waiting for the right moment to tell you."

A wave of emotions flooded him. Joy, fear, surprise. He wasn't sure if he wanted to cry, jump, or run. "So, it's true? You're…?"

Niabi bobbed her head.

He lowered the side of his face against her swollen belly and closed his eyes. She wrapped her arms around him and kissed the top of his head.

"Who told you?" she asked.

Pash pulled himself from her midsection and met her gaze. "My father."

Her eyes flashed in irritation, but she shook the hate from her face, and smiled down at him. "Then it is safe to assume most of the White Keep knows our news."

"I can't leave you," Pash kissed her hand. "Not now. Send someone else to Gomorrah. You need me now more than ever."

"Pash -"

"You will be in more danger than before, Niabi."

"You know as well as I do, the soldiers guarding me are for appearance only." Niabi caressed his cheek. "I am perfectly safe."

"I know you can take care of yourself but…" Pash couldn't finish the thought.

"If it makes you feel better," she picked up where he left off, "I also have Tala and Anaktu to watch out for me." She lifted his chin. "I promise, I'll be alright. We'll be here when you return."

Her smile melted him. She still looked like a queen but the glow of her carrying life inside of her stilled his heart. Somehow, she grew in beauty when he thought that was impossible.

"I thought you would be happy," she tilted her head to the side.

"I am." He exhaled a sad sigh, "I know how you feel about remarrying and I accept that, but will you let me be involved in raising our child or will I be forced to remain a secret?"

Niabi leaned down and gently kissed his lips. "I love you, Pash. And our child will not only know you, but love you, too."

"Please don't make me leave you," he rested his forehead against hers.

"You are the one I trust to lead my men to Gomorrah." She kissed his lips again and this time, he felt her saying goodbye.

"Does Tala know?"

"Yes," she nodded.

He and the Andrago might not like one another but there was one thing Pash knew for certain: Tala would lay down his life to protect Niabi.

"There is nothing to worry about," she squeezed his hand.

"My father -"

Niabi lifted her scarred right palm for him to see. "He cannot kill me without forfeiting his own life. And we both know Gershom loves himself too much to test the blood magic."

Pash kissed her belly and then kissed her, lingering for as long as she allowed. "I will return to you as soon as I can," he whispered.

"We will be waiting."

CHAPTER 31
CRISPIN

The battle raged around him. Blood, soot, and smoke filled Crispin's nostrils as he fought his way closer to Northwind's front gate. An army at his back, Crispin waved them forward to attack with everything they had. Blood that didn't belong to him was splattered across his metal armor and dirt stained his aching hands. As they pressed onward, cutting down enemy soldiers in their path, Crispin heard the laugh that haunted him. Crispin's head whipped to his left where Gershom the Bear stood.

Crispin remembered the Seer telling him his life would be forfeit if he faced Gershom. He should walk away. He should heed the Seer's warning but seeing the man who murdered his mother and his brothers standing less than twenty feet in front of him unleashed a level of hatred he didn't realize he harbored.

Crispin drew his sword and ran toward the warlord. Gershom smiled as Crispin leapt in the air, swinging his sword to slice off Gershom's head, but the Bear deflected the attack, caught the prince by the neck, and began to choke him. Crispin dropped his sword, trying to peel Gershom's massive hand from his throat as his feet dangled in the air like a small child. In a last-ditch effort to free himself, Crispin brought his forehead down, smashing into Gershom's face. The Bear released him and hissed.

As Crispin coughed and stumbled to get to his feet, Gershom kicked him square in his chest, stealing his breath. Lying on his back, Crispin gazed up at Gershom who flashed a sinister smile. Hands stained with blood, Gershom lifted his sword above his head, and with one final cackle brought the blade down, slicing into Crispin's chest.

Crispin shot up from his small cot drenched in sweat. His hand roamed his bare chest, grateful to find himself to be intact. From the sway of the ship, Crispin breathed a sigh of relief to be aboard the *Shadow of Death*. It had been several days since he had that nightmare. But this time, it felt real. He could smell Death. He could feel Gershom's blade rip through his flesh and crush his bones. He could hear the screams of those who loved him as his soul left is body.

Crispin hopped out of his bed, stepped to the wash basin, and splashed lukewarm water on his face. He dragged a soaked wash rag over the back of his neck and chest.

"It was just a dream," he muttered to himself, but when he caught his reflection in the small mirror above the basin, he flinched. He looked weathered. For the first time since he was a boy, he saw fear staring back at him.

A soft knock on his door drew his attention from his horrifying reflection. He didn't move. With his hands resting on either side of the wooden table where the wash basin sat, he waited to see if whoever was at his door would walk away. But a second knock echoed through his narrow sleeping quarters. Whoever was on the other side wasn't going anywhere.

Crispin raked a hand through his messy curls before opening the door just enough to see who was on the other side. Out of all the people he expected to see, he was surprised to see Rahab holding two tin mugs of steaming liquid. The scent of honey, whiskey, and herbs wafted up to his nose and instantly calmed his nerves.

"I thought you could use a drink," she whispered, as if she didn't want anyone to wake up and catch her outside his quarters that late. "And maybe some company?"

If it had been anyone else, he would have declined the drink and slammed the door in their face, but something in him couldn't react that way with her. For one, she might stab him. And two, when he met her gaze, he could tell she was also in need of someone to distract her from nightmares. He pushed the creaky door open as wide as it could go and motioned her in.

Rahab offered him one of the mugs and he gratefully took a sip, letting the warmth and burn of the liquor coat his throat. She sat beside him on his cot and for a few minutes they sipped their drinks in silence and stared directly ahead at the wood panel wall where his wash basin sat.

"I couldn't sleep either," Rahab broke the silence, fingers tapping against her cup.

Crispin stiffened. When he had nightmares in the Tree House Forest, he would sweat, scream, and groan until he shot up in a panic or someone woke him. It's a wonder the pirates hadn't pounded on the adjoining walls to get him to shut up for disturbing their sleep.

As if she could read his mind, Rahab said, "We all have them, you know. The nightmares. We're used to sounds in the night. No one will bother you or mention it tomorrow."

The tension he'd been holding in his shoulders loosened and he slumped forward, rubbing his hand over his forehead. "Did I wake you?"

Rahab shook her head. "I was already up." She took another gulp of her drink, and grinned. "I'm surprised you drank something I handed you."

"I figured poisoning was beneath your stab happy self." Crispin smirked; lips pressed against his mug. "It's actually pretty good. What is it?"

"Something Leeondris showed me." Rahab didn't meet his awaiting gaze. "He told me to drink one whenever I have a nightmare. It helps me sleep."

Crispin straightened, cracking his back. He watched her swirl her mug gently. "Do you have them often?" She glanced up at him. "The nightmares, not the drinks."

Rahab sighed and bobbed her head. "I thought I had them under control. But after seeing the Pirate King…" She chuckled softly, "I suppose I should stock up on honey and whiskey when we get to Northwind."

Her attempt at lightening the mood didn't go unnoticed. Crispin was thankful she'd come to his room. Her presence alone was a huge comfort, and he wasn't sure if he should be happy or worried by that. Master Balor's words kept replaying in his head. If he chose his people, his heirs would rule for an age. But if he chose Rahab…

"What do you dream of?" Her question snapped him free of Balor's words. His brown eyes latched onto hers.

"I dream of how I die." Crispin was surprised when she recoiled, and he stared at his feet to avoid her gaze. "There's a battle outside the gates of Northwind. The man who murdered my mother and brothers is there. I have a choice to fight him or let him go. I choose to fight him every time, and every time his sword plunges into my chest."

Rahab reached over and grabbed his hand. When she squeezed, he looked up at her. "If you find yourself on the battlefield and see that man…" The ache in her voice sent a surge of warmth through his chest. "Let him go."

"I could promise you I would, but I don't know if I could keep my word."

"Your heart is fading, Crispin of Northwind." Amunet, the High Priestess in Numbio, had warned him. *"Do not let the evil that has consumed your enemies, fill your heart. Let your hatred go."*

"My hatred is all I have."

"If you lose yourself," she said, *"then you have already been defeated."*

Crispin's fingers cupped the pendant Amunet had placed around his neck in the Golden Temple. *"As long as you wear this, I will be with you. May this be an everlasting reminder to follow your path and not wish for another's."*

Rahab's hand gently turned his chin to face her. When their eyes met, his heart skipped a beat. The stubborn, fierce, dagger-clutching pirate was gone and a woman with eyes filled with compassion and concern held his gaze. "Let him go, Crispin."

"I don't think I can," he whispered.

"Even if it costs you your life?"

"Could you walk away if you came face to face with Uri again?" Crispin asked, expecting her nostrils to flare in anger or her hand to fly across his face, but she sighed and lowered her hand from his cheek.

"If I die, nothing will change. If you die, your people will miss out on their king." Rahab shrugged, her bottom lip quivering. "You need to let him go so you can live. People need you, Crispin." She stood up and rushed to the door.

Crispin chased her, grabbed her forearm, and spun her around before she could leave. He pinned her against the wooden door, cupped her face in his hands, and thumbed hair out of her face. Tipping her face up to meet his gaze, he whispered, "You think your life is less valuable than mine? That people don't need you? That you wouldn't be missed?"

"You are a prince," Rahab said softly, her weight shifting under his stare. "I am a pirate. We know our lives are not equal."

"I don't even want to think about a life where you aren't in it." Crispin held her chin firmly in his fingers. "If you died, it would break me."

Rahab's eyes bounced from his eyes to his lips. She exhaled a shallow breath before lifting her mouth to his. Crispin kissed her back, tucking his fingers behind her neck. Her hands wandered all over his bare chest, rubbing against the ridges of his abs.

Kissing her felt forbidden; like he was about to ride into a storm that could rip him apart. But kissing her also felt right; like he was supposed to have done it a long time ago. He didn't know if he would be able to stop kissing, her now that he'd had a taste of her lips.

Rahab pushed him gently toward his cot. When the back of his knees hit the edge of his bed, he fell back, and she straddled him. She didn't relent from kissing him as his fingers raked through her shoulder-length hair and trailed down her shoulders, her arms, and landed on her round hips.

"Please," Rahab whispered against his lips, their foreheads touching, "let him go."

With her voice added to Harbona and Amunet's counsel, he was inclined to listen. And what terrified him, was if she asked him to give up his crown, he might do it for her.

He gently flipped her around, so she was lying on her back, and looked down into her hazel eyes. Wrapping his arms around her, their limbs tangled, her walls coming down, he nodded. "I promise."

CHAPTER 32

SALOME

It was nearly midnight when everyone gathered in the circular War Room. Eight high back, wooden chairs were evenly spaced in a circle in the two-story library, with the open archways facing the sea. The room was located at the top of the highest tower and had one way in and out.

Nym sat with her back to the sea, with Zara to her left, and Mika to her right. Although Zara protested that men should not be allowed into their War Room, Nym overruled her because of the special circumstances. Harbona, therefore, claimed the chair to Salome's right and Jinn took the seventh seat next to him. Adonijah and Cato stood slightly behind Salome's seat and Kai took her place by Jinn's side.

Salome wondered why the last chair to her Aunt Zara's left was unoccupied. She glanced to her left at Damaris who sat between her and Mika and caught the oracle staring at the bound Thrak. He was forced to his knees in the middle of their circle where the Myridian sigil was tiled on the floor.

"Who does that seat belong to?" Salome mentally asked Damaris.

The Oracle didn't take her eyes off the monstrosity before them. *"That seat will always be left empty. It was Bilhah's."*

Salome's eyes drifted back to the empty chair, and she was taken aback when she saw her mother sitting in it. Bilhah's back was straight, her head held high, her smile warm and soothing. When Salome blinked, the vision vanished.

Salome shook her head and tore her eyes from her mother's seat. *"I need to talk to you about my magic."*

"What is it you wish to know?"

"How can you hear me? I thought I could only commune with the dead."

Damaris turned her head slightly to Salome, meeting her niece's gaze. *"Your magic is more powerful than you realize."*

"How powerful?"

"Your gift is like a bridge, uniting you to another side. You can commune with the

departed, yes, but you also connect with the living. As long as you reach out, you can communicate telepathically with anyone that shares a bond with you."

Salome shifted in her seat and her eyes zoomed around the room to ensure no one was watching them. *"Jinn said he heard me ask for help in his thoughts. But I didn't address him specifically. I just asked for whoever was listening to help me."*

Damaris dared a brief glance at Jinn across the room. He was whispering something in Kai's ear, oblivious to their eyes on him. *"You two must share a strong connection if he heard you without you reaching out to him."*

"Does that mean," Salome sucked in a breath. *"Does that mean I could talk to Crispin?"*

Damaris glanced around the room before asking, *"You would have to share a bond with him."*

"We share the same blood."

"I am the Oracle of Myr," Damaris explained. *"My magic is what connects us. Us sharing blood is not the determining factor. Crispin might be your blood, but without the right bond, he doesn't have the ability to hear your voice."*

Salome huffed in disappointment. *"What kind of bonds are there?"*

"Magic and marriage."

"Could I hear their thoughts? Like you hear mine?"

Damaris bobbed her head.

Salome glanced at the prince. *"But Jinn and I are nothing to each other. How could he possibly hear me?"*

"Perhaps our prince has magic he doesn't wish for anyone to know about."

Salome and Damaris shifted their focus back to Jinn, but this time, he noticed them staring.

Salome looked at Nym and Zara whispering back and forth. She still had time to find out if Jinn could really hear her or not. Damaris said her magic was like a bridge. She had to initiate contact. She mentally envisioned herself standing on one side of a cavern and Jinn on the other. A swinging rope bridge stretched from her side to his.

"Jinn?"

Jinn crinkled his brow and opened his mouth to say something.

"Don't."

The prince snapped his mouth shut. Keeping as neutral a face as possible, he mentally replied, *"How are you doing this?"*

"It works." Salome was just as amazed as he was.

Realization hit Jinn and his eyes widened. *"So, I did hear you ask for help. I'm not crazy."* Salome bobbed her head an inch to confirm. He scanned the room, and no one seemed to notice them. *"Can you do this with everyone?"*

"Only with someone I share a bond with."

"A bond?" He arched a curious brow. *"What kind of bond?"*

"Magic or marriage."

Jinn's shoulders tensed. They clearly weren't married so there was only one possible explanation. *"I don't -"*

"You don't have to tell me what your affinity is," Salome interrupted him, *"but don't think me to be an idiot."*

"I would never think that." Jinn flashed a wicked smile, tilting his head to the side. *"Especially now that I know you can literally read my thoughts."*

Salome rolled her eyes but before she could respond, Nym and Zara straightened to address the rest of the group.

"From the report I received about what happened in your chambers tonight," Nym's sight darted to Salome, "I am beyond grateful you are alive." Salome nodded and Nym's green eyes turned vicious as she focused on the Thrak crumpled before her. "Are there any more of your kind in the Isles of Myr?" Nym asked sternly with an air of disgust.

The Thrak's eyes shifted, not focusing on anyone in particular. He spat at Nym in a final act of defiance.

In a flash, Mika was on her feet, a dagger drawn and poking against the Thrak's throat. "My queen asked you a question."

"You think I fear your queen more than my own?" The Thrak's gravelly voice trembled. "I would rather spend the rest of my days locked in your darkest dungeon than return to Gomorrah."

"Unfortunately for you," Nym nodded her head at Mika, "we do not harbor enemy soldiers."

The Thrak began to protest but Mika sliced her blade across his neck. He hunched over gurgling, his blood spilling on the Myridian sigil. They silently watched him die before Nym continued.

"So," Nym gazed at Jinn. "It would seem your report this morning was well founded. You have my gratitude."

"That's what you were meeting with her about?" Salome asked through their bond, her eyes drifting over to the prince, though he didn't meet her gaze.

"Had the Myridians discovered our true motive for being here, it could have been seen as an overreach of Eastern power. I let your grandmother know why I was really here, and she agreed to allow me to stay a couple more days to keep an eye on you." Jinn raised a hand to his chest, bowing his head in respect toward Nym. "I am relieved the princess was not harmed."

Salome heard Adonijah mutter something under his breath behind her but couldn't make out the words. If she could mentally chastise him, she would.

"Which brings us to the next matter at hand." Nym tilted her head to the double doors behind Salome. "Bring them in."

Mika opened the doors and Rosalina and Seraphina marched inside shoulder-to-shoulder. They stepped over the Thrak's body, without a second glance, and bowed before the queen and the crown princess.

Salome was confused as to why her ladies in waiting had been called to this meeting. As she observed the twins, she realized they looked different. They weren't wearing the cerulean dresses the palace workers donned. They were wearing pieces of bronze armor and brown fighting leathers. They looked like they were…

"Tell me," Nym folded her hands in her lap. "How did fifteen Thrak get past not one, but two Qata Vishna?"

"Qata Vishna?" Salome blurted without thinking.

"You don't believe I would let my granddaughter roam our halls unprotected, do you?" Nym refocused on the twins, ignoring Adonijah's disgruntled huff. "So, tell us. Why were you not at your posts tonight?"

Rosalina and Seraphina exchanged a side-eyed glance.

Salome caught Cato swaying side to side. She slowly turned her head to watch him and noticed he looked worried and was about to say something. His eyes met hers, and in his panic-stricken face, she realized he was somehow involved with them not being at their posts. She closed her eyes and took a deep breath. He would owe her an explanation.

"It's my fault." All eyes were now on Salome. Even Rosalina and Seraphina dared a glance back at her.

"What's that?" Nym snorted.

"I didn't know they were a protection detail. I wanted time to myself and ordered them to leave me." Salome lied but managed to keep a straight face.

Nym's eyes narrowed. "Is that true, Rosalina?"

Of course, Nym would ask the twin that couldn't keep a straight face.

Rosalina cleared her throat, "Yes, my Queen. The princess gave us an order. We obeyed."

Salome was oddly proud of Rosalina for lying through her teeth but maintained her own neutral expression so not to give them away.

"Had I known they were Qata Vishna," Salome pressed, eyes fixed on her grandmother, "I would not have given them such an order. Perhaps, it is best I am kept in the loop from now on, if we are to avoid these mistakes."

Harbona coughed to cover a laugh. Nym smirked. She could see right through Salome's deception but did not challenge her. There was no proof Salome was lying, so the issue was a mute one.

"Perhaps," Nym settled in her seat, resting her shoulders against the wood, "you should have been informed." She eyed the twins, "This will *not* happen again. You are bound to my granddaughter until I release you or she breathes her last breath. Is that understood?"

Rosalina and Seraphina bowed. "My Queen."

"Unless someone has something they wish to discuss," Nym waved them out, "I believe we are finished here."

As everyone began filing out of the War Room, Salome stopped when her grandmother rose from her seat and sternly said, "Salome, a word."

Salome slouched back into her seat, gearing up for a tongue lashing. Harbona winked at her, drawing a smile from her lips. He ushered a reluctant Adonijah and distracted Cato out of the room.

Jinn sauntered toward her, hands in his pockets, still dressed in his black fighting leathers. His golden-brown eyes danced.

Salome couldn't help herself. *"Why are you looking at me like that?"*

"Can't I just look at you?" Jinn smirked as jet-black strands of hair fell over his forehead.

"Not like that." She crinkled her nose. In an effort not to draw attention to them, she examined her nails, kicking a leg over one of the armrests.

"How am I looking at you?" He seemed amused.

"Like you want something."

"Maybe I do."

Salome couldn't help but look up at him as he passed by. *"And what do you want?"*

"Shut the doors behind you, if you will, Prince Jinn." Nym's voice interrupted them. "My granddaughter and I would like some privacy."

"Sounds like you might be in trouble for that stunt you just pulled." Jinn's voice

echoed in her head as he walked out of the room without a second glance in her direction.

"I'm always in some kind of trouble." Salome rolled her eyes.

"Don't let her bully you."

"Worried about me, Prince Jinn?"

She could hear his warm laugh ringing in her head, and she hated that she liked it. *"Worried for your grandmother. You are quite the handful."*

"I've heard that before, too."

"I think I'm going to enjoy this direct line of communication with you."

"Don't get used to it." Salome snorted a laugh as the doors closed behind them, enclosing her with her grandmother. *"Once I figure out how to use my magic properly, I won't be this accessible."*

"You'll miss me."

Salome huffed aloud before noticing Nym was watching her.

"Do you drink wine?" Nym asked, her hands clasped behind her back.

Salome nodded and her grandmother walked to one of the built-in bookcases. She tapped her foot against the bottom of the shelf and the wall turned around revealing a wet bar. Nym grabbed a bottle of local wine and two glasses. She silently filled them and brought one over to Salome. Nym settled in one of the seats next to Salome. For several minutes they said nothing.

"You do remind me of Niabi." Nym broke the silence. Salome lowered her glass, her attention fixed on the queen. "But you also remind me so much of Bilhah. She pulled stunts like that all the time. Covering for her sisters, the servants. And she knew I knew she was lying."

Salome opened her mouth to protest but Nym held up a hand and she snapped her mouth shut.

"And just like your mother, I can't prove you are lying." Nym smiled, kicking her legs over the armrest like Salome, "I just don't want you thinking you pulled the wool over my eyes. I might be old, but I'm just as sharp as I was when I was your age."

Salome let out a much-needed laugh. "You're not mad?"

Nym shook her head with a wide grin. "I'm not mad. But Zara will be." The queen rolled her eyes and sighed. "I'll be hearing about this for at least a week."

Salome took another sip of red wine and inhaled the salty sea air that wafted through the room.

"Tell me, Granddaughter," Nym swirled the liquid in her glass. "Is it the prince or the sell-sword that has captured your heart?"

Salome coughed, choking on the wine that burned down her throat. "What are you talking about?" Her cheeks flushed, but she could easily blame that on the alcohol.

"They're both handsome, strong, tall, and the way they look at you," Nym slapped a freckled hand to her cheek and smirked. "Oh, what I would give for a man to look at me, the way both of them, look at you."

"I thought Myridians didn't like men." Salome said, hoping to redirect the conversation.

Nym chuckled, her mind clearly replaying a fond memory. "It's true. Some Myridian women hate men."

"You aren't one of them?"

Nym shook her head. "When I was around your age, I had many suitors. I was to be the next queen, so of course, I would be of interest. But there were two men in particular that captured my attention."

"How did you choose?" Salome asked, and when her grandmother met her gaze, she knew she had given herself away.

Nym smiled, "I got to know them both over the course of several months. And when it came time for me to choose a husband, I said a prayer, and went to sleep. When I woke up the next morning, the one that I thought of first, was who I married."

Salome's brows shot up. She didn't know what to say, so she took another sip of wine, finishing her glass. "And it worked?"

"I was happy," Nym nodded. "We had three beautiful daughters and enjoyed each other's company. He was my best friend. There are some in Myr who saw my love for him as a weakness. Zara included. But he brought me joy. And when he passed, I felt lost. Without my crown and my people to care for, I might have been lost completely."

"But you said men of power could not be trusted."

"My husband had no power, no title." Nym polished off her glass of wine and set it on the armrest of her chair. She squared up top her granddaughter. "He was never a threat to me."

"Do you ever wonder what would have happened, if you chose the other man?" Salome's eyes dropped to the floor. "Do you wonder if you made the wrong choice?"

"Why waste time thinking that way?" Nym tsked and rose to her feet. "I followed my instincts. I followed my heart. And I have lived a good life."

"No regrets?"

"Just one." Nym patted Salome's face. "Have you considered my offer?"

Salome rested her hand over her grandmother's. "I would love nothing more than to stay here with you."

Nym's eyes were filled with sadness, "But?"

Salome couldn't say once she killed her sister she would return, so she said, "I will come back to you when I can." A promise she hoped to keep.

Nym placed her forehead against Salome's and whispered, "You will always have a home here, Granddaughter."

Salome wrapped her arms around Nym, and tears streamed down her cheeks. She didn't know what the future held for her. She didn't know what this war would look like, if she would be victorious, or if she would lose everything, including her own life. But to know that she had a place she could call home, meant more than anything to her.

Nym pulled back and looked into Salome's teary eyes. "I'm sorry I wasn't able to provide a home for you before."

"As deep as the sea," Salome whispered the Myridian motto her mother had taught her.

Nym smiled warmly, cupping Salome's face in her withering hands. "As deep as the sea."

~

SALOME MARCHED down the hallway leading back to her chambers. But instead of walking into her room, she burst into the quarters Harbona, Adonijah, and Cato shared.

Cato nearly jumped out of his skin when she stormed in, her eyes filled with fury. She slammed the Stormcrag against the wall, holding him firmly in place with her forearm, and pointed a finger in his face.

"What did you do?" she growled through gritted teeth.

Adonijah hopped to his feet and made his way toward her, but she held a hand up to stop his advance.

"Cato." Salome's nostrils flared. "What did you do?"

Cato's eyes shifted to Adonijah who shrugged. "I'm sorry, I had no idea they would get in trouble."

"I lied to the queen to cover for you," Salome snorted. "I better get some answers and quickly."

"I swore I wouldn't say anything," Cato cast another pleading look Adonijah's way.

"Don't look at him." Salome lightly smacked Cato's cheek. "Look at me. What is going on?"

Cato relented, "At the Festival of Forbidden Fruit, I met a girl. We talked all night long. Then I realized I had seen her before. She was one of your ladies-in-waiting."

"What are you saying?" Adonijah's eyebrow arched.

Cato took a deep breath. "She wasn't at her post because she was with me. In bed."

Salome's jaw dropped. Adonijah rubbed a hand to the back of his neck and Harbona chuckled, not invested enough to put his pipe down and join them inside from the balcony.

"Who is *she*?" Salome asked as calmly as she could.

"I've already told you too much," Cato whimpered, "She'll kill me."

Salome furrowed her brow. "Who are you more afraid of? Me or her?"

"I feel like this is a trick question," Cato squinted.

Adonijah's hand rested on Salome's lower back, and he whispered in her ear, "I think I can help."

Salome side-eyed him but nodded in approval. She eased her grip on Cato's clothes. His eyes shot back and forth between Adonijah and Salome.

"I hate to tell you this, Cato," Adonijah thumbed at his stubbled jaw, "but I kissed Seraphina at the Festival of the Fallen -"

"That's not possible, she was with…" Cato slapped a hand over his mouth.

"The man-hating twin?" Salome laughed, releasing her hold on Cato. "My money would have been on Rosalina."

"I suppose Seraphina isn't as cold as I thought." Adonijah crossed his arms over his chest.

Cato rubbed small circles around his temple. "She's going to kill me," he mumbled.

"She will do nothing of the sort." Salome patted him on the back. "She owes me big time for saving her ass. That doesn't explain why Rosalina wasn't at her post though."

Cato grimaced. "We might have told Rosalina you wanted her to get you some tea before bed, so we could be alone."

Salome wasn't sure if she found this entire situation amusing or irritating. Dealing with Cato felt exactly like how she dealt with Crispin, and it left a soft spot in her heart for the Stormcrag.

"Are you upset with me?" Cato asked, not wanting to meet Salome's gaze.

Salome pushed a fist against his shoulder and laughed. "I was never angry. I just wanted you to think I was, so you'd tell me the truth."

"If that was you pretending to be angry," Cato huffed, wiping invisible dirt off his clothes, "I don't want to see the real thing."

CHAPTER 33
ZOPHAR

Three days after Sheik Ibrahim's men rescued them, Zophar and the Numbio began the rest of their journey north to Oakenshire, with food, water, and what remained of their horses to carry the supplies. They decided to heed Ibrahim's warning and avoided the main roads and headed east toward the Bone Mountains.

Rayma's uncharacteristic silence didn't go unnoticed by Zophar as he tugged Freya and Midnight along the narrow path. He had seen and dealt with this before. When Zophar, Crispin, and Salome escaped Northwind, Salome barely spoke for three months. He wasn't sure how to help her grieve – all he could do was let her know when she was ready to talk, he would be there.

Zophar slowed his pace until he was walking next to Rayma. He whispered, "Is something bothering you, Healer?"

"Leave me alone," she didn't look at him.

The bite in Rayma's voice didn't discourage or intimidate him. If he survived the teenage years with Salome, he could survive anything.

"Whenever you do want someone to talk to, I'll be there to listen." Zophar pressed onward, ignoring Rayma crossing her arms over her chest, and met up with Heru leading their company. Heru, too, seemed to be in a foul mood and if Zophar was a betting man, he'd wager it had something to do with the stubborn healer.

"No sign of the Thrak or the Krazaks." Heru stared at the tree filled Bone Mountains they were approaching.

"You don't sound pleased," Zophar said.

Heru shook his head, running a hand over the nape of his neck. "Forgive me, Zophar. I've had a lot on my mind lately."

"Any of those thoughts about our healer?"

If Heru was offended by Zophar's bold question he didn't show it. The prince shrugged, keeping his eyes on the horizon. "I thought one day she would be my wife – my queen, but… I was a fool to think so. To want her."

"The lady does not return your affections?" Zophar asked, stomping down the narrow, gravelly path.

"The *lady* had other intentions." Heru let loose a wounded breath. "She was sent to kill me."

"She's an assassin?" Zophar found that hard to believe, but Rayma gutting Bantu with Pyke's crystal dagger flashed in his mind. "You know she was sent to kill you and you let her live?"

"She confessed her master's plan. I already sent word to my father about Lord Memucan's treason." Heru pushed a branch out of his way. "We need a healer, and she is the best in Numbio. I told her once the war is over, she will not be allowed home."

"I'm sorry," Zophar scratched his beard. "Perhaps, her unprovoked confession proves she does have genuine feelings for you. It would have been easy for her to have assassinated you by now."

"How can I trust her?" Heru's nostrils flared, and his eyes watered. "No matter what her reasons were, she plotted against the crown. She's lucky to still be breathing."

Zophar felt an urge to defend the healer. He didn't know what her reasons were, but he couldn't help but see similarities between Rayma and Salome. Perhaps, she was a cold-blooded assassin masquerading as a healer, but something deep inside of him wouldn't accept that.

Before Zophar could speak on the topic further, Heru stopped dead in his tracks when a loud bird-like whistle sounded ahead. It was their scout. A low whistle signaled Krazaks. A loud whistle meant they had spotted Thraks headed in their direction.

Heru swiftly waved his hand in a circular motion and flashed a sign, ordering his troops to prepare for battle. Without a second's hesitation, the Numbio warriors unsheathed their weapons, pulled their horses deep into the woods, and hid in the darkness of the trees, waiting for the company of Thrak to walk into their trap.

Zophar drew his axe from his belt and scanned the trees and saw where Rayma was hiding. The only reason he spied her was because the crystal dagger she clutched to her chest reflected the sun's light. If he saw it, it might alert the Thrak to their whereabouts. But it was too late to warn her. Heavy footsteps and low grunts tumbled down the path toward them.

Zophar counted thirty of them, more creature than human. He had seen the Thrak once before, a long time ago, and the image of their sharpened teeth, black eyes, and pointy ears never left his nightmares. He would have preferred to fight the Krazaks. At least the Mountain Men wouldn't resort to eating the flesh clean off their bones.

As long as the Numbio held their position and didn't draw the attention of the monstrous slaves of Gomorrah, there would be no bloodshed. Heru made sure his warriors understood before they left Jannat Sin, they wouldn't initiate any fighting. But if attacked, the Numbio would take no prisoners and leave no witnesses.

Because the Thrak had broad shoulders, they marched down the trail one by one, passing the Numbio, none the wiser. Zophar held his breath as the last of the Thrak appeared around the wooded bend. The biggest and most scarred looking of the bunch was at the rear and when he stopped, Zophar clutched the handle of his battle axe tightly. The Thrak sniffed the air like a wild and hungry animal hunting for his next meal. He stood there for a minute before taking another step toward the line of Thrak in front of him.

Zophar exhaled the breath he had been holding since they started stomping through but winced when he saw the last Thrak cover his face from the reflection of Rayma's dagger.

Damn. Zophar's gaze bounced from the brute to Rayma across the pathway. She must have realized what was happening and tried to hide her dagger underneath her, but it was too late. The Thrak growled and with that one sound the band of thirty monsters armed themselves for battle.

The Thrak turned toward the trees and fanned out to find whoever was lurking in the shadow of the pines. Heru slammed his sword rhythmically against the wooden shield the people in Jannat Sin had given them to replace the ones they had lost in the Caverns of the Undead. A call to arms, a call to battle. The Numbio echoed their prince's battle cry, thudding their weapons against their shields. A ritual to intimidate their enemy and for a brief moment, Zophar noticed the Thrak looked rattled. The Thrak were surrounded, and they didn't know who or how many there were that would come for their necks.

Heru shouted and the Numbio freed themselves from their hiding places, attacking the cannibals. The sound of clashing swords, angry grunts, and thudding bodies filled the normally quiet and empty path. The Thrak were wild in their attack, but the Numbio fought as a unit. They fought as one body that knew exactly what each and every limb was doing. It was structured, it was confident, and it was effective.

Zophar felt alive, like he could battle enemies all day long and not tire of it. He was born and bred for war and felt most comfortable on a battlefield facing monsters of all shapes and sizes. He sliced his way through the Thrak, not a scratch on him, but smeared with the blood of the fallen.

When the last Thrak was defeated, Heru let out a pained groan. Zophar turned around to see a large, fur-clad man standing behind Heru with a knife to his throat.

"Drop your weapons." A female Stormcrag warrior stepped up next to Heru, flipping a dagger around her hand absent-mindedly. "Or your leader gets his throat slit."

"We mean you no harm," Zophar slowly bent to lay his axe on the gravelly ground. "You're Stormcrag, right? We are your friends."

The woman wiped strands of purple hair out of her face and hissed, "Storm-crags don't have the luxury of friends."

"Please," Rayma stepped forward, tears in her eyes as her gaze bounced from the woman to Heru. "Please, we will lower our weapons. Don't hurt him."

A sinister grin flashed across the female Stormcrag's face as she waved a hand in the air, making a spectacle of showing the Numbio they were now surrounded. There were archers with nocked arrows pointed down at them from the tops of the pine trees.

"As long as you don't do anything stupid," the woman scratched at her chest covered in tattoos, "no one needs to get hurt."

"Oifa." The enormous man holding a knife against Heru's throat drew her attention. "They're Southerners. Torrin will want to see them."

Oifa rolled her eyes and clenched her teeth. "Then we take them to the Tears of the Gods." She sheathed her dagger and turned on her heel, starting back up the path. "And no funny business, or I'll let my archers use you for target practice."

All Zophar could hope for as the Stormcrags blindfolded them was that the Mountain Men wouldn't lead them up the mountain to just push them over the side.

CHAPTER 34
NYM

Nym shut the doors to her chambers quickly before anyone passing through the halls could see her come undone. She felt like her throat was closing in on itself. She rushed for the decanter of wine and poured herself a glass, washing it down, coating her dry mouth. Setting the empty glass down on the table, her hand flew up to her chest. Her heart was beating rapidly, and beads of sweat bubbled near her hairline.

Breathe. Just breathe.

These attacks started after Niabi was taken from her. It was worse than losing a granddaughter. She felt like she had failed her. She *had* failed her. And now, she was failing to convince Salome to reconsider launching an attack on her sister. By the time she discovered Niabi's plot to kill her father and usurp the throne, it was too late to save Bilhah and the rest of her grandchildren. Niabi had been willing to send Bilhah's body back to the Isles for a proper Myridian burial, but she refused to meet with her grandmother face to face. The day Niabi sailed from Myridian shores was the last time they had seen one another. If Nym could go back to that day, she would have fought to keep Niabi, even if it meant war with the North.

It was her one regret.

Her ears perked up when she thought she heard someone else in the room. Their rapid breathing gave them away.

"Does your unexpected visit mean my time has come, Marina?" Nym already knew who was watching her from the shadows of her bedroom.

Marina slowly stepped into the light. "How did you know it was me?"

"You and Niabi were inseparable." Nym filled her glass with another serving of wine, sat in her favorite velvet chair, and extended her arm, bidding her granddaughter to sit across from her. "The question was never *if* you would do her bidding but *when*. Tell me, how do you intend to kill me?"

Marina refused to look her grandmother in the eye. "She wants your heart," she whispered.

"I did not ask what she wanted, child," Nym sipped her drink. "I asked how you planned to murder me."

Marina sheepishly pulled a small vile from her cloak. "It will not cause you any pain. I promise."

"Is that supposed to bring me comfort?" Nym was clearly unimpressed. She set the glass down and turned to her vanity. She pulled the pins keeping her hair in place, picked up her comb and began to brush through her tresses.

"I…I…"

"I. I." Nym tsked as she stuttered. "If you intend to kill me, Marina, you might as well have the audacity to speak your peace."

"I did not want you to suffer, Grandmother."

"Poison is a coward's weapon, so it suits you."

Marina slammed her fist on the side table. "I am not a coward!"

"Slamming your fist like that only proves how childish and naïve you are, Marina." Nym finished brushing her hair and began to braid it. "If you intend to take my life, then do so as a warrior. But if you cannot do that, be gone from my sight."

"If I disobey her, my life will be forfeit." Marina fought back tears that welled in her eyes.

"Do you expect my pity?"

"I am not the only Myridian in her service." Marina cleared her throat. "If not by my hand, then it will be by someone else's, and they will not be as merciful."

Over Nym's lifetime, there had been many attempts to take her life. Each assassin's eyes were filled with hatred and contempt, but she did not see that in Marina's eyes. She saw true remorse. She saw fear.

Marina was right about one thing. If not tonight, Niabi would send another and another and another until Nym was dead. Better peacefully than mercilessly.

Her thoughts shot to Salome. She would miss the feisty Mainlander. But knowing Salome, she would add Nym to the list of names she would avenge.

Nym extended her hand, "Be quick about it."

Marina shakily handed her the vile. Nym poured it in with what remained of her wine.

"Tell Niabi I am sorry for sending her back to her father. She is a Myridian, and I failed her." Nym lifted the glass to her lips and downed the liquid before she could change her mind. "And Marina."

"Yes, Grandmother?" Tears streamed down Marina's cheeks.

"As deep as the sea." Nym recited the Myridian motto.

"As deep as the sea." Marina echoed it, wiping her nose with her sleeve. She held her grandmother's hand tightly in hers. "Grandmother?"

Nym closed her eyes. She was finally free of her guilt.

CHAPTER 35
NIABI

With or without Vilora present, Niabi practiced using her fire magic daily. In a short amount of time, she noticed the blackness inching up her arm had stopped spreading. She also noticed her fire wielding skills were improving quickly – as if the power had been dormant underneath her skin for years, hoping, waiting for the day it could awaken.

Playing with small dancing flames in her palm gradually turned into juggling balls of fire which evolved into shooting spurts of fire from her fingers like flying daggers. She incorporated fire into her sword and knife training and relished the fact she now had a new earth-shattering ability her enemies didn't know anything about.

As her belly swelled with new life, her newfound power blossomed into a dark peacefulness that enveloped her soul. The confidence of knowing she once again held the element of surprise. The news of her pregnancy was no longer a secret but this – her fire, her magic – was hers.

"Good," Vilora's voice sliced through the queen's tranquility. A slow clap followed the witch's crooked grin. "You have mastered the flame quicker than I expected."

Niabi detected a hint of jealousy from her aunt's dry lips but chose to ignore it. She stood up straight from her deep lunge, satisfied with the burnt wood and trail of ashes which littered her private training courtyard.

"I was always a fast learner," Niabi flashed the old woman a smile.

Being a fast learner was a truth her father hated. No matter what the task, Niabi always mastered it faster than her brother, Lykos. Her father's son and new heir couldn't measure up to her and it infuriated Issachar. After years of hoping and failing to earn his approval, Niabi knew her father would never be proud of her accomplishments. But what Issachar didn't know about were the late-night sessions and hours Niabi spent teaching Lykos in private.

"I'll never be as good as you," Lykos said during one of their late-night tutoring sessions.

"You're right," Niabi poked him in the ribs with her quill. "You'll never be as good as me. You'll have to be better."

"Why do you care?" He crinkled his nose, slamming the Tome of Northern Military Tactics closed and folding his gangly arms over his chest.

Niabi flipped the book back open and pointed at the page they were studying. "One day you'll be king -"

"It should be you."

Niabi grabbed her younger brother's hand and smiled at him. "It won't ever be me."

"You seem troubled, my Queen," Vilora said, drawing Niabi back to the present.

Niabi shook her head, motioning her Iron Guard, Anaktu, forward. He extended her floor-length coat and draped it over her shoulders. "Not troubled at all. Are you ready?"

Vilora nodded and joined Niabi at her side, with Anaktu following a step behind. As they marched inside the White Keep and turned the corner to follow the length of the hall to Niabi's chambers, the guards posted outside her room bowed and opened the double doors as the two women and the Nephilim swept inside. Tala was already waiting for them with Ziggy seated in a chair, wringing her hands together.

Niabi shrugged her heavy fur coat off, tossed it on a nearby chaise lounge, and sat in the chair opposite the redheaded escort. "Do you have anything useful for me today, Ziggy of Borg?"

Ziggy brushed red curls from her pale, freckled face. "I've been seeing more of Lord Gershom these last few weeks -"

"Do you have information for me or not?" Niabi cut her off with an irritated groan. Ziggy hesitated and Niabi narrowed her eyes. "Remember what I told you in the dungeons, girl. If I find you are keeping secrets, I will let my Shadows keep you as a pet."

Ziggy seemed to snap out of whatever fog she was in and shook her head. "Lord Gershom had an unexpected visitor one evening. I don't know anything about him. I didn't even see him. They talked and then I was told to leave."

"And what was so special about this visitor?" Tala clasped his hands behind his back, circling around from behind Ziggy to Niabi's side. "There must be some reason you found this to be important enough to tell Her Majesty."

Her blue eyes shifted from the Andrago back to the queen. "The man said he was from Numbio. That he had to escape before his king could execute him for treason."

Niabi and Tala exchanged a satisfied grin. "You're sure the man was from Numbio?" Niabi asked.

Ziggy bobbed her head quickly, sweat beading at her hairline. "Yes, my Queen. That is all I know."

"Keep your eyes and ears open," Niabi waved her hand, dismissing the redhead. "Let us know if you hear anything else about this man from Numbio."

Ziggy curtsied before being ushered out of the room and sent on her way.

"You think the man from Numbio is Lord Memucan?" Tala asked the moment the doors closed.

Niabi reclined in her chair, picking at her fingernails with one of her twin daggers. "I would bet my crown it's him. And he's in Northwind. If we can find out where he is, we could get the damning proof of Gershom's treason."

"I can dispatch plain clothed soldiers to scout around the city for him," Tala offered but Niabi shook her head.

"Have one of the new recruits, one Gershom hasn't seen before, stand guard at his chambers." Niabi flashed a deliciously wicked smile. "If Memucan shows his face, we will know about it."

Tala brought his hand to his chest. "It will be done, my Queen."

A knock on the door echoed through the room and had everyone's attention.

"Were we expecting someone else to give a report today?" Niabi asked flippantly, looking bored with the prospect of more royal business.

With a hand on the hilt of his sword, Tala crossed to the door and let a Shadow in tattered black robes inside. Niabi stood slowly, anger raging in her eyes at his disheveled appearance. She knew all of her Shadows and this elite warrior went by the name of Thrice. The other Shadows had given him the nickname when he supposedly sliced three rebels in half with one swoop of his sword. By just looking at him, Niabi knew the expedition to capture the Enchantress of the Swamp had failed. How badly it failed was what she now wanted to know.

"Thrice," Niabi gritted her teeth. "What happened?"

"We found the Enchantress but…" Thrice's throat was dry, as if he hadn't had a drop of water in days. Niabi poured him a cup of water from the glass decanter that replaced her wine and handed it to him. Once he had downed the liquid, he cleared his throat and started over. "We found the Enchantress, but she wasn't alone. She used her magic to summon tree roots that dragged the Shadows into the earth and swallowed them whole. We set the swamp on fire and shot her with an arrow when another magic wielder appeared and extinguished the flames with water."

"Water magic?" Vilora gasped and Niabi didn't know if she was surprised or angered by another magic wielder.

"The other Shadows?" Niabi asked, eyes fixed on Thrice's muddy brown ones. "Did any of them make it?"

Thrice cradled his cracked mask and shook his head. "I'm the only one left."

That was what Niabi didn't want to hear. She had sent some of her best Shadows to capture Odelia and the Enchantress still managed to decimate them. And what was worse, the Enchantress wasn't alone. Whoever the water wielder was, Niabi would now have to deal with them, too.

The queen rested her hand on Thrice's shoulder. "Clean up, eat, and get some rest. We'll talk more tomorrow." Thrice bowed, crossed an arm over his chest in salute, turned on his heel, and left the queen's chambers.

Niabi felt the rage burning from the soles of her feet all the way up to her chest. Her breathing deepened and a lump rose to her throat at the thought of losing men she sparred and trained with. An easy mission. It was supposed to be an easy mission. But the Enchantress was prepared. She brought another magic wielder in to help her.

"Did you know about this water wielder?" Niabi's eyes flashed to meet Vilora's bewildered gaze.

The witch shook her head, plopping down on the chaise lounge where Niabi had thrown her fur cloak. "You think a fire wielder such as me would forget about a water wielder?" Vilora's tone had a bite to it and Niabi was inclined to remind her who she was speaking to but then her aunt said, "If there is a water wielder, we will have to kill them before they can become a real threat."

Tala tilted his head in confusion. "How can a water wielder pose more of a threat than the Enchantress of the Swamp?"

"What extinguishes fire?" Vilora kicked her sandals off her feet and lifted her dirty toes to rest on top of the white linen chaise. "Water. Water can render flame useless."

Niabi flicked her wrist and held a dancing flame in the palm of her left hand. She let the fire wiggle around her fingers before aiming her fingers at the unlit fireplace and sparking it to life.

"What else are you capable of doing?" Tala asked, lifting his head to look at her. "Obviously you can start a fire," he motioned to the crackling fireplace, "but are you powerful enough…"

"To burn cities to the ground?" Vilora finished the question he was too fearful to ask. She grinned. "If she wants to burn a city to the ground, she can."

Niabi shot her aunt a vicious look. "I have no intention of burning any city to the ground. But if my brother and sister think they know everything they need to defeat me, they will be surprised to learn I've got a few more tricks up my sleeve." She rolled her fingers one by one with a tight-lipped smile.

Tala stood; determination etched in his bronze face. "Tomorrow, we will begin the search for Memucan and the water wielder. Neither will pose you any threat as long as I still live and breathe."

Niabi reclined in her chair and rested her hand on her belly. She knew if Tala made a promise, he would keep it. As long as he was hunting her enemies down, they wouldn't step one foot inside the White Keep. And if by some miracle, they made it to her doorstep, then they would be hers for the taking, and she loved playing with her food before devouring it.

"Then we have nothing to worry about," Niabi smiled.

CHAPTER 36
SALOME

Sweat bubbled around Salome's forehead and her sheets were soaked in sweat. She tried desperately to wake up from the nightmares but couldn't. Gripping the blankets and gritting her teeth, she was forced to watch the memory play out.

She saw her brother, Lykos, standing on one of the White Keep's many balconies overlooking the Ignacia Sea. His hands were wrapped around an Immortal woman. Her platinum blonde hair, grey eyes, pointy ears, and white robe, reminded her of Harbona, except she had the Immortal glow.

"Harbona had a vision," Lykos stroked his fingers through the woman's straight, hip long hair. "Niabi is coming."

She scoffed, crinkling her nose. "You trust the word of an exiled Seer? There is a reason the Eldaar banished him."

"Harbona has loyally served the North for generations." Lykos tilted her chin up. "Why would I not believe him?"

"If Northwind is attacked," she sucked in a breath, "I will not leave without you."

"I have a duty to protect my people."

"You really expect me to leave you here?" She grabbed his hands and shook her head. "I am your wife, Lykos."

"And as your husband," Lykos rested his hand on her swollen belly. "I want you and our little one to be safe."

"And if your sister doesn't come?"

"Then you will return to me." He kissed her lips gently.

"By then there will be no questioning my condition," she rubbed her hands in a circular motion around her belly. "Your father will -"

Lykos cupped her face in his calloused hands. "You will be my queen and our child will be my heir. If my father disowns me, so be it. I made my choice the moment I saw you dock in our harbor years ago."

There were tears in her grey eyes. "Are you sure you will not come with me?" She held his hand tightly.

"I am needed here." Lykos cleared his throat, fighting back tears of his own. "I wouldn't be much of a king if I ran at the first sign of trouble."

"I will miss you."

"I will see you again, I promise." He brought her hands to his lips and kissed them.

"If he is a boy," she placed his hand on her belly, "I want to name him Dunlor after your grandfather. He was a great friend to my people."

"And if we have a girl?" His eyes danced in hopeful delight.

"I have not thought of a name yet."

"I like Keeva."

She crinkled her nose in disgust, "Where did you hear that name?"

Lykos grinned sheepishly, "I saw our daughter in a dream and that was her name."

"Let us hope he is a boy," she teased. She wrapped her arms around Lykos and rested her face against his chest. "You are frightened."

"I would be a fool if I wasn't."

"You still wear it," she slipped her hand in his shirt and brought a gold medallion necklace out.

"Of course." Lykos took it off and placed it in her hand. "Give this to our child if I -"

"Do not say it," she covered his lips. "Please. I could not bear to hear those words." A tear slipped down her cheek.

He forced her fingers to enclose the necklace she had given him on their wedding day. "Then take it for safekeeping. I would hate to lose it."

"Come back to me," she wrapped her arms around his neck, fighting back tears. "Promise, you will come back to me."

"I promise."

Salome heard someone scream Harbona's name. She smelled the fire that burned through her city the night they fled. Darkness enveloped her. She couldn't breathe from the ash and soot filling her lungs.

Her mind shot to a city with a palace made entirely of gold. Immortals in golden armor with white feathered wings flying above a glittering city. Lykos' wife's grey eyes flashed before her and held her gaze, refusing to release her.

"Lykos!" Salome screamed. Her eyes shot open to find Harbona sitting on her bed, holding her by the shoulders. She shivered, cold from the sweat dripping down her back. "Harbona?"

"What did you see?" Harbona narrowed his eyes, his hands still gripping her shoulders.

Salome's tears flowed down her cheeks. "I saw my brother with an Immortal woman."

"Is that all?"

She shook her head. "I saw a golden palace and Immortals with golden armor and white feathered wings. There was a battle. I saw ships and explosions," Salome blinked rapidly, wiping away wet hair sticking to her forehead. "Harbona, I heard someone calling for you."

"What else did you see?"

"The Immortal woman. My brother called her his wife." Salome watched him for a reaction, but he remained neutral. "Harbona, there's a child." Harbona's eyes widened. "You didn't know?" Harbona slowly shook his head, lips in a tight line. "What does it mean?" Salome asked.

"You have seen the past." Harbona relaxed his grip on her and rubbed his face. It was still early in the morning, the sun had yet to rise above the horizon. And if Harbona was in her room trying to wake her from the nightmare, she must have woken others. "You have also seen something that has been hidden from my sight."

"How is that possible?"

"A shield."

"You mean magic?" Salome brought her knees to her chest.

Harbona nodded. "This was not an ordinary vision, Salome. This was a message. Lykos wants me to go to her."

"Who is she?"

"Lavena." Harbona smiled but it was followed with what Salome could only identify as dread. "I will have to go."

"Go?" Salome sat up straighter. "Go where?"

"Caelestis."

Salome's mouth dropped. "I thought you were banished."

Harbona reached his hand out. "There is something I need to show you."

Salome looked at his hand wearily. The last time she grabbed his hand, she was rocketed through his past and it left her exhausted and in pain.

As if he could read her thoughts, he said, "Please."

Salome took a deep breath before resting her hand in his palm. She felt her mind sprinting to whatever memory Harbona wanted her to see. She closed her eyes to keep from becoming nauseous but that only made it worse. When she felt the motion stop, she opened her eyes. She was standing in a brightly lit throne room; everything from the floors to the two thrones were made of gold.

"How do you plead, Harbona?"

Salome looked up and saw a man and woman sitting stoically in their golden thrones on a dais ten feet in front of her. They had Harbona's features, but their cold grey eyes made her shiver.

"How do you plead, Harbona?" They asked again in unison. Their voices echoing through the extravagant throne room.

"If by aiding the mortals in an attempt to overthrow their enemy I am considered guilty," she heard Harbona's voice but didn't see him. She realized she was seeing his past through his eyes and his perspective like the previous time she touched him. *"Then I am guilty."*

"Then you leave us no choice, Harbona." The couple said again simultaneously. As if one did not exist without the other. "For attempting to assassinate the brother of the King of Adalore, we find you guilty, and hereby banish you from Caelestis."

Harbona's body convulsed, and he screamed in excruciating pain. His hand flew up to his right eye and covered it.

"You are no longer one of us," the couple continued. "You are no longer allowed to live amongst our kind. You are no longer allowed to have the Glow of Immortality. You are no longer heir to the Eldaar. You are alone."

Harbona's pain ceased, and he slowly stood, facing the Eldaar again.

"We hope your actions were worth your damnation."

Harbona nodded his head. "When faced with a decision to do what is right or do nothing, I will always do what is right. Even if that means I must stand alone."

"You are no son of ours." The man waved a pale hand in the air. "You are no son of the Eldaar."

"Maybe one day you will see, I did what you should have done."

"Should you return to our shores," the woman's grey eyes darted to Harbona's, "your life may be forfeit."

"Then it is forfeit." Harbona bowed and the vision faded.

When Salome blinked, she was no longer in Caelestis, she was in her room with Harbona. "You gave up everything." Salome had so many questions but the first one that flew out of her mouth was, "You are the heir of Caelestis?"

Harbona breathed in deeply. "Was."

"You can't go back there." Salome shook her head in protest. "Your own parents banished you."

"They followed the law of our ancestors." Harbona didn't seem bothered. "In my youth, I was what you would describe as overzealous."

"What was your crime?"

"I had a vision that Phlias would kill his brother, Greygor, for the crown. I told my parents, but they said it was not our place to interfere with the lives of mortals." Harbona sighed, rubbing a hand behind his neck. "I disagreed. I took a small company with me and attempted to assassinate Phlias as he slept. But I failed. And Greygor deemed an Immortal trying to kill his brother as an act of war."

"But Phlias did kill Greygor."

Harbona nodded solemnly. "My parents struck a deal with Greygor for my return. After my banishment, Phlias killed his brother, took the crown, and oppressed Adalorians for seven years. I wandered Adalore during those years until the Almighty gave me a vision of Malachi. The one who would save us from Phlias' tyranny."

"What aren't you telling me?" Salome cocked her head to the side.

"I knew one day I would return to Caelestis to face the Eldaar again." Harbona reached for Salome's hands but stopped short, realizing it could trigger her powers. "Lykos is the only one who could have sent you that vision. There's a reason and I am the only one who can find out what it is."

"Harbona -"

"Listen to me carefully." Harbona interrupted her and whispered his instructions. "Prince Jinn will be leaving for the Mainland, and you, Adonijah, and Cato must be on that ship. The Thrak will be keeping a watchful eye on the ships docking in Port Daelon, so you must not return there. Do not go to Sakurai either. You must have the ship dock where the Bone Mountains and the sea meet. Travel on foot through the mountains, Cato will be your guide. Get to Oakenshire. There, we will meet our allies."

"You will meet us in Oakenshire?"

"The Almighty willing, I will." He was telling her what she wanted to hear.

"The truth." She narrowed her eyes.

"If the Eldaar does not have my head for stepping foot on Immortal ground," Harbona rasped, "I will be in Oakenshire."

"Please don't go."

"I must. If Lykos does have an heir, we need to know."

"You don't think they would want to claim Northwind, do you?"

"I do not know. We have many questions that need answers." Harbona stood.

"Make sure to follow my instructions."

Salome jumped out of her bed and fought the urge to wrap her arms around him and hug him. He stood stoically; hands clasped behind his back.

"What if this is the last time we ever see one another?" Tears welled in Salome's eyes; a lump forming in her throat.

Harbona tilted his head and returned her sad smile, "Then it has been my honor serving you and your family."

A thunderous knock echoed through her chambers before the doors flew open. Adonijah stepped inside, and by the look on his face, Salome knew something terrible had happened.

"What is it?" her voice cracked.

Adonijah's fingers twitched at his sides. "It's the queen."

Salome's heart shattered before he could tell her what happened to her grandmother. "Did she suffer?"

Adonijah's eyes were filled with sorrow. "They caught Marina trying to stowaway on a ship headed for Port Daelon. She admitted to poisoning your grandmother."

Salome stepped toward him, wrapping her arms around herself. "What aren't you telling me?"

"Marina carved out the queen's heart." Adonijah winced when he saw Salome's eyes widen in horror. "She said it was your sister's order."

"Where's Mika?" Salome's nostrils flared and she strutted to the dresser where her fighting leathers were laid out and threw them on over her clothes.

"In the Inner Depths with your aunts." Adonijah stepped to the side of the door to allow Salome a clear path.

Salome holstered her weapons, then whipped around to look at Harbona once more, knowing he wasn't going to stick around for her grandmother's funeral or a potential trial. "I will see you in Oakenshire."

Harbona rested his palm over his heart. "Princess."

Salome's gaze met Adonijah's, and she knew he had as many questions as she did, but she motioned for him to follow her.

When they had rounded the corner Adonijah asked, "Where is he going?"

"Caelestis."

"But -"

"I know." She cut him off, knowing if she dwelled on Harbona's fate, she would melt into a puddle of tears. "He gave us instructions to sail back to the Mainland. We are to travel through the Bone Mountains to get to Oakenshire."

"With Cato as our guide?" He kept his voice low so no one would overhear them.

Salome nodded. She noticed Adonijah had a slight limp from the arrow wound to his thigh, but she didn't mention it. He wouldn't like her gushing over his injuries.

"Will your Aunt Zara grant us passage?"

Salome grimaced. She knew Adonijah was not going to like the next part. "Harbona told us we need to ask Jinn for safe passage."

If Adonijah was angry, he didn't show it. He kept a neutral face and nodded in obedience. "Alright."

Salome stopped and after he took a few more steps, he realized she wasn't by his side, and he turned around to look at her.

"Is something wrong?" Adonijah tilted his head to the side.

"Alright?" Salome rested her hands on her hips. "You don't have anything else to say about us traveling with Jinn?"

"If Harbona said that's what we need to do, then we do it."

Salome looked around as if Adonijah was invisible. "I'm sorry, do you know where I can find Adonijah? Clearly, he's missing."

Adonijah took a step toward her and clenched his fists before composing himself. "Do I like Jinn? No. Do I trust him? No. Do I trust Harbona? Aye. So, if Harbona says that's what we need to do, then we do it."

"So, it does bother you?"

"How can I not be bothered when he looks at you the way he does?" Adonijah narrowed his eyes, but every bit of anger and irritation vanished when he met her gaze. He lifted his hand and stroked his fingers down her cheek. "This isn't about what I like," he said softly. "This is about keeping you safe. I could have lost you to the Thrak last night. And now your grandmother…" He pulled her into his chest and wrapped his arms around her. He kissed the top of her head and whispered, "No matter what happens. I will fight, live, and die by your side."

They were the same words she had sworn to him when they stood shoulder to shoulder against the Thrak. She had never made such a pledge to anyone before and she knew now, how much it meant to him.

Salome kissed his neck and allowed herself a moment to cry in the safety of his arms. Tears she knew she didn't have time for. Nym would not want her crying over her death. She would want Salome to rise like a queen. And she would. Once she let herself be vulnerable in Adonijah's arms for another minute or two.

When she pulled back from his chest, he thumbed the tears from her face. "Are you alright?"

Salome shook her head, sucking in a breath. "No, but I will be. I have to be."

She quickly wiped away any remaining tears from her cheeks, when she heard footsteps approaching from an adjoining hallway. Jinn and Kai walked around the corner and stopped.

Jinn's eyes bounced from Adonijah to Salome. He opened his mouth to say something, but she stopped him.

"We need to talk," she planted her thoughts in his head. *"Meet me in the Great Hall after sunset."*

"Will your bodyguard be with you?"

"No. But keep staring at me like that and I won't be able to keep him away."

Jinn bowed his head toward them and he and Kai kept walking down their hallway. *"I heard about the queen. I'm sorry."*

Salome wasn't sure how to respond, so she just said, *"Don't be late."*

She looked up at Adonijah who was frowning at them.

"You won't be allowed inside the Inner Depths." She continued down the corridor in the opposite direction of Jinn and Kai.

"I'll wait for you outside then."

"Just give Jinn a chance," Salome squeezed his forearm. "You gave Cato a chance and you two are …"

"Careful now." He narrowed his eyes.

"Friends," she finished and smiled.

"Cato doesn't look at you like he's…" He snapped his mouth shut.

"Like he's what?" Salome challenged, as they arrived at the double bronze doors leading to the Inner Depths. She folded her arms across her chest, waiting for an answer.

Adonijah rolled his shoulders back and said, "Like he's wondering what's beneath your fighting leathers."

"I can think of someone else who looks at me that way."

Adonijah's eyes darkened, and his chest rose rapidly. "You should get in there."

Salome nodded, but as she turned toward the door, he grabbed her arm and spun her around. Her hands landed on his chest, and he kissed her.

"What was that for?" She smiled.

He pulled back and whispered, "I couldn't wait to kiss you again."

Salome squeezed his hands. "I'll see you soon."

ZARA SAT on the throne with a silver crown of pearls woven into her dark hair. It was the Queen's Crown.

Salome bowed upon entering the Inner Depths but before she could say a word, she heard the Five Virtues whispering to her.

"She has returned."

"We have been waiting for you."

"Do you think she knows yet?"

"Does she know her fate?"

"Who will she choose?"

Salome's eyes narrowed remembering Harbona and Damaris' advice of asking what the other side wanted from her. *"What do you want from me?"*

"She does not know."

"She does not want to know."

"She will choose me."

"Look at her, she is frightened."

"She is one of us, she will not fail."

"Rise, Cousin," Zara's melancholy voice sliced through Salome's exchange with the Five Virtues. Salome straightened, eyes darting from one Virtue statue to the next, but they had gone silent. "I take it you have heard."

Salome nodded, "What is to be done with Marina?"

"She is locked in the Tower Dungeon where she will remain until her trial." Mika wasn't in her red armor, she was in her red fighting leathers and by the dark circles underneath her eyes, it appeared she hadn't slept all night.

"There will be no trial," Zara said without looking at Mika.

Mika's and Damaris' mouths dropped, simultaneously.

"What?" Mika scoffed. "Anyone accused of a crime receives a trial."

"Marina confessed to her crimes. She is a murderer and a traitor." Zara pressed her back against the high back throne. "No trial will change her fate."

"Zara, that is not our way -"

"At dawn," Zara interrupted Damaris with a vicious glance, "Marina will face the executioner's blade."

"Mother, please reconsider."

"I don't have a choice, Mika!" Zara shouted, slamming her fist on the armrest of her chair. She closed her eyes and rubbed her forehead. "As soon as other kingdoms hear our mother, our queen, was assassinated in her room by her own flesh and blood…" Her voice cracked and she cleared her throat, fighting the tears in her bloodshot eyes. "I will not have them think we are weak or vulnerable. Marina confessed. Marina will die. That is my decision." Zara stood up, ending the discussion, and marched out of the room, Mika trailing her.

For once, Salome agreed with her aunt. Marina murdered Nym and carved out her heart on Niabi's orders. Marina could rot in the dungeons for the rest of her miserable days for all she cared.

Her attention returned to the Five Virtues. They were still silent. She reached out to them, but none answered.

Damaris clamped a hand on Salome's shoulder, startling her. "The Five Virtues. They've been speaking to you?"

Salome bobbed her head, eyes still bouncing from one statue to the next. "What do you think they want from me?"

Damaris tilted her head, "They are the guardians and protectors of the Red Maidens. Once a new one is named, they choose their Virtue."

"I'm not a Red Maiden, though." Salome turned her attention to the Oracle. "So, why are they talking to me?"

"Perhaps, one day, you might lead the Qata Vishna." Damaris shrugged. "Whatever their purpose, they mean you no harm."

"Which Virtue did Niabi choose?" Salome asked.

If Damaris was uncomfortable with the question or the mention of Niabi's name, she did not show it. She extended her arm to the statue on the right. "She chose Rebirth."

"The raven." Salome noted the bird perched on the Virtue's shoulder. "Makes sense."

"I suppose it does." Damaris agreed. "Mika chose Honor."

Salome glanced toward the bronze doors leading out of the Inner Depths. "Will Aunt Zara reconsider?"

Damaris sadly shook her head, eyes glued to the floor. "I'm afraid once Zara has made a decision, no one can sway her."

"What happened to Grandmother's…"

"Her heart?" Damaris' bottom lip quivered as she looped her arm through Salome's arm, guiding her out of the Inner Depths. "Before the Qata Vishna captured Marina, she stashed it somewhere, but refuses to tell us where it is. Marina was always a difficult child, but I never thought she was capable of murder."

Salome patted Damaris' forearm and stopped her before they reached the second set of bronze doors. "Harbona will be leaving today."

"Will you be going with him?"

"No," Salome shook her head. "But he has instructed me to leave in the next couple of days."

Damaris cupped her niece's face in her ringed fingers. "I hope you will return to our shores one day, when the time is right."

Salome smiled, but she didn't know if she would ever return. She had a feeling Death might be interested in meeting her sooner than anticipated.

CHAPTER 37

NIABI

Niabi never liked pirates. With King Uri and his filthy band of misfits standing before her throne with dirt riddled clothes and gold teeth, she liked them even less. Tala disarmed the seafarers before they entered into the queen's presence, their stash of weapons in a pile outside the enormous double doors.

Niabi sat on her White Throne, a glittering crown upon her raven locks fixed in an elaborate updo. Her emerald train stretched the length of the dais and rested upon the marble floor. With Anaktu and Tala on either side of her, and Vilora standing beside the Nephilim, she began the meeting.

Before she spoke, Uri stepped forward with a grin and lust filled eyes, "You're prettier than I imagined, Queen."

Niabi wrinkled her nose. "Perhaps your lack of courtly manners is due to being out at sea far too long."

Uri cackled, slapping a hand against his muscular thigh. "Oh, Your Highness has a sense of humor." He bared his teeth and Niabi wasn't quite sure if it was supposed to intimidate or entice her. It did neither.

"The Sovereign?" Niabi demanded. "Where is he?"

Uri stepped to the side and motioned for Neempo to be brought forward. His arms and feet were shackled, and the chains extended to an iron collar around his neck. He was in what appeared to be nightwear and still had his red wrap around his eyes.

"The Sovereign." Uri's chest puffed out in obvious pride. "Just as you asked, love."

"Show Her Majesty respect," Tala barked, his hand touching the hilt of his sword.

Uri gnashed his teeth and angrily met Tala's judgmental gaze. The Pirate King looked like he was going to say something vicious in return, but a shadowy hand slipped over his shoulder and the woman that slithered from behind him whispered something in his ear that caused him to relax. Niabi had not seen shadow magic before, though she had read about it in her recent study of magic wielders and their abilities. She learned that those with shadow magic had sold their souls to the Grim. Only an idiot would trust a shadow wielder.

"As you can see," Uri finally continued, "he is unspoiled as requested."

Niabi's attention fell on Neempo who stood quietly as he awaited his fate. For being in the company of these ruffians, he looked unharmed. She motioned for Tala to pay them for their services. Tala had two soldiers bring in a chest brimming with gold coins, and they set it in front of the grinning Pirate King.

"One million crowns, as agreed upon." Niabi meant it as a dismissal, but the Pirate King walked toward the dais and knelt on one knee at the foot of the steps leading to her throne. She stared at him with an arched eyebrow. "Is there something else you wish to say?"

Uri raised his head and met her gaze. "If you allow it, I offer our armada to you in the war against your siblings."

Niabi wanted to laugh, but she stifled it, keeping a neutral expression. "A generous offer, King Uri, but one I must decline. Northwind already has a mighty armada and will be ready for any potential attack, though I am certain one won't reach my shores."

"Then I request my crew be allowed to spend a week here in your fair city to rest before we set sail again."

Niabi preferred the pirates be on their way, but knowing their spending habits, and wanting to appease the Merchant and Night Districts, she acquiesced. "You and your crew are welcome to stay the week in Northwind."

Tala shifted his weight but remained silent as the Pirate King swept up to his full height and flashed a malicious grin that Niabi was sure he meant to look friendly.

"A thousand thanks, Majesty," he bowed his head before two of his men grabbed the chest. "Maybe our paths will cross again."

Niabi forced a tight-lip smile and nodded, relieved to see the misfits filing out of her throne room. The woman dressed in shadow whispered something in Neempo's ear before leaving.

"Unshackle him and leave us," Niabi stood and motioned for the guards and the members of her small council to leave her alone with the Sovereign. No one argued with her. A blind man shouldn't pose any danger.

Neempo rubbed his wrists and neck once the iron chains and collar were removed. His skin was raw and blistering red. He didn't move and didn't speak. He seemed resigned to his fate.

Niabi stood in front of him and asked, "Did they mistreat you?"

Neempo smiled warmly and shook his head. "No, they didn't mistreat me. Thank you for your concern."

"It is not my concern for you that makes me wonder of your treatment, Sovereign." Niabi clasped her hands behind her back. "I was curious to know if my orders had been obeyed."

The Sovereign didn't reply, but his smile remained.

"You must know why you're here." Niabi circled him, inspecting him head to toe.

"I suspect you desire my heart to try to resurrect your son," Neempo didn't flinch when she brushed her fingers on the nape of his neck. "But if I may offer you some advice, Your Highness, the Resurrection Spell…"

Niabi leaned close to his ear, her chest resting against his back, and whispered, "Has only worked once. I have heard that before."

"But have you also heard that the person who was resurrected was not the person their loved ones remembered?"

His question surprised her. "What do you mean?" She circled around to stand in front of him, arms folded over her chest.

"Over six hundred years ago, a witch named Hester, grieving the death of the man she loved, ripped out Sovereign Bocatan's heart. Hester drained all her power to bring him back to life using the Heart of the Righteous and it worked. But when he opened his eyes, they weren't the warm golden eyes she loved. They were tinted red and soulless. Gone was the man she had given her heart to, replaced by a monster who didn't remember who she was."

Neempo stopped so abruptly, it rattled her. "What happened to him?"

Even with the red wrap covering his eyes, she could feel the grief they held. "He tried to strangle her, blaming her for his death in the first place. So, Hester did what she never thought she was capable of. She picked up the dagger he had given to her to protect herself and slit his throat."

Niabi shook her head and took a step back, refusing to allow one single tear to stream down her face. "How can I believe you? You could be saying this to trick me into sparing your life."

"You know in your heart I am telling you the truth, Your Majesty." Neempo spoke softly, as if he were speaking to a frightened child. "You are new to this world of magic and spells. I know your heart is in the right place when you wish to revive your son, but if you and the Old Witch of Endor succeed in resurrecting Prince Rollo, it won't be the son you lost. It will be a monster that will destroy you."

Images of Rollo flashed in her mind. Rollo taking his first steps. Rollo picking up a weapon for the first time. Rollo smiling, dancing, and riding through the city. She had failed him. She hadn't protected him.

"Enough!" she yelled. Her left hand was engulfed in flames.

"She hasn't taught you to control your fire magic, has she?" He asked, referring to Vilora. Niabi didn't respond. "If you don't control it, it will control you. I can help you if you'll let me."

Niabi gritted her teeth and willed the fire to extinguish. She called for the guards standing outside the doors and instructed them to take Neempo to his cell.

"I will prove you wrong, Sovereign," Niabi hissed as he was led away. "I will bring my son back."

"I hope for your sake, Your Highness, that you're strong enough to face the consequences."

When the doors closed behind them, Niabi let loose every bit of rage that was bubbling beneath her skin. She let loose a high-pitched scream and fire shot out of her hand, blasting against the wall, and leaving a burn mark.

As much as she hated to admit it, the Sovereign was right about one thing: she needed to learn to control the fire, before it consumed her.

CHAPTER 38
CRISPIN

Crispin's elbows rested against the black railing of the ship, eyes fixed on the white stone buildings of Northwind lit up by the full moon and lanterns scattered throughout the city. It was more beautiful than he remembered. Even at night, the city was humming with life. Music, laughter, and dancing filled the streets nearest the port because that's where the Night District was. Taverns, brothels, and inns picked this location for its quick and easy access to sailors from all over Adalore, as well as Her Majesty's soldiers, looking to lose money on booze, women, and gambling.

The crew had camouflaged their ship with different sails and hid anything that screamed pirate from view. Even their clothes had changed to give the appearance of traveling merchants bringing goods to sell and trade in the northern port. Haldane explained with a proud smile that this wasn't their first attempt at blending in to get supplies from large ports around Adalore. Crispin had to admire their cunning ways.

As they docked at the harbor, Crispin sucked in a breath, hoping their bold plan to rescue Neempo would be worth the risk of being recognized. With the hustle and bustle of the harbor and Night District activities, no one even noticed them.

The heavy wooden ramp was extended and landed with a loud thud. The hooded and cloaked Master Penn led her six Keepers off the ship, securing their position, waiting for Crispin, Rahab, and Corwin to join them.

Crispin hadn't been home in twelve years. Hadn't touched the white stones since he escaped his sister's wrath. Then, he was covered in blood and ash. Tonight, he was clothed in black, a hood over his curls to hide his wanted face, and his longsword swinging at his hip. From a forgotten child to a warrior prince.

He was the last to disembark, following Rahab and Corwin closely. He paused before his foot touched Northern soil. He could do this. It wasn't the homecoming he had imagined, but the one an exiled prince and wanted fugitive deserved.

Penn knew from meetings with Neempo, that Oden ran his underground rebellion, The Order, from the basement of his tavern, *The Whispering Fox*. They kept to the shadows on their trek to finding the bar, walking past drunk sailors and soldiers alike without anyone glancing their way.

Weaving through the Night District, they found *The Whispering Fox*, lit up and open for business. And from the looks of it, this tavern was the place to be to have the best time. Women clad in little clothing draped themselves over men with money to burn, whispering sweet nothings into their ears while robbing them blind. Liquor and ale were poured freely and frequently, and the gambling tables were filled with men willing to try their luck.

Crispin had Master Penn and her Keepers stay hidden in the shadows until he, Rahab, and Corwin could locate Oden. He didn't want to risk word reaching the wrong people about the arrival of warriors from The Sisters in Northwind.

The trio slipped inside the tavern, brushing past the crowd of smiling and dazed faces until Crispin spotted a door at the back of the tavern. It was the only other door they could see that wasn't the front door.

Rahab weaved through the bodies until she reached the door. Once she jiggled the knob and realized it was locked, she motioned for Corwin to get to it. He slid a tiny metal pick from his armband and made quick work of the lock. Making sure no one noticed them, the three of them slithered inside and gently closed the door behind them.

The torches fastened to the stone wall lit the wooden staircase that led to the basement. They tiptoed down the stairs, growing more nervous with each unexpected creak of the wood until they found what appeared to be an office with mismatched chairs arranged in a half circle.

He could hear Rahab breathing behind him and his mind flashed back to when she was lying on his chest, their fingers intertwined. Being tangled together felt like the most natural thing in the world to him. He had woken up before she did and he refused to move, fearing she would panic or pretend nothing happened when she realized she had spent the night in his room. But when her eyes fluttered open and she tilted her head to meet his gaze, she did the one thing he didn't expect. She smiled. Her smile warmed his heart, and he desperately wanted to kiss her, but before he could, she rolled on top of him and kissed him first.

"I told you I'd grow on you," Crispin murmured, his lips pressed against hers.

They spent the rest of the morning together until they had to prepare for their arrival.

Now, she was following him closely into the den of The Order's operations, and it made him nervous. He didn't want her to be in harm's way, but if he told her that, she would be more inclined to stab him than listen.

"Where is he?" Rahab walked around the windowless room before flipping through maps and papers chaotically strewn across Oden's desk.

"If you're looking for Oden," a voice boomed from another doorway they missed. "Then you've found him. But unfortunately for you, I'm not alone." He snapped his fingers and a large man with dark hair and a sword pointed at them, stomped down the stairs.

The trio stood still as Crispin put his hands in the air and turned to face Oden. The door the rebel leader had come through had been hidden behind a tapestry. As soon as Oden saw the prince, his face paled.

"We aren't here to hurt you -"

"It's you," Oden interrupted him, his eyes wide. "It's really you."

"Were you expecting us?" Crispin lowered his arms.

Oden took another step toward the prince and clasped his hands. "Nubis, it's him. Our prince has returned."

The giant man standing at the base of the steps sheathed his sword and watched as his leader extended a hand to Crispin.

"I hoped the rumors were true," Oden whispered, teary eyed. "I hoped I would see Bilhah's son again with my own eyes."

Crispin was used to being called the son of Issachar but being referred to as Bilhah's son threw him. "You know who I am?"

"Oh, yes." Oden rifled through the scattered papers on his desk and grabbed two wanted posters with his and Salome's faces. "Your parents were my dearest friends."

Rahab snatched Crispin's wanted poster and studied it with a smirk. She showed it to him and snorted, "Flattering."

"They managed to capture my good side." Crispin teased.

"It's face forward," Rahab's eyebrow arched.

"Exactly. My good side." He flashed her a smile that promised he'd be spending another night with her in his arms.

Her eyes darkened, and his heart nearly stopped beating when she gnawed at her bottom lip. Before he turned his focus back to Oden, he caught her folding the poster and stuffing it into her pocket. First excursion on land in days, and all he wanted to do was crawl back to his cot on the ship to be alone with her.

Oden cleared his throat, drawing the prince's attention. He still had Salome's wanted poster and Crispin reached for it. He hadn't seen his sister in weeks and missing her was an understatement.

"May I keep this?" Crispin asked, eyes still glued to his sister's face. Whoever described his sister to the artist managed to capture the quiet danger in her eyes and the impish smirk of her lips. Every night before he closed his eyes to sleep, he prayed for her and Zophar. Prayed that they would see each other again and soon. Prayed that they wouldn't forget him, even though he had been out of contact for a while.

"Please," Oden motioned for Crispin to pocket the drawing. "Take a seat. Make yourselves comfortable. I assure you, you are safe to speak freely down here. Nubis will guard the door."

"Master Penn and her Keepers are waiting outside. They should be here for this meeting," Crispin said as he claimed the wooden chair behind him. Rahab and Corwin plopped down in a seater built for two.

Oden nodded and Nubis marched upstairs to fetch them. Rahab nudged Corwin with her elbow, and he stood up and followed Oden's henchman.

Once the two men left, Oden smiled at Crispin. "You favor her."

"Who?"

"Your mother." Tears welled in Oden's eyes and Crispin wondered if there was more to the rebel leader's relationship with his mother that he didn't know about. Maybe didn't want to know.

"You knew her well?" Crispin regretted the question as soon as it spilled out of his mouth.

Oden nodded with a sad smile. "When your mother agreed to marry your father, he sent me to bring her to Northwind. We got to know one another on our journey, and she remained my closest friend until her…" he cleared his throat, not wishing to speak about Bilhah's death. "I swore that night, I would do everything I could to rid the White City of your sister. It's taken me twelve years, but our savior sits before me. Your mother would be so proud of you."

It was odd to think of this stranger knowing his mother better than he did, but he nodded in gratitude for his kind words. Before he could ask how Oden managed to elude his sister for twelve years, one of the walls opened revealing a secret passage. Nubis led Corwin, Master Penn, and her six Keepers into the basement.

"Led them through the back entrance," Nubis leaned against the wall at the base of the stairs. "No one noticed them."

"Good," Oden bobbed his head and bowed before Master Penn who seemed to be aware of his movements. She returned the greeting with a slight nod of acknowledgment. "Welcome to Northwind, Master Penn. I am surprised to see you here."

"Then I will assume you haven't heard," Penn ignored his pleasantries and got straight to the point.

"Heard what?"

"The Sovereign Neempo was captured by the Pirate King and brought here as Niabi's prisoner." Penn sat in a velvet high back chair, her six Keepers stationed around the room, ready for any possible altercation.

By the shocked expression on Oden's face, he had clearly not heard. "What could she possibly need the Sovereign for?"

"His heart." Penn stated.

"She's trying to resurrect her son," Crispin explained, "she needed the Heart of the Righteous to invoke the spell."

Oden pinched the bridge of his nose and exhaled a tired sigh. He reclaimed his seat and leaned back, rubbing his eyes. "There have been reports that her Aunt Vilora is the Old Witch of Endor and is now sitting on her small council."

"This we know," Penn's tight-lipped appearance would seem unfriendly to most, but Oden didn't seem to take offense to her harsh responses.

"Did you also know that Niabi seems to have inherited some of her aunt's power?" Oden asked, his fingers pressed together. "Fire magic."

Crispin's eyes nearly popped out of his head. "She has magic?"

"It would seem so," Oden motioned for Nubis to speak.

"The queen has been practicing with the witch for a couple of weeks. It seems the queen didn't know of her abilities until recently." Nubis shifted side to side, clearly uncomfortable with the attention he was getting. "But there has been chatter of the witch preparing for some kind of ritual. I didn't know what for, but I guess it's safe to assume it's for this resurrection spell."

Crispin's head was spinning. Niabi had fire magic? As if she weren't dangerous enough.

"We need to rescue the Sovereign before they carve out his heart," Rahab finally chimed in.

"We will do whatever you need us to do." Oden rose from his seat when the stairs creaked. Nubis unsheathed his sword and the six Keepers stationed around the room clutched their spears tightly. "Ah, Ziggy, we weren't expecting you tonight."

Ziggy stopped half-way down the steps and clutched her shawl tighter around her shoulders. "Is everything alright?" she flashed a hesitant smile.

Crispin rose to his feet and knew she recognized him when her pouty mouth fell open. "The prince. You found him?" Her blue eyes darted toward Oden who shook his head.

"He found us."

She bowed but Crispin motioned for her to stand back up. "Your name is Ziggy?"

Ziggy nodded, her eyes refusing to meet his gaze. "Yes, Your Highness."

Rahab stifled a giggle at Crispin being referred to as Your Highness.

"It's Crispin," he said with a smile.

Ziggy slowly looked up at him, "Crispin." It felt odd hearing his name roll off her tongue.

"Is there a reason for your late visit?" Oden asked, irritation clear in his tone.

Ziggy snapped out of her stunned stupor and rushed forward, sitting in the wooden chair that Crispin offered. The prince stood behind the two-seat lounge and rested his elbows on the cushion behind Rahab.

"It's about Lord Gershom." Ziggy glanced at the newcomers and waited for Oden to give her permission to speak before continuing. "He had an unexpected visitor the other night. He looked like he was from Numbio."

"From Numbio?" Crispin asked, his interest piqued. "Did you get his name?"

Ziggy nervously bobbed her head. "Gershom called him Memucan. I don't know who he is, but they mentioned something about a plan to overthrow Queen Niabi and the King of Numbio."

"Memucan is here?" Crispin straightened, his hand tickling the hilt of his sword. "Is he in the White Keep?"

"You know him?" Oden's brows furrowed.

"I met him in Numbio. He is King Osiris' advisor." Crispin saw the old man's weathered and wicked face flash before his eyes and he was itching to slit the traitor's throat. "Is he in the White Keep?" He repeated his question, directing it at Ziggy.

"No," she shook her head. "Gershom asked me to find him a room at one of the local inns. He wants Memucan to hide until he is ready to strike."

Crispin's eyes darted to Oden. "We need a plan to rescue Neempo. But first," he looked at Ziggy as she twisted the folds of her skirt with anxious fingers, "I need you to show me where Memucan is."

"Are you going to kill him?" Master Penn asked, her tone ripe with excitement.

"Once I get some answers from him, yes." Crispin didn't try to hide that his mission was to slit Memucan's throat from ear to ear. He had suspected the sandstorm was dark magic and there was only one person who hated Crispin enough to attempt risking discovery to bury him.

"What about Gershom?" Ziggy asked, her cheeks were flushed. "If Memucan ends up dead, he might suspect I had something to do with it."

The room stilled and Crispin reclined against the wall, deep in thought. This was an underground rebellion. Of course, they were spies. They put their lives on the line daily for information to further his ascent to the throne, for his sister's ultimate end.

But he couldn't allow Memucan to live. If he had a hand in the sandstorm, he had blood on his hands. And worse, if he was truly allied with Gershom, he betrayed his king and people. He had betrayed the alliance King Osiris had made with him. Memucan had to be dealt with. Quickly and quietly.

"Does he have soldiers watching over him?" Crispin asked, an idea forming in his mind.

"A handful of Gershom's personal guards are stationed outside the front door, strategically placed as to not draw too much attention." Ziggy seemed rattled so Crispin approached her and knelt in front of her.

"I know you're scared," Crispin grabbed her hand and squeezed it gently. "But I can't let him live. There are too many lives at stake."

"What about my life?" Ziggy's voice cracked.

"We can protect you," Crispin glanced over at Rahab, and she nodded, already knowing what he was going to ask her. "We can get you to safety."

Ziggy's face paled. "You want me to leave with you?"

"Leave?" Oden was surprised. "But you've finally come home. Are you not going to stay?"

"I came here for Neempo." Crispin rose to face Oden. "Once we rescue him, I will have other matters that require my immediate attention."

"More pressing than reclaiming your ancestors' throne?" Oden's smooth voice had more of a bite to it.

"I have given my word to help someone," Crispin stood his ground, sounding more like a king than a fugitive. "When I return, it won't include me slinking in the shadows. I'll have an army at my back and a crown to claim at my front. But if you and I are going to have dealings with one another," he took a breath, steadying his voice, "then you will need to follow my lead."

Oden's shoulders tensed and his mouth trembled, fire clearly raging inside him, as well. "I am here to serve, Prince."

Rahab rose from her seat, "Where's Memucan staying?"

Ziggy had tears in her eyes and Nubis moved to rest his massive hand on her petite shoulder. "You swear you can protect me?"

"Be aboard our ship by tomorrow night," Rahab bobbed her head to reassure the red-headed escort of Crispin's promise. "You'll be out of Gershom's reach when we set sail."

Nubis whispered something in Ziggy's ear that Crispin didn't catch, but whatever it was, seemed to settle her.

"Memucan is staying at *The Black Lotus*," Ziggy said. "I can take you there."

Crispin flashed her a reassuring smile before turning to Master Penn. "I'll leave the rescue planning to you and Oden. I'll be back as soon as I've finished with the Numbio."

Master Penn bowed her head a smidge before turning her attention to Oden. "I believe you owe the Sovereign a favor."

CHAPTER 39

SALOME

Salome strolled into the Great Hall where the Festival of the Forbidden Fruit had been held. Without the floating lights, decorations, music, and mingling couples, it was just another ordinary room. It was still a beautiful space, but the magic of the other night was just that. Magic.

She heard Jinn's voice echo in the empty hall before she saw him.

"Rendezvousing where we first met," he cooed. "Sweet."

Salome turned in a full circle looking around the three-story room. The moonlight poured in through the round hole in the ceiling and made the space sparkle. She spotted him resting his elbows against the railing on the third-floor balcony: the exact spot they first met.

"You seem to have a flair for the dramatic." She climbed the rounding stairs to join him. "Was it really necessary for me to climb all the way up here?"

Jinn turned his back to recline lazily against the railing and shrugged. "When you said to meet you here, I figured you wanted to have a redo of the Festival of the Forbidden Fruit."

"Why, so you can make another bad first impression?" she snorted as she made it to the third floor. "I wanted to meet here because it's private and no one normally comes in here."

Jinn wiggled his eyebrows, "Cozy."

Salome rolled her eyes and stood in front of him, arms crossed over her chest.

"You know," Jinn straightened to his full height and stared down at Salome, "we could have had this private conversation in your chambers."

"Or we could have had this conversation mentally." She cocked her head to the side and smirked.

Jinn laughed and held his hands in the air, signifying his surrender. "What do you need to talk about?"

She scratched her lips, hating herself for loving the sound of his laugh. "Are you still leaving tomorrow night?"

Jinn crossed his arms, "Is this your way of saying you're going to miss me?"

Salome scrunched her nose. "Hardly." She glimpsed around the room to make sure they were still alone. "What would you say, if I asked for passage to the Mainland?"

Jinn's brows lifted, clearly surprised by her request. "You want to come with me?" His voice was soft, expectant.

A tinge of guilt surged through her heart. "Not all the way to Sakurai. Just to where the Bone Mountains and the sea meet. I have business there."

Jinn nodded with a tight-lipped smile. "Whatever you want or need that is within my power to give, is yours."

Salome reached for his hand and squeezed it. "Thank you."

Jinn's golden-brown eyes were glued to hers. "I suppose you haven't considered my proposal?"

Salome didn't want any potential eavesdroppers to hear, so she extended the mental bridge, and said, *"I need more time."*

"Are you afraid to say that aloud because you don't want anyone to hear us or because you don't want to admit to being attracted to me?" His eyes danced in mischievous delight.

Salome's eyes widened and her mouth shot open to deny it, but she snapped her lips closed, and continued their mental conversation. *"You flatter yourself."*

"At least, I'm honest with myself."

She rested her hands on her hips, *"And I'm not honest?"*

Jinn closed the gap between them and smiled down at her. *"Your eyes betray you."*

Salome refused to shrink back and stood her ground. *"What do you mean?"*

"You tell me not to look at you a certain way, but you forget I can see how you look at me, too." His fingers brushed against hers. *"I'm a patient man, Salome, not a stupid one. I know when a woman wants me."*

"Then perhaps, you should ask one of them to be your wife," she narrowed her eyes. *"I'm not looking at you any different than other men."*

"Liar." His gaze drifted to her lips.

Without realizing it, Salome closed her eyes and tilted her head up to him but stopped when she heard him softly chuckle. *"What?"*

"You leaned."

"So?" She snorted defensively.

"I told you, your eyes betray you, and now your body."

Salome took a step back from him, gritting her teeth, despising the itch in her hands to run the tips of her fingers along his perfectly chiseled jaw. *"You're delusional."*

Jinn shrugged, tucking his hands in his pockets. *"And you're in denial."*

"Since you're so determined for us to be honest. Why don't you tell me about your magic?" She knew it was a low blow, but she couldn't help but throw the secrecy of his power in his face. If he was going to accuse her of being dishonest and in denial, then she would gladly remind him that he was a hypocrite.

Jinn twirled one of her curls between his index finger and thumb. *"A secret for a secret."*

She was taken aback by his response. She didn't really think he would agree to tell her. And now, she was afraid of what he might want to know about her.

"Fine. But you go first. Tell me about your magic."

He stepped away from her. *"I think it's better if I show you."*

Salome nodded, but as hard as she tried to keep her expression neutral, anxiety was written all over her face.

"Don't be scared."

And then Jinn vanished.

Salome flinched. She stuck her hand out, but she didn't feel him. *"Where did you go?"*

"I'm right here."

She whipped around to see him leaning against the wall, one ankle crossed over the other, hands in his pockets.

"You're a Cloaker?"

"Does that frighten you?" He cocked his head to the side. She could see the desperation for her to accept him flashing in his eyes.

"I'm not afraid of you." Salome meant it.

"Don't worry," Jinn pushed up and slowly walked toward her. "I don't sneak into your room at night to watch you sleep."

"I wasn't worried, but now I am." She smiled, stifling a laugh.

"That's the first real smile I've gotten from you." Jinn swiped loose hair from her face and tucked it behind her ear. "You have a beautiful smile."

"A secret for a secret." Salome's gaze dropped. Looking him in the eye made her feel as if he could see right through her.

"Are you attracted to me?"

Why did he have to ask her that question? She couldn't lie to him. And even if she wanted to, she was positive her face had already given her away.

Salome sighed. *Yes."*

"Now was that so hard to admit?" Jinn whispered aloud against her ear sending a shiver down her spine.

For the first time in a long time, she was lost for words.

Jinn winked, *"Your secret is safe with me."*

His eyes flicked past Salome's shoulder and when she turned around to see who he was looking at, she saw Kai standing on the landing of the second floor. He nodded in understanding. "I'll expect you and your company at the docks tomorrow night," he said with a princely tone.

"Why the rush?" One of her eyebrows arched.

Jinn flashed a wicked smile and thumbed her chin. "Can't get enough of me, can you?"

Salome pursed her lips and cocked her head to the side. He laughed and it felt like a warm hug.

"Since this was supposed to be a private meeting," he said, "I best be off before your Qata Vishna bodyguards see us together."

He pecked a kiss on Salome's cheek as he passed her. He trotted down the stairs where Kai was waiting. As soon as they left, Seraphina and Rosalina walked in.

"Princess Salome?" Rosalina looked around until she spotted Salome descending the stairs.

"What is it?"

"It's Marina." Salome could hear Seraphina's gulp from the second floor.

"What about Marina?" Salome rushed down the last set of steps.

"She escaped," Seraphina continued, "and Mika took her place."

Salome stopped dead in her tracks. "What do you mean Mika took her place?"

"From what Queen Zara said, Mika helped Marina escape and in accordance with our laws," Rosalina quickly explained, "a life may be given in place of another's, so long as they accept the consequences."

Salome's heart leapt to her throat. "They're going to execute Mika in Marina's place?"

The twins exchanged a quick glance and Salome knew what that look meant.

CHAPTER 40
CRISPIN

As promised, Ziggy led Crispin and Rahab *to The Black Lotus,* the three-story inn where Memucan was staying. The red-head spy's intel checked out when they saw a handful of Gershom's personal guards scattered around the front entrance attempting to blend in with the patrons of the narrow white cobblestone streets. Crispin knew exactly who was on duty by the simple fact that they were the only ones not drinking or chatting up the working women.

"How many are there?" Rahab asked, crouched behind him. They were a block away from *The Black Lotus* and Crispin was peeking around the corner of a bakery that was closed for the evening.

"I counted five." Crispin whispered and turned his attention to Ziggy who was standing a few feet behind Rahab, her arms hugging her torso. "Ziggy." Her frightened eyes darted to meet his. "What room is he in?"

Ziggy brushed the tight curls from her face. "He's on the third floor. Room six."

Crispin nodded. "Thank you, Ziggy. We'll take it from here if you want to go home." She seemed relieved he was letting her go, but he could sense a reluctance too.

"I know it was difficult for you to bring us here, but you've done your job." Crispin shot her a reassuring smile. "Now, it's time for us to do ours."

Ziggy bobbed her head, a silent thank you for not judging her for being fearful, and she stalked back into the dark alleys of Northwind. His eyes rested on Rahab, but she wasn't looking at him. Her gaze was fixed on the sloped roof of *The Black Lotus*.

"We have two options," she started, and Crispin noted her tone was that of a First Mate and not the woman who had curled up to him the night before. "Either we pick the guards off one by one and go in the front door or," her eyes twinkled when they met his, "we go up."

Crispin glanced around the corner again, spying the two guards at the front entrance and all the people walking in and out of the inns, brothels, and taverns on this street, and he shook his head. Too many witnesses. Messy. He looked up at the copper shingle rooftop and turned to face Rahab.

"Not as high as The Sisters," he flashed a grin. "You up for it?"

Her smile was wicked when she said, "Race you to the top."

Crispin didn't know why he let Rahab beat him to the top of *The Black Lotus*, but when she shot him a look over her shoulder, he stopped where he stood. The moonlight hit her icy blue tresses giving her the appearance of an assassin goddess. The unobstructed view of the starry sky above them, twinkling around her seated frame, stole his breath.

"What?" she asked, stretching her legs in front of her.

Crispin slowly approached her on soft feet, not wanting to alert anyone in the rooms below them of their presence. "Are you just as lethal on dry land as you are on the sea?"

She wiggled her eyebrows, "You concerned about me?"

He sat beside her, watching the people in the streets start to stumble their way back to their rented rooms or apartments as the taverns closed a few hours before dawn. "Have you done anything like this before?"

"Sit on a rooftop waiting to assassinate a foreign dignitary? Not recently," she chuckled.

"I meant," he cleared his throat, "have you killed a man before?"

Rahab sighed, bringing one of her knees to her chest, resting her chin on top. "My first kill was at sixteen. Shortly after recovering and joining the *Shadow of Death* crew, our ship was attacked by a rival captain with a vendetta against Haldane." She shrugged, the lights in the city flickering off one by one. "I didn't even know how to wield a weapon. I'd only had a few lessons with Leeondris before Rourke's crew tried to kill us and take our loot.

"Leeondris gave me one of his knives and told me to stay in my room until he came back. Before he made it back, one of Rourke's men kicked in my door. I could see it in his eyes. He was going to kill me but only after he had his fun. I had a choice. I could kill him, or he could kill me. So, I allowed him to get close enough, letting him think I was too afraid to fight back, and as soon as his sticky fingers snatched my wrist and pulled me close, I plunged the dagger deep into his heart. I watched the life leave his eyes and I swore that day, no one would touch me without my permission again."

Crispin soaked in every word she spoke, and a fire raged deep within his soul. She had seen and experienced horrors and atrocities he couldn't even begin to imagine. He had lost his family. He had lost his home. But he had never feared being overpowered or harmed in unspeakable ways.

"What happened to Rourke?" It was all he could ask to steady the anger pulsating through his body.

Rahab flashed a sinister grin and purred, "We stuffed the survivors in burlap sacks, tied weights around their necks, and let them sink to the bottom of the Obsidian Sea."

"Good."

"And you?" She leaned back and placed her palms behind her head. "Have you killed before?"

Crispin bobbed his head as he reclined, looking up into the night sky and seeing

Orion staring back at him. "I killed Shadows that invaded the Tree House Forest and Wagura in the Caverns of the Undead."

"You were in the Caverns of the Undead?" Her voice cracked. He couldn't tell if she was frightened or impressed. "What do they look like?"

"They are the most horrifying creatures I have ever laid eyes on." He wiped the invisible green Wagura blood from his hands, their pale bony figures flashing before his eyes. He hoped Zophar and Heru had led the Numbio out of there. Hoped they were well on their way to Oakenshire to meet up with Salome.

Crispin realized it was quiet and risked a glance over the lip of the roof to see if Gershom's guards were still outside the front door. To his frustration, they were. Now without having to mingle with the crowd, they took up their positions for the rest of the night. Two at the front door, two at the back door, and one that patrolled around the inn at a steady pace.

"Unless we guess which window is Memucan's, we're going to have to use one of the entrances." Crispin didn't want to risk drawing the guards' attention if they entered the wrong room and added screaming civilians to the mix. "We're going to have to take them out."

By the grin stretched across Rahab's face, it looked like she had been waiting for him to come to the same conclusion. "Let the games begin."

They were three stories up. Too high for them to jump and land without injury. But Rahab, being the cunning pirate she was, brought a few supplies buried in her leather satchel.

"You just carry rope with you?" Crispin asked as she tossed him a line.

"Came in handy tonight, didn't it?" Rahab tied her end of the rope around her waist and knotted it. "Alright, when the patrolman passes by the two guards in the back, you'll lower me and let me do the rest."

"Wait, wait, wait." He shook his head with a scowl. "You expect me to lower you down there?"

Rahab snatched the ruby dagger from her hip and nodded. "Headfirst."

"Rahab."

"Crispin." She cocked her head to the side, batting her eyes slowly.

Crispin pinched the bridge of his nose. She was unrelenting. If he didn't lower her, she was liable to tie the end of the rope she'd trusted him with around the chimney and lower herself. "After you kill them, do you want me to pull you up?"

"I'll untie myself for you to climb down." She laid on her belly, overlooking the two guards at the back door. "We'll deal with the other three together."

"And why am I not the one going first?" He knelt beside her after he knotted the rope around the chimney, and she flicked her eyes up at him.

She hesitated, "You weigh too much?"

"Is that a question?" Crispin let out a low chuckle.

"Truthfully," she grinned, speaking to him in a sweet voice meant for babies, "I wouldn't want you messing up that pretty face, Your Majesty."

Crispin wasn't sure if he wanted to push her off the roof or slam his lips against hers, so instead, he leaned back, braced his feet against the gutters, and nodded for her to go. "Go, before I push you off."

"Ah, you'd miss me too much."

"Using my lines?"

Rahab winked before sliding over the edge. He wanted to watch her, to make sure she was alright, but he let the rope gently slip through his fingers as he steadied her descent. He knew she had made it when he heard two quick slices, muffled groans, and two bodies thudding to the ground. When she untied herself, Crispin repelled down the side of the white stone inn until he reached her at the bottom. His eyes darted to the two guards with slits across their throats.

"That was quick." Crispin was both impressed and terrified. Rahab had made quick work of them, leaving little evidence of the assassins having been there.

She propped the guards against the wall and once she was done setting the scene, it looked as if they had fallen asleep from a long drunken night. "What did you expect me to do? Ask them if they wanted to grab a drink?"

Crispin put a finger to his lips, signaling her to be quiet. He heard footsteps approaching at a steady clip. The patrolman was coming. Backing against the end of the building, Crispin unsheathed the dagger Corwin had given him and waited. His heart was racing. The prince had killed in combat, but he had never lurked in the darkness waiting for unsuspecting prey. There was no room for hesitation. Any audible warning would tip off the two guards in the front and that risked Memucan slipping through his fingers. That was not an option.

Taking a deep breath, Crispin listened for the footsteps that grew louder as they neared. As soon as the soldier turned the corner, Crispin clamped a hand over his mouth, slit his throat, and dragged his body toward the other guards.

"Three down," she whispered. "Do we go for the other two? Or take our chances going for Memucan through the back door?"

Crispin's heart was lumped in his throat. The gravity of what he had done weighed on him, but they didn't have time for him to dwell on the blood staining his hands. He pointed at the back door. "Let's worry about the other two guards later."

For once, Rahab didn't argue with him. She faced the door and turned the knob. Luckily it was unlocked, and they slipped inside. There was a long hallway that spanned from the back door to the front door. As quietly as possible, they crept down the corridor until they reached an unattended front desk. The clerk had stepped away making it simple to reach the staircase. They climbed the spiral staircase until they landed on the top floor.

"Room six," Crispin muttered, his eyes darting door to door. Memucan's room was at the end of the hall.

Knives drawn; the duo tip-toed to the Numbio's door. Rahab borrowed Corwin's lock pick since he was told to stay with Master Penn and keep his eyes and ears open on Crispin's behalf. Crispin could have sworn Rahab picked the lock faster than Corwin had at *The Whispering Fox*.

She nodded and Crispin quietly turned the brass knob, opening the door. Slithering inside the dark room, Crispin saw Memucan asleep in the opulent four post bed. The moonlight poured into the best room the inn had to offer and spotlighted the withering advisor wrapped in satin sheets. Crispin put the tip of his dagger against Memucan's throat and watched his eyes flicker open.

"You." Memucan hissed, the flash of fear in his face was gone and malice replaced it. "I had hoped you died in that sandstorm."

"Sorry to disappoint," Crispin crinkled his nose and poked the knife into Memucan's neck, drawing blood. "I have a few questions and you're going to answer them."

"And if I don't?" Memucan asked with a wicked smirk. "Are you going to kill me?"

Crispin was planning to kill him whether he answered his questions or not, but he said, "Maybe I'll just send you back to Numbio for Osiris to deal with you."

A spark lit in Memucan's face, but Crispin wasn't sure what the old man was thinking. "Ask your questions, *Prince*." The way he said prince was like he'd smelled something rotten, and it didn't sit well with Crispin.

"You sent that sandstorm," Crispin accused rather than asked, "with black magic."

Memucan flashed a sinister grin. "A simple incantation."

"Your people lost their lives -"

"Spare me your self-righteous speech," Memucan spat with a snake like hiss. "Their lives mean nothing to me."

That caught Crispin off-guard. "Then why rule them?"

Memucan let out a low chuckle, "I don't intend to rule them. I intend to enslave them. Osiris, Heru… they are weak. Control. Power. Fear. That's what makes a true king. With Gershom reigning in the North and me reigning in the South, we could make all of Adalore bend to our will."

"Was I your intended target? Or was it Heru?" Crispin had to know if his friend was still in danger.

"Oh, don't worry," Memucan bared his teeth, "if the prince managed to survive the Wagura, my servant will finish the job."

"Your servant?"

"You're too late. Heru's death is already set."

Crispin heard a low whistle from the other side of the bedroom door and knew Rahab was warning him of the guards' activity. He didn't have much time before he'd have to clear out of the inn.

"You think you can kill me?" Memucan slowly rose from lying on his back to a seated position, Crispin's hand tightened on the hilt of his blade, holding it against his throat. "You do not have what it takes to be a man wielding great power. You are nothing. You are no one. You will never be -"

Crispin slid the blade across Memucan's throat like a hot knife through butter. He didn't need to hear another word ooze from his crusty lips. Rahab rapped on the door before entering.

"We have to go," she quietly shut it behind her. "They must have found their friends and I heard footsteps coming up the stairs."

Crispin opened the window and motioned for Rahab to slip out. As he was about to follow her, he noticed a black book sitting on Memucan's nightstand. He grabbed it, tucked it under his arm, and ducked out the window.

As Crispin and Rahab made their way down the dark alleyways of the Night District, the alarm of the soldiers who found Memucan's body resounded behind them. Crispin couldn't help the smile of satisfaction that stretched across his face. One enemy was dead, but he knew there were plenty left to face.

CHAPTER 41

SALOME

Salome wished Harbona hadn't left. She needed his guidance on how to save Mika. Rubbing a finger over her drying lips, Salome silently paced around her chambers, deep in thought. Adonijah and Cato had offered several suggestions but none of them would work. And if they were caught, they'd be tossed into the dungeons alongside Mika.

"Could you appeal to your Aunt Zara?" Adonijah was leaning against the wall.

Salome shook her head. "Damaris has been with Zara all night begging for Mika's life to be spared."

"She would execute her daughter for a crime she didn't commit?" Cato had become a stress eater and had eaten both his dinner and Salome's.

"Mika took Marina's place. Meaning Mika accepted Marina's punishment." Salome ran fingers through her hair. "It's legal according to Myridian law."

"Surely, Queen Zara could make an exception," Cato insisted, picking at his teeth with his fork. "She could show mercy, grant her a pardon?"

"Zara was just crowned queen after her mother's assassination," Adonijah chimed in. "She can't afford to look weak in her people's eyes, even to spare her daughter."

"It's too bad Mika can't just fly out of here." Cato huffed, throwing his utensil on his empty plate. He scratched his stomach and pointed at the last remaining wedge of cheese. "Is anyone going to eat that?"

"What did you just say?" Salome turned around to face him, excitement strumming through her body.

Cato's eyes widened; his mouth was filled with cheese. "I asked if anyone was going to eat this."

"No," she waved her hand dismissively. "Before that. What did you say about flying?"

Cato swallowed. "I said it's too bad Mika can't fly out of here."

"That's it!" Salome clapped her hands. "Cato, you're a genius!"

Cato and Adonijah exchanged a look before Cato whispered, slightly terrified, "Can you fly?"

"No," she planted her hands on her hips, her mind racing, "but there is a way we can get Mika out of the Isles of Myr unseen."

Adonijah stepped into the light, arms crossed over his chest. Intrigued, he asked, "How do you propose we do that?"

"I can ask Jinn to get his ship ready to sail tonight, instead of tomorrow. If we can get Mika aboard, she will be safe and on her way to the Mainland."

Adonijah's nostrils flared when Salome mentioned Jinn's name. "Let's say he agrees," he sighed in irritation. "How are we supposed to get her out of that tower," he pointed toward the Tower Dungeon on the opposite side of the Scarlett Citadel, "and past all the Qata Vishna unnoticed?"

"What if you ask Jinn and someone overhears you talking about helping Mika escape?" Cato brought up a valid point. They were thinking about committing an act of treason. "What if Jinn doesn't agree to help and he tells the queen?"

"Jinn wouldn't betray us." Salome countered, surprised at how she defended him.

"Forgive us," Adonijah's tone was icy, "if we do not agree."

She kicked her foot aimlessly in front of her, eyes glued to the floor. She could feel Adonijah's frigid glare.

"You might not trust him, but I do." She held up a hand before either of them could protest. "And no one would overhear us -"

"But anyone could -"

She cut Cato off, "They wouldn't overhear us because Jinn and I can communicate with just thoughts."

"Excuse me?" Cato tilted his head, mouth agape.

"My magic is more than communicating with the dead and having visions of the past." She took a deep breath and met Adonijah's line of sight. "I can have a conversation mind-to-mind with people I share a bond with."

Adonijah seemed to catch on immediately by the frown that creased his brow. Cato needed some clarification.

"Could you talk to me that way?" Cato asked, waving a hand around his head. "With our minds?"

"No," she shook her head, rubbing the nape of her neck. "We need to share a bond of either magic or marriage to mentally speak to one another. Damaris said it's like extending a bridge to connect me to someone else."

"So, Damaris knows?" Adonijah said with a hint of bitterness.

Salome bobbed her head, wrapping her arms around herself. "I can talk to her mentally, too."

"You share this bond with Jinn and Damaris?" Adonijah looked like he could spit fire and Salome's instinct was to shrink back but she forced herself to stay put.

"Yes. Through our magic."

"Jinn has magic?" Cato nearly shouted in excitement. "Wait, does he talk to trees too?"

"I don't talk to tre…" Salome took a deep breath and stroked her palms across her eyes. "Jinn is a cloaker."

"So, he has cool magic." Cato seemed giddy. Impressed would be an understatement.

"I have cool magic," Salome snorted, furrowing her brows.

"Of course, you do." Cato bobbed his head and winked. "How else would we know what the trees have to say?" he snickered.

"You're as irritating as Crispin."

As soon as she mentioned her brother, she felt a lump in her throat. She tried to use the mental bond with him. She had called out to him several times that afternoon, but he never answered. Damaris asked before if he had magical abilities, but as far as she knew, he didn't. If he could see her now, he would be the first person to crack jokes like Cato. Crispin and Cato were probably long-lost brothers. The pranking, the jokes, the constant snacking. She was looking forward to the day they met.

Salome realized by how Cato was staring at her, she had been lost in thought. She plastered a smile on her face, so they wouldn't be able to tell something was bothering her.

"So, are we in agreement?" Salome's gaze drifted from Cato to Adonijah. "We ask Jinn to use his magic to get Mika out of the Tower Dungeon and onto his ship?"

Adonijah shoved his hands into his pockets, refusing to make eye contact. He bobbed his head silently. That was the most enthusiasm she was going to get from him, so she didn't press her luck by arguing.

Cato shrugged his shoulders. "You're in charge. If you say that's the plan, then that's the plan."

"Then I'll reach out to him."

"You do that." Adonijah marched past her to sit on the balcony, lit his pipe, and kicked his feet up on the iron railing.

It was apparent he was furious, but Salome would deal with one problem at a time. Whether he liked it or not, they needed Jinn's help. She plopped onto one of the pillow-infested couches and crossed her legs to get comfortable. With Cato snacking loudly in the room, she closed her eyes to focus.

"I need to ask for a favor." Salome reached out to Jinn.

"Anything."

Her heart was racing. This was going to be one big favor and she was prepared for him to tell her no. *"Before I tell you what it is, I want you to know that if we are caught, we could be tossed into Zara's dungeons."*

Jinn hummed a laugh. *"Sounds like fun. What are we doing?"*

"Could your ship be ready to sail tonight if need be?"

"It's possible, yes. But I fail to see how that could land us in any trouble."

Salome took a deep breath. There was no going back. *"Your magic. Could you cloak more than one person?"*

"How many people are we talking about?"

"You, me," she paused, *"and Mika."*

Salome braced herself when he didn't immediately respond. *"Now, I see how this could land us in Zara's dungeons."*

"You don't have to do this -"

"And let you have all the fun smuggling a fugitive?" He interrupted with a warm chuckle. *"Not a chance."*

"You'll help me get her out?"

"Why do you sound so surprised?" Jinn's voice was silky and danced around her

head. *"I already told you, whatever you want or need that is within my power to give, is yours."*

"I guess I owe you a favor now."

"Spending time with you is all I want."

Salome couldn't help the smile that inched across her face.

"Wow," he purred. *"Two smiles in one day. Must mean you don't hate me."*

She arched an eyebrow, *"How did you know I smiled?"*

"I could sense it."

"More like a lucky guess," she snorted.

"Don't need luck."

Salome could sense him grinning and it made her heart skip a beat.

"Meet me in an hour in the Paraiso Gardens," Jinn instructed. *"I'll leave my watchdog, if you leave yours."*

Salome could picture those golden-brown eyes of his dancing in delight, wiggling his jet-black eyebrows. She refused to give him the satisfaction of sensing her smile, so she cleared her throat and remained tight lipped.

"He's not my watchdog. And if you think he's going to let me wander around that late without back up, you're not as smart as you think you are."

Jinn laughed softly. *"It was worth a shot."*

When Salome opened her eyes, her gaze met Cato's. He was perched in a chair directly across from her, clutching his legs to his chest, watching her intensely.

Salome scrunched her nose. "Can I help you?"

"So, you did it? You did the mind talking thing?" Cato motioned around his head.

"Yes," she smirked, "I did the mind thing." She stood up and glanced toward the balcony. Adonijah hadn't moved. "Was he watching me?"

Cato shook his head. "He didn't seem too interested."

"He's upset with me." Salome rubbed her palms up and down her face.

"Can you blame him?" Cato rested his feet on the floor and snatched some dates from a bowl on the table next to him. "He likes you, you know."

She nodded and cracked her neck. "I should go talk to him."

Cato tossed a date in his mouth. "If you need me, don't. I'll be stepping out for a bit."

"Well, aren't you smitten?" Salome caught the date he threw up in the air and popped it in her mouth.

"Hey!" Cato shook his head trying not to grin. "I guess she's not as scary as I thought she would be."

"Oh, Seraphina is scary. Don't let her fool you."

Cato's eyes widened. He scratched his short cropped, white hair nervously.

"Then again, all women are scary." Salome leaned over and planted a kiss on his forehead. "Have fun."

"Don't kill each other," he called after her.

"I make no promises." She winked.

Adonijah was quietly smoking his pipe. His legs were still stretched out, heels linked to the balcony railing. Salome leaned against the archway, crossing her arms across her chest.

"Is it alright if I join you?"

Adonijah motioned to the seat opposite him, and she sunk into the lounge chair. "All set?" he asked without looking over at her.

She bobbed her head, "We're supposed to meet him in the Paraiso Gardens in one hour."

"Alright," he exhaled a ring of smoke and watched it float away.

The warm ocean breeze wafted Salome's hair in front of her face. She peeled it back and noticed he still hadn't looked at her. "Out with it."

"Out with what?" His gaze was glued on the ships docked in the harbor.

"You're angry." She didn't tip-toe around the issue. "Is this about asking Jinn for his help?"

Adonijah retracted his feet and planted them firmly on the floor. He rested his elbows on his knees and met Salome's awaiting gaze. "Do you trust me?"

"Yes," she smiled, "I do."

"Then why keep your magic, this bond between you and him, a secret from me?"

Salome looked deep into his eyes and wished she could read what was running through his mind. If the pained expression was any indication of what he was feeling, he was not angry. He was wounded. And that was worse.

"I was still trying to figure everything out."

Adonijah rubbed his hands together and shook his head. "That's not what I asked, Salome."

She sighed and straightened her legs. "If I had told you the second I realized I could talk to Jinn with my thoughts, would you have been alright with that?"

Adonijah wiped his brow, gnawing at his bottom lip.

"I didn't tell you because I thought you would be so angry you would discourage me from using my magic anymore."

He ran his fingers through his hair and clicked his tongue. "You like him."

Not a question. An accusation.

"He's not a bad person."

"Please don't act like you don't know what I'm talking about." Adonijah hopped up from his seat and rested his elbows on the railing. "Do you like him?" he whispered, not looking at her.

She joined him at the railing but couldn't look him in the eye. "I would be lying if I told you I didn't like him."

Adonijah nodded. "At least you admitted it."

Salome reached for his arm, "Adonijah -"

He pulled his forearm away before she could grab him. Squaring his shoulders to her, he asked, "So, where does that leave us?"

She mirrored his body position and stroked her fingers down his face. "I care for you, Adonijah. I would die for you if it came down to it." She rested her hand on his chest. "But a war is coming. A war where I will be forced to make difficult decisions for the good of my family, my people, and my allies. You asked if I was considering his proposal. Yes, I am. I can't win a war without an army."

"Crispin could gather an army."

"And if he doesn't?"

Adonijah placed his hand on top of hers and she swore she could feel his heart breaking underneath her fingertips. "We can find another way."

Salome shook her head, "I am being realistic. I might not act like most princesses, but when it comes down to it, it's about power. I have the power to ensure we have a chance at defeating Niabi."

"Would that make you happy?" he whispered, and she felt her own heart shatter.

"What?"

"Offering yourself up to him, so he funds a war to reclaim your home? A home you won't be able to live once you marry him, because you will be expected to dwell in Sakurai. A home where your brother and his descendants will rule, and your name will be forgotten over time." Adonijah caressed her cheek, swiping flyaway hair from her face. "Would that make you happy?"

"You don't get it."

"Why?" he snorted as she stepped away from him. "Because I'm not a prince?"

"You don't have to carry the burden I do," she whipped around, eyes filled with fury. "People are going to die. With the Eastern army, maybe some of those lives can be saved. I can't bear to think about the dead stretched across the battlefield. To have their deaths haunting me for the rest of my life."

"War is ugly, Salome," he rooted his hands on his hips, trying his best to restrain himself from shouting. "No matter what you do, if Death has called them, she will take them."

"I have to try. If I don't, I don't think I could live with myself."

Adonijah froze in place. He looked like he'd been slapped across the face. "It sounds like you've already made your decision."

Tears pricked at her eyes. "That's not fair," she rasped.

Adonijah swept her up in his arms, wiping the tears that slid down her cheeks with his thumbs. He tilted her chin up and she met his gaze. "I want you, Salome. All of you. But I can't share you with him."

"I care for you," she said as his hand caressed her face. "I wish I could say I've made a decision on what to do, but until this war is over, I don't have the luxury of burning bridges."

Adonijah cupped her jaw. "No matter what happens. I will fight, live, and die by your side."

"No matter what happens," she inhaled to keep from sobbing in his arms. "I will fight, live, and die by your side."

CHAPTER 42
HARBONA

As *The Golden Rose* approached the glittering harbor of Caelestis, Harbona breathed in the sight of his city, his once home, with a sad smile. It had been over a thousand years since his banishment, and the sweet hillside breeze filled him with the peace and warmth Caelestis was known for. Though it was technically no longer his home, being back made him feel whole.

Diron, the captain of the ship, stood by Harbona's side with his arms folded over his chest. "Should we be expecting the Ethereals to greet us or the Bellators?"

Harbona had nearly a week to mull over that question and he still wasn't sure which sect of Immortals would be at the dock when they arrived. Ideally, his own sect, the Ethereals would be there to accompany him from the ship. But if his parents, the Eldaar, had any say in the matter, the Bellators would be there instead.

While the scholarly and graceful Ethereals were known for their platinum blonde hair, grey eyes, fair skin, pointy ears, and tall, lean physiques, the Bellators were the opposite. They were gold armor wearing warriors with muscular bronze bodies, golden eyes, dark hair, and birdlike, white feathered wings that made them lethal in battle.

Harbona didn't know if any of the Bellators he knew before his banishment would still be active or retired, but if he were honest, he wouldn't be happy to see them first.

"Let us hope," Harbona flashed his friend the best smile he could muster, "the Eldaar do not know their banished son is coming home."

Diron pulled a spyglass out of his breast pocket and pointed it at the harbor. He hummed before extending it to Harbona.

To Harbona's surprise, the flying warriors were not standing at the wharf, but two Ethereals and three hippogriffs were. It had been such a long time since he'd been home that he'd almost forgotten that was how the Ethereals traveled. The Bellators had their wings, but the Ethereals had their beasts. Harbona loved flying atop the majestic creatures whose front halves resembled an eagle and back halves were horse-like. When he was young, Harbona would sneak out of his room to avoid studying the ancient texts of the Eldaar and would go for a late-night flight instead.

"It would appear that the Almighty is smiling down on us today, Diron." Harbona passed the spyglass back to the seafarer. He breathed a little easier knowing he wasn't going to be dragged from the ship in chains to be thrown at the Eldaar's feet.

As the crew prepared to tether *The Golden Rose* in the marina, Diron extended a hand to Harbona. "We will be docked in Caelestis to conduct some business for a few days. If you need me, let me know."

"Thank you, my friend," Harbona hugged the tan captain before he disembarked.

As soon as his feet touched Immortal ground, Harbona was filled with a joy he never expected to feel again. Though it hadn't been his home in years, he felt a power, a brightness, surge through his body. He felt the weight, worries, and grime of the last one thousand years walking mortal land wash away. He looked down at his hands and saw the Immortal glow he had lost when he sailed away was restored.

"I do not understand," Harbona muttered, thinking his aura had been stripped forever after being exiled. He caught a glimpse of his reflection in the water and all signs of him having aged on the Mainland were wiped away. He still bore the banishment mark around his right eye, but he looked like he was once again in his late twenties, exactly how he looked one thousand years ago. "What is happening to me?"

"Harbona," one of the Ethereals extended him a melodic greeting. "We have been instructed to escort you."

Harbona had so many questions, but he pushed them to the back of his mind, and obediently followed them to the hippogriffs. The one in the center was reserved for him and he was glorious. The Seer gently stroked the creature's bird-like neck before it cocked its head to the side and eyed him. The hippogriff bowed its head and lowered its horse-like body to the ground, granting Harbona permission to mount him. Harbona swung one leg over to the opposite side and sat in the leather saddle strapped to the flying beast.

"What is his name?" Harbona asked the Ethereals.

"Zandaar," one answered with an airy pleasantness. "Do you remember how to fly?"

Harbona smiled. "I believe I do. To the sky, Zandaar." With the command, Zandaar shot into the sky. As they teetered into a glide across the city, Harbona laughed, feeling like no time had truly passed since his last flight.

Zandaar seemed to understand his new rider hadn't been home in a millennium, so the hippogriff soared around Caelestis to give him a tour. The rolling green hillside was pocketed with stone villas. Throughout the city were canals and aqueducts, and the golden brick pathways twisted from one side of the kingdom to the other in serpentine fashion.

Set up on the highest hill was The Holies, a palace constructed entirely of gold. It was where the Eldaar dwelled. Where Harbona had been born and had spent his entire life before... He shook the thoughts of his past free and circled away from the impressive palace.

The Holies not only housed the royal family, but also the Tree of Eternity. When an Immortal was ready to cross over into the Next Life, the Eldaar would open the portal hidden in the tree for them to pass through. Harbona had looked forward to one day experiencing crossing over, but being banished, he wasn't sure that was possible anymore. Perhaps, when he took his last breath, he would join the mortals he loved so much and be buried in the ground to rot and decay.

On the other side of the kingdom, on the second highest hill, sat the grandest villa in Caelestis with a waterfall cascading behind the estate. Harbona knew whose home he had been beckoned to, and though he was relieved he wasn't going to The Holies, he wasn't so sure his reception would be any warmer here.

When they landed, the two Ethereals walked inside the gorgeous stone villa that boasted a new terracotta roof. Led through marble arches and breezeways to a lavish sitting room with views of the lush gardens, Harbona was left to wait for his host to make an appearance.

The Seer waited a few minutes before light footsteps slipped inside the room and stopped. He turned around slowly and when their eyes met, Harbona bowed his head. "It has been a long time, Lavena."

Lavena didn't say anything for several minutes. Her piercing grey eyes refused to release him from her glare. Her hip long, platinum blonde hair wasn't loose like it had been during her romance with Lykos of Northwind, but it was now fashioned in a braided crown.

"How did you break through my shield?" she asked, her hands clasped in front of her.

"I did not break through your shield." Harbona took a deep breath, the memories of his three-thousand-year life, growing up with Lavena, flashed through his mind at warp speed, and he had to quiet them before continuing. "Do you remember Princess Salome of Northwind?"

Lavena barely nodded her head in acknowledgement. "Of course, I remember Lykos' sister. What of her?"

"She is the Hunter." Harbona kept a fixed gaze on Lavena, hoping to get a read on her, but after three thousand years, she had become an expert on keeping a neutral face. "Lykos sent her a vision of the past – a vision about you. And a child."

"Have you come for my child, Harbona?" Lavena's voice used to have a sing-song quality, but now, it was icy.

"I have only come to talk." Harbona raised his hands in silent submission. "Does the child know about their father?"

"Why would I hide Lykos from his child?"

"May I see the child?" Harbona braced himself for a furious refusal, but Lavena glided toward him, and motioned for him to follow her into the gardens.

Quietly, the two Ethereals walked side-by-side through the garden, overflowing with thousands of budding roses, hydrangeas, lilies, and ghost caladium – all white to match the Ethereal essence. Harbona could hear the rushing of the waterfall on the far side of the garden, but they headed away from it.

When Lavena stopped, Harbona glanced at a golden fountain where a twelve-year-old girl knelt, wiggling her fingers through the cool water. She flicked her eyes up from the water and met his curious gaze. He felt as if a bolt of lightning zinged through his chest.

She had Lavena's grey eyes and tall, lean body. Her hair was straight like her mother's, but it was dark brown like Lykos'. Her olive skin, round ears, and smile were also gifts from her late father. Harbona teared up, grateful for the small glimpse of the friend he lost twelve years ago.

"Her name is Keeva," Lavena said softly, her lips slightly upturned. It was as close to a full-blown smile that Harbona was going to see from her.

"Hello, Keeva," Harbona turned his focus back to Lykos' daughter. "I am -"

"I know who you are, Harbona," Keeva interrupted him, and her warm aura washed all his worries and sorrows away. "Welcome home."

"You know who I am?" He exchanged a quick look with Lavena, who was once again stone-faced.

"I told mother you would be coming to visit me." Keeva turned her head to the side but didn't stop playing with the fountain water as she squinted at him. "You looked older in my vision, but I suppose by coming home, the Eldaar restored your aura like I asked them to."

"Is she a ...?" Harbona whispered, so only Lavena could hear him.

Lavena bobbed her head. "The first Seer born to our people since… you."

"And my parents know?" Harbona continued to speak in a hushed tone, as if Keeva didn't know what she was.

"The Eldaar know of her sight." Lavena looked at Harbona. "How else do you think you were allowed to step one foot on our shores and be restored to your former self?"

"She told them I was coming?"

"The Eldaar listen to Keeva. She is a Demi, half-Ethereal and half-mortal. She is rare, but even more so, because she is also a Seer." Lavena let a crack in her armor show, whether she could help it or not, Harbona didn't know. "The Eldaar see her as a sacred being, but she is just a girl, Harbona. And I will fight to give her as normal a life as I can. That's what Lykos would have wanted."

Harbona fought the urge to reach over and grab Lavena's hand to give her an encouraging squeeze. That was a mortal comfort. Ethereals wouldn't take kindly to being touched in that manner and most Bellators would certainly draw their weapons considering it to be a challenge.

Harbona approached Keeva who stood and started to make her way toward him. Before he got close, Harbona heard a flutter, and two loud thuds that shook the ground. He whipped around and saw two Bellators standing on either side of Lavena. She hadn't even blinked when the warriors landed and didn't look surprised by their sudden presence.

"Is it just me, Abba, or has Harbona gotten uglier since the last time we saw him?" The taller of the two muscular Bellators flashed Harbona a crooked grin.

Abba wiped his shaggy, dark hair out of his face, revealing the scars that stretched from his forehead, down the side of his face ending at his neck, barely missing his right eye. "Harbona has always been ugly, Kayven."

Kayven was the first to move toward Harbona. Half of his shoulder-length hair was pulled away from his bronze face, but rebellious strands hovered over his golden eyes. As soon as Kayven reached Harbona, he wrapped his enormous arms around the Seer, and it felt like he was being hugged by a bear.

"Welcome home, Harbona," Kayven whispered.

Harbona smiled with tears in his eyes, "It is good to see you, my friend."

Though Abba wasn't a hugger by nature, he returned Harbona's embrace when he made his way over to him. The scars Abba bore were from the night they attempted to assassinate Phlias – an everlasting reminder of their failure. But at least Harbona was able to keep them from being banished as well. Better him, than all of them.

"How did you know I was here?" Harbona asked, taking a step back from the brothers and fiercest commanders to ever lead the Bellators.

"I told them." Keeva's sweet voice sliced through the circle of testosterone, and Kayven scooped her up in his arms, planting a kiss on her cheek. "Hello, Uncle Kayven."

"Uncle?" Harbona arched a brow in playfulness.

Kayven shrugged. "When a toddler calls you Uncle Kayven, you become Uncle Kayven."

Lavena stepped forward, still wary of Harbona in their midst. "Why are you here, Harbona?"

"The war, of course," Keeva answered before Harbona had a chance.

"War?" Lavena's voice wavered and she narrowed her eyes as she stared at Harbona.

"Crispin and Salome are gathering forces to challenge Niabi for the White Throne," Harbona got straight to the point. "I am not here for aid. Salome had a vision that you and Lykos had a child."

Lavena folded her delicate arms over her chest. "And your precious mortals are worried Keeva will try to stake her claim to her father's throne? How typical of you to look out for the kingdoms and crowns of the mortals, instead of your own people."

"I did not come here to fight, Lavena," Harbona huffed, rubbing a hand over his forehead. "For being so against helping the mortals, you seem to have forgotten that you married one."

"Leave Lykos out of this," Lavena snapped, gritting her teeth.

"I had to see for myself if some piece of Lykos still lived," Harbona looked down at Keeva who took his hand in hers. "You have his smile."

"They will be excited to see you," Keeva said and Harbona tilted his head to the side. "Mother's shield must have prevented you from seeing them."

"Who?" Harbona asked, confused.

"I think the youngling is referring to us."

Harbona turned back toward the fountain and saw Odelia wearing white Ethereal robes, her arm in a sling. Reaper sat faithfully by her side while a younger version of Odelia stood next to her.

"Odelia?" Harbona had never seen Odelia outside of her swamp and his eyebrows shot up in alarm. "The Enchanted Swamp?"

"Shadows came for me," Odelia explained, though she didn't come any closer to them. "Makeda saved me, and the swamp."

Harbona's gaze drifted to Makeda. Other than her grey eyes, she was the spitting image of the Enchantress.

"Harbona," Odelia motioned a hand toward her daughter, "This is Makeda. Makeda, this is Harbona. Your father."

Harbona and Makeda's eyes widened when they heard the last bit of the introduction. The Seer knew Odelia had to be telling the truth. Only one with Ethereal blood had grey eyes, which would make Makeda not only his daughter, but...

"She's a Demi." Lavena stepped forward, a softness in her voice.

Odelia bobbed her head. "And a water wielder."

Harbona took a step forward, eyes fixed on the daughter he never knew existed. His heart was beating fast and hard in his chest, and he wasn't exactly sure what to say. She was a grown woman, and as of that moment, he knew only two things about her. Her name and her magical prowess.

"Makeda, I -"

Makeda's eyes welled with tears. She shook her head before he could say anything else, as if hearing him say her name was too much for her to handle. Snatching her arm from her mother's, and without saying a single word, she retreated into the garden.

"Why did you not tell me we have a daughter?" Harbona viciously spat the question at Odelia. She squinted, slamming her hands on her hips in response.

"And when was I supposed to tell you, Harbona?" She hissed, her accent thicker when she was angry. "You left before I even knew I was pregnant, and I saw you for the first time in almost twenty-five years a few weeks ago. So, please," she waved her uninjured arm wildly in the air, "tell me when would have been a good time to let you know about Makeda?"

Harbona's cheeks flushed in embarrassment. "I am … You are right, Odelia. I am sorry."

Odelia's gaze softened and she sighed. "You will have to give her some time. She has been wanting to know who her father is all her life and didn't know she would be meeting you today."

A silence fell on the group, but after a few moments, Kayven slapped a hand on Harbona's shoulder. "So, tell us more about this war you've gotten yourself into."

CHAPTER 43
SALOME

Salome and Adonijah followed the path through the Paraiso Gardens until they reached a bronze fountain. Her gaze trailed from the perfectly sculpted hedges up to the twinkling stars in the night sky. There were lights strung through the tree branches to illuminate their path, and the smell of jasmine hung in the air, bringing a much-needed smile to her face. The Paraiso Gardens was understandably a wonder of their world and a magical place. She could sit there all night, soaking in the floral scents and peaceful sounds, but that's not why she was there.

Adonijah's fingers tapped the hilt of his longsword hanging at his side. His eyes were alert, darting from one area of the quiet garden to the other. "I don't like this, Salome."

"He'll be here." Though she wondered if maybe he was already there, cloaked, and watching them for his enjoyment. She extended the bridge to Jinn. *"Where are you?"*

"For not being your watchdog," Jinn cooed, and she knew he was hidden nearby, *"he is awfully protective of you. Is it reserved just for me or is he like this with anyone who looks at you?"*

Salome snorted, folding her arms over her chest. "Show yourself." Jinn and Kai appeared out of thin air and were lounging on the other side of the fountain. Kai looked as menacing as the night they first met. She picked at her nails with one of her many knives, barely acknowledging Salome and Adonijah staring at them.

Salome's eyes floated to Jinn and felt a sudden warmth flood her. Her lips parted, but she had nothing to say. If the Prince of Darkness ever took mortal form, he would look exactly like Jinn. She was suddenly aware of how quickly her heart was beating, how her fingers ached with the need to run them through his dark hair.

The prince let out a low, warm chuckle. He uncrossed his ankles and stood from his reclined position. "Forgive the precautions, but we wanted to be sure you came alone."

Adonijah growled, inching closer to speak his mind, but Salome gently grabbed his arm, keeping him by her side. "You've had your fun." Salome narrowed her eyes, although her heart nearly dropped out of her chest when Jinn smiled at her. "We should get going."

"My ship is prepared to launch as soon as I give the order." Jinn approached with a lazy swagger. "I'll cloak us and get us past the guards, but we will need a distraction." He turned his focus to Adonijah. "That's where you and Kai come in."

Adonijah's brows furrowed, and he stepped forward, putting himself between Salome and Jinn. "You think I'm going to let her out of my sight?"

Jinn shrugged, unbothered by Adonijah's stance. "By all means, take her yourself. Let me know how that goes without my magic."

Salome tugged at Adonijah's arm. "I'll be fine. Go with Kai."

Adonijah's shoulders tensed as he turned to face her. "And if this is a trap?" he whispered.

"It's a risk I am willing to take to get Mika out." Salome nodded her head; she had made her decision. Her eyes darted across the small plaza until they settled on Jinn. "Let's go."

CLOAKED, Salome and Jinn waited by the hedges surrounding the tower Mika was being held in. The tower dungeon was not what Salome had expected. It wasn't dark or ominous in appearance, it was merely an extension of the Scarlett Citadel in shape and color. The bronze door was guarded by two Qata Vishna stationed on either side. It was only a two-story tower, so Salome wasn't sure why the Myridians referred to it as Tower Dungeon. It was more like a cylindrical house.

Waiting for the distraction that would spur the guards to leave their posts, Salome and Jinn crouched close to one another. She could feel his steady breathing against the side of her neck. She hadn't been this close to the prince before and found her mind and body dueling. Wanting to put a foot or two of separation between them, but at the same time, wanting to feel his arms wrapped around her. No one would even know with them being cloaked. She shook her head, pinching the bridge of her nose.

She could feel his eyes on her. Not wanting to meet his gaze and give her thoughts away, she mentally shot to him, *"Thank you. I know this was probably a difficult decision. "*

"It was simple."

"Really?"

"You needed me," he smiled at her. *"I will always be there to help you."*

Salome shook her head again, *"I find it hard to believe you don't already have a wife."* She could have slapped herself for being so careless. Her cheeks reddened, and she felt his fingers trail up her jawline, gently forcing her to look at him.

"If I said I wanted to kiss you," he ran the tip of his thumb across her lips, *"would you let me?"*

Salome couldn't help the shiver that ran down her spine when his warm skin touched hers. *"Well,"* she managed, *"you can't* say *it."*

His laugh heated every inch of her body. *"An unfortunate technicality. I might not be able to shout it from the tallest tower, but I've thought about kissing you since I first saw you."*

"Yes, I know, I could see it in your eyes at the Festival of Forbidden Fruit," Salome rolled her eyes in an attempt to release the tension of her rapidly beating heart.

Jinn shook his head slowly, eyes fixed on hers. *"I saw you in the halls once before, when you first arrived to the Isles of Myr."*

Realization hit Salome, nearly robbing her of breath. She *had* seen Jinn in the halls on her way to meet with Zara for the first time. She thought he was one of the most handsome men she had ever laid her eyes on. And now, they were so close she was sure he could feel her longing for him.

"So, you see," he continued, interlocking his fingers with hers, *"you've been on my mind for a while now."* He leaned in to kiss her.

Salome desperately wanted to feel Jinn's lips on hers, and feel his hands grab ahold of her waist, pulling her against his muscular body, but in the corner of her eye she spotted movement. She placed her hand on his chest, *"Jinn."*

He pulled back, raking a hand through his hair, *"Sorry, I -"*

"Look," Salome pointed a finger toward the bronze door. *"They're leaving."*

The two Qata Vishna sprinted from their posts, weapons drawn. Salome watched them and saw smoke rising from the gardens behind them.

"Looks like our distraction worked." Jinn grabbed her hand and tugged her forward. *"Come on."*

Salome wriggled her hand free, *"They set something on fire?"* Her nostrils flared and he raised his hands to calm her down.

"Kai is an expert when it comes to fires. I promise nothing will be damaged."

Salome had no choice but to trust him. They wouldn't have much time to get Mika out before the Qata Vishna returned. She nodded and he focused on the door. He dropped to one knee before he fingered a skinny metal pick out of his sleeve and stuck it inside the lock.

"You pick locks, too?" Salome leaned against the stone walls; arms crossed over her chest. "If I didn't know you were a prince, I'd peg you for a common thief."

Jinn smirked. "I'm flattered." The door unlocked and he pushed it open. "Once you head up those steps," he whispered, "you'll be released from my cloaking. I'll stay here and keep an eye out for the guards."

Salome bobbed her head and sprinted up the stairs, taking them two by two. She reached another bronze door leading to Mika's one room cell. She opened the door and was surprised to see Mika's cell looked more like a lush guest room than a prison. Cushioned furniture, a small fireplace, a bookshelf, an unused bed, and a table with an untouched dinner plate rounded out the room.

Mika's back faced Salome as she entered the room. Her arms were wrapped around her torso as she silently stared out the only window. It wasn't big enough for someone to escape, just large enough for someone to see a sliver of the outside world.

Salome opened her mouth, but snapped it shut when Mika said, "I know what you're going to ask, but I don't know where Marina is. And if I did know, I wouldn't tell you."

"Why, Mika?" Salome rubbed a finger across her forehead. "She murdered our grandmother."

"I went to see Marina after our meeting with my mother. She told me she never wanted to hurt anyone, but if Niabi wasn't obeyed, she would've been killed instead."

"And you believed her?"

"Marina is a lot of things," Mika turned around to look Salome in the eye, "but she is not a liar."

"She's a coward," Salome snorted. "Your mother can't execute you in her place."

Mika nodded, and accepted Salome's tone graciously. "Our laws are clear. A life for a life."

"No," Salome shook her head. "I won't accept that. You are the Red Maiden. You are the heir to the Bronze Throne. You will not be executed."

"It was my choice to switch places with Marina."

"But -"

"Could you watch Crispin die?"

"I could watch Niabi die."

"Despite the person Marina is, and what she has done," Mika sighed, "I can't watch her take her last breath. She is still my sister."

Salome approached her and whispered, "There's a ship leaving for the Mainland tonight. I am going to help you escape."

Mika shook her head, "Salome -"

"I can't watch you die. Not in Marina's place. Not like this." Salome fought back tears. "It's not fair."

Mika grabbed her cousin's hands and squeezed gently. "I will not run. I took Marina's place, and I am willing to accept the consequences. But there is something I will ask of you."

Salome was fighting to keep tears from pouring down her cheeks. "Anything."

"Make sure Utara isn't there to watch." Mika's neutral expression turned into one of sadness at the mention of her ten-year-old daughter. "I couldn't bear for that to be her last memory of me."

Salome nodded. "I swear, from now until I draw my last breath, I will look after her."

Mika hugged her tightly. She took a step back, slipped a pin out of her hair, and clipped it in Salome's curls. "This is given to every Qata Vishna once she has completed training. You are now one of us."

"Please reconsider," Salome's bottom lip quivered. "I can get you out of here. I can help you."

She kissed Salome's forehead, "Make sure Utara knows how much I love her."

Jinn whistled up the stairs signaling their time was nearly up. "I thought we would be fighting side-by-side on the battlefield."

Mika smiled and escorted Salome to the door. "Perhaps we will, in the next life. Goodbye, Cousin." She closed the door and Salome was forced to retreat down the stairs to an awaiting Jinn.

She didn't break stride to wait for him to lock the door. Her breathing was rigid, and her eyes were burning from all the tears she was still holding back until she could reach the privacy of her bedchambers. Mika had made her choice, and Salome would have to accept it.

When she rounded the corner, she realized a second too late, that she hadn't waited for Jinn to cloak her. The two Qata Vishna who had abandoned their posts at the tower stared at her. They exchanged a quick glance before turning their focus back to the princess.

"I…" Salome's throat immediately went dry and any excuse she could think of to explain why she was walking the grounds this late, didn't come to mind.

"There you are. I've been looking for you." Jinn slipped his arm around her waist and slammed his lips against hers. Electricity shot through her body and her knees buckled. She expected him to be smug about finally putting his lips against hers, but she found a gentle longing and an apology before he pulled away. Their foreheads were pressed together, their breathing heavy, and she was ready to ram herself against him once more when one of the Qata Vishna cleared her throat.

Jinn whipped his head toward the guards and acted surprised to see them. "Oh, I see we aren't alone anymore, darling." He kissed Salome's temple, sending another wave of electricity down her spine. "I trust you will keep seeing the princess and myself to yourselves."

The Qata Vishna guards once again exchanged a quiet look, but both nodded their heads in agreement. One said, "If you are looking for a private garden, then try the Rose Garden."

Jinn flashed a charming smile at them, resting his hand on Salome's lower back, ushering her forward. "Thank you both for your discretion. The princess and I appreciate it."

As soon as the Qata Vishna were on the other side of the hedge and back at their posts, Jinn withdrew his hand from her back and shoved both of his hands into his pockets.

"Sorry about -"

Salome waved her hand in the air, "It's alright. It was good thinking on your part. I shouldn't have stormed off without you."

"What happened with…" Jinn wisely didn't say Mika's name.

"She refused to come. She made her choice." Salome wrapped her hands around her body as they silently made their way back into the Scarlett Citadel.

Once they stood outside her chambers, she turned to face him. "I hope I haven't caused you too much trouble tonight." Her eyes darted to the floor to avoid meeting his gaze. The taste of his kiss lingered on her lips, and the ghost of his touch warmed her skin. She craved him, and if she kept looking at him, she was afraid he would see it written all over her face.

Jinn's fingers tenderly lifted her chin, forcing her to make eye contact with him. "Earlier, when I said I was sorry for kissing you -"

She glanced up and down the hall making sure they were still alone. "I already told you, it's alright."

Jinn pressed a finger to her mouth. "I'm not sorry I kissed you. I'm just sorry that was our first kiss." He took another step toward her; her back pinned against the wall.

Before she could respond, a palace worker appeared at the end of the hallway and made her way toward them. Salome wasn't sure how she would explain what they were doing, but the woman walked by them without a word or a curtsey.

"I cloaked us the moment we stepped inside the palace," Jinn whispered. Salome met his gaze. "If I said I wanted to kiss you," Jinn repeated his question from earlier, "would you let me?"

Salome slammed her mouth against his, giving into desire. One hand cupped her face, the other gripped her thigh. She hopped up, wrapping her legs around his torso, and he pinned her against the wall, matching her passion.

It was an odd feeling to be in the middle of the hallway kissing. Ordinarily, anyone could walk by and see them, but with Jinn's magic, they were in a world of their own. They could do whatever they wanted, and no one would ever know. The magnitude of his power struck her, and she craved more of him.

Jinn had been right before. Together, uniting their houses, they could do a lot of good for their people. Their power would be unmatched. The other kingdoms in Adalore would think twice before striking or scheming against them.

Jinn murmured against her mouth, "You're thinking too much."

Salome pushed him away, her hands gripping his shirt so tight her knuckles were white. "You heard what I was thinking?" She hadn't extended the bridge to him.

Jinn shook his head. "I didn't hear your thoughts, but I can tell when you're thinking too much. Your body tenses."

Salome loosened her grip on him, feeling her cheeks brighten in embarrassment. "Sorry."

"Out of curiosity," Jinn kissed her neck, "what were you thinking about?"

Salome smirked and raked her hands through his hair, "I have to keep some thoughts to myself, Jinn."

"A secret for a secret," he whispered in her ear.

"You first," Salome opened their mental bond. Secrets were just for them, and no prying ears would learn them.

"Sometimes at night, you reach out to me in your sleep. I feel you at peace and it helps me sleep."

Jinn's confession nearly brought Salome to her knees. She uncoiled her legs from his body, slipping back to the floor. She cupped his face in her hands and kissed him gently on the lips before admitting, *"Sometimes, I think about what life married to you would look like, and I find myself wanting to accept your proposal."*

He rested his forehead against hers and sighed.

Salome ran her fingers along his jawline. "Did I say something wrong?"

Jinn shook his head and kissed her forehead. His eyes met hers and his smile wasn't as wide as it normally was. "My army will fight for you with or without you accepting my proposal."

"What?" Salome's gaze bounced between his eyes quickly, searching for answers.

"I don't want you to accept my proposal to win a war against your sister." Jinn absentmindedly twisted locks of her curly hair between his thumb and index finger. "I would always wonder if you accepted my proposal for my army or because you loved me. And I would rather you choose me for me."

"Jinn…"

"I don't need an answer tonight." Jinn continued. "I don't even need an answer soon. Whatever, whoever, you choose. I want it to be for the right reasons, and not because you felt you had to put your people before yourself. There will be plenty of difficult decisions for you to make without me adding another to your plate."

"You really mean that?" Her hand trailed down from his chest to his hand gripping her waist and she squeezed it.

"My army is yours. My sword is yours. My life is yours." Jinn kissed her and she wished he didn't pull away. "You should get some rest. I have a ship to delay."

"Thank you." She caressed his face before he pressed his lips against her palm and took off down the hall.

Salome caught her breath before entering her room and stopped when she saw Adonijah on her balcony smoking his pipe. The guilt in the pit of her stomach was back. She knew she cared deeply for Adonijah, but she clearly had feelings for Jinn, too.

She closed the door behind her making enough noise for him to turn his head toward her. "Are you alright?"

"Mika refused to leave." Salome sank in the chair on the other side of the balcony with a thud.

"I know." Adonijah bobbed his head. "Kai said you left the tower without Mika."

Salome's heart skipped a beat. Had he seen her kissing Jinn? "You two were watching us?"

"Kai had eyes on you." Adonijah planted his feet on the floor, squaring his body toward her. "I made sure the Qata Vishna didn't spot us. Once you left, we left."

"Thank you for helping, Adonijah." Salome rubbed the back of her neck. "I just wish she would have…" She inhaled deeply before standing up. "It's been a long day."

Adonijah rose from his seat and nodded. "If you need anything, I'm across the hall." He stepped toward her and wrapped his arms around her. "I'm sorry about Mika."

Salome embraced him, burying her face in the crease of his neck. She wondered if he could smell Jinn on her. She wasn't in a relationship with either man, yet she felt guilty for spending time with one knowing they both had feelings for her.

If Zophar were there, he would have crossed his giant arms across his broad, hairy chest and shook his head mumbling something about not letting either man distract her from what she needed to do. She missed him. Missed his impish blue eyes. Missed his gruff voice. Missed his boorish snoring.

She pulled out of Adonijah's hold and cleared her throat. "I'll see you tomorrow."

"Aye." He took that as her dismissing him for the night and left her room without another word.

Feelings or not, she hadn't come this far to lose herself to a man. She was on this journey for one reason, and that was to defeat her sister. She needed to remain focused, or she might not make it to the battlefield.

CHAPTER 44
CRISPIN

"When I become king, the first thing I'm going to do is change these uniforms." Crispin marched into Oden's office and waved his arms around in childish protest. "How do her soldiers wear this all day long?"

Nubis chuckled, seated in his simple wooden chair, muscular arms crossed over his broad chest. "You get used to it."

"How am I expected to fight in this?" Crispin fidgeted in the black armor. "I'll be glad when I can take this off." He rubbed the nape of his neck and plopped into Ziggy's high-back chair. "I remember when the guards wore navy and white uniforms with the White Wolf sigil on their chests. It seems like anything that reminded her of our father, she's gotten rid of."

"Then you're going to love how she's decorated the White Keep." Nubis chuckled when Crispin's eyes widened.

"She wouldn't."

Nubis shrugged. "Of course, I never saw it before the renovations, but there's a lot of black and white now. Oden gripes about it from time to time. Said your mother was the one to bring the White Keep to life when she arrived to marry your father."

"He seems to have known my mother well." Crispin shifted uncomfortably in his seat. "Do you know if they ever…?"

"I loved your mother with my entire heart and would have gladly given my life in her place," Oden's voice sliced into the underground headquarters with a sharpness that took Crispin by surprise. "But she was faithful to her marriage vows. We never had a relationship of any kind, other than friendship."

"You make it sound as if she didn't want to be with my father at all." Crispin folded his arms over his chest with a scowl.

Oden sat on the edge of his desk facing Crispin and pulled a pendant from under his shirt, holding it in his palm for the prince to see. "This was the last gift she ever gave me before your sister…" He cleared his throat and squeezed the emerald gemstone with teary eyes. "I used to tell Bilhah that her eyes reminded me of emeralds."

Hearing a different side of his mother's life made his heart ache. "She loved you?"

"We knew we could never be together," Oden slipped the necklace underneath his shirt, "but that never stopped me from loving her with all that I am. I wasn't even here when your sister attacked. The king had sent me to the Isles of Myr to meet with Queen Nym. If I had been here, I would have gotten your mother and siblings out of the city."

Crispin was having difficulty breathing. He tried to loosen the heavy pieces of metal weighing him down just to catch a breath.

"I know this isn't something a son wants to hear about his mother," Oden continued, as if he had been waiting for the right moment to confess. "She wasn't happy with Issachar, but she loved you children more than anything in this world."

"You never married?" Crispin asked, his tone edgier than he had intended.

Oden shook his head. "It wouldn't have been fair to another woman to live in your mother's shadow." He stepped toward Crispin and knelt before him. "I swore I would avenge her death. But now, I see I survived all those years ago, so I could serve you now. I swear by my life or by my death, I will help you take back your ancestors' throne."

Crispin rested a hand on Oden's shoulder and nodded. "I only hope to be worthy of such an oath."

Rahab, Penn, and Ziggy entered from the adjoining room. Penn somehow looked like the black armor was tailored for her specifically. She wore the heavy metal pieces as if they were as light as a feather.

Crispin's eyes drifted from Penn to Rahab and nearly choked when he saw her. Not in armor like Nubis, Penn, and himself, but in a dress similar to what Ziggy would wear on one of her late-night rendezvous with Gershom. Rahab planted her hands on her hips and snarled at him.

"Enjoying the view?" Rahab's head tilted to the side; any sign of amusement drained from her face.

Crispin shook his head and stammered, "I… I, uh. I didn't know you were… I didn't realize you were…I didn't expect you to be in a dress…"

"Yikes," Penn tucked the black helmet Nubis handed her under her arm. "I'm blind and even I could see that was the worst experience of your life."

Ziggy chuckled when Crispin blushed. "Nubis couldn't find another set of armor to steal -"

"Borrow." Nubis cut in.

"Nubis couldn't find another set of armor to *borrow*," she flashed Nubis a smile with the amendment. "So, I leant her one of my dresses. Doesn't she look stunning?"

Rahab huffed indignantly. With her waist cinched as tiny as it could go without breaking a rib, and her cleavage on display, Rahab would definitely catch a few wandering eyes tonight. If they needed a distraction, she was their ticket.

"You look beautiful," Crispin offered, trying to hide the flush in his cheeks.

Rahab shifted her weight, tugging at her ear. "As long as I get to slit a few throats, I suppose this will be worth the hassle."

Crispin could have stared at her for hours and not gotten bored, but they had a rescue mission ahead of them that needed his full attention. He turned toward the rest of the group. "Everyone knows their assignment?" Nods from around the room returned in response. "Good. From Nubis' report, the ritual will be happening sometime tonight. With any luck, we'll break into the prison and free Neempo before they come for him."

"And if we don't get there in time?" Rahab asked.

"We don't leave without him." Crispin said, and Penn nodded her head in agreement. "If we run into my sister," the word sister left him with a bitter taste in his mouth, "then everyone is to run as fast as they can. Do not engage her, leave her to me."

"Are you forgetting she has fire magic?" Nubis leaned closer to Ziggy who looked petrified.

"No," Crispin shook his head. "I'm aware of her magic, but if our plan fails, even if that means you leave me behind, get out. She wants me. Not any of you."

"Like hell I'll leave you in there to face her by yourself!" Rahab spat each word and Crispin was taken aback by her reaction.

"You'll have to," he replied as gently and sternly as he could without spurring them to fist fight. "Get Neempo out. If I'm left behind, then you find my sister, Salome. She'll come for me."

"Crispin -"

"Let's go," Crispin interrupted Rahab and motioned for the group to start leaving out the secret entrance. Once Oden, Ziggy, Nubis, and Penn left, Crispin turned to face an enraged Rahab.

"I don't know why you're trying to play the martyr," Rahab fumed, stomping toward him, "but I won't be following any orders that include leaving you behind."

"I don't want anyone getting hurt," Crispin stood his ground, fighting the urge to look down her low-cut gown. "What do you think will happen if she gets her hands on one of you? She'll torture you until you give me up or die. I won't have you or anyone else going through that to protect me."

"But if she captures you..." Rahab sucked in a breath and Crispin realized she was trying to keep tears from rolling down her cheeks.

"You care." Crispin met her watery gaze and smiled.

"If by care, you mean I don't want you to die, then yes, I care." She pointed an accusatory finger at him, but before she could open her mouth to argue further, he cupped her face in his hands and pressed his lips against hers.

"I love you, too," he whispered.

"Then you understand why I can't, why I won't, leave you behind." She raked her fingers through his hair.

Crispin kissed her one more time, before he motioned toward the door. "Then let's hope tonight will be easy."

~

ODEN AND MASTER Penn's six Keepers stayed outside the White Keep, patrolling the streets. Once the others rescued Neempo, they would have backup in escorting him to the *Shadow of Death*.

Ziggy took Rahab through the private entrance Gershom had her use when they would meet. Crispin worried the two guards wouldn't allow a newcomer to pass, but as soon as they saw Ziggy, they motioned the women forward without a second glance.

Crispin and Penn followed Nubis into the soldiers' barracks without a problem. No one questioned them, and it didn't seem like anyone cared as they stomped from one end of the stone building to the other, which was attached to a long hall that led down to the dungeons.

Trying to monitor and regulate his breathing underneath the stifling helmet, Crispin muttered a prayer, and hoped they would make it in time to free Neempo before his sister found out.

As they approached, the guard sitting at the entrance of the dungeons looked up from his desk. "What brings you down here, Nubis?" He checked his paperwork and shook his head. "You aren't scheduled down here tonight."

"I was told to bring the new recruits down for a tour." Nubis lied so effortlessly, Crispin almost forgot why they were there.

The guard narrowed his eyes, "This late?"

Nubis shrugged his massive shoulders, looking bored. "Look, if you want to send us on our way, I'd be glad. I was hoping to get down to the Night District for a drink. But Captain Glenn insisted I bring them down here. Something about putting them into the rotation this week."

At the mention of Captain Glenn, the soldier froze. "Oh, Captain Glenn sent you then."

"That's what I said, Kane," Nubis huffed, and Crispin stifled a laugh. "Now, are you going to let us pass, so I can get this tour over with? If I'm lucky, I'll still be able to make it to the Night District for some fun."

Kane motioned the three of them through and grabbed the giant soldier by the arm. When Nubis cast a judgmental glare down at him, he released him from his grasp. Kane whispered, "You won't tell Captain Glenn of the delay, right? I must have just misplaced the paperwork."

Nubis hesitated before nodding his head. "Sure, Kane."

Once they had gone down a few rickety flights of stairs, Nubis tapped Crispin on top of his helmet, and a clanging rang in his ears. "You can take the helmets off now. No one is stationed all the way down here."

Crispin ripped the helmet from his head, grateful to be rid of it, and took the deepest breath of air he could, only to start coughing. "What is that smell?" Crispin said between chokes.

"What did you expect a dungeon to smell like?" Nubis arched an eyebrow. "Roses?"

Penn chuckled and Nubis cracked the thinnest smile. "You've got a good sense of humor, Nubis."

"He's not that funny," Crispin rolled his eyes.

"According to the manifest," Nubis marched down the damp, sewer smelling hallway, ignoring the whimpers of prisoners behind the solid wooden doors, "he should be in this cell." Nubis pulled a pick out of his hair and went to work on the lock. As soon as it clicked, he swung the door open only to find the cell empty.

"We're too late." Crispin closed his eyes and tilted his head toward the low ceiling.

"They took him a little while ago," a soft voice echoed.

They turned around, looking for who spoke, but found no one.

"Who's there?" Penn asked in a militaristic voice.

A light tapping noise drew their attention to the cell next to Neempo's. "Your friend told me you would come looking for him. Said to tell you they're taking him to the Eastern Courtyard."

"Thank you for your assistance," Penn shucked the helmet back over her head, ready to stomp back down the hall.

"I am one with nothing to offer…" the man's voice trailed off and Penn stopped dead in her tracks.

She turned on her heel and replied, "But I am one with everything to give."

"What is going on?" Crispin looked back and forth between Penn and the prisoner's cell.

"Nubis, open it." Penn ignored Crispin's question and pointed at the wooden door, "He is coming with us."

"What?" Nubis protested. "We don't know anything about this man."

"Only the Sovereign could have told him that phrase," Penn explained. "It's a code. Whoever knows it is protected by The Sisters. This man is coming with us."

Nubis looked at Crispin for direction. The prince nodded for the Stormcrag to set the prisoner free. As quickly as Nubis had opened Neempo's door, he unlocked the second door.

A man not much older than Crispin stumbled out. By his frame, Crispin could tell he was once bulky with muscle, but he was now whittled down to skin and bones. His dark skin and hazel eyes indicated he was originally from Numbio. But how he ended up this far from his home, and in the White Keep's dungeon, was a story for another time.

"Do you need help walking?" Nubis asked as the young man limped, favoring his right leg.

"If it wouldn't be too much trouble," he rasped, as if he hadn't had a drink of water in a while.

"How are we going to get him past the guards in the barracks?" Crispin asked as Nubis wrapped the weary prisoner's arm over his shoulder.

"The same way we would have gotten Neempo out," Nubis puckered his lips toward a second hallway that led into darkness. "None of the guards venture down here. If they did, they'd know there's a grate that leads to the sewers. That's our way back to the city."

Crispin nodded in understanding. "And to get inside the White Keep?"

Penn slammed her palm against Crispin's chest, halting their trek. "You ask, as if you will be going on your own, Prince Crispin."

"You need to get this man to the *Shadow of Death* -"

"I came for the Sovereign." Penn's voice dripped with venom. "I will not leave without him."

"You decided to bring this man along with us," Crispin pointed out as respectfully as he could without riling the Master of Keepers to the point of dueling. "You are now responsible to see that he is safely delivered to the ship."

Before Penn could argue, they heard whispers headed in their direction.

"Soldiers," Penn whispered and began listening intently again. "One sounds like the guard who let us pass, and the man he's talking to is very angry."

"Damn," Nubis growled. "Kane must have alerted Captain Glenn."

"Is this Captain Glenn going to be a problem?" Penn asked, her hand on the hilt of her sword.

"Let's just say, I won't be showing my face around here anymore." Nubis shook his head, still supporting the exhausted and sickly-looking prisoner. "Oden isn't going to like this at all."

"There's just two?" Crispin asked Penn who was still listening.

Penn bobbed her head. "Yes."

"Then you two get him to the ship." Crispin instructed, not taking no for an answer. "I'll handle these two."

"What about the Sovereign?" Penn asked, a hint of alarm in her voice.

"I'll find him and meet you at the docks." The sound of voices grew louder, and Crispin waved the three of them to keep going. "Go."

Nubis nodded and practically carried the prisoner down the tunnel, Penn close in tow. Crispin reluctantly slammed his helmet back over his head and marched toward Captain Glenn and Kane. With his back firmly against the wall that cornered the hallway the two soldiers were walking down, Crispin decided to try to get out of the dungeons without spilling blood. As the two men neared him, Crispin stepped out from his hiding spot, and bumped into a burly, scarred man who he could only assume was Captain Glenn.

"Watch where you're going, soldier!" Captain Glenn bellowed, brushing the imaginary dirt from his pristine uniform.

Crispin straightened and saluted the superior officer. "Apologies, Captain.

Captain Glenn narrowed his eyes at Crispin, not being able to get a good look at him with the helmet hiding most of his face. "What are you doing down here? What's your name?"

"My name is Graves, sir." Crispin lied.

"What are you doing down here, *Graves*?" The captain repeated the name, as if he believed it to be made up.

"I was supposed to be on a tour of the dungeons, but I got sick from the smell and had to stop." Crispin hoped the captain believed that part of the story because it was partially true. "I was separated from the others and got lost."

"Where's Nubis?" Kane interjected, questioning Crispin as if he were a prisoner.

"I'll ask the questions, Kane," Captain Glenn snorted, and Kane took a sheepish step back. "Where's Nubis?"

"I told you, Captain, I got lost. I don't know where Nubis is, sir." Crispin had sweat dripping down his back, tickling his spine. He'd give this another minute before he'd have to slit their throats and find Neempo.

The captain looked Crispin up and down, clearly contemplating if he believed the tale he was being told. "Kane." Kane stepped forward like a dutiful lap dog and bowed his head in anticipation. "Take Graves and lock him up until we can find Nubis and the other guard on this so-called tour."

"Yes, Captain," Kane took a step toward Crispin with a wicked grin.

"I'm afraid that isn't going to work for me," Crispin unsheathed his sword and in the same breath, sliced his blade across Kane's chest. Turning his focus to the middle-aged captain, Crispin pointed the longsword at him. "Let me pass and you won't end up like him."

"I will see you hang for this!" The captain snarled and reached for his sword.

Ordinarily, Crispin would duel the captain for honor's sake, but tonight wasn't about being honorable. Before Captain Glenn could unsheathe his weapon, Crispin stabbed him in his chest. As quickly as he could, the prince stuffed both bodies into Neempo's empty cell and closed the door. Now, he needed to infiltrate the White Keep and find Neempo before someone stumbled upon the bodies. It sounded simple, but then again, the night hadn't been going as smoothly as he had expected. Hopefully, Rahab and Ziggy were having better luck on their end.

CHAPTER 45
RAHAB

"So far so good," Ziggy whispered to Rahab as they strolled through the glistening white halls of the White Keep. It was well past midnight and most people in the castle were tucked in their beds snoring the night away.

"How many more rooms do we have to check?" Rahab tugged and pulled at her corset until Ziggy smacked her hand away. The pirate gritted her teeth, ready to curse at the redhead.

"If you mess with your dress, someone is bound to notice." Ziggy kept her eyes forward, looking for anyone lurking in the halls, ignoring Rahab's menacing glare.

"So?" Rahab snorted.

"So," Ziggy met her irritated gaze, "experienced girls don't fidget the way you do. You'll give us away before I have a chance to lie our way out."

Rahab stiffened. Ziggy had a point. As badly as she wanted to continue scratching at the bone crushing corset, Rahab nodded her head in agreement. "Fine. I'll leave it alone. But I can't promise I won't rip this thing to shreds the second we reach the ship."

"Don't be too hasty." Ziggy flashed the pirate a playful smile and Rahab could have sworn the perky girl's freckles danced across the bridge of her nose. "I think Prince Crispin might want a chance to see you in it again."

Rahab couldn't stifle the laugh that escaped her lips. "You assume too much, Red."

"Red?" Ziggy's eyes softened. "I like it."

"You aren't scared of me, are you?" Rahab asked, as they poked their heads into another empty guest room; checking to see if Neempo was in one of the chambers, instead of a prison cell. The search was becoming tedious and for all they knew, he might already be dead.

Ziggy whipped around in surprise. "Of course, I'm scared of you. You live a dangerous life and from the way you talk, you've killed plenty of people."

Rahab didn't know what to say, but thankfully, Ziggy continued. "I don't mean to be offensive."

"No offense taken." Rahab shrugged. "I know what I am."

"To be fair," Ziggy whispered as they closed the last door on that floor. "I'm scared of everything and everyone. I just pretend not to be."

"But you're a ..." Rahab didn't want to say *spy* aloud, but Ziggy nodded, knowing what she was thinking.

"I've never had a chance to make my own choices." Ziggy shrugged. "Maybe one day, that'll change. Maybe one day, I won't have nightmares of having my throat slit. Maybe one day, I'll be free."

Rahab looked up and down the empty, quiet hallway. She met Ziggy's blue eyes and said, "You should go."

"Go?" Ziggy tilted her head to the side in confusion. "Go where?"

"Get to the ship." Rahab insisted in a hushed voice. "We've finished checking these rooms and there's no sign of Neempo. Get aboard the ship and you can finally sail to freedom."

"I can't leave you here," Ziggy protested but Rahab put a hand up to silence her.

"I'll meet up with Crispin, Penn, and Nubis. We won't be too far behind you."

"You love him, don't you?" Ziggy smiled, and her face lit up like the sparkling night sky.

Rahab motioned for her to go back the way they had come. "Go on, Red. I'll catch up." She couldn't hide her grin when Ziggy mentioned Crispin.

"Thank you." Ziggy hugged Rahab and for once, the pirate didn't push someone away for touching her. In fact, she wrapped her arms around the redhead, returning the embrace.

As Ziggy disappeared around the corner, Rahab felt a swelling in her chest. She'd never had a female friend before. Maybe, she could be friends with the Westerner. She rolled her eyes at the thought. Crispin was going to make fun of her. A pirate of Pulau in love with the Prince of Northwind and declaring friendship with a prostitute from Borg.

"Mainlanders," she muttered.

CHAPTER 46
CRISPIN

Crispin was surprised that after years of being away, he still remembered how to get around the White Keep. Spending his days wandering the castle and getting into trouble wasn't entirely a 'waste of his time' like his mother loved to point out. Nubis was right about the renovations; there was a lot of black and white throughout the keep, but thankfully the changes were mostly cosmetic and not structural. He made his way to the Eastern Courtyard where the Numbio prisoner claimed soldiers had taken the Sovereign.

Tired of being weighed down by the black armor, Crispin ditched the heavy pieces, opting for the black fighting leathers underneath. He also left the shield behind in the dungeon, but kept the crossbow strapped to his back. He hadn't been taught to fight with all that armor, and if he was going to have a chance at succeeding, he would need his mobility.

As he approached the end of the hall, he peeked around the corner, and saw soldiers guarding the entrance to the Eastern Courtyard. He rolled his eyes, resting the back of his head against the wall. Nothing was going according to plan, and the last thing he wanted to do was scale the side of the castle up to the roof in the dark. But that's what he was going to have to do to get a bird's eye view of the courtyard and avoid those guards.

Crispin slipped out one of the windows across from him and slithered up the side of the stone façade. Gripping divots and broken grooves in the wall, he made his way up to the slopped roof. He laid flat on his belly and crawled to the other side of the awning to look down into the courtyard.

Crispin saw Neempo strapped to a thick wooden pole in the middle of the two-story courtyard. Though the Sovereign had been stripped of his red eye wrap and shirt, he didn't look scared, as if he still had faith in being rescued from his cruel fate.

Before the prince could move closer, a weathered hag glided up the wooden steps that led to Neempo's stake. The moonlight streamed in and highlighted her white hair. From description alone, Crispin knew she must be the witch the members of the Order had told him about.

"It is time, Neempo." The witch nearly sang in glee.

"You don't have to do this, Vilora," Neempo remained calm. "You can let me go and all will be forgiven."

Vilora cackled and shook her head. "Righteous of heart until the very end." She leaned in close to Neempo and said, "Queen Niabi thanks you for your sacrifice."

Neempo screamed when Vilora dug her claw-like fingernails into his chest – she was going to rip his heart out with her bare hands. Crispin knew then he wouldn't make it down to the courtyard in time to save the Sovereign.

"If a rescue fails, you must do what needs to be done." Neempo's instructions echoed in his mind, and he finally understood what the Sovereign had been trying to tell him in his office before he was taken by the Pirate King.

Crispin couldn't rescue Neempo, but he could save him from being tortured to death. He nocked an arrow in the crossbow Nubis gave him. Aiming at first for the witch he repositioned his shot for the Sovereign. Even though his breath was labored, and his heart was pounding wildly inside his chest, Crispin let the arrow fly.

Neempo grunted when Crispin's mercy shot pierced his chest, right above Vilora's bloody hand. After a moment of hissed breathing, Neempo's head slumped toward his wounded body.

Crispin dragged his index finger from his forehead down to his chest. He failed to rescue the Sovereign and he felt the burden of his shortcoming perch on his shoulders.

Vilora whipped around, searching for who had killed the Sovereign. The witch snarled when her hateful gaze met his. She opened her mouth and spat fire at him. To avoid the inferno, Crispin slid off the roof, grabbed ahold of the lip of the shingles and flung himself on the second floor that was still open to the courtyard. He sprinted, luckily avoiding the blasts of fire and explosions against the stones. But as he neared the staircase to escape deeper inside the White Keep, a dark figure appeared.

Crispin stopped dead in his tracks. For a split second, he thought he was staring at his mother; her long raven black hair, green eyes, olive skin – but he realized too late it wasn't Bilhah. It was Niabi. Armed with a dagger in her right hand and dancing flames in her left.

"Hello, Crispin." Niabi's voice even sounded like their mother's, and it toyed with his mind.

Crispin drew his sword but was tossed against the wall when a blast from Vilora sent him flying.

"No!" Niabi shouted at the witch, though her eyes were still fixed on him. "He's mine."

Stumbling to his feet as a ball of fire soared toward him, Crispin wished he hadn't discarded the shield that came with his armor. Dodging the incoming fire attack his sister launched, he knew if he didn't find cover, she would succeed in burning him to ash. Bolting away from her, he turned the corner, and ducked behind a column hoping to outrun his sister. But Niabi was quick, ferocious, and unrelenting in her assault.

"You stole from me, little brother." Niabi said calmly, and the wicked chill behind her eyes pierced his soul. "And now you must pay the price."

Rushed footsteps echoed up the second staircase to his left and he was both relieved and terrified to see Rahab pop up. He waved for Rahab to retreat.

"Get out of here!" Crispin warned, but the pirate raced for him instead, determined to help him escape.

Rahab barely managed to reach Crispin before another burst of flame sizzled against the column they were hiding behind.

Niabi let loose a dark and dangerous laugh. "A friend of yours, Crispin?"

"Leave her out of this, Niabi." Crispin shouted; his arms still wrapped tightly around Rahab. "This is between you and me."

"Don't worry," Niabi's voice grew louder as she approached. "You can die together."

They wouldn't make it to the staircase Rahab had come up, and the other set of stairs was blocked by Niabi. She would strike them down with fire if they attempted to escape either direction. There was a window directly in front of them, but being hundreds of feet above the city streets, they would be lucky to die without feeling the excruciating pain of impact first. They were pinned and Crispin was out of options. He would have to face Niabi head on.

Crispin slowly slithered around the column, putting himself between the women. "Why don't you fight me without your magic?" Crispin hissed. "Unless you think you can't beat me in hand-to-hand combat."

A second dagger ejected from Niabi's left sleeve and the flames kissed it. "You want to fight, Crispin?" She flashed a crazed smile. "Show me what you've got."

Crispin clutched the hilt of his longsword tightly as he sprinted toward Niabi. He swung his sword, but she blocked the blow with her right dagger, and sliced at his chest with the blazing weapon in her left. He winced as the hot blade cut through his fighting leathers drawing blood.

Niabi clicked her tongue. "And here I thought this would be a challenge."

She dropped down, swept his legs out from under him, and laughed as Crispin crashed to the floor. The queen approached him as he unsheathed a small dagger in his boot, a trick Salome had insisted would one day save his life and launched it at her chest. Niabi bent backward, avoiding the knife. It was the distraction he needed to get on his feet and sprint back to Rahab.

When he reached her, he wrapped his arms around her torso, and tackled her out of the window behind her. Together they plunged toward the cobblestone streets hundreds of feet below. With the pirate tucked against his chest, he stared at the window they had jumped through and saw Niabi's face. Her hair blew in the light breeze, and he once again saw his mother's face. Would her face really be the last thing he saw before he died?

Rahab didn't scream, nor did she lift her face from his chest to see their fate. She clung to him, trusting him to the very end. But as they neared the city streets, spiraling to their deaths, a blast of air caught them, propelling them upward, before resting them gently on the cobblestones.

Crispin released Rahab from his grasp, and when she opened her eyes, she found herself laying on top of him. Alive. They were alive and sprawled in the street. Rahab glanced up at the White Keep and shuddered at the distance.

She punched his arm. "Don't ever do that to me again!"

Crispin nodded with a weak smile and pulled her to him, planting a kiss against her forehead. "There's no way we should have survived that fall." He pushed up from the ground and helped Rahab to her feet.

"This way, my Prince." A hooded Oden whispered from the darkness of an alley across the street. Obediently, Crispin and Rahab slinked after him. "Where is the Sovereign?"

"He..." Crispin rubbed a dirty hand through his sweaty hair and sighed. "He didn't make it."

Oden didn't turn around to acknowledge his friend's death or that Crispin had failed in rescuing Neempo. He pressed forward to complete the mission of helping them escape Northwind.

"Did you see anything strange?" Crispin asked in a low voice.

Weaving through the labyrinth of the Night District, now closed for business until the next night, Oden only stopped to answer the question once he felt no one would overhear them. "I saw you two falling from the White Keep, if that's what you're asking."

"We shouldn't have survived that fall," Crispin said, "and you were the only one around."

Oden sighed. "No one knows of my magic. Not even the members of the Order."

"You're an Air Manipulator?" Rahab nearly squealed and Oden nodded in confirmation.

"Me saving you; my magic – it needs to stay amongst us," Oden said sternly, his eyebrows knitted together.

"Why?" Crispin pressed as they started down the path again. "Why keep your magic a secret?"

"I haven't lasted this long as an enemy of the crown by speaking of such matters in the middle of the street." Oden whipped around, fire in his eyes. "Magic comes at a price, Prince. And with your sister keeping the company and council of that witch, she is looking to drain magic wielders to harness their power for herself."

"Come with us," Rahab offered as they reached the docks.

"I am needed here." Oden declined, his gaze shifting from her to Crispin. "You will need allies in the city when you return for your crown. Until we meet again, my Prince." He extended his hand and Crispin shook it with gratitude.

"I will return." Crispin said more for himself to hear than anything else.

Oden smiled and bowed his head. "Of this, I have no doubt." The rebel turned on his heel and disappeared into the Night District.

When Oden was out of their sight, Crispin and Rahab made their way to the disguised *Shadow of Death* and hastily boarded the ship as the crew prepared for departure. Haldane greeted them with a curt nod and kept ordering his men to get them out of the harbor before anyone could stop them.

Looking around the deck, Crispin mentally took note to make sure everyone had made it before their launch. Nubis and Corwin were gabbing about their knife collections. Rafi was shimming up to the crow's nest while Ondrej spotted him from below. Phex was giddily showing Ziggy his latest invention. And Rahab was informing Captain Haldane of their failure in procuring the Sovereign. Finally, Crispin spotted Master Penn, the prisoner they had freed from the White Keep dungeons, and her six Keepers huddled together for a drink, and his stomach sank.

He approached Penn, but before he could open his mouth to explain what happened she said, "Did he suffer?"

"How did you -?"

"Your footsteps are heavy, Prince Crispin." Penn stood from her crouched position and offered him a tin mug of what smelled like spiced rum. "Only a man with a burdened heart walks that way."

Crispin accepted the mug and took a sip, letting the rum burn on the way down. "I'm sorry."

"Did he suffer?" Penn asked again softly.

"Not long." Crispin tapped on his mug.

"Thank you for doing what needed to be done." Penn patted him on the shoulder and turned back to her Keepers.

"But I failed," his voice was strained.

Penn shook her head. "The Sovereign might not have survived, but you protected him from suffering a fate worse than death. You did not fail. You did what was asked of you."

"Are we ready to cast off?" Haldane asked Crispin, his arms clasped behind his back.

Crispin glanced up at the White Keep, now crawling with soldiers, smoke rising from the Eastern Courtyard. Despite what Master Penn said, Crispin knew he had failed. He failed to rescue Neempo, and he failed to defeat Niabi. The next time he looked upon the White Keep, he would come out the victor or he would die fighting.

"Crispin?" Rahab's voice brought him back to the present. "Are we ready to cast off?" She repeated Haldane's question and the prince nodded.

"Ready."

CHAPTER 47

NIABI

In a fit of rage, Niabi blasted and burned every inch of the Eastern Courtyard. Smoke wafted up to the sky where streaks of purple, pink, orange, and yellow light glowed from the dawn. She had Crispin cornered and he still slipped through her fingers. He killed the Sovereign, robbing her of her one chance to resurrect Rollo. He would pay. She would make sure of it.

"Are you done?" Vilora's raspy voice grated Niabi's nerves.

The queen looked at her aunt and snarled, "I must speak with the Pirate King."

"For what?" Vilora's question was bordering on insubordinate, but Niabi stomped past her.

Tala burst through the doors of the courtyard, his hair wasn't braided, and he wasn't wearing his armor. He looked like he had heard the explosions, rolled out of bed, and sprinted there. "Niabi? What's going on? Are you hurt?"

She stared at him and hissed, "My brother paid me a little visit."

"What?" Tala's eyes popped open, now fully awake. "Your brother was here?"

"He's gone." Niabi swung the doors open and marched inside the White Keep, beelining for the throne room, Tala and Vilora hot on her heels.

"Gone? As in dead?" Tala asked, his gaze shot to the dirty-faced witch beside him.

"He must be," Vilora said, "he jumped out the window to escape our queen's attack."

Niabi turned around, eyes full of hate. "Crispin is alive! And once the Pirate King gets here, I'll make sure he hunts my brother down and brings him back to me in chains."

"He couldn't have survived that fall," Tala offered, but she interrupted him.

"They have an Air Manipulator." Niabi started her trek to the throne room, not caring if Tala and Vilora were following her. "Right before he and that woman hit the ground, a burst of air saved them. If I hadn't seen it with my own eyes, I wouldn't have believed it."

"An Air Manipulator?" Vilora said in a low, curious voice. "A powerful ally indeed."

Once they reached the throne room she found, Anaktu waiting for her. "Get me the Pirate King. Now!" The Nephilim bowed and thundered from the room.

Niabi sank into her throne and gripped the armrests to calm down and regain her composure before the Pirate King arrived. Crispin's face flashed in her mind, and she grimaced. He looked like a young version of their father, and it made her hate him even more.

She stewed in anger until Uri and his shadow wielder appeared before her.

"Queen," a swift bow from Uri was all Niabi allowed before launching into negotiations.

"How fast is your fleet?" Niabi asked, aware her words were laced with irritation, but she was in a hurry.

Uri flashed a proud smile and pounded a fist to his chest, "The fastest in Pulau."

"I am prepared to offer you double what I paid for the Sovereign, if you capture my brother and return him to me." She got right to it, and by the arch of his eyebrow, he was intrigued.

"Your brother was here?" Uri asked, rubbing his scarred jawline, and exchanging a brief glance with the shadow wielder.

"I don't have time for questions," Niabi shot up from her throne with a vicious growl. "He was headed for the harbor. Hunt him down and bring him to me *alive*. Is that something you can handle, or shall I send someone else?"

Uri raised his hands in surrender, "We can catch him. But what if I wanted another form of payment?"

Tala stepped forward to put the pirate in his place, but Niabi caught him by the forearm. "What is it you want?"

"A partnership." His dark eyes danced in sinister delight. "Unite our kingdoms in marriage. The King of the Seas and the Queen of the Mainland, bound together, we will be unstop -"

"Let me stop you right there," Niabi held up a hand to silence him. "I have no intention of marrying you or uniting our kingdoms. I have offered you a payday unlike anything you, or those filthy pirate scum you call a crew, have seen in your greedy, thieving lives. Take my offer or leave it. You are not the only ship to dispatch."

Uri took a moment to recover from the tongue lashing before nodding. "Double the pay?"

"That's what I said." Every moment she wasted talking to the pirate was another mile her brother gained in escaping her.

Uri whispered something to the blind shadow wielder. He glanced up at Niabi and smiled. "What shall we do with the rest of the ship's crew once we find him?"

Niabi waved a dismissive hand. "Do whatever you want with them. My price is for my brother."

"Then you have a deal. Your brother is as good as yours, Queen." Uri bowed again before strutting out of the throne room, his petite companion following him closely.

"Alive," she reiterated, "and unharmed."

Uri threw his hand up and glanced over his shoulder at the queen. "Yes, yes. Alive and unharmed."

With that, they disappeared and Niabi plopped down onto her throne. Her hand rested on her belly as fatigue set in. Soon, she would have her brother kneeling before her in this very throne room. Soon, she would slice her knife across his throat, making him pay the price for snatching a second chance with Rollo from her grasp. Soon. Just not soon enough.

CHAPTER 48
SALOME

Determined to keep her promise, Salome made sure Utara wasn't anywhere near the executioner's block to watch her mother take her last breath. She had dragged the girl through the Rose Garden until they found a bench tucked underneath an archway of roses.

Utara rubbed her eyes, from lack of sleep or from crying all night, Salome wasn't sure and didn't ask. With the sweet aroma of thousands of roses surrounding them, Salome wrapped her arms around Utara to keep her warm as the morning light broke across the horizon.

Salome closed her eyes, resting her chin on top of Utara's head. Mika was scheduled to be executed at dawn, so she reached for Damaris' mind, knowing the Oracle would be in the arena watching Mika's final moments.

"Damaris," she begged for her to answer, hoping to get a glimpse into what was happening. *"Damaris, please."*

Damaris answered her call, not with thoughts, but with sight. Being the Oracle of Myr, she gave insight into the past and present, and through her eyes, Salome could see what was happening.

Mika held her head high as she emerged from the mouth of the tunnel that led into the depths of the arena. She walked by the Qata Vishna who lined the path to the executioner's block. This arena was where Mika had fought, trained, and bled, and where she would take her last breath. Stripped of her red armor and standing in a loose white shirt and navy pants, Mika nodded her head, giving a silent order for her warriors to stand down. She glanced up to the royal box where her mother, the newly christened queen, and her Aunt Damaris sat.

Zara was pale, and the bags underneath her green eyes were visible from where Mika stood over forty feet away.

Damaris's face was stained with the dried tears she had cried all night. She grabbed Zara's wrist and pleaded for Mika's life once more. "Spare her, Zara."

Zara straightened in her chair and lifted her chin higher. "Mika made her choice. She knows our laws. A life for a life."

"But -"

"My first act as queen cannot be to forgive our mother's assassination. To show mercy would make me look weak."

"Mercy can also show great strength, sister." Damaris knelt before Zara's feet. "Spare Mika. Send the Qata Vishna to find Marina."

"A life for a life." Zara's throat bobbed; eyes glossed over with tears.

Mika closed her eyes. A peace washed over her as she listened to the crash of the waves against the cliffs and felt the light morning breeze dance around her. She could smell the sweet aromatics of the vineyards and the mixture of spices sizzling in the markets.

Surrounded by her sisters in bond and blood, the Qata Vishna crisscrossed their curved blades across their chests, paying their last respects to their Red Maiden.

Mika opened her eyes and met Damaris's teary gaze with a smile. She glanced at her mother who now had tears streaming down her face. Mika bowed her head. A silent goodbye. She knelt before the executioner's block and rested her neck against the wood stained red with blood.

The executioner heaved the scythe above her head. A sad smile tugged at Mika's lips as she whispered, "As deep as the sea." The blade sliced through the air, thudding loudly against the block.

The Qata Vishna slashed their two blades against each other as they whipped them to their sides. The sound echoed through the arena. Their Red Maiden had fallen.

TEARS SLIPPED down Salome's cheeks as she stroked Utara's braided black hair.

"She's gone, isn't she?" Utara whispered, biting her bottom lip, trying not to cry.

Salome tightened her arms around Utara's chest. "I'm sorry."

Utara's body trembled and Salome heard her softly sobbing. "I thought... I thought maybe..."

Salome buried her face in Utara's hair and together they cried until the noonday sun warmed their skin. Salome understood more than most what it felt like to lose a mother. Having to grow up missing her smile, her scent, her voice. She promised Mika she would look after Utara, and she would keep her word. No matter what it cost, she would survive the war, and she would come back for Utara.

"Princess Salome?"

Salome recognized Seraphina's voice, but instead of the icy bite it normally carried, it was solemn, almost broken. She peeled herself from Utara and met the twin's glossy gaze. It was odd to see Seraphina standing alone, her twin nowhere in sight.

"The queen has requested your presence in the Inner Depths."

Realizing Utara had fallen asleep in her arms, Salome lifted the girl to carry her back to her room, but Seraphina stepped forward, blocking her path.

"Please," Seraphina looked down at the child and whispered, "let me."

Salome didn't have the mental strength at the time to note Seraphina's rare usage of the word please. She just nodded, kissed Utara's forehead, and passed her into Seraphina's extended arms.

Grabbing Seraphina's shoulder before she could turn and walk away, Salome cupped the twin's face in her hands. Silently, they stared into each other's watery eyes, until Seraphina bowed her head and vanished into the palace.

Salome knew she was needed, but she took a moment to have a few uninterrupted breaths to settle her frayed nerves. Every time she closed her eyes, she saw the scythe slice through the air toward Mika's neck. The image of seeing her life end, took Salome's breath away. She'd not seen an execution before and she wasn't sure she could stomach another one, even if it was for someone she despised.

Death was close. Salome could sense her presence. Sometimes Salome felt as if Death tailed her day and night, waiting. Biding her time, taking those she loved, until she was ready to snatch Salome's soul too.

"I am not ready," Salome said, somehow knowing Death was listening. *"I have unfinished business."*

She turned on her heel and marched through the halls until she reached the double bronze doors that led to the Inner Depths. The guards opened the doors without her needing to break stride and she marched into the throne room. She expected to find Zara sitting on her throne, but instead, the new queen was crumpled on the floor, staring at her reflection in the small, rectangular pool in the middle of the room.

Her aunt was disheveled. The kohl around her eyes was smudged, and her hair wasn't fashioned in the intricate braids she fancied. Salome's heart shattered at the sight of this woman of great power on her knees, sobbing into the pool.

"It was Mika's last request that these be given to you," Zara didn't look up, but motioned to the table on her right, where Mika's red armor sat.

Mika's ghost. Her identity, her purpose, her passion, displayed on the table and being offered to Salome. She shrunk back a step.

"I don't understand," Salome's voice cracked as her gaze met Zara's bloodshot eyes. "That belongs to the Red Maiden."

"The Qata Vishna will need a commander." Zara reluctantly pushed herself up from the ground. "The Red Maiden must have royal Myridian blood. Mika is dead." The words smacked Salome across the face, awakening a fresh batch of tears. "Even if we found Marina, she is no warrior. And Utara is too young."

"But you -"

"My fighting days are long gone," Zara interrupted her.

Her aunt glanced down at her hands and Salome noticed them shaking. She hadn't noticed before, but when she thought about it, every time they were in the same room, Zara had her hands clasped in her lap.

"I can no longer grip a weapon." Zara admitted. "It has to be you. Mika knew it too. That's why she wanted you to have the armor." Zara stared deep into Salome's eyes. "If we are to go to war with the North, you will need to lead the Qata Vishna."

"War with the North?" Salome was surprised. "You are going to help me?"

"I have already ordered the Qata Vishna to prepare for war." Zara nodded her head and walked toward the table where her daughter's armor laid, she patted the breastplate gently. "We will need time to ready our ships, but know the Qata Vishna, your people, your kin; we are with you."

Salome closed the distance between them. "Why?" she whispered.

"Bilhah. Nym. Mika." Zara tilted her head and Salome saw fire flickering behind those anguished green eyes. "Niabi will answer for their deaths. She will answer for all the blood she has spilled."

Salome slid a finger across Mika's helmet. "What do I need to do?"

"You are intuitive, just like your mother." Zara squared her shoulders to her niece. "If I could grant you the title of Red Maiden, I would, but I can't. No queen can. You must earn it."

Salome nodded. She assumed there would be some sort of task, some duel, that needed to be exacted for the Qata Vishna to see and accept her as their new Red Maiden.

"I have heard of your plans to leave with Prince Jinn tonight." Zara's eyes narrowed.

"I have business on the Mainland, before I reach Oakenshire." Salome offered, "Harbona's instructions."

Zara bobbed her head once Harbona's name was mentioned. She wouldn't question the orders of the Seer. "Can you delay your departure a day or two?"

"Yes." She was sure Jinn would accommodate her if she asked.

"Then you will need to rest tonight. Because tomorrow at dawn, you will face the Trial of Blood and Ash."

"I will not fail you." Salome said.

Zara clasped her hand and whispered, "You are my kin. You are Myridian royalty. You are a Qata Vishna. Failure is not in your blood."

CHAPTER 49

ADONIJAH

After Salome met with her Aunt Zara, she was on edge. Adonijah assumed it had something to do with Mika's execution, but she refused to answer any of his questions, saying she needed everyone to be together, so she only had to explain once. When she said "everyone" he didn't realize she meant Jinn and Kai, as well.

Kai stood in front of the doors to Salome's chambers like a dutiful watchdog. Seraphina and Rosalina sat on the plush, white sofa. Seraphina pretended Cato didn't exist, even though he looked at her like she was the moon to his sun. Cato sat in the chair next to Adonijah, while Jinn took up the armchair directly across from him.

Adonijah could sense Jinn's eyes on him. If a stare off was what the prince wanted, that was exactly what he was going to get from him. Jinn smirked, as if to say he wasn't intimidated by Adonijah. And Adonijah exhaled a puff of smoke from his pipe in the Easterner's direction, not impressed.

Seraphina cleared her throat, drawing their attention. She shook her head with an icy glare as if to say, *"Knock it off, before I throw you both off the balcony."*

The men settled in their chairs and out of fear, or respect, for Seraphina, kept their dirty looks to themselves.

Salome walked into the lounge from her bedroom wringing her hands. She looked pale; like she had been crying for the last hour and was mustering up the courage to face them. She sat on the second couch facing the twins; Adonijah and Cato to one side, and Jinn and Kai on the other. She rubbed her hands up and down her thighs and cleared her throat.

"I figured having everyone together would make this easier on me."

Adonijah cocked his head to the side. "What are you talking about?"

Salome sighed deeply. "I met with my Aunt Zara today. She told me that Mika left me her armor, with the intent I become the next Red Maiden."

The room was quieter than a graveyard. Adonijah's eyes flew to the twins and noticed they had stiffened.

"You say that like it's a bad thing." Cato glanced around at everyone in the room and saw their hunched shoulders and tight-lipped grimaces. "Am I missing something?"

"In order to be the Red Maiden," Salome calmly explained to Cato, who always seemed to be the last to understand, "I will have to face the Trial of Blood and Ash."

Cato swallowed a grape whole and his body twitched. "Well, that sounds like... fun?"

Seraphina scoffed and shook her head. Cato seemed excited she even acknowledged him in public and smiled.

"The trail is at dawn." Salome announced, drawing all eyes, once again.

Jinn sat up straighter in his seat. "That soon?"

Salome looked at the prince, her fingers absent-mindedly tapping the armrests of her chair. "I know you were due to sail tonight -"

"The ship sails when I say it does." Jinn waved his hand in the air. "We leave when you are ready." He smiled at Salome and Adonijah wanted to rip his arms off.

"Thank you," Salome mustered a smile, but it didn't stretch far.

Adonijah crossed his arms over his chest. "What does this trial entail?"

"I'm not really sure," Salome admitted, her eyes shooting to the twins who exchanged a look. "Do I want to know?"

Rosalina nodded her head and Seraphina said, "There's an islet about twenty yards off the coast of Antrope. The candidate for Red Maiden is rowed out there and left to fight the Cornigera."

Cato squirmed in his seat, "What is a Cornigera?"

"It sleeps deep in the sea," Seraphina continued, her eyes filled with fear, "but when someone steps foot on the islet, it awakens and comes to ... eat."

"Is it...?" Salome didn't finish her question.

"Terrifying?" Rosalina filled in the blank and nodded, like she could see the creature in her mind.

"What does it look like?" Cato asked after a brief silence amongst the group.

Seraphina made eye contact with Cato for the first time that evening. She had tears welling up in her hazel eyes. "It has the body of an enormous cat, four legs with razor sharp claws. Its spikes run the length of its spine, starting from its oblong head to its whip for a tail. It is so thin; you can see its ribs from Antrope's shores. It has gills and scales and tiny eyes where a nose should be. But the most frightening thing about it, and the most dangerous, are its rows of jagged teeth. It can open its mouth wide enough to bite a Qata Vishna's head clean off."

While everyone in the room was focused on Seraphina's description of the Cornigera, Adonijah watched Salome. Although, she tried to keep a neutral expression, he knew she was terrified, and it pained him.

"You don't have to do this," Adonijah offered, hoping she wouldn't go through with the fight.

"Zara promised me the Qata Vishna for the war, but only if they have a Red Maiden to lead them." Salome steadied her voice. "Mika is gone. Utara is far too young. Marina is on the run and Zara is the queen. I am the only one left." Her eyes darted to Adonijah, and she shrugged, "I don't have a choice."

"You have other options, Salome." Jinn chimed in and Adonijah saw red.

"Are you seriously bringing up your marriage proposal?" Adonijah growled across the room at Jinn, fists clenched.

Jinn leaned forward; hands clasped between his knees. "I meant she could try to send word to her brother about his progress. Or she could meet with some of the rebels in Northwind." He smirked, "But it's nice to know you are well-informed on my affairs."

"She is none of your concern." Adonijah was itching to fistfight him.

Jinn tilted his head to the side, recognizing the challenge, and willing to accept. "And yet, she has not declined my offer."

Adonijah jumped to his feet and Jinn pushed himself out of his seat, squaring up.

Seraphina hopped up and stood between them, hands stretched out, pressing into their chests. "Stop it. Both of you. How dare you two argue with her in the room? She has more to worry about than your feelings and fragile egos." She pushed them back a step and closed the distance between her and Salome. "You will beat the Cornigera," she knelt before Salome's seat. "You just need to sleep and to keep focused."

Salome was quiet and didn't respond. It was then, Adonijah noticed her eyes were glazed over. Seraphina waved her hand in Salome's face, but there was no indication she noticed. Rattled, she grabbed Salome by the shoulders and shook her. "Your Highness? Princess? Salome!" Salome's eyes fluttered and the glossiness was gone. "Are you ok?"

Salome bobbed her head and whispered, "I know what I need to do."

"Did you have another vision?" Adonijah knelt by her side, grabbing her hand.

"Mika showed me how to beat it."

"How?" Adonijah asked. If Mika had given her insight, that might be the difference between life or death for Salome. And he desperately wanted, needed her to live.

She shook her head. "She told me not to say anything. Bad luck," she shrugged with a forced smile.

Adonijah traced his thumb down her jawline. He was grateful she had missed his encounter with Jinn. Seraphina was right, for once. Salome had more to worry about right now than him. Or Jinn. Adonijah narrowed his eyes as the prince approached Salome.

"If you need anything, let me know." Jinn squeezed her hand.

Seraphina's nostrils flared and she shooed them out. "If there is nothing else, Rosalina and I need to help the princess get ready for bed."

"You don't need to do that," Salome protested softly. "You are Qata Vishna -"

"We are sworn to serve you, to protect you," Rosalina interjected, still pale from Mika's execution. "We will continue to serve you until you die."

"That's not -"

"Please," Rosalina begged Salome once more, her bottom lip quivered. "It was our queen's last command. Our Red Maiden's last assignment. We are to serve until your grandmother releases us or you breathe your last. Please -"

Salome rushed to the couch Rosalina was sitting on and wrapped her arms around her. "It's alright," Salome brushed her fingers through the twin's hair. "I gratefully accept your service."

Seraphina's prickly disposition returned, and she motioned for everyone to leave the room. Adonijah reluctantly left, even though all he wanted to do was wrap his arms around Salome and make sure she was safe. To hold her as she slept and kiss her the moment she woke up. But with Seraphina and Rosalina determined not to leave Salome unattended, any hope for a private moment with the princess was gone.

Cato discreetly squeezed Seraphina's hand by the door right before she slammed it in his face. The Stormcrag turned around with a wide grin. "She likes me." He practically danced across the hallway and into the suite they shared, but before Adonijah could stride in after him, Jinn reappeared, leaning against the wall.

"What do you want?" Adonijah closed the door, so Cato wouldn't overhear them.

"I know you don't like me," Jinn started and Adonijah scoffed.

"An understatement, but please," he motioned for the Easterner to keep talking, "continue."

"I'm not going anywhere." Jinn slipped his hands in his pockets. "You care for Salome. I do, too."

"You only care about her because she's the Hunter." Adonijah snorted and Jinn straightened.

"She's the Hunter?" the prince whispered.

Adonijah rubbed a hand over his forehead. *Damn.* "Stay away from her."

"I already told you, I'm not going anywhere." Jinn tilted his head to the side. "I wanted to be upfront with you. You'll do what you want to do to win her heart. And I will do the same."

"You want to marry her for power." Adonijah's brow furrowed. "She deserves more than that."

"She's a princess," he took a powerful step toward Adonijah. "I am a prince. With our houses united once again, we can do a lot of good for our people."

"Salome isn't good with cages."

Jinn's eyes narrowed. "What is that supposed to mean?"

"She's going to lead armies into battle, and you want her to give up her homeland, her people, and her freedom, to be your prize." Adonijah shook his head in disgust and poked his index finger into Jinn's chest. "She doesn't belong behind stone walls."

"And she would be happy roaming Adalore with you for the rest of her life?" He flicked Adonijah's hand away. "When this war is won, she will have responsibilities you won't even begin to comprehend. Everything Salome does, will be for the benefit of her people."

"Crispin will be responsible for Northwind." Adonijah countered, his blood boiled each time Jinn said Salome's name.

"Crispin will be king, yes," Jinn agreed, "but Salome will be expected to be one of two things. She will either be asked to be an ambassador and travel to the Ten Kingdoms on her brother's behalf, or she will be married to strengthen relations with one of their allies. That is the life of a royal. I am no different."

"You are the heir to the Jade Throne; you can choose anyone to be your wife."

"If Crispin marries Salome to a foreign prince or lord, which he will most likely see as his only option as a new king to solidify alliances, who would you think he would commit her to?" Jinn ticked off his fingers. "There's me, of course. Heru, the heir of Numbio. A good man, but from what I've heard, already has his sights set on another. The Almighty forbid she is promised to that incestuous bastard, Thanos of Gomorrah. I'm sure Benaiah of Borg, that power hungry menace, would love if one of his sons married the Hunter. And then there's the abusive Pirate King. So, you see, there aren't many good options available to her."

"You assume Crispin will be like the rest of the Adalorian kings, but you don't know him." Adonijah didn't know him either, but he refused to believe Crispin would offer his sister up on a silver platter just to make himself look like a powerful king.

"You don't know him either." Jinn flashed a wicked smile. "But maybe you're right. Maybe, Crispin won't be like other kings. Maybe, Salome will break with tradition and pick a sell-sword and roam Adalore on horseback. Power doesn't suit everyone." Jinn shrugged and patted Adonijah's shoulder as he walked by him.

"If it were up to me," Adonijah whipped around to look at him, "you'd be sailing back to Sakurai tonight."

Jinn stuffed his hands in his pockets. "Good thing, it's not up to you." Without waiting for Adonijah to respond, Jinn cloaked himself, and vanished, solidly ending their encounter.

Adonijah didn't care that Jinn tried to size him up and mark his territory. What bothered him was that most of what Jinn said was true. There was a possibility after the war, Salome wouldn't choose him. There was a possibility Crispin would ask or force her to marry a foreign dignitary and from the conversation he had with Salome before, she was prepared to do what was best for her people.

Her people.

They would trump him if it came down to it. Adonijah could spend the next weeks, months, or years fighting by Salome's side and still lose her heart.

CHAPTER 50

SALOME

Dawn was a few hours away and Salome hadn't slept. The last thing she told her friends was that Mika showed her in a vision how to defeat the Cornigera. But that was a lie. She had a vision, but not one she could, or would share with them. She saw the Cornigera. It was everything Seraphina and Rosalina had described. Every time she closed her eyes she saw its scales, its red, oval eyes, and the jagged rows of seemingly endless teeth.

She didn't see how to kill the Cornigera.

She saw how the Cornigera killed her.

If her friends knew the truth, they wouldn't let her step one foot into the Trial of Blood and Ash. But she had to. She knew it deep in her bones.

Salome saw her death, but she wasn't going down without a fight.

Salome stood at the edge of Antrope, the isle where the Qata Vishna trained. There was a slight chill in the early morning air that made Salome cling to her cloak. Or maybe, she trembled because her fate was to be determined on the islet that she was staring at.

An audience had gathered and lined up and down the pebble beach, including Zara, Damaris, Salome's friends, and most of the high-ranking warriors of the Qata Vishna. *An audience to watch her die.* She shook her head, refusing to let that thought take root in her mind.

"Your Highness?" One of the Qata Vishna in a rowboat called out to her, "Are you ready?"

Salome nodded and shrugged off her cloak. She turned and handed it to Adonijah who hadn't said much all morning. She threw her arms around his neck and squeezed.

"No matter what happens..." She wanted to say I will fight, live, and die by your side, but instead she finished with, "...don't interfere."

Before he could respond, she jumped in the boat and was being rowed the short distance to the islet. As soon as Salome stepped foot on the tiny landmass, the Qata Vishna took off for shore.

Her eyes darted around the treeless islet that was less than an acre in size. It was nothing more than a flat, rocky piece of land with nowhere for her to hide. Nothing to pick up and throw in a pinch to buy herself extra time. She felt naked and alone. Images of her dying flashed in her mind. She blinked the negative thoughts free before the water started to bubble behind her.

Salome turned around and braced herself, planting her feet to the ground like Mika had taught her. She grabbed the two curved swords Mika had left her from their holsters on her back and held them at her sides. Her breathing quickened, and she focused on calming down, lest she get the jitters, and make a stupid mistake that could cost her, her life.

Slowly pawing out of the sea, the Cornigera's red eyes and sharp claws were the first things she noticed. She greatly underestimated how enormous the beast was; with his head at least twelve feet above the ground and teeth the length of daggers, Salome knew this would be the most challenging fight of her entire life. *And quite possibly the last.*

All she could do was wait as the creature rose from the watery depths with every intention of ripping her to shreds and swallowing her whole. She narrowed her eyes and held her ground as the monster shook the water from his body like a dog.

Inhale. Exhale. Inhale. Exhale.

Salome stood as still as a statue, watching the creature stalk toward her. His hungry, bloodthirsty gaze was fixed on her, sizing her up. Baring his teeth, Salome suspected the Cornigera didn't see her as much of a threat. A mistake on his part.

The beast circled her, hissing, and puffing hot breath against her skin. She side-eyed the creature; remembering everything Zophar had taught her about defeating a much larger opponent.

"Patience," Zophar had said. *"Let your enemy come to you. And when he underestimates you, use his strengths against him."*

The Cornigera completed his circle around her and stood a few feet in front of her. Their eyes met. It looked like he was smirking, if the beast could even manage that with all those razor-sharp fangs.

He hissed.

She hissed back.

Making sure to keep light on her feet, she knew she would never be able to overpower the beast with brute strength, but she could adapt, and Almighty willing, she would learn how to use the creature's strengths against it.

The Cornigera stood on his back two legs and howled, sending a shiver down her spine. His front paws thudded to the ground, shaking the area between him and Salome. The creature leapt toward her. She side-stepped and deflected his claws with her blades. The beast yelped as blue liquid oozed from his front right leg. She had drawn first blood.

Fire flashed in the beast's eyes. His tail whistled through the air and sliced into her side like a whip, leaving a red lash. She bit back a scream and regained her footing, bracing herself for another attack.

Salome lowered her body, hunching her back to make herself appear like a smaller target. Without warning, the Cornigera sprinted toward her, knocking her off her feet. Before he could slash her face with his claws, she tumbled out of the way, slicing his chest with her blades.

The monster furiously scratched and clawed her swords out of her hands. As the weapons flew in opposite directions and out of her reach, he trampled her, knocking the wind out of her. He turned on his heel and made his way back to run over her again, but she scrambled to her feet, and sprinted to snatch one of Mika's blades.

Salome hit the ground hard, smacking her forehead against the rocky terrain. Before she could touch her face to check for blood, she was dragged backwards. She looked at her left leg; his tail was wrapped around her ankle.

She unsheathed the wolf dagger from her thigh and in a desperate last attempt to escape his grasp, she turned, and sliced through his tail, freeing herself. The beast roared; anger, pain, and revenge were heard in his cries.

Salome pushed up to her feet, but her left knee was throbbing. As quickly as she could, she hobbled to grab ahold of one of the twin curved blades. She could hear the creature chasing her and pure adrenaline propelled her to the sword.

In a flash, the Cornigera was on top of her, his teeth digging into her right forearm which she used to shield her face from his attack. Her scream was piercing, and she heard murmurs and gasps from the shoreline where the crowd was watching.

Salome's blood was splattered all over her bronze fighting leathers. She took the curved blade clutched in her left hand and stabbed the inside of his mouth, forcing him to release his hold on her. To buy herself a moment to breathe, she stuck her fingers into the creature's red eyes, but before she could blind him, he retreated, stomping over her battered body.

Salome laid on the cold, rocky ground, with her eyes closed. She was beaten, exhausted, and was starting to lose consciousness from the blow to her head. Blood was flowing like a river from her mangled arm, and the sting from the saltwater breeze kissing her wounds was almost unbearable. As she started to fade and give into the darkness, she heard Jinn's voice, felt his hands on her skin, his lips on hers.

"Wake up, Salome," Jinn pleaded in a whisper, blowing air into her lungs. "You need to wake up."

"Jinn?" Salome called out through her thoughts, too tired to speak.

"You need to get up." Jinn replied mentally. *"If you don't, that beast will kill you and I can't watch you die."*

Salome's eyes fluttered open. She didn't see the prince anywhere, but she could feel his warm hands cupping her face. *"Jinn?"*

"I cloaked myself," he explained quickly. *"If the Myridians catch me interfering they will disqualify you."*

Salome rubbed the knot developing on her forehead when she spotted the beast. He was about thirty feet away, recovering from his wounds. The curved blade she embedded in his cheek now laid at his feet. Blue blood oozed down his pale scales. As soon as the wounded Cornigera caught sight of her, his red eyes flared in rejuvenated anger.

"Finish this, Salome," Jinn begged, squeezing her hands. He kissed her lips and rested his forehead against hers. *"Survive. I need you."*

"You need to go before it's too late." Salome didn't want to risk reaching out for him, fearful that someone might notice, and suspect Jinn helped her. *"Go. Please."*

She didn't feel Jinn anymore and hoped he listened and swam back to shore. She struggled to her feet. Her right arm was shredded, and she couldn't grip a weapon. Her left knee was already swollen to twice its normal size. Cuts, sprains, and forming bruises were littered all over her aching body. Blood trickled down to her feet, staining her clothes red.

Shaking the ground with each thundering step he took, the Cornigera sprinted toward her.

Jinn had saved her twice now, but if she didn't kill the beast charging for her in the next few seconds, she knew she wasn't going to survive. Her death flashed before her eyes again and she shoved the image away.

"I am not ready," she told Death once more when she felt her presence circling. *"I am not ready to meet you."*

Salome held her ivory, wolf dagger in her left hand tightly. Her last weapon. She stood her ground like the fearsome soldier Zophar trained her to be. Running, jumping, kicking, and leaping were off the table, meaning she only had one option left. Let the creature attack her.

With ten feet between them, the beast leapt into the air, teeth bared, claws out. This was it. The moment she would either live or die. It was her or the Cornigera. She heard gasps and cries echo from the shore, but she refused to take one last look. If she took her eyes off the monster, she would most certainly die.

Salome threw her bloodied right arm up to block the creature's jagged teeth from biting her face. As he landed on top of her, she fell to the ground with it, thrusting her dagger into its bony chest. The creature let out a bloodcurdling screech and Salome screamed as her back smashed onto the rocks.

For a moment, Salome just laid there, drenched with the Cornigera's blue blood. Her body ached; her right arm was too bloody to determine if it was ripped open from the creature's teeth or if it was severely broken. The dead beast wilted on top of her; his weight crushing and preventing air from reaching her lungs. She began to panic when she realized she was suffocating.

Jinn's last words echoed in her mind. *"Survive. I need you."*

Salome thought about her brother. She thought about Zophar, Adonijah, Jinn, and the friends and family she had found along her journey. And one thing was certain: this wasn't how she would leave this life; crushed and suffocated by a sea demon when there were people who needed her to live, needed her to survive.

Broken and bloody, Salome mustered the last bit of strength and tenacity she had to slip out from underneath the beast's carcass.

As soon as she was free, she shot to her swollen knees and sucked in the deepest breath she could, filling her lungs with the salty, sea air. She opened her bloodshot eyes and saw the line of Qata Vishna along the shore crisscrossing their curved swords against their chests. They were saluting her.

Salome forced herself to her feet. She no longer had her curved swords handy, but she crisscrossed her arms over her chest, paying them respect as their new Red Maiden.

The rowboat made it to the islet in a flash. Adonijah jumped out and ran to her, sweeping her battered body in his arms. He clutched her tightly to his chest, drawing a wince from her lips.

Adonijah planted a kiss on her dirty, sweaty forehead. "You did it," he whispered against her temple. "You did it."

That was the last thing she heard Adonijah say before she closed her eyes and drifted into darkness. But before she lost consciousness, she reached out to Jinn.

"Thank you. You saved me."

"You saved yourself." She felt a warmth flood her. *"Rest, Red Maiden. Rest."*

CHAPTER 51

HARBONA

Several days had passed and Makeda seemed to have made it her mission to avoid Harbona at all costs. When he knocked on her bedroom door, she wasn't there. At dinner, she was nowhere to be found. Even strolling through the gardens reaped no reward. If he didn't know any better, he would have guessed Makeda's magical affinity was cloaking, not water wielding.

Odelia told him to give their daughter space, to let her come to him when she was ready to talk, but now that he had a daughter, he wanted to spend as much time with her as possible. He wanted to get to know her and make up for lost time.

Kayven and Abba refused to let Harbona sulk another day, and insisted he show them what mortal fighting tactics he picked up from his one thousand years on the Mainland. Harbona had been involved in more wars, than he cared to remember, and though he was reluctant to join them in the sparring ring, once they started, he was glad they dragged him there.

"So," Kayven wiped sweat from his forehead as they walked back inside Lavena's villa, "do you think your mortals can win this war?"

Harbona sipped from his glass of water and poured his friends a cup, which they gladly accepted. "I believe they can. They have the Hunter on their side."

"Ah, yes," Kayven chuckled, "the all-powerful Hunter. Mortals are delightful in their devotion to a myth."

"The Hunters are not a myth," Harbona shook his head. "I have fought side-by-side with most of the Hunters. They are remarkable beings."

"You really do care for them," Abba said, as he plopped down on the couch.

Harbona smiled, crinkling the sides of his eyes, "They are resilient creatures."

"And dangerous," Lavena's voice sliced through the room like an icy chill. Her grey eyes slid over to Abba, who had his boots kicked up on her marble table in front of the couch, and he immediately planted his feet on the floor.

"Why do you hate them?" Harbona asked, defensive.

"The hearts of mortals are easily swayed." Lavena paced the round room, hands clasped in front of her. "Their allegiance can be bought and sold to the highest bidder. For being called human, they lack humanity. They rule based on fear and they do not know when to show mercy."

"But Lykos was different?" Harbona regretted the question as soon as it left his tongue. Lykos wasn't like his father, Issachar. He was honorable, righteous, noble, kind, and brave: he was everything a king should be and was never given a chance.

Lavena's gaze nearly burned a hole in Harbona's heart. "The truth is, being with Lykos changed my mind about mortals. I began to see what he saw in them. Their capacity to love, grow, adapt, and hope. I knew he would be a great king, if not the greatest king the Mainland had ever seen. And I was willing to give up everything to be by his side: my home, my people, even my immortality."

She stood in front of Harbona, her eyes filled with tears, a rare and unsettling sight. "You asked why I hate mortals? I do not hate them, I pity them. Despite all the good they are capable of, they choose evil. They choose the way of the sword, instead of diplomacy. They choose to seek revenge, instead of pursuing justice. They fill themselves with hatred and wonder why their world burns." Her icy tone was now a rasped whisper. "And they choose to kill good men, so evil men may rule. They strip wives of their husbands and deny children their fathers – all for the sake of wearing a crown stained with the blood of the innocent."

"The good ones are worth fighting side-by-side with. The good ones are worth dying for," Harbona didn't care that it wasn't Ethereal in nature, he reached out and grasped one of Lavena's hands. Her pained gaze met his, but she didn't retract her hand. "Lykos knew before Niabi arrived that Death had called for him. He did not try to run or hide. He stayed to fight for his people and to protect those he loved. Lykos lived bravely and died with a clear conscience. That is the man you loved. And he is not the only good one left."

"What do you want from me?" Lavena asked, her eyes and voice softening.

"Nothing." Harbona smiled weakly. "But Lykos would want you to remember how much he loved you."

A tear slipped down Lavena's pale cheek. Kayven came up behind her and wrapped his arms around her, resting his chin on top of her head. "I am starting to forget what he looked like. If it were not for Keeva, I would have lost him completely."

Harbona lifted his hands to rest against Lavena's temples. "May I?"

Lavena nodded and closed her eyes.

Harbona planted fresh images of Lykos in her mind. As a Seer, he had crystal clear memories and was more than happy to share them with Lavena. When she opened her watery eyes, she smiled as if relieved.

"Thank you for giving him back to me." Lavena whispered. Kayven tightened his embrace around her, and she raised her hands to squeeze his forearms.

Someone cleared their throat by the arched entryway in the hall and the four Immortals turned to see Makeda standing in the opening. She shifted her weight from one foot to the other and twisted one of her braids.

"I'm sorry for interrupting."

Harbona took a step toward her, glad to see her standing there. "There is nothing to apologize for, Makeda."

Makeda's grey eyes shifted from the floor and met Harbona's longing gaze. "I thought maybe we could take a walk. If you're up to it, that is. I'm sure you're very busy -"

"I would love to," Harbona smiled.

Makeda led him through the garden until they came to the hillside cliff where the river disappeared over the edge. They sat on a granite bench and said nothing for several minutes. Harbona allowed her to take the lead. He didn't want to push her to talk. If this was all he would get from her today, it was more than enough. It was a start.

"She never told me who you were," Makeda spat the words out before she could change her mind. "I suppose I should have figured out the Ethereal part based on my grey eyes."

"I know this must be strange for you," Harbona offered.

"It shouldn't be though," Makeda shook her head, twiddling her thumbs in her lap. "I always knew you existed; you didn't know anything about me. This is probably weird for you."

"I left your mother all those years ago without any warning and it was not fair to her. I was a coward. I realized how strong my love for her was and did not think I was worthy of her." Harbona stared toward the horizon, taking in the sweeping views of Caelestis. "I was banished from my home and branded for everyone to know it. Here, I was the heir; the next Eldaar. On the Mainland, I have nothing to offer. I left to avoid the inevitable: the moment your mother realized she was better off without me." Harbona turned to look at Makeda who had tears streaming down her face. "Believe me, Makeda, if I had known about you, I never would have abandoned you."

"Mother never thought you were unworthy of her love." Makeda slid her hand toward Harbona's and hesitated before resting her palm on top of his hand. "If you could only see yourself through her eyes, through my eyes, you would never doubt how loved you are."

"I wish I could go back in time and be the father you deserved."

"If it's alright with you," Makeda exhaled a nervous breath. "I would really like it if we could get to know each other now. Maybe, it's not too late for us to be a family."

"You do not hate me?" Harbona released some of the tension in his shoulders.

"How could I hate you?" Makeda asked, wide-eyed. "I've waited my entire life to meet you."

He smiled. "So, are you really a Water Wielder?"

She bobbed her head with a chuckle. "And a good one, too."

"Well, of course you are a good one." Harbona puffed out his chest. "You are my daughter after all."

She laughed and stood up, motioning to the river. "Would you like to see what I can do?"

Harbona took her extended hand and nodded. "I would love that."

CHAPTER 52
SALOME

Salome's eyes fluttered open, and she stared up at the familiar wood beamed ceiling in her bedroom. Relief flooded her. She survived. But as quickly as relief rushed through her, so did pain. Salome lifted her right arm slowly and saw it was covered in cloth bandages. There was no telling what damage hid beneath all the layers of white wrappings, and honestly, she wasn't in a hurry to find out. Those scars would most likely be the ugliest ones yet.

A groan escaped her lips as she pushed herself up to a seated position. Wanting to get a better look at her appearance in the mirror, she attempted to swing her legs off the side of her bed, but gasped when she heard a voice behind her.

"You're awake."

She turned around and winced from the swift movement. Adonijah was resting beside her. His hair was disheveled and there were dark bags underneath his bloodshot eyes. *Had he been there all night?*

"Always sneaking," Salome shook her head and rubbed her chest, still calming down from the early morning scare.

"It's not sneaking, if I've been by your side the entire time." Adonijah cradled the back of his head in his hands, stretching his legs out.

She hadn't seen him like this before. No leather or weapons adorned his muscular body. No riding boots smeared with dirt. No hood to hide his face or pipe between his lips. Adonijah laid there in a loose white shirt that was untucked from his pants and unbuttoned at the top. She spied a glimpse of his toned chest and averted her gaze with a sharp inhale.

"How long have I been out?" Salome ran fingers through her tangled curls, brutally aware of what horrific shape she must be in.

"Four days."

Salome's eyes popped wide open. "Four days?" Panic flooded her. "The ship?"

Adonijah sat up, reached for her left, uninjured hand, and gently squeezed.

"Breathe, Salome. Everything is fine." His gaze met hers. "Jinn hasn't left. He's kept his word about waiting until you are ready to travel."

Heat flushed Salome's face hearing Adonijah mention Jinn's name without a hint of anger or jealousy. Her mind was racing. *Did Jinn say anything about helping her? Did he come to see her while she was unconscious? Was he cloaked and watching them right now?*

She shook the chaotic thoughts free. Jinn told her once before that he never sneaked into her room to watch her sleep and she desperately wanted, needed, to believe that was true.

Adonijah shifted his weight and brought Salome back to him. "You've been with me the entire time?"

"Where else would I be?" He tilted his head to the side, lifting her hand to his mouth and kissing it. He rubbed small circles with his thumb over the back of her hand.

Salome nearly melted when his lips touched her skin. Lips. Her thoughts shot back to the moment on the islet, when she felt Jinn's lips press against hers. How she wished she had the strength to kiss him back. She thought of his powerful arms holding her as she bled, and all she could think about was hoping he had gotten to safety. If she had died fighting the Cornigera, she didn't want Jinn anywhere nearby.

"Are you alright?" Adonijah asked, once again returning her to the present.

She shook her head a little too quickly to look innocent. "How bad a shape am I in?"

Adonijah's eyes roamed her head to toe before he said, "The Myridian Healer was able to salve and stitch most of your cuts. You sprained your left knee. But the worst of it was your right arm."

Salome's eyes darted from Adonijah's attentive gaze down to her bandaged forearm. "Is it broken?"

Adonijah shook his head. "No, but it'll scar."

"Will I be able to hold a weapon again?" She whispered the question, picturing Zara's shaking hands.

Adonijah slipped out of the bed and walked around to her side. He knelt in front of her, her thighs on either side of his body. Cupping her face in his hands, he gently forced her to look him in the eye.

"You are the only woman I know who could defeat the Cornigera, be unconscious for four days, learn you're going to have a scarred arm, and only be concerned if you're going to be able to wield a weapon again." His smile warmed her belly. "You'll be back to your stab happy self soon enough, Princess."

Salome's gaze slid from his eyes to his lips, and he graciously obliged by leaning closer, and kissing her. He was careful of where he placed his hands, but his kiss was anything but gentle. It was filled with passion, concern, fear, hope.

She twisted her fingers through Adonijah's hair, pulling him closer to her, even though there wasn't much space separating them. She wanted to feel him. Wanted to be wrapped in his embrace. Wanted to feel the weight of him over her. After a brush with Death, she wanted Adonijah to know how much she cared for him. How much she wanted him in her life; needed him in her life.

As if he could read her thoughts, he tucked his arms under her thighs and lifted her off the bed. She wrapped her legs around his torso, only to wince in pain from her swollen knee.

Adonijah pulled his face from hers and whispered, "Are you alright?"

Salome smashed her mouth against his. She wasn't going to let their moment pass again. Her hands roamed down his neck to his chest, and she sucked in a sharp breath. She knew he was muscular but running the tips of her fingers across his chest, ignited a hunger in her.

Adonijah leaned into her touch and spun them around, so he was sitting on the bed, and she was straddling him. He pried his mouth away and rested his forehead against hers. Planting an open mouth kiss to her neck, she shivered, goosebumps rippled through her body.

"I thought I was going to lose you," Adonijah murmured into the crook of her neck.

"You can't get rid of me that easily," Salome whispered, running her fingers through his messy, dark hair.

Adonijah placed his hands on her waist and pulled back to meet her gaze. "I don't want to feel like that ever again." He squeezed her gently. "I thought I was going to watch you die and I just… Salome, I don't see myself living without you. I don't just want you; I need you."

Salome thumbed the stubble along his jawline. He had exposed his soul to her, and when she pictured the future, she saw him in it. But thinking that flooded her with panic.

Jinn's words on the islet rang through her head again, *"Survive. I need you."*

As hard as she tried to purge her mind of the prince, she couldn't rid herself of his smile, his laugh, his warmth, or his powerful presence.

"Did I upset you?" Adonijah's raspy voice sliced through her, and guilt gripped her heart. "I'm sorry -"

Salome placed a finger against his lips to silence him. "I thought I was going to die three days ago. I thought about you, about us." She kissed him again, but they both knew their encounter was over.

"But the war." Adonijah nodded his head, easily piecing together what she was worried about. He tucked pieces of her wild hair behind her ear. "No matter what happens, I will fight, live, and die by your side."

"You deserve more -"

Adonijah kissed her, not allowing her to finish. "Seeing you fight that Cornigera made me realize you're right. You're making hard choices on behalf of your people. I might not like you putting yourself in harm's way, or thinking that what you want doesn't matter, but I understand it. And as much as I want you to say that you are mine and I am yours, I can wait."

Salome wrapped her arms around his neck and hugged him tight. She realized she was falling in love with Adonijah, even though she wanted him, a part of her still wanted Jinn.

~

Salome knelt in the Inner Depths once more before joining her company aboard Jinn's ship. She was well enough to travel and as reluctant as she was to leave the first place she had ever truly felt at home, she knew her journey was pulling her elsewhere.

Damaris and Zara waited silently for her to answer. It was an important decision, and she was focused on making the right one. But concentrating was a monumental task that morning because the Five Virtues were loud in her mind, trying to sway her in their favor. Quieting her thoughts and drowning out their voices, her eyes shot open when she made her choice.

Salome met Damaris' awaiting gaze. "I choose Strength."

Damaris smiled and dipped her index finger into the bronze bowl she held. It contained the blue blood taken from the Cornigera she had slain. The Oracle dragged her blue dipped finger straight down Salome's forehead until she reached her chin.

"May Strength be your protector," Damaris recited the prayer, "and may her eagle guide you on your path."

Zara nodded; pride radiated from her face as she motioned for Salome to rise. "You are our Red Maiden, and we will follow you into battle. As deep as the sea."

Salome crisscrossed her arms across her chest. "As deep as the sea."

Zara embraced her niece and whispered in her ear, "Your mother would be proud."

Salome wanted to believe that was true.

SAILING AWAY from the Isles of Myr ripped through Salome's soul and she had to clutch the railing of the ship to keep her knees from buckling or from diving off the vessel and swimming back to her newfound comfort. Although Adonijah, Cato, Rosalina, and Seraphina had all tried to persuade her to go below deck and get some rest, she had refused to leave her spot until the Isles of Myr was no longer visible across the horizon. No one bothered her for hours as tears slipped down her cheeks.

Salome thought of Niabi sailing away, forced to return to Northwind where she wasn't wanted, respected, or loved, when she had found a home and her place amongst the Myridians. She thought of her mother sailing away, agreeing to marry a man she had never met, to ensure her kingdom had a strong ally in trade and battle. Neither of them saw their home again.

Jinn rested his elbows on the railing next to her, staring out across the sea. He didn't say a word, just remained present in case she needed him.

"Have you ever had the feeling when sailing away from your home, that you might not see it again?" Salome didn't turn to look at him but mirrored his stance by placing her elbows up on the wooden banister.

"Every time." Jinn folded his hands together. "Are you afraid?"

"You will have to be more specific."

"Are you afraid you won't see the Isles of Myr again?"

She sighed, hoping he didn't see how scared she really was. "I'm afraid I won't live to see it again."

Jinn reached for her hand and squeezed it gently. She turned her head far enough to catch a glimpse of his golden-brown eyes. "You *will* survive, do you hear me?"

"I want to believe that, but…"

"But what?"

Salome couldn't tell him that she felt Death following her, watching, and waiting for the right moment to claim her soul. She couldn't, wouldn't, tell any of them.

Salome leaned close enough to rest the side of her face against his shoulder. "Maybe when the war is over, I'll visit Sakurai, and you can show me around."

His eyes were fixed on hers. She knew he recognized she changed the subject, but he wasn't going to pester her for answers. He bobbed his head with a sensual grin, hair falling over his forehead perfectly, making him look even more irresistible than normal.

"It would be my honor."

CHAPTER 53
NIABI

Niabi had seen a heart before, but it was odd to see her grandmother's heart tucked in a box of blue velvet like a newborn swaddled for a nap. Satisfied with Marina's recounting of events that led up to Nym's assassination, she closed the lid, and handed the treasure to their Aunt Vilora. Her wrinkled hands wrapped around the tiny chest with a sinister, yet triumphant, grin.

When Niabi sent orders to Marina to bring her Nym's heart, she felt a pang of guilt tug at her heart. Nym had done more for during her childhood than anyone else, but she had to remind herself that her grandmother failed her. Nym abandoned her to Issachar's abuse. Nym hadn't fought for her freedom like she swore she would when Niabi arrived in the Isles of Myr. Nym gave her up. The moment she left Myridian shores, she never spoke to her grandmother again.

At least, those were the reasons she justified having Nym assassinated. The Myridian Queen's heart for the Resurrection Spell. Her grandmother's sacrifice would pave the way for her son's second chance.

But that opportunity had been stolen from her, too. Crispin had robbed her of another life with her son. Rollo was gone for good, and now Neempo, too, was dead; his heart rendered useless to her. She was so angry, she could feel the flames itching underneath her skin, begging for her to let them loose. The one piece of advice the Sovereign had given her about learning to control her fire magic had genuinely impacted her. She kept the fire at bay, mentally quenching it. Keeping her magic hidden was no longer an option after the debacle with her brother, but as long as she remained in control, she would continue to be lethal and dangerous to anyone who crossed her.

"That will be all, Vilora." Niabi dismissed the witch who silently slipped out of Niabi's office with the box containing Nym's heart tucked underneath her arm.

As soon as the door closed behind their aunt, Marina crinkled her nose and said, "Well, she seems…gross."

Niabi clicked her tongue. "With that attitude you'll end up looking just like her."

"If I end up looking like that, I'll drown myself in the sea."

"Play nice." Niabi's smile didn't stretch far, but it was the best she could offer to her cousin, considering the only reason they were in one another's company again was due to Marina killing their grandmother. "I suppose Northwind will now be your permanent residence. You are welcome to stay here in the White Keep."

Marina looked bored, slumped in the armchair on the opposite side of Niabi's desk. She tore her eyes from inspecting her fingernails and met the queen's gaze. "Seeing as I assassinated the Queen of Myr for you, I would think a room in the White Keep would be the least you could offer."

"Mind your tongue or lose it," Niabi's nostrils flared, and she dispelled the tempting urge to smack Marina across her smug face.

"Apologies," Marina purred. "I didn't realize you were such a stickler on formalities these days."

"It's about respect." Niabi reclined in her chair, sipping from her glass of water. "Something you seem to know very little about."

Marina shrugged lazily. "I stopped caring about respecting my *elders,* a long time ago."

Niabi smirked at the familial dig. "I'm older than you by one year, you witch. That hardly qualifies me to be your elder."

Marina flashed a playful smile and it felt as if no time had passed, since the last time they'd seen one another. Though Marina didn't train as a Qata Vishna like Mika and Niabi, she and her younger cousin were always close. They would stay up late talking, steal late-night snacks from the kitchen, and would play pranks on the staff, not caring about the punishments Zara would hammer down on them if, and when, they were caught.

"I suppose congratulations are in order." Marina rested her chin in her hand.

"You will have to be more specific."

Marina's eyes floated from Niabi's cup of water to her now noticeable belly. "How far along are you?"

Niabi's hand rubbed circles around her bump though her eyes were glued to her cousin. "The healers said, I have a few months left."

"And the father?"

"Is none of your concern."

Marina laughed but her smile quickly faded. Her gaze fell to the floor before she asked, "Any news from the Isles of Myr?"

Niabi knew what she was actually asking – what was Mika's fate for taking her place? Reluctantly, Niabi said, "Mika was… executed."

Marina's lips twitched but any other emotion was buried. "I didn't think mother…" She cleared her throat. "I didn't think she would go through with an execution."

"Zara was always one to follow the law. Even if that meant having her heir executed for a crime she didn't commit."

Marina's brows knitted together in a frown as she sat up straight in her seat. "Mika didn't deserve to die like that. She should have died on the battlefield or at a ripe old age, as queen." She twiddled her fingers aimlessly, her voice was hoarse when she said, "Mika would have been a great queen."

Niabi shifted in her seat. She wasn't wrong about Mika making a great queen. Out of the three of them, Mika had always been the most responsible and the most honorable. No matter what trouble Niabi and Marina found themselves getting into, Mika would always rescue them or clean up their mess. She died the same way she lived, covering for Marina.

"If only life dealt fair hands to those who deserved them." Niabi would never voice it aloud, but when word reached her of Mika's fate, she sat in her room and cried until she didn't have any tears left to shed. Mika was never supposed to be caught up in their scheme. She was never supposed to get hurt. She was never supposed to die.

"What of the Qata Vishna?" Marina's question sliced through Niabi's thoughts, more curiosity than concern in her tone.

"It appears the Qata Vishna has a new Red Maiden." The words left a bitter taste in her mouth. In her mind, she was the rightful Red Maiden, but that, too, had been ripped from her when Nym put her on the ship back to Northwind.

"Who?" Marina's eyes widened.

"My sister."

Marina's nose crinkled in disgust. "Of course, mother would back her as the Red Maiden."

"What's the matter, Marina?" Niabi smirked, a low chuckle escaping her lips. "Did Salome rub you the wrong way?"

"Let's just say," Marina cracked her fingers one by one, "I won't shed one tear when she dies."

Niabi tilted her head to the side. What a curious thing for her cousin to say. "Let's find you a room."

"Or an entire wing," Marina linked her arm in Niabi's and nudged her with a hip. "Whatever is the biggest. You know I have expensive taste."

"I am well aware of your tastes, Marina," Niabi patted her cousin's arm with a laugh. "And I am sure we can find something suitable, even for you."

"It'll be just like old times."

Niabi would give anything to go back to a simpler time, a simpler life. But that wasn't the hand she had been dealt. She'd been given a losing hand and had still found herself on top, as Queen of the North. Even if it cost her what was left of her black heart, she would keep her crown, and would gladly slit her siblings' throats to ensure her reign. No one would steal from her again.

CHAPTER 54

SALOME

Sailing to where the Bone Mountains and the sea met was a smooth and uneventful journey, minus Adonijah's severe seasickness. He was beyond relieved to be back on dry land and nearly kissed the rocky beach the moment his feet thudded to the ground.

Salome had spent the two days aboard *The Jade Warrior* wondering if Jinn and Kai would be continuing to Sakurai once she and her companions had disembarked. But as Adonijah, Cato, Rosalina, Seraphina, and twelve Qata Vishna sent by Zara as a protection detail went ashore, Salome noticed the prince handing the captain a sealed envelope to be given to his father, King Kenji.

Jinn turned to guide his black stallion, Yuki, down the ramp at the fishing village's humble dock, when his eyes met hers.

Salome stroked Snow's mane. "I thought this was going to be goodbye."

"Why would you think that?" He tilted his head to the side and the light breeze blew strands of hair across his face.

"I assumed a busy prince like you would be needed elsewhere." She flashed a coy smile before tugging Snow down the ramp.

"And what exactly do you think a busy prince, such as me, does all day?" Jinn asked, following her. She could hear the teasing in his voice and decided to play along.

"Oh, you know, wave at your people as you ride by on your noble steed, send someone to fetch your slippers, or wink at fancy ladies of your father's court." Salome bit her lip to stifle her laughter.

Jinn's warm laugh rumbled behind her, and although she smiled, she didn't turn around for him to see the effect he had on her.

"I suppose I'll have to find some way to entertain myself, since I won't be waving or winking at my adoring public."

Salome faced him once Snow was on solid ground. "And what do you intend to do with your time, Prince Jinn?"

Jinn closed the gap between them, hiding them from view behind their horses. "I thought I would go for a hike through the Bone Mountains with you."

Salome's heart leapt and her eyes darted to his lips.

"Those eyes of yours betray you again," he whispered, brushing his fingers against hers.

"There's something you should know," Salome said.

"You can tell me anything."

"It's about my eyes."

"And how they betray you?" Jinn chuckled softly.

"My left eye isn't just a different color than the right one." Salome took a deep breath. She hadn't told him before because she was afraid the truth might frighten him. But the way he looked at her now made her want to tell him every secret she had. *"It's a mark. The Mark of Orion. I'm ..."*

"The Hunter?" Jinn offered when she froze.

"You know?" Her eyes shifted from him to the others prepping their horses for the journey. *"How?"*

Jinn hesitated. *"Adonijah told me."*

Fire raged in her eyes. Why would Adonijah tell him? Why was she so upset he had said anything at all? It wasn't supposed to be a secret. She felt Jinn's warm hand tilting her chin back to face him.

"Don't be upset. It's my fault he said anything at all."

"What are you talking about?"

"The night before you fought the Cornigera," Jinn raked his fingers through his hair, looking almost embarrassed, *"he and I talked."*

Her head was starting to pound. She rubbed her fingers in small circles around her temples. *"What did you two talk about?"*

By his sheepish smile, she already knew the answer. *"I told him that I had feelings for you."*

Snow stomped her hooves on the ground alerting Salome that someone was coming. She looked over Jinn's shoulder and saw Kai approaching, the last one off the ship. Salome cleared her throat, but he didn't turn around to look at Kai.

"Are you upset with me?" Jinn asked, eyes fixed on her.

"No."

"But?"

"I don't know what to do," her voice cracked as she looked around to make sure no one was close enough to eavesdrop.

"About what?" His silky voice drew her in, and she wished he'd cloak them, so she could feel his arms wrap around her.

"You. Him." Salome sucked in a breath before turning away from his gaze. "I don't know what to do."

Jinn shrugged, but she could tell he was just as interested in what she was thinking. "It's not something you have to worry about."

"How can I not worry about it?" Salome glanced at the group and caught Adonijah staring at them. "At some point someone is going to get hurt," she whispered, making sure she was completely hidden behind Snow.

"Hey," Jinn grabbed her hand. "Don't focus on us. You have more important things to worry about right now."

"My guardian, Zophar, would have said the same thing," she smirked.

"Well," Jinn smiled, "he sounds like a smart man."

Salome couldn't help the step she took to close the gap between them. She felt drawn to him, like a moth to a flame. When their eyes met, it made her heart leap, and she had an undeniable urge to kiss him, to let him love her, and be her partner in both life and death.

"If I said, I wanted to kiss you," Salome whispered, her lips inches from Jinn's, "would you let me?"

"Using my lines?" He leaned closer.

"It worked for you."

Jinn slipped his arm around her waist, pulling her against him. "If you let me, I would kiss you every day for the rest of my life."

"Is that a promise?" Her fingers trailed down his jawline, brushing over his lips.

"My life is yours," Jinn whispered.

Salome pressed her lips against his and felt him kiss her back. He smelled of cedar and springtime and held her with a confidence and ease that made her feel at home in his arms. *Home*. Maybe home wasn't a place; maybe home was a person.

Heavy and determined footsteps nearing them forced her to tear herself away from Jinn and put a foot of distance between them. Her cheeks flushed when she looked at him and saw the disappointment in his eyes. She was so concerned about hurting Jinn and Adonijah, that she was beginning to think she might be the one to end up crushed and alone.

"Are you ready?" Adonijah's voice sliced between Salome and Jinn, and he didn't try to hide his scowl. Even though she and Jinn were hidden behind their horses, she couldn't help but wonder if Adonijah had seen them kissing.

Kai stepped forward noticing Adonijah's hostile tone, but the prince cleared his throat, halting her approach. Jinn glanced at Salome and smiled. "I think we're ready for that hike now."

~

THE TAYBORNE MOUNTAINS that stretched from the Black Forest through the northern borders of Northwind were rocky and covered in snow, most of the year. The Bone Mountains, however, were riddled with pine trees, creeks, and vegetation. The paths winding up and around the mountains were shaded and provided breathtaking views of Adalore and the Ignacia Sea. The caravan rode horseback most of the day until they reached an adequate clearing to make camp.

Cato was on edge, and Salome thought it was because he was back in the Bone Mountains, but he kept looking into the tree line as if he were expecting someone to pop out at any given moment.

"What is it?" Salome stood next to him.

"We should have run into some scouts by now," Cato didn't look at her but kept focused on the woods.

"You know these paths," Salome offered, "you've been leading us to avoid scouts."

"Yes, but…"

Salome's eyes shot to where he was looking but didn't see anything. "Cato?"

"We're in Krazak territory." He finally met her gaze, arms crossed over his chest. "If I haven't seen them, I'm afraid they've seen us."

Salome patted his shoulder. "I'm sure we're safe. Perhaps a good night's rest -"

"Let me press onward," Cato interrupted her with a fire bubbling in his gut. "I'll see if we're missing something, so we aren't surprised."

Salome knew there would be no arguing with him. He knew these mountains better than any of them, so she had to trust him. "Alright but be back by dawn. Do you need someone to go with you?"

"I should go alo -"

"I will go." Seraphina marched up to them, wearing her bronze armor, with weapons strapped to her back, ready for an adventure. "If that suits you, Your Highness."

"You want to go?" Salome asked, surprised.

"Really?" Cato echoed, his mouth agape.

Seraphina kept a neutral expression. "It is my duty to protect you," she said to Salome. "What if he tries to abandon us or alerts his people of our presence?"

Cato snorted, offended, "I would never -"

"Even so," Seraphina interrupted, sounding bored. "I wouldn't be doing my job, if you were left unsupervised."

Salome bit her bottom lip, stifling a laugh. "Go. But Seraphina." The Qata Vishna twin glanced at her. "Play nice." Seraphina bowed and vanished into the woods with a bug-eyed Cato.

"You sure about that?" Adonijah came up behind her, pipe lit, exhaling a puff of smoke above her head. "They might kill each other."

"They might," she chuckled. "Or they might realize they make a great team – and a cute couple." Adonijah smiled down at her and she smiled back. "What?"

He shook his head. "Nothing."

"That's not fair," she nudged him with her hip. "You can't look at me like that and say it's nothing."

"Fine," he cleared his throat. "When I first met you, I never expected you to be so…"

"Badass? Intimidating? Witty?" She offered with a grin.

"Likeable."

Salome crinkled her nose. "What did you expect me to be? A monster?"

"I don't know," he shrugged, extinguishing his pipe, and putting it back inside his jacket pocket. "Just not… you."

"And now you're stuck with me," she laughed.

"There are worse fates." Adonijah's eyes darted back to the woods where Cato and Seraphina had ventured. "May the Almighty help Cato, if he angers that woman."

Rosalina cleared her throat and they turned around to see her and Kai standing quietly. Salome found it funny that the two quietest warriors had bonded over the last couple of days. What havoc they could wreak if they wanted.

The Qata Vishna bowed her head, "Princess, we are setting up a perimeter around the camp for the night. I will take the first watch unless you have other orders."

Salome shook her head. "Do as you see fit, Rosalina. I trust your judgment."

Rosalina crossed her arms over her chest, saluting her. She and Kai walked to the other side of the camp and Adonijah shuddered.

"What?" Salome asked.

"Those two are dangerous."

"We're all dangerous."

"Women with weapons." Adonijah shook his head and grinned. "It's a wonder we men survive you."

~

SALOME COULDN'T SLEEP that night. Cato and Seraphina hadn't returned, and she was starting to worry that something had happened to them. She sat up and scanned their camp. Twelve Qata Vishna warriors slept on the outskirts, weapons at the ready. She was kept at the center, if anyone attacked, they would have a hell of a time getting to her.

As quietly as she could, she stood up, grabbed her weapons, and walked over to the side of the camp where one of the Qata Vishna was taking her watch.

"Why don't you get some rest, Irena," Salome whispered, clutching her cloak tighter around her. "No reason we both should be up." Irena furrowed her brow, but Salome followed her suggestion with an order. "I will take the rest of the watch."

Reluctantly, the Myridian marched away to her sleeping area and laid down. Salome sat on the stump, bow in hand just in case, and kept her eyes and ears peeled for anyone headed their way. The sun would be rising soon, and she hoped Cato and Seraphina would return by then. Maybe Cato was right to be suspicious.

Thirty minutes passed without an issue, but then Salome heard the rustling of leaves, and the sound of footsteps. They were soft footsteps, but they were loud enough for her to pick up on. She squinted into the tree line and spotted a shadowy figure tiptoeing closer. She tightened her grip on her bow, slowly nocking an arrow. It wasn't Cato or Seraphina. The body was too bulky to be either of her friends. She needed to alert the others without arousing the suspicions of the encroaching figure.

"Jinn," she bridged their bond as calmly as she could. *"Someone is approaching. I don't think he's alone."*

Jinn tapped Kai who was lying a few feet away from him. With three quick hand signals, the Ryoko Naga was armed and ready.

Quickly, but quietly, the rest of the camp was alerted of a possible confrontation and armed themselves. Salome kept her eyes fixed on the moving figure, but when he stopped suddenly, she could sense his gaze on her. He knew he had been made and bellowed a battle cry that sounded like a howl, and to her horror, others echoed in response. By sound alone, Salome knew they were surrounded. The man unsheathed a longsword strapped to his back and charged toward her.

Salome heard dozens of warriors charging their camp and started launching arrows to pick them off as fast as she could before they could reach them. She downed three of them with precision, but the clashing of metal behind her meant they'd reached them.

She shot one more enemy warrior in the neck before she whipped the curved Myridian blades from the holsters on her back and braced herself for hand-to-hand combat. Despite it still being dark, Salome managed to spot their enemies' long braids, furs, and red and black paint smeared all over their bodies.

Krazaks.

One of the brutes jumped out of a tree, battle axe in hand, and sliced his weapon down toward her as he landed on the ground with a giant thud. She deflected his attack with one of her blades and sliced across his midsection with the second. As he fell to the ground, she stabbed him in the neck, letting him bleed out at her feet.

She turned in time to see Kai and Rosalina back-to-back butchering any Krazak that got within a foot of them. Adonijah was right. They were dangerous.

As far as she knew, they hadn't lost anyone in their company. Mika wasn't exaggerating when she said the Qata Vishna were undefeated in battle. They were like dancing assassins. Every movement was graceful and deadly.

"Shield!" Irena yelled.

Salome watched Sabaa drop to the ground, flipping her rectangular shield to cover her back. Irena sprinted toward her, and as soon as her foot hit the shield, Sabaa propelled her up in the air. Flying toward an unsuspecting Krazak, Irena swiped both of her blades in opposite directions, claiming the enemy's head.

Damn. Mika would be beaming with pride.

As mesmerizing as the Qata Vishna were, something twitched in a tree above them, and caught Salome's attention. She spotted an archer perched on a tree branch, his arrow pointed at Jinn in the middle of their camp. The prince was fighting off two Krazaks and didn't look like he'd even broken a sweat.

Within seconds, she snatched her bow off the ground by the stump, nocked an arrow, and let it fly. It pierced the Krazak archer before he had a chance to release his shot.

What Salome didn't see in time, was a second archer hiding in the tree. She slid another bolt out of the quiver hanging from her hip, and dove to avoid his blow, but his arrow slashed her arm. She yelped and fell to her knees. He nocked another arrow; he was going to finish her off. If he had been a better shot, he would have killed her with the first arrow.

With adrenaline pumping through her veins, she launched the arrow nocked in her bow, and watched it slice through the air and pierce the archer's heart. The Krazak fell from the tree, landing on the ground with a heavy thud.

The battle continued to rage around her. The Krazaks were multiplying and coming in endless waves. Though they had slain dozens of Krazaks, it seemed like they were going to lose the battle based on numbers alone.

"Jinn," she whispered in his mind.

The prince stabbed a large Krazak in the chest and turned around to find her. Their eyes met and he paled instantly.

A giant hand grabbed ahold of her by her hair and jerked her head back, poking a knife against her throat. The Krazak behind her shouted, "Drop your weapons or I'll slit her throat!"

Jinn's eyes were filled with rage. If looks alone could kill, he would have massacred the entire lot of them.

"Jinn," she said calmly. *"It's ok."*

"I said, drop your weapons." The Krazak yanked her viciously and she winced, forcing Jinn to lay his tachi swords on the ground, with the others following suit. "Now, what have we got here," the Krazak hissed in Salome's ear. "Looks like trespassers to me."

"We're just passing through." Adonijah stepped forward, hands held at the level of his eyes to show he was unarmed. "We're traveling north and wanted to avoid running into the Thrak."

"Don't we all," the Krazak laughed, his grip on Salome's hair was unyielding.

Salome glanced around their camp and saw they had lost two Qata Vishna, Trin and Valha, and her heart ached. They were sent to protect her. Instead, they died fighting these vicious Mountain Men for no reason other than them being territorial.

Her eyes met Jinn's. She could see the wheels in his mind turning, thinking through any strategy that would work to free her and slaughter the remaining Krazaks. From her count, there were maybe twenty left. They'd killed at least twenty-five.

"Whatever you are thinking," Salome warned, *"don't do anything stupid. I'm rather fond of my neck."*

His gaze softened. *"I'm rather fond of your neck, too."*

"You are trespassing on Krazak territory," the Krazak leader's voice bellowed. "The penalty for crossing into the Bone Mountains is death." The light, morning breeze ruffled the Krazak's furs and Salome could feel his hot breath against the back of her head.

"Parlay," Salome's voice was strained.

The Krazak turned her around to face him. His long, thick, dark braid fell over the front of his chest, and the sides of his head were shaved. Though clean shaven, his face was splattered with red and black paint, and his arms were smeared with ash and clay. Tiny bones protruded through his ear lobes, and his fearsome brown eyes were glued to hers.

"What did you say?" he hissed, pulling the knife away from her throat.

"Parlay," Salome repeated, this time loud enough for everyone in the camp to hear. "I request a parlay."

"You want to meet with King Gerd?" The Krazak looked genuinely surprised.

"I trust you will honor my request.".

He lowered his knife, and the remaining Krazaks lowered their weapons. "Then you shall meet the king."

Before forcing Salome to travel to Fennor to meet King Gerd, the Krazaks allowed Rosalina to patch up her wound. Once she was bandaged, the Mountain Men led them down the twisting pathways to the City of Bones.

Adonijah and Harbona had warned her before of how cruel the Krazaks were and that they would rather slit throats than make deals.

Where were Cato and Seraphina?

If the Krazaks captured or killed them…

She shook the thought free. She couldn't dwell on that possibility.

The Krazak that had held a knife to her throat walked in front of her, glancing back at her occasionally to make sure she wasn't plotting an escape.

"What's your name?" She dared to ask.

"None of your business." He shot back with a snarl.

"You wouldn't do me the honor of knowing my captor's name?" Salome tried once more and to her surprise, he obliged.

"Rune. I am the Commander of the Krazak Militia."

"Rune," she repeated so she would remember it. "I wish I could say it's nice to meet you."

"Save your pleasantries for King Gerd," Rune huffed, shouldering his furs to keep him warm from the early morning chill.

Salome risked a glance behind her to see how her company was holding up. Adonijah was grumbling under his breath, Kai and Rosalina flashed dirty looks at any Krazak who dared look in their direction, and Jinn's eyes were already on her.

"Are you alright?" she asked.

"I'm more concerned about you," his eyes scanned the area she'd been shot.

"I've had worse." She turned her focus forward, her hands bound with rope like the others.

"So," his warmth flooded her mind and she felt like he was wrapping his arms around her. *"A parlay was a nice, unexpected touch."*

"Cato told me a lot about his people. I figured maybe the Krazaks and Stormcrags weren't entirely that different."

"What is the next phase of your plan?"

Salome had an idea but wasn't sure if it would work. Before she could explain her plan to Jinn, Rune announced they had arrived.

From the outside it looked like they were walking into a cave, but as they marched through the tunnel, it opened into a city carved inside the mountain itself. The peak was exposed to let sunlight inside, and Salome's mouth dropped. She never thought the City of Bones would look so beautiful.

Thousands of caves were carved into the rock where the Krazaks lived with their families. They had a market in the open area of the mountain base as well as training grounds, an arena, sheep and goat pens, blacksmiths, and tanners. Torches hung from the rocky walls and illuminated the city, so it didn't feel like they lived inside the mountain. Furs, tapestries, curtains, rugs, and pillows filled the underground city with patterns and color that made it feel cozy and almost homey.

Salome watched some children kick a ball around with broad smiles as the caravan was led to the only freestanding building, other than the arena, which housed King Gerd and the Throne of Skulls.

Rune halted them. "Only three of you may meet with the king. The rest of you will remain outside."

Salome motioned for Adonijah and Jinn to come with her. They followed Rune inside the humble castle made of stone, but they didn't have to walk far before they reached King Gerd who was sitting on his throne made out of the skulls of his enemies.

Gerd was such a large man he made his throne look tiny. He had the same caramel skin tone that Cato did, but his black eyes were filled with lust and malice. His braid was longer than Rune's and hung to his hip. The sides of his head were also shaved, but he had a scraggly beard that rested on his broad, hairy chest. Salome noticed he didn't have a shirt on and spied tiny bones pierced in his nipples. Gerd sported dark pants, worn out boots, and gold rings on all his stubby fingers.

"Who do we have here?" Gerd's gravelly voice boomed in the small throne room. He reclined in his seat, his dirty hands gripping the armrests where two small skulls screamed back at Salome. "Which one of you is the leader?"

Salome stepped forward, fighting the urge to crinkle her nose at the foul smelling ruler. "I am."

Gerd scoffed. "You are a woman."

Salome ignored the disgust rolling off his tongue and said, "My company and I are travelling north. We wish to continue our journey."

The king wheezed out a laugh and shook his head. "You will never leave this mountain. Rune spared your lives; therefore, you will be our slaves. Truthfully, death would have been more merciful." Gerd slipped out of his throne like a serpent and slithered toward Salome. He sniffed her hair and flashed a lustful grin. "Especially, for someone as pretty as you."

"You refuse to let us go?" Salome held her ground, despite every inappropriate glance or touch from the king.

"Like I said," Gerd put his nose against Salome's ear and whispered, "you will *never* leave this mountain."

"Dagaal." Salome rasped, averting her eyes from the king's gaze, not wanting him to notice her two color eyes. Jinn told her the Krazaks would think her to be a witch and she didn't need to add to her list of problems.

"What did you just say?" Gerd hissed, taking a step back.

Did she detect fear in his voice?

"I invoke the right to a Dagaal." Salome said louder. Rune and the handful of Krazak warriors stationed around the room stilled. Their eyes darted to their king.

Gerd stood wide-eyed before a nervous chuckle escaped his lips. He waved a dismissive hand in the air. "You have no rights here. You cannot declare a Dagaal, unless you are a rival attempting to overthrow my rule."

"Then consider yourself challenged." Salome spat, and the Krazaks started whispering amongst themselves. "If we win, you release us to continue our journey."

"And if we win," Gerd's wicked smile beamed, "your companions will be our slaves and you," he twirled a lock of her hair between his scarred fingers, "will belong to me."

Before Adonijah or Jinn could protest, Salome nodded. "Agreed."

Gerd clapped his enormous hands together. "Choose your champion."

"I choose myself." Salome wasn't willing to issue a challenge and back away from a fight, even if she was injured.

Gerd sank into his throne and shook his head, a mocking look inching across his face. "You cannot be your own champion. You must choose one of your own to fight my champion. If no one will fight for you, then you forfeit." His smile sent an unwelcome chill up her spine.

Adonijah stepped forward, "I'm her champion."

Salome slowly turned to face him, her face pale, and her eyes wide. "Adonijah -"

"Done!" Gerd snapped his fingers and Rune approached the throne. "Gather the people. They will want to watch Orn, do what he does best."

Salome stood in front of Adonijah and whispered, "What are you thinking?"

Adonijah brushed hair out of her face and flashed a tight-lipped smile. "I am your best chance, and you know it."

"Adonijah -"

Adonijah bent forward and kissed her forehead. It felt too much like a goodbye kiss for Salome's liking. "I will fight, live, and die by your side, remember?"

Before she could say anything, Rune and two Krazak warriors grabbed Adonijah and escorted him out.

"Where are they taking him?" Salome faced Gerd with a rising rage.

"The arena, of course." For a man that seemed nervous about the mention of a Dagaal, he now seemed awfully confident. "Orn will make quick work of him. Don't worry. He won't suffer. Long."

CHAPTER 55
ADONIJAH

Adonijah stood in the center of the arena where Rune and his men had escorted him. Carved into the mountain, half of the coliseum arches were open to the outside world, boasting some of the most spectacular views of the surrounding mountains. Thousands of Krazaks filled the roofless stadium, ready to see their champion spill the blood of another enemy on the dusty arena ground.

King Gerd ordered his soldiers to carry the Throne of Skulls from his castle to the coliseum and set it on a suspended wooden dais at the end of the arena grounds. With the mountainous view as his backdrop, Gerd raised a hand to silence the deafening crowd. "I have been challenged to a Dagaal. A mistake on our enemy's part." He laughed and the Krazaks echoed his cackle. "But we all know how this will end." He motioned to the Krazak who entered the arena. Our champion, Orn the Bone-Crusher!"

Orn was a seven-foot-tall behemoth of a man. Clay and red and black paint were smeared all over his body, making his broad shoulders and python size thighs seem even bigger. His muscular body was riddled with scars, but the one thing that instantly caught Adonijah's attention was the Bone-Crusher's braid.

Adonijah knew the Krazak warriors grew their braids longer for every battle won. Some of them had shoulder-length braids while others had braids that stretched below their waists. Orn was one of those Krazaks. The giant's braid was dark, thick, and ran the length of his spine, stopping at the back of his knees. Adonijah imagined it was quite possible that Orn had never cut his hair before.

Adonijah had to win, and quickly, because Orn certainly wasn't going into this Dagaal to lose. He would slit Adonijah from neck to navel if he got a clear opening. Strength wouldn't be Adonijah's friend today; he would have to play this smart.

Based on Orn's gait, Adonijah noticed three things. One, the giant favored his right side. Two, from the slightest limp most people wouldn't even notice, he was recovering from a recent leg injury. And three, his legs were so muscular, he could probably stomp someone to death.

The Krazak stood ten feet away from Adonijah, the king sitting behind him, with a devilish grin. The giant brute had the audacity to laugh when he looked at Adonijah. He should have been insulted, but he wouldn't give the Bone-Crusher the satisfaction. He would just kill him instead.

Adonijah caught a glimpse of Salome and the rest of their company sitting in the first row guarded by Krazak warriors. When his gaze met Salome's, he expected to see fear or worry in her eyes, but he didn't see either. He saw a pissed queen staring back at her champion.

No matter what, I will fight, live, and die by your side.

He repeated her promise in his mind. He would fight for her. He would live for a future with her. He would even die for her if it came down to it. But what he wouldn't do, was let Orn win this Dagaal.

Adonijah tuned out the cheers and taunts from the Krazaks and focused solely on the Mountain Man standing between him and freedom.

Rune stomped between them and gave them their choice of weapon. A longsword, a mace, an axe, or a pair of daggers. Orn snatched up the mace without a second thought. It had a long metal shaft and gave him the option to keep Adonijah at a distance. And the heavy, spoked head was perfect for bludgeoning. Not an ideal way to die.

Adonijah was most comfortable with a longsword, and it would normally be his weapon of choice, but knowing his strength would not match Orn's power, he chose the twin daggers. They were lightweight and fit in his palms as if they were forged just for him. He would have to use his speed if he stood any chance of winning.

"Krazaks!" King Gerd raised his fists in the air with a sinister grin. "Who is your champion?"

"Orn! Orn! Orn!" The people chanted, their fists pumping in the air.

"Let the Dagaal begin!"

Gerd nodded his head and Orn took off running, slamming his mace down on the ground, shifting the dirt. Adonijah leapt out of the way and got back up on his feet, clutching the hilts of his daggers tightly. Circling Orn, Adonijah waited for him to make another reckless lunge for him, then he would swipe at the giant's favored side. True to his prediction, Orn raised his weapon over his shoulder to swipe at Adonijah's head. He dodged the blow and sliced the giant's right side, drawing first blood.

Orn yelped, and backhanded Adonijah across the face, sending him tumbling to the ground. "I am going to tear your flesh from your body and wear your bones."

Adonijah had been threatened many times in his life, but this was the first time he felt fear surge through his body in years. Orn didn't mince words, and knowing the Krazak way of life, he knew the giant would proudly wear his bones like a necklace.

Jumping back to his feet, Adonijah parried with the Krazak, hoping to get him off balance to swipe at the back of his knees. If Adonijah could get him to the ground, he might be able to disarm him. But Orn was faster than Adonijah expected, and after letting his guard down before, the Krazak kept a safe watch over his right side.

Orn whipped the mace toward Adonijah's head. He leaned back to avoid the blow and the Krazak jumped at the opening. His gigantic foot landed a firm and heavy blow to Adonijah's chest, launching him into the air.

Adonijah's breath was snatched from him, and it took him a second to recover from the blow. He knew his ribs weren't broken, but another kick like that and he wouldn't be so lucky. Hearing Orn's mace slice through the air forced Adonijah to roll away, narrowly avoiding the shattering thud on the ground.

Adonijah's gaze met Salome's and it was as if everything slowed down around him. She had confidence in him, but as her eyes began to widen in fear, he realized a split second too late that Orn was going to land a solid blow. He scrambled to escape but the spikes of the Krazak's mace ripped across his right thigh, drawing blood.

Gritting his teeth, Adonijah swallowed a scream. The giant loomed over him. Desperate to get back on his feet, Adonijah kicked the Krazak's weapon free from his grasp with his uninjured leg. Now disarmed, Adonijah sliced Orn's arm, and the giant retreated to find his mace.

Adonijah dashed to his feet and ran as fast as his limping leg would allow, toward his opponent. As Orn bent down to pick up his weapon, Adonijah jumped on top of the Krazak's back and shoved one of his daggers into the warrior's chest.

Orn roared. He grabbed Adonijah by his hair and whipped him over his back, slamming him on the ground. A swift punch met Adonijah's wrist when he tried to block Orn's attack, and Adonijah felt his wrist pop from the impact. A second punch followed, and without being able to block it, it landed squarely across his jaw.

Adonijah could taste the blood oozing from his mouth. His eyes watered, blurring his vision. He sensed a third punch coming his way. Gripping his second dagger, he stabbed it into the arm Orn used to pin him to the ground.

Orn released him, but Adonijah quickly realized both of his daggers were now embedded in the giant's chest and bicep. With no weapons to fight with, Adonijah realized defeating his opponent wasn't going to be easy.

As Orn was distracted by the knives protruding from his body, Adonijah caught sight of the long braid dangling behind the Krazak's knees. It wouldn't be a clean death, but without weapons, it was the last chance he had to walk out of that arena alive. Without a second thought to convince himself otherwise, Adonijah dove for the braid and as quickly as he could, wrapped it around Orn's neck several times. He jumped on the giant's back, this time keeping his head out of his reach, and pulled the braid as tightly as he could, strangling the Krazak.

Orn abandoned the daggers in his chest and arm, panicking as he tried to pry the braid from his throat. Adonijah heard him gurgling and gasping for air, but he wasn't going to loosen his noose until he was dead. The giant fell to his knees, desperately trying to claw Adonijah from his back, but failed. The arena of bloodthirsty Krazaks fell silent as they watched their champion die a slow and agonizing death.

Adonijah had never strangled anyone before. He made sure all his killings were swift and clean. But as he felt the Krazak take his last breath and the life leave his body, he felt a heaviness creep into his heart, a weight on his shoulders he had never experienced before.

Slowly lowering Orn to the ground face first, Adonijah checked for a pulse, but there wasn't one. The Krazak was dead. The Dagaal had been won. But the joy and relief of victory didn't flood him.

His eyes darted to Salome. Adonijah wasn't sure what he expected to see in her eyes, but satisfaction wasn't it. She rose from her seat slowly, her gaze now fixed on King Gerd, who was seated behind Adonijah.

Turning just in time to see the Krazak king angrily snap his fingers, Adonijah was suddenly encircled by six archers. He didn't have any strength left to fight the soldiers, and when he saw spears pointed at Salome, something inside of him wanted to snap, but he stilled, when he heard her voice.

"My champion won the Dagaal," she snarled, fire raging in her eyes. "You will honor your word and release us."

Gerd lurched to his feet, slamming his fists against his chest, "You will never leave these mountains!"

Rune stepped to his king's side and whispered something in his ear. Whatever words he used were clearly not the right ones. Gerd unsheathed his sword and held the tip of it against Rune's chest.

"You would seek to undermine me, old friend?" Gerd hissed like a serpent.

Rune spoke loudly enough for all the Krazaks to hear, "You dishonor our people with your refusal to honor the Dagaal. Our ancestors would rip that wicked tongue out of your deceitful mouth if they were alive."

"Well, they're dead." Gerd smirked, his fingers dancing on the hilt of his blade. "So, tell them, King Gerd sends his regards."

Before Gerd could run his commander through with his sword, the sound of a war horn echoed. It sent a chill up Adonijah's spine and goosebumps covered his dirty skin. The Krazaks stilled, as if they were in disbelief of who announced their arrival.

Archers covered in blue ink tattoos, furs, and hair dyed in shades of blue, purple, and white, popped up around the top of the arena. Their arrows nocked in their bows, ready to strike anyone that moved an inch without their approval. The thunder of marching soldiers grew louder as hundreds of Stormcrags stomped into the arena, weapons in their hands, ready for battle.

The man who led the rival Mountain Men clan was well over six feet tall and had ancient runes tattooed all over his bald head. To his right stood a ferocious woman with lavender hair with beads and trinkets strewn throughout her locks. Her neck and upper chest were covered in rune tattoos, and she had the same caramel skin that Cato did.

And that's when Adonijah saw them. Cato and Seraphina stood to the Stormcrag leader's left with hunger in their eyes. Not for food, but for blood. Cato snarled and gritted his teeth, looking like a warrior, and not the scared, skinny boy who had been chained and headed to the Gomorrian gallows.

Unless Adonijah's weary eyes were deceiving him, he swore he saw Numbio warriors gathered with the Stormcrags; their prince and a Westerner leading them.

CHAPTER 56
SALOME

Zophar.

Zophar was in the City of Bones with an army. Tears welled in Salome's eyes at the sight of him but when their gaze met, she felt as if someone had stabbed her straight through her heart. Those impish blue eyes of his didn't dance like she thought they would. They carried pain. *What horrors had he seen these past few weeks?*

Looking through the masses for her brother, she failed to find him. Her eyes darted back to Zophar and a tear slipped down his cheek. Her heart stopped. She wanted to jump over the stone barrier and drop the eight feet to the arena ground to run to him. She needed to see her brother. Needed to know he was safe. Needed to know that tear racing down Zophar's rosy cheek wasn't in memory of someone they both loved deeply but would never see again.

"What are you doing here, Torrin?" Gerd's serpentine voice sliced through her thoughts.

"We have come for our friends," Torrin, the Stormcrag leader, stepped forward, smirking. "And from what I see, they won the Dagaal, meaning you are no longer the rightful ruler of the City of Bones."

Gerd growled through gritted teeth, lowering his sword from Rune's chest, and pointing it at the rival tribesman. "Take your kind and leave my city, before I order my warriors to cut you down and wear your bones."

Torrin's laugh boomed throughout the arena. "I don't think your people will be as dishonorable as you."

"Krazaks!" Gerd shouted. "Kill them all." But not one Krazak moved. Gerd looked around the arena and snarled. No one obeyed his command. No one even looked frightened of him anymore. "I said, kill them!"

"Your champion lost the Dagaal," Rune said again, stepping up to the former king. "You are no longer our leader."

Gerd whipped his sword over his head to strike Rune down, but his body was peppered with arrows.

Salome thought the Stormcrag archers had killed the king, but none of them had loosed an arrow. Her eyes darted to Adonijah in the center of the arena and saw the arrows had been launched by the six soldiers surrounding him.

Rune stepped over Gerd's body and marched toward Salome. When he got within ten feet of her, he lowered his head in respect. "Your champion won the Dagaal, and therefore, we acknowledge you as our new leader. My sword," he lifted his weapon in outstretched hands to Salome, "is yours."

Salome wasn't sure what to say. She didn't want to be their leader, she just wanted to continue her journey north. She looked over at Zophar who seemed just as surprised. But before she could say anything, the Krazaks in the arena bowed their heads, acknowledging the beginning of her reign.

Once the arena had been cleared, and Adonijah had been taken to the medical cavern, the leaders from every group assembled in the castle.

Salome and Jinn entered the dining room where a circular table and eight chairs were. Her eyes found the red-bearded Zophar immediately. They walked toward one another until they stood inches from each other, tears streaming down her cheeks. She had thought about what she would do when she saw her guardian again and pictured herself running into his outstretched arms. Then he would say something about how much he missed her and how he couldn't wait to see her beat Crispin in a sparring match again.

But she didn't run into his arms. Zophar didn't say a word for a full minute as they breathed one another in. He looked as if he had aged years in a matter of weeks.

Salome reached for his scarred and calloused hand, wrapping her pinky around his index finger. "Zophar?" she breathed, a rasp in her throat. It was just his name, but the Westerner knew she was asking about her brother.

"I'm sorry," Zophar whispered as his bottom lip quivered.

Salome took a step back, her knees buckling. She felt Jinn wrap an arm around her waist to keep her from crumbling to the floor. Words failed her. She extended the mental bridge to Crispin, begging him to hear her, to answer her. But she was met with silence; a door that was locked and would remain unanswered. He couldn't be dead. He couldn't be gone.

The man she had seen Zophar standing next to when the Stormcrags entered the arena stepped forward. He placed a hand on his heart and said, "Your brother was lost in the River of Lost Souls, but there is still a chance he survived -"

"Who are you?" Salome interrupted him, her words coming out far sharper than she intended.

"I am Prince Heru." He smiled as widely as he dared. "Your brother was my friend."

Jinn helped Salome to a seat and knelt in front of her. He squeezed her hand, but her eyes were distant. "Salome?"

Salome's gaze settled on his face, and she saw the pain in her eyes reflected in his. "My brother is gone?"

Zophar stood in front of her, arms clasped behind his back. "I have failed you. I have failed your brother, and I have failed your family," his voice cracked. "I will accept whatever punishment you deem worthy, Princess."

Salome's voice cracked, "It's not your fault."

Jinn rubbed small circles in her palm, begging her to let him in. She extended the bridge to him, *"Crispin can't be dead."*

"Heru said there was a chance he survived. We can send some soldiers to -"

"And where would I send them?" Salome stifled a cry. *"What if they bring back his body? Then it will be true, and I don't think… I can't lose him, too."*

Jinn wrapped his arms around her, and she cried into his shoulder. The room was silent and allowed her the moment to grieve in peace. She pulled out of Jinn's embrace and wiped her tears. She would cry herself to sleep that night, but first, there was a room filled with leaders from all over Adalore who needed her to be strong.

Torrin, the leader of the Stormcrags, stepped forward when Salome glanced at him. He crossed a fist over his chest and bowed his bald head. "Your loss is a great one, but if you will permit me an audience, I believe we can help one another."

"You don't have to do this." Jinn cloaked them. She knew the second they vanished from sight because the other leaders, Zophar included, panicked. *"You are allowed to grieve and meet with the Stormcrag tomorrow."*

Salome glanced at Jinn, grateful and humbled he cared enough about her to show everyone else the magic he tried to keep a secret. *"Tonight, I will grieve."* She grabbed his hand and squeezed tightly, not wanting to release him. *"Today, I will carry on."*

Jinn bobbed his head, relinquishing his magical barrier over them, and sat in the seat next to hers. Kai immediately took her place behind her prince's chair, eyes scanning the others, looking for a reason to pull out her knives and poke a few holes into their flesh.

"Are we not going to talk about what just happened?" Torrin's eyes narrowed as he stared at the prince.

Jinn shrugged lazily, "I'm a Cloaker. The end."

Salome could tell by the Stormcrag leader's flared nostrils he felt he had been disrespected, but she didn't need them brawling in the small room. She motioned for Torrin to sit in the seat behind him. "I believe there are more important matters to discuss than Prince Jinn's magic."

Torrin reluctantly sank into a wooden chair across from Salome with Cato and the lavender haired woman named, Oifa, behind him. If Salome thought Kai was intense, Oifa put the Ryoko Naga to shame. There was nothing soft about the warrior, and if Oifa had her way, she would have ripped every Krazak within grabbing distance to shreds.

Heru, the Prince of Numbio, sat to Zophar's left. The healer, introduced as Rayma, stood behind him. Salome spied a crystal dagger hanging from the healer's hip and thought it odd to see someone sworn to save life with a weapon on their person. Whatever the Numbio had seen on their journey through the Sand Lands had impacted them.

Although Zophar protested, Salome insisted the Westerner sit to her direct left. Her Master of War would always have an honored place by her side. The twin Qata Vishna stood behind her and Salome knew Seraphina and Rosalina were just as eager to strike someone down.

There was one leader left that Salome asked to join their inner circle, to the great irritation of the Stormcrags. Rune quickly took his seat next to Jinn with a fierce and devilish looking bowman, Hanzo, taking up watch behind him.

Salome thought she heard Oifa and Hanzo muttering ancient curses against each other's tribes before the meeting had been called to order. Once all the introductions had been made, Salome took a deep breath and began.

"I suppose first thing's first," she exhaled sharply, eyes scanning one leader to the next. "Although my champion won the Dagaal, I have no intention of staying in the City of Bones and ruling the Krazaks."

"Then allow me," Torrin puffed out his hairy chest, "to volunteer."

"Shove that thought back up your ass, Torrin," Rune shot viciously, a clear history between them was beginning to take form in her mind. "The Krazaks will not be ruled by the likes of you."

Torrin bared his teeth like a seething animal. "Do you not see her *eyes*, Rune?" The Stormcrag pointed a stubby finger in Salome's direction. "Do you not remember the prophecy?"

Rune waved his hand in the air, dismissing the religious fanatic. "You have spent too many years up in the Tears of the Gods. You are no longer of sound mind."

"Prophecy does not lie -"

"What prophecy?" Salome asked, confused by their tit for tat conversation. "I thought your people would think me to be a witch for having two different color eyes."

Rune's gaze met hers and he looked into her eyes, as if it was the first time, he truly observed her. "None of us would fear you to be a witch. It's an unfounded rumor and superstition about our people." His eyes shot to Torrin's dirty face. "But *they* are firm believers that a woman with two different colored eyes would come to unite our tribes once and for all, ending the war between brothers."

"Brothers?" Salome asked.

"The Krazaks and Stormcrags are the descendants of King Phlias' soldiers who were exiled for serving the usurper. There were two brothers who led Phlias' armies and when neither would relinquish their rank or claim to lead the exiles, they broke into two tribes." Rune explained quickly, despite Torrin's judgmental looks flashed his way every now and then, as if he could tell the story better. "For a thousand years, we have been at war with one another, fighting over control of the City of Bones. For three hundred years, the Krazaks have lived in this mountain. We have built this kingdom with the blood, sweat, and broken bones of our people." Rune's even-tempered voice started to rise, as if anger was starting to overtake him. "And we will *not* bend the knee to a Stormcrag king. Not now, not ever."

"But you would willingly bend the knee to this outsider from the North?" Torrin snorted, referring to Salome's new reign over the Krazaks.

"You know our laws, Torrin." Rune crossed one leg over the other, not wasting his energy meeting Torrin's gaze. "She declared a Dagaal, saying she was challenging our king. Her champion won. We Krazaks may be a lot of things, most of them cruel and wicked, but what we aren't, and never will be, is dishonorable."

"You wish to speak of honor, but your kind have given Stormcrag men, women, and younglings to the Thrak for generations," Oifa spat at Rune's feet. "You know nothing of honor, only self-preservation."

"And *your* kind has never sacrificed a Krazak before?" Hanzo, Rune's bowman, snarled back. "Both Krazak and Stormcrag blood has been spilled for as long as we can remember, so don't blame us when you are guilty of the same sin."

Oifa launched herself at the Krazak archer. Though she was armed with knives and an axe at her hip, she chose to scratch at his face like a mountain lion protecting her cubs. Hanzo pushed her off him, nocked an arrow, and pointed it at her face. She flashed a vicious grin, daring him to let his arrow loose.

"Enough," Salome barked, and Hanzo lowered his weapon, already listening to his new leader's voice. "There is too much history for this to be resolved in one afternoon."

"So, you just expect us to -"

"Live amongst one another until we figure it out?" Salome interrupted Torrin as if she were separating children from brawling in the street over a toy. "That's exactly what I expect."

"As you wish," Rune folded his arms over his chest, flipping his braid behind him.

Not to be shone up, Torrin mirrored the Krazak's body language, stroking his beard separated in two sections, and nodded. "As you wish."

Salome turned her attention to Zophar and Heru. It was difficult to look at them and not think of her brother failing to return to her. She sucked in a breath, stifling the tears, and swallowing the lump in her throat. She would cry all night long, but not now, not here.

"How did you find yourself in the company of the Stormcrags?" she asked.

Zophar wiggled in his seat; he was never comfortable sitting at a table of leaders when he was better at following orders. "As we were traveling north, we were ambushed by a horde of Thrak. They fought hard and claimed six of our men."

Salome noticed Rayma, the Numbio healer, tense up when Zophar said they had lost six men. Their eyes met, and Salome could sense the animosity she harbored in her heart. She wasn't sure if it was directed at her specifically or the Numbio's involvement in general.

"We defeated the Thrak, but Torrin's men captured us, and took us to their city," Heru picked up on the story. "When we explained who we were and where we were going, Torrin invited us to rest and resupply with his people before continuing north."

"When we were returning from scouting, we saw the Krazaks surround the camp," Cato explained how he and Seraphina fit into the saga. "We wanted to warn you, but we knew we wouldn't be able to get past their ranks in time. I thought it best to find the Stormcrags and tell them of your capture. That's when we met Zophar and realized we were all on the same side."

The puzzle Salome was trying to piece together was complete. She understood how the Stormcrags knew she was in trouble and why Zophar was with them. She knew her business between the Stormcrags and Krazaks was far from over, but at least she knew with her as a buffer between the tribes, there shouldn't be any violence. But she wanted to make sure it was stated plainly in case someone tried to make an excuse for bloodshed.

"Until we figure out what to do next, I don't want any bloodshed or violence between the Stormcrags and Krazaks." Salome's eyes darted between Oifa and Hanzo instead of Torrin and Rune. She knew the latter would obey her words, but she had to ensure the hot-headed warriors standing behind them would understand.

They both reluctantly nodded in agreement. They would comply. For now. Salome would have to figure out how to bring these two tribes together or there would eventually be another war.

"Unless there's something else..." Salome began to rise from her seat when Rayma spoke.

"We were told that you had the Hunter. Is that the case or was that just a ploy to trick the Numbio into fighting your battles?" Rayma's tone was less than cordial and Salome was ready to rip her tongue from her mouth.

Salome might have accepted someone speaking down to her when she was a nobody in the Tree House Forest, but she would be damned if she was spoken to in that manner, with the titles that now followed her name.

Heru jumped to his feet and whipped around to face Rayma. The prince attempted to hide his rage but failed miserably when he snarled at the healer. Normally, a servant of any crown would cower and fumble over an apology for the looseness of their tongue, but Rayma didn't back down. She didn't tremble in fear, nor did she offer an apology. She planted her hands on her hips and her nostrils flared.

Salome knew a standoff when she saw one, but there was something else going on besides a defiant healer and her prince. They must be in a relationship or had been at one point in time.

She just instructed the Mountain Men not to squabble and fight, so she had to squash the tension between her and the healer immediately. They followed her brother into the desert, ready to fight along his side for him to reclaim their family's throne. Crispin trusted them, so she would as well.

"My brother was not one for tricks." Salome's voice cracked when she said *was* and not *is*. Eyes from all around the room shot to her and no one uttered a sound. "My brother was an honorable man, and he was honest to a fault." Salome's eyes were focused on Rayma. "Crispin told you that we have the Hunter, and we do."

Zophar's shoulders tensed. He flashed her a warning look, but she wasn't afraid of the title anymore. There was no turning back, and if people were going to march into battle under her banner as her allies, they deserved to know the whole truth.

"I am the Hunter." Salome said boldly and relished the shock in Rayma's face upon her declaration. "I bear the mark of the Hunter," she pointed to her left eye, "and I will do what all Hunters are expected to do: avenge innocent blood."

"You are the Hunter?" Heru squared his shoulders to Salome's and the awe in his face nearly knocked her off her feet.

Salome nodded, holding her chin higher than before. "I am."

Heru placed a hand over his heart. "I swore to march with your brother and now, I swear the same oath to you. The Numbio will fight with you."

Jinn stood. "The East will fight with you."

Torrin and Rune eyed each other before rising.

"The Stormcrags will fight with you."

"The Krazaks will fight with you."

One by one, everyone in the room pledged their allegiance. Salome was humbled by the four mighty men who swore fealty to her, backing her claim. Whether Crispin was still alive, or Death had swept him into her cold embrace, there was no turning back now. Salome would face her sister with an army that could, and would, rival Niabi's.

"Her name is Salome. Daughter of the White Wolf of Northwind and the Sea Monster of the Myr. Princess of Northwind. Red Maiden of the Qata Vishna. The Hunter of prophecies foretold. Long may she reign." Seraphina presented Salome's titles boldly and proudly.

She was Salome and she would not fail.

CHAPTER 57
CRISPIN

Crispin tossed and turned throughout the night as they sailed west toward The Sisters. Sleep eluded him for the two days since they left Northwind. Neempo's pained face kept flashing in his mind. Every time he closed his eyes, he saw the witch's fingers digging into the Sovereign's chest. He heard his screams until Crispin's arrow pierced him, stealing Neempo's breath, but also ending his suffering.

But it wasn't just Crispin's failure to save Neempo that tormented him. There was an eerie presence that whispered in the darkness of his narrow cabin. At first, he couldn't decipher what the strange, shrilly voice was saying, but tonight, it was clear.

"Open the book. We can make you powerful. Open the book. We can make you powerful."

Crispin elbowed himself up from his cot and planted his feet on the creaky wooden floorboards. He scratched at his chest, the necklace Amunet had given him seemed to be weighing him down, as if it, too, detected the evil lurking in his room.

"Open the book?" Crispin rubbed his bloodshot eyes and threw on a loose white shirt. "Open the book?" He muttered trying to figure out what book he was supposed to open when realization hit him.

Sinking to his knees, he pulled out the leather satchel containing his few belongings from underneath his cot. Rummaging through the folds of the bag, he found the small, black book he had lifted from Memucan's nightstand at *The Black Lotus*. When his fingers grazed the binding of the ancient book, the presence he sensed before seemed to want to touch him back. The pendant started to glow around his neck and Crispin lurched back from the book. The necklace had never reacted that way before and he knew whatever power the book possessed wasn't good. He needed to get rid of it.

Careful not to touch the book again, he wrapped it in a hand towel and beelined for the door. He nearly sprinted to the ship's railing to toss the wicked book overboard when a voice startled him.

"Where did you get that?" The prisoner from the White Keep dungeon approached, his eyes glued to the book wrapped in Crispin's towel.

"You know what this is?" Crispin arched an eyebrow, and he hesitated to throw it overboard.

"That is the Book of Noot. It's filled with black magic."

Crispin stared at his hands, thankful he took the time to wrap the book and avoid direct contact with his skin. "I'm going to throw this overboard, unless you know something I don't....?" Crispin realized he didn't know the man's name. "What's your name?"

His gaze met Crispin's curious and frightened face. "My name is Inaros. I spent the last three years of my life in prison because I stole that book from my master."

"Your master was Lord Memucan?" Crispin didn't know who he had expected the man to be, but that wasn't it.

"You know the master?" Inaros' shoulders tensed hearing Memucan's name. "How did you steal this from him and escape?" Inaros asked in a low voice, not wanting anyone to overhear.

"Memucan is dead." Crispin said in a satisfied, matter of fact way. "I killed him."

"And you took the book?"

Crispin nodded. With every second that passed, he wanted desperately to be rid of the book once and for all. "I didn't know what it was, but it was at his bedside table the night I ..."

Inaros bobbed his head in understanding. "You took a man's life and that must weigh heavily upon you, but believe me when I tell you, not even the Almighty One himself will mar your soul for his death."

"Thanks, but I wasn't concerned about that." Crispin held the book over the edge and took a deep breath. He could sense the book screaming at him, commanding him to open it. Promising him power, promising him what he desired most, promising him victory over all his enemies. Crispin was ashamed to admit it, but he was tempted to keep the Book of Noot and open it to see if it was telling him the truth.

"Do it," Inaros cut into Crispin's thoughts. "Cast it into the water."

Before he could think it over or allow the tempting whispers to change his mind, Crispin let the Book of Noot splash into the seas below.

"It is done." Inaros exhaled a sigh of relief and seemed to stand taller if that were possible. Maybe Crispin was just imagining it.

"How did you end up in the White Keep dungeons? Why not a prison in Numbio?" Crispin asked, leaning against the black wooden railing.

When they freed Inaros, he had a scraggly beard and wild unkempt hair. But once they put Northwind behind them, Inaros was given the opportunity to bathe and clean himself up. Now clean-shaven, with short black curls, he reminded Crispin of someone he had met before.

"Memucan picked me and my sister off the streets and gave us a home after our parents died. Seeing my sister's aptitude for herbs and potions, he sent her to the finest healing school in Numbio, and took me under his wing, educating me in history, politics, economics, and diplomacy. But as I began mastering those subjects, he tried to teach me from that little black book. He said if I wanted to be powerful and follow in his footsteps, I would need to master the fifth subject: magic." Inaros shifted from one foot to the other. "Once I realized the magic he was talking about wasn't light magic like our ancestors wielded, but dark, evil magic, I stole the book, and tried to get my sister to escape with me. But..."

Crispin's eyes widened and he straightened. "Is your sister Rayma?"

It was Inaros' turn to look surprised. "You know Rayma?"

"If the prince managed to survive the Wagura, my servant will finish the job."

Memucan's words floated in his mind as Inaros' story settled. The last piece of the puzzle was finally put in place: Rayma was Memucan's servant. She was the one who was supposed to kill Heru.

"If she hasn't already, I think your sister is supposed to kill Prince Heru." The words spilled out before Crispin had a chance to process them.

"She wouldn't do that," Inaros said nervously.

"Let's hope you know your sister better than Memucan." Crispin glanced at the Mainland in the distance, hoping and praying Heru, Zophar, and the rest of the Numbio survived the Caverns of the Undead.

Before Inaros could say anything else, a giant, blazing ball of fire lit up the night sky and headed straight for them. Crispin grabbed Inaros' arm and dragged him away before the catapulted object grazed the hull of the ship. Crispin's eyes shot back up into the starry night and saw two more spheres of flames soaring toward them.

"We're under attack!" Crispin yelled, stumbling to ring the bell to wake up the crew. "We're under attack!" The two fireballs splashed into the sea directly behind them, splashing water across the quarterdeck.

"There's a fleet behind us," Inaros watched the ships cut through the waves at an alarming speed.

Crispin knew without looking who was pursuing them. "It's the Pirate King."

CHAPTER 58

NIABI

Niabi's eyes flew open the second she heard the scratching of a boot against the stone railing of her balcony. Someone was attempting to sneak into her bedchambers by way of her private office. The queen slipped out from underneath her satin sheets, grabbed her twin daggers from under her pillow, and tip-toed to the door. She pressed her back against the wall and listened as someone made their way to her room.

The steps were light, meaning they belonged to a female assassin or a small male. Either this killer was so confident in their slaying ability they came alone, or they were stupid. Both suited Niabi just fine. She would slice whoever had come for her into pieces and scatter them in the Ignacia Sea.

The assassin's fingers twisted the doorknob and as quietly as possible, the assailant slipped inside the queen's bedroom. Niabi leapt toward the intruder, slicing her knives in fury. The masked assassin whipped around in time to block the surprise attack. The two traded spars, almost a mirror image of one another's movements.

The killer dropped to the floor, attempting to sweep Niabi's legs out from under her, but the queen easily hopped out of danger's way, knowing that move all too well, because she used it often in battle. Suspended in mid-air, Niabi landed a roundhouse kick to the intruder's chest, sending them soaring. Not wasting time for the assailant to catch their breath, Niabi pressed a knee into their breastbone and tucked a dagger against their throat.

"Guards!" She beckoned the clueless soldiers guarding the doors outside her room. They fumbled inside, wide eyed at the queen sitting atop an armed intruder, and they arrested the masked trespasser.

"Wait." Niabi stopped them from dragging the would-be assassin to the dungeons when she caught a glimpse of the assassin's knife. The pearl handle resembled one she had given to a friend as a Name Day gift years ago. Niabi reached a tentative hand up and ripped the mask off. The queen took a step back, shaking her head. "Marina?"

Marina met her cousin's gaze; her eyes raging with hatred.

"Why?" Niabi barely got the one-word question out. She never expected Marina to try to kill her. Hurt was an understatement. Devastated, crushed, shattered. Niabi was flooded with the pain of her cousin's betrayal and felt as if someone had taken one of her precious daggers and plunged it deep into her heart.

Marina spat at Niabi, muttering incoherent curses under her breath as the soldiers dragged her away.

"Take her to the Eastern Courtyard," Niabi ordered. "Have Tala and Vilora meet me there."

Pulling a blue, long-trained coat over her sleepwear, she glided through the empty, cold, white halls to the Eastern Courtyard. The corridor was shaking, and she braced a hand against a wall to steady herself. Only then did she realize the hallway wasn't moving, she was the one trembling. She backed up against the marble and slid down to the floor. Wrapping her arms around her knees, tucked as closely as she could get them without squashing her swollen belly, she cried. Niabi hated crying, but her soul was so wounded, she couldn't help it.

Marina was more than just a cousin to her. She was like her sister. She had picked up the pearl-hilted knife Marina intended to use to slit her throat off her bedroom floor and only realized she had it clutched in her hand when her fingers started to go numb. Niabi had that dagger designed and forged with Marina in mind. It was a Name Day gift that was supposed to remind Marina that even though she wasn't training to be a Qata Vishna, that deep inside, she was a warrior.

Plenty of assassins had tried their hand at taking Niabi out. All of them had failed and were sent to meet Death sooner than they had anticipated. But Marina…

Marina had to be dealt with.

The queen pushed herself up from the black and white tile floor and made her way outside. With torches lighting the crumbling Eastern Courtyard, Niabi could see that Tala, Vilora, Anaktu, and a handful of soldiers were gathered around the wooden platform Neempo had been strapped to before he died. Marina was tied to the stake, her head hanging, avoiding Niabi's glare.

She brushed Tala's extended hand away and walked up to Marina, stopping a few feet in front of her. "Who ordered you to assassinate me?"

Marina slowly raised her head and looked at her with a blank expression. The rage and hatred she had seen in her bedroom was gone. But whatever was racing through Marina's mind remained a mystery to her. "No one."

Niabi didn't believe her. "Who ordered -"

"No one!" Marina shouted, thrashing against the pole. Soldiers went to draw their weapons, but Niabi motioned for them to stand down. "No one ordered me to kill you. I wanted you dead."

She felt a lump in her throat. She wouldn't cry in front of all these people. She wouldn't allow it. "Why, Marina?" The queen took another step forward. "Why?"

"Because I could get close enough to kill you." Marina didn't try to fight the bonds anymore. She rested her head against the wooden pole and sighed. "Mika agreed to take my place, if I agreed to assassinate you when I had the chance."

"So, Mika sent you."

Marina let out a low chuckle and shook her head. "You really have no idea."

"No idea about what?" Niabi narrowed her eyes. Marina's grin sent an eerie shiver up her spine.

"We always knew one day, you would ask me to do something unspeakable," Marina whispered. "I didn't think it would be killing grandmother, but I did it with the end goal in mind."

"What are you talking about?" Niabi asked.

"Have you heard of a rebel group known as the Order?"

Niabi drew a breath. She had heard of the Order before and dismissed them as insignificant. Perhaps, she had been wrong to write them off as disgruntled peasants.

Marina's smile widened at Niabi's reaction. "By the look on your face, you have heard of us."

"Us?" Niabi lurched back as if she'd been stung.

"Mika and I were both part of the Order." Marina's voice grew louder so everyone in the courtyard could hear. "There are more of us than you realize. Magic wielders, royals, commoners. All banded together with one purpose: to see your reign end."

"How could you betray me, Marina?" Rage bubbled within Niabi and she could feel the itch of the magic groaning underneath her skin. "We are blood."

Marina shrugged, "Blood means nothing to you."

"Say what you want about me, Marina," Niabi hissed, inching closer. "But we are guilty of the same sin. We have blood-stained hands, deaths marring our souls."

"And if you don't take my life now," Marina didn't back down from Niabi's intense, wicked glare, "I swear I won't stop until I carve your heart from your chest."

"Then you will die a traitor's death."

"May you never find peace," Marina cursed her. "May you never find happiness. May you die a death worthy of your sins."

"You first." Niabi stepped off the wooden platform and the flames that had been begging to be unleashed, danced in her palm. "Goodbye, Marina." She rested her hand against the wood, and it ignited. Niabi turned on her heel and stomped away, heading toward the doors to enter the White Keep.

Niabi never looked back. Not when she smelled the charring of wood. Not when she felt the heat of the fire licking at her back. Not when Tala pleaded with her to reconsider. Not when Vilora nodded in proud approval. Not even when she heard Marina's screams.

Just before heading inside, she dropped the pearl hilted knife on the ground, swearing she would never step foot in the Eastern Courtyard again.

CHAPTER 59

CRISPIN

Haldane shouted orders at his crew, preparing them for battle. The captain explained that this hadn't been their first explosive encounter with another ship, and it wouldn't be their last. But to know it was the Pirate King assaulting them made Haldane even more excited about sinking the attacking ship.

"Phex!" Haldane barked, and the auburn-haired pirate strutted forward, arms filled with explosive trinkets.

"Captain?" Phex grinned like a beast who knew it was about to be unleashed.

"Light them up." Haldane ordered.

"With pleasure." Phex scrambled up the steps to the back of the quarterdeck. Throwing the explosives as far as he could toward the fast-approaching ships, Crispin thought Phex's inventions didn't work. They didn't come close enough to hit the Pirate King's ships.

"Did they not work?" Crispin came up behind the explosive's expert and leaned over the edge to get a better look at the bobbing bombs. Phex grabbed Crispin by the back of his shirt collar and pulled him away from the railing.

"I wouldn't do that if I were you." Phex shook his head. "Wouldn't want you falling to your death."

"I can swim," Crispin said, but Phex waved a dismissive hand in the air.

"Watch, Prince. Just watch."

Crispin looked at the oncoming ships. As they approached the floating spheres Phex had disposed of, they began exploding as soon as the ships made contact. Loud booms, pirates screaming, and splintering wood echoed in the night. Crispin patted a proud Phex on the back.

"Not bad, Phex." Crispin smiled at the sight of one of Uri's ships sinking. "Not bad at all."

"You haven't seen anything yet." Phex motioned for Crispin to follow him. "I'll need some help with the next one."

"Let's go."

Phex yelled for Corwin, Ondrej, and Rafi to come help him uncover a machine that had been sitting on the deck covered by a tarp. Crispin had wondered what was underneath since he first joined the crew, only to be told several times that he would find out when he needed to. It seemed today was that day. Once the wooden machine had been uncovered, Crispin still didn't know what he was staring at.

"What is it?" Crispin asked as more explosions sounded behind them.

"I call it *The Fist*." Phex was giddy, rubbing his hands together. "Alright, boys, you know what to do."

Crispin watched Corwin, Ondrej, and Rafi attach a few loose pieces into the main mechanism and pointed it toward the stern. Phex hopped into what appeared to be a seat, slapped some goggles on, and gave the others a thumbs up.

The pirates scattered. Corwin grabbed Crispin by the arm and pulled him away. "Keep your distance, unless you want to know how it feels to fly."

Crispin's eye was caught by Rahab on the other side of the ship, making sure Master Penn and her Keepers, Ziggy and Nubis, and Inaros were either armed or updated on battle strategies. She must have felt Crispin's gaze and turned to look at him. Gone was the woman he had kissed and held in his arms. The pirate, the Queen of the Obsidian Seas, was standing there, commanding her crew, readying for the possibility of their ship being boarded. She nodded her head in acknowledgment, before returning to the others.

"Ready!" Phex's scream ripped Crispin's eyes from Rahab and back to the explosives-crazed pirate. "Launch!"

Phex shifted some wooden gears which propelled similar looking spheres to the ones that floated in the water. Except these spheres were bigger and traveled a generous distance. Circling the gears as fast as he could, Phex kept launching different size balls at the Pirate King's fleet. Uri had started with seven ships, including *The Leviathan*, and thanks to Phex's floating minefield, he had lost two of the smaller ships.

Crispin watched in curiosity as the bombs smashed into the Pirate King's ships: the hulls, masts, quarterdecks, and bowsprits. Phex was grinning like a madman and didn't ease up on launching his one-man annihilation. No wonder the Pirate King wanted Phex to work for him.

Corwin elbowed Crispin in the ribs. "Glad he's on our side."

"He's a genius!" Crispin was amazed by the workings of Phex's dangerous mind. Another ship met a watery grave and Phex wasn't even close to finished.

Rafi rang the alarm in the crow's nest. Crispin looked up and the halfling was pointing to three ships in front of them. Rahab joined Crispin as they made their way to the front of the ship to get a better look.

Rahab pulled out her spyglass. "Westerners." She glanced at Crispin. "We can't fight both Uri and the Western Patrol."

Haldane joined them and let loose a string of profanities before realizing Master Penn was standing next to him. "Apologies, Master Penn, I didn't know you were standing there."

"Apologies are not necessary, Captain," Penn waved a hand in the air. "I agree with the sentiment."

"What's the plan?" Rahab looked from Crispin to Haldane.

"We surrender to the Westerners," Crispin said before Haldane had a chance to comment, knowing the pirate was more likely to try to fight everyone and go down with his ship. Despite the pirates' wide-eyed disapproval he continued, "Master Penn and I can vouch for your safety and ask to see King Benaiah. The Westerners won't risk a war knowing Salome is out there amassing an army."

"I don't like it," Haldane snorted. "We can take both the Westerners and the Pirate King."

"I don't like the idea any more than you do," Rahab folded her arms over her chest, wind whipping her blue locks around her face, "but maybe we should let Crispin and Master Penn take the lead on this one."

Master Penn nodded her head. "The Westerners make it a point to keep relations with The Sisters amicable. Prince Crispin and I will do what we need to do to ensure everyone's safety."

"Another one down!" Phex cried in delight, sinking the fourth ship Uri commanded. "You want some more, you bastards?"

Crispin leaned over the railing and saw the Pirate King retreating, salvaging what he had left of his fleet. Whether it was fear of Phex sinking another ship or the sight of the Western Patrol in the distance, Crispin wouldn't know, but he was grateful they would live to see another day.

"Raise the white flag," Haldane ordered, and the words sounded weird coming out of his mouth.

Rafi shouted down from the crow's nest, "Sorry, Captain, I thought you said to raise the white flag."

"I did, you twit!" Haldane barked. "Raise the white flag!"

"Captain." Rafi did as he was ordered, confusion still in his shifty eyes.

"You better be right about this, lad," Haldane said.

DAWN BREACHED the horizon as the lead Western Patrol ship crashed a wooden ramp down, connecting their ship with the *Shadow of Death*. Gathered on the deck, Crispin, and the rest of the crew, new and old, waited as a tall, broad-shouldered captain stomped from his ship to theirs. Two uniformed officers flanked the clean-shaven, redheaded commander. His eyes were the color of the sea and were just as dangerous.

With his arms clasped behind his back, the captain's eyes scanned the group left to right. His eyes stopped when he spotted Ziggy, but he continued until his gaze rested on Haldane. He smiled. "I am Captain Ivar, the commander of this fleet. We have been hunting the *Shadow of Death* for quite some time. King Benaiah will be pleased to know you will no longer be terrorizing the seas."

Haldane muttered under his breath, but Crispin stepped forward before the pirate could say something damaging. "Captain Ivar, I am Prince Crispin of Northwind. I would -"

"Why would the Prince of Northwind keep the company of criminals?" Ivar interrupted him with a calm, threatening tone.

"Would you say the same of me, Captain Ivar?" Penn stepped forward, her feet shoulder-width apart, flanked by her six Keepers.

If Captain Ivar was surprised by her presence, he didn't show it. "Master Penn," he bowed his head in respect. "Have these ruffians kidnapped you?"

"They are friends of The Sisters." Penn said, matching his menacing inflection. "And they will be treated as such."

"Master Penn," Ivar started but stopped when his eyes once again landed on Ziggy. "What is your name?"

"Ziggy," she replied as loudly as she dared.

"Ziggy," he repeated. "Were you taken by this crew?"

She shook her head, "No, they rescued me."

Ivar scoffed, "Rescued. That's not the term I would associate with their kind."

Crispin could sense Rahab's nostrils flaring like a raging bull and squeezed her hand. Their eyes met and she released the anger in her face.

"Captain Ivar," Crispin's focus bounced back to the Westerner. "Unless you want my sister, Princess Salome, to see your aggression toward us as an act of war, I would strongly encourage you to take all of us to meet with King Benaiah. I'm sure he will be inclined to speak with me."

"And me." Penn threw her weight around like a political pro.

Captain Ivar mulled over what they were saying. "Fine." He reluctantly agreed. "I will take all of you to Borg to see King Benaiah. He will determine your fate and I will still be rewarded for the capture of the ever-elusive *Shadow of Death*." His tight-lipped grin barely qualified as a smile. He motioned everyone to board his ship. "Consider yourselves guests of His Majesty until he says otherwise. But while you are passengers on my ship, you will abide by my rules, or I'll happily throw you in the brig. Understood?"

Affirmative grumbling was the closest Ivar was going to get to an enthusiastic response and he allowed it. "Welcome aboard The *Drakkar*."

Crispin didn't need to ask what the name meant. He had learned enough of the ancient Western language from Zophar to know it translated to *The Dragon*. Because of the stories Zophar shared, Crispin always dreamt of visiting Borg after he reclaimed his kingdom. But now, he would be going before the king accused of piracy. Maybe, Benaiah wouldn't be as cut-throat as he'd heard. But with his luck, he was in for a hell of a first meeting.

Rahab's hand slipped into his as *The Drakkar* set course for Borg. He dared a kiss to her forehead as they abandoned the *Shadow of Death* and made their way to the land of battle hungry warriors.

CHAPTER 60
SALOME

Salome slipped inside Adonijah's room the next morning and found him lying in bed flat on his back. He was shirtless and his boots had been placed neatly at the foot of his bed. There were bandages wrapped around his torso, his right wrist, and the cuts on his face and leg were freshly salved. His eyes were closed, so she thought better than to wake him, especially since he had just fought a giant Krazak to the death for her.

For her.

That point had not gone unnoticed. He had fought in the Dagaal she had invoked. It was meant for her. She was prepared to fight it, too. But he volunteered to be her champion and she was angry with him. Angry that he would place himself in that position. Angry that he would risk his life to save hers. Angry. But she wasn't angry anymore. How could she be with him lying there injured?

If she were honest with herself, she might not have been able to defeat the giant he faced with the injuries she was still nursing. She was skilled, but Adonijah bore the brunt of several heavy-handed beatings and still got back on his feet. Had he not volunteered, they might all very well be dead or enslaved. She swallowed hard. She wanted to hug him. To thank him. But it would have to wait. She was going to let him rest.

Salome turned to leave when he asked, "Leaving so soon, Princess?" His eyes were still closed when she whipped around.

"I told you not to call me that," she tried to hide the smirk begging to stretch across her face.

"I suppose I just like riling you up." Adonijah smiled and turned his head to lock eyes with her.

Although he seemed pleased to see her, his bloodshot eyes screamed he needed rest desperately. She could always tell when he was in pain because the corners of his mouth would twitch.

"I should let you rest -"

"Stay with me." Adonijah cut her off with his gentle request.

Salome wanted to stay with him, like he had stayed with her when she was recovering in Myr, so she agreed with a nod. "How did you know it was me?" she sat on the edge of his bed.

Adonijah propped himself up on his elbows as she placed a second pillow behind his back. "I'm not sure how I knew, I just did."

Salome eyes scanned all the cuts, bruises, and bandages covering his lean, muscular body. She then became painfully aware that she was sitting very close to a man only wearing pants. She lifted her gaze from his bare chest to his chiseled jaw, his lips, his eyes… When their eyes met, he seemed to recognize she had been ogling, but he also didn't seem bothered.

"How are you feeling?" she tucked hair behind her shoulders, hoping he wouldn't call her out for staring.

"I feel about as good as I look." He said and she blushed. "So, not great." He motioned toward his bandages.

She released an awkward breath and relaxed her eyebrows. After a moment to compose herself, she asked him what she really wanted to know. "Why did you do it?"

"Do what?" He sat up with a quizzical look on his face.

"Why did you take my place in the Dagaal?" Her gaze swept to the floor, twiddling her fingers in her lap. "It should have been me in that arena."

Adonijah shrugged, flashing a half-smile, "You needed a champion."

"Look at you, Adonijah." She reached out and gently touched the cut along his jawline. "You shouldn't have volunteered. What if you had been…?"

Killed. She wanted to say killed, but she couldn't bring herself to utter the word. Didn't want to think of his lifeless body lying in the dirt of the arena.

Adonijah tipped her chin to look at him. "If I had to, I'd do it again."

"Why?"

He intertwined his fingers with hers and rested them against his chest. "You already know why, Salome."

"Your oath to protect me." She knew as soon as she said it, it was the wrong answer.

Adonijah brought her hand to his lips and kissed it. "My oath had nothing to do with my decision."

Salome brushed her free hand across his chest, and she felt his heartbeat quicken. Her eyes met his again. She leaned forward, touching his face, running her fingers through his loose, shoulder-length hair. His hands reached around her, the pads of his fingers stroking up and down her back.

"I owe you my life, Adonijah."

"All I want," he leaned closer, so their lips were inches from touching, "is your heart."

"You have it," she whispered.

Adonijah kissed her softly, before pulling her closer to him. He flipped her on her back, so she laid underneath him. One of his hands raked up her neck to the back of her head while the other rested on her hip. She cupped his face in her hands, kissing him, unwilling to let him go.

She craved his lips against hers. Shivered as his hands roamed freely over her skin. With every kiss and every moan, she saw their journey flash before her eyes.

Their first encounter in The Hollow; the brawl at the Hidden Tavern; facing their fears in the Enchanted Swamp; fighting the Thrak, freeing the Stormcrags, and their fleeting, private moments together in the Isles of Myr. It had always been him tugging at her heart, whispering his love for her in every smile. Their paths had been destined to cross and she knew, wrapped in his embrace, his mouth pressed against her neck, that he would keep his promise to fight, live, and die by her side.

"Salome," he pulled back. "Salome, wait."

She opened her eyes, "What's wrong?"

He strummed his thumb up and down her jaw. "There's something I need to tell you. Something I should have told you a long time ago."

She propped herself up on her elbows. "What are you talking about?"

"I need to tell you who I really am."

"I know who you are, Adonijah."

His eyes drifted from hers. "I should have told you before, but I was afraid of what you might think of me. Honestly, I'm still afraid."

She kissed his lips once more. "You can tell me anything." She held his hand tightly, even though her stomach was in knots.

Adonijah took a deep breath. His eyes filled with a pain that made her ache. "Salome -"

"Your Highness," Zophar cleared his throat, standing in the entrance with a red tinge spreading across his pale cheeks.

Salome gently pushed Adonijah off her and stood up, trying to meet Zophar's gaze, but he purposely avoided making eye contact with her, knowing he interrupted a very intimate moment.

"You don't have to call me that, Zophar." Salome rested her hands on her hips, not knowing what exactly to do with her hands.

"It's important to use your title now that you command an army." Zophar scratched his face. "Torrin has requested all leaders gather for a meeting. It seems the Stormcrags captured a man claiming to have escaped a Northern camp."

"Northern camp?" Salome's eyes widened as she took a step forward. "There's a Northern camp nearby?"

Zophar held his hands up stopping her approach. His eyes finally meeting hers. "Before you go in there, you should know the man they captured said he knows you."

"Knows me?"

"I didn't get a good look at him," Zophar admitted, "but he has red hair."

"One of the villagers?" Salome's voice cracked; she felt her emotions bubble in her throat. "Take me to him."

Zophar bobbed his head and held the curtains blocking the entrance into Adonijah's cave open for Salome to leave. Adonijah hopped up and said, "I'm going with you."

"You should rest." Salome turned back to him.

"I'll be fine," Adonijah threw a shirt on and fastened his boots, not taking no for an answer. "If there's a Northern camp nearby, I want to know what we are dealing with."

Salome reluctantly nodded, knowing arguing with him would be futile. She found every step she took toward the assembly cavern was heavy and filled with dread. *Which villager had escaped? Were there more villagers that needed help? Was there even a Tree House Forest left for those they rescued to return to?*

Zophar strode inside first but Salome hesitated. Adonijah rested his hand on her lower back.

"You alright?" he whispered in her ear; his chest pressed against her back.

Salome inhaled deeply and rolled her shoulders back. She was the heir to the White Throne. She was the Hunter. She was the Red Maiden. She was the leader of armies and the bringer of rebellion. When she thought about who she used to be, she realized the girl from the Tree House Forest was long gone.

"I'm ready." Salome swooshed the curtains open and walked in with a regality that took some of the other leaders by surprise. All eyes were fixed on her, but her attention was glued to the man standing before them in tattered clothing, with matted red hair, and barely healed scars.

She rounded to her seat in the half circle of leaders and recognized the villager as the baker who once pestered her to teach him to hunt. The villager who declared his intentions of marrying her. And the one she continuously brushed off without a second thought. She nearly gasped at the disheveled sight of Jacobi. The once plump baker with rosy cheeks was thin, bruised, and had hollow cheeks. His wrists were bound with rope, and he swayed on his feet in exhaustion, but she kept her face neutral as she claimed the Throne of Skulls between Zophar and Torrin.

The Stormcrag leader leaned forward, the wooden chair hissing underneath his massive frame. "My warriors found you wandering the mountains. They said you escaped a military camp from Northwind."

Jacobi nodded weakly. "That's true." His eyes floated to Salome. "After you left, more Shadows came to the village." His bottom lip quivered, and Salome's stomach plummeted. "I am the only one left."

"Can you tell us who is in the camp?" The Stormcrag leader didn't care about Jacobi's sentimentality. "Who is their leader? Why are they this far south? How many men are in their company?"

"Prince Thanos of Gomorrah asked Queen Niabi for aid in claiming the Gomorrian throne from his mother." Jacobi explained what he knew, his lips were dry, and his voice was raspy.

"Someone, give him some water," Salome ordered. "Did no one care to help him earlier?"

Kai stepped forward with a sheepskin of water and Jacobi drowned himself in the cool drink.

"Thank you," Jacobi bobbed his head in gratitude.

Torrin huffed an irritated sigh, his fingers tapping the armrest of his chair. "How many soldiers march with them?"

"There are a few hundred soldiers and a company of elite Shadows."

"Which Shadows?" Adonijah straightened from leaning against the entrance threshold, but the villager didn't exert the energy to turn around to look at him.

"The Commander of Shadows leads their entire force."

"Pash? Gershom's son." Heru rubbed his chin, elbow resting on the armrest of his chair.

Jacobi nodded. "His Uncle Ophir rides with him and the one who burned our village to the ground. They call him the Nameless Rider."

Adonijah stiffened at the mention of the Nameless Rider, and it didn't go unnoticed by Salome.

"They have no interest in finding our city?" Rune the Krazak asked, with Hanzo standing behind him. The archer eyed Oifa as she picked her teeth clean with her long nails, grinning at Hanzo as he watched.

"I don't know," Jacobi rolled his shoulders. "All I know is they are preparing to attack Gomorrah within the week."

Heru shifted in his seat, stretching his legs out in front of him. "If we could capture some of their leaders, we could get valuable information about Northwind and their military strategies. Maybe even find a weakness in the White City's walls."

"This sounds too convenient for my liking," Jinn chimed in, lazily lounging in his chair.

"What do you mean?" The Stormcrag leader turned to look at him.

"Tell us," Jinn directed his question at Jacobi, resting his chin in his hand. "How did you manage to escape from the Northerners' camp?"

Jacobi cleared his throat. "When they fell asleep, I bit through my bindings and ran."

"You don't believe him." Salome glanced at him from across their half circle.

"How many people do you know of that have escaped an elite company of Shadows and lived to tell the tale?" Jinn's eyes shifted from the prisoner to her.

"Perhaps we send some scouts to gather information about the camp." Heru suggested.

"Agreed." Torrin nodded. Even sitting down, his biceps bulged, demanding attention. "We will have Cato lead a band of our finest scouts in the morning. We should know more in a couple days."

"I will send Hanzo with these scouts," Rune interjected with a haughty smile. "Just to make sure they are safe, of course."

"If *he* is going," Oifa stepped forward, not stooping to refer to the archer by name, "then I will, too."

Seeing a fight brewing, Salome said, "Hanzo *and* Oifa will accompany Cato. There will be no violence. You are there to protect our scouts if something goes wrong. Is that understood?" Hanzo and Oifa bowed their heads in agreement. "Then it is settled." Salome stood, ending their meeting.

"We never should have sent you away," Jacobi halted the leaders from leaving. His eyes were fixed on Salome. "We never should have sent you away," he whispered sadly.

Salome nodded, her eyes burning as she blinked. She turned to Zophar and said, "Make sure he gets something to eat."

As she turned to leave, Jacobi lunged on bended knee and grabbed her arm. Knives were drawn around the room, but Salome waved them down.

"I..." he whimpered. "I haven't stopped thinking about you. Hoping our paths would cross again. My feelings for you... they haven't changed."

Salome gently pulled her hand from his grasp. "Nor have mine."

She walked out of the room and didn't stop until she entered her private cave. She was shaking. Pouring herself a cup of water, she downed it in one gulp. Tears slipped down her cheeks. She hadn't allowed herself to think of the villagers or what might have happened to the Tree House Forest after they left. But seeing Jacobi, hearing of the devastation and destruction he managed to escape…

Arms wrapped around her from behind. She knew by the scent of cedar and springtime that it was Jinn. He didn't say anything, he just held her until she turned to face him, laying her head against his chest. Jinn stroked her hair and let her soak his shirt in tears. He kissed the top of her head and tightened his arms around her.

"I didn't let myself think about them," Salome's voice cracked. "I didn't want to know what had happened to them…"

Jinn pulled her from his chest and gently lifted her chin forcing her to meet his gaze. "It's not your fault."

"Then why do I feel guilty?" Her lip shook and he swiped her tears away with his thumbs.

"Because you are a good person. Your heart will always feel heavy when the lives of innocents are lost." Jinn took her hands in his and rested them against his chest. "It's cruel, Salome, but good people don't always win the battle. Good people don't always accomplish their goals. And sometimes, good people die before we think they should. You are leading an army to battle your sister. Not all of us are going to make it home when the dust settles. Hell," Jinn tilted his head to the side and dark strands of hair fell over his forehead, "there's a chance I won't even make it."

"Jinn," Salome shook her head furiously, fresh tears streaming down her face, "don't say that."

"I'll still follow you into the blood, ash, and fire of war and not regret it, even if it brings me face to face with Lady Death." Jinn rested his forehead against hers. "We could do everything right and it still not be enough to win, darling."

"Why are you saying these things?" Salome took a step back.

"I don't want you to be unprepared for the reality of war." Jinn said softly. "You have suffered loss. You have felt pain. You have experienced battle, but nothing prepares you for war." His hand slid down her arm, entwining their fingers. "My father and uncles fought against your sister when she first came to power. They were never the same. One of my uncles never made it home."

Salome cupped his face with her free hand, gently rubbing her thumb against his cheek. "You can walk away. I wouldn't fault you for thinking of your people."

"Where you go, I go."

"You are your father's heir. His only son." Salome tried to reason with him.

"And it seems you might be the last of Issachar's children who can avenge your family." Jinn countered.

Salome's thoughts shot to Crispin. Heru told her there was a chance he might have made it, but she also knew there was a possibility her brother was gone.

"A secret for a secret." She sent through their bond.

Jinn nodded. *"You first."*

Salome took a deep breath, maintaining eye contact with Jinn. *"I don't want the crown or the White Throne. If Crispin is gone… He was the one who was supposed to rule Northwind. Not me."*

Jinn squeezed her hand, straightening his shoulders. *"A year ago, I ran away from home because I didn't want to be king. That's when I met Oden and realized I could still be useful. When he asked me to go to the Isles of Myr to see if you might be there, I jumped at the chance."*

"And then you found me."

"And then I found you." Jinn smiled and said, "I understand you, Salome, more than you will ever know."

Salome rested her hands against his chest. "I need you to promise me something."

"What?"

"If things don't go as planned, I want you to cloak yourself and get as far from Death as you can. Even if that means you leave me behind."

Jinn shook his head, "I told you before, if it is within my power to give, I will, but that is something I cannot, will not, promise."

"Why?" Salome furrowed her brow, frustration bubbling inside her. "Your people -"

"I love you," Jinn's confession stole the words from her mouth. "Sakurai stood before I was born, and it will remain even if I fall. But I will not abandon you, even if it costs me everything."

"You love me?" It was all she managed to whisper.

Jinn leaned close, his lips hovering over hers. "With all that I am, I love you, Salome."

"Jinn," she pressed a hand to his chest. He retreated a step, raking a hand through his hair. "I do care for you, but…"

"You chose him." Jinn shrugged with a sad smile. "I knew there was a chance you would."

"I never meant to hurt you," Salome wrapped her arms around herself. It hurt to look into his pained eyes, but she forced herself to maintain eye contact. She owed him that much.

Jinn stuffed his hands into his pockets and tilted his head to the side, clearing his throat. "I meant what I said before. About my armies being yours whether you accepted my proposal or not."

"Jinn…"

"My sword will always be yours, Salome." He bowed his head and turned to leave.

"Survive this war." Her words stopped him, but he didn't look back. "Whatever you have to do, survive."

He walked out and she fought every urge to reach out to him. She had made her choice. But instead of wanting to be in the comfort and warmth of Adonijah's embrace, she found she would rather be alone.

CHAPTER 61

ADONIJAH

Adonijah shook Jacobi awake, holding a finger up to his lips, instructing the villager to keep quiet. Adonijah whispered, "Could you find your way back to the Northern camp?"

Jacobi froze. "Why?"

"Can you find your way back or not?" Adonijah growled and Jacobi flinched. "I won't harm you. I just need to know if you can find your way back."

The redhead reluctantly nodded as he sat up. "I could probably find my way back. Or at least get close enough."

"I need you to take me there tonight."

Jacobi fell to his knees. "Please don't make me go back there. Please. I can't go back. He'll kill me."

Adonijah dropped to one knee to be at eye level with the whimpering prisoner. "I know you don't want to go back, but I need a guide. It's important that I make it there and quickly."

"Why do you want to go?" A fearful tear slipped down Jacobi's cheek. "I told you all I know. Your scouts will confirm it. I swear I told your leaders everything."

"The Nameless Rider – he killed my mother," Adonijah blurted before he had a chance to think it through. The tension in his shoulders vanished and he sat on the ground. "I've been trying to track him for years and I've never gotten this close before. This is my chance, Jacobi. Please." Adonijah met Jacobi's bloodshot eyes. "Will you help me?"

Jacobi puffed out a short, tired breath. "I betrayed them."

Adonijah tilted his head, unsure who he was talking about. "Who?"

"I was scared," Jacobi whispered, wiping a tear with his finger. "He said I could tell him what he wanted to know or I could die with them… I… I…"

Adonijah averted his gaze, not wanting to watch Jacobi suffer with his cowardice. "You can't bring them back. But now, you can try to do what is right."

Jacobi hesitated. "You can kill him?"

Adonijah bobbed his head and met Jacobi's eyes. "Aye."

"Then I will help you," Jacobi agreed.

THE TWO MEN trekked down the mountains for several hours before hearing the clinking of metal, crackling campfires, and the chatter of guards gobbling their mush before heading to bed.

Ducking behind a cluster of boulders, Adonijah popped his head over to have a look at what he was dealing with. Hundreds of white tents were erected at the base of the mountain. Although there were a few guards patrolling, no one was truly expecting an attack. *Who would be foolish enough to attack the Northerners in their own camp?*

Jacobi shivered, his back pinned against the rocks, refusing to look.

"If something happens to me," Adonijah whispered, "then you go back up the mountain until you reach the City of Bones."

"You're not forcing me to go any further?" Jacobi seemed surprised.

Adonijah shook his head. "I only asked you to get me here. You're not a soldier; you have no place here." His eyes scanned the camp again. "If I don't come back in an hour, leave."

"And what do I tell them when I get back?"

Adonijah hadn't thought about him not coming back. In his mind, killing the Nameless Rider wouldn't take him long, and he would be on his way without anyone knowing he'd been there. Of course, there was a possibility he didn't walk out alive, but this was the closest he'd been to finding his mother's murderer. He could go back now, leave the Nameless Rider for another time, but his desire to protect Salome was overshadowed by his need for revenge. Before he met Salome, this had been his life's purpose. He would be lying if he said he didn't have this unquenchable thirst to spill his enemy's blood.

He took a deep breath. "Tell Salome, I'm sorry." Before Jacobi could reply, or he changed his mind, Adonijah skirted around the trees to get to the base.

Eyes darting both directions looking for a passing patrol, Adonijah only came out of hiding to cross into the Northern camp once he was in the clear. It was a wide-open space, no trees, or boulders to take cover behind. He had to be quick if he was going to get into the camp unnoticed. Nearly there, he quickened his soft-footed pace before the patrol could make another pass, but he stopped dead in his tracks when twelve Shadows emerged from outskirt tents and surrounded him.

The Nameless Rider's feet thudded against the ground as he pointed a long sword at Adonijah. "State your business, trespasser."

Adonijah suppressed the rage brewing inside his chest. There was no way he was going to make it out of this alive if he launched an assault. He kept a neutral face and flashed an impish smile. "Sorry. Must have gotten lost."

The Nameless Rider chuckled through gritted teeth. "I see you are going to make this difficult. I like difficult."

Ophir took a step toward Adonijah, an eyebrow arched. Adonijah recognized the old crone he fought in the tavern and saw the moment the Shadow remembered him, too. The bald soldier hissed, "You're that sell-sword from the Hidden Tavern." His eyes darted across the circle, "I saw him escape with the queen's sister."

"Turn around." A familiar voice ordered. "And remember you are surrounded. Don't do anything stupid."

Adonijah slowly turned around, hands at the level of his eyes, and flashed a wicked smile when Pash's eyes widened. "Hello, brother. It's been a long time."

"Brother?" Ophir rasped. "But that would make you…"

"Satara's son," Adonijah finished for him, though he didn't look his way.

Pash lowered his sword and approached his younger brother cautiously. "Is it really you, Adonijah?"

"Better looking than the last time you saw me."

Pash's pace quickened and Adonijah thought his brother was going to take a swing at him. But to his surprise, Pash wrapped his arms around him and whispered in his ear, "I thought you were dead."

"You'd miss me too much if I died." Adonijah tried to keep the conversation light, but he saw the pain in his older brother's eyes when he pulled back.

"Come with me," Pash threw his arm over Adonijah's shoulders. "We have a lot to talk about."

"Pash, he is our enemy -"

"No one is to lay one finger on my brother," Pash hissed, interrupting his uncle, and turning in a circle to meet every Shadow's gaze. "That's an order. Anyone who disobeys will lose their head."

"Wow," Adonijah folded his arms across his chest. "You've trained your dogs well." His eyes drifted to the Nameless Rider's one icy, blue eye. As much as he wanted to slit the Shadow's throat and watch him die in a pool of his own blood, that would have to wait. For now. The last time he was this close to the seven-foot monstrosity was when he was fleeing his mother's burning house.

Pash flashed him a warning look before leading him into the middle of the Northern camp. The commander ushered him inside a large white tent and made sure no one was snooping around to listen to their conversation.

"Wine?" Pash offered, pouring himself a glass from the lavish wet bar.

"Your life must be fancy if this is what roughing it in a military camp looks like." Adonijah sank into a leather chair and kicked his muddy boots up on an end table.

Pash snickered, "Is that why you risked coming to my camp? To mock my lifestyle?" He passed a glass to Adonijah and sat in the chair opposite him.

"Actually, I came to kill one of your men."

One of Pash's eyebrows arched in amusement. "You've got balls, Adonijah, I'll give you that."

"But?" Adonijah sipped his wine with a smirk.

"You know I can't let you do that." Pash rolled his shoulders and sat straighter in his seat.

"Pity."

"When I heard about your mother…" Pash strummed his fingers against his cup. "I went looking for you, but you were gone." He looked at Adonijah, "Where have you been all these years?"

Adonijah shrugged, "Here and there."

"Why didn't you come to Northwind?" Pash's voice cracked, and he cleared his throat, shifting his weight. "I would have helped you."

"We both know what would have happened if I sought you out and Gershom got his hands on me. He would have broken me and molded me into a monster of his own design." Adonijah hated thinking about his father, but over the seven years of being on his own, not a day went by that he didn't think about Pash. "I did miss you though."

Pash nodded in understanding. "I hate him, too, you know."

"Seems like we both have father issues." Adonijah scratched a finger across his forehead.

"You know I have to ask," Pash's tone sharpened. "Are you fighting for Salome?"

"And you know I won't tell you anything of value."

"Well, that answers that question." Pash shook his head with an irritated sigh. "Uncle Ophir is going to push for me to take you to Northwind in shackles. Especially if he sends word to our father -"

"That bald man is our uncle?" Adonijah snorted a laugh. "Seems more like a grumpy old man than a fearsome Shadow."

"Don't let his age fool you," Pash finished his wine and set his empty glass on the table next to him. "He'll gut you for looking at him the wrong way."

"Temper, temper," Adonijah clicked his tongue. His gaze met his brother's, and he could tell the wheels in Pash's mind were racing. "What is it?"

"Who were you here to kill?" Pash tilted his head to the side, "Me?"

"Why would I come here to kill you?" Adonijah was caught off guard by the question. Half-brothers they might be, but Pash had never wronged him. When Gershom would come to visit Adonijah, he would bring Pash along to "get to know his bastard brother." At first, they didn't like one another, but that changed when they realized they both hated their father.

"So, if not me, then who?" Pash furrowed his brow. "Did Salome send you to -"

"She doesn't know I'm here," Adonijah interrupted sharply. "She doesn't know who I really am."

"Interesting." Pash smirked, kicking one leg over the other. "You're in love with her."

"Sounds like we both have a thing for powerful women," Adonijah's eyes danced in delight and Pash barked out a laugh.

"How is it possible you even know about me and -"

"The Monster Queen?"

"Watch it, Adonijah," Pash warned in a big-brother tone.

Adonijah threw his hands up in surrender, "Apologies."

"So, how did you know about us?"

Adonijah met his brother's curious gaze and sighed. "Just because you didn't see me, doesn't mean I wasn't around. I've kept an eye on you since my mother…"

"Do you plan to return to your princess?" Pash asked, sparing him from talking about his mother's death.

"That was the plan." Adonijah nodded. "But my plans haven't been going as smoothly as I had hoped. If things had worked out, I would have killed my mother's murderer, and been on my way. Salome never would have known I was gone."

"And I wouldn't have known you were alive." Pash pinched the bridge of his nose and sighed. "You really won't tell me who you came to kill?"

"If I told you," Adonijah flashed a menacing grin, "would you let me kill him?"

Pash threw his head back and laughed. "Who knows what could happen if you conveniently escaped?"

Adonijah's smile disappeared. "The Nameless Rider."

Pash pursed his lips and rubbed the nape of his neck. "I'm not surprised. He's the worst."

"Then I'll be doing you a favor by killing him."

"As much as I hate him, I can't sanction his assassination." Pash shook his head, leaning forward so his hands dangled between his legs. "But I do have a proposition for you."

Adonijah looked bored. "What kind of proposition?"

"From what Ophir said, you were a bounty hunter before you teamed up with Salome on her ill-advised rebellion."

"Keep Salome out of this."

"Right," Pash rolled his eyes. "Is it true you were a bounty hunter?"

"Are you going to put me in shackles if I say yes?" Adonijah snorted a laugh.

"No," Pash's eyes were lasered on Adonijah. "What would you say, if I asked you to kill someone?"

"If it's not the Nameless Rider, I'm inclined to say no."

"Even if that person were our father?" Pash reclined in his seat, looking victorious, knowing Adonijah wanted Gershom dead just as much as he did.

Adonijah's eyes widened. "You want me to kill Gershom?"

"I want *us* to kill Gershom."

"Why?" Adonijah folded his arms over his chest. "So, you can claim your birthright?"

"I don't give a damn about his titles." He growled through gritted teeth.

"Then why?" Adonijah asked and included, "And if you don't tell me the truth, my answer will be no."

"I think he murdered my mother around the time he had your mother killed." Pash jumped up from his seat and refilled his wine glass. "I would have done it years ago, but he was still in Niabi's good graces."

"And now?" Adonijah slid out of his seat and joined his brother at the wet bar.

"She would dance on top of his corpse if she could." Pash faced his brother. "No one would bat an eye if Gershom was found dead. And I know Niabi wouldn't bother to investigate. We could kill him and not be sentenced to the gallows."

Adonijah would be lying if he denied being tempted by his offer. Killing their father with no repercussions was a bounty hunter's dream. But what about Salome?

"I don't think I could -"

"Here are your options." Pash placed a hand on Adonijah's shoulder. "Either you agree to help me kill our father, and I make sure you don't sit in the White Keep's dungeons for the rest of your life, or Ophir gets his way, and imprisons you in our camp as a rebel, until we head back to Northwind, where I'm sure our father will be most interested in seeing you."

"If I agree, you realize we are still on opposite sides of this war." Adonijah rolled his shoulders back, standing an inch taller than his brother. "Once the job is finished, you'll release me to return to Salome."

Pash smiled. "You have my word."

Adonijah nodded but held out his hand. "Your word would normally satisfy me, brother, but I'm afraid I will need more than that this time."

Pash retrieved the dagger from his hip and sliced the palm of his right hand. Adonijah let him slash his right palm and they shook on it. An agreement in blood. If one of them went back on their word, their life would be forfeited.

"Do me a favor," Pash smirked. "Don't cause any trouble while you're in my camp. I would hate to have to break you out and desert my command to save your ass."

"I'll do my best." Adonijah's heart was pumping quickly in his chest. The chance to kill the Nameless Rider *and* his father was finally within reach. Salome's face flashed in his mind and the guilt of leaving her soured his stomach. He swore to protect her. She chose him. Hopefully, once they found their way back to one another, he could explain, and she would understand why he had to leave. As much as he hated to admit it, even in his absence, Jinn would look out for her. She would be safe until he returned.

"So, when do we start?" Adonijah asked after his brother poured him another glass of wine.

"Once this business with Gomorrah has been settled, we will head back to Northwind."

"You two really are idiots, if you think you'll march into Northwind and kill your father."

Pash and Adonijah whipped toward the tent's entrance where Leoti stood with her arms crossed over her chest.

"Who is this?" Adonijah scanned Leoti head to toe and didn't see any weapons on her person. She wasn't a soldier, but she wasn't dressed like a priestess or servant either.

"This is none of your business, Leoti." Pash huffed. He grabbed her by her upper arm and dragged her further into the tent. "How long have you been listening?"

"How angry would you be, if I told you I was listening the entire time?" Leoti flashed a malicious grin.

"What do you want?" Pash closed his eyes and rubbed his fingers over his forehead.

"I want to join you." Leoti sank into the chair Pash had used and stared at Adonijah sitting in the opposite seat. "As much as you hate your father, I hate him more. He is responsible for my husband's death, and I will fight to my last breath to see him suffer."

Adonijah chuckled. "No disrespect to you, but what do you know about killing?"

"I know the taste of having the man I love die in my arms and being helpless to save him." Leoti met Adonijah's gaze and straightened in her seat. "I have been invisible in the White Keep for years. I know passages even the commander here doesn't know about. I am also a warg, and with my magic, I can make sure our path is clear for the journey ahead."

Pash dropped to one knee in front of Leoti. "This will be dangerous. My father is no fool. He is always prepared for someone to try to assassinate him. Your father -"

"Let's not pretend you care about what my father thinks." Leoti cut him off with a hiss. "You have two options," she used the same phrasing Pash did with Adonijah, "either you let me join you, or I go tell Ophir what you're planning and find a way to kill Gershom myself."

Adonijah barked out a laugh. "Oh, I like her."

Pash smirked. "It seems you have me neatly backed into a corner, Leoti."

"Am I in or not?" Leoti leaned closer until her face was inches from Pash's. She wasn't going to back down and the brothers couldn't afford loose ends.

"You're in." Adonijah took his pipe out of his jacket pocket and lit it, blowing a puff of smoke up toward the ceiling folds of the tent.

Pash nodded in agreement. He extended his hand to her, and she rested her hand in his, palm facing up. He quickly sliced across her right palm, and they shook on it. "Now, we just need to plan the perfect murder."

CHAPTER 62
KAI

Kai hadn't trusted Adonijah the moment she laid eyes on him. Perhaps, it was because he was a rival for Salome's heart or because he was just as comfortable in the darkness as she was, but Adonijah was on her list of people to watch.

When she spotted Adonijah slip into Jacobi's cave, she waited for him to come back out. But when Adonijah and Jacobi emerged from the room and crept to the tunnels, she followed them. She didn't know what the sell-sword was planning, but if the villager was involved, she was determined to find out. Following them against the rocky outskirts of the City of Bones, they easily slipped past the guards who were neglecting their watch. A matter she would absolutely address once she dealt with Adonijah.

Kai knew when they left the city, she should have alerted Jinn, but there wasn't time and she decided it was more important to trail them. She pursued them in the shadows at a safe distance until she caught sight of the villager whimpering behind a cluster of boulders. Occasionally, he popped his head over the rocks, watching someone or something. The sell-sword was nowhere to be seen. She drew two knives from her belt and quietly approached Jacobi.

In a flash, she held a dagger to Jacobi's throat and whispered a warning in his ear. Peering over the boulders, she saw Adonijah standing in a clearing outside the Northern camp, surrounded, with his hands up in surrender.

She muttered a string of curses thinking she would now have to rescue him from being tortured or killed when she spied him turning to face the Commander of Shadows with a smirk.

"Hello, brother," Adonijah said, and it stopped Kai's heart from beating.

The brothers embraced and she watched them wander inside the camp. No shackles or restraints were clamped to Adonijah's body. He walked side by side with Niabi's most trusted sword and disappeared into what she assumed to be Pash's tent.

Another series of expletives poured out of her mouth and her attention refocused to the Shadows in the clearing. They would do a sweep of the area to make sure Adonijah had come alone, meaning she and the villager needed to leave. Now.

Kai gripped Jacobi's upper arm and dragged him away from the boulders. They had to move quickly and quietly, but with the clumsy, exhausted baker in tow, Kai knew it wasn't going to be easy.

She could hear the Shadows beginning their patrol and glared at Jacobi, hoping that would put a pep in his step. But it didn't. She practically carried him back up the mountainside and away from the potential danger of being captured. Once they were a good distance from the Northern camp, Kai let Jacobi take a breather, handing him her flask.

Breathlessly, he nodded his head in gratitude and slurped the contents. "Where are you taking me?"

Kai didn't like talking unless it was necessary, but she also knew this villager wouldn't stop pestering her until he received an answer. "Back."

"Back where?"

Kai rolled her eyes, mentally counting to five so she wouldn't lose her temper. "Back to the City of Bones."

His eyes widened. "Please, I didn't hurt anyone. I didn't want to leave -"

Kai lifted a hand to silence his blubbering. "What were you and Adonijah doing?"

"He asked me to lead him to the camp. He said he wanted to kill the Nameless Rider because he murdered his mother." Jacobi couldn't spit the words out fast enough.

Kai nodded, grabbed her flask from Jacobi, and motioned for him to stand up and follow her. She was right not to trust the sell-sword. But the hard part was going to be telling Salome that the man she loved wasn't her friend.

IT WAS late in the afternoon by the time Kai and Jacobi made it back to the City of Bones and Jinn was waiting for her by the tunneled entrance. He didn't look angry, but he was far from pleased. Once his gaze found Jacobi slinking behind her, his face hardened.

"What is going on?" Jinn asked with a furrowed brow.

"Where is Princess Salome?" Kai asked, wiping the beads of sweat that bubbled around her hairline.

Jinn softened at the mention of Salome but then worry drowned his irritation. "What happened?"

"I think it would be best if I spoke to the princess first, Your Highness." Kai wasn't one to be emotional, but she knew what she was about to tell Salome would be devastating. "It's about Adonijah."

Jinn ordered two Krazak soldiers to put Jacobi in his room and guard him while he walked with Kai to Salome's cave. When they arrived, the curtains were drawn, but they could hear the princess inside.

"Is he…?" Jinn didn't finish with the word *dead,* but Kai knew where his question was leading.

"No," Kai shook her head, "but it would be better news."

Jinn looked like he wanted to go inside with Kai, but he took a few steps back, giving them space to talk. Kai took a deep breath before swooping inside Salome's room. She stood at the entrance and bowed her head.

"Kai?" Salome's face remained neutral, but Kai could see the fear in her eyes. The two of them had never spoken alone before; the princess was right to be leery.

"Princess Salome," Kai met her gaze, "there's something I would like to report."

Salome motioned for the Ryoko Naga to sit with her, so she did. Kai's back was straight and even sitting, she looked deadly.

"What is it, Kai?" Salome asked, offering her a drink which Kai politely declined.

"During my rounds late last night, I noticed Adonijah and the prisoner sneaking out of the city." Kai was going to rush through her story, uncomfortable she had to do this in the first place. "I followed them all the way to the Northern camp. When Adonijah was surrounded by Shadows, I thought I was going to have to rescue him but…"

There were tears welling in Salome's eyes and it honestly pained Kai to finish. "He addressed the Commander of Shadows as his brother and walked with him inside his tent."

Salome didn't say anything. She just stared deep into Kai's eyes, as if she was trying to determine if she was telling the truth.

"I'm sorry." Kai uttered words she hadn't used in years and found she meant them. She never trusted Adonijah, and she never liked him based on her loyalty to Jinn, but she had come to care for Salome as a friend, if she could be as bold to think of herself in that manner.

Salome still hadn't moved, had barely blinked. Tears hadn't streamed down her face, and it struck Kai as odd. Maybe Salome was in shock and her body completely shut down. The princess had been through a whirlwind of emotions in the past week. She had lost her grandmother and her cousin within a day of each other. She had been reunited with her guardian only to be told her brother might be dead. She had declared her love for a sell-sword who swore an oath to protect her, but he turned out to be someone she didn't know at all.

Kai stood to her feet. If she sat there any longer, she would feel like she was intruding. She bowed and made her way to the doorway when Salome finally spoke.

"If he's Pash's brother then that would make him…"

"Gershom's son." Kai cleared her throat, desperate for a drink, but her flask had been drained by that sickly baker.

Salome seemed to snap out of her stupor. She flashed Kai a sad smile and a tear slipped down her cheek. "Thank you," she whispered.

Kai bowed again, knowing she had been dismissed, and marched out. She inhaled a deep breath and Jinn's hands rested on her shoulders as soon as she cleared the cave.

"Are you alright?" Jinn asked and she nodded, straightening to her full height. "What about Salome?"

"She's no longer safe here. We will need to move her as soon as possible." Kai ignored his question. "Adonijah is Pash's brother."

Jinn flinched as if she'd struck him. "His brother?"

Kai nodded in confirmation. "One can only assume that he will divulge the princess' location and we will have a much bigger problem to deal with."

Jinn's gaze darted to the curtains wafting in Salome's doorway. "Tell the others. We will need to make the necessary preparations for our journey to Oakenshire."

Kai bowed and walked away to do as her prince commanded. She still felt an ache in her chest for delivering Salome yet another crushing report, but she knew the princess was strong. She would survive. She had to survive.

CHAPTER 63

SALOME

Even though Salome sat quietly in her room, her mind was racing, her soul was screaming, and her heart was breaking. *Adonijah was Gershom's son? How was that even possible?* She thought about the day before, when he said there was something he wanted to tell her. *Was he about to tell her he was Gershom's son?*

Salome soaked the memory of him in. She felt his arms around her, his lips on hers, his eyes filled with passion. She saw him fighting for her, standing by her side. He had sworn an oath to protect her, but he left. He had broken his word and in turn, he had shattered her already fractured heart.

If Zophar hadn't interrupted them, would he have told her about his father?

Would she have accepted him if she knew the truth?

Did it matter if the truth came from his lips or someone else's?

Gershom killed her mother. Gershom killed four of her brothers. Gershom was her sister's Second in Command, and he was Adonijah's father.

What had he expected her to say once he told her? Once she found out?

How could the man she loved be the son of the man she hated?

The man she loved. Loved. She loved him.

When Salome closed her eyes and pictured Adonijah's face, she didn't see the son of the man that murdered those she loved. She saw the man who swore to protect her. She saw the man who equaled her in both wit and skill. She saw the man who knew every truth about her and stayed because he wanted to. She saw the man she *loved*.

But she also saw the man who had ripped her heart apart, even though she was barely hanging on. She saw the man who had so many opportunities to tell her the truth and didn't. She saw the man she thought she knew, but realized she only knew what he wanted her to know.

Salome's head was pounding, and her chest felt like it was imploding. Tears she was sure were emptied from the last couple of nights of grieving for Crispin flowed down her cheeks. She felt like the walls of her cave were closing in on her and for a second, she forgot how to breathe.

She didn't know how it happened, or how long it took her, but she bolted from her room and sprinted past the guards at the tunnel entrance. She didn't stop running until she reached a small clearing in the pine trees. There was a slab of rock that looked like an ancient altar in the center, and she plopped down on it.

How long she wept, she didn't know. But when she heard the crunch of footsteps approaching, she snapped out of her grief, and swiped her knives from the holsters on her thigh and lower back. She hadn't armed herself with anything else before bolting from her room. Her curved Qata Vishna blades and her bow and arrows had been left behind and for a split second she regretted being so careless.

Zophar stepped into the clearing and stood with his hands buried deep in his pockets. "Are you alright?"

Salome shook her head. If there was one person she would allow to see her vulnerable and broken, it was him. "How many more people will I lose, before I just walk away?"

"War is ugly -"

"The war hasn't even begun," Salome interrupted, nostrils flared. "I don't think I can do this anymore, Zophar."

"And if you don't, who will?" he walked toward her and sat beside her on the slab. After a moment of silence, Zophar said, "I had a wife once. And two sons."

Salome's eyes widened. "I… I never knew that."

"No one did." Zophar shrugged with glossy eyes. "When I lost them, I thought there was nothing left for me to live for. I won't lie to you and say things got better because they didn't. Life got harder and my pain lingered. Although my grief and the pain of losing my wife and my sons has never gone away, I have grown stronger in dealing with my loss."

"I'm sorry, Zophar," Salome whispered, slipping her hand into his.

"Your grief will never end," Zophar swiped tears from her face, "but you will become stronger in walking without them."

Salome sucked in a breath, "Did you hear about…?"

Zophar nodded. "I know how much you cared for Adonijah."

She didn't want to talk about Adonijah anymore. "I don't want the crown," Salome spat before she could change her mind. "I don't want the White Throne. I don't want to rule Northwind. I don't want any of it."

"What do you want?" Zophar asked, without a trace of judgment for speaking her truth.

"Sometimes, I wish I was back in the Tree House Forest where things were simpler."

Zophar shook his head gently. "The Tree House Forest, although simple, was a façade. It was never meant to last forever."

"What do you think I should do?" Salome asked, needing his guidance. She hadn't felt so lost before. She was doing everything she had been asked to do and more, but she didn't feel like she was moving forward. She had suffered so many losses. Was it worth it? Was it worth losing everyone she loved and cared for to sit on a throne she didn't even want?

"Get down!" Zophar grabbed her shoulders and pushed her down to the ground, behind the stone altar. An arrow zipped by and then another. They were being attacked.

Salome muttered curses under her breath. Why had she been so reckless in storming out of the City of Bones not properly armed or protected?

"How many are there?" Salome asked, knowing every second they sat, they were probably being surrounded. It could be Shadows sent by Adonijah and his brother. It could be the Thrak still tracking her. It could be another foe she didn't even know about.

Zophar's eyes darted to hers. "I don't know. But if we're going to get you back to safety, we are going to need help. I don't know how to get reinforcements here in time."

"I do." Salome reached for Jinn and felt herself slam into his mind. *"Zophar and I are surrounded. I need your help."*

"Where are you?" He answered immediately.

"In the woods. We're taking cover behind an ancient altar."

Jinn's response was delayed. *"Rune knows where you are. We're coming. Hold on."*

Salome met Zophar's curious gaze; he was looking for an explanation.

"Short story," Salome risked a glance over the slab only to see an whizzing at her and ducked before it pierced her. "I have magic that allows me to communicate with other magic wielders with my mind."

"What?" Zophar choked on the word. "Have you always been able to do that?"

"No," she grabbed the hilts of her daggers tightly. "I promise to explain everything once we get out of here, but we can't sit here any longer. We have to move, or we might not be able to hold out for help."

"You were able to get help?"

"Jinn." She nodded quickly, her mind racing to formulate a plan of escape. They were a good ten feet from the tree line in front of them. They could hide in the forest, but those ten feet might as well have been a hundred feet. The archers had them pinned. "How do we get out of here?"

Zophar shook his head. "I'm afraid our best option is to wait for reinforcements."

But waiting for reinforcements wasn't going to help them, because crunching through the mulch of the woods, were thirty Thrak who appeared in the clearing. They were indeed surrounded and by the worst of her feared opponents.

The bulkiest Thrak stepped forward, sniffing the air with a grin that Salome wanted to peel off his disfigured face. "We've been looking for you for quite some time."

"Did you get my gift?" Salome cocked her head to the side, knowing she had ordered the heads of all the Thrak who had been sent to the Isles of Myr to fetch her, be delivered to Matildys, as a warning.

The Thrak snarled. "They were my brothers."

"And now, they're dead." Salome knew she was riling him up, but she was trying to buy herself some time for Jinn's reinforcements.

The Thrak didn't take the bait. "Bind and gag them both. Our queen will be excited to finally meet you."

Salome spat at the Thrak's feet. As two Thrak approached her with shackles, rope, and white cloth to gag them, Jinn uncloaked himself standing between her and the Thrak. He sliced off both of their heads in one swift movement.

Jinn held his tachi swords out to his sides, "Who's next?"

A roar came from behind the Thrak, and Rune led a group of Krazak warriors into the clearing, armed to the teeth. The sound of metal on metal clashed through the air as the battle for Salome ensued.

Kai sprinted for Salome, leaping over fallen Thrak, and grabbed her arm. The Ryoko Naga pulled Salome to her feet before the princess had a chance to join the fight. "We need to get you out of here."

"But -"

"I have my orders, Princess," Kai interrupted her, dragging her further toward the trees. She wasn't going to let Salome fight and it enraged her.

Salome glanced over her shoulder and saw Jinn slicing through any Thrak that came within three feet of him. Zophar swung his axe with fury and the eyes of a born warrior burned in his skull. Rune and his Krazaks were vicious and were evenly matched with the monstrous Thrak. They even seemed to be enjoying the bloodshed, which should have unnerved Salome, but didn't.

She wanted to fight, but knew Kai was right in getting her back to the City of Bones. She couldn't fight in every battle, and she needed to be smart. As she turned to face Kai, who still had a firm grip on her forearm, Salome spotted the glint of a couple of arrowheads pointed at Kai's back.

"No!" Salome whipped Kai around, her back taking the two arrows meant for the Easterner. She saw the horror flash in Kai's face as Salome sank to the ground. The pain that shot through her body was excruciating. Kai cried out for someone to help her.

Salome's face hit the ground as Kai unsheathed her daggers and prepared for the wave of Thrak headed their way. Salome glanced up at Jinn and saw him fighting his way to get to her. *Fear*. She saw fear in his eyes and right then, she knew he wasn't going to reach her in time.

Several Thrak surrounded Kai and she started cutting them down, refusing to let them take Salome. Zophar jumped into the mix and started slaying men left and right. Blood was splattered across his beard and the mighty Westerner was ready to add to the tally of enemies killed.

Another arrow sliced through the air, piercing Kai in her chest, and a second cut into her thigh. More Thrak appeared and Salome knew they were going to be overrun. Zophar tossed Kai toward the Krazaks where she would be defended, and perhaps saved by Rayma.

Salome extended the bridge to Jinn, feeling herself giving into the pain riddling her back. *"Get Kai out of here."*

"I'm not leaving you!" He shot back, his golden-brown eyes watering. She could hear the love, the fear, the struggle raging in his mind. *"Don't give up, do you hear me?"*

"They're going to take me."

"No, Salome -"

"I should have accepted your proposal when I had the chance."

Salome saw one of the Thrak hit Zophar over the head, knocking him unconscious. As the soldier threw Zophar over his shoulder, she felt massive hands sweep her off the ground and drape her across broad shoulders. The Thrak started running away from the battle with their prize, their mission complete.

"Salome!" Jinn screamed, before everything went black.

THE RAVEN AND THE WOLF

BOOK THREE

PROLOGUE

NIABI

12 YEARS AGO

As the sun peeked over the horizon after a night of bloodshed, it became evident, the White City of Northwind belonged to another. The stench of blood and burnt rubble was entombed in the city by the looming smoky haze. The Northerners who survived the attack were guarded by the invading soldiers to ensure their submission. Inside the White Keep, the castle attendants were ordered to scrub the blood and ash from the white stone walls and dispose of the dead bodies strewn throughout the halls.

Still in his throne room, Issachar sat with the remains of his loved ones until their bodies were removed. The captured king stared at the pools of blood on the floor and cried until he did not have a tear left to shed. Surrounded by enemy soldiers, he awaited his fate.

The grand wooden doors flew open and she entered. Dressed head to toe in black armor, she slowly walked towards her defeated foe. Protecting her left arm was an intricate metal sheath that perfectly wrapped around her arm and spanned from her shoulder to her fingertips. Underneath her hood, her long raven black hair rested against the back of her neck and the black war paint smeared across her olive face only accentuated her piercing green eyes. Tall and fit, she glided towards her prey with undeniable excitement. The people of the Ten Kingdoms of Adalore knew her as the Green-Eyed-Raven, but Issachar only knew her as Niabi.

With Gershom, Tala, and her nine-foot-tall Nephilim behind her, she marched up to Issachar and stopped a few feet in front of him.

"Hello, Father."

Her icy greeting seemed to rattle him. "After all this time?"

"I told you I would come for you."

His swollen bloodshot eyes met hers. "Why?"

"You know your sins," she snarled, "and now you will pay for them."

"You have murdered my people and ravaged our homeland for power?" Issachar spat at her feet. "The White City burns because of you!"

"The city burns because of you!" She corrected him as she gazed out the floor to ceiling windows. She breathed in the smell of the burning city, but satisfaction eluded her. "Their blood has been spilled for those you stole from me."

"I don't even remember their names." Her father's words stung.

Enraged, she lunged toward him on bended knee and grabbed him by his throat. "You know their names," she gritted her teeth as he gasped for air. "You know their faces. You know I loved them."

"Why did you not let them kill me with the others?" Issachar hissed, eyeing the men that stood silently behind her, with blood still smeared on their hands.

"You are *mine* to kill." Her blood thirsty gaze remained locked on her conquered foe.

"And when I am gone, Gershom will take my throne leaving you with what?"

Niabi laughed, releasing her choke hold. "Surely you do not believe the mastermind who brought your city to its knees was Gershom? It was me. It has always been me." The warrior queen flashed a triumphant smile. "And when my time is up, my son will rule the White City, forever eradicating your name from existence."

"You would have that half-blood sit on the throne of our ancestors?"

"Have you so quickly forgotten that all of your children were half-bloods?" She tilted her head. "Or is it because my son comes from a people you deem lesser than yourself?"

"History will remember what happened here today." Issachar held his head high, indignant to the very end.

"I swear not even the Almighty One himself will be able to find your remains once I have finished with you." She slowly rose from her crouched position and looked down on his tear-stained face. Her twin daggers dropped from her sleeves into her hands, and she clenched them tightly in her palms.

Issachar stared into her ruthless eyes, "You are not as strong as you think you are, Niabi."

"It does not take strength to kill a man," she retorted.

"May the Almighty One have mercy on your soul." Issachar closed his eyes.

With a determined swiftness, Niabi sliced through his throat, nearly decapitating the once King of the North. "Mercy is for the weak."

CHAPTER 1

HARBONA

Harbona had barely slept in days. Looking into Salome's future did not bring him any comfort. Death's presence was strong. He felt her reaching out to him and he heard her cries for help, but when he responded, she did not answer. The one time he spotted her in a vision, she was covered in blood and soot. He wasn't sure if the blood belonged to her or someone else.

Every version of her future varied slightly but ultimately ended the same way. Death was near and she wouldn't be denied this time.

Harbona clung to the hope that there was one way he could save her, but it would take a miracle and he was running out of time.

Pacing Lavena's dining room like a crazed animal, he mumbled and replayed the visions in his mind until he became nauseous. The only reason he had joined Lavena, Kayven, and Abba for breakfast was because Odelia, the Enchantress, dragged him like a defiant child out of his room. He did not notice when she finished her meal and left but the silence of his fellow Immortals in the room did not ease his stomach.

"You are sure about what you saw?" Lavena's voice shattered the silence and Harbona stopped to stare at her. She was sitting at the head of the glass table with the sun's rays beaming through the window behind her making her look more like a goddess than a mere Ethereal.

He nodded solemnly, rubbing the heel of his palms against his bloodshot eyes. "It is the only way to save her."

Her voice did not waver when she said, "Then she is lost."

Harbona refused to let that be the end of it. "If we do not act quickly, Salome will be executed, but not before she is tortured by the Thrak. I cannot and will not let her suffer this fate. Not if I can help it."

"You said you were not here for aid," Lavena nonchalantly raised her cup to her lips, discussing Salome's life as if it were the equivalent to choosing whether or not to add sugar to her tea.

"It was not my intent, but things have changed."

Kayven leaned forward, his elbows resting on the table. Even seated he looked like a battle-ready warrior. "What do you need us to do?"

Before Harbona could say a word, Lavena narrowed her eyes at the Bellator seated to her left. "Until the Eldaar has sanctioned our involvement, you will do nothing."

"It is not just her life at stake, Lavena," Harbona stroked a hand through his disheveled hair.

"You can make me the villain, but unless you want Kayven and Abba to share in your banishment, you will need the Eldaar's blessing."

"Then I shall meet with them."

The room suddenly stilled. The brothers stared at each other across the table before looking at Lavena, who was hastily consuming her meal.

"What is it?" Harbona's gaze shifted from Lavena to the Bellators. "What are you not telling me?"

"The Eldaar do not hold audiences anymore," Kayven began but Lavena hissed his name to silence him.

"Since when?" Harbona took the seat next to Kayven and shoved the plate of food away from him.

"For the last several months" Kayven continued, "they have only granted Keeva an audience."

"Before you ask," Lavena's voice was cold and venomous, "I will not involve my daughter in this matter, Harbona."

"Lavena, please -"

She vehemently shook her head, "My answer is no."

"It is the only way to save Salome," the Seer pleaded. He would do anything to protect the Hunter, to protect Lykos' sister.

"So, your plan is to ask the Eldaar, the parents who banished you, their only son and heir, to send Bellators to fight in a mortal war?" Lavena slapped her linen napkin on her half-eaten plate. "It would be a miracle if they even permit you entry into the Holies."

"Salome is your sister by marriage."

Her nostrils flared."That may be the case, but I will not risk my daughter's future to save her. I am sorry." Harbona noticed a flicker of sorrow behind her cold, grey eyes.

"Then I will meet with my parents with or without their permission," Harbona declared, reclining in his chair.

"They might have you executed," Abba said softly, aimlessly pushing his fruit around his plate with a fork. "Are you willing to risk your life to save this mortal?"

"I would rather die trying to save my friend than live another thousand years with my cowardice." Harbona pushed back from the table and glanced at Lavena, Kayven, and Abba. "I am not asking any of you to come with me."

Kayven and Abba stood. They always had Harbona's back in every situation and this issue was no different.

"You are fools to think you will be allowed before the thrones of the Eldaar." Lavena rubbed her temples in small circles. "They will not see you and if they do, you will not walk out alive," she whispered, worry lacing her words.

"Then it should please you to know that I have already arranged an audience with the Eldaar on your behalf, Harbona." Keeva's young voice sliced through the tension in the room as she walked in.

Lavena rose from her seat, planting her palms on the tabletop. "What is the meaning of this, Keeva?"

Keeva reached in front of Abba and snatched a pear from the spread on the table and took a bite. "The Eldaar have agreed to meet with Harbona as long as I accompany him."

"I cannot allow it," Lavena's voice cracked and Harbona saw the terror in her eyes.

Keeva made her way to her mother and stood before her. "I know you fear for me and my future, Mother, but if I can use my gift to save my aunt from a fate worse than death, how can I not?"

Lavena cupped her daughter's face in her thin fingers. "They will ask too much of you," she whispered as a tear slid down her pale cheek.

"I know," the demi wiped her mother's tear away. "I am willing to pay the price."

Harbona took a step toward the girl. "What are you talking about?"

Keeva looked over at him. "Your father is fading. The Eldaar intend to journey to the After but without an heir…"

Understanding flooded him and it made his heart ache. His eyes shot up to meet Lavena's watery gaze and it served as confirmation. "They want you to take their place. To take… my place."

Keeva nodded. "If that is what they require of me to save my aunt, then that is what I am willing to do."

Harbona knew the high price Keeva had agreed to, but he wasn't sure he could consent to it. To be an Eldaar meant attaching your soul to your partner and ruling the Immortals as one being. Any sense of freedom, autonomy, or choice would be gone, and Keeva would never be able to leave Caelestis. She would endure in the Holies for thousands of years until she bore a son or daughter to take her place when she grew weary of existing and her mate agreed to journey to the After, where they neither lived nor died.

When he was a youngling, Harbona had no interest in ruling, nor any interest in becoming the Eldaar. His banishment was a gift. He now understood why Lavena was unwilling to let her daughter spend time with the Eldaar, why she kept her close, and why she trained the demi never to make deals with the rulers of Caelsetis. They wanted an heir, and who better than the only other Seer in the known world? Harbona had been stripped of power, titles, and responsibilities, but now they would fall on the shoulders of a twelve-year-old girl. Her life would be over before it had a chance to begin.

Keeva grabbed his hand, interrupting his thoughts. She smiled up at him. It was Lykos' smile, and it brought peace and warmth to his soul.

"You need not worry for me, Harbona," she whispered. "It is time to go."

~

WHILE HARBONA and Keeva waited outside the throne room doors, he couldn't help but admire the demi. Even though she was only twelve years old, she was wise for her age. Lykos would be so proud of her, and the seer knew his friend would have doted on her endlessly.

Keeva slowly glanced up at him and smiled. "What troubles you, Harbona?"

"Are you sure about this?" he asked, guilt twisting in his stomach knowing the magnitude of her sacrifice. "I can go in alone."

Keeva gently shook her head and grabbed his hand. "I know what I am doing. Trust me."

"Why are you doing this? Why are you so willing to give up your freedom to save someone you do not even know?"

She crinkled her nose, looking confused. "Why must I know her to want to save her?"

The sides of Harbona's eyes crinkled as he smiled. "You remind me so much of your father."

"Did you know him well?"

"Oh yes," Harbona clasped his hands behind his back. "I was there the day he was born, and I knew him up until the day he…"

"Died."

He nodded sadly, "Yes."

She shifted her weight and asked, "Was he really as wonderful as my mother says he was?"

"I have walked this world for nearly three thousand years." He met her gaze and smiled. "And your father was one of the greatest men I have ever known. It was an honor to call him my friend."

The doors opened before she had a chance to respond. Walking into the throne room with Keeva by his side was humbling. Because of this twelve-year old girl and her selflessness, he was granted an audience with his own parents. He never felt so small and insignificant.

The golden throne room of the Holies had not changed. It was exactly how it was a thousand years ago when he stood before the Eldaar for his sentencing. The floors, the walls, the ceiling, the chandeliers: everything was gold. And the Eldaar, the rulers of the Immortals, sat in their twin golden thrones basking in their glorious glow.

His father, Oleon, didn't appear older. His platinum blonde hair, pointy ears, and clean-shaven face were in pristine condition, but his cold, grey eyes weren't as piercing as they used to be. Keeva was right. He was fading. It wasn't surprising that after ruling for five thousand years, he was now ready to journey to the After.

His gaze fell upon his mother, Soline, who was radiant as ever. Her golden crown fashioned to look like the sun's rays sat upon her long platinum hair, and her golden silks splashed around her thin frame like waves against the shore. Her pointy ears were adorned with the finest glistening jewels, and her straight nose, thin lips, and sharp chin were perfectly sculpted. But when he looked into her calculating grey eyes, he remembered the last time he stood before them, she had been the one to brand him with the banishment mark.

Instinctively, he brushed his fingertips over his right eye where the banishment mark was and felt the Eldaar's judgmental glare.

Regretting his unintentional move, he sheepishly turned to Keeva for direction. Her long dark brown hair, rounded ears and warm smile reminded him of Lykos and it calmed his nerves. She took the lead and stepped toward the dais, tugging

Harbona forward and together they bowed at the waist. They only rose up when the Eldaar, in unison, said, "Rise."

Though a thousand years had passed, Harbona had not forgotten royal etiquette. He knew he could only speak when called upon, so the four of them stood in utter silence until it was nearly unbearable.

"So, you have returned," his father's deep, melodic voice echoed.

Harbona had to remind himself to stand tall, and not shrink before them. The Seer bobbed his head, meeting his father's intense glare. "I have returned."

"Keeva requested this audience," Soline began, her fingers gripping the golden armrests of her throne, "but let it be known that we are not pleased to see you. You sullied these halls and the legacy of our family one thousand years ago and seeing what you have become is pathetic."

The words stung, but Harbona kept a straight face. To react would be mortal and he could not afford to appear weak before his parents.

"It is noted." He nodded his head which seemed to satisfy his mother.

"Why are you here?" Oleon drummed his fingers on his thigh, looking disinterested.

"I had a vision that a dear friend of mine is in need of help," Harbona took a steadying breath. "I have come to ask for your aid."

The Eldaar did not react. They merely stared at their son; that was answer enough. But he couldn't accept anything less than their cooperation.

"I would ask you to send a company of Bellators to the Mainland to save the Hunter from death."

"You want us to send our Bellators to save this mortal?" Oleon scoffed; disgust written all over his pale face. "You are more of an embarrassment than I thought possible. Have you not learned your lesson from a thousand years ago?"

"Those mortals you snub your nose at have more character, courage, and integrity than you can fathom."

Soline held up her slender hand to silence him. "You have no right to come before us as a banished heir and disgraced Ethereal to ask anything of us. You are fortunate to have Keeva for an ally, for she is your only one."

"What must I do -"

"Nothing," she interrupted him. "There is nothing you can do to convince us to help you or those mortals."

"But she will be tortured," Harbona's voice cracked, anger bubbling in his gut. "She will die."

"Such is the way of mortals." Soline laid her hands on her lap. Her movements were graceful, but her eyes were vicious.

All hope he had of convincing them to help was quickly fading. He had nothing to offer them, nothing to barter or trade. In their eyes, he was no longer their son. He was no longer important and had no sway in these halls.

"Then I implore you to make a deal with me," Keeva finally spoke; all eyes fixed on her.

"Keeva?" Oleon tilted his head in confusion. "What are you saying?"

Keeva took a step forward, still paying proper respect and reverence to the rulers. "Send the Bellators to aid Harbona and the mortals in their war and I will be your heir."

The Eldaar both sat straighter in their thrones; a feat Harbona didn't think was even possible. He exchanged a glance with Keeva before she continued.

"There is one more stipulation I require before I agree to be your successor."

Soline scoffed. "You dare request more of us in addition to sending our warriors to fight in a mortal war?"

"If you want me to agree to be your successor, to rule for thousands of years and give up my freedom so you may go to the After, then yes, I require more." Keeva held her ground, tilting her head higher. "With all due respect, Eldaar, I am your only hope of leaving this world for the next."

The Eldaar squinted. Everyone in that throne room knew Keeva was now firmly in charge. With a prince for a father and an ambassador for a mother, Keeva was destined for politics. Harbona had no idea how influential and knowledgeable this twelve-year old was. Every great leader knows to successfully negotiate, you need to possess something the other person desperately wants or needs. Keeva held the fate of the Eldaar in her tiny hands. And they all knew it.

Olean motioned for her to continue. "Speak, Keeva. What is it you desire?"

"I would like to spend the next six years traveling the mortal world. I desire to see my father's homeland before I am forced to remain in Caelestis. On my eighteenth birthday, I will wed a suitable partner and take my vows as the Eldaar."

"You want us to wait another six years to journey to the After?" Oleon asked in disbelief.

"You have ruled for five thousand years," Keeva shrugged one shoulder, "I do not believe six more will make a difference."

Harbona couldn't deny he was impressed with the demi, and became misty-eyed thinking of how proud Lykos would be if he could see her now. She might look like an Ethereal, but her heart was mortal.

The Eldaar exchanged a meaningful glance, as if they were reading each other's mind, before bowing their heads. "We agree to your terms, Keeva."

"Alert Kayven and Abba to ready the Bellators." Soline glared at Harbona. "May our paths never cross again. You are dismissed."

With one final bow, Harbona and Keeva walked out of the Holies. He had entered his ancestral home and walked out alive. He was one step closer to freeing Salome, but instead of feeling triumphant, his heart felt heavier. He knew his parents would never forgive him and he accepted that, but he couldn't stop thinking how Lykos would be heartbroken by the price his daughter paid. He would forever be indebted to Keeva.

CHAPTER 2
SALOME

Salome wasn't sure how long she'd been sitting in the dark and damp cell, but she knew the back wounds she ended up with to save Kai were being treated by the Gomorrian healers and were beginning to mend. By all accounts, she should have died from her injuries, but Death wasn't ready to claim her. Had she not been in the dungeons beneath the Black Tower, she wouldn't have believed she was a prisoner at all. She was given two meals a day and was visited often by the royal healers.

What worried her the most was she hadn't seen Zophar since her capture in the Bone Mountains. She'd been unconscious most of the journey to Gomorrah, partly due to her injuries and partly due to being drugged. The Thrak didn't want her to become a problem on the way, injured or not, so they pulled the arrows from her back, slathered on a salve to ward off infection, and stitched her up. That was the extent of their mercy.

When her thoughts weren't consumed by the impending torture she was sure to endure at the hands of the vicious Gormorrian queen, she thought of Jinn. The fear; the sorrow; the love, she saw in his face and the last words she communicated to him through their bond.

"I should have accepted your proposal when I had the chance."

She wasn't sure why she said it, but at that moment, she meant it. She hurt him by choosing Adonijah over him, rejecting him when he confessed in the City of Bones that he was in love with her.

Her stomach churned at the thought of Adonijah and his betrayal, his lies, and his true identity as Gershom's son. She gave him her heart and her trust, and he'd broken both. She still loved him, but if she were to make it out of Gomorrah alive and encountered him, she wasn't sure how she would react to him.

Tears burned her eyes, so she rubbed the heels of her palms against them. How had she screwed this up so badly? She wasn't one to act impulsively or venture out without being properly armed, but hearing Kai's report about Adonijah felt like a knife to her heart. She had a hard time breathing and being inside the mountain made her feel claustrophobic. Without giving herself a moment to think, she sprinted out of the city and into the forest to find a sense of normalcy. She needed the fresh air, the trees, the sounds of the birds chirping, the crunch of the sticks and mulch under her feet. That was her way of coping with what she had no control over.

But she had been rash, and her actions put her in a life-threatening position.

She tried several times to use her magic to reach out to Jinn and Harbona to ask for help, but neither responded. Whenever she visualized extending the bridge to them, there was no one on the other side. Perhaps, being so far below the city was affecting her in more ways than one.

In a last-ditch effort, she reached out to her mother, but she too was absent, and the only thing Salome could think about was the warning her mother gave her during her time in the Isles of Myr.

"When the time comes and you find yourself standing on your own, you will have a choice to make. Rise from the ashes or crumble into dust."

"Will I be alone for the rest of my life?"

Bilhah smiled, cupping her face, "No, Sweetness, you will not spend the rest of your days alone. But the choices you make during your loneliest moments will determine who you will find on the other side."

Salome was alone. Alone in a cell. Alone to face an enemy she'd never met but had hunted her for weeks. Alone with her fate. Alone with her thoughts. *Alone*. Her worst fear was now her reality.

But she had a choice to make: rise or crumble.

Footsteps behind the wooden cell door interrupted her thoughts. Like she did every time someone came to see her, she stood with her back to the wall. If someone made an attempt on her life, she wouldn't go down without a fight, weapons or not.

Keys jiggled and jangled until the door flew open and instead of the healers or a servant with her meal, she saw two Thrak. The one with iron shackles in his grasp spat on the blood-stained, stone floor.

"The queen wants to see you," said the other Thrak and motioned her forward.

She wanted to deny them, wanted to tell them to go to hell, wanted to demand the queen drag her ass to the dungeons to talk to her, but she wasn't going to press her luck. Stepping forward, she eyed the manacles.

"Are those necessary?" she asked, trying to mask her trepidation. "I have no weapons. You can't believe I am a threat to your queen."

The first Thrak shoved the irons forward with a disgruntled huff. "Queen's orders."

Everything in her screamed not to allow this. She could fight her way out. Disarm them and slit their throats before they knew what was happeneing, but her mind flashed to Zophar. She had no idea if he was dead, alive, or worse, and she couldn't risk harm coming to him if she lashed out.

Reluctantly, she held her wrists out and the Thrak slapped the manacles on. They were heavier than she imagined, and she let her arms fall in front of her dirty, ripped up trousers.

The Thrak that bound her slipped an enormous hand around her bicep to escort her, but she pulled away from his grasp.

"I do believe these," she lifted the irons up for him to see, "are enough to keep me compliant. I can walk without assistance."

The Thrak eyed one another, looking confused and irritated but with a grunt from one and an eye roll from the other, they motioned her to walk forward.

Salome must have been deeper in the dungeons than she originally thought because the trek up the chilly, weaving incline had the back of her thighs screaming in pain. She hadn't been active during her recovery but how could she have gotten so out of shape that she struggled to march up to the main level of the Black Tower?

Once they made it to the Black Tower foyer, she got a glimpse of how the Gomorrian royals lived and it didn't surprise her. Everything was black: black marble floors, black walls, black chandeliers, and small windows to keep it dim. Whoever designed the castle was inspired by death. Salome found it hard to breathe in the stuffy palace, but she swallowed her panic and focused on taking in the details of her surroundings.

The main entrance was closed off by two iron doors with guards stationed outside. At the foot of the black, spiral staircase, stood two, stoic Thrak. They ignored her as she followed her escort up to the third floor where more Thrak patrolled the circular level. Along the far side of the wall were two massive doors guarded by a couple of Thrak, who were waiting for her.

The doors opened and she scanned the throne room. On the dais sat four thrones, two of which were occupied by females with blonde hair. Behind them was a balcony that spanned the width of the room, making it the brightest room in the Black Tower. Mother and daughter, Salome assumed. They shared the same features and were very pale. The only exception was the woman wearing the black crown with spikes had calculating, blue eyes.

Out of the corner of her eye, she saw something shift. It was Zophar, on his knees bearing the same manacles she had. Other than needing a bath, he looked unharmed and she breathed a sigh of relief and thanked the Almighty. He looked her way and offered a feeble smile, before she gave the queen her full attention.

Matildys stared hungrily at Salome which made her skin crawl, but she refused to show her fear. Salome lifted her head and stood tall remembering she was a queen in her own right as she locked eyes with the queen.

After a moment of sizing up one another, Matildys spoke. "So," her eyes ran up and down Salome. "You are the one causing me all this trouble. I imagined you would look more regal."

"And I imagined you'd be more grotesque as the product of incest."

The Thrak who had escorted Salome smacked her for the disrespect, drawing blood, but Matildys shrieked at him to back off. Salome licked the blood from her bottom lip and refocused on the queen. Though her eyes were misty from the slap, she had nothing but rage in her gaze.

Matildys smirked and seemed almost pleased. "You've got spirit. That'll make quite the show when you are executed tomorrow." The queen leaned forward in her throne, her long, black fingernails scratching the onyx armrest. "I look forward to the Thrak breaking you in every sense of the word," she said in a low, predatorial voice.

Salome didn't bat an eye, though her heart pounded in her chest. It all made perfect sense now, why she had not endured torture, why she'd been treated by the healers, and why they fed her twice a day. Matildys wanted her to be in tip top shape when she unleashed her beasts to tear her apart piece by piece for the Gomorrians' pleasure. She shivered at the thought that had she not been injured in the skirmish outside of the City of Bones, she might have already been mutilated for sport.

She needed to show this barbarian queen she was not afraid of her. She would not shrink back no matter how desperately she wanted to beg for mercy because she knew she would receive none.

"Did you receive my gift?" Salome asked knowing it would get under the queen's skin.

Matildys' smirk faded and the girl sitting beside her squirmed in confusion.

"Ah," Salome purred, "I see your daughter has no idea what I'm talking about."

"That's enough," Matildys hissed.

"Did I strike a nerve?"

The queen straightened in her throne, hands gripping the armrests so tightly the whites of her knuckles showed. "You will hold your tongue."

"What gift?" the princess whispered to her mother.

Salome smiled wickedly at the young girl who believed her mother to be all-powerful, a queen to be feared and revered. A faith, she would take great pleasure in shattering.

"Fifteen Thrak were sent to capture me in the Isles of Myr. I sent their heads back to your mother in a sack." Salome smirked at Matildys, feeling stronger with each eye-opening revelation. "They failed *her* mission, and we all know what the penalty for failure is in Gomorrah."

Fury flared in Matildys' eyes but was gone in an instant. "Tell me where the City of Bones is, and I might order the Thrak to go easy on you tomorrow."

A lie if Salome ever heard one. She knewthere was a great possibility the queen would ask her about the Krazak's secret city, but if she was going to die, she wasn't going to give Matildys the satisfaction of knowing she broke her. Salome pursed her lips and shrugged, "Never heard of it."

"We all know the Krazaks came to your aid in the Bone Mountains when the Thrak attacked and captured you. So tell me. Where is Fennor? Where are the Mountain Men?"

Salome lifted her shackled hands to scratch her chin, feigning confusion. "Doesn't ring a bell. Sorry."

"You refuse to tell me," Matildys hollered, "even when I hold your life in my hands?"

"I would rather die."

Matildys rose from her throne and grinned. "You would rather die?"

"It seems that is to be my fate." Salome watched the queen slither down the five steps from her dais to the black marbled floor. By the time she noticed the glint of a small blade clutched in the queen's hand, it was too late. "No!"

Matildys veered away from Salome and lunged at Zophar, plunging her dagger in the Westerner's gut.

Salome knocked down the Thrak standing next to her as she fought to get to her guardian, but the second Thrak yanked her by her hair, keeping her from Zophar. She stared at him with panic-stricken eyes.

"Zophar," she whispered his name as an apology. She'd forgotten he was in the room during her exchange with the queen.

Matildys grabbed Salome's chin forcing her to look at her, instead of Zophar. A triumphant smile spread across her face. "Put them in the same cell. Tonight, you will watch him bleed to death and tomorrow, I will watch you beg for death as I ensure your suffering lasts for an entire week."

"I swear to the Almighty, I swear to Death herself, if it is the last thing I do, I will kill you!" Salome hissed, not backing down from the queen's threats.

Matildys kissed Salome's cheek and whispered in her ear. "Maybe in the next life."

CHAPTER 3
CRISPIN

Captain Ivar, the captain of the *Drakkar,* was personally assigned by the King of Borg to chaperone Crispin and the company of pirates until further notice and he seemed to take his assignment seriously. He made sure every suite the pirates had been offered in Halfrond Keep was guarded by some of the best soldiers in the king's army, and to ensure their obedience, Ivar took it upon himself to stay inside the shared lounge. Crispin figured the captain was either there for information, or he was extremely worried about the pirates doing something stupid on his watch, so he stayed close. But after weeks of waiting for the king to grant them an audience, they were all becoming restless, although they were grateful they weren't sitting in the dungeons.

Most of the crew refused to be in the same room with the Westerner and kept to themselves, but Crispin, Rahab, Ziggy, and Nubis didn't seem to mind the captain's constant presence.

When Crispin thought about it, he could honestly say he'd grown fond of the grumpy seafarer. Ivar was orderly, inquisitive, and from what Crispin could tell, he was quite intelligent coupled with a dry sense of humor. If Ivar and the pirates weren't on opposite sides of the feud between kingdoms, the prince was positive the captain of the *Drakkar* and the captain of the *Shadow of Death* could be great friends.

Ivar let out a groan as he reclined in the same leather chair he sat in every day, with a small plate filled with dried meats and cheese. He glanced over at Ziggy who was sipping a cup of hot tea. As she softly blew the billowing steam, she noticed him staring at her.

Crispin watched as she shifted uncomfortably and observed how tense Nubis was next to her on the couch.

"How long have you two been together?" Ivar asked, lifting a piece of jerky to his mouth, hiding a devilish smirk.

Ziggy and Nubis exchanged a quick glance and Crispin noticed her blush.

"We have been friends for a couple of years," Ziggy answered, running her fingers across her throat where blotch was blossoming.

Ivar quirked his eyebrows, "I see. Just friends then."

"Friends," Nubis repeated the word, but it sounded bitter coming from his lips.

"So, how did a Borgian befriend a Stormcrag and find themselves aboard a pirate ship with the lost prince of Northwind?" Ivar seemed almost giddy with his line of questioning. Although Crispin wanted to come to their rescue, he, too, was curious to hear their answers.

Ziggy cleared her throat before setting her teacup down on the small table in front of her. "My parents were killed when pirates invaded our seaside village." Rahab shifted in her seat, keeping her eyes glued to the wooden floor as Ziggy continued. "Those of us who survived were taken and sold at different ports. I was sold to a ship builder in Northwind until my master offered me up as payment when he lost in cards. The man who won me, freed me."

Ivar and Crispin exchanged a glance. Crispin didn't know slavery was staining his kingdom and by the irritation flaring in the captain's gaze, Crispin knew it had been going on longer than he realized.

"Is *he* the man that freed you?" Ivar looked at Nubis, but Ziggy shook her head.

"No, a man named Oden freed me." Ziggy rolled her shoulders back to sit up straighter. "He is now my employer."

Ivar was quiet for a moment before turning his attention to the Stormcrag. "And you? Do you have a similar story?"

"Oden found me when I was in need. He saved my life." Nubis kept his answers short and vague seemingly on purpose, and Ivar accepted it.

"This Oden," Ivar scratched the two-day old stubble along his jawline, "what business is he in?"

"He owns a tavern in the Night District." Nubis stated in a matter-of-fact tone, suspicion brewing in his eyes.

"The Whispering Fox?" Ivar tilted his head with a gleam in his eyes.

Ziggy and Nubis paled. There weren't many people who knew about Oden since he kept himself hidden and had Makada manage the tavern.

"How do you know about The Whispering Fox?" Nubis demanded to know, a frightening edge in his voice.

Ivar shrugged his shoulders, not bothered by the Stormcrag's tone. "It is my job to know things."

"What kind of things?" Rahab asked, scowling at the captain as she brought her knees to her chest and wrapped herself in a blanket.

Crispin envied that blanket. He wished he were the one wrapping his arms around her. Since they had arrived in Borg, they'd had no time alone, and it was bothering him more than waiting for an inconsiderate king to grant him a meeting. He wanted to toss Rahab over his shoulders, carry her to his room a few doors down the hall, and cradle her in his arms until they fell asleep. He missed her head resting on his chest, the smell of the salty sea in her hair, and her roaming hands. He craved her kiss and missed catching her with a smile on her face, knowing he was the one who put it there.

"Lots of things," Ivar replied, cutting into the prince's daydream. "I am the Captain of the Drakkar. I am the king's eyes at sea. If there is something or someone to know about, I will make it my business to know it."

The room fell silent.

Ziggy mustered the courage to finish her tea which was growing cold.

Rahab tugged her blanket tighter over her shoulders.

And Nubis glared at Ivar across the room, though the Westerner paid him no mind.

When Crispin could no longer tolerate the silence, he shifted in his seat like a petulant child and huffed to draw the captain's attention.

"We've been here for weeks now," the prince griped. "How long do we have to wait until His Majesty grants us an audience?"

Ivar's nostrils flared, but as quick as the irritation flashed, it was gone. He leaned forward and smacked Crispin's boots off the coffee table. "When His Majesty decides he's ready to speak to the likes of you."

"You seem to forget," Crispin placed his hands on the back of his head and reclined in his seat, "that you're mistreating a prince."

"You may be a prince by birth, but a prince of nothing is what you are now. You should consider yourself lucky the king granted you and your *companions*," he said it with an air of disgust, "suites in the Halfrond Keep and did not toss you lot in the dungeons where, quite frankly, you belong."

"And here I was thinking after weeks of playing our nursemaid, you were growing fond of us." Crispin smirked. "Why did they assign you to watch us anyway? Aren't you too important to be with the likes of us?"

Ivar kicked one leg over the other. "Perhaps the king believed me to be the only one capable of keeping you devils in line."

"Or," the prince lifted his index finger, "he hates you and put you on our detail as punishment."

Ivar scoffed when the others snickered. "For a prince, you lack decorum."

Crispin shrugged a shoulder before sinking further into the plush chair. "Exile will do that to a person."

The room fell silent once again.

In the stillness of the room, Crispin sensed Rahab eyeing him, so he looked her way. He could tell she missed him just as much as he missed her. He winked at her and though she tried to hide her grin underneath her blanket, the sides of her eyes crinkled showing him exactly how she felt. One way or another, he would make sure they were alone, and soon.

"Where have you been all this time?" Ivar broke the silence with an oddly personal question and seemed genuinely interested in the answer.

"Not far from here actually." Crispin cracked his neck. "It was a small village called the Tree House Forest."

Ivar paled. "It would seem that village no longer exists."

"It's gone?"

"From the reports we received, Shadows slaughtered the villagers and burned most of the village to ash." Ivar cleared his throat. "Of course, we can't prove it was the Northerners, but it fits their methods, and there were reports they were riding through our lands looking for someone."

Crispin knew exactly who the Shadows were looking for but didn't offer the information to the Westerner. The thought of the village where he'd grown up, spent twelve years of his life, and the people he knew, being destroyed and erased as if they didn't matter, churned his stomach. He never wanted to establish roots there but knowing the tree house he'd call home was gone, pierced his heart.

"Before we could track the Shadows or find out who they were searching for, the raids stopped." Ivar rolled his shoulders back, his military mask back in place. "I guess they found who they were looking."

"I'm sorry to hear the village is gone," Crispin cleared his throat when his voice cracked. "There were good people there."

Ivar nodded, but before he or anyone else could say anything, there was a knock. The captain hopped up and opened the door to find a soldier offering an envelope. He grabbed it, shut the door, and retreated to his chair to read the missive.

Crispin watched the captain's eyes glance over the letter's contents before Ivar read aloud, "His Majesty, King Benaiah of Borg, grants Prince Crispin of Northwind an audience upon receiving this message."

Crispin slowly stood up and cracked his back. It was about time he was granted permission to meet with Benaiah. Perhaps, he could come to a fast resolution with the king so he and his companions could be released by nightfall.

"I suppose we should let Captain Haldane and Master Penn know," Crispin made his way toward the door when Ivar's voice stopped him.

"The king granted *you* permission, no one else." Ivar made his way toward the prince and met his irritated gaze. "I will escort you." He turned back to face the others. "As always, your rooms will be guarded, so please, don't do anything stupid while I'm gone."

Rahab hissed something under her breath that neither Crispin nor Ivar caught.

"What was that, pirate?" Ivar snorted, puffing his chest like a ruffled peacock. "Care to say it a second time?"

Rahab flashed a menacing smile toward the Westerner. "Give the king my regards." Her sing-song voice didn't fool anyone, and Crispin couldn't help but chuckle when Ivar's shoulders tensed.

Ivar refrained from engaging with Rahab further and motioned for Crispin to follow him to the throne room.

The only time Crispin had been able to see the city of Borg was when they first arrived. The lodge style homes and buildings were similar in style and were intricately carved with unique details etched into the wood. The craftmanship reminded Crispin of the toy houses Zophar used to whittle for him when he was a boy. The arched doorways and sloped roofs added to the ancient feel of the city and although, some of the buildings were newly constructed, they looked as if they had been there for a thousand years.

The citizens: men, women, and children alike with their red hair, fair skin, freckles, and blue eyes reminded him of the villagers in the Tree House Forest. But unlike the villagers who were thin and more open to outsiders, the Borgians were built with broad shoulders and prickly dispositions. Their plaited braids, and leather and chain mail garments also differentiated them from the villagers.

Halfrond Keep was impressive and could be seen from the harbor. Pine trees strewn throughout the kingdom made it feel as if he had stepped back into the forest where he'd grown up. Although considered a captive and criminal, Crispin oddly felt at peace in Borg.

Everyone stepped aside when he and his pirate companions were escorted to the Halfrond Keep as guests of the king instead of being thrown into the dungeons as the criminals the Westerners believed them to be. And they weren't wrong.

Crispin wasn't a pirate, but he had blood on his hands. There were times he would close his eyes and flashes of him driving the knife across Memucan's neck disturbed him. He'd killed an unarmed man and although his reasons for doing so were considered righteous and deemed necessary, he was still fighting a twinge of guilt that stung his heart.

When they entered the keep, Crispin was awestruck, because the inside was just as majestic as the outside. Wood beams, high ceilings, iron chandeliers lit with hundreds of candles and beautifully woven tapestries were everywhere, but the animal heads mounted on the wood and stone walls attested to the ruthlessness and hardened ways of the Westerners. He wished Zophar were there to experience the capital city with him, but he'd be thrilled to share his adventures with the old man once they were reunited.

Crispin received his own private quarters while the rest of the crew were ordered to share the remainder of the rooms in the wing available to them. From the outside, the enormous wooden structure didn't look like it had hundreds of rooms inside, but Crispin was pleasantly surprised of the luxury the Borgian royals were accustomed to.

Now marching down the wood paneled halls, walls decorated with artwork depicting the king's accomplishments and bear skin rugs strewn throughout, Crispin wondered what type of man Benaiah was going to be. He'd heard stories of the king from the villagers who ventured into the city to sell some goods or bring back supplies for the harsh winter season, but their reports were never glowing.

Ivar stopped before a large set of doors with two warriors stationed on either side. If Crispin was reading the captain right, he would say Ivar was nervous, but he didn't understand why that could be. As if he could hear Crispin's thoughts, Ivar glanced at him.

"Mind what you say," Ivar whispered so softly Crispin almost didn't hear him. "You are in dangerous territory."

With a nod to the guards, the doors opened slowly. Crispin couldn't even imagine how heavy the doors were. The soldiers pushed with all their might and their muscles bulged with the effort. Crispin waited for Ivar to make the first move before entering the den-like throne room.

At the far end of the room, directly in front of them, sat Benaiah. His once red hair and beard now faded, his blue eyes not kind nor cruel, and his broad shoulders that filled his wooden throne carved into the likeness of a hissing dragon were relaxed. His enormous hands rested on the claw armrests and his feet were firmly planted on the slate floor. Crispin didn't notice a crown on the king's head until they were within twenty feet of the dais. He then saw the simple gold band around the king's head, the only adornment to declare his title. Benaiah's presence alone exuded his power and Crispin forced himself to stand tall, to show he wasn't intimidated by the man who had ruled the Borgians for forty years.

When they were a few feet from the throne, Ivar bowed at the waist and Crispin followed suit. He could at least pay proper respect to the man who held his fate in his hands.

The king ran thick fingers over his braided beard. "So," his voice was coarse, as if he'd been screaming all night long, but there was an undeniable power behind it, "you are Issachar's only surviving son?"

"Yes, Your Majesty. I am Crispin of Northwind."

"Your father prided himself on one thing, and that was the number of sons his wife bore him," Benaiah flashed a crooked smile. "A shame his first born was a disappointment to him."

Somehow, Crispin was offended by the remark about Niabi, and he didn't know why. Perhaps, it was the insult to his blood, but Crispin kept his princely mask in place and smiled. "It seems you and my father knew one another well."

"I'd say. Your father bet his firstborn would be a boy and I bet it would be a girl. He lost a lot of money." The king laughed and the other members of the court in the room laughed with him. Benaiah raised a hand silencing the courtiers. "Now, Prince Crispin, what is this business about you being captured aboard the *Shadow of Death*? Were you kidnapped?"

"No, the crew of the *Shadow of Death* provided me safe passage out of Pulau." Crispin looked at Ivar standing stoically next to him, his hands firmly planted behind his back. "Captain Ivar brought us here because Master Penn of The Sisters and I requested an audience with you."

Benaiah snapped his stubby fingers and a hunched servant scurried toward the throne with a silver tray. The servant took a sip of the wine and once the king was satisfied the drink was not poisoned, he grabbed the goblet and shooed the man away. "Well, as you know, the Pulauans are our enemy. They pillage our outlying villages and have killed more of our people than I care to think about." Benaiah took a long sip, making Crispin wait until he was finished. A classic power move. The king wiped his mouth with his forearm and flashed a toothy grin at Crispin. "I am prepared to make a deal, Prince Crispin."

"You have my attention." Crispin noticed Ivar seemed to tense, as if he was holding his breath.

Benaiah leaned forward. "I assume you have become quite fond of the crew of ruffians you have been traveling with, is that so?"

Crispin wasn't sure if he should truthfully answer that question. Ivar's warning before entering the throne room rang in his head: *Mind what you say. You are in dangerous territory.* He didn't want the knowledge of how he felt about the crew to be used against him. But if he said they meant nothing to him, he was afraid of what Benaiah might do without them as his bargaining chip.

He noticed the king's eyebrow arch and answered, "I hold them in high regard."

Benaiah chewed on that bit of information before continuing. "Normally, we hang pirates on sight, but your *friends* have been given special treatment and housed as guests of the crown because of *you*." The king tugged on his beard. "I can pardon them for their crimes if they swear fealty to me and join the armada under Ivar's watchful command."

Crispin could see Rahab and Haldane slitting their own throats before bending a knee to the Westerner. But the king didn't need to know that. "I can't make that decision for them, Your Majesty. I am not their leader."

"No, but the alternative is finding themselves dangling from the end of a noose." The king's smile sent chills up Crispin's spine. Benaiah most likely knew the pirates would never agree to his terms. The pirates would die, and Benaiah would be seen as benevolent.

Crispin cringed at the thought of Rahab, Haldane, Phex, Corwin, Ondrej, Rafi and the other deckhands hanging lifelessly from the gallows for thousands to gawk and spit upon.

"What is it you want from me?" Crispin decided to play the political game, so he could get out of Borg alive and ensure the safety of his friends. "Surely, you wouldn't pardon pirates, your sworn enemies, and offer them a life amongst your people, if you didn't gain something from it."

Benaiah let out a booming laugh that filled the throne room. "You are definitely Issachar's son. He had a nose like a bloodhound when it came to political dealings." The king seemed proud of that fact, but it made Crispin nauseous. "Word has reached me that you intend to wage a war against Niabi and reclaim your father's throne."

"You've heard correctly."

"I cannot engage in a war with Niabi." The Westerner shook his head sadly, though Crispin could tell it was all an act. "I have too much at risk to anger her, and to be honest, I have no quarrel with her. Your father was a bastard." His words stung. "He was responsible for my son, Antilles', death and I was not sad to hear of his passing."

"That is quite the accusation to put at my dead father's feet." Crispin's nostrils flared.

"There is evidence of his crimes." Benaiah seemed just as angry, but waved a hand in the air. "But no need to worry. Your sister has seen to it that those responsible for assassinating my son, her betrothed, met their deaths gruesomely."

"So, you are asking me not to engage in a war with Niabi? Is that it? To protect your alliance."

"On the contrary, my boy," the king's smile was unsettling. "Wage a war. Kill your sister. It does not matter to me if she survives. She is not my blood nor is she my daughter-in-law."

"But you said -"

Benaiah stood up and made his way toward Crispin. He was much taller and his shoulders boarder than he first appeared, making Crispin feel small.

"*I* will not wage a war against her," the king stopped a foot in front of Crispin and whispered, "but I will not prevent you from starting one. If you lose," he shrugged, "I lose nothing. But if you should win, there is one thing I would ask of you to ensure your friends are granted clemency."

Crispin felt uneasy but asked anyway, "And what is it you want from me?"

"Should you win and become King of the North, I want you to marry my only daughter, Princess Lahki."

Crispin and Ivar both seemed to suck in a breath at the same time. "What?"

"Your father and I made an agreement decades ago that Niabi would wed my second-born son, Antilles. But the idea of my son becoming king didn't sit well with him and he had my son eliminated and married your sister off to the King of Elisor. I have no more sons to marry off. Antilles is dead. Ehrik, my heir, is married, and Ragnar, my spare, is betrothed. But Lahki is available and will make a fine queen."

Crispin's head was spinning. Marry the princess of Borg? His father would have arranged something similar if he were still alive, but Crispin's heart was already set on another. But if it was the only way to ensure his friends survived in enemy territory, he might have to consider it.

"Well?" Benaiah's husky voice sliced through his tormented thoughts. "Do we have an agreement?"

"Might I have some time to consider your offer, Your Majesty? I don't want to rush an important decision." Crispin needed to buy himself some time. He needed to think of how he could get out of this situation unscathed.

The king tried to mask his displeasure but failed. "Take one day. We will reconvene tomorrow, and I expect to be toasting to our newfound alliance."

CHAPTER 4

NIABI

Being pregnant didn't deter Niabi from having Tala and a small host of guards accompany her to Elisor on the sixteenth anniversary of Dichali's death. Her deceased husband's grave was nestled between a meadow of wildflowers and the Ameyalli River. She had never missed paying her respects and this year would be no different, except for the fact, that next to Dichali's marker was a freshly covered gravesite where their son's belongings had been buried.

She cleaned their markers, making sure their names wouldn't fade, and laid fresh flowers at the base. Sitting cross-legged on the grass, she sat in silence as the early morning breeze wisped strands of hair around her face.

In Elisor, she didn't don her royal finery. She wore no crown, no jewels, no expensive dresses. Here she was truly herself. Hair down, make-up free, wearing a traditional Andrago maiden dress, she felt at peace sitting with her departed husband and son. For a moment, she felt whole, until she opened her eyes and saw their tombstones instead of their beautiful faces.

Dichali was unlike any other man she'd ever met. And even though she found love with another man and was carrying his baby, her heart would always belong to the Andrago king.

"Do you remember the day we met?" she whispered, grazing the tips of her fingers across her husband's marker with a small smile. "I wanted so badly to hate you, but I belonged to you the moment you kissed my hand."

She closed her eyes once more, knowing Tala was keeping watch over her. She listened to the rushing water of the Ameyalli River, the chirps of the songbirds welcoming the morning light, and the bleating of a nearby flock of sheep. All the sounds Dichali loved.

Niabi's mind drifted back to the first time they laid eyes on one another.

Her father, Issachar, was seated on his throne, stroking a finger through his salt and pepper beard, as she approached the dais. To Issachar's right was her younger brother, Lykos, with the newly appointed Master of War, Zophar, beside him. Lord

Maon, her father's Second in Command, sat on Issachar's left and next to him was the Immortal Seer, Harbona. The small council, made up entirely of men, summoned her, the rightful heir to the White Throne, as if she were a commoner.

She stood before the council, dressed in black mourning clothes. Her betrothed, Antilles, the Prince of Borg, and his company had been slaughtered in the Black Forest during a hunt. Her father wasn't surprised by the attack, nor did he seem bothered his alliance with the Westerners was now in jeopardy. Her marriage to the prince was the only thing keeping peace between the two mighty kingdoms. She figured her father had summoned her to inform her she was to wed another Westerner.

King Benaiah of Borg, wouldn't allow her to marry Ehrik, his heir, because he was promised to another. And Ragnar, his third born son was only six years old. Though she was against an arranged marriage, when she finally met Antilles, they immediately bonded. She was happy for the first time since her forced return to Northwind from the Isles of Myr. Antilles understood her and accepted her as she was. Her father despised the fact that she learned to wield a weapon in her mother's homeland, but Antilles celebrated it. In Borg, women were not only encouraged to learn the way of the sword but expected to. When Niabi and Antilles weren't attending royal events, they'd steal precious moments in the early morning or late night to spar with one another and share their desires and goals.

Zophar had been Antilles' protector and had seen to it that neither of them were discovered when they were alone. It would have been considered improper, but neither of them cared if they were caught. They were in love and couldn't wait to spend their lives together.

Now Zophar sat next to her brother, Lykos. The King of Borg had blamed him for failing to protect his son. His face was brutally scarred and even the beard he was regrowing didn't hide the smile scars. She could see the pain in his eyes. He, too, mourned for Antilles, but he didn't don black clothes because her father ordered everyone to shed their mourning clothes before the traditional grieving period was supposed to end.

Issachar tilted his head to the side. His judgmental gaze roved up and down her appearance. "Mourning clothes?"

"I mourn my betrothed," she said.

"Antilles is dead," Issachar spat viciously. "Nothing will change that. But today is a joyous occasion for I have found you a husband." His smile was unsettling and normally meant trouble for her.

Niabi quickly glanced at Lykos and saw the fury in his brown eyes. She turned to face their father and straightened to her full height. "Antilles' body has not yet grown cold, and you disrespect his memory by promising me to another?"

"How dare you use that tone with me?" Issachar narrowed his eyes and hissed, "You ungrateful, bitter witch!"

"Your Majesty -"

The king lifted a hand to silence Harbona's protest. "You should be thanking me on bended knees for finding you another suitor. Most men wouldn't touch a bride with a deceased betrothed. It's back luck."

She crinkled her nose but kept her voice steady. "I will not grovel, nor will I thank you for forcing your will upon me. I grieve -"

"A boy who died," he interjected.

"The man I loved. But you wouldn't know anything about love. You are cruel and wicked and selfish."

"Enough, you vile creature!" He slammed his fists on the armrests of his throne and shot down the stairs of the dais.

"Father!" Lykos jumped up to stop him but wasn't fast enough.

Issachar raised a hand to strike her, but she unsheathed the knives hidden in her sleeves and held one to her father's throat and one against his groin. Everyone in the room froze in place. If she wanted to, she could have slit his throat before any one of them so much as blinked, but she held her weapons at bay.

"You will not touch me," Niabi growled, maintaining eye contact with her red-faced father.

"I will have you whipped until there's nothing left of your back but bone," the king hissed.

"If it is your intent to disfigure my future wife, King Issachar, then our agreement will be null and void."

The deep voice sliced through the room, startling everyone. Three Andrago marched into the throne room and Issachar's nostrils flared in irritation at the interruption.

The leader of the trio walked directly to Niabi and stood by her side. "The future queen of the Andrago will not suffer such torture to satisfy your wounded ego."

Issachar reluctantly stepped away from Niabi which surprised her. When she pulled her weapons on her father, she didn't expect to walk out of the throne room alive. She glanced up at the newcomer and found he was already eyeing her. He didn't look angry, he looked amused.

"King Dichali," Issachar cleared his throat. "You arrived sooner than expected." He shot a vicious glance at Niabi. "Put your knives away, girl, and show your betrothed the respect you fail to give your king."

So, this was the King of Elisor. The Leader of the Andrago. The Lord of Horses. She didn't lower or sheathe her weapons but gave him a look over to assess if he was more of a threat to her than her father.

Her lack of obedience infuriated Issachar. "You wicked girl," he seethed. "I ordered you to lower your weapons and show King Dichali respect."

"Why would I show him any more respect than I show you?" Niabi's gaze sliced from her father to the Andrago. "His people are responsible for Antilles' assassination. Do you hate me so much that you would hand me over to his murderer?"

Dichali's face softened. "Despite the malicious rumors circulating that we were responsible for Prince Antilles' death, I can assure you, we are not to blame."

"How dare you speak his name," she wheezed. "I would rather die than marry you, you devil."

"That can be arranged," Issachar fumed, reaching for her, but Dichali raised a hand to block him.

"May I speak with the princess alone?"

Issachar's eyes widened and his cheeks reddened but after a second's hesitation, he reluctantly agreed. The king motioned for everyone to leave the room.

One of the Andrago standing behind Dichali stepped forward. "You sure you want to be alone with her?" He whispered, but not low enough for Niabi to miss it.

She still held her knives and he was wise to question leaving his king alone with her.

Dichali nodded with a smile, his gaze fixed on Niabi. "I'll be fine, Tala. Take Chua and wait outside."

Tala shot her a look that screamed, *touch him and you die,* and she bobbed her head in understanding. He turned on his heel and she watched the two Andrago warriors leave the room. Once they were alone, Dichali circled her. He was sizing her up, so she took a moment to do the same.

The King of Elisor was certainly handsome. His bronze skin and black hair that rested just below his shoulders were Andrago staples. His brown eyes were oddly comforting. He was clean shaven, and his thick, black eyebrows bounced playfully when he stopped in front of her.

They didn't say a word, soaking one another in, maintaining unwavering eye contact that was so intimate it nearly stole her breath. But despite what he said, she was unwilling to believe his people weren't somehow involved in the attack that killed Antilles. The Andrago were known to be fierce and would attack trespassers but slinking into the Black Forest and killing her betrothed was too much for her to forgive or forget.

As if he could read her mind, he said, "I did not order the attack on your departed."

"Andrago weapons were found at the…" she held back the tears and swallowed the knot in her throat. "If you didn't order it, then you are woefully incapable of keeping your people in check."

Dichali smiled, unbothered by her insults. "I see why your father was threatening you when I first walked in. You are fire itself."

"I am more than threatening." She stood her ground, even when he took a small step closer to her, clasping his arms behind his back. "I am a weapon, and he knows it. That is why he fears me."

"Should *I* fear you?" He smirked and she noticed the small, intricate braids plaited against his head.

She fiddled with her daggers and flashed a contemptuous smile. "You would be wise to fear me."

Dichali ate the distance that remained between them. He towered over her and looked down at her. She tilted her face upwards to make eye contact with him and made note that his shoulders were broader than she first thought, and he had dimples that softened the hardness of his masculine jawline.

"I believe we share something in common, Princess."

"Which is?"

His perfect smile sent a shiver down her spine. Being this close to him, she could smell the tobacco and pine clinging to his clothes. It was frustratingly intoxicating.

"We both hate your father," he whispered in glee.

She hadn't expected that response. "Then why ally yourself with him? Why take me for your bride?"

"Because he stole your birthright as his firstborn," he didn't hesitate in answering. "You are destined to rule, not to be in a man's shadow. I want to restore your crown, even if it isn't the one of your ancestors."

"Why?"

He shrugged a shoulder and grinned. "I can't think of a better way to piss him off."

Niabi took a step back and made sure he saw her sheathe her knives up her sleeves. She quirked an eyebrow and crossed her arms across her chest. "What do you gain from marrying me? What do you want from me?"

Dichali walked toward one of the floor-to-ceiling windows that overlooked the White City. "The Andrago have been at war with the North for generations. I do not wish for that cycle of bloodshed to continue. I want my people to live in peace."

"I will never love you."

He turned to look at her, unfazed by her statement. "Maybe you will never love me, but I am being truthful in my desire for peace. I need a woman who is bold and commands attention. I want a queen who will fight for both of our peoples. A wife who will ensure peace. All I ask from you, is your loyalty and your partnership."

"And if I should say no?"

"Then you will never see me again. Unlike your father, I will not silence you or force your hand. In Elisor, women and men are equals. Your choice matters. Your voice matters. Your desires matter. I will not force you to be mine, Your Highness, but I would be honored if you chose a life by my side."

She walked toward him and stood on her tiptoes to whisper in his ear, "How do you know I won't slit your throat the second I have the chance?"

Niabi knew he was smiling without looking at him. "Because you are a warrior and a true warrior is honorable. You won't harm me, just as I won't harm you." She pulled back to meet his gaze and saw a sincerity in his eyes that pierced her heart. "If you want to remain in your father's castle and live under his cruel and crushing will, then I will respect your decision. But, if you want to claim a position of power, ensuring everything he stole from you is restored, then be my queen."

There was something about the king she couldn't figure out. He was charming, but his hellacious reputation that she had heard so much about, now seemed exaggerated. He was speaking from his heart to hers and he was right. If she stayed, her father would crush her in every way.

She met the king's tender gaze. "Children."

He tilted his head to the side. "What about them?"

She jutted her chin, trying to appear taller. "Do you require them?"

"I desire them," he stroked a hand through his dark locks, "but I would not force you to bear them."

"And if I should bear you a daughter?" She held her breath.

Dichali rested a hand over his heart, as if he were swearing an oath. "I will love, protect, teach, and prepare her to rule when I am gone." He lifted his hand and when she flinched his eyes filled with rage and sorrow. Tenderly and slowly, he thumbed loose strands of hair from her face and tucked them behind her ear. "Not all men are like your father, Princess. There are some of us who have compassionate hearts and see the value of a woman. You needn't fear me."

After a moment to think, she said, "I will marry you on one condition."

"Name your terms."

"I want my own horse."

Dichali laughed and it was a deep, melodious sound that set her heart ablaze. "What an odd request from a princess with a stable full of them."

She stared at the white marble floor. "I was never allowed to ride one. I want to learn on my own horse."

The king shook his head, still chuckling. "No." She shot him a look, but he continued before she could lash out. "You want to ensure you have freedom to flee, should you decide to leave me."

Dichali was more intuitive than she gave him credit. A mistake she wouldn't make again. "Is that a bad thing?" she popped a hip to the side and smirked.

"It's a smart thing." He crossed his arms over his chest and even with his breastplate on, she could tell he was muscular. "If there's one thing the Andrago can teach you, it's how to ride." He looked deep into her eyes, clearly seeking the truth behind them. She didn't back down and maintained eye contact until he was satisfied. "I think I have the perfect horse for you, my lady."

Niabi extended her hand. "Are we agreed then, Your Majesty?"

Amused, he took her slender hand in his calloused one and nodded. "As long as you call me Dichali."

Her heart swelled at the contact. "Are we agreed, Dichali?"

He smiled. "We are agreed, Niabi."

"Niabi?" Tala's voice tore her from her memories.

She opened her eyes and tears streamed down her face. He extended his hand to help her up.

"Are you ready to go home?"

She knew he meant Northwind, but Elisor was her true home. And she missed it terribly.

What if she took Pash up on his offer and just left Northwind? Abandoning her kingdom, her crown, her throne. She never truly cared for them. It was always about revenge. Her power wasn't tied to a throne. She was power. Perhaps, she could give it all up. Run and never look back. Start over.

But seeing her father's smug face mocking her reminded her exactly why she would never run away. Why she would never give up what she took with blood and tears. If she retreated, left everything behind for a life of anonymity, she would be proving her father right. She wasn't capable of being queen. And she would be damned if she allowed him to rejoice in the afterlife.

"Niabi?" Tala's eyes were filled with worry, so she flashed a small smile to ease his nerves.

Reluctantly, she accepted his help and stood up. She kissed Dichali's and Rollo's tombstones, whispered her goodbyes and reminded them how much she loved and missed them.

"I am ready." It was time she dealt with Gershom's treason once and for all.

CHAPTER 5
ADONIJAH

After nearly two weeks of being detained in Pash's military camp, surrounded by Shadows like the countless ones he'd slaughtered over the years, Adonijah was growing antsy. He tried thinking of a way to get word to Salome that he was alright, that he was thinking of her, and trying to figure out a way to return to her, but his brother's good graces only stretched so far.

Pash had ensured he wasn't chained or mistreated, but Adonijah saw how the soldiers looked at him. Their hunger to see him hanged was evident. Every time he stepped outside of his brother's tent to smoke, stretch his legs, or get some fresh air, they watched him with hate in their eyes.

His brother was busy most days strategizing and readying his men to launch an attack on Gomorrah. And good riddance to the Gomorrians and the horrific Thrak. Adonijah wouldn't mourn any that died during battle. But observing Prince Thanos skulking about the campgrounds didn't instill confidence the Gomorrians would be any better under his crushing thumb.

Since the night he'd been captured, he hadn't seen the Nameless Rider and Pash reminded him periodically not to get himself into trouble while being his guest. Guest. Prisoner. It all meant the same thing. He wasn't free to leave. He wasn't free to participate in meetings. He wasn't free to wander much farther than a few tents down from his brother's shelter. Pash insisted it was for his safety, but he and his brother both knew Adonijah was instructed to stay in the tent for the safety of Pash's soldiers. Adonijah was lethal. And if he really wanted to, he could try to slip out of the camp, slaughtering a few Shadows on his way out. But he wasn't going to be reckless. That would jeopardize his brother's life and he didn't want to repay his kindness with betrayal. That wasn't his way of doing things.

The only highlight of his long and boring days was at night when he and Pash would stay up late talking. Getting to know his brother again after so many years apart felt fulfilling. He'd been alone so long he almost forgot what it was like to have family. Of course, there was Salome, but that was different. His brother was the only blood relative he had left – other than their father – but Adonijah refused to include him in the family tree.

Leoti, the Andrago maiden, would stop by their tent nightly to eat dinner with them. He thought at first, she and Pash were having an affair, but his brother was far too honorable for that, especially knowing how loyal he was to Niabi. As wretched as Adonijah believed her to be, Pash would light up every time her name was mentioned, and he knew his brother was hopelessly in love with her.

The Andrago maiden was intriguing. She was soft-spoken but bold at the same time. She held her ground when arguing with Pash and didn't bat an eye when challenged. There was a refreshing quality about her that Adonijah couldn't quite put his finger on. There was no denying she was beautiful. Her long black hair was always in an intricate braid and her round eyes and full lips were enticing. But it was her bluntness and calm demeanor that nearly hypnotized him every time she spoke. Whenever she walked into the tent, he felt a wave of peace wash over him and for a second, he would forget all his worries.

That night sitting at the circular dinner table in Pash's tent, despite Leoti's presence, Adonijah didn't feel relaxed and wasn't at peace. He had been stunned into silence and stared at Pash across the table.

"Are you certain?"

Pash took another bite of his venison, the blood sauce dripping back down onto the plate. He nodded. "Our spies are well informed, Adonijah. The Thrak were seen carrying a woman that matches Salome's description along with a middle-aged Westerner. From what we know, they are being held in the dungeons beneath the Black Tower. The square is being prepped for a significant event."

"You mean, they are planning to torture her." Adonijah couldn't eat another bite and pushed his nearly full plate away from him.

"That is what we suspect." Pash glanced at Leoti who sat upright in her chair and hadn't said a word since she entered the tent, nearly thirty minutes ago.

"You have to rescue her." Adonijah leaned forward, tears welling up in his eyes at the thought of Salome being brutalized by the Thrak, while the Gomorrians cheered at her screams.

Pash rested his hands on the table and the look plastered on his face was one Adonijah knew well. It was sympathetic and apologetic, and it enraged him.

"You will sit by and do nothing to save her?" Adonijah fumed. "Does your queen not have a bounty on her head? Surely, she would want you to bring her back to Northwind before letting the Gomorrians have their way with her."

"My orders are to attack the city and claim it for Thanos." Pash wiped his mouth with a linen napkin. "If we can get there in time to extract Salome, we will, but that is not our objective."

"Then let me go," Adonijah pleaded. "Let me go, I can save her."

Pash slowly shook his head. "I'm sorry, Adonijah, but I can't let you do that. If you're captured, it could jeopardize our assault."

"How?" He leapt to his feet, his chair falling to the ground behind him. "You think if they capture me, I'll tell them about you and your army?"

"It's nothing personal," Pash remained calm, straightening in his seat. "We march at dawn. If the Thrak are aware of our plans, I could lose hundreds of men and I am not willing to risk their lives to save one or two people."

"She is not just some random prisoner -"

Pash stood up silencing his brother. "You will stay here. Do not give me a reason to lock you in the pit."

Adonijah flinched. His brother had never sounded so militaristic with him before.

"Please," Pash's voice softened. "I am already sticking my neck out for you by keeping you here, alive, and treated as my guest. If you were any other trespasser, I would have hung you by now." He rounded the table to stand in front of Adonijah and rested a hand on his shoulder. "I swear, I will do what I can to save her when we launch our assault. But I cannot do my job and worry about whether or not you listened to my orders."

"If it were Niabi who had been captured and I asked you to stay put, would you be able to?" He asked, rage coursing through his entire body.

A flash of fear flickered in Pash's eyes, but as quickly as it appeared, it disappeared. "I would want to do everything I could to rescue her."

"Yet, you still expect me to stay behind and do what exactly?" Adonijah shrugged his brother's hand off his shoulder. "If something happens to her -"

"I am asking you to trust me." Pash grabbed the belt that held his weapons and strapped it on. "I have rounds. When I get back, we can talk more." He made his way to the flap entrance and stopped. Looking over his shoulder he said, "My hands are tied, Adonijah. I'm sorry."

Pash left and Adonijah started pacing the room, kicking tables, chairs, and other random objects out of his way. He prowled to the decanter of wine and poured himself a hefty serving. He swallowed the contents in one big gulp and turned back around toward the table where the remainder of his dinner sat. It was then he noticed Leoti sitting quietly at the table, and it startled him. He had forgotten she was in the room. He felt foolish. She'd watched him throw an adult version of a two-year-old tantrum.

"Pash is right," she finally broke the silence, her round, brown eyes fastened on him. "If you get involved, it will give Ophir ammunition to use against not only you, but Pash as well. He might be Pash's uncle, but he's only loyal to himself."

"What is that supposed to mean?" Adonijah picked his chair up and sat back down, kicking his feet up on the table.

"It means, Ophir was passed over as the Commander of Shadows years ago and he hasn't forgiven Pash or Niabi for the insult." Leoti spoke softly, as if she was concerned someone would overhear. "If you interfere with Pash's operation, it will make him look inept and that is the kiss of death for any leader. He stuck his neck out for you when you were captured. Give him a chance to help Salome while fulfilling his duty."

"I'm sure he'll do his best to save her," Adonijah said sarcastically, rolling his eyes.

Leoti smacked his boots off the table and stood in righteous fury. "Your brother and I might not see eye to eye, but no one can accuse him of being dishonorable. If he said he will do his best to save her, you better damn well believe he will fight to his dying breath to get her out of there. Not just for your benefit, but because he cannot fathom an innocent person suffering at the hands of the Thrak." She spat on the ground. "The Thrak are an abomination. A stain on humanity. No one, enemy of the queen or not, should suffer such a fate."

Adonijah was stunned into silence for a second time that evening. This petite woman had humbled him, putting him firmly into his place. He stood up and looked down on her. He was a full head taller than her and to her credit, she didn't shrink back from his encroaching figure.

"I'm sorry," he said, which seemed to surprise her. "You're right."

Leoti flicked her braid behind her with a huff. "Of course I am, and don't you forget it." After a brief moment of maintaining eye contact with him, she took a step back and headed for the tent's entrance. "I know you probably won't, but try to get some sleep, Adonijah."

Once she left and he was truly alone, he sank into one of the leather chairs, pulled out his pipe, and lit it. He exhaled a puff of smoke up to the ceiling folds and groaned. Had he not left Salome, maybe this wouldn't have happened. How had she been captured by the Thrak, anyway?

Pash had never failed to keep his word before, and he had no reason to believe his brother would fail him this time. All he could do now was pray that Pash wasn't too late to save her.

CHAPTER 6
SALOME

Salome and Zophar were dragged back to the dungeons beneath the Black Tower and thrown into Zophar's cell. The Thraks' rough treatment would be evident in the morning. Salome was positive her arms, legs, and torso would be covered in bruises. She could already feel her bottom lip swelling from the smack she received in the throne room. But none of her injuries mattered. She was running on pure adrenaline and the pain did not register. Zophar's groan forced her to lift herself up from the damp prison floor to help him.

"Zophar?" She knelt in front of him and ripped the bottom half of her shirt to press against his wound. "Zophar, I am so sorry. This is all my fault."

He coughed. "No, it isn't. You did what I would have done."

"But you're hurt."

"I've been stabbed worse than this," he flashed a half-smile. He lifted his hand to touch her jaw where a bruise was forming. "Your face."

"I've been struck harder by children," she snorted, drawing a laugh from him.

"You always did have a mouth on you."

Salome pressed the torn piece of cloth against the wound again, making him wince. She looked around the cell to see if there was a way to escape. "I'm sure the guards will come back soon."

Zophar's eyes were filled with pain, but he cleared his throat and said, "You should lie to them about where the City of Bones is to buy yourself some time."

"You know they will never let me walk out of here alive."

"You need to try. When they come back, tell them you want to make a deal."

Salome shook her head. "They will kill you or worse if they find out I've lied."

"I am prepared to die."

"I am not prepared to let you," her voice cracked.

"Salome, please."

"We are both leaving alive, or we are dying together. I will not leave you."

"Our people need you. You cannot die here."

"I will not lose another family member." She pressed his hand to the wound while she took a turn around the cell. "I will not add another band to my arm."

"You need to think of everyone else before me," he said in an oddly calm voice, which rattled her.

"You know me well enough to know I won't." She found a broken piece of rock that fell off the wall, lying on the damp floor. Picking it up, she turned it over in her palm and noticed there was a sharp edge to it. If she needed to, she could use it in lieu of a dagger. Not the cleanest of kills, but it would do the job in her hands. She plopped back down on the floor next to Zophar, resting her head on his shoulder. "How did you get those scars on your face?"

Zophar looked at her, but she didn't meet his gaze. "Why ask me that now?"

"I was always too afraid to ask before."

"The possibility of death brings boldness." He propped himself up as much as possible without groaning. "I was a captain in King Benaiah's army. I swore to protect his son, Antilles, who was betrothed to your sister, Niabi. When it came time for them to meet, they fell hard for one another and were inseparable. We spent a few months in Northwind and once we were ready to return to Borg, we went on a hunting excursion on the way back to the Western Lands. We normally would have travelled by ship, but the pirates of Pulau were aware of the prince's visit. If captured, they could get quite the ransom for him. What we didn't anticipate was being ambushed by the Andrago. Only one of our members managed to make it back to Northwind for aid."

"What happened?"

Salome wasn't sure he would finish the story but then he cleared his throat and continued. "By the time your brother, Lykos, arrived with reinforcements it was too late. My leg was severely broken, and I was unable to get Antilles to a healer. He died in my arms. Your brother helped me bring the fallen bodies to Borg. The king was angry, distraught over losing his son, and sentenced me to be executed."

"But it wasn't your fault."

"The king didn't see it that way. Thankfully, your brother intervened. He broke me out of my cell that same night and took me back to Northwind."

"But the scars?" She looked at his smile scars barely noticeable underneath his bushy beard. Now she wondered if he'd purposely grown it to hide them.

"My punishment before my execution. One to remind me I had failed my king. The second because I had disgraced our people."

"You've never gone back to Borg?"

"If I go back, my life will be forfeited." Zophar reached for her hand and squeezed it. "The Northerners accepted me. Lykos was a better friend than I could have asked for, and I owed him my life. But perhaps, my time has now come."

"Death would have come for us by now, if that were the case."

"She will not be long, I imagine."

Salome stood up and paced. She couldn't sit still anymore. "We need to get out of this cell." She wasn't going to give up that easily. He needed to get to a healer, and she would burn the city to the ground, if that's what it took to save him.

"There is no way out of here, Salome. Gomorrian prison cells are inescapable."

"Then we fight our way out." She whipped around to face him, determination and worry in her face. "We don't end like this. This is not how we die."

Zophar's blue eyes filled with tears. "Your father would be proud of the woman you've become," he whispered.

She knelt in front of him. "Are you proud of me?"

He looked as if the question confused him. "Of course I am."

"Then that is all that truly matters to me." Before he could protest, she continued, "You saved us from our enemies. You raised us, protected us, trained us, and loved us as if we were your own. You have been more of a father to me than Issachar. And if I'm being honest, from what I now know about him, the Almighty blessed me with you."

"Salome, I have been honored to be your guardian," his voice cracked, "but I could never replace your father. Blood is blood."

"Give me your hand." She grasped his outstretched palm and took the sharp rock she'd found earlier and sliced the tip of his finger, then sliced her own. She placed their fingers together letting their blood mix. "Now there is no doubt. We share the same blood. From this day forward, you are my father, and I am your daughter."

"Salome-"

"Say it," she interrupted him.

Zophar's bottom lip quivered, but the burly Westerner's voice boomed with confidence. "From this day forward, I am your father, and you are my daughter. Blood is blood."

She leaned forward and kissed his chilled forehead. "I promise you," she whispered, "you will not die here."

CHAPTER 7

CRISPIN

Crispin and Ivar didn't utter a sound as they trekked through the halls. The captain seemed on edge and even though Crispin was dying to ask why, he kept his mouth shut and his thoughts to himself. There was no way he wanted to agree to an arranged marriage, but he wasn't sure what other options he had to ensure the pirates' safety. To ensure Rahab's safety.

Ivar delivered him to his quarters where two guards were stationed outside, reminding him that even though he was free to roam the designated rooms he and the pirates had been assigned, he was still a prisoner in a foreign kingdom. Still at the mercy of a king who seemed to have held a grudge against his father for two decades.

Once the door to his lavish room closed and he was finally alone, he sat on the edge of his fur-lined bed and hung his head. He rubbed the heels of his palms against his eyes as he listened to the crackling fire in the stone hearth, irritation and exhaustion plaguing him. To agree to the king's demands would go against everything his heart wanted. What would Salome do if she were in this position? He grumbled to himself knowing his sister would do anything in her power to secure an alliance.

But there was something gnawing at him. He didn't trust Benaiah. The king had a sinister look in his eyes. He couldn't have survived as sole ruler for forty years without learning a few wicked and deceitful tricks. What was he missing?

Marry Lahki and he would be free, the pirates would be granted clemency, and no one would be executed. Simple. His ancestors had made alliances forged in marriage countless times. It was politics. But he wasn't sure if the nausea he was battling was because he would be agreeing to marry a woman he'd never met, or he would have to give up the woman he wanted, or if deep in his soul he felt the king wouldn't hold up his end of the bargain.

Crispin flopped down on the soft mattress and laid his forearm over his eyes to block out the bright light pouring in the tall, narrow window.

He could ensure Rahab's safety, the entire crew's safety, if he agreed to Benaiah's terms. It was the most logical choice, but he couldn't convince himself to agree. He would rather plot, destroy, and fight his way out of Borg, if it meant he could be with Rahab. What had that pirate done to him? Had he never met her, he wouldn't have hesitated to marry a princess. If he were still marching through the halls of Northwind, his father surely would have arranged a match similar to this, one that would benefit the North. It was what was expected of him, and in another life, he would have agreed without a second thought. But things were different. He was different.

Consumed wholly by his thoughts, he didn't hear his door creak open, nor did he hear the footsteps approaching him until it was too late. His eyes shot open, and he swung his arm to protect himself but found Rahab standing at the edge of his bed, arms folded over her chest.

"Did I startle you, Your Majesty?" Her left eyebrow arched in teasing, but her smirk vanished when she looked into his eyes. "What is it?"

Crispin sat up and shook his head. "Nothing. I'm just tired is all."

Rahab popped her hip to the side and shot him an angry glare. "You're a terrible liar, Crispin. If you are to be king, you will have to work on that."

"Why would I need to be proficient at lying to be a good king?" He scoffed. "I thought honesty was what made a leader worth following."

Rahab ate the distance between them, her knees bumping his legs planted on the wooden floor. "Honesty is admirable, but it could cost you your life if you aren't careful."

Crispin didn't want to burden her with what he and the king had discussed because he already knew what she would say. She would insist he marry Lahki, reminding him of her lot in life. He refused to let her push him away or make the decision for him. But if their relationship had a chance of working, he knew he'd need to include her in important matters, especially if she would one day be his wife, his queen.

He raked a hand through his hair before snatching her wrists and pulling her on top of him. Once she was straddling him, he wrapped his arms around her hips and stared into her suspicious hazel eyes.

"I spoke with the king."

"And?" she prodded when he didn't offer more information.

"And..." Crispin sighed and decided to tell her the truth. "He made me an offer that would ensure the crew's safety."

"We would be free to go?" Rahab sat wide-eyed before her skepticism kicked back in. "What exactly are you expected to do?"

He bit his bottom lip before breaking eye contact with her. "I must agree to marry his daughter and make her my queen." He felt Rahab's body tense up and he wished he hadn't told her. He forced himself to meet her gaze and was surprised to see the hardened pirate he'd first met in Pulau was staring back at him. She didn't look surprised, she didn't look heartbroken or even angry, and it frightened him.

They stared at one another in silence until Crispin couldn't take it any longer. "Say something, Rahab."

Rahab slid off his lap and stood before him. "What would you have me say? I will not weep when we both knew this was inevitable. You are the future king of the north. I'm a pirate. We had some fun and now it's time for you to marry a princess like we both knew you would."

"Rahab -" He reached for her but she side stepped his advances.

"On behalf of the crew of the *Shadow of Death*, we appreciate you securing our release." She bowed her head slightly, as if dismissing herself from his presence. "I will let the captain know."

She turned on her heel, cold and mechanical, and marched toward the door. Before she was able to touch the doorknob, Crispin was on his feet and upon her. He grabbed her arm and whipped her around to face him. She two-hand shoved him away, but he refused to let that be how things ended between them. She reached for the door again, but he slipped between her and the exit, blocking her path.

"Get out of my way, princeling."

"Rahab, would you stop being stubborn and listen to me for once in your damn life!?"

"What else could you have said?" Rahab's eyes were fiery, and he could feel the pain radiating from her like a cornered and wounded animal. "We both knew this would happen. Why prolong the inevitable?"

"Because I didn't agree to it!" Crispin slammed his fist against the door behind him. "I couldn't agree to it."

"Well, that was stupid." She huffed, backing toward his footboard. He pushed up from the door and stalked toward her.

"You are without a doubt, the most frustrating woman I have ever met. You drive me crazy and half the time we're together, I would like nothing more than to toss you overboard." Crispin closed the gap between them and cupped her face in his hands. "But you are also the one woman I cannot stop thinking about. The only woman I want and need."

"Crispin," she whispered, but he pressed on.

"I am deeply, madly, irrevocably, and helplessly in love with you. I want you. I need you. And I will have you as mine, everyone else be damned."

"Your honesty is going to get us all killed once the king finds out." Rahab rested her hands on his chest.

He bent down so his lips brushed against her ear. "Tell me you do not love me, that you do not want me, that you do not desire me as I desire you, and I will accept the king's offer." He heard her breath hitch and he silently prayed she wouldn't say any of those words. He'd taken a gamble and he needed her to abandon her stubbornness and forget her pride and admit the truth. "Say it," Crispin pressed when she remained silent, "and we will end things between us now."

"I can't say it," Rahab finally whispered, dragging her lips across his stubbled cheek as her hands travelled from his chest up his neck and through his tresses. "Because it is not true."

"Then swear you will be mine," Crispin's lips hovered above hers. "Promise me, when this war is over, you will be my wife, that you will be my queen."

Her eyes widened, as if she was sobering up from a drunken stupor. His heart skipped, thinking she would push him away, or slap him, or flat out reject him. But she planted her hands on his bed, lifted her body over the footboard, and laid back on her elbows. Crispin crawled over her and ran his fingers through her hair.

She gently dragged her thumb over his bottom lip. When he released a shuddering breath, she gripped his chin between her fingers and forced him to look at her. "When this war is over, I will be your wife, your queen, and anything else you require of me. You have ruined me in every possible way, and I intend to live and die by your side, my king."

Crispin claimed her mouth and pressed his chest against hers. They would find another way out of Borg, but he wouldn't sacrifice his love for her to play the political games of kings. He wouldn't be like his father or his ancestors marrying for selfish gain. He would marry the pirate who loved him before he had a throne. He would give his people a queen who would not only fight for them, but alongside them. She was worth the price he would pay for angering the West.

CHAPTER 8
NIABI

Niabi's craving for blood fueled her to drag her aching body out of her soft bed to march to her throne room. She had arrived from Elisor the day before, and although Tala told her the meeting could wait one more day, so she could rest, she adamantly refused. She was looking forward to the meeting and wouldn't miss it for the world.

When she sent written word to Gershom to join her in the White Throne Room, she sealed it with a grin. Tala had asked why she was smiling and all she said was, "One down, two to go."

Her enemies would remember her name. They would regret coming for her crown, her throne, her loved ones. They would beg for mercy but as always, none would be given.

Gershom's treason was now confirmed. His ties to Lord Memucan of the Numbio would be the final nail in his coffin and Niabi couldn't contain the excitement humming through her body as she slipped into her throne and waited for her prey to fall into her trap. Because once he stepped foot into the room, he would be dragged out in chains.

With Tala and Anaktu on either side of her, Gershom entered the throne room with his head held high, but Niabi saw the fear in his shifting eyes as the doors closed behind him. She smiled when she recalled the moment she sliced off his ear months earlier.

Gershom didn't bow before her, most likely because he knew what was about to happen and she relished in the moment she'd dreamt of for years. "You sent for me?"

Niabi ignored his blatant disrespect when he didn't address her by her title. Licking her lips, she flashed her teeth. "We found Lord Memucan's body in the Night District. His neck was slit from ear to ear. Any thoughts on why the Southerner was in Northwind?"

Defeat. She could swim in the despair flooding his muddy brown eyes.

"It seems to me," his voice came out as a raspy hiss, "you already have the answer to your question, Niabi."

"Was it worth it?" she cocked her head to the side, a menacing smile stretched across her face. "Was your failed attempt to usurp my throne worth the years you will spend rotting away in my dungeons? So close to the throne you crave and will never have?"

"When I escape your dungeon, because I *will* escape, I will make sure you suffer greatly, until you beg for a death that will never come."

Nabi stood up from her throne, her hand cradling her swollen belly, and slithered down the steps of her dais to tower over Gershom, who had been forced to his knees by her soldiers. "*If* you escape," she growled. "No one will miss you. No one will mourn you. And soon, no one will remember you. You are a worm and for the rest of your miserable days, you will taste of your failure."

Gershom attempted to fight off the soldiers clamping manacles on his wrists and ankles. "I swear on the Almighty -"

"Oh please," Niabi cut him off and laughed, "your words bear me no threat. You are a broken man with broken dreams." She dragged her fingers over the hole where his ear once was, and said, "To think you had everything and threw it away for nothing."

"Was I supposed to be grateful for your scraps?" he snarled.

She patted his head. "What else would you feed a dog?" She quirked an eyebrow before whistling a laugh. "I would say, until we meet again, but we both know this is the last time we will see one another." Niabi waved her hand and her guards dragged Gershom toward the doors.

"You will pay for this!" Gershom screeched, resisting them. "This isn't the end! This is just the beginning!"

She let out a long sigh. "To think I once thought you mighty."

"Go to hell!"

"You first."

The doors slammed shut once Gershom was dragged out, but she could still hear his screams and curses echoing down the halls. Tala walked to her side and glanced from the doors to her.

"Now what?" he asked.

She met his awaiting gaze. "Prepare for war. My siblings won't be long now I imagine."

CHAPTER 9
SALOME

Salome sleepily opened her bloodshot eyes and lifted her head off Zophar's shoulder when she heard keys clatter outside their cell door. Determined to get Zophar out of Gomorrah one way or another, she laid face down on the floor, geared to ambush their enemy. Her heart was pounding, her hand tightly holding the sharp rock she found in the cell. She wouldn't let Zophar die in a dungeon. She wouldn't let this be their end.

The door squeaked open, footsteps rushed toward her, a hand touched her, and she whipped around forcefully swinging her weapon, but the blow was blocked.

"Jinn?" Salome whispered, tears filling her eyes. "You're here." She touched his face to make sure he was real and not a figment of her imagination. He'd come to rescue her.

"I'm here." The prince thumbed her lip where a fresh bruise sat, as if he could wipe it away.

"I never thought I'd see you again." Salome wrapped her arms around Jinn's neck, feeling his heartbeat against her chest but quickly pulled away. "Zophar is hurt. We need to get him to a healer, and I don' think he can walk on his own. And before you argue with me, old man...." She turned to smile at Zophar and noticed he was slumped over. To anyone walking by, it would look as if he were sleeping, but she knew something was wrong.

"Zophar?" She crawled to him as her heart thrashed in her chest. She could feel it pounding in her ears as she cupped his face. Everything around her slowed, as if frozen in time. "Zophar?" she whispered with tears streaming down her dirt-stained cheeks. When he didn't respond, she rested her forehead against his cold one. Her tears dripped onto his cheeks making it appear as if he was also weeping. "Please, don't leave me. I just got you back."

Hanzo and Oifa entered the cell, cradling a bundle of weapons. She spied her three daggers, including her wolf knife, and the handle of Zophar's battle axe. The Stormcrag and Krazak were silent as they took in the sight of Salome holding her departed. Hanzo dragged his middle finger from his forehead to his chest, paying the Westerner respect.

Jinn knelt next to Salome; eyes filled with sorrow. He hesitantly reached for her hand. "We need to get you out of here."

"I promised him he wouldn't die here," she choked. "I promised to get him out. I failed him."

"This is not your fault." Jinn swiped the tears from her cheeks. "We don't have much time. We need to leave before it's too late."

"I won't leave him here!" She felt the panic rising. "I can't leave him!"

Jinn held her gaze, his golden-brown eyes filling her with warmth amid feeling numb. "We will bring him with us." He motioned for Hanzo to step forward to carry him. "But we need to move quickly before our army launches an assault."

Salome didn't hear a word the prince said. All she saw was Matildys' dagger plunging into Zophar's body. She heard his groans, saw the pain in his eyes, and felt the fear in his shaky hands. Suddenly, her grief turned into a full-blown rage. She felt the fury spark in her toes and spread through her body like a poison. She leapt up, snatched her wolf dagger and Zophar's axe from Oifa's arms, and sprinted out of the cell.

"Salome! Salome, wait!" Jinn called, but she didn't hear him. She was on a mission to cut the queen's black heart out of her chest. Not even the Almighty could stop her now.

She sensed Death's presence. She had come for Zophar, gathering the souls of those Salome loved most, biding her time until she claimed hers.

"Not today." Salome let Death know she would have to keep waiting. She would bring Gomorrah to its knees if it was the last thing she did.

Jinn, Hanzo, and Oifa had killed the Thrak guards in the dungeons on their way to find her, so it made her ascent into the Black Tower easy. As soon as she stepped onto the black marble floor, her eyes zeroed in on the two Thrak stationed at the foot of the stairs which led to the royal sector.

One of the Thrak gurgled a warning, then drew his sword. She couldn't decipher what he'd said, nor did she care. They were between her and revenge, and they wouldn't be able to stop her. She held her weapons tightly and walked with determined steps toward the guards.

The one with his sword drawn ran toward her, ready to strike her down. He swung his blade at her and if it had struck true, she would have lost her head. She ducked, tumbled, and twisted her body like the Qata Vishna had taught her, before she lodged Zophar's axe into his thigh, bringing him to his knees. With cat-like swiftness, she slid behind him, pulled his head back to look into her eyes and slid her dagger across his neck, watching his fear and hatred fade as his life ended.

The second Thrak whipped his mace around, but Salome used the dead Thrak's body as a shield to get closer to her attacker. Bloodied, bludgeoned, and broken, her human shield allowed her to get within striking distance. She threw her wolf dagger at him, but he stepped out of the way to avoid the brunt of the blow. He wasn't fast enough to avoid the blade slicing his arm before it clanged to the floor. He quickly examined his wound and turned to face her with a smirk, but his smile disappeared when Salome, battle axe in hand, leapt at him and two-hand slammed the axe into his head, the crunch of his skull echoing through the rotunda.

She stood over the bodies, blood splattered all over her face, hands, and clothes.

She was the monster parents warned their children about, but she relished the power rushing within her.

"Salome?"

She slowly turned around when she heard Jinn's voice behind her. He stared at her in what she hoped was wonder and not terror. The prince tentatively made his way to her but before he reached her, a boom in the distance rattled the tower.

"What was that?" she asked as dust shook free from the chandelier swinging above them, sprinkling down on them like snow.

"I told you the army was launching an attack on the city," Jinn explained, drawing her attention. "We will have to fight our way out now."

Salome caught sight of Hanzo and Oifa appear in the doorway. Hanzo had Zophar draped over his shoulders like a stag on its way to be skinned. Sorrow and anger once again surged through her. She'd rather die facing the queen than flee the city.

"You go," Salome commanded. "I'll meet you as soon as I can."

"Where are you going?" Jinn grabbed her.

"I have unfinished business."

Jinn turned to Oifa and Hanzo, "Wait here. We'll be back."

"You don't need to come -"

"I came to bring you home," Jinn interrupted her. "I won't leave your side until I do."

Not interested in arguing with the prince any further, she tucked Zophar's axe into her belt loop before sprinting up the stairs, taking them two at a time. The double doors leading to the throne room were within sight and she knew Jinn had cloaked them when the guards didn't notice them. Marching up to the guards, unaware of the danger lurking, and with swift precision, she stabbed them in their chests, and watched them drop to the floor.

She turned to face Jinn, his tachi blades drawn, ready to fight by her side, ready to face any demon hell sent to keep her safe. "When I walk through these doors, don't try to stop me from doing what I must."

Jinn nodded his head in acknowledgement. "I'm with you."

"Uncloak me." Jinn obeyed.

She stepped over the guards, pushed the doors open, and locked eyes with Matildys sitting on her onyx throne with a smugness Salome was itching to wipe off her pale face. If the queen was surprised or fearful to see the blood-stained Salome, she didn't show it.

"Did he die?" Matildys purred. "Did you suffer as greatly as I hoped you would by watching him take his last breath?"

Salome held her wolf dagger in her left hand and Zophar's axe in her right, making sure the queen made note of them as she approached the dais. "I have come to make good on my promise."

Matildys sipped from her goblet of wine, not a care in the world, and waved Salome off. "It seems your *friends* have come for you. Why don't you run off and join them before you die here?"

"You stole from me," Salome kept her approach steady. "You will pay dearly for it."

Matildys glanced around the empty room. All the Thrak were either patrolling outside of the throne room, dead, or at the wall to battle the army Jinn had brought. Apart from Salome and Matildys, Jinn and Ranalda were the only ones in the room.

Ranalda sat at the edge of her throne and when Salome was in reach, she launched herself down the dais and fell to her knees, crying. "Please," she begged, "I did nothing to harm you or your friend. Spare me. Please."

Salome stared at the Gomorrian girl and felt nothing. No compassion, no sympathy, no mercy.

"You are a disgrace, Ranalda!" Matildys hissed.

Salome yanked Ranalda up to her feet, spun her to face her mother, and put a knife against the girl's neck. The princess whimpered, but Salome did not yield. "You killed a good man."

"And I'd gladly do it again," the queen stood up, nostrils flared. "What are you planning to do, *Princess*? Are you going to slit my daughter's throat in my own throne room? Are you going to stoop to my level? Are you -"

Salome ran the blade across Ranalda's throat and let the girl drop to the floor. She reached for her mother for help, but both women knew there was nothing that could be done to save her. Matildys showed a hint of grief and helplessness but quickly returned to her heartless self. When Ranalda's gurgling stopped, Matildys latched her wicked, cruel, hate-filled eyes on Salome.

Salome motioned to the princess sprawled on the floor in a pool of her own blood. "I came here with the intent to gut you, but perhaps I should let you live knowing you will have to bury and grieve your dead for the rest of your miserable days. My army will wipe your filthy city from existence so you can no longer call yourself a queen over anyone but the ashes of the fallen. You stole from me. I am glad to have returned the favor, Matildys."

Matildys stood in utter silence; a silence that would have made Salome's skin crawl, had she not already felt dead on the inside. Salome realized what the queen was about to do before it happened, and then it all happened in slow motion.

The Gomorrian finished her glass of wine and shattered it against the floor. She glided to the balcony, turned to face Salome one last time, anguish and rage brewing in her eyes, and let herself fall backwards to the ground below.

Salome made her way to the banister and glanced over the edge to see a mangled Matildys lying dead in the infamous Square, where thousands of Mountain Men had been tortured and mutilated for generations. The same square where she was to be tortured at dawn the next day. Dogs so skinny their rib cages protruded, found their way to the queen's body and began to lap up her blood. She turned her focus from the dead queen to the fires raging at the city gates. Smoke billowed, people screamed, metal clashed against metal as the battle raged. They'd come for her. Her friends, her allies. They had waged a war to save her.

Remembering she wasn't alone in the throne room, she turned around to see Jinn staring at her. She was suddenly afraid of what he might be thinking of her and what she had done. But the prince extended his hand with compassion in his eyes.

"Are you ready to go home?"

A simple question, but she didn't have a home. She hadn't had one in a very long time and the man who had loved her as his own daughter, who had sacrificed everything to give her a bit of normalcy growing up, was gone. The gravity of

Zophar's death finally gripped her heart and twisted it until it was nothing more than a broken, mangled mess.

She stared at the body on the floor. Ranalda wasn't much younger than her, but there she was, eyes wide open, neck split, dead.

Salome recoiled at the sight of what she had done. The way she let her grief and her anger manifest into a murderous rage. She was the Hunter. She was meant to avenge the blood of the innocent. What if Ranalda wasn't cruel like her mother? Did she take the life of an innocent girl, just to hurt her enemy?

And then it hit her. She'd said it before when talking to her grandmother, Nym, in the Isles of Myr.

"If you were Niabi, what would you have done?" Her grandmother had asked.

"I am *Niabi. We share the same story."*

She judged her sister for seeking revenge for those she'd lost, for all she had suffered. She hated Niabi for what she'd done, and Salome had now done the exact same thing. She and Niabi weren't different at all. They were two sides of the same coin. Perhaps, it was in their nature to be bloodthirsty and in the end, they would share the same fate.

"Salome?" Jinn's honey-smooth voice brought her back to the sight of the body on the floor and she shuddered. Her stomach twisted in knots to the point of needing to wretch. She was grateful she hadn't eaten all day.

She stared at blood-stained hands and broken fingernails, then lifted her gaze to meet Jinn's. "What have I done?" she whispered so softly she didn't think the prince heard her.

But he did, and reached her in three long strides. He wrapped her in his warm embrace; one hand on her back, the other cradling her head.

"I…I killed her. I killed that girl to hurt her mother." Salome sobbed into Jinn's leathers, tucking her forehead into the crook of his neck. "What have I done, Jinn? I'm turning into Niabi."

"Don't say that. You're nothing like her." He rested his chin on top of her head and tightened his grip around her.

She wished that were true, but despite Jinn's words, she knew the truth and had just proven it.

I am Niabi.

CHAPTER 10
PASH

The guilt Pash felt for forcing Adonijah to stay at the camp instead of joining the fight, was eating him alive. He knew his brother, no matter which side of the war he was on, would never betray him or do anything to harm him, but as the commander of Niabi's forces, he needed to think about his men first. If Adonijah had to choose between rescuing Salome or following his orders, Pash knew what his brother's choice would be. He couldn't fault him. If their roles were reversed, he would have burned the enemy campsite to the ground to find Niabi.

One thing was certain, Pash would keep his word to do everything in his power to save the lost princess from the monstrous clutches of the Thrak. No one, not even his worst enemy, should endure such an end.

After hours of riding, Gomorrah was within reach. Once Pash led his army over the tree-lined ridge, the city would be in sight and the battle would begin. The greatest advantage Gomorrah had was its location. The city sat in the middle of flatlands which enabled them to see invaders up to a mile away. Though they may see them approaching, Pash had full confidence in the ability of his soldiers to outmaneuver and outsmart the Thrak. When it came down to it, the Thrak were barbarians with weapons, but Pash and his men were bred for war.

A noise to his right caused Pash to look over at Leoti, who rode by his side in silence. He'd spent enough time with the Andrago to know she was deep in thought, but before he could ask her if she was nervous about the upcoming battle or if something else was bothering her, Thanos' grating laugh pierced his ears.

"By this time tomorrow," the prince flashed a triumphant smile to no one in particular, "I will be King of Gomorrah."

Leoti's reaction didn't go unnoticed. Pash knew they were thinking the same thing. Gomorrah was a stain in Adalore and the Thrak were an abomination. It still didn't sit well that they were there to put this spoiled boy on the throne, but he was a soldier and would serve his mistress well.

"And once I am king," Thanos continued,"I will resume the search for those murderous mountain men and their cave city."

"Murderous are they?" Leoti chimed in with a disdainful chuckle. "Last I checked, the Krazaks and Stormcrags didn't hunt down, imprison, and mutilate *your* people for pleasure."

If looks could kill, Thanos would have killed Leoti eight different ways in the span of two seconds. Pash could have kissed Leoti on the forehead like a proud father would for her retort.

The Gomorrian prince narrowed his blue eyes and licked his dry lips. "Perhaps, I will enlist your services to complete my mission, *warg*. I think you would be a most useful companion in more ways than one."

Pash wanted to wipe the lustful grin off the boy's face. The need to protect Leoti thundered in his chest, but he didn't get a chance to put the would-be king in his place because Leoti straightened in her saddle, doing her best to appear taller than the Gomorrian, and said, "I'd rather bathe in pig slop than be associated with an impudent product of incest."

"Why you little bit-"

"Stay your tongue or lose it," Pash growled, causing the prince to shrink back.

"You will pay for this disrespect, Commander." Thanos promised under his breath. " I will delight in seeing to your punishment personally."

"I am your only hope to claim your throne," Pash met Thanos' cruel gaze, unfazed by the temper brewing within the teenager. "I suggest you mind your manners."

Suddenly a blare rang out, then another, drawing a curse from Pash. There was no way the Gormorrians had already spotted them. His scouts would have decimated any Gomorrian lookout. Pash kicked the sides of his horse to reach the top of the hill to assess the situation. To his amazement, the alarms weren't signaling his army's arrival, but that of another army laying siege to the soot-stained kingdom.

Leoti was by his side a moment later, her mouth agape. "Who is that?"

Pash shook his head in bewilderment. If he hadn't been there to see it with his own eyes, he might not have believed it. "If my eyes aren't deceiving me, that would be the Krazaks and Stormcrags fighting alongside one another. Perhaps, they've finally united to battle the Gomorrians."

Leoti pointed to a small group running alongside the Mountain Men. "Are those warriors from Numbio?"

That didn't make sense. Sure, the Krazaks and Stormcrags had a long-standing feud with the Gomorrians but the southerners had no... Realization hit Pash like a wave crashing against the shore. "They're here for the princess." Relief and satisfaction flooded him. Maybe Salome would be rescued after all, and his brother would be put at ease.

Thanos' horse pulled up and the prince screamed, "What are you waiting for? Attack!"

None of the soldiers moved, waiting for Pash's orders. His mind was racing as to what the best course of action would be. To interfere would put his men at a higher risk. They had come to fight the Gomorrians, but if they attacked, the Mountain Men would believe they were being ambushed and would turn on him and his men. The only ones who would profit from his interference would be the very people he came to destroy.

Pash lifted his hand in the air, silently commanding his troops to stay put. "We wait here."

"What?" Thanos yelled. "You are supposed to-"

"Do not tell me how to command my men," Pash interrupted. "You look stupid." Before the prince could respond, the commander glanced at Leoti. "I need eyes."

The Andrago maiden nodded and dismounted her horse. She took Tiki out from his crate and untied the blindfold. Stroking the bird's feathers, she whispered something to him, and the bird shot into the air. Leoti sat on the ground cross-legged, leaning her back against a tree, and the moment she blinked, her brown eyes were washed over with solid white ones.

Pash's attention bounced from Leoti up to the falcon. All he had to do now was wait.

An unease slithered through Pash as he turned toward Thanos, but the prince's gaze wasn't on him, but fixed on Leoti. Pash knew he'd have to keep an extra eye on the Andrago. If Thanos had his way, he'd kidnap and enslave her to do his bidding and that wasn't going to happen. Not on his watch.

Pash hopped off his horse, spurring his men to do the same and keep themselves hidden behind the tree line. He walked toward Leoti and stood between her and Thanos, blocking his view and garnering a wicked glare. Crossing his arms over his chest, Pash silently willed the boy prince to stand down and to his surprise, Thanos steered his horse in the opposite direction. The Gomorrian might not see a crown upon his head if he kept ogling Leoti in that manner.

Fixing his gaze on the city before them, Pash hoped and prayed he wouldn't have to deliver heartbreaking news to his brother.

CHAPTER 11

SALOME

Salome and Jinn found Hanzo and Oifa exactly where they'd left them in the dark foyer. There were a few more dead Thrak bodies scattered across the room but neither the Stormcrag nor the Krazak looked fazed. Hanzo had placed Zophar's body on the floor, crossing the man's arms over his broad chest; a small gesture of respect, but one that punched Salome in the gut.

Oifa was picking at her fingernails with a dagger, leaning against the wall, as if the battle raging around the city didn't affect her in the least. She glanced up as the duo descended the staircase and straightened to her full height. Though she was slightly shorter than Salome, she was more muscular and broader in the shoulders. A true warrior's frame.

"Ready?" Oifa asked, her pointed gaze roaming over the blood coating Salome's hands and clothes. She didn't make any remark about her appearance and Salome whispered a prayer of thanks for that.

Salome nodded in response to her question and the group readied for their escape. They would more than likely run into more Thrak on their way out of the city, so Jinn would cloak them, but if someone bumped into them, they would be released from his magic. They had to stay together and stay close.

Salome whimpered as Hanzo picked Zophar up and threw him over his shoulders, but she didn't say anything when her eyes collieded with the Krazak's.

"Follow me." Jinn's voice pulled her back and she obediently trailed after him as he led them toward the exit of the Black Tower. Before opening the doors, he turned around to look at Salome. "No matter what you see outside, stay close to me."

"What do you expect us to see?" she asked.

"Death."

His response felt like a bucket of cold water had been dumped over her head. Of course there would be death. She'd never been involved in a true battle before and this would be her first taste in the horrors of war. Jinn's golden-brown eyes were kind, but once she nodded, a hardness washed over his face. She could tell he was prepping himself mentally, emotionally, and physically for what was on the other side of those doors and what was on the other side of the walls surrounding Gomorrah. No one would openly admit it, but those lost lives, their blood, was on her hands.

It was the smell that immediately assaulted her when the doors flew open. Burning wood, sulfur, smoke, blood, and the scent of decomposing flesh filled her nostrils and stung her eyes. Sound followed swiftly. It was incredibly loud and so chaotic in the city streets that it made it difficult to focus. Screams of the citizens, metal clashing against metal, collapsing buildings, Thrak roaring. It was overstimulating. As shocking and nauseating as the smell and sound of battle was, the sights were unmatched. Dirty children hiding behind their mothers' skirts, covering their ears, tears streaking down their ashen faces. Thrak stomping through the city, pushing anyone who got in their way to the ground. Fire raging at the city walls as smoke billowed toward the darkening skies. Hungry dogs feasting on freshly fallen Gomorrians.

It was chaos.

But even with all the dead strewn throughout the streets, she didn't see any of their allies. They were still at the city gates, surrounding the walls to ensure no one escaped but them. So, who was killing the citizens?

And if she hadn't seen it with her own eyes, she wouldn't have believed it. Thrak were killing men, women, and children in their own kingdom. Had they lost their minds? Were they following Matildys' orders? What did they gain in slaughtering their own people?

Jinn was right. War was ugly. But she never imagined the true horror until that moment. The Gomorrians were not just ruthless with their enemies, but with their fellow countrymen as well.

She slapped a hand against Jinn's back and closed her eyes. This was too much for her to take in all at once. She felt trapped, claustrophobic, and was terrified she was going to stop dead in her tracks and panic, giving one of the Thrak the perfect opportunity to stab her through the heart. And they would be right in doing so, because she had blood on her hands as well.

Jinn took her hand in his and squeezed it without looking back at her. A silent comfort. He must have felt her heart thundering in her chest and the anxiety washing over her entire body, but he never once looked back. He kept pulling her forward and she knew the others were right on her heels. Oifa had kicked her calves a couple of times to remain as close as she could to the magical prince.

They weaved up and down the streets for what seemed like an eternity. The Black Tower was in the center of the city, so to get to the wall was quite the hike. She knew Hanzo was getting tired of carrying Zophar's body, she could hear him breathing hard and his footsteps became heavier and slower. Oifa made sure he didn't fall behind and if he needed a break, she'd let Jinn know.

For two people who supposedly hated one another, Salome observed they made quite a good team.

After the fourth or fifth five-minute break, Jinn knelt in front of the others and whispered, "We are almost to the wall. There's a small grate to let sewage out. We'll have to slip out through there."

Salome was already covered in blood, dirt, and sweat. What was a little sewage? She bobbed her head in agreement.

Hanzo picked Zophar back up and his legs wobbled. Jinn volunteered to take over, but as he did the last few times the prince offered, the Krazak archer refused.

Jinn made sure everyone was huddled together before turning the corner, but as soon as he did, he slammed into a bloodied, broad-chested Thrak. The cloaking magic was broken, and a horde of enemy warriors quickly surrounded the group.

With weapons pointed at them, the Thrak leader stepped forward. He had a grotesque scar down the middle of his face and half of his nose was missing. Salome wanted to look away but couldn't. Fear was beginning to take over. Her hands shook as she searched and found her wolf dagger and unsheathed Zophar's battle axe. They would have to fight their way out or die, and she wasn't interested in the latter option.

"Well, well, well," the Thrak leader said in a gravelly voice. "What do we have here?"

Jinn was already armed with his tachi blades and put himself between the Thrak commander and Salome. He tilted his head to the side, looking almost amused by the disfigured soldier. "What happened to your nose?"

The question surprised not only the Thrak soldier but Salome as well. What was Jinn doing?

As the Thrak opened his mouth to speak, Jinn kicked up dust from the street, blinding the Thrak. Taking advantage of the brief moment of confusion, the prince sliced the soldier's head off and watched as it bounced against the street. As intimidating as the move was, the other Thrak were unmoved, and charged as a unit.

Salome gripped her weapons, but as two Thrak approached her, she froze. Every bit of her training seemed to vanish from her mind and her fear overtook her. She felt like she was wading through quicksand and was sinking. Looking around, Oifa and Hanzo had already accumulated a pile of bodies.

Salome was an expert marksman, but Hanzo was quick with his bow, faster than anyone she'd ever seen. And Oifa was ferocious, using her axe to strike any Thrak within arm's-length. Blood was splattered across her face, and she didn't seem bothered. She looked as if she relished the feeling of slaughtering her enemies.

Jinn was holding his own, whipping his blades around effortlessly, almost like an ancient dance. His gaze met hers and she saw her fear reflected in his eyes. "Salome!" he shouted as the two Thrak neared her, swinging their weapons.

Something in her snapped and she ducked, dodged, and eluded their attack. Her muscles ached with the effort. Her back was still healing, and she almost didn't get back up on her feet. Adrenaline was the only reason she jumped up to fight off her attackers. No one was going to be able to help her. They were being overrun with the company of Thrak. She batted her attackers' weapons away, clearly on the defensive.

Salome risked a glance at Oifa when she heard the Stormcrag yelp, and saw she had a slice across her thigh. Hanzo stepped in front of her and whipped out a blade from his belt and shielded her from attack. Oifa bit her bottom lip and forced herself to her feet, putting her back against Hanzo's and defending him from Thrak on the other side.

Jinn was dripping in sweat, his hair falling from its place and sticking to his forehead.

They weren't going to make it. She knew it. All of them knew it.

Salome managed to kill four Thrak, but she was quickly tiring. She'd not had anything to eat in almost two days and her injuries were still not completely healed, and according to the Gomorrian healers, wouldn't fully heal for months.

She heard Jinn hiss and turned around to see blood trickling down his arm. Instead of landing a fatal blow, the Thrak attacking Jinn backed off. The new Thrak leader had thrown his hand up in the air and halted the assault. The four of them were surrounded by the enemy, but it looked as if the Thrak were no longer interested in killing them. Capturing them and torturing them to a slow and painful death was more their speed and Salome was terrified that was in their future.

"I'm sorry," she sent through their bond. It was the first time she'd been able to access her magic since the Gomorrians had imprisoned her. *"This is all my fault."*

Jinn shook his head, pressing his forehead against hers while holding his injured arm. *"In life and death, we go together."*

"Bind them!" the Thrak leader bellowed.

A few Gomorrians stepped forward with manacles but before they were able to slap them on, something large thudded to the ground, shaking the foundation, and knocking everyone off their feet. Several more equally destructive quakes vibrated the ground, toppling buildings, and rattling bodies.

When the dust settled, Salome didn't see angry Gomorrians or bloodthirsty Thrak surrounding them. She found herself in a small crater and saw Zophar's body lying a few feet from her. With a groan, she crawled to his body, tears streaming down her cheeks, dirt itching her eyes. She had just managed to clutch his pale, limp hand in hers when she caught sight of a winged warrior approaching through the smoke. His bronze skin, dark hair, and golden eyes were hypnotizing. His white feathered wings and gold armor shimmered in the streaks of setting sun, signaling he wasn't mortal, but she wasn't sure what or who he was fighting for.

"Who are you?" she asked the warrior now hovering over her.

"I am Kayven, Commander of the Bellators." He extended his hand to her. "It is time to go, my lady."

Salome glanced over at Jinn, Oifa, and Hanzo, all of them injured and trying to find their bearings from the sudden blast. "My friends..."

"Will be coming with us." Kayven smiled and nine Bellators stepped into view, all muscular and battle ready.

"Please," Salome was feeling lightheaded, her hand still in Zophar's lifeless one. "Please don't leave him."

The Bellator Commander motioned one of his winged warriors to collect Zophar's body. Only then did she release him from her white-knuckled grip.

Salome thought she heard Odelia's voice. Glancing around, she squinted at a faint figure in the distance, and saw the Enchantress thrusting her hands into the dirt. She was making the streets and the ground beneath them move. Had Salome hit her head so hard that she was imaging it all? A loud rumble sounded, and screams echoed in a chorus as buildings collapsed and dust rose around them like a sandstorm.

"Princess?" Kayven drew her attention. He was crouched before her, unfazed by the chaos. "Are you ready?"

Salome sucked in a breath and nodded. "I'm ready." She grabbed Kayven's enormous, outstretched hand and once she was cradled in his muscular arms, he said, "Hold on tight," before rocketing into the sky.

She clutched Kayven's neck so tightly she was afraid she'd strangle him. If she was hurting him, he didn't show it. Her stomach churned with each second they climbed higher into the sky. She wasn't sure if she was afraid of the sudden ascent or invigorated by it. Burying her face in the crook of his neck, she took a deep breath of the eucalyptus and leather coating his skin. It was intoxicating enough to ease her upset stomach and calm her frayed nerves.

Mustering the courage to pull her face from his neck, she looked down. A part of her screamed, to be put back down on solid ground, but the other part craved to go higher into the sky to dance in the clouds. From their height, she could see sections of Gomorrah still under siege and sections collapsing into the earth. Odelia was using her magical powers to tear down buildings and she beckoned the earth to do her bidding by swallowing up the unholy city. She was destroying Gomorrah single-handedly. Salome saw a trail of rubble where soot covered buildings use to stand. A ghost of what was. A ghost that would haunt her for the rest of her days.

"You left her!" Salome panicked seeing the other Bellators flying behind them. "You left Odelia, you have to go back for her."

"She is in good hands, my lady." Kayven's voice was soothing, and it instantly calmed her, as if he had cast a spell over her, and she was forced to obey.

When she looked back down, there was a Bellator with shaggy hair standing beside her.

"My brother, Abba, will make sure she escapes unscathed."

Salome nodded, exhaustion beginning to claim her.

What was left of the sadistic Thrak continued to fight the Krazaks, Stormcrags, and Numbio, at what remained of the black stone wall. They had come for her – waged war, shook the very foundation of the entire kingdom, to save her.

Behind her, the Bellators carried her friends and she remembered where she'd heard the term Bellator before. They were in one of the history books her brother, Lykos, used to read to her. They were Immortal warriors. And if they were Immortals, that would mean they knew Harbona.

"Is Harbona…?" She wanted to finish the question with "alive" but wasn't sure she was ready to hear what the Bellator Commander would say.

Kayven met her nervous gaze and grinned. "Who do you think sent us?"

Her bottom lip quivered as tears slipped down her cheeks – a dam broken. He'd survived the Eldaar and answered her plea for help. He was alive. He'd come for her.

"Where are you taking me?" She asked when Kayven and a few of the Bellators headed away from the Bone Mountains.

"Oakenshire." Kayven's grip on her tightened, securing her to his chest for the long journey. "Rest, my lady. You're in safe hands."

CHAPTER 12
ADONIJAH

Adonijah had been driving himself mad with worry since the moment he found out Salome had been taken captive by the Thrak. He should have been there to protect her. He never should have left her side and now, he was a prisoner in his brother's camp, forced to stay put and let other people handle it. He was cursing himself and his reckless decisions for the thousandth time when he heard the pounding hooves of the Northmen returning from Gomorrah. They hadn't been gone long enough to lay siege to the city and he was terrified of getting an update from Pash.

He was pacing back and forth in Pash's tent when his brother entered and beelined for the wine decanter, pouring himself a healthy serving. Before his brother could take a sip of his drink, and before Adonijah could ask him what happened, Prince Thanos stormed in, nostrils flaring like a pissed off bull.

"You failed your mission, *Commander*!" He yelled at Pash with an air of superiority that rubbed Adonijah the wrong way. "You were supposed to conquer my city. Instead, you watched it fall to ruin! You worthless piece of sh -"

Pash drew his sword from the sheathe attached to his hip and pointed the tip against Thanos' chest. He eyed him silently, finally taking a sip of his drink. Once he swallowed, Pash said, "I would choose your next words carefully, *boy*."

Thanos' face reddened. "You dare threaten the Prince of Gomorrah?" he seethed.

"As of a few hours ago," Pash brushed past the whiny prince and slumped into one of the leather chairs, "the Kingdom of Gomorrah no longer exists, thanks to the Immortals."

"The Immortals?" Adonijah's eyes widened and Pash glanced over at him, looking surprised by his brother's reaction.

"Bellators leveled the city to rescue your princess. It would seem she has powerful and timely allies we did not realize she had."

"Your queen will hear of your failure." Thanos hovered above Pash who rolled his eyes.

"Scream of it from the tallest mountain, Thanos, no one will weep for you. No one will mourn the filth that was your kingdom. We should thank the Bellators for ridding Adalore of your cruel and wicked people."

Thanos was going to say something, but Pash waved him off with an irritated huff.

"Now, get out, before my patience and good graces run out." Pash stared at the pouting prince. "You live now because I allow it. You are a prince of nothing. Do not forget it."

Opening his mouth again, but thinking better of it, Thanos marched out of the tent just as furious as when he entered.

Adonijah snickered as he joined his brother for a drink. "I think you made him piss himself."

Pash smirked, "He might lose the appendage required to piss if he speaks to Niabi in that manner."

A silence settled between them as Adonijah downed the contents of his glass in one gulp. "Salome is alive?"

Pash nodded and rubbed his fingers around his temples. "From what we could see, she was in the midst of being rescued, when she was surrounded by the Thrak. The Bellators arrived in time to get them out of the city before it was leveled. All that remains of that unholy and cursed kingdom is the black soot that stained its people and walls."

Adonijah breathed a sigh of relief knowing she had escaped captivity. Her allies had leveled a kingdom to get her back. He wouldn't mourn Gomorrah. In fact, no one would. But he still felt sick to his stomach with the news of how she was rescued. "I should have been there."

"Even if I allowed you to ride with us, you couldn't have done anything to help her." Pash finished his drink and set his glass on the table between them.

"Who rescued her?" Adonijah asked.

Pash's exhausted gaze shot toward his brother. "Were you not listening, brother? The Bellators -"

"No, before," Adonijah cut him off. "You said she was in the midst of escaping when they were surrounded. Who was rescuing her?"

Pash's eyebrow arched as he reclined in his seat. "Is there a name you are hoping or dreading to hear?"

"Indulge me."

"I wish I could, little brother," Pash shook his head. "I don't know names, but I can give you descriptions. There was one male Krazak, one female Stormcrag, and a male dressed in black that Leoti said looked to be from the Eastern Lands."

Adonijah knew based on description alone, Jinn had been the one to rescue Salome and it made his heart ache. It should have been him rescuing her. Not the prince. "How did Leoti know all of that?"

"She's a warg; she's my eyes." Pash closed his eyes and threw a cold rag over his face. Adonijah hadn't seen him soak the towel, but he wasn't paying much attention to anything but the thought of Jinn and Salome together.

Adonijah nodded, having already forgotten the Andrago maiden's affinity. A useful one in battle to be sure.

Pash reached over and smacked Adonijah's chest. "You should be rejoicing that your princess is safe from the Thrak. Yet, here you are looking just as sullen, if not more so. What troubles you?"

Adonijah had a lot troubling him. Salome being captured by the Thrak and him not being the one to rescue her, was eating away at his soul. Jinn vying for her heart and being the one to set her free from captivity, left a bitter taste in his mouth, but he wasn't going to admit any of this to his brother.

"Adonijah?" Pash's voice ripped him from his jealous thoughts. "Is everything alright?"

"Aye." He nodded and pulled his pipe from his jacket pocket. "I need some fresh air. I think I'll take a walk around the camp."

"She's alive. You needn't worry about her safety in your absence."

It wasn't her safety he was concerned with.

Adonijah ducked out of the tent and lit his pipe. He strolled through the camp observing the differences between the Northern army and the Shadows. They kept to their separate groups; to Adonijah's left were the army soldiers and to his right were the Shadows. Both troops were in black armor, but the mercenaries were far more menacing, even while seated, eating and drinking. There was one Shadow he couldn't seem to find in his scanning. He knew he shouldn't be looking for the Nameless Rider because if he found himself alone with the monster, he wouldn't heed Pash's instructions or warnings. He would slit the beast's throat, avenging his mother, and accept whatever punishment his brother dished out.

He walked deeper into the camp, weaving through the different pathways, passing tent after tent, until he saw a large shadowy figure in the corner of his eye. He turned towards it and saw the back of the Nameless Rider. He wasn't alone. Adonijah's curiosity drove him closer. He could hear a muffled groan and high-pitched whimper, but the rider's bulky body was blocking his view. He stopped dead in his tracks when he realized it was a woman.

He hadn't seen many women in their camp. In fact, the only one he could recall was Leoti. He tip-toed closer and heard the Shadow hiss, "You will not deny me, witch."

"You forget who you speak to. I am the queen's daughter-in-law -"

"Your husband is dead. You are cursed. And I don't mind." The Nameless Rider yanked her by her braided hair and tilted her head up. "If you cooperate, you might enjoy yourself."

Leoti spit in his face and the beast smacked her across the jaw, sending her tumbling to the ground.

"I guess we'll be doing this the hard way." He smiled and tugged at his trousers when Adonijah interrupted.

"Lay another finger on her and I will cut your favored appendage off and feed it to the crows."

The monster whipped around, fury and intrigue flashing in his one blue eye. "Ah, the sell-sword. Come to play?"

Adonijah took another step, tossing his dagger haphazardly hand to hand. "Do you remember a woman named Satara?"

If the Shadow was caught off guard by the name or question, he didn't show it.

"Let me refresh your memory, monster. She lived on a farm north of Gomorrah, not far from here, actually. She had blonde hair, freckles, and brown eyes. Gershom ordered you to fetch her son, but instead you murdered her and burned down her cabin."

The beast flashed a sinister grin. "I remember her well. Sometimes, I even dream of her with her hands on my -"

Adonijah threw his dagger, and it pierced the Shadow's groin forcing him to his knees. He squatted in front of the screaming one-eyed man and whispered, "I have been looking for you for quite some time. And even though I shouldn't, I'm going to flay you here in your own camp, consequences be damned. My mother will finally have peace, and you will never terrorize another being again."

The Nameless Rider reached for his sword, blood pooling around his knees, but Adonijah whipped his second dagger out and thrust the blade into the giant's neck. He watched in satisfaction as the monster gurgled, drew his last breath, and keeled over onto the blood-soaked ground.

Adonijah retracted his daggers from the dead man's throat and privates, knowing he'd need to move the body before anyone came looking for the Shadow. But that could wait until he made sure Leoti was alright. She hadn't moved from her position on the ground and held her knees to her chest, eyes wide, and breathing steady. He hesitated before gently resting his hand on her arm. She didn't flinch, but her eyes shot to where his fingers were, then dragged up to meet his gaze.

"Are you alright?"

Leoti nodded, exhaling a breath as if she'd been holding it. "I'm alright."

He maintained eye contact with her as he explained what they needed to do next. "You need to get to your tent. If you aren't comfortable being alone, go to Pash's tent. He'll keep you safe until I come back."

"Where are you going?" A flash of concern lit her brown eyes.

"I need to get rid of the body before someone finds it." Adonijah glanced back at the dead Shadow. "Pash is going to kill me when he finds out."

"He won't find out from me." Leoti promised, releasing her knees from her white-knuckled grip. Whatever fear that had marred her features before was gone and in its place was fury. "Where will we hide his body?"

Adonijah was slightly taken aback but shook his head. "*We* won't be hiding his body. *I* will be hiding it-"

"You can stop with the theatrics. I am more than capable of helping you bury a body."

He furrowed his brow but realized she was going to be stubborn about this and he didn't have the time to waste arguing with her. "Fine. But if Pash finds us, I won't be able to protect you from whatever punishment he inflicts."

"Afraid of your older brother?" she teased.

He narrowed his eyes and huffed, "Hardly. But I am still technically behind enemy lines, so I won't be taking my chances in angering him."

"Enough talk." Leoti stood up and looked down at him. "What's the plan?"

Adonijah lifted from his crouched position, eyes fixed on hers, until he was towering over her. "I was planning to cut him up and scatter his body parts around the outskirts of the camp, but if you're too squeamish at the sight of blood-"

"Please," she puffed, quickly redoing her braid. "I learned as a youngling to hunt, skin, and dismember animals. He will be no different."

Adonijah didn't know whether to be impressed or bothered by her spunk. She was bold, he'd give her that.

"Alright, my lady," he motioned a hand toward the body, "after you."

She brushed past him but before she could get close to the dead man, they heard voices nearing.

"Damn." Adonijah grabbed her forearm and pulled her behind him. He went to unsheathe his daggers, but she tugged him to face her, and shook her head.

"What exactly is the plan here?" Her whisper held a bite to it. "You can't fight every soldier in a military camp. We need to get out of here. Come on." She pulled him to weave behind a row of tents.

She was right and for some reason that irked him. He reluctantly followed her, but before he was behind the tents and out of sight, two Shadows turned the corner, caught sight of their dead comrade and Adonijah creeping in the distance.

"You!" One of them cried, and they both drew their weapons.

Adonijah ducked behind the canvas and sprinted after Leoti. Thunderous footsteps boomed behind them and shouts alerting the other soldiers of what happened echoed through the camp. There was no way to escape unscathed.

Leoti sharply turned to the left and grabbed Adonijah by his shirt and pulled him into a dark corner where the tents met the rocky bottom of the mountain. There wasn't much space between them. Their chests rose and fell against each other and as fast as his heart was beating, so was hers.

Adonijah glanced down at her, his chin skimmed her forehead. Even in the dark, he could feel her gaze piercing him. He leaned forward until his mouth was touching her ear and the stillness of her body sent a shock of electricity through him. He wasn't sure he understood what it meant, but he pushed it to the back of his mind.

"I need you to find Pash and tell him what happened. Don't leave his side."

Leoti tilted her face to look at him. Her breathing was shallow. "What are you doing? You aren't seriously considering giving yourself up to them? They'll demand you be executed."

"Is that concern I hear in your voice, my lady?"

"Someone needs to be concerned about you. Clearly you don't care about saving your own skin."

"Just get to Pash. He'll know what to do."

"We can get out of here." Leoti seemed panicked and he wasn't sure why. "You killed a Shadow. They won't care why. Pash won't have a choice but to give you over to them."

"I guess I'll have to trust you to make sure that doesn't happen." Adonijah glanced over his shoulder to the narrow opening leading to the pathway where footsteps were nearing. "They didn't see you. They only saw me. I promise, I've been in worse situations. Now go. Find my brother."

Leoti clutched his shirt as he tried to leave, and he stared at her. "I didn't thank you for what you did."

"You don't need to." He placed his hand atop hers until she released him and for some reason he couldn't explain, he didn't want to leave her side. His eyes dragged down from her eyes to her full lips. "Find Pash." And then he stepped into the pathway, hands held above his head, a smirk across his face. "Looking for me?"

Shadows and soldiers alike surrounded him. Ophir, the bald Shadow and the man he learned was his uncle, marched toward him, fists clenched.

"You look angry, Uncle. What could possibly be troubling you this fine evening?" He lowered his arms and pulled his pipe out of his pocket. "Smoke?"

"You murdered one of the Shadows. One of our brothers." Ophir stared hostilely at him as he lit his pipe and pressed it between his lips.

"How good of a brother was he though?" Adonijah exhaled. "Were you two close? Should I offer my condolences?"

"You won't be laughing when we riddle your body with arrows."

"You have such a way with words, Uncle."

"Stop calling me that."

"Touchy, touchy." Adonijah tsked. "Pash said you had a temper, but he failed to mention that when you get angry your bald head turns red."

"You're lucky you're Pash's brother. Otherwise, you would have been slaughtered on sight. Chain him. Throw him in the pit." Ophir motioned for two soldiers to slap manacles on his wrists.

Adonijah extinguished his pipe and tucked it in his jacket before offering his wrists. "You really should be careful being out in the sun too long, Uncle. It might scorch your head and you'll look permanently flustered."

Clearly having had enough of Adonijah's taunting, Ophir took the hilt of his sword and struck him on the back of the head, knocking him out cold.

CHAPTER 13

SALOME

It was dark by the time Salome and Kayven hovered above the ancient castle of Oakenshire. In some sections of the walls, there were gaping holes, and what was once a bustling city, the center of the old world, was nothing more than dilapidated houses and deserted businesses. But even in its raw form, Salome could see the potential for it to be an ideal base of operations. The treeline of the Black Forest skirted in the distance around the outer wall of the once capitol kingdom and gave the watchtower a clear view of any approaching parties. On the opposite side of the keep, the Ignacia Sea stretched as far as the eye could see. When their allies arrived, by land or sea, there would be a place for them to stay.

Kayven tightened his grip around her back and underneath her knees, drawing her attention.

"Tired?" she asked, fearing he'd exhausted himself carrying her the distance from what used to be Gomorrah to what remained of Oakenshire.

"No, my lady," he smiled. "Harbona would never forgive me if I dropped you as we descended."

The mention of Harbona's name warmed her. She scanned the bailey for the Immortal's face until she found him standing on the moss-covered steps that led inside the keep.

Kayven landed gently and whispered in her ear, "Are you able to stand, Princess?"

After being off her feet for hours, she hoped she wouldn't fall flat on her face the second her feet hit the stone pavers, but she nodded and the Bellator gently set her down.

When she turned her attention to the steps where she'd seen Harbona, she saw he was already running toward her, brewing a fresh batch of tears to stream down her face. As quickly as she could, she hobbled to meet her friend.

The Immortal Seer crashed into her, wrapping his arms around her, refusing to release her. "Thank the Almighty you're alright," he murmured against her face.

"You're alive." She sobbed into his pristine robes, pulling herself away to get a good look at him. He looked young, not a wrinkle in sight, and the Immortal glow was back, though his banishment mark was still around his right eye.

Harbona nodded, relief washing over him. "Alive and in my true form."

Tentatively, she reached her hand toward his face and trailed a finger down his jaw. "You heard my cry for help."

"I'm just thankful we were able to get to you in time." Harbona said with a sadness that reminded her that not everyone made it.

Her lip quivered. "It's my fault, Harbona. Zophar's dead and it's all my fault." Harbona tried to comfort her, but she shook her head, grief once again ripping her heart in two. "I promised he wouldn't die in that cell. I failed him. I failed to save him. I failed to keep my word."

Harbona wiped the tears from her cheeks as the Bellator carrying Zophar's body arrived. When the warrior's feet thudded to the ground, the pavers beneath her shook. It wasn't a bad dream. Zophar was truly gone, and it was all her fault.

"No," she rasped, crumbling to the ground.

The Seer knelt before her, tilting her chin up to meet his gaze. "We must send him to the ancestors."

Salome's eyes snapped from her friend to the Bellator carrying Zophar's body. The bronze warrior marched to a small boat by the shoreline. It was decked out in furs, weapons, and flowers; then it hit her. It was already made up for a traditional Western burial.

"When did you know he was going to die?" she asked, her gaze fixed on the boat.

"I have many visions, Salome," he replied. "I only knew for sure he was gone, once he passed."

She sucked in a breath, biting her bottom lip to keep from sobbing. "Did you see this when you first came to us?"

"I saw Zophar's death the moment I met him."

That statement caught Salome's attention and she turned to Harbona. "You could have warned him."

"Death is not definite. I have seen Zophar die at least a dozen different ways." He slid bits of his platinum hair out of his face. "There was no way for me to be certain and if I warned him of all the ways he could have met his end, he would have been too afraid to live."

Salome couldn't argue with that logic, although she wished there had been something she could have done to save her guardian. Something she wished Harbona could have done to prevent his death. But it was all wishful thinking and far too late to do Zophar any good. He was gone and she would blame herself for the rest of her days.

Watching the Bellator carefully lay Zophar in the rowboat and slowly push it off into the sea tore at her heart and for a split second, she couldn't bear the thought of never seeing the Westerner again. She pushed Harbona away from her, sprinting toward the sea.

"No!" she cried. "Come back, Zophar! Come back! You can't leave me! I need you!" She waded into the sea, clawing at the water, desperate to get to the boat before he was swept away forever. "You can't leave me!"

The icy water was up to her neck by the time she made it to the boat, gripping the edge to steady herself. She ran her wet hand across Zophar's chest and shoved him, as if he was just in a deep slumber and needed to be woken up.

"Zophar?" Her bottom lip quivered as she rested her head against his chest. There was no heartbeat; she knew she wouldn't hear one, but she couldn't bring herself to let him go. "I'm so sorry, Zophar. It should have been me. It should have been me."

A strong hand clamped down on her shoulder. "Princess?" Kavyen asked softly, spurring her to wiggle out of his grasp.

"Leave me alone!"

"You need to let him go." Kayven didn't attempt to touch her again, but his golden eyes stared so deep into her soul, it almost hurt. "He has returned to the ancestors."

"It's not fair," she whimpered. "I just got him back."

He extended his hand, "We need to get you out of the water. It is far too cold - you will get sick."

"I'm not letting him go!" she howled like a wounded animal, baring her teeth at the warrior.

"Then I am sorry for what is about to happen, my lady."

Before she had a moment to react, the Bellator grabbed ahold of her and dragged her back to shore. All the while, she kicked, screamed, cursed, and clawed at him like a rabid beast.

"Let me go! Let me go!" She watched as Zophar's boat slipped further and further into the distance. "Please," she pleaded, tears flowing like a broken dam. "Please, let me go to him. It's all my fault. It's all my fault."

Once they returned to shore, a small crowd, including a distraught Harbona, had gathered to watch. Kayven held Salome firmly in his arms, not allowing her an opportunity to escape. She fought against him, but he held her close against his body in what could only be described as a hug.

Kayven tilted her chin up to look at him. "Rest, my lady." The Bellator thumbed a golden powder underneath her nose, and everything faded to black.

CHAPTER 14
CRISPIN

The next morning, Captain Ivar escorted Crispin back to the throne room where not only King Benaiah awaited his answer, but the royal family and court did, too. The king was seated in his throne, a mighty figure that exuded power. To his left sat his latest wife who looked to be only a few years older than Crispin.

To the king's right was Prince Ehrik, the firstborn and heir to the throne. Ivar's description of the prince was spot on, even down to the scraggly red beard and cunning blue eyes that narrowed as he approached the dais. He was Benaiah's spitting image and Crispin imagined they were similar in personality as well.

There were two more thrones on either side of the lower level of the dais. Next to Ehrik was Prince Ragnar, the spare. His eyes were blue, but weren't like Benaiah's eyes, they were like the sea, calm and wild all at the same time. His red hair was pulled back in a half knot and he rubbed a ringed index finger across his stubbled face.

Next to the queen lounged a hauntingly beautiful woman with long, wavy red locks that hung loosely right above her hips. Intricately plaited braids weaved along the sides of her head signifying though she was royalty, she too, knew how to wield a weapon. If Crispin were a gambling man, he'd bet she was Princess Lahki.

Crispin and Ivar bowed at the waist when they reached the dais and waited for the king to receive them. Those gathered fell to a hush, all eager to know the prince's answer.

"Prince Crispin," Benaiah motioned for them to stand. Though he smiled, Crispin could sense the venom behind the king's polite words. "Have you considered my generous offer? Agree to marry my daughter," he sliced an enormous hand through the air, pointing at the woman next to the queen, "and your friends will be pardoned of their crimes."

Crispin glanced over at Lahki, who didn't return his gaze. Her brown eyes were looking at Ivar who was standing next to him. Daring a look at Ivar, he found the captain stoically staring forward, his shoulders tense and lips tightly sealed. It appeared as if the captain was holding himself back or stilling his tongue.

"I have considered your offer, Your Majesty." Crispin forced himself to stop reading into Ivar and Lahki's behavior and answer the impatient king. "And I am afraid, I must decline." By the gasps and whispers of the courtiers, Crispin braced himself to incur the king's fury. Even Lahki and Ivar jerked in surprise, or relief, Crispin couldn't tell which.

"You decline my generous and merciful offer?" Benaiah's nostrils flared and his knuckles whitened as he gripped his armrests.

"I am sorry, but I cannot marry your daughter." Crispin turned his full attention to Lahki who met his gaze for the first time, and he realized she was relieved. "I assure you, this has nothing to do with you, Princess, but my own heart. I beg your forgiveness, if I have offended you."

Lahki's lips parted to respond but before she could utter a word, the king jumped from his throne and pointed an accusatory finger at the prince.

"You have not only offended me and my daughter, but you have proven yourself to be no ally of the West. You are like your father in every way, and you shall pay greatly for this dishonor."

Benaiah waved his hand, and the guards surrounded him, pushing Ivar away from the prince. Crispin whipped his head toward Ivar who looked completely caught off guard. The prince protested as soldiers slapped iron shackles on his wrists and bound his hands behind his back, but his cries fell on deaf ears. He was dragged from the throne room and taken to a cell in the dungeons beneath the castle. Once he was thrown into the barred prison, and his eyes adjusted to the dim lighting, he realized the crew of the *Shadow of Death* were already sitting in matching cells around him.

"Crispin?" Rahab's voice sounded to his right. He saw her sitting in a cell next to Ziggy. He was the only one in a holding cell by himself. Haldane, Phex, Corwin, Ondrej, Rafi, Nubis, even Master Penn and her Keepers were stuffed into cages.

Crispin slammed his hands against the bars rattling them. "That bastard!"

Rahab stuck her arms through the bars and Crispin embraced her from his side. He kissed her forehead and whispered, "I'm sorry."

"The king wasn't going to let any of us walk out of here alive." Rahab tilted his chin up to meet her gaze. "We were targets before we even met. If anything, you spared us from being executed on the spot."

"We've been in worse scrapes before," Haldane chimed in from the cell across the hall. "We'll find a way out of here, too." He winked and grinned, but Crispin sensed his panic.

He'd failed them and underestimated Benaiah. Had he agreed to marry Lahki, he'd only be signing his life away to serve the Westerners. He never would have been free to rule the North, not with Benaiah playing puppet master.

~

A COUPLE OF HOURS LATER, footsteps dusted the stone steps leading into the dungeons. Crispin hopped up and made his way to the cell door to see who was coming. His heart was lodged in his throat imagining Benaiah sending soldiers to haul the pirates away and having them hanged in the town square. But when Ivar rounded the corner with a torch in hand, he breathed a little easier.

"Ivar?" Crispin waved at him, and the captain walked toward him. "What are you doing here?"

"His Majesty doesn't know I'm here," Ivar whispered and looked over his shoulder at the stairs. "I don't have much time. The king…" the captain rubbed his forehead and grimaced. "I didn't know what he had planned until it was too late. I assure you I wouldn't have let this happen to you or your friends."

Rahab scoffed from her cell, her back flush against the cold stone wall, legs stretched out across the damp floor. "Oh, I'm sure you're real torn up about it."

Ivar narrowed his eyes at her, but instead of a snide remark the Westerner replied, "I'm sorry. This wasn't supposed to happen. This is not honorable."

"What does the king intend to do now?" Crispin asked, nausea and guilt bubbling in his gut.

Ivar met his gaze and he looked positively exhausted. "It would seem the king has sent word to your sister in Northwind that he has you as his prisoner. He intends to hand you over to her once the ship arrives."

Crispin wasn't surprised by that, but it wasn't his main concern. "And the crew? What of Master Penn and her Keepers?"

"Master Penn and her Keepers will be released in a couple of days and escorted back to The Sisters." Ivar paused and Crispin's heart sank. "He has ordered the crew of the *Shadow of Death* to be executed by the end of the week."

"Why wait?" Rahab growled. "Why not execute the lot of us now?"

"It seems our king -"

"*Your* king." The pirates said in unison which brought a smile to Crispin's face.

Even Ivar couldn't hide a smirk at the blatant defiance. "The king has declared your execution a day of rest for the citizens of Borg. There will be a festival and all Borgians will be in attendance to watch you die."

Crispin rested his forehead against the iron bars. "Why are you telling us this?"

"I found this before the king's soldiers could go through your belongings." Ivar dug through his breast pocket and fished out a rolled-up parchment. Crispin recognized it and it appeared Rahab did too when she leapt up from her lounged position.

She rushed across her cell and hissed,"That's mine!"

Ivar took a step away from the adjoining cell, just out of her reach. He kept an eye on her when he unraveled it and asked, "What do you know of Leeondris?"

"What do *you* know of Leeondris?" She shot back.

"Look," he lowered his voice and once again looked over his shoulder toward the stairs. "I want to help you, but if you don't tell me how you know Leeondris, I won't be able to do anything."

Rahab and Crispin exchanged a glance and the prince nodded for her to tell him. Reluctantly, Rahab explained how the pirates knew Leeondris. How he'd saved her life and after years of being a member of their crew, he just disappeared. When they received word that he was in trouble, they set out to The Sisters to get information from the Witnesses. Rahab hadn't had the heart to open the parchment, fearing he was dead.

"So, you never opened this?" Ivar asked, clearly skeptical.

"Like I told you," Rahab rested her elbows against the bars, "I was afraid it would say he was dead. I wasn't ready to know the truth."

Ivar handed her the note and she nervously read it before gasping. "He's alive?"

"And in Borg." Ivar snatched the piece of paper back, rolled it up, and stuffed it in his pocket. Scuffling at the top of the staircase alerted Ivar to the shift change. "My time is up. I have to go." He turned his focus to Crispin and extended his hand through the bars. "You may be in enemy territory, Prince Crispin, but you have friends."

Crispin clasped Ivar's hand and shook it before the captain pulled away, grabbed the torch, and retreated up the steps.

CHAPTER 15
ADONIJAH

Cold water splashed Adonijah's face, waking him up in an instant. He had no idea how long he'd been unconscious and made a mental note to pay his dear uncle back tenfold for the welt on the back of his head.

"Wake up." A familiar voice barked with a swift kick to his boot.

Adonijah opened his eyes as he wiped the water from his face. His gaze rested on Pash and Ophir's frowns, prompting him to grin. "What a delight to wake up to your smiling faces."

Ophir took a step forward but stopped when Pash held out his arm.

"It appears you're still cross with me, Uncle."

"Shut up, Adonijah." Pash hissed. "Do you know what kind of trouble you're in?"

"Enlighten me, brother."

"The Shadows are demanding your execution." Pash admitted with sadness in his eyes.

"And?" Adonijah motioned for him to continue.

"Show some respect, bastard." Ophir spat at Adonijah's boots.

Adonijah shook his head. "Truly, Uncle, you need to reign in that temper of yours. It'll stop your heart one day."

Ophir muttered a string of curses before Pash ordered him to leave. Reluctantly, the old man left the brothers in silence.

"Someone really should talk to him about his health. He looks unwell," Adonijah smirked.

Pash sat on the ground in front of him and released the tension he'd been holding in his shoulders.

"When am I to be executed?" Adonijah asked.

Pash peered at his brother, raking a hand through his hair. "Why'd you do it? We had a plan."

"Did Leoti talk to you?"

Pash nodded. "She told me."

"Then you know why I did it."

"You didn't have to kill him."

"Was I supposed to ask the monster nicely to leave the lady alone?"

"Damn it, Adonijah, you're not taking this seriously." Pash rubbed a hand down his face. "My hands are tied. You murdered a Shadow, one of the brothers. You are to be executed at dawn."

Adonijah nodded his head. "When you see our father again, tell him, I send my regards."

"That's all you have to say?" Pash scoffed, fury raging in his eyes.

"If you're looking for an apology, I haven't one to offer. If you're looking for an explanation, you've received one." Adonijah leaned forward. "What else would you like me to say?"

Pash stood up and brushed the dirt off his pants. "I can't save you," he said softly, averting his gaze.

"I know." Adonijah bobbed his head in understanding. "Make sure Leoti isn't there to watch."

Pash looked like he wanted to say something else but decided against it. He walked through the flaps, leaving Adonijah chained to a pole in a tent he could only assume was a makeshift prison. He knew when he first left the City of Bones to kill the Nameless Rider that there was a chance he might not make it back to Salome, but with his execution looming, he wished he could hold her one more time to tell her that he was sorry for leaving. Maybe he could make it up to her in the next life.

KNOWING there were only a few hours left before dawn and his inevitable execution, caused sleep to elude him. He was honest when he told Pash he wasn't issuing any apologies, but that didn't mean he was going to accept his fate easily. He'd break free or die trying when the Shadows collected him for punishment.

As his mind plotted any feasible escape, he heard two thuds outside the flaps of his tent. Two figures dressed in black and armed with longswords entered, dragging the two soldiers posted to guard his prison inside.

Adonijah sat straighter. "It's a little early to fetch me, isn't it? Even I can see the sun has yet to make an appearance."

"Are you always this annoying?"

"Pash?" Adonijah tried to get a look at the man beneath the hood.

Pash flipped his cloak back. "We don't have much time."

"You're rescuing me?" Adonijah didn't see that coming.

"You really thought I wouldn't?" Pash almost looked offended.

"We don't have time for this," Leoti hissed. She unlocked Adonijah's manacles with the keys she yanked off one of the unconscious soldiers. The second he was free he twisted his fingers around the raw area of his wrists. "Well, come on. We haven't got all night."

Adonijah hopped up and grabbed her arm, turning her around to face him. "Thank you."

"A life for a life." She bowed her head slightly and Adonijah couldn't take his eyes off of her.

"Oh, it's fine. I'm just the one who hatched the entire plan in the first place. No need to thank *me*." Pash poked his head out of the tent to take a quick look before they darted for the outskirts of the camp.

"I'll thank you once we get out of your camp intact."

Pash grinned, "Oh, we'll get out alright. It's keeping ahead of the Shadows once we escape that'll take some skill."

"We'll manage." Leoti stepped forward to join Pash at the entrance. "With my warging affinity, your Shadow training, and Adonijah's tracking, we'll remain hidden."

"I appreciate your enthusiasm," Pash rolled his eyes, "but don't underestimate Her Majesty's Shadows. They're an elite killing force for a good reason." He handed Adonijah a leather case that held his daggers and tossed him his longsword. "I trust you will only use that if you have to."

Adonijah placed the daggers in their holsters and sheathed his blade. "I will do my best to refrain from slaughtering everyone in sight."

"Ass." Pash shook his head before taking one last look outside and nodded. "Let's go."

Swiftly, but quietly, the trio weaved through the camp. Pash knew exactly where the guards were posted and managed to avoid them. After a few minutes, the outskirts of the camp were within sight. But Pash stopped suddenly, halting the other two.

"What's wrong?" Leoti whispered.

A soldier had crawled out of his tent to relieve himself in the direct path they were headed. Their exit was blocked. They could either wait until the soldier finished and went back to bed, they could eliminate him, or they could try to flee a different way. Adonijah knew what he would do, but followed his brother's lead. Pash had them hide behind tents and wait for the soldier to finish. But instead of going back to his tent, the soldier decided a midnight stroll was what he needed instead.

Pash grumbled something Adonijah couldn't quite make out. The brothers made eye contact and Pash mouthed, "Knock him out."

"Slit his throat?" Adonijah cupped a hand to his ear and feigned confusion.

Pash narrowed his eyes and shook his head. "Knock. Him. Out."

Adonijah smirked and nodded that he understood. As the soldier neared their hiding spot, Adonijah waited for him to pass, then locked his arms around the unsuspecting man's neck from behind. He held him there until he passed out and they deposited him back inside his tent. With nothing blocking their gateway to freedom, the trio slipped out of the Northern camp and headed north until the darkness swallowed them.

CHAPTER 16
SALOME

Salome woke up with a splitting headache. Lifting a palm to her forehead, she could feel the throbbing beneath her fingers. She squinted as she looked around the room, realizing she wasn't in the Gomorrian dungeon. Then she remembered she had been brought to Oakenshire, and the uninhabited castle of King Greygor was now their new base of operations. But that wasn't the only thought that flooded her mind. Everything slammed into her like a crashing wave beating against the rocky cliffs. Zophar was dead. She failed to save him. She thought of her arrival, seeing Harbona again, after weeks apart, only to crumble into a shadow of her former self.

She flashed back to Zophar's funeral and how she lost herself in grief. She swam out to the boat that carried him to the next life but was held back. She fought the Bellator who grabbed ahold of her, wishing she could follow her guardian. The Bellator that saved her apologetically wiped a powdered substance under her nose and that was the last thing she could remember.

Now, she was in a large bed that was nowhere near as comfortable as the one she had in the Isles of Myr, but it beat the damp dungeon floor beneath the Black Tower. She pushed herself up slowly, her head still throbbing. The curtains in her room were closed, shrouding her bedroom in darkness. It reminded her too much of her prison cell. Struggling to get on her feet, she shuffled to the window, gripped the heavy velvet drapes, and ripped them open. She coughed as dust rained down on her but once she was able to see clearly, she stared out her window at the most breathtaking view: The Ignacia Sea. It was so close, she wanted to jump out of her window and feel the cool water swash against her skin.

Her attention turned toward the castle walls. Even though part of the grey-stone wall was crumbling, she saw men and women from different kingdoms in Adalore working together to refortify the former capitol city.

She withdrew her gaze from the people in the bailey back to her room and was pleasantly surprised that after hundreds of years of neglect, it wasn't in complete shambles. There was dust and cobwebs in the corners of the ceiling and the mirror attached to the ornate vanity was so dirty she couldn't make out her own warped reflection. She ran her fingers across the floral wallpaper, a dirty film stained her fingers and she wiped her hand clean against her pants.

It was then she noticed someone had changed her out of the blood-stained, tattered clothing she had worn in Gomorrah, before her escape. She now had a clean pair of brown trousers, a loose white shirt, and sitting neatly at the foot of her bed was a new pair of leather boots. She sat on the edge of her mattress, hearing the creak of her weight sinking, and strapped her boots on.

Curious, she walked over to the mirror and used one of the towels that had been left on the vanity next to the wash basin to wipe the glass clean. It took some effort, but once she saw herself clearly, she started to examine her injuries. Her lip was still swollen and bruised from the Thrak backhanding her in Matildys' throne room. She slipped off her shirt and saw bruises along her ribcage. Slowly, she turned to get her first glimpse of the scars the arrows she'd taken to the back left behind. Two ugly, fresh scars marred her back. She exhaled a deep breath. She really should have died from the injuries.

Death does not want me yet, she thought. That was the only logical explanation. The Gomorrians had put a lot of effort into healing her, making sure she not only survived, but that she was in the best condition possible for her public torture and execution. She shuddered at the thought. Had Jinn not arrived when he did…

Where was Jinn? How long had she been asleep?

She shook her head, rattling the questions free for now and returned to examining her body. Thankfully, apart from the bruises, some cuts on her arms, a busted lip, scars on her back, and exhaustion, she was physically alright. But mentally, the nightmares and flashbacks would take months, if not years, to recover from.

Tears ran down her face when Zophar's face flashed in her head. Her heart ached and she retched, but there was nothing in her stomach to throw up. Overwhelmed with grief and anger, she snatched a candlestick off the vanity and threw it against the wall. The thud echoed in the room and Salome heard feet shuffling toward her wooden door. The doorknob jiggled and she instinctively lunged for her dagger sitting on her nightstand. Whenever she heard footsteps approach her cell in Gomorrah, she wasn't sure if it would be the healers, a servant with her meal, or the Thrak finally coming to harm her.

The door swung open, and her hand shook as she clutched her wolf dagger tightly. But there were no Thrak coming for her. She'd been rescued. The people who entered were ones she recognized, ones she loved. Kai and the Qata Vishna twins, Rosalina and Seraphina, stopped when they took in her appearance.

"Are you alright?" Kai grabbed Salome's shirt from the vanity and slowly approached, offering it to the princess.

Salome opened her mouth to speak but no words came out, only a whimpering cry, and the tears weren't far behind.

"Bring a healer," Kai whispered to Rosalina who immediately turned on her heel to obey.

Salome didn't want Rosalina to fetch anyone looking the way she did, but the twin was gone before she could object.

Seraphina made her way to Salome and helped her sit on the edge of the bed then knelt before the princess. "You are safe, my lady. You can rest."

"Zophar's really gone." Salome's voice was raspy from disuse and a fresh batch of tears dripped down her jawline. "I didn't save him. It should have been me."

Seraphina grabbed Salome's hands and said in a gentle tone that was unlike her, "Do not blame yourself for surviving. I know for a fact your guardian would say the same thing."

"If I hadn't been careless and left the City of Bones without protection, Zophar would still be alive." Salome buried her face in her hands. "This is all my fault."

Kai stepped forward, "You can't do that. You can't blame yourself for his death. Death called -"

"No matter what you say," Salome interrupted the Easterner, "I will always blame myself."

The room fell silent. Kai and Seraphina busied themselves with cleaning and organizing her room until Salome was ready to speak.

"How long have I been asleep?"

"About a week," Kai answered.

"A week?" Salome's eyes widened.

"Harbona believed it necessary for you to rest," Seraphina chimed in with her no-nonsense tone. "You wouldn't have followed the Healer's orders otherwise."

Seraphina was right, but a week? That was far longer than she had originally estimated. She thought she'd been sleeping for a day or two. But an entire week?

"I want to speak with Harbona." By her tone, Seraphina realized Salome meant she wanted to see the Immortal immediately, so she bowed her head and left the room to find him.

Kai was leaning against the wall next to Salome's vanity, arms crossed over her chest.

"Has anyone heard from Adonijah?" Salome bowed her head and stared at the splintered floor.

Kai shook her head. "No."

Her bottom lip quivered, "I'll never understand why he did this to me. Why he left, why he lied."

"I wish I could give you an explanation," Kai said softly, pushing up from the wall, "but I don't know why he left or why he hid his identity from you. Maybe, if your paths cross again, you can get the answers you seek."

"If I ever see Adonijah again, I'll kill him."

Kai reached to touch Salome's shoulder but stopped. "You're angry, you're hurting, and you're grieving, but don't allow that to corrupt the goodness in you." The Easterner shifted her weight from one foot to the other, clearly uncomfortable. "Maybe there is someone who can give you answers."

AFTER THE HEALER examined Salome and gave her a cup of herbal tea to help ease her pain and speed up her recovery, she left the princess so she could speak with her awaiting visitor and promised to check on her again that evening.

Salome sat in the receiving area attached to her bedroom and silently stared at a fidgeting Jacobi. He looked healthier, obviously eating well now that he was out from under the Shadows' thumb. His right knee bounced, and his eyes looked everywhere but at her.

Kai stood in the corner, watching quietly like a predatorial cat and for a second Salome wondered why she was guarding her and not Jinn. She'd meant to reach out to Jinn through their bond but wasn't sure what she'd say to him. 'Thank you' seemed inadequate for what he did to rescue her, and she preferred to tell him in person.

Jacobi coughed and Salome's gaze darted across the coffee table to look at him.

"Kai told me you showed Adonijah the way to the Northern Military encampment." Salome watched him with a calculating stare.

That wasn't the only thing Kai had told her about Jacobi. He'd joined their ranks and, in an attempt to redeem himself for his cowardice in the Tree House Forest, he'd become the head baker in Oakenshire. He took his duties seriously and made sure everyone on castle grounds was well fed. Salome was oddly proud of the redhead, but this wasn't a friendly catch-up session. This meeting was strictly to find out what he knew about the night Adonijah left.

Jacobi nodded his head. "Yes, I showed him how to get there. He told me the Shadow who gave the order to slaughter the people in our village was the same Shadow who killed his mother." The baker swallowed hard before continuing. "He said he could kill him, if I took him."

Salome was oblivious to Adonijah's past and didn't know his mother had been murdered by Shadows. She motioned for the baker to continue. "And once you got him there…?"

"He told me to stay hidden and if he didn't come back, that I should return to the City of Bones and deliver a message to you."

"What was the message?" Her breathing quickened but she steadied herself. What were his last words to her?

"He told me to tell you he was sorry."

Somehow, even with an answer to one of her questions, she didn't feel any better. She almost felt worse. He left knowing there was a possibility he wouldn't return. He left knowing he'd be sorry when she learned the truth. He left knowing he'd lied to her about his past, his true identity, and that he'd leave her shattered in his absence.

He left.

She had to continue to remind herself that Adonijah was Gershom's son, and although that part of his past was hard to swallow, she never would have held it against him. The fact that he hid it from her when he demanded transparency and trust from her made her want to vomit. He didn't trust her. That's what it boiled down to. And where there was no trust, there was no love.

Salome realized Jacobi was watching her in silence and she collected herself, forcing the neutral mask back on her face.

"Thank you, Jacobi." She stood up, signifying their conversation was over and he jumped to his feet, making sure to grab his chef's hat from his lap. "And thank you for joining our company. Kai has raved about your pastries."

Kai stood stoically in the corner, but Jacobi beamed over his shoulder at the Easterner. "She is welcome to have as many as she likes."

The warrior flashed a half-smile which might as well have been her doing a full-blown cartwheel. Jacobi bowed to Salome before Kai opened the door for him to leave.

Salome slumped back into her chair and Kai made her way forward. There was a slight limp in her gait where she'd taken an arrow during the skirmish outside of the City of Bones, but otherwise, you'd never know she'd been wounded. "Should I send for the healer?"

The princess waved the idea off and motioned for the Easterner to sit. Once Kai obliged, taking the spot Jacobi vacated, Salome asked, "Why are you guarding me?"

"What?"

"You're Jinn's protection, his Ryoko Naga." Salome cocked her head to the side, eyes fixed on every slight move or twitch Kai made. "Why aren't you with him?"

"The prince instructed me to guard you while he is away."

Salome's heart sank. She'd hoped to see him, even if she didn't know what exactly to say. "Where is he?"

"Not all of the Bellators flew straight to Oakenshire. Prince Jinn, Oifa, and Hanzo all stayed behind for their minor injuries to be tended to and they were to make the trip with the remainder of the army."

"When will they arrive?" she asked.

Kai shrugged one shoulder. "From our reports, they should be here any day."

"So," Salome's eyes bounced from Kai's face to the leg that had been struck by an arrow. "Are you guarding me because of what happened when the Thrak captured me?"

Kai's body tensed. "I have been meaning to thank you for what you did, Princess -"

"You would have done the same for me."

Kai nodded solemnly. "And that is why I will watch over you, until I am no longer needed."

CHAPTER 17
CRISPIN

Days passed, and they hadn't seen or heard from Ivar. They were given some water and a poor excuse for a meal once a day, but no one seemed to be interested in eating. Any day now, all the pirates would be executed and there wasn't anything Crispin could do about it. He tried asking the soldiers who brought their meals to take him to the king, but they acted like they didn't hear him, as if he were invisible. It was then it hit Crispin, that once again, his title meant nothing. He had no riches, power, throne, crown, or army to back him up. He was just as ordinary as the next person and had little sway in enemy territory.

Even though the pirates tried to keep their spirits up, sharing stories of their adventures, telling crass jokes, or hurling friendly insults at one another, Crispin could tell they were all worried, frightened even.

Crispin had not rested well in days, but when sleep finally summoned him, he laid on the cold, stone floor and shut his eyes. He wasn't sure how long he'd dozed off for, but when Rahab reached through the bars and tapped his foot, he sat up instantly and stared at two cloaked figures standing at the entrance to his cell. He couldn't see their faces, and they didn't immediately identify themselves.

"Who are you?" Crispin tried to mask the fear lacing his voice. "What do you want?"

The two figures exchanged a quick glance before pulling their hoods off their heads. Crispin stood up and rubbed the heels of his palms against his eyes. Surely, he must be imagining them, but then he heard them speak and it confirmed he was wide awake, and they weren't figments of his imagination.

"Prince Crispin." Lahki gripped the bars of his cell. "I apologize on behalf of our father. He does not speak for all Borgians."

"Princess Lahki," Crispin bowed his head in a show of respect and Rahab folded her arms over her chest. His gaze bounced from Lahki to her brother, Prince Ragnar, leaning against the bars lazily. "Prince Ragnar, this is a surprise."

Ragnar brushed a thumb over his jawline before standing up straight. At full height, the prince towered over Crispin's six-foot frame by a few inches. It had been quite a long time since Crispin felt small.

"Captain Ivar told us that we have a friend in common." Ragnar's voice was smooth as honey despite his rugged appearance. Crispin noticed the black tattoos on the prince's wrist and wondered if they extended up his arm.

"It would appear we do," Crispin nodded.

"Then I would like to make a deal with you."

"Forgive me, but I don't know if I believe you will uphold your end of the bargain."

Ragnar's smile crinkled the corners of his eyes. "I am not my father, Prince Crispin."

Crispin was inclined to believe him, his eyes spoke truth, but he was still wary. "What is it you want?"

"We can get you and your friends out of here," Ragnar leaned forward and lowered his voice, "but you will owe me a favor in the future."

"What kind of favor?" Crispin's eyebrow arched.

"I will send word when the time comes." Ragnar reached into his cloak and pulled out a ring of keys, making sure Crispin could see them. "Do we have a deal?"

Crispin wasn't sure he should agree, but what other choice did he have? If the prince had learned of the pirates' relationship with Leeondris from Ivar, clearly, they were friends or at least on the same side. He glanced over at Rahab, then scanned the faces of the weary pirates and relented.

"You get us out of Borg, and I will owe you a favor."

Ragnar flashed a wicked smile and unlocked Crispin's cell door. "Nice doing business with you, *vargr*."

Crispin eyed him suspiciously. "What does that mean? Vargr?"

Ragnar chuckled and offered Lahki the keys to unlock the other cells. "It means 'wolf' in Borgian."

Before Crispin could respond, Lahki had opened all the cells and given the pirates their confiscated weapons before Ragnar led them deeper into the dungeons.

"Stay close," Ragnar ordered as he marched before them, guiding the group with a flaming torch.

"And keep quiet." Lahki added as she walked next to her older brother.

The deeper they traveled through the sloped dungeon halls, the spookier it became. The smell of decay mixed with the humidity made it difficult to breathe. But they continued to follow Ragnar and Lahki, hoping it would lead to their freedom and not an ambush.

After hours of silently trekking forward, Crispin could hear the chirping of birds and could see light. When they reached the end of the tunnel, the prince realized they had been led out of Borg completely underground and were now at the edge of the forest that he had grown up in. Dawn was upon them; they'd walked through the night and were free. Or at least, Crispin hoped they were free.

Ragnar paused at the mouth of the tunnel before motioning the group forward. When they were all standing in the light, hooded figures stepped out from the tree line. A tall man with broad shoulders marched toward them. Every pirate reached for their weapons but Ragnar, held out his arms to embrace the vigilante.

The Western prince turned toward the group, patted the newcomer's chest, and smiled. "I believe, you know one another."

The man removed his hood to reveal himself. The crew of the *Shadow of Death* stood speechless, as if they were seeing a ghost. Rahab slowly approached the red bearded man. She reached a hand out and touched his freckled face.

"Leeondris?" she whispered reverently.

Crispin had always wondered what the mysterious Leeondris looked like and was surprised to find a man not much older than himself. It looked like Leeondris and Ragnar were around the same age, mid-twenties, and his long, red hair and grey-blue eyes identified him as a true Westerner.

"You're a pretty sight for sore eyes, Ray," Leeondris' deep voice boomed, and a set of perfect white teeth flashed. He leaned in to embrace the pirate, but Rahab seemed to snap out of her stupor and punched the Westerner square in the chest. Hooded rebels lurched into attack positions, but Leeondris held a fist up and the vigilantes relaxed. "It would seem you haven't changed a bit." Leeondris smiled.

"That's for leaving," she snorted, popping a hip to the side.

"And what do I get now that you've found me?" His eyes danced as he wiggled his eyebrows.

Rahab nearly tackled the rebel to the ground in a bear hug. "Stars above and seas below. I thought you were dead."

Leeondris smiled against her temple, stroking a large hand through her icy blue locks. "I'm not so easy to kill."

Crispin felt a pang of jealousy pool in his chest at how close – how familiar – they were. He was tempted to clear his throat to remind Rahab he still existed, but she beat him to the punch when she ripped herself from Leeondris' grasp and met his gaze.

"Leeondris, this is Crispin. Prince of Northwind."

"So, you're the man who insulted not only the king, but our princess as well?" Leeondris eyed him with an air of suspicion. "Why did you turn down the chance to marry our princess? Did she not suit your Northern desires?"

Crispin's eyes darted to Rahab before returning to the burly Westerner. He was ready to puff out his chest and put the rebel in his place, when he noticed Ragnar smirking beside Leeondris, his eyes dancing in mischief.

Leeondris bellowed a laugh when Lahki swatted his arm. "You brute. You shouldn't give the prince a hard time."

"Oh, come on, Lahki," Leeondris wiped a tear from his eye, a wide grin plastered on his face. "Did you see the look on the princeling's face?"

"That *princeling* now owes us a favor for helping him and his friends escape." Ragnar's voice hummed in delight, drawing all eyes.

"And when will you be calling in that favor?" Crispin asked, wishing he wasn't in the prince's debt.

"At the proper time." Ragnar's smile reminded Crispin of a fox and it made him nervous. He turned to Leeondris. "I trust you can ensure safe passage for the prince and his company out of our lands?"

Leeondris bobbed his head, a seriousness washed over his features. "Consider it done."

"Good," Ragnar seemed pleased. "This is where my sister and I leave you. We must return to the city before anyone notices our absence."

Crispin extended a hand to the prince who looked at it quizzically. "Thank you."

Ragnar hesitated a moment before snatching Crispin's hand in his. His palm was littered with callouses and proved him to be just as much a warrior as he was a politician. "It was a pleasure doing business with the future King of the North. Our paths will cross again, Crispin." And with that, the prince turned and marched toward a carriage awaiting to take him back to Borg.

Lahki paused in front of Crispin and gave him a peck on the cheek. "Thank you, Prince Crispin. Have a safe journey." Not waiting for him to respond, she turned and quickly followed her brother to the royal carriage and hopped inside. The driver whipped the horses, and they raced back to Borg.

Crispin couldn't shake the feeling that Ragnar would pop up at the most inconvenient moment and he'd have no choice but to honor the Western prince's request.

Leeondris turned to face the group of pirates and lifted his arms out to his sides and said, "Come! We'll get you back to our camp and prepare you for your journey."

CHAPTER 18
ADONIJAH

The trio couldn't stop to rest, if they were going to keep out of the Shadows' reach, but when they became too tired and hungry to continue, they set up camp and sat around the campfire to keep warm from the forest chill. They only had one small tent and the brothers wholeheartedly agreed, Leoti should be the one to have it. She disagreed, but when the distant roll of thunder echoed through the woods, she changed her mind.

Adonijah easily caught three rabbits and Pash had already stoked a roaring fire to roast their dinner. Leoti showed no signs of squeamishness when she took the animals from Adonijah and skinned them, prepping them for their humble feast.

Though they spent the wee hours of the night speaking of their adventures, upbringings, and travels, Adonijah found himself tuning out of the conversation every so often with one person on his mind. He had to keep reminding himself that Salome had escaped. She'd been rescued, despite the fact, he wasn't the one there for her, as he once swore, he would be. His failure, his broken promise to protect her, was slowly eating away at him. But thinking of Jinn being the one to risk everything to get her out of Gomorrah – thinking of the prince with his arms around the woman he loved, and being countless miles away from her, was a new form of pain and torture.

Would she wait for him? Would she even want him anymore? Would he ever see her again?

Though deep in thought, he couldn't shake the feeling he was being watched, so he glanced up and across the campfire, he caught Leoti staring at him.

"You must see something you like, if you're gawking that hard," Adonijah rolled his shoulders back with a devilish smirk.

Leoti didn't look away. "Rollo used to stare off into the distance when he was deep in thought, too."

He shifted uncomfortably. "He's the queen's son?"

"He was."

Adonijah suddenly remembered hearing the prince died unexpectedly and felt like a cad for remarking about him so flippantly. "I'm sorry for your loss."

Something in Leoti's eyes made him feel like she saw Gershom when she looked at him and he hated it. He hated feeling the need to apologize on behalf of his father's transgressions.

As if she could read his mind, she shook her head. "I do not blame you for your father's sins."

"If only everyone saw it that way," he sighed and focused on his rabbit.

"This princess of yours…"

"What of her?" His eyes narrowed, expecting her to attack or slander Salome.

"You said she doesn't know who you really are." Leoti picked up a piece of roasted meat and chewed it. "If you care for her as you claim, why lie to her?"

"I didn't lie to her," he huffed.

"Omitting the truth is still lying." She set her plate on the ground by her feet and leaned forward. "Why did you not tell her?"

He hesitated. "You don't blame me for Gershom's sins, but she might think differently."

"Maybe it isn't her opinion you're frightened of. Maybe it's your own."

He looked up at her. "What do you mean?"

"Has she given you any reason to suspect she would hold an innocent person responsible for someone else's wrong doings? Do you truly believe she would blame you for assassinating her mother and brothers? Has she ever blamed anyone for their deaths, other than Gershom?"

Adonijah smirked, baring his teeth in a predatorial way. "Just your queen."

"Which is understandable," Leoti didn't miss a beat. "If I were in her position, I would blame Niabi, too."

Pash made his way back to the campfire after relieving himself in the woods and plopped down on a stump. "Tread carefully, Leoti. Your words sound treasonous."

"Funny," she scoffed. "My words seem like the last thing we should be worried about, seeing as we are on the run from Her Majesty's Shadows."

Pash shrugged a shoulder. "A misunderstanding."

"Your brother gutted a Shadow," Leoti snapped. "You think our queen will forgive a *misunderstanding*? On top of it, we are helping him evade capture, making us traitors- "

"For the greater good," he interrupted with a bite in his tone. "Once we kill Gershom all will be forgiven."

"So you say."

Pash motioned his hand toward the blackened forest. "You can leave at any time, if this is too much for you to handle."

Leoti looked at Adonijah. "What do you say?"

Adonijah swallowed his food, confusion written all over his face. "What?"

"Do you think I should leave?" Leoti asked.

Adonijah seesawed from the Andrago to his brother. Both were irritated, but he wasn't sure what to say to ease the tension. She was right. She and Pash were now fugitives alongside him. They had committed treason to rescue him and whether the queen loved Pash or not, with her reputation, they might not be forgiven.

"If you want me to leave," Leoti's voice sliced through his thoughts and he met her fiery gaze, "then I will leave."

"Why do you care what I think?" he asked.

There was a mischievous twinkle in her eyes when she said, "I trust you to be honest."

Adonijah knew what she was doing. What she was implying. He hadn't been forthcoming with Salome, hadn't been completely honest. He hadn't lied, but he hadn't been truthful. She was giving him a chance to grow, to redeem himself in a way. Even though Pash would be irritated, they had a better chance of completing their mission if they banded together, instead of pushing her away. And whether he wanted to admit it or not, he hoped she wouldn't disappear in the middle of the night.

"Stay." Adonijah cleared his throat and tried again. "I want you to stay."

Pash rolled his eyes and refocused on his dinner.

With a satisfied grin, Leoti stood up and made her way to her make-shift tent. "Goodnight."

As soon as Leoti disappeared into her sleeping area, Pash flashed a disapproving look at Adonijah. "What is going on?"

"We need her – "

"We don't," Pash interrupted, "but that's not what I'm talking about."

"Then what are you talking about?" Adonijah lit his pipe, bored with his brother's question.

"You have feelings for her."

Not a question. An accusation. A statement.

Adonijah stretched his legs in front of him and scoffed. "Because I told her to stay, I must have romantic feelings or ulterior motives?"

"You can deny it all you like, but I have eyes, and I am very good at reading people," Pash maintained his intense glare. "In fact, I've made a career of it.

"Then I suggest you request a healer examine your eyes, because you are clearly reading into this."

"Am I? I haven't seen Leoti smile in months." Pash sipped water from his sheepskin and wiped the excess from his lips with his sleeve. "And don't think I haven't caught you eyeing her when you think no one is watching."

Adonijah's face flushed, and he attempted to hide it by scratching at his beard. "My heart belongs to another."

Pash tossed the rabbit bones into the fire and set his plate on the ground before standing. "Your heart may belong to Salome, but your attention is fixed on Leoti."

"You're wrong." Adonijah hated that he sounded like a child in his denial.

Pash planted his foot on the stump he'd used for a seat and rested an elbow on his knee. "Let me ask you this. Where do you see yourself in the future? You've killed your mother's murderer and we are on our way to kill our father. Forgetting about this inevitable war between Niabi and Salome; what do you want, should you survive?"

Before answering, Adonijah took a minute to think. Pash was right. His mother's murderer was dead. He and Pash were on their way to kill their father. After that, he had no other passions or goals. His entire life had been so centered on revenge that he never thought about what else he wanted in life.

"I…" Words failed him.

Pash reached forward, clamping a hand on his brother's shoulder. "I'll tell you what I want, should I live through this war. Family. I want Niabi and I to escape the madness of Northwind, to live a life where no one knows us, to live in peace, and to raise our child without fear of someone harming him or her." Adonijah's eyes flashed at the mention of a child and Pash nodded with a smile. "She told me before I left the city. So, what is it you want?"

Adonijah shrugged. "I wish I knew."

"Do you believe Salome would choose a life roaming Adalore with you?"

He knew she wouldn't, and the thought pained him more than he cared to admit.

"She would choose her people before you, then?" Pash asked and it was like a punch to Adonijah's gut.

"How do you do it? Living in your queen's shadow and being second to her crown?"

Pash sank to the ground and sat next to his brother. "You come to realize the woman who bears the crown is different than the woman without it. If you desire a life free from the responsibilities of titles, thrones, crowns, and rulers, then let Salome go. There is no happiness for you there."

"You say that because you do not wish for me to be higher ranking than you, when she wins this war." Adonijah smirked but realized if Salome did win the war, that would mean Niabi would most likely be dead and Pash's dream would be unattainable. That thought didn't sit well with him.

Pash bumped his elbow into his brother's arm playfully. "I say it, because should you choose someone who shares the same goals and desires, you might find yourself content. The Andrago way of life isn't for everyone." He glanced at Leoti's tent. "But it might be perfect for someone like you."

"Were you not just lecturing me about having feelings for Leoti?"

"Not lecturing. Just pointing out my observations."

"Why don't you like her?" Adonijah exhaled a puff of smoke.

"It has nothing to do with her." Pash looked up at the twinkling stars before continuing. "Her father, Tala, and I do not see eye-to-eye. He is Niabi's oldest friend, and he is very protective of her. I don't blame him. Truthfully, I'm grateful he watches over her when I'm not there."

"Are you sure there's nothing more between them?"

Pash shook his head. "She was married to his childhood best friend. They both lost their spouses and rocked the very foundation of Adalore to right Dichali's death. Their bond will always be a strong one, but her heart belongs to me. Of that I have no doubt."

Adonijah shifted his weight. "I wish I had your confidence."

The Shadow patted Adonijah's back as he stood. "Love can be a blessing and a curse." The brothers stared at Leoti's tent again when they heard movement, but she didn't emerge. "A decision like this doesn't need to be made tonight. Get some rest, brother. Tomorrow will be a long day and I have a feeling, Niabi's Shadows aren't too far behind." Pash retreated to his sleeping bag on the other side of the campfire and settled down for the evening.

Once his brother was fast asleep, Adonijah's thoughts flooded him. He thought about Salome and their future together, Pash's goals and desires, Leoti and the

Andrago way of life, and the heartache that one, or both of them would suffer, if they didn't get what they wanted. There was a great possibility that one, or neither of them, would make it out of the war alive, and he wasn't sure which one he'd rather it be.

CHAPTER 19
SALOME

Once the healer cleared Salome to start physical activity again, she jumped at the chance to work out the kinks in her still recovering body. Kai, Rosalina, and Seraphina helped her get ready and escorted her to the section in the bailey that had been set up as a training arena. Numbio, Stormcrags, Krazaks, Easterners, Qata Vishna – they were all exercising and sparring together, learning new tricks and techniques.

"You made it!" Cato's cheerful face instantly brightened Salome's mood and she embraced her Stormcrag friend.

"It's good to see you, Cato."

"I've been wanting to check on you but someone," he rolled his eyes at Seraphina, "forbade me from doing so. Something about you needing rest."

"Well, you can visit me whenever you want now." Salome smiled. "I've been cleared for activity."

"Well, then," Cato scratched his short white hair and took a step back, motioning toward the sparring grounds, "after you, my lady."

"Don't be a fool," Seraphina hissed. "She isn't sparring with you."

"Oh no?" He grinned at the Myridian and playfully bounced his eyebrows. "Does that mean *you* want a piece of me?"

Seraphina whipped out the blades strapped in her back holsters. "I'd prefer *all* of you."

"Gross," Rosalina crinkled her nose and waved them away. "Go on, love birds. Get out of here."

Salome turned to Kai and Rosalina once Seraphina and Cato walked off together, to spar or kiss, she wasn't so sure of anymore. "What was that about?"

"You missed a lot while you were gone," Kai muttered.

"It's almost obscene," Rosalina rolled her eyes. "Seraphina is… *happy*."

"You say that like it's a bad thing," Salome laughed and the Qata Vishna stared at her and shrugged.

"It's weird. I've never seen Seraphina happy." Rosalina scratched her chin. "It's almost unsettling."

"And you don't have your eyes on someone?" Kai's question sounded more like an accusation.

Rosalina blushed and instinctively her eyes drifted to a handsome Numbio warrior across the bailey. "Damn you, Kai, and your Ryoko Naga observations."

Kai shrugged. "I see things."

"And by the looks of it," Salome elbowed Rosalina's arm, "he might think the same about you."

The three of them glanced over at the Numbio Rosalina identified as Obi. With his smooth, dark skin, brown eyes, and muscular body, it wasn't difficult to see why Rosalina found him irresistible.

"You should go talk to him," Salome insisted.

"She won't," Kai snorted. "She will keep watching him from afar wishing he'd make the first move."

Whether Kai was goading the Qata Vishna or just picking on her, Salome didn't know, but either way, it spurred the Myridian to march her way toward Obi. His smile was bright, and though Salome was ecstatic for her friend, it felt like a kick to her gut. She had two men smile at her that way and now, neither one was with her.

"Come on, Kai," Salome nudged the Ryoko Naga to the sparring grounds, refusing to feel sorry for herself any longer. "I guess that leaves you and me."

If Kai was reluctant to spar with her, she didn't show it as they quickly took their stances. The Easterner pulled a couple daggers from her belt and Salome mirrored her by pulling her Qata Vishna blades from her back.

Though her body was sore and seemed rusty from weeks of disuse, muscle memory kicked in and propelled her in the match-up. She suspected Kai was pulling her punches and purposely left herself open to an attack to test her theory. When Kai didn't take the opening, Salome growled in frustration.

"Why are you holding back?"

Kai didn't deny it, nor was she surprised when she was called out. "This is your first session back. I didn't want to hurt you."

"Don't do that," Salome hissed, eyeing her friend. "Don't treat me like I'm fragile. Fight me like you would fight any of them," she motioned around the bailey.

"Princess -"

"Fight me!" Salome wiped sweat from her brow. "Fight me or find me someone who will."

A moment passed and Salome wasn't sure if her friend would do as she asked, until Kai took her fighting stance again. Salome readied herself and when the Easterner flew at her, she braced for impact. As Kai's leg swept through the air, aimed at Salome, something in her slowed. Instead of eluding the blow or blocking the attack, Salome froze. Moments flashed in her mind in the blink of an eye:

Hugging Crispin before they parted ways.

Zophar being stabbed.

Blood gushing from Ranalda's slit throat.

Kissing Adonijah in the City of Bones.

Touching Jinn's face in the dungeons of Gomorrah just to make sure he was real.

Watching Zophar's cold, lifeless body float away.

The stench and chaos of battle raging around her.

Death's presence thick in the air, not quite ready to claim her.

Her hand shaking every time she clutched her weapons, her fighter instinct quiet.

The Easterner's foot slammed into Salome's chest knocking her off her feet. Everyone in the bailey stopped their individual exercises and sparring sessions to gawk at Salome lying on her back, muttering a string of curses under her breath. The princess lifted herself up on her elbows as Kai approached. The Ryoko Naga's normally neutral face was filled with worry which angered Salome.

Kai offered Salome a hand, apologetic for harming her, but Salome waved Kai's hand away and quickly told everyone to get back to their sparring. Before anyone could stop her, she stormed off, embarrassment and rage stewing in her belly. She stared at her hands and noticed them trembling. Balling her hands into fists, she held them tightly at her sides and marched back to the castle, hoping no one noticed.

The moment she crossed the threshold into the castle and turned down the long hallway, a winged warrior stepped out of a dark corridor in front of her, blocking her path. She stopped and stared at Kayven, the Bellator who had rescued her and flown her to Oakenshire. She then noticed no one was around and she wasn't naïve enough to believe it was a coincidence.

"What do you think you are doing, Princess?" Kayven folded his arms over his enormous chest and quirked a dark eyebrow.

"I could ask you the same question, Bellator. Now move." She was not in the mood for lectures or games.

"Move me."

"What?" she growled.

"If you want to get by," Kayven said a bit louder, "make me move."

"I don't have time for these mind games, Bellator." She attempted to side-step the Immortal, but he stepped with her, remaining a huge obstacle in her path.

"I said, make me move."

She looked up at him, tears welling in her eyes from immeasurable anger. "Why are you doing this? Let me pass."

He towered over her and glanced down at her weary face. "Running will not make you stronger."

"Sometimes it's best to retreat before it's too late."

The sternness in Kayven's face softened. "Look, Princess, I know what it feels like to lose a loved one. I know how it feels to see your friends fall in battle. I have lived long enough to taste the bitterness of being the one to survive and wonder why Death called them and not me. I see all the same signs in you, and I beg you not to run."

Salome quickly surveyed the corridor making sure they were still alone. She met his golden gaze and whispered, "I don't think I can do this. I've done terrible things. "

"What are you running from?" he asked.

"I was born with two different color eyes; everyone thought I was cursed," she spoke so softly she was afraid he wouldn't hear her, but she pressed on before she could change her mind. "I didn't want to believe them, but I am starting to. Everyone I love, anyone who gets close to me, ends up dying and I'm left to pick up the shattered pieces of my heart, wondering who might be next. Praying that it's me so everyone else may be spared."

"Death -"

"Comes for us all," she interrupted and rolled her eyes in irritation. "I know that already."

"If you run now, you will not stop." Kayven stepped closer, towering over her. "You are not weak for being afraid," he whispered.

Her bottom lip quivered, and she cleared her throat to keep from weeping. "I'm so tired."

Kayven's feathered wings flared. He wrapped her in his wings giving her privacy in case someone came inside. He gently tilted her chin up to look at him. "That is why you have us. Your friends, your allies. We are here to lift you up when you feel you do not have the strength to go one step farther. Together, we will win. But we need our leader to keep pushing with us." His eyes were burning bright and were filled with hope. "I can help you get through battle fright, but you have to want my help."

"Battle fright?" she asked.

"You have been through things most mortals will never experience. Trauma haunts us all in different ways. I can see it in your eyes. You are having flashbacks even with a weapon in your hand." Kayven lowered his voice, as if he were telling her a secret. "You have stared Death in the face and said, *'not today'*. You survived for a reason. It is time you remember why."

Salome knew the Bellator was right, but she wasn't ready for anyone else to know. "They will all lose faith in me, if they see I can't wield my weapons," she shifted her feet.

"Then we shall practice in secret." Kayven said, matter of fact. "Meet me and Abba at midnight on the practice grounds." He retracted his wings, arms clasped behind his back, the vision of a true soldier.

"Why are you doing this?" She had to know.

Kayven hesitated, and for a moment she was afraid he wouldn't answer, but then he said, "Harbona spoke highly of you mortals. Said he would willingly die by your side than live another thousand years without you. He gave up his birthright, his title, and his home, to walk amongst you. I did not understand why he valued you mortals more than his own people, but seeing you fight, seeing you overcome your deepest fears and fiercest enemies, made me respect you. And if Harbona would willingly lay down his life to save you, then I can make damn sure you are equipped to win your battles."

"And if I can't overcome this? This battle fright?"

Kayven smiled, "I swear on the Eldaar, you will wield your weapons again, my lady." He bowed and turned to leave, but she grabbed his forearm.

"Kayven." He glanced back at her. "Call me Salome."

He bobbed his head. "Until tonight, Salome."

SALOME SPENT the rest of the afternoon in her chambers resting. When darkness fell, she went about her normal bedtime routine, but instead of slipping into her warm, inviting bed, she donned her sparring clothes and crept down to the training grounds. More than once she thought she should just ignore the Bellator and figure out this battle fright on her own, but if Zophar were present, he'd fuss at her for being far too stubborn for her own good. She swallowed the tears that itched to be released and before she could talk herself out of the midnight training, she strutted into the bailey.

Kayven and Abba were already there waiting. How long had they been there? She was five minutes early and they were lounging, as if they had been there for hours.

"Ahh!" Kayven hopped up from the ground and dusted off his pants. "You are finally here."

"What are you puffing on about?" she rolled her eyes. "I'm early."

"Well," the Bellator pulled his shoulder-length hair out of his face, looping a hair-tie around half of his locks. "Show me what I am working with."

She glanced over Kayven's shoulder at Abba, who was leaning against the stone wall, one foot pressed against the castle, arms crossed. She was curious about how he got the scar that ran down the side of his face but kept her questions to herself. She didn't like when people asked her about her two-colored eyes, so she refused to put Abba in that uncomfortable position. "And what is he supposed to be doing? Lurking in the shadows?"

Kayven barked a laugh and turned to look at his brother. "It is better that you spar with me. Abba is too advanced for mortals."

"So, what I'm hearing is he's the better brother," Salome teased, and it was Abba's turn to chuckle.

"Now, I will have none of that," Kayven snorted. "If you are to learn to defeat battle fright, you will have to pay attention."

Salome was trying to make light of the situation but her attempt at humor seemed to offend the Immortal which was not her intent. "I'm sorry," she extended an olive branch. "I didn't mean to upset you."

"Upset me?" Kayven cocked his head to the side, looking more amused than anything. "You will have to do a hell of a lot more than tell a bad joke to hurt me, Princess."

~

"I CAN'T DO THIS ANYMORE!" She flung her hand in the air to stop Kayven's attack. A solid hour had passed, and she was no better than before. Her hands were still shaking, and the flashbacks still haunted her.

"Stand up, Princess." The Bellator motioned for her to rise from her crouched position.

"I'm tired." She shook her head, sweat dripping down her forehead. "It's not working. I'm not getting any better."

"Did you really think you would be back to normal after an hour of training?"

"I at least thought my hands would stop shaking," she snorted. "Or the flashbacks would…" She bit her bottom lip to keep it from quivering and slowly stood up, a foot shorter than the muscular Immortal. His bronze skin glistened in the moonlight, a light film of sweat coated his arms, but he didn't look remotely tired.

"Where are you going?" Kayven asked as she dragged her sore legs toward the castle entrance.

"I'm going to bed." As she brushed past him, she caught Abba's golden eyes.

He didn't look disappointed or surprised – he almost looked as if he'd expected her to give up and she wasn't sure why it bothered her so much.

"We are not finished," Kayven barked. "I told you I would help you overcome your battle fright. It will take some time, but I believe you can do it."

She waved him off, not looking back as she shuffled away. "I'm done."

"What would Zophar say if he saw you like this?" Kayven challenged. "What would he think of you quitting?"

She spun around, fury raging in her eyes. "Don't speak of Zophar!"

"What would he think," the Bellator commander pressed, "of the girl he raised to be a warrior running away from her fear instead of facing it?"

She clenched her fists, her nails digging into her palms. "I said, don't talk about him!"

"You are angry."

"Yes, I'm angry!"

"Good." Kayven smiled and removed his shirt, exposing his bronze, muscular torso. He motioned for Salome to punch him. "Take your best shot. Let go of your anger."

"I'm not going to hit you."

"Your anger will consume you, if you harbor it."

Salome shook her head. "My anger is what fuels me."

"Anger will not win you battles." Kayven took a heavy step toward her and to her credit, she didn't shrink from the Bellator's encroaching figure. "Anger will cost you your life when the dust settles. Anger is an emotion. Emotions are fickle and change from day to night. But your training, your discipline, and your level-headedness is your constant. It is your beacon of light in the darkness. It is your salvation. Training will not fail you at the end of the day. Your emotions will. Now, hit me. Let go of your anger, Salome. Let go of your hatred. Neither will serve you well."

Tears streamed down her cheeks as fire raged in her eyes. Kayven motioned her toward him again with a comforting smile. "Hit me, Salome. I promise, I will not break."

Faces flooded her mind. Zophar. Nym. Mika. Korah. Lykos. Her mother. Her brothers. Ranalda. When Crispin popped into her head, the possibility that he was also gone, caused her to fly into a rampage. She clenched her fists and screamed. She could have sworn the very foundation of the castle trembled beneath her feet. Salome launched herself across the practice grounds, landing blow after blow against Kayven's rock-hard chest. She punched him repeatedly, screaming, crying, wailing, until she was too exhausted to hit him anymore. She threw her head back and yelled again, releasing her fear, her anger, her grief. Her knees gave out and she started to crumble to the ground but Kayven's strong arms caught her and held her against his chest. The Bellator didn't say a word as she released her sorrow and battled her demons. When she opened her eyes, she saw he not only kept her firmly in his embrace, but had shielded her with his wings. She heard his heart beating and the rhythm brought her peace. She pushed away and gazed into his eyes.

"How do you feel?" he asked, retracting his wings.

"Free," she replied. "I feel free."

Kayven smiled. "Choose your weapon."

Abba stepped forward, "Perhaps the mortal needs to rest, Kayven."

The Bellator nodded. "I forget you mortals do not have the same stamina -"

"I choose blades." Salome interrupted him and swiped the Qata Vishna knives from the holsters on her back. She risked a quick glance at Abba who seemed satisfied by her response. As the quiet Bellator leaned against the stone wall, retaking his familiar stance, she turned her focus back to Kayven. "If you are too tired, we can call it a night. I know you're pretty old."

Kayven smirked, cracking his neck. "Some would say, I am in my prime."

"How old are you?" she asked, curiosity getting the better of her.

"I am three thousand years old." He answered without missing a beat and unsheathed a pair of knives.

Salome's mouth dropped open, but she quickly closed it before he could make a snide remark. She flipped her knives around her hands and flashed Kayven a playful grin. "I'll go easy on you this time, old man."

He took his stance and snorted, "Do your worst, mortal."

CHAPTER 20
CRISPIN

The rebel camp was filled with tents and everything they had was meant to be easily packed, in case the group needed to move at a moment's notice. From what Leeondris shared with them that night around the crackling fire, the King of Borg had lost the favor of the people and change was in the air. Leeondris had received word from Ragnar that he needed his help, if he was going to overthrow his tyrant father and provide a better life for his people. But more importantly, Benaiah was planning to launch a thousand ships to destroy the Pulauans once and for all, and Ragnar couldn't – wouldn't – let that happen. So, Leeondris dropped everything and left the pirate life and his Pulauan family behind, to aid and serve his childhood best friend. As Ragnar and Lahki worked in the inner circle of the royal court, Leeondris rallied the people to their side and their cause, and Ivar kept his eyes on the seas. They were a formidable team and serving their people was the highest honor. When the time was right, Ragnar and those loyal to Borg would make the move to overthrow Benaiah and keep Ehrik from taking the throne and following in their father's footsteps. It was a dangerous game they were playing, but one Leeondris said he would give his life for.

With that information planted in his brain, Crispin could only imagine what the rebel prince would ask him to do when he called in his favor. Hopefully it wouldn't cost Crispin something he valued.

Even though Crispin spent most of his life in the Treehouse Forest in the Western Lands, he never kept up with the politics of the capitol. He couldn't blame Ragnar for the coup, and if what Leeondris said about Benaiah was true, he had a gut-wrenching thought that Rahab would band with the members of the crew that planned to join in on the fight to protect their home against the Borgian King. The thought of her not continuing the journey to Oakenshire, pained him.

Ziggy readily agreed to stay with the rebels when Leeondris asked her to help, since she was back in her homeland. And wherever Ziggy went, Nubis was sure to follow. Crispin happily gave them his blessing to fight with the Borgian rebels. He had grown quite fond of the lively redhead and the broody Stormcrag but he wasn't going to drag them to Oakshire to fight for him.

Once everyone had eaten and ushered to their tents for the night, Leeondris bade them goodnight and informed them they would be fully prepared for their journey in the morning. Crispin was relieved when Haldane, Phex, Corwin, Ondrej and Rafi assured him they would be continuing with him until he was seated on the White Throne of Northwind.

"We've come this far," Haldane said, clasping his hand on Crispin's shoulder, "and I believe I've got some unfinished business to settle with a bastard king and conniving witch."

Crispin still bore the weight of Palma's torture and death and he swore he would do everything in his power to help Haldane and his crew get their revenge.

Once he was escorted to his tent, Crispin slipped inside, kicked off his boots, stripped off his shirt, and groaned from exhaustion, before he stretched out on the small cot. He knew they would have to pass through what was left of the Tree House Forest on their way to Oakenshire, and he was terrified of what he was going to find. Or not find.

Korah, his young friend who had been killed by the Shadows months earlier, popped into his head. He remembered the boy's laugh and how excited he was when he agreed to teach him how to use a bow. He missed the freckle-face redhead tremendously and it broke Crispin's heart that the boy was nothing more than a memory.

He ran a hand down his face, swiping a lone tear from his eye and rested his palm on his chest. He'd be a liar, if he said, he wasn't thrilled to be back in the Western Forests, after what seemed like a lifetime of traveling to exotic places. While lying in his tent, he came to realize he was tired and wanted to go home. He wanted to sleep in his own bed, eat Zophar's venison stew and be surrounded by the people who loved him. But that life was gone and the home he took for granted, even cursed on some occasions, no longer existed. How spoiled and selfish he had been months ago when he wished for a life outside of the small village. Now, he would give up just about anything to go back to the comfort of his old life.

His thoughts drifted to Salome. He hadn't seen or heard from her in months. He prayed she was alright and safely waiting for him in Oakenshire. The stories he would swap with her and Zophar put a smile on his face. He couldn't wait to see them. To hug them and maybe feel at home, again. It would only be a few more days before they are reunited, and he couldn't wait.

Exhaustion was setting in and his heavy eyelids closed. He was drifting to sleep when suddenly, lips were pressing against his. Startled, he opened his eyes and there was Rahab, now putting her weight on top of him. Crispin grabbed her hair and gently pulled her back to look at her. She groaned in frustration, and he chuckled.

"I didn't realize we were assigned roommates." He stroked his fingers up and down her tattooed arm.

Rahab flashed him a smile that made his heart flutter. "Thank your lucky stars I'm your bunkmate and not Phex or Rafi."

"I don't know," he shrugged, wrapping his arms around her. "I think it would be fun to cuddle with Rafi. How does he get his mustache to end with such sharp points?"

She giggled and kissed his chin. "Rafi sleeps with his eyes open."

"And how do you know that?"

"Because he tends to sleepwalk, too. It's horrifying."

Crispin barked out a laugh and twisted to his side, pulling Rahab onto the cot beside him. "Well then, I guess I'm lucky the First Mate is sharing my bed."

He couldn't help but think this might be the last time they would cuddle up together. Back in the city, she had promised to be his queen, but after hearing Leeondris' report, he knew there was a good chance she might want to stay and help. Although scared to hear the answer, he had to ask anyway.

"Do you want to stay here?" he whispered.

Rahab tilted her head back and stared into his eyes. "Stay? Why are you asking me that?"

He shrugged, "Because of what Leeondris told us about Benaiah's plans to attack Pulau."

"Do you…" she cleared her throat, "do you want me to stay?"

"No," he shook his head, "but I also don't want to ask you to fight in my war, when your people need you."

"What makes this your war, princeling?" She pushed herself up onto an elbow and glared down at him.

He mirrored her posture and leveled the playing field. "It's about my kingdom-"

"You cannot claim a war, Crispin. This isn't just about you anymore." Rahab's brow furrowed. "Uri and Nezreen are involved now, and they were our enemies long before they were yours. When all is said and done, you will end up on the White Throne, but it's not just about seeing you crowned king. It's about avenging our dead and taking back our freedom." She wiped hair off his face and leaned closer. "Where you go, I go. That's that."

"I can't argue with that."

"Then kiss me already."

Crispin laughed, "Greedy."

"I'm a pirate," she whispered, inching closer to his lips. "I take what I want."

"And what do you want, Rahab?"

"You."

"You have me."

Rahab leaned across his chest and blew out the candle on the small, wooden end table. "I intend to."

BIDDING FAREWELL TO LEEONDRIS, Ziggy, Nubis, and other crew members of the *Shadow of Death*, wasn't easy. Crispin was off to Oakenshire, with Penn and her Keepers and a handful of heavily armed pirates – thanks to their rebel friends. He knew they would have to cut through the Tree House Forest and as they drew closer, his stomach soured. At the rate they were walking, they would be forced to set up camp in the small village and he wasn't looking forward to it.

It was dusk when they finally reached the Tree House Forest and seeing what had become of his childhood home was worse than he imagined. Disaster. That was the best and only word he could use to describe what little remained of the burnt village. The once bustling community was wiped out, and the very spirit and soul of the town had vanished.

Memories of his childhood flashed before his eyes: their first night in their new home; Zophar reading to him and his sister nightly by the fireplace; sparring with Salome as children and seeing their skills improve throughout their teenage years.

He turned and looked from the main square where Korah had been killed and spotted his treehouse. Little remained, but the front steps and first floor were surprisingly intact. His breathing slowed; and for a moment, he felt like he was drowning.

"You hard of hearing, lad?" Haldane slammed his hand down on Crispin's shoulder, freeing him from his thoughts. "Are we to camp here for the night?"

Crispin scanned what remained of his once home and nodded, holding back tears and taking deep breaths. "We'll rest here tonight."

The captain bobbed his head in agreement and began ordering his men to set up camp for the night. Phex volunteered to start the fire, but the pirates unanimously agreed the explosives expert shouldn't be within ten feet of the fire lest they all blow up by mistake. Ondrej and Rafi gathered firewood from some of the dilapidated houses and were in charge of lighting the bonfire. Phex and Corwin set up the sleeping bags that Leeondris had sent with them, and Haldane worked on cooking the food they had in their packs.

Penn and her Keepers pulled their weight during the trek; the fact they were blind didn't hinder nor slow them down and Crispin enjoyed speaking with the Master of Keepers during their walk through the Western Forests. She lived an interesting life and whenever they took short breaks, he insisted she show him some of her fighting moves. She used the vibrations in the ground and her heightened senses, to fight her opponents. Every time they faced off, he got his ass handed to him and loved every second of it. Remarkably, he began to improve and started to hold his own against her.

She must have sensed him watching her because she stopped what she was doing to face him. Her smirk crinkled the black wrap around her eyes. "Another lesson tonight, Prince Crispin?"

"If it's all the same to you, Master Penn, I think I'll let you take a stab at the pirates tonight."

Phex, Corwin, Ondrej, and Rafi all stopped what they were doing and scowled. Penn flashed a wicked smile in their direction and nodded. "Yes, perhaps I will take a stab at the pirates."

"Meaning?" Rafi crossed his arms over his chest.

"Meaning," Penn clasped her hands behind her back and stepped toward the crew, "we will be facing the enemy head on in battle. There will be no ships to keep you at a safe distance and you will need to learn better hand-to-hand combat if you wish to live."

Corwin threw a dagger directly at Penn, but as the knife approached, she kicked up her spear and used it as a shield and blocked the weapon. The dumbstruck pirates stared at Corwin.

"I guess it wouldn't hurt to pick up a few tips." Corwin shrugged and bobbed his head, as if he hadn't tried to kill the Master of Keepers.

"Let's begin then," Penn smiled, stabbing her spear into the ground.

Crispin smiled; grateful the pirates and Keepers were with him on this journey.

But while they laughed, poked fun at one another, and bickered like a true family, Crispin used the distraction to slip away and visit the treehouse where he'd grown up. Despite a few missing boards, Crispin easily made his way across the swinging bridge. The sight from a distance was depressing but stepping onto the front porch where he and Salome used to sit and talk for hours while Zophar puffed on his favorite pipe, pierced his heart.

The prince ran his fingers over the charred wood beams where the front door once stood. Stepping across the threshold, he stood in the main room of their cozy lodging. All of Zophar's books were gone and the chipped plates and mugs Salome used to obsessively clean, were shattered into hundreds of little pieces on the floor. He crouched down, scooped up a kettle Zophar used to make tea, and admired it fondly.

grumbled to Zophar about how much he hated it – how he wished for an adventure that would whisk him away, so he'd never have to return. But now standing in the rumble and remembering how Zophar hid them in the treehouse after losing everything the night Niabi attacked, and how it quickly became their safe haven, filled him with regret. He fought the tears, but he couldn't hold them back, they streamed down his cheeks and he quickly wiped them away with the back of his sleeve.

It was a small mercy that Zophar hadn't been traveling with him – the state of their house, of the village, would have crushed him.

"So," Rahab's whisper startled him, "this is where you grew up."

Crispin thumbed away what evidence remained that he'd been crying and slowly stood up, facing her as she waited in the doorway. "I was six when Zophar brought us here."

"That's a long time to live in the same place," she said.

"All those years, I hated living here. I woke up every morning for twelve years saying one day I'd return to Northwind, to my true home." Crispin dusted the debris from Zophar's favorite armchair and sat in what little remained. "It wasn't until I left that I realized how much of a comfort this treehouse was – how much love filled these creaky walls."

"You can have that feeling again," Rahab assured him and carefully stepped toward him. "Maybe not here, but when you reclaim your kingdom."

He raked his fingers through his hair with a heavy sigh. "I just wish I had appreciated this place more, appreciated everything Zophar did for us. He took two wanted children and raised us as his own. He sacrificed so much for me and my sister. I just… I can't wait to thank him properly when I see him again."

Rahab leaned against part of a wall where the fireplace used to be, twisting a lock of her hair. "What's she like?"

"Who?"

"Your sister."

"Salome?"

She nodded, meeting his gaze. "Is she just as insufferable as you?" she smirked.

Crispin let loose a laugh and it felt good to release the tension in his chest and shoulders. "Oh, even more so, I imagine." He grinned and she offered him a small smile in return. He motioned for her to sit with him and she obliged. She slipped into his lap, and he wrapped his arms around her waist, tugging her close. "Salome is an excellent hunter. She's bold, cunning, and doesn't have a problem speaking her mind. She is also one of the kindest people I know and she's my best friend. If all fails, I know she will be by my side fighting as the world burns around us."

"You miss her."

"More than I thought I would," he caressed her arm and smiled. "We've always had each other. We were born less than a year apart and have wreaked havoc together since we could crawl."

"Do you think she'll like me?" she whispered. It was odd hearing any sort of vulnerability coming from the pirate's mouth.

Gently, he squeezed her hand. "Oh, my sweet pirate queen… no."

"What?"

Crispin chuckled, tightening his hold on her when she tried to wiggle free. "She'll love you."

Rahab punched his chest, nostrils flared. "That's not funny, princeling."

"You know what else she'll love? He honed in on the dagger with the ruby hilt dangling on her hip. "She'll love the hardware. She always carries three knives wherever she goes."

"Sounds like my type of woman," she bounced her eyebrows playfully.

"Should I be worried you'll like my sister more than me?" he teased.

"Oh, absolutely." She smiled and dragged her fingers down the curve of his jaw. Something flashed in her eyes, and he wished he could read her mind.

"Why are you looking at me like that?"

"To think I almost let Kubantu have you."

"You cruel, wicked woman," he shook his head. It seemed like a lifetime ago they'd fought the sea beast in the Obsidian Sea, where he pushed her out of harm's way, sparing her a watery death. She rescued him in return, even though she claimed she felt nothing but hatred for him.

Her laugh filled the empty space and sparked a bit of comfort and joy in him. "Oh, princeling, I don't know what I'd possibly do without you now."

"I told you I'd grow on you."

She ran her thumb over his lips and whispered, "That you did."

Glancing across the bridge, Crispin noticed the pirates had managed to start a fire, but Phex had gotten too close to it, and was told to get away.

"It's cold out here," Phex hissed, slapping his hands on his hips. "You can't expect me to -"

"Empty your pockets!" Rafi shouted, blocking Phex's path.

"I'm not emptying my pockets," the explosives expert grouched. "Captain, tell him I can sit by the fire like everyone else."

"Aye, you got a right to keep warm, same as the rest of us," Haldane bobbed his head as he stirred the stew over the flames.

"See!" Phex whipped his hands around to emphasize the point.

"But," Haldane held the ladle out, blocking Phex from getting too close, "for the safety of the crew, empty your pockets, lad."

"Captain!"

"It's not that we don't trust you, Phex," the captain held firm, "but I'd like to be able to sleep well tonight without worrying one of those inventions of yours will roll into the flames and blow us all to hell."

Phex glanced from the captain to the quiet Corwin sharpening his knives to the giant Ondrej already sprawled out in his designated sleeping area, looking for them to come to his aid. He even dared a glance at Penn and her Keepers, but they sat stoically around the fire, scooping spoons full of stew into their mouths. When no one defended him, he reluctantly, muttering every curse word he knew, emptied his pockets of all its trinkets, and stomped toward a log in front of the fire and plopped down with a huff.

"Happy?" Phex flashed a menacing look Rafi's way and the halfling pirate glared right back.

"And in one piece," Rafi snorted.

"How long do you think it'll take before Phex blows something up just to scare the piss out of Rafi?" Crispin chuckled.

"Phex always gets his revenge when you least expect it," Rahab winked before she slid off of his lap and motioned for him to follow her back to camp. "Best eat and get some sleep, princeling. We've got a long way to walk tomorrow."

CHAPTER 21
SALOME

When Salome was informed Jinn had finally arrived early that morning, she abandoned her breakfast, forgot about the aches and pains of training the night before with Kayven and Abba, and walked as fast as she could toward the room Kai told her he'd been assigned. But when she finally stood outside his door, she felt nervous. What would she say to him? What could you say to someone who'd risked everything to save you from certain death? Someone who'd brought an entire army to rescue you and who slaughtered every Thrak who stood in his way. *Thank you* seemed terribly insufficient.

Before she lost her nerve, she took a deep breath, and pushed the door open to see a shirtless Prince Jinn. The left half of his back was covered in tattoos, as was his entire left arm. When he turned around to see who had burst into his chambers, she saw the tattoos continued to the front left side of his chest and stomach as well. Ancient Eastern runes, dragons, and the history of his ancestors were etched in permanent black ink on his skin. She stopped in the threshold; her heart beating rapidly as their eyes silently roved over one another. His signature black pants hung low on his hips exposing his chiseled abs. She knew he was muscular, but she didn't expect his body to be riddled with scars. Just as her body told a story of brutality and survival, so did his.

Jinn looked as if he wanted to say something, but words failed him. He looked at her as if he'd seen a ghost and she forced herself to speak to slice through the tension.

"I – I'm sorry. I should've knocked." She couldn't hide her blush and forcefully averted her gaze from his half-naked body.

Jinn stared at her as he reached for his shirt. He slipped his arms through the sleeves, but didn't fasten it, leaving the center of his chest exposed.

Salome met his gaze and inhaled deeply to keep from crying at the sight of him. "You came for me."

"I'll always come for you."

She wasn't sure what to do with her shaky hands, so she stuffed them in her pockets. "You've saved my life three times now. I owe you -"

"You don't owe me anything," he whispered, cutting her off.

Once again, silence settled between them. She slowly closed the door behind her, maintaining eye contact with the prince who hadn't moved a muscle.

"Kai told me you tried to see me this morning," she said, "but the twins wouldn't let you wake me."

"Those three don't seem to care I outrank them and insisted I get some rest before seeing you."

His small smile eased her nerves. "You think you would have learned not to question them by now," she teased.

He took a step toward her, hands buried in his black pants pockets. "If I were a smart man, I would have learned by now, but I've been told more than once, that I'm a bit hardheaded." Jinn stopped a few feet from her, soaking her in. He studied her quietly, his eyes scanning her like he wanted to scoop her in his arms but refrained. "I was afraid you were…"

"Dead?" she filled in the blank.

"I tried reaching out to you. I know that's not how our bond works but…" he stared at the floor between them.

"I thought about you," she admitted, earning his gaze. "I was so far beneath the Black Tower; I couldn't seem to access my power."

"Did they hurt you?" he whispered.

"Not as much as we hurt them."

But they had hurt her. They had taken Zophar and in turn, they had taken a piece of her good nature when she slit Ranalda's throat. The nightmares were constant and unrelenting. She blinked and saw Zophar with a knife plunged into his abdomen. She blinked again and saw Ranalda lying in a pool of blood with a gash across her neck. When she blinked a third time, Jinn was watching her with a deep sadness in his golden eyes.

"I'm sorry I didn't protect you that day in the mountains."

She lurched. "Jinn-"

"That moment plays over and over in my head." He raked a hand through his dark locks. "The look in your eyes, as if you knew I wouldn't reach you in time. I see it when I close my eyes. It haunts me when I try to sleep. I don't think I'll ever forget how I felt at that moment. Powerless and afraid. I not only failed to protect you but watched as my entire world crumbled around me."

Salome cupped his face, his smooth skin cool against her warm hands and pressed her forehead against his. Her touch silenced him; his hands rested on her waist, as they drank one another in, falling into a rhythmic breathing.

"I'm sorry I didn't protect you," he whispered again.

"It's not your fault. It's mine." She let him pull her closer until their bodies were flush. "You saved me when I lost hope. Had I not left the City of Bones, Zophar would still be…"

Jinn kissed her forehead and wrapped his arms around her. She rested her head against his chest and listened to his heartbeat, inhaling his scent, and when she realized her cheek was against his bare chest, her face flushed, and her heart skipped a beat.

She pulled away and whispered, "Can I show you where I go when I need peace?"

Jinn nodded as she slipped her hands down his neck and rested them on his exposed chest. His breathing was shallow and his eyes expectant.

She wasn't sure this would work, but she closed her eyes and pictured herself standing in the gardens of the White Keep, extending the memory to Jinn. She and her brother would run around, ducking and dodging all the palace workers, and avoiding their nursemaids. The memory filled her with warmth, peace, and comfort.

"Where are we?" Jinn asked, standing beside her in the frostbitten garden.

Salome gently tapped the frost covered purple crocus and looked over her shoulder at Jinn and smiled. "This was once my home."

"We're in Northwind?" Jinn noticed the white stone walls of the White Keep.

"One of my memories." Salome glided through the crisp snow, pushing it with her foot. "When I was a little girl, there was a late snowfall during spring. It froze the gardens, the flowers, the trees. I remember waking up and seeing the snow on the rooftops in the city and sprinting to this very garden. It was the most magical sight. It felt like I had stepped into a fairytale."

Jinn walked next to her as they toured the snow-covered garden.

"I've always liked the cold. It's one of the things I miss most about Northwind. It's why I named my horse Snow. It's this memory that brings me a sense of peace and wonder. Whenever I feel overwhelmed, whenever I feel lost, I come here." She stopped to breathe in the coolness of the rare, spring snowfall and noticed Jinn smiling at her.

"What?" she asked.

"This is amazing. How is this even possible for me to see?"

"Back in the Isles of Myr, I touched Harbona's hand and was able to see his memories flash before my eyes." She lifted a shoulder. "I thought it might be possible to share a memory of my own with someone I share a bond with." She motioned around the garden. "It reminds me that even in hardship, a flower can flourish. I've lost so many people." She choked up when Zophar came to mind. She reached for a red rose that had icicles nestled between the satiny folds. "This place may not bring you the same peace it brings me, but maybe it will bring you the slightest comfort, and that will be enough for me."

He cupped her face in his hands, forcing her to meet his gaze. "Thank you."

Tears welled up in her eyes and the vision of the frozen garden was lost. When she blinked, they were back in Jinn's quarters.

"What's wrong?" he asked.

She pulled away from him, wrapping her arms around herself. She already felt the heaviness of his absence, missed his hands against her face. "I …" She couldn't seem to get the words out.

"What is it?" he asked again.

"In Gomorrah, in the throne room…" *When I slit Ranalda's throat and watched her die,* is how she wanted to finish that statement but couldn't.

Jinn straightened. By his stance, it was evident he knew what she was referring to, but waited for her to continue.

"If you see me differently because of my sins, I understand, but please know that I regret my actions."

"You don't need to explain yourself to me, Salome."

"But I do."

"Why?" He tilted his head to the side and strands of black hair fell over his forehead.

Because she was afraid he would judge her and distance himself.

"Salome?"

"Forget I said anything." She swatted her hand in the air and headed toward the door.

"Where are you going?"

She grabbed the doorknob and he pressed his palm on top of her hand, preventing her from leaving. She could feel his breath on the back of her neck, his chest rapidly rising and falling behind her. She wanted to lean into him, surrender herself to his embrace, tell him she made a mistake by not choosing him and feel his soft lips against hers, but instead, she turned to face him with her back pinned against the door and said, "I need to meet with Hanzo and Oifa. They're expecting me -"

He planted his hands flat against the door on either side of her. His gaze was unrelenting, searching her eyes for the truth she refused to share. She felt a bead of sweat drip down the center of her back. She didn't know if she was more nervous about him finding whatever he was looking for or the electricity she felt in his presence. She closed her eyes and inhaled his familiar and comforting scent of cedar and springtime. It took every fiber of her being not to jump into his arms and kiss every inch of his body.

"I should probably go," her voice cracked, and Jinn leaned forward so his lips hovered above her ear.

"I'll be here whenever you're done with your meeting." He said *meeting* as if he didn't believe her.

She tried not to shiver at his proximity but failed. "What makes you think I'm interested in your whereabouts?" she fired back.

Jinn pulled back far enough to meet her gaze, if she leaned forward just an inch, they'd be kissing. "Have you already forgotten I can see how you look at me?" He smiled. "I'm inclined not to let you out of my sight, for your own protection, of course."

"Of course." She hid her smile, but her treacherous heart pounded far too quickly for her to appear calm and collected. She cleared her throat. "If you plan to escort me around the castle, I suggest you button your shirt before you catch a chill."

The prince's low chuckle warmed her belly. He pushed up from the door and started buttoning his shirt slowly, eyes still glued on her. She knew he could tell exactly what she was thinking. If she didn't get out of his room and put a few feet of distance between them, she wasn't sure she could keep her hands off of him. Knowing exactly what he looked like without his shirt, his sculpted torso, muscular back and his half-body tattoos would definitely cause her to dream about him later. When he finished looping the last button, he flashed a longing smile at her. She blinked away the hunger in her eyes, but he had already noticed.

"Consider me your bodyguard until further notice." He motioned toward the door behind her.

"You mean my watchdog?" she teased as she twisted the knob, but then Adonijah's face flashed in her mind. Her stomach instantly soured.

What was she doing? She chose Adonijah. But he left her. He'd lied to her. She didn't think she could ever trust him again. But she knew she hurt Jinn when she rejected him. Although she was grateful she and the prince were picking up where they left off in their banter and friendship, she didn't know if his proposal was still on the table or if he had moved on. And she wasn't about to ask, afraid of what he might say.

CHAPTER 22
ADONIJAH

The charred remains of where the cabin used to be, was the ghost that haunted his dreams nightly. This place was what spurred him to dedicate his life to finding his father and those who were complicit in murdering his mother and robbing him of what remained of his childhood. This place marked the beginning and end of everything that molded Adonijah into the man he had become.

"What is this place?" Leoti stopped beside him, eyeing the rubble.

"This used to be my home," Adonijah whispered.

Pash stood silently where the entrance once was with his arms crossed over his chest. He'd been forced to visit the farmhouse a handful of times before the soldiers came and burned it to the ground, forcing Adonijah to flee when the Nameless Rider killed his mother and grandfather.

Leoti dragged her middle finger down the center of her forehead until she reached her chest. "You lost someone?"

His mother's face flashed before his eyes, and he shook the image of her freckled face free. "My mother died protecting me from the Nameless Rider, the Shadow our father sent to find me." Pash seemed to tense at the mention of Gershom. "I've walked Adalore for years alone and never once came back here."

"What happened?"

"Gershom wanted to take me to Northwind, separating me from my mother. She wouldn't let him, so the Nameless Rider broke her neck and set the house on fire. I was able to get away but…"

"Satara was a good woman." Pash sat next to him and patted his back. "She can now rest knowing you avenged her, brother."

Adonijah nodded his head, but he wished he could have done more to save her all those years ago.

"Can I ask why your father never married your mother?"

Pash met Leoti's inquisitive gaze. "Satara was betrothed to our Uncle Ophir before Issachar imprisoned our father in Northwind. When our uncle freed him, he brought him here for his wounds to be treated."

Adonijah cleared his throat and picked up where Pash left off, knowing the next part of the story was gruesome. "Gershom forced himself upon my mother when no one was around. When she told my grandfather what happened, he blamed her. He said she'd defiled herself and the union he arranged for her. I never knew it was Ophir who was betrothed to her, but once she became pregnant with me, Gershom insisted Ophir refuse to marry her because she now belonged to him."

"Your father is a monster." Leoti had tears in her eyes and wiped them away with her thumb.

"One that will be dealt with soon enough," Adonijah bobbed his head. "I would start a fire, but we are out in the open and I don't want to attract any unwanted attention." He glanced at Pash and Leoti. "We'll need to sleep close to keep warm."

Pash and Leoti looked uncomfortable, but eventually nodded in agreement. The cold months were upon them. To survive the trek north, they'd have to do whatever was necessary.

They laid their sleeping bags in a row inside the only tent they had and even though it was cramped, they were out of the blistering cold. Leoti was in the center since she was the smallest and needed the most warmth. But in the middle of the night, she wiggled free from the brothers and before she was able to slip outside, Adonijah grabbed her arm.

"Where are you going?" he whispered.

"I'll be right back."

"Leoti, where are you going?" He glared at her with a seriousness that caused her to narrow her eyes.

"If you must know," she hissed. "I need to relieve myself, if it's alright with you. Or would you like to come watch?"

Releasing her arm, he felt foolish thinking she was going to disappear in the middle of the night. He mumbled an apology as she left and he laid back down. But he couldn't fall back to sleep until she returned. He wanted to make sure she was safe. When a few minutes had ticked by and she hadn't returned, he grabbed the knife underneath his head and made his way to the flap of the ten. It was then he heard a high-pitched scream spurring him and Pash to fly out of the tent. They caught sight of Leoti a few paces away, with Thanos behind her, poking a knife to her throat. As the brothers glanced around, they noticed Thanos' soldiers had surrounded them, and knew they were at the mercy of the deranged boy who wanted to be king.

"Let her go, Thanos." Adonijah sheathed his dagger and raised his hands to show he was unarmed. "She doesn't need to be harmed."

"*You*," the prince seethed, jutting his chin at Pash. "You cost me my kingdom."

"There was nothing to be done to-"

"Shut up!" Thanos interrupted Pash. "You thought you could escape me so easily?"

"Thanos," Adonijah pleaded again, his eyes fixed on the knife at Leoti's neck. "Let Leoti go, she had nothing to do with you losing your crown."

"No, I suppose she didn't." He yanked her head back by her braid, causing her to wince. "But she will help me restore it, once she uses her warging abilities to show me where the City of Bones is. I will take their throne for myself and do what my ancestors couldn't. Destroy the Mountain Men."

"Take me instead," Pash took a step forward.

"Pash," Adonijah growled in warning.

"If you are going to have any chance at restoring your crown, you will need money to fund an army," Pash continued, ignoring his brother. "Take me as your hostage and Niabi will give you what you want. Let Leoti go."

"You raise an excellent point, Commander," Thanos flashed a sinister grin. "But who said I was here to make any deals?"

"Than-"

"We're taking all of you and will use you as I see fit." Thanos tucked his nose against the crook of Leoti's neck and sniffed. He ran his tongue from Leoti's neck up the side of her face, eyeing Adonijah and Pash with a glint of wickedness. "She will be more exciting in my tent, I'm sure."

Adonijah lunged forward, "Why you little-!"

"Ah, ah, ah!" Thanos tsked and his soldiers advanced, weapons drawn. "Not another step, rebel. Any trouble you cause will be taken out on your lover here and believe me, I am not-"

One of Thanos' soldiers screamed before he was launched across the field. Adonijah whipped around and saw a large black bear stampeding the guards, clawing and ripping their limbs from their bodies. He scooped his sword from the tent to attack the beast, but Pash grabbed his arm and held him back.

"Adonijah, don't!" Pash ordered. "It's Leoti! It's Leoti!"

"What?" Adonijah had been so concerned about Pash giving himself up to Thanos that he hadn't realized that his brother was giving Leoti the distraction she needed to warg into the bear who was within distance of her magic. He glanced at her face and noticed her eyes were white. Even in Thanos' grasp, she was destroying his soldiers, bit by bit.

The Gomorrian prince released Leoti from his grasp, unaware she was the one controlling the bear, and attempted to flee the campsite. But the bear didn't give up on the chase and knocked Thanos to the ground, hovering above him, flashing its blood-stained teeth.

"Please," Thanos cried, "spare me."

Leoti cocked her head to the side and the bear mimicked her gesture. Her grin sent a shiver through Adonijah, but before he or Pash could protest, the bear attacked the Gomorrian and mauled him to death.

Once the prince stopped twitching, Adonijah reached for Leoti, but Pash once again prevented him from touching her. "Not while she's in her warg state," Pash shook his head.

His first instinct was to shove his brother away to check on Leoti, but once he took a deep breath, he decided to heed his brother's warning. He nodded his head and Pash released his grip on his forearm.

Once the bear took off and disappeared into the woods, Leoti blinked and her eyes turned brown again. The Andrago slumped to her knees spurring Adonijah to kneel before her. He lifted her chin and the look in her eyes pierced his heart.

"Are you hurt?" he whispered, maintaining eye contact with her.

"No," she shook her head.

"Are you frightened?"

"No." Her voice was raspy. "I've never killed anyone before."

Adonijah gently swiped loose strands of dark hair from her face. "Killing a man is never easy. You did what needed to be done-"

"I enjoyed it," she interrupted him, her eyes hardening, "and I would do it again, if I had to."

Adonijah sat back on his heels. He didn't expect her to say that, and honestly, he had no idea how to respond. When he looked at Leoti he saw a woman full of heartache, a woman who had someone she loved stolen from her, and a woman who wanted revenge. Her peace had been ripped from her and he understood better than most how she felt. When he lost his mother, he set out on a journey to avenge her death, to kill those who had taken her from him. He had killed more men than he cared to admit in his quest, and at this point, he was numb to death. But watching how this woman let her shattered heart and unquenchable rage finally consume her and boil over into using her magic to wipe out nearly a dozen men, was oddly relatable. He wished he could reach out and hold her, to take her heartache and bear that burden himself, but he couldn't. All he could do was help her weather the storm and help her find peace again.

He reached his hand out to her, "Let's get you cleaned up."

Leoti stared at him a moment longer, looking unsure, but when he held steady, she slipped her petite hand into his calloused one and let him hoist her up from the ground. He looked down at her and offered a small smile, hoping she recognized he wasn't judging her, but that he understood.

Adonijah dragged his thumb across her neck where Thanos' blade had been. Her breath quickened and his eyes skipped up to her lips and then her eyes. The need to protect her was strong, but she had not only protected herself, she saved him and Pash as well. The urge to kiss her was consuming his thoughts and without realizing it, he lowered his face as she lifted her head, but the moment was interrupted by Pash clearing his throat.

He glanced at Pash who had his arms crossed over his chest. Adonijah wondered what was going on in his brother's head. Was he trying to keep him from kissing Leoti? Was he being smug about being right that he did have feelings for the Andrago?

As if Pash knew he was silently flipping through questions, he said, "Just wanted to remind you I'm still here."

Adonijah understood what Pash was actually trying to say. He had been so adamant about being in love with Salome and here he was about to kiss another woman. He took a step away from Leoti, rubbing the back of his neck.

"I'm glad you're alright." Adonijah cleared his throat and snatched a piece of cloth from his pocket and handed it to her. "You have some dirt on your face."

"Thank you." Looking as if she too had sobered from what had almost happened between them, she took the cloth, walked toward the sleeping bags, and sat down to wipe herself clean.

The brothers exchanged a quick look. Pash opened his mouth to say something, but Adonijah held up his hand "I already know what you're about to say and it's unnecessary. I know where my heart lies."

Pash slanted his head to the side and smirked. "I was going to say, I owe you an apology. I was opposed to Leoti joining us, but your insistence she stay with us was the right decision." He took a step closer to Adonijah and lowered his voice, "But

I'm glad you're following your heart, brother." By his tone, Adonijah knew his brother didn't believe him.

"We'll have to burn the bodies." Adonijah walked toward Thanos' nearly unrecognizable body and dragged it toward the others. "Then we'll have to move before your Shadows find us."

The Almighty One willing they'd be long gone before those masked riders picked up their trail.

CHAPTER 23
PASH

It took about an hour to gather the bodies, or what was left of them, and toss them into the fire pit. The smell of burning flesh was overwhelming and Pash knew if they didn't get a move on, they were sure to attract the Shadows who were probably not too far behind Thanos' group. Packing up the camp site, they walked northward. Pash was hopeful they would reach the Black Forest before anyone else picked up on their trail.

He glanced behind to ensure his brother and Leoti were still following, because they were undeniably distracted by one another. Even the members of the blind order of The Sisters would be able to see they had feelings for one another. Though Pash should be sickened by the clearly in denial love-struck duo, he found himself secretly rooting for them. Maybe once they killed their father, Adonijah would choose to live in Northwind and abandon fighting in the war. Despite being separated for years, he knew his brother well enough to know he would never turn his back on those he had sworn an oath to.

A soft whistle captured his attention, and he stopped dead in his tracks, glancing around the densely populated forest.

"What is it?" Adonijah was by his side, looking around.

"Did you hear the whistle?" Pash asked.

"Is it a signal?"

Before Pash could answer in the affirmative, several thuds sounded around them as Shadows dropped in from the trees, surrounding them. One of the mercenaries grabbed Leoti but as she fought back, the Shadow hit her on the back of the head, knocking her out. Adonijah growled as he looked at Leoti's limp body dangling in the Shadow's arms, but Pash wrapped his hand around his brother's bicep, keeping him rooted.

"Lower your weapons." Ophir stepped forward, looking angry and disappointed. "Don't make this any more difficult than it has to be, Pash."

Pash shook his head, refusing to obey. "Afraid I can't do that, Uncle."

"I, more than anyone else, understand what it's like to be loyal to your brother," Ophir appealed to him. "That's why I'll give you one more chance to redeem yourself, Pash." He stepped closer. "Lay down your weapons, join us, and all will be forgiven."

"You want me to give up my brother to save myself." Pash shook his head. "My answer is no."

"Think of Niabi, my boy," Ophir played on his emotions. "Think of your unborn child. She need never know of your betrayal."

"Your words sound sweet, Uncle," Pash's eyes watered, "but they're poison. We both know you'll never let me walk free and I won't have my brother's blood on my hands."

The care and sincerity in Ophir's face vanished and his face reddened. "Then you will die together." With a flick of Ophir's wrist, the band of Shadows launched their assault.

Adonijah and Pash unsheathed their weapons and fought their attackers with the same brutality they were shown.

Pash knew if they didn't fend off the men he'd spent most of his life training with, they'd execute him, no questions asked. The men he had led into battle, had fought beside and bled for, were now his enemies and a piece of his heart broke with the understanding that he was going to be the one to steal their last breath. A part of him wanted to lower his sword and let them chain him, if it meant sparing them, but with his back bumping against Adonijah's back, he knew whose life he valued more. So, he swung his sword ferociously against his friends and comrades, striking them down one by one, knowing their faces would haunt him until the end of his days.

Despite their best effort, Pash and Adonijah were simply outnumbered, and it was only a matter of time before they tired and fell to the Northmen.

Pash risked a glance at his uncle and all the warmth had drained from his face. Is that what their enemies saw when they faced Ophir? His muscles were aching; sweat beaded and dripped from his forehead. He didn't have much fight left in him. He was going to fail Adonijah.

Pash watched his brother fend off two Shadows and wished he could have spent more time with him. The truth was: they weren't going to win this battle. He hoped no matter what Ophir told Niabi, she'd remember how deeply he loved her.

One of the Shadows lunged at Pash, and he braced himself for an impact that never came. Two arrows zipped past his shoulder and pierced his attacker square in the chest, downing him. Arrows from different directions flew toward the Shadows, picking them off.

Knowing they were now the hunted, the remaining Shadows, including Ophir, scattered into the woods, escaping the hidden assailants.

Pash turned to face Adonijah, but he wasn't behind him. He was on his knees, cradling Leoti in his arms. Slowly, her eyes fluttered open, but the commander was more concerned with who had saved them, than hovering over his brother and the Andrago.

His question was answered immediately when a group of ruffians stepped into view. They didn't have any armor or banners hailing their kingdom, but from their appearance, they looked to be Puluan. But what were pirates doing this far inland? The man who Pash assumed was their leader pulled his hood back, revealing his face. Pash couldn't believe his eyes. For months, he'd stared at his wanted poster and now, in the middle of nowhere, Pash was standing before him.

"Are any of you hurt?" the man's voice sliced through Pash's thoughts.

Adonijah found his way back to his brother's side, ushering a dazed Leoti with him, and when Pash saw the astonishment on his brother's face, his suspicion was confirmed.

"You're Salome's brother?" Adonijah's question took the ruffian leader by surprise.

"Most people just call me Crispin," he smirked, cocking his head to the side. "You know my sister?"

Pash and his brother exchanged a look.

"Aye," Adonijah finally spoke, drawing a skeptical look from the prince. "I know her."

"Then it seems we have a lot to talk about." Crispin eyed them both suspiciously. "Especially the part about a Shadow fighting off his own men."

The lost prince was no fool and was very observant. Pash bobbed his head, knowing the journey to kill Gershom was now on hold. He was going to be detained as a prisoner in the prince's company, there was no getting around it. And though he desperately wanted to spill the entire story about how they planned to assassinate Gershom, that they were on the same side, he knew at the end of the day, they would never be allies. So, he kept his mouth shut and met Crispin's gaze.

"To free my brother, I turned my back on my men."

Crispin stared at them, giving nothing away in his facial expressions. "A Shadow with a conscience. I never thought I'd see the day."

"So," Pash swallowed his retort. "Are we your prisoners?"

"I prefer the term *unexpected guests.*" The prince smiled and it was oddly comforting even though Pash knew they were talking about the same thing. "What are your names?"

"I am Adonijah."

"I am Leoti."

Crispin fixed his eyes on Pash, and the commander reluctantly said, "My name is Pash."

"By the pin on your chest," he pointed to the raven pin Niabi had awarded him upon his promotion to commander, "it would appear you're a high-ranking Shadow."

The prince really did know too much for his own good. But there was no use in lying, it wouldn't be long before someone recognized him and exposed his true identity.

"I am the Commander of the Shadows."

Crispin grinned and Pash wished he could wipe the smugness off his face.

A woman with blue hair rounded the prince and said in a low voice, "We need to move before they return." Crispin nodded in agreement before glancing at the Andrago.

"Are you able to walk?"

"Yes," Leoti nodded her head.

"Good." The prince pointed in the direction they were headed. "Then we should get moving."

"You aren't going to bind our hands?" Pash quirked an eyebrow.

"With their aim," Crispin cast a thumb at the motley crew behind him and smirked, "you wouldn't get far, if you tried to escape."

And by the hardened looks on the pirates' faces, Pash knew they wouldn't hesitate to shoot him in the back, if he attempted to flee. He was now Crispin's prisoner, and he was well aware wherever he was headed to next was going to put him behind in his quest to assassinate his father and return to his queen. But he was alive, and that was all he could hope for in a situation like this. He was determined not to give his captors any trouble, to earn their trust, and when the moment to escape presented itself, he would jump on it. He would return to Niabi, if it was the last thing he did.

A strange look in Crispin's eyes caused Pash to become paranoid. Had the prince managed to read his thoughts? Had the prince figured out what was running through his head? If he knew, he didn't speak on it. He motioned for the trio to walk with them. East. They were headed east which wouldn't lead them to Northwind, but to the abandoned city of Oakenshire.

"Where are you taking us?" Pash boldly asked his captors.

"I'm sure a man of your military prowess already knows the answer to that question." Crispin slipped his hood back over his head, masking his face in shadows, but Pash saw the prince flash a sinister grin.

"Tell me," the prince's attention honed in on Adonijah, "how does the brother of the Commander of Shadows know my sister?"

Adonijah stiffened but kept a steady hand on Leoti's arm as he helped her trek through the darkening forest. "We met months ago when Harbona found me in the swamplands."

"Are you the Wanderer?" Crispin asked, a twinkle in his eye.

"I was, but that title doesn't seem to suit me anymore."

"Are you no longer wandering then?"

"I suppose you could say that."

Crispin held his arm out, blocking Adonijah's path. "Who are you to my sister and why are you not with her now?"

The need to defend his brother engulfed Pash and he took a step toward the prince, nostrils flared. "He doesn't need to answer your questions."

As if his tone alone triggered the pirates, they all pointed weapons in his direction, reminding him that he was no longer giving orders, he was taking them. Pash took a small step back, raising his hands to show he meant the prince no physical harm.

"When it comes to my sister," Crispin hissed, "any question I ask will be answered." He turned once more to Adonijah and asked, "Why are you not with my sister?"

The brothers exchanged a quick look before Adonijah said, "I left her in the City of Bones to find the man who killed my mother. He was in my brother's camp at the foot of the Bone Mountains."

"And why were you and your Shadows this far south?" Crispin's eyes darted to Pash and Adonijah nodded for him to tell the truth.

"The queen ordered us to aid Prince Thanos in retaking Gomorrah from his mother."

"And did you?"

Pash swallowed hard and shifted from one leg to the other. "My army made it to the outskirts of Gomorrah, but we didn't get the chance to engage the Thrak in battle, because another army had beaten us there."

Crispin's eyes narrowed. It was evident the prince knew he was omitting something in his tale.

Rubbing the back of his neck and again exchanging a look with his brother, Pash continued. "The Stormcrags, Krazaks, a small force from Numbio, and a host of Bellators destroyed the city of Gomorrah, because they were trying to rescue someone."

"Rescue who?"

"Your sister," Adonijah chimed in with a raspy whisper. "After I left, somehow the Thrak captured her and -"

In a flash, Crispin pinned Adonijah against a tree and had a dagger against his throat. Arrows and spears pointed at Pash and Leoti from every angle, keeping them rooted in place.

"Please," Leoti's voice trembled, "don't hurt him."

The prince either didn't hear Leoti's pleas or it fell on deaf ears, because Crispin pressed his forearm in Adonijah's chest, drawing a grunt from him. "You abandoned my sister and let her be taken by the Thrak?"

"She's alive!" Pash shouted, hoping to diffuse the situation. "The Bellators rescued her before they leveled the city. Your sister is safe!"

Crispin cocked his head toward Pash, not releasing his hold on Adonijah. "She might be alive, but can you guarantee she is in one piece?"

The woman with blue hair approached the seething prince and slipped her hand on his forearm, squeezing until he met her gaze. "The sooner we get to Oakenshire, the sooner we can see your sister."

The prince's body relaxed and slowly, he lowered his weapon from Adonijah's neck, releasing him.

"I'm sorry," Adonijah raked a hand through his hair. "Had I not left, maybe I could have protected her."

"You speak of her like you have feelings for her," Crispin's voice had a bite to it.

Pash noticed Leoti's shoulders tense up.

Adonijah bobbed his head. "Aye, she means a lot to me."

"Not enough." Crispin sheathed his knife and motioned the group to lower their weapons. "Move out."

As he traipsed down the path, Pash thanked the Almighty that the prince didn't slit his brother's throat in anger, buh He knew there was a good chance once they set foot in Oakenshire, they would never leave.

CHAPTER 24
SALOME

Salome sat in her makeshift throne with Jinn standing on her right. The prince had kept his word by escorting her everywhere. Clearly, he wasn't going to jeopardize her safety again. And if she were honest with herself, she fully enjoyed having him nearby. She caught herself staring at him, but before she could look away, he noticed her longing gaze. He smiled and winked as the doors to the neglected throne room opened and Oifa and Hanzo entered, a few feet apart but in stride. Once they reached Salome, they bowed.

"I wanted to thank you both for joining Prince Jinn in rescuing me. I am forever in your debt."

Hanzo shook his head, hands clasped behind his back. "You owe us nothing. We volunteered, knowing the risks. I am just sorry we didn't make it to you sooner."

Salome repressed the tears begging to be released. Had they arrived earlier, maybe Zophar would have survived the Gomorrians. She rattled the thought free, dwelling on the what ifs wouldn't bring her guardian back.

"I appreciate you both," Salome forced a smile. "There is another reason I asked you to meet with me."

"And what reason would that be?" Oifa narrowed her eyes, suspicious to her very core. She swatted rebellious strands of her lavender hair from her face.

Salome took a deep breath. She wasn't sure how either one of them would digest what she was about to suggest, but it was the only solution she could think of to unite the two clans. "Are either of you married or betrothed?"

Oifa and Hanzo exchanged an equally hateful and confused glance. Both shook their heads. "No."

"If there is one thing I've learned about politics and the ways of kings and queens," Salome continued before she lost her nerve, "alliances are forged in blood or marriage. I propose you marry to unite your tribes. Rule as king and queen, as equals."

Oifa scoffed, crossing her arms over her chest. "Have you gone completely mad?"

"Show her some respect," Hanzo jumped to Salome's defense, eyes raging. He clearly took her being the new leader of the Krazaks seriously. "She is trying to help our people."

"By suggesting *we* get married?" Oifa shook her head, practically foaming at the mouth. "That will put you in an early grave."

Hanzo looked up at Salome with pleading eyes. "Is there another way for the Krazaks and Stormcrags to have peace?"

"There are a couple ways to conquer a throne. Through war and bloodshed or through marriage and unity. I believe unless you consider marriage, you will continue to have bloodshed between your two mighty clans. You might not like one another, but you make a formidable team. I saw how you worked together in rescuing me. How you protected one another and fought valiantly side by side. If you join forces, you can change everything for your people."

They all stewed in silence. Oifa tapped her foot against the cracked stone tiles, fire raging in her eyes. "You truly expect me to marry *him*?

"Because you're such a prize?" Hanzo spat back, earning a hiss from the Stormcrag.

Salome stood up and walked toward them, shaking her head. "I don't expect anything from either of you. But I will not rule a people I have no business overseeing. The Stormcrags and Krazaks have lived for one thousand years as enemies. You have an opportunity to heal your city. All I ask is that you consider peace and break the cycle of war."

Oifa scoffed, drawing everyone's attention. "You're asking us to agree to an arranged marriage for the sake of peace while we prepare to shed the blood of your sister and your people."

She heard Jinn take a step forward, whether he was offended by Oifa's tone or felt she was a threat to Salome, she didn't know, but she extended her arm to stop him.

Salome locked eyes with Oifa. "You're right. It's hypocritical of me to ask you to choose peace while we prepare for war. Would it mean anything if I told you I never wanted to be involved in this war? That I never wanted the burdens, responsibilities, or scars that titles and power have thrusted upon me? If there was another way to reclaim my home, do you not think I would take it to avoid bloodshed?" Oifa glanced down at the floor. "Like I said before, there are two ways to conquer a throne. Bloodshed or unity. In my future, there is blood. Your future doesn't have to end like mine."

The room stilled and no one said a word. Salome knew she was asking a lot of them, but if she could fulfill her destiny without another person dying, she would jump at the chance. She'd do anything in her power to avoid this inevitable war.

She extended the bridge to Jinn, feeling the anxiety creeping in. *"They're more liable to skin me than agree to this."*

"Don't let them see you sweat. Peace won't come easily. All you can do is steer them in the right direction. That's what a queen does." Jinn's voice calmed her nerves, and she stood a little bit taller.

"I'll do it," Hanzo said, breaking the tension in the crumbling throne room.

"What did you say?" Oifa's eyes were wide, confused.

"She's right." Hanzo turned to the Stormcrag, rolling his shoulders back to make himself appear taller. "Oifa, I think you're crass and rude and lack basic manners -"

She planted her hands firmly on her hips and scowled at him. "Oh, is that all?"

"Even though I may not care for you romantically -"

"Or at all."

Hanzo continued, unfazed by her attitude, "My people mean everything to me. I have lived with Death my entire life. I may not know what peace looks or feels like, but I'd like to try to give it to those who come after me." He met Salome's stunned gaze, "I choose peace. If this woman will agree to the marriage, so will I."

Salome, Hanzo, and Jinn stared at Oifa with expectation. "What say you, Oifa?" the princess asked, hoping her plan would work.

Oifa took a minute to think. Scratching her chin with her long nails until she looked up from her feet. "We would rule as equals." A statement, not a question.

Hanzo nodded. "As equals."

"The Stormcrags will dwell in the City of Bones, if they should so choose." Oifa squared her shoulders to his, looking every bit of a warrior queen even without a crown.

He mirrored her body language, focusing on her as if no one else was in the room. "And the Krazaks will dwell in the Tears of the Gods should they so choose."

Oifa took a step toward her enemy. "I promise not to slit your throat while you sleep."

Hanzo ate the remaining distance between them. "I promise not to raise an unkind hand to you or treat you lesser than myself."

"And do you expect me to warm your bed at night?" She asked with a softness Salome didn't realize the Stormcrag possessed.

"If you should so choose." Hanzo smirked at her; his eyes hazy.

Salome cleared her throat to remind Hanzo and Oifa they weren't alone, drawing scowls from them. Maybe they weren't as opposed to the idea as she originally thought.

"There are two people we need to include in this decision for this to work," Salome said, and by the looks on Oifa and Hanzo's faces, they knew who she was referring to.

AFTER EXPLAINING what they had discussed and agreed upon, Rune and Torrin were oddly and uncharacteristically quiet.

Salome shifted in her throne, poised like a queen, but anxious the two leaders would demand she be flogged for even suggesting the marriage. "What say you, my lords?"

Jinn, Heru, and Harbona were witnesses to the potential peace treaty and held their collective breath.

"Should you both provide your blessing," Salome continued when their silence extended a bit too long for comfort, "your tribes will be united. You will have peace and your children will have a future without bloodshed."

Rune glanced at Hanzo, ignoring everyone else. "Is this what you want?"

Without hesitation, the archer nodded, "To bring our people peace, yes."

Torrin rubbed his bald head before taking a step toward Salome. "Forgive me, my lady, but what will become of our positions amongst our peoples? I have led the Stormcrags for decades."

Salome let loose a breath she'd been holding in for far too long. At least they were talking. "I've thought of that. Though Hanzo and Oifa will rule over a united Mountain Men tribe, the Stormcrags and Krazaks will need spokesmen, ambassadors if you will, during the transition." She maintained eye contact with the Stormcrag, "Torrin, you will remain in the Tears of the Gods and Rune," she met the Krazak's gaze, "will be in the City of Bones. You will maintain the peace and secure the new reign. Together, the four of you can build what your ancestors couldn't."

Rune slammed his hand on Hanzo's shoulder. "I have spent most of my life serving King Gerd. I trust you and Oifa will not follow in his wicked footsteps." Hanzo placed his hand on top of Rune's and nodded. A silent promise.

Torrin turned to Oifa, stroking his long, scraggly beard. After a moment of hesitation, he met Oifa's gaze. "You have served me with a ferocious loyalty since you could walk. May Death take me, if I do not serve you in the same manner."

Salome's heart skipped a beat. Had they all really agreed to unite their clans? "Then we are agreed?"

The four of them nodded their heads in agreement. They had chosen peace.

Salome stood up, clapped her hands together, and smiled, "I think we have a wedding to plan."

CHAPTER 25
CRISPIN

Crispin wanted to throttle Adonijah the night before when he heard that his sister was captured by the Thrak. He heard the pirates' stories about the Gomorrians and the thought of his sister in their cruel hands was more than he could bear. Had Rahab not soothed him, he would have killed the trio for no other reason than they were clearly enemies and deserved to be executed before they could betray him.

Safe.

Salome was safe according to his unexpected guests and he held on to the hope that she was not only in Oakenshire, but had escaped any brutality and torture in Gomorrah. Would he even recognize her when he saw her again? Was it possible she succumbed to her injuries, and he would never get the chance to say goodbye?

He casted out those tormenting thoughts as he sat by the crackling fire the pirates built at their new campsite. Haldane brewed a warm, rum-spiked drink that Crispin welcomed, hoping to drown his anxiety.

Adonijah approached him slowly from across the bonfire and motioned to the area next to the prince. "Mind if I sit?"

Crispin wanted to tell him to piss off, but with eyes on him from around the camp, the prince chose to be diplomatic and patted the ground next to him.

Once the sell-sword made himself comfortable, taking a sip of Haldane's concoction, he cleared his throat and said, "Not a moment goes by that I don't blame myself for failing to protect your sister when she needed me the most."

"I don't want to talk about her."

"Your sister is the bravest woman I know," Adonijah persisted, which irked Crispin. "I've seen her face assassins and bring them to their knees. I've seen her risk her life to free men and women being led to their executions. I've seen her face monsters, both human and creature alike, and come out bloodied, but victorious. I've never met a woman like her -"

"I know how incredible my sister is," Crispin cut him off. "I do not need you to tell me what I already know."

"I failed to protect Salome in her hour of need," Adonijah whispered as he stared at his tin mug, "but I swear, that is not a mistake I will make again. I will live, fight, and die by her side."

Crispin heard the conviction, the sorrow, the truth in the sell-sword's voice and although he desperately wanted to blame him for what happened to his sister, he could hear Salome's voice in his head urging him to give Adonijah a chance. That he wasn't truly at fault for her capture. Adonijah looked broken and then it hit him.

"You're in love with her, aren't you?" Crispin asked. Adonijah stared at him, and by the look on his face, Crispin knew the man was conflicted. "You speak as if you are in love with my sister, but the way you look at your Andrago companion tells me differently." Crispin smiled, but there was nothing kind in the prince's eyes.

Adonijah raked a hand through his dark hair. "I love your sister."

"But?"

Adonijah's eyes fell upon Leoti, who was on the other side of the camp showing the pirates her falcon, Tiki. "Our paths crossed for a reason, but I do not know if your sister and I are headed in the same direction."

"Meaning, she's a princess and you're a sell sword?" Crispin tore a piece of the rabbit from the skewer and chewed it. "If there's one thing my sister isn't, it's a snob. Your title and rank wouldn't make a difference to her."

"I meant no offense to you or your sister," Adonijah corrected himself. "What I meant to say is she has responsibilities I will never truly understand or willingly volunteer to help her with. I am not suited for city living. Not suited for confinement."

"And the Andrago way of life would neither confine you nor thrust you into a life of civil service." Crispin bobbed his head as he glanced across the camp at Leoti, neither angry nor offended.

"That makes me sound selfish."

"Is it selfish to know what would make you happy and to pursue it?" Crispin locked eyes with him, a seriousness in his tone that hadn't been there before. "You would be doing yourself and my sister a disservice by pretending. I don't know you, but I know for a fact my sister deserves better than that."

Adonijah took a bite of his food and chewed silently until Leoti's laugh drew his attention. Crispin watched with great interest as Adonijah's face lit up as he watched the Andrago.

"Does she know how you feel?" Crispin asked, forcing Adonijah to meet his gaze.

"No, and I am not sure what I feel exactly." He rubbed the back of his neck as he stretched his legs out in front of him. "I care deeply for Salome," his eyes found Leoti once more, "but I feel drawn to Leoti and I don't understand why."

Crispin leaned forward and whispered, "I'd make your intentions known, if I were you. And soon."

Adonijah frowned. "Why?"

Crispin jutted his chin toward the group of pirates surrounding Leoti and smirked. "Because if you don't, I guarantee one of those scallywags will."

"Does this mean you won't slit my throat in my sleep?" Adonijah asked as Crispin rose from his seat, cracking his back.

The prince stared at him, his eyes revealing none of his thoughts, but after a moment's hesitation, Crispin pat Adonijah on the shoulder. "Not tonight."

"There's something else you should know." Adonijah tapped the side of his mug rhythmically. "Something I wish I had told Salome but didn't have the courage to."

"And what's that?"

"Pash and I are half-brothers," Adonijah said after taking a deep breath. "We share the same father."

"I already know you are brothers. I learned of it the night we met."

"Our father is Lord Gershom." The confession stole Crispin's breath, and he stepped back. "We were on our way to Northwind to assassinate him when you found us."

Part of Crispin's brain urged him to stab Adonijah through the chest and be done with it, but the other part of him demanded he spare the man. He had willingly confessed who he was – who his father was – and even though Gershom had slaughtered his mother and brothers, Adonijah wasn't responsible for their murders. He even said they were on their way to kill their father – which could be a lie, but when he looked into Adonijah's eyes, he just knew he was telling the truth. He had borne his soul and his true identity to him, and if Zophar were with him, he would insist Crispin give him a chance to prove himself a worthy ally.

The prince once again patted him on the shoulder and mumbled, "We are not our fathers."

He refused to wait for a response. He turned on his heel and walked toward Rahab who was sharpening her knives by her sleeping bag. He knew if anyone would be able to cheer him up, it was her. He felt safe in her embrace, felt seen in her presence, and felt peace when she spoke to him. She was his saving grace, and he needed her now more than ever. The image of what Salome might have endured at the hands of the Thrak was consuming his thoughts, but now Adonijah's confession took up residence in his head.

"Let's hope one of those knives doesn't have my name on it," Crispin smirked as he hovered above the pirate.

She caught his gaze and winked. "Time will tell, princeling."

He laid flat on his back, placing his head on her lap. "I like when you say sweet things to me."

Rahab rolled her eyes but didn't attempt to hide her smile.

"There's that smile I love." Crispin grinned and she swatted at him with a huff.

"You'll have me looking soft to the crew and I can't have that." She shook her head as she ran her fingers through his curls.

"And if they saw me kissing their First Mate?" His eyes danced with mischief and desire.

She pointed one of her freshly sharpened daggers at him and quirked an eyebrow. "Keep your sappy expressions of love to yourself, Your Mightiness."

"Last I checked," Crispin sat up and leaned close to her, even though the tip of her knife poked him in the chest, "we're on the Mainland now."

"Your point?"

"When we're on the seas, I do what you say. When we're on dry land, you do what I say."

Rahab chuckled darkly, "Is that how we're playing this game, Crispin?"

Hearing his name come from her lips excited him and seemed to wash all of his troubled thoughts away. He tilted his head and slowly moved closer. "What say you, Queen of the Seas?" he whispered against her lips.

"I say," she said in a low, raspy voice, "you're in for a heap of trouble once we get back on a ship."

Crispin smiled, "I think I'll take my chances." He pressed his lips against hers and his heart leapt when she kissed him back, running the tips of her fingers along his beard.

Rahab pulled away sooner than he wanted her to, but she gripped his chin between her fingers and said, "I look forward to ordering you around the moment your boots land on the deck of my ship."

"Whatever my queen commands."

She tipped his chin up, forcing him to look into her hazel eyes. "I know you're worried about your sister, but the important thing is she's alive."

A tear slipped down his cheek. "What if she's not the same…"

"Whether she was harmed or not, she will never be the same as she was before." When his bottom lip quivered, she brushed her fingers through his hair and whispered, "Strength will find her. I speak from experience, princeling. When I was left for dead in Uri's dungeons, I knew I would never be the same, if I made it out alive. It's been years, and I'm still not over what happened to me," she cupped his face and leaned her forehead against his. "I survived and she will too."

All Crispin could do was hope and pray she was right.

CHAPTER 26

NIABI

When the army Niabi dispatched to claim Gomorrah for Prince Thanos returned, she demanded for Pash to be brought to her private quarters immediately, to give his report. So, when Ophir, Gershom's brother, entered her office, she was not only confused but irritated. She didn't bother hiding her disregard for the oldest member of the Shadows. She had only permitted him to join the order she founded as a show of goodwill when she first allied herself with Gershom. Now, over two decades later, she still hadn't warmed up to him.

Tala motioned the Shadow inside and he marched up to the queen's desk and bowed.

"I sent for Commander Pash," Niabi eyed the bald man up and down. "Yet, you stand before me. Why?"

Ophir didn't bat an eye at her tone as he straightened to his full height. "I bring sorrowful news, Your Highness." He glanced around the study before suggesting, "Perhaps, my brother should be in attendance for my report?"

"Bold of you to suggest who should be privy to your report, Ophir." Niabi glared at him, fighting the urge to throw him in a cell next to the disgraced second in command just for good measure.

"I meant no offense," Ophir stammered. "I just thought -"

"Lord Gershom has been arrested for treason." Niabi cut him off and motioned for Tala to shut the door as Anaktu took his place standing to her right-hand side.

"Treason?" the Shadow's eyes widened. "Is my brother...?"

"Dead?" She shook her head and straightened in her chair. "Not yet."

"Your Highness, might I ask -"

"You may not." She narrowed her eyes, her patience had run thin, and she wanted to know why Pash hadn't come to give his report. "What is this sorrowful news you bring me instead of your commander?"

"It is about my nephew."

Niabi's heart jolted but she kept her expression unreadable. She perfected her nonchalant glare over the years, and she was grateful it was finally paying off. "What about the commander?"

"While we camped, awaiting to launch our assault on Gomorrah, a sell-sword found his way to our site. It turned out the trespasser was Pash's half-brother, Adonijah."

"Half-brother?" Niabi didn't know about Pash having any siblings.

"Yes, my queen." Ophir nodded. "Bastard born, but a son of my brother, none-theless. I wanted to have him executed for trespassing, but Pash wouldn't allow it, wouldn't listen to reason. He had Adonijah confined to our camp while we left for Gomorrah, but when we arrived, we found another army had laid siege to the city. Krazaks, Stormcrags, Numbio, even Bellators fought to rescue your sister from the Thrak."

"The Thrak had Salome?" She hadn't expected her sister to be a part of Ophir's tale, but then her thoughts drifted to why Matlidys would capture Salome and not try to cash in on the reward money Niabi had offered.

"From what Leoti could see, your sister was rescued, and the city was destroyed. Pash ordered us to return to camp which angered the young Prince Thanos."

Niabi couldn't help but chuckle at the thought of the prince throwing a tantrum over the turn of events. But when Ophir stopped recounting his tale, she rolled her eyes and motioned for him to continue.

"What is this sorrowful news you continue to tip-toe around?" Niabi didn't truly care about Gomorrah's fate. She didn't even care that her sister's army had destroyed the wretched place. But what she did care about was Pash. "Where is the commander?"

"When we returned to our camp, his half-brother killed one of the Shadows and Pash and Leoti helped him escape before his execution," Ophir met her gaze. "We tracked them down. I even asked Pash to rejoin us, that you would be forgiving of his temporary lapse in judgment, but he chose his brother over the crown. We ended up drawing swords against him, but my group was ambushed by vigilantes, and they took Pash with them."

Niabi cocked her head to the side. "Are you trying to tell me that Pash deserted his post?"

"I am trying to tell you, Pash is a traitor. His half-brother serves your sister and if Pash chose to stay with his rebel brother, if Pash chose to desert his command and aid an enemy of the crown, then he has committed treason."

Niabi forced herself to meet Tala's worried gaze. "And Leoti?" she asked. "Did Pash force her to accompany him against her will?"

Ophir shifted side-to-side, most likely feeling the weight of Tala's gaze boring into the back of his skull. "The warg joined the brothers of her own free will."

"Is there anything else you have to report, Ophir?" Niabi could sense Tala's growing anger and didn't want him to say anything about Pash or Leoti in front of Ophir. He was not to be trusted. If anyone would try to usurp Pash's position out of spite, it would be his uncle.

He shook his head. "No, Your Highness."

Niabi waved him away and Tala opened the door to let the Shadow out. "That will be all."

Though he looked like he wanted to say something else, he'd been dismissed, and like a good soldier, Ophir bowed and left. Once the door was closed and he was well out of earshot, Tala took a step toward Niabi.

"Do you believe him?"

Niabi poured herself a glass of water and offered Tala one which he declined. "Ophir is many things, but I do not believe him to be the teller of tall tales."

"So, you believe Pash deserted his command to join up with the rebels? You believe my daughter would abandon us?"

Tala's voice was on the verge of rage and brokenness which spurred the heavily pregnant queen to stand up and approach him. She grabbed his hands in hers and forced him to meet her gaze. "Tala, listen to me. There is more to this story than what Ophir is telling us. I do not believe for a moment that Pash and Leoti are traitors."

"Then what do you intend to do?" he asked, taking a deep breath.

"There is nothing I can do." She reached behind her and grabbed her glass from her desk and took a sip. "All we can do is wait for them to return."

"And what if these ruffians, who supposedly captured them, are torturing them? Or what if they've already killed them?" Tala was unhinged and all Niabi could do was speak softly and hope she soothed his frayed nerves.

"Tala, we will see them again. Pash is the Commander of Shadows and Leoti is a powerful warg. If anyone could escape their captors and make their way back home, it would be them." She squeezed his hand. "And if Pash did desert his post to save his brother, then he must have had a good reason."

Tala stared into her eyes, searching for something. "You trust him that much?"

"He has never given me a reason not to trust him." She cupped his face in her hands and offered a small smile. "We will see them again. I promise."

"You would have me do nothing then?"

It pained her to say it, but she nodded. "Your place is here, with me. If I lose you, I will be vulnerable, and I already have too many enemies to fend off."

She slipped her arms around his neck and hugged him tight. "We will see them again."

She said it again more for her benefit than Tala's. On the outside, she appeared calm, but inside, her heart was breaking. Pash had chosen to save his brother when they were on opposite sides of the upcoming war. He had deserted his command, left his men in the hands of his scheming uncle, and for what? He'd never mentioned this brother to her before, how close could they actually be?

Drawing back from Tala, she cradled her swollen belly and for the first time was nervous that she might raise this child without the man she loved. It felt too much like how she raised Rollo without Dichali. She'd guarded her heart and had always kept Pash at arms-length so she wouldn't get hurt again, but now that she'd let him in, now that they were expecting a child together, she couldn't help but feel like she was drowning, and there was no one there to rescue her.

CHAPTER 27
SALOME

When word was sent to Salome that three war ships from the Eastern Lands had arrived, she quickly made her way to what used to be the throne room, now overrun by greenery and roots protruding through the slate floors and took her place upon her wooden throne.

Jinn took his place at her right-hand side, straightened his clothes, and slicked his hair out of his face. He seemed relieved that his father had sent aid and that they had arrived rapidly, but the second the Eastern delegation entered the room, the prince paled. The elderly man leading the small group shared similar features with Jinn, but while the prince was clean shaven and had dark features, the man using an intricately carved wooden cane to steady himself, had long white hair and a matching mustache.

"Is that...?" Salome started.

"My father," Jinn nodded. "I didn't expect him to come with the reinforcements," he whispered.

"Why do you think he came?" she glanced up at him.

Jinn met her curious gaze but whatever he was thinking, he kept to himself.

"Jinn?" she sent down their bond. *"What is it?"*

She felt a sudden shiver crawl up her spine as Jinn's attention shifted from her to the old man hobbling toward them. The King of Sakurai reached the dais and smiled. He acknowledged his son then fixated on Salome. The way he held her gaze was odd, like he had a deep, dark secret, and she wished she could get him to stop staring at her so unabashedly.

Jinn's shoulders tensed, as if he too was put off by how his father was looking at her. Clearing his throat, the prince drew the king's attention. "Father, I didn't expect you to make the journey from the Jade Palace."

Kenji took a step forward, stretching his hand out for Jinn to grasp. "It's been far too long since I left our shores." The king's gaze once again found its way to Salome. "And I wanted to meet the lost princess for myself."

Salome stood from her throne and made her way toward Jinn's father. Offering a slight bow of her head in respect, Salome said, "It is an honor to welcome you to Oakenshire, Your Highness. Thank you for sending aid."

"Of course," he smiled brightly, crinkling the corners of his eyes.

"You've had a long journey," Salome motioned toward the double doors the king and his entourage had come through. "Perhaps you would like to see your rooms and have refreshments -"

"If it would be alright," the king politely interrupted, causing Jinn to stand straighter. "I had hoped to have a private audience with you, Princess." Kenji's eyes darted to his son but before Jinn could get a word in, he said, "One leader to another."

Salome bobbed her head, even though her heart was thrashing in her chest. Forcing a smile, she motioned them toward the secluded terrace outside of the throne room. "Of course, Your Grace."

Sparring one last glance Jinn's way, Salome led the Easterner outside where a cool breeze was blowing. Once seated at the table, drinks and plates filled with dried meats and fruit were served. Taking a long sip of her wine, Salome waited for Kenji to initiate their meeting. She remembered enough of her lessons on proper etiquette in dealing with other royals to know since the King of Sakurai asked for an audience, it was up to him to bring up the topic at hand. It seemed like a small eternity before he finally set down his glass and spoke.

"Thank you for agreeing to meet with me, Princess." Kenji sat in the seat opposite her overlooking the Eastern ships docked in the harbor.

"It's the least I can do to thank you for bringing aid in our time of need." Salome poured a second glass of wine, offering it to the king who gratefully accepted. After taking another gulp, she placed her glass down on the table, the clink drawing the king's eyes. "What is it you want from me, Your Majesty?

His eyes were filled with confusion. He tilted his head, his white hair falling across his forehead in the same manner Jinn's did. "Want from you?"

She squirmed in her seat, shifting her gaze from his face to the sea. Jinn was the spitting image of his father and in the sunlight, his eyes were the same warm golden-brown. She cleared her throat, lifting the glass to her lips again. "It seems everyone wants something from me these days."

He bobbed his head in understanding. "A crown is a heavy burden to bear."

She shot the king an intrigued look. "Are you saying you aren't here to ask me for something? Money? Promises? An alliance written in blood?"

The king shifted his weight before meeting her gaze, as if what he was about to say was hard for him to bring up. "I want to talk to you about my son."

Her heart raced. "So, you want a formal alliance, then."

He chuckled. "You misunderstand. I don't expect you to marry Jinn, but there is something you should know about him. Something he would never tell you himself."

She was both eager and afraid for the king to continue. She'd already gone through the heartache of Adonijah keeping secrets from her and it cost her dearly. If Jinn had also been lying to her, she didn't know if she would be strong enough to lose him too. "You have my attention."

Kenji leaned closer, as if he was going to share a secret with her. "When Jinn was a little boy, no more than six or seven, he told us he'd been having strange dreams.

Dreams of fire, of ash, of blood. Dreams that scared him, but dreams that he said felt real."

Salome cocked her head to the side. "Are you telling me Jinn used to have nightmares? No disrespect, but it's not uncommon."

"That's what my wife and I thought as well," he held up an index finger to stress his point. "Just nightmares. But he'd have these dreams almost nightly, so we had our Healers examine him. They said nothing was wrong with him. So, we had the oracle speak with him. The only thing Jinn would constantly talk about was a girl. He saw her in a burning city. He saw her in a forest training with different weapons. He saw her riding a horse, watched as she stalked through the woods hunting, watched as she got tattooed."

Salome froze in her seat, her eyes glued to the king.

"As he grew older, so did she. The oracle said he was dreaming of his future love – the woman who would bring peace to his heart. Once he reached the age of marriage, he rejected every suitor to his mother's dismay. He kept saying one day, he'd find her. I am ashamed to say, I never believed he would."

Salome gulped. Even though there was a cool breeze wafting around them, she felt like her skin was on fire. "What changed your mind?" she whispered so softly she was afraid he hadn't heard her.

Kenji reached into his robe and pulled out a folded parchment. A letter by the shape of it. "May I?" Salome nodded and motioned for him to read it aloud. "This is the letter Jinn sent me asking for me to send troops to aid you in reclaiming your ancestral throne." He unfolded it and handed it to her. She warily grabbed ahold of it and let her eyes scan over the neat penmanship. Kenji pointed to the bottom where Jinn signed the letter. "At the end, he said, '*Father, I found her.*' You see, that girl he described had wild curls and two different color eyes."

Kenji pulled out two more sheets of paper from his pocket and flattened them on the table, smoothing them out with care. When Salome glanced at the drawings, it took her breath away. One was of her when she was no more than seven or eight years old, and the other was a recent sketch of her.

"My son never thought he had any talent, but I think he captured your beauty perfectly."

"Jinn drew these?" She didn't dare touch them, fearing she'd smudge the charcoal. She let her hand hover above them an inch or two. Her mouth was suddenly bone dry, so she picked up her wine glass to coat her throat.

The king pointed at the recent rendering with a smile. "He drew this one a year ago. They are yours, if you want them."

"Why are you telling me this?" Her voice came out raspier than she expected.

"For as long as I can remember, he's been searching for you and here you are." Kenji reached for her hand and patted it gently. "Jinn always believed he had a greater destiny than to be King of Sakurai."

"What could be greater than being king?"

The king smiled and it reminded her of Jinn. "Being of service. I have known for years that Jinn was not interested in being my successor. To be fair, he was never meant to be. Jinn is my last son, but he wasn't my only son. I've lost two sons and a daughter. Nobu, my first born, drowned when he was eight. Itsuki was ill, had a cough for months that wouldn't go away and finally succumbed in his teenage years."

Salome fought the urge to get up and hug the man. "I'm sorry. I know about loss."

"It is a heavier burden than a crown, I dare say."

"And Anka?" Jinn mentioned his sister was betrothed to her eldest brother, Lykos, and had died a few years ago. "What happened to her?"

Tears welled in Kenji's eyes. "My sweet daughter was betrothed to your oldest brother, Lykos. When he died, she was devastated. Some of our older citizens believed she was cursed, and no man wanted her, fearing Death followed her. After years of being rejected by suitors, ostracized by our people, losing her two brothers, and her beauty fading, she couldn't defeat the darkness that clouded her mind and poisoned her heart. She..." The king wiped his eyes and cleared his throat before continuing. "She was found days later, washed up on the shore."

"I'm so sorry, I didn't know."

"Jinn is my last born. He was never meant to sit on the Jade Throne."

Salome placed her hand on top of his. "He loves his people, and he knows his duty to them." She meant it to be reassuring but the king shook his head and gave her a warm smile.

"For the first time in years, he is alive, and I know it's because of you." He stood and she jumped up from her seat. "I don't know what your feelings and intentions are for my son, but I thought you should know how deeply he cares for you. How deeply he's always cared for you, even before you officially met."

Salome knew she didn't owe him any explanation, but she felt she wanted to share her thoughts and feelings with him. But before she could, Cato bolted through the arched terrace doorway, breathing heavily, as if he had sprinted the entire length of the castle to bring her a message.

"Cato?" Salome turned her full attention to him. "What is it?"

"Riders approaching from the west." Cato caught his breath, hands perched on his hips.

~

Salome made her way to the watchtower, Cato and King Kenji in tow. Jinn and Heru were already there, watching the approaching group. They waved no flags and gave no indication of who they were or where they hailed from. She knew they weren't Shadows. The northern fighters donned their black uniforms with pride and would never stoop to pretending to be anyone else. She looked through the distant faces, trying to see if she spied anyone she knew. Instead, she saw a woman with icy blue hair, a man who looked like a giant, a halfling, and was that a pirate captain?

"Do we know who they are?" Salome asked Jinn, but he didn't respond. She glanced in his direction and saw him and his father whispering back and forth. Jinn looked rattled. She cleared her throat, drawing their attention. "Do we know who they are?" she repeated her question.

Jinn distanced himself from his father and shook his head. "No. They don't seem to be a large company, but they could be a group sent on someone's behalf to speak with you or give their lists of demands to keep from attacking us."

Salome's nostrils flared. "If they are looking for trouble, they've come to the right place." She scanned the group as they got closer, now starting to make out faces. She didn't recognize anyone, but one man's gait looked familiar. She squinted, as if that would help her identify him. She gasped, her hand covering her mouth. "It can't be."

"Salome?" Jinn reached out for her, but she turned and fled down the steps as fast as her feet could carry her. She sprinted by soldiers and castle attendants, pushing them out of her way if necessary, apologizing as she darted past. She made it to the bailey and shouted at the gatekeepers to open the gate.

"Did you say open the gate?" One of the soldiers from Numbio looked at her wide eyed.

"Open the gate!" Salome stood before the closed entrance, itching to get outside to see if it was really him.

Jinn reached her side. "Do you know them?"

She was so focused on watching the gate lift, listening to the metal gears screech, that she didn't hear Jinn's question. With the prince by her side, they made their way to the lowered drawbridge. On the other side of the bridge, the group stopped. A man stepped in front of the motley crew and pulled his hood off his head.

His teary eyes met her awaiting gaze. For a moment, no one moved or said anything. She sucked in a cool breath; her heart fluttered wildly in her chest. Almighty, was this even possible? Was he really standing a hundred feet in front of her? Was her mind playing tricks on her?

She opened her mouth, but nothing came out. The sting from keeping her emotions in check burned the back of her throat. This time, her voice came out raspy, "Crispin?"

Crispin took off toward Salome and she sprinted to meet him. Jinn motioned for the archers to stand down as Salome jumped into her brother's embrace, wrapping her arms around his neck. Tears streamed down their cheeks as they laughed and cried as if no one was watching them. She felt the tension, grief, worry, and stress leave her body the moment she reached him.

"I've missed you," Crispin whispered in her ear, running his fingers over her intricately braided hair.

"I feared you were dead." Salome pulled back, holding his face in her hands, making sure he was really standing before her. The prickle of his new facial hair tickled her fingers. "This is new," she smiled.

Crispin rolled his eyes and smirked. "Alright, let's have it. Whatever cruel thing you have to say, spit it out while I'm still in a good mood."

She tapped his face lovingly, still overwhelmed that the brother she prayed had survived the Caverns of the Undead, was standing before her. "It suits you."

He grinned, proudly rubbing his fingers across his jawline. "It's not as long and bushy as Zophar's, but I think the old man will still be impressed by it." Crispin looked past Salome, scanning the people for their red bearded guardian. "Where is he? Smoking that pipe of his, I imagine."

Salome's bottom lip quivered, and she swiped tears from her face.

"What is it?" he asked.

"I'm sorry," she whispered, a tremble in her soft voice.

Crispin shook his head. "No." He took a step back. "No, he can't be… But the Numbio…"

"Come inside. There's a lot for us to talk about." Salome extended her hand to him.

As the group he was travelling with made their way across the drawbridge, she caught sight of Adonijah, his hood over his head. Their eyes locked and a wave of anger, surprise, and sadness flooded her heart. She wasn't sure if she wanted to hug him or stab him.

Adonijah stopped next to Crispin, eyes fixed on her. "Hi."

She gritted her teeth, forcing her face to still, to hide the emotions clearly ripping her heart apart. "You're alive."

An awkward tension hovered over the trio until Adonijah cleared his throat and said, "We should talk."

Salome's nostrils flared, but before she could say anything, Crispin chimed in. "Perhaps you can find some time to speak with Adonijah later tonight? Maybe, after we eat and catch up with one another."

Salome reluctantly agreed to meet Adonijah and once he walked away, she quickly put him out of her mind. She grabbed Crispin's arm and led him inside Oakenshire. He was alive and well and finally back home. By the looks of the company he kept, he probably had plenty of stories to share with her and she wanted to hear every single one of them.

CHAPTER 28
GERSHOM

"Wait for me," Gershom called out to Issachar as they ran through the Black Forest.

They had been instructed by their fathers to stay at the hunting campgrounds, but before the sun had fully peaked over the horizon, the wild and reckless Prince Issachar had stirred Gershom from his peaceful sleep and ordered him to come along. Although they were only ten years old, Gershom already knew his place in life. It was the same as his father's. Protect and serve the crown. So, when his best friend gave him an order, he knew to obey, even if it went against his own father's wishes.

"Issachar?" Gershom cried out, hoping to catch up to his friend before one of the fabled monstrosities of the forest found him first. Or worse. His father. "Issachar -"

"Shhh!" Issachar stepped out from a bush and put his index finger to his lips. "I found something."

"We should go back before our fathers realize we've gone missing." Gershom feared disobeying Issachar since he was to be the future king one day, but his father's whippings were in the forefront of his mind. The Commander was not one for foolishness and even though it was Issachar's idea to wander off that morning, his father would state his case that Gershom should have convinced the hot-headed royal to stay put for his own safety. As if Gershom had any sway in the prince's actions. If he had the gift of persuasion, he would have been able to sweet-talk his way out of every unwarranted beating he'd incurred from his father's brutal hands.

"Issachar," Gershom pleaded once more as the prince turned his focus on something he'd spotted down the path. "I don't hear the hounds searching for us, so there's still time for us to return to camp without anyone ever knowing we left."

"Where is your sense of adventure, Gershom?" the prince flashed a mischievous smile at his friend. "Look at what I found."

Gershom wanted to run. Run as far as he could and beg for his father's mercy, but if he left the prince alone, he'd face the king's wrath and that wasn't any better. Reluctantly, Gershom joined his companion behind the bushes and glanced in the direction Issachar pointed, where a small cabin sat nestled in the pines. The sight was odd for sure, since it was well known no one actually dwelled in the Black Forest because of all the creatures and vagabonds rumored to terrorize the woods. But right in front of him, not so much as a stone's throw away, sat a cabin with smoke wafting up the chimney.

"We should go." Gershom's mouth was dry. If someone chose to live in the Black Forest, they were not a person to be trifled with.

"Don't you want to see who lives there?" Issachar wiggled his eyebrows and Gershom quickly shook his head in protest.

"Please, Issachar." His eyes were wide, and sweat was dripping down his back. "We shouldn't be out -"

"I dare you to go inside."

"What?" Gershom stared at him in terror. "No."

Issachar narrowed his eyes, putting his princely mask in place. "I order you to go inside that cabin."

To disobey now was a guaranteed beating that would take him weeks to recover from, so he took a deep breath before slowly making his way to the clearly not abandoned cabin. Even if the house was empty at the present, the owner wasn't too far if they left something cooking in the fireplace. Once he got to the front door, Gershom risked a final pleading look where he knew Issachar was hiding, but when no order to retreat came, he raised his balled-up fist and gently knocked on the door.

Nothing. No answer.

His hand trembled as he grabbed the knob and opened the creaky wooden door. Expecting to find something similar to a torture chamber, he was pleasantly surprised and relieved to see it was just an ordinary cabin. A small cot sat to one side with a table in the center. A cauldron hung upon the open flame in the stone fireplace, but no one was inside the one room hovel. Gershom took another step inside to look around when a strong gust of wind whipped through slamming the door shut. Frightened, he turned and tried tugging the door open, but it wouldn't budge. He was stuck inside. But at least he was alone.

"You've wandered far from your camp," a woman's voice sounded, sending a bolt of fear zinging through his body.

Whipping around, he saw a beautiful woman with long black hair, green eyes, and long black fingernails stirring what he could only imagine was some unholy concoction.

"Please, don't hurt me," he cried out.

Her eyes latched onto his and she smiled. "Oh, child, I do not intend to harm you. I am here to help you."

"Help me?" He pressed his back against the door, keeping the maximum distance between them. "What do you want from me? Who are you?"

"My name is of little importance at the present," she continued stirring her stew. "What is important is that I know who you are, Gershom of Northwind. I know who you serve, and I know that if you do not heed my warning, you will not live to see your glory."

"Glory?" He took a tentative step forward. "You're a witch, aren't you?"

Her side-eyed grin reminded him of a cat that had just toyed with a mouse before swallowing it whole.

"Let me see your hand."

Gulping so loud he was positive the woman heard it, he did as she instructed, walking to her with his palm upturned. Her hands were cold and sent a shiver down his spine the second she touched him. She stroked her thumb up and down his small hand before looking into his eyes.

"You harbor a lot of anger and desire to be the one making all the decisions." Before he could deny her words, she continued. "You will betray your closest friend -"

Gershom ripped his hand away. "That's a filthy lie! I would never betray my friend."

"You will have two sons by two different women," she continued, unfazed by his protests. "Neither will love you."

"Why are you saying these things?" Gershom couldn't help the cry that escaped his lips.

"You will commit many sins, little lord. You will hurt those closest to you and will truly trust no one."

"Stop!" Gershom slammed his hands over his ears, rocking his head back and forth, hoping she would quit talking. "I'm a good boy. I know my duty. I know my place."

"You may know your place," she stood from her stool, fire blazing in her eyes, "but you are not content with it."

"I am to be the next Master of War, like my father. I am to protect the future king. I am to -"

The woman smiled, but he felt no warmth or comfort from her calculating gaze. "The penalty for your betrayal will be the Hunter's blade buried deep in your heart."

His throat tightened, but he mustered the courage to refute her false prophecy. "But there are no Hunters."

She motioned toward the door. "Your friend, the prince, is growing anxious waiting for you in the bushes up on the ridge," she said sweetly. "It is time for you to leave."

He marched to the door, but paused when his hand touched the knob. Without his prompting, it opened, but his hesitancy in leaving hadn't stemmed from wondering if the door would open.

"Ask your question." Her voice echoed behind him.

He didn't turn to look at her, but whispered, "How can I escape this fate?"

"Do not be seduced by the Mistress of Night."

"But who is -" When he looked behind him not only was the woman gone, but the entire cabin had disappeared. He stood in the middle of the Black Forest where the house should have been.

"What happened in there?" Issachar hopped up from his hiding spot and sprinted to him, looking just as confused as Gershom was that the cabin vanished.

Before Gershom could answer the prince's question, pounding hooves and howls of the royal hounds echoed around them. The king and Gershom's father, along with a host of soldiers, appeared from the trees and neither man looked amused.

Gershom hadn't thought about that day in years but sitting in a dark and foul-smelling cell in the dungeons of Northwind, he found he had nothing but time on his hands. Even though he spent most of his life obeying Issachar's commands, he still ended up being seduced by the Mistress of the Night and betraying his childhood best friend. He might be marked for the Hunter's blade, but all was not lost. Not yet. He had years to plan his revenge, to stage his coup. Sure, things looked bleak at the moment, but he had sworn years ago to make Niabi suffer, and he intended to do just that when the moment was right.

Feet scuffed against the stone pavers outside his cell door, but he didn't move from his seated position against his cell wall. If it was that slop that was deemed his dinner, he wasn't in any hurry to lap it up. But the tiny opening at the foot of the door didn't open. The slat where he could see someone's eyes staring at him slid open, and he relaxed, already knowing who the mysterious visitor was.

"What news?" he asked, voice raw from disuse.

"Everything is going according to plan, my King," the silvery voice danced in his cell, drawing a wicked smile from him.

"Excellent, Vilora." He leaned his head against the cold stone wall and glared up at the ceiling, knowing multiple stories above him, sat Niabi, unaware of his schemes. "Vengeance will be mine."

CHAPTER 29

SALOME

After swapping stories of their separate adventures, and how Crispin had faced off with their fire wielding sister, they sat in a comfortable silence, drinking a glass of wine in memory of Zophar. Telling her brother about Zophar's death was the hardest thing she'd ever done. Crispin hadn't cried, he'd just listened intently to each word she spoke until he was all caught up. Months apart but they picked up right where they left off.

He cleared his throat and raised his glass. "To Zophar. The best father and friend."

"To Zophar." She clinked her glass against his and took a long sip. "I miss him."

"I wish I could have had the chance to say goodbye." Crispin swiped a lone tear from his cheek. "The last memory I have of him is in the Cavern of the Undead, when I was swept away, and he looked terrified."

She grabbed his hand and squeezed until he met her gaze. "I'm sorry I couldn't save him."

Crispin pulled her to him, her face resting against his chest. "It's not your fault."

"I wish I could have done more."

"You leveled an entire city on his behalf. I'd say you exacted your justice." Crispin kissed her forehead and held her tighter. "I'm just glad you survived. I don't know what I would have done without you."

She sat up and wiped her eyes with her palms. "Well, now that you're here, you can make all the decisions and I can go and fight a few sea monsters." Her attempt at levity was a welcome one and he laughed.

"As if you could have defeated Kubantu." He elbowed her shoulder and she swatted at him.

"Excuse me, but have you already forgotten that I fought and killed a cornigera and became the Red Maiden?" She snorted when he stuck his tongue out at her. "Maybe I should tell you again. Perhaps your ears stopped working during that part of the story."

"I do believe I missed the part about your relationship with Adonijah." He wiggled his eyebrows playfully, but she recoiled. She didn't want to think about Adonijah, let alone talk to her brother about him.

"I'm sorry," he cleared his throat. "You don't need to talk about him if you don't want to."

"How did you cross paths?"

"After escaping Borg, we ran into a horde of Shadows attacking three travelers. We decided to intervene. I have no qualms in killing Shadows. Turned out, Adonijah was with them and when we introduced ourselves, he told me he knew you." Crispin shrugged. "At first, I thought you would be happy to see him again, especially after hearing how he spoke about you."

"But?"

"I think that's a conversation for you and Adonijah to have."

"You beast." She threw a small pillow at him which he easily dodged. She twirled her curls in her fingers absentmindedly. "I loved him. He left." She shrugged, biting her bottom lip to keep from crying. "He broke my heart and lost my trust." Crispin stretched his arm across her shoulders and kissed her temple. "Did he tell you he's Gershom's son?" she asked, and he nodded.

"We are not our fathers," Crispin whispered.

Silence once again enveloped them. Salome wasn't sure what else to say. They'd both seen and experienced incredible things and suffered tragic losses. She had imagined their reunion including Zophar; the three of them laughing until their bellies hurt and smiling until their cheeks ached. But their guardian, the man who had truly been a father to them, was gone.

"I think -"

Salome didn't get to finish that thought because Crispin let loose a loud snore. He must have been exhausted to fall asleep sitting up. She slithered out from under his arm, carefully ushering his body down to a more comfortable position on the couch. Grabbing one of the blankets from his bed, she covered him, wiped hair from his face, kissed his cheek, and left him to sleep, knowing he would be perfectly safe in the castle.

Slipping out of her brother's room and walking down the hall toward her own chambers, she found she was wide awake and wanted someone to talk to; not wanting to be alone. Her thoughts drifted to Jinn. Seeing him shirtless the other day, having him so close to her, whispering in her ear and sending shivers down her spine. She wondered what it would be like to lay with him, to be wrapped in his warm and protective embrace.

She stopped when she tucked her hand in her pocket and felt the drawings King Kenji had given her. She pulled them out and looked at them, admiring the prince's exceptional talent and being in complete awe of what Jinn's secret had been. Why hadn't he told her? How was it even possible? Damaris had told her in the Isles of Myr that they must have shared a strong bond, but she thought it was because they were both magic wielders. If she had known he'd been searching for her his entire life…

Something shifted in the darkness capturing her undivided attention. Quickly, she tucked the papers back into her pocket and unsheathed her wolf dagger. Salome listened for a moment to see if whoever was lurking in the shadows would reveal themselves.

"I know you're there," she mustered as much courage as she could to sound intimidating. "Either you step into the light, or I'll gut you in the dark."

The hooded figure stepped out from behind a column and her fear vanished. "Did they hurt you?"

"Still lurking in the shadows, Adonijah?" She put her knife back in its sheath strapped to her thigh. "I suppose the darkness suits you."

"What did the Thrak do to you?" Even in the dark, she could sense the pain and grimace his face held. He was bold to ask her that question when he could have probably guessed the terror she endured.

"The question you should be asking is, what did *I* do to *them*?"

He ate the distance between them until they were standing a foot apart. She could see his face clearly once he pushed his hood back. "I cannot even begin to imagine what you must think of me but -"

She crossed her arms, "Try."

"Salome -" He reached for her, but she side stepped his advances.

"I gave you my trust," she hissed, interrupting him. "I gave you my heart. You broke both."

He raked a hand through his hair, regret in his eyes. "I know I hurt you and I'm sorry."

"I hope leaving was worth it."

"I never intended to leave you. Things got complicated." He rested one hand on his hip and the other rubbed the back of his neck. "I swore an oath to avenge my mother's death. Surely, you of all people can understand that."

"I understand loss and have come to know Death quite intimately." Seeing the sorrow in his eyes tugged at her heart and she softened her gaze and voice. Before she could think better of it, she reached out and gently grabbed his forearm. "You leaving wasn't what shattered me. It was that you lied. Lied about who you are, while insisting that I open up to you. Had you told me the truth, I wouldn't have stopped you from fulfilling your oath. I would have helped you."

"I know that now. I was a fool, but I'm back now."

She squeezed his arm. "I will always care for you, but we will never be together."

"It's because of Jinn, isn't it?" He didn't look or sound angry, but Salome still didn't appreciate him dragging the prince into their conversation.

"This has nothing to do with him."

"In my absence, I thought he would look out for you, but now I see he's poisoned you against me."

Her nostrils flared. "I think you did a good enough job of that on your own."

"So, that's it?" His voice was little more than a whisper. "You choose him?

"I choose me."

"I will fight, live, and die by your side." His eyes flicked up to meet hers and she took several steps back.

"It's dangerous to pledge oaths when one does not intend on keeping them."

"I swore to protect you and I -"

"Failed when it counted most," she spat viciously and was surprised when he recoiled, as if he'd been struck. "You failed to protect me from *you*." They stared at one another silently until she approached him, cupping his face in her hands. "I release you from your oath," she whispered as she pressed her forehead against his.

"I release you from whatever responsibility you believe you owe me. I release you, Adonijah."

"I hope one day you will forgive me." He wrapped his arms around her waist and held her close.

She couldn't help the tears that flowed disobediently down her face. He pulled his forehead from hers and wiped her cheeks.

"I will always love you," Adonijah squeezed her hand.

"And I you." Her bottom lip quivered. "But we are on two different paths now. Maybe in another life, we could have been happy together."

"If you will allow it," Adonijah looked into her glassy-eyes and sighed. "I would ask for you to let me continue to fight for you. I may no longer have your heart, but you will always have my sword."

Salome kissed his cheek and nodded in agreement. Before she completely lost all composure, she backed away from him and turned toward her bedroom door. She could feel his devastation, but she pressed onward, not daring to look back.

She closed the door and slipped into her bed, but sleep eluded her. She tossed and turned for hours; her mind restless. Adonijah was fresh in her thoughts, but deep down in her heart, she knew she'd made the right decision in ending whatever was going on between them. Saying she would always love him hadn't been a lie and that's what made her heart ache. If she had stayed in the Tree House Forest, if she hadn't gone on this journey, maybe if their paths had crossed then, they would have been happy roaming Adalore together. And months ago, that's exactly what she thought she wanted.

Turning over on her side facing the window with the moonlight kissing the waves of the Ignacia Sea, Salome replayed the conversation she and Crispin had earlier that evening. He said something that she overlooked at the time, but now she was itching to know more. He faced Niabi in the White Keep and discovered their sister had fire magic. And if she had magic that meant Salome should be able to communicate with her like she could with Jinn and Damaris.

Salome sat up and leaned her back against the cushioned headboard and chewed on the tip of her finger. Crispin would probably be furious if she reached out to Niabi, but she'd be lying if she denied the strong urge to see if it would work, and what her sister would say in response.

Maybe it was all the emotions of the day running wild through her mind, or the fact she just couldn't sleep and needed to talk to someone, but she closed her eyes and reached out to a door that was shrouded in darkness. As she approached, she saw withered flowers covering the archway around the door that belonged to Niabi. This was it. She shouldn't reach out, she shouldn't expose herself or her magic to the sister who was trying to hunt her down and exterminate her, but the temptation was too great.

"Niabi?"

CHAPTER 30

NIABI

Niabi couldn't sleep. All she could think about was Pash. She didn't care about the failure in Gomorrah, but what bothered her was that he had chosen his brother – his rebel brother – over her and their unborn child. She stepped onto her balcony and rested her elbows on the stone railing. The cold, gentle breeze creating goosebumps, the sounds of rushing water, and the barely audible music rising from the Night District, brought her immeasurable peace, though her heart was aching.

She loved Pash. She trusted him. But what if he never made it home to her? What would she do without him? What would she tell their child years from now, when he or she started asking questions?

"Niabi?"

Whipping around, facing her chamber doors, she unsheathed one of her knives, ready to defend herself from the intruder that had managed to sneak up behind her, but to her surprise, and confusion, no one was there. She looked around the balcony area but again came up empty.

She sheathed her dagger and then held her belly, as she inhaled deeply to calm herself down. She could have sworn she heard someone say her name, but she had been so stressed lately she must have just imagined it. But then she heard the soft voice echo in her head again, *"Niabi?"* and she knew she wasn't imaging anything. Who could possess the ability to speak to her through her thoughts? Although she was tempted to ignore whoever was reaching out to her, she decided to soothe the itch of curiosity, and opened the door to the unknown visitor.

"You seem to have me at a disadvantage," she cooed. *"You know who I am, but who are you?"*

"It worked," the voice replied. Niabi detected excitement and hesitancy from whoever was contacting her.

"You seem surprised."

At first, Niabi didn't think the voice was going to respond, but finally, she heard her say, *"You sound so much like her."*

Niabi cocked her head in confusion. *"Like who?"*

"Our mother."

The queen gasped. *"Salome? How are you doing this?"*

"You aren't the only one that possesses magic, sister."

Niabi smirked. The only way she would know about her magic was if Crispin had been reunited with her. *"And how is our dear brother doing?"*

"Alive," Salome's voice held a bite to it. *"No thanks to you."*

"Clearly there's a reason you've gone through the trouble of reaching out to me, Salome." She admired her sister's boldness, but instead of verbally sparring with Salome, Niabi was more curious to understand why she had reached out to begin with. *"So tell me, what do you want from me?"* Her aggressive question was met with silence. After a few moments, Niabi asked again. *"What do you want, Salome?"*

"I don't know," Salome whispered. *"I needed to talk to someone."*

Niabi laughed. *"So you reached out to me? Your enemy?"*

"I saw your past." That caught Niabi off guard. *"I saw what our father did to you and I'm sorry -"*

"Sorry?" Niabi interrupted with a hiss. Her throat tightened as she fought the tears bubbling within her. *"What are you sorry for? Are you sorry the man you called father was cruel and wicked? Are you sorry for looking into my past and seeing how I became your monster? Why are you sorry?"*

"I'm sorry for what happened to you."

"No, you're not." Niabi shook her head, her left hand ignited, and it took great effort to extinguish it. *"You pity me, and there is no greater insult than that."*

"Niabi-"

"What did Damaris show you?"

"How do you know it was Damaris who showed me your past?"

"She is the Oracle of Myr. Or have you already forgotten, I too, dwelled in the Scarlet Citadel?"

"She showed me how father stole your birthright. How he forced you to leave the Isles of Myr and forced you to marry for his gain. I saw how father treated you."

"Did Damaris show you how the monster was born?" Niabi gripped the balcony banister, dragging her fingernails across to soothe her anger. *"Did she show you the night Dichali was murdered?"*

"No."

Niabi saw Dichali's face, his warm smile, the dimples he passed to Rollo. The gravity of everyone she had lost consumed her, crushing her, until she felt as if her heart would burst. Cradling her swollen belly, she straightened, determined to make her sister see the truth. Why she desired for Salome to see this moment in her grief-filled history, she didn't understand, but she was dead set on her truth being made known.

"How does your magic work?" Niabi asked.

"I can communicate mentally with magic wielders and the departed."

"Memories? If I allow you access, can you see my memories?"

"Yes."

"Then I will show you what tipped the scales, sister." Niabi made her way into her

bedroom and sank into her mattress. A light breeze whirled around the room as she closed her eyes.

"Despite Issachar's intentions, I loved my husband deeply, and when our son, Rollo, was born, my desire for the White Throne vanished. I had finally found my place in the world. Ruling by Dichali's side, raising our son to be his heir, accepted by the Andrago as one of their own: I was finally free, and I was finally happy."

Niabi focused on the memory she wanted to share with her sister, mentally opening a door to her traumatic past.

"Dichali kept his promise to me the day I agreed to be his bride and gifted me a magnificent stallion named Nagrom. It was normal for me to go for nighttime rides to clear my head and enjoy the chilly breeze. But one night, when I returned from a late-night ride, I entered our tent and found three assassins making their way toward my sleeping husband and our two-year-old son.

"I unsheathed my knives and screamed for Dichali to wake up. As soon as his eyes opened, he grabbed the knife he had tucked underneath his pillow. I leapt for our son, slitting the throat of the assassin hovering over his crib. Dichali managed to kill one of his attackers, but the second was far too quick for my husband to defend himself. It was in that brief moment, that I realized, I wouldn't be able to save him.

"It all happened so fast. Dichali had taken a blade to the chest by the time the Andrago guards rushed in to arrest the last assassin.

"Tala grabbed my screaming son from his crib, as I sprinted to Dichali and held him in my arms, covered in his blood. His bronze face was draining of color and even though I beckoned for a healer to come at once, my husband reached up and turned my face to meet his gaze."

"It's alright," Dichali whispered.

"Stay with me, Dichali. Stay with me." Niabi sobbed. "I'm so sorry. Please don't leave me."

He weakly pulled her toward him, kissing her forehead. "I will see you again, my love, in the next life. Take care of our son."

"No. Dichali, please, please don't leave me."

She shook him several times when his eyes closed, but despite her screaming and crying, there was nothing she could do. He was gone. She wanted to sit there, holding his lifeless body until she woke up from the nightmare. She rocked him, pressing kisses against his forehead, softly singing Andrago lullabies in his ear.

"My queen," Tala crouched beside her, tears slipping down his cheeks. "My queen, you need to let him go."

"Where is my son?" Niabi didn't bother looking in his direction as she stroked her blood-stained fingers through Dichali's long, black hair.

"He is outside with my wife." Tala slipped his hand around her forearm, finally drawing her attention. "You must let him go, so the healers may prepare his body."

Her bottom lip quivered. "I can't."

"My queen -"

"If I let him go, then it'll be real," she bit back her sobs. "I can't, Tala. I can't let him go."

Tala squeezed her arm gently. "Niabi -"

An Andrago guard slipped into the tent and cleared his throat for permission to speak. Tala kept eye contact with Niabi as he said, "Speak."

"What would you have us do with the assassin?"

All of Niabi's grief turned molten and a fire blazed within her. "Where is he?"

"We have him subdued in the gathering tent, Your Majesty."

Niabi tore her gaze from the Andrago warrior and fixed her attention to Tala. "Take me to him."

"Niabi-"

"Now!"

Reluctantly, Tala led her to the gathering tent and upon entering, she ordered the room to be cleared. Once everyone had left, she and Tala stared upon the remaining assassin and her heart shattered. It wasn't a stranger who had killed her husband, but it was one of his best friends and most trusted soldier.

“Chua?” Niabi gasped as she glared at the familiar face tied to a post in the middle of the room. "Why?"

When Chua didn't respond, Tala growled, "Your queen asked you a question."

Chua spat on the ground before Niabi's feet. "She is *not* my queen."

Before Tala could react, Niabi unsheathed her knives and stabbed Chua in his right shoulder joint. "Why did you kill your king?" she gritted her teeth, beginning her interrogation.

The traitor screamed but refused to answer her, so she took her second dagger and pierced his other shoulder. Holding onto both hilts as his blood spilled down his arms, she said in a low, predatorial voice, "I will destroy you, piece by piece, until I am satisfied. Why did you kill your king? Why did you kill your friend?"

"We were ordered to," Chua hissed in breathless gasps.

"Ordered by who?"

Whimpering, and taking too long to answer her, she retrieved one weapon from his body and stabbed him above the knee. "Who ordered you to assassinate Dichali? Who ordered you to murder my son?" she whispered in his ear.

"Your father," he shouted. "Your father ordered their assassinations!"

Breath stolen, she quickly recovered, twisting the knife still piercing his shoulder. "Why did he order them to be killed?"

Broken, with sweat and blood dripping down his body, Chua confessed. "We were supposed to kill all three of you. Your father didn’t want you or your son trying to claim your birthright. He has never forgotten how you disrespected him the day you agreed to be Dichali's wife."

"You are Andrago. Why do my father's bidding?"

"He promised I would be king, if I obeyed."

Pushing the knife above his knee deeper, relishing in his grunts and screams, she asked, "How long have you served Issachar?"

"He hired us to kill Prince Antilles," he gasped, trying to catch a breath amid the torture. "He didn’t want you marrying him. He didn’t want the West to support your claim to his throne."

Another betrayal. "*You* killed Antilles?"

Chua nodded, "Those were your father’s orders."

Tala stood several feet from them, quiet, his eyes filled with anger and confusion. But Niabi was not done. Not even close. Chua was an extension of Issachar and she would send him a message. One the king would not soon forget.

"Is that all?" She met Chua's weary eyes.

He furiously bobbed his head. "That is everything. I swear it."

Niabi pulled the knife from his shoulder and slammed the blade above his other knee, summoning an ear-piercing scream from him.

"I told you everything!" Chua wailed. "I told you everything I know!"

"I believe you," Niabi acknowledged in a maliciously sweet voice.

Chua's bottom lip quivered, "But you stabbed me. I swore I told you everything."

Niabi leaned close to him, her hands gripping the hilts of her knives, and whispered, "You stole from me. Not once, but twice. You are a traitor, a liar, and a murderer. I promise your death will not be quick. I will bathe in your blood and let the vultures feast on whatever is left of your corpse."

Chua's gaze darted to Tala who did not move to stop their queen from furthering her merciless quest. "Please. Tala, please help me-"

"Beg all you wish," she interrupted his cries with a hateful grin. "No one can save you from me."

Endless screams echoed through the night across the Andrago kingdom. It was rumored, Chua's unearthly howls were heard for miles, as Niabi tore him limb from limb, slowly and methodically. Once the traitor was nothing more than a pile of flesh and bones, she and Tala left the tent. The sun had risen and mirrored the blood red appearance she was sporting.

"The Red Sun," Tala muttered. "The universe mourns the loss of our king."

Niabi shielded her eyes from the sun's glare. "I swear on the blood of my husband, I will destroy my father and everything he holds dear. He will not escape my wrath."

"My queen?" Tala turned to her.

"I am now the monster he always feared me to be." Niabi stared at her hands and tattered clothes covered in so much blood, she wasn't sure what the original color of her dress had been. "Take what is left of the traitor and send it to Issachar with a missive attached."

"What should the note say?" he asked.

"That I will not rest until I claim his head from his body."

Once the memory she cared to share with Salome had come to an end, she forced her sister out of her thoughts and back to the present moment.

"Niabi..." Salome started but either couldn't or wouldn't finish that statement.

"My quarrel has never been with you or our brother," Niabi cut her off. *"All I ever wanted, all I still want, is to live my life in peace. To raise the babe growing within me, away from war and the political dance of the throne."*

"You are with child?"

"I am." Niabi knew better than to reveal so much to her enemy, but despite the warnings blaring in her head, she ignored them. *"And I wish this child could have the peace I was denied. Can you not understand that?"*

"Peace?" Salome's voice was soft and shattered Niabi's heart. *"How can you possibly have peace after what you've done? After the lives you stole?"*

"Our father was cruel, wicked, and selfish," Niabi growled. *"He wouldn't have hesitated to eliminate someone whether they posed a threat or not. You remember him as your protector, your kind and doting father, but that's not who he was. Not really. Had he lived long enough to see you now, he would have sold you to whoever best suited him. Whatever would advance his power, his crown, his throne, and he wouldn't have thought twice about you, once you were gone. He never loved any of us. Had I not helped Lykos in the quiet of*

night to study, father would have deemed him inadequate and found some way to remove him from the line of succession.

"Issachar hated me because of my gender. He hated me because I was smarter, faster, stronger, and bolder than Lykos. He hated me and never hid it. He never said one kind word to me. Never held me, never comforted me, never told me he cared for me. I was the stain on his legacy and a threat to his name.

"Little did our father know that he was the monster, and in his paranoia, anger, and hatred, he created something much, much worse. He molded me into the vengeful and powerful creature that I am. I will not apologize for what I did because I do not hold one inkling of regret."

"But Mother and our brothers did not deserve to be collateral damage in your hostile takeover." Niabi could hear the pain and sorrow in Salome's quiet voice and it tugged at her heart. Her motherly instinct to wrap her arms around her sister and comfort her took her by surprise.

"You of all people should understand that usurpers cannot live." Niabi reminded her of the way of rulers and leaders.

"We were children."

"Children that grew into vengeful adults." Niabi braided her hair, taking a deep breath of the cool breeze that danced around her room. *"Again, that is something you should be well aware of, Salome. I did what I needed to do to ensure my reign, to ensure my son's future reign."*

"And yet your son is dead." The words stung, but Salome was right. Rollo was dead. Niabi had failed to keep him safe.

"Because you lived, he no longer could." The words tasted bitter even as thoughts. *"Again, I ask you one last time. What do you want from me?"*

No answer came and the hollowness in her head confirmed whatever magical door her sister opened to communicate with her, had been slammed shut. Niabi felt empty, drained. She had not allowed herself to relive the day Dichali died, but after sharing it with her enemy, she knew there'd be no resting for her that night. She had more questions than answers when it came to her siblings. She might never know why Salome really reached out to her, she might never know what it was her sister wanted from her, but what she couldn't do was dwell on it. Slowly, she would begin to see Salome as her sister instead of her enemy, and it would make it that much harder to kill her when the time came.

CHAPTER 31

CRISPIN

Crispin hadn't slept so peacefully in weeks. When he woke that morning, his drool was on the red velvet couch where he and Salome had been sitting and swapping stories. He must have fallen asleep while talking to her, obviously more tired than he originally thought. Being on the run from countless enemies had finally caught up with him.

Crispin rubbed his eyes with the heels of his palms, hungrier than ever. He could smell the aroma of freshly baked bread in his room and was thrilled when he remembered what Salome told him about Jacobi the baker. He not only survived the Shadows' massacre, but he had joined their forces and now headed their kitchens. His mouth watered at the thought of sinking his teeth into freshly baked goods, instead of the jerky and dried fruits, Leeondris had sent with them. As if just thinking of food caused it to manifest before him, a knock on the door with a soldier holding a tray of food, put his growling stomach at ease.

He knew there would be countless meetings he would have to attend, and there were dozens of people he wanted to see after weeks apart, but he craved to have a moment to wander the ancient castle alone. He hadn't been by himself in a long time, and before all the chaos was unleashed, and battle plans were formulated, he was determined to have a private moment.

In the quiet of his room, his mind kept flashing back to the sight of Salome standing on the opposite side of the bridge in front of the keep. She was alive. And not only alive, but in one piece. The Thrak hadn't broken her. Before he could even think, he was sprinting to her, tears streaming down his cheeks. It was a memory he would always cherish.

Once he'd had his fill of baked goods, fruit, and meat, Crispin slipped out of his chambers and wandered the halls. Grey stone hallways, red runner carpets eaten by moths, dusty candelabras, and tattered tapestries ushered him down the corridor. On one side of the hall were windows facing the sea, on the other, doors that led to bedrooms. Weaving up and down countless halls, Crispin found himself in what was once known as the largest library in existence. Scrolls, texts, and leather-bound tomes filled with ancient tales and historical accounts of the ancestors of the old world, were stored on hundreds of shelves that spanned from the stone floors up to the dome glass ceiling. There were a few cracks in the ceiling, but nothing too grand to have caused any true damage to the treasured texts.

Memories of helping his mother in the White Keep's library and archives room put a smile on his face. What his mother would have given to stand in this dilapidated room of knowledge.

Running his pointer finger along one of the wooden shelves spurred a tornado of dust to swirl around him, drawing a sneeze from him that echoed throughout the chamber.

"Good morning, my friend." The warm, familiar voice startled Crispin. "I was hoping our paths would cross again." Heru stood with his arms clasped behind his back, a smile on his face.

Crispin grinned and bounded across the space to embrace the Prince of Numbio. "It is good to see you, Heru."

"And you." Heru patted Crispin's back. His eyes were bloodshot, and he looked as if sleep had eluded him for quite some time.

"Are you unwell?" Crispin asked, unable to hide his concern.

Heru's smile didn't stretch far. "A lot has happened since we lost you in the Caverns of the Undead."

"Tell me."

For the next hour, Heru recounted his journey. He told Crispin all about Pyke, the Queen of the Wagura, how they escaped the caverns and how Shiek Ibrahim gave them shelter. Crispin's heart ached hearing stories about Zophar and his final weeks. When Heru told him of Rayma's allegiance to Memucan, which led to the end of their relationship, Crispin could feel how hurt his friend was by the tremor in his voice. What intrigued him the most was Rayma's tale of the Grim and how he demanded she take Pyke's place.

Crispin glanced at the texts scattered on the wooden table. "So, what are you looking for?"

Heru sighed, running his hand down his full, dark beard. "A way to save her from the Grim."

"She was sent to kill you." Crispin furrowed his brow in confusion. Why would Heru even care what happened to her?

"She saved my life in the Caverns of the Undead. I owe her."

Crispin folded his arms across his chest, leaning back in his creaky chair. "You still love her."

"I will always love her," Heru admitted.

"But?"

Heru looked at the prince. "I may not trust her anymore, but she doesn't deserve to wither away for a hundred years serving the Grim. If I can find a way to save her, to outwit the Grim, I will do it."

"You're an honorable man, Heru."

"Or maybe just a very stupid one."

Crispin chuckled, drawing a smile from his friend. As Heru continued to peruse the tomes he had pulled, Crispin's mind wandered to the little black book he'd lifted from Memucan's room the night he killed him in Northwind. Inaros, Rayma's brother, was frightened by it, claiming it was evil. Crispin and Rayma had their differences, but he hoped for Heru's sake, he could find a way to spare her a life with the Wagura. Hopefully, that wicked book didn't contain the secrets his friend needed.

"Have you seen her?"

"Who?" Crispin gave him his full attention.

"Rayma."

He nodded. "I passed Rayma and Inaros as they were reunited when we arrived yesterday."

"Ah yes." Heru clicked his teeth, looking indifferent. "The brother. I'm ashamed to admit, I thought she made him up to save face when she told me of her betrayal." He glanced across the table, a thousand questions swimming in his gaze. "How did you find him?"

"In the dungeons of the White Keep. Memucan had him imprisoned for stealing his book of black magic."

Heru smirked. "It seems you have stories to share."

Crispin gladly shared his encounters with the pirates of the *Shadow of Death*, his run in with Uri and Nezreen, his failure to save Neempo the Sovereign from his sister and her witch. He also didn't hold back any details on how he killed Memucan and tossed his book into the Obsidian Sea.

Had this all happened in a matter of weeks? It seemed like a lifetime ago he was battling Kubantu and scaling one of the towers of The Sisters.

"So," Heru said the word as if he was savoring the thought. "Memucan is dead?"

Crispin bobbed his head. The Southern Lord's face flashed before his eyes as he remembered sliding his blade across the old man's throat. "Yes."

"Then Rayma is finally free of her debt."

"And she has her brother back, after all these years." Crispin playfully wiggled his eyebrows. "She has no reason to make an attempt on your life now."

Heru snickered. "Love is a funny feeling. I want to hate her…"

"But you can't." Crispin thought of Rahab. That feisty, stab-happy pirate had stolen his heart and even though some days he felt like tossing her overboard, he couldn't help but love her.

"We'll find a way to save her," Crispin found himself promising when he noticed Heru's downcast glare.

"Thank you, my friend." Heru stood up, scraping the legs of his chair against the stone floors. "I have training with my men. You are always welcome to join us."

"Perhaps tomorrow. I have some people I need to see first."

"Of course." Heru pressed his hand to his chest. "Crispin."

Once the prince left, Crispin flipped through the manuscripts spread across the table. It was a long shot to defeat or even outwit a Grim when he believed you owed him a life debt, but Crispin couldn't bear the thought of Heru watching the woman he loved suffer. So, he scanned the texts, flipping through dusty page after dusty page, hoping to find a shred of hope to give his friend. But after an hour of searching, he came up empty handed. Maybe Inaros would know of a way, since he trained with Memucan years ago, and had been in possession of the black book of magic.

He let out a defeated sigh as he dragged his hands down his face. He was exhausted. Mentally and physically. And he was hungry. As he contemplated raiding the kitchen for more of Jacobi's freshly baked pastries, he heard footsteps approaching.

"I should have known you'd be hiding in the last place I'd look for you." Salome leaned against one of the bookcases with an impish grin.

"Ah, but you did find me, so not the best hiding place after all," he smirked.

"Speaking of hiding," she welcomed herself to the chair Heru had been using and kicked her boots onto the table. "I just met the most interesting lady pirate with blue hair."

By the look on her face, he knew she was well aware of who Rahab was to him, and instead of denying it, he readily confessed.

"You're too nosy for your own good," he rolled his eyes.

"She's pretty," Salome smiled. "I especially appreciate a woman who loves a dagger."

"I told her you'd like that ruby knife of hers."

"Does she know how to wield it?"

"Too well."

Salome laughed and he hadn't realized until that moment, just how much he'd miss the sound of his sister's voice. How comforting it was when his mind was foggy.

"Do you like her?" he asked.

Salome's stare gave nothing away. "Do *you* like her?"

He nodded, clasping his hands between his knees as he leaned forward. "Very much."

"Is she to be my future queen?"

The question threw him. By the smirk on Salome's face, he knew she was enjoying her teasing far too much.

"Salome," he warned.

She lifted her hands in surrender. "Alright, alright. I yield."

"Never thought I'd hear you say those words," he teased.

Salome's smile faded.

"What is it?"

"Rahab lit up at just the mention of your name." Salome reached for his hand and squeezed. "If you like her, I like her. I look forward to getting to know her as my future sister and my future queen."

"She cannot bear children," he whispered as Salome stood, causing her to stop in her tracks. "How can I be king and not have an heir?"

Salome was silent for a moment. "Would that hinder you from making her your wife?"

"Of course not," Crispin tried not to sound offended.

"Then why -"

"Perhaps you should claim the White Throne," he interrupted. "Produce an heir, keep the House of the White Wolf alive."

She crouched before him, forcing him to look into her eyes. "I do not want the throne. If she cannot bear an heir, then adopt a child or name a successor. You are not the first king to do so, and you won't be the last."

"Would our people accept my heir, if he is not of my blood?"

"Zophar wasn't our kin, but no one could deny that we were family." Salome once again stood, his gaze following her movements. "Your heir will continue our legacy because *you* say so, not because of what others may believe. We are wolves, Crispin, not sheep."

Crispin smiled at her and took her hand and kissed it. "You think Zophar would have approved of Rahab?"

"Absolutely," she grinned. "You need a woman who can kick your ass once in a while."

"You've always had the mouth of soldier."

Salome bowed and winked. "I never was one for the flittering life of the ladies of court, and by the looks of it, your wife-to-be has a fouler mouth than me."

Crispin barked out a laugh. Heaven help the Kingdoms of Adalore with Rahab for his queen and Salome as his right hand. None of the other kings would stand a chance against them.

CHAPTER 32
SALOME

Salome hadn't been able to shake Niabi's memories from her head in over a week. The horror her sister endured was unfathomable and when she slammed their connection shut, she was instantly bathed in guilt. Part of her wanted to hate Niabi, but the other half of her not only sympathized, but understood.

"You do remind me of Niabi." Her grandmother, Nym, had been right.

How could she continue the bloodshed after all the losses both sides had suffered?

Her days were filled with activities: training at night with the Bellator brothers, spending time with Crispin, getting to know the pirates her brother cared about, and preparing for Hanzo and Oifa's wedding to unite the Mountain Men, once and for all. But none of those duties weighed her down. The incredible heaviness she felt, stemmed from harboring her secret conversation with Niabi, and withholding it from Crispin. Although she knew he would angrily disapprove of her actions, something deep within her heart and soul desperately wanted to reach out to her older sister again.

Why, she wasn't quite sure. Maybe to check on her welfare after sharing her dark memory. Maybe to see if she could glean any information that would help further their war. Or maybe, she just wanted to get to know Niabi better, and that was the most frightening reason of all.

She had questions. Lots of questions. But there was no one alive that could answer them, so she reached out to the one person she knew would be honest with her about Niabi.

"Lykos?" Salome closed her eyes as she searched for her eldest brother. *"Lykos, are you there? I need to speak with you."*

The sound of the soldiers sparring in the bailey outside of her bedroom window and the cooks and attendants baking and decorating for the wedding that evening faded and was replaced with the chirping of songbirds and the gentle ripple of a stream. Her eyes flashed open and she saw Lykos standing by the largest wisteria tree she'd ever laid eyes on.

"Hello, Little Wolf," Lykos smiled and the warmth of his voice overwhelmed her.

She took a tentative step forward, closing the gap between them, and took a moment to look around paradise. Grass as far as the eye could see, a light breeze blowing the wisteria branches around them, the sunlight beaming just right casting a halo over Lykos, making him appear otherworldly.

"Where are we?" She finally managed to find her voice.

"The After."

"It's so quiet here," she met his gaze.

"That is called peace," he motioned for her to join him on a white stone bench. "Tell me, Salome, what do you need to speak to me about?"

Once she was seated next to him, she got a whiff of his familiar scent, and fought the urge to melt into his arms like she used to do as a child. Had he lived to see her grow, she was positive he would have continued their secret sparring lessons until she was better than him. He would have been a great king had he had the chance.

"Salome?" He gently squeezed her hand, ending her nostalgia. "Mortals, even a Hunter, do not have much time in the After. I suggest you tell me what you came here for."

"You always knew?"

"About you being the Hunter?" Lykos nodded. "Harbona recognized your mark and told me. He made me promise to protect you at all costs and to keep your identity a secret from father."

"Harbona never told our father?" Salome was surprised the Seer withheld that information from the king he had sworn to advise.

"There is a lot you do not understand about our father." Lykos' brown eyes held a sadness in them that made her want to bear hug him and tell him everything would be alright. "Had our father known of your mark, had he known of your potential magic, I'm not exactly sure what he would have done, but I know without a doubt, he would have used you for his own purpose."

"Niabi said the same thing."

"So, you've spoken to her?" He smiled.

"Tell me about her," Salome whispered, as if she didn't want anyone to overhear, even though they were the only two beings in the area.

"What exactly do you wish to know?"

"Was she always so… vengeful?"

Lykos shook his head. "No. She wasn't born that way. She was created." He met her eager gaze. "Niabi is many things, some of them are not good, but she has suffered much, and loved greatly. Her motivation has always been to protect her loved ones." He sighed, his fingers tugging on the purple wisteria flowers. "She should have been queen all along."

"Are you saying what she did to our family was justified?" Salome spat indignantly.

"Justified in her mind, yes, but wrong nonetheless." Lykos looked at her. "Why are wars started?"

"What?"

"What is the motive for war?" He rephrased the question, a glint in his eyes.

"Power, revenge, money, defense," she listed, and he nodded his head.

"And which of these do you believe fueled Niabi's grab for Northwind?" Lykos stood and strolled around the tree with hands clasped behind his back. "She had willingly given up her birthright to go to the Isles of Myr. She once again gave up her claim to the throne by agreeing to marry King Dichali and become his queen. She showed no signs of being the power-hungry usurper our father feared her to be, and yet, he waged a war against her. So, I ask again. What motivated Niabi?"

Power clearly wasn't the right answer, nor was money. Salome rubbed her hands against her face, "She sought to avenge those who were taken from her. She sought to defend and protect those she still had, against our father."

"You see her as the villain, but she is not so different from you or me."

"I'm not much different in my desire for revenge." Salome stood up and made her way to Lykos. "I've killed in anger because of losing someone I loved dearly. I've joined Crispin in gathering an army to march against Niabi, who lawfully is the true heir to the White Throne. Are Crispin and I..." Salome sucked in a breath, keeping tears at bay. "Are Crispin and I the villains?"

"No one is the villain in their own story, Little Wolf," Lykos cupped her face in his hands.

"I'm the Hunter," her bottom lip quivered. "I am meant to protect the lives of the innocent. I am supposed to defeat Niabi."

"Perhaps, she is not the one you were meant to defeat. Perhaps, she is the one you were meant to save."

"What?"

"Someone is calling you. Your time here is up, Little Wolf." Lykos wrapped his arms around her and squeezed so tightly she gasped for breath. "Your friends are looking for you."

"But I do not know what I am supposed to do," she pulled back from him, staring into his kind, brown eyes.

"You will, when the time is right."

He kissed her forehead and before she could protest, she was sitting on her bed in Oakenshire, as someone knocked on her bedroom door.

"Salome?"

"Yes?" She scurried to answer the door, unsure of how long the visitor had been knocking.

She opened it to Kae and the twins, Rosalina and Seraphina, who had their hands filled with items to prepare her for the wedding festivities. They didn't appear to be frustrated or worried that she'd taken too long to answer their call, so they must have just arrived.

"Is all that necessary?" Salome motioned to their soaps, perfumes, brushes, and towels.

"Did you think you could attend a wedding in your fighting leathers?" Rosalina chuckled as she pushed past Salome to begin setting up.

Seraphina smirked, "I, for one, cannot wait to see you dance."

"Dance?" Salome scoffed. "I don't dance."

"Oh, you will tonight, my lady." Seraphina teased as she helped her twin finish setting up the trinkets and tinctures. "It is expected that the host and hostess of the wedding, dance with the bride and groom."

Salome crossed her arms over her chest and laughed. "You think Oifa and Hanzo are going to dance? They don't care about tradition."

"Ah, but the rest of the kingdoms attending will, Your Highness," Rosalina turned to face Salome with a smile. "First, your bath. Then we will fix you up."

Knowing there was no resisting or fighting the Qata Vishna twins or getting past Kae leaning against the closed door, she nodded her head in agreement. If she was forced to be the center of attention at tonight's reception, she would look ravishing, if her friends had anything to say about it.

~

HER DRESS WASN'T NEARLY AS spectacular as the white silk gown she had worn to the Festival of Forbidden Fruit during her stay in the Isles of Myr, but it was beautiful, nonetheless. When she inquired why they chose the colors navy and white for her outfit, she was reminded they were her House colors. It sparkled like the night sky and even Salome had to admit she liked the feel of the off-the-shoulder, A-line gown.

The twins had pulled her wild curls back in a low bun befitting a royal hosting a wedding and did her make up subtly at her request. With her friends' approval, she made her way down to the renovated ballroom. Weeks earlier, what was overrun with vines, roots, and broken windows, was now plant free, cleaned, and decorated with hundreds of candles, wooden tables, and a designated place for people to dance.

Salome smelled the venison before she saw the magnificent spread Jacobi and his team had put together. His strength was in baking, but once tasked to prepare the feast for everyone staying at Oakenshire, the Westerner rose to the challenge and delivered a buffet kings would covet.

Over the next half hour, she greeted and chatted with guests, royal or not, and waited anxiously to see when her brother would be joining her. He had been ecstatic about attending a wedding, mostly because he loved a good party with food and ale, but he had yet to make his appearance, and it was nearing the time for the ceremony to begin.

"You look beautiful," King Kenji's voice caught her by surprise. "Oh, forgive me, Princess, I didn't mean to startle you."

She smiled at him, looking over his shoulder hoping Jinn was with him.

"My son isn't with me, I'm afraid."

For being as old as he was, Kenji didn't miss a thing. She squeezed his outstretched hand and allowed him to plant a kiss on the back of her hand.

"I'm so glad you could be here to witness the joining of the Mountain Men." She sounded so much like a politician she wanted to kick herself, but Kenji returned her smile and laughed.

"I wouldn't miss this for the world. If you could find a way to unite the tribes after a thousand years of turmoil, then I cannot wait to see what you will do next."

His kind words felt like a punch to the gut. Such a heavy burden – the expectations everyone would have of her was something she thought about often.

"I have offended you?" His eyes were filled with worry, and she shook her head.

"No, Your Highness, you did not offend me," she reassured him, patting his hand still clasping hers. "But there is something I wish to ask you."

"Ask me anything."

"You knew my father." A statement he agreed with. "How well did you know him?"

"If there is something specific about your father you wish to know," he whispered as guests wandered by, "then you may speak candidly."

If Jinn had half the discernment his father had, there would be no way she'd be able to hide anything from him. Not that she wanted to. She shook her head, freeing her thoughts of the prince and refocused on the king.

"Was my father a good man?" The question made her stomach flip. From what she'd learned of her father over the last couple of months, she already knew the answer to her question, but she had to know from a neutral third party who had personally known Issachar, if what she had learned was true. "Was he a good king?"

For the first time since meeting the Easterner, he wouldn't meet her line of sight. Everything seemed to be more interesting at the present moment than answering her question.

She was about to ask again when he finally spoke. "Your father was a strategic king and only pursued tactics that would strengthen his kingdom and further his stretch of power."

"Forgive me, Your Grace," Salome whispered, "but you did not answer my question."

Kenji sighed. "Your father was a good king. He was not a good man."

"How can someone be both?"

"Issachar was so consumed with being the mightiest king the North had ever seen that he forgot to nurture the ones who would come after him." The king led Salome to a table and sat down to relieve his aching feet. "He kept your people safe until the end."

"Do you think my sister is a monster?"

"Why do you ask me that question?" His curious gaze roved across her face.

"Above all else, I seek the truth, Your Majesty." Salome kept steady eye-contact, even though she was desperate to drop her gaze to keep him from seeing how vulnerable she felt. "Do you see Niabi as a villain?"

He took a moment to choose his words carefully, but then nodded his head. "Yes, I see her as a villain, not because of her motives, but how she handled her anger. If I were in her position, I would have sought revenge as well, but not at the price she paid."

"How else would she have defeated my father?"

"She could have rallied support from other kingdoms, staked her claim upon Northwind by the law of your ancestors, brought the King of Elisor's assassination to light -"

"With all due respect," she interrupted him. "Would you have listened to my sister, if she came before your throne accusing one king of assassinating another?"

Kenji stroked his long fingers through his white facial hair and shook his head. "I wish I could say I would have."

"But?"

"I suppose everyone can look back on their life choices and make all the right ones." The king pressed a hand to his chest, bowing his head slightly. "Forgive my judgment."

She reached over and grabbed his hand. "There is nothing to forgive. Thank you for your honesty."

"There you are!" Crispin rushed over to her, whisking curls from his face. "You need to get ahold of those Qata Vishna twins of yours, trying to, as they said, 'fix me up'. What does that even mean? Why do they have so many brushes?" As if he was just now noticing who his sister was with, he bowed slightly at the hip toward the King of Sakurai. "Your Highness, forgive my intrusion."

The old man waved him off, "It is I who have intruded on your sister long enough. Go enjoy yourselves." He smiled at Salome before she stood up and walked away with Crispin.

"What was that about?" he asked her once they distanced themselves.

She wasn't sure how to broach the topic of their sister's past with him, and minutes before Oifa and Hanzo's historic wedding wasn't the proper time, so she lied, which knotted her stomach.

"He was telling me all about Sakurai. They're a very interesting people." She looped her arms in her brother's. "Did you know Sakurai was the first kingdom Malachi the First established once he defeated Phlias?"

Crispin huffed out a laugh, "Forget I asked."

"You better be nice to me."

"Or what?" he teased.

"I'll tell Rosalina and Seraphina to rub kohl around your eyes."

"I don't know," he stopped and faced her, pointing at her eyes. "They might have used it all on you."

She swatted at his chest and laughed, but her face dropped when she looked at the dance floor and remembered what the twins had told her. "Did you know we're supposed to dance with the bride and groom after the ceremony?"

Crispin flashed her an encouraging smile and nudged her chin with his balled-up fist. "It's just swaying back and forth. Here, let me show you." He grabbed her hand and started dragging her to the dance floor, but she panicked and pushed him away.

"What are you doing?" she chastised him, trying to keep her voice low and composure collected, should anyone cast a glance their direction.

He extended his hand to her. "It's just you and me."

"You know I hate dancing."

"That's because you've never had the chance to dance with me." His cocky grin summoned a smile from her. "Dance with me."

Although she wanted to run from the room screaming, she couldn't deny her brother whatever he asked of her, so she bobbed her head and took his outstretched hand. He gently placed one hand on her waist and pulled her close.

"Must we be this close to one another?" she snarled.

"Let's hope you have better manners with Hanzo when the time comes," Crispin rolled his eyes. "Now, all we're going to do is sway back and forth."

Salome could feel the eyes of soldiers, guests, and attendants watching them as they slowly moved side to side, without music.

"Crispin, people are watching us."

"You're going to have to get used to that, *Princess*."

And he was right. They were royalty. Half of royal life was being watched by everyone around you.

"Chin up," he reminded her, and she straightened. "You're doing great."

"I feel silly."

"Why?"

"We're dancing and there's no music."

Crispin smiled, resting his chin against her forehead. He started humming a tune she hadn't heard in years. It was one their mother used to sing to them, one about a great sea monster and the men and women who united to defeat it. It had absolutely nothing to do with the wedding or dancing, but Crispin always had a lovely voice. She closed her eyes and rested her head against his chest, feeling the vibrations as he provided the music she lacked.

Dancing. They were dancing, just the two of them, before everyone in the hall, and for the first time in a long time, she didn't care what any of them were thought or said. It was as if the entire room disappeared, and she and her brother were finally at peace.

"Your Majesties."

Salome and Crispin looked up at Harbona who smiled at them. "It is time to begin."

CHAPTER 33
CRISPIN

Crispin hadn't known the bride or groom long, but within five minutes of meeting them, two things were quite apparent. Oifa was as tenacious, as Hanzo was fearless. They would make a formidable team as King and Queen of a united Mountain Men tribe, if they didn't kill each other first.

This was also the first wedding Crispin had ever attended as an adult and it made him nervous that he was considered the host. He relied heavily on Harbona and Heru's guidance in how to behave, where to stand, how to greet people, and understand the order of festivities.

Once the hand tying ceremony was complete and vows exchanged, the music thrummed to life, signifying the start of the reception. Drinking, eating, dancing. All things Crispin whole-heartedly enjoyed.

After a couple of hours, he wasn't too proud to admit that he truly loved weddings, so much so that he tried convincing other guests not only to get married, but they should invite him to partake in the revelry.

As he looked around the grand hall filled with smiling faces, he couldn't help but wish Zophar was standing next to him, downing a pint of ale as he pointed a turkey leg at whoever he was talking to.

He spotted Salome dancing with King Kenji and beamed with pride at how happy she looked. She had grown in confidence and carried herself as true royalty. Her first dance with Hanzo after the ceremony was sweet to watch as they whispered back and forth and swayed around the dance floor. Her smile brightened the entire room.

His dance with Oifa on the other hand, was in a word: frightening. Not once did she smile. Crispin wasn't entirely sure if she knew how. Despite her answering his questions with one-word answers, he managed to survive the painful ordeal and proceeded to ask some of the older ladies who cooked, cleaned, and mended clothes for the entire camp, if they'd honor him with a dance. In fact, the prince spent most of his time on the dance floor, laughing, and for the first time in months, having a good time.

Crispin attempted to drag Rahab to the dance floor countless times over the span of the evening only to be met with a grumbled, "You're lucky I dressed for the occasion, princeling," before she continued her game of cards with the pirates.

He'd kissed the top of her head, admiring the form-fitting black dress she sported, and laughed at the thought that the foul-mouthed, cigar-smoking, gambling pirate was to be his wife and queen one day.

When he glanced around the room once more, he failed to spot his sister in the sea of jovial faces. But he did happen to notice Heru and Rayma slip out together and watched as Adonijah whispered something into Leoti's ear, before they found their way to the dance floor.

"Do you mind if I have the next dance, Prince Crispin?"

The melodic voice startled him from his shameless people-watching, and he turned to see a beautiful Immortal woman at his side. "It would be my honor, Lady…?"

She offered a tight-lipped smile as she accepted his outstretched hand and followed him to the dance floor. "My name is Lavena."

Crispin wrapped his arm around her. "I do not believe I have seen you in the halls or the bailey, my lady."

"I am an Ethereal, Prince Crispin, I am not designed for war."

"Yet here you are," he stared into her grey eyes, looking for any clue as to what she was thinking. "Who are you?"

"We met once a very long time ago." Lavena did not waver under his scrutinizing glare. "To keep my history brief, I was sent as an ambassador to Northwind, and I fell in love with your brother, Lykos. We were secretly married."

Crispin did his best to hide his surprise but failed miserably. "You and Lykos were married?"

"Before your sister attacked the White City, Lykos put me on a ship back to Caelestis. He wanted to ensure not only my safety, but the safety of our unborn daughter."

He stiffened and narrowed his eyes. "So, you're here to stake your daughter's claim to the White Throne."

Lavena shook her head, her expression giving nothing away. "You misunderstand. My daughter has no interest in claiming your ancestral throne. Her heart and duty now fully lie with the Immortals. She is planning to visit the Mainland after the war, and I wanted you to know about her, since she intends to journey to Northwind. She has so many questions about the White City and about her father, I thought maybe…"

"Maybe I could share some of my memories with her?" He picked up where she trailed off. When she nodded, he felt foolish. "Forgive me, my lady. I rushed to judgment when you reached out to me in peace. If there is ever anything I can do for you or my niece, consider it done."

"That is very generous of you, Prince Crispin."

"Crispin," he squeezed her hand. "You are my sister by marriage and shall be treated as such. You will always have a place in Northwind, should you ever desire it."

Lavena stared at him unabashedly. Whatever thoughts were running wild through her mind, she did not give away through her facial expression. "You remind me of him. There was not a person alive who did not love Lykos."

"Except Niabi," Crispin pointed out and was taken aback when she disagreed.

"No, I dare say, she loved him very much."

"She had him executed."

"If you are to be king, Crispin, there is one thing you will have to learn. It is ugly, but it is the truth." She spoke softly, but her words felt heavy on his soul. "In war there are casualties, familial and stranger alike. As a leader, you will be forced to make the difficult and often heartbreaking decision to put any who would jeopardize your reign to the sword." Lavena's grey eyes narrowed. "Lykos knew the cost of losing. Had he been able to defeat your sister, as much as he loved her, he would have had to put her down like any traitor to the crown."

"You make excuses for her treachery."

The Ethereal halted in place, keeping him rooted where he stood. "Are you not about to march an army to her gates and commit the same sins, my lord?"

"She and I are not the same," Crispin gritted his teeth. "We march to avenge my family's murders. To avenge Lykos' execution!" He angrily whispered, glancing around to see if anyone was watching their interaction. But no one noticed, far too jovial to spot a brewing storm.

"I will love your brother for the rest of my days. And I suspect, I will despise Niabi far longer than that." She slipped her cold hand against his face. "I have seen many kings come and go, Crispin. I have seen their hearts and their motives for why they war against their fellow man. Do not be so filled with pride that you justify your reason to battle your sister, and condemn her for the same."

Crispin lowered his voice, dipping his face closer to her pointy ear, "Are you asking me not to go to war?"

"The question is, are you prepared for the consequences of war?" She cocked her head to the side. "Are you prepared to see your friends fall in battle? Are you prepared to send word to the families of the fallen, that their loved ones will not be returning home? Are you prepared for your sister to claim your head should you fail to defeat her?"

The prince was short of breath and clutched at his collar, trying to loosen the top button. He had only thought of his victory over his sister – he did not once consider the consequences should he fail. It wouldn't just result in his own torment and execution, but for Salome, for Rahab, for all of their friends and allies; their lives too were at stake. Niabi would burn the known world to the ground, before she allowed any of them to escape her wrath.

He needed to find Salome. If anyone could talk him off the ledge of despair, it was her. Glancing around, he once again came up empty. He had almost forgotten he was dancing with Lavena until she spoke.

"You look ill, my lord. Do you need a glass of water?"

Crispin cleared his throat and noticed the song had ended, signifying their dance was over. He bowed. "Thank you for the dance, my lady, and for the stimulating conversation, but there are some matters I must tend to before the night is over."

Lavena barely managed to curtsy in time before Crispin beelined for the door. If he knew Salome, she'd be hiding somewhere no one would think to look. And then it hit him. He knew exactly where she'd be.

CHAPTER 34
RAYMA

Since arriving in Oakenshire, after the Battle of Gomorrah, Harbona set Rayma up in one of the largest rooms in the keep, where he said the apothecary had once been a thousand years ago. Whatever she needed to make her tonics, tinctures, ointments, and bandages, he provided. It was nothing like her shop back in Numbio, but after confessing to Heru about her ties to Lord Memucan and how she was supposed to assassinate him, she knew she would never be able to return to the apothecary in the southern lands. It had been the only place she'd felt safe and in control, and in the blink of an eye, it was gone.

Heru had made it clear their relationship was over and she understood why. But banishing her from her home? Where was she to go after the war was over? She survived the Caverns of the Undead, a run in with the Grim, held captive by Stormcrags, and even managed to keep her cool while healing the wounded as the soldiers battled the Thrak in Gomorrah, but she wasn't sure she would survive being labeled as a traitor and treated as an outcast. Everything she did for her people was for their betterment and even though the original goal was for her to get close to Heru, to hurt him, she secretly fell in love with him and the thought of being his wife, being his queen, brought her great joy. Together, they could continue to uphold the traditions of the Numbio, as well as protect and provide for them.

But that dream was just that. A dream.

And now all she could do was watch him from afar. How strange it was to have been so intimate with someone one minute and the next, be total strangers. She would watch him as he trained with the Numbio soldiers in the bailey. She would watch him as he interacted with the other leaders as they spoke of battle strategies. She even watched him during the wedding festivities, as he twirled with other women on the dance floor and laughed and drank with his fellow men.

Not once did he glance her way and the realization that she meant nothing to him anymore, drove her to the point of insanity. The pain of his rejection was excruciating, and she wished she could concoct a potion to ease her broken heart.

Inaros plopped down in the chair next to her and she smiled at him, thankful he interrupted her self-deprecating thoughts. When she saw him cross the bridge into Oakenshire, she thought she was seeing a ghost. The entire time she served Memucan, a part of her suspected Inaros had been executed years ago, and the old man had been using her love for her brother as leverage without any real proof he was still alive. So, to see him, scrawny, but alive, walking toward her that day, made her forget all her troubles with the Grim and Heru, and was filled with immeasurable relief.

They'd spent the last couple of weeks catching up on the years that had been stolen from them. He spent all his free time helping her in her medical ward. He willingly prepared salves and rolled bandages to prepare for the upcoming battle with the North. She was grateful Inaros was with her during the wedding, otherwise, she might have spent the entire evening alone.

He handed her a glass of wine and sipped his own, eyes fixed on her. "You are awfully quiet tonight, Rayma. What troubles you?"

She wished she could tell him everything about what happened in the Caverns of the Undead and the business concerning the Grim wanting her to replace Pyke, the Queen of the Wagura, she had killed to free her companions, but she didn't want to worry him. She'd just gotten him back and if she was on limited time, she wanted their time to be well spent and filled with happy memories.

Every spare moment she had was spent researching thousands of tomes and scrolls in the dilapidated library, searching for clues on how she could defeat or outwit the Grim, but so far, came up empty-handed. Night after night she dreamed of the Wagura and how she stabbed Pyke and how she killed Bantu, Memucan's spy, in self-defense. How she wished, she could go back to a simpler time in her life, but then she realized she never had a simple life. Maybe, simplicity wasn't meant for her.

"Rayma?"

"I'm sorry," she straightened in her chair, meeting Inaros' gaze. "I am afraid I am not very good company this evening."

"What's wrong?" his brow furrowed.

"I shouldn't be here celebrating." Her eyes latched onto Heru as he laughed at something a lady standing next to him said. She forced herself to look away to keep from tearing up. "I should be making more salves."

Inaros caught her staring at Heru. "How long have you been in love with our prince?"

She wanted to lie. She wanted to deny his keen observations but the truth was, she was tired. Tired of lying. Tired of living in the dark.

"He asked me to marry him after the war."

Inaros' eyes widened but before he could say anything, she lifted her hand to silence him.

"Memucan instructed me to get close to him. To…" she took a deep breath. This was harder to confess to him than she thought it would be. "I was to make him fall in love with me and once I had his unwavering trust, at Memucan's command, I would slip him a poisoned drink and…"

"You were going to assassinate him?" Inaros whispered, leaning closer to her.

"He promised if I did his bidding that he would release you from prison." Tears welled in her eyes, and she swiped them away before they rolled down her cheeks. "But when it came time to do the deed, I couldn't. I saved him from the Wagura -"

"The Wagura?" He gasped. "You were in the Caverns of the Undead and lived?"

"I killed their queen to save the Numbio trapped inside the caves. But the Grim came to me. He wants me to pay him back for the years and souls I stole from him. He is demanding I be their new queen for one hundred years or give up Heru for a shortened sentence." Rayma lowered her head and stared the hands she used to kill, when she took an oath to heal and save. "I confessed everything to Heru once we were out of the caverns."

"You confessed to treason, and he let you live?"

She nodded. She searched for Heru one more time, and found him dancing with the woman who had made him laugh. "He told me when this war is over, I will no longer have a home with the Numbio."

Inaros grabbed her hand and squeezed. "You will always have a home with me, wherever that may be. You will not be alone, and we will find a way to defeat the Grim- "

"There's no way to defeat the Grim," she interrupted, letting out a whimper. "I've already tried finding a way out. There is no hope for me, brother."

"That is not necessarily true." The voice startled the siblings and when they looked up, Harbona was standing on the opposite side of their table with the beautiful woman Heru had just been dancing with. Now that she was closer, she realized she was an Immortal like the Seer, but that didn't ease her gut-wrenching jealousy.

"I don't know what you're talking about, sir," Rayma attempted to deny anything the Seer might have overheard.

"You do not need to be frightened, my dear." Harbona motioned toward the open seats, and she reluctantly waved for them to sit. "Prince Heru has already come to me and Lady Lavena with your predicament and I believe we can help you."

Rayma's narrowed eyes darted to Lavena. "And why would *you* want to help me?"

The Immortal woman tilted her head to the side, a curious but unreadable expression crossed her stoic face. "Rude or not, no one deserves to be indebted to the Grim."

Rayma should have been embarrassed that Lavena called her out for her tone, but she wasn't ashamed. She had nothing left to lose. "Perhaps your time would be better spent with the prince than helping me."

Harbona exchanged a confused look with Lavena. "Rayma, this is Lady Lavena, wife of the late Prince Lykos of Northwind and mother of the future Eldaar. Prince Heru went to her for guidance to help you outwit the Grim because she is the most knowledgeable among the Ethereals.

"I assure you," Lavena added, "there is nothing romantic transpiring between me and your prince."

Rayma felt foolish. Her cheeks burned with embarrassment, and she wished she could take back every word she spewed in jealousy. "I..." she cleared her throat. "I apologize for my tone, Lady Lavena."

"Now that you do not look as if you are going to rip my heart out," Lavena smirked with a twinkle in her grey eyes, "I believe there is the Grim to contend with."

"What can I do?" Rayma asked, hope filled her heart for the first time in ages.

"There is only one thing you can do," the Immortal woman clasped her hands together and set them on her lap. "You will have to sail to Caelestis to live out the remainder of your days."

"What?" the healer's mouth dropped.

"The Grim's reach does not stretch past mortal lands. In Caelestis, you will be able to live out your days until age claims you," Harbona explained.

"But even if I agreed to go to Caelestis, once I die, won't I have to deal with the Grim then?" Her eyes bounced between the Ethereals.

"The Grim makes deals with desperate souls to prolong their lives and once they pass, they must pay off their debt in servitude." Lavena explained. "When mortals pass, they go to the After where Death dwells."

"But the Grim demanded I make a choice. Either I serve him for one hundred years or offer Heru for twenty years as a Wagura."

Harbona leaned forward and whispered, "Have you agreed to either? Have you made an official deal with the Grim?" His eyes were frighteningly serious, and she immediately shook her head in response.

"I have made no deals," she reassured the Immortals. "He hasn't come back to me for an answer. What do I tell him when he returns?"

Lavena smiled. "I have already taken care of the Grim; he will not be visiting you before our departure to Caelestis."

"How?"

"When Prince Heru told me of your predicament, I shielded you from his sight."

"Can you just shield me from the Grim permanently?" Rayma's heart soared. "So I do not have to leave my home?"

Her questions were met with a sympathetic silence, and it extinguished her tiny spark of hope.

"I am afraid," Lavena delivered the final blow, "my abilities only work where I am. I can shield you from prying eyes, but it does not make you invisible. The Grim will not be able to find you while I am here, but once I leave for Caelestis, he will be able to track you down and he will come for you."

Rayma took a deep breath as Inaros snatched her hand in his. "Will she have to go alone?"

"Inaros," Rayma chastised, knowing what he was really asking. "You can't give up everything to follow me. I won't allow it."

"You are welcome to join us," Lavena offered, ignoring Rayma's protests.

"Then I shall go with you." Inaros said without hesitation. "Where she goes, I go."

"Inaros!" Rayma cried. "I can't let you give up your life to follow me."

"I haven't been there to protect you, Rayma," her brother met her teary gaze with one of his own. "I haven't been there during your loneliest days, but I can make up for it now. You will not be alone. Ever."

A tear slipped down her cheek as she lunged for her brother, wrapping her arms around his neck. "Thank you."

Someone behind her cleared his throat and when she turned around, she came face to face with Heru. By the sorrow in his eyes, she knew he was aware of what had to happen. Why he looked forlorn was beyond her. He'd banished her from returning to Numbio, and as reluctant as she was to leave the mainland for a land filled with angelic beings, she now had a place to call home when the war was over.

"Would it be alright, if we spoke privately?" Heru asked.

Without a second thought, she released her brother and stood up. As they walked away, the prince rested his fingers against the small of her back and led her through the crowded hall until they slipped out of the room unnoticed. She hadn't felt his touch in weeks and just the graze of his fingertips sent her soaring.

Once they entered her medical wing, surrounded by everything she had control over, she faced him as he shut the wide, wooden door. It took him a few seconds to turn around and look her in the eye, but when he did, every single wall she'd built up since their break-up, came crashing down. He was broken, and he wasn't even trying to hide it. Tears flowed down her face and there was nothing she could do to stop them. And for the first time in her life, she didn't want to compose herself. They stood in silence, staring at one another as they cried. A tightness in her chest and knot in her throat kept her from speaking and even though she wanted to rush to him and kiss his pain away, she stayed rooted to her side of the apothecary.

"Thank you," she finally managed to whisper.

"For what?"

"The Immortals told me you sought them out for aid in dealing with the Grim. It seems I will now have a place to go when the war is over."

"Rayma." He took a step forward, his voice trembled.

"It's alright." She stepped back, maintaining distance between them. "I'll be alright." But she knew that was only a half-truth. The truth was she would forever miss him.

"I will visit you in Caelestis."

"Why?"

He seemed taken aback, borderline offended by her question. "You truly need to ask?" He ate the distance between them and cupped her face in his hands. "I love you. In spite of everything that has happened, I love you, and I do not wish to see you leave for the Immortal lands."

Raking her hands up and down his muscular arms, she broke their unwavering eye contact before he could see how shattered she truly was.

"It is better this way," she said softly.

"I'll keep looking, Rayma. I swear I will find a way for you to return to Numbio to be my wife, if you will still have me -"

She put a finger to his lips, silencing him. Her lip quivered; she was about to rip his already aching heart into pieces.

"Let me go," she met his eyes and wished she hadn't.

"Rayma -"

"Heru, you must let me go," she interrupted. "One day, you will be King of Numbio. You will need to take a wife and sire children -"

"Don't," he pleaded, horror written across his features. "Please don't ask me to stop loving you."

She summoned a weak smile and stroked his tear-stained cheek with the tips of her fingers. "Our love will never die, but our paths are no longer going in the same direction."

"Don't give up on us." Heru kissed her forehead and it felt an awful like goodbye. "Give me time to save you."

"You already have."

"I'll abdicate -"

"You will do nothing of the kind." She stared into his eyes with a sternness that sobered him. "You will take your rightful place among our people, and you will do what you were born to do."

Heru reluctantly nodded and pulled her to his chest, wrapping his arms around her in a warm embrace. "Is this really how our story ends?"

"I'm afraid we were doomed from the beginning," she whispered into his chest and wished things could have been different for them.

As he pulled away, Rayma tightened her hold on him. He squeezed her in return, and she could feel her heart shatter into a million unfixable pieces. They might not have forever, but they had tonight, and she wasn't ready to let him go.

CHAPTER 35
SALOME

Salome's dance with Hanzo had not only been a success, but a lot of fun. She graced the dance floor a few more times with different men: King Kenji, Cato, Prince Heru, and Harbona. She even managed to convince Kayven to take a spin with her, although Abba was more than happy to stick to the wall he seemed to favor.

As she weaved around the room, greeting guests and sampling food, her eyes stopped on Adonijah, who was across the room. He smiled at her and she started to walk toward him but stopped when his attention was stolen by the Andrago maiden he had arrived with. She was gorgeous for sure, with her silky, black hair, bronze skin, and curvaceous figure, but there was something about the way he looked at the maiden that clicked in her head. For as brief as their attraction to one another had been, Adonijah never stared at her, the way he was admiring the Andrago. For a moment, her heart ached, but she quickly shooed the sting away and happiness filled its place. Though she didn't fully trust him, and they were working on rebuilding a friendship, she believed Adonijah deserved to be happy and there was no denying he'd found his happiness in Leoti.

Drawing her intrusive gaze from the budding lovers, she looked around the hall for Jinn. She'd been hoping to speak with him all evening, but hadn't seen him since the wedding ceremony. Deciding she'd had enough dancing and venison for the evening, she slipped out of the hall and wandered around the ancient keep looking for the prince.

She dared not go straight to his room to knock on his door. She might not care about what people said or thought about her dancing anymore, but she wouldn't have unsavory rumors circulating about her and the prince after a very successful evening of politics.

The kitchens were empty, save Jacobi and a few other cooks cracking jokes and enjoying some sweet treats in private. The bailey was bare, and the library showed no signs of anyone being there. It felt like she'd been wandering the castle for an hour before she thought about the roof. It was the last place she would check before giving up and turning in for the night.

As she climbed the hundreds of steps to get to the rooftop overlook, she stopped, slapping a hand to her forehead in frustration. She had magic that she could have used to ask him where he was, saving her time. *Idiot,* she thought to herself. It was too late now; she was precisely five steps away from pushing the wooden door open that led to the roof.

Muttering a string of curse words under her breath, she opened the door and was relieved to see Jinn leaning against the stone railing. The cool breeze whipped strands of his hair into his face which he swiped away. His gaze was glued to the moonlit sea and the sight of him dressed in his princely attire nearly stole her breath. Or was it the hike up the stairs?

Once she managed to catch her breath, she said, "It's a beautiful view."

He turned around, startled by the voice, but smiled when he saw it was her. "How did you know I would be up here?"

She returned his smile and sauntered over to join him. "I wish I could say it was easy to find you, but to my everlasting shame, it wasn't. I should have known you'd be up here though. It's the same place I'd be, if I were trying to avoid people." Inhaling the saltwater air and feeling the winter chill setting in, she rubbed her bare arms as she rested her elbows on the stone railing next to him.

Jinn took his cloak off and draped it over her shoulders, which she gratefully accepted and tightened around her. She loved that it smelled like him.

"I might not remember much about my childhood home, but I remember that it smelled very similar to this when the cold weather started to blow in." She glanced out over the Ignacia Sea. She turned to look at him and saw he was already admiring her.

"It seems your idea of uniting the Stormcrags and Krazaks has been a success," he bumped her shoulder with his, drawing a grin from her. "If the laughter and music from the wedding downstairs is an indicator, I'm sure Oifa and Hanzo will make a fine couple. I'm surprised they didn't see the potential before."

"They hate each other."

"Hate is a very strong word." He arched an eyebrow.

"But an accurate one," she chuckled. "I just pray Oifa doesn't lose her temper and stab him on their wedding night." She blushed at the thought of a wedding night and cleared her throat to hide her embarrassment. "What are weddings like in Sakurai?"

The prince stiffened a bit and she wished she hadn't asked. She refused his proposal in the Isles of Myr and had turned him down when he confessed his love for her in the City of Bones. She'd chosen to be with Adonijah and knew now it was a mistake. Maybe there was still a chance Jinn would want to be with her, especially after what Kenji had told her about the prince's visions. But he was still free to decide if he wanted to give her another chance. She was just too cowardly to ask for one.

Jinn cleared his throat, "Parents make the arrangements for their children to wed." It warmed her heart that he answered, and she clung to every word that slipped from his tempting lips. "Once an agreement has been reached, the bride and groom meet. The wedding is planned for a month later. There's lots of food and lots of music, very similar to how it sounds downstairs, but I've never been a fan of weddings."

"Why not?" she asked, and his eyes met hers.

"Because I was afraid I would be forced to marry someone I didn't love, when all my life I knew there was someone out there for me, and I just needed the chance to find her."

Salome knew he meant her, and her heart skipped. Maybe there was still a chance for them to be together.

Jinn turned, squaring up with her, and offered his hand. "Dance with me?"

Had he asked hours ago, she might have said no. But with a newfound confidence in the art of dance, Salome reached for his extended hand and let him pull her close to him. His other hand landed on the small of her back and she rested her palm on his shoulder. Together, silently, they swayed with the music that drifted up from the party below. Jinn's chin touched her temple and she shivered.

"Are you cold?" he asked, concern laced his words.

"No," she shook her head, pressing herself against him.

She allowed her thoughts to wander when she closed her eyes. She pictured her future, the future she wanted. Months ago, when her journey began, it never entered her mind that she would find the person she didn't know was missing in her life. She thought it was Adonijah and maybe, in another life, she and Adonijah could have been happy, but she had grown and changed. She was ready to claim her titles, her birthright, and walk in her power. The woman she had become, belonged to Jinn, and she knew deep in her heart that she had found her equal in power and ambition.

Jinn had proposed to her in Myr, breaking a thousand-year tradition in his culture. Call it fate. Call it destiny. She and Jinn were always meant to find one another. They were always meant to be together. He rescued her from the Gomorrians. He kept every promise he made and even when she pushed him away, he never left her side. He nursed her injuries and healed her broken heart.

She tilted her head up and found him already looking down at her.

"What is it?" he asked, his voice raspy.

"Your father and I spoke of you."

His grip on her tightened and she noticed the muscles in his neck tense. Worry. His eyes were filled with it. He didn't need to ask what she was referring to because he already knew.

"Salome, I'm sorry. You were never supposed to find out that way..."

Her eyes cut down to his lips, silencing whatever excuse or apology he was about to issue. She felt his heartbeat quicken against her chest, his breathing was labored, and his eyes hungry. She slid her hand from his shoulder up his neck and cupped his cheek. Her thumb floated across his lips and his fingers pressed against her lower back gripping her dress.

"Jinn?" They stopped dancing and gazed into one another's eyes. "Am I too late?"

Jinn tilted his head, confused. "Too late for what?"

She inhaled deeply when he softly caressed her back. "When this war is over – I choose a life with you. If you will still have me."

His hand stilled, and from his expression, she thought she had made a mistake.

He didn't want to be with her. She'd chosen Adonijah over him. Once the war was over, he'd find someone else, someone better.

Jinn tucked a finger beneath her chin and gently lifted her head.

"I'm sorry, I shouldn't have -"

"If I lived a hundred different lifetimes, I would choose you every time," he said softly.

A tear she had been holding back slipped down her cheek and he wiped it away.

"I have dreamed of you since we were children. I have searched for you all my life," Jinn leaned down, his lips an inch from hers. "I asked you once before and you weren't ready to give me an answer."

"Ask me again," she whispered.

"Marry me?"

"Yes." She smiled a second before his mouth crashed against hers, claiming her as his.

She was flooded with the feeling of completeness. The piece of her heart that was missing was now found. She felt a surge zing through her body, his mouth roamed from her lips down her neck and bare shoulders. She would have to thank the twins for choosing this dress for her. Her fingers plunged into his hair, tugging softly. She arched into him, accepting his loving touch, giving him her heart.

When he finally pulled back from her, he rested his forehead against hers, their breathing rapid, and their lips swollen.

"Why didn't you tell me about your dreams?" she asked, her fingers still tangled in his hair.

"I didn't know how," he answered honestly. "I didn't want you to think I was insane. I wanted to run to you the moment our eyes locked in the halls of the Scarlet Citadel. I knew, after years of hoping you existed, that I had finally found you."

"Damaris told me in Myr we had a strong bond. Now I know what she meant."

Jinn swiped curls away from her face and kissed her again. He opened his mouth to say something but didn't get the chance.

"So, this is where you two are hiding." Crispin leaned against the doorway, arms crossed over his chest, a smirk on his face.

"It's not nice to lurk, Crispin," Salome snorted, painfully aware of her disheveled appearance. Jinn took a step back, allowing her to push away from the wall her back was pinned against.

Crispin winked, "Not to worry, sister, your secret is safe with me."

"Actually," Salome took Jinn's hand and faced her brother. "There's something we want to ask you."

Crispin's eyebrow quirked. "What?"

"Jinn asked me to marry him, and I said yes." Before Crispin could respond, Salome quickly continued. "I love him, and as my brother and my future king, I ask for your permission and blessing for us to wed."

Crispin's mouth dropped. He stood up from his lazy position and took a step toward his sister. All playfulness in his gaze was gone. "You're asking for my permission to get married?"

"Yes," she nodded, "and I hope you approve."

He grabbed Salome's free hand and squeezed. "You don't need my permission to marry the man you love, Salome. I may be the future king, but I won't dare tell you what to do or who to spend your life with."

"You mean that?" Her eyes watered.

Crispin smiled, "Let's not pretend you've ever listened to me before anyways."

Salome threw her arms around her brother's neck. "Thank you!"

Crispin extended his hand to Jinn, and they shook. "She's a handful. I hope you're ready."

Salome smacked Crispin's chest and scoffed.

Jinn snaked his arm around her waist and pulled her close. "I will serve her well."

Crispin smiled at Salome, "Of that I have no doubt."

CHAPTER 36

ADONIJAH

Even though the wedding was still raging, Adonijah slipped out to visit his brother, Pash, who had been confined to his quarters since they arrived in Oakenshire. He'd been treated kindly and hadn't been tortured or thrown into the dungeons, but he hadn't been allowed to leave his room without an escort and his weapons were confiscated. Crispin didn't want to take the chance of Pash spying on their army and resources and managing to escape to inform Niabi of their plans and whereabouts.

Adonijah felt a pang of guilt every time he thought about his brother being locked up, but he'd experienced the same treatment when Pash's men arrested him for trespassing. Pash still treated him with respect and had dinner with him nightly, so Adonijah thought it only fair to return the favor.

Once he approached the door to his brother's quarters, the two soldiers standing on either side of the frame glanced at him and nodded him through. Thankfully, even though Adonijah and Crispin didn't get along when they first met, the prince gave Adonijah free reign of the castle and even allowed him to see his brother whenever he wanted. He was surprised Crispin didn't confine Leoti alongside Pash. Maybe, the prince thought the Andrago wouldn't run away. Even if she managed to slip past the guards, Leoti wouldn't get too far on her own. She was resourceful, but she never travelled alone, so to venture through the Black Forest to get to Northwind would be a monumental task, even for a warg.

Pash on the other hand, could very well make it back to the White City on his own. He was the Commander of Shadows and had traipsed through the Black Forest more than any other man he knew. When Gershom escaped Issachar's dungeons, he and Pash set up their own camp in the middle of the cursed woods. Pash explored the area for years, and knew it like the back of his hand, and he didn't fear the creatures that lurked there. He was born and bred for fighting and had killed many men.

At least Pash was alive. That was more than Adonijah could have hoped for when Crispin and the pirates came to their aid during their altercation with Ophir and his band of Shadows.

As soon as Adonijah walked over the threshold, the guards closed the door, locking him inside. He found Pash in the same place he always found him: the window bench. It didn't matter what time of day or night Adonijah came to visit his older brother, the commander would be staring out the window, watching the waves of the Ignacia Sea slosh around and depending on the training schedule, he'd watch the soldiers from different corners of Adalore sparring together, preparing to war with the woman he loved most.

Adonijah understood that feeling of helplessness. It was only a few weeks ago, he was doing the same thing in Pash's military camp, hoping he would see Salome again. He shook the thought of Salome wrapped in his arms free and made his way toward his brother.

Pash turned at the stomping sound of his boots and smiled. Even being locked in this room hadn't crushed his spirit.

"Sounds like a great party." Pash motioned to the plate Adonijah had in his hand. "What's that?"

"I figured I'd bring you a late-night dinner since you weren't invited to the wedding."

Pash grabbed the plate as he stood and made his way to the humble dining table fit for a party of four, and sat down, motioning for his brother to join him.

"How is Leoti faring?" Pash sank his teeth into a piece of venison.

Adonijah sat across the table from his brother and reclined, stretching his legs out in front of him. "She is doing well. Oddly enough, worried about you."

Pash smirked. "Tell the Andrago, I'll be giving her orders to disregard sooner than she thinks."

The brothers exchanged a look in silence before Pash's smile faded.

"I don't expect I'll be leaving this room for quite some time."

"I'll talk to Crispin again -"

"There's no need, brother," Pash cut him off, shaking his head. "I am fortunate to be confined to this room and not stretched out on a rack in a dark and dank dungeon being tortured for information."

"Has no one questioned you?" Adonijah asked.

"No." Pash leaned back in his seat, breaking the flaky roll apart and tossing a piece into his mouth. "I keep waiting for one of your companions to kick my door in and drag me out in chains to be executed. Waiting is its own sort of torture, I suppose."

"Salome won't let them execute you."

"I hope you're right, Adonijah." Pash chuckled, but his expression remained skeptical. "Men like me are meant to die in battle, not noosed and hanged like a common thief."

Adonijah tapped his fingers on the wooden table, drawing Pash's gaze. "You won't die here. You have a child to raise."

"I am not blind to reality," Pash whispered, tossing his half-eaten roll back on the plate. "My chances of seeing Niabi again are bleak. I may never hold my child or tell him how much I love him."

"Pash -"

"I am a prisoner of war," he interrupted, a bite in his tone. "Do not misunderstand, I am grateful that your friends have been merciful in their treatment of me, but I am still their enemy and at some point, they will understand what they must do."

"They won't execute you," Adonijah's nostrils flared. "I won't allow it."

"I know you would do your best to protect me, but the truth is, if they wish me dead, there is nothing you can do to hinder it." Pash rubbed his fingers across his growing beard. "If that time comes, I need you to promise me something."

"It's not going to happen," Adonijah stood up, scratching the floor with the legs of his chair, "so keep your request to yourself."

Pash jumped up and grabbed his brother's forearm. "If something happens to me, I need you to make sure that Niabi and my child are safe."

Adonijah slowly turned to face him. "You're asking me to commit treason," he whispered.

"I am asking you to ensure the life of my unborn child." Pash lowered his voice and Adonijah didn't miss the brokenness in his tired eyes. "Can I count on you?"

Adonijah was no fool. If something happened to his brother, he wouldn't hesitate to do whatever he had to do to protect his child. But he'd have to betray Crispin and Salome. What he needed to do was secure Pash's release, then he could fulfill his oath to protect and serve Salome and help his brother.

Pash cleared his throat, slicing through Adonijah's hesitant thoughts. He couldn't speak his agreement, but he nodded his head, and that seemed to be enough for Pash.

"I must go," Adonijah pulled his arm from his brother's grasp.

"Tell Leoti I am alright."

He nodded before rapping on the door three times and slipped through once the guards opened it. Marching down the corridors, jovial music from the wedding still wisped around the castle, but Adonijah felt a heaviness weighing on his shoulders. How could he keep both promises? Serve and protect Salome and ensure Niabi and Pash's child's safety?

He raked a hand through his hair and traipsed back to his chambers. Once inside, he ripped his cloak and tunic off and threw them on the bed before sinking into his mattress, not bothering to light any of the candles. He was comfortable in the dark and found it oddly soothing to lay in his room unable to see three feet in front of him. His other senses were heightened when his sight was hindered. He could smell the sweet pastries from the great hall below and could hear light breathing coming from the other side of his room.

Sitting up and grabbing his knife from the holster on his thigh, he growled, "If you wish to remain in one piece, I suggest you state your business."

A match flickered and a candle on his dining table was lit, revealing Leoti staring at him. Even in the dark, he felt as if she could see into his very soul and knew all his deep, dark secrets.

"Do you still intend to cut me to pieces?" she asked, a playful taunt in her voice.

He sheathed his knife and stalked toward her. As he neared, he heard her catch her breath and he realized he was only wearing his trousers and boots. Her eyes roamed the scars littering his chest. He stopped, thinking he should go back to grab his shirt, but when she slowly stood and walked towards him, he froze.

She cautiously lifted her hand and he reached for it and gently led her palm to his chest. Peering into each other's eyes, he was positive she could feel how fast his heart was beating.

"You have so many scars," she finally whispered.

"Aye." He dragged her hand lower where a stab wound he'd received a year ago was, and pressed her palm against it. "Many have tried to kill me and failed."

Leoti didn't say anything, but her gaze slowly moved up from his chest to his lips and then met his eyes.

Adonijah took a deep breath and took a step closer, so their bodies were only inches apart. His heart was racing as he lifted his hand to brush strands of hair that had fallen out of her braids away from her face. His fingers trailed down her cheek, the center of her neck, and stopped just above her breastbone. He could feel her heart pounding beneath his grazing fingertips.

"Why did you come to my room tonight, Leoti?" he whispered.

"I don't know."

He cupped her face in his calloused palms and asked again, "Why did you come to my room tonight, Leoti?"

"I feel safe with you," she confessed. "I feel alive when I'm with you, and I haven't felt this way since…"

"I know I shouldn't," he picked up where she trailed off, "but I have feelings for you."

"What kind of feelings?"

Adonijah pressed his forehead against hers and said, "I know you're still mourning Rollo, but I can't help but want you. I yearn for every bit of you that you are willing to offer. If it's just this moment, I will take it gratefully and die a happy man. But if you would have me, if you would let me, I would love you with every fiber of my heart, soul, and body. I would do everything in my power to bring you joy and to protect you. If you want me, I am yours."

Leoti was silent and he feared he had said something to offend her. She gently lifted his face and looked into his eyes.

"You are mine." Her voice was soft but confident, almost possessive. "And I am yours." Her fingers trailed down his neck and stopped above his heart. "I take all of you, just as you are. I will stand by your side as we fight, build, and grow, until Death claims me for the Great Beyond."

"Leoti." With just her name, he asked permission.

"Adonijah." With just his name, she gave it.

Slowly, he leaned down. Her eyes closed as she tipped her head up, her hands roaming his chest. He hovered over her lips; this was his last chance to turn back. But instead of letting his fear grip him, he pressed his mouth against hers and felt a shock of electricity shoot through his entire body. He'd never experienced a sensation like this when kissing a woman. He'd never had this feeling even when he kissed Salome.

Her hands went from stroking his chest to grabbing his neck and pulling him closer to her. She was intoxicating, an addiction he didn't know he had. Leoti ran her fingers through his hair, tugging to get a reaction out of him. And she got one when she bit his bottom lip, drawing a low growl from him.

He forced himself to pull back to look at her. Though her gaze was hazy, he could still see her longing for him, and his chest swelled. "You are mine," he echoed her words from moments before.

Leoti bobbed her head, "I am yours."

Licking his fingers, he extinguished the candle on the small dining table, shrouding them once again in darkness.

CHAPTER 37
NIABI

The coolness of the winter didn't deter Niabi from making her way to the royal stables where Nagrom, her black steed, was well cared for and housed. She spent as much time with him as she could and once she'd shooed the custodians out of the stable, she picked up the brush and started stroking down Nagrom's muscular body. The quiet solitude was exactly what she needed to clear her foggy mind. Nagrom nudged her with his snout, drawing a smile from her.

"You'll get your snack once I'm done brushing your coat, Nagrom," she tsked. "After twenty years, you should know the routine."

Nagrom shook his head, fluffing his mane, before refocusing on the pile of hay in front of him. She cherished his company and felt so at peace with him that she drifted back to the day Dichali gave him to her. The morning she was to depart to the Andrago lands with her newly betrothed, she found him waiting for her in the courtyard, at the bottom of the White Keep stairs, grinning.

"And what are you smiling about?" Niabi squinted, blocking the sun with her hand as she descended the stairs.

Dichali extended his hand to her once she reached the bottom, and she reluctantly accepted his chivalrous gesture, knowing her father and members of the royal court were all watching her from the top of the stairs. Just another hour and she'd be free from this city and more importantly, free from her father's crushing hand. The Andrago king kissed her hand and winked before leaning closer.

"I'm smiling," he whispered in her ear, "because I have a surprise for you, wife."

"I'm not your wife yet," she retorted, and he chuckled.

"Perhaps not," he pulled back and straightened to his full height, forcing her to look up. "But once you see what I have for you, maybe you will look at me more favorably."

Slipping his hand into hers, as if it was the most natural thing in the world, Dichali led Niabi toward his entourage of Andrago, all suited and seated on their horses for the journey. Their stares didn't go unnoticed, and she was just as wary of them as they were of her. She was the daughter of their enemy, and they were more than likely not happy their king was taking her as his bride. But if she were being honest, this arranged marriage wasn't her idea of a good time either.

Her eyes collided with the one Dichali called Tala and he stared at her unabashedly. He was bold, protective, and confident, she would give him that. He was the one to win over, if she were ever going to be trusted amongst her future husband's people – her future people. She nodded her head in a show of respect, and to her surprise, Tala's eyes softened, and he returned the gesture with a nod of his own.

The one called Chua was a slippery looking fellow. His beady eyes and serpentine smile made her skin crawl, but he was also a member of Dichali's inner circle and unfortunately, she would be seeing plenty of him. She would remain diplomatic, but if he laid one unwanted finger on her, she would claim his whole hand, consequences be damned.

Finally, Dichali stopped pulling her forward and planted his hands over her eyes. She swatted his hands away, gritting her teeth.

"I am not going to harm you, my lady," Dichali said softly, his face a mixture of sympathy and anger.

She shifted her weight foot-to-foot. She did not wish to stir her future husband's anger before they even began their journey and offending him wasn't on her list of things to do either, so she bit down hard on her bottom lip before muttering, "I did not mean to offend you, my lord."

"Offend me?" He flashed a baffled gaze her way. "What are you talking about?"

"You looked upset." Now it was her turn to be confused. "I thought -"

Dichali ate the distance between them, tucked his index finger under her chin and tilted her face upwards. "Any anger you might have seen flash across my face was not directed at you, Niabi. I hate that you flinch when I raise my hand or that your shoulders tense up when I touch you. I would ask for you to give me the names of those who harmed you, but I don't need you to, because I already know. If I could make your father suffer for his sins against you, I would. But freeing you from his prison is the best I can do."

For the first time in a long time, Niabi was truly stunned. She didn’t know how to respond. Part of her wanted to agree with him, keeping her mask firmly in place, hiding any and all weaknesses he could possibly exploit, but the other part of her, the treacherous side, wanted to push up on her toes and kiss him, which was the only way she knew how to thank him. Words meant nothing to her, actions did. How could she thank him enough for all he was risking and willing to do for her. He didn’t truly know her, he shouldn’t even feel obligated to aid her, but here he was, standing before her ready to whisk her to a new home where she would be his queen.

"Niabi?" Dichali's thumb stroked the curvature of her jawline. "Is everything alright?"

She forced herself to nod, banning any thought of kissing him from her mind. "Where is this surprise you promised?"

His cheeks dimpled when he smiled and he motioned towards a black stallion with a saddle and no rider. "This is Nagrom."

Niabi quietly stared at the steed who seemed to almost stare back at her with a gentle strength she was unquestionably drawn to. She felt Dichali's chest settle against her back and she forced herself not to flinch at his soft caress.

"He is yours."

"A horse of my own?"

"That is what my lady requested when we first met, is it not?"

Niabi slowly turned around, missing the feel of his chest against her back. "Thank you."

The words seemed to surprise him just as much as they did to her, but he quickly recovered from his stupor and bobbed his head. "Shall I help you up?"

Niabi smiled and his eyes danced with delight. He cupped her cheek in his hand and whispered, "Do that again."

"Do what?"

"Smile," he dragged his fingers down her face. "I don't believe I've ever seen a more beautiful sight."

"Just wait until you see me riding a horse," she smirked, and he chuckled.

"Safe travels, Niabi." Issachar's menacing voice sliced through their tender moment. Together, the soon-to-be newlyweds glanced up the white stone steps to where Issachar stood with his entourage.

Lykos looked sick to his stomach, and even though she'd wished him farewell, he had spoken to her about helping her get back to the Isles of Myr to avoid their father's arranged marriage. Niabi had assured him she would be alright, that running to the Myridians would only provoke their father to act against their mother's kin, and he reluctantly conceded to her will. She hoped he would make a better king once their father passed. Maybe then she would be welcomed to the White City with open arms.

Dichali slipped his hand into Niabi's hand once more and straightened his shoulders to Issachar. "King Issachar."

"King Dichali" Issachar matched Dichali's tone before he whipped around and reentered the White Keep.

"You ready to go home?" Dichali asked her and she nodded. She was more than ready.

With his help, she mounted Nagrom and though she was frightened, she would rather die than admit her fear to Dichali, who rode by her side the whole way to Elisor. It took several days, but by the end of the trip, she felt more comfortable riding her horse. Dichali was right, the horse lords were the perfect teachers.

It didn't take long after their arrival for them to be wed. With the entire population watching them, Niabi and Dichali had their hands bound with red rope, and at sunset they invoked the traditional vows of the Andrago. The people had been so incredibly welcoming of her and rejoiced when their king not only found a bride but took a queen to rule by his side.

After a night of feasting, drinking, and dancing, Niabi was led to a spectacular tent with bright pattern rugs strewn across the floors, and pillows of all colors thrown on the white canopy bed at the back end of the room. It was well lit with candles, and she couldn't help but admire the wooden case where a host of weaponry was kept. She was more than pleased with her lodging and didn't miss her stark, cold room in the White Keep. For a brief moment, she realized she could find herself quite content amongst the Andrago, and that summoned a rare smile from her.

Someone cleared his throat behind her at the tent's entrance and when she turned around, she was pleased and surprised to see Dichali standing there. She wasn't sure how she was supposed to address him since he was now her husband.

"Am I supposed to bow to you or something?" She squared her shoulders to his. "Is there a certain title I'm supposed to use now that we're married?"

"No special titles, wife," Dichali stepped forward and shook his head. "And you do not bow to me. We are equals in all things."

A comfortable silence fell between them as they stared at each other. She was still waiting for this dream to end, half expecting she'd wake up in the White Keep, and back under her father's thumb. Dichali was nothing like what she expected him to be, but she wasn't sure how to express herself, or if she wanted to allow herself to appear vulnerable.

"I do not have to stay here tonight," Dichali's statement silenced her thoughts. "I can sleep elsewhere, until you are ready for us to…"

"Consummate our marriage." She finished for him and was oddly satisfied to see the King of the Andrago blush. "What will your people think if I ask you to leave?"

"I told you before, Niabi, women are treated as equals here. If you do not wish for me to stay, if you do not wish for me to touch you, I will abide by your wishes."

She should have told him to leave, but something deep down inside of her yearned for him to stay. The walls she'd built up around herself were there to protect her from men like her father, but Dichali made her want to tear the wall down stone by stone until there was nothing that parted them.

"Goodnight, Niabi," Dichali smiled and walked toward the tent flaps to leave.

"Wait," her voice halted him. He slowly turned to face her. "Stay," she whispered.

"What?"

"I want you to stay, Dichali," she rasped again, as if she was in desperate need of a drink of water. He didn't move a muscle. Just stared at her, as if he was the one who wasn't too keen on staying. "Please."

That word seemed to rattle him, and he met her gaze. "I could never refuse you."

As he made his way to her, she forced her feet to move and met him in the middle of their room. He stood stoically, as if he was waiting for her to dictate the pace and what would happen between them. For a second, she panicked and thought it might've been a mistake to have asked him to stay, but when she looked into his kind brown eyes, her fears vanished. Pushing up onto the tips of her toes, she slowly inched her face closer to his. His breath hitched as her lips floated beneath his. Suddenly realizing that was as far as she could go, he lowered his head and met her awaiting lips.

Fire. Ice. Shadows. Light. His kiss was everything and all consuming. Losing control of herself, she snaked her hands up either side of his face, drawing him closer. He tangled his fingers in her hair and tugged gently. Her husband. Her equal in all things.

Before she was ready for him to, he pulled his mouth from hers, but still hovered above her and stared into her eyes, appearing to be a man in search of truth.

"Ask your questions."

"Why did you ask me to stay?" Dichali asked, breathlessly.

"Why did you ask me to be your wife?" She posed a question of her own, still feeling uncomfortable with being vulnerable.

"Because you were drowning and that was the only way to save you."

"You didn't know me. You didn't owe me anything."

"No," he shook his head. "I didn't know you and you're right, I didn't owe you anything. When your father reached out to me asking me to take you as my bride to end the feud between our people, I knew he didn't mean it. I knew he was trying to use me to get rid of you. My counselors tried to dissuade me from traveling to the White City. They tried to convince me not to agree to Issachar's terms. But when I heard how your father spoke to you in the throne room and I saw how you held knives to his throat with every opportunity to kill him, and you restrained yourself - I just knew right then, I had to have you as my wife."

"I don't know how I can ever repay your kindness, Dichali," she stroked a finger through his locks, and he smiled.

"*You* are more than enough."

Their mouths collided again as they stumbled toward the bed. When the back of her legs bumped into the mattress, Dichali whispered, "Are you sure?"

"I'm sure."

Niabi was ripped from her memories when she sensed a presence flooding her head. She knew exactly who it was and although she wanted to be irritated by the sudden interruption, she found herself more curious than anything. *"I didn't think I'd ever hear from you again, sister. Pray, tell me, what is it you wish to talk about this evening?"*

Although Salome was quiet for a moment, she finally asked, *"What was our mother like?"*

The question caught Niabi off guard. She assumed Salome would want to know more about Niabi's past or their father, but to ask about Bilhah – even Niabi didn't allow herself to think about their mother often. It was too painful thinking of how their mother died protecting her brothers when Gershom came and slaughtered them all the night she took the city. She originally wanted to send her mother and siblings to the Isles of Myr, sparing them a gruesome end, but Vilora's prophecy won out in the end. There could be no survivors that would possibly attempt to usurp her reign. If she left them alive, her son would never sit on the White Throne. She supposed none of it mattered in the end since two siblings escaped, and she had to live with the burden that she was the one who signed her mother and brothers' death warrants.

"If you don't want to -"

"She was very kind and had an endless well of patience for her children," Niabi interrupted her as she continued to stroke the brush down Nagrom's back. *"She was wise, had the most beautiful voice, and was the best storyteller at bedtime. When I was sick, she would sit by my bedside, refusing the Healers' offer to care for me themselves. When a nightmare terrified me in the middle of the night, she would cuddle next to me, and when I woke the next morning, she would still be in bed with me. She was a breath of fresh air and revived me every time I felt like I was drowning. She smelled of jasmine and vanilla and when father stripped me of my birthright, she fought for me to be his heir. Ultimately, she was the one who convinced our father to send me to the Isles of Myr. She wanted me to be trained in the ways of her people and he was all too glad to get rid of me. I was so angry with her for sending me away, but it wasn't because she didn't*

want me to be around. It was because in her own way, that was how she could save me from him."

"Why did you not let her go free when you attacked?" The whispered question split Niabi's heart wide open.

"I wanted to," Niabi replied with the quietness of a small child. *"But if I had let her live, let any of you live, it would have cost my son his life. All usurpers had to be dealt with, if I wanted Rollo to sit on the White Throne,"* she explained.

"I don't remember much about her," Salome's voice cracked. *"I have pieces of memories, images, flashes of happiness."*

"But?"

"As I grow older, the moments I hold dear are fading, and I'm afraid and ashamed to admit I am beginning to forget her."

"One day you shall see her again." Though the words sounded threatening, Niabi did not intend for it to come across as menacing. She was trying to comfort her heartbroken sister as best as she could, in spite of the fact she was the reason Salome would never experience more precious moments with their mother. *"Of one thing I am certain, she loved you, Salome. She loved all of us and she didn't deserve to die."*

"I suppose your hatred for our father far outweighed your love for our mother."

The words held a bite to it and rightly so. Niabi deserved that.

She shook her head, even though Salome wasn't there to see it. *"I suppose my grief for Dichali far outweighed my love for any of you. My need for revenge blinded me to all else and I will bear that burden for the rest of my days."*

"You could have let them go. Why didn't you just let us go?"

"We can talk ourselves in circles about why I did what I did, Salome," Niabi issued with a firm hand. *"But talking won't change any of it. It won't bring any of them back. It won't mend my broken heart. It won't convince you to forgive or sympathize with me. So, why bother?"*

"Because unlike you," Salome hissed, sounding more like a wounded animal than anything else, *"I wish to know the truth. I wish to know all the good, the bad, and the horrifying aspects of you, so I can convince myself that we are nothing alike. But the more I discover, the more you share, the more I realize we aren't so different after all and that scares me."*

"Scares you because you fear becoming a monster?"

"Scares me because I fear I no longer wish you dead."

Niabi was too stunned to respond. She stewed in silence for a moment and when she reached out to speak, she felt the coldness of Salome's absence. She'd severed their connection and left Niabi with more questions than ammunition. When she first realized Salome had this magic, she was hoping to garner valuable information about their whereabouts, their plans, or the number of their company, but instead, she was left with a longing to know the sister she'd never met. For the first time in years, she felt seen, felt like someone understood her, and instead of seeing her for the monster she'd allowed herself to become, she saw her for the girl she used to be, the girl she wished she could be again.

CHAPTER 38

SALOME

The Bellators allowed Salome to take a few days off to help prepare and celebrate Oifa and Hanzo's nuptials, but two nights after the wedding, she heard a heavy hand knock on her bedroom door. When she opened it, Kayven stood in the hallway with a giant grin plastered across his bronze face. Abba leaned against the wall behind his brother, and she shook her head.

"We agreed to start back up tomorrow," she folded her arms over her chest in childlike protest.

"And it is a minute past midnight," Kayven motioned for her to grab her stuff. "Officially tomorrow."

Salome rolled her eyes, "Has anyone ever told you -"

"How unbelievably handsome I am?" He wiggled his eyebrows. "All the time."

Abba chuckled but offered her no help in escaping their training session. If she didn't know any better, she could have sworn Abba had grown quite fond of her over their weeks of sparring.

Knowing there was no way she was going to get out of training with the Bellators, she grabbed her weapons, and followed them to the bailey.

It felt good getting back into the routine she'd abandoned the last few days. Over the next hour she took turns sparring with both of the brothers, and even managed to swipe Kayven off his feet, but he avoided falling thanks to his impressive wingspan.

"Dare I say," Kayven smiled at her as she wiped sweat from her temples, "you might be my best student."

She made a spectacle of sweeping her hand down to the ground as she bowed. "What a tremendous compliment, Your Lordship."

"Oh, don't start calling him that," Abba huffed. "It'll go straight to his head."

"Too late," Kayven laughed.

Taking a break to drink some refreshing water, Salome eyed the hippogriffs that the Ethereals had flown to the mainland. She had been curious about the beasts since she first spotted them but didn't dare approach them since Harbona warned her that they tend to bite strangers. Kayven noticed her staring and motioned toward the stables where they were housed.

"Hippogriffs are how the Ethereals travel since they do not have wings. That one there," Kayven pointed at a magnificent looking beast, "is Harbona's hippogriff. He is one of the fastest in the herd."

"Do you have to be an Immortal to ride one?" she asked, eyes fixed on the creature.

"Are you asking to ride one?" Kayven tilted his head, a smirk appearing on his bronze face.

"Mortals aren't used to that form of travel." Abba took a step forward, uncrossing his arms, face serious. "If she should fall off -"

"One of us will catch her." Kayven's eyes danced with mischief.

Salome was excited about the chance to go on a challenging and dangerous adventure with the brothers. "Harbona won't be happy when he finds out."

"Neither will a couple of princes, I imagine." Kayven folded his muscular arms over his broad chest, standing with his feet shoulder width apart. He wiggled his eyebrows when Salome mirrored his stance and narrowed her eyes. "But what Harbona, Crispin, and Jinn do not know, will not harm them."

"You are a terrible influence." Abba shook his head, stretching his wings, as if he already knew what was coming next.

Salome bit her lower lip. She'd be lying if she said she wasn't at least curious to see what flying one of the hippogriffs would be like. If Harbona found out, she'd be on the receiving end of a severe tongue lashing. If Crispin found out, she'd have to explain why she didn't fetch him to join.

"Well?" Kayven cocked his head to the side, already leaning up against the stall where Zandaar pounded his hooves.

Salome grinned. "Let's go."

~

TAKING off was the scariest part, but once she was soaring in the twinkling night sky, with Kayven and Abba flying at her side, she was filled with a sense of freedom, adventure, and peace. She closed her eyes as the wind whooshed around her, taking a deep breath of sea air. Crispin would be envious if he saw her flying Zandaar. He'd demand to have a turn just like a spoiled child.

"Keep your eyes open." Abba instructed. His brow was furrowed, not in anger, she realized, but in concern. He was truly worried about her falling off the flying beast. Or maybe he didn't want to face Harbona's wrath, if something happened to her.

Salome turned to the other side and watched Kayven soar through the starry night sky, looking more like an eagle than a man. She'd seen them fight in Gomorrah and knew how beautifully lethal they were in battle, but seeing them fly without bloodshed on their mind, was a memory that would forever be ingrained in her head.

"Are you alright?" Kayven must have felt her staring.

She bobbed her head and smiled, "This is amazing!"

"Zandaar does not like many mortals," Kayven glanced at the hippogriff who turned his birdlike head to look back at her. "But he seems to like you."

Salome gently stroked Zandaar's feathered head. "And I like him."

In the corner of her eye, Salome noticed a ship. It was still quite a distance from them, but she felt an uneasiness in her gut.

"Do you see that ship?" she asked the brothers.

"Ships," Abba corrected when the fleet sailed out from underneath a cloud and into the unobstructed moonlight.

"Who is it?" Salome had a lump in her throat. Even though a part of her screamed for them to turn around, she had to find out who the fleet belonged to and where they were headed. Oakenshire was as fortified as a ruined castle could be, but unless they patched holes in sections of the wall, they would be easily overrun.

"Abba and I will get a closer look." Kayven veered in front of Zandaar and held up a hand as the beast hovered. "Stay here."

"But -"

"It is for your own protection." The seriousness in Kayven's eyes made her shrink back. This was the Bellator Commander and war hero she'd heard so much about. With her, he was playful and caring. But this wasn't the time for him to make a lighthearted joke. "If something goes wrong, fly as fast as you can back to Oakenshire. Do not try to rescue us if we are captured. Do you understand?"

"I can't just leave you."

"You can and will, should they spot us." Kayven wasn't going to budge an inch on this. "Swear it, Princess."

Even though she wanted to argue with him further, maybe throw her rank in his face, she shut her mouth and nodded. She would obey. This time.

Satisfied with her response, the Bellator brothers flew toward the ships, flying high enough not to draw unnecessary attention to themselves, but low enough to spy. There was a point in which she couldn't see the Immortal warriors anymore, and she sat in complete silence as Zandaar flapped his wings to keep them steady. She listened for any sign the brothers were in trouble. Despite what Kayven made her promise, she wouldn't leave them to die, if something went wrong.

She thought they'd have more time to prepare for war. Some of their promised reinforcements hadn't arrived to Oakenshire yet. And with winter coming, she figured her sister wouldn't mobilize her troops until weather permitted.

One set of wings approaching her snapped her from her thoughts. She scanned the clouds looking for the second warrior, but still only saw one. She wasn't sure if it was Abba or Kayven, but she held her breath as the Bellator approached.

"Glad to see you did not fall to your death."

Abba. She exhaled, relieved her friend was alright, but where was Kayven?

"Where's Kayven?" she asked, terrified of the answer.

Abba grinned and pointed upward. She glanced up toward the heavens and saw a second pair of wings as Kayven lowered himself from the darkness.

"Miss me?" Kayven snickered and Salome wanted to throw something at his smug face.

"I suppose you two thought sneaking up on me would be funny?"

"Sneaking?" Kayven slapped a hand to his breastplate. "She accuses us of sneaking, brother."

"I flew directly at you." Abba crossed his arms across his chest. "How was that sneaking?"

"Valid point, Abba." Kayven purred, aware how scared Salome was and was clearly attempting to lighten the mood.

Salome scratched the side of her face, willing her heart to calm down. "Well, I'm glad neither of you got into trouble."

Kayven tilted his head to the side and grinned. "I think the mortal has grown fond of us."

"We are very likeable." Abba motioned for them to fly back toward Oakenshire.

"And handsome," Kavyen quickly added. "You cannot forget to include how handsome we are."

Salome rolled her eyes and puffed out a breath. It suddenly got chilly and she wished she'd brought a blanket or coat. "Who were they?"

Kayven and Abba exchanged a glance, but she caught the soldier flare in their eyes.

"What is it? Who are they?" Salome demanded answers.

"They fly no banners," Abba started, "but they are equipped for battle."

"The ships look Pulauan." Kayven added. "Whether your sister sent them or not, I am not sure. But they are headed for Oakenshire, of this I have no doubt."

"Are you telling me -?

"To prepare for battle?" Kayven interrupted her with a sorrowful look. "That is exactly what I am saying, Princess."

When they landed in Oakenshire, they were greeted by a group of worried and angry friends. Harbona's face was so red, Salome thought the Seer might explode. Crispin didn't appear upset, but he definitely wanted to get closer to the hippogriff once she hopped off of him. Jinn leaned against one of the stable doorways with an amused look on his face. If he was angered by her disappearance, he didn't show it.

Salome slipped down from Zandaar's back and before she had a second to breathe, Crispin and Harbona started talking at the same time.

"Do you know how risky that midnight ride of yours was?" Harbona's voice boomed. "What if you had fallen off Zandaar or worse, been seen by the enemy?"

"I can't believe you didn't come and get me!" Crispin snorted a laugh.

Jinn smirked when her eyes met his, but once he saw the tension in her face, he straightened up and made his way to her. "What's wrong?"

"We have a problem," she said.

CHAPTER 39

CRISPIN

Once the other leaders had been alerted to the emergency meeting and filed into the dining hall, Crispin took one last breath to steady himself before calling the meeting to order.

Salome sat to his right and squeezed his hand reassuringly under the table. He offered a nervous smile before scanning the faces staring back at him. Around the large wooden table sat Prince Jinn, King Kenji, Master Penn, Kayven, Abba, Harbona, Lavena, Oifa, Hanzo, Prince Heru, Adonijah, Captain Haldane, and Rahab on his left.

Crispin cleared his throat, "We've received a report that a fleet of ships is headed in our direction. The ships appear to be Pulauan and are equipped for war."

The leaders exchanged curious glances around the room, but no one voiced their concerns except Captain Haldane.

"Is King Uri onboard?"

Crispin peered across the table at Kayven and Abba. The former leaned forward, resting his arms on the table.

"My brother and I do not know who this Uri is you speak of, so I cannot say for certain if he is aboard. However, whoever leads the fleet has plenty of weapons and soldiers to overrun us."

Murmurs made their way around the table.

"We are fortunate to have taken the element of surprise out of the equation," Salome added, hushing them.

"They were sailing quickly," Abba revealed, rubbing his chin. "Something is giving speed to their ships."

"Is there a way to know how many soldiers they have at their disposal?" Prince Heru asked.

"We did not have a lot of time to get proper recon," Kayven tapped his fingers against the wood. "I am surprised they did not spot us on a clear night like tonight."

"So, all we know is a fleet of ships is headed our way, but we do not know exactly who we are fighting or how many men we're up against?" Oifa, the newly married queen of the united Mountain Men tribe, flashed a menacing grin as she picked her fingernails clean with a knife. "Sounds like fun."

"As my sister has already stated," Crispin steadied his voice, "we know whoever is coming was banking on ambushing us. Now that we know they're coming, we will be ready to defend ourselves."

From the silence around the room, Crispin sensed the leaders were nervous. He just wasn't sure if they were concerned about fighting an unknown foe, or if they had no faith in him.

Adonijah cleared his throat, drawing Crispin's attention. "There is a way you can get the information you seek."

Crispin quirked an eyebrow. "How?"

~

Leoti stood before the counsel of leaders and stared at them just as curiously and ferociously as they looked at her.

"Adonijah told us you possess certain skills that could help us," Crispin spoke softly, noticing the Andrago's eyes darted to Adonijah.

"What do you want from me?" she asked, refocusing on the prince.

"There is a fleet of ships headed our way. I need to know who is coming and how many soldiers they have."

Leoti cast a glance at Adonijah once more. He stepped up to her and whispered in her ear.

Crispin dared a quick look at Salome, but if she was bothered by her former lover moving on, she didn't show it.

"I will help you on one condition." Leoti's voice drew him back.

The Andrago was bold indeed to think she could bargain with him, but even if she refused to help, he wasn't in the business of torture, so he'd have to find another way to get the information he needed.

"What do you want?"

"Release Pash from confinement, and I will do whatever you ask."

Crispin scoffed. "He is one of Niabi's closest advisors. He's her Commander of Shadows and from what I've heard, her lover. You expect me to allow someone with his title and skillset to roam these halls free?" He shook his head, crossing his arms over his chest. "Your commander is lucky to be alive. Yet, you dare ask me to release him so he might slit my throat in the middle of the night?"

"I did not *ask* you to release him," Leoti took a step forward, her fiery eyes narrowed. "I *told* you to release him, if you want my help."

"You forget your place." Crispin cocked his head to the side. "You may be free to walk around the keep, but you are first and foremost, a prisoner of war."

Adonijah took a heavy step forward and met Crispin's ferocious gaze with one of his own. Salome stood up and joined her brother's side; a lioness protecting her future king. If Crispin wasn't careful in how he handled this situation, they might tear the alliances they'd built to shreds, and they were already stretched thin as it was.

Leoti turned and pressed a hand to Adonijah's chest, stopping his advancement, and stealing his focus. When she faced the siblings again, her eyes had softened.

"We need each other," she exhaled, easing the tension in her shoulders. "Pash is a good man, and he can be an asset when it comes to strategy. At least let him prove himself worthy. Let him help you defend Oakenshire, and I, too, will do my part to help you win this battle."

"And why should I take your word that his advice will be sound?" Crispin asked, surprised he was eager to know her answer.

"Because he has people he loves, that he wants to see again. He will make sure you not only win this battle, but you annihilate your attackers."

"Even if those assailants were sent by his queen?"

Leoti and Adonijah exchanged a quick look before she nodded her head in confirmation. "He gave up his post as Commander of Shadows when he helped Adonijah escape execution. And when the Shadows caught up to us, he fought them, risking his life to defend ours. The simple truth is Pash will help you, if it means he'll be protecting those he loves."

Salome leaned into Crispin's shoulder, and he bent slightly to hear her whisper, "We have never planned for a battle of this magnitude. Perhaps, we should hear the commander out, before we dismiss him."

Crispin knew she was right, but a part of him, the prideful part, wanted to refuse and throw the bold Andrago in a room beside Pash, as a true prisoner. But he had to consider all the people in Oakenshire that were depending on him to make wise decisions. He glanced at Rahab who was still sitting in her seat. Though he expected to see her face hardened at how Leoti had spoken to him, he saw she was already waiting for him to make eye contact with her. With a slight nod, she confirmed what his sister had advised him to do.

He looked at Leoti, "If he betrays us, you will hang alongside him."

The air was sucked out of the room and Adonijah's eyes blazed behind Leoti. Before anyone could protest or interject their opinion, Leoti extended her hand to Crispin and bobbed her head.

"Agreed."

"You trust him that much?" Crispin was surprised she would trust him with her life.

"I do."

Satisfied with her fervent defense of the commander, Crispin shook her hand and ordered for Pash to be brought before the group. Once Crispin had explained what they were up against, and the penalty should he betray them or attempt to flee to Northwind, the commander agreed to aid them. When Crispin asked why he didn't hesitate to agree to his terms, Pash said, "I don't intend to die here."

The first thing they did was have Leoti warg into her falcon and fly toward the incoming fleet. Crispin had instructed her to find out how many soldiers they had, how many ships were in their fleet, what kind of weapons they were armed with, if King Uri and Nezreen the Shadow Witch were on board, and what was giving speed to their ships. Once Leoti was confident she remembered everything the prince needed answers for, she sat down and blinked her brown eyes away.

The leaders sat quietly until Leoti's eyes blinked back to normal and she met Crispin's gaze.

"What did you see?" he asked, while leaders gathered around them.

"There are seven ships," she began, but the worry in her face was unsettling. "From your descriptions, I can tell you King Uri and the Shadow Witch are onboard the largest vessel and they are heavily armed with swords, maces, spears, and bows and arrows."

"How many soldiers?" Adonijah knelt next to her, but she didn't divert her eyes from Crispin.

"They have at least twelve hundred men with them."

Crispin's heart dropped and he had to tune out the whispers amongst the leaders in the room. "How long before they arrive?"

"A couple of days," Leoti whispered. "Maybe less."

"Did you find out how they are traveling so quickly?" Salome crossed her arms across her chest. Not a stitch of worry on her face and that struck Crispin as odd. For their entire upbringing, Salome wasn't one for altercations, but here in this war room, with a fleet of ships coming to destroy them, she was the very picture of calm. Perhaps their time apart had done more than just bring her tragedy.

Leoti nodded in answer to Salome's question, horror visible in her features. "They have a man chained in one of the smaller ships. He is an air manipulator; he's the reason their fleet is so fast."

Crispin's gaze darted to Rahab. They knew of only one air manipulator and since he used his magic to save them in Northwind, he opened himself up for Nezreen's shadows to track him down.

"Oden," Rahab confirmed his suspicions.

"We have to rescue him," Crispin wouldn't budge on that.

"You know him?" Salome chimed in.

"He saved us in Northwind," the prince nodded. "I will not let him be used and tortured for that witch's pleasure."

"But we won't be able to get near him or their ships without Nezreen's shadows knowing about it," Rahab pointed out.

"There has to be a way to get around her magic." Crispin raked his hands through his hair. They had been in the war room for hours and the lack of sleep was starting to wear him down.

"I believe, I can help on that front."

Crispin turned around and saw Jinn had made his way to Salome. They were staring into each other's eyes, and it almost seemed as if they were having an entire conversation by just looking at each other.

"How can you help?" Crispin's voice tugged the lovers from their intense eye contact and the Eastern prince met his awaiting gaze.

"I'm a cloaker."

"You're a cloaker?" Crispin could hear the excitement in Rahab's tone. "How many can you shield with your magic?"

"I've been practicing," the prince scratched his chin, "and I think I can hide a small rowboat."

Crispin turned his attention to Pash. "Let's see how good of a strategist you are, Commander."

Pash bobbed his head with a flash of determination in his eyes as he hunched over the aerial map of Oakenshire and started pointing to areas around the keep. The prince hated to admit it, but Pash had a great mind for military strategy. Within a couple of hours, the leaders hashed out a plan and agreed to Pash's defense positions and ground assault tactics.

Crispin would take the pirates on a rescue mission to retrieve Oden from

Nezreen and Uri's clutches. He'd saved them in Northwind, so he owed him. Jinn readily agreed to cloak the group from Nezreen's shadows as they sneaked aboard the small ship to save the rebel.

With her accuracy as an archer, Salome agreed to join the Stormcrag and Krazak archers with Hanzo on top of the wall. If a ground assault happened, Salome would take her place among the Qata Vishna in the bailey to defend the keep and the castle attendants.

Kayven and Abba were asked to have their Bellators keep the ships busy by launching their attack from the skies, to which both brothers happily agreed.

Even though Crispin was still leery of Pash fighting amongst them, he agreed Pash and Adonijah would fight alongside Prince Heru and the Numbio by the shoreline, to make sure no enemy soldiers penetrated the bailey. If any slipped through, Salome and the Qata Vishna and Master Penn and her Keepers would be ready.

Captain Haldane was more than eager for his pirates to blow up a few of Uri's ships and left the strategy meeting with a twinkle in his eye mentioning he needed to talk to Phex, his explosions expert. Rahab assured Crispin she'd keep an eye on him during the mission to ensure the captain didn't do anything stupid that would result in all of them getting killed before they could extract Oden.

Harbona, Lavena, and King Kenji would stay inside the keep to help Rayma and her team with any fallen or wounded soldiers. The thought of losing any of their bannermen weighed heavily on Crispin, but he couldn't dwell on it, otherwise he'd lose his nerve and that's what would ultimately get him killed in battle.

Crispin was well aware they were still waiting on reinforcements promised from Numbio, the Isles of Myr, and the Immortals, but there was no telling if they'd show up in time. So, they were going to deal with the numbers they had. They had less than twenty Qata Vishna, seven Keepers, a handful of pirates, twenty-five Bellators, and among the Numbio, Eastern warriors, and Krazaks and Stormcrags, they had five hundred men and women. And from the intel Leoti had provided, they were vastly outnumbered.

He rubbed a hand down his face and plopped into his chair once all the other leaders had cleared out of the room. Thinking he was finally alone with his thoughts, he took a moment to release all the tension he'd been holding in his shoulders, cradling his face in his hands. He groaned. How was he going to pull this off? The Pulauans outnumbered them nearly three-to-one, and if Nezreen saw through Jinn's cloaking magic, she'd capture him and the pirates.

Hands slipped around his neck from behind and from the salt water and tobacco scents enveloping him, he knew it was Rahab. He kissed her hand and pulled her around to sit on his lap. Straddling him, she pressed her forehead against his.

"You should get some rest, princeling."

"Even if I tried to lay down, I wouldn't be able to sleep," he shook his head. Kissing the tip of her nose, he reclined in his chair, pulling her with him. He rubbed small circles around her lower back as she stared at him. "What?"

"Tell me what's on your mind."

He sighed and said, "We are outnumbered."

"And?"

"And?" he chuckled; eyes wide. "If we're overrun, we won't make it to Northwind to face my sister."

"One battle at a time, Crispin." She raked her fingers through his curls. "First the Pulauans, then your sister."

"You're rather calm about this," his eyebrow quirked, and he stared deep into her hazel eyes, looking for a crack in her armor. "Are you telling me you're not nervous, my love?"

She grabbed the reefer tucked behind her ear, lit it, and puffed out a cloud of smoke before shaking her head. "I'm terrified."

"But you just said -"

"Come with me," she interrupted him as she hopped off his lap. "There's something I want to show you."

Crispin dragged himself out of his chair and slipped his hand in hers as she pulled him through the corridors.

"Look around and tell me what you see?" she asked, exhaling another puff of smoke away from him.

The prince watched as the other leaders ordered their soldiers to help fortify the city from attack. Castle attendants rushed around helping to prepare the keep and set up areas where Rayma could treat the wounded. Jacobi was in the kitchens getting his staff to double the workload to make sure they had plenty of food before and after the Pulauans arrived.

Rahab tugged him onward and led him out to the back patio where the Ignacia Sea raged.

"You wanted me to look at the sea?"

Rahab shook her head and used her reefer to point at the level beneath them where Salome sparred against Jinn, Kayven, and Abba. She whipped her knives and Qata Vishna blades in fury and her movements were more like a dance. He hadn't taken the time to watch her spar since he'd arrived in Oakenshire, but seeing how much her skills had improved, how much she'd grown as a warrior and a future queen, was impressive.

"You have the Hunter fighting for you, Crispin," Rahab reminded him.

"But she's still mortal," Crispin turned his eyes away from his sister to Rahab. "If she dies -"

"You think anyone will come close to harming her?" Before he had a chance to respond, she motioned toward the Bellators she was fighting off. "Most do not know, but she has been practicing with the Bellator commanders every night for weeks. The people in the keep tell stories about her – how she defeated a cornigera and bathed in its blue blood to become the Red Maiden, how she slayed the Gomorrian royals and had their city destroyed, how she united two warring tribes and fulfilled their ancient prophecy."

"What are you trying to tell me, Rahab?"

Exhaling another waft of smoke, she faced her betrothed with an oddly comforting smile. "She would follow you to the very depths of hell, if it meant putting you on the White Throne. She survived the Thrak, she survived the cornigera, she survived King Gerd in the City of Bones – she will make sure we survive this too."

"It sounds like you have more faith in her than me," Crispin teased, but a piece of him believed it and it made his stomach sink.

"A great king is only as mighty as his warriors and as wise as his counselors." She tucked her finger underneath his chin and tugged his face to look at her. "You are surrounded by the best warriors in Adalore and are armed with the most knowledgeable men and women in the ten kingdoms. We might be outnumbered, but we are united, and that is far more dangerous in battle."

Crispin focused once more on his sister fighting off three skilled warriors at the same time, and a calm washed over him. Rahab was right. He had to have faith that not only his allies would come through for him, but that his sister would fulfill her destiny as the Hunter. Their journey would not end in Oakenshire.

CHAPTER 40

SALOME

Two days of preparation didn't seem like enough time to prepare for an impending attack, but that's all the time they had. Salome walked around the castle grounds one more time to ensure the holes in the walls had been filled. She stopped by the blacksmiths and was pleased they'd been able to forge and sharpen all the weapons they would need for battle. Every soldier was told to eat their fill and rest that evening, because from Leoti's latest warging session, the pirates would be upon them by morning.

Rosalina had made a comment that afternoon that Salome was so calm it was unnerving, but the truth was, she was absolutely terrified. She kept thinking about how Death stalked her, waiting patiently to claim her, but first toyed with her by taking those she loved most. Salome would never admit it aloud, but she looked on her friends' smiling faces and she hoped she would see them again the following day. She made sure to check in on Seraphina, Rosalina, Cato, and Kai that day and hugged them all before they turned in for the evening.

Crispin's time had been occupied by the pirates and their bickering on how they should rescue Oden from Nezreen's clutches. She knew her brother would be protected; his blue-haired lady pirate would see to that, but the fear that he would set off in a rowboat and sail straight into Death's clutches tugged at her heart. She had to remind herself that Jinn would be sailing with him, and his magic was powerful. He'd get them aboard the ship Oden was being held captive in unseen, and he'd make sure they all returned to her.

Salome knew she should be tucked in her warm bed, resting for the day of bloodshed, but her mind was racing, and it took all of her self-control not to reach out to her sister. She still had so many questions, but she had to remind herself that though Niabi shared her blood, she was still her enemy.

Tugging her cloak tighter over her shoulders, she rested her elbows on the patio railing and watched and listened to the waves sprawl across the sandy shoreline.

"You couldn't sleep either, I take it."

Salome smirked as Crispin rested his arms next to hers on the railing. "I'm surprised you aren't visiting with a certain lady pirate on the eve before battle," she wiggled her eyebrows playfully, drawing a smile from him.

"Where exactly do you think I've been this entire time?" He bumped his shoulder into hers and she laughed, feeling a small amount of weight lift from her. "And where is your betrothed this evening?"

"Safe and snug in his bed, I imagine." Salome twisted her body, squaring her shoulders to him. "Are you alright?"

"The truth?" He gazed into her eyes, and she was struck by how sorrowful he appeared.

"Always."

"I wish I could tell you I'm not afraid," he raked a hand through his hair and sighed, "but that would be a lie."

"You aren't weak for being afraid," she squeezed his hand.

"Wise words," he gave her a tight-lipped smile.

"Don't tell Kayven that," Salome snickered. "It'll go straight to his head that you found his words wise."

"I've heard you've been secretly meeting with the Bellators at midnight to train."

"Well, I suppose it isn't much of a secret, if everyone knows about it." Salome twirled a strand of her hair in her fingers. She knew Crispin was waiting for an explanation, and as much as she wanted to keep her battle fright to herself, she couldn't deny him when he'd been vulnerable with her moments before. "After I was rescued from Gomorrah and I was cleared for physical activity, I went to the bailey to spar with Kai and couldn't do it. It was as if my arm was made of stone and my reaction time was non-existent. I kept having flashbacks of my time in Gomorrah, the people I killed, the people I lost..." she cleared her throat. "My hands trembled and I realized there was something wrong with me, but didn't know what."

"What happened?"

"I stormed into the keep like some petulant child that just got her ass whipped and Kayven stopped me in the corridor. He told me he could help me overcome my battle fright, if I let him." Salome smiled, grateful for the Bellator brothers. "Every night after everyone else went to sleep, I would go down to the bailey and spar with them. At first, I had a difficult time. I couldn't get my hands under control and the flashbacks plagued me, but Kayven and Abba didn't give up on me. And now, they're teaching me more tricks. I just wish I had wings, so I could truly be their equal in battle."

"If you had wings, I would legitimately be upset."

"Why?" she laughed.

"Can't have you looking better than me," he dodged her incoming swat and chuckled. "If you had wings that would definitely make you the better-looking sibling."

"What are you talking about?" she snorted. "I'm already better looking than you."

Crispin rubbed his fingers along his beard. When they had parted ways months ago, he looked like a kid. Now, he didn't just look like a grown man, but like a king.

"I don't know. Now that I have this beard, the ladies can't help but look at me."

Salome rolled her eyes, "Delusional to the end." She hadn't meant the words to sound so finite, especially with a looming battle ahead of them, but it put a damper on the evening, no doubt about it. "We'll be alright," she whispered.

"We'll be alright," he echoed softly.

She slipped her hand into his and squeezed, resting her head against his shoulder. "We should at least attempt to get some rest."

"We should." He nodded, but neither of them moved, as if they both just wanted to enjoy one another's uninterrupted company a little while longer.

STANDING with her brother on the eve of battle, in a quiet calm, was a memory that would forever be branded in her mind. Neither alone in their fear. She prayed the Almighty would protect him, even when she couldn't. It was in that hope alone that she was able to rest her head later that evening, but a small knock on her door stirred her from her bed.

Grabbing her robe thrown over the vanity chair, she wrapped it around herself as she made her way to the door. When she opened it, she found Jinn standing on the other side, his palms braced on either side of the doorframe. His head was down, his shoulders tense, as if he was physically restraining himself from stampeding through the door.

"Jinn?" she whispered, quickly glancing up and down the corridor to ensure no one had seen the prince arrive at her bedroom that late at night. "Is everything alrig -"

In a flash, he'd slipped his hands on either side of her face and crashed his lips against hers, swallowing the rest of her question. He was relentless, a drowning man desperate for his last breath. Slowly, tentatively, he grazed his fingertips from her cheeks down her neck, down her arms, until his calloused hands rested on her hips.

Raking her fingers through his already disheveled hair, she bit his bottom lip and twisted her legs around his torso when he hoisted her up into his arms.

Salome craved him; needed him. He was the answer to every riddle, the melody to every song. The stars, the seas, the mountains, they all paled in comparison to the passion of his kiss, the lightness of his touch, the warmth of his eyes. There was no denying her love for him; he was the beginning and end of her beating heart.

Jinn pulled back, but abandoned his retreat when she wrapped her hands around his neck and tugged him closer. He was breathless, his chest rising and falling rapidly, his lips swollen, and eyes hungry. Resting his forehead against hers, he whispered, "I had to see you."

She dragged the tip of her finger along the curvature of his chiseled jaw, drawing a raspy breath from him.

"I couldn't sleep," he said as he grazed his nose along the crook of her neck, breathing her in.

"What troubles you?"

"You."

"Me?" She pulled back, slowly sliding down from his tall frame.

"You have consumed my every waking thought and now infiltrate my dreams."

She smiled but before she could respond, he glided his hand around her neck, cupping her jaw, and said in a low voice that sent a bolt of lightning soaring through her body, "A secret for a secret."

"You first." She ran her thumb across his bottom lip, relishing how he shivered from her light touch.

"I want to marry you." His smile crinkled the corners of his eyes but she rolled her eyes in response. "What?"

"That isn't much of a secret since we are betrothed, my lord."

Her use of the new pet name seemed to ignite a fire in his golden-brown eyes and the way he looked at her made her own heart leap.

Jinn leaned forward, pressing his lips against her ear. His low, sultry voice made her knees buckle. "The secret is, I want to marry you tonight."

"Wishful thinking, my lord."

"Is it?"

Salome's throat tightened. Turning her face to meet his gaze, she found no trace of humor or deception. "You're serious."

"Harbona's room is at the end of the hall," he twisted a strand of her hair between his fingers. "He could oversee an elopement."

"What about a wedding?" She knew his people were extremely faithful to keep their traditions and weddings were a huge part of that. And with them being royals, the future King and Queen of Sakurai, a wedding would be expected, if not demanded.

"After the war, we can plan a traditional wedding," Jinn tucked a strand of her hair behind her ear. "But royal weddings aren't for us, they're for our people." The prince snaked his arm around her waist and tugged her closer, pressing their bodies together. "I would marry you tonight in this rundown castle and be content knowing you're mine."

It was then Salome glanced over Jinn's shoulder and realized they hadn't closed her door when he first arrived, but his low laugh was confirmation he'd already cloaked them.

"You should save your strength for tomorrow, Jinn."

"I will worry about tomorrow when the time comes." The vibrato in his voice sent a welcome shiver down her spine. He planted an open mouth kiss against the crook of her neck. "Tonight, it's just you and me."

She smiled and tilted his chin back up to kiss his lips. "You and me," she echoed.

CHAPTER 41
CRISPIN

Crispin had not gotten much sleep. Even after saying goodnight to Salome, he lay awake in his bed until he was alerted that the fleet had been spotted by the patrolling Bellators. The sun had not peaked above the horizon when the castle hummed to life. Leaders and soldiers alike dressed, prepped, and made their way to their battle positions.

Once Crispin had double checked with each leader and their group, he headed down to the beach where a rowboat filled with what remained of Captain Haldane's pirates awaited. Just to the side of the boat, Salome whispered something in Prince Jinn's ear before embracing him.

At the sound of his boots crunching the sand, Salome turned and met his gaze. The morning light haloed around her, making her appear more like the Goddess of War, than his little sister. With an arms-length of space between them, Crispin halted and offered the best smile he could muster all while battling the thought this might be the last time they ever saw one another.

"Don't," Salome shook her head, eyes tearing up. "Don't look at me like it's the last time."

"You always were too observant for your own good." Crispin kicked at some sand when he teased her. He felt like a giant hand had grabbed ahold of his heart and was crushing it. Reaching for her, he pulled her to his chest for a hug. "Fight hard," he whispered.

She squeezed his torso tight enough to bruise a rib. "I will see you soon, brother."

Reluctantly, Crispin released her and headed toward Jinn to hop into the awaiting boat.

"Take care of him." Salome's voice rang out behind him, spurring him to turn around.

"I promise to keep an eye on your betrothed," he smirked.

"I was talking to Jinn." She motioned toward the prince, eyes now fixed on the Easterner. "Protect my brother and come back to me in one piece."

Jinn bowed his head and winked. "As my lady commands."

Crispin exchanged one last look with his sister before he and Jinn pushed the rowboat away from the shoreline and into the Ignacia Sea. With a nod from Crispin, he signaled Jinn to cloak them as they made their way toward the fleet anchored in the distance.

"How do we know if your magic worked?" Captain Haldane asked Jinn, and all eyes darted to the prince.

"I can sense it," Jinn replied.

"And if it falters?" Rahab quirked an eyebrow which drew a playful grin from the Easterner.

"Then I hope you can swim back to shore, when the Pulauans sink us."

Crispin chuckled, and it seemed to relieve the tension amongst the crew of the *Shadow of Death*. He slipped his hand in Rahab's and squeezed. Her hazel eyes latched onto his and softened a bit before she transformed into the hardened pirate he first met. Mentally, she was ready, and he knew no matter what happened during the battle, he would do everything in his power to make sure she made it out alive.

The moment of truth was upon them. They were within firing range of the Pulauan warships, so if Jinn's magic hadn't worked, it would be seconds before the seafarers launched an assault to sink them. But as they continued to draw closer to the ship Leoti had described as the one Oden was being held captive in, nothing happened. No weapons were aimed at them. No soldiers aboard the ships even gave them a second glance. Their rescue mission was working.

Crispin almost breathed a sigh of relief until he saw pirates emptying from the vessels into smaller boats and rowing straight for them. There was nothing they could do but wait to see if the enemy would sail past them or attack them. They held a collective breath as the invading sailors whooshed by. At least Jinn's magic was powerful and in full effect. But as Crispin did a quick count of how many rowboats filled with enemy soldiers headed toward Oakenshire, his stomach churned. There were easily a thousand warriors making their way toward the castle. He mumbled a quick prayer of protection over his sister, before turning his focus back to the mission at hand. If anyone could lead their troops to victory, it was the Hunter.

With most of the soldiers headed toward shore, there would only be a couple hundred men left aboard the seven vessels to man them. They could easily incapacitate the sailors aboard the ship holding Oden and when they were done rescuing him, sink it. Hopefully, if Phex's trinkets worked, they could sink a couple more ships on their way back to shore. Burn the ships, then their soldiers would be stuck.

They finally made it to the first ship and one by one, slowly boarded. Jinn managed to keep them all cloaked until they were all standing on the deck. But as they were informed during the strategy meeting, the prince wouldn't be able to keep them hidden as they split up and battled the remaining pirates. Once they were ready, Jinn nodded his head, releasing them from his magic and the crew scattered around the warship, making sure to have a partner with them at all times.

Captain Haldane set off with Phex to set up explosives. If they successfully blew up this boat once they extracted Oden, Almighty willing, they'd catch the two ships on either side, burning them to a watery grave.

Ondrej the giant, and Rafi the pint-sized one, took off toward the helm to take control of the ship.

Rahab and Corwin, the quiet, knife-thrower, set off to slit the throats of the seafarers around the deck.

Leaving Crispin and Jinn to find Oden below decks.

With this vessel being the smallest in the fleet, it didn't take long for the enemy to be slaughtered. Crispin and Jinn easily found the room Oden was chained in and while Jinn stood guard outside the entrance, just in case the ship was boarded by a crew from neighboring vessels, Crispin made his way inside to free the Northerner.

"Oden?" Crispin knelt in front of the rebel and gasped when he saw the man's body.

Chained and shackled, his arms were stretched wide, and his legs were rooted to the floor, making him look like a giant X. He'd been badly beaten; his body was riddled with small cuts from his face all the way down to his bare feet. His clothing was stained with blood and had gaping holes. It was cold in the dark, windowless room and Oden's lips were turning blue. His eyes were closed, but when Crispin reached out and touched his shoulder, the man jolted awake, rattling the chains.

"It's me," Crispin held his hands up in surrender. "Oden, it's me."

Oden sighed in relief. "My Prince," his eyes darted around the room. "You shouldn't be here. It is far too dangerous."

"I've come to rescue you."

"You need to go before the witch's shadows sense your presence."

Crispin's heart ached at the fear in Oden's face. What horrors he must have endured being held captive by Nezreen and Uri. Slowly, Crispin extended his hand to the manacles around his wrists, finding the skin underneath raw and bleeding.

"We have a cloaker," the prince explained as he tugged on the chains to see how strong they were. "Once we get you out of here, we'll head back to Oakenshire."

Oden shook his head, a great sadness seeping into his bruised features. "There's no use, Prince Crispin. There is only one key that will unlock these chains -"

"Jinn," Crispin called out and the Easterner slipped inside. If Jinn was horrified by the state Oden was in, he didn't show it, his mask firmly in place. "We need to check every man on this ship for a key to unlock his chains."

Jinn and Oden exchanged a knowing look and Crispin's gaze darted between the two men.

"You know one another?" he asked.

Oden offered a weak smile and nodded. "It is good to see you again, Prince Jinn."

"I wish it were under different circumstances, Oden." Jinn's gaze roved over the chains and then met Crispin's inquisitive look. "Oden asked me to go to the Isles of Myr to see if I could find your sister. He wanted to help her before Niabi or Gershom could get to her."

That answered how the two men knew one another, but it didn't do anything to advance the rescue mission. All Crispin's questions would have to wait until later.

"We need to find the key," Crispin reiterated, but Oden shook his head.

"You don't understand, my Prince. There is only one key and that key hangs from Nezreen's neck." Oden's eyes were filled with a sorrow Crispin knew too well. "There is no saving me."

Crispin refused to accept that and started tugging the chains, hoping he might be able to rip them from the hooks tying him to the room. "I came to rescue you and that's what I intend to do."

"Crispin," Oden's calm voice made his skin prickle with goosebumps. "You need to escape, while you still can. I will buy you time."

"Don't give up," he pulled harder on the chains to no avail.

"I wish I could have been by your side when you swore your oath in Northwind," the rebel met Crispin's teary gaze. "Go. It's alright."

Crispin opened his mouth to refuse the man's plea, but when Rahab ran into the room, he redirected his attention. Apart from some sweat and a small scratch on her left cheek, she was unscathed.

"There's movement from the *Leviathan*," Rahab reported. The *Leviathan* was Uri and Nezreen's ship and was the largest and fastest in the fleet. "They know we're here. We have to go."

Crispin's face hardened as he turned back to Oden.

"You must go," Oden offered a feeble smile. "I knew I was never going to leave this ship alive."

His failure to rescue Neempo the Sovereign from his sister in Northwind weighed heavily upon him. But this. Failing Oden, the man who had saved him and Rahab when certain death was upon them; the man who had loved his mother more than himself; the man who was faithful to his king and country all his days, even as an outlaw. This failure was more than Crispin's heart could bear.

Standing to his full height, the prince rested his forehead against Oden's and whispered, "I'm sorry."

"I'm not," Oden shook his head, tears streaming down his battered face. "I get to see your mother again. Go!"

"Crispin," Rahab's voice sliced through his hesitancy, snapping him into action.

Crispin followed Jinn and Rahab to the door, but he forced himself to look back one more time. "Thank you for your unwavering devotion to my family. You will not be forgotten."

Oden bowed his head. "Long may you reign, my King."

CHAPTER 42

SALOME

Salome watched Crispin, Jinn, and the pirates drift toward the fleet until she noticed enemy soldiers rowing their boats toward shore. They passed her brother, and she was relieved that Jinn's practice had paid off. He had successfully shielded them from the hundreds of seafarers headed her way. Footsteps crunched behind her, but she didn't take her eyes off the dozens of rowboats oaring through the sea.

"How many do you think are coming?" Adonijah asked as he stood by her.

"If I had to take a guess," she turned, "at least eight or nine hundred."

He bobbed his head in agreement.

This had been the first time the two of them had been alone, since his arrival into Oakenshire. It was then, she told him whatever was going on between them was over. She knew she'd made the right decision for herself and after seeing how he interacted with Leoti, she knew her decision was right for him, as well. But she'd be lying if she said she didn't miss their friendly banter and camaraderie.

"Are you afraid?" His voice brought her back to the present and she glanced back at the approaching force.

"Afraid for them," she smirked. "None of them are leaving this place alive."

Adonijah laughed and it filled her with an incredible sense of joy. "Smartass," he crossed his arms over his chest, shaking his head.

"You know me," she bumped her shoulder against his arm. "Thank you."

"For what?"

"Staying."

He cocked his head to the side, confusion written across his face. "Where else would I be?"

"I didn't mean to hurt you," she whispered, the light morning breeze whipping strands of her loose curls across her forehead. She'd let Rosalina braid her hair in the traditional Qata Vishna way, but her hair was stubborn and had a way of sneaking out.

Realization washed over him, and he squared his shoulders to hers. Taking her hand in his, he squeezed and asked, "Are you happy with him?"

Salome smiled. "I am."

"I'm happy too."

"So, are we friends again?" she teased, and he pulled her into his arms for a hug.

"Until Death takes me."

Taking a deep breath, she pulled away from his embrace and turned her attention to the castle they were about to defend. "I suppose it's time."

Adonijah rolled his shoulders back and cracked his neck. "I suppose it is."

Salome patted her palm against his chest. "The Almighty protect you."

He slid his hand above hers. "May Strength and her Eagle guide you."

It warmed her soul that he remembered the Virtue she had chosen as the new Red Maiden: Strength and her Eagle. She cupped his face and thumbed his jawline before turning to head up the embankment to the castle. She would take her place amongst the archers and down any pirate within distance of her shot.

Knowing Adonijah and Pash were joining Heru with the Numbio and Oifa with the united Mountain Men as the first line of defense, she swore she'd make sure they all made it through the battle. She had become deadly in hand-to-hand combat, but archery was still her first love, and she was confident in her ability. She was used to being the hunter and she would make sure all prey suffered the same fate.

Qata Vishna blades strapped to her back, three daggers in their holsters attached to her thigh, lower back, and right boot, her quiver of arrows swinging from her hip, and her bow in her hand, Salome took her place on top of the outer wall facing the Ignacia Sea.

Hanzo had the archers lined up with their bows nocked, ready to rain hell upon the intruders.

Turning to glance into the bailey behind her, the Qata Vishna and Master Penn and her Keepers were armed to the teeth and chomping at the bit, to get a piece of the action.

Although they'd done their best to patch holes and rebuild sections of battered walls, there were still gaps and weak points. That's where the troops, Heru, Oifa, Adonijah, and Pash eagerly awaited the first wave of sailors.

Salome cast her gaze toward Kayven, Abba, and their elite unit of Bellators. Their entire agenda was to destroy ships and keep Uri and Nezreen distracted from Crispin's group rescuing Oden. When the Bellator brothers saw her, she nodded, signaling it was time. They smiled, spread their wings, and rocketed into the sky. They were fast and undeniably beautiful in their lethality. She couldn't help the smirk that snaked across her face as she watched the winged warriors zig-zag through the air, cutting down pirates that attempted to fight them around the decks of the warships.

As the Bellators wreaked havoc upon the fleet itself, the enemy sailors reached the beach and began their assault.

"Archers ready!" Hanzo cried out and all the bowmen aimed their weapons at the invaders.

Salome obeyed the King of Fennor, inhaling and exhaling rhythmically to settle her nerves. They were prey – nothing more.

To her left, Kai readied her own bow, the very picture of calm. She was grateful to have the Ryoko Naga by her side.

"Loose!" Hanzo dropped his hand forward and dozens of arrows soared through the sky, downing their intended targets.

Waves of pirates fell, but many managed to slip through, stampeding toward the gaps in the outer wall and into the awaiting arms of the Numbio and Mountain Men.

"Swords!" Heru bellowed, and his men unsheathed their swords as one.

"No survivors!" Oifa pounded a fist to her chest. "No mercy!"

The Mountain Men howled in response and unleashed hell. The clashing of metal upon metal rang out and drowned all other sounds.

Death was present and she was feasting that morning. Men and women on both sides succumbed to the sword, axe, or arrow, and the grey stone pavers were coated red with blood.

Salome kept a steady pace, each of her arrows meeting its mark, offering another soul to Death. A loud grunt behind her caught her ear and when she whipped around, she saw three Pulauans swinging their cutlasses at Heru. Redirecting her attention, she grabbed three arrows and quickly fired them in rapid succession, striking all three of them dead. Heru flicked his gaze up to the wall and nodded his thanks before jumping back into the fray.

Wave after wave of pirates continued to dock and storm the castle. The marksmen downed as many as they could, but they were running low on arrows.

"I'm out," Kai shouted and motioned toward her empty quiver.

Salome, too, was out and was ready to move to the next phase of her battle assignment. Casting her bow to the side, she unsheathed her Qata Vishna blades and blew two long notes on the horn Seraphina had given her to signal the Myridians and Keepers they were needed. With Kai at her side, armed with her fan of knives, Salome made her way down the stone staircase, setting foot on a real battlefield. Adrenaline pumped through her body and she had to fight the flashbacks that kept wanting to creep into her mind. Training with Kayven and Abba gave her the strength and technique to quiet the battle fright. She couldn't succumb to her fear, not now, when she was needed most.

A small door set inside the gate leading to the bailey opened and the Qata Vishna and Keepers filed out and fell into line behind Salome and Kai.

"Qata Vishna! Keepers!" Salome called out and they stood at attention. "Slay them all."

Blades ripped from the Myridians' holsters; the united unsheathing echoed across the battlefield, alerting everyone they had arrived. As one, they sprinted toward the chaos and once they reached their allies, proceeded to flip, kick, spin, and stab their way through the enemy soldiers.

Salome swiped the legs out from under an enormous Pulauan. The ground shook when he fell. Not wasting time, she drove both her blades into his chest before ripping them back out and moving on to the next one.

"Salome!"

She recognized Adonijah's voice and whipped around. He and a handful of soldiers were surrounded by Pulauans and cut off from the rest of their allies.

"Shield!" She yelled and two Qata Vishna dropped to the ground, bracing their shields above them to propel her as soon as she jumped. Soaring through the air, she decapitated two seafarers as she landed.

Fighting their way out, Adonijah thanked her while wiping blood and dirt from his face. She wasn't sure if the blood belonged to him or not, but there wasn't time to ask as another group darted toward them. As hard as they fought, they were still outnumbered, and it was only a matter of time before they were overrun.

A sudden cold wind stirred, whipping in from the sea. Looking out toward the fleet, she saw a massive storm swirling. Crispin must have gotten to the air manipulator. He's the only one she could think of that could conjure such damaging conditions. But as she looked out and over the expanse of the beach, her heart sank. The endless wave of faces running toward them sobered her to the fact they might not win this battle. Even if Crispin was successful in his rescue mission, he and the Bellators might not make it back in time to help, or worse, they might not be able to do anything to change the outcome.

"Jinn," she couldn't help reaching out to him.

"What's wrong?" He responded immediately.

"We're being overrun. We might not make it," her voice cracked.

"Hold on, darling, we're coming."

"Jinn -"

"Don't you dare give up! Do you hear me?"

"I just wanted you to know that I love you." She slammed their connection closed, sliced a pirate's leg off at the knee, and followed it up with a blade stabbed through his neck.

A horrendous scream pierced her ears and when she turned, she caught sight of Rosalina with a knife stuck in her abdomen. Salome sprinted toward her friend, watching helplessly as Rosalina fell to her knees. The Pulauan that had stabbed her, swung his cutlass, his aim to decapitate the Qata Vishna.

"No!" Salome screamed, pushing people out of her way, but she was blocked.

Rosalina closed her eyes as the blade swung at her neck but at the last second, she ducked, ripped the knife out of her gut, and sliced the inside of both of the sailor's thighs, bringing him to his knees. Now face to face, she took his own knife, covered in her blood, and slit his throat.

Salome reached her as she keeled over, her hand pressed to her wound. Rosalina had lost a lot of blood and was frighteningly pale.

"You're alright." Salome cradled her friend. "I'm going to get you to Rayma. You're going to be alright, Ros."

"I'm sorry, my lady," a tear slid down Rosalina's cheek. "I'm afraid I will not be able to keep my oath to protect you."

Salome shushed her and attempted to lift Rosalina up, but the Qata Vishna fought off her efforts.

"Ros, I am trying to help you."

"I go to the After to join my sisters in arms." Rosalina was having difficulty breathing but met Salome's teary gaze.

"Please don't go," Salome's bottom lip quivered.

"Tell my sister, we will meet again." Rosalina pulled Salome close and kissed her forehead. "As deep as the sea," she whispered.

"Rosalina?" Salome whimpered as the battle raged around her. "Rosalina!?" She shook the Qata Vishna but there was no waking her. She was gone.

It felt like she was wading through quick-sand and she couldn't hear anything or anyone around her. She gently laid Rosalina down on the ground, covered in her friend's blood.

Feeling eyes on her, she looked up and met Seraphina's line of sight. She was frozen in place with several invaders running toward her, swords drawn. It snapped Salome out of her grief. She wouldn't lose both twins. Rushing with her blades out to defend the stricken Qata Vishna, she blocked the incoming blows and fended off the enemy sailors. Once she'd downed them, she shook Seraphina, screaming for her to fight, but her far off gaze was fixed on her dead sister. Seeing no other option, Salome slapped Seraphina, bringing her back.

"Fight, Seraphina," Salome pleaded. "I need you to fight."

The twin dragged her sight from Rosalina's lifeless body; rage replacing her pain. Together, Salome and Seraphina sliced through every pirate in their path, leaving a trail of splattered blood and splintered bones. Scanning for her friends, she was relieved to see Kai, Adonijah, Heru, Oifa, Hanzo, Cato, and Master Penn still standing. They were beaten, bloody, and exhausted, but they were alive, and that's all that mattered. The only thing they could do now was fight for their survival, and hope Crispin and the Bellators could return to aid them before it was too late.

CHAPTER 43
CRISPIN

As soon as his boots hit the deck of the warship, Crispin took in the sight of the chaos and destruction of the Battle of Oakenshire. Dead Pulauans were strewn throughout the deck. Looking up into the sky, the Bellators were zipping in and out of combat with soldiers on other vessels. But when he looked to the Mainland, where his sister was leading the battle against the invaders, his heart lodged in his throat. There wasn't an inch of that beach that wasn't occupied by an enemy soldier. He knew they were outnumbered, but seeing the invasion his sister was facing, sent him into a panic. They needed to get back to help, but what could a handful of people do? They could come up from behind to fight them, but it would still take a miracle for them to win this battle.

"Crispin!" Rahab's voice dragged him back to the present. "We have to get off this ship before it blows."

He followed her to the rope ladder to climb down to their awaiting rowboat, but as he descended, he sensed someone was watching and turned toward the Leviathan and there stood Nezreen with her shadows dancing all around her. He knew she was blind and that she couldn't actually see him, but he swore, she was staring into his very soul. A wicked grin snaked across her pale face, confirming his suspicions. She was well aware of his presence, and it was indeed time for them to escape.

Dropping to the boat, he motioned for them to leave. Pushing against the hull of the vessel that Oden would die in, he whispered, "Rest well, my friend."

Crispin picked up an oar and helped them row back to Oakenshire. He noticed Jinn stiffen, his eyes were filled with concern and his brow was knitted together.

"What is it?" Crispin asked once Jinn was set free from whatever spell he was under.

Jinn met his gaze. "It's Salome. They're being overrun."

"How do you -?"

"Her magic."

Crispin felt stupid. Of course, she could communicate with Jinn through her magic. She had told him about her power when they were reunited, but they hadn't discussed it since. And since Jinn had magic, they had a connection.

"How bad is it?" Crispin refocused and questioned the prince.

Jinn shook his head; a wave of emotions clouded his features. "It sounded like she was saying goodbye."

"Row faster!" Crispin shouted, but Haldane pressed a large hand to his shoulder.

"We're rowing as fast as we can, lad, but the tide is against us," the captain explained.

As if on cue, a gust of wind swept through, propelling them toward the Mainland.

"Oden," Crispin whispered, recognizing the magic in effect.

But the gust of wind that Oden conjured, turned into a funnel and began tearing one of the smaller ships in Uri's fleet apart. The rebel was going to fight until his last breath, once again saving Crispin from Death.

Seeing the storm brewing, Kayven warned the Bellators to avoid the twister, so Crispin took his chance to get the commander's attention by waving and shouting his name.

Kayven heard him and descended, "Prince Crispin?"

"My sister needs your help!"

Hard determination settled into the Bellator's features and the winged warrior nodded in understanding. "Bellators, to Oakenshire!"

"Take me with you!" Jinn called out before the Immortal left. Glancing at Crispin, Jinn said, "I'll make sure she's safe."

Crispin nodded in approval as Kayven extended his hand to Jinn. Once the prince was secure in Kayven's arms, the Bellator rocketed back to the castle, and it gave Crispin hope that Salome and their friends would survive.

Behind him a large explosion sounded. Crispin ducked from the debris flying overhead from the vessel Oden had been on. Phex's trinkets had worked, and the ship was nothing but a pile of floating debris. As Phex hoped, the ship next to it ignited and the flames spread quickly along the hull. The ship sank within minutes.

Crispin looked back at the *Leviathan* and Nezreen still hadn't moved from her position. Her shadows darted toward them, looking for souls to snatch, but suddenly halted and retreated. Her attention was no longer fixed on them, but on something behind her.

A giant harpoon jettisoned out of the fog and splintered the vessel adjacent to the Leviathan. Someone had come to their rescue. When Crispin saw three white ships with golden sails, he jumped to his feet to scream for joy. The Immortal reinforcements had finally arrived, and just in time. Their presence forced Uri and Nezreen to order their fleet to retreat before they lost another ship. But before they could sail away, a wall of water sped toward the vessel next to the Leviathan and crashed into it, toppling it into the sea. Whoever was with the Immortals was a powerful magic wielder, and Crispin was glad to have them on their side.

Crispin glanced around at everyone in the boat and smiled, a second wind filling his lungs. "Let's go help our friends."

CHAPTER 44

SALOME

If she hadn't seen it with her own eyes, Salome wouldn't have believed the wall of water had destroyed one of the Pulauan warships, but that's exactly what happened. She watched as the seafarers retreated, abandoning their soldiers on the Mainland, whom they still had to defeat, but her strength – physically, mentally, emotionally – was waning. Hope stirred within her when she saw the golden sails of the Immortal ships and the hundreds of Bellators taking off from the decks and making their way to shore. Kayven, Abba, and the Bellator elite were leading the charge. Help was on the way, she just had to hold on a little bit longer.

Four Pulauan soldiers rushed and cornered her, bloody weapons drawn. She had to dig deep to muster every last ounce of fight she had left in her to survive. Ducking, dodging, and tumbling, she avoided their attacks, slicing and stabbing as she eluded them. Three fell to the ground, dead, but the fourth and largest Pulauan slapped her wrists, knocking her blades from her grip. Now disarmed, the soldier smacked her hard across the face, drawing blood. She fell to the ground and he swung his cutlass upon her, but she quickly rolled, jumped to her feet and drew her wolf dagger from her thigh, ready to poke holes in his chest. But despite his large size, he moved swiftly and landed another two blows to her face and chest, stealing her breath. He landed a large boot to her stomach and she keeled over. She tried to crawl away, but couldn't move fast enough and suffered a crushing kick to her ribcage, wrenching a scream from her.

This was it. Exhausted and in excruciating pain, she watched as he lifted his weapon over his head to deliver the final blow. "Care to beg for your life? I love when bitches beg for mercy."

Salome flashed her middle finger and spat at him in response.

Enraged, the pirate swung his cutlass at her throat, but Jinn uncloaked himself and blocked the deadly blow.

The prince whipped his tachi swords around, disorienting the Pulauan, but he quickly recovered and sparred with Jinn, landing a punch to the Easterner's chin.

Jinn jumped back, eluding the swipe of the soldier's blade. Their swords clashed ferociously, but Jinn managed to get the upper hand when he elbowed the pirate in the face and quickly plunged a sword into his chest.

With a grunt, the Pulauan dropped dead, and Jinn grimaced, and fell to his knees.

"Jinn!" Salome crawled to him, horrified at all the blood seeping from his abdomen. "No, no, no, no. Jinn, please hang on." She pointed at the nearest soldier, a Stormcrag archer, and ordered him to bring a healer immediately.

"Salome," Jinn's voice was calm and washed over her like rain extinguishing a forest fire. "Look at me." He flashed her a pain-filled smile, "I'm alright."

"Alright?" her voice cracked. "There's a lot of blood, Jinn."

"I've had worse injuries." He cupped her face. "I promise, I'll be alright, darling."

"I can't lose you too," she sobbed. "We lost Rosalina today and I just can't… I can't…"

"I'm not going anywhere." Just as Rosalina had done before she died, Jinn pulled her close and planted a kiss on her dirty forehead, his blood stained her armor. Her breathing hitched and her bottom lip trembled. Noticing she was having a panic attack, Jinn tilted her chin to force her to look into his eyes. "I'm not going anywhere," he whispered in a tone that began to soothe her. "It's you and me. Say it."

"It's you and me," she echoed softly, returning to herself. She ran her fingers through his sweaty hair, hovering above him. "You saved me again."

"It's becoming a habit," he chuckled softly, his free hand covering his wound.

Salome scanned the bailey and was relieved to see with the Bellators' help, they were able to push the Pulauans out of the city and cut them down as they fled to their rowboats, not knowing they'd already been put to the flame. Despite the odds, they had won. They had won the Battle of Oakenshire, although she still didn't know how many lives this victory had cost them.

Jinn groaned as he pulled his breastplate off and tried to sit up, spurring Salome to slip behind him and guide his head onto her lap. "Don't move." She glanced toward the keep where all the injured were being taken but didn't see anyone from Rayma's team coming. "Where is the healer?"

When footsteps approached, she snatched one of Jinn's swords and pointed it at whoever was coming. Adonijah raised his hands, and she lowered the weapon. His gaze bounced from her to the bloody prince as he knelt beside them.

"How badly are you hurt?" Adonijah asked.

Jinn gritted his teeth as he pulled his blood-soaked shirt up revealing a slash across his lower abdomen. There was a lot of blood and Salome was finding it difficult to mask her panic. Adonijah took his canteen and poured a little bit of water over the wound to get a better look. The prince hissed, but Adonijah nodded and the tension in his shoulders vanished.

"It looks worse than it is." Adonijah started ripping pieces of fabric from a dead Pulauan's cloak to wrap around Jinn's torso. "It will need to be cleaned, stitched, and bandaged, but you'll live."

Once Adonijah and Salome wrapped Jinn's gash to stop the bleeding, the sell-sword helped the prince to his feet. With Jinn's arm over Adonijah's shoulders, they walked to the keep where Rayma and her team were tending to the wounded. The great hall where they'd celebrated Hanzo and Oifa's wedding a week ago, was now riddled with bodies, dead and alive, friend and foe. It reeked of blood, sweat, and death. Adonijah set Jinn down when he found an open spot on the floor and marched over to where Rayma was, got some supplies, and returned. Salome watched Adonijah silently take a needle and thread and look up at the prince.

"If you would prefer someone else do this -"

Jinn shook his head and motioned for Adonijah to do what needed to be done. "Try not to enjoy this too much," the prince smirked.

"I'll do my best." Adonijah grinned, then focused on the gash. After cleaning it, he carefully stitched up the wound. Salome held onto Jinn's hand tightly, grateful Adonijah was there to help him.

"That should do it." Adonijah cut the string and tied it. "I can help you to your room. You'll need to rest."

The trek to Jinn's chambers was long and somber. Salome was so relieved Jinn was safe, but her heart was heavy, knowing so many of their comrades didn't make it through the battle. She would need to give Rosalina a proper Myridian burial out at sea. She feared seeing who else might not have made it through the day.

"You should get checked out yourself," Adonijah's voice sliced through her thoughts.

Consumed with worry for Jinn, she had forgotten she, too, suffered injuries, but it wasn't anything she couldn't handle herself, knowing Rayma and her staff were busy tending to more serious wounds.

She shook her head, "I look worse than I feel." A lie, and by the look on Adonijah's face, he knew it, but he nodded and let the issue go.

Once they made it to the prince's chambers, Adonijah helped him into his bed and quickly headed for the door. Salome clasped Adonijah's forearm before he left and said, "Thank you."

Adonijah kissed her forehead. "You're welcome." And then he turned on his heel and disappeared down the hall.

Salome stood in the threshold of Jinn's chamber door, conflicted. Should she leave him to rest, so she could find the other leaders to get updates? Or should she watch over him for a little while, until someone else could take her place?

"Salome?" She closed the bedroom door slowly, before turning to face him. "Are you alright?"

"I should let you rest," she averted her gaze from his bandaged abdomen, guilt weighing heavily on her shoulders that he had been injured protecting her.

"Stay with me?" His voice was soft, his eyes expectant.

She knew she needed to meet with her brother the moment he and the pirates returned, but she couldn't bring herself to deny his humble request. Perching herself on the edge of his mattress, she gently caressed his bruised knuckles.

"What am I going to with you?" Salome's questioned seemed to catch him off guard.

"What do you mean?"

Her eyes latched onto his and there was no hiding her fear. "Jinn, promise me you won't risk your life for me again."

"You should already know I won't agree to that."

"I would never be able to forgive myself if you died protecting me," she interrupted him. "Promise me, please, promise me, you won't jeopardize your life for me again. Do not value my life above your own."

Jinn winced as he sat up, ignoring Salome's protests for him to remain in a comfortable position, and cupped her face in his hands. When she met his gaze, tears she'd been holding back slipped down her smudged cheeks. He swiped his thumb over her lips and offered a weak smile.

"I told you before, darling, if it is within my power to give, I will give you whatever you want or need," he tilted her chin up, forcing her to look at him, "but you already know I will not promise to abandon you when you need me most." She opened her mouth to argue, but he pressed his lips to hers, silencing her. When he pulled back, he whispered, "Whether in life or death, we go together. That is my promise."

Salome bobbed her head, "In life or death, we go together." Resting her forehead against his, rubbing her forearm where the freshly tattooed band in Zophar's honor sat, she knew she'd be adding more bands before the end of the war, and the thought shattered her heart.

CHAPTER 45
CRISPIN

The second the rowboat hit the sandy shore, Crispin and the pirates hopped out and stormed the beach, slicing and stabbing all enemy soldiers in their path. The Bellators were making quick work of the stragglers around the keep and when Uri's pirates saw they were surrounded, they attempted to flee to their boats, but Ondrej and Rafi had already torched them. Even if they had been able to reach their boats, Nezreen and Uri retreated, leaving them to die or face execution.

Crispin had one goal in mind, get inside Oakenshire and make sure his sister had survived. He cut off arms and legs of enemy Pulauans, leaving them bleeding in his wake, knowing one of his companions would finish them off. It took so much longer than he'd hoped to reach the bailey, but once he was there, he was struck by the smell. Covering his nose with his sleeve, he glanced around at the dead bodies lying in puddles of blood. Some eyes of the fallen were still open, forever staring upwards in terror or pain. He scanned the bodies, sifting through some of them to see if his sister's body was among them, to see if he saw any of his friends blankly staring back at him. To his relief, he didn't see Salome or any of his close companions. What he did see were faces that had been smiling around the bailey during training, and citizens from each corner of Adalore that had celebrated Hanzo and Oifa's wedding a week ago.

Dragging a hand down his face, he turned toward the keep and made his way to the grand hall where he knew the wounded were being taken care of, and exhaled a sigh of relief when he still didn't see his sister. The longer it took to find her, the more hope he had that she'd survived and was helping others.

As soon as he stepped over the threshold into the make-shift infirmary, all eyes darted to stare at him. Men were groaning and screaming as Rayma's team helped stitch them up, or in some cases, amputate limbs that could not be saved. Blood was everywhere. Tears flowed and he could sense the shattered hearts of those grieving friends and loved ones.

"She's not here," a familiar voice stated, spurring him to turn around.

Rayma wiped her bloody hands on what used to be a white apron tied around her waist.

"What?"

"Your sister," she clarified. "She's not here. She and Adonijah helped an injured Prince Jinn to his room to rest."

"Prince Jinn was injured?" Crispin had been with him less than an hour ago and it was unsettling that in that short amount of time, the prince, who was tasked with ensuring Salome's safety, found himself in need of help.

"The prince will live. Adonijah stitched and bandaged him," Rayma tilted her head to the side, pressing her hands to her hips. She looked him up and down, examining him as if to see if the blood staining his armor and face belonged to him or not.

"I'm uninjured." Crispin wiped the splattered blood she was staring at off his cheek.

"I'm glad to hear it."

He never thought he'd hear concern or genuine joy for his well-being come from the Healer from Numbio. When they had first met all those months ago in the Southern Lands, she hated him and didn't attempt to hide it. But now, something was different. Something had changed between them.

"Don't look so surprised," she huffed, as if she could read his mind. "I might not be your best friend but I'm hardly a monster."

"I didn't think you were," he offered. "Do you need help?" He looked around the room, knowing he didn't possess skills Rayma could use, but he'd do whatever he needed to do to aid her and her team.

She slipped her hand around his bicep, dragging his gaze to meet her exhausted eyes. "You should rest, Prince Crispin. You will be needed tonight."

"Tonight?"

She nodded her head sadly. "For the funerals."

Crispin could have sworn someone had taken a knife and sliced his chest wide open. "How many?"

"So far, by my count, we lost around eighty men and women today."

His head was spinning, so he sat down on the nearest bench and scraped his fingers through his sweaty, tousled hair. His bottom lip quivered, but he looked up when Rayma knelt in front of him, her normally stone-cold eyes were filled with sorrow.

"We lost good men and women today, my lord." Tentatively, she reached for his hand and squeezed gently. "We won this battle, but we will need you to be strong, if we are to win this war."

"You sound awfully close to being kind to me," he offered her a tight-lipped smile, as a tear slipped down his cheek.

Rayma flicked the lone tear from his face and smiled in return. "You freed my brother from the dungeons in Northwind. You were willing to help Heru find a way to outwit the Grim. You killed Memucan, setting me free from my prison." She held his stare and her eyes softened. "You are a good man, Crispin of Northwind. I am sorry I did not see it before."

"I don't feel like a good man right now," he whispered.

"You hurt because you care." She stood from her crouched position when someone called her name. "There are many leaders who look at their soldiers as expendable, but not you. You grieve our losses and that is what sets you apart from the rulers that came before you."

"Rayma," he hopped to his feet when she turned to leave. "I know you only came on this journey because of Heru, but I want you to know, I'm grateful you're here."

"If I didn't know any better," she smirked, "I would think we're becoming friends."

With a nod of his head, Rayma walked off to help more wounded men and women and he set off to find a quiet place where he could be alone.

Crispin's first stop was the kitchens, not for food, but for a bottle of rum. Snatching one, he stomped out and made his way to the library where he knew he'd find some peace and quiet. He didn't want to be near anyone, fearing he would look weak and vulnerable. Plopping into a wooden chair, he uncorked the liquor bottle and took a shot, welcoming the burn.

The sun was beginning to set and gave the records room a heavenly glow. This is where he found peace amidst the chaos, surrounded by ancient tomes and scattered candles. It brought back memories of his mother and how he loved helping her in the library in Northwind. *Knowledge is power.* That had been branded into his brain since he was three. Now, as the future king, he was determined to surround himself with books and wise counselors, but no text or person could have prepared him for the heaviness war brings. The death, the destruction, the loss; he wasn't sure he could manage it.

"Oden's death isn't your fault, Crispin."

He should have known Rahab would find him sooner or later. Not bothering to look up, he took another sip of rum and offered it to her, but she didn't take it.

"If it isn't my fault, then whose fault is it?" he asked, his voice hoarse.

Rahab leaned her hip against the table, crossing her arms over her chest. "He used his magic and Nezreen's shadows tracked him -"

"He used his magic to save us when I shoved us out of a window," he hissed, raking a hand through his sweaty hair.

"He could have let us die. He didn't -"

"It wouldn't be in his nature to shield himself and watch us die." Crispin reluctantly met her gaze knowing at some point he was going to have to face her. "I know you're trying to help, but his blood is on my hands. I failed to save him in the end."

She frowned and shook her head. "You dishonor his sacrifice by claiming responsibility for Oden's decisions. He knew the risks – he risked it anyway. He knew what his magic was capable of – he used it anyway."

Crispin didn't want to be on the receiving end of yet another lecture and hopped up from his seat and started to stomp away, but Rahab wouldn't be dismissed so easily. She followed him and grabbed his forearm, whipping him to face her. His nostrils flared, but she didn't relent.

"Rahab, don't -"

"He gave his life to save hundreds of lives today," her voice had a bite to it, which didn't surprise him. "He died a hero, not a victim. Do not disrespect him by feeling sorry for yourself. Mourn the dead. Thank them for their sacrifice. Live to fight another day."

A tear slipped down his cheek and he rubbed the heels of his palms against his eyes. Groaning, he pressed his back against one of the wooden bookcases and gently banged the back of his head a couple times.

"These people, men and women alike, are here to follow your lead." Rahab slipped her hand against his cheek and forced him to meet her gaze. "They will look to you for strength. Be their fortress, Crispin."

"Has anyone ever told you that your bluntness is irritating?"

"All the time," she smiled. Reaching for the bottle of rum on the table behind her, she took a swig and offered it to him. "Hail to the dead."

Crispin gulped another shot and nodded his head in agreement. "Hail to the dead."

HOURS LATER, when the sun had set, and the wounded had been tended to, Crispin joined the others as they sifted through the bodies strewn from the beach to the bailey of the keep, searching and sorting through the bodies of the fallen, friend and foe. The enemy soldiers were piled and set to the flame, but when it came to their fallen companions, each leader oversaw their traditional burial rituals.

King Kenji murmured the ancient prayers of the Easterners as the bodies of his fallen warriors were burned on separate pyres. In accordance with their people, the ashes of the lost would be placed in decorative urns and sent back to their families to be placed in the crypts of their ancestors.

Hanzo and Oifa sent their dead wrapped in linens in a cart back to the Bone Mountains where their bodies would be buried in caves. They believed for a tribesman to go to the After, they would need to be close to the heavens, and there was no higher burial ground than the mountains.

Heru joined the surviving Numbio to bury their dead in the ground. They were formed from the earth and to the earth they would return.

The Bellators did not have traditions to follow since they were not accustomed to death in Caelestis. An Immortal, Ethereal and Bellator alike, would choose when they were ready to cross into the After and pass on to the next life. So, when Kayven and Abba had to make a decision on how to deal with the three men they lost, they opted to adopt the water burial the Myridians and Westerners cherished.

The Myridians lost two warriors, including Seraphina's twin sister, Rosalina. Salome helped wrap her friend's body and set her in a rowboat dressed in her armor, helmet, and armed with her Qata Vishna blades laid across her chest. Seraphina placed two gold coins on top of her sister's eyes before she and Salome set the boats carrying the Myridian warriors adrift.

In Northwind, the departed were buried in the mountain crypts with their ancestors. But they weren't in Northwind, nor did Crispin have Oden's body to wrap and bury, so he whispered prayers his mother had taught him, helping to usher his soul from his watery grave to the After.

Master Penn and her Keepers managed not to lose one of their own during the battle, but that didn't stop the blind warriors from offering their hands to help prepare the dead.

Once each leader had assisted their departed to the After, Crispin stood before those who remained and lifted his glass of wine. "We thank the dead for their sacrifice."

Everyone in the bailey lifted their drinks, then drank in memory of the victorious dead. Crispin knew some of the men and women gathered together wouldn't survive the war, and that thought weighed heavily on him.

CHAPTER 46
SALOME

Several days had passed since the Battle of Oakenshire, but Seraphina still wasn't interested in leaving her chambers for training. Losing her twin was more than she could handle and even though she lashed out and pushed Salome and Kai away, they made sure she received food three times a day and forced her to bathe, even going so far as trying to braid the Qata Vishna's hair, but it just made them think of Rosalina and her impressive skills with hair and make-up.

The Qata Vishna allowed Cato to stay every night with her since the battle, so Salome's mind was put to rest knowing Seraphina was in good, caring hands with the Stormcrag. But that didn't relieve Salome of the grief and angst pent up inside her, so she dragged Kai down to the bailey to spar.

This time, Kai didn't go easy on her and gave her quite the challenge. Spinning, flipping, kicking, they began to gather a crowd who watched them spar to perfection. They'd fought one another countless times over the last several weeks and had learned one another's moves, so their sparring sessions lasted much longer than the ordinary pairing. But after going back and forth, sweat glistening across their foreheads despite the low temperatures, Salome faked Kai out and took the opportunity to land a blow to the Ryoko Naga's chest.

Salome walked over to the fallen Kai and extended her hand to pull her up. Kai flashed a rare smile and accepted the help.

"Not bad, my lady," Kai bowed her head.

"I dare say, you're a tougher opponent than Kayven," Salome chuckled.

As if mentioning the Bellator's name conjured him, the brothers sifted through the dispersing crowd and Kayven tsked.

"I dare say, I have been too easy on you, Princess," the Bellator's grin was unsettling. "What do you think, Abba? Should I show my true strength?"

Abba shrugged, "If the Princess is looking for a more challenging sparring partner, I volunteer."

Salome rolled her eyes. "Leave it to you two to get your feathers all ruffled."

"We are not birds," Kayven scoffed. "Our wings do not ruffle."

A soft voice cleared behind them and everyone turned to see Leoti standing in the bailey, her hand crossed over her chest gripping her other arm. "I was wondering… I was wondering, if I could join you?"

Salome's face softened at the sight of the Andrago who had captured Adonijah's heart and motioned her forward. "You're Leoti, right? The warg?"

Her eyes brightened and she nodded. "Yes, Your Highness."

"Call me Salome."

Leoti's doe-eyes scanned all the weapons the four of them had strapped to them and said, "I'm afraid I do not know much about weaponry and feel ill-prepared for the battle that lies ahead."

"From what I've heard about you, you are quite powerful without swords and daggers." Salome sheathed her Qata Vishna blades in the holsters on her back. "I heard you killed Prince Thanos of Gomorrah, along with his guards." The Andrago's gaze fell to the stone pavers and Salome feared she'd said something wrong. "I didn't mean to offend you, Leoti."

"Oh, no," Leoti flicked her eyes up from the ground and shook her head. "You didn't. It's just…"

Salome stepped toward her and smiled, "You may speak freely."

"I want to learn how to fight," she confessed. "I want to learn how to fight with weapons like the rest of you."

"I'm sure Kai or the Bellator commanders would -"

"I would prefer if you taught me," Leoti interrupted her which surprised Salome.

"Why me?"

"You've heard tales about me," the Andrago fiddled with the braid that hung over her shoulder and down her chest, "but I have also heard tales about you. Adonijah told me all about your time together."

In an instant, Salome stiffened as her mind flashed back to battling the Thrak on multiple occasions with Adonijah, defeating the Cornigera, and Adonijah volunteering as her champion to fight Gerd in the City of Bones. She couldn't help remembering their intimate moments as well, how his lips felt pressed against hers and how he used to look at her.

Leoti smiled, "I know he loved you."

Salome could sense Kai and the Bellator brothers backing up to give them space, but she wished they would interrupt this ambush, and sweep her away from the awkward conversation she knew she was about to have.

"I was married before I met Adonijah, but he… died." Leoti pressed on, unfazed by Salome's discomfort.

"I'm sorry for your loss," she offered.

"I've mourned Rollo and I know a piece of my heart will always love him, but that doesn't mean I cannot find love again."

"What are you trying to say?" Salome rubbed her hand along the back of her neck, shifting her weight.

"You and Adonijah cared for one another, there's history between you two, but I want you to know that I am not intimidated by that." Leoti smiled and reached for Salome's hand. "I know a part of him will always care for you, but if you would be open to it, I think we could be good friends."

The Andrago maiden surprised Salome yet again. She'd assumed she was going to stake her claim on the sell-sword or tell Salome to keep her distance from Adonijah, but instead she acknowledged their past and didn't allow it to hinder building a friendship with her. Salome immediately felt shame creep into her cheeks as she had jumped conclusions.

"I'd like that," Salome bobbed her head and smiled. "Adonijah is happy with you. It is obvious his heart is yours."

"And my heart belongs to him." Leoti pointed at the wolf dagger strapped to Salome's thigh. "So, will you teach me how to fight?"

Salome unsheathed it and handed it to her. "It would be an honor."

AFTER SPENDING a couple of hours teaching Leoti basic self-defense moves and how to protect herself should she be attacked, Salome made her way to her room so she could soak in a warm bath, but when she turned the corner of the hall leading to her chambers, she saw Adonijah leaning against the wall waiting for her.

"Looking for someone?" Her question spurred him to straighten from his reclined position.

"I saw you and Leoti sparring in the bailey."

She couldn't tell if he was pleased or irritated, so she marched up to him and squared her shoulders to his. "And?"

"Thank you."

"For what?" She cocked her head to the side.

"Being kind to her." His eyes met hers. "I didn't know how you would react to me and her..."

Salome slipped her hand over his forearm and squeezed. "Adonijah, I'm happy for you. She is wonderful and she suits you."

He exhaled, and the tension in his shoulders vanished. "Well, I'll take my leave then."

She nodded as he started walking down the corridor she'd just come from. "Adonijah." He turned to face her. "I'm glad you've found happiness. You deserve it."

With a smile, he bowed his head, and turned the corner, disappearing from view. And she found she meant it. She wanted him to be just as happy with Leoti, as she was with Jinn.

Slipping into her chambers, she stripped her sweaty clothes and fighting leathers off and walked into her bathroom where a hot bath was already awaiting her. She dipped her fingers in the water and sighed at the warmth. She took a breath before plunging her body into the steaming water. After the initial sting of the heat kissing her flesh, she adjusted to the temperature and leaned her head against the porcelain lip.

Her mind was restless, and even though she knew she shouldn't reach out to Niabi, especially after she'd sent the Puluans to attack them, she couldn't resist the temptation. She closed her eyes and mentally ventured to the door that belonged to her sister and instead of gently pushing the connection open, she kicked it in, like she was stampeding through a door.

"For someone who desires peace as much as you do," Salome barged into her sister's

mind, vengeance and wrath fueling her, *"you certainly don't know how to pursue it."*

"What are you talking about?" Niabi's voice swam in her head, grating her already frayed nerves.

"The fleet of Pulaun ships you sent to attack us in Oakenshire," Salome gritted out. *"You speak of wanting peace for you and your unborn child, yet you send the Pirate King and his Shadow Witch after us, instead of coming yourself. You're not only a monster, but a coward as well."*

"Salome -"

"I lost someone very dear to me," Salome interrupted her sister. *"You say your quarrel was never with me or our brother, but this seems awfully personal and yellow-bellied, even for you. I thought you were a warrior queen, but I suppose those are exaggerated stories since you prefer hiring pirates to do your dirty work."*

"I have no idea what you're talking about!" Niabi's voice rumbled in her head. She could sense her sister's anger and confusion and it made her stop to think. How could she be so surprised by the attack she sanctioned? *"I never sent a fleet of Pulaun ships to Oakenshire. Up until this moment, I had no idea where you were hiding."*

Salome was now the one left confused. *"You didn't send them?"*

"No, I didn't send them." Niabi didn't hesitate and by her tone, Salome believed her. And then realized she'd just given away their position.

"If you didn't," Salome asked, *"then who did?"*

"That is a very good question," Niabi's words were laced with worry.

"What will you do?" Salome didn't want to have to admit her blunder to Crispin, but if Niabi now knew where they were, they'd have to either move quickly to prepare for war with the North or be prepared for another strike.

"If you are concerned I am going to send my soldiers to attack you in Oakenshire, you can put that thought to rest," Niabi said with a calculating tone. *"If someone ordered the Pulauans to Oakenshire, then they are within my court and will be dealt with swiftly."*

"You expect me to believe you won't attack us, now that you know where we are?"

"Only a fool would move troops in the winter months," Niabi scoffed, as if Salome was an idiot for suggesting such a thing. *"By the time they made their way to you, they'd be frost-bitten and fatigued. You might not believe me, sister, but I truly do not wish for a war. I've had enough bloodshed to last me a thousand lifetimes and I am weary."*

"Why are you telling me this?"

"Because, I meant what I told you before. All I want is to raise my child in peace."

"You will never have peace if you remain on the White Throne," Salome countered. *"Crispin will have it, whether he has to kill you to get it or not."*

Niabi chuckled sadly and it tugged at Salome's heart. *"It would seem war is in our blood. None of us ever stood a chance."*

Salome wanted to ask her more, but she felt Niabi tearing away from the connection. She'd not had anyone do that to her before. She'd always been the one to end the connection, but Niabi was putting up a tremendous fight to escape.

"As fun as this chat has been," Niabi purred, *"there are matters that require my attention. Goodbye, Salome."*

Before Salome could protest, she felt as if two hands shoved her out of Niabi's mind and when she opened her eyes, she found she wasn't alone in her bathroom.

"What are you doing in here?" Salome slipped lower beneath the water, attempting to hide her naked form, and scowled at Kai standing in the doorway.

"I knocked several times, and you didn't answer," Kai stated, as if she didn't notice Salome sitting in the bath.

"As you can see," Salome made a sweeping motion around the room, "I am occupied. What couldn't wait?"

"Harbona has requested you and Prince Crispin meet with him." Kai offered her a towel and Salome reluctantly grabbed it, motioning for the Easterner to leave.

"I know Jinn wants you to watch me, but you can at least let me get dressed in private."

Kai smirked. "Nothing I haven't seen before, my lady."

"Kai," Salome warned and the Ryoko Naga put her hands up in surrender.

"I will be in the hall to escort you when you are ready."

"Kai," Salome called out, halting her from leaving. "When Jinn and I are married, who will you be sworn to obey?"

The Ryoko Naga shrugged a shoulder. "I will serve you both. But if you wish to be technical, I am sworn to protect Prince Jinn. When you become his wife, you will be assigned a protector of your own."

Salome smiled. "Thank you for protecting him, Kai."

"It is my honor to protect and serve you both," Kai bowed her head slightly before walking out of the room.

Once Salome heard the door click, she hopped out of the tub, dried herself, and dressed quickly. The last thing she wanted was to keep Harbona waiting longer than he deemed necessary. A grumpy Harbona was not her favorite person to deal with. But once she readied herself and joined Crispin in Harbona's quarters, she was surprised to find the Seer sitting with a woman who looked a lot like Odelia. Her stunning grey eyes didn't go unnoticed, and Salome knew only Ethereals had such eyes.

Harbona must have sensed her question because he quickly introduced them to his daughter, Makeda, and Salome chuckled when Crispin's mouth fell open. After arriving with the Immortals who aided them in defeating the Pulauans, Makeda was preparing to journey south to the Enchanted Swamp to look after Odelia, as she recovered from her stint away from her home. She'd overexerted herself by destroying Gomorrah with her magic.

Over dinner, Makeda explained how she was a member of Oden's team and was saddened to learn of his death. She offered her magical services during the upcoming battle with Northwind, but Harbona insisted she be with Odelia and reconnect with her. If another attempt on the Enchantress' life was made, he felt better with his water wielding daughter being by her side. Salome knew Harbona was trying to fit into his new fatherly role and keep his daughter safe. She didn't blame him. She would have done the exact same thing.

It was odd to see Harbona so at ease, when Salome knew him for being serious and overprotective. It filled her heart with joy seeing him interact with his daughter. She hoped after the war was won, that Harbona would finally take time to make himself happy, instead of putting the whims and wills of kings and queens before his own family, now that he had one.

After they'd eaten dinner with Harbona and wished Makeda a fair journey, Crispin and Salome made their way to their own rooms and settled in for the evening. Her body ached, her mind was exhausted, and her spirit was empty. As soon as her head hit her pillow, she closed her eyes, and dreamt of nothing, which suited her just fine.

CHAPTER 47

NIABI

Niabi didn't care the members of her small council had turned in for the evening. She wanted to know who attacked Oakenshire, and she would get those answers one way or another. Comfortably seated around the wooden table in her study, the queen carefully eyed Tala and Vilora. Anaktu stood in front of the doors ensuring no one could come in or out.

Vilora picked food from between her snaggleteeth with her pinky fingernail, not bothered by Tala's disgusted glare "My Queen, will you tell us what this is all about or will you continue to give us the evil eye until we guess what you're thinking?"

Niabi's penetrating gaze shifted to her aunt, not sure if the witch had just rolled out of bed or if the disheveled look was a personal choice, she crinkled her nose and began the meeting. "A fleet of ships attacked my siblings in Oakenshire. I want to know who ordered the assault."

Neither Tala nor Vilora said a word. Niabi watched them intently, waiting to see who would speak first.

"How do you know Oakenshire was attacked?" The Andrago finally spoke, clearly confused.

"I have my sources." Niabi didn't want to reveal Salome's magical connection with her, especially not with Vilora in the room. She'd give her life for Tala, but the witch couldn't be trusted. "Someone has betrayed me, and I want to know who."

Vilora met Niabi's accusatory gaze and whispered, "No child of your womb will sit on the White Throne of Northwind, until all other usurpers have been vanquished. But I warn you, you will pay a heavy price for victory and an even heavier price for failure."

"What?" Niabi cocked her head to the side. That was the prophecy the old witch foretold almost twenty years ago.

The hag smirked, no longer lounging lazily in her chair. She squared her shoulders to the queen. "You think yourself so wise, Niabi, but you are a fool."

Tala hissed, "Watch your tongue, witch, before I claim it."

Vilora pointed at Niabi's swollen belly, "You think *that* child will sit on the throne -?"

"My siblings shall be dealt with- "

"Whether your siblings were killed the night you took Northwind or not, your heirs will never claim the White Throne," Vilora interrupted.

"What are you saying?" Niabi leaned forward, cradling her belly.

Vilora chuckled, batting scraggly hair from her weathered face. "I thought you would have figured it out by now. For your children to live, *you* must die."

Realization that she had usurped the throne from her father slapped her across the face. The old witch had tricked her with her riddles and craftily phrased prophecy, but the truth was, she had doomed Rollo the second she killed her father. "You deceived me!"

"I am the Old Witch of Endor," Vilora threw her hands up and cackled, thoroughly enjoying her moment. "Did you really think I cared what happened to you when we first met? You wanted so desperately to believe you could right the wrongs inflicted by your father that you condemned yourself."

"It's you," Niabi slowly stood from her seat, narrowing her eyes at her betrayer. "You're the one who sent the ships."

Tala hopped to his feet, unsheathing his sword and pointing it at the witch.

Vilora sighed, waving a lazy hand in the air. "I told you not to underestimate him, deary."

"Gershom," Niabi growled. "You are working for him."

"With," she corrected with a wicked grin. "I am working *with* the king."

"You mean the queen's prisoner," Tala scoffed, his brow furrowed.

"You've never been safe, Niabi," the witch rose to her feet, unfazed by Tala's weapon aimed at her chest. "And now, everything you have will be taken from you," she said so softly that it sent an unwelcome shiver down Niabi's spine.

"Or I can have you executed and put an end to your treasonous schemes." Niabi held her head high, but Vilora's hoarse laugh diffused her short-lived victory.

"It is already too late," the witch said. "Your Shadows have been poisoned against you and now serve Ophir. Your precious commander chose his brother over you and isn't here to help you." Vilora tilted her head to the side, giving the appearance of a feral animal. "You are alone."

Niabi snarled and was flirting with her knives sheathed in her sleeves, when Thrice burst into the room. Anaktu grabbed the unmasked Shadow by his throat and slammed him against the wall. Thrice reached out to Niabi, gurgling his words.

"Release him," Niabi commanded, and the Nephilim immediately dropped him. "What is it, Thrice?"

"The Shadows," Thrice's voice was raspy, but he pushed through with his message. "They have sworn loyalty to Ophir. They've freed Gershom from his prison and Ophir is on his way here to kill you. We need to get you out of the city."

Without hesitation, Vilora and Niabi launched fireballs at each other. Tala and Thrice were armed with their blades, but with fire being shot across the study, all they could do was to jump out of the way, before being struck. Niabi unsheathed her daggers, her left arm still ablaze, and kicked her desk at Vilora. Though she was a witch with fire magic, Vilora was old, and her reflexes slow, so she couldn't move fast enough to avoid the blow of the heavy, wooden desk, and Niabi took advantage of the opportunity and ran out with Tala, Thrice, and Anaktu.

"We won't be able to get you out through the main gate," Thrice stalked down the corridor, keeping his eyes peeled for any Shadows headed their way.

"I know a way out." Niabi grabbed Thrice's arm and pulled him down a different hallway. "We'll have to be quick about it."

The four of them sprinted down the hall, remaining vigilant to a potential attack, but if there was a coup being staged, it was a quiet one. She didn't hear any screams coming from the castle staff, didn't detect the sounds of metal against metal indicating soldiers fighting other soldiers. It was deathly silent and that is what made her worry. How had she been so blind to Gershom's schemes? She was so focused and angry about him garnering foreign allies and support, for his quest for her throne, she was oblivious that he had used her own men against her.

She would make Gershom and Vilora pay if it was the last thing she did, but first, she needed to survive to fight another day.

Once they zig-zagged through the castle, they came upon a door that led through the staff's quarters. At the very end of the wing, there was a humble, wooden door that allowed passage into the city streets. Thrice had given her his black cloak to not only protect her from the chill of winter, but to help disguise her from citizens. They already had a Nephilim with them, the last thing they needed was for people to start bowing and drawing attention to them.

Niabi knew there were tunnels that led to the castle, but she was nervous about spending more time inside the keep with cold-hearted assassins on her tail. So she immediately thought of the safe house at the southeast end of the city wall. An entrance to the tunnels could be accessed beneath the house floorboards and it would lead them to safety. They just had to make it there before her enemies spotted them.

Thankfully, darkness shrouded them and the only people still out and about at that hour, were the revelers in the Night District. She would have preferred sneaking aboard an outbound ship and hatching her plan for revenge as they sailed away, but ships did not leave the harbor at night. The sailors were far too drunk or up to their necks in women to sail to the next kingdom. Instead, they'd have to make their way through the Black Forest, which didn't bother her, because she knew it like the back of her hand, but Gershom and Vilora also knew it well, and if they came looking for them there, they'd be sure to find them.

Niabi clutched her belly, and as they were scrambling toward the southeast side of the kingdom, a terracotta shingle fell from one of the rooftops and smashed on the stone road in front of them. Glancing up, she sensed them before she saw them. The Shadows, the mercenaries she'd founded and trained with for nearly two decades, had tracked them down. Slipping down from the roofs, the Shadows surrounded the four of them, successfully cutting them off from the house that was just down the street.

"Would you turn against your queen? You swore an oath to me. You bear my sigil on your arms." Niabi looked at each masked warrior one-by-one. "Would you truly commit treason knowing the penalty?"

She knew there was no use talking them down once they'd been given the order to assassinate her, but she turned in a circle appearing to plead her case only to get an accurate count of how many they were up against. By her quick count, there were fifteen of them. Fifteen to four. Not great odds, but she had faced worse. Slowly, she unsheathed her knives underneath the large cloak Thrice had given her, ready to strike the moment one stepped too close. She'd trained with these men, bled with them, and now, she would kill them without remorse. That was the way of the Shadows.

Niabi heard someone clapping and when she whipped around, she saw Vilora and Ophir appear from the darkened street. Vilora stopped clapping once she met Niabi's gaze and flashed a malicious grin. "Leaving so soon, Niabi?"

"Enough talk." Niabi slipped her hands through the cloak, revealing her knives and left arm ablaze. She whipped a blast of fire at the unsuspecting Vilora and it smashed into her chest, launching her into the air.

That was signal enough for Tala, Thrice, and Anaktu to wage war against the Shadows that surrounded them. Being severely pregnant didn't hinder Niabi from sparring with her friends-turned-enemies and she cut them down with righteous indignation. She managed to dodge a fireball. Vilora was back on her feet and the witch looked like a hornet that had been swatted one too many times. She was angry, and just like Niabi, she was out for blood. Back and forth the fire wielders went, landing blows and singeing hair and clothing. With sheer determination to see the witch burn to ash, Niabi fought on, knowing her three companions would have her back.

A chorus of footsteps stomped down the street and when Niabi looked beyond Vilora, she saw a group of about fifty armored soldiers marching toward them. They weren't going to make it out alive if those soldiers reached them, so she opted for a reckless option. She stopped firing at Vilora and aimed at the buildings surrounding them. The thought of burning a citizen's business or home made her sick, but if she was going to have her revenge, she was going to have to escape. Beams from the burning buildings fell between her and the army, but the Shadows were already scrabbling up to nearby roofs to cut them off from behind.

They had to run. She motioned for the others to follow her; they could make, it if they hurried. But someone grabbed her forearm, forcing her to stop. She looked up into Anaktu's masked face.

"Anaktu," she hissed.

The Nephilim raised his scarred hand to his mask and pulled it off his face. It had been nearly two decades since she had seen him without it and although he had aged, he hadn't changed.

"Anaktu," she whispered gently, tugging him forward. "We need to go."

Without his tongue, he couldn't speak, but he signed to her and her eyes widened.

"No," she choked up. "I will not allow it. I order you to -"

He signed with more fervor than she'd ever seen from him before. With a giant finger, he pointed for her to run, and she once again shook her head in protest, but she couldn't hold back her tears.

"I said, no!" She pulled him, but he didn't budge. "I will not leave you here. I will not -"

Anaktu wrapped his enormous arms around her and held her tightly. A whimper escaped her lips and when he pulled back, he offered a rare smile. Tala grabbed her arm and tugged her down the street.

"Niabi, we need to move, now! They're going to catch us."

"Anaktu!" She tried to fight Tala, but Thrice grabbed her other arm and together the men dragged her down the dimly lit street. "Anaktu!"

Anaktu had been captured by Andrago scouts and brought before Dichali and Niabi. The Nephilim, the last of his kind, was forced to his knees before the royals and his eyes shifted around the room in terror. It was obvious he had been mistreated while in Chua's care.

Anger flared in Niabi and she clutched the wooden armrests of her throne to keep from attacking Dichali's friend for his barbaric treatment of the creature.

"A gift for Your Majesty," Chua beamed, raising his arms in victory. "The Last Nephilim."

"What is your name?" Dichali's soft voice silenced everyone in the gathering tent, but when the Nephilim didn't answer, Chua chuckled and said, "It would be hard for him to answer without his tongue."

Niabi couldn't help herself; she shot up from her chair and hissed, "You cut out his tongue?"

"What if he mumbled curses against us?" the Andrago warrior narrowed his eyes at her. "We couldn't take that chance."

"And the slashes and bruises all over his body?" she pointed out, stepping down from her dais to approach them.

Chua shrugged lazily, "The monster is clumsy."

"As far as I can tell, you're the only monster that stands before me," Niabi spat. Before Chua had a chance to defend himself, she turned to face her husband and said, "My love, give this Nephilim to me. Spare his life and I promise he will be a loyal member of our court."

Chua balked, "You cannot be serious!"

Niabi whipped a dagger out from her sleeve and held it against Chua's neck when he got too close to her. "Friend of the king or not, you will remember your place, or your queen will remind you."

"Enough," Dichali waved his hand and Niabi lowered her weapon but her gaze on Chua didn't waver. "The Nephilim is yours, my love. But if he does not abide by our laws, then he will be executed." Niabi bowed her head in understanding. The king's glare was now directed at his best friend. "We do not maim and torture prisoners, Chua. Next time, there will be swift punishment for the offense. Am I clear?"

Chua nodded, though his eyes burned. "My King."

Dichali motioned for everyone to leave and once they had, Niabi knelt before the Nephilim and slowly stretched her hand to his face. When he flinched, it broke her heart. She whispered, "You need not fear me. I will protect you."

"Niabi!" Tala's voice jostled her from her memories of Anaktu. "Tell us where to go!"

The Last Nephilim's eyes were filled with nothing but love as he slipped his mask back onto his face and drew his sword, nodding a silent goodbye. He turned to face the enemy soldiers dousing the fire she'd started and waited for them to attack.

She had sworn to protect him, to save him, but he was the one who had always protected her and now he was laying his life down to save hers. She couldn't allow him to do it. She broke free from Tala and Thrice's hold and darted toward him, but Tala wrapped his arms around her, halting her.

"Anaktu!" she cried, but the Nephilim stalked away, deeper into the flames to face the soldiers who had once called her master.

"He's gone, my Queen," Tala pressed his cheek against hers, her back flush with his chest. "Tell us where the tunnel is so we can get you out. Do not let his sacrifice be in vain."

Reluctantly, she pointed to the small house and once they opened the secret door underneath the rug, they descended into the tunnel. She swore she heard one final roar echo from Anaktu, but then it was snuffed out and she knew he was truly gone. Her friend and protector was dead. She swore on every dead soul she'd lost that she would make sure all those responsible would beg for Death before she exacted her revenge.

~

NIABI, Tala, and Thrice ran through the Black Forest as quickly as their tired legs could carry them. They escaped Northwind but hadn't had the time to grab supplies or horses. But with their skills as Shadows, they had the skills to survive the bitter winter.

The guilt of leaving Anaktu behind weighed heavily on Niabi. Other than Tala, he'd been her constant companion and silent comfort for two decades. She'd sworn to protect him and she failed. She could still hear him roaring as he darted to his certain death to give her time to get away. She would never be able to say goodbye, she would never be able to thank him for his love, friendship, and ultimate sacrifice. Everyone saw him as a monster, a beast, an unfeeling creature, but Anaktu was gentle, caring, loving, and deserving of happiness.

Tears slipped down her rosy cheeks as they trudged through the snow with only the moon illuminating their path.

Suddenly a sharp pain ricocheted through her abdomen and stole her breath. She slammed her hand against the trunk of one of the many pine trees and waited for the pain to pass. She knew what was happening, she'd been having the contractions for the last couple of hours, but now, it was becoming unbearable.

As Tala brushed by her, she grabbed his arm and through gritted teeth said, "The baby is coming."

"Right now?" Thrice whipped around from leading the pack and caught Niabi's feral gaze.

"As inconvenient as it might be, Thrice, yes," she hissed, riding out another wave of labor pain.

Tala didn't question her but got straight to work. They were in the middle of the forest and not within walking distance of any house or village. Niabi knew the Black Forest well and knew her baby was going to be born outside on a bitter winter's night.

The Andrago helped her lay down in a comfortable position and draped his cloak over her. "I know you will shoot daggers at me when I say this, but you will need to bite down on my leather belt when you're in pain." Tala took off his belt and gave it to her. "If they hear you scream, they'll find us and Thrice and I won't be able to defend you."

Niabi knew he was right, but she wasn't sure she'd be able to do what he was asking. As wonderful as her pregnancy with Rollo had been, she remembered how excruciating birthing him was and a spark of fear flickered in her heart. Either way, she would have to do as Tala asked. Bobbing her head in agreement, she took the leather belt he offered and bit down on it hard.

Tala glanced at Thrice who looked as if he was going to be sick and ordered him to, "Keep watch and keep out of sight." Thrice nodded, not needing to be told twice, and disappeared into the dark, cold woods.

"I don't think I can do this, Tala," Niabi mumbled, biting the belt as another contraction hit her. Sweat beaded around her brow and she mentally willed herself to be quiet.

He clasped her hand and she squeezed tightly. Once the pain subsided, she opened her eyes and stared at him. "You can do this, Niabi," he said gently before adding, "and you will. Keep your eyes on me and I'll get you through this."

Niabi bobbed her head. Even though they escaped the city, her enemies would never stop hunting for her, especially knowing she'd give birth to an heir that would pose a threat to their reign.

She had two options once her baby was born. Disappear and let her enemies have her kingdom, but live in fear that history would repeat itself, and one day they'd find her and kill everyone she loved, or she could face them and protect not only her newborn, but the Andrago too. Whether she sought sanctuary from the Andrago or not, Gershom and Vilora would assume she'd be hiding there and would attack Elisor. They would kill every citizen and burn every house to the ground to find her. She wouldn't have innocent blood on her hands.

"Push," Tala whispered and her focus returned to him. "You're almost there, Niabi. You can do this."

Niabi took a deep breath of chilly air and pushed with all the strength she had left. Her head fell back in exhaustion and when she thought she wouldn't be able to push again, she heard a small, angry cry sound in the darkness.

Her eyes snapped toward Tala who held a tiny newborn wrapped in the cloak that had been draped over her. Tears filled her eyes knowing she did the impossible and after nine long months, she was finally able to meet her child.

Tala smiled as he handed her the bundle. "It's a boy."

Niabi stroked her son's rosy cheek and wiped her own tears away. "Hello, Ivaylo."

Footsteps approached and Tala jumped up, drawing his sword, but relaxed when he saw Thrice returning.

"Soldiers?" Tala asked.

"We're clear for now," Thrice reported. "I set some traps. That'll buy us some time just in case they catch up." The Shadow glanced at his queen. "We will need to move at first light. You just need to tell me which way to head."

Niabi glanced down at her son nuzzling against her chest and the choice was clear. She couldn't disappear. She would have to face her enemies, but she wouldn't do it alone. She would go to the only place Gershom and Vilora wouldn't think to look for her.

"Oakenshire," she said, and although Tala and Thrice exchanged a confused look, they didn't question her. "We are going to make a deal with my siblings."

CHAPTER 48
CRISPIN

It'd been a couple of weeks since the Battle of Oakenshire and reinforcements and supplies were slowly trickling in. Crispin had managed to get some rest, although nightmares of the battle plagued him. He kept seeing Oden's drowned body. He was dealing with his trauma on his own, but when he heard the clashing of metal against metal coming from the bailey, he panicked, thinking they were under attack. He bolted to his window and looked outside not only to find they weren't under attack, but that his sister was once again up late sparring with the Bellator commanders.

Quick to put his fighting leathers and boots on, he made his way to the sparring grounds and hid in the shadows to watch up close how his sister and the Bellators fought. He only caught the last few movements between Salome and Kayven and was impressed with how Salome slid on her knees, bent backwards, to avoid Kayven's incoming blow. The Bellator seemed surprised by the extra effort to elude him and barked out a hearty laugh.

"Well done, Princess." Kayven nodded his head in approval as he sheathed his weapon. "You'd make a fine Bellator."

Salome bowed, a wide grin across her face. "If only I had wings, I might actually beat you," she teased.

Abba scoffed as he stepped out of the shadows. "You are far too generous, my lady. You do not need wings to beat him, just a mirror. Kayven cannot resist the opportunity to admire himself."

Salome's laugh filled the bailey and drew a smile from Crispin. He hadn't heard her laugh like that in weeks. He had only come to watch, but seeing how much fun they were having made him want to join, so he stepped out of his hiding spot, surprising them.

Salome looked him up and down and grinned. "How long have you been there?"

Crispin shrugged a shoulder. "Long enough to see you've picked up a few new moves."

Salome waved him forward, wiping sweat from her brow. "Care to step in the ring?"

His eyes danced. The siblings hadn't sparred with one another in months, and after seeing her new tricks, he was itching to face off with her again. He shrugged off his jacket and unsheathed his longsword. As he took his stance, he could see she held herself differently – with more confidence. From swapping tales of their journeys, he knew she'd trained with the Qata Vishna, and she'd been training with the Bellator commanders for weeks, so this wasn't going to be the same Salome he sparred with in the Tree House Forest. But he had also picked up a few moves. Granted his were more in the stealth department, learning from both the pirates and the Keepers during their travels, but he was confident he could still hold his own against his sister.

As they stood on opposite sides of the sparring ring, staring at one another, it gutted Crispin to realize that he'd been waiting for Zophar to count them down. Something flashed across Salome's face that let him know she'd been thinking the same thing. If only Zophar could have lived to see this day – they were back together with new skills under their belts. He would have been so proud and excited to see his wards face off. He'd probably still be secretly rooting for Salome, like he always did.

"I miss him too," Salome acknowledged.

Crispin offered a tight-lipped smile. "Commander Kayven," he didn't take his eyes off his sister, "would you start us off?"

Kayven counted them down before releasing them.

Salome used to be more defensive in nature, but she initiated the duel by running toward him. He used his sword to block the blow of her Qata Vishna blades and shoved her back.

"You learned to be defensive," she smirked and nodded in approval.

"And you learned to attack first," he took his stance again. "Let's see what else you've learned."

Both siblings had not only grown stronger, but they were faster as well. Faster in their movements but quick in their reaction time. Granted, Salome was far more flexible and agile than him, but he adapted to her movements and had more force behind his blows.

Sweat dripped down his forehead as they sparred: blocking, dodging, tumbling, kicking, punching… it was chaotic, and Crispin loved every bit of it. He wondered how she managed to survive the Battle of Oakenshire when they were being overrun by the Pulauans, but seeing her in action made him realize she was no longer the girl he grew up with in the Tree House Forest. She was a force to be reckoned with and could shake the very foundation of their world, if she truly wanted to.

"I grow bored with this back-and-forth nonsense," Kayven bellowed, a playful grin plastered across his bronze face. "We need a victor!"

"My money is on my lady," Abba said, garnering a scoff from Kayven.

"Well, of course she will win," Kayven pounded a fist to his chest. "I trained her."

"You're not even going to give me a chance to prove you wrong?" Crispin barked out a laugh.

The Bellator brothers exchanged a look before shrugging their shoulders.

"It is not because we do not believe you are a skilled fighter, Prince Crispin," Kayven began, but Crispin waved his hand in the air, cutting him off. Salome's laugh was so infectious that it spurred Crispin to laugh with her.

"Don't listen to them, Crispin," she said between giggles. "You're just as skilled -"

"Don't you start with me," Crispin pointed his sword at her, failing to hide his grin. "Best two out of three?" He wiggled his eyebrows, remembering their sparring sessions in the Tree House Forest, always trying to best the other in battle. They'd grown so much, he almost wished they could go back and enjoy those precious moments they spent together, without the titles and responsibility currently weighing them down.

Salome took her stance once more, eyes filled with mischief. "Best two out of three it is."

As he took his position, heavy boots marched toward them. He turned to see an Eastern warrior bow and say, "Your Highness, someone has arrived at the gate and claims to know you."

Crispin and Salome exchange a puzzled look. Everyone they knew was already in Oakenshire. "Who is it?"

"We aren't sure, Your Majesty," the soldier shrugged his shoulders. "She wouldn't give a name. Just said she would speak with you and Princess Salome tonight on an urgent matter."

"Bring this mysterious guest to the throne room," Crispin instructed, sheathing his sword. "Make sure they come in under a heavily armed escort."

The soldier bowed and turned on his heel to deliver the message to the guards at the gate.

"Do you know who it might be?" Salome stalked toward him, sheathing her Qata Vishna blades in their holsters.

"No, but we're about to find out." Crispin glanced at the Bellator brothers. "Would you have Harbona, Prince Jinn, and Rahab join us?" Seeing the curious look on Salome's face, he explained, "I would imagine our betrothed would want to be included in this secret meeting, don't you?"

She nodded with a knowing smile. "Let's go meet this mysterious woman of yours."

Crispin rolled his eyes and sighed. "Now don't go saying things like that around Rahab. She won't take too kindly to that introduction."

Salome snaked her arm around his and pulled him toward the keep. "You'll need someone to keep you in line when I'm not around."

He stopped, forcing her to face him.

"Crispin?" she cocked her head to the side. "What's -"

"What do you mean by that? When you're not around?" His heart was thundering in his chest; the image of her perishing in battle flashed before him and he felt his throat constrict.

She grabbed his hand, drawing his gaze to meet hers. "When this war is over, I will marry Jinn and one day be his queen. Surely, you didn't believe I would marry the future King of Sakurai and remain in Northwind with you?"

In truth, Crispin hadn't thought about it. He was so focused on the battles that lied ahead of them, that he hadn't considered what life after a victory would look like. He'd be king, yes, but he always imagined Salome by his side, heading up his small council. He felt like stomping his feet like a petulant child and demand she stay in Northwind forever, but when he thought about how Jinn and Salome looked at one another and the love they held for each other, he knew he could never impose his selfish will upon her.

"I'll still be around," she whispered. "Just not as much as we both would like."

He hugged her, her wild curls brushing against his face. "You think Harbona would give you a hippogriff so you can fly to Northwind whenever you want?"

She chuckled and he could hear the slight tremor in her voice signaling she was holding back tears. "He won't have a choice. I'll steal Zandaar if I need to; he likes me more anyway."

Crispin pulled back from her and flashed the best smile he could muster. "Of that I have no doubt."

ONCE CRISPIN WAS SEATED in the wooden throne with Salome and Jinn on his right and Rahab and Harbona on his left, he motioned for the Bellator brothers guarding the doors to open them. Escorted inside by a heavily armed group of Bellator Elite, the woman shrouded in a black hood and cloak strutted forward. Her gait seemed familiar but without seeing her face, Crispin couldn't be sure who was walking toward him. Two men followed closely behind her; one bore the resemblance of the Andrago, and the other Crispin couldn't place. He knew for sure he'd never seen them before.

The mysterious woman stopped several feet before the slightly elevated dais but didn't bow or kneel before him.

"Who are you and why have you come before me at this late hour?" His stern voice would have unnerved most guests, but the figure before him did not flinch.

"I have come to make a deal."

Her voice was eerily familiar and by Salome's reaction, he was positive she knew who stood cloaked before them.

"That's impossible," Salome whispered.

Crispin refocused on the stranger, and thought he saw a smirk beneath the shadowed hood. "Who are you? Show yourself."

The woman slowly reached up and pulled the hood back, revealing her jet-black hair and piercing green eyes. "Hello, little brother."

"You!?" He jumped to his feet and pointed at her. "Bellators, arrest her!"

The Immortal warriors leapt into action, surrounding the trio with pointed weapons, but Niabi was unfazed, and did not bother raising her hands in surrender. She held fast to her position and stared at Crispin with the same smirk snaked across her face.

"Is this how you treat your potential allies, Crispin?" she tsked as her gaze slid to the Seer. "I assumed Harbona had taught you better than that."

Harbona didn't respond, instead turned his attention to a nearby Bellator to whisper his orders and shooed him away to do his bidding.

Crispin's nostrils flared as he gritted out, "You have three seconds to give me a good reason why I shouldn't have you executed on the spot."

"Gershom staged a coup," Niabi's voice was steady and calm, unlike his own, "and I escaped before I was assassinated."

"So, your first thought was to come here?" He scoffed, crossing his arms over his chest.

"Why are you here, Niabi?" Salome chimed in with a tone of intimacy that surprised Crispin. As far as he knew, his sisters had never met, but the way they looked at one another debated that fact.

Niabi met Salome's gaze and the hardness in her face softened. "I believe we can help one another."

"Have you come to surrender the White Throne?" Crispin tilted his head up and looked down his nose at her.

His sister's green eyes bounced back and forth between him and Salome. It unnerved him at how much she resembled their mother. "I am no longer in possession of it, therefore, I cannot surrender it to you."

"So," Crispin cleared his throat, "you lost our ancestral home and what? You came here to ask us to fight for you? To harbor you? Are you delusional?"

"You want the White Throne, you can have it," she hissed. "I never wanted it; I never wanted any of it."

"You truly expect me to believe that?" He shook his head.

"What do you want from us?" Salome asked. Crispin recognized her attempts to diffuse the tension and was grateful she was his right hand.

"Let's join forces to reclaim Northwind," Niabi stared at Crispin.

"Why would we agree to that?" Crispin frowned. "Take it back yourself, *sister*."

"I swore a blood oath years ago that Gershom would not die by my hand." Her eyes drifted to Salome. "But that doesn't mean *you* can't kill him."

"So, we kill your enemy and -"

"*Our* enemy, dear brother," Niabi matched his belligerent tone. "Or have you forgotten, he too, played a role in the deaths of our mother and our brothers?"

"On your orders!" Crispin shouted and it stilled everyone in the room.

Salome slid her hand over his shoulder and squeezed, bringing him back to himself. He straightened and rolled his shoulders back.

"No apology I give will satisfy you," Niabi's voice was low, and he almost didn't hear her. "No reasoning I give will convince you that if I could go back and do everything over, I would." She met his fiery gaze with one of her own. "So, let's make a deal instead. The crown, the throne, the kingdom – take it. I don't want it."

"What do you want in return should we agree to unite?" Salome's question angered Crispin. Considering their sister's deal was insane.

"You should already know the answer to that, little sister," Niabi flashed a wicked smile. "I've told you several times over the last few weeks."

Crispin spun to look at Salome. "What is she talking about?"

Salome met his eyes and though she did not ask for forgiveness, the look in her eyes begged for it. "With my magic – I can communicate with other magic wielders. When you told me she had fire magic -"

"How long?" he cut her off.

She reached for him, "I should have told you sooner, Crispin, but -"

He slapped her hands away. "How long?"

"Since the night you arrived in Oakenshire."

"You lied to me," he whispered; betrayed didn't even begin to describe how he felt.

"Would you have been accepting of our conversations, if she had told you sooner?" Niabi posed, which only added fuel to an already raging fire.

He pointed his index finger at her, "Do not speak to me as if we are equals."

Niabi took a bold step forward, "The way I see it, we're both rulers of nothing at this point."

"You lost your crown," he hissed, squaring his shoulders to hers.

"And without my help, you'll never gain yours."

"Crispin, let's hear her out," Salome pleaded.

"Would you side with her?" He glared at Salome like a wounded animal. "Would you turn against me after everything we've been through?"

"I'm not turning against you," Salome reached for him but he eluded her grasp. "I've seen what kind of man our father was, what he did to her, and I cannot say I don't understand."

"You would have never done what she did -"

"But I have!" she shouted. "I *have* done what she has done." Tears welled in her eyes. "When Zophar died, I slit an innocent girl's throat to hurt her mother. I didn't shed a tear when Gomorrah was destroyed and if I had been on the opposite side of the wall leading the charge, I would have instructed they all be put to the sword for what they did to Zophar. I have done things I am not proud of in my anger and grief." Her gaze shifted from him to Niabi. "And if could change what I did, I would."

"She should be executed for what she's done. Not given a chance to join our ranks, so she can slit our throats in the middle of the night." He was baffled that Salome would stand up for Niabi.

Rushing down the dais, Salome positioned herself between him and Niabi. "If you order our sister to be executed for her sins, then you will have to hang me beside her, because I have committed the same crimes."

Crispin froze in place. Salome tentatively stepped toward him, slowly slipping her hands on either side of his face. "You are my king. I would give my life for you. But I have seen things, I have seen what our father did, and he was not a good man. She is not so different from us."

"Do not ask me to forgive her for the lives she stole from us."

"Crispin," she shook her head. "I am not asking you to forgive her, I am asking you to think of our people. Think of our allies. Think of the countless lives that could be spared with her help. We do not know the White Keep's layout. We don't know anything about the city, nor do we truly know Gershom and what we are facing. She does. She can give us all the information we need to take the city."

Crispin wanted nothing more than to watch Niabi hang for her crimes, but deep down, he knew Salome was giving him the counsel he needed to make the best choices to win the war and reclaim the White Throne. Despite the fact he hated her, Niabi was a force to be reckoned with and with her magic, skillset, and knowledge of both their enemy's tactics and Northwind itself, she could prove to be a powerful ally, if she didn't betray them first.

He glanced over Salome's shoulder and found Niabi waiting patiently for his decision. "What kind of deal are you proposing?"

"You can have the kingdom, but you will need to defeat Gershom and the two witches who fight for him," Niabi approached, now within an armslength of him. "I will join your ranks and battle those who betrayed me, but once the war is over, I want to be left alone to raise my son. You will never hear from me nor see me again after you become king. I wish to live out my days in the peace our father stole from me."

"You truly expect me to believe, you will freely give up the kingdom?" Crispin eyed her suspiciously and because of her proximity, he spotted her infant tucked inside of a cloth strapped across her chest.

"I'm here, aren't I?" Her voice drew his gaze from the baby. "I could have disappeared and skipped this little family reunion, but I'm here to help you. I'm here to make things right for all of us."

"I don't believe you."

"I do," Salome said, drawing a scoff from him. "I will go."

"Salome, you can't be serious."

"I'm the Hunter," Salome spun around to face him and Niabi's face flashed with surprise. "I am destined to kill those who have spilled innocent blood. Gershom's hands are stained with their blood." She glanced at Niabi. "I don't remember the White Keep."

Niabi nodded. "I can help with that."

"And me?" Crispin spat. "You would willingly ignore me?"

"I know you don't trust her -"

"That's an understatement, Salome. She killed our entire family!"

"And I will never forget it, but they're gone, Crispin. Nothing we say or do will change that," Salome grabbed his hand. "We have a chance to join forces and get our home back. Isn't that what we want?"

"If it quenches your thirst for punishing me," Niabi's silvery voice sliced through the tension in the air. "I have suffered greatly for my sins. I've lost almost everyone I have ever loved and know their deaths are my burden to bear, until I breathe my last."

"You have not suffered nearly enough." Crispin glared at her, unmoved by her speech.

"Hate me all you want, Crispin," she clasped her hands behind her back. "But to be king, one must put their grievances aside for the greater good."

He grinded his teeth, hating every second of being in Niabi's presence. "What are we up against?"

"Gershom has control of not only the Northern army, but the Shadows as well. Ophir saw to that," she revealed. "He also has two witches at his side, the Old Witch of Endor who has fire magic, and Nezreen who has her shadows."

Witches. He hated both of those witches with every fiber of his being.

Crispin rubbed the heels of his palms against his bloodshot eyes. If he didn't get some decent rest soon, he would collapse. "So, that's who attacked us."

"I found out about the Battle of Oakenshire after it occurred," Niabi nodded, looking at Salome. "And by then, I was running for my life."

"What of Uri the Pirate King?" Salome asked, arms crossed over her chest.

"A pawn in their game." Niabi sneered. "Pirate scum."

Rahab, who had remained quiet the entire time, cleared her throat drawing the siblings' attention. "Say that again."

Niabi's signature grin snaked across her face. "You're the girl my brother was so eager to defend in Northwind." She slowly and disdainfully examined Rahab from head to toe. "I would say it's good to see you again, but why lie?"

"I know pirates who possess more honor in their little finger, than you do in your entire body," Rahab hissed, tickling the hilt of the dagger on her hip.

"Honor gets you killed." Niabi kept her eyes glued on the pirate, but before Rahab could reply, the doors opened again allowing two new members to join the room.

"Father?"

Everyone turned to see Leoti sprinting toward the Andrago who had arrived with Niabi. He rushed to her and swept her into his arms.

"You're alive!" the man cried, touching Leoti's face. "I feared the worst when you didn't return."

"I'm so happy to see you!" She cupped his face and stared at him. She suddenly noticed Niabi standing with a baby strapped to her chest. "My queen, what are you doing here?"

"Niabi?" Pash's voice silenced everyone in the room as Niabi turned to face him.

CHAPTER 49

NIABI

Pash was here. Standing less than thirty feet from her. She knew she should remain stone-faced in front of her siblings but something within her broke loose. Seeing him, not only alive, but again, spurred her to sprint to him. He, too, took off running and threw his arms around her when they met in the middle of the throne room.

Pash kissed her, then planted kisses on her forehead, cheek, and neck. "I didn't know if I was ever going to see you again," he whispered, resting his head on her shoulder.

Running her hands through his hair, a tear slipped down her cheek, and for once, she didn't care about looking weak. Ivaylo stretched in the wrap, startling Pash. He took a step back and glanced down at the bundle. He opened his mouth to speak but words failed him. Tears welled in his eyes as he met her gaze.

"This is Ivaylo, your son," she whispered, swiping her thumb against the tears that trickled down his face.

"He's perfect." Pash slipped his hand into the wrap and had to catch his breath when the babe grabbed his finger. "I'm sorry I wasn't there."

Niabi kissed him, silencing his apology. "We lost Anaktu," her voice cracked remembering the Nephilim.

"Wait," Pash glanced from Niabi to Crispin and Salome behind her. "What's going on here?" He looked at Niabi for answers. "Why are you here?"

"Gershom staged a coup," she explained, and his face dropped. "I've come here to make a deal with my brother and sister." She turned to face them, cupping her hand around the swaddled baby attached to her. "And do we have a deal? I help you take Northwind, and I can raise my son in peace."

Crispin and Salome exchanged a look. Niabi hoped that after their talks, Salome would be more open to her and her cause. She was well aware, especially after their run in at the White Keep, that Crispin would be less forgiving and opposed to merging, but as she watched and waited for one of them to speak, she prayed she hadn't made a huge mistake by asking them for help. There was still a chance Crispin would ignore Salome's advice and execute her on the spot. She wouldn't go down without a fight, her blades were safely tucked up her sleeves, since the guards at the front gate failed to check her thoroughly for weapons. Plus, she had fire magic and would easily watch the place burn to the ground.

Crispin cleared his throat. "You aid us in taking Northwind back from Gershom and the witches, and I will allow you to disappear and raise your son in peace."

Her heart leapt. Her gamble had paid off. Before she could respond, her brother narrowed his eyes and cut her off.

"If you step out of line, if I detect a hint of betrayal on your part, I'll cut you down where you stand. Are we agreed?"

Niabi felt Pash tense up beside her and he opened his mouth, most likely to defend her, but she flashed him a look, stifling whatever choice words he was about to spew. Looking back at her siblings, she smiled and bobbed her head. "We are agreed."

Salome descended from the dais and Niabi straightened her shoulders and waited for her sister to approach. Once they were face to face, Niabi looked her over. She had their father's curls, but their mother's skin tone and features. Her different color eyes were a surprise, and she couldn't stop staring at the intricate, green specks in her left eye.

"I will show you to your rooms," Salome said. "Unless you prefer to stay with the commander?"

Niabi glanced up at Pash and the pleading in his eyes was answer enough. "I'm sure the commander and I have much to discuss in private."

Salome nodded. A man walked up behind her, took her hand and placed it on his forearm.

"You make a lovely couple," Niabi offered a rare compliment. They looked at her. "Don't look so surprised. I recognize a couple in love when I see one. I'm not blind."

"This is Prince Jinn of Sakurai," Salome introduced them, and Jinn bowed his head, though his eyes were narrow and vigilant. As if to say, if you hurt her, you'll deal with me. And she couldn't fault him for it.

"Prince Jinn," Niabi said politely.

"Queen Niabi," he returned her tone, but she shook her head.

"Just Niabi," she corrected. "I have no throne anymore." She met Salome's softened gaze and motioned toward the door. "Shall we?"

Snapped out of her momentary stupor, Salome nodded and began the trek through the keep.

Her siblings and their allies had worked wonders in resurrecting the ancient castle. She was impressed with how well organized and heavily manned their rebellion was. She didn't think they were capable of amassing an army, but here she was, walking in the lion's den, grateful she wasn't facing them in battle.

"How did you escape?" Salome asked.

The question conjured Anaktu's face, and it rattled her, but she shook the image free. "Tala, Thrice, and I had to fight our way out. I lost a dear friend of mine during our flight."

"I'm sorry to hear that." Niabi was surprised to hear genuine sorrow in her sister's voice.

"Why do they call you Thrice?" Salome turned to look at the Shadow stalking behind them and he flashed a menacing grin.

"I once killed three men with one swing of my sword." He held up three fingers, "Hence, Thrice."

If Salome was impressed or intimidated, she didn't show it. "Well, Thrice, I assume you will want to be near my sister, so this is your room. Commander Pash's room is right next door."

Thrice looked to Niabi for permission to be dismissed and with a flicker of her eyes, he bowed and slipped into his quarters. "Leoti's room is across the hall from Commander Pash's chambers."

"I hope my presence hasn't created a wedge between you and our brother," Niabi said, halting Salome's departure.

Salome turned back around and gave an insincere smile. "If driving a wedge between us is your goal, I'd give it up. We have been through far too much to let you divide us."

"But you defended me," Niabi cocked her head to the side, rubbing small circles around Ivaylo's cradled form. "He wanted to execute me, and you stood up for me."

"Do not think for one second I won't strike you down, if I feel you are a threat to Crispin." The friendliness was gone from Salome's voice, replaced with an iciness Niabi knew all too well. "But I will help him make the right choices for the good of our people and allies, not the easy decisions based on emotion and grudges. He is my king, and I will die before anyone touches him."

"Let us hope, dear sister," Niabi cooed, "it does not come down to that."

"Rest well, Niabi." Salome stalked down the hall, Jinn beside her like a dutiful lapdog.

Once the couple turned the corner, Niabi closed the bedroom door and while Pash stared at her, she cast a quick glance around the space and took note of all the entrances, exits, and windows. The wardrobe wasn't large enough for anyone to hide in and there was no space underneath the wooden bedframe for an assassin to lie in wait. The fireplace was lit preventing anyone from slipping in that way. From her quick assessment, there was no real threat to worry about and with Pash in the room and Thrice next door, she knew she'd be able to rest. She needed a good night's sleep after the days of roughing it in the cold, dark forest.

"I don't know what you've heard about me," Pash's voice sliced through her thoughts, drawing her gaze, "but I am no traitor."

"Ophir told me of your brother," Niabi tilted her head in curiosity. "A brother I didn't know you had."

"He's my half-brother," Pash explained. "We share the same father."

"Why didn't you tell me about him?"

"I swore I'd never speak of him to anyone in order to protect him." Pash sat on the edge of his bed, twiddling his thumbs between his thighs. "My father ordered men to burn his childhood house to the ground which killed his mother and grandfather. I didn't know if Adonijah had survived, but if by chance, he was alive, I knew, he would want to remain hidden."

Niabi approached him on soft feet, squeezing next to him on the mattress. "Why did you save him? You hardly know him."

Pash met her eyes and smiled. "He's my brother. I do not need to know him well to save him."

She scoffed, looking at the door and making a mental note to lock it before going to sleep.

"Why did you come here of all places, Niabi? You could have been executed on the spot."

"A calculated risk," she said without hesitation.

"You could have gone to Elisor to be with the Andrago -"

"Your father betrayed me," her eyes lit up with a fiery rage. "He stole my throne, my crown, my home. I underestimated him. A mistake I do not intend to make again." Her face softened when he placed his hand on her bouncing knee. "I did not go to Elisor because that is the first place Gershom would have expected me to go. I did not wish to bring further harm to the Andrago."

He lifted her hand to his lips and pressed a loving kiss to her skin. "We could leave this place tonight. I've been plotting my own escape for weeks."

"Why were you trying to escape?"

"To get back to you." He said it with such conviction it made her heart leap.

"Well, I do not intend to run like a whipped dog with my tail between my legs," she shook her head. "No, my love, I intend to bring Gershom to his knees for his treachery."

"Did you mean what you said to your siblings? They could have the kingdom and you'd disappear to raise our son?"

She brushed her hand down his cheek and nodded. "I've been given a second chance. I do not intend to squander it."

"So, after this war is over…?"

"We will go to Elisor and start over. You, me, and Ivaylo," she bobbed her head. "I've already spoken to Tala, and he's agreed to welcome you into the Andrago fold as long as you swear fealty to them."

"Where you go," he kissed her hand once more and smiled, "I go."

She smiled back and for the first time in months, she felt true joy and hope. Ivaylo wiggled in his wrap, letting loose a small cry.

"Would you like to hold him?" She unwrapped the newborn strapped to her chest and offered him to Pash who carefully accepted the tiny bundle.

The warmth on Pash's face filled the entire room with a palpable love that brought a tear to her eye. Gently, he kissed Ivaylo's head and whispered, "My son, you are so desperately loved. I can't wait to teach you everything I know."

Niabi leaned closer, resting her head on Pash's shoulder. Taking a deep breath, she closed her eyes, and dfited to sleep for some much needed rest.

CHAPTER 50
SALOME

Niabi and her humble entourage had arrived in Oakenshire weeks ago and Salome was relieved her siblings hadn't attempted to kill each other. Reinforcements and supplies trickled in and as they did, the leaders met daily to exchange pertinent information about the war they were going to wage against Gershom and his allies, but every day, they left the room more frustrated than the day before. If Crispin and Niabi didn't start seeing eye to eye, and soon, she was going to lock them up until they swore on their lives that they would at least attempt to work together.

Although her daily routine had changed, Salome's nightly routine remained the same: training with the Bellators. Some nights, Leoti would join her to keep practicing the techniques she'd learned, but the Andrago asked for a reprieve so she could spend time with her father and broach the subject of marrying Adonijah after the war.

Tala was surprisingly kind and generous for someone who was Niabi's closest companion and most trusted advisor, but despite her initial judgment, Salome took quite the liking to him and even spent a few early mornings with him, devouring fresh pastries Jacobi had baked before the rest of the castle stirred. She listened to his stories of the Andrago and their way of life and she found his traditions and culture fascinating. She secretly hoped that one day she might be able to visit Elisor, and see for herself the beauty the Andrago offered. In a way, Tala reminded her of Zophar, and she knew, deep down, they would have been the best of friends had they had the chance to meet.

But once midnight struck, she made her way to the bailey where the Bellators were always waiting for her. An hour of drills and sparring flew by, and her strength, speed, and stamina had greatly improved since their first lesson. She wasn't sure battle fright was still an issue for her, but she didn't have the courage to ask Kayven if he thought she was ready to end their sessions. She didn't want him to tell her she no longer needed them, because that would be the farthest thing from the truth. Even if she didn't need to train with them anymore, she found their companionship not only soothing, but their presence brought her immeasurable joy when all she was surrounded by was talk of war, politics, and death.

Another thirty minutes passed, but instead of pushing through the pain, Salome motioned to Kayven and Abba that she needed a break.

"There will not be time for breaks in war, my lady." Kayven speared his sword between the pavers and leaned his weight upon it. "If you keep demanding we prepare you for what is to come, you must fight through your exhaustion. It could mean the difference between life or death."

"And if I don't get a drink of water this very moment, you'll have to explain to not only my brother, but to Jinn and Harbona as well, why you pushed me to the point of passing out," she teased as she sipped from her cup.

Kayven rolled his eyes as Abba puffed out a laugh.

"For being the Hunter," Kayven quipped, "you certainly need a lot of breaks."

"I might be the Hunter," Salome shot back with a smirk, "but I'm still mortal."

Once Salome had finished her drink and wiped the sweat from her brow, she motioned for the Bellators to resume their session, but their eyes weren't on her. Their gaze was fixed on someone behind her.

"Mind if I join you?"

Salome turned to look at Niabi sauntering into the bailey, flashing a pair of daggers in her palms. The night Niabi arrived, she learned that Salome was the Hunter, but the revelation didn't seem to faze her. Most of the leaders assumed Niabi would be on Salome's kill list but if Niabi was worried, she didn't show it. She kept her face neutral and carried herself like a true warrior queen when the other leaders rained their complaints and accusations against the Green-Eyed-Raven. Rightfully so, they didn't trust her, and they didn't want her amongst their ranks. Some, but mostly bloodthirsty Oifa, demanded they just execute her and be done with it.

Salome found it exhausting to defend her sister on a daily basis, but she didn't fault their allies for their concerns. Truthfully, she had her uncertainties, but above all else, she wished to end the vicious cycle her father started. Niabi sought a second chance to raise her family in peace and to be left alone. Would she have sought her siblings out before war came to her doorstep? Most likely not, but when she had a chance to escape and live the life she desperately wanted, she willingly put her life at risk by coming to Oakenshire. Niabi was as cunning as she was dangerous, but over the last few weeks, she'd come to learn that her sister was bold in the face of adversity and spoke her mind freely without fear of those who would oppose her.

But deep down in Salome's gut, she felt a tug, an undeniable urge to listen to what Lykos had told her when she'd reached out to him in the After. *Maybe she is not the one you are meant to defeat. Perhaps, she is the one you are meant to save.* She'd tried to shake his words from her mind, but it was impossible, as if Lykos was whispering it to her every morning when she woke up and every night before she closed her eyes. If nothing else, she owed it to Lykos to try to set things right, since their father unleashed his chaos.

As her sister approached, Salome couldn't keep her eyes off of her. There was something truly unsettling about Niabi that Salome couldn't quite put her finger on, but she was curious to see the queen in action. Maybe she would even learn a few moves from the lethal warrior. Crispin would be furious, and Jinn wouldn't be too excited to hear about their private sparring session either, but she wasn't concerned about the Bellators ratting them out.

"You sure you should be sparring so soon after having your son?"

Niabi smiled and it reminded Salome so much of their mother it stopped her dead in her tracks. "Thank you for your concern, but I've been cleared by your healers, and after weeks of inactivity, I could use the practice." She circled her blades around her hands, not at all looking out of practice.

Salome took her stance and nodded. "Show me what you've got."

Kayven and Abba stepped out of the designated training area, leaning against the wall to keep an eye on the two women and to be lookouts in case Harbona or any of the others came snooping.

Niabi stood several feet from her younger sister, her daggers in her grasp at her sides. The warm smile that had graced the queen's face moments earlier was wiped clean, and a hardened assassin stood in her place. The intensity in her green eyes sent an unwelcome shiver down Salome's spine but when her sister's left hand ignited in flames, she jumped back in surprise. She knew about Niabi's fire magic, but she hadn't anticipated seeing it in action at the beginning of a friendly sparring session.

They stared at one another silently, waiting, mentally willing the other to make the first move, but neither did. Instead, they soaked one another in, eyeing their stances, their choice of weaponry, even making eye contact at one point to feel the other out. Finally, Salome struck first, launching herself at her sister, using all the techniques she'd learned over the years. She implemented all the lessons Zophar had taught her, the Qata Vishna movements she learned from Mika, and even the few moves the Bellators had shown her. She wielded a weapon unlike any warrior Adalore had ever seen – taught by some of the most cunning warriors to take down her own blood.

But Niabi moved with the same lethal elegance having trained with the Qata Vishna, and being a Red Maiden in her own right. Her blades were extensions of her arms, and she sliced around the sparring grounds like the Andrago and Shadows. If Salome hadn't been impressed with her sister before, she was mesmerized by her now.

Salome wielded weapons – Niabi was a weapon. No wonder their father didn't stand a chance when she invaded.

"You're thinking too much," Niabi's voice cut into her thoughts. "If you don't harness your mind, you will lose every time." She dropped to the ground to sweep Salome's legs out from under her, but she had anticipated the move and hopped over effortlessly.

"Maybe you should focus on yourself more than me." Salome leapt in the air, attempting to land a roundhouse kick to her sister's chest, but only met the air when Niabi tumbled out the way.

They danced around one another, landing a few well-timed blows, but doing no true damage. It wasn't until Niabi flipped toward her that she was thrown off balance. When Niabi landed on her feet, she slammed her flaming hand against Salome's chest sending her flying and singeing her shirt.

Kayven flinched, ready to strike, but Salome held out a hand, halting him. Niabi walked over and hovered above her.

"You fight well, little sister." Niabi extinguished her hand and extended it to help her up. "You could be even better, if you let me teach you."

"Unless you can teach me how to wield fire like you, I don't think I could get any better." Salome accepted her help and planted her feet on the stone pavers.

"My fire magic doesn't make me a better fighter. It makes you believe that I am, because it's a distraction." Niabi cocked her head to the side, retracting her blades into her sleeves. "Win the battle of the mind, and you've already defeated your enemy."

"And how exactly am I supposed to do that when I don't even know my enemy?" Salome asked. She knew of Gershom and his crimes, but she didn't know the first thing about him or what would distract him enough to better her odds of defeating him in combat.

"Oh, but you do know your enemy, Salome," Niabi cooed, "and you already know what the perfect distraction will be. Us."

"Us?"

"Gershom knows he's wronged me and that I always have my revenge." Niabi sat on one of the wooden boxes used as stools and Salome perched on the one next to her. "He also knows that Vilora failed to eliminate me. He knows I'll be back, it's just a matter of when. What he won't anticipate is me joining forces with the very siblings I ordered him to hunt down. We have the element of surprise and that in itself will throw him off. He will be reckless in his decisions and in his desperation to keep the crown, he will make mistakes. That's when we strike. That's when you take your shot and kill that bastard. That's when you fulfill the prophecy and become the Hunter you were meant to be and avenge the blood of the innocent."

Salome scoffed. "For a while there, I thought I'd be killing you."

"You still might."

"Why do you say that?"

Niabi offered her a sad smile. "I am far from a hero, Salome. I have blood on my hands and though right now we have the same goals, there may come a time when you turn on me."

"I won't."

Niabi met Salome's confused gaze and stared deep into her eyes. "You and I are very similar."

"You say that like it's a bad thing," Salome whispered. "And what does that have to do with me turning on you?"

"Because if our roles were reversed and I was the Hunter, I would consider your past and what havoc you could possibly wreak in the future. Killing you would be at the forefront of my mind – just like it is on yours."

"That's -"

"Please don't insult me by lying about it. I can see it in your eyes."

Salome looked away from her, twiddling her fingers. "I have considered it."

"But?"

"But," Salome met her gaze, "you remind me too much of our mother."

"Looks can be deceiving."

"If you could go back and do things differently, would you?"

Niabi peered into Salome's eyes. "If you're asking, would I have spared our father if I had a chance to rethink my choices, my answer would be no." Her answer surprised Salome. "Had Issachar left me alone, let me live my life in peace with my husband and my son, I never would have come for him. But what he did, who he stole from me, that was something I could not, would not, forgive or forget." Before Salome could respond, Niabi continued. "Let me ask you something."

Salome bobbed her head and waited for the question.

"This prince of yours, Jinn."

"What of him?"

"What would you do, if someone murdered him before your eyes?"

Salome recoiled, but then her nostrils flared. "Is that a threat?"

"No," Niabi shook her head and patted her sister's hand to reassure her. "I am asking, if he was taken from you, what would you do?"

Salome knew exactly what Niabi was trying to get her to understand, what she was trying to get her to admit, and she was ashamed to say, she didn't blame her sister one bit, because that's exactly what she would have done. But she didn't need to admit it aloud for Niabi to guess what her answer would be.

"Am I really that much of a monster for avenging the man I loved?" Niabi asked, her eyes tearing up. "I turned my back on the White Throne and everything Issachar stood for long before I met Dichali, but he just couldn't let me be free, let me be happy. He never would have stopped hunting me, tormenting me, until I either lied down like a rodent and died, or fought back. He pushed me too far by taking Dichali. He underestimated my devotion to my husband and it cost him everything."

Salome stared at her sister, touched by the pain that filled her eyes, and realized behind that gaze was a hurting and broken woman. Maybe, just maybe, Salome could do as Lykos asked and save her before it was too late.

"I suppose I should be heading inside," Niabi broke the silence first and Salome nodded in agreement. "Until next time, little sister."

Kayven and Abba joined Salome once Niabi left.

"You trust her?" Abba asked once she was out of earshot and Salome bobbed her head, wrapping her arms around herself as the blistering cold wind whisked around.

"I hope she's wrong."

"Wrong about what?" Kayven's eyes darted to hers, clearly confused.

"I hope I'm not forced to turn on her."

CHAPTER 51

CRISPIN

Although the general consensus was to wait until winter had passed to move the troops towards Northwind, Niabi pleaded her case to the leaders that Gershom would only amass a greater army and strengthen his hold on the White City if they didn't move quickly. When Salome noted that during one of their private conversations, Niabi had said it would be foolish to move an army in the cold months, Niabi acknowledged her statement and said, "It's a risk I wouldn't have taken, but with Gershom trying to establish his reign, he's currently at his weakest. The time to strike is when he would least expect it, and in the middle of winter after staging a coup, would be the time to do it."

So, despite the heavy snow they would encounter the further north they'd travel, the leaders all agreed they'd strike hard and fast, hoping to have the element of surprise on their side and keep Gershom from strengthening his hold on the city.

Crispin hated to admit he agreed with Niabi's suggested strategy, but it was the best course, so he ordered their allies to be ready to travel in the morning.

After the meeting was adjourned, Crispin slipped out virtually unnoticed and went to the stables where Freya, the horse Zophar had purchased for him years ago, was housed. He hadn't spent much time with her and was honestly surprised to see her in Oakenshire when he reunited with Salome. Zophar had cared for her and Midnight even after Crispin had been swept down the River of Lost Souls and presumed dead. Now it was his turn to take care of Freya and Midnight. He brushed them, fed them, and made sure he swiped a couple apples to give them a sweet treat. Snow, Salome's horse, glanced over her pen and stared at him when she heard the crunching of apples, and he offered her one. Greedily, she accepted his offering and a few pets before she huddled back into her area, ignoring him for the remainder of his visit.

He chuckled and rolled his eyes. Snow was exactly like Salome. If she knew you had snacks, she would drop everything to get some and then she'd go back into her own little world and ignore you.

Midnight was just like Zophar. There was a quiet strength and kindness in his eyes that reminded him of his guardian.

When he kissed Freya's snout, she nuzzled into his neck, giving him the unspoken love and understanding he was longing for. Sometimes Crispin preferred the company of horses over people. They didn't confuse him, nor did they make him compromise what he knew to be right, for the betterment of other people.

Crispin pinned his back against the door to Freya's pen and slid down, stretching one leg out and pulling the other against his chest. He played with the hay poking out of Freya's stable before he rested his head against the door and closed his eyes. Winter's chill was brutal that afternoon. Whipping around the keep mercilessly. Certain parts of the castle were uninhabitable since they hadn't been able to repair all the damage in the outer walls. But at least the stable was intact and the horses were well cared for. They would need all the strength they could muster to make the trip north in the morning.

It would take them a few days to reach the designated location the leaders had agreed upon and set up their military camp before launching their attack on Northwind.

After weeks of planning, months of adventures, and a lifetime of waiting, his moment was coming. In a week, he could be king. The thought was as jarring as it was exciting. His life had changed drastically from the moment he stepped foot outside of the Tree House Forest. He just hoped he would lead his allies to victory.

"I know you do not trust me," the female voice he dreaded hearing disturbed his tranquil space and instantly grated his nerves, "but if we do not show a united front, your allies will waver."

Crispin's eyes narrowed as he met Niabi's gaze. "Surely you didn't drag yourself out to the stables to risk angering me."

She smirked; her boots clicked against the stone pavers as she made her way toward him. No, not toward him. Toward Freya. He was about to warn her that Freya was a biter, but as she stretched her hand toward the mare, Freya the Betrayer, tucked her snout underneath Niabi's palm, accepting her pat. If Crispin hadn't seen it with his own eyes, he wouldn't have believed it. Freya, to this day, would try to bite Salome if she got too close, so the fact that she allowed this stranger, this monster, to touch her, made him sick to his stomach.

"You're always angry, brother," Niabi's voice sliced through his thoughts, further irritating him.

"What's in your hand?" His question seemed to surprise her.

"What?"

"What's in your hand?" he repeated.

Slowly, she lifted her hand from Freya's nose and showed him her empty palm. "Is something wrong, brother?"

"Quit calling me that," he hissed, stalking past her toward the exit.

"I know there's nothing I can do or say that will earn your forgiveness, nor am I asking for it." That halted his retreat, but he didn't turn around to face her. "I have blood on my hands. I have loved fiercely and lost tragically. I tried to take the higher ground with our father, but he struck me so deeply in the heart that had I not acted, he never would have stopped hunting me."

He didn't hear her approach him until she was upon him. He turned around, half-expecting her to stab him in the chest since he'd been foolish enough to turn his back to her, but he found her unarmed with glossy eyes.

"I remember receiving news that you had been born. Even though you were father's fourth son, the kingdom rejoiced and celebrated for an entire week." Niabi's voice was soft and despite fighting it, her words drew him in. "My own son was born around the same time, but I did not send word to our mother or father, fearing what Issachar's reaction would be with me producing an heir for the Andrago throne. A baby's birth is a miraculous and joyous occasion, but for me, it reminded me that even though I was a queen in a different kingdom, out from under our father's thumb, I was still fearful of what he could do to me. He learned quickly that physical beatings and torment had zero effect on me. I was trained by the Qata Vishna, I was battered and bruised in training for years. But he was a cunning king and cruel man and knew the only way to truly hurt me was to harm those I loved most."

"Why are you telling me this?" Crispin looked at her and searched for a crack in her armor and found just a broken woman with scars that ran so deep it choked him.

"I realize you see me as I see him." Niabi tilted her head to the side, a playful curiosity. "You see me as the monster and not the wounded wife and mother who lost her husband and son. You see me as the villain, and I do not blame you. In my quest to avenge my dead, I didn't realize until it was far too late, that in order to defeat him, I'd become him." She took another step toward him, eating the remaining distance between them. Slowly, tentatively, she raised her hand and cupped his face and the touch felt like a punch to his gut. "I'm sorry I became your villain, dear brother. My quarrel was never with you. See me for what I am and swear you will never be like me. It is a terribly lonely existence."

Withdrawing her hand from his cheek, she slipped by him, headed for the door, when he suddenly grabbed her arm and yanked her back against his chest.

"Your pathetic story might work on Salome," he hissed into her ear, fire raging in his soul, "but I am not so easily swayed." Her body tensed, but he did not relinquish his hold on her. "I will never forgive you. I will never forget that you are a monster of your own making. When this war is over, dare not show your face again, lest I take the revenge I've dreamt of since the day I escaped your villainous clutches twelve years ago."

Releasing her, he pushed past her, and stomped out into the bailey. Snow flurries danced around as he strode toward the keep, bypassing anyone who looked like they might want to speak with him. He needed to get to his room and have a moment to be alone, otherwise he was afraid of what might come flying out of his mouth.

How dare she try to plead her case with him? Was she looking for forgiveness? Mercy? Was this just part of her scheme to suck him into her story of victimhood, only to wait like a snake in the grass for her moment to betray him?

He raked his hand through his hair, exhaustion settling in, even though it wasn't nearly time to sleep. Tripping up the stairs as he sprinted toward his bed chambers, he waved off castle attendants who offered to help him up. *Unhinged*. That's what he saw reflected in their stares. The future king of the north was stampeding through the keep like he was afraid someone was after him.

Finally pushing his door open, he slammed it shut, rattling the sconces attached to the walls. Cupping his face in his hands, he trembled. His rage turned into tears that slipped down his rosy cheeks. Swiping them away, his frozen hand felt like he was scraping his face with a knife. A bath. That's what he needed. A hot bath.

Stripping as he made his way toward his bathroom, he blessed the castle attendants who had just filled his tub before sinking in, relishing the burn against his frozen skin. He tipped his head against the rim and closed his eyes.

If all went according to plan, in a week's time, he would be crowned King of Northwind. But first, he had to make it through the four-day journey to the next military camp without breaking Niabi's neck, which would be no easy feat.

He hated how much Niabi resembled their mother. Down to the tone of her voice, she was every part Bilhah, and it pained him to look upon his enemy's face and see his mother staring back at him. Crispin and Salome inherited their mother's skin tone and some of her personality traits, but they were born with Issachar's curly, brown hair, brown eyes, and obsessive need to crush their enemies.

Allowing himself to wallow for a brief moment, he thought about what his life would look like had his father been a good king and a kind father. Niabi never would have lashed out, taking those he loved. She would have inherited the White Throne, as was her birthright according to their laws, and the rest of his brothers would be alive.

Crispin glanced out the frosted window at the Ignacia Sea and it called out to him. Oh, how he loved being aboard the *Shadow of Death*, sailing across the seas, and living out every adventurous dream his childhood heart longed for. Had his father followed the laws of their ancestors, Niabi would have been queen, Lykos would have been her Master of War, Mosgalath would have found his place amongst the scholars in Northwind, Elias would have gladly accepted a position in the elite forces that protected the crown, and Crispin would have been given a command in the naval fleet. Salome and Jepthudar, the youngest of the seven, would have been given positions of high honor, although they all would have been expected to marry for power and not love.

A sudden knock on his bedchamber door throttled him from his daydream. "Enter," he shouted as he hopped out of the tub and wrapped a towel around his waist.

"Oh, seven hells, Crispin!" Salome slapped her hands over her eyes. "How are you going to tell someone to come in when you're in this state? Put a shirt on."

He rolled his eyes and slipped his clothes on and threw the damp towel at her. "You're a child."

"Moody today?" she teased and welcomed herself to sit cross-legged on his bed, wrinkling the sheets. "Are you disappointed it's me and not a certain lady pirate visiting you?"

Crispin opened his mouth to say something snarky, but nothing came out. His heart was hurting, and his stress was at an all-time high, but he wasn't sure how to tell his sister all of that when he knew she carried her own set of heavy burdens.

"What is it?" she asked, her tone now sharp.

"It's nothing," he lied.

"One of the maids told me you were running through the halls in a panic."

"I tripped up the stairs," he scoffed, waving a hand in the air to emphasize his point, "that hardly qualifies as me running through the castle in a panic."

Salome patted the spot next to her, beckoning him to come sit with her, which he reluctantly did. As soon as his body hit the mattress, she wrapped her arms around him, pulling him into a hug.

"Salome -"

She shushed him. "This is happening."

Crispin leaned into her and released a sigh that shook his entire body.

"Are you alright?" she asked and he shook his head.

"No, but I will be."

"You don't have to talk about it," she pulled away from him, eyeing him with concern, "but I'm right down the hall, if you need me." She planted a kiss on his forehead before hopping off the bed and slipping out the door. "Goodnight," she offered him one last smile before disappearing.

Crispin threw himself back onto the bed, covering his eyes with his forearm. Tomorrow morning, they would start their journey north, bringing him one step closer to Death or destiny. Without realizing it, he'd drifted off to sleep and didn't stir until first light.

CHAPTER 52
ADONIJAH

Leaving Oakenshire and trekking north for four days was surprisingly uneventful.

Pash and Leoti brought Adonijah up to speed on the state of Northwind. How Gershom staged a successful coup and how Niabi found, joined, and became an ally to her siblings in their fight to reclaim the White Throne. Adonijah even met the former queen and Tala, her Andrago bodyguard and father of Leoti. He hated that he was nervous meeting the Andrago, but when asked about his intentions for the future, he happily poured his heart out about wanting to build a life with Leoti. She'd accepted Adonijah, and in doing so, Tala welcomed him into the fold. Especially when he found out Adonijah had been willing to die in Pash's camp for killing the Shadow that attempted to assault his daughter.

Even though he now found himself betrothed, Adonijah found everything else around him confusing. He wasn't certain if Niabi could be trusted, but he rejoiced with his brother that he had he been reunited with the love of his life, and he was now a proud father of a little boy that had his nose and Niabi's piercing green eyes.

What bothered him most about Niabi wasn't that her very presence was threatening, but that watching her interact with those she loved made her so human. He'd heard the stories about her; how she was lethal in battle and her weapons were extensions of her body. He remembered tales of how she slaughtered her enemies and purged the Black Forest of vagabonds that terrorized travelers passing through. But seeing her cuddle her newborn and kiss Pash with nothing but pure love in her eyes made his heart ache. He wanted happiness for them, but he knew the prophecy of the Hunter, just like everyone else in that camp. Salome was destined to avenge the blood of the innocent. Niabi might have had just cause to want her father dead, but she still had blood on her hands. There was a good chance Salome would still be expected to execute her sister, even though they'd come to an agreement in Oakenshire to fight together to defeat Gershom.

Over the course of the four-day journey, Adonijah observed Crispin glaring at

Niabi countless times, and recognized the look of a man with murderous intent. Not even Salome would be able to prevent Crispin from driving his sword through Niabi's chest, if he set his mind to it. And he thought his family was complicated.

"You ready?" Salome asked, plopping down beside him by the campfire, startling him from his thoughts.

He bobbed his head but by the skeptical look on her face, he knew he couldn't hide his true feelings from her. She knew him far too well.

"What is it that troubles you, Adonijah?" She snatched a piece of venison off his plate, drawing a smile from him.

"Little thief."

Her smile faded when he evaded the question. "Are you worried we won't win tomorrow?"

Adonijah lowered his head.

They'd set up their military camp a couple miles outside of Northwind, still shielded by the trees of the Black Forest. They were a large and mighty host of some of the greatest soldiers in Adalore, and just off the coast, their ships awaited those who would fight by sea.

"I haven't seen my father since I was a boy," he admitted, "I'm afraid I might freeze once I see him again."

Salome slipped her hand onto his. "I know you fear his blood runs through your veins, but you are nothing like him."

"I should have told you months ago when we first met," he lamented. "I was afraid I'd lose you if I revealed my identity," he chuckled softly. "I guess I never really had you to lose." When she said nothing, he looked at her and asked, "Did I ever stand a chance?"

Salome smiled. "Had we met under different circumstances, I think we could have been happy together. But I'm no longer that girl from the Tree House Forest. And you're far more than just being The Wanderer."

"I meant what I said before, about protecting you." His eyes bore into hers, silently hoping to get his message across. "My sword will always be yours."

"All I want," she whispered, "is for you to survive this war. I want you to be happy with Leoti and maybe you'll find the peace you have so desperately been seeking."

"You were my light when all I expected was darkness. I will cherish you for the rest of my days for saving me."

She slipped her arms around his neck and embraced him. "You have been the best friend I could have ever hoped for, Adonijah." She pulled away from him and smiled. "Leoti is a far better match for you than I ever was. The way you look at one another is how great love stories begin."

"She admires you as well," he added. He felt like a weight had been fully lifted off his shoulders. Salome was right, Leoti was the best suited partner for him, and he was happier than he'd ever been.

"Well," she slapped his knee and stood up, "we better get going."

"Going? Where?" He quirked an eyebrow.

"I came to bring you to the war tent," she smiled down at him. "The leaders have gathered to finalize strategy, and I want you in there with me."

"Why?" he asked as he motioned around the camp. "I lead no army to give you input."

"There is no one I trust more to give sound advice in that room," she said without question or hesitation. "War will be waged in that room and I need to know that those with sound minds will prevail."

"I take it you're worried about your brother and sister." He snickered, drawing a labored chuckle from her.

"I'm afraid with their tempers, one will be tempted to stab the other."

"Seems like a family trait," he tossed one last piece of food in his mouth before standing up, towering over her. He motioned toward the large white tent in the middle of their encampment. "Lead the way, my lady."

As they made their way toward the tent, they spotted Niabi and Pash passing a bundled Ivaylo into Tala's arms.

"Take him to Elisor and keep him safe," Niabi instructed. Tala attempted to hand the baby back, but Niabi squeezed his forearm. "Please, my friend."

"I should be fighting alongside you," Tala's voice trembled, and Adonijah thought it sounded awfully close to a goodbye on Niabi's part.

"Should we fail to return -"

"Niabi -"

She cupped his face in her hands, forcing him to meet her gaze and listen. "Should we fail to return, I am trusting you to make sure he knows who he is and how much we loved him." Pash slipped his hands on Niabi's shoulders and nodded his head in agreement. "Promise me, you will keep Ivaylo safe and train him in the ways of the Andrago."

A tear slipped down Tala's cheek and his lip quivered as he bobbed his head. "I swear he will be safe in my charge."

Niabi embraced the Andrago and as she pulled away, she kissed his cheek. "Now, go. Get my son as far away from here as you can."

Tala cradled Ivaylo in his arms and reluctantly walked away.

Adonijah watched as the Andrago fought brimming tears, before returning his attention to his brother and Niabi. They were somber and didn't move a muscle until Tala hopped on his saddled horse and took off into the forest with their son and a couple guards as an escort. Pash wrapped his arms around Niabi's waist, and she rested the back of her head against his chest. Adonijah couldn't imagine how difficult it must have been for them to send their son away with the thought that they might not live to see him again. Pash met his gaze but didn't say anything as he clutched Niabi.

He'd nearly forgotten Salome was with him until she made her way toward them and reached for Niabi's hand. "You don't have to stay here, Niabi. You can go with your son."

Niabi shook her head and rubbed Salome's arm. "I gave you and Crispin my word and I intend to see this through to the end."

"But -"

"I was not raised to run away from adversity, no matter how tempting it might be," Niabi gently cut her off. "We are wolves, and we will take back our home." Without another word, she freed herself from Pash and marched toward the war tent, her head held high, ready for battle.

Pash scowled at Salome, which was so unlike him, it was unsettling.

"Pash?" Adonijah stepped closer to Salome, his eyes fixed on his brother. "Is everything alright?"

The commander didn't tear his gaze from Salome, but he didn't say anything. Something was clearly bothering Pash, but if he chose not to address it, then Adonijah wouldn't force him to. Without saying a word, or even acknowledging Adonijah's question, Pash stormed off to the war tent.

"I don't think your brother cares for me," Salome whispered.

"He's probably stressed. He is not acting like himself." Adonijah raked a hand through his hair and grimaced. "I hope you won't hold it against him."

Salome shook her head. "If I got mad everytime someone gave me a nasty look, I would be in a perpetual state of rage." She laughed, and it relaxed him. "Come on, we need to get in there."

"Right," Adonijah nodded.

"Leoti?" Salome called out to the Andrago and motioned her to come forward. "Join us."

Without hesitation, Leoti smiled and joined their ranks as they sauntered into the lion's den, hopefully coming out with a sound plan and without injuries.

CHAPTER 53
SALOME

They'd been at it for hours. Arguing back and forth, leaders from all over Adalore offered their best strategy for effectively bringing Gershom and his allies to their knees, all while the other leaders poked holes in their plans. Salome rubbed her temples, feeling a splitting headache coming on. She hadn't offered any ideas because quite frankly, she didn't have any. At this point, she could have sneaked into the White Keep on her own and driven her blade into Gershom's heart and returned to find them all in the same positions arguing over their next course of action.

Niabi stood up and placed her hand on the map of Northwind and the surrounding areas, frustration and exhaustion riddled in her features. Salome swore every time Niabi looked at her, she saw her mother staring back. It was as equally comforting as it was unsettling.

"I can lead a small team into the city undetected," Niabi raised her voice above the rest of the leaders, drawing their undivided attention, "but the majority of your army will have to attack by land and sea."

Crispin scoffed, removing his palms from the table and straightening to his full height. "You are truly a fool, if you think I'm going to let you out of our sight during battle."

"I won't be out of sight," Niabi flashed a coy smile at Salome. "Our sister will be going with me."

"Out of the question." Crispin shook his head, folding his arms across his chest.

"Crispin -" Salome attempted to protest but was cut off.

"I will not allow you to be alone with her."

"I'll go with them," Adonijah stepped forward and everyone stared at him. "From what we've already discussed," he motioned toward the map on the wooden table with figurines scattered around, "Prince Crispin, Prince Heru, Pash, Leoti, King Hanzo, Queen Oifa, the Numbio, and the Mountain Men will attack the main gate. Prince Jinn,

Rahab, the rest of the pirates, Master Penn and her Keepers, the Qata Vishna, the Eastern forces, and the Bellators will attack Nezreen and Uri by air and sea. That leaves Salome and Niabi to infiltrate the White Keep and assassinate Gershom. Thrice and I can go with them and give them the backup they need, as well as keep them safe."

"I need you at the front lines," Crispin insisted. "I need all the best swordsmen battling at the main gate."

"Then I will go with them."

Salome turned around and saw Leoti holding her arm. She looked nervous, but she held her head high, mustering every bit of courage she could.

"What did you say?" Crispin asked.

"I said, I will go with them. I will be their fourth." Leoti's voice grew stronger the more she spoke, and Salome couldn't help but feel a sense of great pride that the woman who had never wielded a sword before, was now volunteering for a stealth assassination mission. Her knife skills had improved by leaps and bounds since their first sparring session and she would be more than happy for the Andrago to join them.

"Leoti," Adonijah took a step toward her, his face twisted with concern. "It's a dangersous mission, are you sure you want to go?"

Leoti furrowed her brow. "I've been training with Salome for weeks. My warging abilities would enable us to see what we might be up against on our way to the tunnel entrance, and I know the White Keep like the back of my hand. I would be an asset." Her eyes trailed away from her intended and met Niabi's stare. "And I have a no qualms in poking some holes in Gershom's chest."

Niabi grinned and nodded. "I say she goes."

Crispin opened his mouth, looking like he was going to argue just because Niabi liked the idea, when Salome cut him off. "I agree."

Leoti had made a compelling argument and she was right, she would be an incredible asset and it would free Adonijah to be where he needed to be, by Crispin's side. She knew no matter what, Adonijah would protect Crispin when she couldn't.

"What say you, brother?" Salome held his irritated glare until he conceded.

"It is agreed." He reluctantly declared. "Inform your warriors of the plan," Crispin ordered. "And get some rest. We're going to need it."

The contentious strategy meeting was finally over and the leaders were wearily trickling out of the war tent. Salome spotted Jinn across the room and his smile made her heart leap. She would never grow tired of how he looked at her. He made her feel like she was more stunning than all the twinkling stars in the night sky. His attention was stolen when Crispin engaged him in conversation.

She noticed Adonijah and Leoti on the other side of the table, whispering back and forth. Salome figured Adonijah's instinct to protect Leoti was in full swing and from what she knew about Leoti, he didn't stand a chance at talking her out of joining the assassination mission. They really were a great match.

As she was about to make her way to Jinn and her brother to join in on their conversation, she felt a calloused hand grab her bicep and yank her back.

"If you harm Niabi," Pash whispered gruffly against her ear, "you will answer to me."

Salome attempted to pull her arm from his iron grip but failed. She glanced around the room, but most of the leaders had already left or were on their way out, and Jinn and Crispin were lost in their exchange.

"Let go of me," she hissed.

"Niabi means everything to me," Pash's tone was wild, and she knew there would be no reasoning with him. She didn't want to harm him and risk jeopardizing her fragile alliance with her sister, so she kept calm and attempted once more to wiggle free of his grasp. "If you betray her, no man, woman, or deity will keep me from driving my knife straight through your heart."

Suddenly, Pash's hold on her was broken and he was thrown across the room. A loud clanging sounded through the tent as Pash fell to the fur-lined ground, pulling the map and all the figurines off the table. Crispin, Adonijah, and Leoti immediately turned to see what was going on, and some of the leaders that had left the tent reentered to see what was happening.

Jinn stood between Salome and the commander and glared at Pash viciously. Fire raged in Jinn's eyes as he growled, "Touch my wife again, and I'll gut you."

"Wife?" Crispin asked, surprised. His gaze bounced between her and Jinn. "Salome, is that true?"

The night before the Battle of Oakenshire, Harbona answered his bedroom door groggily to find Salome and Jinn. When they explained why they had disturbed his sleep, he happily waved them into his chambers. On his balcony, facing the Ignacia Sea, Harbona led the couple in their vows and bound their hands with the same rope Oifa and Hanzo had been married with.

Gazing into one another's eyes, Salome and Jinn promised themselves to one another. The moonlight lit the prince's face perfectly, and she knew, this would be an image she would never forget. A secret marriage – a secret they could share for the rest of their days.

When their lips met, something deep within her hummed and she realized her magical bond with Jinn had grown more powerful. Married magic wielders. Their connection would be deeper, stronger, clearer.

Jinn smiled against her lips. "My wife," he whispered, and she felt whole.

They spent the rest of the evening before battle together, cuddled in bed. Jinn laid on his side and stroked her hair as she ran her fingers up and down his tattooed arm and chest. They didn't get much sleep, but they laughed, cried, and shared their dreams and fears with each other until it was time to report for duty. Jinn kissed her one last time before he cloaked himself and slipped out of her room, no one the wiser.

"Salome?" Crispin's voice sliced through her memories, bringing her back to the tent full of prying eyes.

Looking up at Jinn, his face filled with apology for spilling their secret, she smiled, slipping her hand into his. "Yes," she nodded, "I'm his wife."

Stunned congratulations flooded in as their friends surrounded them, embracing them.

Adonijah helped Pash up off the ground and whispered something harshly in his ear. Pash stormed out of the tent, and Adonijah watched him leave before he turned his attention to Salome and Jinn. As he approached the newlyweds, eyes from around the room darted to them. It was no secret Adonijah and Salome had cared for one another, some thought they might eventually get married, but when Adonijah finally reached the couple, he smiled and issued his congratulations.

With a cheer, and Oifa calling for a celebration, wine was brought in, and a toast was given to bless the union between Jinn and Salome. Jinn assured them they would have a royal wedding in due time, and they were all invited to share in the revelry.

As Salome sipped on her glass of wine, a quiet sadness filled her heart as she looked around at the wondrous faces filling the tent. She wasn't naive enough to believe they would all be attending her wedding, not because they didn't want to, but because some of them wouldn't survive tomorrow's war. She used to imagine that Zophar would walk her down the aisle, that Rosalina would style her hair just right for the occasion, that her grandmother, Nym, would be there to share a piece of marital wisdom before being whisked away to the bridal suite, but they were all gone, and after tomorrow, they might have company in the After.

"You're thinking too much again," Jinn's teasing voice pulled her from her thoughts and brought a smile to her face. She hadn't noticed when everyone trickled out of the tent, but she was happy it was just her and her husband now, grateful for a moment of privacy with him.

"A dangerous thing, I'm told," she teased. "Thinking too much."

"Better to think too much," he leaned close and whispered against her lips, "than not to think at all."

She closed the gap between them and kissed him. She rested her forehead against his. "Stay with me tonight?"

"There's nowhere I'd rather be," he smiled, tilting her chin up so he could meet her line of sight. "I love you."

"I love you, too," she said softly, running her fingers through his hair.

She wanted to tell him to survive, but there was no use in stating the obvious. They'd be separated in their missions tomorrow, but the end goal was the same. If fate was on their side, and the Almighty with them, they would see another day together.

What would she do if Jinn didn't survive? She hated the thought, but hated even more that Niabi's words kept flooding her mind. What would she do if Jinn was taken from her? She had demonstrated how far her wrath extended with Zophar's death. She couldn't imagine the destruction she would be capable of, if Jinn didn't make it out alive.

Forcing her fearful thoughts out of her mind, she and Jinn walked to her tent, and didn't come out again until he had to join the others headed for the ships. With one final kiss, she watched her husband, her love, disappear into the chilly night.

CHAPTER 54
CRISPIN

Crispin was up and dressed before the sun peeked the horizon. His boots crunched through the fresh snow as he made his way to the edge of camp, facing north, the direction he'd soon be leading an army to battle Gershom. The stillness of the Black Forest reminded him of the Tree House Forest, but instead of peace, he felt an emptiness that chilled him down to the bone. Or maybe, it was just the extreme drop in temperature that had him nervous and chattering his teeth. He had forgotten how cold Northwind got during the winter months and because it was the middle of the season, it was bitter and biting. He shimmied the white fur draped over his shoulders tighter around his body, attempting to, but failing, to harbor any little body heat he had.

The team launching the attack via sea and air left last night and he had to say goodbye to Rahab. He was uneasy. This was the first time they'd been apart since meeting a few months ago, and he wouldn't be there to have her back. But the truth was she probably didn't need his protection; she was a force to be reckoned with. He just wished he could be there to see Uri's face as she plunged her daggers deep into his scarred chest.

"Don't do anything stupid," Rahab had whispered against his lips a second before she kissed him. Her eyes were sharp, and her tone carried both warning and pleading and he knew exactly what she was trying to say without actually saying the words: I love you.

His nightmare had plagued him for weeks without fail. He felt Gershom's sword plunge into his chest; he saw the smug, victorious look on his face; he heard the screams of those he loved as he took his last breath. It ended the same way, every time, and he would wake up drenched in sweat.

"Nothing stupid." He smiled against her mouth. *"Just a little reckless."*

He slept with his arm stretched across her side of the bed, wishing she were next to him. It'd been twelve hours and he felt her absence terribly.

"You'll have to keep your wits about you today, Crispin."

Salome's voice spooked him. He whipped around and saw she was bundled up in her coat, her blue hood slipped over her braided curls, very much prepared for war.

"I've got my wits about me." He offered the best smile he could, and she shook her head, a teasing grin spreading across her face.

"Then how come I was able to sneak up on you so easily in a freshly laid batch of snow?"

"You were always the better hunter."

She pointed a finger at him, triumph in her voice, "Ah ha! You finally admit I'm the better hunter."

"Did you need me to admit it?" he chuckled, rolling his eyes. "You consistently brought food to the table when we lived in the Tree House Forest."

"It's nice when a man can be humble about his shortcomings," she giggled, elbowing his ribs playfully.

A comfortable silence fell between them as they stood side by side looking through the pine trees dusted with snow. On the other side of the ridge, the battlefield in front of the city of Northwind awaited them.

"Wife, huh?" He broke the silence and she side-eyed him.

"Are you terribly angry?"

"No." Crispin snaked his arm across her shoulders and pulled her close. "Just mad you thought of it first," he winked, drawing a laugh from her. Though it wasn't her infectious giggle, it was something and it counted.

"I won't be there to cover your ass, so make sure you watch your back," Salome cleared her throat, swiping a finger under her eye.

Squeezing her tight, he kissed her forehead and nodded. "Don't let your guard down around Niabi," he whispered. "She's not to be trusted."

"I'll be careful," she agreed, but something in her voice gave him trepidation.

"Your Majesties." Harbona bowed at the hip and when he straightened, there was a warm, familiar smile on his face. When his aura was restored, it rejuvenated his weathered appearance to smooth, youthful skin, and Crispin was still getting used to seeing him in his true Ethereal form. "The men and women are assembled and are ready to go when you command."

"And the ships?" Crispin asked.

"Leoti warged this morning and said they have set their course for the harbor."

"Good." He turned and gave his sister one more hug. "Be quick. Be safe. Come back to me in one piece."

Salome nodded, her smooth skin rubbing against his short beard. "Don't do anything I wouldn't do."

Reluctantly, he pulled back to get one more look at her. He prayed this wasn't the last time they would see each other, but before she could see any kind of crack in his facade, he motioned for her to join her small team back at camp. They wouldn't be traveling together to Northwind. She, Niabi, Leoti, and Thrice would cut east toward the coast to find the tunnel entrance into the keep. If they were successful in assassinating Gershom and Vilora, the battle wouldn't last long. What they needed was time, and a good distraction at the main gate. He would give them that and hopefully his tricks and strategy would pay off in the end.

~

CRISPIN, alongside Heru and the Numbio, Hanzo, Oifa, and the united Mountain Men, Rayma and her team of healers, and Harbona, made their way through the Black Forest. Once they breached the perimeter, the White City was within sight and it stole the prince's breath. The white spires of the White Keep built on a hill in the center of the city captured his gaze as they stretched toward the heavens. The tears welling up in Crispin's eyes could have been from the blistering cold wind that whipped around him the second he left the pines trees' protection, or it could have been spurred by the fact he'd finally made it home.

Twelve years. Twelve very long years. The last male heir of Issachar had finally come home.

"It is quite impressive." Heru trotted up to Crispin, enthralled by the sight.

"I dare say, Numbio is far more impressive." Crispin quickly wiped the tear from his cheek before his friend could notice.

"Maybe so," Heru grinned, "but you have snow."

"Is it your first-time experiencing snow?" he asked, grateful for the lighthearted conversation. Heru was good at lifting his spirits when he felt the looming shadow of despair creep over him.

"Yes, and I love it." The Numbio nodded, dragging a hand down his black beard. "But I do not believe Oifa likes it."

Both of them risked a quick glance behind them to catch a glimpse of Oifa, who appeared even more prickly than normal, flipping her lavender locks behind her shoulders.

"I don't know what would make that woman happy," Heru chuckled. They turned around before the Stormcrag noticed them staring.

"I imagine killing a few dozen enemy soldiers would put a smile on her face." Crispin laughed, but the joviality was short lived when alarm bells tolled alerting the citizens of Northwind of their presence.

The main gate was sealed shut as archers and soldiers scurried back and forth on top of the white stone wall. It glistened as the sun continued to rise high above them and appeared even more brilliant against the snow. But soon, that pristine white snow would be stained red with blood. Crispin wasn't naive to believe anything different. It would be a hard battle to win, especially since the Northmen knew how to defend their walls, but with Niabi and Pash's insight into the tactics of their military, he hoped it would give them the slight advantage they needed to come out victorious.

The night before, Cato and a small group of Mountain Men sneaked through the forest to head to the city wall. Their mission was dangerous but if done right, they'd force the Northmen to come out and face their army on level ground. Cato was instructed to take his team and tunnel underneath the main gate. Once they reached the entrance to the city, they were to put the explosives that Phex had engineered there, and once they were free from the mine, they were to detonate the explosives. If everything went according to plan, the explosion would splinter the gate, giving them a way inside and past the stone walls.

Niabi and Pash assured the leaders when they formulated these plans, that no citizens lived at the front end of the city and that the explosion would only tear down one of the military's garrisons.

As long as Crispin and his company kept the soldiers at the main gate distracted, they wouldn't notice what would truly bring their city to its knees.

Lined up on the battlefield, a hundred yards from the main gate, Crispin kicked at Freya's sides beckoning her forward. With the other leaders following up behind him flying their banners, Crispin rode as close as he dared before yelling up at the gatekeepers, not missing the hundreds of archers with their bows nocked and ready to strike staring down at him.

"I am Crispin, son of Issachar, and heir to the White Throne. Lay down your weapons or die by mine."

"Archers ready!" The commander atop the wall commanded and the bowman held their weapons taut. "Take aim!"

"Fall back," Crispin ordered, pulling Freya's reins and galloping back to his troops. "Prepare for battle!"

Hanzo and his archers readied their arrows in response to the hailstorm the Northmen unleashed, as Crispin retreated to a safe position. A smile snaked across Hanzo's face. "Let's give them our answer!" He sliced his hand through the air, "Fire!"

The marksmen let loose their arrows. While the Northmen's arrows had riddled the battlefield, the Stormcrag and Krazaks were known for their long-distance range, and easily found their targets along the stone walls.

Crispin bobbed his head at Heru and Oifa, signaling them to prepare for a ground assault. The Numbio lifted their enormous shields and as a unit began the steady trek forward, covering the Stormcrags and Krazak warriors pushing a battering ram. Hanzo and his archers fired away behind them. While camped in the Black Forest, they had used the resources provided by their allies to construct several siege towers, ladders, and ballistae. Although Crispin hated seeing his kingdom's walls damaged, he intended to use every piece of equipment they had to bring his enemies to their knees.

Hanzo had three ballistae at his disposal and had his most accurate marksmen launch enormous arrows afire at the men lining the city walls.

The stone walls held firm, but with the barrage of their persistent assault, cracks and small openings began to snake across the city's facade. Little by little, they laid siege to the White City and though the Northmen shot arrows at them, they pushed their way to the main gate and slammed their battering ram against the wood, rattling it. The Numbio held their shields in place, protecting the soldiers operating the ram, but the gate was solid and wasn't showing any signs of breakage.

Crispin whispered his prayers under his breath, as he hoped Cato and his crew had made their way underneath the gate and planted their explosives. Phex had been specific in his instructions on how to handle them and set them off. Cato nodded in understanding during the exchange, but Crispin had spent some time with the Stormcrag and knew he wasn't the fastest learner. Hopefully, they hadn't run into any problems, or worse, blow themselves up in the process. Seraphina would never forgive him, if Cato's blood was on his hands.

It wasn't long before the fresh batch of snow that glistened that morning was nothing more than slosh and mud. Crispin couldn't do anything but watch as the Northerners threw stones and boiling water down from their walls and murder holes at the soldiers doing their best to break down the main gate. Crispin knew if Cato and his team weren't successful, his army would have to find another way to take the city, hence the battering ram, but the bloodcurdling screams of his allies echoed across the battlefield, tearing his heart to pieces.

Crispin turned to Harbona. "Any word from Cato?"

Harbona shook his head. "We are waiting for his signal."

"Signal them to fall back," Crispin instructed the soldier standing next to him with a horn.

Without hestitation, the man blew the prince's command. Oifa whipped around, glaring at Crispin. Retreating wasn't in her nature, but if she didn't obey, she and her soldiers might not survive the assault from above. Crispin narrowed his eyes and told the soldier to repeat the signal. The soldier blew his horn and finally, albeit reluctantly, Oifa echoed Crispin's instructions and she and her warriors pulled the battering ram back, the Numbio shielding them as they retreated.

The Northmen let out a cry of victory, having fended off the battering ram. Arrows flitted through the sky in both directions, killing soldiers on the wall and field.

This was going to be a bloodbath. Gershom might not have had time to get reinforcements, but in truth, he didn't need the help. He had a large army at his disposal and the pirates of Pulau guarding his harbor. Perhaps, it was unwise to attack in the winter, but it was far too late to turn back now.

CHAPTER 55
SALOME

It took Salome, Niabi, Leoti, and Thrice about an hour to trek through the snow until they arrived at a large tree that looked completely ordinary. But this tree was actually the entrance to the tunnels under Northwind and led directly to the White Keep. Niabi circled the trunk until she found the spot she was looking for and pressed her hand against it. A section of the tree slid open, allowing them to descend a set of creaky wooden steps. She motioned her hand toward the tunnel.

"This is our way in," Niabi stated.

Salome flashed back to the night Zophar helped her and Crispin escape through the tunnels. They'd come out through a tree, but she hadn't thought about it in years. She ran her fingers across the bark and knew it was the same one from her childhood.

Zophar's smiling face consumed her thoughts; tears welled up in her eyes. She wished he could be here. If she hadn't put him in jeopardy – if she hadn't failed to save him –

"You alright?" Leoti's voice sliced through her masachistic thoughts, and she bobbed her head.

"You've been here before," Niabi's eyes narrowed. It was unnerving that she was so incredibly observant.

"It's how Crispin and I escaped you all those years ago," Salome confessed, seeing no harm in admitting the truth.

Niabi didn't say anything in response, her face stone-cold and neutral. She waved for them to follow her and for a split second, Salome hesitated. What if this was a trap? Salome wanted to believe her sister would hold up her end of their bargain, but there was always a chance she would betray her when, and if, the right opportunity presented itself. Maybe this was a huge mistake, and she should have listened to Crispin after all.

Leoti pressed her hand to Salome's shoulder. "If you've changed your mind, say the word and I'll get you out of here."

"What do you mean?" Salome turned to look at her and the Andrago shrugged her shoulders and flashed a sheepish smile.

"Adonijah made me promise I'd watch over you. Said he swore an oath to protect you and didn't want to fail you."

Salome let out a breath. That was typical Adonijah behavior. Always looking out for those he cared about. But she'd come too far to turn back now. Their friends, her brother, her betrothed – they were all counting on her to cut off the head of the snake and end the war before it truly had a chance to begin.

"No," she shook her head. "We have to go."

Although she looked as if she had something to say, Leoti conceded and motioned with her head toward the tunnel that Niabi and Thrice had already gone into.

Salome slipped inside the tree and followed the steps down, down, down into the darkness. It was cold and the only source of light was the torch that Thrice held. Niabi had explained beforehand that the tunnels had been dug out hundreds of years ago, but that over time, most Northerners had forgotten all about them. As children, Niabi and Lykos would go exploring and found their way through the ancient passageways. Built into the earth, their ancestors had fortified the tunnels with the same white stones they used to build the White City.

Silently, the four of them walked through the cobweb-filled hallways. They passed a rickety ladder and Niabi commented that they had reached the city wall. Immediately, Salome realized where that particular ladder led. The small house on the southeast side of the city that Zophar had taken them to, the hole in the floor – it was directly above her. Twelve years ago, that little house had been part of her salvation. It was all coming back to her, waves of emotions flooded her, but she pushed it to the back of her mind. Distraction would get her killed. It was a lesson Zophar had taught them in the Tree House Forest.

"Focus on your goal," Zophar would say, "Distractions will get you killed."

After another thirty minutes of walking in complete silence, Niabi stopped and turned to look at her.

"When we push through this wall," she threw her thumb over her shoulder at the dead end, "we will be inside the White Keep. Stay close to me and don't make a sound."

Nerves bubbled within her, but she steadied her breathing and nodded in agreement.

Thrice put out the torch and pushed the wall open. Light beamed into the slit as the fake door slid. Salome was the last one to slip inside the White Keep and when she did, she couldn't breathe. It had been twelve years since she'd wandered the white halls. Glancing down at the white marble floors, she could see her reflection and remembered the last time she'd done so, she was staring back at her five-year-old self.

She'd come home.

She'd come home as a warrior.

She'd come home as the Hunter.

Niabi made a sharp sound, drawing Salome's attention. With a quick nod, the four of them made their way down the corridor. There was a lot of commotion in the castle as well as the city around them. When they came upon the hallway that had windows flanking either side, one facing the Ignacia Sea, the other facing the

Taybourne Mountains and the main gate, Salome stopped and glanced both ways. To her left, her brother's battlefield. To her right, Jinn at sea. She said a quick prayer before catching up with the others on the other side of the bridge.

As they approached one of the main courtyards that led to the throne room, Niabi stopped and looked around, a wariness in her green eyes.

"What is it?" Salome stood next to her and whispered.

"There aren't any soldiers posted here." The Green-Eyed Raven met her gaze.

Salome's stomach churned, an unease sinking deep into her bones.

"Where are they?" Leoti asked, her hand tickling the hilt of her sword.

Thrice turned in a complete circle, even leaning forward to look up at the second floor balcony but shook his head when he came up empty. "I don't like this."

Commotion coming from down the hall echoed their way and Thrice hissed for them to hide behind the columns positioned around the courtyard. As Salome pressed her back against a marble column, she sucked in a breath to keep quiet. The heavy footsteps of soldiers thundered through the space and she could hear the battle raging around them from both the main gate and the sea. They needed to find Gershom and they needed to do it fast, if they wanted to spare their friends.

A group of fifteen foot soldiers marched down the corridor, their leader waving them forward.

Niabi quietly unsheathed her daggers from her sleeves and nodded for Salome to arm herself. She pulled her Qata Vishna blades from the holsters on her back while Leoti and Thrice both readied themselves with their swords.

Once the soldiers were in the middle of the courtyard and within striking distance, the four of them jumped out of their hiding places and launched their speedy assault.

The soldiers didn't stand a chance as the lethal warriors sliced through them before they were able to react. In the midst of the chaos, Thrice refrained from killing one, forcing the soldier to his knees and poking a knife to his throat. Pulling his head back with a fist-full of the guard's hair, Niabi stood in front of the patrolman, her hands clasped behind her back.

"Where is Gershom?" Niabi asked, a hardness in her features.

The soldier's eyes shifted amongst them, trepidation in his gaze.

Niabi snapped her fingers in his face, motioning for him to focus on her. "I will only ask once more." Flames licked up her left hand, drawing his attention and several whimpers. "Where is Gershom?"

"The king led his troops to the battlefield at the main gate," he answered, sweat dripping down his brow.

Salome and Niabi exchanged a disappointed look. They sneaked into the White Keep to assassinate Gershom. What they hadn't planned for was Gershom having the balls to lead his army into battle and face Crispin head on.

"Please," the soldier begged, tears welling in his eyes. "I don't want to die. I have a family, please."

Thrice looked eager to slit the soldier's throat, but Salome was determined not to let that happen. Before she had a chance to tell the former Shadow to stand down, Niabi extinguished her hand and waved Thrice down.

Crouching down in front of the guard, Niabi tipped his chin up and glared at him. "Tell me where I can find the witch."

If he was fearful before, he was downright horrified now. He began to tremble, but Niabi stroked a hand down his face, soothing him. "What's your name?"

"T-T-Tobias, my lady," he stuttered.

"Tobias," she repeated so gently it even calmed Salome's nerves. "I need to find Vilora. Tell me where she is so I can kill her."

Hope. There was a glimmer of hope in the soldier's face. He nodded, "She is in the East Wing."

"Thank you." She patted his cheek and pointed down the hallway. "Go home to your family, Tobias. Do not speak of what you have seen." He bobbed his head as he scurried down the corridor and out of sight.

"You realize he might alert the others of our presence." Thrice crossed his arms over his chest and leaned lazily against a column.

Niabi stood up slowly. "I am not here to kill my people, Thrice." She glanced at Salome and flashed a malicious grin. "But I am here to kill a witch."

Salome returned the smile and an energy pulsated through her body at the thought of striking down one of Gershom's allies.

It didn't take them long to make their way to the East Wing of the White Keep and there weren't many soldiers patrolling the halls, most were called to fight at the main gate.

Niabi told them they were headed to a lounge area where she used to greet her guests upon their arrival. That's where Vilora would most likely be, considering the fact she thought herself to be of queen status now that Niabi had been run out of her kingdom. Once the guards standing watch outside the doors leading into the chamber were taken out, the four of them marched inside, and were met by a lounging Vilora and a host of twenty soldiers. Any surprise in her face at their sudden and unexpected arrival was short-lived.

"I see you have returned, niece."

Salome didn't mean to flinch. Seeing the Old Witch of Endor after learning of her description and past life from her sister was one thing but hearing her speak was another thing entirely. Her voice sounded eerily like her grandmother, Nym's. Had she taken better care of herself, not spent so much of her life harboring her anger and letting her need for revenge ravage her body, Vilora might have managed to look as elegant as Nym. But instead, the hag was wrinkled and fed off the misery and spite of anyone who drew near.

Niabi took a step forward, not looking intimidated in the slightest by the witch reclining in the ornate chair that once belonged to her. "Only one of us is walking out those doors, Vilora."

"You fool," she cackled. "You should have disappeared when you had the chance." She slowly rose from her seat, exposing her bare feet with long, cracked toenails. "Now, you will die."

CHAPTER 56
RAHAB

Saying goodbye to Crispin had been the hardest thing Rahab had ever done, but she made sure to keep a brave face, even though her heart was pounding inside her chest.

Once the group, consisting of the pirates of the *Shadow of Death,* Prince Jinn, Kai, the Eastern army, Master Penn and her Keepers, and the Bellators, reached the fleet, they began their short sail to the shores of Northwind to face the Pulauan armada.

Rahab noticed Prince Jinn standing by the railing overlooking Northwind, and though she wasn't one for chit-chat, she felt compelled to talk to him. Maybe it was nerves, maybe it was because they were in love with siblings and would one day be family, but she walked up to him and plopped her elbows down on the railing next to him.

"Are you scared, princeling?"

Jinn glanced at her and smiled. "Not for myself."

She nodded in understanding. "It's funny, isn't it?"

"What is?"

"Love," she smirked. "I used to be afraid I wouldn't live through a battle. Now, I'm afraid of what life would look like if Crispin doesn't survive."

"I won't be able to help her if she needs me," Jinn's eyes were fastened on the White Keep. "That's what scares me more than anything."

"Then let us make quick work of the witch bitch and that bastard she serves." She uncorked her flask and took a shot of rum before passing it to the prince.

Jinn smiled, the corners of his eyes crinkling, as he took a shot. "You will make a fine queen, my lady."

"Every lion needs his lioness," she slipped the flask back into her pant pocket.

"We are approaching where the fleet should be." Kai stomped toward them.

They glanced out into the mist, but the fog was so thick, they couldn't see anything in the open water. Rahab didn't like it.

"Maybe the pirates abandoned the city?" Kai presumed, but Rahab knew Uri better than that.

"No," she shook her head. "They're here. We just haven't found them yet -"

"Look out!" A soldier bellowed from the crow's nest, but it was too late to avoid the crash.

Out of the mist, the Leviathan, fashioned with a metal bowsprit, speared into the hull of the ship Rahab was on, splitting the ship in half, the splintering wood echoing throughout the harbor. Soldiers jumped out of the way and Rahab leapt out of the direct path of the ship, but ended up falling into the freezing Ignacia Sea with hundreds of soldiers. She surfaced and waded, looking all around for Jinn, but the prince was nowhere to be found.

The men and women who weren't able to avoid the blow from the Pulauan ship, floated in the blood darkened waters.

Once more, she tried to find Jinn, but when she realized there was a good chance the prince was dead, her heart sank. Not only would Salome be devastated, but Rahab had lost her Cloaker and her best chance at sneaking up on the Shadow Witch.

"Damn it!" She slapped the water.

Screams from the other ships in Rahab's fleet sounded, drawing her attention. Pulauan pirates were swinging from their ships and boarding the rebel fleet. Metal clashed against metal, bodies fell into the sea, splashing all around her and those who had survived the first ship attack.

Kayven and Abba led the Bellators into the sky and they dodged the explosives and battled the shadows Nezreen threw their way. When Rahab noticed which ship the shadows were coming from, she spotted Nezreen and knew if she could cut off the head of the snake, then they might be able to salvage this battle.

Swimming toward the Leviathan, she grabbed her knives and stabbed them into the hull of the ship, making her way up the side. It was grueling and tiring and by the time she made it to the deck, she was shivering and exhausted. Pure adrenaline was the only thing that kept her going. She kept seeing Crispin's face flash in her head, she felt his lips pressed against hers, and his hands roaming her body. She would make it back to him, if it was the last thing she did.

A loud explosion knocked her off her feet. When she pulled herself up to the railing, she was relieved to see Phex's trinkets were working and giving the rebels a fighting chance. The auburn-haired pirate had his reefer in his mouth and he was shouting commands for the Eastern soldiers to follow. As a unit, they launched wave after wave of concentrated explosives and managed to poke enough holes into one of the smaller ships that it began to sink, causing the pirates to abandon ship.

Hope. There was still hope.

She dragged herself to her feet, dripping along the deck as she sneaked behind unsuspecting pirates and slit their throats or stabbed them in the back. Slowly, and stealthily, she made her way from the quarterdeck to the staircase leading up to the sterncastle where Nezreen was launching her shadow assault against the Bellators.

Rahab couldn't do anything but watch as Nezreen speared her shadows as weapons. One sliced into a Bellator's chest and shredded his white wings. He plunged into the sea, dead before he hit the water. She slammed a hand over her mouth, stifling her horrified gasp. Though they'd lost one of their elite warriors,

Kayven and Abba continued to lead their men and fight hard to defend the mortals they'd come to care for. Launching another round of attacks, Nezreen was fully engaged and distracted by them. It was now or never.

She sprinted up the steps, weapons drawn, ready to cut the witch down, mentally prepared for the possibility it might end up being a suicide mission, but before she could get within reach, a large fist collided with her cheek, knocking her off her feet. She hit the deck so hard her weapons flew out of her hands. Her vision was blurred, and her ears were ringing. Planting her palms on the floor and pushing herself up onto her knees, she blinked several times hoping her hazy vision would clear up before whoever hit her finished her off.

Heavy steps approached her as she crawled away, but her retreat was short-lived as she backed up into the wall, and two scuffed leather boots stopped in front of her. She squinted as she looked up and her heart sank.

"Well, well, well," Uri the Pirate King bared his teeth. "It looks like you've lost your weapons."

She spat at him. "Go to hell."

"I was hoping to see you again." He cocked his head to the side. "The one who escaped me."

Rahab found it hard to breathe. All this time, she thought he'd forgotten all about her, but he remembered her as the one who got away. She'd dyed her hair and changed her name. The girl she used to be was dead.

"If you know who I am," though she was terrified, she willed the fear from her face, "then why didn't you say something at The Sisters?"

"You've done a good job of disguising yourself, little one, but I never forget a face. Especially the face of the bitch that gave me this." He pointed to the scar she'd left across his face. "It took me a week to place you, but once I did, I knew I'd see you again. You wouldn't be able to stay away."

"Enough talking," she snarled, defiant until the end. "Slit my throat and be done with it."

"Oh, I will," he flashed a malicious grin. "But first, I think I'll take my time with you since I was robbed of that privilege years ago."

"Touch me and I'll -"

"You'll what?" Uri hissed, taking his blade and slicing her thigh, drawing blood and a muffled scream from her lips. "You have no weapons and no one here to save you." He knelt before her, grabbing her neck and squeezing, forcing her to meet his crazed eyes.

Rahab slid her hand into her pant pocket and slipped her brass knuckles on. Gasping for air as the pirate king strangled her, she used the little bit of strength she had left to punch him in the ribs. Uri roared, releasing her from his grasp. He back-handed her and she could taste the iron in the blood he'd summoned. His boot stomped down on her injured leg and even though she tried to fight it, when he ground his toe in her wound, she screamed.

Crispin's face flashed in her head, a cruel reminder of everything she was about to lose. Death had come for her before, and she defied her. Perhaps her stolen time had finally run its course, but if she was to die, she wouldn't go out sniveling in the corner like prey. She'd bare her claws and show her fangs; she wouldn't be the only one to take their last breath that day: Uri would be gutted right alongside her.

As he lowered his face toward her, a smug grin snaked across his face. Uri pressed his knee into her injured thigh. She bit her lip, refusing to give him the satisfaction of prying another howl from her.

"Yield," he whispered. "And I will make your death a quick one."

"I yield to no one."

Without hesitation, Uri slowly slid his blade down her arm, leaving a trail of blood from the tip of her shoulder down to her wrist.

Sweat dripped from her hairline, but she still refused to yield. She would rather die, than bend the knee to this monster.

"So brave," Uri cooed. "But even the brave die, deary." His eyes shifted from her gaze to her other arm. "Should I do the other one or do you yield?"

The thought of feeling his dagger slice through her skin again, made her heart tremble. She quickly glanced around to see if any of her friends were coming to rescue her, but she saw no one, and Uri laughed knowing all too well who she was looking for.

"You're all alone," he purred, a look of smug satisfaction graced his scarred face. "Your friends will not come for you. They will die here, just like you."

"She's not alone."

Rahab and Uri's focus darted toward the steps. Captain Haldane made his way up, blood streaked across his rugged face, cutlass drawn, and revenge rooted in his gaze.

"Ahhh," Uri stood up, relieving Rahab of his weight on her thigh. "The fortune teller's husband. "He straightened his shoulders to mirror Haldane's stance. "You know, I can still hear her screams. I remember the sweet taste of her blood as she agonized for hours."

"Haldane, go!" Rahab ordered through gritted teeth, but the captain refused to listen.

"I plan to kill you." Haldane said plainly. "And when I do, I'll cut you limb from limb and feed what's left of you to the sharks."

The pirate king tapped his cutlasses together, clanging the metal loudly, and stomped toward him. "I'd like to see you try."

As if someone had urged them to begin, the two pirates launched themselves at each other. She knew Haldane was skilled with his cutlass, but Uri was ruthless and significantly bigger than her friend. If she didn't get to her feet to help him, she was afraid Haldane wouldn't be a match for the Pirate King.

CHAPTER 57
CRISPIN

"Get those siege towers moving!" Crispin motioned to Oifa and Heru. "Maintain a distance from the main gate, just in case Cato pulls through."

Heru darted to the tower to the left and Oifa sprinted to the right one. Shouting their commands, the leaders had the two siege towers they'd constructed in the Black Forest, pushed toward the wall. There was a high probability that the Northmen would set the towers ablaze, but with Phex's input, they had put as much metal around the front of the tower as possible. It made the tower much heavier, but it gave them a fighting chance at getting to the wall where they could infiltrate the city wall.

Crispin was itching to jump into the fray, but he knew his orders, and his mission was to lead the ground assault, once they got the main gate open or destroyed. He was restless, he didn't like the fact men and women were dying and he wasn't there to help them.

"Patience," Harbona whispered, probably knowing what was flooding Crispin's mind.

"They're dying out there." He raked a hand through his hair, fighting to maintain composure in front of the men and women that were in his charge.

"It's war, my Prince. Lives are lost, but if you do not hold fast to the plan you agreed to, you will lead your men to slaughter."

Crispin knew Harbona was giving him sound advice, but it didn't relieve the guilt in his heart. If Cato didn't give them the signal soon, he was going to have to regroup on the fly and aid his allies one way or another. He paced up and down the line, hands clasped behind his back.

Heru's tower made it to the wall first. He dropped the top so his men could fight the Northerners on the wall. Oifa's tower was struck with several flaming arrows and caught fire. Crispin could hear Oifa shouting orders for the men to put out the fire, knowing they were so close to laying siege to the wall, but they weren't quick enough to extinguish the flames and she ordered the soldiers to retreat. Crispin knew that order must have been difficult for her, since retreating went against everything she believed in, but with so many lives in her hands, she had made the right decision. They sprinted back from the wall, some falling dead with arrows lodged in their backs. But once they were out of firing range, Oifa nabbed some water from a sheepskin Crispin handed her. She had dirt and blood smeared across her face and arms and she smelled like sulphur.

"Stay here," Crispin met her furious gaze. "I'll lead the next wave with the battering ram. With Heru on the wall -"

Oifa pointed a tattooed finger in his face, her eyes blazing. "The only way I won't be fighting is if I'm dead and gone. Is that clear?"

"You should rest -"

She pounded on her chest and grunted. "I will rest when the battle is won. Now get out of my way, I have Northerners to kill."

Crispin grabbed her wrist, "Wait!"

Oifa swung around, looking like she was going to punch him, but he held up a hand and pointed to the tree line. "It's the signal. Cato's ready."

She narrowed her eyes at him, ripping her arm from his grasp. "You're lucky. Men have lost hands for less."

"Forgive me," he lifted his hands in surrender. "Once the gate explodes, we will hit them fast and hit them hard. Are you with me?"

Nodding, Oifa smiled and tapped her axe. "Aye."

Crispin exhaled in relief. The signal had been given and now they had to wait for the explosion to take place. Heru had kept his men clear of the main gate and they fought valiantly atop the wall. They'd slaughtered the archers, giving them a fighting chance at getting close to the city once the gate was destroyed.

And then it happened. A thunderous boom rattled the ground beneath them and tore through the main gate, splintering the wooden doors, and flung sections of the stone wall, as if it weighed nothing. When the dust settled, Crispin saw a gaping hole for him and his men to run into the city.

The horn blew a different signal, spurring the foot soldiers to unsheathe their weapons, and with Crispin and Oifa leading, they stormed the city.

The Northerners didn't waste any time. Their soldiers bolted through the billowing smoke and charged at Crispin and his army. Now, he would get his wish to be in the thick of battle, winning back his homeland, and protecting his friends fighting by his side.

As they approached the stampeding soldiers, Crispin glanced up and caught sight of Heru and the Numbio holding their ground on top of the wall. Finally, the soldiers converged in a great crash of metal on metal. Blood sloshed in the muddied snow. Men lost their footing and slipped. Agonizing screams and final breaths flitted around Crispin. It was chaos. Adrenaline coursed through his body, spurring him to fight any enemy soldier that crossed his path. A part of him wished he didn't have to strike down his countrymen, didn't have to claim so many lives in order to take back his father's throne, but when it came down to it, it was him or them, and he was determined to walk away from the battlefield alive.

Crossbowmen let their arrows fly, downing men all around Crispin. He attempted to side-step one of his attackers, but in doing so, his enemy took an arrow to the back and fell on top of Crispin. The prince pushed the dead soldier off of him, but more fighters, both friend and foe, fell down dead or slipped in the slosh of snow and blood. Before he knew it, he was buried beneath a stack of bodies and had to claw his way out.

He thrashed through the piles of bodies, trying to get out from underneath those trampling him, because he couldn't catch his breath. He had no room to move. Suffocating. He was suffocating underneath dozens of fallen soldiers and the thought that this was how he was going to die, awakened his fight. He'd felt this sensation of drowning before when he shoved Rahab out of Kubantu's grasp and was dragged beneath the waves of the Obsidian Sea. She had saved him and breathed life back into him, but this time, he would have to save himself, if he wanted to see her again.

Slowly but methodically, he wiggled free from the arms and legs entangling him and broke through to the surface. His face was kissed by the sun and chilly air filled his lungs. He never felt more alive.

"Crispin!" Oifa shouted, pushing bodies to the side. She extended her hand and pulled him out. "You're alive!"

Crispin embraced her. Even though the battle was raging all around them, he couldn't help thanking the stubborn Stormcrag for rescuing him.

"Gershom has been spotted," Oifa pulled back and grabbed Crispin's shoulders. "He is here with the troops. If we can get to him, we can end this!"

Crispin glanced in the direction she pointed and just like in his nightmares, he saw The Bear swinging his sword, slicing down any and all in his path. He was tall with broad shoulders and looked every bit as menacing in reality, as he did when he visited Crispin in his sleep. But what was he doing on the battlefield? He was supposed to be in the White Keep, not leading his soldiers in battle. Salome was the one prophesied to kill Gershom, even Harbona had said so months ago in the Tree House Forest. But if he was down here and she was in the White Keep looking for him, this battle would be far from over.

"Let's go," Oifa persisted. "What are we waiting for?"

Crispin grabbed the hilt of his sword and took a step in Gershom's direction, but the sting of The Bear's blade and the crack of Crispin's ribcage echoed in his head, thwarting his attempts to fight him.

"I can't." Crispin shook his head. "I can't fight him."

"What do you mean?" Oifa looked baffled and glared at him with disdain. "He's right there! We could end this war right now."

"Harbona told me if I fight him, I won't survive." Crispin hated to admit it aloud and hoped Oifa didn't think him to be a coward. "Salome is the only one who can kill him. It's the prophecy."

At that, Oifa's face softened, and she nodded which shocked him. "Then we will find another way."

As Oifa glanced around, Crispin caught sight of Adonijah sprinting toward Gershom, longsword clutched in one hand and a dagger in the other. He looked like a man willing to lay down his life to settle a score.

"Damn it," Crispin hissed. He couldn't fight Gershom and live, but he couldn't watch Adonijah duel him and meet the end of The Bear's blade. He was going to have to help him.

"Push our men forward," Crispin pointed at the section of wall that had exploded. "I'll meet you there." With a nod from Oifa, Crispin jogged across the battlefield, cutting enemy soldiers down, and praying he wouldn't be too late to save his friend.

CHAPTER 58

NIABI

Vilora's short stature and her non-threatening stance didn't tame the adrenaline pulsing through Niabi's veins. She knew the power her aunt harnessed, but she also knew the same power hummed through her. She would destroy that deceitful witch with the very magic she unwittingly stole from her all those years ago, in the cabin that appeared out of nowhere. She'd been a fool for listening to Vilora. The witch had played on her fears and in allowing her emotions to control her, Niabi didn't decipher the witch's double-sided prophecy and paid a hefty price. Rollo deserved better. Dichali deserved better. She deserved better. And now, after all this time, looking into the face of the woman who had set her up for defeat and deceived her into believing she had an ally who understood her pain, she was itching to strike her down and tear her limb from limb.

With a snap of her fingers, Vilora unleashed the Shadows guarding her. They pointed their spears and swords at the four invaders, who had also unsheathed their weapons. They were clearly outnumbered, and Niabi knew some of the soldiers; she's sparred with a handful of them on a daily basis for years. They were skilled warriors and could generate quite a fight, but Niabi wasn't accustomed to losing and knew her sister wasn't either.

In the blink of an eye, the assault was launched. Niabi ignited her left arm and fired, roasting two Shadows. Their screams would undoubtedly haunt her nightmares, but she didn't give them a second glance as she whipped around, flying around the room like a twister of flames, slicing and stabbing anyone who crossed her path. She knew Salome, Thrice, and Leoti would handle the Shadows. Her eyes were fixed on her own prize: Vilora.

Vilora's glared at Niabi and smirked, both her hands ablaze. "Has my student come to play?"

"No," Niabi snarled. "I've come for your head."

"Then come and take it!" Vilora blasted two enormous fireballs at Niabi, but she tumbled away, dodging the attack.

Launching her own flamed attack at the witch, Vilora was forced to hide behind her chair, taking cover as best she could. Niabi was skilled with her blades, but the witch didn't know how to wield a sword. She relied heavily upon her magic, albeit strong magic, but that wouldn't stop Niabi from chopping her to pieces for her treachery.

Niabi integrated her magic along with sword play so she was confident in her abilities. Slamming her hand down on the tile, she zipped a blast of fire toward the chair Vilora was crouched behind and lit it up. The witch screamed as she scrambled from her hiding place, which was exactly what Niabi wanted her to do. With a quickness, Niabi sprinted toward her aunt, weapons drawn, ready to strike her down, but Vilora laughed and shot a blast of fire that nailed her square in the chest.

There was blood all over the white marble floor and the room smelled like death.

"You thought you could defeat me, Niabi?" Vilora's voice drew her distracted gaze. "You really thought you were stronger than the Old Witch of Endor?"

Niabi lifted herself up onto her elbows and stared up at Vilora. Her hands were cradling balls of fire and the smirk on the witch's face meant only one thing. She was aiming for the kill.

"Any last words, niece?"

But before Niabi could respond, Thrice sprinted toward the witch, his sword in hand, but at the sound of his rushed footsteps, Vilora turned one hand toward him and blasted an orb of fire into his chest, knocking him off his feet. Thrice screamed as his leathers ignited, but Leoti ran up quickly to help him.

Enraged, Niabi took advantage of Vilora's distraction and hopped up, landing on her feet. The witch spun around and placed her hand against Niabi's chest and issued her flames to consume her. Niabi grabbed Vilora's throat with her own flaming hand. "Have you forgotten, Vilora?" she hissed, relishing the fear in her aunt's eyes. "Fire doesn't burn fire." Niabi plunged her dagger into the old woman's chest.

Vilora gasped for air as Niabi released her, letting her crumble to the floor in a pool of her own blood. "I should have known you would be my undoing," she rasped, meeting Niabi's gaze one last time. "You are cursed. Anyone close to you ends up dead."

Those words stung Niabi more than she would ever admit. She didn't offer a response. She just stood over Vilora and watched as the life drained from her face. Her eyes were glossed over, and she stared blankly at the ceiling. Grabbing Thrice's longsword, she slammed it down across Vilora's neck, claiming the witch's head.

Thrice groaned, wrenching Niabi from her aunt's lifeless body. She slid over to him and grabbed his hand. Leoti had managed to put out the fire before it consumed him, but he was badly burned, and parts of his flesh were welded to the clothing that remained around his torso.

"He needs a healer," Leoti whispered as Thrice dipped in and out of consciousness. "There is nothing more I can do for him."

Salome knelt beside them, her eyes roving across his charred chest. She stared at Niabi and she shook her head. Niabi was all too aware of what that meant. Thrice wasn't going to make it. He was in bad shape. His death would be slow and painful and the thought that her friend, one of her most loyal protectors, wasn't going to make it out of the White Keep as a victor, soured her stomach.

Leoti's eyes bounced back and forth between the sisters, silently reading into their exchanged looks. "We can't leave him here to die," her voice cracked. "He needs a healer."

"He won't make it in time." Niabi spoke the truth, but it didn't sting less.

"We have to try to save him," Leoti was indignant. "We need to get him to one of the medical bays. I can make a salve that will help him until we can get him to a healer."

Niabi wanted to put her foot down and remind her they had more important matters to tend to, especially with a war raging all around them, but when she heard Thrice hiss in pain, her heart shattered. She'd known him for years and he'd risked his life to help her escape the coup Gershom had ignited. She owed him.

Niabi glanced at them, gaging the interest in the new mission. "If we all carry him, we can get him to a medical bay."

Salome bobbed her head in agreement, sheathing her weapons, and grabbing one of his legs.

Together, the trio carried Thrice as quickly as they could down the twisting corridors. If there was a chance to save Thrice, they would do everything they could to do so.

When they finally reached the apothecary, Niabi and Salome hoisted Thrice's heavy body up onto a wooden table in the middle of the room. There were jars filled with liquids and creatures, even eyes and bones and teeth. Salome looked around the room with upmost horror, but Leoti weaved around the room as if it were a second home. She speedily examined the shelves, grabbing different glass containers to concoct the salve for Thrice's gooey chest.

"You'll have to hold him down." Leoti rolled her sleeves up and grabbed a glob of the balm, spreading it across her palms. "This will sting him at first and I don't want him to move."

Niabi pressed down on Thrice's shoulders and Salome put all her weight across his legs. With a quick nod of affirmation, Leoti started applying the salve, and just as she predicted, Thrice started jostling around. Even in his unconscious state, he fought them as if they were torturing him. He let out a scream and the three of them glanced at the entrance, hoping no one heard him.

Leoti grabbed a piece of cloth and stuffed it in his mouth. "I'm almost finished." She went back to slathering the salve across his chest and abdomen.

If he survived, he would have severe burn marks, but knowing Thrice, he'd probably give himself another nickname to gloat of his brush with Death.

Once Leoti was finished applying the balm, she wiped her hands clean before taking the cloth out of his mouth. He wasn't shaking or fighting them anymore, the worst of the sting over. Thrice laid so still Niabi feared he was dead, but the slight rise and fall of his chest gave her hope that her friend might make it.

"Now what?" Salome asked, leaning against a wall of shelving, pointing at the bag Niabi had stuffed Vilora's head in. "Gershom isn't in the White Keep. The witch is dead, but we still failed our mission."

Niabi rubbed the heels of her palms over her eyes. "Then we make our way to the battlefield."

"And what? Hope we spot him amongst thousands of soldiers?" Salome shook her head.

"We'll rest here for a little while." Niabi brushed hair out of Thrice's face. She didn't see his face often. Shadows always hid behind their masks, but once he abandoned the Shadows, he ditched the uniform. He was quite handsome with his dark locks and facial hair. She wished he would open his hazel eyes and promise he would be alright. She had lost so many friends and loved ones already. Did she really have to lose him too?

"And then?" Salome questioned, stealing her from her thoughts.

"Then we find Gershom, one way or another."

CHAPTER 59
ADONIJAH

The second Adonijah caught sight of his father across the battlefield, hacking his allies to pieces, he didn't hesitate to chase after him. Gershom was bold to leave the White Keep, but he had always been a vain man. Adonijah knew the only reason the old man was fighting amongst the troops was to establish his dominance and have his men spread tales of their victorious king. But Adonijah didn't particularly care why Gershom was fighting, he was just elated to set his eyes on him, after all these years of plotting. For it would be the last time he saw his father, his mother's murderer, whether he gutted Gershom or fell prey to his sword, it would be over one way or another.

Northern soldiers and Shadows blocked his path, and he was forced to battle several soldiers before he came within striking distance of Gershom. He clanged his blades together, making a loud noise, which captured his father's attention. Slowly, The Bear turned around, blood smeared across his face. His hair was the same, shaved on the sides with a chestnut bun streaked with white hair. He was missing an ear, which was surprising, but those eyes – no matter how desperately he tried, he couldn't forget how haunted and enraged Gershom's eyes were. The Bear flashed a menacing smile as Adonijah pointed his sword at him.

"Do you remember me?" Adonijah circled, keeping pace with Gershom as he moved, maintaining a safe distance between them.

Gershom cocked his head to the side, "Should I, boy?"

"I am Adonijah, son of Satara," Gershom's eyes widened as Adonijah continued, "and I'm here to kill you."

Gershom laughed. "After all these years, you've finally come home, my son."

Adonijah spat on the ground, taking his fighting stance. "I am not your son."

"Oh, but you are, Adonijah. My blood flows through your veins and whether you like it or not, you will always be mine." Gershom circled his sword around his hand, not looking remotely interested in a fight. "Lay down your weapons, Adonijah. Join me and I will make you my heir."

"If memory serves me correctly, you already have an heir."

Gershom barked a laugh. "Pash is nothing more than a disappointment. That's why I sent for you all those years ago. I was going to make you my heir and teach you everything you needed to know to one day take my place and rule in my stead. Your brother is useless to me. Has too much of his mother's southern blood in him to make him a well-suited successor. But *you*," Gershom took a step toward him. "You were special and I knew I'd finally gotten it right." He was now within striking distance, but something about the way he spoke and moved gave Adonijah pause from striking him down. "What happened to your mother was a pity. She wasn't supposed to get hurt."

As if snapping out from some hypnotic spell, Adonijah snarled and swung his sword at his father who blocked the blow. "But she did," Adonijah stilled, meeting Gershom's gaze. "And I've waited all these years to avenge her."

Gershom sighed. "Have it your way then."

Gershom pushed Adonijah back and whipped his longsword around, forcing Adonijah to be on the defensive. He blocked blow after hammering blow, until he tripped over a fallen soldier's leg and tumbled to the ground. Still fighting his father's barrage as he tried to scramble to his feet, he found himself in an extremely vulnerable position. Gershom kicked a batch of muddy snow at Adonijah, temporarily blinding him. It gave The Bear enough time to disarm his son and point the tip of his blade to Adonijah's chest, just above his heart.

"I would tell you to yield, but we both know I won't spare you," Gershom smirked.

"Then run me through," Adonijah spat viciously. "Do it!"

A wicked gleam flashed in Gershom's eyes as he thrust his sword forward. Only the tip broke through Adonijah's flesh before Gershom was tackled to the snow, dragging his weapon along with him.

Adonijah winced in pain as he put his hand to his wound. He pulled away and his hand was coated in blood. He glanced over at Gershom, searching for whoever pushed him in time to save him. His stomach dropped when he spotted Pash hopping up next to their father.

"You!" Gershom growled, grabbing his sword and rushing toward Pash. "I should have killed you years ago!"

Adonijah got up with every intention to help his brother, but Ophir suddenly stepped between them with a vicious wrinkle creasing his bald head.

"Frowning ages you, Uncle." Adonijah couldn't help himself and relished seeing Ophir's head redden in rage.

"I'll enjoy gutting you like a pig." Ophir swung his sword, initiating their duel.

Adonijah had to hand it to his uncle. Despite his age, he was still light on his feet. Harbona had warned him at the Hidden Tavern months ago, that he'd meet the Shadow who he had brawled with again. He just didn't expect the bald man he exchanged punches with would turn out to be his blood relative. But blood or not, Adonijah wouldn't lament striking him down.

Risking a quick glance at Pash battling with their father, Adonijah knew he would have to make quick work of Ophir, if he was going to help his brother take their father down. Adonijah and his uncle's swords clashed loudly, and Ophir grimaced at the contact. Sweat beaded around his head and his arms shook. Capitalizing on Ophir's rare show of fatigue, Adonijah used his sword to parry Ophir's away and rammed his shoulder into his uncle's chest, knocking the wind out of him. Ophir threw a punch, but Adonijah dodged it as he snatched his dagger from his belt and lodged it into the Shadow's chest.

A grunt escaped his uncle's lips as he sank to his knees. Adonijah grabbed the knife and began walking past Ophir, but his uncle grappled for the small blade in his boot, spurring Adonijah to slip behind him and with a swiftness, placed his hands on the man's head and snapped his neck, letting him fall to the bloodied snow in an odd position.

One down. One to go.

Adonijah rushed toward Pash, but fighting Ophir had not only delayed him, but distanced him from the fight. Pash and Gershom fought with fervor, anger, and a deep-rooted animosity that it was difficult to tell who the better swordsman was.

Pushing people out of his way, Adonijah stormed toward them, but when Gershom landed a well-timed blow to Pash's weapon and plunged his sword into Pash's chest, Adonijah's world slowed. Gershom's mouth moved, but he didn't hear what his last words to his brother were. Gershom retrieved his sword and marched toward the main gate, signaling his personal guards to surround him.

Adonijah sprinted to his brother and cradled his head. "Pash, I'm here. I'm here." Pash's hazy eyes met his and it was at that moment, Adonijah knew he wouldn't be able to save him.

"Tell Niabi, I love her." Pash strained to get that final message out as his breathing turned ragged. Adonijah wasn't an expert, but by the way he sounded, he was positive Pash's lung had collapsed and was slowly filling with blood.

"I'm sorry, Pash," Adonijah whimpered, tucking his head against his brother's. "I'm so sorry." But Pash didn't respond and Adonijah couldn't feel him moving, couldn't hear him breathing.

Reluctantly, he pulled back and saw Pash was gone. Overwhelmed with grief, Adonijah roared up into the sky, before turning his tear-stricken face toward the fleeing Gershom. Adonijah lowered his brother down and grabbed his sword. He was going to drive his blade straight through his father's back. He would make him suffer for what he'd done to Pash. He would -

Arms grabbed him from behind and without looking to see who it was, Adonijah swung his sword, barely missing Crispin's chest.

"Let him go!" Crispin shouted before pushing Adonijah out of the way of an incoming blow from a Northern soldier. Crispin stabbed the guard before turning back to him. "I need you to fight, Adonijah. Leave Gershom to Salome. If you go after him again, I can't follow."

Adonijah wanted to disobey, wanted to rebel, wanted to knock Crispin out of his path and charge after his father, but he knew the prophecy. He knew if anyone could kill Gershom, it was Salome. He had to trust her. Had to give her a chance to set things right. Him bolting after Gershom put him and Crispin in a precarious position, and they were going to have to fight together, if they were going to make it back to their allies. So Adonijah let his father go and allowed his grief and anger to fuel him, becoming a wrecking ball on the battlefield.

CHAPTER 60
RAHAB

Attempting to stand, Rahab felt the full extent of the wounds she'd sustained. Her thigh had a nasty gash across it and her pants were soaked in her blood. Her sleeve had been shredded and the long cut that ran the length of her left arm was leaving a puddle of blood next to her.

Haldane groaned when Uri sliced his inner thigh.

"Get up!" Rahab commanded herself.

Uri slashed Haldane's other leg, bringing the pirate captain to his knees.

She was about to watch her friend, her captain, be murdered. But something snapped inside of her, propelling her to pull herself to her feet, using the wooden railing as an anchor. Pure adrenaline and hatred fueled her, and like a caged animal that had been freed, Rahab ran toward Uri whose cutlass was pointed at Haldane's chest and jumped on his back. She didn't wait for the pirate king to react to her assault because if he got the drop on her, she and Haldane would both die. Wrapping her hands around Uri's head, she twisted with all her strength until she heard a loud snap. Then she and the pirate fell to the wooden floorboards.

She rolled onto her back in excruciating pain. She couldn't hold back the tears any longer as Haldane dragged himself over to her.

"He's dead." She breathed a sigh of relief when she saw the pirate king lying a foot away, eyes glossed over, neck twisted in an unnatural angle.

Haldane stroked her face, tears in his eyes. "Aye, lass. You saved my life."

"How disgustingly touching," Nezreen hissed. Her attention and shadows fully fixed on them. "You might have killed the king," the shadows twisted around their limbs, pinning them to the floor, "but you will not live to tell the tale."

Rahab fought against the shadowy bonds but to no avail. There was no breaking free from the blind witch's dark magic.

"Any last words, pet?" Nezreen waved her hand in the air, summoning one of her shadow tendrils to stroke Rahab's cheek like a passionate lover would.

Before Rahab could answer, several blades sliced through the air toward

Nezreen, but her shadows alerted her to the attack, and she ducked out of the way. Blinking twice, Rahab didn't understand where the knives had come from. No one else was on this level of the Leviathan. But it was then, Master Penn and Kai stepped out of thin air, weapons drawn and ready.

"Oh, it's you," Nezreen sounded bored. "I thought you would have crawled back to The Sisters like a whipped dog by now, Penn." She cocked her head to the side, her sightless gaze fixed on Kai. "And who is your friend?"

"Fight me, you bitch," Master Penn growled, baring her teeth at Nezreen.

The witch's shadows flared around her, all pointed at the ends like spears. "Gladly." With a wave of her hand, the shadow spears sliced down toward the women, forcing them to duck and dodge as they tried to get closer to the witch.

Rahab was wholly transfixed by the duel and how incredibly graceful Master Penn moved, not being struck once by Nezreen's shadowy attack. Kai was death itself, dancing around the ship, slicing pieces of shadow like she would a sea monster's tentacles. She was so distracted she didn't realize that Jinn was kneeling before her until he grabbed her and hoisted her up into his arms.

"We need to get you out of here," he whispered and tucked his arm underneath her knees.

"It's about damn time you showed up," she hissed with his movements.

"My apologies. Battle delayed me." Jinn flashed a wicked smile before he glanced at Haldane. "Captain, can you walk?"

Haldane nodded, pain rippling through his features, though he refused to acknowledge it. "Aye, I can walk."

"Seraphina and the Qata Vishna are waiting for you below. They will get you to safety and to a healer." Jinn started walking toward the steps but stopped when Kai screamed.

Nezreen cackled as she wrapped her shadow tentacles around Kai's body. She was squeezing her, cutting off her air. Kai's face was turning blue, and her weapons were on the floor, just out of her reach. Master Penn attempted to help the Ryoko Naga but in her moment of distraction, Nezreen struck. Pinning the Master of Keepers to the floor with her shadows, Nezreen flashed a malicious smile.

"Your fear is delicious," the witch cooed, breathing in as if she could indeed taste their fear.

"Help them," Rahab ordered Jinn.

"You've already lost a lot of blood, Rahab."

"Put me down and help them!" She punched his chest. "I swear I'll gut you the second I have the chance if you let them die."

Jinn gently placed her on the floor, eyes glued to hers. "Keep out of sight."

Nezreen stalked around the two women being strangled by her shadows and crowed, "I look forward to destroying The Sisters next. Those who do not swear fealty to me, will be put to the sword, and I do enjoy it when they refuse to bend the knee. I have learned to crave the sound of pained screams and tortured souls."

"You won't -" Penn's voice was cut off when the shadow around her neck tightened.

"Goodbye, Penn," Nezreen smiled, closing her fingers together, forcing her shadows to squeeze. "Tell Neempo I said -"

But she didn't get to finish that sentence because Jinn uncloaked himself standing directly in front of her and whipped his tachi blades across his chest, beheading her. As soon as her severed head bounced on the wooden floorboards, her shadows disappeared, releasing both Kai and Master Penn.

Rahab rubbed the heels of her palms against her eyes. It was over. They'd actually defeated both the pirate king and his witch. Tears rolled down her cheeks.

Someone's hand swiped at her cheeks. Opening her eyes, she met Haldane's equally relieved gaze. Everyone they had lost, everything that had been stolen from them – they'd had their revenge. It was over. She slipped her arms around his neck and pulled him into a full-blown hug. The captain's shoulders tensed, but a split second later, he wrapped her in his arms and laughed.

"Why are you laughing?" she mumbled into his shoulder.

"I never thought I'd get a hug from the likes of you," he smiled against her cheek.

"I knew the princeling would make me soft."

Haldane barked out another hearty laugh as he pulled away from her. "Aye, but being soft doesn't make you any less fearsome. It just makes you more human."

Two thuds hit the deck, rattling the floor beneath her. Kayven and Abba, their faces and arms streaked with blood and glistening in sweat, glanced around at their injured comrades and surveyed the two dead monsters.

Abba made his way to her, dropping down to one knee. Tossing his head to the side to remove his dark hair from covering his eyes, he smiled and extended his hand. "You look like you need to see a healer, my lady."

"Captain Haldane is also injured," Rahab motioned to the blood on the pirate's pants.

Abba nodded in understanding as several more Bellators landed onto the deck. A smug smile crossed his bronze features, as if to say, I'm already a step ahead of you.

Rahab huffed and accepted his outstretched hand. "If you bolt into the sky and make me sick, I'll be forced to fight you."

A small laugh escaped the Bellator's lips as he lifted her in his arms and held her tightly against his armored chest. "Are all mortal women as feisty as you and Salome?"

She grinned, "Is that your way of saying you like us?"

"I suppose it is." Abba looked up into the sky, wings stretching for take-off. "Hold on tight, my lady."

CHAPTER 61

NIABI

Niabi wasn't sure how long they'd been hiding in the apothecary, but Thrice still hadn't stirred. At least he wasn't groaning or screaming in agonizing pain. His chest was angry looking, but Leoti assured her he would survive, as long as they weren't discovered. Thrice was an easy target and wouldn't be able to defend himself should soldiers burst through the doors.

Salome paced back and forth; her hands perched on her hips. Her boots crunching against the floors was an irritating sound that grated Niabi's nerves, but after a while, she tuned her out and sat in a comfortable silence, drowning in her own thoughts.

She prayed Tala and Ivaylo had crossed into Andrago territory. She hoped Pash was still holding strong on the battlefield, even though she currently felt like a complete failure in her mission. She and Salome were tasked with finding and eliminating Gershom. Though they'd killed Vilora, their expectation in ending the war quickly was dashed. Niabi racked her brain, trying to formulate the best strategy to get them to the front lines without having to battle soldiers scattered throughout the city streets. There wasn't a tunnel that would take them to the main gate, and they didn't have horses to speed their journey. And of course, there was the issue with Thrice. They couldn't leave him behind, but they also couldn't stay held up with him, hoping their allies would come for them.

"Someone is coming." Salome's voice ripped Niabi from her thoughts.

Niabi unsheathed her daggers from her sleeves, ready to kill anyone who walked through that door. But the footsteps that neared, passed by and continued down the corridor. She and her sister exchanged a look before Salome slowly opened the door an inch to peek at who was marching by. Salome's shoulders stiffened and she waved Niabi forward. When Niabi glanced out, she understood why her sister's body posture had changed so abruptly.

"Is that -?

"Gershom," Niabi hissed softly. He and his small entourage were headed in the direction of the throne room. He had blood and dirt smeared all over his armor and for a moment, Niabi believed maybe luck was finally on their side. She whipped around to meet Leoti's gaze. "You stay here and watch over Thrice. We will deal with Gershom and come back for you."

Leoti's brow furrowed and Niabi could sense the Andrago was itching to disagree and argue her case, but for whatever reason Niabi didn't quite understand, the warg nodded her head in agreement. "Be quick about it," Leoti said and clutched the hilt of her longsword tightly.

Niabi's eyes collided with Salome's. "Are you ready?"

Salome grabbed her Qata Vishna blades off her back and smiled. A wolf, if Niabi ever saw one. "Let's finish this."

When the coast was clear, Niabi and Salome slipped out of the room and waited until they heard the click of the latch behind them before slipping down the hallway. Stealthily, the sisters made their way toward the throne room. The irony hadn't escaped Niabi that the very same place she had been given to Dichali in marriage as a death sentence, the same place she'd killed her own father, was the same place she'd face off with The Bear and claw his eyes out for his treachery.

Niabi and Salome crept behind statues and columns until they came upon the double doors that led into the throne room. Four soldiers stood guard outside the room. Easy pickings for her and Salome. With a quick nod, she and Salome threw daggers across the hall and downed the four men, ensuring they were all dead by slitting their throats.

As Salome bent down to grab her daggers lodged in the chests of two soldiers, Niabi kicked the doors open like a battering ram against the main gate. Sauntering inside what used to be her throne room, she caught Gershom's stunned look as he reclined in her throne.

"You!" he seethed.

Niabi smirked. "Afraid you're down a witch." She tossed Vilora's head on the floor before flexing her left hand, igniting it. "Nothing to say? How unlike you, Gershom." She cooed and cocked her head to the side.

Seeming to regain himself, he snarled, "We both know you can't kill me without forfeiting your own life, Niabi. Perhaps, we should quit with the theatrics."

She flashed a wicked smile. "It's not me you should fear."

Salome walked in as if on cue, Qata Vishna blades drawn, blood splattered across her face, arms, and fighting leathers.

Gershom had the audacity to laugh, swatting his hand around like he was shooing a pesky fly. "You think this *girl* can defeat me, Niabi? I killed my own son for power – this girl won't stand a chance."

Niabi couldn't help the gasp that escaped her lips causing Gershom to grin in great satisfaction.

"Oh yes," he crowed. "Pash is dead."

Flames licked up Niabi's arm with every intention to burn him to ash, but Salome stepped between her and Gershom, blocking her from attacking him. Niabi knew Salome was trying to prevent her from breaking her blood oath, but it did nothing to quench her rage.

"I am Salome." She narrowed her eyes, making sure he noticed her blades held out to her sides. "I've been looking for you for quite some time."

Gershom turned to look at her and his face paled when he noticed her two different color eyes, one containing the mark he'd spent the majority of his life afraid of. Salome smirked. "And I hear you've been dreading to meet me."

"You're the Hunter?"

Salome nodded. "Unfortunately for you, you won't be leaving this room alive."

"Just like your sister, you've underestimated me." He whistled, and Shadows stationed in an adjoining room filed in, surrounding the sisters, weapons drawn.

Niabi and Salome wielded their weapons, back-to-back, and when the Shadows launched their assault, they fought together. They flipped, spun, dove, kicked, sliced, and struck the shadows, battling them down dead. Oddly, it felt right fighting side by side with Salome. They fought as a unit, using their combined skills to take down a host of highly skilled Shadows.

Bodies were scattered around the throne room, staining the white marble floors red. Salome and Niabi were the only two that remained unscathed. Standing face to face, Niabi smiled, proud of how effortlessly she and her sister fought together. She knew in accordance with their agreement, once Gershom was defeated, Niabi would disappear and never show her face again, but getting to know Salome had her rethinking living a life of obscurity. She found herself wanting a friendship with Salome and maybe, just maybe, once the dust settled, they could have that. She wouldn't be so lonely thinking she was the last of the White Wolves of Northwind. Perhaps, in time, Crispin too would come around and they could wash the slate clean.

Movement from over Salome's shoulder caught Niabi's attention, ripping her from her brief moment of hope. Gershom stood on the dais, a bow drawn taut, with an arrow nocked and aimed directly at Salome. With a wicked and triumphant grin, The Bear released the arrow. Niabi grabbed Salome by her shoulders and spun them, so they switched positions. The arrow pierced Niabi's back, lurching her forward into her sister's arms. The horror written across Salome's face echoed the pain that ricocheted through Niabi's entire body. She'd been shot before and stabbed countless times, but this was by far the worst pain she'd ever experienced.

Gershom hissed and Niabi could hear him nocking another arrow, either to finish her off or strike his true intended target. Salome lowered Niabi to the ground quickly and carefully before launching an attack on Gershom before he had a chance to take another shot.

Crawling to one of the columns to lean against, Niabi couldn't do anything but watch as her sister battled Gershom. Despite his age, he still moved like a warrior in his prime and landed several punches to Salome's gut and chest, knocking her weapons out of her hands and bringing her to her knees.

"Get up," Niabi commanded, though she was positive Salome was too far away to hear her strained voice.

Gershom hovered over Salome, grabbing her hair and tugging her to meet his gaze. With her neck exposed, Gershom took the sword clutched in his right hand and swung with all his might, but Salome punched him in the groin and wiggled free from his grasp, escaping the blow. Tumbling away, she hopped to her feet, grabbed Gershom's head and slammed it down on her rising knee. With a howl, Gershom fell to the floor, his nose broken and bloody.

"You bitch!" he screamed, snatching his sword and stalking toward Salome.

She was light on her feet, dodging his reckless blows, allowing the old man to tire himself. Niabi knew Gershom trained for hours almost daily so his stamina was excellent, but Salome too had been endlessly training for this very moment, and if Niabi was a betting woman, her money would be on her sister to come out victorious.

Salome unsheathed the white wolf dagger attached to her hip and blocked what would have been a lethal blow. Using his momentum against him, Salome danced out of his way, spinning to his back and slicing his side as she passed. He hissed, fire raging in his eyes. Niabi knew that look: desperation. He was tiring and instead of adapting to his enemy, he fell prey to her.

"I shall never yield to you!" Gershom stood to his full height, towering over Salome by several inches.

"I never asked you to yield." Salome snatched her Qata Vishna blades up from the floor where she'd dropped them and spun them around her hands, beckoning him forward. "I will take no prisoners and leave none alive."

Niabi coughed, drawing Salome's attention. Her eyes were hazy and blood trickled down her back and pooled underneath her.

Taking advantage of the distraction, Gershom charged at Salome, his sword swinging down at her. Shoving her blades up just in time to block his attack, she kicked him square in his chest, and knocked his sword from his hand, making sure it wasn't within reach. He crawled away from Salome, but Niabi noticed he'd pulled a small knife out of his belt, but before she had a chance to warn her sister, he whipped around and stabbed Salome in the side, drawing an ear-piercing scream from her.

"No," Niabi teared up at the grimace crossing Salome's face.

Gershom once again towered over Salome. He retrieved his knife from her body and pointed it against her throat. "I will finally put an end to Issachar's line after all these years."

"Crispin -"

"Can't kill me, foolish girl," he interrupted, flashing a wicked grin. "Only the Hunter can kill me, and it doesn't look like you'll be doing that. You failed." Poking the dagger into her neck, drawing a bit of blood, he whispered, "Do tell your father who sent you."

With surprising quickness, Salome smashed her arm against his, pushing the knife away, leaving a small slice against her throat. She jumped up and took the small dagger she kept hidden in her boot and stabbed it into the side of his neck. "Tell him yourself," she growled in his ear before letting him fall to the floor, clutching at the hole in his neck.

As he gurgled on the floor, writhing in pain, the life slowly draining from him, Salome picked up Gershom's longsword and with a mighty swing, she claimed his head from his shoulders.

Niabi sighed in relief, but when a wheezed cough escaped her, it drew Salome to her. Salome clutched her side, blood staining her clothes.

"You need to get out of here," Niabi motioned toward the doors leading out of the throne room. "You need to get Leoti and Thrice."

Salome knelt next to Niabi and gently pulled her from the column to look at the injury she'd sustained. The arrow was still stuck in her back and when Salome reached up to touch it, Niabi winced and shook her head. The way Salome looked at her, Niabi knew she looked just as bad as she felt.

"Tell me what you see," Niabi instructed.

"There's purple splotches veining from the wound."

Nightshade. The tip of Gershom's arrow was poisoned. That's why she felt as if life was slipping away from her. Niabi rested against the column and glanced around at the sea of dead bodies. This throne room had seen more death than any other room in the White Keep. Niabi was starting to believe the room was cursed.

Salome grabbed her arm and with an exhausted groan, she attempted to help Niabi to her feet. "We need to get you out of here. Rayma will -"

"It's too late for me, Salome."

"We can -"

"Salome," Niabi's voice was calm but firm. "The arrow was poisoned. There's no saving me." Niabi saw the desperation to save her deep in Salome's eyes, but Niabi offered her a loving smile. "It's ok, Little Wolf."

The tears Salome was holding hostage finally escaped at the use of the nickname Lykos coined for her. "You took the arrow meant for me."

Niabi coughed, resituating herself even though it didn't ease her pain. "Surprising, I know. The villain has a heart after all."

"You aren't my villain." Salome grabbed her hand and squeezed. "Not anymore."

A tear slipped down Niabi's face. "Tell my son, I love him."

"I swear he will be cared for, Niabi." Salome sliced her hand and let her blood drip onto the marble floors. "I swear to you, Ivaylo will know of you and Pash. He will know you loved him and that you both fought courageously."

"And died with honor?" she whispered, and Salome nodded. Niabi's bottom lip quivered, the burning pain consuming her, drawing a small groan from her. She grabbed her sister's hand, not caring of the blood that now seeped onto her. "Stay with me?"

Salome bobbed her head. "Until the end."

"I need you to do something for me."

"Name it."

"Bury me in Elisor with Dichali and Rollo." Her eyes welled up. "And tell Crispin that I'm sorry. For everything. He will make a fine king."

Salome swiped a tear that slipped down her dirt-stained cheek. "Consider it done," she whispered.

Niabi painfully reached over and embraced Salome. "I wish we could have had more time, sister."

She closed her eyes, taking a deep breath as her body numbed to all the pain she'd been battling a moment before. When she opened her eyes, she found herself lying in a field of wheat. A light breeze whisked through, guiding her to stand up and walk through the farmlands. The sun was beginning to set and hues of purple, pink, and orange streaked across the sparsely clouded sky. For miles, all she could see was row after row of honey-golden barley dancing side to side as the wind led her forward. After what seemed like a small eternity, Niabi finally reached the edge of the field and came upon a grand white tent. She'd never seen this place before, but she instinctually knew where she was: The Great Beyond. And this tent flooded her with a familiarity that spurred her heart to leap within her chest.

Could it be?

She forced her feet to move closer, to see if the hope ricocheting through her was well warranted. The nearer she drew to the humble abode, the more at peace she felt. Before she reached the flapped entrance, a man stepped outside and the sight of him made her fall to her knees as tears streamed down her cheeks.

"My heart and my soul." The gentle voice washed over her like waves across the sand.

Slowly, she looked into Rollo's green eyes. Her son stroked his hand down her cheek and flicked her tears away. "I've missed your face," he smiled.

"Rollo," she threw her arms around his neck and squeezed. Wildly, she raked her hands through his hair, over his face, and kissed both of his cheeks. "My moon and my stars."

Rollo rested his forehead against hers and he whispered, "We've been waiting for you."

"We?" Her eyes met his and he nodded. His smile was punctuated by his dimples and gave him that boyish look she'd longed to see one more time.

"We."

Niabi glanced over Rollo's shoulder and saw Dichali standing at the entrance of the tent. Her breath was stolen at the sight of her late husband and with Rollo's help, she scrambled to her feet and ran toward the former Andrago king. Wrenching his arms open, she leapt into his awaiting grasp, and laughed. She kissed his lips, his cheeks, his forehead; she laughed, she cried, she nearly screamed.

"It's you," she whispered against his lips. "Oh, how I've missed you, my love."

"We will never be parted again," Dichali smiled, and it filled her heart with a happiness that she had yearned for years to feel again. "We can be a family again."

She bobbed her head. "We can finally be at peace." Wrapping her arms around Dichali again, she closed her eyes and inhaled his pine and tobacco scent. She had made it back to them. She'd finally made it home.

CHAPTER 62

SALOME

Salome held onto Niabi and didn't release her until she couldn't feel her sister moving anymore. After a minute of cradling her, she reluctantly leaned Niabi back against the column, resting her forehead against hers.

"May Death guide you to those you loved and lost. Until we meet again, sister." She dragged her middle finger from her forehead down to her chest.

It was then her own breathing became labored. Remembering she too had been injured, she placed her hand against the stab wound in her side, drenching her fingers in blood. If she didn't get it taken care of soon, she might be seeing her sister sooner than she expected. Her heart ached as she looked at Niabi's lifeless face once more before she struggled to her feet. Grabbing Gershom and Vilora's severed heads, she stuffed them in the same bag, and dragged it with her as she made her way down the hallway.

Though she'd killed Gershom, and Niabi had put an end to the Old Witch of Endor, no one else knew, so the battle raged on at the main gate as well as at sea. As she trapsed through the corridor that had windows on either side giving her views of both the mountains and the sea, she was relieved to see the Bellators still flying around, giving her the hope that their forces were holding their own against the ruthless Pirate King and his Shadow Witch. But as she took a closer look at the winged warriors, she noticed they weren't fighting, but patrolling. Had they defeated the pirates?

She whipped her head in the other direction where her brother led the foot soldiers and saw that the battle continued to rage, and flames licked up the white stone walls. She needed to get to Crispin, she needed to show everyone that the city was now under a new rule, with the death of their masters. Feeling lightheaded, she sat down on the floor before she fell and hurt herself. Steadily taking slow, deep breaths, she calmed her nerves and purged her fear of dying, to think through her options. She would never make it through the city to the battlefront on foot and she didn't have Snow to get her there either.

"Jinn?" She extended the bridge between them, hoping he answered. If he was silent, if he didn't respond, she wasn't sure if she could handle losing him after watching her sister die in her arms. *"Jinn, my love?"*

He wasn't answering; he was always quick to respond. The deafening silence made her head spin. He couldn't be dead. Her husband couldn't be dead. Dragging herself up to peer out the windows overlooking the sea, she stared at the ships. There were some on fire, there was one that was sinking, and if her eyes weren't deceiving her, there was one ship that was completely split in half and inoperable. How could that be.

She couldn't give up. She had to get to Crispin somehow to deliver Gershom's head, even if she got there pale, frail, and on Death's doorstep, she would come through for her brother.

As she shakily stood to her feet, she felt a warmth flood her head.

"Salome?"

"Jinn?" Her bottom lip quivered at the sound of his voice. *"You're alive. I thought when you didn't respond that you..."*

"I'm here, darling." He picked up when she trailed off, and her heart was filled with relief. *"Where are you?"*

"I'm still in the White Keep." She couldn't help the pained groan that escaped her lips.

"You're hurt."

"Where is Kayven? Or Abba?" She didn't confirm or deny her injury to him, he couldn't get to her fast enough to help, so there was no need to worry him. *"I need them to get me. I'm sitting in a long corridor of windows."*

There was a brief pause before Jinn answered. *"Abba is taking Rahab to see the healers."*

"Is she alright?" Her heart dropped. If the pirate didn't make it, her brother would be devastated.

"She'll be fine." Jinn's voice soothed her. *"Kayven is making his way to you now."*

"Thank you." She clutched her side.

"How bad is it?" he asked. *"And before you tell me you're fine, I can sense your pain through our bond."*

She leaned her head back against the wall. *"Gershom stabbed me, but I'll be ok."* Why did that sound like a lie?

"Is he dead?"

"Yes." Her lip quivered, Niabi's dead body flashed in her mind. *"Niabi is dead. She took an arrow meant for me and I couldn't..."* She sucked in a breath before explaining, *"It was poisoned, and she was gone before I could save her."*

"I'm sorry," his voice soothed her, wrapping around her as if he were sitting next to her.

"Are you safe?" she asked.

"The Pulauans have been defeated and though we suffered casualties, both the Pirate King and Shadow Witch are dead." She sensed a bubbling pride stirring within him and couldn't help but smile.

Another groan escaped her lips as the burning in her side started to throb. She felt cold. Perhaps the hallway filled with windows was lettingthe chill in, or perhaps she'd lost too much blood and was dying. She looked up and down the hallway, feeling someone's presence. When she didn't see anyone, she realized Death was with her, standing in wait to claim her soul and usher her away.

"Salome?" Jinn attempted to mask the panic in his voice but failed. *"Don't. Don't give up."*

"When we first met," Salome shifted into a more comfortable position, stretching her legs out in front of her, *"I thought you were the most handsome man I'd ever laid my eyes on. There was something about you, how you looked at me, how you spoke, how you moved that hypnotized me and drew me to you. I tried to fight it, tried to fight falling for you, but it was like fighting to breathe or refusing to eat. It was impossible for me not to love you, Jinn."*

"Why does it sound like you're saying goodbye?"

"I have loved you in this life, and I will love you in the next." A tear slid down her cheek. She shivered, feeling like her fingers and toes were submerged in ice, and noticed her hands were turning blue.

"Stay with me," Jinn's voice rang out. *"Salome, stay with me! Please!"*

Death was near. She had bided her time, she'd been patient in claiming Salome's soul by shepherding other souls to the After, leaving Salome for last, and now, she could sense Death closing the gap between them. She closed her eyes, taking in a deep breath to steady herself, knowing this was the end for her. Quietly, she slipped into darkness and Jinn's voice was snuffed out.

CHAPTER 63
RAHAB

"Ouch!" Rahab winced, fighting the urge to slap the needle out of Rayma's steadily working hand. "I'd prefer if you didn't enjoy inflicting so much pain on me, Healer."

"For being a fearsome pirate," Rayma shot back, flicking her eyes up for a fraction of a second, before returning to her work stitching up Rahab's thigh, "you complain an awful lot."

Abba cleared his throat and took a step forward. Since he'd flown her to the medical tents, he had refused to leave her side, which both touched and irritated her. "Would holding my hand help?"

Rahab glared at the Bellator's extended hand and shook her head. "Not necessary. I've been through worse."

"By all that grumbling, you wouldn't know it." Rayma rolled her eyes as she finished the last stitch. "You'll be back on your feet in no time, but you'll have to use a cane for a few days to let your leg heal properly."

Rahab scoffed and crossed her arms over her chest. "I won't be using a cane."

Rayma cleaned her hands before packing up her medical kit. "Then I suppose you'll really resemble a pirate when you start limping around like one."

"That's a vicious stereotype," the pirate narrowed her eyes, but Rayma didn't back down.

"Then prove me wrong. Use the cane."

The tent flap opened and when Rahab looked up, relief flooded her seeing Crispin standing there.

"Hello, princeling," she smiled, a tease embedded in her tone, "or should I call you king now?"

He huffed a chuckle, her comment seemed to rattle him from his stunned silence. It was then she noticed he was carrying a head by the hair, it hung by his side and its face was frozen in horror for the rest of eternity. She jutted her chin toward the severed head and said, "Most men bring flowers or sweet treats for the woman they love, but I suppose this head will do."

Crispin's eyes flared, mischief and warning dancing in his expression. "That mouth of yours."

"Tempting, I'm sure," Rahab smirked.

"Is she alright?" Crispin ignored her comment and addressed Rayma. Once the Healer nodded, his body seemed to relax.

"She'll have to use a cane to help her walk until she's fully healed," Rayma narrowed her eyes at the pirate, making sure she understood these were non-negotiable instructions. "But she'll be back to seafaring and plundering before you know it."

"You don't have to talk about me, as if I'm not in the room, Rayma," Rahab straightened, cracking her back, as the Healer gathered her medical supplies.

"Ah, so you do listen?" Rayma griped and Crispin laughed.

"And what's so funny?" Rahab glared at Crispin, fire flaring inside her chest.

Crispin dropped the head, his eyes glued to the pirate. "Leave us, please."

Rayma and Abba left without pause or argument. Once the flap of the tent swooshed back into place, Rahab opened her mouth to say something snarky, but Crispin's lips crashed against hers, and whatever insult she was about to spew was forgotten. They'd had their fair share of passionate encounters, but the way he kissed her this time was raw, wild, and filled with relief. She cupped his face, dragging him closer to her, but when she winced from her freshly mended injuries, he jumped back, raking a hand through his disheveled hair. His lips were swollen, his eyes hungry, but there was a tentativeness in his posture that made her heart ache.

"I'm fine, Crispin," she said softly.

Gently, he caressed her thigh, seeing the stitches holding the red, angry flesh together. "Who did this to you?" His fiery gaze met hers. If there had been an army between them and the person who had maimed her, she had no doubt Crispin would have torn them all to pieces to avenge her.

Pressing her hands to his face, dragging the tips of her fingers down to his chest, she said, "There is no one for you to harm. I took care of it myself."

The storminess in his expression seemed to subside, but only by a fraction. "Who did it?"

"Uri." She smiled, the realization that the pirate king was dead suddenly impacted her. "He won't ever hurt anyone again."

Crispin nodded, beaming with pride. "When they told me you'd been injured…" he sucked in a breath, steadying himself, "…I thought the worst."

"You think you'd get rid of me that easily?" She tsked, drawing a much-needed laugh from him. "You'd be bored without me."

He swiped pieces of her sweaty blue hair away from her face. "Of that I have no doubt." With an impish grin, he slipped one arm carefully underneath her knees and cradled her back with the other. Lifting her up into his arms, he kissed her forehead and said, "I think you'd be far more comfortable in my tent."

"Is that so?" she snickered, slithering her arm around his neck.

"I'll make sure you get all the rest you need," he winked.

"Prince Crispin." Kayven's voice sliced through the room and drew their attention. The warrior's face was forlorn, and Crispin's breathing quickened. She could feel his heart thrashing against her waist.

"What is it, Commander?" Crispin asked, though his voice seemed shaky.

"It's your sister," Kayven whispered, a scratchiness in his throat.

"What about my sister?"

"The Healers are working on her, but they can't seem to wake her." Kayven straightened his shoulders back, but it didn't mask his fear or his watery eyes.

"Go to her," Rahab patted Crispin's chest. When their eyes met, her heart nearly ripped out of her chest. If she could relieve him of his pain, she would have jumped at the chance. "Go," she nudged him gently, spurring him to action.

Crispin set her back down on the table and kissed her forehead before he motioned for the Bellator to show him where his sister was. Rahab wasn't the praying sort, but she whispered to the Almighty, hoping He was listening, hoping that He would spare Salome and let her live.

CHAPTER 64
CRISPIN

Crispin followed the Bellator commander to a tent very similar to the one he'd been visiting Rahab in. Neither man spoke a word as they walked a few tents down but as soon as Kayven stopped and pointed to the flap, Crispin couldn't seem to make himself walk inside. He just watched the flap waft in the light breeze, catching glimpses of Rayma's feet scurrying around the table where he knew his unresponsive sister was lying.

"Prince Crispin?" Kayven's voice brought him back from the depths of his mind.

"What happened?" It was all the prince could think of asking, buying himself some time to avoid looking upon his sister.

"She reached out to Prince Jinn through their bond, said she needed someone to come get her." Kayven rubbed a hand against the back of his neck. "She needed a way to get to the front lines, to bring you Gershom's head and to end the bloodshed. But when I got to her..."

"What?" Crispin pressed, his chest constricting his air flow.

"I expected her to be waiting for me with a triumphant smile, but she was lying on the floor, clutching her side. She had been stabbed and by the looks of it, lost a lot of blood." Kayven swiped a single tear that slipped down his bronze cheek and cleared his voice. "I tried to wake her, but she did not stir. I had Durmas fly Gershom's head to you, and I brought her here, hoping Rayma could help her before it was too late."

Crispin patted Kayven's shoulder, not knowing how to respond. He knew Kayven and Abba had grown quite fond of Salome, seeing as they spent a lot of time together in Oakenshire, but he never thought he'd see a mighty Bellator shed a tear for a mortal. Either Kayven was terrified and was trying to mask it, or he knew there truly was no hope of Salome living and Crispin was here to say goodbye.

"And Niabi?" Crispin found himself asking. The thought she was the one to stab Salome crossed his mind.

"Dead." Kayven met his gaze. "We found her body in the throne room, a poisoned arrow in her back."

Hearing Niabi was dead didn't flood him with relief or joy like he expected it to. Instead, he felt a deep sorrow squeeze his heart. For a moment, he thought Niabi was invincible, that no one could kill her. But knowing she fought for him to be king, knowing she gave up the throne for a life of obscurity, humbled him for some reason. He might not have cared for her, and he certainly hadn't forgiven her, but in the end, she'd earned his gratitude.

Rayma whipped the tent flap behind her as she stomped outside. Her sudden presence startled Crispin.

"How is she?" He dared to ask, but she shook her head slowly.

"I've done everything I can for her," Rayma wiped her bloody hands on her apron. "I'm sorry."

Crispin's bottom lip quivered as he rubbed the heels of his palms against his eyes. Rayma slipped her hands around his wrists, bringing them down from his face, forcing him to meet her compassionate gaze.

"Go to her."

"I failed her."

Rayma shook her head. "Your sister did what she promised to do. She saved hundreds, if not thousands of lives today." The Healer motioned for him to go inside the tent. "I cannot promise she will make it through the night, but I will do everything in my power to help her. I suggest you say your goodbyes, just in case."

How could he say goodbye to his best friend? How could he say goodbye when they still had so much left to accomplish together?

Crispin dug deep within his soul to force his feet to move. He moved the flap and took a deep breath before plunging into the tent and resting his eyes on his sister's still form. Her breathing was light, the only sign she still had a fighting chance to wake up. She'd been stripped of her armor and fighting leathers and had a piece of cloth covering her chest and another one concealing her lower extremities. She looked so much like a corpse being prepped for burial than a warrior fighting for her life. Her body was bloody, and dirt stained her paling face. He noticed multiple bruises beginning to form on her face, hands, and torso and a deep-rooted rage stirred within him. He approached her body and gripped the edge of the table, hovering above her.

"Wake up," he whispered, his voice breaking. "Please, Salome, wake up."

Nothing happened. She didn't move, her breathing didn't change, her eyes didn't flutter. Oh, what he would give to see her look up at him and smile, say something snarky, and wrap her arms around him. But she didn't. She didn't respond at all.

I suggest you say your goodbyes, just in case.

Crispin batted Rayma's words from his mind as grief and hopelessness settled within him. He shook his head and slammed his hand on the table, rattling Salome's body. "Wake up!" he shouted. He grabbed her by her shoulders and shook her a little bit, his tears raining down on her. "Salome! Salome! Wake up, Salome! You can't leave me! I can't lose you," he sobbed.

His knees gave way and the soft ground broke his fall. He didn't care that everyone outside could hear his cries. He didn't care that they would think he'd come undone, because the truth was, he had.

Flashing back months ago when he and Salome were first approached by Harbona, she didn't want to go to war. She was content with the Tree House Forest, but he forced the issue. He wanted them to battle their enemies and come out with the kingdom, crown, and throne. It had been his obsession for twelve years and now that they'd won the war, now that he would bear the crown, sit on the White Throne, and rule over the Kingdom of Northwind, he realized he hadn't considered what it would cost him. They'd already lost Zophar but losing his sister too – his heart just couldn't bear it. She didn't deserve an end like that.

If he could go back, he would have left her in the Tree House Forest. He would have made sure he kept both Zophar and Salome safe and more importantly, alive. But he couldn't go back. He couldn't change their fates. He didn't protect them, and in the end, couldn't save them.

"Please," Crispin grabbed Salome's cold hand and kissed it. "Please, wake up. Come back to me."

Rushed footsteps entered the tent and stopped as the flap whipped opened and closed. Crispin turned to see who had interrupted his private moment with his sister and saw both Adonijah and Jinn gawking at her body.

Jinn stepped forward; his eyes fixed on his wife. If he noticed Crispin crouched on the ground, he didn't acknowledge him. The prince cupped Salome's face and rested his forehead against hers, tears unapologetically streamed down his face. He whispered something to her that Crispin couldn't hear but knew just like he had his moment with his sister, Jinn would need his time as well.

Crispin pulled himself to his feet and proceeded to leave the tent but stopped next to Adonijah. He put his hand on his shoulder. "Rayma said we should say our goodbyes," Crispin whispered. "She might not last the night."

Adonijah's teary gaze met Crispin's and he shook his head. "Your sister is far too stubborn to leave us behind."

"I'm having her taken to the White Keep," Crispin explained, glancing over his shoulder as Jinn cradled Salome's body. "If nothing else, she will be in the home of our ancestors one last time."

Without waiting for Adonijah to respond, Crispin stomped out, and unless it was important, everyone left him alone.

It was going to be a long, sleepless night.

CHAPTER 65
SALOME

When Salome opened her eyes, she was no longer in the white stone corridor. She was sitting at a long white table and across from her was the most beautiful woman she'd ever seen. Her white, long braid draped over her pale shoulder. Her purple eyes were zoned in on Salome, and even though she looked young, there was no mistaking who she was and that she had roamed Adalore for an eternity.

"You've been following me for quite some time," Salome initiated the conversation. "It looks like your patience finally paid off, Lady Death."

Death smiled and it was laced with a friendly familiarity that surprised Salome. Every time she thought about Death, she fought it, but sitting before her now, she was flooded with peace.

"I've been watching you, Hunter," Death spoke and her voice was melodious. "I wanted to see for myself, if you were worthy."

"Worthy of what?"

"Living."

"What does that mean?" Salome tilted her head to the side before scanning the stark room she was in. She visited her brother, Lykos, in the After before, and this didn't look remotely like the same place. "Where am I?"

Death motioned her hand around the space that had no windows or doors or furniture other than the table and two chairs. "This is the Void. This is my home."

"Why am I here?" She refocused on Lady Death. "Am I not dead?"

It was Death's turn to look confused. "Your soul has not decided whether to release you or not."

"You mean, I could go back?" Salome didn't want to get her hopes up, but she couldn't help it. If there was a chance she could see Jinn again, see her brother again, she would do whatever she could to find her way back to them.

"Those who come to the Void are between life and death," the goddess explained like a mother would speak to her child. "Your body is in need of healing.

If your friends are able to find you in time, this door will open, and you will be free to return to the mortal world." She motioned toward a door on her left that hadn't been there before.

"And if my friends don't find me in time?"

"Then the other door will open, and you will be welcomed to the After to see those who came before you." A second door, this one to Death's right, appeared.

Salome dragged her gaze from the door and stared into Death's violet eyes. "Why not just claim me? I've felt your presence for months. What is it you want from me?"

"I do not want anything from you. I have been your constant companion since the day you were born." Death pushed her seat back and slid to her feet. She floated toward Salome and only stopped once she was before her. "I have followed each Hunter since Malachi and have ushered them all to the After when their mortal lives came to an end. But you," she smiled, "you were the first Hunter who fought me; the first Hunter who defied my presence. You did not welcome me, nor did you let your fear of me deter you from risking your life to save others. You surprised me, mortal."

A rattling sound from one of the doors drew Salome's attention. She could hear her name being called. Walking toward the doors, she found the one leading back to the land of the living shook. Light flickered behind it.

"Salome!" the voice cried out again. "Salome!"

She recognized the voice, and she slammed her hand on the door and cried out, "Crispin! I'm here! I'm here!"

"He can't hear you." Death was now standing beside her, arms clasped behind her.

"But I can hear him."

"He's trying to wake you from your slumber." Death turned to face Salome and she mirrored her stance. "Should you sense my presence again, Salome the Strong, know that I've come as your friend and protector. Not your enemy."

"What did you call me?" Salome cocked her head in confusion.

"When the mortals sing their ballads and tell their tales of your great victories, they will refer to you as Salome the Strong, the first female Hunter, and in time, when another Hunter is needed," Death met her gaze with a bright smile, "hopefully they are just as worthy as you are to bear the title."

Salome shot back to when she was in the Isles of Myr and had become the newest Red Maiden. She was instructed to pick one of the Five Virtues and though all of their voices were pleading their case, it was Strength that she chose.

May Strength be your protector and may her eagle guide you on your path.

"Salome, come back to me, darling." A gentle whisper wisped through the room, drawing Salome's attention. "Come back to me."

"Jinn?" She touched the door and felt a growing warmth beneath her palm.

"They're waiting for you," Death said.

The door leading to the mortal world grew brighter, so bright, Salome was forced to squint, and Death began to fade from view.

"We will meet again, Salome the Strong," Death's voice rang out around her. Though the words seemed ominous, Salome felt a wave of peace wash over her and she knew the next time she met Death, she would greet her like an old friend.

SALOME'S EYES SHOT OPEN, and she found she was lying in a bed that felt like she had been resting on a cloud. Scanning the room, she recognized the white stone walls and the window that looked out over the White City. She didn't hear the sounds of battle raging around Northwind, nor did she smell the burning wood from the ships in the harbor. Scooting up so she was leaning against the white oak headboard, she finally noticed Jinn and Crispin on the other side of the room, slumped on the couch against the wall, sleeping. They didn't look like they'd even taken a moment to bathe or scrub the evidence of battle from their armor.

She pulled the blankets off her and noticed she was in a plain white smock. Her body was clean and when she lifted the smock to examine her stab wound, she found an angry, swollen wound that had been stitched to perfection. Another scar to add to her ever-growing list, but she was alive, and that's all that mattered.

She wasn't sure how long she'd been unconcious, but her back ached, and all she wanted to do was stretch her legs. Draping her legs over the side of her bed, she slowly put her feet on the cold tile floor and applied her weight, making sure she didn't fall flat on her face. With some difficulty, she made her way toward her balcony, grabbing a fur tossed over a chair, and wrapped it around herself before slipping out the door. The cold burned her lungs as she breathed in the salty sea air whipping through the city. Snow was peppered across rooftops in the city below her and memories of her growing up in the White Keep flooded her. As she scanned the surrounding areas, she caught sight of the gardens she loved running through as a child and made note to visit as soon as she could.

"Thinking of escaping, Princess?"

Salome turned to see Kayven perched on the railing of her balcony. She hadn't noticed him at the far end of the patio and smiled. He tucked his wings behind him and returned her smile with a bright one of his own. His hair was pulled back in his typical half-up, half-down style and he had fresh cuts and bruises on his face and arms, but other than that, he was in prime shape.

"It is good to see you on your feet." He hopped up and walked toward her.

As soon as he was within reach, she wrapped her arms around him and to her delight and surprise, he gently squeezed her back.

"You mortals with your physical displays of affection," he teased, though he didn't release her until she pulled away.

"Admit it. You've grown fond of our ways," she grinned, attempting to hide the wince she whimpered from straining her injured side.

"You should not be out of bed when you clearly need rest," he chided, but she waved him off.

"I needed some fresh air." She brushed wild strands of her hair from her face. "How long have I been out?"

"Two days." He rested his elbows on the railing and she did the same. "Those two in your room refused to leave your side even though we begged them to. Thank the Almighty you woke when you did. Everyone in the keep was beginning to smell them."

Salome barked out a laugh. "It's nice to know they care." She bumped him with her shoulder, drawing his golden gaze. "What happened after I passed out?"

"Once I found you, I flew you to Rayma. I knew by your coloring that I might be too late, but I had to try." Kayven's face darkened. She rested her hand on his forearm, bringing him back from whatever memory haunted him. "I made sure one of my men delivered Gershom's head to your brother at the front lines and the fighting ended. The city surrendered seeing Gershom was dead and the people welcomed Crispin as their true king. Apparently, rumors had spread through Northwind over the last few months that Issachar's son lived, and they were relieved he'd come to defeat Gershom, who had always been seen as an enemy of the people."

Resting her head against his shoulder, she said, "Thank you for saving me."

In a rare display of affection, the Bellator pecked her head before snaking his arm across her shoulders and tugging her close. "Out of all the mortals I have met, you are by far my favorite."

"And out of all the Immortals I've met, Abba is by far my favorite." She tried and failed to hide her smirk and before long they were both laughing.

"Salome!?"

Footsteps thundered inside her chambers as Crispin and Jinn had woken up and noticed her empty bed. Kayven opened the door, and she stood in the threshold as her husband and brother rushed around the room frantically, until they noticed her. Their faces were filled with relief and Jinn rushed to her, slipping his arms around her and gently picking her up, kissing her. She raked her fingers through his hair, pulling back from his kiss, swiping the tear slipping down his cheek.

"I thought I had lost you," he whispered.

She shook her head. "I heard you calling for me."

There would be a time when she explained the Void, and everything she talked to Death about, but all she wanted to do now was kiss him, and by the look in his eyes, she knew he felt the same way.

Jinn's lips met hers and she could feel his longing for her, she could sense his stress melting from him, and she deepened their kiss until Crispin cleared his throat, reminding them they weren't alone. With care, Jinn set Salome back on her feet and she walked toward her brother who still had dirt smeared across his face.

She sniffed the air around him and crinkled her nose. "You could have at least bathed in the two days I was asleep," she teased and the tension he was holding in his shoulders loosened.

"Brat," he chuckled and wrapped his arms around her, kissing her forehead.

"We did it," she whispered, and he nodded.

"We did it."

Remembering Rahab had been injured and Abba had flown her to Rayma, she asked, "How's Rahab?"

"Bandaged and having to use a cane until she heals, which she gripes about, but she's recovering." Crispin pulled back from her and slipped his hands around her face. "You scared me. What happened to you?"

Salome, Crispin, Jinn, and Kayven spent the next couple of hours catching up on their versions of the battle. They reflected on those they'd lost and that's when Salome informed Crispin of how Niabi died. How she sacrificed herself to save her and that her last request was to be buried with her kin in Elisor. Crispin agreed without question and even teared up a little bit when she delivered Niabi's last words to him. Salome planned to fulfill her promises to her sister as she took her last breaths; she would make sure Ivaylo was cared for and that he grew up knowing who his parents were.

Once she was dressed and able to walk more than a few feet without needing to catch her breath, Salome reunited with her friends. She swapped stories with Adonijah, Seraphina, and Cato. She hugged Kai and kissed Abba on the cheek. She danced with Harbona, laughed with Oifa and Hanzo, and drank her fill with her future sister-in-law, Rahab. As a group, they toasted their dead and buried them in the mountain crypts, honoring their sacrifice.

Crispin's coronation and wedding to Rahab was celebrated across Adalore and the people of Northwind feasted for a week in their honor. Although Rahab wasn't a huge fan of the title of queen, she was extremely excited when Crispin made her the Commander of Northwind's armada and ensured the crew of the *Shadow of Death* had high ranking positions in the fleet and enticing pay to keep them in the White City. All of them readily accepted, except Captain Haldane, who returned to Pulau and became the new Pirate King, swearing he'd right Uri's wrongs in honor of his late-wife, Palma.

Adonijah and Leoti journeyed to Elisor, where they were determined to help Tala raise Ivaylo. Salome promised to visit as soon as she could and if Ivaylo needed anything, he would have it. She knew her nephew would be in good hands with the Andrago, and Crispin offered Tala an ambassadorship to Northwind, should he ever wish to return.

Oifa and Hanzo took the united Mountain Men tribe back to the Bone Mountains where they established a peaceful world for their people. Within a few weeks of being in Fennor, Oifa and Hanzo discovered they were expecting a child and the couple that used to loathe one another, rejoiced, knowing with their child, a new age had truly dawned. Equally Stormcrag and Krazak, their heir would continue the work of unity between the ancient peoples.

Heru and Rayma tearfully said goodbye to one another before the prince returned south with the Numbio. With Harbona and Lavena pulling some strings, they ensured Heru could visit Rayma and Inaros in Caelestis whenever he wanted, and that the Immortals would keep Rayma protected from the Grim, breaking the curse.

Though the Qata Vishna bid their Red Maiden farewell and sailed back to the Isles of Myr, Seraphina remained with Salome, fulfilling her oath to Nym to protect her granddaughter. And wherever Seraphina went, Cato went as well.

Harbona remained with Crispin and Rahab as their advisor. Once Odelia was well, she and Makeda joined him in the White Keep, finally mending their familial bond.

The Bellator commanders returned with Lavena to Caelestis, but as a parting gift and with Harbona's blessing, Salome got to keep Zandaar, the hippogriff. Kayven and Abba made her promise that she wouldn't fly alone at night. She only conceded to those terms once they agreed to visit her in Sakurai, whenever they had the chance. She owed the Bellator brothers everything; they saved her when no one else realized she was drowning. They would always hold a special place in her heart.

Master Penn and her Keepers hitched a ride with Captain Haldane and returned to The Sisters where they christened a new Sovereign. Penn and Haldane had grown quite fond of one another during the course of their journey and as the pirate established his new reign in Pulau, the Master of Keepers did everything in her power to aid him and improve relations between their kingdoms.

Though it was difficult saying goodbye to the friends who had become her family, Salome knew they'd all join her and Jinn in Sakurai for their royal wedding the following year. But what she'd been dreading for weeks, what she had refused to think about until that moment, was having to say goodbye to her brother before she boarded Jinn's ship to Sakurai.

Standing face to face on the docks, the winter chill gone and the crisp, floral air replacing it, the siblings stared at one another in complete silence. She wasn't exactly sure how to say goodbye to her best friend.

"Make sure you don't let that crown go to your head," she teased, pointing at the silver crown resting upon his curls.

He rolled his eyes and clicked his tongue. "You're worried about *my* head getting inflated? What about you, Salome the Strong? I've already heard two different ballads about your victory in the North."

She shrugged a lazy shoulder, feigning indifference. "Three, but who is counting?"

"Brat," he laughed and pulled her to his chest, squeezing her tightly. "How am I supposed to say goodbye?" he asked softly, tears filling his eyes. "How am I supposed to be happy for you, when my heart is breaking?"

"Out of everyone I have known and loved, you will always be my favorite." She hugged him, not wanting to let him go. "Take care of him, Rahab." The pirate queen nodded, stretching her hand across Crispin's chest once Salome released him.

"I will," Rahab promised and Salome knew she would keep her word.

"I will see you both soon."

With a final kiss and hug, Salome walked up the gangplank with Jinn and boarded the *Jade Warrior*. Sailing out of the harbor, taking one last, long look at Northwind, she let loose the breath she'd been holding onto, and waved at Crispin and Rahab until she couldn't see them anymore. Jinn slipped up next to her and rested his elbows on the railing.

"We will visit them often," he smiled. "You might be the future queen of Sakurai, but I know where your heart lies."

Salome tunneled her hand into his and squeezed. "My heart is with you, my lord."

"You flatter me," he raised her hand to his mouth and kissed it. "I swear to you, we will come back. This is your home, and I wouldn't dare take that from you."

Salome pushed up on her toes until her lips met his. "A secret for a secret?" she said softly against his mouth.

He flashed a crooked smile and nodded, wrapping his arms around her waist and pulling her to his chest. "You first."

ACKNOWLEDGMENTS

Holy Guacamole, the trilogy is complete!!! I started writing this story when I was fourteen and honestly, gave up on my dream of being a published author. Thank God, my husband, Brad, convinced me to give it another go. My fourteen-year-old self would be in awe of us at thirty-two.

If you have a dream, pursue it! If you gave up, it's not too late to try again. If I can do it, you can do it.

Thank you, the reader, for giving my work a chance. I appreciate YOU! Thank you for your support and for reading (and hopefully loving) my work. It has been such a dream come true to put all the stories running wild in my head down on paper. I am so excited for you to follow my career and fall in love with the characters who take up all my free time.

Be on the lookout for my new books! And don't worry, one day soon, we will return to the Ten Kingdoms of Adalore on a new adventure!

And as always, I want to thank God. Without Him, I would be lost and on a different path.

To my husband and best friend, Brad. Thank you for every bit of encouragement, support, and love you send my way. Without you, I would have given up on my dream years ago.

To my daughter, Remi, thank you for telling me how much you love me. You will never know how much that means to me.

To my son, Archer, thank you for your hugs throughout the day. They are my favorite interruptions.

To my daughter, Roux, thank you for bringing all the sass and smiles. It fueled me.

To my Mom and Dad, thank you for all your love and support. Mom, thank you for encouraging me to read and write from such an early age and for helping me edit my work! Dad, thank you for seeing my talent before I saw it myself.

To my sister, Logan, thank you for playing video games with me whenever I needed a break from work!

To my brother-in-law, Matt, thank you for your friendship, and for believing in my success before I published a single word.

To my friend, Mercedes. Thank you for your past ten years of friendship and for being the godmother to my three children. I love you, girl, and I'm so grateful for our talks.

To my book loving, writing sound board of a friend, Pier! You are an amazing friend, and I appreciate all your encouragement, support, and for being the best hype woman around!

To my Midnight Tide Publishing family, THANK YOU for welcoming me into the fold! Elle, thank you for your help and answering all my random questions like the true Mama Bear that you are! Brindi, thank you for our light-hearted chats when I'm feeling down! Jenny, thank you for brightening my day and hyping me up! Lou, Hannah, Whitney, Nicole, Stephanie, and everyone else at MTP, you rock!

And to my incredible street team! Thank you for encouraging me, supporting me, and loving my characters and books! It's a dream come true!

ABOUT THE AUTHOR

Morgan Gauthier lives in East Tennessee with her husband and best friend, Brad, and with their three children, Remi, Archer, and Roux (who are 4 years old and younger!). If five people wreaking havoc in the same house wasn't enough, Morgan also has three dogs, Potter, Skye, and Bubba, and one grumpy bird named Titus.

Her first book, *Wolves of Adalore*, was published in 2021 and is the first book in a YA Epic Fantasy Trilogy. The second book, *The Red Maiden*, was published in 2022, and the third book, *The Raven and the Wolf*, is due for publication in 2023.

Morgan also published *Aloha, Seattle* in November of 2021. It is her first Contemporary Romantic Comedy and she is planning on writing more in the genre.

If Morgan isn't writing or reading, she can be found binge watching Netflix shows, playing video games, attempting to cook like Gordon Ramsay (not even close to his level), and practicing archery.

You can follow her on:

- facebook.com/authormorgangauthier
- instagram.com/authormorgangauthier
- tiktok.com/@authormorgangauthier
- pinterest.com/authormorgangauthier
- amazon.com/stores/Morgan-Gauthier

Also by Morgan Gauthier

Fantasy:

Wolves of Adalore

The Red Maiden

The Raven and the Wolf

Contemporary Romance:

Aloha, Seattle

The Maine Attraction

ALSO BY MIDNIGHT TIDE PUBLISHING

During the month of Amira, the silver moon emerges, and the kingdom of Zyra comes alive with anticipation for its annual ball. Mellana Goodwick, finally at the rightful age of sixteen, receives her first invitation, but when unexpected events take place, immediate regret sets in. Mellana finds herself caught in a strange storm—casting down green lightning and filling the sky with ear-splitting thunder. To make matters worse, the kingdom comes under attack by Prince Lorian, a man removed from the line of succession for murdering his sister, the future queen, and her newborn child.

After escaping the attack with her best friends, Mellana stumbles upon a box left by a woman named Rose. With the power to see glimpses of the future, Rose warns Mellana of hidden powers the kingdom has covered up and Lorian's desire to unleash them all. Rose instructs Mellana to gather the sacred article from each of the seven kingdoms before Lorian and his deadly group can gain access to them. Together, the items unlock a barrier that is meant to stay shut.

Available Now

www.ingramcontent.com/pod-product-compliance
Lightning Source LLC
Chambersburg PA
CBHW020345310726
48979CB00015B/2512/J

* 9 7 8 1 9 5 8 6 7 3 3 1 7 *